HELLO TEMPTATION

KELSIE HOSS

Editing by Tricia Harden of Emerald Eyes Editing.

Cover design by Najla Qamber of Najla Qamber Designs.

Sensitivity Reading by Kelsea Reeves.

Have questions? Email kelsie@kelsiehoss.com.

For info on sensitive content, visit https://kelsiehoss.com/ pages/sensitive-content.

This book was previously titled Confessions of the Funny Fat Friend.

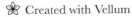 Created with Vellum

For anyone who's ever felt like the funny fat friend. You deserve to take center stage. <3

CONTENTS

A QUICK NOTE FROM THE AUTHOR

Dear Reader,

This book is full of humor, romance, and sexy scenes. Readers 18+ only, please!

Love,
Kelsie Hoss

HENRIETTA

Confession: I'm a 28-year-old virgin.

I WAS BACK IN VESTIDO, bridesmaid dress shopping for my best friend's wedding, and I was starting to see a pattern. A pattern I didn't like.

I met Birdie and Mara two years ago. We'd become fast friends, all single girls in our late twenties, transitioning into our thirties. It helped that we had a mutual love of breakfast food and mojitos.

Then, I witnessed Birdie fall in love with a hot single dad and stood by her side a year later as she got married.

I'd never really been the kind of person to have a lot of girlfriends, always being a loner who was more worried about school and work than fun. It didn't help that my grandma couldn't drive anymore and took up lots of my free time with her appointments and outings.

Or maybe that was just an excuse.

Because after Birdie got married, Mara, a famous

romance author and the self-proclaimed eternally single woman, fell in love.

She got engaged.

And now she was six months from getting married.

And me?

You guessed it.

Still. Single.

Still a virgin.

I'd never had a boyfriend in high school, and I'd been too busy working in college to ever make time for a guy. At least that's what I told myself. But the truth was, the guys I met in person just weren't interested in me like that. And online dating at my size? I'd rather help my mom weed her massive garden or... be single for the rest of my life.

Before I knew it, they'd be printing my face on the back of a set of Old Maid cards.

Mara held up a deep-green dress that pinched in around the waist and flowed to the ground. She smiled at the gown, making her brown eyes crinkle at the corners. "What do you think about this one? It would look beautiful on all your body types and skin tones."

Birdie laughed. "I love it. It might actually make me look like I have a waist."

I laughed with her. Even though we'd all been friends for two and a half years now, I was still getting used to the way she and Mara so easily accepted themselves. I hoped I'd get there someday.

While Birdie was what my gran described as "apple shaped," I was built like a brick shit house. (That's what my grandpa used to call it, before he passed a few years back.) Square and strong enough to throw down on the football field with my brothers and bigger than half the guys I came into contact with.

This dress would look pretty on me, but I wished it had straps to hold up the girls. They did not play well with a lack of support. "Do you think we can get straps added?" I asked.

Mara nodded. "I bet Jonas's tailor could sew some on. She does incredible work." She winked.

I laughed. That boy did fill out a suit better than most. "Then let's get it," I said. It wouldn't really matter which one we got, at the end of the day. I would feel uncomfortable in my body whether I was wearing sweat-pants, business casual, or a beautiful dress worth hundreds of dollars.

Mara left, taking the dress to the saleswoman, prob-ably to order enough for all of us bridesmaids. In just a few months, Birdie and I would be standing beside Mara on her big day, along with her future sister-in-law, Tess.

Tess's wedding, just shy of a year ago at Emerson Trails, had been so beautiful that Jonas and Mara had taken the first opening the park had available when she wasn't writing for TV in Atlanta. Bonus that it was during Birdie's summer break from school, and I had enough PTO saved up to take a few days off for the event.

My phone rang, and I pulled it from my purse seeing my boss's name on the screen. Stepping away from Birdie and Tess, I answered the call. "Hey, Janessa," I said. "How are you doing?"

"Great! I just wanted to let you know that the head contractor's plane just landed, and he'll be at the building in an hour to get his keys."

"I'll be there," I promised. Even though it was a

Saturday. Even though I was supposed to be dress shopping. Even though I'd been looking forward to a late afternoon dinner at Waldo's Diner with my friends. I couldn't afford to lose this job.

I put my phone in my purse, and Birdie touched my arm, her wide blue eyes on me. "You have to go to work?"

I pouted. "Yeah, I have to get this contractor some keys. I'm not sure how long it'll take. I might have to miss dinner."

She shook her head, her blond curls bouncing. "We'll wait for you."

"You sure?" I asked, looking to Mara, who was busy chatting with the dress salesperson. Of the three of us, she was easily the most extroverted. "I feel guilty, like I'm already failing my bridesmaid's duties."

"Don't worry about it. She'll understand. And you call us when you get done, okay?"

"You'll fill her in?" I asked.

Birdie smiled. "Of course."

I left Vestido and went to my car in the parking lot. It was cheap and in regular need of repairs, but my dad had taught me enough about cars that I didn't often have to spend money on a mechanic, which helped me tuck away that much more. With my new promotion, I was less than a year away from my savings goal. After that, I had no idea what I would do.

As I drove away from the store, I tried to imagine what life would look like when I finally had the savings I wanted after eight years of scrimping and living with my parents. I'd probably keep my job—I loved managing an apartment building and giving tenants good care and a safe place to live. There were so many shady rental companies out there, and luckily, I didn't work for one of them.

They'd hired me as a move-out cleaner back when I was in community college, getting a business degree. When a manager spot opened, I applied, and they promoted me. Now that the company was developing a completely new apartment building, they'd given me a raise to liaise with the head contractor on the build, and I'd eventually manage the new complex.

It was exciting.

Even if it was a little inconvenient today.

But this would be my first time working with a construction company, my first time having a hand in something from the ground up. I couldn't wait to see how it came to be. (And the extra pay wasn't bad either.)

I reached Blue Bird Apartments and unlocked the main office. The building was fairly old, but I'd spiced up the office and its whitewashed wood paneled walls with lots of plants and some artwork from my mother's studio. She worked at Brentwood University, teaching art classes to college students.

My favorite piece she'd created for me was a colorful chicken in my namesake. *Hen*rietta. It was kind of an inside joke at this point, and my family's entire home was decorated in chicken décor, from our kitschy salt and pepper shakers to the metal napkin holder shaped like a rooster.

At least we'd been able to talk Dad out of putting a weathervane on top of our suburban home.

Since I was already at the office, I worked on printing off some new unit applications, as we had a few coming available soon.

The bell rang over the door, and I stood up to greet the head contractor. Unfortunately, this wasn't him. This guy couldn't have been more than thirty, and he had thick black tattoos swirling down one of his tan arms. Part of me wondered how much his tattoo covered under his tight white T-shirt and jogger sweatpants, but I quickly shut down that thought. He did *not* look like the kind of guy in charge of a multi-million-dollar operation, and I had a diner to get to.

"Sorry," I said. "The office isn't open right now."

"You're here, aren't you?" he replied, the slightest hint of a southern drawl in his voice.

I raised my eyebrows, so not in the mood for sass from a walk-in on a Saturday afternoon.

"Janessa told me to come this way to get my keys?" he said.

My eyes widened. "Janessa?" She was my boss stationed in the corporate office in LA and didn't work with regular tenants... *Shit.* "You're the head contractor?"

"That's me. Tyler Griffen."

"Henrietta Jones. But everyone calls me Hen."

He extended his hand for me to shake.

My cheeks felt hot as I slipped my hand into his. It was large and warm and calloused. So freaking hot. Not to mention his grip was just the right firmness. "Sorry," I said, turning and looking for a key in the lock box as I tried to calm my thoughts. "I thought you were someone else."

When I turned back to him, he had an amused look on his chiseled face. Now that I looked a little closer, I could tell he worked outside. His white skin had a deep tan, like he spent a lot of time in the sun, and his strong jaw had a light cover of stubble. Not to mention, there were flecks of paint on his hands as he reached for the key. Interesting. This head contractor wasn't just a stand-by-and-tell-everyone-what-to-do kind of guy. He must have been highly involved in the work. And that made me even more interested than the tattoos or his defined biceps.

I tilted my gaze down as I realized I was ogling. Clearing my throat, I tucked my relaxed hair behind my ear and said, "Why don't you let me show you around the unit?"

"That would be great," he replied with a crooked smile. "Thanks, Hen."

God, the way my name sounded off his lips. "Is that a Texas accent I hear?" I asked as we pushed out the door and stepped outside.

He chuckled. "It's that obvious? I'm from the Fort Worth area."

"It's subtle," I replied. Cute, I didn't add. "I thought you Texans weren't fans of California."

He laughed. "You can get us to come here from time to time—if the price is right."

I smiled, stopping in front of Unit C. "This is the building you'll be in. There's a laundromat downstairs with a few coin-operated washers and dryers. Your apartment's on the third floor, so we have a bit of a climb. But it is nice and quiet up there, and you have an amazing view of the park from the balcony off your living room."

Usually people weren't so happy about all the stairs, but he rubbed his hands together and said, "Can't wait to see it."

As we hoofed it up the flights, him with ease and me

trying not to breathe hard and embarrass myself, I wondered why he was staying here at all. He had to be making hundreds of thousands of dollars a year, and this place definitely wasn't the best he could afford. But I'd already been rude enough for one day, so I didn't pry.

We reached unit 303, and I said, "This is it. Why don't you test the keys?"

He leaned forward, slipping the key into the lock and turning. It opened easily, and he walked in, examining the two-bedroom unit. "It's nice," he said, setting down his duffel bag beside the couch.

He was full of surprises. "I keep trying to talk corporate into replacing the carpets," I admitted, "but they've been freshly cleaned by a great local company. Most units aren't furnished, but they gave me a small budget and I personally picked out some pieces for you so you'll be comfortable while you're here. If you get situated and realize you don't have something you need, give me a call. I'll make sure to get it for you right away."

He turned from his examination of the apartment and laid his eyes on me. They were captivating, a mix of green and gold and brown that I'm sure my mother would have loved to paint. "That's real nice of you, Hen."

God, could he stop saying my name so my heart would slow down?

"Of course," I said, straightening my blouse. I found myself lost without something to do with my hands. "I'll let you get settled in."

I turned to leave his apartment, but he said, "Wait up."

Standing in the hallway, I faced him again. "Did I miss something?"

"Your number," he said with a smooth smile. My heart skipped a beat, and I was about to say something stupid before he added, "In case I need anything?"

"Oh, right." Of course he wanted my number for business, not for any other reason. I reached into my purse hanging from my shoulder. I always kept some business cards with my cell number written on the back, just in case. "This is the office number, but you can use my cell on the back if I'm not in there. My office hours are eight to five, Monday through Friday."

"Great. And we're meeting at the building site Monday at four," he confirmed.

I nodded. "That's Pacific time. In case your phone isn't set to change time zones automatically."

"Good thinking," he said, and damn, why did that compliment have my cheeks all flushed? Good thing my dark skin hid things like that. I could always tell when my white friends were embarrassed just by the color of their cheeks.

"Well, I'll let you get settled in," I said again, turning and walking away.

"See you Monday," he replied.

I walked down the stairs, trying my damnedest not to trip. That was the last thing I needed to do, embarrass myself yet again in front of this person I'd be working so closely with for the next several months. I needed this experience to go off without a hitch. If all went well, Janessa had already hinted I could be traveling around the country, managing new builds for Blue Bird, Inc. *Me*, with my little associate degree that everyone said would never be enough.

I bit my lip, worried if I'd made a good impression.

I'd been a little harsh at first. And there was no time like the present to make things better.

On the second landing, I turned myself around and marched back up the stairs, knocking on Tyler Griffen's door.

2

TYLER

I was about to sit down in front of the TV when a knock sounded on my door. After a long flight to yet another place where I knew no one, I'd planned to order takeout, zone out with a show I'd seen a million times before, and fall asleep. But when I opened the door and saw Hen there, my mind went crazy, just like when I'd first seen her moments ago.

She had these sharp eyes that cut straight to the point like she did with her words. Her relaxed, raven toned hair curled past her shoulders and drew my attention down to luscious curves and legs that went on for miles. I knew I couldn't date her—I never dated anyone when I was on location. It would be unprofessional, not to mention futile with me leaving once the project was done—but damn was she something to look at.

"Is there something I forgot?" I asked.

"I was wondering..." She hesitated, chewing on her lip, and I had to force myself to look away from her mouth "Have you eaten yet? I would feel bad leaving you here and not showing you around a little bit. There are a few fast food places nearby, a Chinese place I love down the road, and if you're missing home, I think there's a Texas Roadhouse a few blocks past that."

I let out a laugh. Cute and funny. "Texas Roadhouse has nothing on my dad's grill."

Her laugh was contagious but quiet, like she didn't want to take up too much space. "So, what do you say?"

I wanted to... But I didn't want to give her the wrong impression either. "No better plans on a Saturday afternoon?"

"I was actually on my way to supper with my friends. You can join if you want?"

Relief loosened my shoulders. She wasn't coming on to me—she was helping me feel less lonely. Something I really appreciated, especially in a new town. "If you're sure it's not any trouble..."

"Of course not. It'd be good to get to know each other a bit since we'll be working so closely together." She added, "But it is just a diner. Nothing fancy."

"If it's good enough for you, it's good enough for me," I said, reaching for my duffel bag. "Mind if I change?" She had looked so pretty in her flowy sundress, and I didn't want to look like a schlub in front of her and her friends. Because for some reason... it mattered. She was right. If we'd be working together, it would be good to start things off on the right foot. And if there was one thing I learned from my sister, Liv, it was that if you didn't pass the girlfriend test, you wouldn't be making much progress with the kind of girl that mattered.

"Do you want to ride with me," she asked, "or should I send you the address?"

"A ride would be nice," I said, selfishly wanting more time to talk to her. "I'll be down in a sec."

I couldn't wipe the smile from my face as I threw on the jeans and a fresh shirt. I wanted to get to know her better—for work.

I jogged down the stairs, the memory of her hips as she walked up distracting me. Those hips had looked so fine swaying side to side. I tried to remind myself I shouldn't be thinking of her that way and found her in the parking lot next to the kind of car my mom would call a puddle jumper. She opened her own door and said, "It's unlocked."

I grinned. "You know my dad would have my head for not getting your door."

"Your secret's safe with me, Tex." She shook her head with a small smile and got in, and me? I was grinning like a damn fool. It had been a long time since I'd bantered with a woman I wasn't related to.

When I opened the door and got in, I was immediately surrounded by her perfume. It was like a mix of spring bluebonnets and sugar cookies, and it took all I had not to breathe in deeply.

"The lever's under the seat," she said. "If you want to scoot your chair back."

I'd been so distracted by her fragrance that I hadn't even noticed my knees bumping against the dash.

"Where is it if I don't want to scoot it back?" I teased.

"Ha ha," she said, backing out of the parking spot.

I reached down to the lever, giving myself a little more room. My siblings and I got our height from my dad, who'd hit six-four at fourteen years old. I was six-three, and each of my brothers stood over six feet tall. My sister was taller than most girls at five-nine. I guessed her and Hen at about the same height.

When I chanced a glance around Hen's car, I noticed how nice it looked on the inside. Even though it was an older model, there wasn't a stain or rip in the interior to be seen, nor a crumb in any crevice.

Catching my examination, she said, "I'm saving for a house. A new car's pretty low on the list."

"It's nice," I said, but all I could think was how ridiculous it was that the woman who was "single handedly running this place," according to the Blue Bird corporate office, couldn't afford a newer car along with a decent home of her own. But then again, California real estate was a beast, from what my brother Gage told me. And coming from a billionaire real estate mogul, that was saying something.

She paused at the stop sign before the main road.

"Let me text the girls." She tapped on her phone with its cracked screen for a moment and then set it face up in the console. Interesting. She either wanted me to see a text from some other guy or... she had nothing to hide. As she pulled onto the highway, she said, "It's probably a good thing you came along so we can get to know each other. We'll be spending a lot of time together on this project."

"I'm looking forward to it," I said honestly. "I want to hear about this house you're saving for."

She turned onto the road, quiet for a moment. "I don't need anything fancy..." She took a breath. "But I'm hoping for something big enough that I can stay in for a lot of years to come. Three beds, two baths, a nice backyard but not too big. Of course, it has to have a nice front porch to sit on with my girlfriends. And a garage to hold my tools."

"Tools?"

She nodded. "I'm not the kind to sit by the phone and wait for someone to help."

Damn was that hot. Especially in the way she said it—not bragging, only stating the facts.

"What about you?" she asked. "Do you have a home base, or is it apartments and hotels all the time?"

I shifted, leaning my shoulder against the door so I could face her more. "I have a house back home, but I've had renters in it for the last five years. Don't really have much need for one with all the traveling."

"What's after this?" she asked.

"I've got some ideas."

She raised her eyebrows. "Yeah?"

"I always thought I'd be settled by now, starting a family. It's hard to do when you're moving all the time."

"Hard to do when you're staying in the same place—at least for me."

I was about to ask what she meant, how a catch like her could possibly still be single if a relationship was what she wanted, but instead, she turned into the parking lot of a chrome diner building.

"This is it," she said.

I looked at the sign, taking in the retro design.

Waldo's Diner.

For the first time, California reminded me of home.

Back in my hometown of Cottonwood Falls, this was the kind of place where old men would grab morning coffee and sit and talk about cattle prices for hours. I got out of the car, seeing couples and families through the large windows.

She reached for the door, but I stepped ahead and held it for her. At her questioning look, I said, "Making up for last time. A man never lets a lady open the door."

"Who says I'm a lady?" she teased. Her soft, raspy voice made my pulse quicken.

Steeling myself, I said, "No one needed to."

With a small smile, she stepped through the door and into the aisle that went down the diner between the barstools and booths. Even though we'd just come in, a group of women and one older man waved at her from the other end of the diner, smiles on their faces and a few assessing gazes sent my way.

I straightened my shoulders, mentally preparing myself to meet new people. I used to be shy as a kid, and it had taken a lot of practice to get comfortable meeting and working with strangers.

The first woman to slide down the circular booth to make room for us had light skin with dark brown hair and even darker eyes. "Hen, introduce us to your friend." A ring sparkled on her finger as she waved at me.

Hen got into the booth next to her and corrected, "This is my *colleague*, Tyler Griffen."

Ignoring the confounding sting of her correction, I extended my hand to her friend. "Nice to meet you."

She shook it, an impish grin on her face. "I *adore* your accent."

I chuckled. "That obvious?"

She nodded, then gestured at a curvy blonde next to her. "This is our friend Birdie," then she pointed at a thin woman with black hair, olive skin, and a large smile. "My sister-in-law, Tess." I shook their hands.

Then the man at the other end of the booth extended his weathered hand. "I'm Chester. This one's grandpa." He pointed at Birdie.

"Pleasure, sir," I said, shaking his pale weathered hand, spotted with freckles.

He nodded, then grinned at the girls. "Good handshake. I like him."

They laughed, and when all was said and done, I got into the chair next to Henrietta. Everything was going well, until I was enveloped by her scent. Intoxicated was more like it. And damn was it hard to think with her thick thigh brushing up against mine.

Between ordering our food, her friends asked me all the regular questions. Where are you from, how many siblings do you have, what is your job like, and then I got the surprising question from Mara.

"Are you single?" she asked.

Henrietta said, "*Mara*, that's private."

"It's okay," I said, taking a sip from my sweet tea. "Haven't found the one yet. Still looking." I inadvertently glanced toward Hen, who was looking anywhere but at me.

Birdie smiled and said, "You'll find her when you least expect it."

Chester nodded. "And then you'll never be able to let her go."

"Maybe someday," I replied, thinking that was years down the road, when I could afford to stay in Cottonwood Falls and invest in my dream.

Our food came out, and a waitress named Betty set

our dishes in front of us, along with all the condiments we could wish for. "I'll refill your drinks," she said. "Let me know if you need anything else."

The service was great, and then when I took a bite of the burger, I knew I'd be frequenting Waldo's Diner while I was in town. "This place is amazing. I mean the service is great, and the food... Tastes like home."

Birdie and Chester smiled at each other, and Chester said, "I'll be sure to tell the owner."

Mara and Tess laughed, and I asked, "What am I missing?"

Henrietta gestured toward Chester. "He's being humble. He owns the place. But it would be our favorite either way."

Chester blushed as much as an old man could and batted his hand at the women. "I'm just good at quality testing the coffee."

"Well, I'm going to get good at testing the burgers," I replied, taking another bite.

Out of the corner of my eye, I saw Mara mouth to Hen, *I like him.*

I focused on my food, desperately hoping this dinner hadn't gone amiss and I hadn't sent Hen the wrong signal. Best not to mix business with pleasure, no matter how beautiful and curvy that pleasure was.

3

HENRIETTA

Confession: My grandma is just as invested in my happily ever after as I am.

THE MORE I got to know Tyler throughout dinner, the more I liked him. He had a tight-knit family like mine. The same number of siblings, except he had one sister and two brothers instead of three brothers like me. He was second born, where I was the second youngest. Since his family's farm wasn't big enough to support him once he grew up, he learned a trade and worked his way up in Crenshaw Construction until they trusted him enough to lead major projects around the country.

But he didn't brag. On the contrary, he acted like it was no big deal and asked questions of each of my friends. In fact, watching the way he blended in intrigued me that much more. He didn't act like a boss—he acted like a friend. And I wondered how that would change on the job.

He walked with Chester to the register, insisting he pay for each of our meals, while the girls and I finished up our drinks.

Mara nudged my side and said, "Hen, you have to get on that!"

My cheeks were just as hot as Tyler's backside. "He's working with my company."

"And?" Birdie demanded. "You're both still answering to your boss, so technically it wouldn't be a huge conflict of interest."

"Maybe a tiny one then?" I deadpanned. Because even though I *maybe* had a crush on Tyler, there was no way a guy like him would ever want a twenty-eight-year-old plus-sized virgin like me. And did I mention I still lived with my parents? Not exactly a great look, especially to a guy like that.

Tess glanced toward him and Chester. "He's a great guy. I mean if I wasn't married with a baby... I'd be getting his number."

Birdie gave her a coy look. "Or building a weak chair for him to sit on."

We all laughed at the joke of how Tess met her husband while she rolled her eyes at us.

Mara shook her head. "I think you need to keep your eyes, and your legs, open."

"Oh hush," I said, swatting her hand. "I'm giving him a ride home. Which is where I *work*. I will see you all Wednesday for breakfast."

They waved goodbye, and I walked toward the register just in time to hear Tyler and Chester talking about the build for the second Blue Bird apartment complex. Chester shook Tyler's hand again and gave me a hug before we left.

Tyler and I walked to my car, and he stopped on his side, looking at me over the roof. "That was great, Hen. Thanks for letting me crash dinner."

I nodded, all my friends' thoughts echoing in my head. "I had fun," I admitted, getting in the car. And my friends were right. He was cute. From the strong edges of his stubbled jaw to the ridge of his nose and the fullness of his lips that revealed a breathtaking smile. And God, the way my name sounded with his accent. If I moved to the South, I'd be in trouble. Pining for men just for the way they spoke.

But Tyler would be my coworker, and I knew better than to chase men who would only break my heart.

I focused on driving, at least until he said, "I feel like I didn't learn much about you at dinner."

"What do you want to know?" I asked cautiously. I had to be careful—revealing too much could be a liability, especially as a woman in the workforce. I'd seen my sister-in-law get shoved out of her job after announcing her pregnancy. Not to mention my younger brother's fiancée constantly got called 'emotional' since her line of work was heavily male populated.

"Did you always want to be in property management?" Tyler asked, drawing me out of my thoughts.

The question seemed innocent enough, minus the way he watched me. It was like he wanted to genuinely hear my answer. And with his eyes on me, it was hard putting two words together. "Not really," I admitted. "I went to college after high school and got my associate degree in business, but I had to work full-time to pay for everything. Once I got a full-time job I liked, it seemed silly to spend all that money to go back."

He nodded. "So you like this line of work?"

"I do," I admitted. When he was quiet, I felt like I had to fill the silence. "Home has always been a special place for me. Somewhere I could go back to after a hard day and always feel safe, loved. Helping other people create that kind of place... it's the dream."

When I glanced his way, there was a small smile on his lips. "I'm excited to build that with you. Especially knowing you'll be the one in charge of the new building."

I couldn't help the grin that spread on my face. Getting this promotion—it was a huge affirmation for me. It meant I'd been right to follow my gut and stop after an associate degree. It meant that my work mattered and was valued by the people I served. And it meant I'd finally be able to reach my savings goal that had always seemed so far away.

Maybe I'd even find someone to share it with.

Someday.

The apartment building came into view, and I parked along the curb closest to his unit. Instead of immediately getting out, he smiled over at me. Not a forced smile, but a real one that took all the air out of the car.

"Thank you for letting me crash your dinner," he said.

I smiled. "Around here, we call it supper."

His laugh was infectious. "Supper," he corrected. "Let's do it again sometime?"

With a silent nod, he opened his car door and got out, then bent down to look at me again. "See you Monday."

I waved, pressing my lips together so I wouldn't squeal. As soon as I got out of the parking lot, I started a group call with Mara and Birdie. But I ended it before I hit send. How juvenile did I look, getting all giddy because a guy I worked with mentioned the potentiality of having supper together again.

I needed to remember who I was—his plus-sized tomboy virgin coworker with less of a chance of hooking up with Tyler Griffen than the Brentwood Badgers had of playing in the finals this year.

With a sigh, I continued toward home.

My family lived on the line between Emerson and Seaton in a smaller ranch-style house with a big backyard. But with so many of us living there, Dad had converted the garage into an extra bedroom, keeping all of our tools in the shop out back.

The light blue house came into view, and I parked under the carport next to Dad's old Buick. That thing had seen more years than I had, but it ran like a dream. No way would he leave it completely exposed to the elements.

When I got out, I noticed a car I didn't recognize along the curb. "Great," I muttered, hoping with all my heart this wasn't another setup. But when I got inside, my fears were confirmed.

A guy around my age, with short coiled hair sat at the table with my mom and grandma while my dad cooked at the stove. He had the distinct look of someone who didn't know exactly how they'd gotten there, but also didn't know how to leave.

At the creak of our front door, all eyes landed on me, and my grandma waved me over. She stood behind her latest attempt at Prince Charming, rubbing his shoulders like a boxer about to go into the ring. "Henrietta, dear, look who I met at the grocery store today! His name is Deshawn, he works at a bank, and he has a *401k*!"

When he waved at me, she pointed at his ringless finger.

Oh dear lord.

Dad gave me a look over Grandma's shoulder that said, *be good*. This wasn't the first time Grandma had brought a respectable stranger over to sweep me off my feet, and it wouldn't be the last. But we all put up with it because she was such a romantic, and well, arguing with her was about as useful as gassing a car in park.

"Hi, Deshawn," I said, hanging my purse up and wishing for the millionth time that I had my own home with my own key and multiple locks. "Which bank?"

"First Bank of Emerson."

"Free cash bags—that's a nice perk," I said. It really did help not to carry around a paper envelope stuffed to the brim with bills.

He nodded, and I took him in. He looked like the kid in school who only showed up so his parents wouldn't pull his keys. With his white sleeves rolled up and half his shirt untucked, he'd clearly been in the mood to relax when Grandma caught him.

She patted his leg. "Tell her about your car. She likes cars."

"My car?" He looked confused. "It's, uh... five years old."

"What kind of engine?" Dad asked.

"Um... gas?"

It took all I had not to snicker at the pained look on Dad's face.

"It's a V4," I said, taking pity on this stranger.

Deshawn gave me an impressed look. "How did you know that?"

"That model brags about good gas mileage. Wouldn't make sense to have any higher." I went to the fridge and got a hard, fruity seltzer, then opened it on Dad's novelty bottle opener before sitting at the table. "That gets, what? Twenty-eight in the city? Thirty-four highway?"

Suddenly Deshawn seemed a lot more interested and a lot less trapped. "Thirty-five..."

Dad and I nodded at each other, and Mom waved her hand, annoyed with us both.

Grandma said, "Enough about cars. Tell me, Deshawn. How many children do you want to have?"

4

TYLER

When my alarm went off Monday morning, I scrubbed my face and got out of bed to hit the apartment gym. I'd checked it out the day before, and it wasn't much. Just a treadmill, an exercise bike, and a rack of dumbbells, but I could make that work. After growing up on a ranch where I had to do chores upon waking, working out seemed the closest thing now. It steadied my nerves and gave me a sense of purpose until it was time to start my workday.

An hour of exercise circuits later, I went back to my place, checking for Hen's car in the parking lot. The instant hit of disappointment I felt at not seeing it there surprised me. Why was I looking forward to seeing her so much?

Blue Bird corporate was meeting Crenshaw Construction leaders at the job site for a groundbreaking ceremony and photo opportunity before the real work began tomorrow.

I showered off the workout and then went to my dresser to retrieve my Crenshaw Construction shirt and a pair of khaki pants. I wouldn't wear this set for an actual day of work, but CC's publicist preferred I wore this outfit for public events.

My phone rang, and I scanned the caller ID. James Crenshaw, my boss and owner of Crenshaw Construction. "Hi, Jim," I said. "Y'all downstairs?"

"Yessir," he replied. "You about ready, or do you need some more beauty work done to that face of yours?"

I snorted. "I'm good, but I could give you a few pointers."

He let out a mix between a grunt and a chuckle. "See you in a few."

I grabbed my wallet from my bedside table and shoved it in my pocket with my phone before jogging downstairs where a black car was waiting. The driver held open the back door for me, which still made me uncomfortable, and I slid in next to Jim. He wore a suit that probably cost more than my first truck, and his salt and pepper hair was combed over to the side.

I shook his extended hand. "Good to see you, sir."

"Same, but I have to say, son, I don't understand your insistence on the cheap accommodations. I pay you enough to stay in a five-star hotel, and you choose a one-bed apartment?"

I followed his eyes, trying to understand why the gray building wasn't good enough. It wasn't the custom-built mansion he and his wife shared back in Dallas, not even close, but the property was well-kept and there were a few modest planter boxes around. "Good enough for a few months," I finally said.

As the driver pulled out of the parking lot, Jim asked,

"How are you feeling about the build? Ready to meet the new crew?"

Subcontracting out crews in new locations brought on its own challenges, but I'd discovered a method to make things go more smoothly. "Pizza for lunch and beer after hours always does the trick," I said.

"I've taught you well. Keep it up and you'll be taking over once I retire."

"Retire?" I said.

"When you get to being my age, you think about resting once in a while... And you think about who's going to take over your legacy when you're gone, especially when you don't have any children."

"Jim, I couldn't possibly——"

"Nothing's official. Just the musings of an old man."

I studied him a little closer as he looked out the window. Jim was getting older—well into his sixties with a thinning head of gray hair and plenty of wrinkles and sunspots. I'd only worked closely with him the last four years, but his age was beginning to show. Was he really hinting that I could be the one to take over? I'd thought I'd grown as much as I could in his company, but now? The possibilities were endless.

"It's exciting, isn't it?" Jim said as we pulled up to a vacant lot sporting a giant sign with a mock-up of the building that said FUTURE HOME OF BLUE BIRD LUXURY APARTMENTS.

I nodded in agreement. There was always a buzz that came with groundbreaking. It was full of potential, but if I was being honest, I felt more at home in the day to day of making the project run smoothly than I did in the planning stage or at photo ops.

The driver stopped the car, and while he got Jim's door, I let myself out, taking in the small group of people. A few news vans lined the property, along with sleek cars like the one we'd arrived in. And then there was Henrietta's red car. The sight of it, so different from the rest, brought a smile to my face, and I began scanning the crowd of suits for her.

I spotted her immediately, the sunlight glancing off her dark hair. The blue dress she wore clung to her curves, and I found myself wishing I could be just as close. She was clearly in her element, talking freely with her colleagues, a stunning smile on her face.

Jim put his hand on my shoulder, jerking me away from the thoughts I shouldn't have had. "Ah, there she is. Let me introduce you to the woman you need to meet." He began walking toward Henrietta, but then stopped short and said, "Tyler, this is Janessa Vogul. She's head of operations of Blue Bird's properties in southern California."

I caught Henrietta looking at me for a moment, but then I heard Janessa say, "Pleased to meet you, Tyler." Her smile fell perfectly in place like she'd practiced it a hundred times before. But the expression didn't meet her green eyes—they were just as calculating, assessing as her smile. I felt like a piece of meat being examined at the butcher shop.

Thanking my lucky stars that Henrietta would be working more closely with me instead of Janessa, I said, "Nice to meet you, Mrs. Vogul."

"Ms.," she corrected with a wink. "And you can call me Janessa."

Jim clapped my shoulder. "Janessa, you'll have to

excuse me. I see our publicist. I need a chat with her before we get called for photos."

"That's okay. I'll keep Tyler company," she said.

Jim chuckled, but I wished he would have brought me with him. Instead, Janessa stood just a little too close, like a shark who smelled blood in the water.

"How did we get so lucky to work with you?" she asked, folding her white arms over her chest, like she wanted me to look there.

An uncomfortable chuckle escaped my throat. "I believe Mr. Crenshaw met with the CEO," I said.

She forced a laugh. "I trust you moved in alright. I know it gets lonely, traveling so much for work. I'd love to give you a little company after this. Perhaps get some dinner together? Or a nightcap?"

I raised my eyebrows, shocked at how quickly this woman worked and wishing Jim would come back and save me. I didn't think I could handle dinner, much less an evening with someone who clearly had more than business on her mind. "Ms. Vogul, that's a kind offer, but I'm sorry I have to decline for the sake of professionalism."

She gave me an amused grin. The first expression she made that seemed natural. "Hard to get? I can appreciate that. Let the games begin."

Jim and our publicist, Nancy Finnagan, saved me the challenge of replying. Nancy called out and said, "Can we get the C-suite and property manager in hard hats?"

I hurried away from Janessa, fearing she might be the kind to slap my behind on the way out, and in my hurry, bumped into Henrietta. She swayed in her heels, and I reached to catch her, my hands landing on her curvy hips.

But the feel of her under my palms caught me off guard. She was soft, but solid. And my mind went places it shouldn't have gone in public. "I'm so sorry," I said, quickly righting her and pulling my hands away.

She wouldn't meet my eyes and muttered something about it being okay before grabbing a hat from Nancy.

Great.

Two days in and I'd already made things awkward by practically fondling her on the job site. I'd apologize to her later, maybe with lunch, and hope it would patch things up.

"Over here, Tyler," Nancy said.

I nodded, going to stand beside Jim in the middle of the empty lot. It was mostly mowed weeds and grass underfoot, but soon it would be dirt, a foundation, framing, a building, a home. I couldn't wait to see the transition.

With our hard hats on, Nancy lined us up and began passing out shovels to signify the groundbreaking. Janessa squeezed in next to me, and I had to suppress a cringe. Thank god LA was an hour away, probably more with traffic. Otherwise, I had a feeling she'd be one to make frequent pop-ins.

A professional photographer began snapping photos while the news stations got their shots and filmed B-roll. And then it was time for my least favorite part of any new project—live interviews. I always felt so uncomfortable, preferring hands-on work to talking about work.

But here I was, standing next to a man in a suit with a microphone in his hand. "This is Tim Dugan from Channel Five News, and I'm here with Tyler Griffen, the head contractor on this apartment complex. Tyler, can you tell us a little about the environmental and community outlooks for this project?"

In the background, I heard Henrietta talking with another reporter, and even though I wished I could listen to her, I spoke into the microphone. Time to focus on work.

5

HENRIETTA

Confession: I hate standing next to skinny girls.

EVEN WHEN TYLER was out of sight, I could *feel* his presence. He had a way that drew people to him, commanded attention. Including the attention of my boss. She was as high-strung and confident as they came, and my chest ached when I saw her speaking with Tyler. What little chance I may have had with him was long gone. Not that him feeling the girth of my body during his rescue hadn't sealed my hopeless fate.

When we bumped into each other and he'd reached out to catch me, his large hands had landed on my hips, steadying me. His touch had sucked all the air from my lungs, and I'd stared at him, stunned at his strength. But I could see the moment he realized just how big I was. His eyes had clouded over, and he stepped away, immediately apologizing.

I tried to walk away from him as quickly as possible because I just couldn't handle seeing the rejection. But adding insult to injury, we all had to stand in line for photos. Me right next to all of the thin, attractive executives at Blue Bird corporate. All the men were slimmer than me. Even Tyler's aging boss.

And even though they could have been thinking about the weather, I worried they were silently judging me. Most people thought being fat was a moral failing—a lack of willpower against fatty foods. But I'd been fat my whole life, even though half our food came from Mom's massive backyard garden. I was just a big girl. Always had been, always would be.

My friends would kill me if they knew that I was speaking about myself in this way. Mara and Birdie were so much more confident than me, but it was easy for them to be that way. They both had landed men that were obsessed with them. Me on the other hand? My grandma was still trying to set me up at twenty-eight years old, and I'd yet to have a serious adult relationship.

And I knew my grandma's heart was in a good place. She was just trying to get me the same kind of love that she and Grandpa had experienced. But when I walked into the house and she had some guy there, I could see it the instant they laid their eyes on me. What little hope they'd had for a random blind date was quickly replaced with disappointment.

It hurt every time. I tried to keep my mind off of it all as I focused on the television interviews. The corporate publicist gave me talking points, and I'd spent the week memorizing them. But soon, it was time for me to get back to the office.

I didn't bother telling Tyler goodbye before I began walking toward the parking lot with Janessa. She had her hard hat under her arm and a slight grin on her face. "That contractor's something to look at. I'm a little jealous you get to see him every day."

I didn't argue with her because Tyler was handsome in every single way. In fact, I'd never really been that into guys in polo shirts, but the Crenshaw Construction shirt hugged his biceps perfectly, and the collar dipped down to his chest where I could see just the slightest hint of chest hair. For a split second, I wondered what it would be like to feel the crisp curls underneath my fingertips, but I quickly shut down that thought. "He's all yours," I said.

Janessa shook her head. "It's against company policy to have romantic relations with contractors while they're employed by us."

"Oh?" I hadn't even realized that.

She nodded, stopping by her car. "The shareholders wouldn't be happy if they thought we only hired someone because of a romantic relationship. Do you remember Frances?"

"Frannie?" I asked. "I kind of thought we weren't allowed to talk about her anymore." I couldn't remember exactly why she'd been let go from her position managing a complex further south in California, only that it hadn't been on good terms.

Janessa nodded. "She hooked up with a window cleaner, and they had to let her go."

I cringed. How had I been so reckless to think about dating Tyler? I needed this job.

"Her mistake was getting caught," Janessa added with a wink.

I shook my head at her. "It'll be all business around here," I said. "Besides, I don't really foresee him needing a lot from me."

Janessa nodded, opening the door of her car. "Any of the big problems should go up to corporate, but I think you'll be fine with the day to day here."

"See you around," I replied, going to my car. Emotion clogged my throat as I drove back to work. Even though I had been really happy to earn this promotion and a little bit of extra income, I was already wishing this project could be over. Tyler's clear disinterest had only reminded me of my failure in the romance department.

Maybe when I finally had enough money to afford my own place, I would just have a big ol' chicken coop in the backyard and help my nephews and nieces sell eggs. It sounded nice, if not a bit sad. Because if I was being honest, I wanted a man to look at me the adoring way that Cohen looked at Birdie or the proud way Jonas looked at Mara.

Before Mara fell for Jonas, she used to say, "Some people just don't get happily ever after, at least not in the traditional sense."

And I was starting to think she was right. I was twenty-eight, after all. Shouldn't I have kissed a few frogs by now if I were on the way to a prince?

It was depressing. So I spent the rest of the day at the office trying to avoid those thoughts by doing my normal daily tasks, from offering tours, handling leases, emptying the change in the laundry machines, and so on.

At the end of my shift, I called Tyler while locking up the office. It rang once before I saw his pickup pull into the parking lot. There was a twinge in my chest as I saw him open the heavy black door and step out. Instead of khakis, he was wearing jeans smudged with dirt and a dark blue T-shirt that clung to his muscled chest and arms. With that tattoo peeking out...I almost forgot to hang up the phone.

Not to mention the Griffen Farms hat that was on his head made him look younger, more relaxed. I much preferred this look on him to the khakis and polo from earlier.

"Hey," he said with a smile that outshone the California sun.

I made myself busy tucking my keys in my purse to hide my own smile. "How was the first day on the site?"

"It was great," he said. "We always start off a little slow to get the guys used to working with a new crew. I always bring in plenty of pizza for a long lunch and have a beer at the end of the day—in the parking lot, of course."

"Clever." If I was being honest, I completely appreciated the taste of a beer at the end of a long day's work. My dad and brothers had made sure of it. "You'd win me over pretty fast with beer and pizza," I admitted.

"Well, I don't have any plans for supper, and I can always go for a second beer," he said.

"Nice use of supper. You're catching on," I teased, but then my mind immediately went to what Janessa had said about dating Tyler being off limits. I needed to be more professional. Not that I had to worry. I remembered the way he looked at me earlier. A romantic relationship was never in a million years going to happen between us. This was work and friendship only.

I was so lost in my thoughts I missed his reply, so I

said, "Supper sounds good, but we don't have to do pizza and beer again. If you don't want to."

"Dealer's choice," he replied with a grin. "But I should probably get showered first. Do you want to wait in my apartment?"

"Oh," I said, "no. I can just wait in my car."

He looked around. "It's nearly ninety degrees outside. The air conditioning in my unit is pretty nice. And it doesn't cost you your gas."

At this point, arguing would just make me seem rude, especially since he knew my car AC was on the fritz from the night before. So I followed him up the steps to his apartment. It looked almost the same as it had a couple days ago. But I noticed there were several books and magazines spread out on his coffee table.

"Are you a reader?" I asked, slightly impressed. My mom had to pay my brothers to get their reading done in high school. Literally. Each book report earned them five dollars, and they never made more than twenty in a year.

"From time to time." He gestured at the table. "Feel free to look through them. I don't have anything weird in there."

I laughed. "I hadn't really been worried until you mentioned it, but then again, having brothers should have prepared me for anything."

Chuckling, he said, "There are some things we never grow out of." Tipping his head toward the bathroom, he added, "Should take me about ten, fifteen minutes."

I nodded and sat on the couch I'd picked out myself. It was just as comfortable as I remembered. Add that to a good book and the smell of his cologne that was lingering in the apartment already... Well, it was a great way to pass a quarter of an hour. I reached forward, thumbing through the books and magazines, seeing titles about retirement living bed and breakfasts and interior design. I picked up the first one that caught my eye, *The Homiest Bed and Breakfasts in North America.*

I flipped to the first page and stared in awe at beautiful photography of a bed and breakfast in Montana. It looked like a giant white farmhouse with a chicken coop and a garden with rows of leafy green vegetables out back. With the sun setting over the scene, it looked like heaven on earth.

A block of text flowed beside the picture of the owners. They hadn't been able to have children of their own. So instead, they turned their big home into a bed and breakfast and renovated it over the years to become a great place for guests to stay. They said it was their way of building a family. My heart melted for the ways two people could make a home.

A cute colonial home in Georgia covered the next page. It was magnificent, with giant pillars and vines creeping up the sides of the building. This one had lots of planned activities for the guests, from drives around the Georgia countryside to classes on classic southern cooking. I pictured myself there, running an inn like that, and smiled. It would be idealistic to go along and see their joy at a new experience.

That was one of my favorite parts about working for the apartment company. Getting to see how proud people were of their apartments when they moved in for the first time and knowing I had a part in that... Incredible.

Curious about Tyler's other interests, I set the book down and picked up the one about retirement living. The title, *How Seniors Can Thrive in Community Living*, stared back at me from the cover, alongside a group of women sitting around a table, playing cards.

Why would Tyler have this? His parents couldn't possibly be old enough to need this. But as I opened the book, it opened to a page with a light-yellow sticky note. This section talked about how gardening could be really good for older people. Helping something grow, having regular responsibilities, and enjoying the fruits of their work positively impacted mental health in multiple studies.

My heart ached for the people who didn't have that. I would never let my grandma go to a nursing home, not when she could stay with us. She deserved more than reruns of fifty-year-old TV shows on full volume and six o'clock bedtimes.

The bedroom door opened, and I looked back to see Tyler running a towel through his wet hair. With his arms lifted, his shirt pulled up, showing a sliver of his abs and a trail of hair into his waistband that practically had me salivating.

"That's a good one," he said.

My brain short-circuited. "What?"

He nodded toward my hands. *The book!*

I stood, setting it back on his coffee table. "What got you interested in senior living? Doesn't seem like a normal topic of interest for a construction worker."

There was a laugh in his eyes as he said, "What type of things do you think construction workers are interested in?"

"Oh, I don't know," I teased. "Beer and pizza?"

Laughing, he opened the door for me so we could leave his apartment. "Can I let you in on a secret?" He seemed to sober at the end, like there wasn't another joke or small talk coming next.

"Sure," I replied, making sure to let him go down the stairs first this time.

He glanced back up at me as he easily took the stairs. "My grandpa moved into senior apartments, and he's having a really hard time with it."

"What do you mean?" I asked.

"Well, you remember me mentioning I grew up outside of Fort Worth?"

"Yeah," I said.

"It's a really small town, and there isn't much for older people there. At a certain age, their homes are too much to take care of, but even assisted living is a little too much. Most people put their relatives in homes in Fort Worth or Dallas and have to drive a long way to see them or they keep them at home with them. But it makes it kind of hard for the family. I know it's been hard on my mom as my grandpa got to that age."

I nodded as we reached the bottom steps and went outside.

"I keep thinking there has to be something to make the assisted living where he is better, so I've been doing some research to pitch to the building's owners."

I couldn't quite find something to say because, honestly, I was breathless. Most men didn't really give two cares about what happened to their grandparents, or their parents for that matter, but here Tyler was reading research books on his time off to make a better home for his grandpa and everyone else. It was incredible.

He held up his keys and said, "Mind if I drive?"

Looking at his pickup compared to my rickety red car, I grinned. "Of course not."

6

TYLER

Henrietta put directions into her phone and told me we were going to an Italian place. It had been a long time since I'd been to a nicer restaurant, usually opting to have food delivered, so I was excited. But to be fair, I was more excited for her company than anything.

Being on the road all the time got lonely. Most of the guys I worked with had families, lives, and not a lot of time to hang out with someone who'd be leaving in a few months. But conversation flowed easily between Hen and me, and I never felt her coming on to me like Janessa had earlier. Even when I went home, it felt like everyone was pressuring me to couple up.

Back in Cottonwood Falls, most people thought marriage and family were the biggest success you could have. So the fact that I was over thirty without so much as a divorce or an illegitimate child under my belt made me the number one bachelor in town, aside from my brothers. The youngest, Rhett, was a perpetual playboy, and my older brother cared more about his Dallas-based business than dating.

And me? I had my job. I could hardly imagine a serious relationship with how much I traveled, and if I was promoted to Jim's position, I'd have more work than free time.

Henrietta pointed at a restaurant with twinkle lights under an awning. "That's it."

I looked at the red sign with swirling white letters spelling La Belle.

Hen said, "Don't ask for pizza or the waiters will laugh at you."

I chuckled. "Thanks for the warning."

We pulled alongside the building, and I gave my keys to the valet driver. As I got out and met her on the sidewalk, she said, "The food really is amazing here. I think you'll like it."

"As long as they serve beer on draft, I'm not too picky," I admitted.

"Not a wine guy?" she asked.

I pulled the hat off as we walked into the building. "I do drink wine from time to time. Just don't tell my dad."

We fell into line behind other parties waiting to talk with the hostess.

"I'm guessing he's a real meat and potatoes kind of guy?"

"Oh yeah. If the food doesn't come off his grill, it's already at a disadvantage."

"My dad's the same way," she replied. I noticed the way her eyes crinkled around the corners when she talked about her family. "Mom's been trying to sneak spinach into his meals for years."

"Does it work?" I asked.

She laughed. "About as well as an engine without gas."

A server led the group ahead of us toward the dining area, and the hostess gave me a warm smile from behind her podium covered in ivy. "Are you waiting on someone?" she asked.

Confused, I glanced toward Henrietta, confirming she was standing beside me. Her eyes were focused on the floor, so I answered, "It's us two."

The hostess let out a surprised, "Oh," but quickly wiped the look from her face. "Follow me." She reached for a pair of menus and silverware rolled in a black napkin.

When we were alone at the table, I asked Hen, "What was that about?"

She kept her eyes on her menu. "She didn't believe that someone like you would be here with someone like me."

I nearly choked on my spit. "What? That's crazy."

Henrietta gave me a look with a tinge of annoyance. "Guys like you don't exactly go out with girls like me. Especially not to a fancy place like this."

I studied her for a moment in utter disbelief, wondering what Henrietta had seen. What would make her think that a guy like me wouldn't be interested in her? I knew plenty of guys who liked their girls with curves— myself included.

Any guy, or woman for that matter, should be able to see that Henrietta was a catch. She smelled amazing, had a sexy swell of breasts under her blouse that gave just a peek at her cleavage. And the curve of her hips underneath her pencil skirt was practically kryptonite. Most of all, I liked her smile. It transformed her whole face, lighting it up completely.

"Maybe she smoked some dope before her shift," I said. That was the only explanation.

Henrietta burst out laughing, and the sound was music to my ears. "Dope?" she said with another laugh. "No one calls it that anymore."

"I do." I lifted my menu, glad to see her smile, and said, "What's good here?"

"Everything," she replied honestly. "And be sure to save enough room for the tiramisu after *supper*. It is to die for."

"Good looking out." I flicked my gaze to the drink menu, seeing a decent selection. "Do you want to share a bottle of wine?"

She raised her eyebrows at me. "Wine? What if your dad finds out?"

I shot her a smile. "I usually prefer reds, but we can get whatever you'd like. Perhaps champagne to celebrate our first official day working together?"

She smiled. "I'm fine with either one. I don't really drink much at all unless I'm out at the bar with my friends. One of my friends married the owner so we get free drinks."

"Well, that's the best kind of friend to have," I said.

Henrietta nodded. "That and my dad has a refrigerator full of beer in our garage for after we're finished with projects. But if I had my choice, it would be Cupcake wine."

"Cupcake wine it is," I agreed, just in time for the waiter to come by and get our orders. As he walked away, his notepad full of our choices, I asked, "What kind of projects?"

"Anything, really," she said. "One year we restored an old car. Another year, we built an entire raised garden bed for my mom so she didn't have to stoop so low anymore. And the year after that, we were restoring some of Grandpa's old furniture. You never know what kind of wild-hare idea Dad's going to get. Anything to do with his hands, he'll learn how to do it and be amazing at it."

This woman in front of me was so intriguing. The thought of her restoring a car when I'd only ever seen her in dresses made me want to know even more. "What's been your favorite project?" I asked.

"I think the furniture," she said. "For a while, I would pick up furniture along the road and restore it and then sell it online to make some extra cash. When I was in college it was kind of a nice side hustle."

"You don't do it anymore?" I asked.

She looked thoughtful, like she'd almost forgotten she worked with furniture. "No, I think I just got busy with work and family and let it go. But I should start looking for projects again."

I nodded. "Then what about the garden? What does your mom like to grow?"

"A *lot* of tomatoes." Hen chuckled. "She's always giving away tomato sauce because she says it goes great with just about everything. But my personal favorite is her bed of tulips. She keeps them each year in every color and makes the prettiest little bouquets for our table."

An image of Hen with her nose nestled in tulip petals warmed me in a way I didn't quite understand. And I didn't have time to think about it either, because the server walked up to our table, holding two glasses and a cooler of wine.

We watched as he popped the bottle, and when he poured Hen's glass, she said a sweet, "Thank you."

I thanked him too and took a sip. I stared from the cup to her. "Oh my gosh, this is really good."

Her laugh was contagious. "Why do you sound so surprised?"

"With a name like Cupcake?"

"Fair," she said. Then her mouth dropped, and she slumped low in her chair, lifting a hand to cover the side of her face. "Please don't see me."

"What?" I asked, looking around.

Her eyes darted around, a battle raging internally that I could only see a piece of. Finally, she whispered, "That guy that just walked in. My grandma tried to set me up with him a couple of nights ago."

I did a double take, realizing she'd been talking about the couple who'd just walked inside. The guy was handsome enough, with dark skin and the kind of girl the hostess probably expected me to be with on his arm.

"Did he see me?" Henrietta whispered.

I cringed the moment I saw him noticing. "Yeah."

She sat up, her expression grim. "This is so embarrassing."

I was about to ask for the backstory when the guy walked over with his date and said, "Hey, Henrietta." He glanced at me and said, "Looks like your grandma found someone else to set you up with after all."

God, I already hated this guy. And his date seemed just as stuck up.

Hen opened her mouth, probably to correct him, but

I hurried up and said, "Actually, I saw her walking by my work and couldn't let her go without taking her on a date. We've been together about a month now. Although, I don't know how you let a chance with her go." I winked, extending my hand. "Tyler."

"Deshawn." He gripped my hand harder than necessary. No doubt trying to prove dominance. That and the way his eyes were calculating me had the hairs on the back of my neck rising. He was jealous, but only because another guy was interested. It pissed me right off. He had no right to be jealous, especially since he'd turned her down once and then made a joke at her expense. Not to mention he was here with a different girl.

He glanced from Henrietta to me again, completely forgetting about his date. "Your grandma hadn't mentioned anyone else." Then he mumbled, "Not exactly normal conversation in the produce aisle."

Hen smiled at his date, who was growing progressively more stink-eyed. "Sorry, we're being really rude. Deshawn met my grandma at the grocery store the other day. She's getting older, so she forgot I was involved. Hope you two have a good dinner."

Deshawn's date didn't even reply, instead giving Henrietta another annoyed look, and said to Deshawn, "Let's go sit down."

The second they turned around, I could see the air deflate from Henrietta.

Part of me wanted to look away and deny the sadness in her deep brown eyes. I'd only known her two days, and it fucking sucked seeing this strong, beautiful woman brought down by a man who would hardly give her a second look and a woman who clearly thought appearance was the only thing that mattered.

I gave her a second to gather herself, and then I said, "I hope you don't mind me stepping in."

"Not at all," she deadpanned, taking another drink of her wine.

I waited for more info, then finally I couldn't hold myself back. "So what was this about your grandma and the grocery store?"

She gave me a pained look. "I don't know if your family's this way, but mine is bound and determined to keep me from becoming an old maid. It's not working out."

"Old maid?" I laughed. "You're what? Twenty-six?"

"Twenty-eight," she replied, "but I think they can feel my biological clock ticking. Every time my grandma goes to the grocery store, she comes back with some guy she thinks is going to be my happily ever after."

"Just any stranger?" I asked, thinking my mom could probably take notes from her grandma. She'd been trying to set me up with every single mom who had a child in her fifth-grade classroom.

"Oh no," Hen said, taking another drink. "Grandma gets his credentials first, of course. She only brings home people with a 401k and decent employment of more than two years." She shook her head, an amused look in her eyes.

"What's the rush?" I asked, refilling her glass of wine. I expected that kind of push in small-town Texas but not here, just an hour from LA, where people were getting married and having kids later and later in life.

Our server came back, bringing plates full of buttery,

herbaceous food. My mouth watered before I even unrolled my silverware.

As we began eating, Hen said, "My grandma and grandpa had the best marriage ever. They were so close, and I know she just wants me to find something like that. But every time she brings someone by..." She shook her head and continued swirling spaghetti around her fork.

"What?" I asked.

She let out a heavy breath, setting her fork down. "I can see the look in their eyes when they realize who I am." She swallowed hard, looking down at the table again to hide the moisture shining in her eyes.

It took all I had not to get up and walk to Deshawn's table, just across the room, and shake him. What was wrong with these guys that they couldn't see what was right in front of them?

Without thinking, I reached across the table, covered her hand with mine, a strange sense of protection rushing through me. Maybe it was because my sister was full-figured, maybe it was the wine, but I needed her to know she deserved better.

"Do me a favor?" I asked.

She tilted her head in question.

"Don't let those guys make you feel bad about yourself." Her eyes flickered toward our joined hands and then toward me.

She nodded, and it took all I had to pull my hand away.

7

HENRIETTA

Confession: I'm not used to accepting help.

THE WALDO'S Diner sign appeared in my windshield, and relief swept through me as I pulled into a spot next to Birdie's car. I needed to talk to my friends, to get their help sorting through the jumbled mess of my thoughts. The run-in with Deshawn the other day and what Tyler had said to me had my mind spinning the rest of the night and into the day. Maybe it was just my lack of any male interaction for the last few years, but I could have sworn I saw something in his eyes...

Shaking off the thought, I turned off my car and walked into the diner. Chester wasn't in yet, but Mara and Birdie both sat at our usual booth. When they saw me, they got up to hug me, and my favorite waitress, Betty, promptly put a mug of coffee in front of me.

"Extra cream, just like you like," she said.

I grinned at her. "That's why you're the best."

She smiled back. "I put a ticket in for the usual. Should be ready to go soon."

"Thanks," I replied.

Mara wasted no time getting to the point. She leaned forward and said, "*Please*, tell us something salacious has happened with the Texan."

My cheeks warmed, but I teased, "Are you looking for more material for your next romance novel?"

She batted her hand. "I'm already fifty percent done with the story. All I need is a good dark moment."

Birdie laughed, "Of course, you have to torture the characters now.

"Right." Mara nodded, taking a sip of her coffee. "They have to suffer a little before their happily ever after. But stop deflecting. He's had to have taken you up to his apartment by now. Right? Maybe flirted a little?"

My mouth fell open. "How did you know that?"

She had a smug grin as she shrugged. "It's a talent. So what did he say?"

I bit my lip, hoping I didn't sound too juvenile. "We went to dinner together last night to celebrate his first day on the job. And he had me wait in his apartment while he showered." At the excited look in Mara's eyes, I added, "*Alone.*"

She pouted, and Birdie said, "You can learn a lot about a guy from his apartment."

"He hasn't been there long enough to have any skeletons in the closet, but he did have an interesting selection of books. He says that he wants to open a senior living apartment in his hometown someday.

Birdie seemed impressed. "That's admirable."

"It is," I agreed, trying to keep the swoon out of my voice.

"Tell us about the dinner," Mara said, a twinkle in her eyes. "Anything happen?"

"Yeah, one of the guys my grandma tried to set me up with walked in with a very hot mean girl on his arm. I'm sure Tyler was wishing that she would have been there with him instead of me."

Mara scrunched up her face. "Why on earth would he want to be with a mean girl when he was sitting across from you?"

I didn't want to say the obvious, so I only said, "The whole encounter was super awkward, and I wish I could have disappeared into the booth."

Birdie asked, "How did Tyler handle it?"

I wrapped my hands around my mug, holding on to it as I searched for the right words. "He rescued me."

With a smile, Mara said, "This is the part I was hoping for."

I shook my head at her. "I think he took pity on me— he pretended to be my boyfriend and made the guy totally jealous in front of his date. He was really sweet about it after too. There was a moment..." I paused, my throat catching with emotion. Tyler had seemed so sincere, and my hopes were getting far too high. But this was the part I needed help sorting through, so I continued.

"He put his hand on mine and looked me in the eyes and said not to let them make me feel any less beautiful than I am. And it seemed like he really meant it."

Both of my friends covered their hearts with their

hands and made *aww* sounds like he was some kind of sweet puppy dog.

"He felt sorry for me, right?" I said.

Mara gave me a sad look. "Can I give you some advice?"

Trying to keep from crying, I teased, "I know it's coming anyway, so I don't know why you're asking."

Birdie chuckled as Mara continued. "Let him choose his intentions."

"What do you mean?" I asked.

"You're already assuming you know the 'why' behind what he did, but the truth is, Tyler's the only one who knows."

Her words settled over me for a moment, and I realized she was right. I had already pegged him as just another hot guy who would never be interested in a plus-sized girl like me. What if he had other reasons for doing what he'd done?

Betty saved me from replying by bringing three plates full of pancakes, eggs, and bacon. The three of us dug into our breakfast, eating our way through the food and moving on to other subjects. Birdie told us about their plans for her stepson, Ollie's, senior year, and Mara shared about the condo she and Jonas were buying in Atlanta for when she had to go there for work.

Catching up with them over comfort food really was a great way to start the morning.

With our food and drinks mostly gone, we all waved goodbye and left the diner. As I got in the car, I realized my mind had settled somewhat. Stewing over the "why" behind Tyler's actions had driven me crazy. Mara's advice gave me permission to simply... enjoy.

I drove toward the job site since I was supposed to check in every day and see if they have all that they needed or if I could get them anything. Janessa had told me that there would be errands to run and communication between Crenshaw and Blue Bird to handle. I was excited to start this new part of my job... when a thump sounded underneath my car and it started pulling to the right.

I groaned as I gently tapped the brakes and pulled onto the shoulder of the highway. That couldn't have been good. Cars rushed by me as I got out and walked around my car, trying to determine what damage there was. And then I found the culprit. I must have hit a rock or something with my tire because it was already completely flat.

I tilted my head back, letting out a frustrated grunt toward the sky. I didn't have time for this, nor did I have the desire to be late on my very first day checking in on the build site. I was *not* dressed for changing a tire, but I had to get to work at a decent time.

I opened the trunk, trying to ignore the fact that I'd worn my best formfitting green dress and knowing that it would probably be completely ruined by the time I got to the job site. I lifted the storage flap and got out the tire iron, jack, and my spare tire. Thankfully Dad had made me practice changing a tire before I ever got behind the wheel.

I quickly had the lug nuts loosened and the car jacked up. I positioned the tire iron over the lug nuts to take off the punctured tire. Gravel crunched under slowing tire treads on the shoulder, and I looked up to wave them off. I was no damsel in distress.

But the sight of Tyler's pickup and his concerned face through the windshield had me freezing. Now I was really embarrassed. I straightened, wiping gravel off my knees and pulling my dress down.

He hopped out of his truck, his work boots crunching dirt beneath him. My eyes trailed from his boots up his muscular, denim-clad legs, over his green Crenshaw Construction T-shirt, and to the concern in his hazy eyes. "Flat tire?" he asked.

I folded my arms across my chest and nodded. "Bad timing also."

"Can I help you change it? I'd hate to see you ruin that pretty dress."

He thought my dress was pretty? I bit back a smile. "I can handle it. I wouldn't want us both being late to work."

He glanced at his watch. "If we work on it together, I bet we can get there on time."

Everything in me screamed that I needed to be independent. That I didn't want him to see me as any more of a charity case than he probably already did. But then Mara's words came to mind. *Let him choose his intentions.* "If you're sure," I finally said.

His grin was crooked as he stepped closer to me, taking the tire iron. "My dad would whoop me upside the head if I didn't stop to help." He glanced toward all the cars on the road. "I'm surprised someone hasn't already."

"That's not the way out here," I said.

"It should be," he replied simply and quickly spun the tire iron on the nuts. I watched as he easily removed the tire and reached for the donut. I passed it to him, watching his muscles move as he slid it over the bolts.

He tightened the lug nuts in a star pattern, just like my dad taught me. Then he lowered the jack, setting the car firmly on the ground. Tyler knew what he was doing; that much was clear. And if I was being honest, watching his muscles do the job was more than a little attractive.

He finished the bolts, making sure they were secure, and said, "You should be good to go."

"Thanks," I said, taking the jack and the tire iron.

"No problem." He picked up the wounded tire. "Do you want me to take this to get it patched?"

I shook my head. "My brother works at a dealership, and he always gets our tires fixed free."

Tyler nodded, bringing my tire to the back of my car. Once it was in place, he closed the flap over it and shut the trunk. With the job done and us standing on the side of the highway, cars whizzing by, I had no idea what to say. I was used to being alone, used to taking care of myself, but him stopping and helping, inconveniencing himself, I didn't know how to react, how to let him know that it meant the world to me.

So I only said, "Thank you," and moved toward the driver's side of my car. But he reached out, touching my hand to stop me. Just that simple touch sent a jolt of electricity up my arm.

His eyes were warm on mine as he said, "If you ever get in trouble like that again, you can call me."

I was about to tell him I had it handled, but he added, "Can I have your phone?"

"Why?" I asked, completely confused.

"So you can call me next time you're stopped on the side of the road."

My heart quickened. This was a fantasy—someone

like Tyler demanding he cared for me. It couldn't be true. But he extended his hand, waiting like there was no world in which he wouldn't get exactly what he wanted.

And maybe it was what I wanted too, so I reached into my purse, which was still around my shoulders, and handed my phone to him. When he returned it, his name was saved in my contacts with a hammer beside the letters.

Chuckling, I said, "I like the emoji."

He winked. "Just in case there are any other Tylers in your life."

"You're the only one," I said without thinking, and at the dimming in his eyes, I was worried I said too much.

He cleared his throat. "We better go or you'll be late."

A fraction of the light in his eyes returned as he said, almost to himself, "I think I was right on time."

8

TYLER

As I pulled onto the highway, I could not get the image of Henrietta bent in front of her car out of my mind. How the fuck had no one stopped to help her? Where I was from, if you saw a lady on the side of the road, you stopped. You helped. You made sure she didn't get so much as a finger dirty.

But the knees of her dress weren't the only dirty thing around here. I was having less than honorable images of her bent like that in front of me. My mind had me pulling up that dark green dress, seeing the fabric slide over her full thighs.

Someone honked at me, and I realized I'd almost drifted into the next lane. *Fuck*, I needed to focus. My hardening cock was already aching against my jeans, for a colleague I'd barely met. I shifted to give myself some relief and did my best to focus on the road and the job at hand.

We had a lot of work to do to get started pouring the foundation for the project. It would be a lot of moving pieces, and I needed to be at my best. Playing sports in high school had helped me learn how to zone out the crowd and focus on the task in front of me, so that's exactly what I did for the rest of the day. It was harder during lunch when I had less to distract me, and even more difficult on the drive back to the complex.

Was I a creep for hoping to see her car in the parking lot? Or better yet, alongside the road? Probably. If not a creep, then, at the very least, a moron. Nothing could happen between us, I reminded myself for the millionth time that day.

And still, I was more than a little disappointed when I noticed it was already gone. Hopefully she was getting her tire fixed and wouldn't be changing any more tires on the road.

After showering, I got out my tablet and called Mom like I always did on Wednesday nights. When we all lived in Cottonwood Falls, it was our family's tradition to get together Wednesday nights and have supper. Mom always made a delicious meal, and when it was nice outside, Dad grilled the meat to go with it.

On those nights, we'd sit around a table on the cement patio overlooking our family's pasture. I missed that when I was on the road. Especially now, in this apartment with a view of a family playing in the park between buildings. So when Mom's face surrounded by a mop of frizzy blond hair appeared on the screen, it was like a breath of fresh air. A breath of home.

"Hey hon, how you doing?" she asked, setting her phone on the windowsill and washing her hands in the sink.

"Just got settled in here. First couple days have gone well," I answered. "How's everything there?"

She turned the sink off and squinted at the camera, then my view flipped to the window. She showed Dad at the grill, Rhett at the patio table, and my sister, Liv, sitting across from him. My older brother, Gage, was nowhere to be seen. Since his falling out with Dad, he hadn't been around much. But we didn't speak about his absence because it broke Mom's heart.

The camera wobbled as she stepped outside, and I heard her announce, "Tyler's on the phone!"

"Hey, what's that grilling?" I asked.

She turned the camera on the grill, showing blackened steaks and foil packed with what I assumed were peppers and onions fresh from the garden.

"Now you're being mean," I said. I could feel my accent growing heavier the longer I talked to them.

Mom laughed, turning the camera back on her. "You know you can come home any time, right? We miss you like crazy."

"I miss you too," I admitted, that homesick feeling back full force.

She moved again, and I saw her sitting next to Liv. "How's California?" Mom asked. "Are you liking it out there?"

My mind drifted to my new colleague, the one who had occupied far too many of my thoughts as of late.

"That's a smile I see on your face. Did you meet someone?"

I swore my mom could read minds. I didn't want to answer, but my hesitation was all she needed to let out a joyous squeal. "Do you hear that, Liv? Tyler met someone out there!"

My sister waggled her eyebrows at me, and I heard Dad grumble something about California. Rhett added something offensive about bleach-blonde girls in bikinis, and I could hear his protest as my sister slugged him.

I laughed, despite the homesick feeling in my chest. I knew Jim was counting on someone like me to handle the business, but I didn't know how much longer I could stay away from home. Every time I came out on a job like this, I felt like something was missing. But there wasn't anything for me in Cottonwood Falls—not without me coming up with a lot of money. Because I would never ask my older brother for money no matter how much he had to spare or how quickly he'd give it. My pride wouldn't let me do that.

"So when do we get to meet her?" Mom asked.

"I don't date girls when I'm on location," I reminded her, "especially not ones I work with."

"You work with her!" Rhett said in the background. "You dirty dog."

I rolled my eyes. "I do. And even if I didn't, I don't think she's the kind who would move back to Texas with me, and there's no way I'd fit in out here. There was a girl on the side of the road this morning changing her tire, and no one even stopped to offer her help."

"Typical city folk," Dad grunted off-camera. "They're always in a rush. No time to help."

I could feel the rant coming on. Dad loved Cottonwood Falls almost as much as he loved his family, and he never understood why anyone would want to leave town, most of all his oldest two sons. "The job's going well," I said, cutting the rant short. "We got the foundation going today and everything seems to be on track. One of the guys invited me out for a beer Friday night so I think that should be a good time."

"Good deal," Dad said, back to his quiet self.

"How's everything at the school?" I asked Mom. She'd be starting her tenth year of teaching in just a couple weeks. She always said teaching was her second career, since she'd stayed at home until all us kids were in school and then went back to college to get her own degree.

"We got new books for the classroom, so that's good. Although I will miss one student showing me their book that has Tyler Griffen's signature along with a big butt drawn next to it, written in pen no less."

My ears heated at the memory. I'd been such a dumb kid, leaving stupid drawings in all the books. "Maybe I can finally live that down," I said.

She chuckled, and Dad said, "Dinner's ready."

Mom quickly said, "Remember to book your flights for Thanksgiving before prices go up on them."

"Already have one booked," I said. I didn't tell her that Gage had used his extra miles to get it for me.

She smiled. "Good. And hey, maybe buy an extra ticket for that girl."

Mom could dream. Because that's where thoughts like that belonged.

9

HENRIETTA

Confession: I've gone so long without a relationship that sometimes I have a hard time believing anyone would want to date me.

WHEN I CAME HOME from work on Thursday night and saw a different car in the driveway, I steeled myself for another one of Grandma's setups. I ran through the way I knew it would go—he'd see me, look disappointed, suffer through an awkward meal with my family, then he'd go home and I'd never have to see him again. (Hopefully.)

I'd been through it before, and I could do it again. And hey, maybe someday, I'd have a real boyfriend when I ran into one of these setups in the wild.

Just as I'd expected, I walked into the house to find another guy sitting at our kitchen table. Even sitting down, I could tell he was tall. He had broad shoulders, a solid chest, a short thick beard, and nearly black eyes that unapologetically studied my body. It was different. And to my surprise, it was nice to have someone so clearly appreciate me.

Grandma stood and walked behind him to pat his shoulder. "Henrietta, this is Houston."

He stood and shook my hand. His skin was a little darker than mine, and his hand was so large, it enveloped mine completely, and I was pleased to find out he was a good six inches taller than me. Just as tall as Tyler.

Shaking that last thought, I sat across the table from him. While Dad finished cooking, Mom asked him about his work. He said he supervised workers at a factory that made glass syringes. But as soon as he was done answering, he asked Mom about her garden. Talked to Dad about his work as a journeyman. Had Grandma telling stories about her first car.

He was checking all the boxes—tall, decently handsome, interested enough to ask my family about themselves, and he seemed to be listening to what they had to say. He even complimented my dad on the sautéed squash that we'd been eating from Mom's garden almost every day for the last month and a half.

And when he asked me about work, I told him about my job, steering clear of the hot new contractor who Janessa had forbid me from dating. Ever since he'd rescued me at La Belle, then helped me change my tire the day before, I couldn't stop thinking about him. The way his muscles had worked under his shirt as he made quick work of the job. The way he'd so easily stepped in to help without worrying about how it inconvenienced him. And most of all, the way he put his number in my phone. I pulled it up every few hours the last couple of days, just looking at the numbers, memorizing them, wondering if I would ever get the courage to do something with them.

I was so lost in my thoughts, I almost missed Houston speaking. "Henrietta?"

I looked up from my plate. "Sorry, yes?"

"Would you do me the honor of going on a date with me tomorrow night?"

My grandma was smiling bigger than I'd ever seen, and even my parents seemed pleased, even at how formal the request sounded to my ears. And to be honest, I didn't really have a reason to say no. He seemed decent enough. My grandma liked him. He was single. And, unfortunately, so was I.

So I said, "Okay."

While my mom worked on dishes, Grandma said I should walk Houston to his car. So I did.

The evening sun was hot on us as we walked down the sidewalk. It was a newer Hyundai. Nothing flashy, just... okay.

When we reached his car, he took my hand and said, "I'm glad I got off work early to stop by the pharmacy tonight."

I laughed. "I think my grandma's overjoyed as well. I know they're a lot, so it's okay if you don't want to follow through on the date. I can make up something about you being in an accident or getting transferred from work at the last minute."

His full lips quirked to the side. "Why would you say that? I want to go out with you."

Now it was my turn to be confused. None of the guys Grandma brought home actually wanted to go out with me. "Are you sure?"

He pulled me a little closer. "Your body is bangin', girl. Of course I want to take you out on the town."

Flustered didn't even begin to cover it. No one had ever told me that my body was "bangin'" or even acted like they wanted to show me off. The couple of boyfriends I'd had when I was younger only took me to dark movie theaters or secluded restaurants. It didn't take long to figure out that they were embarrassed to be seen with me.

"If you're sure," I said, smiling slightly.

"I am. I'll pick you up here tomorrow at eight."

That seemed a little late, but I figured he might need to catch up on work since he'd said he left early today. "I can meet you at the restaurant," I offered.

"I like my dates to ride with me."

I shrugged, not mad about saving on gas. "See you tomorrow."

"I'll be here." He kissed my hand, leaving a small wet spot behind.

I waited until he'd driven away to wipe it off.

When I came in the house, everyone stopped what they were doing to congratulate me. Grandma wrapped her arms around me and said, "I am so excited for you! What a charmer!"

Mom nodded. "Can I take you out to buy a new dress?"

Dad said. "Need something good to wear with that car."

I laughed at his last comment. "It wasn't anything special, Dad. I'd be more impressed by a..."

"A what?" Dad asked.

I realized I'd been about to say "a truck." More

specifically, a truck like the one Tyler drove. I'd only ridden in it once, but I liked the way it sat high off the ground and I could feel the power of the engine as we drove. But Tyler was off limits, and I had a perfectly decent guy coming to pick me up tomorrow night.

"You know what, Mom? I think I could use a new dress."

10

TYLER

I looked up from the paperwork on my desk to see Henrietta coming into the trailer/office we had set up at every job site.

"Hi there," she said with a smile. She stepped the rest of the way in, handing me a paper to-go cup. "Might not be beer, but coffee's pretty good too."

I smiled, thanking her as I took it. One sip and sugary, creamy liquid filled my mouth. I coughed at the surprising taste. "What is this?"

"A latte," she said, confused. "Do you not like lattes?"

At this moment, I had two choices. Lie and get lattes delivered the rest of the project or tell her the truth. "I'm sorry. I'm more of a black coffee kind of guy. I really appreciate this though. It was awful nice of you to think of me."

She chuckled. "Not that nice, considering I didn't ask your coffee order. I just can't believe it."

"Believe what?"

"That I've met my first person with horrible taste in

coffee," she teased.

I let out a surprised laugh. "If you need to fill it with sugar and cream, the coffee must not be very good."

"What kind do you like?" she asked.

I shrugged. "I'm not that picky. Whatever Chester had at the diner was good enough for me."

"Noted," she replied with a smile, then looked down at my desk. "Seems like you're swamped."

"Yeah, it's always heavy at the beginning of a project. Plus, one of the guys tripped yesterday and rolled his ankle. Had him get an X-ray done, so I need to fill out an incident report."

"Was it broken?" Hen asked, genuine concern in her look. "Should I get an ice machine on site for injuries?"

"That's not a bad idea," I said, frustrated I'd never thought of it. We had to use ice from the drink cooler yesterday.

She got out her phone, tapping on the screen. "I'll have one by the end of next week. What else can I help with?"

The way she'd buckled down and gotten to work the last few days was admirable. "It won't set you back at the other apartments?"

She shook her head. "I don't have an appointment for a tour until eleven, so I'm yours until then."

A strange silvery feeling filled my chest at those words, and I found myself searching for a reason to keep her around. I wanted to know her better, understand what this strange draw was all about.

"If you wanted to make copies for me, that would be a huge help," I said, even though I definitely could have made time to do them myself.

"Of course," she replied. "Let me know what needs copied."

I passed her a stack of papers to copy and then sort in the filing cabinets. (James Crenshaw was nothing if not old-fashioned.)

We both got to work, me filling out the lengthy incident report and her moving between the copier and the cabinets. For a while, we worked in tandem—well, she did. I couldn't seem to focus with her delicate, wildflower smell filling the trailer. So I gave up.

"Any plans for the weekend?" I asked, using one of the questions I'd practiced as a kid.

She paused, and I immediately regretted the intrusion.

"Sorry," I said. "It's none of my business." I focused on the report again, forcing myself to read each letter. *Cause of incident.*

"I have a date tonight," she said.

I looked up, finding her standing against the printer table. She nibbled on the side of her full bottom lip, and my eyes drifted from there to her wide brown eyes.

"Yeah?" My voice sounded rough, even to me.

She nodded. "Another one of my grandma's setups."

That fact made breathing only slightly easier. "Ah."

"Yep. But he seemed nice enough."

Even I knew she deserved more than "nice enough." But if I wasn't willing or able to give it to her, what more was there to say? "I hope you have a good time." Lies. Right through my clenched teeth.

"Thanks," she said. And then the sound of the copier resumed. But it had nothing on the thoughts raging in my head.

11

HENRIETTA

Confession: I had no idea how I'd react to this kind of guy until I encountered him in real life...

"YOU LOOK BEAUTIFUL," my mom said when I walked into the living room in my new shimmery green dress. I hadn't been sure about the way it showed off my cleavage and barely skimmed my knees, but Mom and Grandma both assured me I looked beautiful in the store.

Now, with my hair done up and my makeup on, I looked for my dad's approval. His lips stretched to a sweet smile, and he stood, taking me in a hug. "You look beautiful, baby girl. But please," he whispered in my hair, "wear a jacket with that dress."

I let out a laugh as I pulled back. "I'm not so little anymore."

"You'll always be my little girl," he supplied.

A knock sounded on the door, breaking up our moment. Grandma shot me a thumbs-up, and Mom shooed me toward the entrance. With my heart beating quickly, I opened the door to see Houston holding a gaudy bouquet to match the silver shirt he wore with the top showing off ungodly amounts of chest hair.

From behind me, Mom said, "We'll take those flowers and put them in a vase, honey. That was so kind of you, Houston."

I nodded, snapping out of my stupor as Mom reached past me for the flowers.

"Thank you, Houston," I said, his name sounding strange on my lips.

As Houston and I said goodbye, I realized I couldn't wait for the day when I had my own house and wouldn't have the whole family looking over my shoulder and peeking through the curtains at me.

Houston didn't seem to notice as we got to the car. He didn't open the door for me, which I realized I've been coming to expect after only a week with Tyler. And we weren't even dating.

I needed to get a grip. I couldn't date Tyler, and even if I could, he clearly couldn't care less that I was going on a date with someone else. In fact, he'd barely even looked up from his paper long enough to tell me "have fun."

No, I was here with Houston. He'd gone through the trouble of picking me up and bringing me flowers, and I needed to give him a real chance.

I got in, and the car smelled nice. It was clear Houston cared a lot about it by how clean it was. That, at least, was something we had in common.

He took me out to dinner at a steakhouse I hadn't been to before near his work. The food was good, and Houston kept the conversation going, talking about his job, the investment property he owned in eastern California, his family, and basically anything a person could want to know about him. I tried to give him some slack for talking so much because first dates can be awkward. And some people got chatty when they were nervous. But then his foot bumped mine under the table. And when I pulled my foot away, he moved his again so our ankles were touching.

I glanced up at him, wondering if he was having a spasm. Instead, there was a suggestive glint in his eyes.

Houston wasn't nervous at all.

He was playing footsie with me.

And that made me even more nervous. I thought footsie was something that only happened in movies. Yet, here I was, on a first date, with Houston's ankle rubbing against my leg.

Was this supposed to be hot?

Because I didn't feel turned on. In fact, I felt... his ankle on my leg. Just like the way he kissed my hand yesterday, there was no spark. No excitement like there had been when Tyler gripped my hand on the table.

Oh god.

Did I have a complex?

Was I only attracted to unavailable men?

I was mid-spiral when Houston asked, "Do you want to go get a drink? There's a bar I like near here."

And just to prove I wasn't pathetically attracted to a man I could never be romantically involved with, I took him up on the offer.

We drove to a bar nearby, the kind I'd only ever gone to with my brothers to play pool. Smoke made the air hazy, even though indoor smoking had been outlawed ages ago. A few pool tables lined the back area and a small dance floor, and an untouched jukebox that charged $5 per song cast colorful beams over the dimly lit area.

Houston walked up to the bar, and he ordered two rum and Cokes before I had a chance to order my usual mai tai. But I'd drunk Cuba libres before, so it wasn't the end of the world. He started a tab, and the bartender handed him two drinks that were more rum than Coke.

He brought them to a standing tabletop and said, "Let's dance."

I cringed, the drinks sounding good for the first time. "I really have two left feet," I said. The most words I'd said all night, really.

"You just have to follow me." He took my hand, swinging his hips as he pulled me toward the postage-stamp-size dance floor. Then he dragged my hand to his shoulder and made himself far too comfortable, gripping low on my hips.

My stomach churned. Someone braver would grab his hands and pull them back up to where they belonged. But he was bigger than me, stronger, and I didn't want to set him off. That was until he grinded his hips against mine, biting his bottom lip suggestively.

Did he really think I was going to be some cheap date? That he could buy me some flowers and hook up with me in a seedy bar?

I wanted to go home, but I didn't have my car, and the odds of him giving me a ride to anywhere but his bedroom were nonexistent.

"I have to pee," I blurted.

He chuckled low. "Eager for me to join you in the bathroom?"

The greedy way he studied me made me want to puke.

"I'll just be a few minutes," I said and hurried to the bathroom at the back of the bar. I slid the lock shut, and taking a few deep breaths, I had to plug my nose at the stench. It clearly hadn't been cleaned in a long time, and I doubted any amount of cleaner would even touch this smell regardless.

For good measure, I locked myself in a stall in case he decided to follow me, and then I quickly pulled up my messages to text my friends. Hopefully Mara or Birdie could come rescue me, and soon.

Henrietta: This date is horrible. He's getting really handsy, and I think he's going to try something. Can you come get me?

I sent a map pin to my location and then held my phone to my chest, praying they would get here soon. I thought about ordering a rideshare, but waiting outside this place at night seemed just as dangerous as spending more time with Houston.

If they didn't text me back in fifteen minutes, I'd suck it up and get an Uber. See what happened when I told him no. It wasn't like he could force me to do anything with all these people around. As strange as it sounded, as long as I was here, I would be okay.

When I walked out of the bathroom, I nearly bumped into Houston, who was standing in the hallway.

"Took you a while in there," he said.

What kind of a comment was that? "Takes girls a little longer," I muttered.

"But not with me." He winked.

When I realized what he was alluding to, I almost excused myself to go throw up. "Can you get me another drink?" I asked instead.

"Sure." He walked toward our table. "But you barely touched this one?"

Desperate to get some time away from him, I tried my hand at seduction, licking the plain rim. "I'm thirsty."

It must have worked, because his jaw went slack for a moment. He cleared his throat. "I'll get that for you."

As soon as his back was turned, I got out my phone. No new text messages.

Shit.

I quickly typed in my location for a rideshare, but we were farther away from my house than I thought. It would take at least thirty minutes for a ride to get here. That was too long. I needed to be gone five minutes ago.

I ordered it anyway, hoping I could stall long enough before he suggested we leave together.

He came back with the drink, holding it up. "Why don't you finish these and I'll take you back to my place?"

Shit. Think fast.

"Let's dance," I rushed out. "You—I mean, we were having so much fun doing that." I just had to suffer through, what, five songs? I could do anything for five songs.

"Anything for my sexy girl."

Barf.

He led me to the dance floor, his hands resting even lower on my butt, and began grinding his hips into me. My eyes widened in shock, because I could feel him growing hard.

"Do you feel that, baby?" he said. "You turn me on so much."

My instincts took over, and I shoved him as hard as I could. "Get away from me," I snapped. But he might as well have been a brick wall for all the effect my efforts had.

He chuckled. "Playing hard to get?"

I closed my eyes, wishing I could be anywhere but here when I felt his body pull away from me. I snapped my gaze up, wondering why he would give me space for the first time all night.

And then I saw him. *Tyler.*

He had Houston pushed up against a wall, his hands clenched into Houston's silvery shirt. Even though Houston outweighed Tyler by at least fifty pounds, he cowered away from him.

Tyler jerked his hands and growled, "If you touch her again, you'll die."

Terror was clear in Houston's eyes as he held up his hands and said, "I don't want her anyway."

Tyler shook his head, a vein in his neck throbbing. "Get the hell out of here."

He watched Houston stumble away, out of the bar past everyone who acted like this was just another night.

And then Tyler turned his eyes on me.

12

TYLER

White-hot rage slowly dissipated from my body as I turned to face Henrietta. The sight of that bastard with his hands all over her—I could have fucking killed him. It took all I had to let him leave the bar, sprinting away like the worthless son of a bitch he was.

My hands were still shaking as I approached her, my eyes running up and down her body for any hint of injury. I palmed her shoulders, taking an inventory of her face, her eyes. "Are you okay?" I asked, terrified she'd been hurt in some way before I got here.

She nodded slowly, as if she wasn't quite sure. "How did you know to come?"

Had he drugged her? I searched her eyes, but they seemed clear, as usual. "You texted me."

She shook her head. "I—I meant to text my friends for a ride." She left me, going to her purse at the table and looking through her phone. A stricken look crossed her face. "God, Tyler I'm so sorry. I didn't mean to ruin your evening."

Ruin my evening? She'd been assaulted and she was worried about my Friday night? "Do you remember what I said earlier? If you ever need anything, that means a tire change, a rescue driver, a fucking pack of gum, you call me, okay?"

She nodded slowly again, and then her lips trembled. "I'm just so glad you came," she said, her voice cracking on the last word.

Without thinking, I took her in my arms, holding her as she shook with tears or adrenaline or maybe a mixture of both. I didn't know. I just knew that I wanted to keep her close. Keep her safe. She deserved so much better than this.

When her tears slowed, I asked, "Do you want me to take you home?"

"Not like this," she said, wiping tears from her cheeks. "My mom and grandma were so excited for me to go on this date. And I don't want to disappoint them."

The fact that she was thinking about everyone else at a time like this just showed how selfless she really was. I got pissed all over again at this guy who hadn't seen what he had right in front of him.

"Where do you want to go?" I asked. "I'll take you wherever you want to go."

She pushed her lips thoughtfully to the side. "I have an idea."

I walked her to my truck, keeping my arm around her shoulders to make me feel better about her safety. At least that's what I told myself. Not that it felt good to have her tucked under my arm, her warmth against my side.

I opened the door for her and held her hand as she

got inside. Once she was securely in, I grabbed the belt and reached around her to buckle her in.

She started to protest, but I paused. "Let me have this," I breathed. "I need to know you're safe."

She nodded. The belt latched in place, and I let my hands linger for a second. Fuck, seeing her like that, shoving that guy away and the laugh on that sick fuck's face... it had broken something in me.

I pulled my hand away and walked to my side of the truck, my eyes scanning the parking lot for any type of danger. Seeing none, I got in and locked the door.

She looked over at me, a frown pulling at her lips. "You must think I'm pathetic."

"Why would I think that?" I asked, genuinely confused. I thought a lot of things about this girl—more than I should—and none of them included the word pathetic.

"You're always rescuing me."

"What's pathetic is how much I want to," I admitted. Then I cleared my throat. "Where's this place you want to go?"

She tapped an address into my phone. Collie's Bar. It wasn't too far away from the apartments and only about twenty minutes from here. We drove in silence until we reached a building with a glowing green sign with a black and white border collie.

The brightly lit parking lot immediately made me feel less sketchy than that seedy back-alley bar.

I parked and walked to her side, opening the door for her. Although I didn't have my arm around her this time, I walked close to her, determined to help her feel safe.

As we reached the door, she warned, "It's going to be a little loud in here."

I grinned. "How old do you think I am?"

She pretended to think on it. "Fifty?"

I rolled my eyes. "Minus twenty." I pulled the door open for her, and we stepped inside. I gazed around at the big wooden dance floor that had couples swinging about. The bar along the back wall was busy with customers, and barstools lined the dance floor like they were waiting for people to take a break from dancing.

"I'm impressed," she said, tilting her chin up to speak closer to my ear. "Only thirty and in charge of an entire build."

I didn't like to brag, but I gave her what I felt comfortable saying. "I worked hard to get here."

"I believe it," she said.

We reached the bar, and I waited for her order before asking for a beer for myself. I reached into my back pocket to pay for our drinks, but the bartender said, "Henrietta and her friends don't pay here."

The guy turned away to make the drinks, and I gave her a questioning look." Do you have a secret life I don't know about?"

She laughed, the sound music to my ears. "One of my best friend's husbands owns the place." She looked around. "He might be here, actually."

"Oh, nice," I said, glad that I was wearing decent clothes. When I'd gotten Henrietta's text, I hadn't even thought, just got up from my seat in the movie theater and ran.

For some reason, what Hen's friends thought... it mattered to me.

"There he is," she said.

She passed a glass full of beer to me, then held her mai tai and led me down the bar toward silver saloon doors. Standing near the end of the bar was an older guy in a dark green Collie's shirt. He was fit, but his mostly brown hair was sprinkled with some silver streaks, especially around the temples.

He was talking to another employee in a green shirt but paused when he saw us, giving Hen a warm smile and me a calculating look.

Henrietta was definitely well-loved and protected, when her friends were around.

"Cohen," Henrietta said, "this is my coworker, Tyler. Tyler, this is my best friend's husband and the owner of this bar."

He reached out to shake my hand and gave me an assessing smile. "I'm assuming you're here for a work meeting."

I couldn't help but feel like I was taking my first girlfriend to prom and her dad was telling me to keep my hands to myself. I forced a chuckle and took a deep swig of my beer. I needed to calm all the rage that was still in my body. It was making me jumpy. If I ever came across that guy in a dark alley, I didn't know what I would do.

Henrietta explained, "Blind date gone wrong. Tyler kind of saved the day."

Cohen seemed to loosen up a little at that. "Let's turn your night around."

Hen smiled. "Thanks, Cohen."

He nodded. "How long have you been in town, Tyler?"

"Just a little over a week." I said. "Hen's been a life-saver, showing me the ropes around the office and helping me get settled in."

"How long are you here for?"

"Nine months," I answered.

"Must suck being on the road all the time," he said. "The guys and I play poker on Thursday nights if you need some people to hang out with."

The thought of a regular poker night made me happier than I wanted to let on. Because guys just didn't do giddy. But I did smile. "That sounds great."

Henrietta offered to send me his number, then she said, "We'll let you get to work, Cohen."

He nodded, and we left him for a two-person table near the dance floor. She slid into her seat and took a deep drink of her mai tai, her eyes tracing the couples dancing.

"Do you dance?" I asked.

She gave me one of her shy grins. "I do the macarena with the best of them."

I couldn't help but laugh.

"What about you?" she asked.

"Two stepping is like a religion in Texas," I said. "Everyone from my hometown knows how to do that and a little swing dancing."

She seemed impressed. "I don't think I've ever been dancing with a guy."

"I'm surprised none of your boyfriends brought you out to dance," I said. I loved taking my girlfriend out on the weekends, when I had one.

Her eyes downturned slightly, and I realized I'd hit a

nerve. I just didn't know which one. Had her last boyfriend broken her heart? Or was it about the monster she'd just escaped? I shuddered to think what might have happened if no one had been there to rescue her.

A country song came on before she answered, and I said, "Looks like it's time to learn."

She looked at me in surprise. "Oh, you don't have to do that. I'd hate to crush your toes."

I'd grown up on a farm dealing with thousand-pound animals and this dime piece thought I couldn't handle her size? "Nonsense," I said.

Hesitatingly, she slipped her hand in mine, heat leeching through her skin and slowly up my arm. A thrill went through me at the thought of putting my hands on her hips.

Back in Texas, guys put their arm over their partner's shoulder during a two-step, but I never really liked that. So I settled my hand just where her hip met the curve of her waist and began talking her through the moves. "Slow, slow, quick, quick. Slow, slow, quick, quick."

Despite her talk of two left feet, she was already catching on. "You're doing great," I said honestly.

Still focusing on her feet, as if she could will them into submission, she said, "I just needed someone good to lead."

Good thing she couldn't see my dopey fucking grin.

As she slowly got the hang of the moves, we kept better pace with the song. By the time it ended, she had the most adorable grin on her face. "I think I'm getting it!"

"You're a natural," I replied, loving the way her body felt pressed to mine. Her hand in mine, her flesh under my other hand, moving to the music... it was almost like the song had been made just for us. For this moment.

A new song started, and she smiled up at me. "Thank you for teaching me, but I think I could use some more practice."

I grinned at her, more than willing to help.

13

HENRIETTA

Confession: Sometimes, I wanted a hero to rescue me.

IT WAS NEARLY midnight when Tyler pulled up to my house. The porch light was on, but it looked like the bedroom lights were off. I breathed a sigh of relief. At least there would be no questioning until I had time to work out a story that would satisfy my grandma without breaking her heart.

Blue shadows from the dash danced across the ridges of Tyler's arm as he put the truck in park. When I looked up to his face, his eyes were on me.

He'd caught me staring, but I couldn't bring myself to look away. I could hardly bring myself to breathe.

I swallowed, breaking eye contact. "Thank you for coming to the rescue," I managed, reaching for my seat belt. "I only wish you wouldn't have to do that so often."

I peeked up to see his response, and he wore a smile

on his lips, his eyes taking me in. "What if I said I enjoyed it?"

"Then that would make one of us. I mean, the damsel-in-distress part. I actually had fun tonight at Collie's."

"Actually?" he said, feigning offense.

I playfully narrowed my eyes, unable to hide my smile. "I had fun. And maybe I enjoyed all the jealous looks I was getting too. Everyone wished they would have been on your arm."

He covered his chest with his hand. "Henrietta. Cohen is a married man."

I rolled my eyes, laughing. I adored this playful side of him. Which was dangerous. Adoration was nothing I should be feeling for a coworker. Especially when it could cost me my job. But with Tyler? I couldn't help it. He had this aura of joy around him, and I wanted to bask in the glow.

Which was exactly why I needed to leave, and fast. I reached for the door handle to get out, but he said, "Wait."

I gave him a curious look, and he added, "Let me get that for you."

"That's not necessary. It's not like you were my date." Although Houston certainly wouldn't have opened the door for me.

The quiet before his response unsettled me, but then he said, "I want you to see how you deserve to be treated."

My heart was a puddle on his truck floor.

Without waiting for my response, he opened his door,

passing through the headlights to my side. I allowed myself a moment to watch him, the way his arms pulled around his muscles. The strong profile of his face. The contrast of his dark brown hair to his tanned white skin.

But then my door was opening, and he was waiting with one arm up, showing a tattoo on the inside of his bicep. He followed my gaze to the black ink swirling around his muscular arm.

"Is there a story for the tattoo?" I asked, wishing it wasn't midnight. Wishing that he had been the one to ask me on the date. Wishing that the walk to my house was miles instead of minutes.

"A long one," he replied, extending his hand to help me down.

I slipped my hand into his, my heart speeding just as it had when we'd danced before. But now there was no loud music, no other couples to distract me from the heady rush of this man in front of me. Only the pale glow of the streetlights and the soft summer breeze caressing my skin.

He walked beside me to the sidewalk lined with tulips my mom carefully planted from bulbs each year. "Have you ever thought about getting a tattoo?" he asked.

"I've thought about it. There's just never been anything I wanted to look at for the rest of my life."

"So perhaps one on your back?" He winked.

I laughed, gently shoving his arm.

My front porch was approaching way too quickly. We were close enough now to read the embroidery on the porch swing's decorative pillow. *Home Sweet Home.*

Desperate to keep him here a little longer, I asked, "What would a gentleman do on a date now?"

His eyes looked golden in our porch light as he reached for my hands. He held both of them in his, gently pressing my fingertips with his thumbs. "On a proper date, he'd tell you what a great time he had."

The breeze picked up, circling our porch and freeing a strand of hair from behind my ear. He reached up and gently pressed it back.

Between the wind and his touch and the look in his eyes, my breath was gone.

His voice was honey, just as sweet as his words. "This is when a regular guy would lean in and kiss you goodnight."

Involuntarily, I swallowed, flicking my gaze to his lips.

"But you don't want a regular guy," he finished.

"I don't?" I breathed. Because right now, nothing sounded better than a kiss goodnight from Tyler Griffen.

He shook his head, resolute. "You deserve a hero. Someone who would take care of you, even though you're capable of caring for yourself."

My lips parted. Was he saying...

"A hero would lean in, kiss your forehead, and walk away, because, with a girl like you, he'd know the best is yet to come."

Tyler stepped closer, pressing his lips to my forehead, and with one final sweep of his eyes over me, he turned and walked away.

Shivers prickled down my skin as I turned to the door, fingers shaking on my keys as I pushed them into the deadbolt lock.

Feeling eyes on me, I looked over my shoulder, seeing Tyler smiling at me—*me*—before he opened his pickup door and got inside.

Unsure my heart could take any more, I let myself in and leaned back against the door, smiling wider than I ever had and feeling tears burn my eyes.

Every feeling. Hope. Worry. Longing. Despair. I felt them all as his engine fired up and then faded away.

14

HENRIETTA

Confession: I want to make my grandma happy. I just don't know if that's possible.

I TIPTOED TO MY ROOM, where I was in danger of hanging a Tyler Griffen poster on my ceiling like some kind of fifteen-year-old fangirl. This had gone from the worst to the best night of my life, all thanks to him.

Standing in front of my dresser, I pulled out my hoop earrings, hanging them back on my jewelry tree. With them out, I looked in the mirror. My cheeks still felt warm, my hair was slightly askew, and there was a light in my eyes that hadn't been there before.

I wondered what Tyler saw when he looked at me. The small mole on my cheek? The fullness of my lips? The perfect shape of my waxed eyebrows (the one splurge I regularly allowed myself.) Or did he notice my broad shoulders? My full hips or the extra flesh on my stomach?

The line of questioning was driving me nuts, because

I had to know what he had seen that no other guy had noticed.

My door clicked open, and I nearly jumped out of my skin, stumbling backward.

Grandma stepped into my room, wearing her gold and black silk robe, pink silk cap, and a sly grin.

"Grandma!" I hissed at her. "You nearly scared me to death!"

"Seems like the date went well," she said anyway.

I shook my head at her, continuing my routine of unclipping my necklace. The date had been incredible, for reasons she didn't understand.

"Well?" she prompted, leaving room for me to fill in the rest.

I glanced at her. "Aren't you supposed to be in bed?"

"I'm old, not an invalid," she replied, sitting on my bed and crossing her legs. "I had a good feeling about this one."

The hope in her voice nearly undid me. Grandma thought she had done me a favor, but I had to tell her the truth. I hung my necklace on the jewelry tree, then went to sit beside her.

"Grandma, I know you want me to be happy like you and Grandpa, but I have to tell you... I felt really uncomfortable with Houston tonight."

Worry deepened her wrinkles. "What happened? If your father finds out he tried anything..."

"He did," I said. "I actually had to call a friend to rescue me."

Grandma covered her mouth with her weathered hands. "Henrietta, did he—"

"No, no, I'm fine. I just don't think I can do the setups anymore, Grandma."

There was so much sadness and compassion in her eyes as she covered my knee with her hand. "Honey, I never meant to put you in danger. I only mean to help you find someone like my Harold."

"I know you loved Grandpa, but what you two shared, it was magic, Grandma. Maybe…" My throat tightened, and I had to swallow to speak my biggest fear. "Maybe that's just not in the cards for me."

She shook her head, gently running her thumb over my knee. "A partner, a true partner, can change every-thing. They'll bring out the best in you, force you to acknowledge your weak spots, help you grow faster than you ever could on your own. I'd hate for you to miss out on that because you don't think you deserve it."

My eyes watered again, and I tried to hide the emotion from my eyes.

Grandma didn't miss anything. "You seemed so happy when I came in, and I made things worse. Oh, I feel terrible."

I gripped her hand. "It's not that."

"What is it?" she asked. "Did your friend say some-thing that upset you? You were on the porch for a long time with her…"

"Him," I corrected, and the light of hope in her eyes made me instantly regret it.

"Him?"

"He's a colleague, Grandma. From Texas. Nothing can happen."

"So he's from out of town and has no one to keep him company other than a pretty thing like you?" Her sly smile was back. "He must be lonely then. Invite him over for Kenner's birthday next Saturday.

"I don't think—"

"It's the least we can do to thank him for taking such good care of you," Grandma said. Then she stretched out and yawned. "You know, it is getting late. I think I'll get some shut eye, now that I know you're home safe." She hugged me tight, and I squeezed her back.

"I love you," I said, only the slightest edge of exasperation creeping into my voice.

"I love you too," she replied, giving me an extra tight squeeze before releasing me. "I can't wait to meet..."

"Tyler," I supplied.

"Tyler next Saturday," she finished. "Goodnight, darling."

"Goodnight."

15

TYLER

Growing up on a ranch, I could always count on some hard physical labor to occupy my mind, but now I had to make my own solutions. I worked out the next morning, hoping it would take care of my buzzing thoughts.

But this time, it didn't help like it usually did. No matter how many times I bench-pressed, squatted, or pulled myself up on the bar, I could still see that asshole pressed up against Henrietta. Still feel the soft skin of her forehead underneath my lips.

And most of all, I could feel the pit of guilt growing in my stomach. I shouldn't have taken things as far as I did.

I got on the treadmill and turned it to full speed, sprinting as hard as I could. As if I could forget my own personal rule or the situation we were in. I knew better than to start something I couldn't finish. Yet here I was, ready to break my rule just a couple of weeks into this assignment. I needed a kick in the ass.

I needed to talk to my older brother.

Gage had always been one who knew when to follow the rules and when to break them. He'd pushed my siblings and me to do better and work harder, regardless of who was watching. On top of that, he'd taught us patience—the importance of making the right move at the right time and being certain when we did. It was part of what led to his success in business and made him one of my most trusted advisors.

And even though I didn't want him telling me to back off from Henrietta, I knew I needed him to.

I slowed the treadmill and draped a towel around my sweaty neck. After taking a few deep breaths and drinking a slug of water, I picked up my phone and dialed his number.

After a few rings, he appeared on my screen, dressed in a suit with the blue sky behind him. I'd asked him once why he turned his desk away from the panoramic view he had of downtown Dallas, and he said he wasted too much time looking at the city instead of his work.

"Hold on," he said, not yet looking at the phone.

I continued walking toward my apartment, waiting for him to finish up whatever had his attention.

When I crested the stairs, he said, "Sorry, I'm acquiring a self-storage facility and had to move some things around to make it happen."

"Self-storage?" I asked, my interest piqued. "Is there any money in that?"

"Ridiculous amounts. Everyone's been sleeping on them, including myself."

"Interesting." I pressed my key into the lock and walked into my empty apartment.

"I'm assuming you didn't call me to discuss investment opportunities," he said. "Although, your portfolio is doing well, by the way."

"Of course it is. You're managing it."

"Tyler."

I sat on the couch, still unable to forget the image of Henrietta sitting there, flipping through my books, her eyes lighting with questions, her lips turning into a smile at my answers.

"I'm in deep shit," I said.

A crease formed between his eyebrows. "Do you need money?"

Of course he would jump to the one thing he could solve. "No, I need advice." I propped my phone against a stack of books on the coffee table and leaned my elbows on my knees.

"What's going on?"

I let out a sigh, looking away from my brother. After my dad, he was the person I admired most. "I met a girl."

His lips curled into a smile. "Considering they make up fifty-one percent of the population, it was bound to happen at some point."

I hadn't expected to laugh, but I did. "They're not like this one."

The lift of his eyebrows told me he was listening.

"She's smart and funny, driven, selfless, loves her family and friends, has a smile that makes you forget how to breathe, and her curves..." I closed my eyes. "She's the total package, Gage. But she works for the company we're building for... I can't date her. I *can't*."

When I opened my eyes again, he had a devilish grin on his face, not too dissimilar from when we were kids and he had a prank planned for us.

"What?" I asked.

"You're in deep shit."

"Why do you think I called you!" I half laughed, half cried. I was a drowning man, and damn, if he didn't rescue me soon, I was in danger of sinking.

His background shifted as he stood, pacing his office. "You've never dated women on the job, which I've respected. Makes sense not to rile things up, especially when you're looking for a promotion... Are there any rules against it?"

I shook my head. Waited for him to throw me a raft.

"Honestly, Ty?"

I nodded.

"I don't see the problem."

My jaw clenched. "Don't see the problem? She's from California; I'm from Texas."

"People move all the time."

"Not her. She's saving for her own house."

"And I have so many miles you know you could fly her back and forth every day if you wanted to."

Gritting my teeth, I said, "How's that supposed to work with a family? With children?"

"You're already planning for children with her? How serious is it?"

The tips of my ears got hot, because I was placing a lot of pressure on a woman I hadn't even officially asked on a first date.

Gage asked, "I know you said it's technically allowed, but does Jim have something against it? Or her company? Is it the kind of thing that would be frowned upon?"

"Jim doesn't care as long as I keep things professional.

And her boss was practically begging me to take her out, so I doubt there are any rules there."

Gage took a deep breath. "Tyler, I know you're responsible. That's why you went out and made a career for yourself outside the farm. Lord knows Rhett could use some of those brains. But you can't read the future. No one can. Say you go on a couple dates with this girl and it fizzles. That's better than sitting around, beating yourself up over a fictional breakup that may or may not ever happen."

Okay, so maybe he had given me a kick in the pants, but not the kind I had expected. "What if we don't break up?" I asked. "I can't ask her to move to Texas, and I can't move here."

Gage shook his head. "It sounds like you're asking the wrong question."

"What do you mean?" I asked.

He laughed softly, his eyes turning down. "I think the question is, 'How could I miss out on a girl like that?'"

16

HENRIETTA

Confession: I can't stop thinking about him.

I STOPPED by Seaton Bakery on my way into work to get donuts and coffee for all the construction workers. Corporate had given me a budget to help manage things like this because they knew happy workers meant a job well done.

Gayle, the owner at the bakery, helped me load up all of the supplies into my trunk. "Are you getting excited for Mara and Jonas's wedding?" she asked.

I nodded. "Knowing them, it's going to be a night to remember. And I hear someone incredible is making the cakes."

She laughed. "We just want to do a good job for them. They're such a sweet couple."

"I'm sure you will," I said. "The cakes at Tess's wedding were fabulous. I had to stop myself from eating everything at the table."

Laughing, she said, "Thanks for saying that." She bumped my elbow. "Who knows? Maybe I'll be making a cake for your wedding soon."

"I love your sense of humor," I teased. "I'm closer to a house full of cats than I am a house full of kids."

"You'd be surprised. Love can always be right around the corner."

Hoping she was right, I replied, "I'll see you at the wedding."

"See you then."

On my drive to the construction site, I may or may not have fantasized about Tyler standing at the end of the aisle, looking incredible in a black and white suit. He was a classic kind of guy—he wouldn't wear any other color. He'd smile at me as I walked down the aisle, wipe a tear away from his face as I got close.

But as I neared the construction zone, I realized I'd just indulged myself in the adult equivalent of writing *Mrs. Tyler Griffen* on my notebook. So I shook all thoughts of marriage and babies from my mind and pulled up next to Tyler's truck.

I couldn't believe how much progress they had already made, taking it all in through the chain-link fence. In a matter of two weeks, they'd begun pouring the foundation. Now, gray cement and a steel frame occupied the space that was dirt and weeds just days ago.

I got out of my car and went to the trunk, grabbing two boxes of donuts. As I walked toward the office trailer, Tyler opened the door and came out. He didn't see me at first, so I had a moment to take him in. The way his tight T-shirt pulled against his biceps. The peek of a tattoo on his arm. The way the morning sun hit his skin, making him look almost golden.

All of it combined was enough to make me drool more than the donuts. But then he saw me, and his smile was even more dazzling.

Catching my breath, I lifted the box of donuts. "I brought breakfast for everyone."

"Well, that was mighty nice of you."

I shook my head. "I don't think I'll ever be used to that Texas accent."

He laughed, taking the box from me. "Here. Let me help you."

I nodded. "I have a few more in the car and some coffee thermoses."

"Great," he said. "I have a folding table in the office. I could set that up in front of the trailer."

"Perfect," I replied. I went to the car and carried back another box. Some of the workers were already beginning to line up around the table, looking at the spread. Seeing them dig in made me feel better—I knew how hard a day of work could be. Sometimes a little thoughtful gesture went a long way.

Tyler came beside me on my way back to the car to get the coffee, and he said, "It may not be pizza and beer, but I think you're winning them over."

I looked over my shoulder to see the guys chatting it up and snacking. "I have my ways," I said.

He replied, "You only needed that smile."

If he wasn't right in front of me, I would have done a happy dance on my two left feet. But since he was, I looked at my trunk to hide just how happy that comment made me. With my facial expression somewhat managed,

I handed him a thermos and a stack of Styrofoam cups before grabbing the other thermos for myself.

With everything organized and set up on the table, Tyler poured himself a cup of coffee—black.

"Is there anything you're needing from us this week?" I asked him after a sip of my heavily doctored cup.

"Actually," he said, "if you could bring some paperwork by the city, that would be really helpful."

"No problem," I replied. "I'm really impressed by how much work you guys have done already. I almost can't believe this used to just be an empty field."

He held the Styrofoam rim on his lips as he said, "That's one of my favorite parts of the job."

"What do you mean?" I asked, trying not to be distracted by those lips.

His hazel eyes on me were just as distracting. "In a lot of jobs, you do the work and then you have to do it over and over again. With construction, you can actually see the effects of all the work that we're doing and the lasting results. Fifty years from now, I'll be driving my kids by this building and saying, 'When I was your age, I built this.'"

I pictured Tyler with children, and my mind went haywire. And speaking of children... "So I told my grandma about how you rescued me on Friday. And she wants to thank you personally at my nephew's birthday party on Saturday."

Tyler grinned, his eyes crinkling at the corners. "She does?"

I nodded. "In fact, I'm pretty sure if you don't come, she will call a senior ride and track you down herself."

"Well, I can't disappoint Grandma." He pretended to be at a loss of what to do. Adorable.

I bit my lip, smiling. "I don't think so."

"What time?" he asked.

"It starts at five. Dad will grill hamburgers and hot dogs. We'll put on some TV for the kids and play card games. It'll be fun."

"Sounds like it. Any tips on the gift? How old is he turning?"

"He's four, and you don't need to get a gift," I said. "You've done more than enough."

"There's no way I'm showing up empty-handed." I got the feeling he wasn't going to be talked out of this one, so I said, "Anything Paw Patrol is always a win with Kenner."

"That's a show, right? I don't have any nieces or nephews, so I'm not really up on the kid stuff."

Teasing him, I said, "Are you sure you're not fifty?"

He laughed. "My mom would lose her mind if I reached fifty without a single grandchild for her to spoil rotten."

"I know the feeling."

"The setups?" he asked.

"Yep, not to mention the sad looks at every family get together."

He groaned. "And the wallet photos of every niece/cousin/daughter/cocker spaniel."

I laughed. "Dogs too?"

"Can't have a boatload of kids without a dog," he replied.

"Fair. But I would go with something a little meatier for Texas. Maybe a Saint Bernard?"

"We had one when we were kids. Bernie."

"Cute," I said.

He was about to reply when one of his colleagues called him over.

While he was occupied, I went and refilled my coffee, chatting casually with the construction guys. Most of them didn't give me a second glance, but there was an older guy named Rich who was really kind and got me talking about my work.

I heard Tyler's voice above the chatter as he said, "A few more minutes, guys, then we need to get back to work."

"That's my cue," Rich said.

"Mine too," I replied. "Nice to meet you."

He tipped his ball cap off his head. "You too, Miss Henrietta."

Tyler called me over to the trailer, and I walked into the small space with him. It couldn't have been more than eight by fifteen, but there were a couple of desks and filing cabinets, and even a bathroom in the corner.

Just like the last time we were here together, our aloneness felt so palpable. I could smell his cologne, something earthy and light at the same time. I wanted to reach him to feel his lips on my forehead again. Maybe even on my mouth.

Logically, I knew he was off limits. But that didn't stop my mind and my body and my heart from wanting more with him.

He handed me a couple of manila envelopes and said, "These need to go to the environmental planning office." His fingers brushed mine, leaving a jolt of electricity in their wake.

I quickly took the envelopes and pulled away, not wanting him to see how much of an effect he had on me.

In a matter of weeks, he'd consumed my every thought and replaced them with fantasies I shouldn't be having.

"I'll see you tomorrow," he said.

I couldn't wait. And that would be the end of me. I could feel it in my bones.

17

HENRIETTA

Confession: I still struggle with my self-esteem.

AFTER WORK, I drove to meet my friends at Vestido for a dress fitting. Mara's wedding was just a couple weeks away, and we needed to make sure that all the alterations had been done correctly.

As I turned into the parking lot, I wished I could ask their advice with Tyler, but this was Mara's time. For the millionth time, I cursed myself for not being more experienced. If I'd dated more, maybe I would know how to make the next move with Tyler. Or maybe I wouldn't be so desperate for love that I was even thinking about jeopardizing my job.

It was a good thing I couldn't ask for advice tonight while my willpower was nonexistent. I needed to remind myself that I couldn't lose this job. That no man, even one as handsome and sweet as Tyler Griffen, was worth giving up all I'd sacrificed on the way to my goal.

I parked my car and walked to the dress shop, seeing my friends toward the back of the shop. Tess stood on the platform, looking absolutely gorgeous in her dress. I pushed through the door and walked back. "That's amazing on you," I said.

My friends turned to look at me, and Mara got up, giving me a hug. "This is exciting, isn't it? I never thought anything like this would happen for me."

I squeezed her back. "The rest of us did."

She laughed. "Of course you did."

The saleswoman, Venitia, poured me a glass of champagne. I thanked her and took a drink, letting the bubbles warm my mouth and throat on the way down. For the first time today, I felt like I could... breathe.

While the seamstress worked around Tess, I asked Mara, "Getting excited?"

"Honestly?" she said. "I'm looking forward to the honeymoon more than anything. I already feel like Jonas and I are married, with or without the ceremony."

"I could see that." The two of them had been a perfect match from the moment they started their fake relationship—even if neither of them could see it. He kept her feet on the ground, and she kept his feet on the clouds.

Birdie added, "A week in Mexico does sound fabulous."

Mara nodded. "I'm thinking we should all do a girls' trip there next summer, maybe when the show wraps up filming."

I thought through my finances, wondering if I could spare a thousand dollars (or more) to go on a trip. I hadn't been on a vacation in so long, and I needed one, for sure.

But I couldn't. My goals were bigger than little frivolities. I had to stay focused.

"Who's up next?" the seamstress, May, asked.

I raised my hand, partially to avoid any more conversations about vacations.

She walked me back to the fitting room and showed me the dress with a little name card on it that said Henrietta. It looked just as beautiful on the hanger as it had the day we picked it out. My problem with clothes was never with the shopping, only with the trying on.

"Let me know if you need any help," May said.

I nodded, steeling myself for any possible outcome. I didn't check the scale anymore, aside from the once a year I went to the doctor—and endured a rant about my BMI that left me crying for days. So there was a decent chance I'd gained or lost since they took my measurements.

I gave myself a mini pep talk and slipped it over my head, surprised at how soft the fabric felt against my skin. Usually when I dressed up, it felt more like being squeezed into a sausage casing, but this gown felt amazing. Even the straps that had been added after the fact looked like they were meant to be part of the dress.

I gaped at myself in the mirror, my eyes watering. I felt beautiful, and it had been so damn long since I'd seen myself that way.

"Henrietta?" May called. "Everything okay?"

"Be out in a sec," I said, trying to hide the emotion in my voice. I pressed the corners of my eyes, stemming the flow of tears, and then I lifted the hem and walked to the podium.

As soon as the girls saw me, they began squealing and

clapping. Birdie said, "Oh my gosh, that dress was made for you!"

Tess nodded and bumped Mara's arm. "Aren't bridesmaids dresses supposed to be ugly?"

Smiling, I shook my head, turning and looking at myself in the trifold mirror. Even though I tried to fight it, the tears came anyway. For once in my life, I could see what Tyler saw.

"Oh, Hen," Mara said, coming up and putting her arms around me. "What's going on?"

I shook my head, wiping at my eyes again. "I'm so sorry. This is supposed to be your time."

Birdie said, "She gets a whole wedding for that. Tell us what's going on?"

I bit my lip but finally gave in, telling them about my horrible date and Tyler saving me and the fact that if anything happened between us, I could very well lose my job.

Mara and Birdie exchanged a glance, and Birdie said, "I wouldn't have gotten my happily ever after without breaking a rule."

I shook my head, sitting down on the edge of the podium. "I don't have a thousand students who would be devastated to see me go. They could find someone else in a heartbeat. But it feels silly to even worry about it. I don't know if Tyler feels that way about me or if he was just being nice."

Tess gave me a look like I was being absolutely insane. "Henrietta. He left his plans on a Friday night because you sent him a text message. He threatened to kill a guy, and then kissed you on the forehead saying, and I quote, *'the best is yet to come.'* I don't know what you could possibly be missing here."

"I just—" I swallowed down the lump in my throat, trying to speak. "I never thought something like that could happen to me." I closed my eyes, embarrassed by my low self-esteem. I was almost thirty. Shouldn't I be feeling good about myself by now?

Mara wrote romance novels for curvy women. Birdie was a guidance counselor, helping teens with their self-worth, and Tess was happily married to the love of her life with the most adorable child. And yet here I was, a twenty-eight-year-old virgin, feeling like the kid in gym class who always got picked last.

Mara put her hands on either side of my face and made me look her in the eyes. "Henrietta Jones. You are absolutely beautiful, but you don't have to see that for someone else to realize it."

My eyes watered as I nodded.

Birdie rested her hand on my shoulder. "There are hundreds of jobs out there. There's only one Tyler."

That was a thought that echoed in my mind as I waited for what was to come next.

18

TYLER

I had the Saturday birthday party so firmly planted in my mind that I almost forgot the poker night Henrietta's friend Cohen invited me to. Luckily, he texted me his address about an hour before it was set to start, giving me just enough time to shower off, change, and grab a case of beer from the liquor store on my way over.

I wasn't sure what kind they liked, so I picked a local brew kept in the refrigerated section and hoped for the best.

The directions on my phone led me to a neighborhood with big yards, tall shade trees, and brightly colored houses. The one Cohen had directed me to was a soft yellow, and the yard was decorated with quirky planter pots filled with colorful blooms.

As I got closer, I noticed the garage door pulled up to show a table surrounded by a few guys. They looked my way, and I lifted my hand in a wave before parking along the curb.

I'd had so much practice getting to know new people

that it usually didn't faze me anymore. But now? My stomach felt like it used to before an important football game.

And judging by the protective way Cohen had acted at the bar last Friday, this would be an important game. Especially if I followed Gage's advice and gave a relationship with Henrietta a chance.

I took a couple deep breaths as I grabbed the case of beer from the bed of the truck and walked up.

A guy with dark hair, wearing dress clothes with the sleeves rolled up, said, "He brought beer! I like him already."

Cohen lifted an eyebrow and said, "You didn't have to —I have plenty from the bar."

Another guy at the table with gray hair and tanned skin said, "You don't need to buy all the drinks all the time." He stood up and walked toward me, extending his hand. "Name's Steve. I work with Cohen—I'm the bar manager."

"Tyler," I replied, shaking his hand. "I'm working on that new build for Hen's apartments."

"That's what I heard," he said, a slight twinkle in his eyes. "And a little more."

The guy with dark hair took the case from me, setting it in an old refrigerator in the garage.

"Thanks," I said.

He looked over his shoulder. "Nice to meet you, Tyler. I'm Jonas, Mara's fiancé. She said she met you the other day at Waldo's?"

"Yep. Hen was nice enough to let me tag along."

Cohen had a knowing grin on his lips that had me feeling embarrassed. Was I *that* obvious?

"What type of poker do y'all play?" I asked, hoping for a change in subject.

Cohen said, "You'll like it. We play Texas Hold'em."

Laughing, I replied, "Sounds like I'll be right at home."

Jonas pulled out the chair next to him and passed me the deck to cut. I sat down and tapped the top card. He took it back, passing out the cards to each of us. "What part of Texas are you from, Tyler?"

"Cottonwood Falls, a little town outside of Dallas."

Steve said, "Does your family farm?"

I almost laughed, because everyone assumed that I lived on a farm. But I nodded, because I did fit the stereotype, my Griffen Farms hat giving me away. "My family has a beef cattle operation with a small feed yard, and then we grow a few crops to help feed the cattle."

Jonas looked deep in thought. "Does beef come from somewhere other than cattle?"

I laughed for real this time. "No, we say beef cattle, because there can be dairy cows too."

"Makes sense," Steve said. "My grandparents had a farm we went to every summer. It was fun, except the billy goats were assholes."

That made me laugh out loud. "One year my dad got it in his head that goat milk was gonna make us rich. They lasted a year before Mom said it was her or them."

Cohen cracked a smile. "I'm guessing he chose her?"

I nodded. "They've been together thirty-six years. And I don't think she'll ever forgive the goat hoofprints on the top of her car."

Jonas set the deck in the middle of the table and flipped over five cards. "You're first," he said to me.

I looked to my hand... not bad. I swapped a seven for a jack, hoping to make a straight. We went around the table for a while, and I studied each of them, getting a feel for how they played. Cohen was the hardest to read, never giving much away whether he had a good or bad hand.

Steve, on the other hand, kept his good cards close to his chest, removing the smile that was always on his lips otherwise. And Jonas was clearly a terrible liar. His hands twitched when he had good cards, and his jaw tightened with the bad cards.

After a couple hours, Steve and Jonas had dwindling stacks of chips, and between Cohen and me, we knocked them out within a few rounds of each other.

Steve grumbled something about promising his wife he'd get home when he lost, so he said goodbye to all of us before telling me, "You better beat Cohen. He's not used to losing."

Cohen snorted. "Good luck."

It just made me want to win all that much more.

"I'm staying to see this one," Jonas said. "Besides, the girls have taken over my house with wedding craft projects, so I'm in no rush to get home." He shuddered. "So much glitter."

The girls... I'm assuming he meant Henrietta, Birdie, Mara, and Tess. Those four seemed thick as thieves.

But the distraction of Henrietta cost me a couple rounds before I focused back in on the game and won one against Cohen.

"I'll just say it," Cohen said as he shuffled the deck over and over again. "What are your intentions with Henrietta?"

Jonas gave him a look but then watched me for my answer.

"My intentions?" I hedged. Fuck, I was a couple beers in and about to admit that dating her was the worst idea ever—but I still wanted to.

He finished dealing and then flipped the cards over. "You were pretty close on the dance floor."

"She had a bad date, didn't want to go home," I replied, glancing from my cards to Cohen. This hand was good, but was it good enough to win?

Cohen tossed a couple of chips in the pile growing in the middle of the table. "You're in town on contract, right? Just here for a few months?"

"Nine," I replied, as if it made a difference.

Another round.

"So you're leaving soon," Cohen said.

Jonas's eyes tracked between the two of us.

Instead of answering, I matched his bid and raised it.

Cohen looked from my chips to me. "Henrietta doesn't date. Not seriously, anyway."

"Maybe she hasn't found the right match yet." I traded a card from the pile and replaced one in my hand.

He raised an eyebrow. "And you're saying you could be that match?"

"I'm saying I'm all in," I replied, pushing all my chips to the center of the table.

Cohen studied me before matching my bid with all of his.

When we turned our cards over, I won.

19

HENRIETTA

Confession: My ovaries have a mind of their own.

MY STOMACH WAS a ball of nerves Saturday morning. Tyler and I hadn't spoken much outside of work since I dropped off the donuts Monday. But if his forehead kiss the weekend before meant anything, today would be one to remember.

I got up early, taking extra time on my hair and makeup, and then helped my mom peel and boil potatoes for the potato salad. After that, we made deviled eggs, and I ran to the grocery store for chips, soda, disposable plates and silverware, and of course, the cake with the puppy's face printed on top.

As we were putting food into dishes, Grandma sat at the kitchen island and said, "Is your male friend coming today, Hen?"

All eyes swiveled on me, making me very aware that I hadn't told my parents Tyler was coming over.

Dad's hands stalled over the piping bag he used to fill the deviled eggs. "Male friend?"

Despite the heat in my cheeks, I kept my voice even. "He's a *colleague* who rescued me from that horrible date last Friday. Grandma insisted I invite him."

With a cunning smile, she said, "You know how I love a good Prince Charming, Murph."

Before Dad could reply, the doorbell rang.

"Saved by the bell," I muttered, wiping my hands on a rag to go and answer it.

As soon as I opened the door, my brother Bertrand and his fiancée, Imani, came inside, carrying ridiculous amounts of presents for a birthday Kenner probably wouldn't remember. Mom immediately put Bertrand to work on the potato salad, and I stepped outside to help my other brother Justus, who had just pulled up.

He and Raven had driven a slick red convertible he no doubt borrowed from the car dealership where he worked. Driving new cars, even with the giant stickers on the front, was just a perk of the job.

He popped the trunk and walked to Raven's side of the car. She was eight months pregnant and no doubt needed some help up from her seat. I went to the trunk, grabbing a big wrapped box. "How are you two doing?"

Raven groaned. "If this baby doesn't get here soon, I might lose my mind."

Over the present, I caught sight of her wearing Crocs. "I thought you hated those shoes! You must be hurting bad to have those on."

"You have no idea," she grunted, making her way toward the house with her hands supporting her back.

Justus took the gift from me and followed her to the

door. As he passed me, he whispered, "These hormones are killing me, sis."

"Seems like a fair trade—she carries your baby, and you deal with a few mood swings and cravings."

He stuck his tongue out at me, and I patted his back as I walked toward the house, a minivan pulling up.

My oldest brother, Johmarcus, was there with his wife, Laila. They got out of the car, grabbing the kids. She held their nine-month-old, A'yisha, and Kenner bounced up and down with a balloon.

"Look what I got!" Kenner said, waving his arm around to show the string tied around his wrist.

"I love that balloon! And it's red! Your favorite color!"

His smile couldn't have been any bigger as he jumped into my arms for a hug. He wrapped his little arms around my neck, and I squeezed him back, saying, "Happy birthday, four-year-old!"

He let me go before running into the house as Laila futilely asked him to tell me thank you.

"Don't worry about it," I said, reaching for the baby. That's what we did when they came. I took the kids and gave them a break, and by the way their shoulders instantly relaxed, I knew they needed it. I'd do the same for Justus and Raven when their baby came.

Laila and Johmarcus passed me, going into the house while I slowly trailed after them, holding my niece. A'yisha was only nine months old, but she had the most beautiful dark curls and these big black eyes that constantly sparkled. This had to be my favorite age.

"Hi, baby!" I said to her, smiling wide.

"I usually go by Tyler, but baby will do."

My eyes widened as I looked away from my niece to

see the most handsome guy ever walking up the sidewalk. I hadn't heard his truck in all the chaos, but there he was in dark wash jeans, cowboy boots, and a plaid shirt tucked in, showing off his narrow hips and broad shoulders. The bag in his hand with a puppy's face on it and tissue paper sticking out made me swoon that much more.

Damn. I was completely unprepared.

I focused my eyes back on A'yisha and said, "Sweetie, this is Tyler. Tyler, this is my favorite niece, A'yisha."

"Nice to meet you, A'yisha." He reached for her little fingers, and she wrapped her fist around his pointer finger, hanging on. There was the sweetest smile on her lips, showing off her two bottom teeth.

"You are the cutest," he said, his eyes crinkling at the corners.

She babbled back at him, and I swear, my ovaries were screaming at me, GET A MOVE ON, HENRIETTA! HE WILL NOT LAST LONG! My grandma would probably say the same thing as soon as she met him.

I cleared my throat, hoping for the millionth time he couldn't read my mind, and said, "This is home."

We walked closer to the front door, taking our time. As he took in the simple ranch-style house where I grew up, I wondered what he thought. If it was anything like his home in Texas.

"It's nice," he said. "And tulips." He gestured at the flowers lining the sidewalk. "Your favorite."

My lips turned up. "You remembered that?"

"Of course," he said.

"Henrietta! Who is this?" my grandma asked, her

voice as sweet as pie as she watched us from the front door.

A'yisha squealed at the sight of Grandma, and I bounced her on my hip. Grandma was strong, but not that steady. "Grandma, this is Tyler Griffen, my *coworker*."

Tyler extended his hand to her, and she shook it, hearts in her eyes as she sized him up. "We heard all about your heroic rescue last week. I was quite impressed."

Was that a blush on Tyler's cheeks? "I was happy to help."

Her eyes narrowed playfully. "I'm sure you were." Instead of letting go of his hand, she maneuvered him so she could wind her arm through his elbow. "Come now, let's meet the rest of the family."

I nuzzled my nose against A'yisha's ear, making her giggle, and whispered, "When you're my age, I promise I won't make it this difficult."

We followed them inside, and I swear, the entire house went silent at Tyler's entrance. Grandma cleared her throat, as if she didn't already have everyone's attention, and said, "This is Tyler, Henrietta's new male friend."

As if "male friend" wasn't embarrassing enough, my brothers stared him down, three wolves to Tyler's sheep. They didn't know he could bare his fangs when needed. And then there were my sisters-in-law, both pretending they didn't find him attractive. And my mom, all moony eyed, just like her mother.

Dad was the first to speak. "Welcome to our home, Tyler. We're happy to have you."

Thank you, I wanted to shout.

And then Kenner yelled, "I'm FOUR!"

It broke the tension just enough to spur some laughter while Grandma marched Tyler around the room, dutifully introducing him to everyone in our family. And since I didn't want to stare in horror, I went to stand by the island with Mom. "How can I help?"

She gave me a knowing smile and leaned against the island. "So this is why you've been so distracted lately?"

"I haven't been distracted."

"Please, I've asked you to take the trash out every day this week and you've forgotten just as many times," she said.

"That was on purpose," I deadpanned.

"And that date you went on last week? I've seen you primp every day for work for longer than you took getting ready for that date."

Okay, so maybe she was right, but, "Was I really that obvious?"

She nodded. "But I can't blame you. He is gorgeous."

Her giggle made me laugh too. "He is. Grandma's going to be real upset when she finds out I'm not allowed to date him."

"What does that mean?"

"My boss, Janessa, said I can't date him, or I could lose my job."

Mom pressed her lips together. "If it doesn't affect your quality of work, what you do in your free time is none of her business. Especially when you don't have anyone in town supervising you."

I was about to argue, but Grandma paraded Tyler our way and said, "Tamica, this is Tyler. Tyler, this is the backbone that holds this family together."

"You can call me Tam," my mother said, smiling as

she reached for Tyler's hand. "We're so happy to have you here. Can I get you a lemonade or maybe a beer?"

"A lemonade would be real nice, Tam. Thank you."

"Of course," she said, reaching for the pitcher. I grabbed a red Solo cup for him, feeling Tyler's eyes on me. When I chanced a glance his way, there was a warm look in his eyes and a half smile on his lips.

Warmth flooded my chest as I fluttered my eyelids down and wrote his name on the cup. Giving him a labeled cup felt like giving him a place in our family. And my family was everything to me. No matter how crazy it got when all my brothers were home, no matter how over-bearing my grandma's search for my mate could be, I couldn't imagine getting serious with anyone they didn't love.

Dad came out of the garage, carrying a tray of hot dogs and burgers, and said, "Tyler, why don't you come help me with the grill?"

20

TYLER

My stomach was a ball of nerves as Tam loaded my arms with spices and I followed Murphy out to the backyard. Of course, Henrietta's brothers had given me the stare down, just as Cohen and Jonas had, but it was her dad who made me on edge.

He had an easy smile, but eyes that didn't miss anything. Just from our short meeting, I could tell he was the kind of guy who would give you his trust until you broke it, and I wasn't going to give him a reason not to trust me.

As we walked to the grill, I glanced around the yard, seeing garden beds all around the perimeter, filled with lush plants and fruit trees. Catching my gaze, Murphy said, "Will you go grab a few zucchinis from that bed over there? Maybe pull a couple onions. This time of year, it's all we can do to keep up with Tam's green thumb."

"Sure thing," I said, walking to the beds he pointed out. This garden was really something. I was sure if Tam and my mom got together, they'd talk for hours about soil amendments and growing seasons.

"Hose is over there," Murphy said, pointing his tongs to the side yard.

I grabbed the hose and used the spray nozzle, turning it to the center setting to rinse off the plants.

When I returned to the outdoor kitchen area with the produce, Murphy said, "Tam's going to be impressed."

"These are looking really good," I said about the vegetables.

"No, she always says you can tell a lot about a person by the hose setting they use. She'd approve of your choice for cleaning."

I laughed. "She's into garden psychology then."

He cracked a smile of his own. "Something like that."

While he began heating the grill with propane—my dad would approve—he had me chop the vegetables and wrap them in a foil sheet. I was halfway through the first sweet onion when he began talking.

"Henrietta's our only daughter, our baby girl."

I stalled my knife for a little while, then began chopping more slowly. I listened carefully for his words, despite the fact that I could hear my heartbeat pounding in my ears, the sound of child's laughter coming from inside.

"She's got three brothers who would drop anything to be there for her, but she's independent as hell and has a stubborn streak to match. She's fiercely loyal, unendingly kind, and if you take her to a baseball field, she's got a swing that won't quit."

I found a smile on my lips. He was naming a lot of the things I liked about her—except for the baseball swing. I needed to see that for myself one of these days.

Murphy grew quiet, and I found the courage to meet his eyes. When I did, I saw his wrinkles first. The concern for his daughter, but the fierce protection was there in his stare.

"If you hurt my daughter or plan to drop her for another girl the second you go home, I'd appreciate it if you just went back to being coworkers only."

"We are only coworkers," I said.

A humorless smile twitched at the corner of his lips. "Either you're lying to me or yourself. Which one is it?"

My throat felt thick, and I swallowed. "Sir, where I come from, we do things a little differently when we meet a girl, a woman, we really like. I wouldn't dream of getting serious with your daughter unless I first asked your permission. If it's alright with you, I'd like the chance to date your daughter."

Another peal of laughter broke through the silence while I waited for Murphy's answer. He gave me one of those easy smiles again and said, "You have my blessing." I was about to celebrate when he added, "But Hen's opinion is the one that matters."

He turned back to the grill, and I got the distinct feeling our conversation was over. I began salting and peppering the veggies in my foil pouches. Murphy picked up a seasoning container and said, "Son, there is one thing you need to know. When we cook here, we add the flavor." As he added an ungodly amount of spices to the food, the back door swung open.

Kenner sprinted to the trampoline in the corner of the yard, and Hen's two sisters-in-law followed behind. They stood by the trampoline, watching as he tried, and failed, to do a front flip.

"Mind if I cut out?" I asked, nodding toward his grandson. "I think I could give him a few pointers."

He set the foil-wrapped vegetables over the heat. "Not at all, but Kenner's never done well with strangers. Don't let him hurt your feelings."

"I was the same way when I was a kid." I wiped my hands on a dishrag, then walked across the yard. Laila was cheering on her son while Imani checked something on her phone. I asked Laila if she minded me giving Kenner a few pointers.

"That's fine with me," she said, "but Kenner's pretty shy with strang—"

"Cowboys can do flips?" Kenner asked me, coming to the opening in the safety net.

"Only the good ones," I replied with a wink. "I used to do flips off the horses every summer." Not on purpose, but I'd keep that part to myself.

"Off horses?" he cried, putting both of his hands to his head and falling over.

I chuckled. What a character. "But I started on the trampoline like you."

His eyes went wide. "Prove it."

"Okay, but only because it's your birthday." I kicked off my cowboy boots, set my cowboy hat on the edge of the tramp, and climbed up, hoping I wouldn't embarrass myself too much in front of the adults outside. But then the back door opened again, and I glanced over to see Henrietta walking her grandma out to the table and her brothers close behind with dishes.

Great. Her whole damn family was going to see.

Oblivious to my nerves, Kenner said, "I'll sit off to the

side like this. That's what Mama says you have to do
when someone else is doing a trick."

"Your mama's right," I said, feeling Henrietta's eyes
on me. "So all there is to flipping is tucking your chin and
trusting yourself, okay?"

He nodded.

I gave myself a couple warm-up jumps, wishing I
wasn't so damn rusty, and then flipped through the air like
it was just yesterday that my siblings and I were spending
hot summer days with a sprinkler under the trampoline. I
landed on my feet, bouncing a couple times, and looked
back at Kenner.

"Whoa!" he pealed. "Can you teach me how to do
that? My daddy said he's too big to do it."

I laughed, thinking of Johmarcus, who was built like a
lineman to my running back. "Well, we all have different
talents."

"And flipping is yours?" Kenner said.

Henrietta's voice came. "One of many."

"I have to keep up with my *coworker*," I teased.

Raven called from the folding table, "Keep it up, you
two. That's how this happened," she pointed at her belly.

I laughed and got on my knees in front of Kenner.
"Can you do a somersault?"

He nodded.

"Show me?" I asked, just like he'd done me.

He bent over and rolled, coming quickly to his feet. I
put my hand up for a high five.

"So try jumping before you do that. And put your
hands out so they land first."

He gave me a questioning look, but then his little face
set with determination, and he jumped a few times before

flipping and landing on his hands. Just as he got scared mid-jump, I reached for his legs and flipped him the rest of the way over.

He came back up grinning. "I did it!"

"You did! I barely helped at all!"

"Did you see that?" he asked his mom.

Laila had a proud smile on her face. "You did amazing, honey!"

He turned back to me and said, "I want to try again."

I nodded. "Whenever you're ready."

He did it a few more times with help, and then when he looked up, he grinned. "Everyone's watching me."

I glanced around seeing most of Henrietta's family circled around the trampoline, except for her dad, who was still grilling, and her grandma, who was leaning against a support pole of the pergola.

I focused back on Kenner and said, "You've got this, buddy." I scooted back to give him room, and he balled his little fists at his sides, pursing his lips with determination.

He jumped, swinging his arms to give him extra height, and then used all his force to propel himself forward. He tucked his head, and his hands barely skimmed the trampoline as he flipped over and landed on his bottom.

Everyone cheered as he scrambled up, and then he sprinted into my arms, squeezing me.

"Thank you!" he cried.

I grinned at him. "You did it all on your own, buddy." I climbed off the trampoline and let him bask in all the congratulations and cheering happening around him. But

then I felt a hand brush against my arm, and I looked to
see Henrietta.

She still had A'yisha on her hip, clearly a natural with
the littles in her family.

She smiled up at me, her eyes warm in the summer
sun. "That was pretty heroic."

"Nah." I folded my arms over my chest to keep it
from puffing up too big. "He was just scared—had to get
out of his own way." I thought of me, not asking her out
yet. Now that I had her father's permission... there was
nothing holding me back. "Actually, speaking of being
afraid—"

"Who's ready for lunch?" Tam called. "Gotta eat
some good cookin' before we can have cake!"

"CAKE!" Kenner screamed, jumping off the trampoline and running past us.

Henrietta giggled at him, and the sound hit me
straight in the chest. I loved her laugh. She nodded
toward the table. "Let's grab some food—before Bertrand
eats all the deviled eggs."

"Sounds like it'll benefit us and Imani," I said, making
her laugh again. "We wouldn't want her to call off the
wedding due to excessive flatulence."

"I'll remind her to thank us later." She walked across
the grass beside me to the little outdoor kitchen area.

"Why don't you let me hold A'yisha so you can get a
plate?" I offered.

She seemed surprised by the gesture. "Are you sure?
You are the guest."

"And you're the lady." I extended my hands for her
niece.

As she passed the little girl to me, Henrietta said, "If

she starts crying, I can trade."

"You think I'm incapable of handling a child?" I asked, eyebrows raised. I already had her tucked against my side. A'yisha fit easily into my arms, light as a feather and so soft. Instinctually, I put my nose to her crown, smelling her sweet baby smell. None of my siblings had children yet, but my friends who had always welcomed a break.

Hen looked me over for a moment before saying, "I'll be right back."

"How you doing, darling?" I asked A'yisha, smiling big.

She cooed back, and I put my hand up to cover my face. When I moved it away and made a face, she squealed happily. I did it a few more times before Henrietta came back holding two plates.

"I got one for you," she said, holding up a plate packed to the brim with home cooking. I was more excited than I should admit to have food that wasn't cooked in a borrowed kitchen or a restaurant. Plus, it smelled amazing with all those spices.

We sat beside each other at one of the folding tables, and Bertrand and Imani sat with us. Bertrand's plate was half full of deviled eggs, and I nudged Hen's leg under the table. As soon as I nodded toward his plate, she burst out laughing.

"What?" Bertrand asked, his mouth stuffed.

Imani said, "Tyler, will you be around long enough for the wedding?"

Henrietta shook her head. "He's set to go home in May."

"That's a shame," she said. "If you find your way

back here in August, we'd love to have you."

I thanked her for the invitation, trying to ignore the reminder about the fleeting nature of my stay here. "How did you two meet?" I asked.

They launched into the story, and I held A'yisha in my lap, wondering if someday, Henrietta and I would be telling the same story with a child of our own.

After dinner, there was cake and candles and singing. And when that was over, Kenner watched TV in the living room while everyone else sat around a long table playing Rummikub, her grandma, Cordelia's, favorite game. Henrietta's family partied like my family did—long and relaxed with plenty of beer and laughter.

I hadn't ever felt so at home on a work trip, but now, with Henrietta by my side, I felt it.

But when Cordelia announced she was tired, that was everyone's sign to go home. Johmarcus picked up a sleeping Kenner, who hung over his shoulder like a sack of potatoes. Laila retrieved A'yisha from the Pack 'n Play, while Bertrand and Justus helped carry out presents. Imani and Raven helped Tam pack up the food and throw out empty beer cans, and then they were gone too. It was clearly a practiced routine.

"Can I walk you to your truck?" Henrietta asked at my side.

I nodded, sad the night had come to an end.

As we walked down the sidewalk, barely lit by a lone streetlight, I said, "You know, I'm the one who's supposed to be walking you to your door."

Johmarcus waved out the window as they drove the van away, and it was quickly followed by the other two vehicles. Hen and I waved back, smiling as we did.

We paused by my pickup, and she looked up at me, moonlight sparkling in her eyes. "Is it bad if I say I wanted a few seconds longer?"

My heart sped at her admission, because I felt the same way. I could have stayed here all night, well into the next morning, and it still wouldn't be long enough. "Henrietta, I have a question to ask you."

Her lips lifted slightly, and I smiled, realizing I was learning all her smiles, all her laughs. This one was shy, patient.

"Will you go on a date with me?" I asked. Never before had I been so nervous to ask, so anxious for the answer... so crushed when her features fell.

There was a war happening on her face, and I didn't know why. Had I read her signals wrong?

"Tyler, I'd love to," she said, "but Janessa said dating contractors is strictly forbidden. I like spending time with you, but... I can't lose my job."

My chest ached as all hope fled my body. With the way Janessa came on to me at the build site, I knew it was a lie, no matter how earnestly Henrietta delivered it. She even seemed genuinely regretful to say no. But I should have known better than to plan an imaginary future with a girl I'd just met. No matter how beautiful and intriguing she was. I'd let myself get invested before I even knew her true feelings.

And arguing the point now would only disrespect her, disrespect her father in saying it was her choice, and her choice alone.

So I dipped my head, attempting to recover, and smiled back at her. "I completely understand. Thank you for inviting me to the party. I'll see you on Monday."

21

HENRIETTA

Confession: I haven't really been saving for a house...

THE WALK back to the house was the longest of my life. It took all I had to keep my shoulders square and not show Tyler how much this decision was killing me on the inside. I managed a smile and a wave as his truck drove by, and then I walked inside, expecting to make a quiet escape to my bedroom.

Instead, my mom, dad, and grandma were waiting in the living room. I froze in the doorway, feeling like a goldfish in the bowl. "Why are you all staring at me?"

"Well!" Grandma said. "Did he ask you out?"

My features fell. That's what this was about? "Why would you think he asked me out?"

She glanced at Dad who admitted that Tyler had asked his permission.

I shook my head at the both of them. "I already told you I can't be with him. My job—"

"Your job?" Mom said. "Why are you so devoted to a job when you know you have the skills and experience to do that anywhere else?"

"I just got that promotion, and I'm saving for a house so I can get out of your hair, Mom. I can't be frivolous with my money."

"Stop," Dad said, his tone disappointed. He scrubbed his hand along his chin, not yet meeting me in the eyes. "Henrietta, we need to talk."

My stomach dropped. "What?"

"Sit," he ordered.

Feeling like I was sixteen years old and missing curfew, I crossed from the entryway to the living room, sitting on the chair as the three people I loved and respected most stared at me. And I didn't know how, but I could tell I'd let them down.

Dad said, "Henrietta, I'm no math genius, but your stories aren't adding up. You pay us two hundred a month for utilities, ninety dollars for your car insurance, and your phone is free through our family plan. Your car is paid off, and you fix everything for free at home. You buy all your clothes from the thrift store. Accounting for taxes, gas, and going out with your friends once a week, you have to be putting away, what, two thousand dollars a month? At least fifteen hundred for the last six years since paying down your student loans... Either I'm very confused about the kind of house you're saving for, or you're hiding something."

Busted.

"What if I do want a showstopper house?" I asked, lifting my chin.

They all saw right through it.

Mom asked, "Honey, are you in trouble of some sort?"

The worry in her voice almost undid me. I wanted to tell them the truth of why I'd saved so diligently. Why I was determined to put as much away as quickly as possible. But I couldn't without ruining the whole plan.

Grandma said, "Just because Johmarcus got upside-down in a business venture doesn't mean you have to be afraid of money."

"Mom and Dad had to take out another mortgage on the house to help him, Grandma," I said. "If that's not reason enough to be cautious, I don't know what is."

Dad cut his hand through the air. "That was our decision, what your mother and I were willing to do for our child. It was our choice to make, and we made it. That should have nothing to do with your saving habits."

Frowning, Mom said, "Are you waiting to buy a house until you find a boyfriend to move in with? Because times are different now. A real man won't be intimidated by a woman owning her own property and making her own mark in the world."

Seeing my opening, I hung my head. "I am waiting for a man," I admitted, but not in the way they thought I was. I raised my eyes to meet theirs, and my dad shook his head, a heavy expression on his face.

"You just let a good one walk right out that door," he said.

I replied, "I know, but that was my decision to make, and I made it." Then I stood up and walked to my room.

♥•♥•♥•♥

I TRIED to avoid my parents and Grandma for the rest of the weekend, because if they got too close, they'd see that my heart was breaking.

Tyler was the first man in my life who had asked me out, asked my father's permission no less. He'd proven his character when he respected my no without a single argument. He was one in a million, and I was losing him. Had lost him.

I tried to remind myself that I would have lost him when his job was over, but the truth? I'd imagined happily ever after. I'd imagined moving to Texas and celebrating Thanksgiving with his family and Christmas with mine. I'd imagined little children with my skin tone and his hazel eyes pattering through our house.

No amount of logic could take away the ache of that dream gone unrealized.

I kept things strictly business with Tyler at the beginning of the week, hoping he wouldn't see how turning him down had been the hardest thing I'd ever had to do.

But no matter how cheery I tried to be Wednesday morning, my friends knew it instantly.

Birdie took me in, concern in her eyes. "You look... awful. What went wrong?"

Mara nodded. "Did something happen this weekend with Tyler? You haven't replied to any of our messages."

I stared at my coffee and let out a sigh. I couldn't hide this from them just because I was embarrassed. So I told them the story, including my parents' interrogation after I turned Tyler down.

"But I want to know the same thing," Birdie said. "I thought he was the dream guy?"

Mara frowned. "And why is it taking you so long to

save for a house? Do you have a gambling problem or something?"

I almost laughed at the absurdity of it. "No, I don't have a gambling problem."

"Then what is it?" Mara asked. "You've been saving as long as I've known you and living with your parents to save costs. Even if you wanted twenty percent down, you'd easily have enough for a smaller house out here." She wasn't judgmental about it. Just confused.

If I told my parents and grandma the real reason I'd been saving, they would talk me out of it, and I didn't want anyone to do that. But my friends could respect my choices. I trusted them. Still, I asked, "If I tell you the truth, can you promise to keep it a secret?"

Birdie and Mara each offered their word.

I took a breath.

I hadn't ever voiced my plan aloud. But I knew I needed to get it off my chest. I needed someone to understand and tell me I wasn't completely insane for letting a guy like Tyler walk away.

"When my grandpa got colon cancer six years ago, it was the worst year of my life. He was diagnosed at stage IV, and he got so horribly sick, he was gasping for air with every breath for months. He deteriorated to skin and bones, but there was so much fluid in his body that his stomach was the size of a beach ball." I choked on my words, on the memory. He'd been such a strong, proud man, but this disease reduced him to nothing.

Birdie reached across the table and held my hand.

"Grandma had to sell her house just to pay for his hospice care. It wiped out all of their savings. The care wasn't great either. The hospice house was so sterile, and turnover was so high you couldn't count on the same workers being there every day. And then the walls were so thin, you could hear all those people suffering around him." My voice cracked, and I hung on to Birdie with all I had. "He kept begging to come home so he could go peacefully in his bed, but Grandma couldn't tell him she'd sold the house. There was nowhere else for him to go. I felt so powerless, watching him suffer and not having the money to do anything about it, especially after all he and Grandma did for me."

My friends waited silently, so I took a deep breath, revealing my biggest secret of all.

"So, I promised myself that I would save all the money I could to keep my grandma from suffering the same fate he did."

Mara covered her mouth, tears in her eyes. "That's why you've been so frugal? Hen, why didn't you tell us?"

I wiped at my own teary eyes. "I got so used to telling the house story around my family, I guess it was easier to keep up the lie."

Birdie squeezed my hand. "That's so selfless of you, Hen, to do that for your grandma. Does she know?"

I shook my head. "If she knew, she'd try to talk me out of it."

"How much do you have saved?" Mara asked.

I bit my lip, knowing the exact number. "Almost a hundred thousand."

Birdie let out a low whistle. "I knew end-of-life care was expensive, but not that expensive…"

"They say to budget for five thousand dollars a month," I said, "and I want to give her two years of really good care in our home, if she ever needs it. I should be able to save the last twenty thousand dollars this year, but by the time I do..."

"It'll be too late for Tyler," Birdie said.

I nodded. "But if I risk my job to be with Tyler and shit hits the fan, then I have to look for a new job, which could take months. Especially if I want to find one that pays as much as this one."

My friends and I were quiet as the weight of what I admitted hung over us. Because the truth was, some things were more important than following a potential love.

Mara tilted her head, smiling softly. "You know, in business they say short-term loss can lead to long-term gain. It's kind of like with you and Tyler. Even if you're set back a few months, you could gain experience at the very least."

Birdie nodded. "You could find your person, Hen. Tyler could turn out to be nothing—but you'll never know if you don't give him a chance. And if you'd go through all of this for your grandma, don't you think the potential love of your life deserves a date?"

22

TYLER

Gravel crunched under Henrietta's tires as she approached the construction site. I'd love to say it didn't hurt like hell to hear her pulling up, but it did. And maybe I did the immature thing of hiding out in the trailer because I wasn't quite ready to see her yet this morning. She'd been so stoic with me all week, only talking about work and not bantering with me like she usually did. It hurt almost as bad as her rejection.

Rich, an older guy on the construction crew, with white hair and a red face from years of working in the sun, came in and got a couple of folding tables. "Hen brought treats again. I'm really coming to love that girl."

The laugh that passed my lips felt strangled. "She's one of a kind."

He nodded and brought the tables out while I sat down at my desk, bracing myself to see her. I knew when to accept defeat, and I wanted to respect her answer, but man, it was hard. I was already counting down the days until it was time to go back home so I didn't have to suffer in silence anymore.

The door to the trailer opened again, and this time I heard a different voice. "Hey," Henrietta said gently.

I looked up to see her holding up a giant cinnamon roll on a paper plate and a steaming cup of coffee.

"Want some breakfast?" she asked. "The coffee's black this time."

I couldn't say no to her, not when she was smiling at me like that. "I'd love some."

She passed me the plate, and I was careful not to let my fingers touch hers, not to let the heat transfer from her skin to mine. I'd be a burning man with no way to save myself from the flames.

I set the cinnamon roll on my desk and took a burning sip from the Styrofoam cup. "Is this from Waldo's?"

She nodded. "The girls and I go every Wednesday before work. It's kind of a tradition."

"Nice," I said, wondering why we were making small talk. Why it hurt so fucking much to be in her presence and know I wasn't enough.

"Tyler, there was one thing I wanted to talk to you about..."

My gut dropped. "Yeah? What's up?" This couldn't get any worse than rejection, right? Because I'd made countless moves on her, and now I knew all of them had been unwelcome. I felt like such a creep, reliving the kiss on her forehead, two-stepping at the bar, telling her she was beautiful... A dumb creep at that for misreading all the signs.

"About the question you asked me the other night." She took a breath, her eyes looking everywhere but at me.

"I'm really sorry about that," I began. "I shouldn't have crossed a line, and I promise it won't happen again."

Her eyes snapped to mine. "What if I want it to happen again?"

"What?" I asked, my mind fumbling for a possible explanation.

"I would be honored to go on a date with you, if you're still interested, that is," she said. There was so much vulnerability in her features, and even though I was overjoyed that she'd changed her mind, I had to ask... "What changed?"

She smiled, as if to herself, and said, "Circumstances changed."

That was all I needed—I wasn't about to look a gift horse in the mouth. "Are you free on Friday night?"

She nodded, smiling.

"I'll pick you up from your place at seven?"

"It's a date."

THE NEXT TWO days passed so slowly, I wished I would have asked her out for Wednesday night, but Friday finally, *finally* came. As I got ready to pick her up, I realized just how long it had been since I'd gone on any sort of date at all.

It had to be two years ago... when I realized dating on the job was idiotic.

Not dating Hen felt even crazier, though. Despite how nervous I was.

In fact, I was wearing some of my best clothes, had on new cologne, and I hardly felt prepared to walk out the door. So I stood in my living room, got out my phone, and video called my brother Rhett who had been on so many dates, he had to be an expert by now.

He answered within a few minutes, and I saw his front yard behind him.

"Hey, what's up?" I asked.

"Watering these damn flowers," he said. "Mom planted them last spring, and I know if I let them die, it'd kill 'er." He moved the phone to show the sunflowers in full bloom.

I laughed. "I guess that is one of the benefits of not living back home anymore. No surprised redecorations."

He snorted in agreement. "What's up with you? Job going well?"

"It's fine. Actually, I... uh. I have a date tonight."

"Hot damn," Rhett said, grinning ear to ear. The look instantly made me regret calling. "It's been what? Two years since Sheridan?"

I lifted my eyes toward the sky, trying to forget my crazy ex-girlfriend. I'd been up-front, telling the girl, Sheridan, that I was only in town for a few months. I'd thought we were just having fun together, but she'd been completely heartbroken and even showed up to my next job site, trying to win me back. Jim had been pissed, calling it a liability. So my no-dating rule commenced.

I cleared my throat. "Two years. Which means I'm rusty as hell. Any tips?"

"On getting laid? I have a few tricks up my sleeve."

"Okay, now I'm really regretting this call."

Rhett laughed. "Girls always loved you. You have that mama's boy charm no one can resist."

I rolled my eyes. "I'm hanging up now."

"Girls like it when they feel like the most interesting thing in the room," he said. "That hot waitress walks by? Don't give her a second glance. Eyes on your date. She says something about her boring job? Ask her questions about it like it's the most intriguing thing you've ever heard. She talks about how her nephew blew his first spit bubble, you're in awe. Got it?"

I nodded, although it seemed easy. Henrietta was like a puzzle, and each new thing I learned about her felt like a piece that would get me closer to the full picture.

"But if you like the girl, which I'm guessing you do because you've never asked me girl advice before..."

I didn't argue.

"You want her falling for the real you and not some lame tip your brother gave you five minutes before the date. Just be yourself, okay? It's enough. I promise it's enough."

I cracked a smile at that. "Thanks, Rhett."

"Any time."

We hung up, and I took a deep breath before leaving the house.

Tonight was going to be big. I could feel it.

23

HENRIETTA

Confession: No one in my family has any chill when it comes to first dates... especially me.

BOTH OF MY best friends sat on my bed while I looked at myself in the mirror above my dresser. Birdie had helped with my makeup while Mara picked out my outfit, and even though I was all dressed and ready, I was more nervous than I'd ever been in my life.

I turned toward my friends and said, "Are you sure this is the look?"

We'd gone with an olive-green dress, a denim jacket, white and cheetah print sneakers, and a white headband tied around my hair to match. It was cute, but was it enough for the firework show picking me up tonight?

Mara got up from the bed and put her hands on my shoulder. "Hen, you look amazing, but Tyler already knows what you look like! He already likes you! Remember, this is just for you two to spend more time together and see what happens. No pressure at all."

Birdie nodded from where she sat on the bed. "I totally agree. You two are going to have so much fun tonight. Wherever you go."

I tried to stifle my giddy smile. Tyler was surprising me with the destination of our date, and if I was being honest, I loved surprises. I loved that he was thinking of me enough to plan something he thought I'd love.

I glanced at my watch and saw I only had fifteen minutes until the date. "You guys should probably go so he doesn't find out I needed my besties to help me get ready."

Birdie winked. "Playing it cool, I like it."

I snorted. "Cool is about the furthest thing from how I feel. I need all the help I can get."

Mara hooked her purse around her shoulder. "So not true. Tyler's not going to know what hit him."

I smiled, following them out of my room to the living room. But our quick exit quickly turned into my mom and grandma squealing about my outfit and hair and how excited they were that I was going out with Tyler.

Tears shone in my grandma's eyes, and she put her hand to her mouth. "I remember going on my first date with your grandpa. I wore a dress my mama made for me —little pink and blue flowers on the fabric. He took me to a barn dance out in the country, and we spent the whole night dancing with each other."

Mara asked, "How old were you?"

"Seventeen," Grandma answered, her eyes in her memories. "He borrowed his daddy's car to drive me. We thought we were styling."

The doorbell rang, jerking us out of memory lane. I glanced at my watch and said, "Crap! He's ten minutes early!"

Mom nodded approvingly. "That's the sign of a good man."

"Or an eager one," Mara said with a wink.

I would have laughed if I wasn't so panicked. "He's going to think I'm pathetic if he sees everyone in here! Go hide!"

Grandma raised her eyebrows. "I ain't about to hide behind no couch."

"Please? Just until he gets me to his truck?"

Mom had an amused smile on her lips. "Come on, everyone. We can go out back. I want to show you my verbena."

I waited until they were all safely in the backyard to walk to the front door. I placed my hand on the knob, knowing minutes had already passed since he rang the bell, but I took my time, allowing myself a deep breath.

I'd gotten my associate degree, worked as a professional for eight years... I could do this. I could go on a date with Tyler Griffen.

I opened the door, and the sight of him standing there took my breath away. He held a full bouquet of purple blooms of all kinds, interspersed by greenery and baby's breath. So tasteful and beautiful.

I covered my mouth with my hand, never expecting this. "These are beautiful, Tyler. Are they for me?"

"Unless you know another Henrietta," he said, a teasing smile on his lips.

He held the flowers out for me, and I breathed in the

floral scents. Regardless of how things ended, I wanted to remember this moment when I was my grandma's age. I wanted to reminisce on the fact that this handsome man had thought of me, cared for me, in a way that was so unexpected, so wholesome.

"I'll get a vase for these," I said.

Tyler chuckled, pointing toward the back window just in time for me to see Grandma hide again. "Looks like you'll have some help."

My cheeks felt hot as I set the bouquet on the counter. "I'll let them take care of these."

He walked beside me out the door and down the side-walk, his hand resting gently on my middle back, reminding me he was there but not suggesting any more. I liked it, especially mingled with the smell of his cologne and the fresh sunshine-filled air.

He opened the door for me, helping me in, and then when we were on the road, I asked the question. "Where are we going?"

Glancing my way, he replied, "Not too much longer until you find out."

I watched out the window, practically vibrating with excitement. I was on a date. With Tyler Griffen. The cute contractor with a smile that could replace the sun, muscled arms that would make any woman drool, a laugh that melted my insides, and enough ink to make him interesting without scaring off my parents. How could this be my life?

"What?" he asked, smiling my way.

"Nothing. This just doesn't feel real," I admitted.

And just when I thought the night couldn't get any

better, he reached across the center seat, sliding his fingers through mine. "I feel the same way."

I stared at our intertwined fingers, my skin dark against his pale. There were a few freckles on the back of his hand, and a small bit of hair on his fingers. This was a masculine hand, one that spent hours on hard labor. But the tender way he held me... this man was full of so many surprises.

Soon he pulled into the parking lot at the Brentwood Marina, and I said, "The date's *here?*"

"What?" he asked. "You weren't expecting a fine-dining nautical experience?"

I relaxed my brow. "It doesn't seem very Tyler Griffen, farm boy from Texas with the cutest southern twang."

He chuckled, the sound melting me from the inside out. "It's Tyler Griffen, formerly landlocked redneck who wants to impress the most beautiful girl in California."

My eyelids drifted closed with my smile, and I shook my head. "You are no redneck, you southern charmer."

"On that note, let me keep up my good streak and get your door."

He got out and walked to my side of the truck, and once I was on the pavement, he offered his elbow to me. I looped my hands through, linking my fingers around his solid arm. For a moment, I leaned my temple against his strong shoulder and pretended I was one of those girls who'd been doing this all the time. The kind of girl who had no lack of dates for Friday night and was always treated like a gem. That's how Tyler made me feel, and I was high on the experience. High on him.

He led us to a boat with cursive writing on the front. It said *The Daydreamer*. I smiled at the name. How apt.

A worker dressed in a white suit extended his arm in a welcoming gesture and said, "Welcome aboard."

24

TYLER

As we stepped aboard the yacht I'd reserved for our first date, there was plenty to draw my attention, but all I could focus on was Henrietta. Her eyes were awestruck at the splendor of the boat. And me? Well, I was enamored with her. Seeing everything through her eyes made it feel like the first time.

The maître d', who introduced himself as Jacob, led us to an elaborately decorated table on the deck overlooking the water. Sailboats dotted the horizon, interrupting the space where turquoise water met soft orange sky.

I missed Texas sunsets, all the bright colors meeting waving prairie grass, but this view, reflected in Henrietta's eyes? It had to be my favorite.

"It's beautiful out here," she said as she sat down. "I don't think I've been on a yacht except for my ten-year reunion."

"They had it on a yacht?" I asked. "My class's

reunion was in the school parking lot and involved coolers full of beer."

She nodded with a smile. "Had to make sure we wouldn't escape."

"You'd want to escape? Seems like high school would have been a breeze for you. You're so easy to talk to."

She laughed. "Being just as tall and bigger than most of the guys at my school didn't do me any social favors."

I shook my head, hating to admit it probably would have been the same at my high school. "When you're young and dumb, different things seem important. And then you grow up."

"True," she said, scrunching her nose in the cutest way. "I'm sure you were the star at your school."

I laughed. "In Cottonwood Falls, you go to school with the same kids from the time you're in kindergarten to graduation. They all remembered my awkward younger years."

"We all have awkward younger years," she replied.

"My mom had to drive me to Dallas for therapy because I was so shy, I wouldn't even talk to the teacher."

Now it was her turn to be surprised. "You seem so confident, easygoing."

"Three decades of practice," I replied.

Jacob brought out some wine for us, pouring our glasses full of rosé. They hadn't offered Cupcake on the menu, but I hoped this would be close enough.

She took a cautious sip, her expression thoughtful.

"As good as Cupcake?" I asked.

She hesitated before shaking her head, and I laughed.

"I was worried it would be awkward," she admitted. "Being somewhere so fancy."

"You don't go out much?"

"No, I'm pretty frugal. Pancakes at Waldo's and free drinks at Collie's is about as high-class as I get."

"You'd love Cottonwood Falls," I said. "Everything is like that. If you want fancy, you have to go to the city."

"Do you miss home?" she asked.

I took a drink of my own wine, the bitter liquid sliding down my throat. "I thought I would get used to it, being away, but after four years, I think feeling out of place has just become the norm for me."

"Are you planning on moving back sometime?"

It was too soon to be thinking about how things like this would affect our relationship, but I had to be honest. "If my boss promotes me, I'd be able to move back home and work there full-time. There would be travel for different projects, but I'd have a home base."

Jacob came back with our first course. A salad with a mixture of fruits and vegetables I hadn't encountered. Which left me with a dilemma. I leaned forward and asked Henrietta, "Which fork do I use?"

She giggled, covering her mouth. "I was waiting for you to go first so I would know."

I racked my brain, trying to remember the etiquette lessons I had in sophomore home economics. "I think you go from the outside in."

"Let's do that," she said. We both picked up our outside fork and tasted the salad.

As Hen chewed, her eyes drifted to the water. The sun was sinking quickly. When she looked back at me, she said, "It's funny—you can't wait to get home and I need to leave mine."

I chuckled, wiping at the corners of my mouth with my white napkin. "Your family seems close."

"We are. My brothers come over almost every weekend, and when my grandma can't catch a ride on the senior bus, I take her out. It's nice. But we're *all* ready for me to move out and live my own life. I've been living at home for far too long."

"Have you found a house you like yet?" I asked. The food in my stomach settled heavily. If Hen bought a house here, that would be it. Our fates would be sealed... separately.

"I haven't really looked. I still have quite a ways to go."

"What do you mean?"

She chewed her lip, that same warring expression from the night she turned me down present yet again. "Can I tell you a secret?"

"Of course," I said.

Our main course came out, and as we ate, she launched into this story about saving for her grandma that made me see her in a whole new way.

When I didn't respond right away, she said, "What? You're thinking I'm crazy."

Sure, I already knew she was kind, hardworking. But to know how much she'd sacrificed for her grandma without anyone ever asking... it was amazing. "I'm speechless, Hen," I breathed. "The girls back home— they think of having babies, doing the same thing their parents did before them. What you're doing, what you've done... no one does that. Only you."

She glanced down at her lap like my praise made her uncomfortable.

"You don't like compliments," I observed.

She met my eyes again. "I'm not used to them."

A little rip formed in my chest at the way Henrietta had been made to see the world. "If we make it to another date, I'll give you plenty of practice."

Her laugh tinkled amongst the lap of waves on the boat. "If the food is this good, you know I'm there."

AS WE DROVE BACK to her family's home, her fingers tangled with mine, I couldn't help but think it had been the perfect first date. The food and scenery were good, but getting to know Hen outside of work? Even better. I could talk to her for hours or sit silently beside her for the same amount of time.

I didn't want this date to end. Didn't want to walk her to the end of the sidewalk and say goodnight. But there was something I'd been wondering. And I couldn't stop myself from asking.

I put my truck into park along the curb and turned to her. She looked beautiful with the light from my dash reflecting off her skin, her dark eyes on mine.

"Can I ask you a question?" I asked.

"Another one, you mean?"

I gave her an exasperated shake of my head.

She giggled, nodded, leaning her head back against the headrest.

"When I asked you out... you told me your job had a rule against it. What was really holding you back? I only ask because I wouldn't ever want to do something that made you uncomfortable..."

Two lines formed between her eyebrows. "What do you mean?"

"After the way Janessa came on to me at the build site, there's no way there's a rule against dating contractors."

Her lips parted. "What did Janessa do?"

At the disbelief in her voice, I felt like I should tread carefully. "That first day... she asked me out to dinner and implied we should spend some time together, if you know what I mean."

Henrietta pressed her lips together and shook her head. "That same day, she told me that I could lose my job if I dated you. I've been fretting over my attraction to you for weeks because of her."

That made so much more sense, the way Hen held me at arm's length. The sincerity when she said no to dating me.

"Why would she do something like that?" Henrietta asked, hurt clear in her voice.

"She saw the way I was looking at you after I told her no." It was the only thing that made sense. "She was threatened by you."

"Threatened by me." Hen snorted. "The girl's a size two, and she felt like she had to threaten my job to keep me away from you."

"You know size isn't the only thing a guy sees," I said.

She raised her eyebrows. "Maybe it's not the only thing *you* specifically see, but that's not my experience with most men."

"What do you mean?"

"Do you know what it feels like to have people make fun of you at the beach for simply existing at your size? Do you know how it feels to walk by magazines and have headlines shouting at you that you need to change? Do you know how it feels to always be the funny fat friend?"

I studied her for a moment, hating anything and everyone that had made her feel like that. "I've never seen you that way."

"How do you see me?" she asked.

I took her in, and only one word came to mind. "Beautiful."

25

HENRIETTA

Confession: For a woman named Hen, I have a hard time not counting my chickens before they hatch.

ALL THIS TIME, I'd been so worried about my job, worried about my grandma, worried about my future. When in reality, I'd just been missing out on an incredible guy, all so my boss could call dibs on him, like a child licking a cookie to make it their own. Kenner had more maturity than her, and he was still wearing Pull-Ups to bed.

Tyler was only here for nine months, and I'd missed so much of it just by following the "rules." Well, I was done wasting time, especially when it came to Tyler.

I unbuckled my seat belt and leaned closer.

His eyes flicked from mine to my lips.

A question.

I nodded.

A promise.

My eyelids slid closed, and I felt his lips against mine, felt the slight stubble on his chin as our skin brushed. Electricity, lust, desire, longing, it all swept through me as I got lost in our kiss, tasting the mint on his tongue, feeling his hand grip the base of my neck, holding me in place so he could deepen the kiss.

A small whimper escaped my lips, one I hadn't been expecting or holding in, and that only encouraged him more. Our tongues tangled, removing all the breath from my body as I tried to feel him, taste him, get lost in him.

Tyler was a gentleman, but the way he was holding me, his hand dancing up my hip, barely touching the side of my breast, he was holding himself back. Every part of me wanted to find out what more he could do, discover the ways he wanted to touch me.

I fisted my hand in his shirt over his stomach and kissed him hungrily. I'd made out with guys before, but it had never been like this—so all-consuming, so addicting to where I cared more about his lips on mine than my next breath.

Moisture soaked my panties, and even though I'd never had sex before, my body knew I wanted it. Was ready for it. With him.

He pulled back, his heavy breathing matching my own. I studied his hooded eyes, feeling all the passion I saw there.

His voice was husky as he said, "I should get you inside."

"What if I don't want to go?" I whispered.

A heated grin hit his lips. "Does this mean I get a second date?"

My smile came all on its own. I nodded. But then my lips turned down.

"What?" he asked.

"It's wedding week."

"And?"

"I'm a bridesmaid. It's a lot of responsibility, and I don't want to drag you along to it if..." I couldn't bring myself to finish the sentence. It was too much too soon.

But Tyler said, "If what?"

"If this wasn't something that's going to last."

His expression grew serious as he took my hand in his. "I can't predict the future, Hen, but until we figure out what this is..." He gestured between us. "I'm in. All in."

I bit my bottom lip, holding back a smile. "In that case, will you be my date to the rehearsal dinner and the wedding?"

He cupped my cheek with his hand and kissed me again, softer this time, only stirring the embers instead of lighting a flame.

A curtain in the front window of my house cracked, letting out enough light for me to know my family was waiting on me. They were just as excited to hear about my date with Tyler as I was to tell them and my friends.

"We're being watched," I whispered.

"Then I should get you to the door like a gentleman instead of doing everything else I'm imagining right now."

A swoop of desire went through my stomach.

This could be it, I realized.

The guy I lost my virginity to.

The guy I loved.

But I couldn't get ahead of myself right now.

Instead, I let him open the door for me. We walked together down the sidewalk, and he kissed me on the cheek at the house, an unspoken promise in the air.

The best was yet to come.

26

HENRIETTA

Confession: I felt betrayed.

AS I DROVE to the office Monday morning, I couldn't stop thinking about the bomb Tyler had dropped on me. Had Janessa really lied to me? We'd worked together for eight years, and at this point, I'd considered her a friend. A close colleague at the very least. Would she really have felt threatened enough to lie?

There was really only one way to find out.

When I reached the apartment parking lot, I put my car in park and began searching through my contact list. One of the benefits of never updating your phone? I had every single contact from as far back as I could remember.

Midway through the Fs, I found Frannie's number. Hoping she hadn't changed it in the last few years, I pressed call.

"Henrietta!" she answered. "Long time no talk."

I could hear her car running in the background. Maybe she was driving to work. "I'm sorry about that," I said. "Have you been doing alright?"

"Great, actually! I ended up marrying that contractor I met on the SoCal build, and we have a kid now. I'm on my way to drop her off at daycare as we speak."

"Congratulations!" I told her. I hadn't been invited to the wedding, but then again, that didn't surprise me. The events of her leaving Blue Bird had been really hush-hush. "I was wondering... whatever happened back then? Do you mind sharing why you left?"

She was quiet for a moment, and I half expected her to tell me to fuck off. I wouldn't blame her one bit. I needed to be a better friend that way. I was about to apologize for interrupting her day when she said, "They didn't tell you?"

"No," I answered. "Well, Janessa said it had something to do with that contractor. What was his name?"

"Jeremy," she answered.

"Right."

"Janessa's full of hot air, but you know that," Frannie said. Her daughter cried, and she shushed her for a moment before saying, "I kept showing up to work late because I was so nauseous in the mornings, so they let me go. If I would have known the reason for my 'stomach bug' was morning sickness, I would have sued them for all they had."

I shook my head, processing it all. "I'm sorry they did that to you. Being pregnant sounds miserable." If I got pregnant, I'd only know the signs because of my sisters-in-law, who way overshared.

"It is, and then you get the best gift ever at the end."

I smiled at the love I heard in her voice. "So it wasn't against the rules for you to date Jeremy?"

"Corporate only cares what you do on company time. They don't give a shit who you're dating off the clock."

"Right." My jaw tensed. So Janessa really had lied to me, just to get Tyler.

"Hey, I'm at the daycare, but if you're ever in Chula Vista, let me know. I'd love to get some drinks with you, catch up sometime."

"I'd love that too," I replied honestly. "I'll talk to you later?"

"Sure thing."

We hung up, and I gripped my phone tightly as I lowered it from my ear. I felt sickened, betrayed. If Janessa had so easily lied to me about Tyler, what else had she lied to me about? I thought back over what I once believed had been a friendly working relationship, rethinking everything.

She'd only been looking out for herself. And maybe it was time I did the same, starting with enjoying this wedding week and spending the weekend with Tyler. I had felt so guilty for submitting my time-off request for Wednesday through Friday since it meant Janessa would have to drive from LA to Emerson.

But now, I didn't feel guilty at all. In fact, the only thing I regretted was having to call and remind her that I'd be off work. I went into the office, putting my sack lunch in the fridge and then checking voicemails.

With my blood at a simmer instead of a boil, I dialed her number on the office phone. It rang a few times before her perky voice came on the line. "Hey, Hen! How's it going this week?"

I stood to pace my office as far as the phone cord would allow. "Construction is still on track. Tyler says we're good on all the permits, and so far, there have been no delays."

"I knew he was amazing," she said, a wistfulness to her voice.

I scowled. "I just wanted to remind you I'll be out Wednesday through Friday. I'm meeting with the maintenance crew tomorrow to make sure they can handle any emergencies that come up, and I'll set up the phone to forward calls to you."

"Have I told you that I love how on top of everything you are? You've always done such a good job for us."

Her words were just another slap to the face. Did she mean any of them? We'd been colleagues for eight years, and suddenly, this office didn't feel like a second home anymore. It felt like a cage. A lie. One I had to stay trapped in to keep my job and save enough for Grandma.

"Thanks," I said, carrying on the act. "I'll call you first thing Monday to touch base on anything I missed."

"Perfect. Have a great day, girlie!"

She hung up, and I sat back down in my chair, defeated.

I really had loved this job, loved this company. I'd put years of my life toward it. Maybe it really was time for a change of scenery.

Since I didn't have any tours scheduled this morning and I didn't have to run rent checks to the bank until this afternoon, I clicked onto the computer and began looking for new jobs. By lunchtime, I had printed off my résumé to go over, along with a few listings I thought would be a good fit for me.

I ate my packed lunch at my desk, crossing out words on my résumé and replacing them with keywords from the job listings like I'd learned to in a professional development class. But I was so busy marking red, the sound of the door opening nearly scared me to death.

I hurriedly swiped my papers aside, setting them beneath a stack of apartment layouts, and smiled up at the intruder.

It was a young guy, barely twenty if I had to guess. "Hey," he said, "I'm here for the tour?"

I nodded, getting back to business. "Come with me."

27

TYLER

The third time in Cohen's garage was far more comfortable than the first time. Especially when Cohen started the conversation by raising his beer to me. "Birdie said you and Hen had a great first date."

Steve crooned happily and Jonas grinned at me, making my ears feel hot.

"How was it?" Steve asked. "Tell me you brought her flowers."

Okay, now my neck and cheeks were red too. "Can't show up to a first date without flowers."

"Sheesh," Jonas said. "You're going to make the rest of us look bad. Better step up my game before Mara calls off the wedding."

"Speaking of the wedding," I said, "Henrietta invited me as her plus one. Are you sure it's okay that I come?"

"Of course. Any friend of Hen's is a friend of ours. And if you keep beating Cohen at Hold'em, you'll be replacing him as best man."

Cohen scowled at him. "Couple weeks of bad luck and all of a sudden I'm getting demoted."

Steve tilted his head back and laughed. "You always were a sore loser."

Cohen good-naturedly brushed off the heckling. "Your deal, Ty."

I smiled slightly at the nickname, beginning to shuffle the deck. The sound mixed with the flutter of cardstock against my fingers was strangely settling. "Any plans for the bachelor party?"

I glanced up in time to see Jonas shrug. "That's more of Mara's thing."

I raised my eyebrows. "A bachelor party?"

"The whole"—he waved his hand through the air—"stripper, drinking, penis-shaped-candy, party thing. We'll be here, having a beer and playing poker if you want to join."

I thanked him for the invitation, and we got back to the game. Drinking, gambling, all the things that would make my late grandma shudder. "Sounds like a good time," I replied, continuing with the game.

When the night was over, with another win for me, Jonas and Steve left, but Cohen held me back.

"What's up?" I asked as the garage door slid shut, blocking us from the outside world.

He scratched the back of his neck. "Well, here's the deal. I don't want to just drink beer and play poker for Jonas's bachelor party, but I have no idea what else to do."

"Steve didn't have any ideas?" I asked.

"We're all pretty laid-back guys. We didn't want strippers or a party bus or anything like that, and going to the bar I own just feels like a cop-out."

I grinned, thinking of the party bus I'd been on for my high school best friend's wedding. There had been more beer than common sense on that thing. "Y'all live minutes away from the ocean. Why not do some deep-sea fishing or a kayak tour or something active like that? Get away from the city and clear your head for a day."

Cohen nodded. "Steve's shit on motorboats—gets seasick—but a kayak could be fine. We can always do beer and poker afterward if Jonas wants... Hell, it's just a couple hours to San Diego..."

I patted his shoulder. "Now you're thinking."

He grinned. "Thanks. I guess I've lived here so long I've forgotten what we have." He opened the side door leading into his kitchen, gesturing for me to follow him.

"Dallas is pretty landlocked, so I'm trying to enjoy the water while I can. We have lakes, but it's not the same." I followed him into a well-lit kitchen area that was far fancier than anything I'd grown up with. They had matching dishes, glass cups, and herbs in kitschy containers.

"Nice place," I said.

He grinned my way. "It's all Birdie."

"How long have y'all been together?" I asked on the way to the front door.

"Almost three years now. One year married. Best years of my life."

The comment made me smile. I hoped to find that someday. Soon.

28

HENRIETTA

Confession: There are some things even I can't plan for.

WAKING up Wednesday morning and not having to go to work was a huge relief. I hardly ever took time off, but I had vacation days saved up, and I was excited to spend them with my best friends.

Before meeting Birdie and Mara a few years back, I never really had girlfriends. I was always that girl who hung around my brothers or read books by myself. Then when my brothers started dating, I got girl time with their girlfriends (now wives and soon-to-be wife) when they came over. Now that I had best friends, I wouldn't trade them for anything.

Mara wanted to start wedding week off with a relaxing day at the beach, so I put on my one-piece, then slipped my cover-up dress over my head, packed a beach bag and left my room to help Grandma with her morning medications.

She wasn't in the living room, reading her Bible like she usually did in the mornings. So I checked the kitchen, thinking maybe she'd gotten her toast, but still came up empty. Worry settled in my gut, making it hard to move. I walked to her bedroom and found her lying on the floor by her closet, her pants half on and her arms covering her face.

"Grandma?" I choked out.

When she moved her hands, I saw the tears on her cheeks.

I hurried to her, kneeling next to her on the floor. "Grandma, are you hurt?"

She slowly nodded. "I fell getting dressed, and my hip... I think it might be broken."

"Why didn't you call for me?"

"I didn't want to bother anyone."

If I wasn't so worried, I would have scolded her. "I'm calling an ambulance," I said, getting my cell from my purse. I tried to keep my voice from shaking as I spoke with the dispatcher and gave them directions to my house.

The person on the phone said not to sit her up until the medics arrived in case there was a spinal injury. And then it was on us to wait.

"Can you help me put a skirt on?" Grandma asked.

I gave her a look. "You trying to get fancy for the EMTs?"

"I can't be seen like this. So... frail." Her voice sounded frail as she said it. Frail, but stubborn. "Please, Hen?"

I couldn't argue with her, so I carefully slid her pants off without moving her legs and then got the most forgiving skirt I could find and carefully shimmied it up her hips. She cringed when I slid it under her backside, but as soon as it was on, she seemed to settle.

"When are they getting here?" she demanded. "Did they send a student driver?"

I let out a relieved laugh as I checked my phone. That was the grandma I knew. "Average response time for our area is seven minutes. It's been five."

As if on time, the front door rang, and I said, "I'm going to let them in, but I'll be with you every step, okay?"

Her eyes watered as she held my hand. "I'm sorry to ruin your day with your friends."

"They're my friends; you're my *family*." I held her weathered hand in mine. "I would do anything for you, Grandma."

She squeezed my hand and then let go so I could answer the door. There were three paramedics in blue uniforms, one carrying a gurney. It all happened in a flash, showing them where she was, following them out the door, and getting into the ambulance with my grandma strapped to a board and her trying not to make a sound with each bump the ambulance hit.

As we drove, I called my mom and dad, telling them we were on the way to the hospital, then I texted Mara to let her know I wasn't coming this morning.

When we reached the hospital, they wheeled Grandma back to imaging and told me which ER room to wait in. I paced the small space, the fluorescent lighting hurting my head just as much as Grandma's helplessness had hurt my heart.

I'd expected, prepared for, Grandma to struggle for a

year, maybe two, like Grandpa had, but I hadn't considered a broken bone. If it was bad, she could be in a wheelchair for years. And my parents couldn't help her all day every day to get the things she needed. The thought of my vibrant, spirited, opinionated grandma being relegated to a cold, impersonal nursing home... it made my stomach churn.

I was about to break when the doors pushed open and Grandma was wheeled into the room. They transferred her onto the bed and then helped her get comfortable before saying a doctor would be in to let us know the results of her X-rays, along with her next steps. I just hoped she'd be able to make them at home.

29

TYLER

Since I knew Henrietta wouldn't be by this morning, I ordered coffee and donuts for the guys. She was right—beer and pizza were a great way to make friends, but breakfast was the best way to start the day.

I set up the table myself and then helped the delivery person lay out the food and drink. With it all ready to go, I called the guys over. "Grab some breakfast! We've got a long day of work ahead!"

"You're in a good mood, boss," Rich said, coming up beside me with a donut in hand.

I was beginning to like this guy, even though he still called me boss despite all my protestations. "I *am* in a good mood," I admitted. It's not like I could deny it. I'd worn a smile on my face since my first date with Henrietta, and the thought of going to a wedding with her as her date... It meant we were moving forward. Together.

But then I saw a slick car pull up to the job site. And a heeled leg extend from the cab and settle on the ground.

"Shit," I muttered.

Rich followed my gaze and murmured, "Corporate. Good luck."

It wasn't my kind of corporate. Jimmy was laid back, and anyone else he hired to work with him had the same down-to-earth attitude.

No, this was Janessa, dressed to kill. She had on a sleek black dress that hugged her toned body. Her blond hair was curled, her lips blood red, and her heels the expensive, pointy kind my sister would never wear.

At the sight of me, her lips curled into a deadly, seductive smile, and she crooned, "Tyler Griffen, aren't you a sight for sore eyes?" She was looking at my Crenshaw Construction T-shirt like she wanted to rip it off my body.

I folded my arms over my chest as she neared. "Janessa, we weren't expecting to see you here."

She touched my arm with her hand, decorated with pointy red nails. "Henrietta's out of the office this week, so I wanted to check in. See if there was..." She slowly wet her lips. "Anything you needed?"

I suppressed a shudder. Maybe I would have been into this even a few months ago, but now it made my skin crawl. I wanted to send the clear message that our relationship would remain professional. "We're making great progress here. Pouring the foundation for the second floor this week, and when it cures, we'll be on to the third."

Her eyes traveled over the job site, all my guys back to work with a suit on site. "You have quite the team here, Tyler."

"I do," I agreed. I was happy with everyone and their work. "I think Blue Bird will be pleased with the build when it's all said and done."

"That's why we hired Crenshaw," she said. "James's reputation is stellar. Getting you with the deal was just a perk." She winked.

I studied her for a moment. This was a woman who was used to getting what she wanted, and she had no qualms doing so by any means necessary. That much was apparent from what she'd told Henrietta. I tried not to be annoyed that her lie had nearly cost me an incredible woman.

"Since I'm in town, I was wondering if you might want to get lunch, professionally speaking, and talk over the project?"

I was on a tight rope; I could feel it. If I said no, I'd offend someone very important to Crenshaw Construction. But if I said yes, I'd risk her twisting more words to Henrietta. But at this point, Henrietta had to know I wasn't interested in Janessa, so I nodded and said, "Sure. Where would you like to go?"

She rattled off the name of a restaurant I didn't recognize and said, "I'll be back at noon to pick you up."

I nodded. "See you then."

Giving me a wicked grin, she spun on her heels and turned to walk away. Shaking my head, I walked up to the site where they were starting to pour concrete. This was going to be a long day.

JANESSA WAS BACK at twelve o'clock on the dot, just as she'd promised, and there was nothing I could do to worm my way out of it. So I washed my hands in the on-site bathroom, threw on a polo I kept in the office, and followed her to her car.

It was one of those small, sleek things that made me feel like I was riding in a clown car. I reached for the button and pushed my chair back so my knees wouldn't be knocking the dash as she whipped out of the parking lot.

"How was your morning?" she asked.

"Good, and yours?"

"Learned something new about Henrietta. Turns out she's been fronting rent for people at the beginning of the month."

"She pays their rent?" I asked.

Janessa nodded. "And then they'll pay her on the fifth or sixth when their check comes in."

My eyebrows rose. "For how many people?"

"A couple every month as far as I can tell." She shook her head as if Hen's generosity was unbelievable. Or stupid. "Her money, though."

"Why not move the rent payment back for those renters if it's the same people every month?" I asked.

"Makes accounting's job harder, and they have enough on their plate as it is," Janessa said, whipping around another corner.

Thankfully, I wasn't driving, because that news about Hen knocked me back. Even though she was saving for her grandma and living frugally herself... she was still helping how she could. The charitable giving part of Gage's business should take notes from her.

"Here we are," Janessa said. She pulled up along a restaurant with big glass windows overlooking a downtown park, then let the valet open her door.

I got out on my side and walked to the restaurant with Janessa at my side. "Are you sure I'm not underdressed for this place?"

She studied me for a moment. "Maybe."

With all that reassurance, I felt like I was a socially awkward child all over again. We walked inside, and I certainly was not dressed fine. I was surprised they didn't kick me back by the dumpster to be rid of me. The hostess stared me down, the server stayed as far away from me as possible, and they sat us at the worst table, way back by the kitchen where basically no one could see us except staff.

Which, unfortunately, gave Janessa an excuse. "I'm going to sit by you so I can stay out of the way," she said, getting up and moving her chair. Right. By. Mine.

Her perfume, almost clinically strong, wafted over me, and my stomach turned at the scent combined with all the seasonings from the kitchen.

"Tell me, Tyler, how are you liking California?"

My mind immediately went to Henrietta. "It's better than I expected." In every possible way.

"If you think Emerson is great, there's a vineyard farther north I *have* to take you to. They have the most romantic weekend retreats, beautiful rooms overlooking miles of grape vines... It's quite the aphrodisiac."

I tucked the idea away for a weekend with Hen and said, "There are a few vineyards in Texas."

She laughed like that was the funniest thing she'd ever heard.

Thankfully, a waiter came and saved me. I ordered the daily special, and Janessa picked something off the menu, making a million adjustments "to protect my figure," she explained after he left.

My phone began ringing, and I thanked whoever it was on the other end.

Seeing Hen's number, I smiled slightly, then said to Janessa, "Sorry, I have to take this."

30

HENRIETTA

Confession: I made a mistake.

TYLER'S VOICE was warm over the receiver. "Am I happy to hear from you."

My lips cracked a smile before quickly falling. I'd hoped calling him would cheer me up, but now it was taking all I had not to cry. I walked farther down the hallway away from the waiting room and stood at a window overlooking the parking garage.

It was full of cars. I wondered how many of those cars belonged to hospital employees. How many belonged to family like me, their world turned upside down.

"Henrietta? I can't hear you."

"I'm here," I said, barely a whisper.

"Are you okay?"

Okay? Not even close. It felt like everything was falling apart. "My grandma fell this morning." I sniffed in a heavy breath, but the hospital smell didn't help anything. "She fractured her hip, Tyler. They moved her to the trauma unit of the hospital."

"Oh no, that's awful," he said. "Did they say what next steps were?"

My voice went on autopilot, relating the same story I had called all my siblings with this morning. Both my parents had been at the hospital almost immediately after we arrived. "Lots of physical therapy. She'll be in a walker once she gets out of here. Mom's already trying to figure out how to get another credit card to have the carpet replaced. I could dip into my savings to replace it, but that would set me back months..."

"I can do that."

I turned away from the window, staring at the white cinder block wall as I attempted to process what he said. Had he really just offered to replace all of our flooring? "Tyler, that's too much."

"It's the least I could do," he said. "I can get supplies cheap, and I've installed hundreds of floors before. Done. What else do you need?"

I racked my mind, wondering what else there was to do. The list had seemed so insurmountable before this call. "We need a rail installed in the bathroom and another rail and a seat in the shower."

"Easy. What else?"

Now hot tears were rolling down my cheeks. A nurse walked by, and I turned toward the window to hide my emotions. I'd felt so alone this morning before everyone arrived, and now I knew I wasn't. "I was supposed to be going away to an overnight spa with Mara tomorrow, but someone needs to take care of Mom's garden."

"I can hoe with the best of them."

The smile in his voice made me laugh for the first time all day. "You're amazing."

"I'm *here*," he said. "Do you want me to come to the hospital?"

The sound of clashing dishes came from the background. "Where are you? It sounds like you're in a kitchen."

"Almost. I'm at lunch with Janessa. She insisted."

My stomach instantly soured. "What is she doing in town so early? I had everything prepped already. Was there an emergency at the apartments?" It would be just my luck.

"I suspect she wanted to make another pass at me without you around. Which, she has, and trust me, it's not working. Although she has been poking around the office."

"Shit," I muttered, then looked down the hallway to make sure no small ears had overheard. I was still alone. I had left my updated résumé and printed off job listings at the office. If Janessa found them, I'd be out a job before I was even close to ready.

"What's wrong?" he asked.

"I need to get back to the office. Can you stall Janessa?"

"Not a problem. I have a feeling she'll be dragging this out as long as possible."

"My hero," I said, a slight smile on my lips.

"Thanks for letting me rescue you for once."

I hung up and hurried back to the room to tell Mom I had an errand to run. Grandma was sleeping, her hands folded peacefully over her chest. Dad had gone to the cafeteria to bring lunch back.

"Hey, you can stop looking at credit cards," I said with a smile.

She looked up from her phone, surprised to see me. "Oh, Hen, what do you mean?"

I told her about Tyler's offer, and his insistence to follow through on it.

Mom put her hands over her heart. "He is one of the good ones."

"I think so," I agreed. "I have to run an errand for work real quick, and then I'll be back for the night. Are you sure it's okay that I go away with the girls tomorrow? I feel bad for leaving her."

Mom glanced at Grandma. "She wants you to go."

"She's not thinking of herself."

A coy smile crossed Mom's lips. "Well now we know where you get it."

Shaking my head, I took the keys from Mom's purse and left the hospital. It took precious minutes to find her car in the massive parking garage, and my nerves were starting to fray. Tyler had said he would stall, but if Janessa got to those papers before I did...

I didn't want to think about it. I hadn't yet reached my savings goal, and losing this job... I pressed my foot down on the gas and finally, finally reached my office. I parked in front of the main door, one mission on my mind: in and out as quickly as possible.

I fumbled with shaking hands to unlock the door and yanked it open. I quickly crossed the worn blue carpet to the spot behind my desk. Janessa had clearly messed with some papers, but my stack was safely at the bottom of an untouched pile.

Breathing a sigh of relief, I folded the papers in half.

The bell above the door jangled, and I jumped backward, seeing Janessa come inside, followed by Tyler speaking rapidly about a deck that needed structural repair on the opposite side of the complex.

"Henrietta," Janessa said, her eyes narrowing. "What are you doing here? It's your day off!"

"I, uh…" I searched desperately for an excuse and accidently walked into my hanging plant, the pothos leaves tickling my shoulder. Thankful beyond belief, I reached for it, pulling it down. "I just had to bring my plant home! Didn't want it to feel all abandoned and wilt while I was gone." As I had my back to Janessa, I tucked the papers between the two inside pots. Mission complete.

When I looked back at them, Tyler had a small smile for just the two of us. Janessa shook her head, looking around the office. "I have no idea how you keep all these things alive. They'd be dead within a week if I were taking care of them."

"Which is why I wanted to bring it home," I teased. "This one has an attitude."

Tyler laughed. "You and your mom with your plant psychology."

I smiled, but Janessa asked, "You've met Henrietta's mom?"

Shit. Shit. Shit. I had to think fast. But I was coming up blank.

Tyler quickly supplied, "Henrietta's mom brought lunch to the office one day while I came to ask Henrietta a question. I think she loves these plants as much as Hen does."

Janessa eyed us suspiciously. Then she turned to Tyler and said, sickly sweet, "No need to come by the office,

Tyler. Henrietta should be coming to you. And if she's unavailable, I'd be happy to make a trip out here."

I closed my eyes, biting back rage. How dare she tell me dating was against the rules when her words were full of innuendo.

"Actually," Tyler said, "I need to get back to the job site. Henrietta, can you give me a ride? I know Janessa is so busy with work. That's one of the things I admire about you, J. So dedicated to your role."

Janessa barely concealed her giddy smile at his compliment and the nickname. "Are you sure? I don't mind taking some extra time. So Hen can have her day off."

"It's on my way," I offered. "No big deal."

Before Janessa could argue, Tyler said, "Thanks, Hen. Janessa, thanks for lunch. Hope you have a great day."

He hurried us out of the office and got into my car so fast, you'd think Janessa was a cheetah on a hunt instead of a thirty-something blonde in middle management.

As soon as we pulled out of the parking lot, he was laughing.

"Your plant needed to come home?" he teased.

I glared at him. "The deck needed looked at?"

He reached across the console and grabbed my hand. "I still feel like I win for getting an extra few minutes with you today."

Butterfly wings tickled my insides.

"How are you?" he asked, bringing me back down to earth.

"I feel guilty," I answered honestly. "On one hand, I'm letting down my grandma by going away with my friends, and on the other hand, I'm missing out on my best friend's wedding week. There's no winning."

"I know I just met your family, but I can tell she won't be alone for even a minute at that hospital."

A smile touched my lips. "You're right."

"So go with your friends and have a good time." He drew my hand to his lips, making it hard to focus on the road. "Although selfishly, I do wish you could stay so I could take you out before the wedding."

My cheeks warmed. "I'd like that too."

He glanced toward the clock. "I do have a few minutes before I have to be back..."

"What did you have in mind?"

31

TYLER

"Pull over up there," I said, gesturing toward a stand of trees I'd noticed before on my drives to work. As far as I could tell, it was an empty lot, and right now, I couldn't stop thinking of kissing Henrietta senseless. Of helping her forget her worries for the day, if only for a few stolen moments.

She swiveled the wheel, following the overgrown trail into a space between tall sycamore trees. With the car parked, I could hear the music more clearly. I reached for the keys and twisted them off. "So we don't start a fire in the grass," I explained.

Her dark eyes were on me as she nodded, her breasts moving up and down with her breath. It was sexy as hell, especially with the lacy dress she had on over a swimsuit.

I trailed my finger from her shoulder to the spot where her suit began to dip into her cleavage. "I like this."

Her voice was quiet as she said, "I meant to wear it to the beach."

"I'd like to see that," I said, coming closer, pressing my lips to hers.

She softened into my kiss, her hands coming to my head and weaving through the short hair above my neck.

Already turned on, I kissed her cheek, tipped her chin back and kissed along her jaw, her neck, the top of her breasts where they began to swell. She kept her hands in my hair, her breath coming in a gasp as I gently bit down.

"Tyler," she breathed.

It was enough to spur me on, to drive me wild. I pulled back on her top, sliding her black suit back until I could see the dark, puckered skin of her areola, the full, hard tip of her nipple. I took it in my mouth, sucking and licking in tandem with my other thumb, swiping over her other nipple.

She let out a moan that made my cock harden. I covered her lips with mine, kissing her deeply, tangling my tongue with hers. I wanted more, these clothes out of the way, her skin against mine.

But I had to back off before I couldn't stop myself. She deserves more than me taking it further in the car. Our first time together was going to be something she'd remember as perfect. "Fuck," I moaned against her lips. I moved her clothes back in place and kissed her gently. "You are irresistible."

"Irresistible?" she asked, a slight smile on her lips.

They were so kissable, I kissed them again. "Irresistible, incredible, the whole damn package," I said. "And this weekend is going to be amazing. For you and your friends. And your grandma should know how much you love her if she doesn't already."

Hen closed her eyes, nodding, and I slipped my fingers through hers.

There was an unspoken understanding in the car. I needed to get back to work, and Hen had things to take care of at home. But the best was yet to come, and damn, was I looking forward to it.

She drove the last couple minutes to the job site, and then when she parked in the small dirt lot, I didn't want to get out.

"Text me if you need anything while you're out of town," I said.

She nodded, biting her lip.

"And call, if you want to talk."

Now she smiled. "Do you like talking on the phone?"

I shrugged, not wanting to give myself away. "When you live on the road so long, you get plenty of practice."

There was awe in her eyes as she looked at me. "I can't believe you're interested in me."

But the words sounded so wrong. I took her face in my hands, not caring if any of the workers saw me. She needed to hear this. "Hen, there are billions of women on the planet, and none of them have ever amazed me the way you continue to do. Please, believe me."

Her eyes softened as she took in the words, and I couldn't stop from kissing her one more time.

"I'll see you at the wedding," I said.

"I'll be the one in the purple dress, walking down the aisle."

"And I'll be the guy sitting there, wondering how in the hell he got lucky enough to be your date."

32

HENRIETTA

Confession: I'm done keeping secrets from my friends.

I TOOK a drink from my own bottle of champagne, my toes dangling in the hot tub, a terry cloth robe wrapped around me. Mara, Birdie, and Tess sat with me around the hot tub, in pure heaven as the sun sank down a sky of orange and gold.

A spa day for the bachelorette party had been brilliant. We'd spent the day drinking cucumber water, soaking in mud tubs, getting waxed, having our nails painted and our hair done. Even the bride-to-be seemed relaxed, which was the exact opposite of how my sisters-in-law had been prior to their weddings.

Birdie raised her bottle of champagne toward Mara. "A toast to your last moments as a single woman. Can you believe you're getting married Saturday? *One* penis for the rest of your life?"

Mara giggled, swinging her feet through the water. "One *amazing* penis. You forgot that word."

Tess covered her ears and started humming, and I giggled so hard my stomach hurt.

Okay, so maybe we were getting a little tipsy.

Birdie laughed. "It must be amazing for you to feel so happy about settling down."

Mara reached out to uncover her sister-in-law's ears and smiled as she rolled the champagne bottle in her hands. "You know, I used to think that settling down was a bad thing, like it was an act of giving up. Settling for less than you wanted. But this feels so much different."

I tilted my head to the side. "What do you mean?"

She set down her half-empty bottle and leaned back on her hands, resting her head on one shoulder. "Settling down is not the same as settling for less. It's resting where you know you belong. Not needing to run and chase and search anymore. It's the best feeling ever."

My heart swelled at the description. I wanted that. I wanted to feel at peace with someone I loved. I wanted to know that my heart was where it belonged. But there was something I still didn't understand. "What about the passion, Mara? You were always about the hot sex and exciting adventures."

"Cover your ears, Tess," she laughed out. Tess chugged some more champagne instead as Mara said, "The sex is still hot. And let me tell you, there's something to experimenting with someone who makes you feel safe."

Safe? With Tyler, I felt terrified. Terrified of not being enough. Of being disappointing. Exhilarated. Electrified by his touch and the words he spoke about me. and then there was the fear—that all of it was too good to be true. None of that felt safe.

"What is it?" Tess asked, studying me.

I looked up at them, realizing there was one big secret I'd kept from my very best friends. Maybe it was the champagne, or maybe I was tired of the secrets, because I blurted my biggest one: "I'm a virgin."

Champagne flew from Mara's mouth into the hot tub, and if I wasn't so embarrassed, I would have cackled at the stunned expression on her face.

"You're a virgin?" she gasped. "Like you've never done anal before?"

Okay, now my feet and face felt hot. "I haven't passed second base before."

Birdie's jaw dropped. "There's never been anyone? Not even a high school boyfriend or a summer fling?"

I shook my head.

Tess asked, "Are you saving it for marriage?"

The laugh that passed my lips was almost bitter. "No one's ever gotten close enough for that to be an option."

My friends were quiet for the first time that night, and I felt shame washing over me. I was undateable. Unlikable. Cursed to be the funny fat friend for the rest of my life. And not only that, I'd taken away from Mara's moment, yet again.

Not seeming to mind, Mara asked, "Do you think Tyler could be the one to pop that cherry? Take your v-card. Deflower that perfect little pus—"

"Mara!" I cried, laughing through my horror. Birdie and Tess were laughing too, the sound blending with the hot tub jets. But they quieted, and the question was still there. Could Tyler be the one to take my virginity?

And I nodded, because I had a feeling he could be more than my first time.

He could be the one.

Birdie's eyes widened at a spot behind me, and she muttered, "Finally!"

I twisted to see what she was looking at and saw a guy walking toward the pool area in a suit...with silver buttons on the side of his pants.

TYLER

Cohen had booked a kayak tour at La Jolla Beach for Jonas's bachelor party, and I was honored to be included. The fact that the guys treated me like one of the crew meant more than they knew.

There were five of us total, including Jonas's brother-in-law, Derek. I could definitely see myself hanging out with someone like him back home. We rode in Derek's minivan, which Jonas teased him mercilessly for. Apparently, Derek only had one kid, but there were hopes for more on the way soon.

We rolled up to a crowded parking lot near the beach and Cohen led us to a stand farther down the sand. They had racks of long kayaks, paddleboards, and surfboards.

When we reached the place, looking like a bunch of tourists in our swim trunks and T-shirts, a guy walked out of the shack. "Cohen?"

Cohen lifted his hand.

"Right on, right on," he said. He looked like a complete California surf bro stereotype, from his sun-streaked hair to his tanned skin and shell necklace. "I'm Geoff—with a G—and I'll be leading the tour today. Five singles, right?"

"We're all married, or about to be," Derek said. "Well, except him."

I felt like I was in fifth grade again, the only kid without a little crush to call my own.

Geoff with a G laughed. "I meant single kayaks." He winked at me. "Although, I have a friend I could hook you up with."

"That won't be necessary," I grunted.

"Right on. So pick a yak and let's get on the water."

Steve looked at the kayaks like they were wild animals. "I'm going to need an extra life jacket."

Jonas patted me on the back with an apologetic grin before taking a kayak off the rack. Geoff had us carry them toward the water's edge, and I stood by mine, feeling the rough brush of sand under my feet, the sun on my skin.

I worked so much, I didn't take a lot of time to enjoy or relax. I should change that, I thought. Ask my brothers to go on a trip with me. Maybe they'd agree to Vegas. At least, I knew Rhett would.

Geoff interrupted my thoughts, going through a safety spiel, which Steve listened very intently to, before helping us get our kayaks out on the ocean. We paddled out, following Geoff away from the crowded beach. Steven's knuckles were white on his oar.

The late afternoon sun glanced off the dark blue water, and here, away from the city, there was a sense of peace and quiet I hadn't found since leaving Texas. Between the cool saltwater soaking my skin to the powerful feel of my paddle ripping through the waves, I couldn't help the grin on my face. I felt like a kid riding go-karts for the first time, except this was better because I could have beer after.

Another wave approached, and I paddled to angle my kayak so it wouldn't tip. Geoff pointed out cliffs on our left with million-dollar houses on top. He said the land eroded each year, getting closer and closer to making those houses cave in. The thought that someone could build their home on such shaky foundation baffled me. But then again, a tornado could hit any time in Texas— maybe it was better to know when the end would come so you could be prepared.

Geoff pointed his paddle to a spot north of Cohen's kayak. "Look down there! Three sea lions swimming by."

I paddled forward, careful to give Cohen some space, and spotted three darker spots deep below the water. I wished Henrietta could see this with me.

"We should take the girls next time," I said. "They'd love this."

Cohen splashed me with his paddle.

Wiping saltwater from my face, I said, "What the hell was that for?"

Wearing a grin that looked like one of Rhett's, he said, "You're in trouble! Already thinking of her when you're on a guys' trip?"

Steve grunted from his kayak. "Next thing you know, you'll be looking at dolphin souvenirs for your three-year-old."

Jonas said, "He's speaking from personal experience."

"Obviously," Steve said. "And can I just say, magnet prices are ridiculous these days."

I shook my head at the three. I may have been the only 'single' one here, but I couldn't deny all those thoughts had been on my mind. "Shit, you're right."

Cohen rested his paddle in his lap. "Nothin' wrong with that."

I didn't know if I agreed. Because it meant six months from now, I'd have an impossible choice to make.

At my hesitation, the guide said, "What's with the face? You fall for someone unavailable?"

All the guys looked at me, waiting for my answer. "I fell alright. Now let's find some more of those damn seals."

Geoff said, "Sea lions," and continued on his way.

34

HENRIETTA

Confession: I'm... beautiful.

MAGIC WAS in the air as we got ready for Mara's wedding.

The event center at Emerson Trails had separate dressing rooms for the bridal party, and this one had big skylights in the ceiling, bathing us in soft natural light. Mara wore a silk white robe as we had our hair and makeup done, and each of the bridesmaids wore similar robes in black. It was picturesque and beautiful and... inevitable. Like this day was meant to happen exactly this way.

And as I watched Mara get eyeshadow patted on and lipstick painted across her lips, I couldn't help but hope it would be me soon. Me next. Because I was ready for that feeling she described. I wanted to settle. I wanted peace. I wanted my own family for Saturday afternoon barbeques and sports games on the weekends and home-cooked dinners on weeknights. And most of all, I loved the idea of writing my future with a partner at my side. Someone who would lift me up when I was weak and someone I could provide shelter to in any storm.

But today wasn't about me. It was about my best friend. I got her mimosas whenever she ran empty, added polish to a nail that chipped, and when it came time, I'd hold her wedding dress so she could pee. That's what friends did.

The wedding planner, a woman younger than us by a few years, came in and said, "It's time to start getting your dresses on, ladies. Twenty minutes to showtime."

Mara, Tess, Birdie, and I all exchanged glances. Today was the day, and now was the time.

We helped Mara into her dress first, sliding the tulle skirts over her head and shoulders, then flaring them out to the natural-toned wood floor. The hairdresser slipped the veil in her hair, and we stared.

She looked beautiful.

But more than that, she looked *happy*.

With the time left over, we put on our bridesmaid dresses, taking turns zipping up the backs. Birdie handed me my bouquet of white and green flowers and foliage. And I stared at my reflection.

The woman looking at me in the mirror wasn't the funny fat friend.

She was beautiful.

She was happy.

And she smiled. Because now I knew when Tyler looked at me and saw something beautiful, I wouldn't disagree.

35

TYLER

Gravel crunched underfoot as I walked across the parking lot with other guests toward a tall glass building. Past the eaves, I could see acres of rolling grass and trees. The sun shone down from overhead—the perfect day for a wedding.

I'd been to tons of weddings in Texas, and most of them were more casual than this. Everyone around me was dressed in black-tie attire. Back home, most of the grooms wore jeans and boots. Their good jeans, but still. Lots of the ceremonies happened in little churches and the receptions were moved to a shop building that had been cleaned up for the event.

When I walked inside, Derek greeted me, holding his little baby in a light purple dress.

"Got wrangled into being an usher?" I asked.

He grinned. "It's not so bad with my little helper." The baby couldn't have been much older than A'yisha, except his little girl had far less hair.

"She's beautiful," I said honestly.

"I think so too," he said. People were piling up behind me, so he added, "Either side, my man. We're all family today."

I grinned, walking past him. I sat on the edge of a row toward the back so I wouldn't take up the spot of someone more important than me and waited, listened, watched people filter into the seats around me and talk about the bride and groom.

I picked up snippets about the television show Mara was writing for, heard about how Jonas's virtual accounting firm continued to grow. And most of all, I waited to see Henrietta.

And then the music started, cutting all chatter. A man holding a Bible walked to the front, followed by Steve and Cohen. Then Jonas walked up the aisle, an older woman dressed in a purple gown on his arm. He kissed her cheek before leaving her sitting in the front row.

As if my body sensed her, I turned, looking to the aisle. Henrietta approached, moving purposefully in a floor-length dress. Soft fabric swished around her perfect hips with each step, and the bouquet she held at her chest only accentuated her cleavage. But her face stole the show. She had a soft peach blush on her cheeks and her full lips were glossy. And the light in her eyes, in her smile, made her shine.

Our eyes met, and her smile grew, deepened, and for a moment, all the air was gone from the room. All the people had vanished. It was her and me and the sound of the pounding in my chest.

And then she passed me, and the view got even better.

Shit, my girl looked like a million bucks.
My stomach dropped. My girl.
She wasn't my girl. Not officially.
I'd never asked her to be. And I needed to fix that.
Immediately.

36

HENRIETTA

Confession: I'm not jealous, but I don't mind claiming my territory.

THE CEREMONY HAD BEEN ABSOLUTELY beautiful, but after taking about a million and one pictures with the bridal party, my feet hurt and I had to pee like a racehorse. I made it to the bathroom and took the best restroom break of my life, then checked myself in the mirror. Only a few hairs needed brushed back into place, and I reapplied gloss to my lips, even though doing this in front of other women in the bathroom usually made me nervous.

Two women came in, a little younger than me, and each took a stall.

"Did you see that hottie in the boots?" one said.

I smirked in the mirror. I only knew one guy who'd arrived in cowboy boots.

"Think he's single?"

"Didn't see a ring," the other replied.

I zipped my clutch shut. "He's here with someone," I told them, smiling to myself as they groaned before leaving the restroom.

I planned to walk to the reception area, find Tyler, and ask him to spin me on the dance floor like he had that night he rescued me. Instead, I felt a calloused hand grab my wrist and pull me backward into a dark room.

I was about to scream when another hand covered my mouth. "It's me, Hen."

Tyler's warm voice mixed with his rough grip already had my skin tingling. "What are we doing in here?" I looked around, my eyes adjusting to the dim lighting. "Is this a coat closet?"

"It's a closet no one has entered for the last half hour, and it locks from the inside." His hands skimmed my bare arms, sending goosebumps rising on my skin.

As far as I was concerned, we could stay in here all day. But I wasn't bold enough to say so. Not that forward or sexy. So I swallowed and tried not to let my shallow breathing give me away.

"You were great up there," he said. "I couldn't take my eyes off you."

I grinned, the compliment meaning everything, especially after overhearing those girls. "Thank you."

"But there was one issue," he said, his fingers toying with the thin strap of my dress.

"And what was that?"

He brushed his nose over my neck, making me catch my breath, and said, "I wanted everyone to know you were mine, and we haven't had that talk yet."

"Oh," was all I could manage to say with his lips trailing kisses and nips down my neck.

"Any objections?"

"None." To anything he was doing. "None at all."

His hand tightened around my waist, pulling me closer to him, and I leaned into his kisses, working my fingers through his hair and tugging. He palmed my ass, pressing us together, and—oh my—I felt something hard at his waist. He was turned on by me. *Me.*

Feeling bold, I reached down, rubbing it with my hand, and he moaned in my ear. Heat pooled between my legs, readying me for him.

"Fuck, Hen, if you keep this up, I'll have to take you right here."

I froze, realizing he was ready for that step. And I was too, but I didn't want to lose my virginity in a closet.

Sensing the change, he stepped away from me, his hands completely gone from my body. "I'm sorry. Did I overstep?" he asked.

Guilt immediately racked me. For the secret of my virginity. For the fact that I wanted to keep it a secret. That he thought for one moment I didn't want every single thing he was doing to me and all the ways my body reacted.

"That's not it," I said, stepping closer and placing a kiss on his jaw. On his chin. "What are you doing tonight?"

I already knew the answer.

He smiled underneath my lips. "Any ideas?"

"I'd like to check on your apartment, make sure it's still in good shape—you know, for my job."

"For your job," he repeated, kissing my cheek, nipping the shell of my ear.

I let out a shaky breath. "We should get back..."

And in five minutes, we did.

37

TYLER

Weddings might be my new favorite date with Henrietta. Although she sat at the bridal party's table for the meal, I loved watching her, seeing her smile, meeting her eyes across the room.

And knowing she was officially mine... it made it that much better.

After the meal, Mara and Jonas shared their first dance. They held each other close, Mara gently playing with the hair at the back of his neck as they swayed back and forth. Then the DJ invited other couples to the dance floor.

I crossed the room to Hen. "May I have this dance?"

She smiled up at me. "I'm not sure what my 'male friend' will think."

I laughed, remembering how heady and nervous I'd felt to be introduced to Hen's entire family as her male friend. But now I wouldn't want to be known as anything else. "I think your male friend will be mighty disappointed if he doesn't get to spin you around the dance floor."

Her chocolate eyes warmed. "I'd love that."

I extended my hand, and she slipped hers in mine. The perfect fit. As we walked away from the table, I spun her twice, and she giggled, her dress flaring around her. On the third spin, she fell into my chest, breathless and smiling.

"I wasn't ready for that," she said with a laugh.

"Well you looked damn good doing it," I said, two-stepping with her. We fell into rhythm together, just like we had that first night I taught her to dance.

She leaned her head close. "Thank you for coming. I know weddings aren't for everyone."

I kissed her crown. "I love being here with you. And you might be surprised—I think weddings are fun."

"Yeah? What do you like about them?"

"Other than the leap of faith it takes to commit in front of everyone you know?"

She chuckled. "Yeah, other than that."

"Hmm." I thought it over for a moment, letting the music wash over us. "I like the cake cutting, and not just because I inherited my grandpa's sweet tooth."

Smiling, she said, "What is it then?"

"You know how they hold the knife together? It's ridiculous and adorable at the same time. And then you get to see their personalities on full display by the way they feed each other."

"What do you think of shoving cake in each other's face?" she asked.

"A waste of perfectly good cake." I winked. "Unless you get to lick it off."

The music slowed, and the DJ came over the speakers. "It's time for our bride and groom to cut the cake."

We walked closer to the table with the cake, getting a better view of Mara and Jonas. The cake was stunning—lots of creamy frosting, decorative frosted flowers, and multiple tiers so everyone would have plenty to eat.

Just like every other wedding, Mara and Jonas approached the cake. A little couple mirroring them stood on the top tier, holding hands. Mara grabbed the topper first and licked the bottom, making me laugh along with everyone else.

"What? I'm not wasting perfectly good frosting," she said.

"Hear, hear," I called, raising my beer. (The open bar was a nice touch.)

Hen giggled. "That's my girl."

Jonas grinned adoringly at Mara, picking up the knife as the photographer's camera sounded with each new picture. She placed her hands atop his, and they cut a chunk from the bottom layer. Jonas put a small piece in her mouth, and she sucked his finger suggestively.

Everyone whooped, cheering and making comments about the honeymoon.

"That sums up their personalities," Hen confirmed with a laugh.

Then Mara held out the cake for Jonas, and after he ate it, he kissed a stray bit of frosting from her lips. I tightened my grip around Hen's waist, and she smiled up at me, that ever-present light in her brown eyes. Feeling like my heart couldn't get any bigger, any fuller, I bent my neck and placed a kiss on her lips.

She smiled up at me, and it was good.

It was so fucking good.

We danced for the rest of the reception, held up

sparklers as Jonas and Mara walked away from the venue, and cheered along with everyone else as their car drove toward the airport, cans rattling on the ground behind them.

People around us began dissipating, getting into their cars and lighting the dark parking lot with headlights and taillights.

"Did you drive here?" I asked.

She nodded. "I can follow you to your place?"

I kissed her, hard. "I'll see you soon."

38

HENRIETTA

Confession: Cleaning supplies turn me on.

AS I DROVE to Tyler's place, all I could think was... I'm about to lose my virginity. My heart was beating fast and my hands were shaky on the steering wheel, but when I saw him standing against his truck in the parking lot, my worries faded. He'd been the dream guy since I met him —sex wouldn't change that.

I got out of my car, acutely aware of his eyes sizzling over me like no man had ever looked at me before. His gaze wasn't greedy or hungry... It was... appreciative. And oh so sexy.

I noticed something sticking out of the truck bed behind him, and I nodded toward it. "Bring your work home?"

"Oh this?" He turned toward the boxes as I walked beside him, looking at them.

My eyes instantly watered at the labels.

Engineered hardwood flooring, oak brown.

"Tyler, that stuff is so expensive. We have fifteen hundred feet to cover."

He ran his hands over my hair, my shoulders, and hugged me from behind. His breath feathered my hair as he said, "Can you believe me when I tell you it's no big deal?"

I shook my head, the memory of my mom begging with credit card companies fresh on my mind. I turned to face him, linking my hands behind his neck. "It's a huge deal, Tyler. A very, very big deal."

He leaned his head forward, resting his forehead against mine. "Then would you believe me when I told you that you're worth it?"

Butterfly wings tickled my insides, replacing nervous jitters with syrupy sweet emotion. And since there weren't words to show him just how much it meant to me, I tilted my chin up and met his lips with mine. His touch mingled with the breeze against my skin and sent tingles down my spine.

"Come on," he said, his voice a whisper. His lips a smile.

I nodded, biting my bottom lip, and slipped my fingers through his. Going to his place with him, with our fingers linked, was so different than the first time. I'd been so nervous, insecure, but now he made me feel beautiful, desired, and I was high on the feeling.

He let go of my hand to get his keys and slipped them into the lock before leading me in. His scent hit my nose even stronger, a fresh mix of leather and linen that was just as sexy as the man before me.

"Did you spray your cologne as air freshener?" I asked. "Because I'll gladly buy some off you."

Chuckling, he said, "My sister sells candles, so I bought a few off her. She did a whole scent profile for me and everything."

I closed my eyes, savoring the smell. "She's got some real talent."

"I'll let her know you said so," he replied as he slipped off his suit jacket and went to hang it up in the coat closet. There were three other coats in there—a rain jacket, a Northface outer shell and then a thicker winter coat. Everything he needed and nothing more. I liked that about him too.

I kicked out of my heels, breathing a sigh of relief as my feet flattened on the carpeted floor. "That feels so good."

"I can give you a foot rub," he offered.

"And make me fall in love with you?"

He laughed. "That's the goal."

I shook my head, still smiling, and said, "Can I borrow a pair of socks? I'd hate for you to be disgusted by my feet."

Acting exasperated, he took my hand and pulled me onto the couch with him. He sat opposite me and took my feet in his lap. I knew I'd hoped for sexy times, but the way this man rubbed my foot... It had to be orgasmic. "That feels so good," I sighed, leaning my head back against the couch cushion.

"You've had a long few days," he said. "With your grandma and the wedding... I bet you're exhausted."

With his words, I felt down to my bones how true that was. "I am. When you're a woman in business, you start to feel like you can't show any emotions, any weakness, or people won't take you seriously. And at home—I know I have it good, being able to live there basically rent free. It feels wrong to complain."

"You have every right to feel however you feel. I love my folks, but I couldn't share a sink with them. My mom's so particular about dishes that she rewashes the plates my dad cleaned after he goes to bed."

"Seriously?" I laughed. "I would just be happy someone's doing the dishes who isn't me."

"You don't like dishes?"

I shook my head. "It's the worst. And knowing all that dirty water is soaking into your skin. Yuck."

"You know they have this fancy contraption called rubber gloves."

"And have my hands soak in their own sweat? No thank you. And god forbid some of that dirty water gets in there and starts growing something. No, no, no."

He chuckled, reaching for my opposite foot. "As long as you're with me, I'll do the dishes."

I bit my lip. "So. Freaking. Sexy."

Waggling his eyebrows, he said, "You should see me with a toilet brush."

"Talk dirty to me." I winked, resting my head back on the couch.

39

TYLER

Henrietta's eyes slid closed, and her breathing slowly evened out. I smiled, feeling her completely relax in my hands, her legs growing heavy in my lap. I'd wanted to please her tonight, but this, knowing she felt safe enough to let her guard down with me... it was just as good.

I looked at her feet in my hands, soft from the spa day, and her toes were painted with a shiny olive-green paint. For a moment, I sat, watching the rise and fall of her chest, gliding my palm over her shins, just enjoying the peace that came with her presence. Something about having her here made my apartment feel less lonely than it usually did, and I dreaded the moment she'd eventually have to go.

But I didn't want to think of that now. I carefully lifted her legs from my lap and went to my room to get a spare pillow and blanket. When I returned, I gently moved her into a more comfortable position and then covered her with the blanket.

She shifted slightly, nuzzling her head into the pillow,

and then settled again. I stood back, folding my arms across my chest. "You're one hell of a woman, Henrietta Jones."

Smiling to myself, I walked back to the bedroom and began taking off the rest of my suit from the wedding. As I slid down my pants, my phone fell out of my side pocket, and I picked it up, seeing a text from the group chat I had going with her brothers.

Johmarcus: I'll be there at seven. See you then.
Justus: Me too. Thanks for this.
Bertrand: I'll be there at half past eight with the lumber delivery.

I texted them back.

Tyler: See y'all soon.

Then I set my phone on the dresser, threw the clothes in the hamper, and walked back to the shower. These apartments weren't fancy, but one thing I could say, the water pressure was top-notch.

I stepped under the heavy stream, letting the pressure wash away all the tension from the day. I'd wanted to take things to the next step with Henrietta, make her scream my name until she clenched around me, but once I saw how tired she was, I couldn't ask that of her.

That memo hadn't reached my dick yet, though. I was so fucking hard for her. I ran my hand down my length, wishing it was her hand instead.

Fuck. I didn't want to masturbate with her in the next room, but this situation wasn't going away any time soon... especially with how good she looked tonight, how fucking sexy she was pressed against the coat closet wall.

I gripped my cock, holding it tight in my hand and closing my eyes. Her breasts would bounce as she worked me faster and harder. Her lips would part, ready for me to enter her mouth so she could taste me on her tongue.

Fuck, she was so hot. And those tits. I'd knead them, slather them with oil and thrust my cock in her cleavage. Harder and faster, her throat humming with pleasure as I tit-fucked her.

Just as I got close to coming, she'd take me in her mouth, hold my thighs with her hands so I had no choice but to nut down her warm throat. And she'd look up at me as she swallowed every. Last. drop.

My cock throbbed one last time before I came all over the shower floor. The next time, it would be with her.

40

HENRIETTA

Confession: There's not a lot that Grandma's hugs can't fix.

WHEN I WOKE UP, Tyler's apartment was dark except for a bright slit of light shining through the blackout shades in his living room. And then it hit me: I'd fallen asleep on his couch, in my bridesmaid dress, still a virgin.

I sat up and let out a groan. Gah, I was so pathetic. I couldn't even stay awake to bone my hot boyfriend.

I cringed internally at my use of the word bone. That was such a virgin word to use. Which made sense because... Flower? Still there.

I stood up, wondering where he was and what time it was. A paper crunched between my leg and the coffee table. I picked it up, then went to the shades, drawing them back and squinting at the bright reflection of sun on notebook paper.

Sorry I had a work thing to get to. The coffee pot is on, and there's a to-go cup you can use. Creamer is in the fridge, and sugar's in the cabinet—help yourself to anything. I had your friend Birdie get an extra outfit for you too, and it's sitting on the counter.

I glanced toward the counter, seeing a reusable grocery bag there.

Take a shower, make yourself at home, maybe visit your grandma. I'd love to take you to dinner tonight.

- Tyler

Still stunned at his thoughtfulness, and Birdie's involvement, I went through the tote bag. Everything was there, from toiletries to a fresh pair of *lacy* underwear, a cotton dress, socks, and slip-on sneakers.

I opened up my clutch, which was on the coffee table, and pulled out my phone, seeing a few new texts in the group chat.

Birdie: HENRIETTA! PLEASE TELL ME IT HAPPENED LAST NIGHT!
Mara: Did you get deflowered?! Details!! (For book purposes of course ;))
Birdie: It was so sweet of him to have me get your stuff for you. *swoon*
Mara: The suspense is killing me, girl!

I smiled at my friends' messages. They were so excited for me. I should have opened up sooner about my virginity. But for now, it was still intact.

Henrietta: I fell asleep before we could do anything. So freaking lame.
Mara: Was he bad in bed?
Henrietta: I wouldn't know! He gave me a foot rub and I basically passed out on his couch.

I glanced at my clock, and my jaw dropped open. How had I managed to sleep past eleven o'clock? I must have needed the extra sleep. And I promised myself I'd make the most of my renewed energy tonight.

Birdie: There's still time. You should have seen the way he was looking at you last night. That boy's not going anywhere.

I smiled at the text.

Henrietta: Fingers crossed.
Henrietta: Now get back to your honeymoon, Mara.
Mara: Fine, but text me when it happens. I'll drink a margarita to celebrate. Extra cherry on top. ;)
Henrietta: Gross lol and promise

I WALKED into the hospital carrying three sweet teas. A raspberry flavored one for Mom, peach flavored for Grandma, and blackberry for me. Usually we made flavored teas at home, and we'd sit on the back patio sipping away and chatting about the day.

Today was different.

We weren't at home. We were in the hospital, and I felt the weight of that fact as soon as I got underneath the harsh fluorescent lights. Even though I'd had fun at the wedding, everything was different now, and the future was more uncertain than ever.

When I was younger and had worried thoughts like that, Grandma would say, "Stop with your stinkin' thinkin'." I tried to do that now, taking a deep breath to clear my mind before walking into the room.

Mom smiled at me, taking her tea, and Grandma grinned. "I was just thinking I needed some sweet tea," she said.

I handed her the clear cup with ice crackling against the plastic. "I had them add some extra sugar for you."

"You're bad," she said, giving me an appreciative yet scolding smile.

I took the other open chair by her bed and drank from my straw. Sweet liquid flooded my tongue, making me relax a bit. "How has it been, Gran? I still feel guilty for not being here this weekend."

"Don't be silly," Grandma said. "You can't stop living your life because I'm getting old."

I gave her a look. "Getting?"

She batted her hand at me, and I laughed. "Can't you just let me worry about you?" I asked, exasperated.

"If it involves pittea, then yes," she replied. "Get it? Pitty-tea?"

I rolled my eyes letting out a laugh. "You've done better."

"Well excuse me. My humor lately is almost as bad as the hospital food."

Mom smiled at us, shaking her head. "How was the wedding?"

"Beautiful," I began, telling them all about the event, from the vows they wrote themselves to the best-man speech Cohen gave that had me crying I was laughing so hard. And then, of course, I had to tell them how amazing Tyler had been on the dance floor. "I overheard multiple women saying they hoped he was single when I was in the bathroom."

Mom said, "That's exactly how your dad was. Every girl had their eyes on him, but we've been together thirty-eight years now."

Grandma said, "Well now I do feel old. I remember you bringing Murph home that first time to meet us."

Mom covered her face with her hand not resting on a magazine. "I'd rather forget it."

Grandma cackled and put her hand on my arm. "That boy dressed up, had on suspenders even."

"Suspenders?" I gasped. "I've never seen Dad out of jeans."

Grandma nodded. "Suspenders and these shiny black shoes. Your grandpa gave him one look and shook his head." She lowered her voice. "'Not for my daughter. I need a man who can get some dirt on his hands. I'm not going to be able to run over to fix every leaky faucet and change every tire forever.'"

I dropped my head back and laughed. Of all the stories I'd been told of my parents' youth, I hadn't heard this one.

Mom said, "Murph was absolutely floored. He was stumbling over his words, and Grandpa gave him the side-eye. 'You tongue-tied boy?'"

My stomach shook with laughter. "Poor Dad."

Grandma said, "The next day he drove the car he restored over to the house, wearing his work clothes, and got his second chance at a first impression. Harold loved that boy once he got to know him. You're lucky to have him as your daddy."

After hearing Mara's horror stories and seeing how

strained things had been between Birdie and her parents, I knew she was right. "I'm lucky to have all of you as my family." My voice cracked. "I love you."

"Oh, honey," Grandma said. She extended her arms for me, and I stood over her bed, letting her give me one of those hugs that makes everything better even though you're falling apart. As I sat back in my chair, she said, "We are *so* proud of you, baby girl. And we're happy you've found Tyler. I have a good feeling about that boy."

"Me too," I said.

"In fact," Mom said, looking at her phone.

"What?" I asked.

"Nothing," she said quickly. "I just need you to head by the house in an hour. I want to make some more macramé hangers and all my stuff is there."

I gave her a suspicious look, but she was already flipping back through her magazine, a small smile on her face.

41

HENRIETTA

Confession: I don't know what I did to deserve this.

I SENT a text to Tyler before leaving the hospital, letting him know it would be another hour or so before we could meet up for dinner. I needed to get Mom her rope and rings to make those hangers. I should have asked her why Dad or my brothers couldn't do it, since I hadn't seen them at the hospital, but I'd honestly forgotten.

Tyler: No worries. I can pick you up from the hospital.

I smiled at my phone before tucking it in my purse and driving to my parents' house. I needed to ask him when we'd be able to get to work on the new flooring. According to Mom, we had a couple weeks, since they wanted Grandma to do physical therapy in the hospital and get stronger before coming home. The fracture was small enough they hoped it would heal naturally, and she could use a walker until she felt more confident. If not, we'd have a whole ramp to install as well, adding the question of someone around to help her

Grandma's life could be a lot longer, and harder, than I had planned for. And that put a knot of worry in my gut. I could be working for another ten years to keep her at home... unless I could find a remote job to stay at home with her?

But that thought was quickly wiped from my mind as I pulled up to the house. All of my brothers' vehicles were there, along with Tyler's pickup, and there was a brand-new ramp leading up to the front door.

Completely speechless, I got out of the car, seeing my brothers and Tyler spilling out the front door onto the porch.

"What do you think?" Dad called, grinning ear to ear.

"You built a ramp!" I barely registered my feet carrying me down the front sidewalk.

Dad clapped Tyler's shoulder. "Wait 'til you see the inside."

Our eyes locked from feet away, and I gave him a disbelieving look. "What's inside?"

Tyler nodded, answering my unspoken question.

It was taken care of. All of it.

I walked up the ramp, and Johmarcus put his arm around my shoulders. "Check this out, sis."

We walked inside, and it was like a new house. The flooring gleamed under the lights, completely beautiful, and all the furniture and trim boards were already back in place. There was even a new recliner in our living room.

"We got a new chair too?" I asked.

Justus said, "Imani's mom had an extra chair with a

built-in lift. We thought it might make things easier for Grammy."

I let go of Johmarcus and hugged Justus, his earring scratching my cheek. "Guys, it looks incredible."

Bertrand said, "We did the living room and all the bedrooms."

"How did you work so quickly?"

Tyler grinned and said, "I've asked them if I can hire them for my crew at least ten times. They made the job go so fast."

Dad shook his head and said, "Tyler's being modest. He put this all together, got us here at seven in the morning. Ordered all the materials. This wouldn't have been possible without him."

Feeling my eyes well up, I went and wrapped my arms around Tyler's middle. He held me close while my brothers and dad stayed silent, giving us this moment. I hoped Tyler understood how big of a difference this would make to Grandma coming home and life hopefully getting back to normal. Or at least the newer version of it.

Then it hit me, and all the blood drained from my face. "Does that mean you all went through my room?"

Tyler chuckled, and Dad said, "Don't worry. We hid all your unmentionables."

Unmentionables? Now I was really embarrassed. I let go of Tyler and walked into my room, staring at how all my furniture looked on the new flooring. It was like an entirely different space.

"Well, it does look good," I said.

Tyler huffed, "You sound so surprised."

Laughing, I hit his chest. "It wasn't very clean before I left for the wedding." I frowned. "Speaking of leaving, I was supposed to get Mom stuff to make her macramé plant hangers."

Johmarcus spoke up. "That was just an excuse to get you here. We're all going to the hospital now for a visit. Why don't you stay and enjoy the new floors?"

Dad nodded. "I'm spending the night there with Grandma. No one should be back here tonight. Just eat some vegetables, please. We're up to our ears."

There wasn't any insinuation behind his words, but the meaning was clear. Tyler and I had the house to ourselves for the entire night to do whatever we chose. Trying not to blush, I nodded. "Want me to make you all some supper before you leave?" I didn't want to seem too eager to jump Tyler's sexy bones.

Dad shook his head and clapped his hand on Tyler's shoulder. "I have to get your mom some food anyway. I'll see you tomorrow, baby girl."

And just like that, they were walking out of the house, getting into their cars, and driving away.

Tyler and I were alone.

42

TYLER

Henrietta faced me, a slight smile on her lips. "I'm sorry," she said, "I still can't believe you did all this."

"I mean, it wasn't just me. Your brothers and dad did most of the work."

She shook her head, stepping closer and taking my face in her hands, kissing me deep. Her kiss drew all the air from the room, made me forget anything else but the two of us.

I wrapped my arms around her waist, deepening our embrace. Yesterday, she'd said this was all too much, but she was wrong. I wished I could show her just how special she was, how any guy worth his salt would have done the same thing I had.

Her hands traveled from my neck, to my chest, and then down to my belt. My dick twitched in response, already growing hard.

But then my fucking stomach growled.

She giggled as she pulled away, and I tried not to look annoyed at my traitorous stomach. I was already planning my next meal anyway, and it was going to include Henrietta, on her back, screaming my name.

"Let me make you some supper," she said. "I'm kind of hungry anyway."

Well there went my response. If she was hungry, she should eat. "Can I help?" Anything to get my mind off my aching balls.

"You've done more than enough. Sit at the island. I'll get you a beer."

If this girl wasn't perfect already... "That sounds amazing."

She smiled at me before reaching into the fridge and handing me an icy can. "Beer always tastes better after a long day of work."

I nodded. That first-sip feeling always got me. I thumbed the top, and it cracked loudly as it opened. She got herself a beer from the fridge as well and opened it. I held my can out to her, and the aluminum made a soft bumping sound as she tapped her can to mine.

She took a drink and set her beer down on the island before reaching to the vegetable basket. "Do you like bell peppers?"

"Love 'em," I answered.

She grabbed a couple from the basket, along with an onion and garlic clove, then got a cut of meat from the fridge. She cut the meat first, slicing it in methodic motions.

"Do you like cooking?" I asked.

"Love it. I can't wait to have my own kitchen someday. I want a double oven where I can cook loaves of zucchini bread every summer and a big island where everyone can sit when I make Christmas dinner."

I loved the way she talked about her dreams, like they were this fantasyland where anything was possible. I wanted those dreams to come true for her so damn bad. "You like hosting?"

She nodded. "You just got a taste of it at Kenner's birthday party. My family's always coming over and hanging out."

"Same here," I said. "Except there's usually a dumb prank involved. I kind of think that's why I was so awkward. I was used to my close circle of people and new faces made me nervous."

She nodded. "I always felt like I had plenty of friends in my family. It only got lonely at school."

I totally got it. Hen was quiet as she chopped, giving us both time to get lost in our memories.

"You never told me about the bachelorette party," I said.

She grinned. "There was a stripper involved."

I nearly snorted. "A stripper?"

She nodded. "He came in wearing a suit, since Jonas is an accountant." She shuddered slightly. "He did things with a calculator I never would have dreamed of."

I tried to imagine what he must have done and came up blank. But judging by Hen's reaction, that was a mental image to avoid.

"What about the bachelor trip?" she asked. "Mara said you went with them?"

I couldn't believe I'd forgotten to tell her. "We went to La Jolla and did a kayak tour, then one of those bike and beer tours. It was pretty fun. Especially since Steve asked for an extra life jacket in case his first one failed."

Her tinkling laugh mingled with the smell of food in the air. "Sounds like swim lessons are in order."

"If you could get Steve back on the water, that's probably a good idea," I said, watching her liberally season the meat before tossing in the vegetables. While they sizzled in the pan, she got tortillas from the fridge and started some rice in another pot. "Tell me about your mom," she said. "What does she do?"

"She's a teacher, a good one. She won teacher of the year last year."

"That's amazing. I like kids, but I couldn't imagine watching twenty of them all day every day."

"My mom's always been talented that way. She could be in an empty room and still find something fun for everyone to do. And she's one of those people who never makes you feel stupid about having questions. My sister wasn't very good in school, but Mom worked with her every night on her homework because she was too embarrassed to ask for help in class. Helped her self-esteem a lot."

Henrietta tilted her head. "She sounds amazing. My mom's main strategy for homework was to sit us at the kitchen table and stand over us with a wooden spoon." Hen laughed. "Johmarcus especially needed the motivation."

"My brother Rhett was the same way. But Johmarcus seemed to have plenty of motivation today," I said.

"He's grown a lot." She stirred the meat. "Back when he was younger, he was always about to become rich on some scheme. It cost him and my parents a lot."

I nodded. "Some lessons are harder to learn than others."

"True." She turned and retrieved two bowls from the cabinet, then dished them for us. The smell wafting from the dish she passed to me made my mouth water. "This looks delicious, and you made whipping it all together seem so effortless."

She smiled. "You flatter me, Tyler Griffen."

"You make it easy."

43

HENRIETTA

Confession: I'm terrified of losing my virginity.

WE'D EATEN OUR FAJITAS. We'd drunk our beer.

I was warm and buzzing with electricity.

And I'd never been more nervous in my life.

I pushed abruptly back from the island and said, "I'm going to use the bathroom."

"Sure, I'll take care of the dishes." He winked.

I shook my head at him because, gah, he wasn't allowed to be sexy *and* kind *and* do the dishes because he knew I hated them.

My breath picked up as I walked to the bathroom and shut myself inside. Was I really going to lose my virginity to Tyler? Tonight? And what would he think when he saw me naked? Would he change his mind? Had he been with big girls like me before? Would he know to expect the stretch marks and dimples and rolls? Or would it all scare him away?

I wished I was more like Mara and Birdie, confident in my size. But even if I didn't have their confidence, I did have them at my fingertips, so I sent them a text.

Henrietta: SOS. I'M ABOUT TO HAVE SEX WITH TYLER AND I'M FREAKING TF OUT!
Mara: What happened? What's wrong?
Birdie: I'm here too. <3
Henrietta: What if he doesn't like my body?
Mara: Henrietta. You're fat. Your clothes don't hide that.

I cringed at her calling me fat. I knew to her it was just a word, a descriptor, but when people had used those three letters to insult you your entire life, it was hard to get used to thinking of the word any other way.

Mara: And being fat isn't a bad thing.
Birdie: Exactly. Cohen loves my curves. Honey, I don't think Tyler would be so into you if he didn't like your size.
Mara: ^^^ I know it sounds cliché, but there's literally more of you for him to love... and play with. ;)

My cheeks were getting hot. Was I really ready for this? What if...

Henrietta: What if I'm bad in bed?
Birdie: I don't think Tyler will mind practicing with you. ;)

Practice. I could do that.

There wasn't a text from Mara right away, so I locked my phone and set it on the sink. If I stayed in here too long, Tyler would think I was having stomach problems and that would totally kill the mood. And I wasn't about to *almost* have sex for the second time. No, tonight was the night.

I reached into the cabinet and dabbed on some expensive perfume my grandma got me for my birthday a few years back. Then I ran my fingers through my hair, making sure it was perfect. And, of course, I dabbed on just a little bit of lip gloss.

I looked at myself in the mirror and whispered, "You can do this. You have a hot guy who likes you. The whole house is yours for the night. And if it doesn't go well... you can try again. If it doesn't work with Tyler, there will be someone else."

But I already knew that last part was a lie. I may not have known Tyler long, but I knew him well enough to understand that there was no one else like him.

I pushed back from the sink, put my hand on the doorknob, and took a deep breath. Henrietta Jones was not going to be a virgin anymore.

44

HENRIETTA

Confession: It's time.

"TYLER?" I called from the bathroom doorway.

"Yeah?"

"Meet me in my room?"

The sink immediately turned off, and I smiled to myself. Maybe that meant he was just as excited as me.

I met him in my bedroom doorway, and we were squeezed into the space, our bodies pressed against each other. He palmed the side of my neck, his hand big enough to cover my jaw too. "Have I told you how beautiful you are?" he breathed, his voice husky.

I looked from his eyes, a dreamy mix of dark green and brown, to his lips. Full. Pink. And I kissed him. Slow at first, then harder as we walked to my bed.

He lowered me down, straddling me on the bed as he feathered kisses from my lips to my cheek and jaw. His five o'clock shadow scratched against my skin as he worked his way to my neck, my collarbone. And then his hands slid under my dress, his palm running over my thighs, my side, my breasts. His thumb flicked over my nipple, already pebbling in anticipation.

He parted my legs with his and pressed his knee against my center. Moisture pooled between my legs, soaking my lacy underwear as I rode his thigh.

"Tyler," I moaned.

"I know, baby," he breathed, pulling at my dress. He lowered himself until his face hovered over my vagina, and he pulled my underwear aside, rubbing his thumb over my clit. The sensation was so strong, I clenched and moaned.

I'd touched myself before, spent time with toys, but this was already so much better. So much *more*. His thumb kept pressure on my clit as he slid a finger inside me. "You're so wet." His voice was husky before he replaced his thumb with his mouth.

Knowing he was tasting me... savoring me. Fuck, it was hot. My hips bucked, and I moaned, gripping the blanket we lay atop. I might not be good in bed, but Tyler was already surpassing every expectation, meeting every need I didn't know I had.

His tongue worked slow circles around my sensitive spot as he caressed my insides with his fingertips, hitting all the right places that I hardly knew could feel that way.

And then he hummed against my clit, and I nearly came undone.

"Tyler," I gasped.

He hummed, moving his fingers in and out, sweeping them around.

I tightened around his digits, so close to the edge, until

he worked me over the top, and I came undone around his finger, on his mouth. He continued licking it all until the waves slowly faded.

"Tyler," I said again. I was at a loss for words, only able to speak his name. But that was more than enough for him. He got up and took a tissue from my nightstand, wiping his face, and then took off his shirt.

I sat up, still quivering from his touch, and stared at his shirtless body. He was perfect, all hard lines, a dusting of short brown hair, and now I could see all of his tattoos. There was the one on the inside of his bicep and then a pattern that changed from prairie to sun that covered one of his shoulders almost to his neck.

He caught me staring, and I let myself look. He reached for his jeans, undoing the button and slowly lowering the zipper. His cock strained against his black underwear, the tip full, hard under the fabric.

I wanted to feel it, to touch it.

I moved to the edge of the bed, reaching for his underwear, but he caught my hand. When I looked up at him in question, there was a salacious smirk on his lips.

"You, Henrietta Jones, are wearing far too much clothing."

A laugh passed my lips, surprising even me. This, with Tyler, was sexy, hot, incredible, and... fun.

He reached for my hands, pulling me to stand next to him. And then he raised my dress over my head. Blinded by fabric, I could only feel him against me, my stomach brushing against his.

When the dress left my head, I could see him again. He looked in my eyes, his hazel ones so captivating. So open. He was letting me see him, the real him.

And I was letting him see me.

Stretch marks.

Cellulite.

My apron belly and my thighs that rubbed together and my breasts that strained against my size G bra.

It was me.

All of me.

But he didn't look away or step back. Instead, he kissed me. Not like I was something to be devoured or fetishized, but instead, someone to be worshiped. He reached to my shoulder, fingering the white strap of my bra.

"I like this," he said.

I reached behind me, undoing the clasps, freeing my breasts, and handed it to him. "It's yours." I took a breath. "I'm yours."

He stared at my breasts, then lifted one into his hand, drawing the nipple into his mouth.

I closed my eyes as he sucked. "That feels so good."

He drew his mouth away and said, "I want to make you feel good, baby." He lowered himself, pulling my panties over my thighs, and I kicked them aside as he stood, fully bare to this man I cared so much about.

Who'd given me more than he'd ever know. And I wanted to return the favor.

45

TYLER

Henrietta lowered herself to her knees in front of me. She gave me a coy smile before hooking her hands on the waistband of my underwear and bringing them down, releasing my cock. It was thick and veiny, waiting for her, and when she saw it, she licked her lips.

Fuck, it was hot.

She took it in her hand, giving it a few soft pumps.

"Harder, baby," I said.

She tightened her grip, pumping it for another few seconds before bringing her lips to the tip. Moving her hands to my hips, she slowly took me into her mouth. The soft warmth of her tongue on the underside of my tip, the stretch of her lips around my shaft, was almost too much.

I dropped my head back, moaning. "You know how to make me feel good, baby."

She moaned against my cock, and it took all I had to stay still, not to ram it the rest of the way into her mouth. Instead, I weaved my fingers through the hair at the back of her head, holding it away from her face as she moved over me, sucking and moaning and driving me fucking crazy. And when she looked up at me, like she was checking to see if she was doing a good job...

"Good girl," I encouraged.

She moved faster over my cock, and I could feel my precum sliding into her mouth. I was getting close. Too close. There was no way I was coming on her tongue when I hadn't felt what it was like to be inside her.

I took her hands from my ass and pulled her up, turning her so I could lay her back on the bed. Her tits spread, lulling to the side, so full I couldn't even hold them in one hand. Her stomach flattened into a brown pillow. And don't even get me started on the sexy girth of her thighs. I wanted her on top of me, riding me, pressing me into the bed. But first, I wanted her like this, face to face, with me in control.

Her eyes stayed on me as I lowered myself over her, my cock pressing into her stomach. "You're so fucking sexy, Henrietta," I breathed.

Her lips quirked slightly. She was nervous—I could tell—so I worked my way down, kissing her neck, her collarbone, sucking on one nipple while kneading her other breast, working a hand down to rub her sensitive spot. I was more than fine with taking my time with this beautiful woman despite how hard I was for her. She was worth the wait. And I needed her to *need* me. To beg for me. Because I wouldn't have her any other way.

She ran her hands down my back, digging her nails into my skin, holding on, until she was gasping for air.

"Tyler," she rasped. "I want you closer."

46

HENRIETTA

Confession: I love Tyler Griffen.

HE ROLLED a condom over his length and then propped himself up over me. I held on to his shoulders, feeling him press his tip to my entrance. This was it, the moment I would no longer be a virgin. But it was so much more, seeing Tyler's face, inches from mine. Watching him search my eyes as he pressed inside.

I'd heard it could hurt the first time, and I had prepared myself for that. But it was more of a stretching sensation as he sheathed his thick cock inside me. He was slow at first, drawing himself almost all the way out, then pushing all the way in. Pressure built inside me with each thrust.

His lips curled into a sultry smile. "You feel so good, baby."

All the emotions were there, happiness, surprise,

delight, and so much more. I hardly had words, so I took his face in my hands, drawing his mouth to mine. He kissed me, hard, as he continued a steady rhythm, in and out. It was all so surreal. My first time. With Tyler Griffen.

I couldn't have asked for anything better. My heart swelled as he continued his pace, filling me in a way I'd never known before. Emotion clogged my throat, and I swallowed, feeling tears sting my eyes.

"I know, baby," he said as tears dripped down my cheeks. He lowered his hips to mine as he ground inside me, then cupped my face with his hand, brushing a tear away from my cheek. His voice was hoarse. "It's never been like this for me before either."

I felt more vulnerable, more seen, than I ever had in my life, with this man holding me. He wasn't shying away from my feelings, from my size, from me. No, he'd embraced me and all that I was.

The swell in my heart grew with the build of my orgasm. "Tyler, I'm coming," I gasped in shock. I never thought I would come with my first time, but the waves were growing. "I'm coming."

"Yes, baby, that's it," he said, pushing harder, faster, until he shuddered over me. Inside me. I whimpered as my orgasm milked his cock, and when we stilled, he lowered himself to lie beside me, his breaths slowing from the gasps he'd taken earlier.

Plastic snapped as he freed himself of the condom. I watched as he tied it in a knot, pulled the plastic to check for holes. Seeing none, he set it in the trashcan by my bed.

I rolled to my side, facing him, as I assessed my body. I felt different, not because I'd had sex, but because I'd been claimed as his. And he'd let himself be mine in the most intimate way. Somewhere in the back of my mind, I wondered if I was bleeding, but I doubted it. My hymen had probably already been broken by a toy or a tampon.

"That was amazing," he said.

I smiled slightly and nodded. "I'm sorry for crying."

He laughed, and I found myself laughing too. "Don't worry about that," he said. "You were so beautiful with your eyes shining."

I covered my heart. "You're perfect. Tell me there's something wrong with you."

"Well, I did have some unwholesome thoughts when you had your mouth on my cock."

I sputtered, laughing. "I mean, that's about the most 'unwholesome' sentence I've heard. What were you thinking?"

He took my hair, twirling it around his finger, then tugging gently. "I thought about taking your head and making you take all of me, as deep as you could, until you gagged on my cock."

Even though I'd already come twice, my vagina clenched. "That sounds sexy."

"Yeah? You're into the dominating type?"

I bit my lip. "I think I am."

"We'll have to try it next time."

My lips lifted with a smile. "There will be a next time?"

"If I have a say in it, there will be a next time, and a next time, and a next time." He nuzzled his chin into my collarbone, tickling me and making me giggle.

I hugged his head to stall him and kissed his crown. "Good. I want that too."

He spread his arms so I could rest on his shoulder, and I curled into the nook, pulling the sheets over my chest. I loved the warmth of his naked body against mine under a cocoon of sheets and blankets. With his arm behind his head, I could see the tattoo on his bicep more clearly. It looked like a windmill, but just the blades... I traced my fingers over the spokes.

He watched my hand, then looked back at the ceiling. "My siblings and I got them together, after Gage's falling-out with my parents."

I watched him, taking in his beautiful eyes. "What was their fight about?"

"Gage wanted to take over the ranch and help Dad grow it so it could be big enough to support our entire family."

"And your dad didn't want that?"

He shook his head. "Dad thought Gage's idea was a pipe dream, something that would drain all our money and break their hearts in the process. And Gage told Dad that he was just scared and using money as an excuse. So, of course, Dad punched back, with his words. Said Gage was greedy and needed to stop talking about land grabbing from other families like us."

My heart already ached for Gage, for the rift all of it must have caused their family.

"Rhett was only twenty, too young to have much of a say, and my sister told Gage to stop arguing. I was already set on getting a job, and nothing I said could convince Dad to change his mind or take it back. So Gage was going to leave, join the military and never come back."

"Wow," I said. "It must have been awful."

"It was. Mostly because it was the beginning of the

war in Afghanistan. He would have gotten sent abroad, and so many people were dying. I was selfish—didn't want him to be one of them."

I nodded. "I would have done the same thing if one of my brothers had wanted to enlist."

Tyler took a deep breath. "So I told him to prove Dad wrong. To build a business from nothing and buy a ranch twice the size of Dad's out of sheer spite." He laughed. "Now he's a billionaire with the biggest real estate investment company in Texas."

"Has he bought the ranch?"

Tyler shook his head. "It was never about the ranch. It was about keeping our family together, rescuing them. And now that the family's all split up, well..."

I trailed the path of his tattoo with my fingertip. "Not really much of a point anymore."

He tapped my nose, making me smile. "But the four of us siblings all got tattoos. My sister's idea. She was only twenty-two, but I think she could sense all of us drifting apart."

"Why windmills though?"

"Because they always move but never leave." He kissed my temple. "You can count on them, day in, day out, to give you water, life. And you can never miss them. Even in a big pasture, it's like a country lighthouse telling you to come back home."

"That's beautiful," I said.

"It is, isn't it?" The slight smile on his lips touched his eyes. "Willa Cather always said anyone could love the ocean or the mountains. It takes a special person to see the beauty in the plains."

"I hope I can see it someday," I said.

"You will," he promised, shifting to get up. "I'm going to use the bathroom. Be right back." He kissed my forehead and got off my bed, walking that beautiful naked body to the door.

As soon as it shut behind him, I rolled and put my face in the pillow, squealing. I'd just had my first time, and it had been *amazing*.

After allowing myself a few moments of celebration, I rearranged myself on the bed, fixing my hair and pulling the sheets and blankets neatly up over my breasts like the women always did in the movies, waiting for him to come back.

As he walked back through the door, I smiled at him, until I noticed the frown on his lips, the crease between his eyebrows. And then I saw my phone in his hands.

"Henrietta, what the hell is this?" He held up my phone, showing a text I couldn't make out. But I could certainly imagine what was on the screen.

"What does it say?" I asked.

He held it up, reading from the screen. "'You should tell him you're a virgin. It will make ravaging you that much more fun for him.'"

I cringed, wishing I could sink below my bed and hide next to the boogeyman. Instead, I lay there, facing Tyler and his critical gaze.

"Is this true?" he asked.

"That you'd have more fun ravaging me? I think you're the only one who can answer that."

His frown only deepened. "Henrietta."

My cheeks warmed, and I felt like a little kid being caught with my hand in the candy jar. But I couldn't lie to him, couldn't keep the secret anymore. "That was my first time."

His jaw went slack, and he scrubbed his hand over his chin as if in disbelief. "There's never been anyone else? You *are* twenty-eight, aren't you? I didn't accidentally hook up with some teenage intern?"

Now it was my turn to glare at him. "Does this body look like a teenager's?"

A small flame sparked in his eyes, but he quickly put it out, coming to sit next to me and speaking gently. "Why didn't you tell me?"

"I was embarrassed!" I cried. "It's not exactly the best pickup line. 'Hi, my name's Henrietta. I live with my parents, and no one's ever been interested enough to round home base.' You would have run away screaming."

He reached for my hands. "Not true. Especially after I found out how good you could cook."

The joke would have made me laugh if my chest wasn't feeling so tight.

Running his thumbs over the back of my hands, he said, "If I would have known, I would have... I don't know, been more careful with you. Were you crying because you were hurt? Are you bleeding?"

I bit down on my lip, considering my words. "I was crying because I've never felt closer to anyone else than I have to you today. I'm so lucky to know you, Tyler. To be loved by you."

His eyebrows lifted, and I instantly backtracked. "Not saying you're in love with me, but——"

He stopped my words with a kiss, and when he pulled back, he held my face in his hand. "I do love you, Henrietta Jones. I love you."

Tears filled my eyes again for completely different reasons. "I love you too, Tyler."

He kissed me again, and with both of us naked in bed, it quickly became heated. He pulled back, still close enough for me to feel his breath on my cheek. "I'll make sure you never want anyone else."

47

TYLER

We spent all night in bed, drifting between sleep and lustfulness, exploring each other's bodies and making each other feel so damn good. It was heaven, and I knew I'd been a damn fool to think I would ever be okay with goodbye. So when Henrietta was sleeping, around two in the morning, I ordered plane tickets for us to visit home for Thanksgiving, just a couple months away now.

I wanted to convince her that Cottonwood Falls could be home. Show her all the trees that lined the creeks as their leaves changed to orange and gold. Introduce her to my mama and have her drive around to check cattle with my dad. Yell at my brother Rhett for flirting with her and my sister, Olivia, for sharing too many embarrassing secrets. I wanted to show her the high-rise where Gage worked and the incredible view from his office at night.

And most of all, I wanted her to fall in love with Texas like I'd fallen for her, because this feeling I had? Just the *thought* of it ending ripped me to shreds. But I wouldn't focus on that. I'd focus on this beautiful girl and the feeling I had in my chest. Like I had everything I needed right in front of me.

I rolled to my side, taking her in. She slept so peacefully, just like she had on my couch the night before. I loved her awake, but this quiet, serene side of her was beautiful too. If she woke up now, I knew she'd laugh at me for staring, but I enjoyed this immensely. Just as much as I liked lying next to her as I slowly fell asleep.

♥·♥·♥·♥

NORMALLY I'D GO for a run when I woke up, but this was a special morning, and my girl was getting a special breakfast. Even if I had to look through every drawer and cabinet in this kitchen to find what I was looking for.

That yellow box I used to make pancakes at home was nowhere to be found, so I used my phone to look up ingredients for pancakes and got to mixing. I was halfway through the batch when I heard a yawn behind me.

Henrietta was shuffling into the kitchen, her black robe tied at the waist and her gray slippers swishing against the new vinyl floor. With her hair tied in a messy bun atop her head and her eyes half closed, she still looked half asleep.

"Not a morning person?" I asked.

She hmphed. Maybe it was supposed to be a laugh. "Coffee?" she asked.

I nodded toward the pot, still tending to the pancakes. "Did you know your mom keeps coffee in a cookie jar?"

That got her laughing. "It's decorative."

"It's *hidden*," I retorted. "If the can isn't red or blue, I have no idea what to look for."

She stirred in cream and sugar, took a long sip, then said, "All a part of my mom's evil plan to see how we'd handle a relationship decaffeinated."

"Now there's a test," I replied, taking a drink of my own coffee. "But I am a morning person. I like to get my workout in before work, or I'd be too tired afterward."

She shook her head at me. "I knew there had to be something wrong with you."

I tossed my head back and laughed. "You're so grumpy when you first wake up."

Smiling slightly, she said, "Only after I've been kept awake all night."

I winked at her. "I'm more than happy to stay up for those reasons."

"Me too."

I leaned in and kissed her, her tongue tasting like sweet coffee, and then got back to cooking.

She leaned against the counter, watching me. "I was thinking I'd go visit my grandma real quick before work."

I glanced at the clock. It was only six fifteen. "Do you mind if I come along?"

Her smile grew. "I'd love that."

"There's my sunshine," I said. "Just needed some coffee."

She shook her head at me and took another drink. I finished dishing up the pancakes, and we ate in companionable silence before she needed to shower and get dressed. I'd brought a change of clothes to wear, so I put those on, and we made quick work of getting out the door and into my truck.

"It's fun, riding to work together," she said with a smile.

I smirked. "It's fun, knowing I'm your only ride so you'll be forced to stay with me."

She snorted. "As if you'd do that. You're too nice."

"Too nice?" I pretended my chest was hurting. "You wound me."

"It's a compliment. Most guys I know feel like they have to put on this tough guy act, never show an emotion. The way you handle things is... refreshing."

"I'll take that compliment," I said.

She pointed out another turn, and soon we were at the hospital, walking toward her grandma's room. As we approached, I could hear someone talking to her grandma. Hen listened quietly at the door and said, "Sounds like the doctors are here."

She knocked, and the talking paused as we walked into the room. Cordelia lit up at the sight of Henrietta and grinned even bigger when she saw me behind her.

"Hi, you two! Sounds like Tyler was quite the hero yesterday." Cordelia said to the doctor, "He installed vinyl floors and a ramp so I could get around the house easier."

The woman in a white coat smiled at me. "That's great. I was just telling your grandma here that things are on the right track. Inflammation and pain seem to be down, so we'll focus on the steroid regimen and some strenuous physical therapy, since Cordelia says she's up for the challenge."

Hen squeezed her grandma's hand. "Gran's the toughest person I know."

"When will I be able to go home?" Cordelia asked.

The doctor glanced at the chart in her hand. "Other than the hip, you're looking very healthy. Once you're able to make it around this unit with your walker, without anyone assisting, I don't see why we wouldn't release you. I'll recommend outpatient PT three times a week, but there may be an option to have someone see you at home."

Henrietta let out a quiet cry, covering her mouth with her hand. "That's great," Henrietta said. "I'm so happy."

I put my arm around her, holding her close, and she rested her free hand on my chest.

I smiled. "That is great news. But we all knew Cordelia was too stubborn to stick around here long."

Cordelia smirked. "Damn straight."

"Grandma!" Henrietta said at the same time the doctor said, "Right on."

48

HENRIETTA

Confession: So maybe I'm not as professional as I thought...

WHEN I GOT BACK to my office, everything felt right. Except for the plant I forgot to bring back with me. The room did feel a little bare without it. And the fact that Janessa had clearly messed with some papers while she was here. It took about an hour to get things back to the way I liked them.

I was glad I remembered those papers when I did. From now on, my searches would be purely digital and on my phone. For the rest of the day, I gave tours, managed the clean out of one apartment and had to serve an eviction notice to someone I'm pretty sure had already abandoned their unit.

But most of all, I looked forward to after work. Tyler and I hadn't made plans specifically, but as he mentioned, he was my ride, in more ways than one. *Wink.*

During the last ten minutes of work, I shut myself in

the bathroom and refreshed my makeup, then added a little perfume to my wrists and neck. And when I walked back out, I saw Tyler standing by the door, his hand on the knob.

We both froze, but Tyler's eyes moved first, traveling over my body, something heated in his stare.

Then he slid the lock shut and said, "Close the blinds, and get on your desk."

Goosebumps erupted over my skin.

"Now," he growled.

I fought the giddy smile taking over my face and went to the windows, pulling down each of the cordless blinds. This was something out of a fantasy, and here I was, experiencing it in real life.

A million worries popped up—what if someone came by, or worse, what if Janessa did a surprise drop in? But knowing we could get caught and being too overcome with desire to care made this even hotter.

With the blinds down, I did as he asked, walking around the counter to sit on my desk. His hooded eyes followed my every step. And when I sat on the desk, my skirt riding up, he said, "Good girl."

Did I have a praise kink? Maybe. Because hearing those words just made me want to do whatever he asked of me that much more.

With a sizzling look in his eyes, he lowered himself to his knees, separating my legs with his shoulders. Just like the night before, he pulled my panties aside and began feasting. The scrape of his five o'clock shadow on my delicate skin was just as sexy as what he was doing with his tongue.

I raked my fingers through his hair as he continued his assault, each second better than the one before.

"Tyler," I moaned as silently as I could, but it was hard to hold back. I gripped the edge of the desk and held on for dear life as he pushed me higher, harder, with just his mouth. And then he added his fingers to the mix, and I came undone, clenching hard and screaming with my mouth closed.

But there wasn't time to recover after my orgasm because he slid me off the desk, roughly turned me and bent me over, and then rammed into me from behind, the pain of his sudden entrance deliciously hot against my sensitive vagina.

He held on to my skirt, using it to pull my hips back to meet his, the slap of his front against my thighs filling the office.

"I love that fucking sound," he growled. "Tell me what you like."

I was nervous to speak out loud, to tell him what I liked when I'd never done that before, but I leaned into the moment, focused on the sensations in my body. How he made me feel. "The slap of your sack against me," I gasped.

"Fuck. And the way your ass jiggles with each thrust? So fucking sexy."

"Mhmm." My moan is almost a whine. All of him felt so good.

He reached up and grabbed my ponytail, yanking my head back. "Tell me more, baby."

The pain was exquisite, only adding to all the other sensations I felt. "I love it when you take control," I said. "When you tell me what to do and make me yours."

"You are mine," he said. "No one else's." He pulled out, turning me around so my ass was pressed against the desk, then hooked his arm under one of my legs. As he came back into me, we were face to face, nose to nose, eye to eye.

"You're mine," he said again.

And that, being claimed by Tyler, was everything.

"I'm yours," I said, my voice shaking with an oncoming orgasm.

"Come with me, baby," he said.

And I had no choice but to listen. My body would obey his every command. I held on to his shoulders as I tightened around him. He shuddered against me, filling me with the warmth of his come.

As we slowed, he kissed me, hard, then smiled against my mouth. "That was sexy as hell."

I never thought those words would ever be used to describe me, or anything I did, but I agreed. "I think my office is better with you in it."

Grinning, he released my leg and helped me stand, straightened my skirt and my blouse and buttoned his pants. Then he brushed back hair that had fallen from my ponytail, tucking it behind my ear. "We'll have to see if that theory holds true everywhere else." He held up his fingers, ticking them off. "My office, my truck, your car, my apartment..."

I couldn't wait to find out.

49

TYLER

If I could only use one word to describe the last month with Henrietta, it would be... *right*.

Spending time with her, getting to know her and exploring how our bodies fit together... I'd never done anything that came so naturally but felt so electrifying at the same time.

We spent almost every day together, and a lot of nights, she stayed over at my place, quickly turning it from a temporary stay to a home. On Wednesday mornings, she had breakfast with the girls, on Thursday nights, I played poker with the guys, and on the weekends, we hung out with her friends or her family. Her family had a *huge* party when Cordelia came home.

But most of all, I couldn't wait for her to meet my family, see my home. Because each day in Emerson felt like a grain of sand falling to the bottom of the hourglass on our relationship, and there was no way I could ever let her go.

I just hoped she'd be okay with spending Thanksgiving in Texas instead of California like she normally did. We were just a couple weeks away, and I needed to ask soon.

Wanting the request to be special—and to stack the odds in my favor—I printed out the tickets and had them wrapped in a beautiful box with a necklace that had a windmill charm hanging at the end of it.

I stashed the items in my office this morning so when she did her afternoon check-in at the build site, I could give them to her and ask her to come along. That would give us two weeks to prepare for the trip. And to meet my family. They could definitely be a lot.

The build was going along smoothly. We'd only had one permitting delay, and that was back on track now, thanks to a guy on my team whose wife worked at city hall. A few papers may or may not have been moved to the top of the review pile.

With the foundation poured, we were working on framing the first level. I liked this part, where it started looking more like an actual building and not like a big mess of concrete, metal, and broken ground.

I checked my watch again and saw it was about time for Henrietta to get here, but when I told the guys I was going back to the office trailer, I found her already standing outside the building, grinning at me. When we got out of earshot of the workers, she said, "You look sexy working like that." She fanned herself. "Should I be worried that I like the sight of you handling wood?"

I snorted. "I like the sight of me handling you better."

She giggled. "I enjoy that also." The fall sun hit her hair, sending rays bouncing off her black waves.

"You look beautiful today," I said, using all my

restraint to keep my hands off her. We tried to keep things professional during the workday, but damn was it hard when I knew how hot she could get for me.

"Thank you," she replied.

We stepped inside my office, and she said, "Is there anything I need to bring by city hall?"

"Not today. Our next checkpoint with the inspectors isn't for another few weeks, so things should be light on your end until then."

She pretended to pout. "Does that mean I don't need to come visit you?"

"If your hot ass isn't on the job site every damn day, we're going to have a problem," I growled.

She laughed. "Where's nice guy Tyler?"

"Right here." I pulled her in, kissing her lips. "And I'll stay that way as long as I have my girl at my side."

"Gosh, you're perfect," she replied. And even though I knew I was far from perfect, I liked hearing the word roll off her tongue.

"Hey, there was something I wanted to talk to you about," I said.

Worry instantly formed a crease between her eyebrows.

"It's nothing bad," I reassured her. "Actually, I'm excited about it."

"What is it?" she asked, the crease disappearing.

I walked around my desk and opened the drawer, pulling out the decorative red box.

"What is this?" she asked, taking it gingerly in her hands.

"I've loved spending these last months with you, Hen, and getting to know your family has been incredible. But my family wants me to go home for Thanksgiving, and I can't stand the idea of going without you."

She watched me, a small smile playing on her lips.

"I want you to meet my parents and get annoyed by my siblings and stare at my brother's office and spend a night under the Texas stars with me."

She bit her bottom lip. "Camping? Won't it be cold in November?"

"Makes cuddling that much better."

Her smile grew, and the suspense was killing me.

Not able to take it any longer, I asked, "Will you go?"

She nodded and wrapped her arms around my shoulders. "I'd love to, Tyler!"

I held her close, breathing in her delicate perfume and loving every damn second. Until the door opened. The only time I'd ever jumped apart from a girl faster was when I got caught making out with my girlfriend in high school.

Rich grinned between the two of us, but didn't say anything about what he'd caught us doing. Instead, he said, "We're at the point where starting the next step would keep the guys here for another hour. Do you want to have them keep going or let them out a little early?"

I glanced at my watch, seeing there were about fifteen minutes left in the workday. "You can send them home. I need to show the boss here what we've been up to."

Rich winked. "I'll tell them to get the show on the road." He turned around and left the trailer, and I shared a guilty smile with Henrietta.

"We should be more careful when the guys are on site," I said.

She nodded. "Definitely."

"But in the meantime." I lifted the lid from the box she was holding. "I thought you should have a piece of home to look forward to."

Her eyes softened as she took it in. "Tyler, it's beautiful."

My lips lifted, her reaction to the necklace was like an acceptance of me, my family. "Can I put this on you?"

She nodded, turning and lifting her hair off her neck. I draped the delicate silver chain around her and clasped the back. It fell against her dark skin, and it took all I had not to place a kiss there.

Instead, I let it go and stepped back. As she turned, she held her hand to the pendant. And when she removed her fingers so I could get a good look, I smiled. "It's beautiful on you."

"Thank you," she said. "Now why don't you show me the site? It's so different every day."

We walked out of the trailer together, saying goodbye to the workers when they passed us toward the small gravel parking lot. As we approached the building, I started pointing out the foundation, how many steel bars had been laid within the concrete to make sure the building would withstand age and weather and even earthquakes.

Then I showed her the steel framing, long beams that would maintain structural integrity, even in hurricane-force winds. She asked really astute questions, and when I was done, she leaned against one of the walls that had been framed in, shielded from the road.

"It's amazing to think people will live here someday. Hundreds maybe."

"Do you think you'll be working here to see it?" I

asked. Because I didn't want to ask the real question—will you move to Texas with me? Would you give up everything you have here so we can build a life together there?

"I don't know yet," she answered. "I've applied for a few jobs, but nothing's come back that would match my salary, and I still have eighteen thousand to save."

Not quite the answer I was hoping for, but it was something.

"You know," she said, "it really was sexy, seeing you working earlier." She trailed her fingers up my polo and undid the top button.

My heart was already speeding. "Yeah?"

She nodded, looking up at me before undoing the next button. "I can see your muscles moving under this shirt when you're working. It's hot knowing my man's so strong and capable with his hands."

My dick twitched, already getting hard. Henrietta, here, in her work dress she knew I loved, was a fucking fantasy. But we'd almost been caught in the office just moments before. I needed to make sure everyone had left first.

"Hold on," I whispered to her. Then I stepped away from the small enclosure and looked outside. The job site was like a ghost town. No one was here to see us, and our vehicles were the only ones in the lot.

Excitement ripped through me as I walked back to her. She gave me a questioning look, and I answered by crossing the small space between us and taking her in a kiss.

But instead of letting me continue to kiss her senseless, she dropped to her knees in front of me.

"Hen..." I said.

She only answered by wrapping her mouth around my cock. And I was gone, lost in the feel of her mouth around me, lost in the grip of her hands on my thighs, lost in the sexy suckling sounds she made on my cock and the gagging sound she made when she took me too far in.

And then I was lost in my orgasm, in the heady rush of knowing my cum was spilling down her throat.

She licked her lips and smiled up at me, fire dancing in her eyes. "How was that?"

"Unbefucklinglievable," I said, my voice hoarse.

She laughed. "Good. Now let's go get some supper. Although I am feeling a little full." And then my girl winked.

God, I loved her.

50

HENRIETTA

Confession: This trip had me more nervous than I'd ever been.

GRANDMA SAT on her walker by my bed while I packed for my trip to visit Tyler's family. "Are you excited?" she asked.

"Nervous is more like it. I'm going to be meeting his entire family for the first time, and I'm all in my head about it," I replied, taking a dress out of my suitcase for the third time. "I've checked the weather forecast about ten times, and I still can't decide if it'll be warm enough to wear a dress while we're there."

"Then wear pants," Grandma said. "It's not like they're going to see you in slacks and say, 'Nope. Not good enough for our son.'"

I gave her a look. "Is it just me or are you sassier since you got home from the hospital?"

"Why don't you wear some of those leggings with a longer dress shirt? You look so cute in those outfits."

I nodded. She was right. And I was definitely over-thinking this. "But what if his family doesn't like big girls?" I asked. "It'll be a long five days if they're disgusted by me."

Grandma said, "You're not asking the right question."

I faced her, waiting for her to explain. She knew it was true—some people thought being overweight was a moral failing. They judged people like me to no end.

She lifted her hands, her elbows resting on the walker, and said, "You need to be asking, 'What if they are warm, kind, loving people? What if I love Texas? What if this brings Tyler and me that much closer together?'" She smiled. "And if you must be negative, you can ask, 'What if I can't stand them?' Because you are incredible, my dear. If they don't like you, there's clearly something wrong with them. Enough with the stinkin' thinkin'."

I set down the shirt I was folding and went to give her a hug. "Thanks, Grandma." But there was still something holding me back… "I feel like I have to address the elephant in the room."

"And what is that?" she asked.

"I'm a Black woman from California, and Tyler's a white man from outside of Dallas, Texas, one of the most conservative places in the country. What if we don't fit in together there? What if the community doesn't welcome me?"

She twisted her lips to the side deepening her wrinkles. "You know the world's changed so much since I was younger. I lived through the Loving case, and some people still think the courts got it wrong…"

My chest got tight in the way it always did thinking about racist people, the bias some people had against me and people like me. Most of the time I tried to ignore it, but now? It was all I could think about.

"You know, it's hard to believe you two have only been together for a few months. It feels like he's been a part of our family from day one." She shrugged. "Seems to me a man like that wouldn't take you anywhere that could cause you harm. And if for some reason, an issue did arise, a man like that would nip it in the bud faster than you could blink."

I nodded, feeling light enough to get back to folding some blouses to put in my suitcase. Tyler would keep me safe, just like he'd protected me that night from Houston. "He's so easy to be around. I wonder if his family is the same way."

"There you go," Grandma said with a wink.

"What are you going to do without me here to boss around?" I asked in a teasing tone, but part of me was worried about her. I wanted her to be safe when I was gone, and I had been filling in the gaps here lately, especially since it was hard to get on the senior ride with her walker. I'd been taking her to appointments and the store when Mom and Dad couldn't.

"It's only a week," Grandma said. "And besides, you know they have special buses for *old, feeble* people like me. I just need to get signed up."

"I didn't call you feeble."

"You didn't deny the old part," she retorted.

"Didn't need to." I winked.

She rolled her eyes.

I scanned my suitcase, deciding I had everything I needed and probably a lot more. "I think that's it."

From the doorway, I heard Tyler's voice say, "Good timing."

He looked so handsome, changed out of his work clothes into a pair of jeans that fit him so well it should be a crime. And with his arm propped up against the door-frame, I could see a sliver of his fit stomach. If he stood like that much longer, I'd need a mop to wipe up all this drool.

Grandma looked between me and him. "I hope you have a great Thanksgiving with your family, Tyler. Although, we call the next one."

I loved the way she assumed we'd be together, because I was hoping the same thing. Even though I had no idea how it would work with him at his next job site, wherever it would be, and me in California. In fact, I tried not to think about it at all.

I'd wanted to move out from my parents' house, but now that Grandma needed so much extra help... I just didn't know how that would work. Would my family be able to pick up the slack if I moved all the way to Texas? Would I be able to forgive myself if they did?

Tyler said, "Can I carry your bags for you, Hen?"

I nodded, passing him my suitcase and picking up my purse filled to the brim with the essentials.

Grandma extended her arms for another hug, which I gladly took.

"Give my brothers hell for me," I said.

"You know I will," she replied, squeezing me just a little tighter before letting me go.

Mom and Dad said goodbye to us in the living room, wishing us well, and soon we were on the road to Tyler's apartment. It was easier for me to stay with him so we could get up early for our drive to LA.

Instead of eating out, we grabbed some takeout on the way and walked up the steps to his apartment. As soon as we walked through the door, the smell of his leather and linen candles enveloped me, making me smile. "I need to ask your sister to make me some of these candles so I can light them in the office."

"I'm sure she'd love that," Tyler said, squeezing my hand.

He set up dinner at the table, and we ate while he gave me all the details and quirks I might need to know about his family. He said his brother Rhett would flirt with me, his sister would probably want to take me horseback riding (which sounded like a ton of fun), and his brother Gage would probably spend way too much money on whatever we did. But then he said his mom would love me, and I already felt more at ease. He loved his mom more than anyone in the world, and if I passed her test, I had no doubt this relationship would be something that would last.

With dinner done and Tyler doing what was left of his dishes, I excused myself to take a shower. The water pressure here was incredible. I took my time, shaving my legs, brushing out my hair, and then rubbing coconut oil all over my body. I loved using it as a natural moisturizer, and it smelled amazing. Plus, I knew Tyler liked it too.

I walked to his bedroom and reached into his closet for the oversized T-shirts he kept especially for me because he thought they were sexy. I slipped one over my head, no underwear or bra underneath, and walked to the living room.

Where Janessa was edging her way into the apartment.

My mouth fell open, and I quickly turned to leave, but it was too late. We'd been caught.

51

TYLER

I clenched my jaw, mentally cussing Janessa for being so damn pushy. She'd literally invited herself into my apartment to "make sure it was up to par", even though I'd said, multiple times, that I wasn't feeling well.

Of course, now I was caught in the lie, and Henrietta had been caught half naked.

Janessa's eyes widened as she looked between Henrietta and me, processing what she saw, and then her gaze narrowed with recognition. "What do we have here?" she asked.

Henrietta chirped, "I'll be right back." She pulled the hem of her shirt down and hurried to the bedroom, leaving Janessa and me standing alone.

"Well, now I know why you've been turning me down," Janessa said. "Not that I understand the allure."

Protective rage quickly rose in my chest, spewing out my mouth. "Watch it."

She lifted her eyebrows, an amused smile on her lips. "Look at those claws coming out."

My jaw twitched with bitten-back words. If she uttered one more negative comment about my girl, she'd regret it.

But her smile fell back into place, and she said, "Henrietta, how nice to see you in your clothes."

I looked over my shoulder to see Henrietta walking down the hallway toward us. Her hair was still wet, but now she had on a cotton dress and house shoes.

"Janessa, I wasn't expecting to see you here," Hen said, a smile on her face that didn't reach her eyes.

"I could say the same." She stepped farther into the apartment, brushing her fingers along the back of my couch and thumbing away the dust. "I thought we had a talk about dating Tyler being against the rules."

The audacity of this woman, pushing her way into my home and then shaming Henrietta for doing the same thing she had wanted. My voice was tight as I said, "I informed Henrietta of your very direct, and failed, attempts at flirting with me."

Janessa's smile only faltered for a minute. "That was only banter, Tyler."

Henrietta narrowed her gaze. "I called Frannie. She told me the truth—she was fired for coming to work late *because she had morning sickness*, not for hooking up with Jeremy."

"Same difference," Janessa said as if her lies were no big deal.

Henrietta said, "I'm sure the shareholders wouldn't be happy that Blue Bird only hired Crenshaw Construction for your own selfish crush on Tyler."

"That wasn't at all the plan," Janessa sputtered.

Henrietta lifted her chin. "You met with Tyler and his

boss prior to hiring. I doubt your denial will prove anything."

Changing tactics, Janessa stepped between Hen and me. "Henrietta, I thought we were friends. Are you really going to let some guy come between us?"

My gut sank, waiting to hear Hen's answer.

"I thought we were friends too," Hen said, a quiver in her voice. "We've worked together for eight years, and you had no problem lying to me because I told you he was cute. That's *not* what friends do. You are no friend of mine."

Any hint of Janessa's fake smile was gone. "Fine. Enjoy each other. Although I have no idea how that's possible."

Henrietta's jaw fell, and I stepped forward, holding my hand on the door so Janessa couldn't open it. She needed to hear this—and Henrietta did too.

"You want to know why I chose Henrietta when you were so clearly interested? I chose her because I could have a conversation with her without feeling like a piece of meat. Henrietta is intelligent and kind and clearly cares about the people who live here and making them feel safe and comfortable. And I don't know if you've seen her curves, but they're sexy as hell. So I will not be having any more negative talk about her from a desperate, jealous woman like you. Especially not in my own damn home."

Janessa grit her teeth before ripping open the door and leaving the apartment. "You'll regret this," she said in the hallway. "I'll make sure of it."

I shut the door in her face.

I turned toward Henrietta, gripping her shoulders in

my hands. "Are you okay? I'm so sorry about what she said."

Henrietta lifted her chin and kissed me. "Thank you for standing up for me like that."

"Of course."

"But are you freaking crazy?" she asked, hitting my shoulder. "Janessa is a powerful woman, and she's clearly not above lying. What if she gets the CEO to fire Crenshaw?"

"She can't. We have a contract in place saying we finish the project unless there are legitimate safety or quality concerns. We do everything by the book on site. She's all talk." I wrapped my arms around Henrietta's waist. "Now, can you go put that shirt back on?" I bit the shell of her ear. "I want to see you bent over the couch with nothing underneath."

Her voice was rough as she said, "Whatever you tell me to do, it's done."

52

HENRIETTA

Confession: I'm still trying to remind myself that I'm not too big for certain things—they are just too small for me.

MOST OF THE time I could forget my size. But there were certain things that made me hate the way fat people were treated in this world. Clothes shopping was number one—most people relegated you to one tiny corner of the store, and it was even harder when you tried to thrift most of your clothes.

And then there was basically anything that included chairs. Being forced to stand in waiting rooms because you knew you couldn't squeeze your butt between the arms of the chair. Forget amusement parks—the shame of having to exit the ride because you can't fit and then hearing people whisper, or even talk loudly about you as you walk away. It's a form of torture no one deserves.

But then, there's getting on an airplane. Walking

down the rows and every person looking away because they don't want you in their row. People skipping by you because they don't want to sit next to you.

This time, though, I had Tyler with me. We'd sit side by side, and he'd already offered to take the middle seat so I could see Texas from the air. I hadn't traveled much, but he said when you flew over the Midwest, you could see little squares of farm ground below. I couldn't wait.

I walked ahead, since he insisted on carrying my bags, and found us a seat a few rows behind the wings. I scooted into the seat and reached for my belt, and then it hit me.

No matter how much I sucked, squeezed, or adjusted myself, my seat belt would not reach all the way around my waist. My eyes stung as I let loose of the clip and looked out the window. I felt Tyler's shoulder brush against me, but I kept my eyes away.

I was so embarrassed. He knew I was a big girl, had seen me naked and told me I was sexy, but this felt way too much like reality compared to the blissful fantasy we'd been living in. This was part of dating a big girl, and I didn't want to find out that he actually couldn't handle it.

He leaned over, resting his chin on my shoulder. "It's kinda nice that the seats are small so we can cuddle the whole way."

"Yeah," I said, but my voice cracked. I really freaking wish it hadn't cracked.

"Hen, are you okay?"

I tried to blink back tears. "I'm fine." Was there a way to fold my belly over the belt so the flight attendant couldn't see if it was buckled?

"Baby, look at me. What's going on?"

I closed my eyes, wishing for a moment that I could be smaller. That this wouldn't be an issue I had to worry about.

"Do you not want to meet my family anymore?" he asked.

The worry in his voice gutted me. And I hated to make him worry when it wasn't his problem; it's mine.

"The belt doesn't fit," I whispered, blinking back hot tears. One slid down my cheek, and I wiped it away.

"Oh, that's no big deal," he said. He turned away from me, and when he spotted a flight attendant walking by, he said, "Excuse me, sir, can I get a belt extender for my girlfriend?"

"Of course," the guy said, like it was no big deal. He handed one to Tyler, and then Tyler passed it to me, and I held the clip in my hand, staring at it.

"Here," he said gently. He took it back and hooked it on his side of me, then he reached across my midsection, finding the other side of my belt. Once it was all clipped into place, he kissed my cheek. "Look, you're all belted in. No need to be embarrassed."

I looked at him, studying his molten hazel eyes and wondering what he saw in me. If he ever wished he was with someone who would... fit better into the way the world expected beautiful people like him to live.

He held my face in his hands and kissed me softly.

And it was better. Already it was better. And he hadn't even said a word. I knew I had to talk to him about something else, to help the worry that hadn't quite left my system since my talk with Grandma.

"Maybe there is something else," I admitted, biting my lip.

"What is it?" he asked.

I ran my hands over my legs, trying to remove the sweat from my palms. "Tyler, I'm Black."

He chuckled slightly. "I know that."

"Does your family know that?"

He seemed confused by my question. "Well, yeah. I sent them a picture pretty soon after I bought plane tickets. My sister thinks you're gorgeous, by the way."

I smiled slightly. "It's just... Texas isn't always well-known for being welcoming to different kinds of people. With you being from a small-town... Not that I'm saying every person who comes from a small town in a red state is racist, but maybe if they don't see a lot of people like me." My eyes were stinging again as I struggled to get out the words, struggled to express my fears. I wiped at my tears. "I don't want to feel out of place when I'm there, and I don't want you to change your mind," I whispered.

Tyler held my face in both of his hands. "I need you to hear this."

I nodded.

"What other people think about you will never change the way I see you, right now. You are perfect, kind, sexy as hell, *and* Black. It's a part of you, just like your family and your heart and that beautiful brain in your head. And *if* we come across anyone who judges you, they have another fucking thing coming. I promise, I won't let anyone tear you down without ripping out their ass hole and pulling it over their head."

I couldn't help but laugh at his violence. Tyler was

always a gentleman, but when it came to me, I knew he'd defend me, no matter what it took.

"I'm serious," he said. "But I also want you to know that Cottonwood Falls is different from what you see on the news. The people there look out for each other, no matter if you've been there five days or fifty years. They're going to love you."

"Thank you," I said, my chest finally relaxing. "I needed to hear that."

"Of course. Is there anything else? I want you to be excited, not scared."

"Not at all. It just helps knowing you have my back."

He kissed my forehead. "Of course I do."

I lifted the armrest between us and leaned against his shoulder. "What do you usually do on flights?" I asked, trying to distract myself. "I haven't been on one since I was little."

"I usually just find a movie on the airline's list and watch that." He got out his phone, going to the in-flight Wi-Fi. My eyes widened in horror as he paid the eight dollars for advanced access.

"What are you doing?" I asked. "We can go a few hours without internet."

"But what if you want to watch something they don't have?"

I laughed and shook my head. "We haven't even been through the list yet!"

"Yeah, but what my baby wants, my baby gets. That's worth way more than eight dollars to me."

Tears of a new kind found my eyes. "How did I get so lucky with you?" Because really, I felt like the luckiest girl in the world—he wasn't ashamed of my size, he supported my dreams, and he was even flying me across the country because he wanted me to see his hometown.

He kissed me again, making butterflies dance in my stomach. "I've been asking myself the same question ever since you agreed to that first date." Then he kissed the top of my head. "So, what do you want to watch, baby girl? We have the internet at our fingertips."

53

TYLER

We were midway through our second movie when the pilot said we'd crossed the Texas border. Hen looked away from my phone and leaned close to the window.

"Look at the little squares!"

The joy in her voice made me smile so damn big. I looked over her shoulder, seeing all the farmland below. My chest swelled with pride, knowing that less than two percent of the population was growing food for all of the US and then some. My family was part of that number.

"What are the squares with circles?" Hen asked.

"Those are the ones with center pivots. They're like giant sprinklers that spin around the field."

"Way cool," she said, looking back at me for a moment. "I've seen some farmland in California, but not like this." We watched the landscape go by as it gave way from open space and farmland to the bustling city streets of Dallas.

The pilot announced our descent, and she smiled over at me.

"Will your parents pick us up?" she asked.

I shook my head. "I have a truck in long-term parking. We'll get lunch, and then I'll drive you out to the farm. Everyone's excited to meet you."

Her nervous smile wrenched my heart. But if she knew how much I cared for her, she'd know how little she had to worry. My parents weren't the kind to judge—if we kids were happy, then they were happy. (Even if Rhett had them shaking their heads from time to time.)

We grabbed our suitcases from the baggage claim and then went out to the parking lot. It had been a few months since my truck had been driven, but it was nice and clean and fired right up.

"Why do you keep a truck out here?" Henrietta asked.

"It's just easier not to bother anyone when I come to town. Cottonwood Falls is about two hours from the airport."

"Oh wow," she said. "You really are from the boonies."

"Hey," I laughed.

We joked and talked until we got to the restaurant for lunch, and then we talked some more, and then it was time to take her to the farm. On the drive, I pointed out every special place to me. There was the turnoff that led to a cornfield where I lost my virginity in the back of my truck. (Original, I know.) And then there was the rival school our football team always beat despite having half as many guys on the team. We drove past the movie theater where we took all our dates.

Then I saw something that caught me off guard. A for-sale sign in front of the old schoolhouse. Both of my parents had gone to school in this building, but they built a new school before my siblings and I started. For the last thirty years, the local hardware store had used it for extra storage.

I stopped in front of the building, staring from the sign to the building.

They were selling it.

"What is this?" Hen asked, looking at the brick facade through the window. "Did you go to school here?"

I shook my head. "My parents did... I always thought it was stupid that they filled it with junk instead of using it."

"Using it for what?" Hen asked.

"With all that square footage, it would make a great apartment building. People would go crazy over the historical details inside—if they haven't been completely ruined."

Hen got out her phone, tapping on the screen.

"I know it's not that interesting but—"

She held up her finger, putting her phone to her ear. After a couple seconds, she said, "Hey, we were wondering if we could take a tour of the schoolhouse?... I mean, we're here now.... Great! I'll see you in a few minutes."

I stared at Hen. "What did you do?"

She laughed, pushing her door open. "I wanted to see inside. Why don't we look around until the agent gets here?"

Shaking my head, I followed Hen out of the truck. Life with her was certainly an adventure.

She walked over the unkempt buffalo grass to the big front stoop. "This would be a beautiful common area for an apartment building—you could set up some benches and people could actually get to know their neighbors."

I pictured the peeling paint over the cement done up freshly, maybe even covered with a wooden deck, and rocking chairs lined along the building. Add some hanging plants, and it could be a beautiful place to pass an afternoon with a glass of sweet tea.

She walked to the side of the porch, looking around the back. "The playground is dangerous, but if you took it out, there would be plenty of room for a big community garden and maybe even another sitting area?"

I put my arm around her, loving the way she dreamed. "Imagine it being a senior living building," I said. "Grandpa would love it here, closer to home."

"I love that!" she said, twisting in my arms to give me a kiss.

Tires crunched on gravel, and we looked over to see Linda Macomb walking our way. I lifted a hand and said, "Hi, Linda."

She peeled off her black sunglasses, revealing light blue eyes. "Tyler Griffen, is that you? I haven't seen you since you were scoring touchdowns!"

I chuckled, turning to Hen. "Linda, this is my girl-friend, Hen."

Hen smiled, shaking Linda's pale hand. "Nice to meet you."

"You too, darling. Let me show you around."

We went into the school, and it was about as rundown as I'd expected. Even though the hardware store had taken out most of their stuff, there was a layer of dirt on the floor an inch thick. All the windows were dirty and cobwebbed. But I'd been right—this place had been built in the early 1900s. So much detail had gone into wood-work back then, before the minimalism trend hit.

As we walked outside, Linda asked, "Thinking of buying it?"

Hen glanced at me, her eyes full of curiosity.

"It's a pipe dream," I said. "I travel too much to ever be able to do it justice."

"That's a shame," Linda said. She reached into her purse and handed me a business card. Her photo on it had to be from ten years ago. "Call me if anything changes."

I assured her I would, and then Hen and I got in the truck. From the schoolhouse, it was a right turn and an easy shot out of town.

"It's so different from Emerson," Hen said, gazing around as we drove down the dirt road that led to Griffen Farms. It was a beautiful fall day, low sixties, and the sun was shining. All the cottonwood trees had brown and yellow leaves, and even the grass was turning from green to yellow. Something about this place just made my heart feel lighter.

"It's home," I said.

"I bet you get so homesick when you're on the road."

I nodded, squeezing her hand. "The air's just different here."

She smiled, then her look changed to surprise. Pointing out the windshield, she asked, "Are those llamas?"

"Alpacas," I said. "When I was about five, the Deans decided alpacas were better than cattle. They've had ostriches, emus, even camels one year. It's always fun to see what they've got going."

Hen giggled. "Who would have thought? Camels in Texas."

"We're full of surprises."

"Any camels on your farm?"

I shook my head. "But Dad did buy a goat one year because he was tired of mowing the lawn."

She laughed. "Don't mention that to my dad. He would actually buy one."

"It's all fun and games until you see goat hoofprints on your car."

"They jump?" she asked, seemingly surprised and amused.

"Oh yeah. And they'll headbutt you if you're not paying attention."

She covered her mouth as she giggled. "I'm imagining a little goat running up on you before school."

"You're not too far off." The metal arch leading to my family's farm appeared on the side of the road, and I pointed it out. "That's us."

I slowed and watched her smile as she read the letters. *Griffen Farms*

Then she gazed at the white farmhouse farther down the road. "Tyler, it's beautiful! Like something out of a picture book."

I followed her gaze, trying to see it with new eyes. This place had always been home, but it certainly was beautiful. Mom and Dad lived in a two-story white farmhouse with red shutters and a wraparound porch Mom kept decorated with hanging planters full of flowers and spider plants. The grassy yard spilled into a buffalo grass prairie, and just beyond the house, you could spot the red barn and the horse pen.

"It was fun to grow up here," I said. "Like the whole world was my backyard."

She gazed out the window toward the black and red cattle dotting the hillside. One of my favorite views. With the windows down, you could hear the occasional moo. That, mixed with the breeze rustling the grass, was one of my favorite sounds.

We parked in the gravel drive alongside the house where Rhett and Liv's cars were already parked.

"Do we need to get our bags?" Hen asked.

"I can grab them later." I smiled over at her and said, "I can't wait for you to meet them. They're going to love you."

"As long as you love me," she said.

I gave her a quick kiss to let her know that hadn't changed and got out of the truck to open her door. As we walked to the house, I kept my arm around her shoulders, and she hooked hers around my waist.

I was so proud to bring this woman home. Her wit, her humor, her heart... she was the complete catch.

Before we reached the door, Mom pushed it open and greeted us on the porch. "Honey!"

I let go of Hen to hug my mom, then stepped back, my arm around my mom's shoulders, and said, "This is her."

Mom covered her mouth with her hands. "Henrietta, you're just as beautiful as he said you were." She extended her hand to shake Henrietta's. "My name's Deidre. It's so nice to meet you."

Hen shook my mom's hand. "You can call me Hen."

"Love it," Mom said, holding on to Henrietta's hand. "Come meet the rest of the family."

54

HENRIETTA

Confession: I love a family man.

DEIDRE HAD her hand linked with mine as she led me into their home. It was beautiful, with what looked like original hardwood floors, big picture windows with a view of the prairie, and the people inside were just as good-looking.

The one woman in the room close to my age was beautiful with curvy hips and a sweet, heart-shaped face. She had long, brown hair with natural curl, and her eyes were the same shade of green as Tyler's. I liked her instantly.

She said, "I'm Tyler's sister, Olivia, but everyone calls me Liv."

"Nice to meet you," I said, shaking her hand.

A guy who stood a couple inches taller than Tyler's six-foot height stepped forward, laying hazel eyes with thick brown lashes on me. "I'm Rhett, the good-looking one."

Tyler snorted behind me. "More like the cocky one."

"That too," Rhett said, extending his hand. "Pleased to meet you, Hen."

I shook his rough hand and smiled at him. "Same here."

Tyler put his arm back around my waist as the elder Griffen stepped forward. His dad looked so much like him, tall and strong, except he had a brown mustache peppered with gray hairs, and his tanned face was full of wrinkles.

"Jack," he said as he shook my hand. "Glad to have you on the farm."

"It's stunning," I said. "Tyler's told me all about it and how much he loved growing up out here."

Deidre smiled. "He was a good kid when he wasn't hiding in the trees, trying to get out of doing chores."

I laughed, remembering Tyler telling me about that. "There are more places to hide out here than there are in the city."

"One of the many benefits," Tyler said.

Deidre shook her head with a smile. "I thought Tyler, Rhett, and Liv could take you on a tour of the farm while Jack and I get dinner ready. We have some Griffen select steaks we'd love for you to try." She glanced at Tyler. "She does eat meat, right?"

"As if I'd bring home a girl who couldn't house a steak," Tyler said.

Olivia laughed. "He knows better than that."

The banter between them made me smile. I'd only ever seen Tyler around my family or on his own, but seeing him so close with his siblings and parents brought out another side of him that only made me love him even more. I'd always wanted to be with a family man, and Tyler delivered that and so much more.

Deidre asked, "Do you need to get freshened up before you go out?"

Tyler said, "Let me show her the room and bring our bags in."

"Good idea," his mom said.

"I'll get the bags," Rhett offered. "Are they under the shell?"

Tyler nodded and then led me toward the stairs in the corner of the living room. They had a beautiful oak railing, and as we walked up, I imagined all the mornings Tyler had come down these stairs, all the touches that had worn this rail smooth. It was like the house had a history all its own.

"Are we staying in your old room?" I asked as we crested the stairs.

"We are," Tyler said. "I hope my mom hid my 'unmentionables.'"

I elbowed him in the stomach with a laugh. "I'm pretty sure I've seen all of those already."

The wood floors creaked under foot as we walked down the hall. Tyler tapped on one door, opening it to a bathroom that had clearly been remodeled with black and white floor tile and a walk-in shower backed with pretty green tile. "This is the bathroom. You can imagine it was fun to share before school with four kids."

"Just about as fun as ours was to share," I said. I loved that we both had big families, so we understood each other in that way.

He stopped at the bedroom at the end of the hall and pushed the door open. "Home sweet home." I stepped through the doorway, taking it all in, from the full-size bed on a wooden frame to the west-facing windows that gave him a stunning view of the barn and everything that lay beyond it. You could see forever here, and something about that set my heart at peace.

Tearing my gaze away from the view, I saw mostly bare walls. "Where are all the posters of naked ladies?" I teased.

Tyler leaned against his wooden dresser and said, "I told you it's not much."

He must not be a decorator. In fact, I only saw a calendar from nearly ten years ago hanging by his dresser. It was open to a page of a boy standing with a calf on a leash.

"Oh my gosh, is that you?" I walked closer, grinning giddily at the little Tyler. "Oh my gosh, you were so cute! That plaid shirt was way too big on you, but you rocked those Wranglers!"

"I was fifteen and wore Gage's hand-me-downs half the time," he protested. "But I got on the calendar for winning grand champion with my bucket calf."

"I only understood about half of that," I admitted.

He folded his arms across his muscular chest. "It means I was the best."

"Looking to replace Rhett with the cocky-brother title?" I teased.

"No way," Rhett said, pushing in the door with two rolling suitcases and both of our duffel bags. "Plus, you're losing at the strongest title."

Tyler rolled his eyes. "You're a child."

Rhett stuck out his tongue. "A strong one."

I laughed at the two of them. "Is it always like this?"

"Most of the time," Tyler answered at the same time Rhett said, "When he's home."

While Rhett helped Tyler get our bags unpacked and they teased each other mercilessly, I excused myself to the bathroom. I took my time, looking in the mirror and making sure my hair was okay and none of my makeup had gotten messed up on the plane.

When I came out of the bathroom, I walked down the hall, hearing voices in the bedroom. Rhett said, "Did you see the way Mom looked at her? I think she's already in love."

"It's impossible not to love Hen," Tyler said.

"I get where you're coming from," Rhett replied. "Not in a 'steal yo' girl' way, but a 'man, my brother is lucky way.'"

I smiled at their conversation and made sure the floorboards creaked on my next step.

They went silent, and I reached the doorway. "Ready when you are."

55

TYLER

The second we got outside, Liv ran to the pickup and reached the front door. "I'm driving!"

"Shotgun!" Hen called.

Rhett and I stared at each other, stunned, as our sister and my girlfriend got in the front of the ranch truck.

Liv fired up the truck and craned her head out the open driver's side window. "You snooze, you lose!"

"I feel like I'm five again," I muttered.

Rhett patted my shoulder. "Can't win 'em all."

We walked to the truck, and I got in the seat catty-cornered to Hen, wanting to see all her reactions to the ranch as we drove along. After Rhett climbed in, Liv put the truck in drive and started down the rutted trail toward the barn.

Liv pointed out Hen's window. "This is the barn up here, and we keep the horses in the pen right next to it, especially this time of year, so we can supplement their feed. That black and white horse is Rhett's. The reddish-brown one is Dad's. And then that darker brown one is kind of like the family horse. Whoever's helping out gets to ride it because it's the oldest and the easiest."

"I call that one," Hen said with a smile.

"We'll take you out on a ride to the creek tomorrow," I said, excited to show her one of my favorite spots.

Liv stopped in front of the gate to the main pasture and said, "Rhett, you grab the gate."

"No way," he said. "Hen's shotgun; she gets it."

"She's our guest," Liv said.

Rhett shrugged, a smirk on his lips. "Rules are rules."

"Come on, Hen," I got out of the truck, and she climbed down too.

"What's this shotgun rule?" she asked, walking to the gate with me.

"When we were younger, we always argued about who got to ride up front, so Dad's rule was whoever sat shotgun had to open the gates. Made it a little less appealing. Especially because some of these are hard to open."

"How do you do it?" she asked, a look of determination on her face.

That's my girl.

I walked up to the barbed-wire fence and pointed at the pole looped through with wire to hold the fence up. "You push your shoulder against that, then move the wire up over the post. After that, you should be able to slip it out and move it to the side. But you're in that dress. I can do it."

"No way will I give Rhett more ammo to tease me with," she said.

I laughed, hands up. "I knew you would fit right in."

She grit her teeth and carefully lifted her arm over the barbed wire, pushing the gate post, and then lifted the wire over the top. "Easy peasy," she said, pulling the gate to the side so Liv could drive the truck through.

"Hen's a baddie!" Liv called on her ride past us.

Hen grinned, and damn, I was grinning too.

We slid back into our seats, and Rhett said, "Hen, if this dumbass doesn't marry you, I will."

He might have been joking, but I punched him in the shoulder just in case. No way was he coming anywhere near my girl.

She tossed her head back and laughed, and with the wind fluttering through her hair, she looked like she'd descended straight from heaven's gates.

Hen held on to the oh-shit handle as we bumped over the pasture, and Liv pointed out everything around us. She told Hen about our neighbors who had been renting their grass to us for the last fifty years so our cattle would have plenty to graze. Then she showed Hen the copse of trees in the corner by the creek that ran in the summer or after heavy rains in other times of year.

As we crested another hill, the feedlot came to view. "This is where we feed cattle in the winter and after weaning," Liv explained. "Since the grass has been eaten down, it gives us a chance to make sure they're getting good nutrition and are well taken care of."

Hen nodded, taking it all in. "It sounds like a lot of work."

Rhett said, "Twenty-four-seven, three-sixty-five."

Liv nodded. "It's like having three hundred thousand-pound kids."

Laughing, Hen said, "I imagine finding a sitter is difficult."

"We trade off on the weekends," Rhett said. "That way Dad can get a break from time to time."

I tried not to feel guilty for not being around—being a part of this family had always meant helping out—but I reminded myself that it was Dad's choice to keep the ranch small. One call to Gage and he'd have an investor to help expand the operation. They were both just too damn proud.

I must have been deep in my thoughts, because I jerked back when Hen said, "Windmill!"

I looked where she was pointing and saw our windmill in the corner of the far pasture. Its dark iron silhouette stood out against the background of the pasture, its spokes spinning quickly in the breeze.

Liv drove us up to it, parking on the worn-down dirt several feet away from the tank. She stopped the engine and got out. The country played its own kind of music. The drop of water into the tank. The clod of cows' hooves on the dirt. The rustle of wind against the grass. It was my favorite song.

As we got closer to the cows, they backed away. Hen watched them with wonder. "I don't think I've ever seen a cow this close up."

"That's crazy," Liv said. "They should put them in zoos or something so people can see them."

"Yeah," Hen agreed. "I've only ever seen goats, chickens, and rabbits in a petting zoo. Never a cow."

She looked away from the cows to the tank, tipping her head back to take in the windmill. "How tall is it?"

"About twenty feet," I said.

Hen approached the tank and trailed her fingers through the water.

Liv did the same and said, "In the summers when the creek was dry, we'd come over here to cool off."

Hen laughed. "I bet the cows love Griffen-flavored water."

Rhett nudged my arm, whispering loudly, "Funny too? Get a move on, man."

I shook my head at him. For someone who was so... free with his relationships, he certainly was pressuring me to settle down. But I couldn't blame him. I'd been having the same thoughts myself, in between the fears of what would happen when my time was up in Emerson.

"Come on," Liv said. "We should show her the hay loft."

56

HENRIETTA

Confession: If I'm being honest, I have no idea how we'll figure this out.

"NO." I stared at the wooden boards nailed to the wall of the barn, then stared at Tyler. "No way are those holding me up."

While I hesitated, Rhett easily took the ladder up and disappeared through the hole in the ceiling of the dusty barn. It was dim in here, just a few plexiglass windows offering light filled with dust motes. The whole place smelled like dust and composting earth and something else I couldn't quite place.

Liv winked at me. "They're stronger than they look. See?" She reached for them and started climbing up. The wood bowed a little under her weight, but it held steady.

In my ear, Tyler teased, "I'm here to catch you."

"More like break my fall," I retorted, reaching for a rung at shoulder height. Very aware that a dress was not the best idea for this, I put my foot up on a rung and hoisted myself up, not breathing for fear of falling.

Tyler whistled below me and said, "Beautiful view down here."

I sent him a glare over my shoulder but couldn't help my smile. I faced the ladder again, climbing until I crested the hole in the ceiling. Or floor, depending on your perspective. I kept my eyes forward, seeing tiny cobwebs and even a couple of brown spiders hanging out on the wooden wall. Then when I was high enough, Rhett said, "Here, take my hand."

I let go of my death grip on the wooden rung and squeezed his hand. He easily pulled me closer to him so I fell against his chest. He waggled his eyebrows, and I rolled my eyes at him.

I stepped back, brushing dust off my dress, and looked around in awe just as twinkle lights came on. Liv walked away from the outlet to stand beside me. "What do you think?" she asked.

My eyes were glued to the building. There was a rough wood plank floor, light green and yellow hay bales stacked along the walls, a rope swing in the middle, and even a wooden couch and a refrigerator back against the wall.

"This is like every kid's dream," I said.

Tyler put his arm around me—he must have come up without me even noticing. "We hung out here all the time. Snuck beer out here too when we were teenagers."

"Mom and Dad totally knew," Liv said.

"Don't they always?" I cringed internally, thinking of my first encounter with alcohol when Bertrand bought a bottle of vodka off some guy in the streets of LA. We both drank so much one night when Mom and Dad were out that we puked all over the bathroom. Of course Mom and Dad knew, and our punishment was cleaning vomit hungover. Never would I ever drink that much again.

Tyler said, "I think they were just happy we were getting drunk out here and not going anywhere else and driving afterward."

Rhett tapped his nose. It was fun to see Tyler's gesture on his brother. I wondered what my brothers and I had in common—if Tyler had noticed.

"Check this out," Liv said. She walked to the front wall of the barn, unhooked the latch, and swung the door open. As I approached the opening, I first noticed how high we were—at least ten feet in the air. And then I saw the view. From here, you could see the horses in the grazing pen, cattle on the hillside, and the beautiful farmhouse they grew up in.

"Wow," I breathed. No wonder Tyler loved growing up here. It was incredible, and I couldn't believe I'd gone my whole life up until now without experiencing it.

I looked over at him and laced my fingers through his. He smiled at me, happier than I'd ever seen him. "I'm so glad you came," he said.

"Me too."

Liv glanced at the smart watch on her wrist and said, "We should probably get back and wash up for dinner."

We all made our way to the ladder. Liv went down first, and I gave the loft one last look before following her down to the floor of the barn. While she and Rhett took the truck back to the house, Tyler and I walked the few hundred-yards distance, with our arms around each other.

With the sun sinking down, it was getting cooler, but I felt so warm with the excitement of the day. And as we got closer, I could smell the most heavenly scents coming from the house. "It smells amazing," I said.

"Dad's the best on the grill," Tyler said. "Mom told me they're setting up the heaters outside and we'll eat on the porch."

I smiled. "That sounds so fun. And I love your siblings. Liv is so beautiful and nice, and Rhett, well, he's a handful."

Tyler laughed. "That's one way to put it."

"At least I know he likes me," I teased. Rhett's comments about putting a ring on my finger had been all in good fun. But despite the fact that Tyler and I had been together just a short while, I hoped that's where this was heading. It was like Grandma said with Grandpa— she just knew he was the one.

There was a knowing in my heart that this man beside me was meant to be in my life. Not just for a little while, but forever.

Tyler opened the door to the house for me, and we went upstairs to wash up for supper. Since we were eating outside, I changed into a pair of leggings and a sweater so I'd be nice and warm. When I came out of the bathroom, Tyler was still in his jeans and T-shirt, and damn, did he look good.

"Have I ever mentioned how sexy you are with that tattoo peeking out from under your sleeve?" I asked.

He came to me, putting his arms around my waist. "If tattoos turn you on, I'll get more."

I laughed, running my arm over the swirling pattern. "I like these just fine."

"Come on," he said. "Let's get downstairs."

As we reached the kitchen, I saw Deidre balancing a big dish of mashed potatoes in her arms. Tyler hurried to get the back door for her, and seeing a few dishes still on the island, I grabbed them to walk them outside.

Deidre smiled at me. "You are so sweet, Hen. You didn't have to do that."

"No worries," I said, setting the gravy and corn on the table. "It all looks so good."

Jack lowered a platter full of charred steaks to the table. "Wait until you cut into these. Best steak of your life, I promise."

Tyler chuckled. "One thing I love about my dad is his modesty."

Jack held up his hand, flashing a greasy spatula. "No harm in confidence—where its due." He stared at Rhett as he said that last part.

Rhett said, "I don't know why you're looking at me." And everyone laughed.

"So, Hen, tell us about yourself," Deidre said. "Tyler says you work in property management?"

I nodded. "I've been managing an apartment complex in my hometown for about eight years now. I love it."

"She's being humble." Tyler said, "All the renters there love her, and she won over the guys on my crew faster than I've ever seen."

My cheeks warmed at the compliment. "I think coffee and donuts have more to do with that than anything else."

Deidre smiled between the two of us. "What's the

plan when Tyler moves to his next job? Will you do long distance, or—"

Liv gave Diedre a look. "*Mom.*"

She lifted her hands. "Sorry, was that off limits? I was just asking."

Despite the heaters around us, it felt like all the warmth had been sucked out of my bones. The one thing Tyler and I had both been avoiding was staring us in the face. But Tyler squeezed my hand under the table and said, "We'll figure it out. Right, babe?"

I nodded, giving him a grateful smile. "Right."

But for the rest of dinner, there was a sinking feeling in my gut. Some things were easier said than done.

57

TYLER

Hen and I didn't talk much after dinner. Instead, she said she was tired and excused herself up to her room, but she encouraged me to spend time with my family. I stayed up with my siblings for a little while, talking and catching up, but soon I went to join her.

Mom's question had dampened the whole evening, not that I was mad at her. It was a fair question—one I didn't have an answer to. I hoped Hen would be up to talk a little bit, but the bedroom lights were off, and her breathing was slow and steady.

So I slipped out of my clothes, down to my underwear, and slid into bed with her, pressing my front to her back and loving the way her curves felt against me. She was so solid, steady, and I couldn't imagine ever living without her again.

I slept through the night with her at my side and woke with sunlight shining through the sheer curtains. She stirred against me and then rolled over in my arms to face me, her face only inches away.

I dropped a kiss on her nose. "Happy Thanksgiving, beautiful."

She smiled. "Happy Thanksgiving."

"How'd you sleep?"

"Much better after you got in here," she said.

"I hope you didn't mind me staying up."

"Not at all. Family time is important. Especially when you've been away from them for so long." She blinked sleepily and yawned. "Your mom missed you like crazy. I can tell."

I nodded. "What do you want to do today?"

"Eat and watch football? Isn't that what everyone does?"

I chuckled at her response. "We usually do that after chores. I thought we could ride the horses around the pasture this morning. Check in on the cattle that aren't in the feedlot."

Her expression fell. "I know I said I was interested in horseback riding, but isn't there a weight limit? I was too big to go on a trail ride with Kenner last year."

An ache grew in my chest. I hated that she had to worry about these kinds of things. "Our horses are really strong—made for hard work. You'll be fine."

"Are you sure?"

I nodded. "Of course. Plus, I want to see that ass in some jeans." I reached around and grabbed a handful, already turned on.

She shook her head at me. "You're such a horndog."

"Maybe. But I have a gift for you. Go use the bathroom, and I'll leave it for you on the bed."

While she used the bathroom, I set the gift I'd special ordered for her, with some help from her mom, and then got dressed and went downstairs. Mom was in the kitchen, cooking breakfast, coffee gurgling in the pot.

"Morning," I said.

"Morning." She reached for a mug and poured me some coffee. "Still take it black?"

I nodded, reaching for the cup. That first sip tasted amazing. No matter where I went or where I ordered it, coffee never tasted like it did brewed from the well water at home.

"What are your plans for the day?"

"After the game, we're going to the city to see Gage," I said.

A dark look crossed Mom's face. "Can you bring him a loaf of the lemon zucchini bread for me? I have some in the freezer."

"Sure thing." My heart ached for her, caught up in a war between her husband and her son. Mom's rule was always to put her marriage first, but I could tell it was hurting her.

Footfalls sounded on the stairs, and we both looked to see Hen coming in jeans, a flannel shirt, and her brand-new cowboy boots. I'd gone with square toes and tan coloring with intricate leather work up the wide calves. With her jeans tucked into the boots and her buffalo plaid shirt, she looked absolutely adorable.

I whistled loudly, and Mom clapped her hands together.

"You fit right in on the farm," Mom said.

Hen smiled, doing a spin in her boots. "I can't believe you got these for me, Tyler. How did you know my size?"

"Had a little insider help," I answered with a grin. "Do you like them?"

She nodded, coming to sit beside me. She placed a kiss on my cheek and said, "Thank you so much. That was so thoughtful of you."

"We couldn't have you riding horses in tennis shoes," I said.

Mom offered Hen coffee, and soon we were both done with breakfast and walking to the barn. Liv was already there, riding Fred, the paint horse, around the pen. She trotted easily, perfectly at home in the saddle.

We Griffen kids had to be, growing up with our parents. Dad expected nothing less than our best, and if we ever got thrown off the saddle, we had to get right back on.

When Liv spotted us, she waved and easily slid out of the saddle. As she got closer, Hen said, "You look like a natural up there, Liv! Such a baddie."

"Thanks, girl," Liv said. "We'll have you doing the same in no time."

"I'm willing to try it," Hen said with a hint of doubt in her voice as she nervously rubbed her hands together.

We walked her to the horses lined up in front of the barn and introduced her to Star. She was a pretty chestnut mare, eleven years old with a white blaze running from her nose to her forehead, covered with her shiny mane.

Hen gently patted Star's neck. "That's the smell from the barn. Horses." She breathed in deeply. "I love that smell."

I grinned. Seeing Hen take so easily to my life... it was just that much more proof that we belonged together.

We told Hen about the parts of the saddle, how to use the reins to lead the horse, and then it was time for her to get on. She looked nervous at the size of the horse, so Liv brought out a five-gallon bucket for Hen to stand on to give her some more height.

With the extra lift, we had Hen on Star's back in no time. She gripped tightly to the saddle horn as she slipped the toes of her boots into the stirrups.

I held on to the reins, leading her around the pounded-down dirt of the pen. She rocked atop the horse, slowly getting used to the movements. Liv held up her phone, pointing it at Hen. "Smile big!"

Hen gave her a cheesy grin that made my heart soar.

"How are you feeling about it?" I asked. "Ready to take the reins?"

With a determined look, Hen nodded, and I handed her the leather straps. I went to go stand by Liv, and we both gave her directions from time to time until she was walking in steady circles around the pen.

"Time to speed it up!" Liv challenged. At the nervous look Hen gave her, Liv said, "You're ready, girl! Go for it!"

Hen carefully tapped her heels to Star's sides, and Star walked a little faster.

"Bit harder," Liv called.

With the extra nudge, Star took off at a trot, Hen's legs clinging to the horse's sides.

"I'm doing it!" she cried.

"That's right, baby!" I yelled, pumping my fist in the air. "You're fuckin' doing it!"

58

HENRIETTA

Confession: I like my men sweet, and their talk dirty.

MY LEGS FELT like rubber as I stepped on land for the first time. "Okay, now I know why all those cowboys walk funny in the movies."

Liv laughed. "It's a bit awkward at first, but you get used to it with some practice."

Frowning, I said, "No way to practice where I'm from. I don't think I could convince Mom to let a horse have part of her garden."

Smiling, Liv said, "You're welcome back for a practice run any time. I'm sure Ty's already told you about Gage's frequent flyer miles."

"Your whole family is so generous."

Liv smiled. "When you grow up out here, you learn that everyone needs a leg up from time to time, including us."

Tyler was busy unsaddling the horses, but when he

was done putting the saddles away and brushing them down, the three of us walked back to the house. Even though the sun was right overhead, the clouds were thick enough to keep the sky a pale gray. The air prickled like there might be rain later.

In a similar way to the ocean, the entire country landscape changed with the weather—it was a sight to behold. The golden grass had a deeper hue, the dirt trails took on a somber feel, and even the wind was subdued.

When we walked inside the house, my senses were completely overwhelmed. Jack was carving the turkey, and Deidre's face was red with heat from baking. Sports commentary played from a radio with an antenna sitting on the buffet table.

"It smells wonderful," I said. "I wish I had enough room in my suitcase to bring this all back with me."

Deidre chuckled, and Jack asked, "How were the horses?"

"Star was a great horse to learn on," I answered. "It was so much fun."

Liv said, "We'll have her running barrels in the rodeo in no time."

I laughed at the thought. "Not a chance."

Deidre said, "Why don't y'all go wash up, and we'll sit down to eat."

We went up the stairs, the insides of my legs already burning. Riding horses was a heck of a workout (and probably the only one I didn't mind). In the bedroom, Tyler sent me a sexy stare.

"Did I mention how hot it was to see you on that horse? I wish I was the one you were riding." He trailed his hands along the waist of my jeans, then linked his fingers through the belt loops, pulling me closer.

A swoop of desire went through my stomach, sending heat between my legs. His mouth was already on my neck, working his way down the slit of my shirt, unbuttoning the top button.

"Tyler," I gasped. "Your family is downstairs."

He ground his hips into me, and I felt his erection, turning me on that much more.

I was beginning to forget the four very specific reasons why I should say no. "What if they hear us?" I breathed, already lifting the hem of his dark gray Henley shirt.

He took his shirt the rest of the way off and spun me, pushing my face into the pillows of his bed. Excitement rippled across my skin as he yanked my jeans down. I loved it when he got rough with me, and mix that with my kink of risking being caught?

There was no turning him down.

I arched my back, wishing he wasn't still out of me. "Hurry," I whispered.

"I'm getting a condom."

"Don't worry about it," I said, my chest tight with the knowledge of what I was saying. What I was offering. "I'm on the pill." But nothing was a hundred percent effective.

He was quiet for a moment. "Are you sure?"

"I am."

Then I heard the teeth of his zipper come apart before he pressed inside me all the way. I bit back a cry from my body adjusting to him, to the delicious pain of his girth, and tried not to moan as he slowly backed out.

He pressed one hand on the back of my head,

shoving me deeper into the pillows as he pounded into me again, and my eyes rolled back in pleasure. I could still hear the hum of voices downstairs, oblivious to all the ways Tyler was claiming me above their heads.

He picked up the pace, and when the headboard rattled, he shifted—I assumed to still it with his other hand—and continued his relentless drive into my body.

I reached down, rubbing my sensitive spot as his thrusts continued, and between the force of his hand on me, the pace of his thrusts, and the pressure on my clit, I was close. So fucking close.

"Fuck," Tyler hissed. "I'm coming."

And that was all I needed to push me over the edge. My orgasm racked my body, and I tightened around his cock, raking my hands across the comforter for anything that would keep me from crying out.

As the waves slowed, Tyler bent over me, his torso pressing into my back, and he whispered in my ear. "My cum's going to be dripping out of you in front of my whole family. Because you're *my* good girl."

My sensitive vagina clenched again around his softening cock. Fuck, he was hot, and he knew exactly what to say to me to drive me wild.

He pulled out of me, handing me a tissue to help me clean up, and then we both got dressed, sending each other heated smiles as we did.

Before we went downstairs, I relieved myself in the bathroom and did the best I could to make sure my hair wasn't wild. There wasn't much I could do about the added brightness in my eyes or extra color in my cheeks.

When I reached the main floor, Tyler was already

tucked into the table, an empty seat across from him. I slid into the chair, and he winked at me. Reminding me.

My cum's dripping out of you in front of my whole family.

I shuddered, already looking forward to round two.

But I did the best I could to act like I wasn't constantly turned on by their son and brother. Instead, we talked about football, something my brothers had prepared me for with endless hours of conversation.

My phone buzzed in my hip pocket. (Side note: leggings with pockets are the absolute best.) I drew it out below the table and saw my mom was calling me. Probably just to wish me a happy Thanksgiving. I pushed the button to send the call to voicemail.

My phone vibrated again, I assumed with the voicemail notification. But then there was another buzzing. A call from my dad. Were they really that worried about me being away from home?

I pressed the end button again, but then there was a fresh call. From my mom again.

I looked up at Tyler across the table, and he had a worried look on me. "Sorry," I said. "I need to take this."

His family was really sweet about it, and I stepped out on the back porch to answer the call. "Mom, what's going on? Is everything okay?"

Mom's voice shook as she said, "Your grandma fell again. She's back in the hospital, but this time the break was bad. They think they'll need to do a full hip replacement."

My chest froze. I couldn't breathe. Could hardly speak. "A hip replacement? At her age?"

"They think it will help with her pain and maybe her

mobility, but the odds of her coming home this time aren't looking great."

I dropped into a chair at the patio table, shivering from the cold, from the news. This couldn't be true. Grandma had been doing great on her walker. "What happened?"

"It was an accident. She tripped over one of Kenner's toys."

Anger made me grit my teeth together. Had no one been paying attention to Grandma? She'd barely gotten out of the hospital, and the second I left, she was back in. I knew what hip surgery meant, especially for someone her age. It meant more health risks, including pneumonia, which could be deadly.

My voice was raw. "I'll find a flight and have Tyler—"

"No, you absolutely will not," Mom said. "You are there with his family, and we have more than enough people here to help if needed. You can come back on Sunday like you had planned."

"Mom, I—"

"Honey, you can't fix this," she said softly.

And that was the thing that broke me the most. My grandma probably wouldn't be coming home. I'd missed her last Thanksgiving.

I glanced through the windows, seeing Tyler laughing with his family. I should have been home, but I wasn't.

I was here.

"Tell Grandma I'll see her as soon as we get back."

"I will, honey," Mom said.

And then she hung up, and I was alone on the porch, filled with worry and fear and something even worse...

Regret.

59

TYLER

"Hey, is Hen okay?" Liv asked.

I turned in my seat to see Hen on the patio, her elbows resting on the table, her head in her hands. My heart dropped to my stomach, and the smile lingering on my lips quickly fell. "Excuse me," I said, pushing back from the table in complete silence and walking to the sliding door that led to the porch. As soon as I got outside, Hen turned to face me, the porch light catching the tears streaking down her cheeks.

I hurried to her, dropping to my knees beside the table. "What's going on? What happened?"

"Grandma—" Her voice broke and she sniffed, looking down at the table at her phone. "Grandma fell again. They think she has to have a hip replacement and she—and she—" Hen began sobbing, and through each cry, she sputtered, "She won't be able to come home."

"Oh my god," I whispered, pulling her into my arms as she continued shaking. I wanted to fix all the pain I could feel rolling off of her. "Hen, I'm so sorry. Do we need to find a way to fly back? I'm sure I could book us something tonight if we need to go."

She shook her head, pulling back to wipe her eyes. "My mom told me I should stay here, that Grandma has plenty of people around, but I feel so guilty. Like I should have been there for her, like I could have prevented it somehow."

"What-if is a dangerous game," I said, accentuating each word so she understood how much I meant what I was saying. "Even if you could have prevented this fall, there's no guaranteeing it wouldn't have happened another time when you were at work or busy with friends. We can only focus on *now*. So tell me, what feels right in this moment? I'll do whatever *you* need. Not what your mom wants you to do."

She bit her lip, her eyes still full of tears. "I don't want to ruin your family's dinner."

"It's just food. It'll keep."

"I don't want to miss out on meeting Gage. I know how much he means to you."

"A million points, remember? He could fly us back tomorrow if we wanted to."

She shook her head at me. "Sitting here and pretending to be happy when my grandma's lying in a hospital bed feels wrong."

I nodded, already knowing the answer. "Let's go."

We went back inside, and I explained what was going on to my family. Hen apologized a million times, but my mom hugged her and said, "Honey, you don't need to apologize to us. Family is everything."

I could have sworn my dad's eyes misted over when she said that.

Hen hugged my mom back, uttering a quiet, "Thank you."

Liv came upstairs with us, helping pack our bags back up, and then Hen and I were in the truck, rushing to Dallas. After five minutes on a call with Gage, we had seats on the evening's last direct flight to LA.

It was the waiting that was the hardest. Watching Hen lean her head back on the truck seat and close her eyes, picturing god knows what.

I reached across the console to hold her hand, but it felt limp in mine, like she was somewhere else entirely. Selfishly, I ached to be closer to her, to be needed and leaned on, but I was doing the best I could, and that had to be okay.

The three-hour flight to LA was almost as torturous as the hour drive to RWE Memorial Hospital in Emerson. We parked in the parking garage, and I had to lengthen my strides to keep up with Hen's quick pace. We had to go through the emergency entrance since it was nearly midnight, and Hen quickly said to security, "I'm here to see Cordelia Jones."

The guard looked from Hen to me. "Are you family?" he asked.

Hen nodded.

"Trauma unit, room 1431. Follow the red lines."

Trauma. The word sounded harsh on my ears. Cordelia was in a trauma unit from her fall? She was tough, but this... it was a lot.

The side door automatically opened with the sound of metal sliding against metal.

Hen took the visitor sticker from the security guard and said, "Let's go."

I followed her, the halls mostly empty around us save for the sounds of the night shift. But the smell was there —chemical and sweet at the same time. It made my stomach turn. The fluorescent lights were even harsher at night, slightly orange, and eerie against the painted cinderblock walls.

The sound of talking grew louder as we turned the corner and came to the trauma unit's waiting area. Almost all of Hen's family was there. Imani and Raven were there, but I assumed Laila had taken Kenner and A'yisha home for bedtime.

When they saw us, Johmarcus looked up and said, "What are you two doing back here?"

Hen was looking straight at her mom as she choked out, "I'm sorry, Mom. I had to be here."

Tam got up, taking Hen in her arms and patting her back. "I know, baby. I know."

Her dad got up, standing with us, and Hen pulled back from her mom's embrace. "Is there any news?"

Murphy repeated what Hen already knew—that it was a bad break and that there would be an emergency hip replacement the next day. Other than that, it would be a waiting game to see how well she recovered from surgery and which "skilled nursing" facility would take Cordelia.

Hen and I exchanged a look. We both knew that last part wasn't going to be an option.

"I need to see her," Hen said.

Tam replied, "It's just Bertrand in there now. She's allowed two visitors at a time."

I reached for Hen's hand. "Do you want me to come with you and see if he'll trade?"

Hen shook her head, patting my hand with hers. "I'll be okay. You can go home if you want."

My eyebrows drew together. That wasn't even something I'd considered, leaving her when she was going through this. Why would she have thought that's what I would want? "I'll be right out here," I replied.

She nodded and slipped her hand from mine, the absence of her touch making me feel cold all over. Then she left the room and was gone.

I felt a hand on my mid back and looked to see Tam standing next to me. "Don't take it personal, honey. She's always been close with her grandma. I tried to get her to stay there in Texas, but you know how she is."

A faint smile touched my lips. "She loves her family more than anything."

And for a guy who claimed to love her, I was being unforgivably selfish for hoping to take her away.

60

HENRIETTA

Confession: I can't do this anymore.

THIS WING of the hospital set me on edge. I could hear moaning down the hall, beeping from various monitors within the rooms. The nurses I walked past didn't say anything, barely met my eyes.

I counted down the numbers until I reached Grandma's room, then slowly pushed the door open. Bertrand sat at the chair next to our sleeping grandma's bed, holding her hand that wasn't hooked up to an IV.

There were two bags there, dripping fluid into her veins. And she looked so frail, her brown skin and silver hair a deep contrast to the stark white blankets and pillow behind her head.

At the sound of my footsteps, Bertrand turned to look at me, surprise clear in his face. "I thought you were in Texas."

"I was," I whispered, folding my arms around my

middle to hold myself together. My legs felt weak, seeing Grandma like this again when I thought we were in the clear. It was so much like Grandpa lying in that hospice bed, fighting for each breath.

"Here," Bertrand said, reaching for the wheelchair behind him and wheeling it next to the bed.

I sat in the chair, locking the wheels for stability.

"It was crazy, Hen," he said, his voice low. "All of a sudden we heard this crash and then a scream. I can't get that scream out of my head."

I leaned my head against his shoulder. It must have been awful to witness. "I should have been there to make sure the walkways were clear." Bitterness leached into my voice. We shouldn't have been here on Thanksgiving night.

"It was a freak thing, truly. Kenner was trying to get a toy to come apart, and it slipped from his hands and flung back toward Grandma just as she was getting up to use the bathroom. Johmarcus and Laila feel awful, and Kenner was crying so bad to see his great-grandma hurt."

My anger didn't dissolve at the knowledge that it was a true accident and not just carelessness. It changed. I was mad at myself for not being there to support my family when shit hit the fan. I'd been off galivanting in Texas, riding horses, having sex, being *selfish*. What other moments, tragedies, would I miss if I moved away to be with Tyler?

Bertrand slowly removed his hand from Grandma's. "I'll give you two some time."

"Thank you," I said.

"Of course." He patted my back one more time before leaving the room.

With his footsteps growing quieter, I turned my attention on Grandma. I sat in Bertrand's seat and reached gently for her hand, her palm soft against mine. The skin on the back of her hand looked papery, slightly glossy and cracked with age. When I was little, she'd hold my hand, and I'd press into her fingertips, watching the indentations formed there slowly bounce back in place.

These hands had loved us so well, from cooking treats to serving her husband on his deathbed to holding us when we were down. Grandma had always been there for us. Every football game, every scholar's bowl competition, every graduation and dance recital, she had been there.

And I'd abandoned her.

A tear slipped down my cheek at the pull I felt between my new love and my family who had always been there for me. I'd only known Tyler for months, and I loved him with all my heart. But my family had been there for *life*.

What future could there be with Tyler when he had a job that required such extensive travel? When he wanted to settle in a state over a thousand miles from California? I couldn't ask him to give that up to move here, even if I had a house for us to share. Just like he couldn't ask me the same question.

It was reckless to let my heart become so invested in him when this was the inevitable answer.

So I cried.

I cried for my grandma lying in this hospital bed, her life forever changed.

I cried for my first real love, the man of my dreams.

And I cried for the future we could never have together.

61

TYLER

My phone vibrated in my pocket, waking me up from where I'd slept in a waiting room chair the whole night. All of Hen's brothers had gone home, but her mom and dad were here too, leaning against each other as they slept. My neck protested as I slowly stood, reaching into my pocket to see who was calling.

Jim Crenshaw's name filled the screen, and my eyebrows drew together. He knew I was off work, and we didn't have a meeting scheduled until the following Tuesday. And it was only nine in the morning. I swiped to answer, wondering what he could possibly want.

"Hello?" I asked, my voice rough from a poor night's sleep. Hen hadn't come out all night, and I wanted to know if she was okay.

"You really shit the bed on this one," Jim growled.

My chest instantly tightened. In my ten years of working with him, Jim *never* talked to me like that. "What's going on?"

"Don't play dumb with me, Tyler. I understand

needing to get your dick wet, but I never would have thought—"

"Whoa, whoa, whoa," I said, walking away from the waiting room and into the hallway so Hen's parents wouldn't overhear this conversation that had already turned into an explicit yelling match on Jim's end. "Jim, I don't know what you're talking about."

He cleared his throat, and it sounded more like a growl. "I get a call this morning from a suit at Blue Bird, and you know what she tells me? She thinks that you have been acting inappropriately on the job site."

Ice filled my veins. My knees buckled, and I leaned against the cinderblock wall for support.

"But I tell her that's impossible," Jim railed on. "I've been working with Tyler for ten years, and he's the best damn employee I have. So good, in fact, that I'm considering training him up to run the damn company once this project's done. But she demanded a review of the security footage anyway."

I raked my hands through my hair. The fucking cameras. I never thought much about them because we never reviewed footage unless there was vandalism. But Janessa had given him all the cause he needed. *Clients first* was Crenshaw Construction's motto. The first line of our company mission statement. If a client wanted a video review, they got one.

"Imagine my surprise when our security guy sends me a clip of you getting *fucking blown on the job site* BY THE WOMAN WHO'S SUPPOSED TO BE HELPING THE CONSTRUCTION PROCESS RUN SMOOTHLY."

I held the phone away from my ear, easily hearing him shouting even from a distance.

"Now what you do in your free time is your damn business. You can fuck whoever you want. Man. Woman. I don't give a shit. But the second you step on the job site, it's about the project. I can't believe you would jeopardize our reputation like this and risk a *multi-million-dollar project!*"

Fuck, fuck, fuck. "Did they let us go?"

"I saved the deal on one condition. You're off the job, Tyler. You need to pack your shit and go home by Sunday. They're done with you, and so am I."

"Jim, I—" I began, but the call ended.

I stared at the lock screen on my phone, the picture of Henrietta on the horse. I'd had Liv send it to me, and it made me smile so much, I'd put it there. But now I didn't feel like smiling. I felt like an asshole.

I'd never been fired before in my life. Not when I was a teenager baling hay. Not when I was working at a sandwich shop while in carpentry school. And not in the ten years of my professional career. Ten years of hard work, moving around the country, giving all I had to this business.

What was I supposed to do now? Pack up my bags and share Hen's bedroom? Take over a guest bedroom in her family's home while they dealt with the very real changes coming in their beloved grandma's life?

I had savings, but that would get eaten up quickly with rent going the way it was in this town. But I'd do it. I'd spend every last dime and work any grunt job I could find—if Hen would be my last just like I'd been her first. But that was a lot of pressure to put on a new relationship, on someone whose worst fear had just been confirmed.

But I had to ask.

Love isn't convenient. I just hoped she'd think it was worth it.

62

HENRIETTA

Confession: I wish I could go back to being the funny fat friend.

I'D BEEN in and out of sleep throughout the night, and when I was awake, I watched the rise and fall of Grandma's chest. The part in her lips as she breathed. The drip of liquid through her IV. All signs of life to be lived.

Grandma blinked her eyes open around nine in the morning. She looked at our linked hands, then at me. Her voice was raspy as she said, "Baby girl, shouldn't you be in Texas?"

Fresh tears slid down my cheeks as I shook my head. "I'm right where I need to be." I opened my mouth to say more, but a nurse walked in saying, "Great, you're awake! I have orders to take you back to pre-op so we can get started on your hip replacement." Another nurse followed behind her, giving me a smile.

Grandma nodded. "Have you reviewed my advanced directives? I have a DNR in place."

"DNR?" I asked.

The nurse answered, "It means do not resuscitate. It's a common request from older patients."

I stared at my grandma, saying these words so casually to a nurse before a major surgery.

"And, yes, we have all of those orders in place," the nurse said. Then she looked at me. "You're free to wait in here or in the waiting area, but it will be several hours before she's back."

I nodded and squeezed Grandma's hand. "We'll be praying for you, Grandma. See you soon."

She patted my hand and nodded to the nurse who began the process of wheeling her away.

Moments after she left, I realized I'd never said I love you.

I fought tears, hoping she'd come back so I could say it out loud.

I sat in her empty room for a moment, looking out the window that only faced a brick building. Part of me wanted to sit here forever, never face the conversation that I knew was coming. I didn't want to have it. Didn't want to face it.

But if Grandma could suffer a broken hip, go under the knife knowing they wouldn't resuscitate her if something happened, I could survive a heartbreak. Especially if it meant Tyler could have the kind of life he wanted without my selfish needs getting in the way.

I stood on shaky legs and left the room, walking down the long hallway to the waiting area. As I walked in, I noticed my parents sipping coffee, eating takeout. Where was Tyler?

My mom said, "Hen! How was she? Did you get to talk to her?"

I nodded, redirecting my attention to my parents. "I can tell she's in pain, but she woke up right before they came to take her for surgery. Did you know she has a DNR?" The betrayal in that statement hit me in the gut. "Why wouldn't she do everything she could to stay with us longer?"

Mom and Dad exchanged looks.

Mom tilted her head. "Watching your grandpa suffer was so painful. She doesn't want that for herself, honey."

Dad nodded. "It's difficult to understand now when you're young and in love and have your whole life ahead of you. But someday, if you're lucky, you will have a new perspective on Grandma's wishes."

It felt like a punch to the gut, that they were all okay with just letting her go. But I didn't want to fight. I didn't know what I could say that wouldn't cause irreparable harm, so I said, "Did Tyler go home?"

Mom shook her head. "He took a call in the hallway."

I left the waiting room, finding Tyler leaning against a wall. At the sound of opening doors, he glanced over and quickly straightened when he saw it was me.

"Tyler." I allowed myself a selfish moment, falling into his hug as tears fell down my cheeks. Would this really be the last time I felt his arms around me? The last time his lips feathered kisses on my forehead.

"How is she?" he asked, stepping back.

I wrapped my arms around myself, trying to stay strong. "She's going for surgery. And she has a DNR, Tyler."

He didn't seem surprised. "My grandpa has one too."

"Why would she do that?" I asked, hoping he would see my side.

Instead, he replied, "Maybe she misses her husband."

Emotion swelled within me, taking over my every thought. "How could you say that? She's better off dead with her husband than alive with us? No one even knows what happens after you die! What if you're just supporting her to go into oblivion for eternity?"

I stopped, my chest heaving as I waited for his response. The kindness in his green eyes just made me that much angrier.

"It's her decision, Hen."

"It's a bad one," I snapped.

His voice was gentle. "In your opinion."

I glared at him. "What are you doing here anyway? I said you could go home."

A crease formed between his brow, and I hated how tired he looked with circles under his eyes and scruff on his chin. "I couldn't leave you here, Hen. I wanted to be here for you."

"Why?" I demanded, my voice breaking. "Why are we doing this? Someday, your job is going to be done here, and you'll be on the road again. Were you just expecting me to follow you wherever you go? Give up on being here for my family and my career so I could be some sort of housewife? Why did you do it?" I demanded.

"I couldn't stay away from you," he yelled, his voice tortured. He put his hand on the wall by my shoulder, holding the other against his chest. "I love you, and I don't want this to end. I meant what I said when I told my mom we'd figure it out. I know it's hard to see an answer right now, but if we put our heads together, we can—"

"We can *what?*" I argued, tears streaming down my cheeks. Why was he so fucking perfect and understanding? Why couldn't he be like every other asshole who my grandma tried to set me up with? Why did he make saying goodbye so damn hard?

"We can be together!"

"Until the job is done," I bit back.

He shook his head. "Hen, I got fired this morning."

The words took the air out of my chest. "What?"

"Janessa had them look at security footage of us, and they found some incriminating video. Jim let me go to keep the contract with Blue Bird. I'm supposed to be out of the apartment by Sunday."

My mouth fell open and closed as the words hit my brain, one after another, like hail shattering on a sidewalk. He'd lost his job—and would be moving out of Emerson in two days.

He took my hands in his, my arms feeling wooden as he spoke. "I can get an apartment here, try to find a job. Or I could bring you back to Texas, we could start a life, a family. I know it's soon, but I love you, Hen. I don't want to live without you. I don't want to fuck around with long distance and video calls and seeing each other on the weekends. And I know you have a job here, but Janessa won't stop at me. Not when she has video proof. You could find a job in Cottonwood Falls. Or I could support you. I know the timing isn't great with your grandma being in the hospital, but I know Gage would help us with flights to visit her. You could come visit every weekend if you wanted to. I just want to be with you." His voice cracked at the end because he knew what he was asking. He was asking the impossible.

"We can't live with my parents," I said.

"I'll pull my investments."

"You can't do that," I said.

"Then come with me," he begged, his molten hazel eyes on mine.

"I can't do that," I cried. Our relationship was ending. Right here in the hospital hallways, with families walking by and workers in scrubs acting like my world wasn't falling apart. But it was. Piece by fucking piece. "My grandma could live for years with a broken hip, Tyler. I have savings, but I can't afford to take a gap in employment if I still have a job on Monday. My family's going to need me around to help. My parents still work. My brothers have jobs, families. They can't do it all on their own. They need me."

Tyler's gaze darted over me. "Do they really need you? Or are you looking for a reason to run?"

"You're the dream guy, Tyler, but if you move here, you'll resent me. Maybe not today, maybe not a year from now, but someday you'll look around at your city life and know there's something missing."

His voice was a whisper as he said, "Something will be missing if you're not with me."

My lips quivered. He was taking all the fight left in me. "Tyler, tell me you'd be happy here."

He hesitated. "I'd give it up, for you."

"I can't ask you to do that."

"Then what are you saying?" he asked, his eyes red.

"I'm saying you're a windmill, Tyler, and we both know you don't belong here."

His Adam's apple slid down his throat as he swallowed. "Don't do this, Hen. Please don't do this."

Tears rolled down my cheeks as I shook my head. "We both knew how it was going to end."

"I thought you loved me." His hoarse whisper broke every last unshattered part of me.

"I do," I said. "But it's not enough."

Then I turned and walked back where I belonged, with my family. Tyler was behind me, in my past. And even though I loved him with every broken piece, that's where he needed to stay. After all, if you loved something, you needed to set it free.

63

TYLER

I wasn't waiting around until Sunday. Not when everywhere I looked reminded me of her. Not when all I saw was her face telling me there was no future, nothing I could do to change her mind.

Not when I'd lost everything that mattered to me.

I packed up all my things, shoving them in the suitcases I moved here with, then I texted Gage.

Tyler: Can you get me a flight back to Dallas for tonight?
Gage: For you and Hen?
Tyler: Just me.

There was a pause before he replied.

Gage: Booked.

He sent me a screenshot of the boarding pass, and I locked my phone, holding it tightly in my hand. I was leaving Emerson. Without Henrietta by my side.

64

HENRIETTA

Confession: I've been preparing for this moment for the last eight years, and I'm still not ready.

I GAVE my parents an excuse about Tyler needing to change and shower at his apartment, and they let my red eyes and smeared makeup pass without further questioning. It had been a long night for all of us.

While my grandma was in surgery, Birdie called me. I didn't answer. But then she sent me a text.

Birdie: Just checking in to see how it's going with Tyler's family. Are they as sweet as he is?

A small huff of air came out my nose.

Henrietta: They were incredible.

His sister was warm and welcoming, Rhett was funny,

and even though I didn't get to meet Gage, I knew he'd be just as generous and gracious as Tyler was. And his parents had this quiet agreement about them, like after so many years, they naturally knew how to exist together and keep a home running. I knew they weren't perfect, but Cottonwood Falls could have been named Paradise and it still would have been accurate.

My phone pinged with another notification.

Birdie: Were? Did something happen?

I closed my eyes, not wanting to admit what I'd done. Because it was stupid; I already knew it was stupid to let Tyler go. But I had to stand true to the people who had given me everything. If that meant saying goodbye to the love of my life, I'd do it. If it meant working a job under a woman I now knew was truly evil, I'd grit my teeth and make it through.

No matter how much it hurt.

I took a breath and sent Birdie another text.

Henrietta: My grandma was admitted to the hospital last night. She's getting hip replacement surgery. And because everything has to go wrong at the same time, Tyler was fired for... indecent activity on the job site. I ruined his job for him and I feel awful, but I couldn't stay with him. He's always said he wants to settle in Texas, and I can't leave my grandma here.

My vision blurred by the end of the message, and I took a shaky breath as I blinked away the ever-present tears. Three bubbles appeared on the screen, and I watched them, waiting for Birdie to tell me how stupid I was, to chase him down and keep him. But then her message came through.

Birdie: I am so sorry, Hen. That's so much to deal with. What hospital are you at? I'll bring you all supper tonight, and I'm sure Mara will help too with anything you need. I love you.

Gratitude poured through me as I typed out my reply.

Henrietta: We're at RWE Memorial.
Henrietta: I love you too.

The door from the trauma unit opened, and a doctor came out in scrubs and a white lab coat. "Are you the family of Cordelia Jones?"

My stomach clenched with nerves as my mom said, "We are."

We circled around him, desperate to hear the news, praying that it was good.

"The surgery went well. With her age, it's hard to tell how recovery will go, but I'm hoping with good PT she can make a decent recovery and walk again with a walker when needed, but it's more than likely that she'll be in a wheelchair long term, despite our best efforts." He frowned, reaching into his pocket and retrieving several brochures. "Our team is recommending advanced nursing care. These are all state-sponsored facilities that Medicare will cover. Once you decide, they typically have someone on staff who will coordinate discharge from the hospital and get her admitted there."

Mom nodded, taking the brochures. "Thank you, doctor."

I looked up from the brochures and asked, "When can we go see her?"

"I recommend we let her rest for the next few hours as she comes off the anesthesia, but there's no reason you can't go sit with her quietly now until she wakes up."

"Thank you," I said.

He nodded, walking back through the doors. Mom, Dad, and I exchanged a glance.

Mom said, "Why don't you two go sit with her in case she wakes up? I'll call the boys and let them know she's alright."

I took a shaky breath. "I need to talk to you both about something first."

Mom and Dad exchanged a glance, then Mom said, "Here, honey, let's sit down."

I took one of the cramped hospital chairs and looked across the coffee table at them. "A while back, Dad asked me what I was doing with my money. The truth is, I've been saving for something like this so Grandma wouldn't have to go to a home."

Dad looked dumbfounded while Mom said, "That's really sweet of you, but in-home care is very expensive. Even ten thousand dollars would only get us a couple months of care, three at most."

I nodded. "I've done my research, and I've saved a hundred and eight thousand."

Now Dad's jaw was on the floor. "I knew the numbers weren't adding up, but Hen, this is crazy. You've been living at home all this time so you could save for Grandma?"

I felt embarrassed to admit it, but I nodded. "I know it was hard on you and Mom to help Johmarcus, and we didn't have the money for private care when Grandpa was so sick... I just didn't want to see Grandma's life end like Grandpa's did."

They sat in a stunned silence for a moment, and Mom said, "Honey, you're twenty-eight years old. I'm sure Grandma will understand if you put your life savings toward a home, a family, a wedding."

The realization struck me that two of those things were not in my cards anymore. But I'd decided my course of action at twenty and had been staying the course for eight years. No way would I let my grandma down now, in her moment of need.

"This is what I want to do," I said. "But I'd rather not tell Grandma that I'm the one paying for it. I don't want her to feel guilty or try and talk me out of it. We all know she's so persuasive she'd win."

Dad chuckled, but it was a sad sound. He put his arms around me and held me close. "I love your heart," he said. "Sometimes I wish you would care a little more about yourself. It's good that you have Tyler now. That boy thinks you hung the moon and all the stars."

Mom gave me a small smile. "I noticed he has a picture of you on a horse as his phone wallpaper. It's adorable."

Each word was another twist of the knife in my heart.

About to break down, I said, "I'm going to sit with Grandma."

I walked back to her room, and when I saw her in the bed, her chest rising and falling with the oxygen cannulas in her nose, I covered my mouth to hold back a sob. She'd made it through surgery. I knew this was only the beginning of her recovery, but she'd made it through the first step.

I went and sat by her bed, just thinking. Looking out the window. Wondering what was next for me. Hoping that if I kept my job, Janessa would somehow get fired or leave. And then I felt a hand on my hand.

I looked up, seeing Grandma looking back at me. "Hi, sweetheart," she rasped.

I got up and hugged her gently. "Grandma, I'm so glad you're okay."

"I am," she said tiredly, resting her head back on the pillow.

"Do you need anything?" I asked. "I can ask a nurse to bring more pain meds?"

"I'm a little hungry," she rasped out.

I pressed the call button and asked for some food and a new drink for grandma, and we sat for a couple hours, not talking much as the anesthesia wore off and she became more coherent.

Mom came in and told us she was getting supper and then left. When I glanced back at my grandma, I saw tears streaming down her cheeks.

My heart stalled. "Grandma? Are you hurting? I can ask for more medicine."

"It's not that... It's just, I've enjoyed living with your family more than you'll ever know. The idea of moving to a place I've never been and being away from you all..." She put her fist to her lips, tears sliding down her creviced cheeks.

"Grandma?"

She looked my way.

My voice was shaky as I said, "That's not going to

happen. There's a Medicare program that will pay for a home health aide. You can stay with us."

Her lips parted. "You can't be serious."

"I am," I said, crying with her. "You can come home."

Her smile was wide, and she cried happy tears. "Give me a hug, baby girl. That's the best news I've heard all day."

I hugged her tight, hanging on for dear life. "I love you, Grandma."

She smiled at me as I sat back down and said, "Me too. But I want to hear about you. How was your time in Texas?"

"It was amazing," I answered honestly. "If my whole life wasn't here, I'd move there in a second and stare at the prairie all day long."

Grandma laughed. "My little hen wants to live on a farm."

I smiled.

"Maybe you and Tyler will move to Texas together one day," she said, so much hope in her eyes.

I fought back tears and smiled. "Let's just focus on today."

65

HENRIETTA

Confession: I can do hard things... as long as there's an end in sight.

IT TOOK ALL I had to leave the hospital to get ready for work on Monday morning. Partly because I didn't want to leave my grandma's side, but also because I had no idea what would greet me at the office.

Janessa had been on radio silence all weekend. I kept waiting for her to call me, tell me Tyler was fired, that they had hired a new site manager, but... nothing.

So I went home, walked up the ramp Tyler had helped my family install, treaded on the brand-new flooring Tyler had donated, and cried in the shower. He was everywhere. From the renovations on the house to the photobooth strips of pictures I hung up on my mirror. Not to mention the stabbing ache in my heart.

I missed him so much already it was hard to breathe. But I had to be okay with my decision. Okay with the fact that I needed to let him go because I needed to be near my family, and he needed to be near his. He'd offered to move here, but I didn't want him resenting me down the road because he'd given up what I couldn't.

I wore a black dress to work and drove my car down the freeway. When the heat gauge popped up to the danger zone, I got pulled off to the side of the road, waiting for the radiator to cool off so I could add some water. Tyler wasn't there to drive by and save me.

I parked in front of the office, but noticed through the window that there were two people inside... Janessa and a man I didn't recognize. Dread filled my gut. Janessa hardly ever came out here. Especially not this early on a Monday morning. This couldn't be good.

Taking a steady breath to steel myself, I pushed through the door, bells chiming overhead. Janessa turned toward me, an evil smile curling her lips. I'd never really considered her a friend, but we'd worked together for eight years, and I'd never seen this side of her. Just another knife, this one twisting in my back.

"Right on time," Janessa said.

I glanced at the clock on the wall. I was five minutes early. "I wasn't expecting you," I said, still not sure who this guy was. He was muscular, nearly six feet tall, dressed in all black. "Are you the new site manager I'll be working with?" I asked, extending my hand. "I'm Henrietta."

The guy looked at my hand, his brown eyes cold.

I lowered my hand, and Janessa said, "Pierce is a security guard. It's company policy to have two people present during a reprimanding."

"A... reprimanding?" I asked. The word rolled around in my head, still not registering. She wasn't firing me?

Janessa let out a cold chuckle. "Did you really think

you could blow the construction manager on site with no repercussions? Corporate was very interested in your unprofessionalism, not to mention your lack of safety gear —and I don't mean condoms. My 'flirtation' with Tyler is *nothing* compared to what you did."

Pierce stood stone-faced, not even flinching at her vulgarity.

"Unfortunately, they said your record has been so good over the last eight years, they didn't want to fire you. Yet. You will be demoted from overseeing the construction process, which also means a cut in your pay. I'll be here every day though to check in on construction—and you."

My mouth opened and closed. I'd been all but ready to get fired and then beg on my knees for my job back. I'd been ready to swallow my pride, show up to work, and do my job, despite the way Janessa had spoken about me in Tyler's apartment, and despite the fact that she clearly had no problem destroying his life out of sheer jealousy. But now I'd have to see her every day? And for how long?

There were a million bitten-back words I wanted to say to her. I wanted to tell her she was lewd, coming on to people who had no desire in her. That she was as fake as vegetable oil butter, treating me kindly until I did something to make her jealous. That she was fatphobic for considering herself the better pick based purely on looks.

But I closed my eyes, thinking of my grandma. How happy she had been when she found out she could come home... I could do this. For her.

66

HENRIETTA

Confession: I'm afraid I'll forget what it feels like to be loved by him.

I LIED TO MY FAMILY.

I told them I was spending a couple weeks with Tyler, but the truth was, I was staying with Mara and Jonas. Hiding out in their guest room was more like it. My heart was breaking, and I couldn't hold in my pain all day long, go to work like I hadn't just let go of the best thing that had happened to me, then continue to hold it together once I got home too.

I considered myself lucky to be born into the family I was, but meeting Tyler... it was once in a lifetime. And now that I'd let him go, I couldn't flip the script and beg him back. I'd already broken that trust.

My life fell into a survival pattern.

Sleep in as long as I could.

Go to work.

See Grandma at the hospital.

Go back to Mara's.

Say hello.

Go to sleep.

Mara tried to be there for me, and Birdie even came over to watch movies one night, but I just couldn't. Pretending everything was okay for Grandma took all my energy. I even missed Wednesday morning breakfast because I knew it would be just my friends and me and they'd ask the question: Why? Why did you let him go?

I'd gone over all my reasons in my head, every single day, trying to convince myself I'd done the right thing. If they argued, it would be too easy to do the selfish thing and take him back, ask him to stay somewhere he didn't belong. But I couldn't leave either. Not with my grandma here. Not with my savings goal still unmet.

I planned to spend the entire weekend in bed, save for a couple hospital visits, but Saturday evening, Mara and Birdie both came into my room.

"Get out of bed," Mara said.

I squinted at the bright light. "Thanks for knocking."

"It's my house, and it's for your own good!" she said. Which really made me wish I'd sucked it up and stayed at home.

Birdie sat on my bed. "I know you're sad, honey, but can you let us have a chance at cheering you up?"

I sat up against the pillows, blinking. "I don't want to feel better."

Mara and Birdie exchanged a glance.

Birdie rubbed my shoulder, asking, "What do you mean?"

I took the extra pillow and held it in front of me. "I

feel like I deserve to be in pain."

Mara frowned. "That's not true, honey."

"It is!" I cried, frustrated. "You didn't see him as he was walking away, but I did. I ruined everything for him —I cost him his job, pushed him away, because I'm not ready to leave my family, and I'm afraid he'd resent me if he stayed."

Both of my friends wore matching looks of pity. I hated it, mostly because I *was* pitiful. I was a mess.

"And you know the worst part?" I asked them.

They waited for me to continue.

"In a sick way, I want to feel the pain, all of it, because it reminds me of him."

Mara said, "He was your first, Hen. He'll always be on your heart."

"But what if he isn't?" I asked. "What if I'm fifty and I forget what it feels like to be loved by him?"

Birdie pinched her lips together, thinking. "Can you write something? Maybe have a journal you can look back on?"

"Yeah," Mara said. "Or a note on your phone?"

"Not permanent enough," I said.

A small smile grew on Mara's lips. "I have an idea."

We left the house, me still in my sweats, and then she drove up to a strip mall, parking in front of a store with a sign that said TATTOO in bright red letters. There was a sign in the window too. *Walk-ins welcome.*

"A tattoo?" I said.

"You said you wanted something permanent," Mara replied.

Birdie looked over at me in the back seat. "You don't have to do this, Hen."

I shook my head. "I want to."

Without waiting for someone to talk me out of it, I pushed the door open and got out of the car, walking to the tattoo parlor's door. There was a guy in a ball cap at the front counter, scrolling through his phone. At the sound of jingling bells, he looked up, seeming bored.

"Got an appointment?"

I shook my head. "Can I get a tattoo?"

He studied me. "You eighteen?"

"Do I look like I'm eighteen?"

"You drunk?"

"I wish."

He shook his head, reaching under the counter, and then handed me a clipboard. "Fill this out, and then come back to my chair."

Birdie and Mara whispered back and forth as I filled out the form, and when I was done, I turned to them. Birdie looked concerned, and Mara seemed annoyed.

"Look, I know you're worried about me doing something impulsive," I said, more to Birdie. "But people get tattoos all the time. And if I hate it in a year, I can put a black square over it. Okay?"

"But your job..." Birdie said. "It's already on thin ice."

"They don't care about tattoos," I said.

Birdie pressed her lips together, nodding. "If you're sure this is what you want."

I nodded. Then I followed the guy's directions and sat in his chair.

"Do you know what you want?" he asked.

I nodded, reaching for my phone. I got out a picture and showed it to him.

He studied it for a moment and said, "I can do that."

TYLER

I stared at the ceiling of the guest bedroom in Gage's downtown condo, hearing hushed voices in the living room. I closed my eyes, wishing I had it in me to care who his guests were. But I didn't.

I'd lost my job. Lost my apartment. Lost my girl.

My life was looking like a bad country song with no royalty income to go along with it.

And it wasn't about the money—I had savings. I was willing to work hard until I found another good paying job. No, it was the way Hen looked at me and said with all certainty that it was never going to work.

I'd put my whole heart in her despite my fears and doubts. I was willing to work at it and fight until we found something we both liked. And if I was being honest, I would have done whatever it took to have her. Because I was back in Dallas now, and it didn't feel like home anymore. Not without her.

The door to my bedroom opened, and I glared toward the light coming through the door. The first couple days Gage checked in on me, but after that, he let me have my space. I was about to tell him to go away, like a petulant teenager, but then I realized it was more than just him in the doorway.

Rhett was already moving to the big window wall, using a remote to open the blinds. Liv came to me, shaking her head exactly like our mother would. "When is the last time you showered and shaved? Up. Now."

I threw my arm over my eyes to block out the light. "Why's it matter?"

She ripped the blanket and sheets off me—a move my mom used on me in middle school when I was going through puberty and could never get enough sleep.

"I'm not a child," I growled.

"Good, then you can shower yourself," she said.

Knowing Liv would never back down and she could get her other brothers to do whatever she wanted, I got out of bed and stumbled in my boxers to the bathroom. I needed to piss anyway.

Outside of the bathroom door, Gage said, "He's been like this for two weeks. Just leaves the room to get food, and then it's back to lying around. He must sleep fourteen hours a day. At least."

"I can hear you," I yelled, feeling like absolute shit from all the time spent in bed. But he was right. Sleeping was easier than being awake with the pain of what I lost. At least sleep was black. In my waking hours, all I could see was her face.

Her face.

Telling me it could never work.

Her face.

Pushing me away no matter how much I begged her to let me stay.

Cohen, Jonas, and Steve had texted me, saying they were sorry about the split, telling me to give Hen some time, but I hadn't replied. Hen had spoken. And I'd heard her. The gaping hole in my chest was proof enough of that.

Liv yelled, "I don't hear the shower going!"

I shook my head and got off the pot, flicking the shower handle. Water poured from the rainfall shower-head, and I stepped in. Cold water pricked at my skin, but it quickly warmed. I felt just as tired, just as hollow in the shower as I'd felt outside of it, but now that I was in, I might as well make use of it.

I finished showering and used the disposable razor and travel-size shaving cream to shave my face. When I was done, there was a fresh pair of gray sweats on the bed, which had been completely stripped of sheets, along with new underwear and a white T-shirt.

My siblings weren't going away. Not until we talked.

So I got dressed and walked out of the room into Gage's open-space living area that had a view of the entire city. The three of them sat at his glass table, looking right at me.

"Join us," Gage said, and Rhett shoved a Styrofoam box and plastic silverware toward the open seat.

"Eat," he ordered.

"You're just as bad as Liv," I muttered, dropping into the seat and opening the box. Inside was some of my favorite food—a pulled pork sandwich and coleslaw. I forced myself to take a bite, but it tasted like mushy cardboard.

They watched me stomach three mouthfuls before Gage said, "Tyler, you can't live like this."

I looked up to him, the hollow ache in my chest bigger than ever. "I don't know how to live without her anymore. It's like the second I met her, she became my air. Every morning, I woke up, waiting for the second I'd see her at work, hear her voice. And now that she's gone, I don't know how to look forward to the next day or how to even have the motivation to get up anymore."

"It's fucking hard," Rhett said, pain ghosting in his eyes. "But you get your ass up and you do it anyway because she's not the only person you love." He tapped at the windmill tattoo on his inner bicep. "We're here too, and it hurts like hell to see our brother like this."

I pushed the box of food away and scored my fingers through my hair. "Shit, guys. I'm sorry."

Liv reached over, putting her hand on my forearm. "We know you're hurting like hell, but you're not alone. Whatever you need to get back on your feet again, we're here."

I didn't have a plan, not even close. But I would find a way to get up and go. If not for me, if not for Hen, then for them.

68

HENRIETTA

Confession: I miss him.

THEY SAY time heals all wounds, but it had been two months, and I missed Tyler more than ever before.

Instead of seeing him every day, Janessa made her rounds in the office, watching everything I did and pointing out everything she thought I was doing wrong. It was exhausting. And miserable.

I've never hated my job more or dreaded going to work in the mornings. I hit all my snooze alarms and practically forced myself to roll out of bed each day, praying one of the jobs I applied to would call me back. I only hoped that Tyler had landed on his feet better than I had. I tried to check his social media accounts every so often, but all I'd seen was a picture Liv tagged him in with their other two siblings.

It hurt to see him smiling at the camera, his eyes crinkling in the corners and his perfect teeth on full display.

He had his arms easily draped around Liv and Rhett's shoulders, and I would have given anything—almost anything—to trade places with them and feel his arms around me just one more time.

Weekends were easier, though. I could spend the day with my family, which was exactly why I made the choices I did. This weekend, we were sitting around the table, celebrating Bertrand's birthday.

Grandma was in her wheelchair at the table and asked, "Where's Tyler?"

I frowned, aching at the mere sound of his name. I'd been lying to all of them—telling them he was busy with the build or traveling to see his family, but the lies had been harder to keep up with. More painful to tell. "I need to tell you all something."

The table grew quiet.

"Tyler and I... we aren't together anymore. He went back to Texas a couple months ago, and I was just too embarrassed to say anything."

The table burst out into a million questions. Johmarcus wanted to know if he needed to beat him up—typical older brother. Bertrand asked if that meant Tyler wouldn't be coming to the wedding. And Justus wanted to know if he'd left me for another woman, which stung. But nothing hurt more than the disappointed look in Grandma's eyes.

"I thought he was the one," she said.

My lips trembled. "He was." I knew that much for sure.

Everyone was quiet for a moment until Dad graciously changed the subject, saying, "Bertrand, how many spankings is it this year? Twenty-six?"

A look of terror crossed Bertrand's face. "I'm too old for this shit!"

"Language!" Laila hissed.

Dad shook his head. "You're still my child."

Bertrand got up, running from the table, quickly followed by Johmarcus and Justus.

Some things never changed.

69

TYLER

I lay on my childhood bed after a long day of work with a neighbor who needed help building a fence. The labor had been freeing, with hours spent under the warm spring sun, pounding away at the rain-softened earth.

But when the work was done, the pain came back. I always ate dinner at the table with Mom and Dad, not speaking much, and then I went upstairs, took a shower, lay in my bed, and prayed sleep would come quickly.

For the most part, my parents let me be. But tonight, there was a knock on the door.

"About to go to sleep," I called.

"Like hell you are," Rhett said, shoving open the door.

I propped myself on my elbows, staring at him in the dim lighting. "What the hell are you doing here?"

"I'm taking you out."

"On a Wednesday night?"

"Ladies drink free on Wednesday's. Now up."

I shook my head, lying back down. "No way in hell."

"I will drag you out of this house myself, and you know I could do it. So why don't you make this easy on both of us and leave of your own free will." He went to the closet, rifling through the clothes.

"Free will," I muttered. "Doesn't count if you're coerced."

He tossed a pair of jeans and a button-up shirt at me. "Wear this." He walked to the door. "If you're not down in five minutes, I'll come up and get you."

I shook my head. Why were my siblings so damn stubborn?

The door clicked shut, and I let out a groan. I didn't want to go to a fucking bar and have Rhett try to set me up with random women to get my dick wet. I wanted to go to sleep and forget how much it still fucking hurt to know I'd never see Henrietta again.

And I knew it wasn't healthy—you weren't supposed to make someone your whole world, but damn it, she was mine. She was more than that. She was the air that I breathed, the sun on my skin, the ground underneath my feet, and the clouds I loved to get lost in.

If I died still heartbroken, it would be a price I'd pay. Because it was proof that once I had been loved by her. Once I'd been a part of her dreams.

But I could see it in the quiet glances my parents shared across the table. The way my siblings checked on me throughout the week. I was scaring them. So I quit thinking about myself for a second, got off my ass, and put on the clothes.

Before I knew it, I was riding shotgun in Rhett's truck, praying this night would go quickly.

♥ ⋅ ♥ ⋅ ♥ ⋅ ♥

RHETT PULLED UP TO NOWHERE, the only pool hall in town. It was a big wooden building with a dance floor, rows of pool tables, and enough liquor to drown an army. And since Cottonwood Falls was surrounded by a few other small towns, there was enough business to keep it going. Dad used to say people forgot about liquor when they said death and taxes were the only two certainties in life, and this town proved him right.

And judging by all the trucks in the parking lot, it was just as true on a Wednesday night as it was any other day of the week.

Rhett parked in the lot and rubbed his hands together. "Ready for a little fun?"

I gave him a look. "We both know this is my last idea of fun."

Ignoring me, he got out and started walking toward the building. Heaving a sigh, I followed him into the dusky bar. My first thought was it wasn't as nice as Collie's. My second? That I missed dancing with Henrietta.

"I need a drink," I muttered.

Rhett clapped my shoulder. "On it." We walked to the bar, and he ordered four shots of whiskey. I expected him to take two, but he slid all four to me.

I gave him a look.

"I'm driving," he said.

"And?" I'd done my best to avoid alcohol, because I knew if I started it would be too easy to spiral. Too easy to try and drown out all this pain. But that was all I had left connecting me to her.

"One night," Rhett said.

"Fine, then you take one," I replied.

He picked up a shot glass, easily dropping it back. I stared at the shots on the counter, preparing myself for the buzz of liquor. The dulling of my emotions. And the hangover I knew I'd have the next day.

And then I downed the shots, one after another. I came up coughing, and Rhett patted my shoulder, laughing. "That's how you do it."

I raised my hand and asked for a beer, which the bartender quickly brought. I reached for my card, but Rhett said, "Drinks are on me tonight."

I gave him a look before drowning half of one. The liquid slid down my throat, warming me right along with the whiskey.

"Now," Rhett said. "I see a table right over there."

Nodding, I walked toward the booth on the edge of the dance floor, wishing I wouldn't be able to see the spinning couples so well. I sat down and rolled my cup around in my hands. I was tired, but not physically. Deep in my soul.

"Hey, baby," a woman's voice said, and I looked up to see Rhett extending his hand to a blond-haired, blue-eyed girl, with her shirt low on her chest.

Rhett gave her his signature flirtatious grin. "Look what the cat dragged in."

It took all I had not to roll my eyes.

"Oh hush," she said, sliding in next to him.

Another woman stood by the table, looking a little uncomfortable and far more clothed.

"This is my friend Darletta," the blonde said. She never gave me her name.

Darletta smiled at me. "Is it okay if I sit by you?"

No. "Actually, I need to piss."

I got up, my legs feeling far less solid than earlier, and made my way to the bathroom. But as soon as I got inside and took a good look at myself in the dingy mirror, Rhett joined me.

"What the fuck, Ty?"

I turned to him. "I didn't want a setup, Rhett. I'm not ready to date anyone else."

He swore at the ground, then faced me, putting his hands on my shoulders. "Look, Mom and Dad, hell, all of us, are worried about you. It's been three months, and nothing's any better. Mom's talking about having you go in-patient for a little while."

My eyes widened. "In-patient? Like psychiatric care?"

He nodded. "And honestly, Ty, I'm not so sure I disagree with her."

"I'm not mental, Rhett. I'm fucking heartbroken," I said, my voice rising. A guy walked into the bathroom then, going back to the urinals. I lowered my voice. "You wouldn't understand."

"The fuck I wouldn't. You remember Mags?"

"The girl you dated in high school?" I asked. I barely remembered him taking her to the prom. I was already out of the house at the time.

His jaw clenched as he nodded. "I get it, Ty; I do. But that pain? It can't be all of you. You gotta turn it into a piece." He clenched his chest, right above his heart. "It won't take the hurt away, but if it's all of you, it takes away those parts of your life you do enjoy."

My jaw trembled, and I clenched it, attempting to

swallow back the lump in my throat. "What do you want me to do, Rhett? Go fuck Darletta?"

A ghost of his crooked smirk was back. "I don't think it could hurt. But maybe just get used to looking at another person like you're not seconds from falling part."

I glared at him. "I hate you... but thanks."

He nodded, resting his forehead against mine. "You've got this."

HENRIETTA

Confession: I'm twenty-eight years old, and I still need my mom's permission sometimes.

I HURRIED DOWN THE SIDEWALK, trying not to get completely drenched by this spring rain. I pushed through the door, lowering my denim jacket and sliding it off my arms. But I stopped in the doorway, seeing half a dozen suitcases lined up against the living room wall.

Grandma sat in her wheelchair in the living room, and I was about to ask her what was going on when I heard wheel casters rolling over vinyl. Mom rolled another suitcase into the living room, freezing when she saw me.

"Are you going on vacation?" I asked, my smile fading.

She and Grandma exchanged a look I didn't like at all.

"What's going on here?" I asked.

Mom let out a sigh. "One thing led to another, and the nurse let on that they don't, in fact, take Medicare. Only private payment. Grandma called me and asked for an explanation, and I couldn't lie to her."

Feeling something close to shame, I turned my eyes toward the ground, but Grandma said, "Henrietta, I need you to come here." She patted the couch next to her chair.

Knowing I'd been caught, I went and sat beside her.

She took my hand, holding it in her lap. "Honey, why would you use all your savings on this?"

I met her murky brown eyes, so full of love and affection and... questions. My throat was already tight as I said, "I wasn't able to do anything for Grandpa. But I can do this for you."

"Oh, honey." She met my eyes, then looked over her shoulder at my mom. "The end of your grandpa's life would have been hard no matter where he was. It was better that his last days were spent in a place we didn't have to come home to."

Her words surprised me. "He was so uncomfortable there. He wanted to come home so badly."

She reached up and cupped my face, her wrinkled palm smooth against my skin. "He did go home, honey."

My throat stung, straining against the ball of emotions growing there.

"But wouldn't it have been worth it, to have given him that wish?"

Grandma pressed her lips together thoughtfully. "Generosity is always a virtue, until the cost is your own peace. And don't take that to mean you should never feel discomfort in this life, only that certain sacrifices will haunt you and lead to resentment down the road."

I took in her words, feeling them hard in my heart. "I would never resent you, Grandma."

She shook her head. "Maybe not now. But when you learn you've missed out on the love of your life to stick around here and slave away at a job you clearly don't enjoy anymore?"

My eyes watered at the mention of Tyler. I missed him like I'd miss my right arm. He was a piece of me forever, no matter where we lived.

"It was never going to work between Tyler and me," I reminded both of us. "His family, his home is in Texas. And mine is here, with my family."

Grandma and Mom exchanged another glance, and Mom came to sit by me on the couch.

Mom said, "Hen, you've always been our baby bird, here when we need you, but it's time for you to leave the nest. You are the child, and it is not your job to take care of any of us. It's time you took care of yourself, thought about what *you* want."

I sniffed away liquid and said, "I want Grandma to be happy and know how much we love her. You've always been here for us, Grandma. You deserve the same."

Grandma smiled at me, her eyes watery. "I've lived the best life, Hen. I met the love of my life, raised a *beautiful* family with him, and gave him my whole heart for fifty-two years. I have children I'm proud of, grandchildren I love to pieces, and great-grandchildren who bring me more joy than I know what to do with. I am happy. And I want you to be happy too."

Mom rubbed my back as I shook with tears. "Tyler

made you so happy, honey. I've never seen you so light as you looked with him."

I shook my head. "It's too late with him. He hasn't called me or texted me once since he left."

Grandma laughed. "That boy is head over heels for you. I'd bet he's been moping around just as much as you have."

I laughed through my tears. "I haven't been moping."

"Have too," Mom and Grandma said at the same time.

A car pulled into the driveway, and I looked out the window to see a big white van with *Emerson Senior Living* on the side.

"That's my ride," Grandma said. "Your father is meeting us there to help me move. I want you to stay here and think about yourself for once. But please come visit me before you leave for Texas."

"Leave for Texas?" I asked, just as a knock sounded on the door.

Mom went up to get it as Grandma said, "You need to follow your heart, and I'm pretty sure that's where it is."

71

HENRIETTA

Confession: I can't believe he remembered.

I MUST HAVE OPENED my phone a million times to send a text to Tyler. To call him and beg his forgiveness, but I always came up empty.

My family didn't need me. They were setting me free, or rather, shoving me out of the nest, even though the idea terrified me.

I had ninety-eight thousand dollars in a savings account and nowhere to go. I was lost.

After a restless night, I got up to go to work. Not because I needed to, but because I had no idea what else to do. I went to my desk, began drafting the script that was now required of me to write and turn in before every potential tenant toured the building. It was humiliating and tedious, just like Janessa wanted.

Taking a deep breath, I looked out my window, seeing the signs of spring. Buds were blooming on the trees, and the grass had greened up nicely. It was probably time for me to go to the store and see if there were any clearance annuals I could put in the flower box outside my office window that overlooked the small courtyard between apartment buildings.

I studied it, expecting to see plain dirt, but instead...

My mouth fell open, and I pushed up from my desk, running outside. I hurried around the building to the box outside my window. And then I saw them.

Tulips.

The flowers had opened into a beautiful shade of pink petals. My eyebrows drew together. How had they gotten there? I knew there was no way the grounds crew had planted them...

But then I remembered a conversation I had with Tyler only days after he moved here. Would he have remembered that? It was the only thing that made sense.

Forgetting my hesitation from the night before, I took a picture of the blooms and sent it to him.

Henrietta: Did you plant these?

I looked at my phone for a moment, wishing he would reply, but the sound of Janessa's voice interrupted me.

"What are you doing out here?" she asked, her pointy heels sinking into the grass as she walked toward me. "Shouldn't you be working? You know, you are on proba- tion. If we see you lazing around, there's a good chance..."

I didn't hear the rest of her words because my phone vibrated. I stared at the screen.

Tyler: I hope they made you smile.

My heart filled, and I covered my mouth, tears stinging my eyes. It wasn't a confession of love, but it was a glimmer of hope. The last shred I had left.

"Henrietta!" Janessa trilled. "Are you really on your phone while I'm trying to talk to you?"

I looked up at her from my phone. "I quit."

"*What?*"

I gripped my phone in one hand, holding it at my side. "You heard me. I quit. I am *done* working under a jealous, controlling, *vile* person." I clenched my jaw in anger. "You had an incredible worker in Tyler. This new guy doesn't care half as much about his crew as Tyler did —that's why turnover has almost *quadrupled* since he left and why production is already a month behind. And now you'll see how much I did for this place." I walked past her, going straight for the office. "Have a nice life."

She followed behind me as I grabbed the few belongings I kept here and threw them into my purse.

"If you walk out that door, there's no coming back," Janessa threatened.

I stood in the doorway, looking at the office. At the kitschy paintings my mom had done for me, at my flourishing hanging plants, and I realized none of it mattered to me. Not if I couldn't spend my time with the people, the person, I truly loved. "The plants need watered twice a week," I said, and then I walked out the door.

72

TYLER

"Something from a job?" Dad asked as we drove down the pasture to build a temporary fence around some corn stalks. We'd move the heifers there once the fence was built to get them some extra nutrition.

I only shook my head. That hollow feeling in my chest was stronger than ever as I realized Henrietta wasn't going to reply. Just like Rhett had said, I moved that pain to a part of me, right at my sternum, but it bloomed now, threatening to take over again. I'd forgotten that I planted those bulbs after our conversation when she told me she liked them.

But the fact that she had texted me after months of silence… I'd been so excited. And now I just wanted to go back to the house and hide all over again.

I'd done well since my talk with Rhett a couple weeks ago, doing gig work with farmers and ranchers in the area while I decided my next move. I wanted to work in construction again, but a lot of employers thought I wouldn't be a good grunt worker since I'd spent so much time in management. And Jim was a big name in construction around Dallas. The second any employer saw my name on an application for a higher-up position, they called him, and I never heard from them again.

Gage offered me a job on one of his maintenance crews—he wanted to fix everything for me—but my pride turned him down. I'd been the one to mess up my career, and I was the one who needed to put it back together. How? I had no fucking clue.

I felt stuck. Trapped. I wished I would have fought with Hen to stay in Emerson. Rented an apartment and worked whatever job I could get. But it was too late. Months stood between us now. Months and a single text message. And that fact haunted me every single day.

Even home didn't feel like home. It all reminded me of Henrietta, the joy in her eyes as she saw everything for the first time. I knew in my heart she belonged here. That we belonged together.

But I had no doubt she'd find another man there locally. One who wouldn't take her away from the people she loved most. I just hoped he'd love her the way she deserved.

And me? It was looking like our family would have three perpetual bachelors in my brothers and me.

Dad and I spent the day building temporary fence, and after that, I went into Dallas to have dinner with Gage. Even though I was staying in my old room with Mom and Dad, he wanted to meet up once a week for dinner. I think to make sure I was okay. He wouldn't admit it, but I'd scared him.

Hell, I'd scared myself. I was barely climbing out of that hole, hanging on to the edge with my fingertips bleeding in the dirt. But I could see some light. And that hope... it was everything to me.

Gage and I sat in a high-end restaurant and ordered off a menu that didn't even have prices listed.

After the server left, I said, "I need to get a job."

Gage looked at me across the table, annoyance making his lips twitch just like they always did when we were kids.

"What?" I asked.

"You don't want a job. Why the fuck haven't you bought the schoolhouse yet?"

I really fucking regretted telling him about that. He'd called me the night we were at the hospital, and I'd filled him in on our brief trip to Texas. And he'd brought it up every couple of weeks since I moved out of his guest bedroom. Feeling like I was under a magnifying glass, I said, "What did you say about unsecured debt?"

"It's a trap that never pays off. And if you want to argue with me, I'll point you toward the student loan crisis."

"Right. So tell me what lender would want to work with me when I haven't had a pay stub for months. Hell, half the people I've worked for still owe me."

"You could take a home equity loan—"

"And risk keeping a roof over my renters' heads?" I said. "They have children."

"If you'd just let me—"

I glared at him, cutting him off.

"Fine," he mumbled. "But for the record, you're being fucking stupid. And someone's going to buy that place if you don't get a move on it."

"Noted. But I think you're wrong. It's been for sale for almost six months. I've got time."

He folded his hands on the table. "Number one mistake."

"What do you mean?" I asked.

"You know how I've been able to grow my company so quickly?"

"You're smart," I said easily. "You can always spot a good deal."

"You can be smart as Einstein, but if you don't move, it means nothing. I've grown my business because I don't sit on a good opportunity. When I see something I want, I make it mine."

I looked down at the beer in my cup and took a deep drink. "I think that's enough life advice for one day."

73

HENRIETTA

Confession: My grandma is my hero.

I WALKED through the double glass doors Emerson Senior Living. My heart beat quickly, and my stomach turned with fear. Mom had told me move-in went well yesterday, but I wanted to see for myself that it was good enough for my grandma.

The front lobby area was cozy with gilded art, cushy chairs, and plants growing in pots along the wall. As I walked a little farther in, a woman walking by in scrubs greeted me.

"Hi there! Can I help you find something?" she asked.

I picked at my thumbnail as I nodded. "I'm looking for Cordelia Jones. I can't remember what her room number is."

"She just moved in, right?"

I nodded.

"She's in the room on the right at the end of the hall. Just walk down that way and take the second hallway."

Great. She smiled at me and continued the opposite way. I walked down the tile hallway, breathing in the disinfectant smell. But they also had some type of cinnamon air fresheners going, so it wasn't as harsh as a hospital smell. As I walked farther down the hall, I saw a big room on the left. Half of it was filled with dining tables. A few women sat around a table playing cards.

My eyebrows drew together. "Grandma?" I called. "Is that you?"

Grandma perked her head up, looking over her cards and grinned at me. "Henrietta! What are you doing here?" As I walked toward the ladies, Grandma said, "This is my favorite granddaughter, Henrietta."

The women greeted me, complimenting me profusely and making me feel like a million bucks.

"You're too sweet," I said. "What are you playing?"

Grandma held up the backs of her cards. "Skip-Bo."

"She's a natural," the white-haired lady on her left said.

Batting her hand, Grandma said, "Beginner's luck. But you'll have to excuse me. I need to show my grand-daughter around!"

The women waved at her, and Grandma stacked her cards for them, putting them at the bottom of the draw pile. I got behind Grandma's wheelchair, backing her from the table and pulling her away.

"Go this way," she said, pointing toward the rec area. "They have a TV over here, and then there's an instructor that comes in and does aerobics once a day. My physical therapist came in this morning and said I can do all the exercises sitting down until I get stronger."

My throat felt tight, seeing it all. One day here, and Grandma already had friends her age. A place to go work out. A routine.

"Wait until you see the salon," she said with a wink.

"There's more?" I asked.

She directed me down a hall that had a small salon, including chairs where they could get pedicures if they made appointments. Then she showed me the back courtyard with a small community flower garden and a heated pool with sparkling blue water.

"Some people do water therapy," she explained. "I should be able to start that here in a few weeks."

I fought happy tears for her as we walked to her room. It was small inside, but my parents had set her framed photos on the dresser and nightstand, and even hung some on the walls. There was a big window out to the street so she could get sunshine. And she had her own bathroom and mini fridge.

"What do you think?" she asked.

"It's incredible," I said, sitting on the chair across from her. And I meant it. It wasn't perfect, by any means, but so much better than what I had feared. "Grandma, you're so brave."

"What do you mean?"

I looked around her new home. "You're on your own now, in your own place, meeting all new people, even after all the bad things people say about places like this. It's so brave."

She tilted her head, smiling softly. "You'd be surprised how brave you can be for the people you love."

I wished with all my heart I had been braver for Tyler. Brave enough to trust my family to take care of my grandma. Brave enough to let go of my safety net and build a life with the man I loved. Brave enough to ask for what I really wanted and let him give it to me.

Grandma asked, "Did you come all this way over your lunch break just to check on me?"

I bit my lip. "Actually...I quit my job."

Her face lit up with a smile, and she patted her hands happily on her lap. "Baby girl, that's huge! Congratulations!"

"Thank you." I couldn't help the smile I wore. It had felt so freaking good to stick it to Janessa and tell her what I truly thought.

"So when are you going to Texas?"

"How did you know..."

"Lucky guess." She had a sly grin. "So, you are going, right?"

I nodded. "I booked the first flight out of LA tomorrow morning. Mom's dropping me off so my car doesn't break down on the way."

Grandma laughed. "Please tell me you're getting rid of that hunk of junk."

"I'm selling it online. Bertrand told me a regular dealership wouldn't take it," I said with a laugh.

"This is so exciting," she said, her eyes shining.

I nodded. "It's exciting *if* it works out. We haven't even talked for months."

"A few months apart is nothing compared to the lifetime you could have together." She smiled over at a picture of her and Grandpa. "All you have to do is show him that you still care about him. That you're dreaming *with* him now."

I lifted a corner of my mouth. She was so right. It was scary to put myself out there, to go big when he could tell me to go home, but I had to. Because the thought of feeling this ache for him every day for the rest of my life... it was pure misery.

I never should have let him go. I knew that now. It had been a massive mistake, but I couldn't go back in time and fix all my worries, fear, and false sense of responsibility. All I could do now was show him that I'd never make the mistake of losing him again and pray he'd take me back.

74

HENRIETTA

Confession: I've never been so scared in my life.

AS I DROVE my brand new (to me) SUV away from the Dallas dealership, my heart was racing. I hoped I wouldn't be driving this car back to California any time soon.

A call came through on Bluetooth, and I tapped the green button on the screen, feeling fancier than I ever felt in my puddle jumper. I answered it, and my dad's voice filled the car.

"Hey, Hen. I just got off the phone with our lender, and they're sending you a pre-qual letter. You're good to put in an offer if that's what you decide to do."

My heart lurched, and I took a few deep breaths to focus on this busy Dallas traffic. Even driving out of town, the roads were packed. I definitely hadn't timed my trip well, leaving the dealership around five.

"Are you sure you're okay with co-signing for me?" I asked.

Dad quickly replied. "Of course we are. I know you'll never need us to help with a payment with how frugal you are."

I laughed. "The vote of confidence is nice."

"Did you splurge on your car?" he asked.

"Yes! We're actually talking on my new-car phone! I went with a Cherokee like Johmarcus suggested. Runs like a dream, and hopefully, I won't be changing tires on the side of the road anymore."

"Good," Dad said. "You deserve to have something nice."

"Thanks, Daddy," I said.

I heard the smile in his voice as he said, "Go get 'em, tiger. Call us after to tell us how it went."

"Pray for good news," I asked.

"We already are."

We hung up, and then I tapped through to call the only romance author I knew. She answered after a few rings, and I said, "Mara, I need some advice."

"Anything. How can I help?"

My cheeks warmed, but I barreled ahead with my embarrassing question. "Well, since you're kind of the expert on grand gestures and couples making up... I wanted some tips on how to do that with Tyler."

Her squeal rang throughout my car. "You're trying to get him back?"

My smile grew. "I'm in Texas right now."

"Oh my *gosh*!" she pealed.

I bit my lip, realizing I should have stopped by to tell my friends goodbye before I dropped everything to start a new life here (hopefully). But thinking of myself was new, and I didn't want to lose my nerve.

"What changed your mind?" she asked.

"He planted tulips in my flower box."

"Is that an innuendo?"

I laughed and filled her in on the whirlwind of the last couple of days.

"Does that mean we won't see you on Wednesday mornings when I'm home?" she asked. She usually videoed in with Birdie and me when she had to be in Georgia to help write for a body positive TV show.

"It means we'll be doing virtual breakfasts, I hope."

"Awesome," she said. "So here's what you do..."

I PULLED up to the old school building on the outskirts of Cottonwood Falls. It was just as impressive as I remembered it. There was traditional brick, big white columns, and big windows wrapped around the building. It would take some work to make my dream come true, but I was ready for work. I was ready to build a life with Tyler from the ground floor.

Soon after I parked, a white pickup pulled in next to me, and through the tinted windows, I recognized Linda from Thanksgiving. She had a new short haircut that accentuated her pointed chin.

I got out of my car to talk to her, giving her a big smile and a wave. "I love that new haircut on you!"

"Henrietta, you are just so sweet," she said. The sad look in her eyes told me otherwise.

A sinking feeling filled my gut. Had word of my

breakup with Tyler gotten around town? Was there something, or someone else, I didn't know about?

I shoved aside my fear and said, "Should we go inside
and look around? Or can I make the offer now?"

She wrung her thin hands. "I'm so sorry, but the
building sold."

Punch to the face. The chest. The gut. "*What*? We
talked on the phone this morning. Why didn't you
call me?"

"I tried to get ahold of you, but it went straight to
voicemail. I left a message."

I must have missed the notification in all the rush of
getting off the plane and car shopping. "What
happened?"

"We had a cash offer over asking price that the seller
couldn't turn down. I'm so sorry. I know you were excited
about this."

Despair washed over me. This had been my grand
gesture. My way to show Tyler that I was committed to
him, to building a life together regardless of where we
were. That I wanted *him* to be my family.

But then I remembered where I came from. My
grandma taught me that a stubborn streak can move
mountains. My mom taught me anything can grow with a
little care. My brothers taught me to go down swinging.
And my dad? He taught me how to get my hands dirty
and find my own solution instead of sitting around and
waiting for a hero.

I was *not* losing this sale.

"Who bought it?" I asked.

She frowned. "I'm really not at liberty to say. You'll be
able to search the public records once they're updated."

I reached into my purse, pulling out a hundred-dollar bill.

She eyed it, then me, then took the money. Wordlessly, she tucked the bill in a zipper pocket of her purse, then pulled out a business card.

I held the black cardstock in my hand, desperately reading the information, and my jaw fell to the floor.

Gage Griffen, CEO

75

GAGE

My desk phone beeped, and I pressed the button. "Yes, Mia?"

"You have a call from a 'Ms. Jones.' I told her you were busy, but she said it was an urgent family matter."

My shoulders tensed with dread. No matter how hard of a line I'd drawn between my parents and myself, the thought of them passing before we had a chance to make amends... it was a fear that haunted me every damn day.

"Send it through," I said, closing my eyes and hoping like hell it wasn't bad news.

The phone rang, and I gripped the receiver, holding it to my ear. "This is Gage Griffen."

A clear voice came through the phone, strong and in control. "This is Henrietta Jones."

I blinked at the name. "Tyler's Henrietta?"

"I have to know why you bought the schoolhouse. I know for a fact he would never accept a handout from you. Are you trying to take it out from under him?"

I bristled at the harshness in her tone. "I bought it so

someone else doesn't do what you're accusing me of. I thought I would hold on to it until he gets his head out of his ass and buys the place himself." In fact, the ink had barely dried on the papers. "How did you find out?"

"I..." She hesitated for the first time since barreling into this call.

"What?" I demanded.

"I'm in Cottonwood Falls. I was going to put in an offer."

"You're *where?*"

"Standing in front of the school right now," she replied.

I reached for the blazer hanging over the back of my chair. "I'll meet you there in an hour and a half."

And then I did something I hadn't done in over a decade—I left the office early for a personal matter.

I rushed past the reception area, and Mia called, "Everything okay?"

The relief I felt throughout my body had me smiling. "More than okay."

I got in the elevator and took it all the way down to the parking garage. My Tesla waited for me in a reserved spot near the door. The car unlocked as I neared, and I got in, tossing my jacket in the passenger seat. The engine quietly revved as I whipped out of the parking garage and onto the road. The sky was already dusky, but I raced through traffic, driving to Cottonwood Falls as quickly as I could. Usually the drive took a good two hours, but I could shave off thirty minutes.

As I flew down the interstate, I dialed Tyler's phone number.

"What's up?" he answered.

"I need you to meet me at the schoolhouse tonight."

"What? Why? I already told you I'm waiting until I find a steady job."

"Indulge me," I said.

I could practically feel him rolling his eyes. "Only if we hit the diner after. I'm fucking starving."

The idea of sitting in the diner where I used to hang out in high school made my skin crawl, but I had a feeling when he found out what was waiting for him, he wouldn't hold me to it.

"Fine," I said. "Be at the school in an hour."

"See you then."

We hung up just as I reached the city limit sign of Cottonwood Falls. Incorporated. Population 8,432.

An unpleasant mixture of anger, guilt, and regret flooded my body at the familiar sights. My life would have been so different if my dad didn't have his head up his ass. I would have been working on the family farm, growing something that had been built over generations.

Instead, I worked in an office, had employees working for me that I'd never even met before. I hadn't even come into town to buy the damn building, but I needed to see Henrietta for myself. I had to make sure she was honest about her intentions before I did what I wanted to do.

I turned down the streets so familiar they'd been buried into an automatic part of my memory. As I reached the school, I saw a red SUV parked out front, temporary tags on the back. Then my eyes drifted to the front entrance of the school.

A woman with dark skin and ample curves sat on the porch steps, her elbows on her knees and her chin in her hands. An orange security light cast a halo around her, making her black hair appear almost golden. This was Tyler's Henrietta.

Part of me wanted to hate this woman. Wasn't she the one who had broken my brother to the point he wouldn't get out of bed? The one who caused that ever-present glint of pain in his eyes, even months later?

But the way he loved her made me care for her too. I wanted this to work for them—if she was here for good. I couldn't watch my brother go through this again.

Clearing my throat, I turned off the car and got out, walking toward where she sat. With Tyler on the way, we didn't have much time, and I had plenty to say.

She eyed me wearily as I approached. "Are you Gage?"

I nodded.

"You look just like him. But you have your mom's hair color."

"Except mine doesn't come from a box for six ninety-five," I said.

A small smile formed on her lips, but her expression quickly turned serious. "Gage, I want to buy the school-house from you. I have a significant down payment, and even though I don't have a job here yet, my parents co-signed with me on the loan. I'm hoping Tyler will help me turn this into his dream come true.... together."

I studied her, looking for any hint of inauthenticity. In my line of work, most of my decisions were analytical, but there also came a time to trust your gut. And this woman, with her wide brown eyes and lips pulled down with worry? She was the real deal.

"I'm not selling it to you," I said.

Her mouth fell open. "Gage, you have to know how

much this would mean to us." Her eyes grew shiny with tears. "Unless he's found someone else." She put her head in her hands. "Oh god, I'm so stupid. I should have called before I—"

I stepped closer, putting my hand on her shoulder. "I'm not selling the schoolhouse to you, because I'm giving it to you."

All her pain was replaced with shock, so easily visible in each of her features. "What?"

"You said you had a down payment. I want you to use that money, and the money Tyler has saved, to build this business. And if Tyler's pride requires him to pay me back, I'll take a cut of the profits over time as an investor. Even if it's annoying."

Now a smile played across her lips. "Gage... that's amazing. Are you sure?"

I chewed the inside of my cheek, not sure how much to give away. "I've never seen my brother happier than when he was with you... or more devastated than when it ended. I'd give everything I have never to see him like that again."

I studied her, waiting to see her response, already knowing I'd be able to read her.

"I may have ended things, but it was the worst mistake I've ever made. If he gives me another chance, I promise you both I'll never waste it."

I saw something in her face, heard it in her words. The truth.

Headlights panned over us, and we looked over to see Tyler's truck pulling up to the school.

76

TYLER

I blinked at the windshield because I couldn't be seeing straight. Gage stood on the front steps of the school with Henrietta.

Seeing her was like a punch to the gut and a drink of fresh water after months in the desert. She was beautiful, even in the dim lighting. The light yellow dress she wore hugged her curves, and her hair fell down her back in soft curls. I wanted to kiss her, I wanted to hold her, I wanted to pool her hair in my hands and breathe in her scent I'd missed so damn much.

But I was hurt too, and that pain kept me sitting in the truck, staring at my brother and the woman I loved.

How long had Gage been talking with her? How long had he known her?

What were they doing here? Together?

Movement made me refocus my gaze, and I saw Gage walking toward me, quickly striding across the distance still in his work clothes. He reached my window and rolled his finger through the air.

My arm felt stiff and heavy as cement as I reached for the button and pushed it down. A fresh blast of cool spring air and Gage's cologne came into the truck.

"What are you doing?" he asked, a slight smile on his face. "Get over there!"

"Gage, I'm gonna need a little more explanation than that. What the hell is going on?"

"I think Henrietta needs to be the one to explain that to you. Call me tomorrow. I'll take you both out to eat somewhere better than the diner."

Despite my protests, he walked to his car and pulled away, leaving just a red Jeep in the lot.

It was just Henrietta and me. She looked at me. I looked at her. She waited on the steps. I waited in the truck. But with my window rolled down, I felt more exposed than I had in the safety of my enclosed truck cab.

She tilted her head, a question in her eyes. *Will you hear me out?*

I had to. Because all the pain this woman had caused me had been from her absence, not her presence. With my body feeling different than my own, I pushed the door open, stepping down and feeling every bit of gravel under my boots.

I kept my eyes on her, silence, pain, distance filling the space between us, no matter how close I got. I stepped onto the porch with her, enveloped by the harsh glow and buzzing of the safety lights.

"Hi," she whispered.

That little box I'd been keeping my pain in for the last two weeks? It completely shattered with that one word. "Hi," I managed, my voice sounding strangled.

I watched her a second longer, not knowing how to ask the question on the tip of my tongue.

What are you doing here?

Instead, I asked something different. "Is that your car?"

She looked around like she'd forgotten completely how she'd arrived. When her gaze landed on the red vehicle, her eyes widened slightly in recognition. "I bought it today," she said. "After I got to Dallas."

"You bought a car?"

A small smile played along her lips. "It turns out my grandma didn't want me to sacrifice the love of my life for her to stay at home."

Those words... they assaulted my heart, pulverizing the already tender muscle. "She didn't?"

Hen shook her head. "My grandma requested to move into a senior living center, and it's great. She already has friends she's beating at cards." Hen smiled softly at the cracked cement beneath us. "And seeing those flowers you planted for me... I realized I wanted to grow something just as beautiful... with you."

It was everything I'd ever wanted her to say, but my life was a mess. And her family was still in California. "Hen, I love you."

She smiled up at me. "You do?"

It took all the strength I had to keep my hands at my sides. I wanted to hold her face and kiss her just to show her how much love I had for her. I only wanted her to be happy with the life she wanted to live. And she'd chosen one without me. "Of course I love you. I love you in a way I've never loved another woman. But you love your family. And even though I miss you like crazy, I can't

promise forever to someone who'd put me second. I
barely made it through you turning me away the last
time. I couldn't make it through another."

"I'm not going anywhere, Tyler," she said stubbornly.

Didn't she get it? We had our window. Our opening
where my job wasn't an issue. I'd offered to stay! But my
savings were lower now. "I don't have anything for you
here!" My voice echoed off the bricks. "I don't have a job.
No one in construction will hire me with my reputation,
and I don't have the capital for my own business. I'm
living with my parents now because I can't kick out my
renters. I have nothing, Hen."

She turned toward the school. "What if I do?"

It was like she was speaking in riddles, and the anger
and pain in my chest had me letting out a mix between a
laugh and a cry. "What do you mean?"

Facing me again, she said, "The reason why my
grandma wouldn't accept my help was because of the life
she had with my grandpa. She knew I could have that
kind of life... with you."

The buoyancy in my chest was dangerous. The kind
that could end a guy if he didn't watch out.

She reached out for my hand, her touch instantly
making a lump grow in my throat. "Tyler, I've spent my
whole life with my family, being loved and cared for by
them. And part of me thought I didn't deserve it, no
matter how freely they loved me. I thought I had to earn
it, thought I had to protect them because of how they
cared for me. But that's not what they wanted for me.
And it turns out... that's not what I wanted for myself."

She held her other hand to my cheek, wiping away an
errant tear I hadn't realized was there. "Tyler, I want to

build a life with you, a family, a home. This building? It's so much more than four walls and a roof. It's a place where we can make our own mark, serve others the way they deserve, and grow our life, *together*."

The dream she was speaking of was everything I'd wanted for us. But I had to tell her the truth. "I can't give that to you, Hen. I don't have a job, no way to get financing for a project this size."

"Now that my grandma's care is covered, I have enough to invest. My whole life savings is ready to create this with you."

I held her face in my hand, tears falling unapologetically down my cheeks. "I can't ask that of you. To give everything you have to me."

Her voice cracked. "Tyler, I already have. My heart? It's yours. My body? My life? Yours. There will never be anyone else like you, no one to replace you, Tyler." She held her hand to her chest. "If I have to renovate this thing by myself until I can prove to you how committed I am, I'll do it."

As she gesticulated, I noticed something on her wrist I hadn't seen before. I took her arm and held it up, giving me a clear view of her skin in the light.

"What are you doing?" she asked.

"Hen, what is this?"

She looked from my eyes to her wrist. South of her thumb, right below the crease, was a windmill. Just like mine.

"When did you get this?" I asked.

She bit her lip, tears filling her eyes. "A week after you left."

My voice was hoarse as I whispered, "Why?"

"Because I knew no matter how much I moved, my heart would always be with you. You're the one, Tyler."

I couldn't hold myself back anymore. I wrapped my arms around her middle and pulled her close to me, kissing her with all I had. Every ache, every tear, every broken dream from the last several months, I poured into our embrace.

"Marry me," I said against her lips.

She looked up at me, her eyes wide. "What?"

"I'm not going another day in this life without you by my side," I said. "Be my wife."

Tears fell down her cheeks as she nodded.

I covered her yes with my kiss, filled with dreams of forever.

77

HENRIETTA

Confession: I still can't believe I'm getting my happily ever after.

TYLER WIPED AWAY my tears with his thumbs. "I'm so happy you came here. I never knew how much I was missing in my life before I met you."

I smiled up at him, my lips trembling with emotion. "I knew what was missing. I just didn't know love could be as incredible as it is with you."

He lifted my hand to his lips, kissing my palm, and then he placed his lips over the windmill at my wrist. "Let's get out of here?"

I nodded, despite the worry filling my heart. "Will your family forgive me for the way I hurt you?"

"They love you, Hen. When I first came home, I stayed with Gage because I knew my parents would tell me to get my ass back to California and win you back."

What would have happened if he had come back? I wondered. Would I have accepted him?

No, I decided. I never would have asked him to give up his home for me. Tyler's dreams existed here, and my family would always be there for me. I'd never cared where I was, as long as I was with the people I loved.

"Is it okay for me to stay at your parents' house tonight, on such short notice?" I asked, biting my lip.

"It would be... except I have another idea."

Tyler drove me to one of the three hotels in town, lifting his middle console so I could slide over and sit tucked against his side. After so long apart, we weren't wasting a minute together. He insisted my car would be fine at the schoolhouse overnight, but that was the last thing on my mind.

We walked down the hallway over green and gold carpet to room 106. Tyler held the keycard against the reader, and we stepped into the room. Together. A million missed moments and painful memories filled the space between us.

For a moment, I stood, looking at the bed. He slipped off his cowboy boots, the leather worn with hard work. My own white sneakers were a contrast in almost every way.

That was us. We were different. Him, a tall, strong country boy from Texas. Me, a curvy city girl who'd always been under her family's wing. But together? We created something different entirely. A pair of people who led with love, who served with our whole hearts, and who fumbled through life until we finally got something right. Each other.

"Lie down with me," he asked, lifting the blanket.

I nodded, walking around the other side of the bed to curl in next to his warm body. He was so solid against me, and I slid my hand under his shirt, running it over the ridges of his stomach, the crisp of his chest hair, the slope of his collarbone, the divot at the base of his neck and back down again.

He pressed a kiss to my temple, drawing emotion to my eyes again. It was like my heart had barely scabbed over the last few months apart, and being here with him now pulled me all the way open, leaving me more vulnerable than ever before.

I lifted my face to him, kissing him slowly. Refamiliarizing myself with his taste, the swirl of his tongue against mine, the scratch of his five o'clock shadow over my chin. And then I needed to remember more, to feel more.

I gripped the hem of his shirt, pulling it up, and he helped me, slipping it over his head before moving to my dress, pulling it off. And then we were back together.

Kissing.

Savoring.

Loving.

Our middles pressed together, his skin warm against mine. His hands gentle on my hips, my shoulders.

With each second that passed, our kiss intensified, our hands explored. His palm slid against my ass, lifting my thigh so it crossed over his hip, and then there was space for him to gently slide my thong aside, to run his thumb along my slit.

My breath caught as he slipped a finger inside and then lifted it to his lips. He drew his finger in his mouth, closing his eyes. "I missed the way you taste."

Moisture pooled between my legs. "I missed the way you feel," I breathed.

"Not much longer, baby," he breathed, kissing me

again, bringing his hand back down and circling his fingers around my clit.

As the sensation grew between my legs, I bucked against his hand. Tears filled my eyes, dripped over my nose and down my cheek as my orgasm built. Tyler was back, he was with me, he loved me.

And then I came into his hand, crying out his name.

With my orgasm still rocking my body, he rolled me to my back and unzipped his pants. Pulled them down just enough to plunge into me.

I stretched around him, my body having tightened up in his absence.

"Baby," he breathed against my lips.

"I love you," I cried, tears flowing freely. "I love you so damn much, Tyler."

"I love you," he said, pumping fast. "I love you."

"I love you."

Our words slowly transformed into breathless pants until his orgasm came and he pumped harder into me, letting go of all he had and filling me completely.

He lay on top of me, letting his orgasm dwindle, then he rolled to the side, opening his arms for me to lie in my nook. I kissed the bulge of his shoulder muscle and then lay in his arms. He wrapped them around me, tracing his fingers gently up and down my side, and one word came to mind.

Home.

This was home.

"I can't believe I get to be your wife," I said, a smile stretching my lips.

"I can't believe you said yes." He froze, then rolled away from me.

His swift distance made my heart stall. "Tyler? Are you alright?" I asked, when really what I needed to know was *are we okay?* Did he realize getting back together with me was a mistake?

There was a deep crease between his eyebrows and his mouth was pinched as he kicked off his jeans the rest of the way and paced the room.

"I fucked up, Hen."

My heart sank, on the precipice of sheer destruction. "What do you mean?"

He shook his head angrily.

"Tyler, you're scaring me."

Almost as if he remembered I was in the room, his expression softened and he came closer to me, kissing my forehead. "You didn't do anything wrong. It was me." And then he was back to pacing. "I asked you to marry me without asking your dad first. How could I have been so stupid?"

All the worry let out of me like a balloon releasing air, and I laughed. "That's what you're worried about?"

A tortured expression pained his face as he looked at me. "That's not how I do things, Hen. I want to do them the right way with you."

I bit my lip, shaking my head. "My dad's happy if I'm happy. And I am, Tyler. So, so happy."

His features lightened a little bit as he knelt by the bed next to me. "I love you. But please don't tell him until I have the chance to ask for his blessing."

I'd do anything for this man, but hiding my excitement from our families? "Okay, but only if you promise to ask him soon."

♥ ♥ ♥ ♥

WOODY'S WAS no Waldo's Diner, but their pancakes were delicious, and they had a table in the back corner perfect for Wednesday morning brunches with my best friends. Only this time, I had news. Big news.

I sat with my pancakes ordered and my coffee steaming and pressed *call* to be on Birdie's table. Within a few rings, they answered, Birdie and Mara sitting on the same side of the booth with their own pancakes.

Mara jumped right into it. "Tell us how it went!"

I grinned at them, holding up my hand to show them the silver engagement ring on my finger with an oval diamond set in the middle. Classic, modest, beautiful, just like the man who had given it to me.

Their screams came through my phone, making a few of the regulars around me turn their heads.

"You're getting married?!" Birdie cried.

I nodded, smiling so hard my cheeks almost closed my eyes. "He asked me that night I came back. We just got the ring yesterday!"

"That was fast!" Mara said. "The grand gesture must have been really good."

I laughed and filled them in on the confusion of the day, hearing that Tyler's brother had bought the schoolhouse and then talking with Tyler on the porch.

Birdie had her hands laced under her chin, practically swooning. "That is so romantic."

"It's been amazing these last couple days, just catching up on everything we missed."

Mara winked. "And the make-up sex."

My cheeks heated as someone in the booth next to me

gave me the side-eye. I scratched my neck nervously, looking down. "That too."

"I'm so happy for you," Mara said.

Birdie nodded but had a frown on her lips. "Does this mean you're there permanently?"

My heart tugged at the question. Birdie had been my first real adult girlfriend. Her moving into the apartments and introducing me to Mara had changed my life in so many ways. Saying goodbye would be too hard. So I'd have to settle on see you soon. "I'll be back," I promised. "Frequently. Apparently, Tyler's brother has a ton of flight miles from his business credit card that he's practically begging everyone to use. And of course I want you all to come and visit us." I told them all about the schoolhouse and our plans for the building.

Birdie said, "I'll take you up on that. Is there even a hotel in that town?"

I laughed. "Two, actually. And a motel."

"Fancy," Birdie said with a laugh.

"Where are you and Tyler staying?" Mara asked. "With his family?"

"For now," I answered. "But we're working to renovate a living space for us at the schoolhouse for us first. We're going to be staying there and managing the property on site so we can give better help to the residents. Tyler thinks he can have it livable in a month, since this is our full-time job now. Bertrand even offered to take a week off work to come help us get settled."

"Your family's all on board?" Birdie asked.

"Oh yeah." I laughed, twirling my engagement ring around my finger. "They practically shoved me out the door to get him back. They all love him as much as I do."

Mara bumped her shoulder against Birdie's. "We love him too."

Birdie nodded. "If I could have hand-designed a guy for you, even he wouldn't have been half the man that Tyler is."

"He is pretty amazing." I took a sip of my coffee that was already cooling down. "I do have a question though."

"What's up?" Mara asked.

I bit my lip, holding back a smile. "What are you doing a month from now?"

Birdie and Mara exchanged a glance.

"Because I'd love for you to stand by my side when I say 'I do'," I finished.

Another round of squealing had people sending me more looks. In a town this size, I was bound to have a reputation before our wedding announcement hit the local paper.

Birdie said, "That's so soon. Are you worried about planning the wedding?"

"We would have gone to city hall yesterday, but Tyler wants to ask my dad for his blessing before we tie the knot," I admitted. "And Tyler's mom and sister begged for us to have a wedding for our families to get a chance to celebrate and meet each other. So, this was the compromise." My grin spread across my entire face. It was crazy, getting married this soon to the man I lost my virginity to, but on a soul level, it didn't feel crazy at all.

It felt right.

Perfect.

Inevitable.

I just couldn't wait.

78

TYLER

A week after Hen came to Cottonwood Falls, I drove to DFW Airport to pick up Bertrand. The second Hen told him about our project, he said he wanted to come and return the favor for helping his family with their home. Even though I told him he didn't need to, he insisted, and it was probably a good thing he had.

The only problem? I still hadn't called Hen's dad to ask his blessing. I'd already fucked up, and I knew this was a conversation we needed to have in person. But with how hard we'd been working on the schoolhouse, I hadn't had the time to fly to California.

For the last week, Hen and I had worked all day every day to get the top part of the schoolhouse up and running so we'd have our own place to stay, hopefully by our wedding night. But at this rate, we were still a couple weeks behind. And with my chicken-shit behavior, the wedding would have to be pushed back too unless I found a way to talk to her dad.

Except with Bertrand coming, I wasn't sure how

much longer we could keep our engagement a secret. What if Bertrand told their parents before I had a chance?

I reached the airport and exited into the cell phone lot to wait until Bertrand texted me that he was ready. My hands were jumpy on the steering wheel with nerves. In an hour, he'd see the ring on his sister's finger. He'd know I'd done things in the wrong order.

Bertrand: I'm here. Hope you have extra room in your truck. Brought a lot of baggage.

I laughed at the phone, his text breaking the tension.

Tyler: You must pack like your sister.

I put the truck in drive and pulled around the curb, taking deep breaths. Bertrand came into view, standing next to a single duffel bag. Rolling down the window, I said, "What happened to all your bags?"

He nodded his head over his shoulder, and two other Joneses came through the airport doors. My jaw dropped at all of Hen's brothers being in Dallas.

"What the hell?" I laughed out, grinning wide as I got out of my truck. I hugged Bertrand, Johmarcus, and Justus. And then I saw Murphy walk out the door.

My blood went cold. I had two hours between here and Cottonwood Falls before he saw the ring on his daughter's hand and found out I was a coward.

My knees buckled, and I knelt in front of Murphy. "Can I marry you?"

He stared at me, confusion scrunching up his nose. "You okay, son?"

I shook my head, standing up. "Sorry, I fucked up. Shit. Sorry for cussing. *Shit*." I was *really* fucking this one up. I ran my hand over my face, trying to give myself an internal pep talk.

"I asked Henrietta to marry me." Shock raised his eyebrows, but I pressed on. "I know I should have asked you first, but I was so excited she wanted me back that my heart spoke before my mind thought. And now that I asked, and she said yes, I can't take it back from her. But I wanted to know if we could have your blessing, despite my lapse in judgment."

Murphy shook his head, grinning. "Her yes was all the blessing you needed." He wrapped his arms around my shoulders. "Welcome to the family."

Hen's brothers joined in the celebration, patting my back and whooping it up. Until a security guard yelled, "HEY! Get a move on."

The guys were still laughing as we piled into the truck and headed toward home.

I PARKED the truck at the schoolhouse in between the plumber's truck and the electrician's van. Gary Johnson, the plumber, had been working around town since I was in diapers, and he'd been thrilled to get his hands on this school to turn it into something of use. He'd been working with us the last week to plumb a new kitchen and bathroom upstairs. When that was all done, he'd plumb bathrooms and kitchenettes in the units downstairs.

Grant Arnold, the electrician, had worked with me on projects in Dallas back when I was starting out on a construction crew. He was cutting us a special price to upgrade the wiring in the entire building. He'd also hang new ceiling fans and decorative lights for each room.

Meanwhile, Hen and I had worked on framing out the bedrooms, hanging up drywall and repairing cracks that had formed in the ceiling over the years. This week, I had hoped Bertrand would help us lay flooring and maybe even install some stock cabinets from the nearest box store, but now that the four of them were here, I couldn't wait to see how much we'd accomplish. I knew firsthand how hard and fast these guys could work.

As we got out of the truck and walked toward the front entrance, excitement rushed through me. Maybe we would get this all done on time for our wedding, which could happen now—with her father's blessing.

Everything was finally falling into place.

79

HENRIETTA

Confession: I used to think moving meant leaving my home. I couldn't have been more wrong.

I SCRAPED the drywall knife over a seam, making it disappear in one quick movement. I'd helped Dad with drywall patches around the house, but Tyler had to show me how to hang big sheets of drywall, making walls appear where there had been none. It was heady, seeing something this big come together thanks to the work of my own two hands. I couldn't wait for Bertrand to get here so we could show him all we'd already done.

From downstairs, Tyler called out, "Babe! We're here!"

I grinned, setting down my bucket of joint compound and wiped my hands on my work overalls. I put my hand on the oak stair railing and went down the stairs, excited to wrap my brother in a big hug and show him this life I was building.

But when I got halfway down the stairs and the entrance came into view, I froze. Not only was Bertrand in the entryway, but so were Johmarcus, Justus, and my dad.

My mouth fell open. "What are you doing here?"

Grinning, Dad said, "Came to help you out, but it sounds like we'll be celebrating your engagement too."

I looked from Dad to Tyler, and Tyler nodded.

"Come here, baby girl," Dad said.

I jumped down the rest of the stairs, running to my dad and letting him wrap me in his arms. We rocked back and forth as he spoke into my hair. "I'm so happy for you, honey. He's one of the good ones."

"Thanks, Daddy," I said, stepping back. "I can't wait for you to see it."

He slipped his hand in mine and said, "Show us around."

We walked through the ground floor, which had barely been touched except by Grant to upgrade the wiring. There were six classrooms down here and a massive kitchen. All of it would be converted to six apartments and a common area for mail, laundry, and a small office space.

Then we went upstairs, where there were another six classrooms. Tyler and I had demoed half of them to make room for our future kitchen, living room, and primary bedroom with an en suite bathroom.

We also introduced my brothers and dad to Grant, who was working in the kitchen to wire all the plugs we'd need, and Gary, who was in the bathroom, building plumbing for all the fixtures.

"Holy crap," Johmarcus said as we all stood in the open living area. "You've been busy the last week."

I laughed, looking around at the walls that had been taken down and the walls that were already built up, joint compound drying on the drywall. "It's been a whirlwind. Gary and Grant are helping a bunch, and now that you're here, it'll move so much faster! Thank you for doing this. It means the world." I looked at all the men in my life. It seemed like I'd been crying constantly the last several months between sad and happy tears, but these were happy tears.

I'd been so afraid to move, afraid of losing my family, but seeing them here in my new home, I knew I'd been so wrong to worry. I hadn't lost my family—it had grown. My life was so much better for it.

"Do we need to take you to the hotel to get you settled in?" I asked.

Justus pulled his head back. "Hell no. Girl, you need all the help you can get."

I laughed. "Then let's get to work."

TYLER and I had also made a tearfully happy video call to Grandma and Mom, who celebrated our engagement with us and were already planning what they wanted to wear to our wedding. Mom asked for Deidre's number, and they had quickly started talking by video call, planning the wedding and getting to know each other while Tyler and I worked on the house with my brothers and dad.

In five days, the guys had all the drywall up in the

main living areas and had laid hardwood floors with lots of soundproofing so we wouldn't disturb future tenants below. Now Dad and I were on the way to the nearest box store to pick up my cabinet order. The kitchen was going to be kitschy and cute with light blue cabinets, vinyl countertops with a Calcutta marble pattern, and a big island in the middle with room for family, just like the kitchen at home in California.

Tyler's parents had loaned us a horse trailer to carry all the cabinets from the store, and I had to smile at the way my life had changed. At least Dad had rented a trailer way back when I was a teenager to teach me how to pull one; otherwise I'd be completely lost.

He sat in the passenger seat of Tyler's truck, music playing softly through the speakers as the sun shined down on us.

"The skies seem bigger in Texas," he said, gazing out at the landscape blurring past, blue skies before us, dotted with puffy white clouds.

"Haven't you heard? Everything's bigger here," I teased.

He chuckled. "You seem happy here. Like you were always meant to be here."

I felt that way, but it made me happy that my dad noticed, that he didn't hold it against me that I'd decided to move here. "It felt like home the moment I arrived." I'd already met so many people. Apparently, in a small town, any major project called for random visits just to see what was going on.

I'd met the hairdresser, two bank tellers, some teachers, and a handful of other townspeople. They all welcomed me warmly and were so happy to hear that

Tyler was back for good. Not to mention Liv had already invited me to go out with her and her friends. My community here was growing so quickly. But most of all, I had Tyler by my side.

We reached the store, and I pulled up along the big garage doors for pickup. An employee came out and took my order number and ID and said he'd be back to load them up in just a little bit.

I smiled and nodded, then sat back to wait with my dad. When I glanced at him, he had a thoughtful expression on his face.

"What are you thinking about?" I asked.

"I'm realizing this might be one of our last chances to talk before you get married next month."

My heart wobbled at the truth. I was getting married in May and then Bertrand would be married in August, just a couple months from now. All of us kids were grown, out of the nest, even if it was later than most. "It'll be just you and Mom in the house."

He nodded. "It just hit me that there's so much that I haven't told you about marriage, about life."

I reached across the middle console, covering his hand with mine. "I'm only a phone call away, Dad. You can call and tell me any time."

He glanced my way with a somber smile. "But there are some things I want to tell you *before* you get married."

"Sure," I said. "I think I need all the advice I can get."

His chuckle rumbled in his chest, and then he sobered. "Mom and I always saved our big arguments for after you kids were asleep, but I don't want you to think we never had any fights."

"You were never that coy," I replied. "Mom would always burn your toast the day after."

He laughed. "A small price to pay for some of the dumb stuff I've done. But you know, I'm thankful for those arguments. Everyone thinks that getting married is supposed to be a happily ever after where you feel only love and never pain, but it's not."

My eyebrows drew together. My parents were some of the happiest, most in love people I knew. "What do you mean?"

"Do you remember when Justus tore his ACL playing football? After the surgery, the doctor told him that his left leg would be stronger than his right, even though that was the one that had been injured. Because the strength, the healing, comes in the repair."

I nodded, understanding what he meant.

"When you and Tyler have arguments, because you will, don't look at it like a break from the ideal life you want to live. Look at it as a chance to make things stronger than they were before."

"Of course," I managed.

"And forget about all that nonsense everyone wants to sell you about marriage being fifty-fifty. People get so caught up in making things equal that they forget marriage isn't just a contract on a piece of paper. It's a commitment to serve each other in sickness and in health. Richer and poorer. There will be times Tyler's too sick to do the dishes." Dad winked. "That means you'll have an opportunity to serve him by finishing them up. There will be times when you've had a hard day with the kids, if you decide to have children, and he'll be there to pick up the slack, even if the bedtime routine is usually your task.

Don't get caught up in keeping score, because in a marriage, you're both on the same team."

"Oh, Dad..."

He smiled, reaching across the cab to bump my chin with his thumb. "He's lucky to have you, Hen. Don't you ever forget that."

"I promise, I won't."

80

TYLER

A bachelor party hardly seemed necessary when I'd been ready to marry Hen a month and a half ago, but here I was, riding around a lazy river outside of Waco with my brothers and Cohen, Jonas, and Steve.

This place was really cool, actually. Some couple had bought property and dug out a massive lazy river and a pond with slides that launched you ten feet in the air before plunging you in the murky water. You could bring your own floats and coolers of beer, and it kind of felt like a high school party with legal alcohol.

After smacking my face and ass in the pond a few times, I decided I much preferred the lazy river where we could float on inner tubes and drink beer at the same time.

Gage said, "Is this your first day off since Hen came back?"

I took a drink, thinking it over. "Actually, yeah..."

"Dang," Steve said. "Tell your boss to give you a day off more often!"

I laughed. Henrietta and I weren't the boss of each other. We were a team, equal partners, just like it was always meant to be. "It's hard work; don't get me wrong, but it doesn't feel like work when I'm with her."

Rhett splashed me with water. "Whipped!"

Cohen and Jonas laughed, and Steve said, "There are advantages to being whipped."

Rhett just shook his head, drinking his beer. "I'll take my wet and wild weekends, thank you very much."

Gage rolled his eyes at our brother, then changed the subject. "I have the sign scheduled for delivery, by the way."

"Perfect," I said.

Cohen asked, "Does she have any idea that you're doing this?"

"Not a clue," I replied with a smile.

Jonas lifted his own beer toward me. "Hats off to you, man. We knew you were a good guy, but this seals the deal."

My chest swelled with pride. Almost a year ago, I'd met these guys and wanted to impress them, wanted to show them that I was worthy of Hen. Earning their approval, along with their friendship, meant the world to me. Because in one day, I'd be giving Hen my last name and every last breath I had as her husband.

81

HENRIETTA

Confession: Maybe I'm a glutton for pain.

"WHERE ARE YOU TAKING ME?" I demanded of my two best friends. They had me blindfolded in the back seat of my car. I'd agreed to a surprise, but that was before I'd been back here for thirty minutes.

Birdie laughed. "We're almost there."

I shook my head. "If you guys brought me to some weird strip club that's open in the middle of the day..." We had all agreed to bypass the stripper since Liv and all three of my sisters-in-law were coming over later for a grown-up slumber party, but Mara was kind of a wild card. Especially since they asked me to go on a pre-bache-lorette-party party with them.

"We're here," Mara squealed.

I reached up and pulled off my blindfold. "No fucking way."

Birdie and Mara were both giggling, but my mouth was open. "What are we doing at a tattoo parlor?"

"Well, you made the last one seem so fun that we thought it was time for a repeat."

"I cried like a baby the whole time," I deadpanned. It turned out I was *highly* averse to pain.

Birdie smiled. "You're not the one getting the tattoo today."

I looked around, wondering who else was here. "Is Tyler getting another tattoo?"

"Nope," Mara said. "Jonas texted me a few minutes ago and said they're all in Waco."

That still didn't answer my question. I gave them both a confused look. "Who is it then?"

With a nervous shrug of her shoulders, Birdie said, "It's us."

"Both of you?" I asked. "I know Mara has ink, but I thought you didn't like tattoos!"

"It's not that I don't like them," Birdie said. "It's just that I've never known what to get before."

"What are you getting?" I asked.

Mara grinned, holding up her phone. On the screen was a cute line drawing of a chicken.

My mouth fell open in a surprised smile. "You're joking, right? This is a prank and we're all going to get margaritas?"

Birdie laughed. "I'll say yes to a margarita after this if it's half as bad as you made it look." She grabbed her purse, reaching for the door handle. "Come on. We have an appointment."

The three of us walked into the tattoo parlor. It was a bit nicer than the one I'd been to for my windmill tattoo, but the tattoo artist up front seemed just as disinterested. I wondered if that was a thing they were taught or if I was just two for two.

The guy with sleeves covering his arms led us back to a chair, and one at a time, my friends got tiny little hens on their ankles. When they were done, the black ink permanently on their skin, I said, "Wait."

Birdie chuckled. "It's a little late for that."

I looked at the tattoo artist—his name was Gabe. "Can you give me one too?"

He shrugged. "Sure. My next appointment flaked."

I grinned. "Great."

Mara took my arm. "Are you sure?"

"I can handle a little pain," I replied with a smile. "And besides, I want to remember my best friends forever."

82

TYLER

"Not like that," Liv said, gesturing her arms at us as we set up white folding chairs behind the house for the wedding. "It has to be a semicircle so everyone can see you two."

Rhett grumbled, but the rest of us adjusted the chairs for the third time until it fit Liv's expectations. With the chairs in place, Liv, Mom, and Tam flitted around the chairs, adding small bundles of flowers to the ones on the aisles.

We'd all decided to go with a wildflower theme, and with all the blooms thriving in Texas, we had plenty to choose from. It was already looking incredible. Dad had paid for a tent rental so there'd be some shade, and then he'd put up twinkle lights around the tables for the reception area.

In true Texas fashion, we had a hog roasted for barbecue, and some of the ladies from town volunteered to bring sides as a gift. There would be plenty of beer and soda covered in ice, resting in tin tanks.

But I didn't give a shit about any of that as long as Hen was happy when we left for our honeymoon in Cancun tomorrow. According to Mara, it was *the* place to go.

With the chairs set up, Liv had us roll out a burlap aisle and stake it to the ground so it wouldn't blow away if the wind picked up. But she had nothing to worry about. It was a perfect July day with crystalline blue skies and the sun gently setting. It was like the whole world knew this moment was always meant to be.

I kept moving chairs, but I didn't get as much yelling from Liv. "Pretty quiet over there," I said, looking up. Then I realized why everyone had stopped talking. Gage stood at the back of the house. Mom was frozen with flowers in her hand, staring at him. Liv and I looked between the two, waiting to see what would happen. And Tam? She looked like a woman slowly backing away from a rattlesnake.

Gage cleared his throat and said, "How can I help?"

Mom let out a strangled cry and walked inside.

All of Gage's features pinched as he watched our mom rush into the house. "I should..." His sentence trailed off.

"I'll handle it," I said.

He and Liv nodded, and I put a hand on Tam's shoulder just to let her know everything was okay before following our mom inside. I followed the sound of her quiet crying to hers and dad's bedroom on the main floor off the living room.

She sat on her bed, one leg bent on the mattress and the other dangling over the edge. Her curly hair fell in her face, and she had her hand pressed to her mouth, trying —and failing—to quiet herself.

She looked up at me for a moment, then back at the bed, her shoulders shaking.

I took a breath and sat beside her, rubbing a hand on her back. This was the woman who'd lain next to me after every bad dream, made sure I always had a hot meal at night, who pretended she didn't see me cry the day I moved into an apartment away from home.

She was the strongest person I knew, and I hated seeing her like this. "Mom..."

Her eyes were red as she looked at me. "I'm sorry."

I shook my head, rubbing her shoulder. "Don't be sorry."

"It's just... I... his hairline changed."

"Don't tell him that," I teased.

She laughed despite herself, but then her expression fell again. "How many years is it going to be before we make amends? Will I be old and gray before I get to have my boy over for dinner again?"

"You'll never be gray," I told her, brushing back a curl. "There's hair dye for that."

She gave me a look.

"Maybe today will be a chance for him and Dad both to get some perspective. But no one ever said you had to join in on their fight."

She reached to the nightstand for a tissue and blew her nose. With it clear, she said, "I know I'm supposed to be giving you advice today, but I don't think you're the one who needs it."

I chuckled. "I've messed up plenty of times."

"You have, because that's what people do, but it's more than that."

"What do you mean?" I asked.

"You remember when you were younger and you had such a hard time meeting people?"

I nodded.

"One day in therapy, I don't know if you remember this, but you said something I've thought about for years. You said, 'It's not that I'm afraid to meet people. It's that I don't know if I have enough room.'"

I smiled slightly, the memory fuzzy.

"You were so worried that if you met too many people you wouldn't be able to give them all of yourself. You wanted to remember their names, their favorite colors, have enough time to play with them all on the playground... It made you so anxious that you choked up every time you met someone new. And then it happened at school and kids picked on you for being shy, and it all snowballed from there."

Her fingers toyed with the tissue, rolling it in a ball. "I always knew you'd make the best partner to someone, because anything you do, you give all of yourself."

My eyes felt hot with tears. I felt seen in a way I rarely did. "That's exactly what I want to give to Hen."

She reached up, hugging me close. "I love you and your big heart, Tyler Jay."

"I love you too."

83

HENRIETTA

Confession: Everyone talks about cold feet on their wedding day, but mine were toasty warm.

I STOOD in the hotel conference room where we were all getting ready and looked at myself in the mirror.

I was a *bride*.

The wedding dress I'd bought in Dallas with my mom, grandma, and best friends just a couple days ago couldn't have been more perfect. Everyone had told me it was crazy to wait until the last minute and buy a dress off the rack, but if I was being honest, I didn't care what I wore as long as Tyler was standing at the end of the aisle, ready to say *I do*. Our marriage and the people celebrating Tyler and me were so much more important than having the "perfect" dress.

But despite the last-minute trip, we'd found *the* dress. It had been tucked at the very back of a sale rack as if someone had stowed it away there for me. It was a pure white, floor-length gown with off-the-shoulder straps and lacy fabric that nipped in at my waist and flowed out, giving the illusion of an hourglass figure I'd never had before.

Underneath the dress, I wore the boots Tyler had given me. The intricate leather design matched the dress perfectly, and I couldn't pass up the chance to wear a gift from my husband-to-be.

Grandma appeared in the mirror, pushing her wheel-chair behind me. "You are a beautiful bride," she said.

"Thanks, Grandma." I turned to smile at her and noticed something in her hands. A velvet blue box. "What is that?"

Her weathered hands rested atop it, her gold wedding band still shining on her left hand. I came from a long line of happy, meaningful, fruitful marriages, and I couldn't wait to carry on the tradition.

"You know the saying," she said. "Something old, something new, something borrowed, something blue?"

I nodded. I hadn't thought about it much in the rush of the last couple months. Just having my friends and family here and knowing I'd be married to the man of my dreams had been more than enough for me.

But she pulled the box open, showing a beautiful hair comb made of what I guessed was sterling silver. Several blue jewels rested in its ornate design. "My grandma gave this to me on my wedding day, and I want to pass it on to you. So it won't be borrowed, but it is old and blue."

I covered my heart with my hands. "Grandma... it's so precious. Are you sure you don't want to keep it?"

Her lips trembled as she shook her head and said, "May I?"

"Of course," I breathed. I knelt next to her, resting my hand on the arm of her chair. Her fingers were featherlight as she pressed the clip at the back of my hair, above the intricate bun Liv had done for me.

"Perfect," she said, removing her hands.

I hugged her tight, then turned to look in the mirror. My mouth fell open as I saw myself, really saw myself. I may not have been small in any way. I may not have the perfect smile or a high-level corporate job.

But I looked every bit worthy of the woman to be Tyler's wife. And I was so glad he agreed.

The door to the conference room opened, and Mara, Birdie, and Liv came back in from taking bridesmaids photos. Mom followed them in with the photographer we hired. She posed me in front of the window and snapped photos of me with my wildflower bouquet picked directly from the pasture behind the Griffens' family home.

When the photographer lowered her camera, Mom smiled at me, tears in her eyes. "It's time."

I'd never been more ready for anything in my life.

84

TYLER

Mom stood in the doorway of my childhood bedroom. "It's time."

All of the groomsmen had changed up here, then gone outside to help with last minute details or directing guests to the best places to park and sit. It was just me up here now, and I still couldn't get this handmade boutonniere Liv made to rest straight on my lapel.

"Let me," Mom said, replacing my hands with hers and easily maneuvering the pin into place. "There you go."

I gave her a grateful smile. "Thanks."

She put her arm around me, looking in the mirror above my dresser. "You look very handsome. I'm glad you decided to go with suits."

"I think Hen's family would have been horrified if I walked down the aisle in jeans." I chuckled. But the truth was, I wanted to look my best for her. When she saw me today, I wanted her to see a man who loved her, who cared for her, and who would always put his best foot forward.

Mom looped her arm through mine. "Let's get down there."

We walked together down the stairs, and my brothers waited for us in the living room. I could already hear the guitar playing outside. My best friend from high school had a way with the guitar, and it sounded beautiful even from in here.

I walked Mom down the burlap aisle to her chair, giving her a kiss on the cheek as she sat next to Dad. I stood at the front of the aisle next to the pastor. Matthew Cole had gone to school with me, and now he preached at the cowboy church outside of Fort Worth.

I looked over the guests in folding chairs. There were about fifty people, half friends, half family, all here to witness me tie my life to Hen's forevermore.

And then the music on the guitar changed.

Laila nudged Kenner out the door, and he sprinted down the aisle to me, the ring pillow waving in one hand. A gasp went throughout the crowd, and then a chuckle when he reached me.

"Hey, buddy," I said to my nephew-to-be.

"I can run really fast in these shoes. Did you see?"

I chuckled. "Yeah. I saw. Are the rings still there?" I really hoped they'd tied them good, because I didn't want to be searching for gold bands in the grass.

Seeming to remember his job, Kenner held the pillow up to his face. "Yep." He handed the pillow to me, and I double-checked, just in case.

Still there.

"Great job, Kenner. Mission accomplished." I stuck

my fist out for him, and he tapped his little knuckles to mine, blowing it up afterward. As he sprinted back to his mom, the guests chuckled too.

Mara and Rhett walked out of the house next, her hand on his arm. The deep blue dress flowed around her as she stepped down the aisle holding a small bouquet of wildflowers. Birdie and Gage stepped out after, both smiling as they followed along.

And then everyone stood. The back door to the house opened, and my heart stopped.

Henrietta walked outside, her arm looped around her dad's. There might have been music playing still, but I couldn't hear it.

The woman I loved, the woman of my dreams, was walking toward me. Her long white dress fit her perfectly, and were those...? I grinned, seeing the toes of her boots peeking under her dress. But it was her smile that captivated me.

Her beautiful brown eyes were shining in the Texas sun, and her smile was even brighter. This woman was mine. And this day?

It was ours.

I barely dragged my eyes off of her long enough to hear her dad say, "Take care of her, son."

"I will," I promised.

He put her hand in mine, and I held her other hand too, running my thumbs over the back of her hands.

"Hi," I whispered.

"Hi," she said with a smile.

My throat felt tight, and I couldn't get any words out as the pastor started talking about weddings, about love and matrimony and the holy bond that tied us together.

We exchanged rings.

Henrietta repeated her vows, each promise a balm to my heart.

And then Matthew said, "The groom wishes to say something before he speaks his vows."

Henrietta whispered, "Tyler, I thought we weren't writing our own vows."

"This is something extra," I replied before taking the microphone from Matthew. I reached into my jacket pocket and held up the piece of paper I'd been staring at ever since she said yes. But instead of looking at her, I faced our guests. I faced her family.

"The second I met Henrietta, I knew there was something different about her. Something special. And that knowing kept me chasing after her, made me want to learn everything about her. The time we spent together, the more I could see her heart for you all, the people she loves most. I knew anything between us would require a sacrifice. I could give up on my dreams of settling here to be with her. Or she would have to move away from the people she loves so much to be with me." My throat got tight, guilt eating at me even though I knew we'd both made the right choice. Even though our location could change, our love for each other, and our families, would not.

"I think you know what decision we made together. And even though this union is between myself and my beautiful bride..." I smiled at Henrietta, and her smile in return settled me again. "I'd be remiss to think it didn't involve all of you too. I've seen the way Henrietta loves you, and through her eyes, I've come to love you just as much. I want to promise you that even though Hen is becoming my wife, she'll always be your friend, your sister, your daughter and granddaughter too. I promise to always make time for your bond and value it just as much as she does. I am so grateful to be joining your family today, just as Hen is joining mine."

I saw tears streaming down her mom and grandma's cheeks. Even her brothers' and dad's eyes were red. As I turned back to Hen, I noticed tracks of moisture streaking from her eyes.

I passed the microphone back to Matthew and reached up with my thumbs, wiping her tears away. She held my wrists, whispering, "I love you."

My jaw trembled as I rested my forehead against hers. "I meant every word."

"I know," she replied.

Matthew continued the ceremony, and I put all my heart into the vows as I promised my life to the woman across from me.

And when he said, "I now pronounce you man and wife. You may kiss the bride," I wrapped my arms around my wife and made our first kiss as a married couple one we'd remember for the rest of our lives.

HENRIETTA

Confession: I may always be a funny fat friend... but I'm also so much more.

SPARKLERS LIT our path as Tyler and I left the reception to his truck that Liv had decorated. Flowers lined the truck bed, and the back window said JUST MARRIED surrounded by hearts.

He opened the door for me and helped me in, making sure my dress was fully inside before closing the door. When he got in, he leaned across the middle seat and gave me a kiss before pulling away.

I watched out the window, seeing the twinkle lights fade away. Tyler turned right out of their drive, and my eyebrows drew together. "Weren't we supposed to go that way to get to Dallas?" We had a one-night stay before our flight tomorrow at a place Tyler described as a "ritzy mix of character and culture."

A smile danced along his lips, illuminated by the green dash lights. "We have a stop to make first."

My eyebrows drew together. "Did you forget something at the school?"

"Something like that," he replied, turning down another dirt road.

I shook my head at him, smiling. "Married for four hours, and you're already keeping me on my toes."

He squeezed my hand, lifting my knuckles to his lips. "I hope you're ready, because I plan to do that every day for the rest of my life."

"Of course, Mr. Griffen," I said, loving the way *our* name sounded on my tongue. "But is it okay if I change there? I'd rather not waltz into a fancy hotel still in my wedding dress."

"You can get naked any time you want," he said, his voice husky with desire. The wedding night was something we'd both been fantasizing about for the last month and a half.

I bit my lip. "Keep looking at me like that, and we won't make it to the hotel."

His eyes were hot on mine for a moment before he looked back to the road. We pulled into town and took the familiar city streets to the schoolhouse. We still hadn't decided on a name for it. I thought it should be something like Cottonwood Estates, but he'd wanted to make it more personal to us.

Luckily, we had a few months left of construction to get the units completed, and that was plenty of time to decide.

He parked in front of the schoolhouse, and I got out, going to the tailgate to get my bags from the truck bed.

"Are you insane, woman?" Tyler chastised, coming beside me. "Let me get your suitcase. You go inside."

Shaking my head at him, I lifted the hem of my skirt and walked toward the school until my eyes caught something different.

Underneath the new antique security light, there was a sign.

The Hen House

I stared at the letters, my jaw slack, until Tyler came to stand beside me, wrapping his arm around my shoulders.

"What is this?" I asked.

"It's our home," he replied. "What do you think of the name?"

I looked from him to the sign and back again. "You want to name it after me?"

He palmed my cheek, cradling my face in his hand. "*You* are what makes this place a home. You did it at Blue Bird, and I have no doubt you'll do the same here. You're done fading into the background, baby. It's time to have you front and center, right where you belong."

Tears came to my eyes for the millionth time that day. All my life, I'd thought I was destined to be the funny fat friend. Always taking a back seat to other people and their needs, their stories. But this man, my husband, had shown me, every single day, that I could be so much more.

I kissed his lips, rejoicing in my role, not as the funny fat friend, but as his wife, as the main character of my own happily ever after.

EPILOGUE
HENRIETTA

Confession: I love the life we're building together.

CHRISTMAS

TYLER and I walked up the sidewalk to my parents' house, wheeling a suitcase packed to the *brim* with presents for my family.

Instead of knocking, I opened the door and walked inside. Even if I lived in Texas now, this place would always be home, and my parents made sure I knew their door would always be open.

"UNCLE TYLER!" Kenner yelled, running to Tyler and wrapping his arms around his legs. A'yisha toddled behind him, saying, "Unca Tya."

I shook my head, scooping her up and saying, "What

am I? Chopped liver?" I tickled her sides and she giggled, making me grin.

Our other greetings may not have been as enthusiastic as Kenner's, but they were filled with love all the same. My parents hugged me tight, Raven's pregnant belly pressed into me as she gave me a side hug, and I kissed my new nephew, Tevon, on the forehead. "You are just precious," I said, setting A'yisha down and taking the five-month-old in my arms. A'yisha toddled away, going to play with Kenner.

The party continued, as if we hadn't missed a beat in our relationships, with eggnog being passed around, cartoons playing on TV for the kids, and a competitive card game going on at the table. Grandma was winning.

"Dang, Cordelia," Tyler said. "Those ladies at the home must be whipping you into shape."

Grandma kept her poker face as she reached for another card from the stack. "It's the other way around. Someone needs to keep them on their toes."

"Speaking of keeping people on their toes," I said...

Everyone turned to me, and I grinned. I'd been bursting to tell everyone the news since we walked in, and I couldn't wait any longer.

"I'm getting another grandbaby?" Mom cried.

I laughed, shaking my head. "Not yet." I exchanged a grin with Tyler, who'd been very eager to practice the act, even if we planned to enjoy marriage just the two of us for a little while.

"What's going on then?" Johmarcus asked.

I grinned, saying, "We're opening up other locations of The Hen House!"

"What!" Bertrand said. "That's awesome!"

I nodded excitedly. We'd opened our location just a few months ago, but the concept of boutique senior living in a small town had taken off with the media. Turned out people loved the idea of having a homey, comfortable place for their parents and grandparents to live where they could have their privacy and enjoy activities like gardening while still having a nurse check in on them from time to time.

"We caught the eye of an investor," Tyler said. "They cut us a deal to find and restore five older buildings across Texas, and if this goes well, they want to partner with us to make it a nationwide franchise."

My family cheered for us, and Dad got up from the table to walk around and hug us both. "I'm proud of you two."

"Me too," I admitted. After stopping college with an associate degree and working the same job for so long, I thought just being a property manager was my future. But Tyler had shown me there could be more to life. Especially with my best friend, my partner, my husband, my *home* at my side.

WANT to see where Henrietta and Tyler are three years down the road? Get their free bonus scene today!

Everyone thought Gage Griffen would be the eternal bachelor, but he'll find his happily ever after in **Hello Billionaire**! Grab your copy now! Or save when you purchase the Hello Series Bundle from Kelsie.

Access the free bonus content!

Start reading Hello Billionaire today!

Get the series bundle!

AUTHOR'S NOTE

Being the funny fat friend is *hard*.

I remember boys befriending me. I thought they might like me... until then asking for one of my classmate's numbers.

I remember going out to bars with my college friends and watching all of them get asked to dance while I stood on the sidelines, holding purses and drinks like a dutiful friend.

It hurt, every time. It made me look at myself and then look at them and ask... Why are they so much better than me?

I used to wish that once, just once, a guy would approach me first, because he was interested in *me*.

I got lucky, as I started dating my now husband in my senior year of high school. I wasn't single for long. But I imagine, if I had been single until twenty-eight, being the funny fat friend would have been even more difficult. Add in online dating, with the instant rejection of swiping at a picture, and you have a recipe for low confidence.

When you're the friend that is always overlooked, you start wondering things about yourself, and then you start assuming things about other people.

He wasn't interested in me because of my size.

He's only paying attention to me to get to my friend.

He wants to take me out because he has a fat fetish.

A guy like that would never be seen with a girl like me.

These thoughts are there to protect you, to make sense of rejection and loneliness. But soon the voice in your head isn't so nice. And when a guy like Tyler shows you genuine interest, it can feel suspicious.

That's why I love what Mara said to Henrietta.

Let him choose his intentions.

When you place the responsibility for someone else's feelings or perspectives on your shoulders, you lose every single time. Just because you have grown up in a society conditioned to scorn fat people and view them as less than, just because you've navigated life in a bigger body and struggle to love yourself, doesn't mean you're not worthy of love.

You deserve love and affection at any size, even if you're having a hard time loving yourself.

Self-love isn't a lightning moment where all of a sudden it all comes together and years of self-deprecation are undone.

Instead, it's a puzzle. You put little pieces together, one at a time, until you realize you were building a picture of yourself. Even when there are holes, pieces missing, you can start to see yourself for who you are. Who you could be.

For Henrietta, there were lots of little pieces that

came together. She had friends with great advice. A love interest who told her how beautiful she was. A family to support her. A beautiful moment at a friend's wedding in her bridesmaid dress. And finally, the freedom to be herself, without the expectations she'd picked up along the way.

And I'm here to tell you, it's okay if you only have a few pieces of the puzzle. It's okay if you look at a photo of yourself and have a negative reaction or opt for sleeves on a summer day. It's normal not to have it all together.

But I also want you to look for those little pieces that will show you more of your true, beautiful, worthy self.

Because you deserve to see the full puzzle, no matter how long it takes.

ACKNOWLEDGMENTS

Oh my goodness! This last part of the book is always so fun, and I'm going to savor a few minutes thanking all these wonderful people who helped bring the book to you!

As always, I want to thank you for reading this story. The reason I write is to make readers like you feel beautiful, exactly as you are. I hope you felt the love in every page.

My family is my biggest supporter and biggest motivator. Although my boys would rather I write more children's books about poop and farts, they make me feel like a rock star when they brag about their mom being an author. My husband and I are likely qualified for a circus act at this point with all the juggling we do. I'm so glad he believes in me and my business, even when I have doubts. My siblings have always encouraged me and helped spread the word about my books. I love them for believing in me and my work.

The group members in the Kelsie Stelting: Readers Club who read my YA books and then encouraged me to write curvy adult stories... thank you! I was so terrified of writing spice, but I've found so much fun and freedom in these last three stories. You've changed the trajectory of my career, challenged me, and encouraged me to be an even better writer. Thank you times a million.

I'm dedicated to writing a cast of diverse characters that reflects the real world, and as a white woman, I couldn't do that without tons of help. Thank you to my sensitivity readers, Kelsea Reeves and Angela Leafi, for helping me get Hen and her family right. You make the world of fiction better with your voices.

My writer friend, and soon to be partner in crime, Sally Henson, has encouraged me to write adult books and throw myself into these stories. I love how she pushes me as a person, a mom, and a writer. Love you Sal Gal.

Two other writer friends have chatted consistently with me about promoting my books and spreading the curvy girl love to the world! Anne-Marie Meyer and Judy Corry, thanks for being a sounding board and source of encouragement!

My editor, Tricia Harden, has seen me from sweet country YA romance to spicy and tender adult books, and I have loved having her walk beside me every step of the way! She is the best cheerleader, friend, and mentor with the biggest heart and most wonderful soul. Thank you for being you.

The cover on this book came to life thanks to Najla Qamber and her team. I love how responsive, understanding, and creative she is. She's so dedicated to helping my vision become a reality, and I absolutely adore her for that! Thank you much!

Maddie Zahm, although I don't know you, I loved listening to your song. It was an inspiration to see you help curvy girls feel seen and heard with your words.

To all the lovely ladies in Hoss's Hussies, I adore you. Thanks for making such a fun space for adult women to hang out and lift each other up. You help me see the good in people and are the kind of friends I love to write about.

ALSO BY KELSIE HOSS

The Hello Series

Hello Single Dad

Hello Fake Boyfriend

Hello Temptation

Hello Billionaire

Hello Doctor

Hello Heartbreaker

Hello Tease

JOIN THE PARTY

Want to talk about Hello Temptation? Join Hoss's Hussies today!

Join here: https://www.facebook.com/groups/hossshussies

ABOUT THE AUTHOR

Kelsie Hoss writes sexy romantic comedies with plus size leads. Her favorite dessert is ice cream, her favorite food is chocolate chip pancakes, and… now she's hungry.

You can find her enjoying one of the aforementioned treats, soaking up some sunshine like an emotional house plant, or loving on her three sweet boys.

Her alter ego, Kelsie Stelting, writes sweet, body positive romance for young adults. You can learn more (and even grab some special merch) at kelsiehoss.com.

facebook.com/authorkelsiehoss

instagram.com/kelsiehoss

Made in United States
Orlando, FL
25 May 2024

pantoprazole, pemetrexed, pentobarbital, phenobarbital, phenytoin, rituximab, sargramostim, sodium bicarbonate, SMZ/TMP, thiopental, trastuzumab, TPN.

ADVERSE EFFECTS CNS: Dizziness, fatigue, light-headedness, *headache, sedation.* GI: *Diarrhea,* constipation, dry mouth, transient increases in liver aminotransferases and bilirubin. **Other:** Hypersensitivity reactions.

INTERACTIONS Drug: Do not use with **apomorphine** due to risk of hypotension. Do not use with **hydroxyhloroquine, mifepristone,** and other agents affecting QT interval due to risk of QT prolongation.

PHARMACOKINETICS Peak: 1–1.5 h. **Metabolism:** In liver (CYP3A4). **Elimination:** 44–60% in urine within 24 h; ~25% in feces. **Half-Life:** 3 h.

NURSING IMPLICATIONS

Assessment & Drug Effects
- Monitor fluid and electrolyte status. Diarrhea, which may cause fluid and electrolyte imbalance, is a potential adverse effect of the drug.
- Monitor cardiovascular status, especially in patients with a history of coronary artery disease. Rare cases of tachycardia and angina have been reported.

Patient & Family Education
- Be aware that headache requiring an analgesic for relief is a common adverse effect.

OPICAPONE
(oh-pik'-a-pone)

Ongentys
Classifications: ANTIPARKINSON AGENTS, CATECHOLAMINE O–METHYLTRANSFERASE (COMT) INHIBITOR
Therapeutic: ANTIPARKINSON
Prototype: tolcapone

AVAILABILITY Tablet

ACTION & *THERAPEUTIC EFFECT*
A reversible and selective inhibitor of COMT, a major degradation pathway for levodopa resulting in more sustained serum levodopa levels. This provides for increased concentrations available for absorption across the blood-brain barrier thereby providing for increased CNS levels of dopamine, the active metabolite of levodopa. *Provides for increased CNS levels of dopamine.*

USES Adjunctive to levodopa/carbidopa to treat Parkinson's disease

CONTRAINDICATIONS Concomitant use of nonselective monoamine oxidase inhibitors; pheochromocytoma, paraganglioma, or other catecholamine secreting neoplasms.

CAUTIOUS USE Risk for CNS depression, dyskinesia, hallucinations, hypotension, impulse control disorders; hepatic impairment; renal impairment; psychotic disorders; pregnancy (in utero exposure by cause fetal harm); lactation.

ROUTE & DOSAGE

Parkinson's Disease
Adult: **PO** 50 mg once daily

Hepatic Impairment Dosage Adjustment

Child-Pugh class B: 25 mg once daily
Child-Pugh class C: Avoid use

ADMINISTRATION

Oral

- Administer at bedtime; do not eat for 1 hour before and at least 1 hour after dose.
- Store at < 30° C (< 86° F).

ADVERSE EFFECTS CV: Orthostatic hypotension, hypotension, increased serum CK, syncope. GI: Constipation. Musculoskeletal: Dyskinesia.

INTERACTIONS Drug: Do not combine with nonselective MAO inhibitors (phenelzine, isocarboxazid); **Dobutamine, dopamine, epinephrine, isoetharine, isoproterenol, methyldopa, norepinephrine** may increase heart rates, possible cause arrhythmias, excessive changes in BP. May enhance effects of CNS deppressants.

PHARMACOKINETICS Peak: 2 h. Distribution: 99% protein bound. Metabolism: Primarily through sulphation. Elimination: 70% excreted in feces Half-Life: 1–2 h.

NURSING IMPLICATIONS

Assessment & Drug Effects

- Monitor baseline and periodic BP.
- Monitor lab tests: Liver function tests; renal function tests.

Patient & Family Education

- Avoid driving or doing other tasks that require alertness until you see how this drug affects you.

- To lower the risk of feeling dizzy or passing out, rise slowly from lying or sitting positions. Be careful going up and down stairs.
- Notify your doctor or get medical help right away if you have any of the following signs or symptoms of allergic reaction such as rash, hives, itching; red, swollen, blistered, or peeling skin with or without fever; wheezing; tightness in the chest or throat; trouble breathing, swallowing, or talking; unusual hoarsenses; or swelling of the mouth, face, lips, tongue, or throat; or any dizziness or passing out.

OPIUM, POWDERED OPIUM TINCTURE (LAUDANUM) ⚠

(oh'pee-um)

Classification: NARCOTIC (OPIATE AGONIST) ANALGESIC; ANTI-DIARRHEAL
Therapeutic: NARCOTIC ANALGESIC; ANTIDIARRHEAL
Prototype: Morphine
Controlled Substance: Schedule II

AVAILABILITY Tincture

ACTION & *THERAPEUTIC EFFECT*

Contains several natural alkaloids including morphine, codeine, papaverine. Antidiarrheal due to inhibition of GI motility and propulsion; leads to prolonged transit of intestinal contents, desiccation of feces, and constipation. *Antidiarrheal activity due to inhibition of GI motility.*

USES Diarrhea.

CONTRAINDICATIONS Diarrhea caused by poisoning (until poison is completely eliminated).

CAUTIOUS USE History of opiate agonist dependence; asthma;

severe prostatic hypertrophy; hepatic disease; pregnancy (category C); lactation; children.

ROUTE & DOSAGE

Acute Diarrhea
Adult: **PO** 0.6 mL qid (max: 6 mL/day)

ADMINISTRATION

Oral
- Do not confuse this preparation with camphorated opium tincture (paregoric), which contains only 2 mg anhydrous morphine/5 mL, thus requiring a higher dose volume than that required for therapeutic dose of Deodorized Opium Tincture.
- Give drug diluted with about one third glass of water to ensure passage of entire dose into stomach.
- Store in tight, light-resistant containers.

ADVERSE EFFECTS CV: Bradycardia, hypotension. **Respiratory:** Respiratory depression. **CNS:** CNS depression, dizziness, drowsiness. **GI:** Constipation, stomach cramps. **GU:** Decreased urine output. **Musculoskeletal:** Weakness.

INTERACTIONS Drug: Alcohol and other CNS DEPRESSANTS add to CNS effects.

PHARMACOKINETICS Absorption: Variable absorption from GI tract. **Distribution:** Crosses placenta; distributed into breast milk. **Metabolism:** In liver. **Elimination:** In urine.

NURSING IMPLICATIONS

Assessment & Drug Effects
- Withhold medication and report to prescriber if respirations are

12/min or below or have changed in character and rate.
- Discontinue as soon as diarrhea is controlled; note character and frequency of stools.
- Offer small amounts of fluid frequently but attempt to maintain 3000–4000 mL fluid total in 24 h.
- Monitor body weight, I&O ratio and pattern, and temperature. If patient develops fever of 38.8° C (102° F) or above, electrolyte and hydration levels may need to be evaluated. Consult prescriber.

Patient & Family Education
- Be aware that constipation may be a consequence of antidiarrheal therapy but that normal habit pattern usually is reestablished with resumption of normal dietary intake.
- Note: Addiction is possible with prolonged use or with drug abuse.

OPRELVEKIN
(o-prel've-kin)
Neumega
Classification: BLOOD FORMER; HEMATOPOIETIC GROWTH FACTOR
Therapeutic: HEMATOPOIETIC GROWTH FACTOR
Prototype: Epoetin alfa

AVAILABILITY Solution for injection

ACTION & *THERAPEUTIC EFFECT*
The primary hematopoietic activity of oprelvekin is stimulation of production of megakaryocytes (precursors of blood platelets) and thrombocytes by the bone marrow. *Effectiveness indicated by return of postnadir platelet count toward normal (50,000 or higher). Increases platelet count in a dose-dependent manner.*

USES Prevention of severe thrombocytopenia following myelosuppressive chemotherapy (not effective after myeloablative chemotherapy).

CONTRAINDICATIONS Hypersensitivity to oprelvekin; myeloablative chemotherapy; myeloid malignancies; lactation.

CAUTIOUS USE Left ventricular dysfunction, cardiac disease, CHF, history of atrial arrhythmias, or other arrhythmias; electrolyte imbalance, hypokalemia; respiratory disease; papilledema; thromboembolic disorders; older adults; cerebrovascular disease, stroke, TIAs; pleural effusion, pericardial effusion, ascites, ICP, brain tumor, visual disturbances; hepatic or renal dysfunction; pregnancy (category C); children.

ROUTE & DOSAGE

Thrombocytopenia

Adult: **Subcutaneous** 50 mcg/kg once daily starting 6–24 h after completing chemotherapy and continuing until platelet count is 50,000 cells/mcL or higher or up to 21 days

Renal Impairment Dosage Adjustment

CrCl less than 30 mL/min: 25 mcg/kg

ADMINISTRATION

- Note: Do not use if solution is discolored or if it contains particulate matter.

Subcutaneous

- Reconstitute solution by gently injecting 1 mL of sterile water for injection (without preservative) toward the sides of the vial. Keep needle in vial and gently swirl to dissolve but do not shake solution. Without removing needle, withdraw specified amount of oprelvekin for injection.
- Give as single dose into the abdomen, thigh, hip, or upper arm.
- Discard any unused portion of the vial. It contains no preservatives.
- Use reconstituted solution within 3 h; store at 2°–8° C (36°–46° F) until used.
- Store unopened vials at 2°–8° C (36°–46° F). Do not freeze.

ADVERSE EFFECTS CV: *Tachycardia,* vasodilation, palpitations, syncope, atrial fibrillation/flutter, peripheral edema, capillary leak syndrome. **Respiratory:** *Dyspnea, rhinitis, cough, pharyngitis,* pleural effusion, pulmonary edema, exacerbation of preexisting pleural effusion. **CNS:** *Headache, dizziness, insomnia,* nervousness. **HEENT:** Conjunctival injection, amblyopia. **Skin:** Alopecia, *rash,* skin discoloration, exfoliative dermatitis. **GI:** *Nausea, vomiting, mucositis, diarrhea,* oral moniliasis, anorexia, constipation, dyspepsia. **Hematologic:** Ecchymosis. **Other:** *Edema, neutropenic fever, fever,* asthenia, pain, chills, myalgia, bone pain, dehydration.

INTERACTIONS Drug: No clinically significant established.

PHARMACOKINETICS Absorption: 80% from subcutaneous injection site. **Onset:** Days 5–9. **Duration:** 7 days after last dose. **Distribution:** Distributes to highly perfused organs. **Elimination:** In urine. **Half-Life:** 6.9 h.

NURSING IMPLICATIONS

Black Box Warning

Oprelvekin has been associated with allergic or hypersensitivity

Common adverse effects in *italic;* life-threatening effects <u>underlined;</u> generic names in **bold;** classifications in SMALL CAPS; ✤ Canadian drug name; ◐ Prototype drug; △ Alert

reactions, including anaphylaxis. Oprelvekin should be discontinued if patient develops an allergic or hypersensitivity reaction.

Assessment & Drug Effects
- Monitor carefully for and immediately report S&S of fluid overload, hypokalemia, and cardiac arrhythmias.
- Monitor persons with preexisting fluid retention carefully (e.g., CHF, pleural effusion, ascites) for worsening of symptoms.
- Monitor lab tests: Baseline and periodic CBC; platelet count at nadir and until adequate recovery; periodic serum electrolytes.

Patient & Family Education
- Review patient information leaflet with special attention to administration directions.
- Report any of the following to the prescriber: Shortness of breath, edema of arms and/or legs, chest pain, unusual fatigue or weakness, irregular heartbeat, blurred vision.

ORITAVANCIN
(or-ita-van′sin)
Orbactiv
Classification: ANTIBIOTIC; LIPOGLYCOPROTEIN
Therapeutic: ANTIBIOTIC
Prototype: Vancomycin

AVAILABILITY Lyophilized powder

ACTION & *THERAPEUTIC EFFECT*
Binds to components required for the bacterial cell wall preventing cell wall synthesis. *It is bactericidal against Staphylococcus aureus, Streptococcus pyogenes, and Enterococcus faecalis.*

USES Treatment of adult patients with acute bacterial skin and skin structure infections (ABSSSI) caused or suspected to be caused by susceptible isolates of designated gram-positive microorganisms.

CONTRAINDICATIONS Known hypersensitivity to oritavancin; IV unfractionated heparin sodium contraindicated for 48 h after receiving oritavancin; oritavancin induced *Clostridium difficile* associated diarrhea; oritavanicn induced osteomylitis.

CAUTIOUS USE Hypersensitivity to other antibiotics; concomitant warfarin use; colitis; severe renal or hepatic impairment; pregnancy (category C); lactation. Safety and efficacy in children younger than 18 y not established.

ROUTE & DOSAGE

Skin and Skin Structure Infections
Adult: **IV** 1200 mg one time dose

ADMINISTRATION

Intravenous

PREPARE: **IV Infusion:** Three 400 mg vials are need for a single 1200 mg dose. Reconstitute each 400 mg vial with 40 mL of SW for injection to yield 10 mg/mL. Swirl vials gently until completely dissolved. Do not shake. Must be further diluted as follows: Withdraw and discard 120 mL from a 1000 mL bag of D5W; then withdraw 40 mL from each reconstituted vial and add to the D5W bag to bring volume to 1000 mL with a concentration of 1.2 mg/mL.
ADMINISTER: **IV Infusion:** Infuse over 3 h. Flush line before/after with D5W if line used for other drugs or solutions.

INCOMPATIBILITIES: Do not mix or infuse with any other drugs or solutions.

- Storage: Bag for IV infusion should be used within 6 h when stored at room temperature, or within 12 h when refrigerated at 2–8° C (36–46° F). The combined storage time (reconstituted solution in the vial and diluted solution in the bag) and 3 h infusion time should not exceed 6 h at room temperature or 12 h if refrigerated.

ADVERSE EFFECTS CV: Tachycardia. **Respiratory:** Bronchospasm, wheezing. **CNS:** Dizziness, headache. **Endocrine:** Hyperuricemia, hypoglycemia, increased ALT and AST, increased bilirubin. **Skin:** Angioedema, erythema multiforme, leucocytoclastic vasculitis, urticarial. **GI:** Clostridium difficile-associated diarrhea, diarrhea, *nausea*, vomiting. **Musculoskeletal:** Myalgia, tenosynovitis. **Hematological:** Anemia, eosinophilia. **Other:** Hypersensitivity reaction, infusion site reaction, limb and subcutaneous abscess, osteomyelitis, peripheral edema, pruritus, rash.

DIAGNOSTIC TEST INTERFERENCE
Drug: Oritavancin has no effect on the coagulation system; however, prolongs *aPTT* for 48 h and *INR* for up to 24 h.

INTERACTIONS Drug: Oritavancin may increase the levels of other drugs requiring CYP2C9 or CYP2C19 for metabolism (e.g., **warfarin**) and may decrease the levels of other drugs requiring CYP2D6 or CYP3A4 for metabolism (e.g., **aripiprazole, axitinib, hydrocodone, ibrutinib, saxagliptin, simeprevir**).

PHARMACOKINETICS Distribution: Widely distributed with 85% plasma protein bound. **Metabolism:** Not significantly metabolized. **Elimination:** Slowly excreted unchanged via renal and fecal elimination. **Half-Life:** 245 h.

NURSING IMPLICATIONS

Assessment & Drug Effects
- Monitor patients for any infusion-related reactions.
- Monitor for S&S of superinfection, including *C. difficile*-associated diarrhea (CDAD) and pseudomembranous colitis, that may develop within days or up to several months after completion of therapy.
- If superinfection is suspected, withhold drug and contact prescriber.

Patient & Family Education
- Report promptly to prescriber if you develop frequent watery or bloody diarrhea.
- Consult with prescriber if you are a female who is or plans to become pregnant.
- Do not breast-feed without consulting prescriber.

ORLISTAT
(or'li-stat)
Alli, Xenical
Classification: ANORECTANT; NONSYSTEMIC LIPASE INHIBITOR
Therapeutic: ANORECTANT
Prototype: Diethylpropion

AVAILABILITY Capsule

ACTION & *THERAPEUTIC EFFECT*
Nonsystemic inhibitor of gastrointestinal lipase. Reduces intestinal absorption of dietary fat by forming inactive enzymes with pancreatic

and gastric lipase in the GI tract. *Indicated by weight loss/decreased body mass index (BMI). Reduces caloric intake in obese individuals.*

USES Weight loss and weight maintenance in conjunction with diet and exercise.

CONTRAINDICATIONS Hypersensitivity to orlistat; malabsorption syndrome; cholestasis; gallbladder disease; hypothyroidism; organic causes of obesity; anorexia nervosa, bulimia nervosa; pregnancy (category X).

CAUTIOUS USE Gastrointestinal diseases including frequent diarrhea; known dietary deficiencies in fat soluble vitamins (i.e., A, D, E); history of calcium oxalate nephrolithiasis or hyperoxaluria; older adults; lactation; children younger than 12 y.

ROUTE & DOSAGE

Weight Loss

Adult/Adolescent (older than 12 y): **PO** 60 or 120 mg tid with each main meal containing fat

ADMINISTRATION

Oral

- Give during or up to 1 h after a meal containing fat.
- Omit dose with nonfat-containing meal or if meal is skipped.
- Store at 15°–30° C (59°–86° F). Keep bottle tightly closed; **do not** use after the printed expiration date.

ADVERSE EFFECTS

CV: Hypertension, stroke. **CNS:** *Headache, dizziness, anxiety.* **Skin:** Rash. **GI:** *Oily spotting, flatus with discharge,*

fecal urgency, fatty/oily stool, oily evacuation, increased defecation, fecal incontinence, *abdominal pain/discomfort,* nausea, infectious diarrhea, rectal pain/discomfort, tooth disorder, gingival disorder, vomiting. **GU:** Menstrual irregularity. **Other:** Fatigue, back pain, infection.

DIAGNOSTIC TEST INTERFERENCE

Monitor PT/INR in patients on chronic stable doses of **warfarin**.

INTERACTIONS

Drug: Orlistat may increase absorption of **pravastatin**; may decrease absorption of fat soluble VITAMINS (A, D, E, K), **amiodarone**, THYROID HORMONES, **cyclosporine**. Taking **orlistat** with **atazanavir, ritonavir, tenofovir disoproxil fumarate, emtricitabine, lopinavir; ritonavir**, and **emtricitabine; efavirenz; tenofovir disoproxil fumarate** may decrease HIV control.

PHARMACOKINETICS

Absorption: Minimal. **Metabolism:** In gastrointestinal wall. **Elimination:** In feces. **Half-Life:** 1–2 h.

NURSING IMPLICATIONS

Assessment & Drug Effects

- Monitor weight and BMI; closely monitor diabetics for hypoglycemia.
- Monitor BP frequently, especially with preexisting hypertension.

Patient & Family Education

- Take a daily multivitamin containing fat-soluble vitamins at least 2 h before/after orlistat.
- Remember common GI adverse effects typically resolve after 4 wk therapy.
- Avoid high-fat meals to minimize adverse GI effects. Distribute fat

calories over three main meals daily.

- Monitor weight several times weekly. *Diabetics*: Monitor blood glucose carefully following any weight loss.

ORPHENADRINE CITRATE
(or-fen'a-dreen)
Classification: CENTRAL ACTING SKELETAL MUSCLE RELAXANT
Therapeutic: SKELETAL MUSCLE RELAXANT
Prototype: Cyclobenzaprine

AVAILABILITY Sustained release tablet; solution for injection

ACTION & *THERAPEUTIC EFFECT*
Tertiary amine anticholinergic and central-acting skeletal muscle relaxant. Relaxes tense skeletal muscles indirectly, possibly by analgesic action or by atropine-like central action. *Relieves skeletal muscle spasm.*

USES To relieve muscle spasm discomfort associated with acute musculoskeletal conditions.

CONTRAINDICATIONS Narrow-angle glaucoma; achalasia; pyloric or duodenal obstruction, stenosing peptic ulcers; prostatic hypertrophy or bladder neck obstruction; urinary tract obstruction; myasthenia gravis; cardiospasm; tachycardia.

CAUTIOUS USE History of cardiac disease, arrhythmias, coronary insufficiency; asthma; GERD; hepatic disease; renal disease; renal impairment; older adults; pregnancy (category C); lactation; children.

ROUTE & DOSAGE

Muscle Spasm
Adult: **PO** 100 mg bid; **IM/IV** 60 mg q12h, convert to PO therapy as soon as possible

ADMINISTRATION
Oral

- Ensure that sustained release form is not chewed or crushed. It **must be** swallowed whole.

Intramuscular

- Give undiluted deep into a large muscle.

Intravenous

PREPARE: Direct: Give undiluted. Protect from light.
ADMINISTER: Direct: Give at a rate of 60 mg (2 mL) over 5 min with patient in supine position.
- Keep supine for 5–10 min post-injection.

ADVERSE EFFECTS CNS: *Drowsiness*, weakness, headache, dizziness; mild CNS stimulation (high doses: restlessness, anxiety, tremors, confusion, hallucinations, agitation, tachycardia, palpitation, syncope). **HEENT:** Increased ocular tension, dilated pupils, blurred vision. **GI:** *Dry mouth*, nausea, vomiting, abdominal cramps, constipation. **GU:** *Urinary hesitancy* or *retention*. **Other:** Hypersensitivity [pruritus, urticaria, rash, anaphylactic reaction (rare)].

INTERACTIONS Drug: Propoxyphene may cause increased confusion, anxiety, and tremors; may worsen schizophrenic symptoms, or increase risk of tardive dyskinesia with **haloperidol**; additive CNS depressant with ANXIOLYTICS,

Common adverse effects in *italic;* life-threatening effects <u>underlined;</u> generic names in **bold;** classifications in SMALL CAPS; ♣ Canadian drug name; ◑ Prototype drug; ⚠ Alert

1230

SEDATIVES, HYPNOTICS, **butorphanol, nalbuphine**, OPIATE AGONISTS, **pentazocine, tramadol, cyclobenzaprine** may increase anticholinergic effects. **Herbal: Valerian, kava** potentiate sedation.

PHARMACOKINETICS Absorption:
Readily from GI tract. **Peak:** 2 h. **Duration:** 4–6 h. **Distribution:** Rapidly distributed in tissues; crosses placenta. **Metabolism:** In liver. **Elimination:** In urine. **Half-Life:** 14 h.

NURSING IMPLICATIONS

Assessment & Drug Effects

- Report complaints of mouth dryness, urinary hesitancy or retention, headache, tremors, GI problems, palpitation, or rapid pulse to prescriber. Dosage reduction or drug withdrawal is indicated.
- Monitor elimination patterns. Older adults are particularly sensitive to anticholinergic effects (urinary hesitancy, constipation); closely observe.
- Monitor therapeutic drug effect. In the patient with parkinsonism, orphenadrine reduces muscular rigidity but has little effect on tremors. Some reduction in excessive salivation and perspiration may occur, and patient may appear mildly euphoric.

Patient & Family Education

- Relieve mouth dryness by frequent rinsing with clear tepid water, increasing noncaloric fluid intake, sugarless gum, or lemon drops. If these measures fail, a saliva substitute may help.
- Do not drive or engage in potentially hazardous activities until response to drug is known.
- Avoid concomitant use of alcohol and other CNS depressants; these may potentiate depressant effects.

OSELTAMIVIR PHOSPHATE ⊙
(o-sel'tam-i-vir)
Tamiflu
Classification: ANTIVIRAL; NEURAMINDASE INHIBITOR; ANTI-INFLUENZA
Therapeutic: ANTI-INFLUENZA

AVAILABILITY Capsule; oral suspension

ACTION & *THERAPEUTIC EFFECT*
Inhibits influenza A and B viral neuraminidase enzyme, preventing the release of newly formed virus from the surface of the infected cells. Inhibits replication of the influenza A and B virus. *Effectiveness indicated by relief of flu symptoms. Prevents viral spread across the mucous lining of the respiratory tract.*

USES Treatment of uncomplicated acute influenza in adults symptomatic for no more than 2 days; prophylaxis of influenza.

UNLABELED USES H_1N_1 influenza.

CONTRAINDICATIONS Hypersensitivity to oseltamivir; development of allegic-like reaction(s) from drug including anaplaxis and serious skin reactions; severe hepatic impairment or severe hepatic disease; viral infections other than flu. Use within 2 wk of receiving a live vaccine; ESRD. Safety in immunosuppression not established.

CAUTIOUS USE Hereditary fructose intolerance; cardiac disease; COPD, children with asthma; mild or moderate hepatic impairment; psychiatric disorders; renal impairment; pregnancy (category C); lactation; infants younger than 1 y for propylaxis or neonates younger than 2 wk old for influenza treatment. Safety and efficacy in chronic cardiac/respiratory disease not established.

ROUTE & DOSAGE

Influenza Treatment

Adult/Adolescent/Child (over 40 kg): PO 75 mg bid × 5 days *Child (1–12 y, weight 20–40 kg):* PO 60 mg bid × 5 days; *weight 16–23 kg:* 45 mg bid × 5 days; *weight less than 15 kg:* 30 mg bid × 5 days *Infant:* PO 3 mg/kg bid × 5 days

Influenza Prevention

Adult/Adolescent/Child (1 y or older and weight over 40 kg): PO 75 mg daily × 10 days; begin within 2 days of contact with infected person *Child (weight 23–40 kg):* PO 60 mg daily × 10 days; *weight 15–23 kg:* 45 mg daily × 10 days; *weight less than 15 kg:* 30 mg × 10 days

Renal Impairment Dosage Adjustment

CrCl 10–30 mL/min: **Treatment:** 30 mg daily × 5 days; **Prophylaxis:** 30 mg every other day

ADMINISTRATION

Oral

- Give with food to decrease the risk of GI upset.
- Start within 48 h of onset of flu symptoms.
- Take missed dose as soon as possible unless next dose is due within 2 h.
- Store at 15°–30° C (59°–86° F); protect from moisture, keep dry.

ADVERSE EFFECTS Respiratory:
Bronchitis, cough. **CNS:** Dizziness, headache, insomnia, vertigo. **GI:** Nausea, vomiting, diarrhea, abdominal pain. **Other:** Fatigue.

PHARMACOKINETICS Absorption:
Readily absorbed, 75% bioavailable. **Distribution:** 42% protein bound. **Metabolism:** Extensively metabolized to active metabolite oseltamivir carboxylate by liver esterases. **Elimination:** Primarily in urine. **Half-Life:** 1–2 h; oseltamivir carboxylate 6–10 h.

NURSING IMPLICATIONS

Assessment & Drug Effects

- Monitor ambulation in frail and older adult patients due to potential for dizziness and vertigo.
- Monitor children for abnormal behavior such as delirium or self-injury.

Patient & Family Education

- Contact your prescriber regarding the use of this drug in children.

OSIMERTINIB

(oh'si-mer'ti-nib)

Tagrisso

Classification: ANTINEOPLASTIC; KINASE INHIBITOR; EPIDERMAL GROWTH FACTOR RECEPTOR INHIBITOR
Therapeutic: ANTINEOPLASTIC
Prototype: Erlotinib

AVAILABILITY Tablets

ACTION & *THERAPEUTIC EFFECT*

An irreversible epidermal growth factor receptor (EGFR) tyrosine kinase inhibitor. It preferentially binds to mutant forms of EGFR as compared to the normal wild-type EGFR. It also exhibits anti-tumor

Common adverse effects in *italic;* life-threatening effects underlined; generic names in **bold;** classifications in SMALL CAPS; ♣ Canadian drug name; ◐ Prototype drug; ▲ Alert

1232

activity against cell lines with EGFR-mutations, such as the T790M resistance mutation. *This mutation can cause resistance to other EGFR tyrosine kinase inhibitors.*

USES Treatment of patients with metastatic EGFR T790M mutation-positive non-small-cell lung cancer (NSCLC) who have failed treatment with other EGFR tyrosine kinase inhibitor (TKI) therapy.

CAUTIOUS USE Interstitial pulmonary disease/interstitial lung disease (ILD) or pneumonitis, including fatalities, have been reported. Permanently discontinue use in patients with confirmed, treatment-related ILD or pneumonia. Use cautiously in patients with cardiac disease or other conditions that may increase the risk of QT prolongation including cardiac arrhythmias, congenital long QT syndrome, heart failure, bradycardia, myocardial infarction, hypertension, coronary artery disease, hypomagnesemia, hypokalemia, hypocalcemia or in patients receiving medications for long QT interval. Treatment should be held with an ejection fraction of less than 50% or with more than a 10% decrease from baseline. Geriatric patients (older than 65 y) are at a higher risk of adverse effects. There are no adequate well-controlled studies in pregnant women. It is not known if osimertinib is present in human milk. Recommendations are to discontinue breast-feeding during treatment and for 2 wk after the final dose.

ROUTE & DOSAGE

Non-Small Cell Lung Cancer
Adult: **PO** 80 mg once daily

Adverse Reaction Dosage Adjustment

Interstitial lung disease (ILD)/ pneumonitis: Permanently discontinue
QTc interval greater than 500 msec on at least 2 separate ECGs: Withhold until QTc interval is less than 481 msec; resume at 40 mg
QTc interval prolongation with signs or symptoms of life-threatening arrhythmia: Permanently discontinue
Decrease in LVEF of 10% from baseline and below 50%: Withhold up to 4 wk; resume if improved to baseline; if not, permanently discontinue
Symptomatic congestive heart failure: Permanently discontinue
Other Grade 3 reaction: Withhold for 3 wk; resume at 40–80 mg once daily if resolved to Grade 0–2; if not, permanently

ADMINISTRATION
Oral
▪ Take without regard to food.

Extemporaneous Compounding Oral
▪ Disperse tablet in 15 mL of non-carbonated water only.
▪ Stir until tablet is in small pieces, it will not completely dissolve.
▪ Administer immediately.
▪ Rinse the container with 4–8 oz (120 mL–240 mL) of water and immediately drink.
▪ Store between 15°–30° F (59°–86° F).

ADVERSE EFFECTS CV: Prolonged QT interval. **Respiratory:** Cough, dyspnea, upper respiratory infection. **CNS:** Fatigue, headache. **Endocrine:** *Hyperglycemia, hypermagnesemia, hyponatremia,* hypokalemia. **Skin:** *Skin rash, xeroderma, nail disease, pruritus.* **Hepatic/GI:** Increased serum AST, increased serum ALT, hyperbilirubinemia, *diarrhea, stomatitis,* decreased appetite, constipation, nausea, vomiting. **Hematologic:** *Lymphocytopenia, anemia, thrombocytopenia, neutropenia.* **Other:** Fever.

INTERACTIONS Drug: Strong CYP3A inhibitors (e.g., **itraconazole, nefazodone, ritonavir, telithromycin**) may increase the levels of osimertinib. Strong CYP3A inducers (e.g., **carbamazepine, phenytoin, rifampicin**) may decrease the levels of osimertinib. Do not use with other agents that prolong QT interval. Osimertinib may alter the plasma levels of **carbamazepine, cyclosporine,** ERGOT ALKALOIDS, **fentanyl, quinidine,** and **phenytoin.** Do not use with LIVE VACCINES. May enhance effect of **deferiprone, dipyrone, pazopanib, pimecrolimus, tacrolimus. Herbal: St. John's Wort** may decrease the levels of osimertinib.

PHARMACOKINETICS Peak: 6 h. **Metabolism:** Hepatic oxidation by CYP enzymes. **Elimination:** Fecal (68%) and renal (14%). **Half-Life:** 48 h.

NURSING IMPLICATIONS

Assessment & Drug Effects

- Hazardous agent (meets NIOSH 2016 criteria for handling and disposing)—double glove, wear a gown if there is a chance of vomit or spit up, eye/face protection for administration of a liquid.

Crushed tablets should be prepared in a controlled device.
- Perform respiratory assessments being alert to complaints of shortness of breath and any pain in lower extremities or jugular veins that could be related to thrombosis. Hold drug and notify prescriber if symptoms develop.
- Perform oral exams for inspection of oral mucosa and complaints of pain.
- Monitor daily weight.
- Monitor lab tests: CBC with differential, monitor ECG, ejection fraction, and serum electrolytes.

Patient & Family Education

- Contact medical provider for shortness of breath, new or worsening cough, or pain, edema or warmth in extremities or neck.
- Women should use effective contraception during therapy and for 6 wk after the last dose. Males with female partners of reproductive potential should also use effective contraception during therapy and for 4 mo after the last dose.
- Report any changes in balance, confusion, weakness, severe dizziness or fainting.

OSPEMIFENE
(os-pem'ih-feen)
Osphena
Classification: ESTROGEN AGONIST/ANTAGONIST; SELECTIVE ESTROGEN RECEPTOR MODIFIER (SERM)
Therapeutic: ESTROGEN AGONIST/ANTAGONIST
Prototype: Tamoxifen

AVAILABILITY Tablet

ACTION & *THERAPEUTIC EFFECT* A selective estrogen receptor agonist/antagonist that activates estrogenic pathways in some

tissues (agonist) and blocks the pathways in other tissues (antagonist). *Exerts an estrogen-like effect on the vaginal epithelium thus reversing vulvovaginal atrophy and decreasing dyspareunia.*

USES Treatment of moderate to severe dyspareunia, a symptomatic estrogen-like effect on the vaginal epithelium of vulvar and vaginal atrophy, due to menopause.

CONTRAINDICATIONS Undiagnosed abnormal genital bleeding; known or suspected neoplasia; endometrial cancer; history of breast cancer; history or active VTE, pulmonary embolism (PE), or history of these conditions; active arterial thromboembolic disease (e.g., stroke, MI, or history of these conditions); severe hepatic impairment; known or suspected pregnancy (category X); lactation.

CAUTIOUS USE Risk for DVT, PE, or history of stroke; hypertension; smoking; DM, hypercholesterolemia; obesity, SLE, mild or moderate hepatic impairment.

ROUTE & DOSAGE

Dyspareunia
Adult: PO 60 mg once daily

Hepatic Impairment Dosage Adjustment
Severe hepatic impairment (Child-Pugh class C): Do not administer

ADMINISTRATION
Oral
- Give with food.
- Store at 15°–30° C (59°–86° F).

ADVERSE EFFECTS Skin: Hyperhidrosis. **GU:** Genital discharge,

vaginal discharge. **Musculoskeletal:** Muscle spasms.

INTERACTIONS Drug: Coadministration of CYP2C9 and CYP3A4 Inhibitors (e.g., **fluconazole, ketoconazole**) may increase the levels of ospemifene. Coadministration of CYP2C9 and CYP3A4 inducers (e.g., **rifampin**) may decrease the levels of ospemifene. Coadministration with other drugs that are highly plasma protein bound may cause displacement reactions resulting in increased levels of either ospemifene or other drugs. **Food:** Food increases the bioavailability of ospemifene.

PHARMACOKINETICS Peak: 2–2.5 h. **Distribution:** 99% plasma protein bound. **Metabolism:** Hepatic oxidation. **Elimination:** Fecal (75%) and renal (7%). **Half-Life:** 26 h.

NURSING IMPLICATIONS

Black Box Warning

Ospemifene has been associated with increased risk of endometrial cancer in women who are not receiving a progestin, and with increased risk of DVT and CVA.

Assessment & Drug Effects
- Monitor for and report persistent or recurring genital bleeding.
- Monitor closely those with risk factors for cardiovascular disease and thromboembolism (e.g., hypertension, DM, tobacco use, hypercholesterolemia, obesity, history of SLE).

Patient & Family Education
- Notify prescriber immediately if you become pregnant.

- Report promptly all instances of vaginal bleeding.
- This drug may cause or increase the occurrence of hot flashes.

OXACILLIN SODIUM ℗ℝ
(ox-a-sill'in)

Classification: PENICILLIN ANTIBIOTIC; PENICILLINASE-RESISTANT PENICILLIN
Therapeutic: ANTIBIOTIC

AVAILABILITY Solution for injection

ACTION & *THERAPEUTIC EFFECT*
Oxacillin inhibits final stage of bacterial cell wall synthesis by preferentially binding to specific penicillin-binding proteins (PBPs) located within the bacterial cell wall, leading to destruction of the cell wall of the organism. *It is highly active against most penicillinase-producing staphylococci, and is generally ineffective against gram-negative bacteria and methicillin-resistant staphylococci (MRSA).*

USES Infections caused by staphylococci.

UNLABELED USES Catheter-related infections, skin/soft tissue necrotizing infection.

CONTRAINDICATIONS Hypersensitivity to oxacillin, penicillin, or any component of formulation.

CAUTIOUS USE History of or suspected atopy or allergy (hives, eczema, hay fever, asthma); history of GI disease; hepatic or renal impairment; CHF; older adults; pregnancy (maternal use of penicillins has generally not resulted in an increased risk of adverse fetal effects); lactation (may cause infant diarrhea); premature infants, neonates.

ROUTE & DOSAGE

Staphylococcal Infections
Adult: **IV** 2 g q4h
Adolescent/Child: **IV** 100–150 mg/kg/day in divided doses q6h (max: 4000 mg/day)

ADMINISTRATION
Note: The total sodium content (including that contributed by buffer) in each gram of oxacillin is approximately 3.1 mEq or 71 mg.

Intramuscular
- Administer into muscle; avoid sciatic nerve injury.

Intravascular
Note: Verify correct IV concentration and rate of infusion/injection with prescriber before IV administration to neonates, infants, and children.

PREPARE: Direct: Reconstitute each 1 g or fraction thereof with 10 mL with sterile water for injection or NS to yield 250 mg/1.5 mL. **Intermittent:** Dilute required dose of reconstituted solution in 50–100 mL of D5W, NS, D5/NS, or LR. **Continuous:** Dilute required dose of reconstituted solution in up to 1000 mL of compatible IV solutions.
ADMINISTER: Direct: Give at a rate of 1 g or fraction thereof over 10 min. **Intermittent IVPB:** Give over 30 min.
INCOMPATIBILITIES: Solution/additive: Cytarabine Y-site: Amphotericin B, calcium, dantrolene, diazepam, diazoxide, diphenhydramine, dobutamine, doxycycline, esmolol, ganciclovir, gentamicin, haloperidol, hydralazine, inamrinone, metaraminol, minocycline,

netilmicin, pentazocine, phenytoin, polymixin B, promethazine, protamine, pyridoxine, quinidine, succinylcholine, SMZ/TMP, tobramycin.

ADVERSE EFFECTS GI: *C.difficile-associated diarrhea*, hepatotoxicity, elevated liver enzymes. **GU:** Interstitial nephritis, acute renal tubular disease. **Hematologic:** Eosinophilia.

DIAGNOSTIC TEST INTERFERENCE
Oxacillin in large doses can cause false-positive **urine protein tests** using **sulfosalicylic acid methods**; may interfere with **urinary glucose tests**.

INTERACTIONS Do not administer with LIVE VACCINES.

PHARMACOKINETICS Peak: 30 min IM; 15 min IV. **Distribution:** Distributes into CNS with inflamed meninges; crosses placenta; distributed into breast milk, 90% protein bound. **Metabolism:** Enters enterohepatic circulation. **Elimination:** Primarily in urine, some in bile. **Half-Life:** 0.5–1 h.

NURSING IMPLICATIONS

Assessment & Drug Effects

- Ask patient prior to first dose about hypersensitivity reactions to penicillins, cephalosporins, and other allergens.
- Hepatic dysfunction (possibly a hypersensitivity reaction) has been associated with IV oxacillin; it is reversible with discontinuation of drug. Symptoms may resemble viral hepatitis or general signs of hypersensitivity and should be reported promptly: Hives, rash, fever, nausea, vomiting, abdominal discomfort, anorexia, malaise, jaundice (with dark yellow to brown urine, light-colored or clay-colored stools, pruritus).
- Withhold next drug dose and report the onset of hypersensitivity reactions and superinfections (see Appendix F).
- Monitor lab tests: Periodic serum LFTs, CBC, BUN, creatinine, and urinalysis.

Patient & Family Education

- Take oral medication around the clock; do not miss a dose. Take all of the medication prescribed even if you feel better, unless otherwise directed by prescriber.

OXALIPLATIN
(ox-a-li-pla′tin)

Classification: ANTINEOPLASTIC; ALKYLATING AGENT
Therapeutic: ANTINEOPLASTIC
Prototype: Cyclophosphamide

AVAILABILITY Solution for injection

ACTION & *THERAPEUTIC EFFECT*
Oxaliplatin forms inter- and intrastrand DNA cross-links that inhibit DNA replication and transcription resulting in cell death. *Antitumor activity of oxaliplatin in combination with 5-fluorouracil (5-FU) has antiproliferative activity against colon carcinoma that is greater than either compound alone.*

USES Metastatic cancer of colon and rectum.

UNLABELED USES Advanced prostate cancer, non-Hodgkin lymphoma, ovarian cancer.

CONTRAINDICATIONS Hypersensitivity to oxaliplatin or other platinum compounds; myelosuppression; pregnancy (may result in fetal harm); lactation.

CAUTIOUS USE Renal impairment, because clearance of ultra-filterable platinum is decreased in mild, moderate, and severe renal impairment; hepatic impairment; older adults; children.

ROUTE & DOSAGE

Metastatic Colon or Rectal Cancer
Adult: IV 85 mg/m² once every 2 wk until disease progression or unacceptable toxicity; adjust for toxicities (see package insert for adjustments)

Renal Impairment Dosage Adjustment
CrCl less than 30 mL/min: Reduce initial dose to 65 mg/m²

ADMINISTRATION

Intravenous
Premedication with an antiemetic is recommended.

PREPARE: IV Infusion: NEVER reconstitute with NS or any solution containing chloride. ▪ Reconstitute the 50 mg vial or the 100 mg vial by adding 10 mL or 20 mL, respectively, of sterile water for injection or D5W. ▪ MUST further dilute in 250–500 mL of D5W for infusion.

ADMINISTER: IV Infusion: Do not use needles or infusion sets containing aluminum parts. ▪ Flush infusion line with D5W before and after administration of any other concomitant medication. ▪ Give over 2 hours with frequent monitoring of the IV insertion site; extend infusion time to 6 hours for acute toxicities. ▪ Discontinue at the first sign of extravasation and restart IV in a different site.

INCOMPATIBILITIES: Solution/additive: **dexamethasone.** Y-site: **cefepime, cefoperazone, dantrolene, diazepam.**

▪ Store reconstituted solution up to 24 h under refrigeration at 2°–8° C (36°–46° F). ▪ After final dilution, the IV solution may be stored for 6 h at room temperature [20°–25° C (68°–77° F)] or up to 24 h under refrigeration.

ADVERSE EFFECTS CV: Chest pain, peripheral edema. **Respiratory:** *Dyspnea, cough,* upper respiratory tract infection. **CNS:** *Fatigue, neuropathy, headache,* insomnia, dizziness, rigors. **Endocrine:** Hypokalemia, dehydration. **Hepatic/GI:** *Diarrhea, nausea, vomiting, anorexia, stomatitis, constipation, abdominal pain,* dyspepsia, dysgeusia, increased liver enzymes. **GU:** Increased serum creatinine. **Hematologic:** *Anemia,* leukopenia, thrombocytopenia, neutropenia. **Musculoskeletal:** Arthralgia. **Other:** *Fever,* back pain, injection site reaction.

INTERACTIONS Drug: MYELOSUPPRESIVE and IMMUNOSUPRESSIVE AGENTS have increased risk of adverse effects; increases risk of adverse effects with **topotecan.** Do not use with LIVE VACCINES

PHARMACOKINETICS Distribution: Greater than 90% protein bound. **Metabolism:** Rapid and extensive nonenzymatic biotransformation. **Elimination:** Primarily in urine. **Half-Life:** 391 h.

NURSING IMPLICATIONS

Black Box Warning

Oxaliplatin has been associated with anaphylactic reactions within minutes of administration.

Assessment & Drug Effects

- Monitor for S&S of hypersensitivity (e.g., rash, urticaria, erythema, pruritus; rarely, bronchospasm and hypotension). Discontinue drug and notify prescriber if any of these occur.
- Monitor insertion site. Extravasation may cause local pain and inflammation that may be severe and lead to complications, including necrosis.
- Monitor for S&S of coagulation disorders including GI bleeding, hematuria, and epistaxis.
- Monitor for S&S of peripheral neuropathy (e.g., paresthesia, dysesthesia, hypoesthesia in the hands, feet, perioral area, or throat, jaw spasm, abnormal tongue sensation, dysarthria, eye pain, and chest pressure). Symptoms may be precipitated or exacerbated by exposure to cold temperature or cold objects.
- Do not apply ice to oral mucous membranes (e.g., mucositis prophylaxis) during the infusion of oxaliplatin as cold temperature can exacerbate acute neurological symptoms.
- Monitor lab tests: Before each administration cycle, CBC with differential, electrolytes, and blood chemistries (including ALT, AST, bilirubin, and creatinine). Baseline and periodic renal function tests. INR and PT in patients on oral anticoagulation therapy. Evaluate pregnancy status.

Patient & Family Education

- Use effective methods of contraception while receiving this drug.
- Avoid cold drinks, use of ice, and cover exposed skin prior to exposure to cold temperature or cold objects.
- Do not drive or engage in potentially hazardous activities until response to drug is known.
- Report any of the following to a health care provider: Difficulty writing, buttoning, swallowing, walking; numbness, tingling or other unusual sensations in extremities; non-productive cough or shortness of breath; fever, particularly if associated with persistent diarrhea or other evidence of infection.
- Report promptly S&S of a bleeding disorder such as black tarry stool, coke-colored or frankly bloody urine, bleeding from the nose or mucous membranes.

OXANDROLONE

(ox-an′dro-lone)

Oxandrin

Classification: ANDROGEN/ANABOLIC STEROID

Therapeutic: ANABOLIC STEROID

Prototype: Testosterone

Controlled Substance: Schedule III

AVAILABILITY Tablet

ACTION & *THERAPEUTIC EFFECT*

A synthetic derivative of testosterone that promotes weight gain after weight loss following extensive surgery, chronic infections, or severe trauma. It offsets the protein catabolism associated with prolonged administration of corticosteroids, and relieves bone pain frequently accompanying osteoporosis. *Promotes weight gain and relieves bone pain caused by osteoporosis.*

USES Adjunctive therapy to promote weight gain, offset protein catabolism associated with prolonged administration of corticosteroids, relieve bone pain accompanying osteoporosis.

CONTRAINDICATIONS Hypersensitivity or toxic reactions to androgens; severe cardiac, hepatic, or renal disease; possibility of virilization of external genitalia of female fetus; polycythemia; hypercalcemia; known or suspected prostatic or breast cancer in males; benign prostatic hypertrophy with obstruction; patients easily stimulated sexually; asthenic males who may react adversely to androgenic overstimulation; conditions aggravated by fluid retention; hypertension; pregnancy (category X); lactation.

CAUTIOUS USE Cardiac, hepatic, and mild to moderate renal disease, hypercholesterolemia, heart failure, peripheral edema, arteriosclerosis, coronary artery disease, MI; cholestasis; DM; BPH; prepubertal males, acute intermittent porphyria; older adults; children.

ROUTE & DOSAGE

Weight Gain
Adult: **PO** 2.5 mg bid to qid (max: 20 mg/day) for 2–4 wk
Child: **PO** 0.1 mg/kg/day

Bone Pain
Adult: **PO** 2.5–20 mg bid to qid for 2–4 wk

ADMINISTRATION

Oral
▪ Individualize doses; great variations in response exist.
▪ Store at 15°–30° C (59°–86° F).

ADVERSE EFFECTS CNS: Habituation, excitation, insomnia, depression, changes in libido. **Endocrine:** Gynecomastia, deepening of voice in females, premature closure of epiphyses in children, edema, decreased glucose tolerance.

Skin: Hirsutism and male pattern baldness in females, acne. **Hepatic:** Cholestatic jaundice with or without <u>hepatic necrosis and death, hepatocellular neoplasms, peliosis hepatitis (long-term use)</u>. **GU:** *Males:* Phallic enlargement, increased frequency or persistence of erections, inhibition of testicular function, testicular atrophy, oligospermia, impotence, chronic priapism, epididymitis, bladder irritability; *Females:* Clitoral enlargement, menstrual irregularities.

DIAGNOSTIC TEST INTERFERENCE May decrease levels of thyroxine-binding globulin (decreased total T_4 and increased T_3 RU and free T_4).

INTERACTIONS Drug: May increase INR with **warfarin**. May inhibit metabolism of ORAL HYPOGLYCEMIC AGENTS. Concomitant STEROIDS may increase edema. **Herbal: Echinacea** may increase risk of hepatotoxicity.

PHARMACOKINETICS Half-Life: 10–13 h (increased in elderly patients).

NURSING IMPLICATIONS

Black Box Warning

Oxandrolone has been associated with hepatic dysfunction, liver failure, liver cell tumors, and increased risk of atherosclerosis from blood lipid changes.

Assessment & Drug Effects
▪ Monitor weight closely throughout therapy.
▪ Assess for and report development of edema or S&S of jaundice (see Appendix F).

- Withhold and notify prescriber if hypercalcemia develops in breast cancer patient.
- Monitor growth in children closely.
- Monitor lab tests: Periodic LFTs, lipid profile, Hct and Hgb.

Patient & Family Education
- Women: Report signs of virilization, including acne and changes in menstrual periods.
- Men: Report too frequent or prolonged erections or appearance/ worsening of acne.
- Report S&S of jaundice (see Appendix F) or edema.
- Monitor blood glucose for loss of glycemic control if diabetic.

OXAPROZIN
(ox-a-pro′zin)
Daypro
Classification: ANALGESIC, NON-STEROIDAL ANTI-INFLAMMATORY DRUG (NSAID)
Therapeutic: NONNARCOTIC ANALGESIC, NSAID; ANTIRHEUMATIC; ANTIPYRETIC
Prototype: Ibuprofen

AVAILABILITY Tablet

ACTION & *THERAPEUTIC EFFECT*
Long-acting NSAID agent, which is an effective prostaglandin synthetase inhibitor. It inhibits COX-1 and COX-2 enzymes needed for prostaglandin synthesis at the site of inflammation. *Has anti-inflammatory, antipyretic, and analgesic properties.*

USES Treatment of osteoarthritis and rheumatoid arthritis, juvenile rheumatoid arthritis.

UNLABELED USES Ankylosing spondylitis, chronic pain, gout, oral surgery pain, temporal arteritis, tendinitis.

CONTRAINDICATIONS Hypersensitivity to oxaprozin, salicylates, or any other NSAID; UGI bleeding; complete or partial syndrome of nasal polyps; angioedema; CABG perioperative pain; pregnancy (category D third trimester); lactation.

CAUTIOUS USE History of GI bleeding, alcoholism, smoking; history of severe hepatic dysfunction, renal insufficiency; cardiac disease; coagulopathy; photosensitivity; older adults; pregnancy (category C first and second trimester). Safety and efficacy in children younger than 6 y not established.

ROUTE & DOSAGE

Osteoarthritis, Rheumatoid Arthritis
Adult: **PO** 1200 mg daily (max: 1800 mg/day or 26 mg/kg, whichever is lower)

Juvenile Rheumatoid Arthritis
Adolescent/Child (6 y or older, weight over 55 kg): **PO** 1200 mg qd; *weight 32–54 kg:* 900 mg qd; *weight 22–31 kg:* 600 mg qd

ADMINISTRATION
Oral
- Give with meals or milk to decrease GI distress.
- Divide doses in those unable to tolerate once-daily dosing.

- Use lower starting doses for those with renal or hepatic dysfunction, advanced age, low body weight, or a predisposition to GI ulceration.

ADVERSE EFFECTS CV: Edema. **CNS:** Confusion, depression, disturbed sleep, dizziness, drowsiness, headache, sedation. **HEENT:** Tinnitus. **Skin:** Pruritis, skin rash. **Hepatic/GI:** Increased liver enzymes, abdominal pain, anorexia, constipation, dyspepsia, flatulence. **GU:** Dysuria, urinary frequency. **Hematologic:** Anemia, prolonged bleeding time.

DIAGNOSTIC TEST INTERFERENCE
May cause false-positive reactions for BENZODIAZEPINES with *urine drug-screening* tests. May lead to false-positive aldosterone/renin ratio.

INTERACTIONS Drug: May attenuate the antihypertensive response to DIURETICS. NSAIDS increase the risk of **methotrexate** or **lithium** toxicity. Use caution with ANTICOAGULANTS, PLATELET INHIBITORS. May increase **aspirin** toxicity. Do not use with **cidofovir** or **ketorolac**. **Herbal: Feverfew, garlic, ginger, ginkgo** may increase risk of bleeding.

PHARMACOKINETICS Absorption: Readily from GI tract. **Peak:** 125 min. **Onset:** 1–6 wk for maximum therapeutic effect. **Distribution:** 99% protein bound. Distributes into synovial fluid, crosses placenta. Distributed into breast milk. **Metabolism:** In the liver. **Elimination:** 60% in urine, 30–35% in feces. **Half-Life:** 40 h.

NURSING IMPLICATIONS

Black Box Warning

Oxaprozin has been associated with increased risk of serious, potentially fatal, GI bleeding and cardiovascular events (e.g., MI & CVA); risk may increase with duration of use and may be greater in the older adult and those with risk factors for CV disease.

Assessment & Drug Effects

- Monitor for S&S of GI bleeding, especially in patients with a history of inflammation or ulceration of upper GI tract, or those treated chronically with NSAIDs.
- Monitor patients with CHF for increased fluid retention and edema. Report rapid weight increases accompanied by edema.
- Auditory and ophthalmologic exams are recommended with prolonged or high-dose therapy.
- Monitor lab tests: Baseline and periodic CBC, LFTs and renal function tests.

Patient & Family Education

- Report immediately dark tarry stools, "coffee ground" or bloody emesis, or other GI distress.
- Avoid aspirin or other NSAIDs without explicit permission of prescriber.
- Stop taking drug and report promptly to prescriber if you experience chest pain, shortness of breath, weakness, slurring of speech, or other signs of a cardiac or neurologic problem.
- Be aware of the possibility of photosensitivity, which results in a rash on sun-exposed skin.
- Report immediately to prescriber ringing in ears, decreased hearing, or blurred vision.

- Do not exceed ordered dose. The goal of therapy is lowest effective dose.

OXAZEPAM
(ox-a′ze-pam)
Ox-Pam ♦, Zapex ♦
Classification: ANXIOLYTIC; SEDATIVE-HYPNOTIC; BENZODIAZEPINE
Therapeutic: ANTIANXIETY; SEDATIVE-HYPNOTIC
Prototype: Lorazepam
Controlled Substance: Schedule IV

AVAILABILITY Capsule; tablet

ACTION & *THERAPEUTIC EFFECT*
Benzodiazepine derivative related to lorazepam. Effects are mediated by the inhibitory neurotransmitter GABA, and acts on the thalamic, hypothalamic, and limbic levels of CNS. *Has anxiolytic, sedative, hypnotic, and skeletal muscle relaxant effects.*

USES Management of anxiety; control acute withdrawal symptoms in chronic alcoholism.

CONTRAINDICATIONS Hypersensitivity to oxazepam and other benzodiazepines; respiratory depression; psychoses, suicidal ideation; acute alcohol intoxication; acute-angle glaucoma; pregnancy (category D); lactation.

CAUTIOUS USE Impaired kidney and liver function; alcoholism; addiction-prone patients; COPD; history of seizures; history of suicide; mental depression; bipolar disorder; older adults and debilitated patients; children younger than 6 y.

ROUTE & DOSAGE

Anxiety
Adult/Adolescent/Child (6 y or older): PO 10–30 mg tid or qid

Acute Alcohol Withdrawal
Adult: PO 15–30 mg tid or qid

ADMINISTRATION
Oral
- Give with food if GI upset occurs.
- Store in a tightly closed container at 15°–30° C (59°–86° F) unless otherwise specified.

ADVERSE EFFECTS CV: Hypotension, edema. **CNS:** *Drowsiness*, dizziness, mental confusion, vertigo, ataxia, headache, lethargy, syncope, tremor, slurred speech, paradoxic reaction (euphoria, excitement). **Skin:** Skin rash, edema. **GI:** Nausea, xero-stomia, jaundice. **GU:** Altered libido. **Hematologic:** Leukopenia.

INTERACTIONS Drug: Alcohol, CNS DEPRESSANTS, ANTICONVULSANTS potentiate CNS depression; **cimetidine** increases oxazepam plasma levels, increasing its toxicity; may decrease antiparkinsonism effects of **levodopa**; may increase **phenytoin** levels; smoking decreases sedative and antianxiety effects. **Herbal: Kava, valerian** may potentiate sedation.

PHARMACOKINETICS Absorption: Readily absorbed from GI tract. **Peak:** 2–3 h. **Distribution:** Crosses placenta; distributed into breast milk. **Metabolism:** In liver. **Elimination:** Primarily in urine, some in feces. **Half-Life:** 2–8 h.

NURSING IMPLICATIONS

Assessment & Drug Effects

- Observe older adult patients closely for signs of overdosage. Report to prescriber if daytime psychomotor function is depressed.
- Monitor for increased signs and symptoms of suicidality.
- Note: Excessive and prolonged use may cause physical dependence.
- Monitor lab tests: Periodic LFTs and WBC count.

Patient & Family Education

- Report promptly any mild paradoxic stimulation of affect and excitement with sleep disturbances that may occur within the first 2 wk of therapy. Dosage reduction is indicated.
- Consult prescriber before self-medicating with OTC drugs.
- Do not drive or engage in potentially hazardous activities until response to drug is known.
- Do not drink alcoholic beverages while taking oxazepam. The CNS depressant effects of each agent may be intensified.
- Contact prescriber if you intend to or do become pregnant during therapy about discontinuing the drug.
- Withdraw drug slowly following prolonged therapy to avoid precipitating withdrawal symptoms (seizures, mental confusion, nausea, vomiting, muscle and abdominal cramps, tremulousness, sleep disturbances, unusual irritability, hyperhidrosis).

OXCARBAZEPINE

(ox-car′ba-ze-peen)
Oxtellar XR, Trileptal
Classification: ANTICONVULSANT
Therapeutic: ANTICONVULSANT
Prototype: Carbamazepine

AVAILABILITY Tablet; extended release tablet; oral suspension

ACTION & *THERAPEUTIC EFFECT*

Anticonvulsant properties may result from blockage of voltage-sensitive sodium channels, which results in stabilization of hyperexcited neural membranes. *Inhibits repetitive neuronal firing, and decreased propagation of neuronal impulses.*

USES Focal onset seizures.

UNLABELED USES Trigeminal neuralgia.

CONTRAINDICATIONS Hypersensitivity to oxcarbazepine including skin reactions; suicidal ideation or behavior; drug induced agranulocytosis, pancytopenia, leukopenia; pregnancy—fetal risk cannot be ruled out; lactation—infant risk cannot be ruled out.

CAUTIOUS USE Renal impairment; renal failure; severe hepatic impairment; patients at risk for hyponatremia; history of hypothyroidism; Asian ancestry; infertility; suicidal tendencies; CNS effects including somnolence and gait changes; older adults; children younger than 2 y. **Extended Release:** Use in children 6 y or older.

ROUTE & DOSAGE

Focal Onset Seizures

Adult: **PO** Immediate release 300–600 mg/day in divided doses (max: 2.4 g/day) *Extended release:* 600 mg daily, may increase at weekly intervals to 2.4 g/day
Child (4–16 y): **PO** Initiate with 8–10 mg/kg/day divided bid, gradually increase weekly to

---

Common adverse effects in *italic*; life-threatening effects underlined; generic names in **bold**; classifications in SMALL CAPS; ✦ Canadian drug name; ◐ Prototype drug; ⚠ Alert

1244

target dose (divided bid) based on weight: *Weight 20–35 kg:* 600–1200 mg/day; *weight 35.1–50 kg:* 900–1500 mg/day; *weight greater than 50 kg:* 1200–2100 mg/day

Renal Impairment Dosage Adjustment

CrCl less than 30 mL/min: Initiate at ½ usual starting dose

ADMINISTRATION

Oral

- NIOSH recommends use of single gloves by anyone handling intact tablets or capsules or administering from a unit-dose package. If cutting, crushing, or manipulating, or handling of uncoated tablets, use double gloves and protective gown. During administration, eye/face protection is needed if the patient may resist or if there is a potential to vomit or spit up.
- Ensure that extended release tablet is swallowed whole. It should not be crushed or chewed.
- Extended release: Take a single daily dose on an empty stomach, at least 1 hour before or 2 hours after a meal.
- Immediate release: Can be taken with or without food.
- Immediate release suspension: Shake well and prepare dose immediately using the oral dosing syringe. Can be mixed in a small glass of water just prior to administration or may be swallowed directly from the syringe.
- Initiate therapy at one-half the usual starting dose (300 mg/day) if creatinine clearance is less than 30 mL/min.
- Do not abruptly stop this medication; withdraw drug gradually when discontinued to minimize seizure potential.
- Store at controlled room temperature of 25° C (77° F), with excursions permitted between 15 and 30 degrees C (59 and 86 degrees F). Protect extended-release tablets from moisture and light. Use suspension within 7 weeks of first opening the bottle.

ADVERSE EFFECTS (≥ 5%) CNS:

Headache, dizziness, somnolence, ataxia, nystagmus, abnormal gait, drowsiness, tremor, abnormal coordination. **HEENT:** *Diplopia, abnormal vision,* nystagmus. **Endocrine:** Hyponatremia. **GI:** *Nausea, vomiting, abdominal pain,* dyspepsia. **Other:** *Fatigue.*

DIAGNOSTIC TEST INTERFERENCE

May decrease serum T4.

INTERACTIONS Drug: Carbamazepine, phenobarbital, phenytoin, valproic acid, verapamil;

CALCIUM CHANNEL BLOCKERS may decrease oxcarbazepine levels; may increase levels of **phenobarbital, phenytoin;** may decrease levels of **felodipine,** ORAL CONTRACEPTIVES. Do not use with transdermal **selegiline, cobicistat, dolutegravir, doravirine, elvitegravir, eslicarbazepine, ledipasvir, selegiline, simeprevir, sofosbuvir, tendofovir, dasabuvir/ombitasvir/paritaprevir/ritonavir. Herbal: Ginkgo** may decrease anticonvulsant effectiveness. **Evening primrose oil** may decrease the seizure threshold.

PHARMACOKINETICS Absorption: Rapidly and completely from GI tract. Peak: Steady-state levels reached in 2–3 days. Distribution: 40% protein bound. Metabolism: Extensively metabolized in liver to

0

active 10-monohydroxy metabolite (MHD). **Elimination:** 95% in kidneys. **Half-Life:** 2 h, MHD 9 h.

NURSING IMPLICATIONS

Assessment & Drug Effects

- Monitor for and report S&S of: Hyponatremia (e.g., nausea, malaise, headache, lethargy, confusion); CNS impairment (e.g., somnolence, excessive fatigue, cognitive deficits, speech or language problems, incoordination, gait disturbances).
- Monitor phenytoin levels when administered concurrently.
- Monitor lab tests: Periodic serum sodium; plasma level of the concomitant antiepileptic drug during titration of the oxcarbazepine dose.

Patient & Family Education

- Notify prescriber of the following: Dizziness, excess drowsiness, frequent headaches, malaise, double vision, lack of coordination, or persistent nausea.
- Report any worsening depression, suicidal ideation, or unusual changes in behavior.
- Exercise special caution with concurrent use of alcohol or CNS depressants.
- Use caution with potentially hazardous activities and driving until response to drug is known.
- Advise against sudden discontinuation as this may lead to seizures.
- Use or add barrier contraceptive since drug may render hormonal methods ineffective.

OXICONAZOLE NITRATE

(ox-i-con'a-zole)
Oxistat
Classification: AZOLE ANTIFUNGAL

Therapeutic: ANTIFUNGAL
Prototype: Fluconazole

AVAILABILITY Cream; lotion

ACTION & THERAPEUTIC EFFECT

Topical synthetic antifungal agent that presumably works by altering the cellular membrane of the fungi, resulting in increased membrane permeability, secondary metabolic effects, and growth inhibition. *Prevents growth of fungi that cause tinea pedis, tinea cruris, and tinea corporis.*

USES Topical treatment of tinea pedis, tinea cruris, and tinea corporis due to *Trichophyton rubrum* and *Trichophyton mentagrophytes;* also used for cutaneous candidiasis caused by *Candida albicans* and *Candida tropicalis.*

CONTRAINDICATIONS Hypersensitivity to oxiconazole.

CAUTIOUS USE Hypersensitivity to other azole antifungals; pregnancy (category B); lactation.

ROUTE & DOSAGE

Tinea and Other Dermal Infections

Adult: **Topical** Apply to affected area once daily in the evening

ADMINISTRATION

Topical

- Apply cream to cover the affected areas once daily (in the evening).
- Treat tinea corporis and tinea cruris for 2 wk; tinea pedis for 1 mo to reduce the possibility of recurrence.
- Store at 15°–30° C (59°–86° F).

Common adverse effects in *italic;* life-threatening effects <u>underlined;</u> generic names in **bold;** classifications in SMALL CAPS; ✦ Canadian drug name; ○ Prototype drug; ⚠ Alert

ADVERSE EFFECTS Skin: Transient burning and stinging, dryness, erythema, pruritus, and local irritation.

PHARMACOKINETICS Absorption: Less than 0.3% is absorbed systemically.

NURSING IMPLICATIONS

Patient & Family Education
- Use only externally. Do not use intravaginally.
- Discontinue drug and contact prescriber if irritation or sensitivity develops.
- Avoid contact with eyes.
- Contact prescriber if no improvement is noted after the prescribed treatment period.

OXYBUTYNIN CHLORIDE ⊙

(ox-i-byoo′ti-nin)

Ditropan XL, Gelnique, Oxytrol

Classification: ANTICHOLINERGIC; ANTIMUSCARINIC; GU ANTISPASMODIC
Therapeutic: GU ANTISPASMODIC

AVAILABILITY Tablet; extended release tablet; oral solution; transdermal patch; topical gel

ACTION & *THERAPEUTIC EFFECT*

Exerts a direct antispasmodic effect on smooth muscle and inhibits the muscarinic action of acetylcholine on smooth muscle. *Relaxes bladder smooth muscle and increases bladder capacity.*

USES To relieve symptoms associated with overactive bladder.

CONTRAINDICATIONS Hypersensitivity of oxybutynin; narrow-angle glaucoma, myasthenia gravis, partial or complete GI obstruction, gastric retention, paralytic ileus, intestinal atony (especially older adult or debilitated patients), megacolon, pyloric stenosis, severe colitis, GU obstruction, urinary retention, unstable cardiovascular status; pregnancy—fetal risk cannot be ruled out; lactation—infant risk cannot be ruled out. **Extended Release:** With renal impairment or pediatric patients that cannot swallow a tablet whole.

CAUTIOUS USE Autonomic neuropathy, hiatal hernia with reflex esophagitis; gastric obstructive disorders due to risk of gastric retention; gastric motility problems, hepatic or renal dysfunction; urinary infection; hyperthyroidism; CHF, coronary artery disease, hypertension; myasthenia gravis, Parkinson disease; prostatic hypertrophy; older adults; children 5y and older.

ROUTE & DOSAGE

Overactive Bladder

Adult/Adolescent: **PO Immediate release** 5 mg 2–3 × day (max: 20 mg/day) **Sustained release** 5–10 mg daily, may adjust as needed (max 30 mg/day); **Topical** Apply 1 patch twice weekly; or apply contents of 1 10% gel package once daily
Geriatric: **PO Immediate release** 2.5–5 mg bid (max: 15 mg/day); use adult dosing for topical or sustained release products
Child (5 y or older): **PO** 5 mg bid; increase as necessary (max: 5 mg qid)

ADMINISTRATION

Oral

- Ensure that sustained release form is not chewed or crushed. It **must be** swallowed whole. May be given without regard to meals and should be given at the same time each day with plenty of fluids.
- Store syrup, tablet, extended release tablet, at controlled room temperature between 15 and 30 degrees C (59 and 86 degrees F). Protect from light. Store extended release tablets at controlled room temperature at 25 degrees C (77 degrees F), excursions permitted to 15 to 30 degrees C (59 to 86 degrees F). Protect from light.

Topical

- Ensure that old patch is removed prior to application of new patch.
- Gel may be applied to abdomen, upper arms/shoulder, and thigh. Rotate site application and avoid using the same site on 2 consecutive days. Squeeze entire contents of the gel packet onto application site. Wear gloves and gently rub into skin until dried.
- Avoid exposure to open fire or smoking until gel has dried.
- Avoid contact with eyes, nose, open sores, recently shaved skin, and skin with rashes.
- Do not shower or immerse area in water for 1 hour after gel application.
- Cover application site with clothing if skin-to-skin contact is anticipated.
- Storage variances for each trade drug. All can be stored at controlled room temperature at 25 degrees for other variances see package insert. Protect from moisture.

ADVERSE EFFECTS ($\geq$ 5%) CNS:
Drowsiness, dizziness headache. **HEENT:** *Blurred vision.* **GI:** *Dry mouth,* nausea, *constipation,* diarrhea, indigestion, bloated feeling.

DIAGNOSTIC TEST INTERFERENCE
May suppress the wheal and flare reactions to skin test antigen.

INTERACTIONS: Drugs: Do not use with, ANTICHOLINERGIC AGENTS. CYP3A4 inhibitors may increase serum concentrations.

PHARMACOKINETICS Absorption: Diffuses across intact skin. **Onset:** 0.5–1 h. (oral immediate release) **Peak:** 3–6 h. (PO Immediate); 3 days (PO Extended) **Duration:** 6–10 h (PO immediate). 96 h transdermal. **Metabolism:** In liver (CYP 3A4). **Elimination:** Primarily in urine. **Half-Life:** 2–5 h.

NURSING IMPLICATIONS

Assessment & Drug Effects

- Periodic interruptions of therapy are recommended to determine patient's need for continued treatment. Tolerance has occurred in some patients.
- Keep prescriber informed of expected responses to drug therapy (e.g., effect on urinary frequency, urgency, urge incontinence, nocturia, completeness of bladder emptying).
- Monitor patients with colostomy or ileostomy closely; abdominal distention and the onset of diarrhea in these patients may be early signs of intestinal obstruction or of toxic megacolon.

Patient & Family Education

- Do not drive or engage in potentially hazardous activities until response to drug is known.

Common adverse effects in *italic;* life-threatening effects <u>underlined</u>; generic names in **bold**; classifications in SMALL CAPS; ♣ Canadian drug name; ○ Prototype drug; ⚠ Alert

1248

- Exercise caution in hot environments. By suppressing sweating, oxybutynin can cause fever and heat stroke.
- Review adverse effects with patient and/or caregiver.
- Report hallucinations, agitation, and confusion especially during the first few months of therapy and with dose increase.
- Avoid alcohol as it will increase drowsiness.

OXYCODONE HYDROCHLORIDE

(ox-i-koe'done)

Oxaydo, OxyContin, Roxicodone, Roxybond, Xtampza

Classification: NARCOTIC (OPIATE AGONIST); ANALGESIC
Therapeutic: NARCOTIC ANALGESIC
Prototype: Morphine
Controlled Substance: Schedule II

AVAILABILITY Tablet. **OxyContin:** Sustained release tablet; oral solution

ACTION & *THERAPEUTIC EFFECT*

Semisynthetic derivative of an opium agonist that binds with stereo-specific receptors in various sites of CNS to alter both perception of pain and emotional response to pain. *Active against moderate to moderately severe pain. Appears to be more effective in relief of acute than long-standing pain.*

USES Relief of moderate to moderately severe pain, neuralgia. Relieves postoperative, postextractional, postpartum pain.

CONTRAINDICATIONS Hypersensitivity to oxycodone and principle drugs with which it

is combined; bronchial asthma; known gastrointestinal obstruction; significant respiratory depression. pregnancy (category D for prolonged use or high doses at term); lactation.

CAUTIOUS USE Alcoholism; renal or hepatic disease; viral infections; Addison's disease; cardiac arrhythmias; chronic ulcerative colitis; history of drug abuse or dependency; gallbladder disease, acute abdominal conditions; head injury, intracranial lesions; history of seizures, hypothyroidism; BPH; respiratory disease; urethral stricture; peptic ulcer or coagulation abnormalities (combination products containing aspirin); older adult or debilitated patients; children.

ROUTE & DOSAGE

Moderate to Severe Pain

(Dose individualized per opioid tolerance and patient response)
Adult: **PO** 5–15 mg q4–6h prn; **Controlled release** 10 mg q12h (reserved for opioid tolerant patients)

Hepatic Impairment Dosage Adjustment

Start initial therapy at ⅓ to ½ normal dose and titrate carefully

ADMINISTRATION

Oral
- Ensure that sustained release form is not chewed or crushed. It **must be** swallowed whole.
- Administer with approximately the same amount of food to ensure consistent plasma levels.
- May be administered via gastrostomy or nasogastric tube. Flush the tube with water, pour capsule

contents into the tube with 15 mL of water; flush tube 2 more times with 10 mL of water per flush; milk or nutritional supplements may be used for flushing instead of water.

- Store at 15°–30° C (59°–86° F). Protect from light and moisture.

ADVERSE EFFECTS
CV: Bradycardia, flushing, edema, orthostatic hypotension. **Respiratory:** Shortness of breath, cough, respiratory depression. **CNS:** Euphoria, dysphoria, abnormal dreaming, agitation, abnormal thinking, anxiety, lightheadedness, *headache, dizziness, sedation.* **Endocrine:** Hyperglycemia, hyponatremia. **Skin:** Pruritus, skin rash. **GI:** Anorexia, nausea, abdominal pain, vomiting, *constipation,* jaundice, hepatotoxicity (combinations containing acetaminophen). **GU:** Dysuria, frequency of urination, urinary retention. **Ocular:** Miosis. **Other:** Unusual bleeding or bruising, arthralgia, back pain, fever, blurred vision.

DIAGNOSTIC TEST INTERFERENCE
Serum amylase levels may be elevated because oxycodone causes spasm of sphincter of Oddi. *Blood glucose determinations:* False decrease (measured by *glucose oxidase-peroxidase method*). *5-HIAA determination:* False positive with use of *nitrosonaphthol reagent* (quantitative test is unaffected).

INTERACTIONS
Drug: Alcohol and other CNS DEPRESSANTS add to CNS depressant activity. Monitor closely if used with **amiodarone.** Use caution with CYP3A4 INHIBITORS due to increased risk of toxicities. Serotonin syndrome could occur when used with TRIPTANS.

Do not use with BENZODIAZEPINES due to increased risk of sedation. **Herbal: St. John's wort** may increase sedation. **Food:** Grapefruit juice can increase adverse effects.

PHARMACOKINETICS
Absorption: Readily from GI tract. **Onset:** 10–15 min. **Peak:** 30–60 min. **Duration:** 4–5 h. **Distribution:** Crosses placenta; distributed into breast milk. **Metabolism:** In liver by CYP3A4, CYP2D6. **Elimination:** Primarily in urine. **Half-Life:** 3–5 h.

NURSING IMPLICATIONS

Black Box Warning

Oxycodone has been associated with high abuse potential, and life-threatening respiratory depression, neonatal opioid withdrawal, Cytochrome P450 3A4 interaction.

Assessment & Drug Effects
- Monitor respiratory status. Withhold drug and notify prescriber if respiratory depression occurs.
- Monitor patient's response closely, especially to sustained-release preparations.
- Consult prescriber if nausea continues after first few days of therapy.
- Note: Lightheadedness, dizziness, sedation, or fainting appears to be more prominent in ambulatory than in nonambulatory patients and may be alleviated if patient lies down. Monitor blood pressure.
- Evaluate patient's continued need for oxycodone preparations. Monitor effectiveness of pain relief. Psychic and physical dependence and tolerance may develop with repeated use. The potential for drug abuse is high.

0

Common adverse effects in *italic;* life-threatening effects <u>underlined</u>; generic names in **bold;** classifications in SMALL CAPS; ♣ Canadian drug name; ◑ Prototype drug; ⚠ Alert

- Be aware that serious overdosage of any oxycodone preparation presents problems associated with a narcotic overdose (respiratory depression, circulatory collapse, extreme somnolence progressing to stupor, coma, or death.) After long term use, discontinuation should be tapered. Monitor for signs of opioid withdrawal.

Patient & Family Education

- Do not alter dosage regimen by increasing, decreasing, or shortening intervals between doses. Habit formation and liver damage may result.
- Avoid potentially hazardous activities such as driving a car or operating machinery while using oxycodone preparation.
- Do not drink large amounts of alcoholic beverages while using oxycodone preparations; risk of liver damage is increased.
- Check with prescriber before taking OTC drugs for colds, stomach distress, allergies, insomnia, or pain.
- Inform surgeon or dentist that you are taking an oxycodone preparation before any surgical procedure is undertaken.

OXYMETAZOLINE HYDROCHLORIDE

(ox-i-met-az'oh-leen)
Afrin, Dristan, Nafrine ♣, Neo-Synephrine 12 Hour, Nostrilla, Rhofade
Classification: NASAL PREPARATION; DECONGESTANT
Therapeutic: DECONGESTANT
Prototype: Naphazoline

AVAILABILITY Intranasal solution; cream; ophthalmic drop

ACTION & *THERAPEUTIC EFFECT*
Sympathomimetic agent that acts directly on alpha receptors of sympathetic nervous system resulting in relief of nasal congestion. *Constricts smaller arterioles in nasal passages and has prolonged decongestant effect.*

USES Relief of nasal congestion in a variety of allergic and infectious disorders of the upper respiratory tract; ocular pruritis (ophthalmic drops); acne rosacea (cream).

CONTRAINDICATIONS Closed-angle glaucoma.

CAUTIOUS USE Within 14 days of MAO inhibitors, CAD, hypertension, hyperthyroidism, DM; lactation; children younger than 2 y.

ROUTE & DOSAGE

Nasal Congestion

Adult /Adolescent/Child (6 y and older): **Intranasal** 2–3 drops or 2–3 sprays of 0.05% solution into each nostril bid for up to 3–5 days

Acne Rosacea (cream only)

Adult: Topical Apply thin layer once daily

ADMINISTRATION
Topical

- Prime the pump. Apply a smooth and even layer across entire face (forehead, each cheek, nose, and chin). Avoid eyes and lips. Do not apply to open wounds or irritated skin. Wash hands after application.

Instillation of Nasal Spray

- Place spray nozzle in nostril without occluding it and tilt head slightly forward prior to instillation of spray; instruct patient to sniff briskly during administration.

- Rinse dropper or spray tip in hot water after each use to prevent contamination of solution by nasal secretions.
- Wash hands after administration.

ADVERSE EFFECTS HEENT: *Burning,* stinging, dryness of nasal mucosa, *sneezing.* **Other:** Headache, lightheadedness, drowsiness, insomnia, palpitations, *rebound congestion,* exacerbation of acne rosacea, application site erythema, and pain (topical).

PHARMACOKINETICS Onset: 5–10 min. **Duration:** 6–10 h.

NURSING IMPLICATIONS

Assessment & Drug Effects
- Monitor for S&S of excess use. If noted, discuss possibility of rebound congestion (nasal).
- Monitor for improvement of facial erythema due to rosacea (topical).

Patient & Family Education
- Wash hands carefully after handling oxymetazoline. Anisocoria (inequality of pupil size, blurred vision) can develop if eyes are rubbed with contaminated fingers.
- Do not to exceed recommended dosage. Rebound congestion (chemical rhinitis) may occur with prolonged or excessive use (nasal administration).
- Systemic effects can result from swallowing excessive medication (nasal administration).
- Report any development of facial acne.

OXYMETHOLONE
(ox-i-meth'oh-lone)
Anadrol-50
Classification: ANDROGEN/ ANABOLIC STEROID

Therapeutic: ANABOLIC STEROID
Prototype: Testosterone
Controlled Substance: Schedule III

AVAILABILITY Tablet

ACTION & THERAPEUTIC EFFECT
Mechanism of action in refractory anemias is unclear but may be due to direct stimulation of bone marrow, protein anabolic activity, or to androgenic stimulation of erythropoiesis. *Stimulates formation of red blood cells in the bone marrow. Stimulates bone growth, aids in bone matrix reconstitution.*

USES Aplastic anemia.

CONTRAINDICATIONS Hypersensitivity to oxymetholone; prostatic hypertrophy with obstruction; prostatic or male breast cancer; carcinoma of the breast in women with hypercalcemia; hepatic decompensation; hepatic carcinoma; nephrosis or nephrotic stage of nephritis; females of childbearing age; pregnancy (category X); lactation.

CAUTIOUS USE Prepubertal males; older males; DM; history of cardiac, renal, or hepatic impairment; CAD; atherosclerosis; children.

ROUTE & DOSAGE

Aplastic Anemia
Adult/Adolescent/Child: **PO** 1–2 mg/kg/day (may require doses up to 5 mg/kg/day)

ADMINISTRATION

Oral
- For treatment of anemias, a minimum trial period of 3–6 mo is recommended, since response tends to be slow.

Common adverse effects in *italic;* life-threatening effects <u>underlined;</u> generic names in **bold;** classifications in SMALL CAPS; ♣ Canadian drug name; ⚫ Prototype drug; ⚠ Alert

- Store at 15°–30° C (59°–86° F). Protect from heat and light.

ADVERSE EFFECTS CV: *Edema,* skin flush. **Endocrine:** Androgenic in women: Suppression of ovulation, lactation, or menstruation; *hoarseness or deepening of voice* (often irreversible); *hirsutism; oily skin; acne;* clitoral enlargement; regression of breasts; male-pattern baldness. Hypoestrogenic effects in women: Flushing, sweating; vaginitis with pruritus, drying, bleeding; menstrual irregularities. Hypercalcemia. **GI:** *Nausea, vomiting, anorexia,* diarrhea, jaundice, hepatotoxicity. **GU:** Bladder irritability. **Hematologic:** Bleeding (with concurrent anticoagulant therapy), iron deficiency anemia, leukemia. **Other:** Premature epiphyseal closure, phallic enlargement, priapism. Postpubertal: Testicular atrophy, decreased ejaculatory volume, azoospermia, oligospermia (after prolonged administration or excessive dosage), impotence, epididymitis, gynecomastia; increased risk of atherosclerosis.

INTERACTIONS Drug: May enhance hypoprothrombinemic effects of **warfarin. Herbal: Echinacea** may increase risk of hepatotoxicity.

PHARMACOKINETICS Absorption: Readily from GI tract. **Metabolism:** In liver. **Elimination:** In urine. **Half-Life:** 9 h.

NURSING IMPLICATIONS

Black Box Warning

Oxymetholone has been associated with hepatic dysfunction, liver failure, liver cell tumors, and increased risk of atherosclerosis from blood lipid changes.

Assessment & Drug Effects

- Monitor patient with a history of seizures closely because an increase in their frequency may be noted.
- Monitor periodically for edema that may develop with or without CHF.
- Monitor for and report jaundice or other S&S of hepatotoxicity (see Appendix F). Withhold drug at first sign of liver toxicity.
- Monitor for hypercalcemia (see Appendix F), especially in women with breast cancer.
- Monitor lab tests: Periodic Hgb and Hct, serum iron and iron binding capacity, and LFTs.

Patient & Family Education

- Monitor blood glucose for loss of glycemic control if diabetic.
- Stop taking drug and notify prescriber if jaundice appears.
- Women: Notify prescriber of signs of virilization.

OXYMORPHONE HYDROCHLORIDE

(ox-i-mor'fone)

Numorphan, Opana, Opana ER

Classification: NARCOTIC (OPIATE AGONIST); ANALGESIC
Therapeutic: NARCOTIC ANALGESIC
Prototype: Morphine
Controlled Substance: Schedule II

AVAILABILITY Solution for injection; suppository; extended release tablet; tablet

ACTION & *THERAPEUTIC EFFECT*
The precise mechanism of the action is unknown; however, specific CNS opioid receptors for endogenous compounds with opioid-like activity have been identified throughout the

CNS and play a role in the analgesic effects of this drug. *Effective in relief of moderate to severe pain.*

USES Relief of moderate to severe pain, preoperative medication, support of anesthesia.

CONTRAINDICATIONS Hypersensitivity to oxymorphone; pulmonary edema resulting from chemical respiratory irritants; ileus; respiratory depression without appropriate monitoring; acute or severe bronchial asthma; upper airway obstruction; hypercapnia; moderate and severe hepatic function impairment; status asthmaticus.

CAUTIOUS USE Alcoholism; biliary tract disease; bladder obstruction; severe pulmonary disease, respiratory insufficiency, COPD; head injury; circulatory shock; history of seizures; renal impairment; depression; older adults and debilitated patients; pregnancy (category C); lactation; children younger than 18 y.

ROUTE & DOSAGE

Moderate to Severe Pain

Adult: **PO** 10–20 mg q4–6h prn; **Extended release** 5–10 mg q12h; **Subcutaneous/IM** 1–1.5 mg q4–6h prn **IV** 0.5 mg q4–6h then switch to alternate route **PR** 5 mg q4–6h prn

ADMINISTRATION

Oral

- Give on an empty stomach at least 1 h before or 2 h after eating.
- Extended-release tablets must be swallowed whole with enough water to ensure immediate, complete swallowing. Tablets must not be crushed or chewed.

Subcutaneous/Intramuscular

- Give undiluted.

Intravenous

PREPARE: **Direct:** May be given undiluted or diluted in 5 mL of sterile water or NS.
ADMINISTER: **Direct:** Give at a rate of 0.5 mg over 2–5 min.

- Protect drug from light. Store suppositories in refrigerator 2°–15° C (36°–59° F).

ADVERSE EFFECTS CV: <u>Cardiac arrest</u>, circulatory depression. **Respiratory:** <u>Respiratory depression</u> (see morphine), apnea, <u>respiratory arrest</u>. **CNS:** *Dizziness,* lightheadedness, sedation. **GI:** *Nausea, vomiting, euphoria.* **Other:** Sweating, coma, shock.

INTERACTIONS Drug: Alcohol and other CNS DEPRESSANTS add to CNS depression; **propofol** increases risk of bradycardia.

PHARMACOKINETICS Onset: 5–10 min IV; 10–15 min IM; 15–30 min PR. **Peak:** 1–1.5 h. **Duration:** 3–6 h. **Distribution:** Crosses placenta. **Metabolism:** In liver. **Elimination:** In urine. **Half-Life:** PO 7–9 h; extended release 9–11 h.

NURSING IMPLICATIONS

Black Box Warning

Oxymorphone has been associated with high abuse potential, respiratory depression, accidental overdose (especially in children), and death with co-ingestion of alcohol.

Assessment & Drug Effects

- Monitor respiratory rate. Withhold drug and notify prescriber if rate falls below 12 breaths/min.

- Supervise ambulation and advise patient of possible lightheadedness. Older adult and debilitated patients are most susceptible to CNS depressant effects of drug.
- Evaluate patient's continued need for narcotic analgesic. Prolonged use can lead to dependence of morphine type.
- Medication contains sulfite and may precipitate a hypersensitivity reaction in susceptible patient.

Patient & Family Education
- Use caution when walking because of potential for injury from dizziness.
- Do not consume alcohol while taking oxymorphone.

OXYTOCIN INJECTION
(ox-i-toe'sin)
Pitocin
Classification: OXYTOCIC
Therapeutic: OXYTOCIC

AVAILABILITY Solution for injection

ACTION & *THERAPEUTIC EFFECT*
Synthetic polypeptide identical pharmacologically to natural oxytocin released by posterior pituitary. By direct action on myofibrils, produces phasic contractions characteristic of normal delivery. Uterine sensitivity to oxytocin increases during gestational period and peaks sharply before parturition. *Effective in initiating or improving uterine contractions at term.*

USES To initiate or improve uterine contraction at term, management of inevitable, incomplete, or missed abortion; stimulation of uterine contractions during third stage of labor; stimulation to overcome uterine inertia; control of postpartum hemorrhage and promotion of postpartum uterine involution. Also used to induce labor in cases of maternal diabetes, preeclampsia, eclampsia, and erythroblastosis fetalis.

CONTRAINDICATIONS Hypersensitivity to oxytocin; significant cephalopelvic disproportion, unfavorable fetal position or presentations that are undeliverable without conversion before delivery, obstetric emergencies that favor surgical intervention, fetal distress in which delivery is not imminent, prematurity, placenta previa, prolonged use in severe toxemia or uterine inertia, hypertonic uterine patterns, conditions predisposing to thromboplastin or amniotic fluid embolism (dead fetus, abruptio placentae), grand multiparity, invasive cervical carcinoma, primipara older than 35 y, past history of uterine sepsis or of traumatic delivery; pregnancy (category C).

CAUTIOUS USE Preeclampsia; history of seizures; history of mental hypertension.

ROUTE & DOSAGE

Labor Induction
Adult: **IV** 0.5–2 milliunits/min, may increase by 1–2 milliunits/min q15–60 min (max: 20 milliunits/min); dose is decreased when labor is established; **High dose regimen** 6 milliunits/min, may increase by 6 milliunits/min q15–60 min until contraction pattern established.

Postpartum Bleeding
Adult: **IM** 10 units total dose; **IV** Infuse a total of 10–40 units at a rate of 20–40 milliunits/min after delivery

---

Incomplete Abortion
Adult: **IV** 10–20 milliunits/min

ADMINISTRATION

Intramuscular

- NIOSH recommends the use of double gloves and protective gown. During administration, if there is a potential that the substance could splash or if the patient may resist, use eye/face protection.
- Give 10 units IM after delivery of the placenta.

Intravenous

PREPARE: **IV Infusion:** When diluting oxytocin for IV infusion, rotate bottle gently to distribute medicine throughout solution. **IV Infusion for Inducing Labor:** Add 10 units (1 mL) to 1 L of D5W, NS, LR, or D5NS to yield 10 milliunits/mL. **IV Infusion for Postpartum Bleeding/Incomplete Abortion:** Add 10–40 units (1–4 mL) to 1 L of D5W, NS, LR, or D5NS to yield 10–40 milliunits/mL.

ADMINISTER: **IV Infusion:** Use an infusion pump for accurate control of infusion rate. **IV Infusion for Inducing Labor:** Initially infuse 0.5–2 milliunits/min; increase by 1–2 milliunits/min at 30–60 min intervals. **IV Infusion for Postpartum Bleeding:** Initially infuse 10–40 milliunits/min, then adjust to control uterine atony. **IV Infusion for Incomplete Abortion:** Infuse 10–20 milliunits/min. Do not exceed 30 units in 12 h.

INCOMPATIBILITIES: **Y-site: Amphotericin B, ampicillin, chlorpromazine, dantrolene, diazepam, diazoxide, dimenhydrinate, haloperidol, hydralazine, inamrinone lactate, indomethacin, insulin, methohexital, pantoprazole, phenytoin, sulfamethoxazole/ trimethoprim.**

ADVERSE EFFECTS CV: <u>Dysrhythmia</u>, fetal bradycardia, hypertensive episodes. **CNS:** <u>Brain injury, central nervous system deficit, coma, convulsion.</u> **Endocrine:** Water intoxication. **GI:** Nausea, vomiting. **GU:** Pelvic hematoma. **Hematologic:** <u>Afibrinogenemia.</u>

INTERACTIONS Drug: vasoconstrictors cause severe hypertension; **cyclopropane anesthesia** causes hypotension, maternal bradycardia, arrhythmias. **Herbal: Ephedra, ma huang** may cause hypertension.

PHARMACOKINETICS Duration: 1 h. **Distribution:** Distributed throughout extracellular fluid; small amount may cross placenta. **Metabolism:** Rapidly destroyed in liver and kidneys. **Elimination:** Small amounts excreted unchanged in urine. **Half-Life:** 3–5 min.

NURSING IMPLICATIONS

Assessment & Drug E†ffects

- Start flow charts to record maternal BP and other vital signs, I&O ratio, weight, strength, duration, and frequency of contractions, as well as fetal heart tone and rate, before instituting treatment.
- Monitor fetal heart rate and maternal BP and pulse at least q15min during infusion period; evaluate tonus of myometrium during and between contractions and record on flow chart. Report change in rate and rhythm immediately.
- Stop infusion to prevent fetal anoxia, turn patient on her side, and notify prescriber if contractions are prolonged (occurring

at less than 2-min intervals) and if monitor records contractions about 50 mm Hg or if contractions last 90 sec or longer. Stimulation will wane rapidly within 2–3 min. Oxygen administration may be necessary.

- If local or regional (caudal, spinal) anesthesia is being given to the patient receiving oxytocin, be alert to the possibility of hypertensive crisis (sudden intense occipital headache, palpitation, marked hypertension, stiff neck, nausea, vomiting, sweating, fever, photophobia, dilated pupils, bradycardia or tachycardia, constricting chest pain).
- Monitor I&O during labor. If patient is receiving drug by prolonged IV infusion, watch for symptoms of water intoxication (drowsiness, listlessness, headache, confusion, anuria, weight gain). Report changes in alertness and orientation and changes in I&O ratio (i.e., marked decrease in output with excessive intake).
- Check fundus frequently during the first few postpartum hours and several times daily thereafter.

Patient & Family Education
- Be aware of purpose and anticipated effect of oxytocin.
- Report sudden, severe headache immediately to health care providers.

OZENOXACIN
(oz-en-ox′a sin)
Xepi
Classification: QUINOLONE ANTIBIOTIC
Therapeutic: ANTIBIOTIC
Prototype: Ciprofloxacin

AVAILABILITY Topical 1% external cream

ACTION & *THERAPEUTIC EFFECT*
Similar to other quinolone antibiotics, inhibits DNA gyrase A and topoisomerase IV, enzymes responsible for bacterial DNA replication. *Bactericidal against S. aureus and S. pyogenes which treats common impetigo infections.*

USES Treatment of impetigo.

CAUTIOUS USE Prolonged use may result in overgrowth of resistant bacteria or fungi; only for external topical use.

ROUTE & DOSAGE

Impetigo
Adult and Child: **Topical** Apply a thin film 2 × day for five days to the affected areas

ADMINISTRATION
Topical
- Apply a thin film of cream 2 × day to the affected area.
- Wash hands after application. Treated area may be covered with a sterile bandage or gauze dressing.
- Store at 20°–25° C (68°–77° F).

ADVERSE EFFECTS Skin: Rosacea, seborrheic dermatitis.

PHARMACOKINETICS Absorption: Due to topical application, negligible systemic absorption. Elimination: Not metabolized.

NURSING IMPLICATIONS
Assessment & Drug Effects
- Assess for effective use and severe skin irritation.

Patient & Family Education
- Apply medication topically only.
- Report any skin irritation to your provider.

PACLITAXEL ⊕

(pac-li-tax'el)

Abraxane, Taxol

Classification: ANTINEOPLASTIC TAXANE

Therapeutic: ANTINEOPLASTIC; ANTIMICROTUBULE

AVAILABILITY Solution for injection; powder for injection (with 900 mg human albumin)

ACTION & *THERAPEUTIC EFFECT*

During cell division paclitaxel acts as an antimicrotubular agent that interferes with the microtubule network essential for interphase and mitosis. This results in abnormal spindle formation during mitosis. *Interferes with growth of rapidly dividing cells including cancer cells, and eventually causes cell death. Additionally, the breakup of the cytoskeleton within non-dividing cells interrupts intracellular transport and communications.*

USES Ovarian cancer, breast cancer, Kaposi's sarcoma, non–small-cell lung cancer (NSCLC).

UNLABELED USES Squamous cell head and neck cancer, small-cell lung cancer, endometrial cancer, esophageal cancer, gastric cancer, testicular cancer, germ cell tumors, and other solid tumors, leukemia, melanoma.

CONTRAINDICATIONS Taxol: Hypersensitivity to paclitaxel, or taxanes; baseline neutrophil count less than 1500 cells/mm^3; thrombocytopenia; with AIDS-related Kaposi's sarcoma baseline neutrophil count less than 1000 cells/mm^3; pregnancy (category D); lactation (infant risk cannot be ruled out).

For **Abraxane:** Baseline neutrophil count less than 1500 cells/mm^3.

CAUTIOUS USE Cardiac arrhythmias, cardiac disease; impaired liver function; alcoholism; older adults; peripheral neuropathy. Safety and efficacy in children not established.

ROUTE & DOSAGE

Ovarian Cancer, NSCLC

Adult: **IV** 135 mg/m^2 over 24 h infusion repeated q3wk

Breast Cancer

Adult: **IV** 175 mg/m^2 over 3 h q3wk

Abraxane: **IV** 260 mg/m^2 over 30 min q3wk

Kaposi's Sarcoma

Adult: **IV** 135 mg/m^2 infused over 3 h q3wk or 100 mg/m^2 infused over 3 h q2wk

ADMINISTRATION

Intravenous

- NIOSH recommends double gloves and a protective gown when handling. If there is a potential for a splash or the patient may resist, use eye/face protection. Note: Premedication is required (except with **Abraxane**) to avoid severe hypersensitivity. ▪ Follow institutional or standard guidelines for preparation, handling, and disposal of cytotoxic agents.

***PREPARE:* IV Infusion: Dilution of Conventional Paclitaxel:** Do not use equipment or devices containing polyvinyl chloride (PVC) in preparation of infusion. ▪ Dilute to a final concentration of 0.3–1.2 mg/mL in any of the following: D5W, NS, D5/NS, or D5W in Ringer's injection. The prepared solution may be hazy, but this does not indicate a loss of potency.

Abraxane Vial Reconstitution: Slowly inject 20 mL NS over at least 1 min onto the inside wall of the vial to yield 5 mg/mL. ▪ **Do not** inject directly into the cake powder. Allow vial to sit for at least 5 min, then gently swirl for at least 2 min to completely dissolve. If foaming occurs, let stand for at least 15 min until foam subsides. ▪ If particulates or settling are visible, gently invert vial to ensure complete resuspension prior to use. ▪ Remove the required dose and inject into an empty sterile, PVC or non-PVC type IV bag.

ADMINISTER: **IV Infusion:** Because tissue necrosis occurs with extravasation, frequently assess patency of a peripheral IV site. ▪ **Conventional Paclitaxel:** Infuse over 1–24 h through IV tubing containing an in-line (0.22 -micron or less) filter. Do not use equipment containing PVC. ▪ **Abraxane: Do not** use an in-line filter. Infuse over 30 min.

INCOMPATIBILITIES: Solution/additive: **PVC bags** and **infusion sets** should be avoided (except with Abraxane) due to leaching of DEHP (plasticizer). ▪ Do not mix with any other medications. Y-site: **Amiodarone hydrochloride, amphotericin B, amphotericin B cholesteryl sulfate complex, chlorpromazine, diazepam, digoxin, doxorubicin liposome, gemtuzumab, hydroxyzine, idarubicin, indomethacin, labetalol, methylprednisolone, mitoxantrone, phenytoin, propranolol.**

▪ **Conventional paclitaxel** solutions diluted for infusion are stable at room temperature (approximately 25° C/77° F) for up to 27 h. ▪ Reconstituted **Abraxane** should be used immediately but may be kept refrigerated for up to 8 h if needed.

ADVERSE EFFECTS CV: *Flushing,* *edema,* hypotension. **CNS:** *Peripheral neuropathy.* **Skin:** *Alopecia,* rash. **Hepatic:** Increased serum alkaline phosphatase, increased serum AST. **GI:** *Diarrhea, inflammation of mucous membrane, nausea, vomiting.* **Musculoskeletal:** Weakness. **Hematologic:** *Anemia, lekopenia, neutropenia, thrombocytopenia.*

INTERACTIONS Drug: Increased myelosuppression if **cisplatin, doxorubicin** is given before paclitaxel; **ketoconazole** can inhibit metabolism of paclitaxel; additive bradycardia with BETA-BLOCKERS, **digoxin, verapamil;** additive risk of bleeding with ANTICOAGULANTS, NSAIDS, PLATELET INHIBITORS (including **aspirin**), THROMBOLYTIC AGENTS. Do not use with LIVE VACCINES, **conivaptan, deferiprone, dipyrone, natalizumab, pimecrolimus, tacrolimus.**

PHARMACOKINETICS Distribution: Greater than 90% protein bound; does not cross CSF. **Metabolism:** In liver (CYP3A4, 2C8). **Elimination:** Feces 70%, urine 14%. **Half-Life:** 1–9 h.

NURSING IMPLICATIONS

Black Box Warning

Paclitaxel has been associated with severe hypersensitivity, anaphylaxis, and neutropenia.

Assessment & Drug Effects

- Monitor for hypersensitivity reactions, especially during first and second administrations of the paclitaxel. S&S requiring treatment, but not necessarily discontinuation of the drug, include dyspnea, hypotension, and chest pain. Discontinue immediately and manage symptoms aggressively if angioedema and generalized urticaria develop.
- Monitor vital signs frequently, especially during the first hour of infusion. Bradycardia occurs in approximately 12% of patients, usually during infusion. It does not normally require treatment. Cardiac monitoring is indicated for those with severe conduction abnormalities.
- Monitor for anemia, neutropenia, and thrombocytopenia.
- Monitor for peripheral neuropathy, the severity of which is dose dependent. Severe symptoms occur primarily with higher than recommended doses.
- Monitor lab tests: Periodic CBC with differential and platelet count, and Hct & Hgb throughout course of treatment.

Patient & Family Education

- Immediately report to prescriber S&S of paclitaxel hypersensitivity: Difficulty breathing, chest pain, palpitations, angioedema (subcutaneous swelling usually around face and neck), and skin rashes or itching.
- Be sure to have periodic blood work as prescribed.
- Avoid aspirin, NSAIDs, and alcohol to minimize GI distress.
- Be aware of high probability of developing hair loss (greater than 80%).

PALBOCICLIB
(pal-bo-cyc'lib)

Ibrance

Classification: ANTINEOPLASTIC; KINASE INHIBITOR; CYCLIN-DEPENDENT KINASE (CDK) INHIBITOR

Therapeutic: ANTINEOPLASTIC

AVAILABILITY Capsules

ACTION & *THERAPEUTIC EFFECT*

Inhibits an enzyme (cyclin-dependent kinase) that is essential for cancer cells to progress through the cell cycle at the G1/S phase. *Reduces proliferation of breast cancer cells by preventing progression through the cell cycle.*

USES Treatment of postmenopausal women with estrogen receptor (ER) positive, human epidermal growth factor receptor 2 (HER2) negative advanced breast cancer in combination with letrozole.

CONTRAINDICATIONS Pregnancy; lactation.

CAUTIOUS USE Concomitant use of moderate or strong CYP3A4 inhibitor; grapefruit products; bone marrow suppression; infection; thromboembolic events including pulmonary embolism.

ROUTE & DOSAGE

Breast Cancer

Adult: **PO** 125 mg once daily in combination with letrozole for 21 days, followed by 7 days with letrozole only; repeat cycle until progressive disease or unacceptable toxicity occur

Hematologic Toxicity Dosage Adjustment

Grade 3: Withhold initiation of next cycle until recovery to Grade 2 or less

Grade 3 with ANC (less than 1000 to 500/mm³) and Fever 38.5° C (101.3° F) or greater and/or infection: Withhold until recovery to Grade 2 or less (at least 1000/mm³); resume at 100 mg once daily if first occurrence or 75 mg once daily if second occurrence

Grade 4: Withhold until recovery to Grade 2 or less; resume at 100 mg once daily if first occurrence or 75 mg once daily if second occurrence

Non-Hematologic Toxicity Dosage Adjustment

Grade 3 or higher: Withhold until recovery to Grade 2 or less depending on toxicity; resume at 100 mg once daily if first occurrence or 75 mg once daily if second occurrence

Co-Administered Strong CYP3A Inhibitor Dosage Adjustment

Decrease dose to 75 mg once daily

ADMINISTRATION

Oral

- Give with food at approximately the same time each day.
- Capsules must be swallowed whole. They must not be crushed, chewed, or opened prior to swallowing (do not administer if capsules are broken, cracked, or not fully intact).
- Do not administer with grapefruit juice.
- Store at 20°–25° C (68°–77° F).

ADVERSE EFFECTS Respiratory: Epistaxis, <u>pulmonary embolism</u>, *upper respiratory infection.* **Endocrine:** Decreased appetite. **Skin:** *Alopecia.* **GI:** *Diarrhea, nausea, stomatitis,* vomiting. **Hematologic:** *Anemia, leukopenia, neutropenia,* thrombocytopenia. **Other:** Asthenia, *fatigue,* peripheral neuropathy.

INTERACTIONS Drug: Concomitant use of strong CYP3A inhibitors (e.g., **clarithromycin, indinavir, itraconazole, ketoconazole, lopinavir/ritonavir, nefazodone, nelfinavir, posaconazole, ritonavir, saquinavir, telaprevir, telithromycin, verapamil,** and **voriconazole**) increases the levels of palbociclib. Concomitant use of strong CYP3A inducers (e.g., **phenytoin, rifampin, carbamazepine**) decreases the levels of palbociclib. Concomitant use of moderate CYP3A inducers (e.g., **bosentan, efavirenz, etravirine, modafinil, nafcillin**) may decrease the levels of palbociclib. Palbociclib increases the levels of midazolam. Palbociclib may increase the levels of other drugs requiring CYP3A isozymes (e.g., **alfentanil, cyclosporine, dihydroergotamine, ergotamine, everolimus, fentanyl, pimozide, quinidine, sirolimus, tacrolimus**). **Food: Grapefruit** or **grapefruit juice** may increase the levels of palbociclib. **Herbal: St John's wort** decreases the levels of palbociclib.

PHARMACOKINETICS Absorption: 46% bioavailable. **Peak:** 6–12 h. **Distribution:** 85% plasma protein bound. **Metabolism:** In liver. **Elimination:** Fecal (74.1%) and renal (17.5%). **Half-Life:** 29 h.

NURSING IMPLICATIONS

Assessment & Drug Effects

- Monitor for and report promptly S&S of infection; report fever of 101° F or greater.
- Monitor for S&S of pulmonary embolism (e.g., shortness of breath, anxiety, chest pain, hemoptysis, fainting, irregular or rapid HR).
- Monitor lab tests: Baseline CBC with differential, repeat q2wk for first 2 cycles, then prior to each cycle or more often if indicated.

Patient & Family Education

- Report immediately to prescriber any of the following S&S: Fever, chills, dizziness, weakness, increased tendency to bleed and/or bruise, shortness of breath or rapid breathing, chest pain, or rapid heart rate.
- Do not consume grapefruit or grapefruit juice while taking this drug.
- Women should use effective contraception during treatment and for at least 2 wk after the last dose.
- Do not breast-feed while taking this drug.

PALIFERMIN

(pal-i-fur'men)

Kepivance

Classification: BIOLOGIC RESPONSE MODIFIER; KERATINOCYTE GROWTH FACTOR; CYTOKINE

Therapeutic: KERATINOCYTE GROWTH FACTOR (KGF)

AVAILABILITY Powder for injection

ACTION & *THERAPEUTIC EFFECT*

Naturally occurring keratinocyte growth factor (KGF) is produced and regulated in response to epithelial tissue injury. Binding of KGF to its receptors in epithelial cells results in proliferation, differentiation, and repair of injury to epithelial cells. Palifermin is a synthetic form of KGF; thus it enhances replacement of injured cells. *Reduces the incidence of severe oral mucositis that interferes with food consumption in the cancer patient.*

USES Reduction of the incidence and duration of severe oral mucositis in patients with hematologic malignancies who are receiving myelotoxic therapy requiring hematopoietic stem cell support.

CONTRAINDICATIONS Hypersensitivity to *Escherichia coli*-derived protein, palifermin; nonhematologic malignancies; within 24 h of chemotherapy; lactation.

CAUTIOUS USE Use contraception for females of childbearing age; pregnancy (category C); children.

ROUTE & DOSAGE

Mucositis Prophylaxis

Adult: **IV** 60 mcg/kg/day for 3 days before and 3 days after myelotoxic therapy (total: 6 doses)

ADMINISTRATION

Intravenous

Do not give within 24 h before/after or during myelotoxic chemotherapy.

PREPARE: **Direct:** Use double gloves and protective gown while preparing and administering. If there is any chance that the patient may resist, wear eye/

Common adverse effects in *italic*; life-threatening effects underlined; generic names in **bold**; classifications in SMALL CAPS; ✦ Canadian drug name; ⊙ Prototype drug; ⚠ Alert

face protection. Reconstitute powder with 1.2 mL sterile water **only** to yield 5 mg/mL. Gently swirl to dissolve but do not shake. ▪ Powder will dissolve in about 3 min. Should be used immediately. *ADMINISTER:* **Direct:** Give as a bolus dose. ▪ If heparin is used to maintain the IV line, flush before/after with NS. ▪ If diluted solution was refrigerated (max refrigeration time: 24 h), may warm to room temperature for up to 1 h but protect from light. *INCOMPATIBILITIES:* Y-site: **Heparin.**

▪ Store powder vial at 2°–8° C (36°–46° F). Protect from light. ▪ If needed, may store reconstituted solution refrigerated for up to 24 h. ▪ Discard any reconstituted solution left at room temperature for longer than 1 h.

ADVERSE EFFECTS CNS: *Dysesthesia.* **Endocrine:** *Elevated serum amylase, elevated serum lipase.* **Skin:** *Erythema, pruritus, rash.* **GI:** *Mouth/tongue thickness or discoloration, taste alterations, abdominal pain, anorexia, vomiting.* **GU:** Proteinuria. **Musculoskeletal:** *Arthralgia.* **Other:** *Edema, arthralgia, fever, pain.*

INTERACTIONS Drug: Should not be administered within 24 h before, during infusion of or within 24 h after administration of ANTINEOPLASTIC agents.

PHARMACOKINETICS Distribution: Extravascular distribution. **Half-Life:** 4.5 h.

NURSING IMPLICATIONS

Assessment & Drug Effects
▪ Monitor for improvement in mucositis.

▪ Monitor for S&S of oral toxicities and skin toxicities.

Patient & Family Education
▪ Report any of the following to a health care provider: Alteration of taste, discoloration or enlargement of the tongue, lack of sensation around the mouth, skin rash, itching, or edema.

PALIPERIDONE

(pa-li'per-i-done)
Invega

PALIPERIDONE PALMITATE

Invega Sustenna, Invega Trinza
Classification: ATYPICAL ANTI-PSYCHOTIC
Therapeutic: ANTIPSYCHOTIC
Prototype: Clozapine

AVAILABILITY Extended release tablet; solution for injection

ACTION & THERAPEUTIC EFFECT While the mechanism is unknown, its proposed action interferes with binding of dopamine to dopamine type 2 (D2) receptors, serotonin (5-HT2A) receptors, and alpha-adrenergic receptors. *Effective in controlling symptoms of schizophrenia as well as other psychotic symptoms.*

USES Treatment of schizophrenia, schizoaffective disorder.

UNLABELED USES Agitation associated with dementia, bipolar disorder.

CONTRAINDICATIONS Hypersensitivity to paliperidone, risperidone; concurrent administration with drugs that produce QT_c prolongation; severe GI narrowing (pathologic or iatrogenic); drug induced

P

NMS; older adults with dementia-related psychosis; pregnancy—fetal risk cannot be ruled out; lactation—infant risk cannot be ruled out.

CAUTIOUS USE History of cerebrovascular events; hypovolemia, dehydration; cardiovascular disease; QT prolongation; history of cardiac arrhythmias; risk factors for hypotension; renal impairment; CNS pathology; history of seizures; systemic infection; DM; hyperglycemia; obesity; Parkinson's disease; Lewy bodies dementia; older adults; children younger than 12 y.

ROUTE & DOSAGE

Schizophrenia

Adult: **PO** Initially 6 mg/day; may adjust up/down in 3 mg increments; at least 5 day intervals needed for dosage increments (max: 12 mg/day); **IM** 234 mg on day 1, then 156 mg on day 8, then monthly dose of 117 mg (dose may vary based on patient response)
Adolescent: **PO** 3 mg daily

Schizoaffective Disorder

Adult: **PO** 6 mg daily, dose adjusted at intervals of more than 4 days (max: 12 mg/day); **IM** 234 mg on day 1, then 156 mg on day 8, then monthly dose of 117 mg (dose may vary based on patient response)

Renal Impairment Dosage Adjustment

CrCl 50–79 mL/min: Max: **PO** 6 mg/day; **IM** 156 mg on day 1 and 117 mg 1 wk later, then monthly 78 mg injections; *CrCl 10–49 mL/min:* Max: **PO** 3 mg/day; **IM** not recommended

ADMINISTRATION

Oral

- Extended release tablets **must be** swallowed whole. They should not be chewed or crushed.
- Give in the morning with or without food.
- Store extended release tablets at 25 degrees C (77 degrees F), with excursion permitted to 15 to 30 degrees C (59 to 86 degrees F). Protect from moisture.

Intramuscular

- Give as a single injection; do not administer in divided doses. Must be administered by a healthcare provider.
- First 2 doses on day 1 and 1 wk later: Inject slowly, deep into the deltoid muscle.
- Monthly maintenance dose: Inject slowly, deep into the deltoid or gluteal muscle.
- Store extended release tablets at 25 degrees C (77 degrees F), with excursion permitted to 15 to 30 degrees C (59 to 86 degrees F).

ADVERSE EFFECTS (≥ 5%) CV: *tachycardia.* **Respiratory:** Nasopharyngitis. **CNS:** *Akathisia, anxiety,* dystonia, dyskinesia, extrapyramidal disorder, Parkinsonism, *somnolence,* tremor. **Endocrine:** Hyperprolactinemia, weight gain. **GI:** Dyspepsia, constipation.

INTERACTIONS Drug: Enhanced CNS depression with **alcohol** or CNS DEPRESSANTS. Paliperidone may enhance the effects of ANTIHYPERTENSIVE AGENTS. Paliperidone can diminish the effects of DOPAMINE AGONISTS **(levodopa, cabergoline, pergolide, pramipexole, ropinirole);** ANTIPARKINSON AGENTS. **Carbamazepine** decreases effectiveness. Avoid with agents that increase QT interval (e.g., **bepridil, ziprasidone**).

Common adverse effects in *italic;* life-threatening effects <u>underlined</u>; generic names in **bold;** classifications in SMALL CAPS; ♣ Canadian drug name; ♦ Prototype drug; ⚠ Alert

Avoid CYP3A4 inhibitors (e.g., AZOLE ANTIFUNGALS). **Amisulpride** may increase risk of adverse effects. **Food:** High fat/high caloric meal increases paliperidone levels.

PHARMACOKINETICS Absorption: Bioavailability is 28%. **Peak:** 24 h. **Distribution:** 74% protein bound. **Metabolism:** In liver (26–41%). **Elimination:** Urine (major, 50–70% unchanged) and stool (minor). **Half-Life:** 23 h.

NURSING IMPLICATIONS

Black Box Warning

Paliperidone has been associated with increased mortality in older adults with dementia-related psychosis.

Assessment & Drug Effects
- Baseline ECG recommended to rule out congenital, long-QT syndrome.
- Prior to initiating therapy, hypokalemia and hypo-magnesemia should be corrected.
- Monitor weight.
- Monitor CV status and monitor orthostatic BP especially in those prone to hypotension.
- Reassess patient periodically in order to maintain on the lowest effective drug dose.
- Monitor closely neurologic status of older adults.
- Supervise closely those with suicidal ideation.
- Monitor closely those at risk for seizures.
- Assess degree of cognitive and motor impairment, and assess for environmental hazards.
- Monitor diabetics for loss of glycemic control.
- Monitor lab tests: Baseline and periodic serum electrolytes; periodic renal function tests, LFTs, lipid profile, thyroid function tests, blood glucose, and CBC.

Patient & Family Education
- Exercise caution with hazardous activities until response to drug is known.
- The capsule should be swallowed whole.
- Risk of orthostatic hypotension. Encourage rising slowly from sitting/supine position.
- Use caution when participating in activities leading to an increased core temperature such as strenuous exercise, exposure to extreme heat or dehydration.
- Do not be surprised by seeing the tablet shell and core components in the stool because they are insoluble.
- Avoid alcohol while taking this medication.
- Carefully monitor blood glucose levels if diabetic.
- Be aware of the risk of orthostatic hypotension.
- Monitor for signs and symptoms of suicidal ideation.
- Be aware of the possibility of seizure activity.

PALIVIZUMAB
(pal-i-viz'u-mab)
Synagis
Classification:
IMMUNOMODULATOR; MONOCLONAL ANTIBODY; IMMUNOGLOBULIN
Therapeutic: IMMUNOGLOBULIN (IGG)

AVAILABILITY Solution for injection

ACTION & *THERAPEUTIC EFFECT*
Exhibits neutralizing and fusion-inhibitory activity against the respiratory syncytial virus (RSV). *Provides passive immunity against respiratory syncytial virus. Indicated by*

prevention of lower respiratory tract infection.

USES Prevention of serious lower respiratory tract infections in children susceptible to RSV.

CONTRAINDICATIONS Hypersensitivity to palivizumab.

CAUTIOUS USE Hypersensitivity to other immunoglobulin preparations, blood products, or other medications; kidney or liver dysfunction; acute RSV infection; pregnancy (category C).

ROUTE & DOSAGE

RSV
Child: **IM** 15 mg/kg qmo during RSV season

ADMINISTRATION

Intramuscular

- Give IM only into the anterolateral aspect of the thigh. Volumes greater than 1 mL should be divided and given in different sites.

ADVERSE EFFECTS Respiratory: *URI, rhinitis,* pharyngitis, cough, wheeze, bronchiolitis, asthma, croup, dyspnea, sinusitis, apnea. **Skin:** *Rash.* **GI:** Increased AST, diarrhea, nausea, vomiting, gastroenteritis. **Other:** *Otitis media,* pain, hernia.

PHARMACOKINETICS Half-Life: 20 days.

NURSING IMPLICATIONS

Assessment & Drug Effects

- Monitor carefully for and immediately report S&S of respiratory illness including fever, cough, wheezing, and chest retractions.
- Assess for and report erythema or indurations at injection site.

Patient & Family Education

- Contact prescriber for S&S of respiratory illness, vomiting, diarrhea, or if redness develops at injection site.

PALONOSETRON

(pal-o-no′si-tron)
Aloxi
Classification: SEROTONIN 5-HT₃ RECEPTOR ANTAGONIST; ANTIEMETIC
Therapeutic: ANTIEMETIC
Prototype: Ondansetron

AVAILABILITY Solution for injection

ACTION & *THERAPEUTIC EFFECT* Selectively blocks serotonin 5-HT_3 receptors found centrally in the chemoreceptor trigger zone (CTZ) of the hypothalamus, and peripherally at vagal nerve endings in the intestines. *Prevents acute chemotherapy-induced nausea and vomiting associated with initial and -repeat courses of moderately or highly emetogenic chemotherapy.*

USES Prevention of acute and delayed nausea and vomiting associated with highly emetogenic cancer chemotherapy; postoperative nausea/vomiting.

CONTRAINDICATIONS Hypersensitivity to palonosetron.

CAUTIOUS USE Dehydration; cardiac arrhythmias, QT prolongation; electrolyte imbalance; pregnancy (category B); lactation; children younger than 18 y.

Common adverse effects in *italic;* life-threatening effects <u>underlined</u>; generic names in **bold;** classifications in SMALL CAPS; ♣ Canadian drug name; ⊙ Prototype drug; ⚠ Alert

ROUTE & DOSAGE

Prevention of Chemotherapy-Induced Nausea and Vomiting

Adult: **IV** 0.25 mg infused over 30 sec 30 min prior to chemotherapy; do not repeat for at least 7 days
Child: **IV** 20 mcg/kg Infused over 15 min prior to chemotherapy

Post-Operative Nausea/Vomiting

Adult: **IV** 0.075 mg single dose administered over 10 sec immediately before anesthesia

ADMINISTRATION

Intravenous

PREPARE: Direct: Do not dilute and do not mix with other drugs.
ADMINISTER: Prevention of chemotherapy-induced nausea and vomiting. **Direct:** Give 30 min prior to start of chemotherapy. Adults: Give over 30 sec. Children: Give over 15 min. Flush IV line with NS before and after administration. Prevention of nausea and vomiting; infuse over 10 sec prior to anesthesia induction.
INCOMPATIBILITIES: Do not mix with other drugs.

• Store at room temperature of 15°–30° C (59°–86° F). Protect from light.

ADVERSE EFFECTS CNS: Headache, anxiety, dizziness. **GI:** Constipation, diarrhea, abdominal pain. **Cardiac:** Prolonged QT interval. **Dermatologic:** Pruritus.

INTERACTIONS Drug: Can cause profound hypotension with **apomorphine**. May cause serotonin syndrome with other serotonergic drugs (e.g., SSRI).

PHARMACOKINETICS Metabolism: In liver (CYP2D6, 1A2, 3A4). **Elimination:** Primarily renal. **Half-Life:** 40 h.

NURSING IMPLICATIONS

Assessment & Drug Effects

• Monitor closely cardiac status especially in those taking diuretics or otherwise at risk for hypokalemia or hypomagnesemia, with congenital QT syndrome, or patients taking antiarrhythmic or other drugs that lead to QT prolongation.

Patient & Family Education

• Report promptly any of the following: Difficulty breathing, wheezing, or shortness of breath; palpitations or chest tightness; skin rash or itching; swelling of the face, tongue, throat, hands, or feet.

PAMIDRONATE DISODIUM

(pa-mi′dro-nate)

Classification: BISPHOSPHONATE
Therapeutic: BONE METABOLISM REGULATORY
Prototype: Etidronate

AVAILABILITY Powder for injection; solution for injection

ACTION & *THERAPEUTIC EFFECT*

A bone-resorption inhibitor thought to absorb calcium phosphate crystals into bone. May also inhibit osteoclast activity, thus contributing to inhibition of bone resorption. *Reduces bone turn-over and, when used in combination with adequate hydration, it increases renal excretion of calcium, thus reducing serum calcium concentrations.*

USES Hypercalcemia of malignancy and Paget's disease, bone metastases in multiple myeloma or breast cancer.

UNLABELED USES Primary hyperparathyroidism, osteoporosis prophylaxis.

CONTRAINDICATIONS Hypersensitivity to pamidronate; breast cancer, severe renal disease, hypercalcemia, hypercholesterolemia, polycythemia, prostatic cancer; pregnancy (category D); lactation (infant risk cannot be ruled out).

CAUTIOUS USE Hypersensitivity to pamidronate or other bisphosphonates; heart failure, nephrosis or nephrotic syndrome, moderate renal disease, chronic kidney failure; hepatic disease, cholestasis; peripheral edema, prostate hypertrophy; cancer patients with stomatitis; older adults. Safe use in children not established.

ROUTE & DOSAGE

Moderate Hypercalcemia of Malignancy (corrected calcium 12–13.5 mg/dL)

Adult: **IV** 60–90 mg may repeat in 7 days

Severe Hypercalcemia of Malignancy (corrected calcium greater than 13.5 mg/dL)

Adult: **IV** 90 may repeat in 7 days

Paget's Disease

Adult: **IV** 30 mg once daily for 3 days (90 mg total)

Osteolytic Metastases

Adult: **IV** 90 mg once/mo

ADMINISTRATION

Intravenous

PREPARE: NIOSH recommends the use of double gloves and protective gown. During administration, if there is potential that the substance could splash or if the patient may resist, use eye/face protection. **IV Infusion:** Add 10 mL sterile water for injection to reconstitute the 30 or 90 mg vial to yield 3 or 9 mg/mL, respectively. Allow to completely dissolve. **IV Infusion for Hypercalcemia of Malignancy:** Withdraw the required dose and dilute in D5W, NS, or 1/2NS as follows: Use 1000 mL. **IV Infusion for Paget's Disease and Multiple Myeloma:** Withdraw the required dose and dilute in D5W, NS, or 1/2NS as follows: Use 500 mL. **IV Infusion for Breast Cancer Bone Metastases:** Withdraw the required dose and dilute in D5W, NS, or 1/2NS as follows: Use 250 mL.

ADMINISTER: **IV Infusion:** Regulate infusion rate carefully. Rapid infusion may cause renal damage. **IV Infusion for Hypercalcemia of Malignancy:** Infuse over 2–24 h. **IV Infusion for Paget's Disease and Multiple Myeloma:** Infuse over 4 h. **IV Infusion for Breast Cancer Bone Metastases:** Infuse over 2 h.

INCOMPATIBILITIES: Solution/additive: Hetastarch, CALCIUM-CONTAINING SOLUTIONS (including **lactated Ringer's**). Y-site: **Amphotericin B, caspofungin, dantrolene, diazepam, gemtuzumab, leucovorin, phenytoin.**

Common adverse effects in *italic*; life-threatening effects <u>underlined</u>; generic names in **bold**; classifications in SMALL CAPS; ✦ Canadian drug name; ☺ Prototype drug; ⚠ Alert

• Refrigerate reconstituted pamidronate solution at 2°–8° C (36°–46° F); the IV solution may be stored at room temperature. Both are stable for 24 h.

ADVERSE EFFECTS CV: Hypertension. **Respiratory:** *Dyspnea, cough.* **CNS:** *Fatigue,* hypercalcemia, *headache, insomnia,* anxiety, pain. **Endocrine:** Hypophosphatemia, hypokalemia, hypocalcemia, hypomagnesemia. **GI:** *Nausea, vomiting, anorexia,* abdominal pain. **GU:** UTI, increased creatinine. **Musculoskeletal:** Muscle pain, weakness, joint pain. **Hematologic:** Anemia. **Other:** Fever.

DIAGNOSTIC TEST INTERFERENCE May interfere with diagnostic imaging agents such as technetium-99m-diphosphonate in bone scans.

INTERACTIONS Drug: Concurrent use of **foscarnet** may further decrease serum levels of ionized calcium.

PHARMACOKINETICS Absorption: 50% of dose is retained in body. **Onset:** 24–48 h. **Peak:** 6 days. **Duration:** 2 wk–3 mo. **Distribution:** Accumulates in bone; once deposited, remains bound until bone is remodeled. **Metabolism:** Not metabolized. **Elimination:** 50% excreted in urine unchanged. **Half-Life:** 28 h.

NURSING IMPLICATIONS
Assessment & Drug Effects
• Assess IV injection site for thrombophlebitis.
• Monitor for S&S of hypocalcemia, hypokalemia, hypomagnesemia, and hypophosphatemia. Continue monitoring for hypo-calcemia at least 2 wk after treatment completed.

• Monitor for seizures especially in those with a preexisting seizure disorder.
• Monitor vital signs. Be aware that drug fever, which may occur with pamidronate use, is self-limiting, usually subsiding in 48 h even with continued therapy.
• Monitor I&O and hydration status. Patient should be adequately hydrated, without fluid overload.
• Monitor lab tests: Baseline and prior to each treatment serum creatinine; frequent serum electrolytes; periodic CBC with differential.

Patient & Family Education
• Be aware that transient, self-limiting fever with/without chills may develop.
• Generalized malaise, which may last for several weeks following treatment, is an anticipated adverse effect.
• Report to prescriber immediately perioral tingling, numbness, and paresthesia. These are signs of hypocalcemia.

PANCRELIPASE ⊕
(pan-kre-li'pase)
Creon, Pancreaze, Pertzye, Ultresa, Viokace, Zenpep
Classification: ENZYME REPLACEMENT THERAPY
Therapeutic: PANCREATIC ENZYME REPLACEMENT THERAPY

AVAILABILITY Tablet or capsule containing lipase, protease, and amylase

ACTION & THERAPEUTIC EFFECT
Pancreatic enzyme concentrate similar to natural pancreatin but on a weight basis has 12 times the lipolytic activity and at least 4 × the

trypsin and amylase content of pancreatin. *Facilitates hydrolysis of fats into glycerol and fatty acids, starches into dextrins and sugars, and proteins into peptides for easier absorption.*

USES Replacement therapy in symptomatic treatment of malabsorption syndrome due to cystic fibrosis; management of exocrine pancreatic insufficiency due to pancreatectomy.

CONTRAINDICATIONS None listed in the manufacturer's labeling.

CAUTIOUS USE Hypersensitivity to pancrelipase or porcine; GI disease, gout; hyperuricemia; renal impairment; Crohn's disease, short bowel syndrome; pregnancy (category C); lactation.

ROUTE & DOSAGE

Pancreatic Insufficiency

Various brands are not interchangeable, see package insert for interchangeability
Adult /Adolescent/Child (4 y or older): **PO** 500 lipase units/kg/meal; titrate based on symptoms
Child (1–3 y): **PO** 1000 lipase units/kg/meal; titrate based on symptoms
Neonate/Infant (younger than 12 mo): **PO** varies per brand, see package insert

ADMINISTRATION

Oral

- Give capsules with food and sufficient liquid. Do not crush or chew capsules or capsule contents; capsules should be swallowed whole.
- May open capsule and sprinkle contents on soft acidic food, which should be swallowed without chewing. Follow with a full glass of water or juice.
- Determine dosage in relation to fat content in diet (suggested ratio: 300 mg pancrelipase for each 17 g dietary fat).

ADVERSE EFFECTS CV: Peripheral edema. **Respiratory:** Nasal congestion, cough. **CNS:** Dizziness, headache, otalgia. **HEENT:** *Ear pain.* **Endocrine:** Hyperuricosuria, hyperglycemia. **GI:** Anorexia, *abdominal pain,* nausea, vomiting, abdominal pain, dyspepsia diarrhea. **Hematologic:** Lymphadenopathy.

INTERACTIONS Drug: Effectiveness can be decreased by concurrent ANTACID use.

PHARMACOKINETICS Distribution: Acts locally in GI tract. **Elimination:** Feces.

NURSING IMPLICATIONS

Assessment & Drug Effects

- Monitor I&O and weight. Note appetite and quality of stools, weight loss, abdominal bloating, polyuria, thirst, hunger, itching. Pancreatic insufficiency is frequently associated with steatorrhea, bulky stools, and insulin dependent diabetes.
- Monitor uric acid levels in patients with hyperuricemia, gout or renal impairment.
- S&S of colon stricture (cramping, abdominal pain, constipation, vomiting, inability to pass gas or stool).

Patient & Family Education

- Notify prescriber if breast-feeding or intending to breast-feed during treatment.

PANCURONIUM BROMIDE

(pan-kyoo-roe'nee-um)

Classification: NONDEPOLARIZING SKELETAL MUSCLE RELAXANT
Therapeutic: SKELETAL MUSCLE RELAXANT
Prototype: Atracurium

AVAILABILITY Solution for injection

ACTION & THERAPEUTIC EFFECT

Produces skeletal muscle relaxation or paralysis by competing with acetylcholine at cholinergic receptor sites on the skeletal muscle endplate and thus blocks nerve impulse transmission. *Induces skeletal muscle relaxation or paralysis.*

USES Adjunct to anesthesia to induce skeletal muscle relaxation. Also to facilitate management of patients undergoing mechanical ventilation.

CONTRAINDICATIONS Hypersensitivity to the drug or bromides.

CAUTIOUS USE History of severe anaphylactic reactions to other neuromuscular blocking agents requires appropriate emergency treatment. Debilitated patients; dehydration; MG; neuromuscular disease; pulmonary, liver, or kidney disease; fluid or electrolyte imbalance; pregnancy (category C); lactation; neonate less than 1 mo.

ROUTE & DOSAGE

Skeletal Muscle Relaxation

Adult/Child/Infant: **IV** 0.04–0.1 mg/kg initial dose, may give additional doses of 0.01 mg/kg at 30–60 min intervals
Neonate: **IV** 0.02 mg/kg test dose

ADMINISTRATION

Intravenous

Plastic syringe may be used for administration, but drug may adsorb to plastic with prolonged storage.

PREPARE: Direct: Give undiluted.
ADMINISTER: Direct: Give over 30–90 sec.
INCOMPATIBILITIES: Solution/additive: Allopurinol, amphotericin B (conventional and lipid), caspofungin, dantrolene, diazepam, furosemide, gemtuzamab, lansoprazole, mitomycin, pantoprazole, phenytoin.

■ Refrigerate at 2°–8° C (36°–46° F). Do not freeze.

ADVERSE EFFECTS CV: *Increased pulse rate and BP,* ventricular extrasystoles. **Skin:** Transient acneiform rash, burning sensation along course of vein. **Other:** Salivation, skeletal muscle weakness, <u>respiratory depression</u>.

DIAGNOSTIC TEST INTERFERENCE

Pancuronium may decrease ***serum cholinesterase*** concentrations.

INTERACTIONS Drug: GENERAL ANESTHETICS increase neuromuscular blocking and duration of action; AMINOGLYCOSIDES, **polymyxin B, clindamycin, lidocaine,** parenteral **magnesium, quinidine, quinine, trimethaphan, verapamil** increase neuromuscular blockade; DIURETICS may increase or decrease neuromuscular blockade; **lithium** prolongs duration of neuromuscular blockade; NARCOTIC ANALGESICS possibly add to respiratory depression; **succinylcholine** increases onset and depth of neuromuscular blockade; **phenytoin** may cause resistance to or reversal of neuro-muscular blockade.

PHARMACOKINETICS
Onset: 30–45 sec. **Peak:** 2–3 min. **Duration:** 60 min. **Distribution:** Well distributed to tissues and extracellular fluids; crosses placenta in small amounts. **Metabolism:** Small amount in liver. **Elimination:** Primarily in urine. **Half-Life:** 2 h.

NURSING IMPLICATIONS

Assessment & Drug Effects
- Assess cardiovascular and respiratory status continuously.
- Observe patient closely for residual muscle weakness and signs of respiratory distress during recovery period. Monitor BP and vital signs. Peripheral nerve stimulator may be used to assess the effects of pancuronium and to monitor restoration of neuromuscular function.
- Note: Consciousness is not affected by pancuronium. Patient will be awake and alert but unable to speak.

PANITUMUMAB
(pan-i-tu-mu'mab)
Vectibix
Classification: ANTINEOPLASTIC TYROSINE KINASE INHIBITOR
Therapeutic: ANTINEOPLASTIC
Prototype: Erlotinib

AVAILABILITY Solution for injection

ACTION & *THERAPEUTIC EFFECT*
Epidermal growth factor receptors (EGFRs) are overexpressed in many human cancers, including those of the colon and rectum. EGFRs control the activity of intra-cellular tyrosine kinases that regulate transcription of DNA molecules involved in cancer cell growth, survival, and proliferation. *Panitumumab inhibits over-expression of EGFRs in cancer cells, decreasing their proliferation, survival, and decreasing their invasive capacity and metastases.*

USES Treatment of EGFR-expressing metastatic colorectal carcinoma in patients with disease progression on or following fluoropyrimidine-, oxaliplatin-, and irinotecan-containing chemotherapy regimens.

CONTRAINDICATIONS Pulmonary fibrosis; interstitial lung disease; pregnancy (fetal risk cannot be ruled out); lactation (infant risk cannot be ruled out).

CAUTIOUS USE Photosensitivity with drug use; electrolyte imbalances, especially hypomagnesemia, and hypocalcemia; lung disorders; older patients. Safe use in children not established.

ROUTE & DOSAGE

Metastatic Colorectal Carcinoma
Adult: **IV** 6 mg/kg q14days

Dosage Adjustments for Infusion Reactions and Dermatologic Reactions
Mild or moderate infusion reactions (Grade 1 or 2): Reduce infusion rate by 50%
Severe infusion reactions (Grade 3 or 4): Discontinue permanently
Intolerable or severe dermatologic toxicity (greater than Grade 3): Withhold drug. If toxicity does not improve to at least Grade 2 within 1 mo, permanently discontinue. If toxicity improves to at least Grade 2 and patient

P

is symptomatically improved after withholding no more than 2 doses, resume at 50% of original dose. If toxicities recur, discontinue permanently. If toxicities do not recur, subsequent doses may be increased by increments of 25% of original dose until 6 mg/kg is reached.

ADMINISTRATION

Intravenous

PREPARE: **IV Infusion:** Dilute doses up to 1000 mg with NS to a total volume of 100 mL. ▪ Dilute higher doses with NS to a total volume of 150 mL. ▪ Final concentration should not exceed 10 mg/mL. ▪ Mix by gentle inversion and do not shake. Solution will contain small translucent particles that will be removed by filtration during infusion.
ADMINISTER: **IV Infusion:** Infuse doses less than 1000 mg over 60 min. ▪ Infuse doses greater than 1000 mg over 90 min. ▪ Use an infusion pump and a 0.2 or 0.22 micron in-line filter. ▪ Flush the line before/after infusion with NS. ▪ Discontinue infusion immediately if an anaphylactic reaction is suspected (i.e., bronchospasm, fever, chills, hypotension).

▪ Store unopened vials at 2°–8° C (36°–46° F). Protect vials from direct sunlight. ▪ Use diluted infusion solution within 6 h if stored at room temperature, or within 24 h if stored at 2°–8° C (36°–46° F).

ADVERSE EFFECTS CV: Peripheral edema. **Respiratory:** Cough, dyspnea. **HEENT:** Eye irritation, abnormal eyelash growth. **Endocrine:** hypomagnesemia. **Skin:** *Acne,* fissures, dermatitis, *nail changes, pruritis, rash.* **GI:** *Abdominal pain,* constipation, *diarrhea,* nausea, mucositis, stomatitis, vomiting. **Other:** *Fatigue.*

INTERACTIONS Drugs: Do not use with **aminolevulinic acid.**

PHARMACOKINETICS Half-Life: 7.5 days.

NURSING IMPLICATIONS

Black Box Warning

Panitumumab has been associated with frequent, sometimes severe, dermatologic toxicities, and severe infusion reactions.

Assessment & Drug Effects
▪ Monitor for S&S of a severe infusion reaction; check vital signs q30min during infusion and 30 min post infusion.
▪ Monitor for and report S&S of dermatologic toxicity such as acne-like dermatitis, pruritus, erythema, rash, skin exfoliation, dry skin, and skin fissures; inflammatory or infectious sequelae in those who experience severe dermatologic toxicities.
▪ Withhold drug and notify prescriber for any signs of drug toxicity.
▪ Monitor lab tests: Periodic serum electrolytes during and for 8 wk following completion of therapy.

Patient & Family Education
▪ Immediately report any discomfort experienced during and shortly after drug infusion.
▪ Wear sunscreen and limit sun exposure while receiving panitumumab.
▪ Report any of the following to a health care provider: Any signs of

irritation, inflammation, or infection of the skin, nails, or eyes; shortness of breath or any other breathing difficulty.
- Women of childbearing age should use reliable means of contraception during and for 6 mo after the last dose of panitumumab.

PANTOPRAZOLE SODIUM
(pan-to'pra-zole)
Protonix
Classification: PROTON PUMP INHIBITOR; ANTISECRETORY
Therapeutic: ANTIULCER
Prototype: Omeprazole

AVAILABILITY Delayed release tablet; solution for injection; delayed release oral suspension

ACTION & *THERAPEUTIC EFFECT*
Gastric acid secretion is decreased by inhibiting the H^+, K^+-ATPase enzyme system responsible for acid production. *Suppresses gastric acid secretion by inhibiting the acid (proton H^+) pump in the parietal cells.*

USES Short-term treatment of erosive esophagitis associated with gastroesophageal reflux disease (GERD), hypersecretory disease.

UNLABELED USES Peptic ulcer disease, dyspepsia, stress ulcer prophylaxis, heartburn, duodenal ulcer.

CONTRAINDICATIONS Hypersensitivity to pantoprazole or other proton pump inhibitors (PPIs).

CAUTIOUS USE Mild to severe hepatic insufficiency, cirrhosis; concurrent administration of EDTA-containing products; elderly (avoid

after 8 wk); history of lupus erythematosus, history of osteoporosis; pregnancy (category B); lactation (infant risk cannot be ruled out). Safety and efficacy in children younger than 5 y not established for uses other than erosive esophagitis. There is no commercially available dosage formulation appropriate for children younger than 5 y.

ROUTE & DOSAGE

Erosive Esophagitis
Adult: **PO** 40 mg daily × 8 wks
IV 40 mg daily × 7–10 days
Adolescent/Child (5 y and older, weight 40 kg or more): **PO** 40 mg daily × 8 wk; *weight 15–39 kg:* 20 mg daily × 8 wk

Hypersecretory Disease
Adult: **PO** 40 mg bid (doses up to 240 mg/day have been used)
IV 80 mg bid; adjust based on acid output

ADMINISTRATION
Oral
- Do not crush or break in half. **Must be** swallowed whole with or without food.
- Granules for oral suspension should be given 30 min before meals. Granules should be put into apple juice or applesauce, not water and given within 10 min of preparation.
- *NG tube administration:* Add granules for suspension to a catheter tip syringe inserted into a 16 French catheter (or larger). Add 40 mL of apple juice in 10 mL increments to fully suspend granules and ensure that all of the drug is washed into the stomach.
- Store tablet and oral suspension at 20°–25° C (66°–77° F),

but room temperature permitted. Excursions permitted to 15°–30° C (59°–86° F).

Intravenous

PREPARE: IV 15 Min Infusion: Reconstitute each 40 mg vial with 10 mL NS to yield 4 mg/mL. ▪ The required dose of 40 or 80 mg may be further diluted to a **total volume** of 100 mL in D5W, NS, or LR to yield 0.4 mg/mL or 0.8 mg/mL, respectively.

ADMINISTER: IV Infusion: Give through a dedicated line or flushed IV line before and after each dose with D5W, NS, or LR. ▪ Give the 4 mg/mL concentration over at least 2 min. ▪ Infuse the 0.4 or 0.8 mg/mL concentration over 15 min.

INCOMPATIBILITIES: Solution/additive: Nefopam, solutions containing **zinc, nefopam hydrochloride. Y-site: Acyclovir sodium, alemtuzumab, alfentanil, amikacin, amiodarone hydrochloride, amphotericin b, atenolol, atracurium, atropine, aztreonam, blinatumomab, bretylium, buprenorphine, butorphanol, caffeine, calcium salts, caspofungin, acetate, cefazolin sodium, cefepime, cefoperazone, cefotaxime, cefotetan disodium, cefoxitin, ceftazidime, ceftobiprole medocaril, cefuroxime, chloramphenicol, chlorpromazine, cimetidine, ciprofloxacin, cisatracurium, cisplatin, clindamycin phosphate, cloxacillin sodium, cyclosporine, dacarbazine, dactinomycin, dantrolene, daptomycin, daunorubicin, dexamethasone sodium phosphate, dexmedetomidine hydrochloride, dexrazoxane, diazepam, digoxin, diltiazem, dimenhydrinate, diphenhydramine, dobutamine, dolasetron, dopamine hydrochloride, doxacurium chloride doxorubicin, droperidol, enalaprilat, ephedrine, epinephrine hydrochloride, epirubicin, esmolol, estrogens, etoposide, famotidine, fenoldopam, fentanyl, fluconazole, fludarabine, furosemide, gatifloxacin, gemcitabine, gemtuzumab, gentamicin sulfate, glycopyrrolate, haloperidol, heparin, hydralazine, hydrocortisone, hydromorphone, hydroxyzine, idarubicin, ifosfamide, indomethacin, insulin, isoproterenol hydrochloride, isavuconazonium, ketorolac, labetalol, leucovorin, levofloxacin, levorphanol, lidocaine, linezolid, lorazepam, magnesium sulfate, mannitol, mechlorethamine, melphalan, meperidine, meropenem, methotrexate, methylprednisolone, metoclopramide hydrochloride, metoprolol, metronidazole, midazolam hydrochloride, milrinone, minocycline, mitomycin, mitoxantrone hydrochloride, mivacurium chloride, morphine sulfate, moxifloxacin, multiple vitamin injections, mycophenolate, nalbuphine, naloxone, nicardipine, nitroglycerin, nitroprusside sodium, norepinephrine bitartrate, octreotide acetate, ondansetron, oxytocin, palonosetron, pancuronium, pemetrexed, pentamidine isethionate, phenobarbital sodium, phenytoin, piperacillin sodium–tazobactam sodium, polymyxin B, potassium acetate, potassium**

P

phosphate, prochlorpera-zine, promethazine, propo-fol, propranolol, quinidine, quinupristin/dalfopristin, remifentanil, rocuronium, salbutamol, sodium ace-tate, sodium bicarbonate, sodium phosphate, strep-tozocin, sulfamethoxazole-trimethoprim, tacrolimus, thiopental sodium, thiotepa, tobramycin sulfate, tolazo-line hydrochloride, topo-tecan, trimethobenzamide hydrochloride, vancomycin, vecuronium, verapamil, vin-blastine, vincristine, vinorel-bine, voriconazole.

▪ Reconstituted IV solutions may be stored for up to 6 h at 15°–30° C (59°–86° F) before further dilution.
▪ The diluted 100 mL solu-tion should be infused within 24 h or infused within 24 h of reconstitution.

ADVERSE EFFECTS CNS: *Head-ache*. GI: *Diarrhea*.

DIAGNOSTIC TEST INTERFERENCE
May cause false–positive **urine tet-rahydrocannabinol (THC) test**; may increase CgA levels, which may interfere with neuroendocrine tumor detection.

INTERACTIONS Drug: Contra-indicated with **atazanavir** or **rilpivirine**. Do not use with **acala-brutinib, dacomitinib, dasatinib, delavirdine, erlotinib, nelfina-vir, neratinib, pazopanib, rilpi-virine, risedronate, velpatasvir**. May decrease absorption of **ampi-cillin**, IRON SALTS, **itraconazole, ketoconazole**; increases INR with **warfarin**. May decrease concen-tration of CEPHALOSPORINS. **Herbal: Ginkgo** may decrease plasma levels.

PHARMACOKINETICS Absorp-tion: Well absorbed with 77% bioavailability. **Peak:** 2.4 h. **Dis-tribution:** 98% protein bound. **Metabolism:** In liver (CYP2C19). **Elimination:** 71% in urine, 18% in feces. **Half-Life:** 1 h.

NURSING IMPLICATIONS
Assessment & Drug Effects
▪ Monitor for and immediately report S&S of angioedema or a severe skin reaction.
▪ Monitor for improvement in gas-troesophageal comfort.
▪ Monitor lab tests: Vitamin B_{12} and magnesium with long-term therapy.

Patient & Family Education
▪ Contact prescriber promptly if any of the following occur: Peeling, blistering, or loosening of skin; skin rash, hives, or itching; swell-ing of the face, tongue, or lips; difficulty breathing or swallowing.

PAPAVERINE HYDROCHLORIDE
(pa-pav'er-een)

Classification: NONNITRATE VASODILATOR
Therapeutic: VASODILATOR; SMOOTH MUSCLE RELAXANT
Prototype: Hydralazine

AVAILABILITY Solution for injection

ACTION & *THERAPEUTIC EFFECT*
Exerts nonspecific direct spasmolytic effect on smooth muscles unrelated to innervation. Acts directly on myo-cardium, depresses conduction and irritability, and prolongs refractory period. *Relaxes the smooth muscle of the heart as well as produces relax-ation of vascular smooth muscles.*

USES Smooth muscle spasms.

UNLABELED USES Impotence, cardiac bypass surgery.

CONTRAINDICATIONS Parenteral use in complete AV block.

CAUTIOUS USE Glaucoma; myocardial depression; QT prolongation, angina pectoris; recent stroke; pregnancy (category C); lactation.

ROUTE & DOSAGE

Smooth Muscle Spasm
Adult: **IM/IV** 30–120 mg q3h as needed

ADMINISTRATION

Intramuscular

- Aspirate carefully before injecting IM to avoid inadvertent entry into blood vessel, and administer slowly.

Intravenous

- IV administration to children: Verify correct IV concentration and rate of infusion with prescriber.

PREPARE: **Direct:** Give undiluted or diluted in an equal volume of sterile water for injection.
ADMINISTER: **Direct:** Give slowly over 1–2 min. Avoid rapid injection.
INCOMPATIBILITIES: Solution/additive: **Aminophylline, heparin, lactated Ringer's.** Y-site: **aminophylline, amphotericin B, ampicillin, bumetanide,** CEPHALOSPORINS, **clindamycin, dantrolene, diazepam, diazoxide, furosemide, heparin, indomethacin, ketorolac, methylprednisolone, phenobarbital, phenytoin, piperacillin.**

ADVERSE EFFECTS CV: Slight rise in BP, paroxysmal tachycardia, transient ventricular ectopic rhythms, AV block, arrhythmias. **Respiratory:** Increased depth of respiration, respiratory depression, fatal apnea. **CNS:** Dizziness, drowsiness, headache, sedation. **HEENT:** Diplopia, nystagmus. **Skin:** Pruritus, skin rash. **GI:** Nausea, anorexia, constipation, diarrhea, abdominal distress, dry mouth and throat, hepatotoxicity (jaundice, eosinophilia, abnormal liver function tests); with rapid IV administration. **GU:** Priapism. **Other:** General discomfort, facial flushing, sweating, weakness, coma.

INTERACTIONS Drug: May decrease **levodopa** effectiveness; **morphine** may antagonize smooth muscle relaxation effect of papaverine.

PHARMACOKINETICS Absorption: Readily from GI tract. **Peak:** 1–2 h. **Duration:** 12 h sustained release. **Metabolism:** In liver. **Elimination:** In urine chiefly as metabolites. **Half-Life:** 90 min.

NURSING IMPLICATIONS

Assessment & Drug Effects

- Monitor pulse, respiration, and BP in patients receiving drug parenterally. If significant changes are noted, withhold medication and report promptly to prescriber.

Patient & Family Education

- Notify prescriber if any adverse effect persists or if GI symptoms, jaundice, or skin rash appears. Liver function tests may be indicated.
- Do not drive or engage in potentially hazardous activities until response to drug is known. Alcohol may increase drowsiness and dizziness.

PAREGORIC
(par-e-gor'ik)

Classification:
ANTIDIARRHEAL; NARCOTIC
(OPIATE AGONIST) ANALGESIC
Therapeutic: ANTIDIARRHEAL
Prototype: Loperamide
Controlled Substance: Schedule III

AVAILABILITY Liquid

ACTION & *THERAPEUTIC EFFECT*
Decreases GI motility and effective propulsive peristalsis while diminishing digestive secretions. *Delayed transit of intestinal contents results in desiccation of feces and constipation.*

USES Short-term treatment for symptomatic relief of acute diarrhea.

CONTRAINDICATIONS Hypersensitivity to opium alkaloids; diarrhea caused by poisons (until eliminated); COPD; children; pregnancy—fetal risk cannot be ruled out; lactation—infant risk cannot be ruled out.

CAUTIOUS USE Asthma; liver disease; severely impaired renal function; GI disease or hemorrhage; history of opiate agonist dependence; severe prostatic hypertrophy; Addison's disease; hypothyroidism; atrial flutter and other supraventricular tachycardias; low blood volume; history of respiratory depression or emphysema; elderly.

ROUTE & DOSAGE

Acute Diarrhea
Adult: **PO** 5–10 mL after loose bowel movement, 1–4 × daily if needed

Child: **PO** 0.25–0.5 mL/kg 1–4 × day

ADMINISTRATION
Oral
- Give paregoric in sufficient water (2 or 3 swallows) to ensure its passage into the stomach (mixture will appear milky).
- Extra precaution in double-checking dose and administering. A 25- fold difference in morphine content exists between paregoric an opium tincture.
- Store tincture at controlled room temperature between 15 and 30 degrees C (59 and 86 degrees F)

ADVERSE EFFECTS CNS: *Dizziness, lightheadedness, sedated.* **GI:** *Nausea, vomiting, constipation.*

INTERACTIONS Drug: Alcohol and other CNS DEPRESSANTS add to CNS effects.

PHARMACOKINETICS Distribution: Crosses placenta; distributed into breast milk. **Metabolism:** In liver. **Elimination:** In urine.

NURSING IMPLICATIONS
Assessment & Drug Effects
- Paregoric may worsen the course of infection-associated diarrhea by delaying the elimination of pathogens.
- Be aware that adverse effects are primarily due to morphine content. Paregoric abuse results because of the narcotic content of the drug.
- Assess for fluid and electrolyte imbalance until diarrhea has stopped.

Patient & Family Education
- Adhere strictly to prescribed dosage schedule.

Common adverse effects in *italic;* life-threatening effects <u>underlined;</u> generic names in **bold;** classifications in SMALL CAPS; ♣ Canadian drug name; ◎ Prototype drug; △ Alert

- Avoid activities requiring mental alertness or coordination until the drug effects are realized.
- Review adverse effects with patient and/or caregiver.
- Maintain bed rest if diarrhea is severe with a high level of fluid loss.
- Replace fluids and electrolytes as needed for diarrhea. Drink warm clear liquids and avoid dairy products, concentrated sweets, and cold drinks until diarrhea stops.
- Observe character and frequency of stools. Discontinue drug as soon as diarrhea is controlled. Report promptly to prescriber if diarrhea persists more than 3 days, if fever is higher than 38.8° C (102° F), abdominal pain develops, or if mucus or blood is passed.
- Understand that constipation is often a consequence of antidiarrheal treatment and a normal elimination pattern is usually established as dietary intake increases.
- There are many drugs that paregoric interacts with. Consult healthcare professional prior to new drug use (including over-the-counter drugs).

PARICALCITOL

(par-i-cal′ci-tol)
Zemplar
Classification: VITAMIN D ANALOG
Therapeutic: VITAMIN D ANALOG
Prototype: Calcitriol

AVAILABILITY Vial; capsule

ACTION & *THERAPEUTIC EFFECT*

Synthetic vitamin D analog that reduces parathyroid hormone (PTH) activity levels in chronic kidney failure (CRF). Lowers serum levels of calcium and phosphate. Decreases parathyroid hormone release as well as bone resorption in some patients. *Effectiveness indicated by iPTH levels less than 1.5–3 × the upper limit of normal.*

USES Prevention and treatment of secondary hyperparathyroidism associated with CRF.

CONTRAINDICATIONS Hypersensitivity to paricalcitol; hypercalcemia; evidence of vitamin D toxicity; concurrent administration of phosphate preparations and vitamin D.

CAUTIOUS USE Severe liver disease; abnormally low levels of PTH; pregnancy (fetal risk cannot be ruled out); lactation (infant risk cannot be ruled out). Safety and efficacy in children younger than 5 y not established.

ROUTE & DOSAGE

Secondary Hyperparathyroidism
Adult: **IV** 0.04 mcg/kg–0.1 mcg/kg (max: 0.24 mcg/kg), no more than every other day during dialysis; adjust based on serum iPTH **PO** based on baseline iPTH level divided by 80 and administered 3 × weekly, no more than every other day

Renal Impairment Dosage Adjustment

Stage 5 Chronic Kidney Disease (CKD): **See package insert**

ADMINISTRATION

Oral
- Give no more frequently than every other day when dosing 3 × wk.

- Store at 15°–30° C (59°–86° F).

Intravenous

PREPARE: **Direct:** Give undiluted.
ADMINISTER: **Direct:** Give IV bolus dose anytime during dialysis.

- Store at 25° C (77° F). Discard unused portion of a single dose vial.

ADVERSE EFFECTS CV: Edema, hypertension, hypotension. **Respiratory:** Rhinitis. **CNS:** Dizziness, insomnia, headache. **Endocrine:** hypervolemia. **Skin:** Rash. **GI:** Diarrhea, *nausea,* vomiting, <u>gastrointestinal hemorrhage,</u> peritonitis, constipation. **GU:** Urinary urgency. **Other:** Sepsis.

INTERACTIONS Drug: Hypercalcemia may increase risk of **digoxin** toxicity; may increase **magnesium** absorption and toxicity in renal failure. Do not use with **vitamin D analogs. Herbal:** Be cautious of **vitamin D** content in herbal and OTC products.

PHARMACOKINETICS Distribution: Greater than 99% protein bound. **Metabolism:** Via CYP3A4. **Elimination:** In feces. **Half-Life:** 15 h.

NURSING IMPLICATIONS

Assessment & Drug Effects
- Monitor for S&S of hypercalcemia (see Appendix F).
- Withhold drug and notify prescriber if hypercalcemia occurs.
- Coadministered drugs: Monitor for digoxin toxicity if serum calcium level is elevated.
- Monitor lab tests: Serum calcium, serum phosphorus, and serum or plasma intact PTH at least every 2 wk for 3 mo, then monthly for 3 mo, and every 3 mo thereafter. Increase frequency of lab tests

with coadministration of strong CYP3A inhibitors.

Patient & Family Education
- Report immediately any of the following to the prescriber: Weakness, anorexia, nausea, vomiting, abdominal cramps, diarrhea, muscle or bone pain, or excessive thirst.
- Adhere strictly to dietary regimen of calcium supplementation and phosphorus restriction to ensure successful therapy.
- Avoid excessive use of aluminum-containing compounds such as antacids/vitamins.

PAROMOMYCIN SULFATE

(par-oh-moe-mye′sin)

Classification:
AMINOGLYCOSIDE ANTIBIOTIC;
AMEBICIDE
Therapeutic: AMEBICIDE

AVAILABILITY Capsule

ACTION & *THERAPEUTIC EFFECT*
Aminoglycoside antibiotic with broad-spectrum antibacterial activity. *Exerts direct bactericidal and amebicidal action, primarily in lumen of GI tract. Ineffective against extraintestinal amebiasis.*

USES Acute and chronic intestinal amebiasis; adjunctive therapy for hepatic coma/encephalopathy.

CONTRAINDICATIONS Aminoglycoside hypersensitivity; intestinal obstruction; impaired kidney function.

CAUTIOUS USE GI ulceration; renal failure, renal impairment; older adults; myasthenia gravis; parkinsonism; pregnancy (category C); children.

ROUTE & DOSAGE

Intestinal Amebiasis

Adult/Child: **PO** 25–35 mg/kg divided in 3 doses for 7–10 days

Hepatic Coma

Adult: **PO** 4 g/day in divided doses for 5–10 days

ADMINISTRATION

Oral

▪ Administer with meals.

ADVERSE EFFECTS CNS: Headache, vertigo. **HEENT:** Ototoxicity. **Skin:** Exanthema, rash, pruritus. **GI:** *Diarrhea, abdominal cramps,* steatorrhea, *nausea, vomiting, heartburn,* secondary enterocolitis. **GU:** Nephrotoxicity (in patients with GI inflammation or ulcerations) oliguria, proteinuria, pyuria. **Other:** Eosinophilia, overgrowth of nonsusceptible organisms.

DIAGNOSTIC TEST INTERFERENCE

Prolonged use of paromomycin may cause reduction in ***serum cholesterol.***

INTERACTIONS Drug: May decrease absorption of **cyanocobalamin.** Do not use with **cidofovir** or **gallium.** Use caution with other AMINOGLYCOSIDES or agents that may increase risk of nephrotoxicity.

PHARMACOKINETICS Absorption: Poorly from intact GI tract. **Elimination:** In feces. **Half-Life:** 2–3 h.

NURSING IMPLICATIONS

Assessment & Drug Effects

▪ Monitor therapeutic effectiveness. Criterion of cure is absence of amoebae in stool specimens examined at weekly intervals for 6 wk after completion of treatment, and thereafter at monthly intervals for 2 y.

▪ Monitor for appearance of a superinfection during therapy (see Appendix F).

▪ Monitor closely patients with history of GI ulceration for nephrotoxicity and ototoxicity (see Appendix F). Drug absorption can take place through diseased mucosa.

Patient & Family Education

▪ Do not prepare, process, or serve food until treatment is complete when receiving drug for intestinal amebiasis. Isolation is not required.

▪ Practice strict personal hygiene, particularly hand washing after defecation and before eating food.

PAROXETINE

(par-ox'e-teen)

Brisdelle, Pexeva, Paxil, Paxil CR

Classification: ANTIDEPRESSANT; SELECTIVE SEROTONIN 5-HT REUPTAKE INHIBITOR (SSRI)

Therapeutic: ANTIDEPRESSANT; SSRI; ANTIANXIETY

Prototype: Fluoxetine

AVAILABILITY Tablet; sustained release tablet; suspension; capsule

ACTION & THERAPEUTIC EFFECT

Antidepressant that is a serotonin 5-HT reuptake inhibitor. It is highly potent and a highly selective inhibitor of serotonin reuptake by neurons in CNS. *Efficacious in depression resistant to other antidepressants and in depression complicated by anxiety.*

USES Depression, obsessive-compulsive disorders, panic attacks, excessive social anxiety, generalized anxiety, post traumatic stress disorder (PTSD), premenstrual dysphoric disorder (PMDD), hot flashes.

UNLABELED USES Diabetic neuropathy, myoclonus, bipolar depression in conjunction with lithium, chronic headache, premature ejaculation, fibromyalgia.

CONTRAINDICATIONS Hypersensitivity to paroxetine; suicidal ideation; concomitant use of MAO inhibitors or within 14 days of stoppage; bipolar disorder; alcohol; pregnancy (category D and X for **Brisdelle**).

CAUTIOUS USE History of mania, suicidal tendencies; history of drug abuse; anorexia nervosa, ECT therapy; MDD; seizure disorder; renal/hepatic impairment; history of metabolic disorders; volume-depleted patients, recent MI, unstable cardiac disease; abrupt discontinuation; older adults; lactation. Not FDA approved for children and adolescents.

ROUTE & DOSAGE

Depression

Adult: **PO** 20 mg/day may increase by 10 mg weekly (max: 50 mg/day); 25 mg sustained release daily in morning, may increase by 12.5 mg (max: 62.5 mg/day); use lower starting doses for patients with renal or hepatic insufficiency
Geriatric: **PO** Start with 10 mg/day (12.5 mg/day sustained release), [max: 40 mg/day (50 mg/day sustained release)]

Panic Disorder

Adult: **PO** 10 mg daily then increase to 40 mg/day; **Sustained release** 12.5 mg daily, may increase (max: 75 mg/day)

Social Anxiety Disorder

Adult: **PO** 20–60 mg/day

Generalized Anxiety, PTSD, OCD

Adult: **PO** Start with 20 mg once daily, may increase by 10 mg/day at weekly intervals if needed to target dose of 40 mg once daily (max: 60 mg/day)
Geriatric: **PO** Start with 10 mg once daily, may increase by 10 mg/day at weekly intervals if needed (max: 40 mg/day)

Premenstrual Dysphoric Disorder

Adult: **PO** 12.5 mg once daily (up to 25 mg once daily) throughout the month or daily for 2 wk before menstrual period

Hot Flashes

Adult: **PO** 7.5 mg daily (Brisdelle formulation); **Extended release** 12.5 mg daily may titrate up to 25 mg daily

Pharmacogenetic Dosage Adjustment

Poor CYP2D6 metabolizers: Start with 65% of dose

ADMINISTRATION

Oral

- Ensure that sustained release form is not chewed or crushed. **Must be** swallowed whole.
- Usually administered every morning. Administering with food will decrease GI adverse effects. Do not administer concomitantly with antacids.

Common adverse effects in *italic;* life-threatening effects underlined; generic names in **bold;** classifications in SMALL CAPS; ♣ Canadian drug name; ○ Prototype drug; ⚠ Alert

- Be aware that at least 14 days should elapse when switching a patient from/to an MAO inhibitor to/from paroxetine.

ADVERSE EFFECTS CV: Postural hypotension. **CNS:** *Headache,* tremor, agitation or nervousness, anxiety, paresthesias, dizziness, insomnia, *sedation.* **HEENT:** Blurred vision. **Endocrine:** Hyponatremia in older adults. **Skin:** Diaphoresis, rash, pruritus. **Hepatic:** Isolated reports of elevated liver enzymes. **GI:** *Nausea,* constipation, vomiting, anorexia, diarrhea, dyspepsia, flatulence, increased appetite, taste aversion, *dry mouth.* **GU:** Urinary hesitancy or frequency, change in male fertility, decrease in libido. **Other:** Bone fracture (in older adults), weakness.

INTERACTIONS Drug: Do not use with **pimozide. Activated charcoal** reduces absorption of paroxetine. **Cimetidine** increases paroxetine levels. MAO INHIBITORS, **selegiline** may cause an increased vasopressor response leading to hypertensive crisis or death. Use with other serotonergic agents (e.g., SSRIs) or MAOIs can cause serotonin syndrome. **Phenytoin** can cause liver enzyme induction resulting in lower paroxetine levels and shorter half-life. **Warfarin** may increase risk of bleeding and **thioridazine** levels, and prolong QT_c interval leading to heart block; increase **ergotamine** toxicity with **dihydroergotamine, ergotamine.** May reduce the efficacy of **tamoxifen. Herbal: St. John's wort** may cause serotonin syndrome (headache, dizziness, sweating, agitation).

PHARMACOKINETICS Absorption: 99% from GI tract. **Onset:** 2 wk. **Peak:** 5–8 h. **Distribution:** Very lipophilic. 95% protein bound. Distributes into breast milk. **Metabolism:** Extensively in the liver to inactive metabolites via CYP2D6. **Elimination:** Less than 2% is excreted unchanged in urine. 65% of dose appears in urine as metabolites. Metabolites of paroxetine are also excreted in feces, presumably via bile. **Half-Life:** 24 h.

NURSING IMPLICATIONS

Black Box Warning

Paroxetine has been associated with suicidal ideation and behavior in children, adolescents, and young adults.

Assessment & Drug Effects

- Monitor for worsening of depression or emergence of suicidal ideation. Closely monitor those younger than 18 y for suicidal thinking and behavior.
- Monitor for adverse effects, which include headache, weakness, sedation, dizziness, insomnia; nausea, constipation, or diarrhea; dry mouth; sweating; male ejaculatory disturbance. These occur in more than 10% of all patients and may result in poor compliance with drug regimen.
- Monitor older adults for fluid and sodium imbalances.
- Monitor for significant weight loss.
- Monitor patients with history of mania for reactivation of condition.
- Monitor patients with preexisting cardiovascular disease carefully because paroxetine may adversely affect hemodynamic status.

Patient & Family Education

- Monitor children, adolescents, and young adults for changes in behavior that may indicate suicidal ideation.

P

- Use caution when operating hazardous machinery or equipment until response to drug is known.
- Concurrent use of alcohol may increase risk of adverse CNS effects.
- Adaptation to some adverse effects (especially dizziness and nausea) may occur over a period of 4–6 wk.
- Do not stop drug therapy after improvement in emotional status occurs.
- Notify prescriber of any distressing adverse effects.

PATIROMER
(pa-tir'oh-mer)
Veltassa
Classification: CATIONIC EXCHANGE POLYMER; POTASSIUM BINDER
Therapeutic: POTASSIUM BINDER

AVAILABILITY Powder for oral suspension

ACTION & THERAPEUTIC EFFECT
A nonabsorbed, cation exchange polymer that binds to potassium in the lumen of the gastrointestinal tract and increases its fecal elimination. *The binding of potassium reduces the concentration of free potassium in the gastrointestinal lumen, resulting in a reduction of serum potassium levels.*

USES Treatment of hyperkalemia. Due to its delayed onset of action, it should not be used in the emergency treatment of life-threatening hyperkalemia.

CONTRAINDICATIONS Hypersensitivity to patiromer. Avoid use in patients with severe constipation, GI obstruction, fecal impaction, including post-operative bowel motility disorders.

CAUTIOUS USE Use cautiously in patients with a history of hypomagnesemia. Maternal use during pregnancy is not expected to result in fetal risk. According to the manufacturer, breast-feeding is not expected to result in risk to the infant. If an infant does experience adverse effects, it should be reported to the FDA.

ROUTE & DOSAGE

Hyperkalemia
Adult: **PO 8.4 grams once daily; may increase to 25.2 grams once daily**

ADMINISTRATION
Oral
- Administer patiromer 6 h before or 6 h after other orally administered medications to prevent patiromer from binding to other oral medications.
- Administer with food.
- Do not administer in its dry form.
- Do not heat or add to heated food or liquids.

Oral Liquid Formulation
- Prepare each dose immediately before administration.
- Measure 1/3 cup of water. Pour half into the cup and then empty the entire contents of the packet into the glass. Stir thoroughly and add the remaining water. Stir again, the particles will not completely dissolve. The mixture will look cloudy. Add more water if needed for desired consistency.
- Drink immediately, rinse the glass with more water and drink again. Repeat as needed to ensure that the entire dose has been given.
- Store at 2°–8° C (36°–46° F). If stored at room temperature 25° C (77° F), use within 3 mo of being taken out of refrigeration. Avoid

exposure to excessive heat above 40° C (104° F).

ADVERSE EFFECTS CNS: Nausea. **Endocrine:** Hypokalemia, hypomagnesemia. **GI:** Abdominal discomfort, constipation, diarrhea, flatulence.

INTERACTIONS Drug: Patiromer can bind to other coadministered oral drugs and reduce their absorption. Oral drugs should be taken at least 6 h before or 6 h after patiromer.

PHARMACOKINETICS Absorption: Not orally absorbed.

NURSING IMPLICATIONS

Assessment & Drug Effects
- Older adults may experience more gastrointestinal adverse reactions.
- Monitor lab tests: Serum magnesium and potassium levels.

Patient & Family Education
- Immediately report to prescriber for any of the following: Mood changes, muscle pain, weakness, muscle cramps or spasms, seizures, lack of appetite, severe nausea or vomiting, or an abnormal heart beat.
- Report signs of a significant reaction: Wheezing, chest tightness, itching, swelling of face, lips, tongue, or throat.

PAZOPANIB
(pas-o'pa-nib)
Votrient
Classification: ANTINEOPLASTIC; KINASE INHIBITOR
Therapeutic: ANTINEOPLASTIC
Prototype: Erlotinib

AVAILABILITY Tablet

ACTION & THERAPEUTIC EFFECT
A multityrosine kinase (i.e., multikinase) inhibitor that limits tumor growth by inhibiting cell surface vascular endothelial growth factor receptors and other receptors needed for tumor angiogenesis and growth. *Pazopanib inhibits growth of advanced renal cell carcinoma.*

USES Treatment of advanced renal cell carcinoma; soft tissue sarcoma.

CONTRAINDICATIONS Hepatotoxicity; severe hepatic impairment; ALT elevation greater than $3 \times$ ULN concurrently with bilirubin elevation of greater than $2 \times$ ULN; cerebral or GI bleeding within last 6 mo; GI perforation or fistula; uncontrolled hypertension; drug induced left ventricular ejection fraction (LVEF); wound dehiscence; stop drug 7 days before surgical procedures; patients who have had an arterial thrombotic event within 6 mo; reversible posterior leukoencephalopathy syndrome; nephrotic syndrome; pregnancy—fetal risk cannot be ruled out; lactation—infant risk cannot be ruled out.

CAUTIOUS USE Risk for QT prolongation or history of QT prolongation; electrolyte imbalance; CHF; cardiac dysfunction; risk for or history of thrombotic event; risk for or history of GI perforation or fistula; moderate hepatic impairment; history of hypothyroidism; infection; older adults; children younger than 18 y.

ROUTE & DOSAGE

Renal Cell Carcinoma/Soft Tissue Sarcoma

Adult: **PO** 800 mg once daily reduce until disease progression or unacceptable toxicity

P

Hepatic Impairment Dosage Adjustment

See package insert for details

ADMINISTRATION
Oral
- NIOSH guidelines recommend single gloves by anyone handling intact tablets or capsules or administering from a unit-dose package.
- Give without food at least 1 h before or 2 h after a meal.
- Ensure that the tablets are swallowed whole. They should not be crushed or chewed.

ADVERSE EFFECTS (≥ 5%) CV:
Hypertension, **Respiratory:** *Dyspnea.* **CNS:** *Headache.* **Endocrine:** *Alterations- in glucose, anorexia, AST and ALT elevation, decreased magnesium, decreased phosphorus, decreased sodium,* decreased weight, *elevated bilirubin,* hypothyroidism, lipase enzyme elevation, proteinuria. **Skin:** Hair color change. **Hepatic:** Increase alkaline phosphatase. **GI:** *Abdominal pain, diarrhea, nausea, vomiting.* **Musculoskeletal:** Myalgia, pain, weakness. **Hematologic:** <u>Leukopenia, lymphocytopenia, neutropenia, thrombocytopenia.</u> **Other:** *Soft tissue sarcoma, cancer pain.*

INTERACTIONS Drug: Multiple
significant interactions exist, consult a drug interaction database for most complete information. Strong INHIBITORS OF CYP3A4 (e.g., **ketoconazole, ritonavir, clarithromycin**) may increase pazopanib levels. INDUCERS OF CYP3A4 (e.g., **rifampin**) may decrease pazopanib levels. Pazopanib may increase the levels of other drugs that require CYP3A4, CYP2D6, or CYP2C8 for their metabolism. Do not use with agents that prolong QT interval (e.g., **bepridil, cisapride, dofetilide, quinidine, ziprasidone**). Do not use with LIVE VACCINES. **Food: Grapefruit juice** may increase pazopanib levels.

PHARMACOKINETICS Peak: 2–4 h.
Distribution: Greater than 99% plasma protein bound. **Metabolism:** Hepatic oxidation by CYP3A4, minor metabolism via CYP1A2 and CYP2C8. **Elimination:** Primarily fecal. **Half-Life:** 31 h.

NURSING IMPLICATIONS

Black Box Warning

Pazopanib has been associated with severe, sometimes fatal, hepatotoxicity.

Assessment & Drug Effects
- Monitor BP closely. Consult prescriber for desired parameters and report promptly BP elevations above desired levels.
- Monitor cardiac status, especially in those at higher risk for QT interval prolongation. ECG monitoring as warranted.
- Withhold drug and notify prescriber immediately if ALT exceeds 3 × ULN and bilirubin exceeds 2 × ULN.
- Monitor lab tests: CBC with differential. Baseline LFTs, then q4wk for 4 mo, and periodically thereafter; periodic thyroid function tests, urinalysis for proteinuria; baseline and periodic serum electrolytes, pregnancy test before starting therapy.

Patient & Family Education
- Report promptly any of the following: Unexplained signs of bleeding, jaundice, unusually

Common adverse effects in *italic;* life-threatening effects <u>underlined;</u> generic names in **bold;** classifications in SMALL CAPS; ♣ Canadian drug name; ⊙ Prototype drug; ⚠ Alert

- dark urine, unusual tiredness, or pain in the right upper abdomen.
- Do not take OTC drugs, herbs, vitamins or dietary supplements without consulting prescriber.
- Women of childbearing age should use adequate means of contraception to avoid pregnancy while on this drug and for at least 2 weeks after discontinuing the drug.
- Take a missed dose as soon as possible, but if the next dose is less than 12 hours skip the missed dose.

PEGFILGRASTIM

(peg-fil-gras'tim)
Neulasta, Fulphila, Udenyca
Classification: HEMATOPOIETIC GROWTH FACTOR; GRANULOCYTE COLONY-STIMULATING FACTOR (G-CSF)
Therapeutic: HEMATOPOIETIC GROWTH FACTOR; G-CSF
Prototype: Filgrastim

AVAILABILITY Solution for injection

ACTION & THERAPEUTIC EFFECT Endogenous G-CSF regulates the production of neutrophils within the bone marrow; primarily affects neutrophil proliferation, differentiation, and selected end-cell functional activity (including enhanced phagocytic activity, antibody-dependent killing, and increased expression of some functions associated with cell-surface antigens). *Increases neutrophil proliferation and differentiation within the bone marrow.*

USES To decrease the incidence of infection, as manifested by febrile neutropenia, in patients with non-myeloid malignancies receiving myelosuppressive anticancer drugs

associated with a significant incidence of severe neutropenia with fever.

CONTRAINDICATIONS Severe hypersensitivity to perfilgrastim, filgrastin, or any component of the formulation; myeloid cancers; splenomegaly; ARDS from drug.

CAUTIOUS USE Sickle cell disorders; neutropenic patients with sepsis; leukemia; pregnancy (category C); lactation. Safety and efficacy in children not established.

ROUTE & DOSAGE

Neutropenia

Adult (weight greater than 45 kg): **Subcutaneous** 6 mg once/chemotherapy cycle at least 24 h after chemotherapy

ADMINISTRATION

Subcutaneous
- Do not administer pegfilgrastim in the period 14 days before or 24 h after cytotoxic chemotherapy.
- Use only one dose/vial; do not reenter the vial.
- Prior to injection, pegfilgrastim may be allowed to reach room temperature for a maximum of 6 h. Discard any vial left at room temperature for longer than 6 h.
- Aspirate prior to injection to avoid injection into a blood vessel. Inject subcutaneously; do not inject intradermally. Recommended injection sites include outer area of upper arms, abdomen (excluding 2-in. area around navel), front of middle thighs, and upper outer areas of the buttocks.
- Store refrigerated at 2°–8° C (36°–46° F). Do not freeze. Avoid shaking.

ADVERSE EFFECTS Musculoskeletal: *Bone pain*, limb pain.

DIAGNOSTIC TEST INTERFERENCE
May interfere with *bone imaging studies.*

INTERACTIONS Drug: Can interfere with activity of CYTOTOXIC AGENTS; do not use 14 days before or less than 24 h after CYTOTOXIC AGENTS; **lithium** may increase release of neutrophils. Do not use with **tisagenlecleucel.**

PHARMACOKINETICS Absorption: Readily absorbed from subcutaneous site. **Half-Life:** 15–80 h.

NURSING IMPLICATIONS
Assessment & Drug Effects
- Discontinue pegfilgrastim if absolute neutrophil count exceeds 10,000/mm³ after the chemotherapy-induced nadir. Neutrophil counts should then return to normal.
- Monitor patients with preexisting cardiac conditions closely. MI and arrhythmias have been associated with a small percent of patients receiving pegfilgrastim.
- Monitor temperature q4h. Incidence of infection should be reduced after administration of pegfilgrastim.
- Assess degree of bone pain if present. Consult prescriber if nonnarcotic analgesics do not provide relief.
- Monitor lab tests: Baseline CBC with differential and platelet count; then CBC twice weekly during therapy; regular Hct and Hgb, and platelet count.

Patient & Family Education
- Report bone pain and, if necessary, request analgesics to control pain.

- Note: Proper drug administration and disposal is important. A puncture-resistant container for the disposal of used syringes and needles should be utilized.

PEGINTERFERON ALFA-2A ☺
(peg-in-ter-fer'on)
Pegasys
Classification: BIOLOGIC RESPONSE MODIFIER; IMMUNOMODULATOR; ALPHA INTERFERON
Therapeutic: ANTIVIRAL; ANTIHEPATITIS

AVAILABILITY Solution for injection

ACTION & *THERAPEUTIC EFFECT*
Interferon-stimulated genes modulate processes leading to inhibition of viral replication in infected cells, inhibition of cell proliferation, and immunomodulation. *Induces antiviral effects by activation of macrophages, natural killer cells, and T-cells, thus boosting cellular immunity and suppressing hepatic inflammation and replication of hepatitis C virus.*

USES Chronic hepatitis B.

CONTRAINDICATIONS Hypersensitivity to peginterferon alfa-2a or any of its components; drug induced life-threatening neuromuscular, autoimmune, ischemic or infectious disorder(s); severe immunosuppression; autoimmune thyroid diseases (e.g., Graves' disease, thyroiditis); autoimmune hepatitis; encephalopathy; history of significant or uncontrolled cardiac disease; dental work; sepsis; *E. coli* hypersensitivity, neonates and infants because it contains benzyl alcohol;

Common adverse effects in *italic*; life-threatening effects <u>underlined</u>; generic names in **bold**; classifications in SMALL CAPS; ✦ Canadian drug name; ☺ Prototype drug; ⚠ Alert pregnancy—fetal risk cannot be ruled out; lactation—infant risk cannot be ruled out.

CAUTIOUS USE History of neuropsychiatric disorder; alcoholism, substance abuse; risk of pulmonary failure; bipolar disorder, mania, psychosis, history of suicides; bone marrow suppression; cardiac arrhythmias, history of MI, cardiac disease, heart failure, uncontrolled hypertension; pulmonary disease, including COPD; thyroid dysfunction; DM; autoimmune disorders; ulcerative and hemorrhagic colitis; pancreatitis; pulmonary disorders; liver impairment; HBV or HIV coinfection; retinal disease; history of depression, renal impairment with creatinine clearance less than 50 mL/min; organ transplant recipients; older adults;. Safe use in children younger than 3 y not established.

ROUTE & DOSAGE

Chronic Hepatitis B

Adult: **Subcutaneous** 180 mcg once weekly × 48 wk

Hematologic Parameters, Adverse Effects, Renal Impairment, and Hepatic Impairment Dosage Adjustments

See package insert

ADMINISTRATION

Subcutaneous

- Give dose on the same day of each week. Consider night time administration to increase patient's tolerance. Administer subcutaneously in the abdomen or thigh and rotate injection sites.
- Warm refrigerated vial by rolling in hands for about 1 min. Do not use if particulate matter is visible

in the vial or product is discolored. Discard any unused portion.
- Withhold drug and notify prescriber for any of the following: ANC less than 750/mm³ or platelet count less than 50,000/mm³.
- Store in the refrigerator at 36°–46° F (2°–8° C), do not freeze or shake. Protect from light. Vials, prefilled syringes and autoinjectors are for single use only. Discard unused portions. Do not leave out of the refrigerator longer than 24 hours.

ADVERSE EFFECTS Respiratory: *Cough, dyspnea.* **CNS:** *Headache, irritability, insomnia, dizziness, impaired concentration.* **Endocrine:** Increased serum triglycerides, decreased weight. **Skin:** *Alopecia, pruritus, dermatitis, rash, injection site inflammation.* **Hepatic:** Elevated ALT/SGPT. **GI:** *Nausea, diarrhea, abdominal pain, anorexia.* **Musculoskeletal:** *Arthralgia, myalgia.* **Hematologic:** Thrombocytopenia, neutropenia. **Other:** *Fatigue, flu-like symptoms, rigors, fever.*

INTERACTIONS Drug: additive myelosuppression with ANTINEOPLASTICS. Do not administer LIVE VACCINES.

PHARMACOKINETICS Peak: 72–96 h. **Half-Life:** 50-160 h.

NURSING IMPLICATIONS

Black Box Warning

Peginterferon Alfa-2A has been associated with fatal or life-threatening neuropsychiatric, autoimmune, ischemic, and infectious disorders.

Assessment & Drug Effects

- Monitor for S&S of hypersensitivity (e.g., angioedema,

broncho-constriction) and, if noted, institute appropriate medical action immediately. Note that transient rashes are not an indication to discontinue treatment.

- Withhold drug and notify prescriber for any of the following: Severe neuropsychiatric events (e.g., psychosis, hallucinations, suicidal ideation, depression, bipolar disorders, and mania), severe neutropenia or thrombocytopenia, abdominal pain accompanied by bloody diarrhea and fever, S&S of pancreatitis, new or worsening ophthalmologic disorders, or any other severe adverse event (see CAUTIOUS USE).
- Monitor respiratory and cardiovascular status; report dyspnea, chest pain, and hypotension immediately; perform baseline and periodic ECG and chest X-ray.
- Baseline and periodic ophthalmology exams are recommended.
- Monitor lab tests: Baseline creatinine clearance, uric acid, CBC with differential, platelet count, Hct and Hgb, TSH, ALT, AST, bilirubin, blood glucose; CBC with differential, platelet count, Hct and Hgb after 2 wk and other blood chemistries after 4 wk. Serum HCV RNA level after 24 wk of treatment.

Patient & Family Education

- If you miss a drug dose and remember within 2 days of the scheduled dose, take the dose and continue with your regular schedule. If more than 2 days have passed, contact prescriber for instructions.
- Instruct and provide opportunity for return demonstration of proper subcutaneous injection technique and placement of injections.
- Notify prescriber immediately for any of the following: Severe

depression or suicidal thoughts, severe chest pain, difficulty breathing, changes in vision, unusual bleeding or bruising, bloody diarrhea, high fever, severe stomach or lower back pain, severe chest pain, development of a new or worsening of a preexisting skin condition.

- Follow up with lab tests; compliance with lab testing is extremely important while taking this drug.
- Review adverse effects with patient and/or caregiver.
- Do not drive or engage in other potentially hazardous activities until reaction to drug is known.
- Report any visual disturbances.
- Avoid drinking alcohol.
- Women should use reliable means of contraception while taking this drug and up to 6 months after therapy ends. Notify prescriber immediately if they become pregnant. Adverse effects to the fetus may be caused by either male of female patients receiving this drug in combination with ribavirin.

PEGINTERFERON ALFA-2B

(peg-in-ter-fer'on)
PegIntron, Sylatron
Classification: BIOLOGIC RESPONSE MODIFIER; IMMUNOMODULATOR; ALPHA INTERFERON
Therapeutic: ANTIVIRAL; ANTIHEPATITIS
Prototype: Peginterferon alfa-2a

AVAILABILITY Powder for injection

ACTION & *THERAPEUTIC EFFECT*

Binds to specific membrane receptors on the cell surface, thereby initiating suppression of cell proliferation, enhanced phagocytic activity of macrophages, augmentation of specific cytotoxic lymphocytes for target cells, and inhibition of viral replication in virus-infected cells. *Induces antiviral effects by activation of macrophages, natural killer cells, and T-cells, thus boosting cellular immunity and suppressing hepatic inflammation and replication of hepatitis C virus.*

USES Adjuvant therapy of melanoma.

CONTRAINDICATIONS Hypersensitivity to peginterferon or interferon alfa; autoimmune hepatitis; decompensated liver disease {Child-Pugh (class B and C)} in cirrhotic chronic hepatitis C patients before or during treatment; pancreatitis; persistently severe or worsening S&S of life-threatening neuropsychiatric, autoimmune, ischemic, or infectious disorders; history of significant or unstable cardiac disease; uncontrollable DM or hypo- or hyperthyroidism; pregnancy – fetal risk cannot be ruled out; lactation – infant risk cannot be ruled out. **Sylatron:** Hepatic decompensation. {Child-Pugh (class B and C)}.

CAUTIOUS USE History of neuropsychiatric disorder; suicidal tendencies; substance abuse disorders; bone marrow suppression; ulcerative and hemorrhagic colitis; pulmonary disorders; HBV or HIV coinfection; thyroid dysfunction; DM; cardiovascular disease; autoimmune disorders; pulmonary disease, COPD; retinal disease; renal impairment with creatinine clearance less than 50 mL/min; older adults; Safety and efficacy in children younger than 3 y not established.

ROUTE & DOSAGE

Melanoma (Sylatron only)

Adult: **Subcutaneous** 6 mcg/kg/wk × 8 doses then 3 mcg/kg/wk for up to 5 y

Renal Impairment Dosage Adjustment

CrCl 30–50 mL/min: reduce initial dose to 4.5 mcg/kg/week; then 2.25 mcg/kg/week; CrCl less than 30 mL/min: reduce initial dose to 3 mcg/kg/week; then 1.5 mcg/kg/week

ADMINISTRATION

Subcutaneous
- Give dose on the same day of each week.
- *Vial reconstitution:* Be aware that two Safety Lok™ syringes are provided in the drug package: One for reconstitution and one for injection. Reconstitute with only 0.7 mL of supplied diluent and discard remaining diluent. Enter the vial only once as it does not contain a preservative. Swirl gently to produce a clear, colorless solution. Use solution immediately.
- Store dry vial at 15°–30° C (59°–86° F). If necessary, store reconstituted solution up to 24 h at 2°–8° C (36°–46° F).

ADVERSE EFFECTS (≥ 5%) CNS:
Headache, dizziness. **Skin:** *Alopecia.* **Hepatic:** *Increased liver enzymes.* **GI:** *Nausea, anorexia, diarrhea,* vomiting. **Musculoskeletal:** *Arthralgia, myalgia.* **Hematologic:** <u>Thrombocytopenia</u>, neutropenia. **Other:** *Fatigue, inflammation at injection site, rigors, fever.*

INTERACTIONS Drug: additive myelosuppression with ANTINEO-PLASTICS; **zidovudine** may increase hematologic toxicity; i increase neurotoxicity with **telbivudine; aldesleukin (IL-2)** may potentiate the risk of kidney failure. Do not administer LIVE VACCINES.

PHARMACOKINETICS Peak:
15–44 h. **Elimination:** 30% in urine. **Half-Life:** 40-50 h.

NURSING IMPLICATIONS

Black Box Warning

PegIntron has been associated with fatal or life-threatening neuropsychiatric, autoimmune, ischemic, and infectious disorders. Sylatron has been associated with serious depression with suicidal ideation, completed suicides, and other serious neuropsychiatric disorders.

Assessment & Drug Effects

- Monitor for S&S of hypersensitivity (e.g., angioedema, bronchoconstriction) and, if noted, institute appropriate medical action immediately. Note that transient rashes are not an indication to discontinue treatment.
- Monitor for and report immediately S&S of neuropsychiatric disorders (e.g., psychosis, hallucinations, suicidal ideation, depression). Every 3 weeks during the initial 8 weeks of treatment, every 6 months thereafter while on therapy, and for at least 6 months after discontinuing therapy.
- Regular dental exams.
- Monitor respiratory and cardiovascular status; report dyspnea, chest pain, and hypotension immediately; baseline and periodic ECG and chest X-ray.
- Withhold drug and notify prescriber for any of the following: Severe neuropsychiatric events, severe neutropenia or thrombocytopenia, abdominal pain accompanied by bloody diarrhea and fever, S&S of pancreatitis, or any other severe adverse event (see CAUTIOUS USE).
- Baseline and periodic ophthalmology exams are recommended.
- Monitor lab tests: Baseline and periodic creatinine clearance, serum uric acid, CBC with differential, platelet count, Hct and Hgb, TSH, ALT, AST, bilirubin, blood glucose; triglycerides; serum HCV RNA level after 24 wk of treatment, pregnancy test immediately prior to initiation of therapy and monthly during therapy and for 6 months after therapy.

Patient & Family Education

- Drink fluids liberally while taking this drug, especially during the initial stages of therapy.
- Instruct, and provide opportunity for return demonstration of subcutaneous injections.
- Learn reasons for withholding drug (SEE ASSESSMENT & DRUG EFFECTS).
- Use effective means of contraception while taking this drug. Women should not become pregnant. Use 2 forms of birth control during therapy and for 6 months after the last dose.
- Review adverse effects with patient and/or caregiver.
- Immediately report chest pain, lightheadedness, fainting episode, or racing heartbeat.
- Follow up with lab tests; compliance with lab testing is extremely important while taking this drug.

PEGINTERFERON BETA-1A

(peg-in-ter-fer'on)
Plegridy
Classification: BIOLOGIC
RESPONSE MODIFIER;
IMMUNOMODULATOR; BETA
INTERFERON
Therapeutic: IMMUNOMODULATOR
Prototype: Peginterferon alfa-2A

AVAILABILITY Prefilled solution for injection

ACTION & *THERAPEUTIC EFFECT*
Exact mechanism of action in the treatment of multiple sclerosis is unknown. Interferon beta-1A alters the expression and response to surface antigens and enhances immune cell activities. *Improves symptoms and functionality in patients with relapsing MS.*

USES Treatment of patients with relapsing forms of multiple sclerosis.

CONTRAINDICATIONS History of hypersensitivity to natural or recombinant interferon beta or peginterferon, or any other component of the formulation; suicidal ideation or other severe psychiatric symptoms.

CAUTIOUS USE Severe renal impairment; seizure disorder; hepatic impairment; depression, history of suicidal thoughts; seizure disorder; myelosuppression; CHF; cardiomyopathy; serious injections site reactions; older adults; pregnancy (category C); lactation. Safety and efficacy in children younger than 18 y not established.

ROUTE & DOSAGE

Multiple Sclerosis

Adult: **Subcutaneous** 63 mcg on day 1; 94 mcg on day 15; 125 mcg on day 29 and 125 mcg every 14 days thereafter

ADMINISTRATION

Subcutaneous
- Allow prefilled syringe or pen to warm to room temperature (approx. 30 min) prior to injection; do not use external heat sources (e.g., hot water) to warm.
- Inject into the abdomen, back of the upper arm, or thigh; rotate injection sites; do not inject into area where skin is red, irritated, bruised, or scarred.
- Store in the closed original carton to protect from light, at 2°–8° C (36°–46° F). Do not freeze; discard if frozen.

ADVERSE EFFECTS CNS: *Headache.* **Endocrine:** Increased ALT and AST, increased gamma glutamyl transferase. **Skin:** Pruritus. **GI:** Nausea, vomiting. **Musculoskeletal:** Arthralgia, *myalgia.* **Hematologic:** Decreased white cell counts. **Other:** *Asthenia, chills,* hyperthermia, *influenza-like illness,* injection site edema, *injection site erythema,* injection site hematoma, *injection site illness, injection site pain, injection site pruritus,* injection site rash, injection site hematoma, pain, *pyrexia.*

INTERACTIONS Drugs: Use with NRTIS should be done with caution as it may impact antiviral clearance. Avoid use with **vigabatrin.**

PHARMACOKINETICS Peak: 1–1.5 days. **Distribution:** Well distributed to tissues. **Metabolism:** Not extensive. **Elimination:** Primarily renal. **Half-Life:** 78 h.

NURSING IMPLICATIONS

Assessment & Drug Effects

- Monitor for injection site reactions (e.g., erythema, pain, pruritus, edema, necrosis).
- Monitor for and report promptly any of the following: S&S of hypersensitivity or hepatic injury; S&S of myelosuppression (e.g., infections, bleeding, anemia); new onset or worsening signs of CV disease (i.e., CHF); mental status changes.
- Monitor for increased seizure activity with a preexisting seizure disorder.
- Monitor lab tests: Baseline and periodic CBC with differential and platelet count, LFTs, renal function tests; periodic thyroid function tests.

Patient & Family Education

- Report promptly to prescriber if you develop signs of infection or bleeding.
- Consult your prescriber if you experience mental status changes (e.g., depression, suicidal ideation, anxiety, emotional instability, illogical thinking).
- Notify prescriber immediately if you experience worsening symptoms of heart failure such as shortness of breath, swelling of your lower legs, or excessive weight gain.
- Notify your prescriber if you are pregnant or plan to become pregnant.
- Do not breast-feed without first consulting your prescriber.

PEGLOTICASE

(peg-lo'ti-case)

Krystexxa
Classification: ANTIGOUT; URIC ACID METABOLIZING ENZYME
Therapeutic: ANTIGOUT

AVAILABILITY Solution for injection

ACTION & THERAPEUTIC EFFECT
Pegloticase is a recombinant uric acid specific enzyme that catalyzes the conversion of uric acid to a water soluble, inert metabolite readily eliminated by the kidney. *It lowers the serum uric acid, thus reducing uric acid induced inflammation.*

USES Treatment of chronic gout.

CONTRAINDICATIONS Established G6PD deficiency; lactation.

CAUTIOUS USE African or Mediterranean ancestry; consider discontinuing if uric acid level above 6 mg/mL; retreatment with pegloticase following discontinuation of therapy for longer than 6 wk; CHF; pregnancy (category C); children younger than 18 y.

ROUTE & DOSAGE

Chronic Gout

Adult: **IV** 8 mg over 2 hrs q2wk

ADMINISTRATION

Intravenous

- Note: Premedication with antihistamines and corticosteroids is required to minimize the risk of anaphylaxis and infusion reactions. ▪ Pegloticase should only be administered in a health care setting and by health care providers trained to manage anaphylaxis and infusion reactions.

Common adverse effects in *italic;* life-threatening effects underlined; generic names in **bold;** classifications in SMALL CAPS; ♣ Canadian drug name; ◑ Prototype drug; ⚠ Alert

PEGLOTICASE

***PREPARE:* IV Infusion:** Do not shake vial. ▪ Withdraw 1 mL of pegloticase from the 2 mL vial and inject into 250 mL of NS. Do not mix or dilute with other drugs. ▪ Invert IV bag to mix but do not shake. ▪ Discard unused pegloticase remaining in vial.

***ADMINISTER:* IV Infusion:** If refrigerated, bring to room temperature prior to infusion. **Do not give IV push or bolus.** Infuse over NO LESS THAN 120 min. ▪ Monitor closely throughout infusion and for 2 h post-infusion for S&S of anaphylaxis or an infusion reaction (e.g., urticarial, erythema, dyspnea, flushing, chest discomfort, chest pain, and rash). ▪ If S&S of anaphylaxis or an infusion reaction occur, stop infusion and immediately notify prescriber. ▪ If anaphylaxis is ruled out and infusion is restarted, it should be run at a slower rate. ▪ Infusion bags may be stored refrigerated for 4 h after dilution.

***INCOMPATIBILITIES:* Solution/additive:** Do not mix with another drug. **Y-site:** Do not mix with another drug.

▪ Store unopened vials in refrigerator at (2°–8° C or 36°–46° F) and protect from light. Do not shake or freeze.
▪ Diluted solution may be stored up to 4 h at 2°–8° C (36°–46° F). Warm to room temperature before administration. Diluted solution is also stable at room temperature for up to 4 h, but should be protected from light.

ADVERSE EFFECTS CV: Chest pain. **Respiratory:** Dyspnea, nasopharyngitis. **CNS:** Headache. **Endocrine:** Anemia. **Skin:** Erythema, urticaria. **GI:** *Nausea* vomiting, constipation **Other:** Anaphylaxis,

contusion, ecchymosis, arthralgia, gout flare, infusion reaction, pruritus.

INTERACTIONS Drug: Potential interaction with other pegylated products (**pegfilgrastim, peginterferon alfa-2a**). Do not use with **allopurinol, febuxostat, probenecid, sulfinpyrazone.**

NURSING IMPLICATIONS

Black Box Warning

Pegloticase has been associated with anaphylaxis and infusion reactions during and after administration. G6PD deficiency-associated hemolysis and methemoglobinemia.

Assessment & Drug Effects
▪ Monitor closely during infusion and for 2 h postinfusion for S&S of anaphylaxis (see Appendix F) or an infusion reaction (see IV ADMINISTRATION).
▪ Assess vital signs frequently during and for 2 h postinfusion.
▪ Monitor cardiac status, especially with preexisting congestive heart failure.
▪ Notify prescriber if uric acid level is 6 mg/mL or above. Two consecutive readings above 6 mm/mL may indicate need to discontinue treatment.
▪ Monitor lab tests: Baseline and periodic serum uric acid level.

Patient & Family Education
▪ Report promptly any discomfort (e.g., wheezing, facial swelling, skin rash, redness of the skin, difficulty breathing, flushing, chest discomfort, chest pain, rash) during or following IV infusion.
▪ Gout flares may increase during the first 3 mo of therapy and are not a reason to discontinue pegloticase.

Common adverse effects in *italic;* life-threatening effects underlined; generic names in **bold;** classifications in SMALL CAPS; ♣ Canadian drug name; ⊙ Prototype drug; ⚠ Alert

PEMBROLIZUMAB
(pem-bro-li'zu-mab)
Keytruda
Classification: IMMUNOMODULA-TOR; MONOCLONAL ANTIBODY; PROGRAMMED DEATH RECEPTOR-1 BLOCKER
Therapeutic: IMMUNOSUPPRESSANT
Prototype: Basiliximab

AVAILABILITY Lyophilized powder

ACTION & *THERAPEUTIC EFFECT*
Activation of programmed cell death (PD-1) receptors found on T cells inhibits T cell proliferation and cytokine production. Increased activation of PD-1 receptors occurs in some tumors and can contribute to inhibition of active T-cell immune response to tumors. Pembrolizumab binds to the PD-1 receptor and blocks its activation thus removing inhibition of the immune response, including the antitumor immune response. *Blocking PD-1 activity results in decreased tumor growth.*

USES Treatment of patients with unresectable or metastatic melanoma and disease progression following ipilimumab and a BRAF inhibitor (for those patients who have a BRAF V600 mutation), metastatic non–small-cell lung cancer; head/neck cancer; colorectal cancer; Hogkin's disease, urothelial cancer.

CONTRAINDICATIONS Any life-threatening adverse reaction; drug induced Grade 3–4 renal failure, hepatitis, or infusion-related reactions; drug induced life-threatening immune-mediated colitis; pregnancy (category D); lactation.

CAUTIOUS USE Renal or hepatic impairment; drug induced pneumonitis; asthma; COPD; prior thoracic radiation; inflammation of the pituitary (hypophysitis); DM; thyroid disorders; colitis; organ donor recipients; women of child bearing age. Safety and efficacy in children younger than 18 y not established.

ROUTE & DOSAGE

Metastatic Melanoma
Adult: **IV** 200 mg every 3 wk until disease progression or unacceptable toxicity

Non–Small-Cell Lung Cancer/ Head/Neck Cancer
Adult: **IV** 200 mg q3w for up to 24 mo until disease progression or unacceptable toxicity

Toxicity Dosage Adjustment
See package insert

ADMINISTRATION
Intravenous

PREPARE: IV Infusion: Reconstitute by adding 2.3 mL SW for injection along vial wall to yield 25 mg/mL. Slowly swirl vial; do not shake. Allow up to 5 min for bubbles to dissipate. Withdraw required volume from vial and dilute in IV NS to a final concentration of 1–10 mg/mL. Mix by gently inverting bag. Discard unused portion of the vial.
ADMINISTER: IV Infusion: Infuse over 30 min through a 0.2-0.5 micron sterile, nonpyrogenic, low-protein-binding inline or add-on filter.
INCOMPATIBILITIES: Do not mix or infuse with any other medications.

▪ Store intact vials at 2°–8° C (36°–46° F). Reconstituted and solutions diluted for infusion may be stored at room temperature for up to 6 h (infusion must be completed within 6 h of reconstitution) or refrigerated at 2°–8° C (36°–46° F) for no more than 24 h from the time of reconstitution.

ADVERSE EFFECTS CV: Peripheral edema. **Respiratory:** *Cough,* dyspnea, pneumonia, upper respiratory tract infection, pleural effusion. **CNS:** Dizziness, headache, insomnia. **Endocrine:** *Decreased appetite,* hyperglycemia, hypercholesterolemia, hypertriglyceridemia, hypoalbuminemia, hypocalcemia, hyponatremia, increased AST. **Skin:** Pruritus, *rash,* vitiligo. **GI:** Abdominal pain, *constipation, anorexia, diarrhea, nausea,* vomiting. **GU:** Renal failure. **Musculoskeletal:** *Arthralgia,* back pain, myalgia, pain in extremity. **Hematologic:** Anemia. **Other:** Cellulitis, chills, *fatigue,* immunogenic response, peripheral edema, pyrexia, sepsis.

INTERACTIONS Drug: If used with **clozapine** monitor ANC.

PHARMACOKINETICS Half-Life: 26 days.

NURSING IMPLICATIONS

Assessment & Drug Effects
- Monitor for S&S of hypersensitivity or infusion-related reactions.
- Monitor for S&S of drug toxicity including pneumonitis, colitis, hepatitis, pituitary disorders, nephritis, thyroid dysfunction.
- Monitor lab tests: Baseline and periodic LFTs, renal function tests, thyroid function tests; periodic lipid profile and serum electrolytes, blood glucose levels.

Patient & Family Education
- Report promptly to prescriber if you experience signs of pulmonary toxicity such as new or worsening cough, chest pain, or shortness of breath.
- Report signs of colitis or liver damage such as diarrhea, severe abdominal pain, jaundice, severe nausea or vomiting, or easy bruising or bleeding.
- Report signs of endocrine dysfunction including persistent or unusual headache, extreme weakness, dizziness or fainting, or vision changes.
- Women of childbearing potential should use highly effective contraception during and for 4 mo after the last dose of this drug.
- Do not breast-feed while taking this drug.

PEMETREXED
(pe-me-trex'ed)
Alimta
Classification: ANTINEOPLASTIC; ANTIMETABOLITE, ANTIFOLATE
Therapeutic: ANTINEOPLASTIC
Prototype: Methotrexate

AVAILABILITY Powder for injection

ACTION & THERAPEUTIC EFFECT
Suppresses tumor growth by inhibiting both DNA synthesis and folate metabolism at multiple target enzymes. *Appears to arrest the cell cycle, thus inhibiting tumor growth.*

USES Treatment of malignant pleural mesothelioma that is unresectable or in patients that are not surgery candidates in combination with cisplatin; treatment of locally advanced or metastatic non–small-cell lung cancer (NSCLC).

UNLABELED USES Solid tumors, including bladder, breast, colorectal, gastric, head and neck, pancreatic, and renal cell cancers.

CONTRAINDICATIONS Mannitol hypersensitivity; creatinine clearance is less than 45 mL/min; renal failure, active infection; vaccines; pregnancy (category D); lactation.

CAUTIOUS USE Anemia, thrombocytopenia, neutropenia, dental disease; older adults; hepatic disease, renal impairment; hypoalbuminemia, hypovolemia, dehydration, ascites, pleural effusion; children younger than 18 y.

ROUTE & DOSAGE

Malignant Mesothelioma, Non–Small-Cell Lung Cancer

Adult: **IV** 500 mg/m² on day 1 of each 21-day cycle

Renal Impairment Dosage Adjustment

CrCl less than 45 mL/min: Not recommended

ADMINISTRATION

Intravenous

Pre/posttreatment with folic acid, vitamin B₁₂, and dexamethasone are needed to reduce hematologic and gastrointestinal toxicity, and the possibility of severe cutaneous reactions from pemetrexed.

This drug is a cytotoxic agent and caution should be used to prevent any contact with the drug. Follow institutional or standard guidelines for preparation, handling, and disposal of cytotoxic agents.

PREPARE: IV Infusion: Reconstitute each 100 mg or 500 mg vial with 4.2 mL or 20 mL, respectively, of preservative-free NS. ▪ Do not use any other diluent. Swirl gently to dissolve. Each vial will contain 25 mg/mL. ▪ Withdraw the needed amount of reconstituted solution and add to 100 mL of preservative-free NS. ▪ Discard any unused portion.

ADMINISTER: IV Infusion: Do not give a bolus dose. ▪ Infuse over 10 min.

INCOMPATIBILITIES: Solution/additive: Solutions containing **calcium, lactated Ringer's. Y-site: Amphotericin B, calcium, cefazolin, cefotaxime, cefotetan, cefoxitin, ceftazidime, chlorpromazine, ciprofloxacin, dobutamine, doxorubicin, doxycycline, droperidol, gemcitabine, gentamicin, irinotecan, metronidazole, minocycline, mitoxantrone, nalbuphine, ondansetron, prochlorperazine, tobramycin, topotecan.**

▪ Store unopened single-use vials at room temperature at 15°–30° C (59°–86° F). ▪ The reconstituted drug is stable for up to 24 h at 2°–8° C (36°–46° F) or at 25° C (77° F).

ADVERSE EFFECTS CV: Chest pain, thromboembolism. **Respiratory:** *Dyspnea.* **CNS:** Neuropathy, *mood alteration, depression.* **Skin:** *Rash, desquamation,* alopecia. **GI:** *Nausea, vomiting, constipation, anorexia, stomatitis, diarrhea,* dehydration, dysphagia, esophagitis, odynophagia, increased LFTs. **GU:** *Increases serum creatinine,* renal failure. **Hematologic:** Neutropenia, leukopenia, anemia, thrombocytopenia. **Other:** *Fatigue, fever,* hypersensitivity reaction, edema, myalgia, arthralgia.

INTERACTIONS Drug: Increased risk of renal toxicity with other nephrotoxic drugs (**acyclovir, adefovir, amphotericin B,**

AMINOGLYCOSIDES, **carboplatin, cidofovir, cisplatin, cyclosporine, foscarnet, ganciclovir, sirolimus, tacrolimus, vancomycin**); NSAIDS may increase risk of renal toxicity in patients with preexisting renal insufficiency; may cause additive risk of bleeding with ANTICOAGULANTS, PLATELET INHIBITORS, **aspirin,** THROMBOLYTIC AGENTS.

PHARMACOKINETICS **Metabolism:** Not extensively. **Elimination:** Primarily in urine. **Half-Life:** 3.5 h.

NURSING IMPLICATIONS

Assessment & Drug Effects
- Withhold drug and notify prescriber if the absolute neutrophil count (ANC) is less than 1500 cells/mm^3 or the platelet count is less than at least 100,000 cells/mm^3, or if the CrCl is less than 45 mL/min.
- Notify prescriber for S&S of neuropathy (paresthesia) or thromboembolism.
- Monitor lab tests: Baseline and periodic CBC with differential; monitor for nadir and recovery before each dose (on days 8 and 15, respectively, of each cycle); periodic LFTs, serum creatinine and BUN.

Patient & Family Education
- Report promptly any of the following to prescriber: Symptoms of anemia (e.g., chest pain, unusual weakness or tiredness, fainting spells, lightheadedness, shortness of breath); symptoms of poor blood clotting (e.g., bruising; red spots on skin; black, tarry stools; blood in urine); symptoms of infection (e.g., fever or chills, cough, sore throat, pain or difficulty passing urine); symptoms of liver problems (e.g., yellowing of skin).

- Do not take nonsteroidal anti-inflammatory drugs (NSAIDs) without first consulting the prescriber.

PENBUTOLOL
(pen-bu'tol-ol)
Levatol
Classification: BETA-ADRENERGIC ANTAGONIST; ANTIHYPERTENSIVE
Therapeutic: ANTIHYPERTENSIVE
Prototype: Propranolol

AVAILABILITY Tablet

ACTION & *THERAPEUTIC EFFECT*
Synthetic beta$_1$- and beta$_2$-adrenergic blocking agent that competes with epinephrine and norepinephrine for available beta receptor sites. Lowers both supine and standing BP in hypertensive patients. Hypotensive effect is associated with decreased cardiac output, suppressed renin activity as well as beta blockage. *Effective in lowering mild to moderate blood pressure.*

USES Mild to moderate hypertension.

CONTRAINDICATIONS Hypersensitivity to penbutolol; cardiogenic shock, acute CHF, sinus bradycardia, second and third degree AV block; bronchial asthma, acute bronchospasm; Raynaund's disease; COPD; abrupt withdrawal.

CAUTIOUS USE Cardiac failure; PVD; chronic bronchitis; diabetes; mental depression; myasthenia gravis, cerebrovascular insufficiency, stroke; renal disease; major surgery; hyperthyroid; older adults; pregnancy (category C); lactation. Safety and efficacy in children not established.

ROUTE & DOSAGE

Hypertension
Adult: **PO** 20 mg daily, may increase to 40–80 mg/day

ADMINISTRATION
Oral
- Discontinue by reducing the dose gradually over 1 to 2 wk.

ADVERSE EFFECTS **CV:** AV block, bradycardia. **Respiratory:** Cough, dyspnea. **CNS:** Dizziness, fatigue, *headache,* insomnia. **GI:** Nausea, diarrhea, dyspepsia. **GU:** Impotence.

INTERACTIONS **Drug:** DIURETICS and other HYPOTENSIVE AGENTS increase hypotensive effect; effects of **albuterol, metaproterenol, terbutaline, pirbuterol,** and **penbutolol** are antagonized; NSAIDS blunt hypotensive effect; decreases hypoglycemic effect of **glyburide; amiodarone** increases risk of bradycardia and sinus arrest.

PHARMACOKINETICS **Absorption:** Readily from GI tract. **Peak:** 2–3 h. **Duration:** 20 h. **Metabolism:** In liver. **Elimination:** In urine. **Half-Life:** 5 h.

NURSING IMPLICATIONS
Assessment & Drug Effects
- Take apical pulse before administering drug. If pulse is below 60, or other established parameter, hold the drug and contact prescriber.
- Take a BP reading before giving drug, if BP is not stabilized. If systolic pressure is 90 mm Hg or less, hold drug and contact prescriber.
- Check BP near end of dosage interval or before administration of next dose to evaluate effectiveness.
- Monitor therapeutic effectiveness. Full effectiveness of the drug may not be seen for 4–6 wk.
- Watch for S&S of bronchial constriction. Report promptly and withhold drug.
- Monitor diabetics for loss of glycemic control. Drug suppresses clinical signs of hypoglycemia (e.g., BP changes, increased pulse rate) and may prolong hypoglycemic state.
- Monitor carefully for exacerbation of angina during drug withdrawal.

Patient & Family Education
- Do not discontinue the drug without prescriber's advice because of the possible exacerbation of ischemic heart disease.
- If diabetic, report persistent S&S of hypoglycemia (see Appendix F) to prescriber (diabetics).
- Avoid driving or other potentially hazardous activities until response to drug is known.
- Make position changes slowly and avoid prolonged standing. Notify prescriber if dizziness and lightheadedness persist.
- Comply with and do not alter established regimen (i.e., do not omit, increase, or decrease dosage or change dosage interval).
- Avoid prolonged exposure of extremities to cold.
- Avoid excesses of alcohol. Heavy alcohol consumption [i.e., greater than 60 mL (2 oz)/day] may elevate arterial pressure; therefore, to maintain treatment effectiveness, either avoid alcohol or drink moderately (less than 60 mL/day). Consult prescriber.

PENCICLOVIR
(pen-cy′clo-vir)

P

Denavir
Classification: ANTIVIRAL
Therapeutic: TOPICAL ANTIVIRAL
Prototype: Acyclovir

AVAILABILITY Cream

ACTION & *THERAPEUTIC EFFECT*
Antiviral agent active against herpes simplex virus type 1 (HSV-1) and type 2 (HSV-2). HSV-1 and HSV-2 infected cells phosphorylate penciclovir utilizing viral thymidine kinase. Competes with viral DNA, thus inhibiting both viral DNA synthesis and replication. *Effectiveness is measured in decreased viral load.*

USES Treatment of recurrent herpes labialis (cold sores).

CONTRAINDICATIONS Hypersensitivity to penciclovir or famciclovir.

CAUTIOUS USE Acyclovir, or related antiviral hypersensitivity; pregnancy—fetal risk minimal; lactation—infant risk minimal. Safety and efficacy in children younger than 12 y not established. Safety in immunocompromised patients not established.

ROUTE & DOSAGE

Cold Sores
Adult: **Topical** Apply q2h while awake × 4 days

ADVMINISTRATION
Topical
- Apply as soon as possible after developing lesion.
- Do not apply to mucous membranes or near the eyes.
- Store at 20 to 25 degrees C (68 to 77 degrees F).

ADVERSE EFFECTS No adverse effects with occurrence of 1% or greater.

PHARMACOKINETICS Absorption: Minimally absorbed from cold sore.

NURSING IMPLICATIONS

Assessment & Drug Effects
- Monitor the extent of lesions and treatment effectiveness.

Patient & Family Education
- Wash hands before and after application. Avoid contact of drug with eyes.
- Start using treatment at the earliest sign of a cold sore.
- Apply sunscreen to lips; may minimize recurrence of lesions.

PENICILLAMINE
(pen-i-sill′a-meen)
Cuprimine, Depen
Classification: DISEASE-MODIFYING ANTIRHEUMATIC DRUG (DMARD)
Therapeutic: CHELATING AGENT; ANTIRHEUMATIC (DMARD)

AVAILABILITY Capsule; tablet

ACTION & *THERAPEUTIC EFFECT*
Combines chemically with cystine to form a soluble disulfide complex that prevents stone formation and may even dissolve existing cystic stones. Forms stable soluble chelate with copper, zinc, iron, lead, mercury, and possibly other heavy metals and promotes their excretion in urine. Mechanism of action in rheumatoid arthritis appears to be related to inhibition of collagen formation. *With Wilson's disease, therapeutic effectiveness is indicated by improvement in psychiatric and neurologic*

symptoms, visual symptoms, and liver function. With rheumatoid arthritis, therapeutic effectiveness is indicated by improvement in grip strength, decrease in stiffness following immobility, reduction of pain, decrease in sedimentation rate and rheumatoid factor.

USES To promote renal excretion of excess copper in Wilson's disease (hepatolenticular degeneration); cystinuria.

UNLABELED USES Scleroderma, primary biliary cirrhosis, porphyria cutanea tarda, lead poisoning.

CONTRAINDICATIONS Hypersensitivity to penicillamine or to any penicillin; history of penicillamine-related aplastic anemia or agranulocytosis; rheumatoid arthritis patients with renal insufficiency or who are pregnant; renal failure; concomitant administration with drugs that can cause severe hematologic or renal reactions (e.g., antimalarials, gold salts); pregnancy; lactation.

CAUTIOUS USE Allergy-prone individuals; DM; renal disease; renal impairment; hepatic impairment, hepatic disease; history of hematologic disease; children.

ROUTE & DOSAGE

Wilson's Disease
Adult: **PO** 750–1,500 mg/day in divided doses (max: 2000 mg/day)

Cystinuria
Adult: **PO** 250–500 mg qid, with doses adjusted to limit urinary excretion of cystine to 100–200 mg/day

Child: **PO** 20–40 mg/kg/day in 4 divided doses with doses adjusted to limit urinary excretion of cystine to 100–200 mg/day

Renal Impairment Dosage Adjustment
CrCl less than 50 mL/min: Avoid use

ADMINISTRATION

Oral
- Give on empty stomach (60 min before or 2 h after meals) to avoid absorption of metals in foods by penicillamine.
- Give contents in 15–30 mL of chilled fruit juice or pureed fruit (e.g., applesauce) if patient cannot swallow capsules or tablets.
- Drink copious amounts of water, about 1 pint at bedtime and another pint once during the night.
- Store in tight, well-closed containers.

ADVERSE EFFECTS Skin: Rash. **GI:** *Diarrhea, loss of appetite, loss of taste, nausea, vomiting,* ulcers in the mouth. **GU:** Proteinuria.

INTERACTIONS Drug: ANTIMALARIALS, CYTOTOXICS, **gold** therapy may potentiate hematologic and renal adverse effects; **iron** may decrease penicillamine absorption.

PHARMACOKINETICS Absorption: Readily from GI tract. **Peak:** 1 h. **Distribution:** Crosses placenta. **Metabolism:** In liver. **Elimination:** In urine. **Half-Life:** 1–7 h.

NURSING IMPLICATIONS

Black Box Warning

Penicillamine has been associated with serious hematological and renal adverse reactions.

Assessment & Drug Effects

- Monitor for and report promptly S&S of granulocytopenia and/or thrombocytopenia such as fever, sore throat, chills, bruising, or bleeding.
- Monitor skin, lymph nodes, and body temperature, during the first month of therapy, every 2 wk for the next 5 mo, and monthly thereafter.
- Withhold drug and contact prescriber if the patient with rheumatoid arthritis develops proteinuria greater than 1 g (some clinicians accept greater than 2 g) or if platelet count drops to less than 100,000/mm^3, or platelet count falls below 3500–4000/mm^3, or neutropenia occurs.
- Monitor lab tests: Baseline WBC with differential, direct platelet count, Hgb, LFTs (every 6 months), and urinalyses prior to initiation of therapy and twice weekly during the first month of therapy, then every 2 wk for the next 5 mo, and monthly thereafter.

Patient & Family Education

- Note: Clinical evidence of therapeutic effectiveness may not be apparent until 1–3 mo of drug therapy.
- Take exactly as prescribed. Allergic reactions occur in about one third of patients receiving penicillamine. Temporary interruptions of therapy increase possibility of sensitivity reactions.
- Take temperature nightly during first few months of therapy. Fever is a possible early sign of allergy.
- Observe skin over pressure sites: Knees, elbows, shoulder blades, toes, buttocks. Penicillamine increases risk of skin breakdown.
- Report unusual bruising or bleeding, sore mouth or throat, fever, skin rash, or any other unusual symptoms to prescriber.

PENICILLIN G BENZATHINE

(pen-i-sill'in)

Bicillin, Bicillin L-A, Permapen

Classification: BETA-LACTAM ANTIBIOTIC; NATURAL PENICILLIN
Therapeutic: ANTIBIOTIC
Prototype: Penicillin G potassium

AVAILABILITY Solution for injection

ACTION & *THERAPEUTIC EFFECT*

Acts by interfering with synthesis of mucopeptides essential to formation and integrity of the bacterial cell wall. *Effective against many strains of Staphylococcus aureus, gram-positive cocci, gram-negative cocci. Also effective against gram-positive bacilli and gram-negative bacilli as well as some strains of Salmonella, Shigella, and spirochetes.*

USES Infections highly susceptible to penicillin G, such as streptococcal, pneumococcal, and staphylococcal infections, venereal disease such as syphilis (including early, late, and congenital forms), and nonvenereal diseases. Also used in prophylaxis of rheumatic fever.

CONTRAINDICATIONS Hypersensitivity to penicillins; IV administration.

CAUTIOUS USE History of or suspected allergy (eczema, hives, hay fever, asthma); hypersensitivity to cephalosporins or carbapenems; history of colitis; IBD; renal disease, renal impairment; GI disease; pregnancy (category B); lactation; infants, neonates.

ROUTE & DOSAGE

Mild to Moderate Infections

Adult: **IM** 1,200,000 units once/day

Child (weight greater than 27 kg): **IM** 900,000 units once/day; *weight less than 27 kg:* 300,000–600,000 units once/day

Syphilis

Adult: **IM** Less than 1 y duration: 2,400,000 units as single dose; greater than 1 y duration: 2,400,000 units/wk for 3 wk
Child (younger than 2 y): **IM** 50,000 units/kg as single dose

Prophylaxis for Rheumatic Fever

Adult: **IM** 1.2 million units q4wk
Child: **IM** 1.2 million units q3–4wk

ADMINISTRATION

Intramuscular

- Do not confuse penicillin G benzathine with preparations containing procaine penicillin G (e.g., Bicillin C-R).
- Make IM injection deep into upper outer quadrant of buttock. In infants and small children, the preferred site is the midlateral aspect of the thigh.
- Shake multiple-dose vial vigorously before withdrawing desired IM dose. Shake prepared cartridge unit vigorously before injecting drug.
- Select IM site with care. Injection into or near a major peripheral nerve can result in nerve damage.
- Inadvertent IV administration has resulted in arterial occlusion and cardiac arrest.
- Make injections at a slow steady rate to prevent needle blockage.
- Store at 15°–30° C (59°–86° F).

ADVERSE EFFECTS **Skin:** Pruritus, urticaria, and other skin eruptions. **Hematologic:** Eosinophilia, hemolytic anemia, and other blood abnormalities. Also see PENICILLIN G POTASSIUM. **Other:** *Local pain,* tenderness, and fever associated with IM injection, chills, fever, wheezing, anaphylaxis, neuropathy, nephrotoxicity; superinfections, Jarisch-Herxheimer reaction in patients with syphilis.

INTERACTIONS **Drug: Probenecid** decreases renal elimination; may decrease efficacy of ORAL CONTRACEPTIVES.

PHARMACOKINETICS **Absorption:** Slowly absorbed from IM site. **Peak:** 12–24 h. **Duration:** 26 days. **Distribution:** Crosses placenta; distributed into breast milk. **Metabolism:** Hydrolyzed to penicillin in body. **Elimination:** Excreted slowly by kidneys.

NURSING IMPLICATIONS

Black Box Warning

Penicillin G has been associated with serious adverse reaction due to inadvertent IV administration.

Note: See penicillin G potassium for numerous additional clinical implications.

Assessment & Drug Effects

- Determine history of hypersensitivity reactions to penicillins, cephalosporins, or other allergens prior to initiation of drug therapy.
- Monitor lab tests: Baseline C&S and repeat at completion of therapy.

Patient & Family Education

- Report immediately to prescriber the onset of an allergic reaction. There is great risk of severe and prolonged reactions because drug is absorbed so slowly.

Common adverse effects in *italic;* life-threatening effects <u>underlined;</u> generic names in **bold;** classifications in SMALL CAPS; ♣ Canadian drug name; ❍ Prototype drug; ⚠ Alert

1304

PENICILLIN G POTASSIUM ⊙

(pen-i-sill'in)

Megacillin ✦

PENICILLIN G SODIUM

Classification: BETA-LACTAM
ANTIBIOTIC; NATURAL PENICILLIN
Therapeutic: ANTIBIOTIC

AVAILABILITY Vial; solution for injection

ACTION & *THERAPEUTIC EFFECT*

Acid labile, penicillinase-sensitive, natural penicillin that acts by interfering with synthesis of mucopeptides essential to formation and integrity of bacterial cell wall. Antimicrobial spectrum is narrow compared to that of semisynthetic penicillins. *Highly active against gram-positive cocci (e.g., non-penicillinase-producing* Staphylococcus, Streptococcus *groups) and gram-negative cocci. Also effective against gram-positive bacilli and gram-negative bacilli as well as some strains of* Salmonella *and* Shigella *and spirochetes.*

USES Moderate to severe systemic infections caused by penicillin-sensitive microorganisms. Certain staphylococcal infections; streptococcal infections. Also used as prophylaxis in patients with rheumatic or congenital heart disease. Since oral preparations are absorbed erratically and thus **must be** given in comparatively high doses, this route is generally used only for mild or stabilized infections or long-term prophylaxis.

UNLABELED USES Skin/soft tissue infection.

CONTRAINDICATIONS Hypersensitivity to any of the penicillins or corn for dextrose solution prep; cardiospasm; viral infections; patients on sodium restriction.

CAUTIOUS USE History of or suspected allergy (asthma, eczema, hay fever, hives); history of allergy to cephalosporins; GI disorders; kidney or liver dysfunction, cardiac or vascular conditions; electrolyte imbalance; renal disease or renal impairment; MG; older adults; pregnancy (category B); lactation; young infants; neonates.

ROUTE & DOSAGE

Moderate to Severe Infections

Adult: **IV/IM** 2–24 million units divided q4h
Child: **IV/IM** 250,000–400,000 units/kg divided q4h

ADMINISTRATION

Note: Check whether prescriber has prescribed penicillin G potassium or sodium.

Intramuscular

- Do not use the 20,000,000 unit dosage form for IM injection.
- Reconstitute for IM: Loosen powder by shaking bottle before adding diluent (sterile water for injection or sterile NS). Keep the total volume to be injected small. Solutions containing up to 100,000 units/mL cause the least discomfort. Adding 10 mL diluent to the 1,000,000 unit vial = 100,000 units/mL. Shake well to dissolve.
- Select IM site carefully. IM injection is made deep into a large muscle mass. Inject slowly. Rotate injection sites.

Intravenous

PREPARE: Intermittent/Continuous: Reconstitute as for IM injection then withdraw the required

P

dose and add to 100–1000 mL of D5W or NS IV solution, depending on length of each infusion.

ADMINISTER: Intermittent: *Adults:* Give over at least 1 h; *Infants and Children:* Give over 15–30 min. **Continuous:** Give at a rate required to infuse the daily dose in 24 h. ▪ With high doses, IV penicillin G should be administered slowly (usually over 24 h) to prevent electrolyte imbalance from potassium or sodium content. ▪ Prescriber will often prescribe specific flow rate.

INCOMPATIBILITIES: Solution/ additive: Dextran 40, fat emulsion, aminophylline, amphotericin B, cephalothin, chlorpromazine, dopamine, hydroxyzine, metaraminol, metoclopramide, pentobarbital, prochlorperazine, promazine, sodium bicarbonate, TETRACYCLINES.

▪ Store dry powder (for parenteral use) at room temperature. After reconstitution (initial dilution), store solutions for 1 wk under refrigeration. ▪ Intravenous infusion solutions containing penicillin G are stable at room temperature for at least 24 h.

ADVERSE EFFECTS

CV: Hypotension, circulatory collapse, cardiac arrhythmias, cardiac arrest. **Respiratory:** Bronchospasm, asthma. **Endocrine:** Hyperkalemia (penicillin G potassium); hypokalemia, alkalosis, hypernatremia, CHF (penicillin G sodium). **Skin:** Itchy palms or axilla, pruritus, *urticaria,* flushed skin, *delayed skin rashes* ranging from urticaria to exfoliative dermatitis, Stevens–Johnson syndrome, fixed-drug eruptions, contact dermatitis. **GI:** Vomiting, diarrhea, severe abdominal cramps, nausea, epigastric distress, diarrhea, flatulence, dark discoloration of tongue, sore mouth or tongue. **GU:** Interstitial nephritis, Loeffler's syndrome, vasculitis. **Hematologic:** Hemolytic anemia, thrombocytopenia. **Other:** Coughing, sneezing, feeling of uneasiness; systemic anaphylaxis, fever, widespread increase in capillary permeability and vasodilation with resulting edema (mouth, tongue, pharynx, larynx), laryngo-spasm, malaise, serum sickness (fever, malaise, pruritus, urticaria, lymphadenopathy, arthralgia, angioedema of face and extremities, neuritis prostration, eosinophilia), SLE-like syndrome, injection site reactions (pain, inflammation, abscess, phlebitis), superinfections (especially with *Candida* and gram-negative bacteria), neuromuscular irritability (twitching, lethargy, confusion, stupor, hyperreflexia, multi-focal myoclonus, localized or generalized seizures, coma).

DIAGNOSTIC TEST INTERFERENCE

Blood grouping and compatibility tests: Possible interference associated with penicillin doses greater than 20 million units daily. **Urine glucose:** Massive doses of penicillin may cause false-positive test results with **Benedict's solution** and possibly **Clinitest** but not with **glucose oxidase methods** (e.g., **Clinistix, Diastix, TesTape**). **Urine protein:** Massive doses of penicillin can produce false-positive results when turbidity measures are used (e.g., **acetic acid** and **heat, sulfosalicylic acid**); **Ames reagent** reportedly not affected. **Urinary PSP excretion tests:** False decrease in urinary excretion of PSP. **Urinary steroids:** Large IV doses of penicillin may interfere with accurate measurement of *urinary 17-OHCS* (*Glenn–Nelson technique* not affected).

INTERACTIONS Drug: Probenecid decreases renal elimination; penicillin G may decrease efficacy of ORAL CONTRACEPTIVES; **colestipol** decreases penicillin absorption; POTASSIUM-SPARING DIURETICS may cause hyperkalemia with penicillin G potassium. **Food:** Food increases breakdown in stomach.

PHARMACOKINETICS Peak: 15–30 min IM. **Distribution:** Widely distributed; good CSF concentrations with inflamed meninges; crosses placenta; distributed in breast milk. **Metabolism:** 16–30% metabolized. **Elimination:** 60% in urine within 6 h. **Half-Life:** 0.4–0.9 h.

NURSING IMPLICATIONS
Assessment & Drug Effects
- Obtain an exact history of patient's previous exposure and sensitivity to penicillins and cephalosporins and other allergic reactions of any kind prior to treatment with penicillin.
- Hypersensitivity reactions are more likely to occur with parenteral penicillin than with the oral drug. Skin rash is the most common type allergic reaction and should be reported promptly to prescriber.
- Observe all patients closely for at least 30 min following administration of parenteral penicillin. The rapid appearance of a red flare or wheal at the IM or IV injection site is a possible sign of sensitivity. Also suspect an allergic reaction if patient becomes irritable, has nausea and vomiting, breathing difficulty, or sudden fever. Report any of the foregoing to prescriber immediately.

- Be aware that reactions to penicillin may be rapid in onset or may not appear for days or weeks. Symptoms usually disappear fairly quickly once drug is stopped, but in some patients may persist for 5 days or more.
- Allergy to penicillin is unpredictable. It has occurred in patients with a negative history of penicillin allergy and also in patients with no known prior contact with penicillin (sensitization may have occurred from penicillin used commercially in foods and beverages).
- Be alert for neuromuscular irritability in patients receiving parenteral penicillin in excess of 20 million units/day who have renal insufficiency, hyponatremia, or underlying CNS disease, notably myasthenia gravis or epilepsy. Seizure precautions are indicated. Symptoms usually begin with twitching, especially of face and extremities.
- Monitor I&O, particularly in patients receiving high parenteral doses. Report oliguria, hematuria, and changes in I&O ratio. Consult prescriber regarding optimum fluid intake. Dehydration increases the concentration of drug in kidneys and can cause renal irritation and damage.
- Observe closely for signs of toxicity, especially in neonates, young infants, older adults, and patients with impaired kidney function receiving high-dose penicillin therapy. Urinary excretion of penicillin is significantly delayed in these patients.
- Observe patients on high-dose therapy closely for evidence of bleeding, and bleeding time should be monitored. (In high doses, penicillin interferes with platelet aggregation.)

P

- Monitor lab tests: Baseline C&S; periodic LFTs, kidney function tests, and serum electrolytes with high-dose therapy.

Patient & Family Education
- Understand that hypersensitivity reaction may be delayed. Report skin rashes, itching, fever, malaise, and other signs of a delayed reaction to prescriber immediately (see ADVERSE EFFECTS).
- Notify prescriber if following symptoms appear when taking penicillin for treatment of syphilis: Headache, chills, fever, myalgia, arthralgia, malaise, and worsening of syphilitic skin lesions. Reaction is usually self-limiting. Check with prescriber if symptoms do not improve within a few days or get worse.
- Report S&S of superinfection (see Appendix F).

PENICILLIN G PROCAINE
(pen-i-sill'in)
Classification: BETA-LACTAM ANTIBIOTIC; NATURAL PENICILLIN
Therapeutic: ANTIBIOTIC
Prototype: Penicillin G potassium

AVAILABILITY Solution for injection

ACTION & *THERAPEUTIC EFFECT*
Long-acting form of penicillin G. The procaine salt has low solubility and thus creates a tissue depot from which penicillin is slowly absorbed. Slower onset of action than penicillin G potassium, but longer duration of action. It inhibits the final stage of bacterial cell wall synthesis by binding to specific penicillin-binding proteins (PBPs) located in the bacterial cell wall. This results in cell death of bacteria. *Same actions and antibacterial activity as for penicillin G potassium and is similarly inactivated by penicillinase and gastric acid.*

USES Moderately severe infections due to penicillin G-sensitive microorganisms that are susceptible to low but prolonged serum penicillin concentrations. Commonly, uncomplicated pneumococcal pneumonia, uncomplicated gonorrheal infections, and all stages of syphilis. May be used concomitantly with penicillin G or probenecid when more rapid action and higher blood levels are indicated.

CONTRAINDICATIONS History of hypersensitivity to any of the penicillins.

CAUTIOUS USE History of or suspected allergy, hypersensitivity to cephalosporins, carbapenem; asthmatics; procaine; history of seizures; asthmatics; GI disease, renal disease; severe renal impairment; pregnancy (category B); lactation; children.

ROUTE & DOSAGE

Moderate to Severe Infections
Adult: **IM** 600,000–1,200,000 units once/day
Child: **IM** 300,000 units once/day

Pneumococcal Pneumonia
Adult: **IM** 600,000 units q12h

Uncomplicated Gonorrhea
Adult: **IM** 4,800,000 units divided between 2 different injection sites at one visit preceded by 1 g of probenecid 30 min before injections

Syphilis
Adult: **IM** Primary, secondary, latent: 600,000 units/day for

Common adverse effects in *italic*; life-threatening effects underlined; generic names in **bold**; classifications in SMALL CAPS; ✦ Canadian drug name; ⊙ Prototype drug; ⚠ Alert

8 days; late latent, tertiary, neurosyphilis: 600,000 units/day for 10–15 days
Child: IM 500,000–1,000,000 units/m^2 once/day

ADMINISTRATION

Intramuscular

- Shake multiple-dose vial thoroughly before withdrawing medication to ensure uniform suspension of drug.
- Use 20-gauge needle to avoid clogging.
- Give IM deep into upper outer quadrant of gluteus muscle; in infants and small children midlateral aspect of thigh is generally preferred. Select IM site carefully. Accidental injection into or near major peripheral nerves and blood vessels can cause neurovascular damage.
- Aspirate carefully before injecting drug to avoid entry into a blood vessel. Inadvertent IV administration reportedly has resulted in pulmonary infarcts and death.
- Inject drug at a slow, but steady rate to prevent needle blockage. Give in two sites if the dose is very large. Rotate injection sites.

ADVERSE EFFECTS Other: Procaine toxicity [e.g., mental disturbances (anxiety, confusion, depression, combativeness, hallucinations), expressed fear of impending death, weakness, dizziness, headache, tinnitus, unusual tastes, palpitation, changes in pulse rate and BP, seizures. Also see PENICILLIN G POTASSIUM.

INTERACTIONS Drug: Probenecid decreases renal elimination; may decrease efficacy of ORAL CONTRACEPTIVES.

PHARMACOKINETICS Absorption: Slowly from IM site. **Peak:** 1–3 h. **Duration:** 15–20 h. **Distribution:** Crosses placenta; distributed into breast milk. **Metabolism:** Hydrolyzed to penicillin in body. **Elimination:** By kidneys within 24–36 h.

NURSING IMPLICATIONS

Assessment & Drug Effects

- Obtain an exact history of patient's previous exposure and sensitivity to penicillins, cephalosporins, and to procaine, and other allergic reactions of any kind prior to treatment.
- Test patient by injecting 0.1 mL of 1–2% procaine hydrochloride intradermally if sensitivity is suspected. Appearance of a wheal, flare, or eruption indicates procaine sensitivity.
- Be alert to the possibility of a transient toxic reaction to procaine, particularly when large single doses are administered. The reaction manifested by mental disturbance and other symptoms (SEE ADVERSE EFFECTS) occurs almost immediately and usually subsides after 15–30 min.

Patient & Family Education

- Report any skin reaction at the site of injection.
- Report onset of rash, itching, fever, chills, or other symptoms of an allergic reaction to prescriber.

PENICILLIN V
PENICILLIN V POTASSIUM
(pen-i-sill'in)
Apo-Pen-VK ♣, Nadopen-V ♣, Novopen-VK ♣
Classification: BETA-LACTAM ANTIBIOTIC; NATURAL PENICILLIN
Therapeutic: ANTIBIOTIC
Prototype: Penicillin G potassium

P

AVAILABILITY Tablet; suspension

ACTION & *THERAPEUTIC EFFECT*
Acid stable analog of penicillin G with which it shares actions. It binds with the necessary penicillin-binding proteins (PBP) in cell wall of bacteria interfering with cell wall synthesis and resulting in cell lysis. *Penicillin V is bactericidal and is inactivated by penicillinase. Less active than penicillin G against gonococci and other gram-negative microorganisms.*

USES Mild to moderate infections caused by susceptible *Streptococci, Pneumococci,* and *Staphylococci.* Also Vincent's infection and as prophylaxis in rheumatic fever.

UNLABELED USES Bite wounds, cutaneous anthrax, pharyngitis.

CONTRAINDICATIONS Hypersensitivity to any penicillin.

CAUTIOUS USE History of or suspected allergy (hay fever, asthma, hives, eczema) reactions; hypersensitivity to cephalosporins, beta-lactamase inhibitors, or carbapenem; GI disease; cystic fibrosis; renal impairment; hepatic impairment; pregnancy (category B); lactation; children.

ROUTE & DOSAGE

Mild to Moderate Infections
Adult: **PO** 250–500 mg q6h
Child (younger than 12 y):
PO 15–50 mg/kg/day in 3–6 divided doses

Rheumatic Fever Prophylaxis
Adult: **PO** 125–250 mg bid

Endocarditis Prophylaxis
Adult: **PO** 2 g 30–60 min before procedure, then 500 mg q6h for 8 doses
Child (weight less than 30 kg): **PO** 1 g 30–60 min before procedure, then 250 mg q6h for 8 doses

ADMINISTRATION
Oral
- Give after a meal rather than on an empty stomach; drug may be better absorbed and result in higher blood levels.
- Shake well before pouring. Following reconstitution, oral solution is stable for 14 days under refrigeration.

ADVERSE EFFECTS Other: Nausea, vomiting, *diarrhea,* epigastric distress. *Hypersensitivity reactions* (e.g., flushing, pruritus, urticaria, or other skin eruptions, eosinophilia, anaphylaxis; hemolytic anemia, leukopenia, thrombocytopenia, neuropathy, superinfections).

INTERACTIONS Drug: Probenecid decreases renal elimination; may decrease efficacy of ORAL CONTRACEPTIVES; **colestipol** decreases absorption. **Food:** Food increases breakdown in stomach.

PHARMACOKINETICS Absorption: 60–73% absorbed from GI tract. **Peak:** 30–60 min. **Duration:** 6 h. **Distribution:** Highest levels in kidneys; crosses placenta; distributed into breast milk. **Elimination:** In urine. **Half-Life:** 30 min.

NURSING IMPLICATIONS

Note: See penicillin G potassium for numerous additional nursing implications.

Assessment & Drug Effects

- Obtain careful history concerning hypersensitivity reactions to penicillins, cephalosporins, and other allergens before therapy begins.
- Monitor lab tests: Baseline C&S; LFTs, and hematologic studies at regular intervals in patients receiving prolonged therapy.

Patient & Family Education

- Take penicillin V around the clock at specific intervals to maintain a constant blood level.
- Do not miss any doses and continue taking medication until it is all gone unless otherwise directed by the prescriber.
- Discontinue medication and promptly report to prescriber the onset of hypersensitivity reactions and superinfections (see Appendix F).
- Use specially marked measuring device to ensure accurate doses of oral liquid preparation.

PENTAMIDINE ISETHIONATE

(pen-tam'i-deen)
Nebupent, Pentacarinat ✦, Pentam
Classification: ANTIPROTOZOAL
Therapeutic: ANTIPROTOZOAL

AVAILABILITY Solution for injection; aerosol

ACTION & *THERAPEUTIC EFFECT*

Blocks parasite reproduction by interfering with nucleotide (DNA, RNA), phospholipid, and protein synthesis. *Effective against the protozoan parasite* Pneumocystis carinii *in AIDS patients.*

USES Pneumocystis jirovecii pneumonia (PCP).

UNLABELED USES African trypanosomiasis and visceral leishmaniasis. (Drug supplied for latter uses is through the Centers for Disease Control and Prevention, Atlanta, GA.)

CONTRAINDICATIONS QT prolongation, history of torsades de pointes; lactation (infant risk cannot be ruled out).

CAUTIOUS USE Hypertension, hypotension; hyperglycemia; pancreatitis; hypoglycemia; hypocalcemia; blood dyscrasias; liver or kidney dysfunction; diabetes mellitus; pancreatitis; asthma; history of smoking, cardiac arrhythmias; pregnancy (category C); children.

ROUTE & DOSAGE

Treatment of *Pneumocystis jirovecii* Pneumonia
Adult/Child: **IM/IV** 4 mg/kg/day for 21 days

Prophylaxis of *Pneumocystis jirovecii* Pneumonia
Adult: **Inhaled** 300 mg/nebulizer q4wk
Child: **Inhaled** 300 mg/nebulizer monthly

ADMINISTRATION

Inhaled

- Reconstitute contents of one vial in 6 mL sterile water (not saline) and administer using nebulizer.
- Do not mix with any other drug.

Intramuscular

- Dissolve contents of 1 vial (300 mg) in 3 mL sterile water for injection.
- Give deep IM into a large muscle.
- The IM injection is painful and frequently causes local reactions (pain, indurations, swelling).

P

Select alternate sites for daily doses and institute local treatment if indicated.

Intravenous

PREPARE: **IV Infusion:** Dissolve contents of 1 vial in 3–5 mL sterile water for injection or D5W. ▪ Further dilute in 50–250 mL of D5W.
ADMINISTER: **IV Infusion:** Give over 60–120 min.
INCOMPATIBILITIES: **Y-site:** Extensive list of incompatibilities, do not administer with other medications.

▪ Note: IV solutions are stable at room temperature for up to 48 h. Protect solution from light.

ADVERSE EFFECTS **Respiratory:**
Bronchospasm, *cough, dyspnea, wheezing.* **CNS:** *Fatigue dizziness.* **Endocrine:** Hypoglycemia. **GI:** *Decreased appetite.* **GU:** *Nephrotoxicity, renal impairment,* increased serum creatinine. **Hematologic:** Leukopenia.

INTERACTIONS **Drug:** AMINOGLYCOSIDES, **amphotericin B, cidofovir, cisplatin, ganciclovir, cyclosporine, vancomycin,** other nephrotoxic drugs increase risk of nephrotoxicity.

PHARMACOKINETICS **Absorption:** Readily after IM injection. **Distribution:** Leaves bloodstream rapidly to bind extensively to body tissues. **Elimination:** 50–66% in urine within 6 h; small amounts found in urine for as long as 6–8 wk. **Half-Life:** 6.5–13.2 h.

NURSING IMPLICATIONS

Assessment & Drug Effects
▪ Monitor BP and HR continuously during the infusion, every half hour for 2 h thereafter, and then every 4 h until BP stabilizes.

Sudden severe hypotension may develop after a single dose. Place patient in supine position while receiving the drug.
▪ Measure and record I&O ratio and pattern.
▪ Be alert and report promptly S&S of impending kidney dysfunction (e.g., changed I&O ratio, oliguria, edema).
▪ Characteristics of pneumonia in the immunocompromised patient include constant fever, scanty (if any) sputum, dyspnea, tachypnea, and cyanosis.
▪ Monitor temperature changes and institute measures to lower the temperature as indicated. Fever is a constant symptom in *P. carinii* pneumonia, but may be rapidly elevated [as high as 40° C (104° F)] shortly after drug infusion.
▪ Monitor lab tests: Periodic serum electrolytes, renal function tests, LFTs, CBC with differential, platelet count, BUN, creatinine, and blood glucose.

Patient & Family Education
▪ Report promptly to prescriber increasing respiratory difficulty.
▪ Monitor blood glucose for loss of glycemic control if diabetic.
▪ Report any unusual bruising or bleeding. Avoid using aspirin or other NSAIDs.
▪ Increase fluid intake (if not contraindicated) to 2–3 qt (L)/day.

PENTAZOCINE HYDROCHLORIDE ○
(pen-taz′oh-seen)
Talwin
Classification: NARCOTIC (OPIATE AGONIST–ANTAGONIST); ANALGESIC
Therapeutic: NARCOTIC ANALGESIC
Controlled Substance: Schedule IV

AVAILABILITY Solution for injection

ACTION & *THERAPEUTIC EFFECT*

Synthetic analgesic with potency approximately one-third that of morphine. Opiates exert their effects by stimulating specific opiate receptors that produce analgesia, respiratory depression, and euphoria as well as physical dependence. *Effective for moderate to severe pain relief. Acts as weak narcotic antagonist and has sedative properties.*

USES Relief of moderate to severe pain; also used for preoperative analgesia or sedation, and as supplement to surgical anesthesia.

CONTRAINDICATIONS Hypersensitivity to sulfite; head injury, increased intracranial pressure; seizures; emotionally unstable patients, respiratory depression, or history of drug abuse.

CAUTIOUS USE Impaired kidney or liver function; cardiac disease; COPD, asthmas; GI obstruction; biliary surgery; patients with MI who have nausea and vomiting; pregnancy (category C); lactation; children younger than 12 y.

ROUTE & DOSAGE

Moderate to Severe Pain (Excluding Patients in Labor)
Adult: **IM/IV/Subcutaneous** 30 mg q3–4h (max: 360 mg/day)

Anesthesia
Adult: **IM/IV/Subcutaneous** 30 mg dose; may repeat q3–4h as needed (max: 360 mg daily)
Adolescent/Child: **IM** 0.5 mg/kg single dose (max: 30 mg)

Pain during Labor
Adult: **IM** 30 mg dose; **IV** 20 mg dose may repeat q2–3h (total: 2–3 doses)

Renal Impairment Dosage Adjustment
CrCl 10–50 mL/min: **Give 75% of dose;** *less than 10 mL/min:* **Give 50% of dose**

ADMINISTRATION

Subcutaneous/Intramuscular
- IM is preferred to subcutaneous route when frequent injections over an extended period are required.
- Observe injection sites daily for signs of irritation or inflammation.

Intravenous

PREPARE: **Direct:** Give undiluted or diluted with 1 mL sterile water for injection for each 5 mg.
ADMINISTER: **Direct:** Give slowly at a rate of 5 mg over 60 sec.
INCOMPATIBILITIES: Solution/additive: **Alemtuzumab, aminophylline,** BARBITURATES, **sodium bicarbonate, glycopyrrolate, heparin, nafcillin.** Y-site: **Alemtuzumab, aminophylline, amphotericin B, ampicillin, atenolol, azathioprine, aztreonam, bivalirudin, cefamandole, cefazolin, cefoperazone, cefotaxime, cefotetan, cefoxitin, ceftizoxime, ceftriaxone, cefuroxime, chloramphenicol, dantrolene, daptomycin, diazepam, diazoxide, foscarnet, furosemide, gallium, ganciclovir, gemtuzumab, indomethacin, ketorolac, methylprednisolone, mitomycin, nafcillin, nitroprusside, oxacillin, pemetrexed, penicillin G, pentobarbital, phenobarbital, phenytoin, piperacillin, SMZ/TMP, ticarcillin, nafcillin.**

ADVERSE EFFECTS CV: Hypertension, palpitation, tachycardia. **Respiratory:** Respiratory depression. **CNS:** *Drowsiness,* sweating,

P

dizziness, lightheadedness, euphoria, psychotomimetic effects, confusion, anxiety, hallucinations, disturbed dreams, bizarre thoughts, euphoria and other mood alterations. **HEENT:** Visual disturbances. **Skin:** Injection site reactions (induration, nodule formation, sloughing, sclerosis, cutaneous depression), rash, pruritus. **GI:** *Nausea, vomiting,* constipation, dry mouth, alterations of taste. **GU:** Urinary retention. **Other:** Flushing, allergic reactions, shock.

INTERACTIONS Drug: Alcohol and other CNS DEPRESSANTS add to CNS depression; NARCOTIC ANALGESICS may precipitate narcotic withdrawal syndrome.

PHARMACOKINETICS Onset: 15 min IM, Subcutaneous; 2–3 min IV. **Peak:** 1 h IM, 15 min IV. **Duration:** 3 h IM, 1 h IV. **Distribution:** Crosses placenta. **Metabolism:** Extensively in liver. **Elimination:** Primarily in urine; small amount in feces. **Half-Life:** 2–3 h.

NURSING IMPLICATIONS

Assessment & Drug Effects

- Monitor therapeutic effect. Tolerance to analgesic effect sometimes occurs. Psychologic and physical dependence have been reported in patients with history of drug abuse, but rarely in patients without such history. Addiction liability matches that of codeine.
- Monitor vital signs and assess for respiratory depression. Keep supine to minimize adverse effects.
- Monitor drug-induced CNS depression.
- Be aware that pentazocine may produce acute withdrawal symptoms in some patients who have been receiving opioids on a regular basis.
- Monitor I&O as drug may cause urinary retention.

Patient & Family Education

- Avoid driving and other potentially hazardous activities until response to drug is known.
- Do not discontinue drug abruptly following extended use; may result in chills, abdominal and muscle cramps, yawning, runny nose, tearing, itching, restlessness, anxiety, drug-seeking behavior.

PENTOBARBITAL

(pen-toe-bar′bi-tal)

PENTOBARBITAL SODIUM

Nembutal, Novopentobarb ♦
Classification: ANXIOLYTIC; SEDATIVE-HYPNOTIC; BARBITURATE; ANTICONVULSANT
Therapeutic ANTIANXIETY; SEDATIVE-HYPNOTIC; ANTI-CONVULSANT
Prototype: Secobarbital
Controlled Substance: Schedule II

AVAILABILITY Solution for injection

ACTION & THERAPEUTIC EFFECT Short-acting barbiturate with anticonvulsant properties. Potent respiratory depressant. Initially, barbiturates suppress REM sleep, but with chronic therapy REM sleep returns to normal. *Effective as a sedative and hypnotic and anticonvulsant.*

USES Sedative or hypnotic for preanesthetic medication, induction of general anesthesia, adjunct in manipulative or diagnostic procedures, and emergency control of acute convulsions.

CONTRAINDICATIONS History of sensitivity to barbiturates; parturition, fetal immaturity, uncontrolled pain; ethanol intoxication; hepatic encephalopathy; porphyria; suicidal ideation; pregnancy (category D); lactation.

Common adverse effects in *italic*; life-threatening effects underlined; generic names in **bold**; classifications in SMALL CAPS; ♦ Canadian drug name; ❍ Prototype drug; ⚠ Alert

CAUTIOUS USE COPD, sleep apnea; heart failure; hypertension, hypotension, pulmonary disease; alcoholism; mental status changes, suicidality, major depression; neonates; renal impairment, renal failure; children.

ROUTE & DOSAGE

Preoperative Sedation

Adult: **IM** 150–200 mg in 2 divided doses
Child: **IV** 2–6 mg/kg (max: 100 mg)

Hypnotic/Insomnia

Adult: **IM** 150–200 mg
Child: **IM** 2–6 mg/kg (max: 100 mg)

Status Epilepticus

Adult: **IV** 5–15 mg/kg loading, then 0.5–3 mg/kg/h
Child: **IM** 5–15 mg/kg loading, then 0.5–5 mg/kg/h

ADMINISTRATION

Note: Do not give within 14 days of starting/stopping an MAO inhibitor.

Intramuscular

- Do not use parenteral solutions that appear cloudy or in which a precipitate has formed.
- Make IM injections deep into large muscle mass, preferably upper outer quadrant of buttock. Aspirate needle carefully before injecting to prevent inadvertent entry into blood vessel. Inject no more than 5 mL (250 mg) in any one site because of possible tissue irritation.

Intravenous

PREPARE: Direct: Give undiluted or diluted (preferred) with sterile water, D5W, NS, or other compatible IV solutions.

ADMINISTER: Direct: Give slowly. Do not exceed rate of 50 mg/min.
INCOMPATIBILITIES: Solution/additive: Atropine, butorphanol, chlorpheniramine, chlorpromazine, cimetidine, codeine, dimenhydrinate, diphenhydramine, droperidol, ephedrine, fentanyl, glycopyrrolate, hydrocortisone, hydroxyzine, inulin, levorphanol, meperidine, methadone, midazolam, morphine, nalbuphine, norepinephrine, TETRACYCLINES, **penicillin G, pentazocine, perphenazine, phenytoin, promazine, prochlorperazine, promethazine, sodium bicarbonate, streptomycin, succinylcholine, triflupromazine, vancomycin. Y-site: Amphotericin B cholesteryl, fenoldopam, TPN.**

- Take extreme care to avoid extravasation. Necrosis may result because parenteral solution is highly alkaline. - Do not use cloudy or precipitated solution.

ADVERSE EFFECTS CV: Hypotension with rapid IV. **Respiratory:** With rapid IV (respiratory depression, laryngospasm, bronchospasm, apnea). **Other:** Drowsiness, lethargy, hang-over, paradoxical excitement in the older adult patient.

INTERACTIONS Drug: Phenmetrazine antagonizes effects of pentobarbital; CNS DEPRESSANTS, **alcohol,** SEDATIVES add to CNS depression; MAO INHIBITORS cause excessive CNS depression; **methoxyflurane** creates risk of nephrotoxicity. **Herbal: Kava, valerian** may potentiate sedation.

PHARMACOKINETICS Onset: 10–15 min IM; 1 min IV. **Duration:** 15 min IV. **Distribution:** Crosses placenta. **Metabolism:** Primarily in liver. **Elimination:** In urine. **Half-Life:** 4–50 h.

P

NURSING IMPLICATIONS
Assessment & Drug Effects
- Monitor BP, pulse, and respiration q3–5min during IV administration. Observe patient closely; maintain airway. Have equipment for artificial respiration immediately available.
- Observe patient closely for adverse effects for at least 30 min after IM administration of hypnotic dose.
- Monitor for hypersensitivity reactions (see Appendix E) especially with a history of asthma or angioedema.
- Monitor for adverse CNS effects including exacerbation of depression and suicidal ideation.
- Monitor those in acute pain, children, the elderly, and debilitated patients for paradoxical excitement restlessness.
- Concurrent drug: Monitor warfarin and phenytoin levels frequently to ensure therapeutic range.
- Monitor lab tests: Periodic pentobarbital level. Note: Plasma level greater than 30 mcg/mL may be toxic and 65 mcg/mL and above may be lethal.

Patient & Family Education
- Exercise caution when driving or operating machinery for the remainder of day after taking drug.
- Avoid alcohol and other CNS depressants for 24 h after receiving this drug.
- Women using oral contraceptives should use an additional, alternative form of contraception.

PENTOXIFYLLINE
(pen-tox-i'fi-leen)

Classification: HEMATOLOGIC; RED BLOOD CELL MODIFIER; BLOOD VISCOSITY REDUCER

Therapeutic: RED BLOOD CELL MODIFIER; BLOOD VISCOSITY IMPROVER

AVAILABILITY Sustained release tablet

ACTION & *THERAPEUTIC EFFECT*
Maintains the flexibility of RBCs, increasing erythrocyte cAMP activity, thus allowing erythrocyte membranes to maintain their integrity and become more resistant to deformity. Improvement in blood viscosity results in increased blood flow to the microcirculation and enhanced tissue oxygenation. *Results in increased blood flow to the extremities, reduced pain and paresthesia of intermittent claudication.*

USES Intermittent claudication associated with occlusive peripheral vascular disease; diabetic angiopathies.

UNLABELED USES To improve psychopathologic symptoms in patient with cerebrovascular insufficiency and to reduce incidence of stroke in the patient with recurrent TIAs.

CONTRAINDICATIONS Intolerance to pentoxifylline or to methylxanthines (caffeine and theophylline); intracranial bleeding; retinal bleeding; lactation.

CAUTIOUS USE Angina, hypotension, arrhythmias, cerebrovascular disease; peptic ulcer disease; renal failure; renal impairment; risk of bleeding; pregnancy (category C); children younger than 18 y.

ROUTE & DOSAGE

Intermittent Claudication
Adult: **PO** 400 mg tid with meals

Common adverse effects in *italic;* life-threatening effects <u>underlined</u>; generic names in **bold;** classifications in SMALL CAPS; ♣ Canadian drug name; ○ Prototype drug; ▲ Alert

ADMINISTRATION

Oral

- Give on an empty stomach or with food; be consistent with time of day and relationship to food in establishing the daily regimen.
- Store tablets at 15°–30° C (59°–86° F).

ADVERSE EFFECTS CV: Angina, chest pain, dyspnea, arrhythmias, palpitations, hypotension, edema, flushing. **CNS:** Agitation, nervousness, *dizziness,* drowsiness, headache, insomnia, tremor, confusion. **Skin:** Brittle fingernails, pruritus, rash, urticaria. **GI:** Abdominal discomfort, belching, flatus, bloating, diarrhea, *dyspepsia, nausea, vomiting.* **Eye:** Blurred vision, conjunctivitis, scotomas. **Other:** Fever, flushing, convulsions, somnolence, loss of consciousness. Earache, unpleasant taste, excessive salivation, leukopenia, malaise, sore throat, swollen neck glands, weight change.

INTERACTIONS Drug: Ciprofloxacin, cimetidine may increase levels and toxicity, **warfarin** may have additive effects. Do not use with **ketorolac. Herbal: Evening primrose oil, ginseng, ginkgo** may increase bleeding risk.

PHARMACOKINETICS Absorption: Readily from GI tract; 10–50% reaches systemic circulation (first pass metabolism). **Peak:** 2–4 h. **Distribution:** Distributed into breast milk. **Metabolism:** In liver and erythrocytes. **Elimination:** Primarily in urine. **Half-Life:** 0.4–0.8 h.

NURSING IMPLICATIONS

Assessment & Drug Effects

- Monitor therapeutic effectiveness which is indicated by relief from pain and cramping in calf muscles, buttocks, thighs, and feet during exercise and improves walking performance (time and duration).
- Monitor BP if patient is also on antihypertensive treatment. Drug may slightly decrease an already stabilized BP, necessitating a reduced dose of the hypotensive drug.

Patient & Family Education

- Consult prescriber to determine CV status and capacity before reestablishing walking as exercise.
- Pay particular attention to care of the feet because of arterial insufficiency (diminished perfusion to feet).
- Be aware that bleeding and prolonged PT/INR associated with this treatment have been reported. Report promptly unexplained bleeding, easy bruising, nose bleed, pinpoint rash to prescriber.
- Avoid driving or working with hazardous machinery until drug response has stabilized because of potential for tiredness, blurred vision, dizziness.

PERAMIVIR

(per-a-mi'vir)

Rapivab

Classification: ANTIVIRAL; NEURAMINIDASE INHIBITOR
Therapeutic: ANTI-INFLUENZA
Prototype: Oseltamivir

AVAILABILITY Solution for injection

ACTION & THERAPEUTIC EFFECT

Inhibits influenza A and B viral neuraminidase enzyme, preventing the release of newly formed viruses from the surface of the infected cells. Inhibits replication of the influenza A and B virus. *Relieves flu symptoms and prevents viral spread across the mucous lining of the respiratory tract.*

USES Treatment of acute uncomplicated influenza in patients 18 y or older who have been symptomatic for no more than 2 days.

CAUTIOUS USE Serious skin reactions; abnormal behavior including hallucinations and delirium; renal impairment; pregnancy (category C); lactation. Safety and efficacy in patients younger than 18 y not established.

ROUTE & DOSAGE

Influenza

Adult: **IV** Single 600 mg dose within 48 h of symptoms

Renal Impairment Dosage Adjustment

CrCL 30–49 mL/min: Reduce to 200 mg
CrCL 10–29 mL/min: Reduce To Whom It May Concern: 100 mg

ADMINISTRATION

Intravenous

PREPARE: **IV Infusion:** Dilute required dose in NS, 0.45% NaCl, D5W, or LR to a max volume of 100 mL.
ADMINISTER: **IV Infusion:** Give over 15–30 min.
INCOMPATIBILITIES: **Solution/additive:** Do not mix with other IV medications. **Y-site:** Do not co-infuse with other IV medications

• Store refrigerated at 2°–8° C (36°–46° F) for up to 24 h if not administered immediately. If refrigerated, allow solution to reach

room temperature then administer immediately.

ADVERSE EFFECTS CV: Hypertension. **CNS:** Insomnia. **Endocrine:** Hyperglycemia, increased ALT/AST, increased creatine phosphokinase. **Skin:** Exfoliative dermatitis, rash, Stevens–Johnson syndrome. **GI:** Constipation, *diarrhea*. **Hematological:** Neutropenia.

PHARMACOKINETICS Distribution: 30% plasma protein bound. **Metabolism:** Minimal. **Elimination:** Primarily renal (90%). **Half-Life:** 20 h.

NURSING IMPLICATIONS

Assessment and Drug Effects

• Monitor for and report promptly skin rash, dermatitis, erythema.
• Monitor for neuropsychiatric events, especially in children.
• Monitor lab tests: Baseline serum urea nitrogen and serum creatinine.

Patient & Family Education

• Seek immediate medical attention if a skin reaction occurs.
• Contact prescriber for any signs of abnormal behavior including illogical thinking, altered speech, hallucinations, or delusions.

PERINDOPRIL ERBUMINE
(per-in'do-pril)

Classification: ANGIOTENSIN-CONVERTING ENZYME (ACE) INHIBITOR; ANTIHYPERTENSIVE
Therapeutic: ANTIHYPERTENSIVE
Prototype: Captopril

AVAILABILITY Tablet

ACTION & *THERAPEUTIC EFFECT*
Inhibits the renin angiotensin-converting enzyme (ACE) that

Common adverse effects in *italic;* life-threatening effects underlined; generic names in **bold;** classifications in SMALL CAPS; ♣ Canadian drug name; ◑ Prototype drug; ⚠ Alert

P

catalyzes the conversion of angiotensin I to angiotensin II, a potent vasoconstrictor substance. Also reduces aldosterone production causing a potassium-sparing effect. In addition, it decreases systemic vascular resistance (afterload) and pulmonary capillary wedge pressure (PCWP), a measure of preload, and improves cardiac output as well as activity tolerance. *Effective in lowering blood pressure by vasodilatation resulting from inhibition of ACE. Improves cardiac output as well as activity tolerance in CAD.*

USES Hypertension, reduce the risk of myocardial infarction in patients with stable CAD.

UNLABELED USES Heart failure, ST elevation acute coronary syndrome.

CONTRAINDICATIONS Hypersensitivity to perindopril or any other ACE inhibitors; history of angioedema induced by an ACE inhibitor, patients with hypertrophic cardiomyopathy, hepatoxicity; renal artery stenosis; concomitant use with aliskiren in patients with diabetes mellitus; concomitant use or within 36 hours of switching to or from a neprilysin inhibitor; pregnancy (exposure to an ACE inhibitor during the first trimester of pregnancy may be associated with an increased risk of fetal malformation); lactation.

CAUTIOUS USE Renal insufficiency, volume-depleted patients, severe liver dysfunction; autoimmune diseases, immunosuppressant drug therapy; hyperkalemia or potassiumsparing diuretics; surgery; neutropenia; febrile illness; older adults. Safety and efficacy in children not established.

ROUTE & DOSAGE

Hypertension
Adult: **PO** 4 mg once daily, may be titrated to 16 mg daily

Stable Coronary Artery Disease
Adult: **PO** 4 mg daily × 2 wk, then 8 mg daily

Renal Impairment Dosage Adjustment
CrCl 30–79 mL/min: Start at 2 mg daily; *CrCl less than mL/min:* not recommended

ADMINISTRATION
Oral
- Manufacturer recommends an initial dose of 2–4 mg in 1 or 2 divided doses if concurrently ordered diuretic cannot be discontinued 2–3 days before beginning perinodopril. Consult prescriber.
- Give on an empty stomach 1 h before meals.
- Dosage adjustments are generally made at intervals of at least 1 wk.
- Store at 20°–25° C (68°–77° F) and protect from moisture.

ADVERSE EFFECTS **CV:** Edema, *angioedema.* **Respiratory:** Cough, upper respiratory infection, sinusitis, rhinitis. **CNS:** Headache. **GI:** Diarrhea. **GU:** Urinary tract infection. **Musculoskeletal**: Weakness, back pain, leg pain. **Other:** Infection.

DIAGNOSTIC TEST INTERFERENCE
May lead to false negative aldosterone/renin ratio.

INTERACTIONS **Drug:** POTASSIUM SPARING DIURETICS (**amiloride, spironolactone, triamterene**)

may increase the risk of hyperkalemia. POTASSIUM SUPPLEMENTS increase the risk of hyperkalemia; **lithium** levels can be increased; ANTIHYPERTENSIVES may increase risk of hypotension; use with **azathioprine** may cause anemia and leukopenia; may increase adverse effects of **iron**.; may increase risk of nephrotoxicity with **sodium phosphate**. **Pregabalin** may increase risk of angioedema. **Food:** Food can decrease drug absorption 35%.

PHARMACOKINETICS Absorption: Readily from GI tract, absorption significantly decreased when taken with food. **Peak:** 1–2 h. **Metabolism:** Hydrolyzed in the liver to its active form, perindoprilat. **Elimination:** Primarily in urine. **Half-Life: Perindopril:** 0.8–1 h, **perindoprilat:** 30–120 h.

NURSING IMPLICATIONS

Black Box Warning

Perindropril has been associated with fetal injury and death.

Assessment & Drug Effects

- Monitor BR and HR carefully following initial dose for several hours until stable, especially in patients using concurrent diuretics, on salt restriction, or volume depleted.
- Place patient immediately in a supine position if excess hypotension develops.
- Monitor closely kidney function in patients with CHF.
- Monitor serum lithium levels and assess for S&S of lithium toxicity when used concurrently; increased caution is needed when diuretic therapy is also used.

- Monitor lab tests: Periodic serum potassium, BUN, and creatinine; periodic CBC with differential.

Patient & Family Education

- Discontinue drug and immediately report S&S of angioedema (i.e., swelling) of face or extremities to prescriber. Seek emergency help for swelling of the tongue or any other signs of potential airway obstruction.
- Contact prescriber immediately if you become pregnant.
- Be aware that light-headedness can occur, especially during early therapy; excess fluid loss of any kind (e.g., vomiting, diarrhea) will increase risk of hypotension and fainting.
- Avoid using potassium supplements unless specifically directed to do so by prescriber.
- Report S&S of infection (e.g., sore throat, fever) promptly to prescriber.

PERMETHRIN ○

(per-meth′rin)

Nix, Elimite, Acticin
Classification: SCABICIDE; PEDICULICIDE
Therapeutic: SCABICIDE; PEDICULICIDE

AVAILABILITY Cream; liquid

ACTION & THERAPEUTIC EFFECT
Inhibits sodium ion influx through nerve cell membrane channels, resulting in delayed repolarization of the action potential and paralysis of the pest. *It prevents burrowing into host's skin. Since lice are completely dependent on blood for survival, they die within 24–48 h. Also active against ticks, mites, and fleas.*

USES Pediculosis capitis.

Common adverse effects in *italic;* life-threatening effects underlined; generic names in **bold;** classifications in SMALL CAPS; ◆ Canadian drug name; ○ Prototype drug; ▲ Alert

CONTRAINDICATIONS Hypersensitivity to pyrethrins, chrysanthemums, sulfites, or other preservatives or dyes; acute inflammation of the scalp; lactation.

CAUTIOUS USE Children younger than 2 y **(liquid),** and less than 2 mo **(lotion);** asthma; pregnancy (category B).

ROUTE & DOSAGE

Head Lice

Adult/Child (2 y or older):
Topical Apply sufficient volume to clean wet hair to saturate the hair and scalp; leave on 10 min, then rinse hair thoroughly

ADMINISTRATION

Topical
- Saturate scalp as well as hair with the lotion; this is not a shampoo. Shake lotion well before application.
- Hair should be washed with regular shampoo before treatment with permethrin, thoroughly rinsed and dried.
- Rinse hair and scalp thoroughly and dry with a clean towel following 10 min exposure to the medication. Head lice are usually eliminated with one treatment.
- Store drug away from heat at 15°–25° C (59°–77° F) and direct light. Avoid freezing.

ADVERSE EFFECTS Skin: *Pruritus, transient tingling,* burning, stinging, numbness; erythema, edema, rash.

PHARMACOKINETICS Absorption: Less than 2% of amount applied is absorbed through intact skin. **Metabolism:** Rapidly hydrolyzed to inactive metabolites. **Elimination:** Primarily in urine.

NURSING IMPLICATIONS

Assessment & Drug Effects
- Do not attempt therapy if patient is known to be sensitive to any pyrethrin or pyrethroid. Stop treatment if a reaction occurs.

Patient & Family Education
- When hair is dry, comb with a fine-tooth comb (furnished with medication) to remove dead lice and remaining nits or nit shells.
- Be aware that drug remains on hair shaft up to 14 days; therefore, recurrence of infestation rarely occurs (less than 1%).
- Inspect hair shafts daily for at least 1 wk to determine drug effectiveness. Contact prescriber if live lice are observed after 7 days. Signs of inadequate treatment: Itching, redness of skin, skin abrasion, infected scalp areas.
- Resume regular shampooing after treatment; residual deposit of drug on hair is not reduced.
- Be aware that drug is usually irritating to the eyes and mucosa. Flush well with water if medicine accidentally gets into eyes.

PERPHENAZINE
(per-fen'a-zeen)
Classification:
PHENOTHIAZINE ANTIPSYCHOTIC; ANTIEMETIC
Therapeutic: ANTIPSYCHOTIC; ANTIEMETIC
Prototype: Chlorpromazine

AVAILABILITY Tablet

ACTION & *THERAPEUTIC EFFECT*
Affects all parts of CNS, particularly the hypothalamus. Antipsychotic

effect is due to its ability to antagonize neurotransmitter dopamine by acting on its receptors in the brain. Antiemetic action results from direct blockade of dopamine in the chemoreceptor trigger zone (CTZ) in the medulla. *Has antipsychotic and antiemetic properties.*

USES Schizophrenia, symptomatic control of severe nausea and vomiting.

CONTRAINDICATIONS Hypersensitivity to perphenazine and other phenothiazines; preexisting liver damage; suspected or established subcortical brain damage, comatose states, CNS depression; dementia-related psychosis; hepatic encephalopathy; QT prolongation; bone marrow depression; hematological disease; pregnancy (jaundice has been observed in newborns following maternal use of phenothiazines); lactation.

CAUTIOUS USE Previously diagnosed breast cancer; liver or kidney dysfunction; renal impairment; cardiovascular disorders; drug or alcohol abuse; epilepsy; psychic depression, patients with suicidal tendency; cardiac and pulmonary disease; glaucoma; history of intestinal or GU obstruction; older adults or debilitated patients; children younger than 12 y.

ROUTE & DOSAGE

Schizophrenia
Adult/Adolescent: **PO** 8–16 mg/day in divided doses; titrate to response (max: 64 mg/day)

Nausea
Adult: **PO** 8–16 mg daily in divided doses (max: 24 mg/day)

ADMINISTRATION
Oral
- May be taken with or without food. Administer with food, milk, or full glass of water to minimize gastric irritation.
- Storage: Store at 20°C to 25°C (68°F to 77°F).

ADVERSE EFFECTS CV: *Orthostatic hypotension,* bradycardia, ECG changes. **CNS:** *Extrapyramidal effects (dystonic reactions, akathisia, parkinsonian syndrome, tardive dyskinesia), sedation,* convulsions, bizarre dreams, catatonic-like state, cerebral edema. **HEENT:** Mydriasis, blurred vision, corneal and lenticular deposits. **Endocrine:** Hyperprolactinemia, galactorrhea, weight gain. **GI:** Constipation, *dry mouth,* increased appetite, adynamic ileus, abnormal liver function tests, cholestatic jaundice. **GU:** *Urinary retention,* gynecomastia, menstrual irregularities, inhibited ejaculation. **Hematologic:** Agranulocytosis, thrombocytopenic purpura, aplastic or hemolytic anemia. **Other:** Photosensitivity, itching, erythema, urticaria, angioneurotic edema, drug fever, anaphylactoid reaction, sterile abscess. Nasal congestion, decreased sweating.

INTERACTIONS Drug: Alcohol and other CNS DEPRESSANTS enhance CNS depression; ANTICHOLINERGIC AGENTS add to anticholinergic effects including fecal impaction and paralytic ileus; BARBITURATES, ANESTHETICS increase hypotension, excitation and may increase risk of QT prolongation; PHOTOSENSITIZING AGENTS may have additive effect; ANTIPARKINSON AGENTS may decrease efficacy of perphenazine; may increase ulcerogenic effect of **potassium. Herbal: Kava** increased risk and severity of dystonic reactions.

Common adverse effects in *italic;* life-threatening effects underlined; generic names in **bold;** classifications in SMALL CAPS; ✦ Canadian drug name; ◐ Prototype drug; ⚠ Alert

1322

PHARMACOKINETICS Absorption: Poorly absorbed from GI tract; 20% reaches systemic circulation. **Onset of action:** 2–4 weeks. **Duration:** 6–12 h. **Distribution:** Crosses placenta. **Metabolism:** In liver (CYP2D6). **Elimination:** In urine and feces. **Half-Life:** 9–12 h.

NURSING IMPLICATIONS

Black Box Warning

Perphenazine has been associated with increased mortality in older adults with dementia-related psychosis.

Assessment & Drug Effects

- Monitor mental status and report promptly suicidal ideation, significant changes in mood, behavior, or functional ability.
- Monitor vital signs periodically and report significant changes in HR or BP (especially with marked dosage increases).
- Report restlessness, weakness of extremities, dystonic reactions (spasms of neck and shoulder muscles, rigidity of back, difficulty swallowing or talking); motor restlessness (akathisia: inability to be still); and parkinsonian syndrome (tremors, shuffling gait, drooling, slow speech).
- Withhold medication and report immediately to prescriber S&S of tardive dyskinesia (i.e., fine, wormlike movements or rapid protrusions of the tongue, chewing motions, lip smacking).
- ECG and ophthalmologic examination are recommended prior to initiation and periodically during therapy.
- Suspect hypersensitivity, withhold drug, and report to prescriber if jaundice appears between weeks 2 and 4.

- Monitor urine and bowel elimination pattern especially with daily doses greater than 24 mg.
- Monitor ophthalmic screening at onset of therapy and periodically throughout.
- Monitor lab tests: Periodic CBC with differential, LFTs, renal function tests, serum electrolytes, fasting blood glucose, HgA1C, and lipid panel.

Patient & Family Education

- Make all position changes slowly and in stages, particularly from recumbent to upright posture, and to lie down or sit down if lightheadedness or dizziness occurs.
- Do not drive or engage in potentially hazardous activities until response to drug is known.
- Discontinue drug and report to prescriber immediately if jaundice appears between weeks 2 and 4.
- Avoid long exposure to sunlight and to sunlamps. Photosensitivity results in skin color changes from brown to blue-gray.
- Adhere strictly to dosage regimen. Contact prescriber before changing it for any reason.
- Drug should be discontinued gradually over a period of several weeks following prolonged therapy.
- Avoid OTC drugs unless prescriber prescribes them.
- Be aware that perphenazine may discolor urine reddish brown.

PERTUZUMAB

(per-tu'zu-mab)

Perjeta

Classification: MONOCLONAL ANTIBODY; HUMAN EPIDERAL GROWTH FACTOR RECEPTOR 2 PROTEIN (HER2) ANTAGONIST; ANTINEOPLASTIC

Therapeutic: ANTINEOPLASTIC; HER2 ANTAGONIST

Prototype: Trastuzumab

P

AVAILABILITY Solution for injection

ACTION & *THERAPEUTIC EFFECT*
Inhibits kinase-mediated intracellular signaling pathways by blocking HER2 receptors which results in cancer cell growth arrest and apoptosis; stimulates antibody-dependent cell-mediated cytotoxicity (ADCC) of cancer cells. *Inhibits proliferation of tumor cells with HER2 receptors.*

USES Indicated for the treatment of patients with HER2-positive metastatic breast cancer (with trastuzumab and docetaxel).

CONTRAINDICATIONS Hyersensitivity to pertuzumab; severe infusion reaction; clinical significant decrease in left ventricular function due to drug; pregnancy (category D); lactation.

CAUTIOUS USE Hepatic impairment; severe renal impairment; prior use of anthracycline or radiation; uncontrolled hypertension; recent MI, serious cardiac arrhythmias; CHF. Safety and efficacy in children younger than 18 y not established.

ROUTE & DOSAGE

Metastatic Breast Cancer
Adult: **IV** Initial dose of 840 mg; follow q3wk with 420 mg in combination with trastuzumab and docetaxel. Withhold or discontinue if trastuzumab is withheld or discontinued.

Dosing Interruption Due to Decreased Left Ventricular Ejection Fraction (LVEF)
Decreased LVEF to less than 45% or LVEF between 45%–49% with a 10% or greater absolute decrease below pretreatment values: **Withhold pertuzumab and trastuzumab for at least 3 wk.** *If the LVEF recovers to greater than 49% or to 45%–49% with less than 10% absolute decrease from baseline:* **Resume pertuzumab therapy.** *If the LVEF does not improve or declines further within approximately 3 wk:* **Discontinue pertuzumab and trastuzumab.**

ADMINISTRATION

Intravenous
This drug is a cytotoxic agent and caution should be used to prevent any contact with the drug. Follow institutional or standard guidelines for preparation, handling, and disposal of cytotoxic agents.

PREPARE: **IV Infusion:** Dilute required dose in 250 mL NS in a PVC or non-PVC polyolefin bag. Invert to mix but do not shake. Prepare just before use.
ADMINISTER: **IV Infusion:** Infuse initial dose of pertuzumab over 60 min; infuse subsequent doses of pertuzumab over 30–60 min. If trastuzumab is given concurrently with initial dose of pertuzumab, infuse trastuzumab over 90 min; give subsequent doses of trastuzumab over 30–90 min.
INCOMPATIBILITIES: **Solution/ additive:** Do not mix with other drugs. Do not mix/dilute with dextrose (5%) solution. **Y-site:** Do not mix with other drugs.

▪ Observe closely during first 60 min after initial infusion and for 30 min after subsequent infusions. Slow or stop infusion for significant infusion-related reactions.

Monitor vital signs and other parameters frequently until complete return to baseline. ▪ Store vials at 2°–8° C (36°–46° F). Store IV infusion refrigerated for up to 24 h.

ADVERSE EFFECTS Respiratory: Dyspnea, cough, nasopharyngitis, URI, epistaxis. **CNS:** Asthenia, dizziness, *fatigue*, headache, insomnia, *peripheral neuropathy*. **Skin:** *Alopecia*, dry skin, nail disorder, pruritus, *rash*. **GI:** Constipation, decreased appetite, *diarrhea*, dyspepsia, dysgeusia, *nausea*, stomatitis, vomiting. **Musculoskeletal:** Arthralgia, myalgia, weakness. **Hematological:** Anemia, <u>febrile neutropenia</u>, <u>leukopenia</u>, <u>neutropenia</u>. **Cardiac:** Decreased left ventricular ejection fraction. **Other:** Hypersensitivity, increased lacrimation, mucosal inflammation, peripheral edema, pyrexia.

PHARMACOKINETICS Half-Life: 18 d.

NURSING IMPLICATIONS

Black Box Warning

Pertuzumab has been associated with a significant decrease in left ventricular function, and with fetal death and birth defects.

Assessment & Drug Effects

▪ Monitor vital signs and cardiac status closely during drug administration and for 60 min after initial infusion and 30 min after subsequent infusions.
▪ Assess frequently for infusion-related reactions. Slow or stop infusion for significant infusion-related reactions. Institute appropriate support therapies.
▪ Assess for and report S&S of peripheral neuropathy and infection.
▪ Monitor lab tests: Baseline and periodic CBC with differential.

Patient & Family Education

▪ Report promptly S&S of infection.
▪ Use effective means of contraception during and for 6 mo following end of therapy.
▪ Report promptly to prescriber if you become pregnant.
▪ Do not breast-feed while taking this drug.
▪ Monitor weight daily and report greater than 2 lb weight gain in a day, swelling in the lower extremities, or shortness of breath.

PHENAZOPYRIDINE HYDROCHLORIDE

(fen-az-oh-peer'i-deen)

Azo-Standard, Baridium, Geridium, Phenazo ♦, Phenazodine, Pyridiate, Pyridium, Pyronium ♦, Urodine, Urogesic

Classification: URINARY TRACT ANALGESIC
Therapeutic: URINARY TRACT ANALGESIC

AVAILABILITY Tablet

ACTION & *THERAPEUTIC* EFFECT
Azo dye that has local anesthetic action on urinary tract mucosa, which imparts little or no antibacterial activity. *Effective as a urinary tract analgesic.*

USES Symptomatic relief of pain, burning, frequency, and urgency arising from irritation of urinary tract mucosa, as from infection, trauma, surgery, or instrumentation.

CONTRAINDICATIONS Renal insufficiency, renal disease including glomerulonephritis, pyelonephritis, renal failure, uremia; hepatic disease; glucose-6-phosphate dehydrogenase deficiency, severe hepatitis.

CAUTIOUS USE GI disturbances; older adults; pregnancy (category B); lactation; children.

ROUTE & DOSAGE

Cystitis
Adult: **PO** 200 mg tid
Child: **PO** 12 mg/kg/day in 3 divided doses

ADMINISTRATION
Oral
▪ Give with or after meals.

ADVERSE EFFECTS Endocrine: Methemoglobinemia, hemolytic anemia. **Skin:** Skin pigmentation. **GI:** Mild GI disturbances. **GU:** Kidney stones, transient acute kidney failure. **Special Senses:** May stain soft contact lenses. **Other:** Headache, vertigo.

DIAGNOSTIC TEST INTERFERENCE
Phenazopyridine may interfere with any urinary test that is based on color reactions or spectrometry: *Bromsulphalein* and *phenolsulfonphthalein* excretion tests; urinary *glucose* test using *Clinistix* or *TesTape* (*copper-reduction methods* such as *Clinitest* and *Benedict's test* reportedly not affected); *bilirubin* using "foam test" or *Ictotest; ketones* using *nitroprusside* (e.g., *Acetest, Ketostix,* or *Gerhardt ferric chloride*); *urinary protein* using *Albustix, Albutest,* or *nitric acid ring test;* urinary *steroids; urobilinogen; assays* for *porphyrins.*

PHARMACOKINETICS Absorption: Readily absorbed from GI tract. **Distribution:** Crosses placenta in trace amounts. **Metabolism:** In liver and other tissues. **Elimination:** Primarily in urine.

NURSING IMPLICATIONS
Assessment & Drug Effects
▪ Monitor for therapeutic effectiveness as indicated by relief from pain and burning upon urination.

Patient & Family Education
▪ Drug will impart an orange to red color to urine and may stain clothing.

PHENELZINE SULFATE ☺
(fen'el-zeen)
Classification:
ANTIDEPRESSANT; MONOAMINE OXIDASE (MAO) INHIBITOR
Therapeutic: ANTIDEPRESSANT; MAO INHIBITOR

AVAILABILITY Tablet

ACTION & *THERAPEUTIC EFFECT*
Antidepressant action believed to be due to irreversible inhibition of MAO, thereby permitting increased concentrations of endogenous epinephrine, norepinephrine, serotonin, and dopamine within presynaptic neurons and at receptor sites. *Antidepressant utilization is limited to individuals who do not respond well to other classes of antidepressants.*

USES Atypical or nonendogenous depression.

CONTRAINDICATIONS Hypersensitivity to MAO inhibitors; suicidal ideation; pheochromocytoma; untreated hyperthyroidism; cardiac arrhythmias, uncontrolled hypertension; increased intracranial pressure; intracranial bleeding; atonic colitis; glaucoma; frequent headaches; bipolar depression; accompanying alcoholism or drug addiction; paranoid schizophrenia; older adults or debilitated patients; lactation.

CAUTIOUS USE Epilepsy; pyloric stenosis; DM; manic-depressive states; agitated patients; schizophrenia or psychosis; seizures; suicidal tendencies; chronic brain syndromes; pregnancy (category C); children and adolescents.

ROUTE & DOSAGE

Depression

Adult: **PO** 15 mg tid, rapidly increase to at least 60 mg/day, may need up to 90 mg/day

ADMINISTRATION

Oral

- Avoid rapid discontinuation, particularly after high dosage, since a rebound effect may occur (e.g., headache, excitability, hallucinations, and possibly depression).
- Store in tightly covered containers away from heat and light.

ADVERSE EFFECTS CV: <u>Hypertensive crisis</u> (intense occipital headache, palpitation, marked hypertension, stiff neck, nausea, vomiting, sweating, fever, photophobia, dilated pupils, bradycardia or tachycardia, constricting chest pain, intracranial bleeding), hypotension or hypertension, <u>circulatory collapse</u>. **CNS:** Mania, hypomania, confusion, memory impairment, delirium, hallucinations, euphoria, acute anxiety reaction, toxic precipitation of schizophrenia, convulsions, peripheral neuropathy. **HEENT:** Blurred vision. **Skin:** Hyperhidrosis, skin rash, photosensitivity. **GI:** *Constipation, dry mouth, nausea,* vomiting, *anorexia,* weight gain. **Hematologic:** Normocytic and normochromic anemia, <u>leukopenia</u>. **Other:** Dizziness or vertigo, headache, *orthostatic hypotension,* drowsiness or *insomnia,* weakness, fatigue, edema, tremors, twitching, akathisia, ataxia, hyperreflexia, faintness, hyperactivity, marked agitation, anxiety, seizures, trismus, opisthotonos, <u>respiratory depression, coma</u>.

DIAGNOSTIC TEST INTERFERENCE

Phenelzine may cause a slight false increase in ***serum bilirubin.***

INTERACTIONS Drug: TRICYCLIC ANTIDEPRESSANTS may cause hyperpyrexia, seizures; **fluoxetine, sertraline, paroxetine** may cause serotonin syndrome (see Appendix E); SYMPATHOMIMETIC AGENTS (e.g., **amphetamine, phenylephrine, phenylpropanolamine**), **guanethidine** may cause hypertensive crisis; CNS DEPRESSANTS have additive CNS depressive effects; OPIATE ANALGESICS (especially **meperidine**) may cause hypertensive crisis and circulatory collapse; **buspirone,** hypertension; GENERAL ANESTHETICS, prolonged hypotensive and CNS depressant effects; hypertension, headache, hyperexcitability reported with **dopamine, methyldopa, levodopa, tryptophan; metrizamide** may increase risk of seizures; HYPOTENSIVE AGENTS and DIURETICS have additive hypotensive effects. **Food:** Aged meats or aged cheeses, protein extracts, sour cream, alcohol, anchovies, liver, sausages, overripe figs, bananas, avocados, chocolate, soy

---

sauce, bean curd, natural yogurt, fava beans—**tyramine**-containing foods—may precipitate hypertensive crisis. Avoid **chocolate** or **caffeine. Herbal: Ginseng, ephedra, ma huang, St. John's wort** may cause hypertensive crisis.

PHARMACOKINETICS Absorption: Readily absorbed from GI tract. **Onset:** 2 wk. **Metabolism:** Rapidly metabolized. **Elimination:** 79% of metabolites excreted in urine in 96 h.

NURSING IMPLICATIONS

Black Box Warning

Phenelzine has been associated with increased risk of suicidal thinking and behavior (suicidality) in children, adolescents, and young adults.

Assessment & Drug Effects

- Monitor children, adolescents, and adults for changes in behavior that may indicate suicidality.
- Prior to initiation of treatment, evaluate patient's BP in standing and recumbent positions.
- Monitor BP and pulse between doses when titrating initial dosages. Observe closely for evidence of adverse drug effects. Thereafter, monitor at regular intervals throughout therapy.
- Report immediately if hypomania (exaggeration of motility, feelings, and ideas) occurs as depression improves. This reaction may also appear at higher than recommended doses or with long-term therapy.
- Observe for and report therapeutic effectiveness of drug: Improvement in sleep pattern, appetite, physical activity, interest in self and surroundings, as well as lessening of anxiety and bodily complaints.
- Observe patient with diabetes closely for S&S of hypoglycemia (see Appendix F).
- Patients on prolonged therapy should be checked periodically for altered color perception, changes in fundi or visual fields. Changes in red-green vision may be the first indication of eye damage.

Patient & Family Education

- Maximum antidepressant effects generally appear in 2–6 wk and persist several weeks after drug withdrawal.
- Avoid self-medication. OTC preparations (e.g., cough, cold, hay fever remedies, and appetite suppressants) can precipitate severe hypertensive reactions if taken during therapy or within 2–3 wk after discontinuation of an MAO inhibitor.
- Report immediately to prescriber the onset of headache and palpitation, or any other unusual effects which may indicate need to discontinue therapy.
- Do not consume foods and beverages containing tyramine or tryptophan or drugs containing pressor agent. These can cause severe hypertensive reactions. Get a list from your care provider.
- Avoid drinking excessive caffeine and chocolate beverages (e.g., coffee, tea, cocoa, or cola).
- Make position changes slowly, especially from recumbent to upright posture, and dangle legs over bed a few minutes before rising to walk. Avoid standing still for prolonged periods. Also avoid hot showers and baths (resulting vasodilatation may potentiate hypotension); lie down immediately if feeling light-headed or faint.

- Check weight 2 or 3 × wk and report unusual gain.
- Report jaundice. Hepatotoxicity is believed to be a hypersensitivity reaction unrelated to dosage or duration of therapy.

PHENOBARBITAL ⊕
(fee-noe-bar′bi-tal)
Solfoton

PHENOBARBITAL SODIUM
Luminal
Classification: ANTICONVULSANT; SEDATIVE-HYPNOTIC; BARBITURATE
Therapeutic: ANTICONVULSANT; SEDATIVE-HYPNOTIC
Controlled Substance: Schedule IV

AVAILABILITY Tablet; capsule; liquid; solution for injection

ACTION & *THERAPEUTIC EFFECT*
Sedative and hypnotic effects appear to be due primarily to interference with impulse transmission of cerebral cortex by inhibition of reticular activating system. Limiting spread of seizure activity results by increasing the threshold for motor cortex stimulation. *Effective as a sedative, hypnotic, and an anticonvulsant with no analgesic effect.*

USES Long-term management of tonic-clonic (grand mal) seizures and partial seizures; status epilepticus, eclampsia, febrile convulsions in young children. Also used as a sedative in anxiety or tension states; in pediatrics as preoperative and postoperative sedation and to treat pylorospasm in infants.

UNLABELED USES Treatment and prevention of hyperbilirubinemia in neonates and in the management of chronic cholestasis; benzodiazepine withdrawal.

CONTRAINDICATIONS Hypersensitivity to barbiturates; manifest hepatic or familial history of porphyria; severe respiratory or kidney disease; history of previous addiction to sedative hypnotics; alcohol intoxication; uncontrolled pain; renal failure, anuria; pregnancy (category D).

CAUTIOUS USE Impaired liver, kidney, cardiac, or respiratory function; sleep apnea; COPD; history of allergies; patients with fever; hyperthyroidism; diabetes mellitus or severe anemia; seizure disorders; during labor and delivery; patient with borderline hypoadrenal function; older adult or debilitated patients; lactation; young children and neonates.

ROUTE & DOSAGE

Anticonvulsant
Adult: **PO/IV** 1–3 mg/kg/day in divided doses
Child: **PO/IV** 4–8 mg/kg/day in divided doses

Status Epilepticus
Adult: **IV** 300–800 mg, then 120–240 mg q20min (total max: 1–2 g)
Child: **IV** 10–20 mg/kg in single or divided doses, then 5 mg/kg/dose q15–30min (total max: 40 mg/kg)
Neonate: **IV** 15–20 mg/kg in single or divided doses

Sedative/Hypnotic
Adult: **PO** 30–120 mg/day; **IV/IM** 100–320 mg/day
Child: **PO** 2 mg/kg/day in 3 divided doses **IV/IM** 3–5 mg/kg

P

Common adverse effects in *italic;* life-threatening effects underlined; generic names in **bold;** classifications in SMALL CAPS; ♦ Canadian drug name; ⊕ Prototype drug; ⚠ Alert

Renal Impairment Dosage Adjustment

CrCl less than 10 mL/min: Dose q12–16h

Hemodialysis Dosage Adjustment

20–50% dialyzed

ADMINISTRATION

Oral

- Give crushed and mixed with a fluid or with food if patient cannot swallow pill. Do not permit patient to swallow dry crushed drug.

Intramuscular

- Give IM deep into large muscle mass; do not exceed 5 mL at any one site.

Intravenous

Note: Verify correct IV concentration and rate of infusion for neonates, infants, children with prescriber. Use IV route ONLY if other routes are not feasible.

PREPARE: **Direct:** May be given undiluted or diluted in 10 mL of sterile water for injection.

ADMINISTER: **Direct:** Give no faster than 60 mg/min in adults and 30 mg/min in children. Give within 30 min after preparation.

INCOMPATIBILITIES: Solution/additive: **Ampicillin, cephalothin, chlorpromazine, cimetidine, clindamycin, dexamethasone, diphenhydramine, erythromycin, ephedrine, hydralazine, hydrocortisone sodium succinate, hydroxyzine, insulin, kanamycin, levorphanol, meperidine, methadone, methylphenidate, morphine, nitrofurantoin, norepinephrine, pentazocine, pentobarbital, phytonadione, procaine, prochlorperazine, promazine, promethazine, sodium bicarbonate, streptomycin,** TETRACYCLINES, **vancomycin, warfarin.** Y-site: **Amphotericin B cholesteryl complex, hydromorphone, TPN with albumin.**

- Be aware that extravasation of IV phenobarbital may cause necrotic tissue changes that necessitate skin grafting. Check injection site frequently.

ADVERSE EFFECTS

CV: Bradycardia, syncope, hypotension. **Respiratory:** Respiratory depression. **CNS:** *Somnolence,* nightmares, insomnia, "hangover," headache, anxiety, thinking abnormalities, dizziness, nystagmus, irritability, paradoxic excitement and exacerbation of hyperkinetic behavior (in children); confusion or depression or marked excitement (older adult or debilitated patients); ataxia. **Endocrine:** Hypocalcemia, osteomalacia, rickets. **Skin:** Mild maculopapular, morbilliform rash; erythema multiforme, Stevens–Johnson syndrome, exfoliative dermatitis (rare). **GI:** Nausea, vomiting, constipation, diarrhea, epigastric pain, liver damage. **Musculoskeletal:** Folic acid deficiency, vitamin D deficiency. **Hematologic:** Megaloblastic anemia, agranulocytosis, thrombocytopenia. **Other:** Myalgia, neuralgia, CNS depression, coma, and death.

DIAGNOSTIC TEST INTERFERENCE

BARBITURATES may affect *bromsulphalein* retention tests (by enhancing liver uptake and excretion of dye) and increase *serum phosphatase.*

INTERACTIONS

Drug: Alcohol, CNS DEPRESSANTS compound CNS depression; phenobarbital may decrease absorption and increase metabolism of ORAL ANTICOAGU-LANTS; increases metabolism of CORTICOSTEROIDS, ORAL CONTRACEP-TIVES, ANTICONVULSANTS, **digitoxin,** possibly decreasing their effects; ANTIDEPRESSANTS potentiate adverse effects of phenobarbital; **griseoful-vin** decreases absorption of phenobarbital; **quinine** increases plasma levels. **Herbal: Kava, valerian** may potentiate sedation.

PHARMACOKINETICS **Absorption:** 70–90% slowly from GI tract. **Peak:** 8–12 h PO; 30 min IV. **Duration:** 4–6 h IV. **Distribution:** 20–45% protein bound; crosses placenta; enters breast milk. **Metabolism:** In liver (CYP2C19). **Elimination:** In urine. **Half-Life:** 2–6 days.

NURSING IMPLICATIONS

Assessment & Drug Effects

- Observe patients receiving large doses for at least 30 min to ensure that sedation is not excessive.
- Chronic use in children or infants requires continuous assessment related to normal cognitive and behavioral functioning.
- Keep patient under constant observation when drug is administered IV, and record vital signs at least every hour or more often if indicated.
- Check IV injection site very frequently to prevent extravasation of phenobarbital. It could result in tissue damage requiring skin grafting.
- Monitor serum drug levels. Serum concentrations greater than 50 mcg/mL may cause coma. Therapeutic serum concentrations of 15–40 mcg/mL produce anticonvulsant activity in most patients. These values are usually attained after 2 or 3 wk of therapy with a dose of 100–200 mg/day.

- Expect barbiturates to produce restlessness when given to patients in pain because these drugs do not have analgesic action.
- Be prepared for paradoxical responses and report promptly in older adult or debilitated patient and children [i.e., irritability, marked excitement (inappropriate tearfulness and aggression in children), depression, and confusion].
- Monitor for drug interactions. Barbiturates increase the metabolism of many drugs, leading to decreased pharmacologic effects of those drugs.
- Monitor for and report chronic toxicity symptoms (e.g., ataxia, slurred speech, irritability, poor judgment, slight dysarthria, nystagmus on vertical gaze, confusion, insomnia, somatic complaints).
- Monitor lab tests: Periodic LFTs, CBC with differential, Hct and Hgb, and renal function tests.

Patient & Family Education

- Be aware that anticonvulsant therapy may cause drowsiness during first few weeks of treatment, but this usually diminishes with continued use.
- Avoid potentially hazardous activities requiring mental alertness until response to drug is known.
- Do not consume alcohol in any amount when taking a barbiturate; it may severely impair judgment and abilities.
- Increase vitamin D-fortified foods (e.g., milk products) because drug increases vitamin D metabolism. A vitamin D supplement may be prescribed.
- Maintain adequate dietary folate intake: Fresh vegetables (especially green leafy), fresh fruits, whole grains, liver. Long-term therapy may result in nutritional

P

folate (B₉) deficiency. A supplement of folic acid may be prescribed.

- Adhere to drug regimen (i.e., do not change intervals between doses or increase or decrease doses) without contacting prescriber.
- Do not stop taking drug abruptly because of danger of withdrawal symptoms (8–12 h after last dose), which can be fatal.
- Report to prescriber the onset of fever, sore throat or mouth, malaise, easy bruising or bleeding, petechiae, jaundice, rash when on prolonged therapy.
- Avoid pregnancy when receiving barbiturates. Use or add barrier device to hormonal contraceptive when taking prolonged therapy.

PHENTERMINE HYDROCHLORIDE

(phen-ter'meen)
Adipex-P, Lomaira
Classification: ANOREXIANT
Therapeutic: APPETITE SUPPRESSANT
Prototype: Diethylpropion
Controlled Substance: Schedule IV

AVAILABILITY Tablet; capsule

ACTION & THERAPEUTIC EFFECT
Sympathetic amine with actions that include CNS stimulation and blood pressure elevation. *Appetite suppression or metabolic effects along with diet adjustment result in weight loss in obese individuals.*

USES Short-term (8–12 wk) adjunct for weight loss.

CONTRAINDICATIONS Known hypersensitivity to sympathetic amines; glaucoma; moderate to severe uncontrolled hypertension, advanced arteriosclerosis, cardiovascular disease, cardiac arrhythmias, stroke; hyperthyroidism; agitated states; history of drug abuse; during or within 14 days of administration of MAO inhibitor; glaucoma; pregnancy (category X); lactation.

CAUTIOUS USE Hypertension, DM; seizures; renal impairment; older adults; children younger than 16 y.

ROUTE & DOSAGE

Obesity
Adult/Adolescent: **PO** 15–37.5 mg each morning; 8 mg tid (Lomaira)

ADMINISTRATION
Oral
- Ensure that at least 14 days have elapsed between the first dose of phentermine and the last dose of an MAO inhibitor.
- Give 30 min before meals.
- Do not administer if an SSRI is currently prescribed.
- Store in a tight container.

ADVERSE EFFECTS CV: Palpitations, tachycardia, arrhythmias, hypertension or hypotension, syncope, precordial pain, pulmonary hypertension. **CNS:** Overstimulation, nervousness, restlessness, dizziness, insomnia, weakness, fatigue, malaise, anxiety, euphoria, drowsiness, depression, agitation, dysphoria, tremor, dyskinesia, dysarthria, confusion, incoordination, headache, change in libido. **HEENT:** Mydriasis, blurred vision. **Endocrine:** Gynecomastia. **Skin:** Hair loss, ecchymosis. **GI:** Dry mouth, altered taste, nausea, vomiting,

Common adverse effects in *italic;* life-threatening effects underlined; generic names in **bold;** classifications in SMALL CAPS; ◆ Canadian drug name; ❍ Prototype drug; ⚠ Alert abdominal pain, diarrhea, constipation, stomach pain. **GU:** Dysuria, polyuria, urinary frequency, impotence, menstrual upset. **Musculoskeletal:** Muscle pain. **Hematologic:** Bone marrow suppression, agranulocytosis, leukopenia. **Other:** Hypersensitivity (urticaria, rash, erythema, burning sensation), chest pain, excessive sweating, clamminess, chills, flushing, fever, myalgia.

INTERACTIONS Drug: MAO INHIBITORS, **furazolidone** may increase pressor response resulting in hypertensive crisis. TRICYCLIC ANTIDEPRESSANTS may decrease anorectic response. May decrease hypotensive effects of **guanethidine.**

PHARMACOKINETICS Absorption: Absorbed from the small intestine. **Duration:** 4–14 h. **Elimination:** Primarily in urine. **Half-Life:** 19–24 h.

NURSING IMPLICATIONS

Assessment & Drug Effects

- Assess for tolerance to the anorectic effect of the drug. Withhold drug and report to prescriber when this occurs.
- Monitor periodic cardiovascular status, including BP, exercise tolerance, peripheral edema.
- Monitor weight at least 3 × wk.

Patient & Family Education

- Do not take this drug late in the evening because it could cause insomnia.
- Report immediately any of the following: Shortness of breath, chest pains, dizziness or fainting, swelling of the extremities.
- Tolerance to the appetite suppression effects of the drug usually develops in a few weeks. Notify prescriber, but do not increase drug dose.

- Weigh yourself at least 3 × wk at the same time of day with the same amount of clothing.

PHENTOLAMINE MESYLATE

(fen-tole′a-meen)

OraVerse

Classification: ALPHA-ADRENERGIC RECEPTOR ANTAGONIST; VASODILATOR
Therapeutic: VASODILATOR; ANTIHYPERTENSIVE
Prototype: Prazosin

AVAILABILITY Solution for injection

ACTION & THERAPEUTIC EFFECT Alpha-adrenergic blocking agent that competitively blocks alpha-adrenergic receptors, but action is transient and incomplete. Causes vasodilation and decreases general vascular resistance as well as pulmonary arterial pressure, primarily by direct action on vascular smooth muscle. *Prevents hypertension resulting from elevated levels of circulating epinephrine or norepinephrine.*

USES Diagnosis of pheochromocytoma and to prevent or control hypertensive episodes associated with pheochromocytoma; management of extravasation of norepinephrine.

UNLABELED USES Extravasation of sympathomimetic vasopressors

CONTRAINDICATIONS Hypersensitivity to phentolamine; MI (or history of MI), CAD; coronary insufficiency; angina; peptic ulcer disease.

CAUTIOUS USE Gastritis; pregnancy (adverse effects have been observed in some animal reproduction studies); lactation; children.

P

ROUTE & DOSAGE

Diagnosis of Pheochromocytoma

Adult: **IV/IM** 5 mg
Child: **IM** 3 mg; **IV** 1 mg

To Treat Extravasation

Adult: **Intradermal** 5–10 mg
diluted in 10 mL of normal saline
injected into affected area within
12 h of extravasation
Child: **Intradermal** small amount
of a 0.5 to 1 mg/mL solution
injected into affected area within
12 h of extravasation

ADMINISTRATION

Note: Place patient in supine position when receiving drug parenterally. ▪ Monitor BP and pulse q5min until stabilized.

Intramuscular

▪ Reconstitute 5 mg vial with 1 mL of sterile water for injection.

Intravenous

***PREPARE:* Direct:** Reconstitute as for IM. May be further diluted with up to 10 mL of sterile water. ▪ Use immediately.
***ADMINISTER:* Direct:** Inject rapidly. Monitor BP immediately after injection, every 30 seconds for 3 minutes, then every minute for 7 minutes.
***INCOMPATIBILITIES:* Y-site:** **Amphotericin B (conventional), carmustine, cefamandole, cefazolin, cefoperazone, cefotaxime, cefotetan, cefoxitin, cefuroxime, clindamycin, dantrolene, diazepam, diazoxide, ganciclovir, gemtuzumab, insulin, ketorolac, phenobarbital, phenytoin, sulfamethoxazole/ trimethoprim.**

ADVERSE EFFECTS CV: *Orthostatic hypotension, bradycardia, flushing.* **Respiratory:** Nasal congestion. **CNS:** Mouth pain, headache, weakness, dizziness. **Other:** Pain at injection site.

INTERACTIONS **Drug:** May antagonize BP raising effects of **epinephrine, ephedrine;** may increase antihypertensive effects of other ANTIHYPERTENSIVES.

PHARMACOKINETICS **Peak:** 2 min IV; 15–20 min IM. **Duration:** 10–30 min IV; 30-45 min IM. **Elimination:** In urine. **Half-Life:** 19 min.

NURSING IMPLICATIONS

Assessment & Drug Effects

Test for pheochromocytoma:

▪ *IV administration:* Keep patient at rest in supine position throughout test, preferably in quiet darkened room. ▪ Prior to drug administration, take BP q10min for at least 30 min to establish that BP has stabilized before IV injection. ▪ Record BP immediately after injection and at 30-sec intervals for first 3 min; then at 1-min intervals for next 7 min.
▪ *IM administration:* Post-injection, BP determinations at 5-min intervals for 30–45 min.

Patient & Family Education

▪ Avoid sudden changes in position, particularly from reclining to upright posture and dangle legs and exercise ankles and toes for a few minutes before standing to walk.
▪ Lie down or sit down in headlow position immediately if lightheaded or dizzy.

PHENYLEPHRINE HYDROCHLORIDE

(fen-ill-ef'rin)

AK-Dilate Ophthalmic, Alconefrin, Isopto Frin, Mydfrin, Nostril, Rhinall, Sinarest Nasal, Sinex

Classification: EYE AND NOSE PREPARATION; ALPHA-ADRENERGIC AGONIST; MYDRIATIC; VASOPRESSOR; DECONGESTANT

Therapeutic: VASOCONSTRICTOR; DECONGESTANT; MYDRIATIC

Prototype: Dexmedetomide

AVAILABILITY Tablet; nasal solution; ophthalmic solution; solution for injection; suppository

ACTION & THERAPEUTIC EFFECT
Potent, synthetic, direct-acting sympathomimetic with strong alpha-adrenergic cardiac stimulant actions. Elevates systolic and diastolic pressures through arteriolar constriction. Reduces intraocular pressure by increasing outflow and decreasing rate of aqueous humor secretion. *Effective antihypotensive agent. Topical applications to eye produce vasoconstriction and prompt mydriasis of short duration, usually without causing cycloplegia. Nasal decongestant action qualitatively similar to that of epinephrine but more potent.*

USES Parenterally to maintain BP during anesthesia, to treat vascular failure in shock, and to overcome paroxysmal supraventricular tachycardia. Used topically for rhinitis of common cold, allergic rhinitis, and sinusitis; in selected patients with wide-angle glaucoma; as mydriatic for ophthalmoscopic examination or surgery, and for relief of uveitis.

CONTRAINDICATIONS Severe CAD, severe hypertension, atrial fibrillation, atrial flutter, cardiac arrhythmias; severe organic cardiac disease, cardiomyopathy; uncontrolled hypertension; ventricular fibrillation or tachycardia; acute MI, angina; thyrotoxicosis; cerebral arteriosclerosis, MAOI; labor, delivery, infants, neonates. **Ophthalmic preparations:** Narrow-angle glaucoma.

CAUTIOUS USE Hyperthyroidism; DM; heart failure; thyroid disease; BPH; 21 days before or following termination of MAO inhibitor therapy; older adults; pregnancy (category C); children younger than 6 y. **Ophthalmic:** Lactation.

ROUTE & DOSAGE

Hypotension

Adult: **IM/Subcutaneous** 2–5 mg (initial dose not to exceed 5 mg) q10–15min as needed; **IV** 0.2 mg (range: 0.1–0.5 mg) every 10–15 min as needed

Supraventricular Tachycardia

Adult: **IV** 0.25–0.5 mg bolus, then 0.1–0.2 mg doses (total max: 1 mg)

Vasoconstrictor

Adult: **Ophthalmic** See Appendix A-1; **Intranasal** 2–3 drops or sprays of 0.25–0.5% solution q3–4h as needed
Child (6–12 y): **Intranasal** 2–3 drops or sprays of 0.25% solution q3–4h as needed

ADMINISTRATION

Instillation

- Nasal preparations: Instruct patient to blow nose gently (with both nostrils open) to clear nasal passages before administration of medication.

- Instillation (drops): Tilt head back while sitting or standing up, or lie on bed and hang head over side. Stay in position a few minutes to permit medication to spread through nose. (Spray): With head upright, squeeze bottle quickly and firmly to produce 1 or 2 sprays into each nostril; wait 3–5 min, blow nose, and repeat dose. (Jelly): Place in each nostril and sniff it well back into nose.
- Clean tips and droppers of nasal solution dispensers with hot water after use to prevent contamination of solution. Droppers of ophthalmic solution bottles should not touch any surface including the eye.
- Ophthalmic preparations: To avoid excessive systemic absorption, apply pressure to lacrimal sac during and for 1–2 min after instillation of drops.

Subcutaneous/Intramuscular
- Give undiluted.

Intravenous
Note: Ensure patency of IV site prior to administration.

PREPARE: **Direct:** Dilute each 10 mg (1 mL) of 1% solution in 9 mL of sterile water. **IV Infusion:** Dilute each 10 mg in 500 mL D5W or NS (concentration: 0.02 mg/mL). *ADMINISTER:* **Direct:** Give a single dose over 30 sec. **IV Infusion:** Titrate to maintain BP.
INCOMPATIBILITIES: **Y-site:** **Acyclovir, amphotericin B (conventional and lipid), azathioprine, dantrolene, diazepam, diazoxide, ganciclovir, indomethacin, insulin, lansoprazole, minocycline, mitomycin, pentamidine, phenytoin, SMZ/TMP, propofol.**

- Protect from exposure to air, strong light, or heat, any of which can cause solutions to change color to brown, form a precipitate, and lose potency.

ADVERSE EFFECTS CV: Palpitation, tachycardia, bradycardia (overdosage), arrhythmia, hypertension. **HEENT:** *Transient stinging,* lacrimation, brow ache, headache, blurred vision, allergy (pigmentary deposits on lids, conjunctiva, and cornea with prolonged use), increased sensitivity to light. *Rebound nasal congestion* (hyperemia and edema of mucosa), *nasal burning,* stinging, dryness, *sneezing.* **GI:** Nausea. **Other:** Trembling, sweating, pallor, sense of fullness in head, tingling of extremities, sleeplessness, dizziness, lightheadedness, weakness, restlessness, anxiety, precordial pain, *tremor,* severe visceral or peripheral vasoconstriction, necrosis if IV infiltrates.

INTERACTIONS Drug: ERGOT ALKALOIDS, **guanethidine,** TRICYCLIC ANTIDEPRESSANTS increase pressor effects of phenylephrine; **halothane, digoxin** increase risk of arrhythmias; MAO INHIBITORS cause hypertensive crisis; **oxytocin** causes persistent hypertension; ALPHA-BLOCKERS, BETA-BLOCKERS antagonize effects of phenylephrine.

PHARMACOKINETICS Onset: Immediate IV; 10–15 min IM/Subcutaneous. **Duration:** 15–20 min IV; 30–120 min IM/Subcutaneous; 3–6 h topical. **Metabolism:** In liver and tissues by monoamine oxidase.

NURSING IMPLICATIONS
Assessment & Drug Effects
- Monitor infusion site closely as extravasation may cause tissue necrosis and gangrene. If

extravasation does occur, area should be immediately injected with 5–10 mg of phentolamine (Regitine) diluted in 10–15 mL of NS.

- Monitor pulse, BP, and central venous pressure (q2–5min) during IV administration.
- Control flow rate and dosage to prevent excessive dosage. IV overdoses can induce ventricular dysrhythmias.
- Observe for congestion or rebound miosis after topical administration to eye.

Patient & Family Education

- Be aware that instillation of 2.5–10% strength ophthalmic solution can cause burning and stinging.
- Do not exceed recommended dosage regardless of formulation.
- Inform the prescriber if no relief is experienced from preparation in 5 days.
- Wear sunglasses in bright light because after instillation of ophthalmic drops, pupils will be large and eyes may be more sensitive to light than usual. Stop medication and notify prescriber if sensitivity persists beyond 12 h after drug has been discontinued.
- Be aware that some ophthalmic solutions may stain contact lenses.

PHENYTOIN ⊙

(fen'i-toy-in)
Dilantin-125, Dilantin

PHENYTOIN SODIUM EXTENDED

Dilantin, Phentek

PHENYTOIN SODIUM PROMPT

Dilantin

Classification: ANTICONVULSANT; HYDANTOIN
Therapeutic: ANTICONVULSANT

AVAILABILITY Capsule; sustained release capsule; chewable tablet; suspension; solution for injection

ACTION & THERAPEUTIC EFFECT
Anticonvulsant action elevates the seizure threshold and/or limits the spread of seizure discharge. Phenytoin is accompanied by reduced voltage, frequency, and spread of electrical discharges within the motor cortex. *Inhibits seizure activity. Effective in treating arrhythmias associated with QT prolongation.*

USES To control tonic-clonic (grand mal) and complex partial seizures; treatment of status epilepticus; (injection only) seizure prophylaxis due to specific neurologic conditions.

UNLABELED USES Treatment of trigeminal neuralgia (tic douloureux).

CONTRAINDICATIONS Hypersensitivity to hydantoin products; rash; seizures due to hypoglycemia; sinus bradycardia, complete or incomplete heart block; Adams-Stokes syndrome; pregnancy (category D).

CAUTIOUS USE Impaired liver or kidney function; alcoholism; blood dyscrasias; hypotension, severe myocardial insufficiency, impending or frank heart failure; pancreatic adenoma; DM, hyperglycemia; respiratory depression; acute intermittent porphyria; older adult, debilitated, or gravely ill patients.

ROUTE & DOSAGE

Status Epilepticus
Adult: **IV** 20 mg/kg at a max rate of 50 mg/minute; if necessary, may give an additional

dose of 5–10 mg/kg 10 min after the loading dose *Adolescent/ Child/Infant:* **IV** 20 mg/kg

Non Emergent Seizures

Adult: **PO** 100 mg tid; **Extended release** 100 mg tid adjust dose *Adolescent/Child:* **PO/IV** 5 mg/ kg/day in divided doses (max: 300 mg/day)

ADMINISTRATION

Oral

- Ensure that sustained release form is not chewed or crushed. **Must be** swallowed whole.
- Do not give within 2–3 h of antacid ingestion.
- Shake suspension vigorously before pouring to ensure uniform distribution of drug.
- Note: Chewable tablets are not intended for once-a-day dosage since drug is too quickly bioavailable and can therefore lead to toxic serum levels.
- Use sustained release capsules ONLY for once-a-day dosage regimens.

Intravenous

Note: Verify correct rate of IV injection for administration to infants or children with prescriber.

- Inspect solution prior to use. May use a slightly yellowed injectable solution safely. Precipitation may be caused by refrigeration, but slow warming to room temperature restores clarity.

PREPARE: **Direct:** Give undiluted. Use only when clear without precipitate.

ADMINISTER: **Direct for Adult** Give 50 mg or fraction thereof over 1 min (25 mg/min in older adult or when used as antiarrhythmic).

Do not give more rapidly. ▪ Follow with an injection of sterile saline through the same in-place catheter or needle. **Do not** use solutions containing dextrose.

Direct for Child/Neonate: Give 1 mg/kg/min. **Do not** give more rapidly. ▪ Follow with an injection of sterile saline through the same in-place catheter or needle. **Do not** use solutions containing dextrose.

INCOMPATIBILITIES: **Solution/ additive: Do not administer with other medications. Y-site: Do not administer with other medications.**

- Observe injection site frequently during administration to prevent infiltration. Local soft tissue irritation may be serious, leading to erosion of tissues.

ADVERSE EFFECTS **CV:** Atrial conduction depression, bradycardia, hypotension. **CNS:** Ataxia, confusion, dizziness, drowsiness, headache, insomnia, mood changes, nervousness, paresthesia, slurred speech, twitching, vertigo. **HEENT:** Nystagmus. **Endocrine:** Hyperglycemia, vitamin D deficiency. **Skin:** Dermatitis, rash, Stevens-Johnson syndrome, injection site reaction, local tissue necrosis. **Hepatic/GI:** Acute hepatic injury, increased ALP, constipation, gingival hyperplasia, nausea, vomiting. **GU:** Peyronie disease. **Hematologic:** Agranulocytosis, leukopenia.

DIAGNOSTIC TEST INTERFERENCE

Phenytoin (HYDANTOINS) may produce lower than normal values for T4 and T3, *dexamethasone* or *metyrapone* tests; may increase serum levels of *TSH, glucose, BSP,* and *alkaline phosphatase* and may decrease *PBI* and *urinary steroid* levels.

INTERACTIONS

Drug: Alcohol decreases phenytoin effects; OTHER ANTICONVULSANTS may increase or decrease phenytoin levels; phenytoin may decrease absorption and increase metabolism of ORAL ANTICOAGULANTS; phenytoin increases metabolism of CORTICOSTEROIDS, ORAL CONTRACEPTIVES, and **nisoldipine,** decreasing their effectiveness; **amiodarone, chloramphenicol, omeprazole,** and **ticlopidine** increase phenytoin levels; ANTITUBERCULOSIS AGENTS decrease phenytoin levels. Closely monitor if used with ANTIRETROVIRALS. May impact serum concentrations of other medications metabolized by CYP3A4. **Food: Folic acid, calcium,** and **vitamin D** absorption may be decreased by phenytoin; phenytoin absorption may be decreased by enteral nutrition supplements. **Herbal: Ginkgo** may decrease anticonvulsant effectiveness.

PHARMACOKINETICS

Absorption: Completely from GI tract. **Peak:** 1.5–3 h prompt release; 4–12 h sustained release. **Distribution:** 95% protein bound; crosses placenta; small amount in breast milk. **Metabolism:** Oxidized in liver to inactive metabolites; induces CYP 3A4. **Elimination:** By kidneys. **Half-Life:** 22 h.

NURSING IMPLICATIONS

Black Box Warning

Phenytoin has been associated with severe adverse cardiovascular effects when administered too rapidly.

Assessment & Drug Effects

- Monitor infusion site closely as extravasation may cause tissue necrosis.
- Continuously monitor vital signs and symptoms during IV infusion and for an hour afterward. Watch for respiratory depression. Constant observation and a cardiac monitor are necessary with older adults or patients with cardiac disease. Margin between toxic and therapeutic IV doses is relatively small.
- Be aware of therapeutic serum concentration: 10–20 mcg/mL; toxic level: 30–50 mcg/mL; lethal level: 100 mcg/mL. Steady-state therapeutic levels are not achieved for at least 7–10 days.
- Observe patient closely for neurologic adverse effects following IV administration.
- Monitor for gingival hyperplasia, which appears most commonly in children and adolescents and never occurs in patients without teeth.
- Make sure patients on prolonged therapy have adequate intake of vitamin D-containing foods and sufficient exposure to sunlight.
- Monitor diabetics for loss of glycemic control.
- Monitor for S&S of hypocalcemia (see Appendix E), especially in patients receiving other anticonvulsants concurrently, as well as those who are inactive, have limited exposure to sun, or whose dietary intake is inadequate.
- Observe for symptoms of folic acid deficiency: Neuropathy, mental dysfunction.
- Be alert to symptoms of hypomagnesemia (see Appendix E); neuromuscular symptoms: Tetany, positive Chvostek's and Trousseau's signs, seizures, tremors, ataxia, vertigo, nystagmus, muscular fasciculations.
- Monitor lab tests: Periodic serum phenytoin concentration, CBC, LFTs.

P

Patient & Family Education

- Be aware that drug may make urine pink or red to red-brown.
- Report symptoms of fatigue, dry skin, deepening voice when receiving long-term therapy because phenytoin can unmask a low thyroid reserve.
- Do not alter prescribed drug regimen. Stopping drug abruptly may precipitate seizures and status epilepticus.
- Do not request/accept change in drug brand when refilling prescription without consulting prescriber.
- Understand the effects of alcohol: Alcohol intake may increase phenytoin serum levels, leading to phenytoin toxicity.
- Discontinue drug immediately if a measles-like skin rash or jaundice appears and notify prescriber.
- Be aware that influenza vaccine during phenytoin treatment may increase seizure activity. Consult prescriber.

PHYSOSTIGMINE SALICYLATE

(fi-zoe-stig'meen)

Classification:
CHOLINESTERASE INHIBITOR
Therapeutic: ANTICHOLINERGIC
ANTIDOTE, CHOLINESTERASE
INHIBITOR
Prototype: Neostigmine

AVAILABILITY Solution for injection

ACTION & THERAPEUTIC EFFECT
Inhibits the destructive action of acetylcholinesterase and thereby prolongs and exaggerates the effect of the acetylcholine on the skeletal muscle, GI tract and within the CNS. *Effective in reversing anticholinergic toxicity.*

USES To reverse anticholinergic toxicity.

CONTRAINDICATIONS Asthma; DM; gangrene, cardiovascular disease; mechanical obstruction of intestinal or urogenital tract; peptic ulcer disease; asthma; any vagotonic state; closed-angle glaucoma; secondary glaucoma; inflammatory disease of iris or ciliary body; lactation.

CAUTIOUS USE Epilepsy; parkinsonism; bradycardia; hyperthyroidism; seizure disorders; hypotension; pregnancy (category C); children.

ROUTE & DOSAGE

Reversal of Anticholinergic Effects

Adult: **IM/IV** 0.5–2 mg (IV not faster than 1 mg/min), repeat as needed
Child: **IV** 0.02 mg/kg/dose, may repeat q5–10min (max total dose: 2 mg)

ADMINISTRATION

- Use only clear, colorless solutions. Redtinted solution indicates oxidation, and such solutions should be discarded.

Intramuscular
- Give undiluted.

Intravenous
Note: Verify correct rate of IV injection for infants or children with prescriber.

PREPARE: Direct: Give undiluted.
ADMINISTER: Direct for Adult: Give slowly at a rate of no more than 1 mg/min. Rapid administration and overdosage can cause a cholinergic crisis. **Direct for Child:** Give 0.5 mg or fraction

Common adverse effects in *italic*; life-threatening effects <u>underlined</u>; generic names in **bold**; classifications in SMALL CAPS; ♣ Canadian drug name; ○ Prototype drug; ⚠ Alert

thereof over at least 1 min. ▪ Rapid administration and overdosage can cause a cholinergic crisis.

INCOMPATIBILITIES: **Solution/additive: Phenytoin. Y-site: Dobutamine.**

ADVERSE EFFECTS CV: Irregular pulse, palpitations, bradycardia, rise in BP. **Respiratory:** Dyspnea, bronchospasm, respiratory paralysis, pulmonary edema. **CNS:** Restlessness, hallucinations, twitching, tremors, *sweating,* weakness, ataxia, convulsions, collapse. **HEENT:** Miosis, *lacrimation,* rhinorrhea. **GI:** *Nausea, vomiting, epigastric pain, diarrhea, salivation.* **GU:** Involuntary urination or defecation. **Other:** *Sweating,* cholinergic crisis (acute toxicity), hyperactivity, respiratory distress, convulsions.

INTERACTIONS Drug: Antagonizes effects of **echothiophate, isofluorphate.**

PHARMACOKINETICS Absorption: Readily from mucous membranes, muscle, subcutaneous tissue; 10–12% absorbed from GI tract. **Onset:** 3–8 min IM/IV. **Duration:** 0.5–5 h IM/IV. **Distribution:** Crosses blood–brain barrier. **Metabolism:** In plasma by cholinesterase. **Elimination:** Small amounts in urine. **Half-Life:** 15–40 min.

NURSING IMPLICATIONS

Assessment & Drug Effects

▪ Monitor vital signs and state of consciousness closely in patients receiving drug for atropine poisoning. Since physostigmine is usually rapidly eliminated, patient can lapse into delirium and coma within 1 to 2 h; repeat doses may be required.

▪ Monitor closely for adverse effects related to CNS and for signs of sensitivity to physostigmine. Have atropine sulfate readily available for clinical emergency.

▪ Discontinue parenteral or oral drug if following symptoms arise: Excessive salivation, emesis, frequent urination, or diarrhea.

▪ Eliminate excessive sweating or nausea with dose reduction.

PHYTONADIONE (VITAMIN K₁)

(fye-toe-na-dye'one)

Mephyton

Classification: VITAMIN K; ANTIDOTE

Therapeutic: VITAMIN K; ANTIDOTE

AVAILABILITY Tablet; solution for injection

ACTION & *THERAPEUTIC EFFECT* Fat-soluble substance chemically identical to and with similar activity as naturally occurring vitamin K. Vitamin K is essential for hepatic biosynthesis of blood clotting Factors II, VII, IX, and X. *Promotes liver synthesis of clotting factors.*

USES Drug of choice as antidote for overdosage of coumarin and indandione oral anticoagulants. Also reverses hypoprothrombinemia secondary to administration of oral antibiotics, quinidine, quinine, salicylates, sulfonamides, excessive vitamin A, and secondary to inadequate absorption and synthesis of vitamin K (as in obstructive jaundice, biliary fistula, ulcerative colitis, intestinal resection, prolonged hyperalimentation). Also prophylaxis of and therapy for neonatal hemorrhagic disease.

P

CONTRAINDICATIONS
Hypersensitivity to phytonadione, benzyl alcohol, or castor oil; severe liver disease.

CAUTIOUS USE
Biliary tract disease, obstructive jaundice, pregnancy (category C). **IV:** Older adults.

ROUTE & DOSAGE

Anticoagulant Overdose
Adult: **PO/Subcutaneous/IM** 2.5–10 mg; rarely up to 50 mg/day, may repeat parenteral dose after 6–8 h if needed or PO dose after 12–24 h; **IV** Emergency only: 10–15 mg at a rate of 1 mg/min or less, may be repeated in 4 h if bleeding continues

Hemorrhagic Disease of Newborns
Infant: **IM/Subcutaneous** 0.5–1 mg immediately after delivery, may repeat in 6–8 h if necessary

Other Prothrombin Deficiencies
Adult: **IM/Subcutaneous/IV** 2–25 mg
Child/Infant: **IM/Subcutaneous/ IV** 0.5–5 mg

ADMINISTRATION
Oral
- Bile salts must be given with tablets if patient has deficient bile production.
- Store in tightly closed container and protect from light. Vitamin K is rapidly degraded by light.

Intramuscular/Subcutaneous
- Subcutaneous route is preferred. IM route has been associated with severe reactions.

- Apply gentle pressure to site following injection. Swelling (internal bleeding) and pain sometimes occur with injection.

Intravenous
Note: Reserve IV route only for emergencies.
PREPARE: **Direct:** Dilute a single dose in 10 mL D5W, NS, or D5/NS. ∎ Protect infusion solution from light.
ADMINISTER: **Direct:** Give solution immediately after dilution at a rate not to exceed 1 mg/min.
INCOMPATIBILITIES: **Solution/ additive: Ascorbic acid, cephalothin, dobutamine, doxycycline, magnesium sulfate, minocycline, phenobarbital, vancomycin, warfarin. Y-site: Dantrolene, diazepam.**

- Protect infusion solution from light by wrapping container with aluminum foil or other opaque material. ∎ Discard unused solution and contents in open ampule.

ADVERSE EFFECTS
Respiratory: Bronchospasm, dyspnea, sensation of chest constriction, respiratory arrest. **CNS:** Headache (after oral dose), brain damage, death. **HEENT:** Peculiar taste sensation. **Endocrine:** Hyperbilirubinemia, kernicterus. **Skin:** Pain at injection site, hematoma, and nodule formation, erythematous skin eruptions (with repeated injections). **GI:** Gastric upset. **Hematologic:** Paradoxic hypoprothrombinemia (patients with severe liver disease), severe hemolytic anemia. **Other:** Hypersensitivity or anaphylaxis-like reaction: Facial flushing, cramplike pains, convulsive movements, chills, fever, diaphoresis, weakness, dizziness, shock, cardiac arrest.

Common adverse effects in *italic;* life-threatening effects underlined; generic names in **bold;** classifications in SMALL CAPS; ✤ Canadian drug name; ⊙ Prototype drug; ⚠ Alert

DIAGNOSTIC TEST INTERFERENCE

Falsely elevated **urine steroids** (by modifications of **Reddy, Jenkins, Thorn procedure**).

INTERACTIONS Drug:

Antagonizes effects of **warfarin; cholestyramine, colestipol, mineral oil** decrease absorption of oral phytonadione.

PHARMACOKINETICS Absorption:

Readily from intestinal lymph if bile is present. **Onset:** 6–12 h PO; 1–2 h IM/Subcutaneous; 15 min IV. **Peak:** Hemorrhage usually controlled within 3–8 h; normal prothrombin time may be obtained in 12–14 h after administration. **Distribution:** Concentrates briefly in liver after absorption; crosses placenta; distributed into breast milk. **Metabolism:** Rapidly in liver. **Elimination:** In urine and bile.

NURSING IMPLICATIONS

Black Box Warning

Phytonadione has been associated with severe reactions (resembling hypersensitivity or anaphylaxis) during and immediately after IV and IM administration.

Assessment & Drug Effects

- Monitor patient constantly. Severe reactions, including fatalities, have occurred during and immediately after IV and IM injection (see ADVERSE EFFECTS).
- Frequency, dose, and therapy duration are guided by PT/INR clinical response.
- Monitor therapeutic effectiveness which is indicated by shortened PT, INR, bleeding, and clotting times, as well as decreased hemorrhagic tendencies.

- Be aware that patients on large doses may develop temporary resistance to coumarin-type anticoagulants. If oral anticoagulant is reinstituted, larger than former doses may be needed. Some patients may require change to heparin.
- Monitor lab tests: Baseline and frequent PT.

Patient & Family Education

- Maintain consistency in diet and avoid significant increases in daily intake of vitamin K-rich foods when drug regimen is stabilized. Know sources rich in vitamin K: Asparagus, broccoli, cabbage, lettuce, turnip greens, pork or beef liver, green tea, spinach, watercress, and tomatoes.

PILOCARPINE HYDROCHLORIDE ⊙

PILOCARPINE NITRATE

(pye-loe-kar′peen)

Adsorbocarpine, Isopto Carpine, Minims Pilocarpine ◆, Miocarpine ◆, Ocusert, Pilo, Pilocar, Salagen

Classification: EYE PREPARATION; MIOTIC (ANTIGLAUCOMA); DIRECT-ACTING CHOLINERGIC

Therapeutic: ANTIGLAUCOMA

AVAILABILITY Ophthalmic solution; ophthalmic gel; ocular insert; tablet

ACTION & THERAPEUTIC EFFECT

In open-angle glaucoma, pilocarpine causes contraction of the ciliary muscle, increasing the outflow of aqueous humor, which reduces intraocular pressure (IOP). In closed-angle glaucoma, it induces miosis by opening the angle of the anterior chamber of the eye, through which aqueous humor exits. *Decrease in IOP results from stimulation of ciliary and papillary sphincter muscles, thus facilitating outflow of aqueous humor.*

USES Open-angle and angle-closure glaucomas; to reduce IOP and to protect the lens during surgery and laser iridotomy; to counteract effects of mydriatics and cycloplegics following surgery or ophthalmoscopic examination; to treat xerostomia.

CONTRAINDICATIONS Secondary glaucoma, acute iritis, acute inflammatory disease of anterior segment of eye; uncontrolled asthma; lactation. **Ocular therapeutic system:** Not used in acute infectious conjunctivitis, keratitis, retinal detachment, or when intense miosis is required, or with contact lens use.

CAUTIOUS USE Bronchial asthma; biliary tract disease; COPD; hypertension; pregnancy (category C).

ROUTE & DOSAGE

Acute Glaucoma

Adult/Child: **Ophthalmic** 1 drop of 1–2% solution in affected eye q5–10min for 3–6 doses, then 1 drop q1–3h until IOP is reduced

Chronic Glaucoma

Adult/Child: **Ophthalmic** 1 drop of 0.5–4% solution in affected eye q4–12h or 1 ocular system **(Ocusert)** q7days

Miotic

Adult/Child: **Ophthalmic** 1 drop of 1% solution in affected eye

Xerostomia

Adult: **PO** 5 mg tid, may increase up to 10 mg tid

ADMINISTRATION

Oral

- Give with a full glass of water, if not contraindicated.

Instillation

- Note: During acute phase, prescriber may prescribe instillation of drug into unaffected eye to prevent bilateral attack of acute glaucoma.
- Apply gentle digital pressure to periphery of nasolacrimal drainage system for 1–2 min immediately after instillation of drops to prevent delivery of drug to nasal mucosa and general circulation.

ADVERSE EFFECTS CV: Tachycardia. **Respiratory:** Bronchospasm, rhinitis. **CNS:** Oral (asthenia, headaches, dizziness, chills). **HEENT:** Ciliary spasm with brow ache, twitching of eyelids, eye pain with change in eye focus, miosis, *diminished vision in poorly illuminated areas,* blurred vision, reduced visual acuity, sensitivity, contact allergy, lacrimation, follicular conjunctivitis, conjunctival irritation, cataract, <u>retinal detachment</u>. **GI:** *Nausea,* vomiting, abdominal cramps, diarrhea, epigastric distress, *salivation.* **Other:** Tremors, *increased sweating,* urinary frequency.

INTERACTIONS Drug: The actions of pilocarpine and **carbachol** are additive when used concomitantly. Oral form may cause conduction disturbances with BETA-BLOCKERS. Antagonizes the effects of concurrent ANTICHOLINERGIC DRUGS (e.g., **atropine, ipratropium**). **Food:** High-fat meal decreases absorption of pilocarpine.

PHARMACOKINETICS Absorption: Topical penetrates cornea

rapidly; readily absorbed from GI tract. **Onset:** Miosis 10–30 min; IOP reduction 60 min; salivary stimulation 20 min. **Peak:** Miosis 30 min; IOP reduction 75 min; salivary stimulation 60 min. **Duration:** Miosis 4–8 h; IOP reduction 4–14 h (7 days with Ocusert); salivary stimulation 3–5 h. **Metabolism:** Inactivated at neuronal synapses and in plasma. **Elimination:** In urine. **Half-Life:** 0.76–1.35 h.

NURSING IMPLICATIONS

Assessment & Drug Effects

- Be aware that hourly tonometric tests may be done during early treatment because drug may cause an initial transitory increase in IOP.
- Monitor changes in visual acuity.
- Monitor for adverse effects. Brow pain and myopia tend to be more prominent in younger patients and generally disappear with continued use of drug.

Patient & Family Education

- Understand that therapy for glaucoma is prolonged and that adherence to established regimen is crucial to prevent blindness.
- Do not drive or engage in potentially hazardous activities until vision clears. Drug causes blurred vision and difficulty in focusing.
- Discontinue medication if symptoms of irritation or sensitization persist and report to prescriber.

PIMAVANSERIN

(pim-a-van'ser-in)

Nuplazid

Classification: ATYPICAL ANTIPSYCHOTIC
Therapeutic: ANTIPSYCHOTIC
Prototype: Clozapine

AVAILABILITY Tablets

ACTION & *THERAPEUTIC EFFECT*

An inverse agonist and antagonist with a high binding affinity for the serotonin 5-HT$_{2A}$ receptor and a lower binding affinity for the 5-HT$_{2C}$ receptor.

USES Treatment of hallucinations and delusions associated with Parkinson's disease.

CONTRAINDICATIONS Avoid use in patients with cardiac disease or other risk factors for prolonged QT intervals, torsade de pointes, and/or sudden death such as cardiac arrhythmias, congenital long QT syndrome, heart failure, bradycardia, myocardial infarction, hypertension, coronary artery disease, hypomagnesemia, hypokalemia, hypocalcemia, or in patients receiving medications known to prolong the QT interval. Females and elderly patients are also at risk for QT prolongation. Pimavanserin is not recommended for patients with severe renal impairment (CrCl less than 30 mL/min), including renal failure. Not recommended for patients with mild, moderate or severe hepatic disease or impairment. Drug has not been evaluated in this population. Not approved for patients with dementia, related psychosis and delusions associated with Parkinson's disease.

CAUTIOUS USE Cautious use for older adults. No data on use in pregnant or lactating women.

ROUTE & DOSAGE

Hallucinations and Delusions

Adult: **PO** 34 mg once daily

Hepatic Impairment Dosage Adjustment

Not recommended in patients with hepatic impairment

Renal Impairment Dosage Adjustment

CrCl less than 30 mL/min: Not recommended

Concomitant Use with CYP3A4 Inhibitors Dosage Adjustment

Decrease dose to 17 mg once daily if used with a strong CYP3A4 inhibitor

ADMINISTRATION

Oral

- May be administered without regard to food.
- Store at 15°–30° C (59°–86° F).

ADVERSE EFFECTS CV: QT interval prolongation. **CNS:** Confusional state, hallucinations. **GI:** Constipation, nausea. **Other:** Gait disturbance, peripheral edema.

INTERACTIONS Drug: Concomitant use of drugs that prolong the QT interval (e.g., **amiodarone, chlorpromazine, disopyramide, gatifloxacin, moxifloxacin, procainamide, quinidine, sotalol, thioridazine, ziprasidone**) may be additive to the QT effects of pimavanserin and increase the risk of cardiac arrhythmia. Concomitant use with a strong CYP3A4 inhibitor (e.g., **clarithromycin, indinavir, itraconazole, ketoconazole**) increases the levels of pimavanserin. Concomitant use with a strong CYP3A4 inducer (e.g., **carbamazepine, phenytoin, rifampin**) may decrease the levels of pimavanserin. **Herbal: St. John's wort** may decrease the levels of pimavanserin.

PHARMACOKINETICS Peak: 6 h. **Distribution:** 95% plasma protein bound. **Metabolism:** Hepatic oxidation to active and inactive metabolites. **Elimination:** Renal and fecal. **Half-Life:** 57 h.

NURSING IMPLICATIONS

Assessment & Drug Effects

- Monitor ECG: Prolonged QT interval has been reported.
- Monitor vital signs.
- Assess for peripheral edema and perform daily weights.
- Assess cognition and gait, patient at risk for confusion, hallucinations, and altered gait that impact safety.
- Monitor lab tests: LFTs, serum creatinine, and electrolytes.

Patient & Family Education

- No data on use in pregnant women; contraceptive measures should be taken.
- Check with provider before taking any over the counter medication and make sure to tell healthcare providers the patient is currently taking this medication.
- Avoid drinking alcohol while taking this medication.
- Report any swelling noted in hands or feet.
- Report a fast or pounding heartbeat, chest pain, confusion, or severe dizziness.

PIMECROLIMUS

(pim-e-cro-lim'us)
Elidel
Classification: BIOLOGIC RESPONSE MODIFIER; IMMUNOMODULATOR
Therapeutic: IMMUNOSUPPRESSANT; ANTI-INFLAMMATORY
Prototype: Cyclosporine

AVAILABILITY Cream

ACTION & *THERAPEUTIC EFFECT*
Selectively inhibits inflammatory action of skin cells by blocking T-cell activation and cytokine release. It appears to inhibit the production of IL-2, IL-4, IL-10, and interferon gamma in T-cells. *Produces significant anti-inflammatory activity without evidence of skin atrophy.*

USES Shortterm intermittent treatment of mild to moderate atopic dermatitis, eczema.

CONTRAINDICATIONS Hypersensitivity to pimecrolimus or components in the cream; Netherton's syndrome; immunocompromised individuals; application to active cutaneous viral infection; occlusive dressing; artificial or natural sunlight (UV) exposure; continuous long-term use; lactation; children younger than 2 y.

CAUTIOUS USE Infection at topical treatment sites; history of untoward effects with topical cyclosporine or tacrolimus; skin papillomas; immunocompromised patients; pregnancy (category C).

ROUTE & DOSAGE

Atopic Dermatitis

Adult/Adolescent/Child (older than 2 y): **Topical**
Apply thin layer to affected skin bid (avoid continuous long-term use)

ADMINISTRATION

Topical
- Do not apply to any skin surface that appears to be infected.
- Limit application to areas of involvement with atopic dermatitis.

ADVERSE EFFECTS Respiratory:
Sore throat, *upper respiratory infection, cough,* nasal congestion, asthma exacerbation, rhinitis, epistaxis. **CNS:** Headache. **HEENT:** Ear infection, earache, conjunctivitis. **Skin:** *Burning,* irritation, pruritus, skin infection, impetigo, folliculitis, skin papilloma, herpes simplex dermatitis, urticaria, acne. **GI:** Gastroenteritis, abdominal pain, nausea, vomiting, diarrhea, constipation. **Other:** Flu-like symptoms, infections, fever, increased risk of cancer.

PHARMACOKINETICS Absorption: Minimal through intact skin. **Metabolism:** No evidence of skin-mediated metabolism, metabolized in liver by CYP3A4. **Elimination:** Primarily in feces.

NURSING IMPLICATIONS

Assessment & Drug Effects
- Assess for and report persistent skin irritation that develops following application of the cream and lasts for more than 1 wk.

Patient & Family Education
- Minimize exposure of treated area to natural or artificial sunlight.
- Immediately report a new or changed skin lesion to the prescriber.
- Stop topical application once signs of dermatitis have disappeared. Resume application at the first sign of recurrence.
- Continuous, long-term use of this cream is not recommended.
- Wash hands thoroughly after application if hands are not the treatment sites.
- Report any significant skin irritation that results from application of the cream.

P

PIMOZIDE
(pi'moe-zide)
Classification: ANTIPSYCHOTIC
Therapeutic: ANTIPSYCHOTIC;
CNS DOPAMINERGIC RECEPTOR
ANTAGONIST
Prototype: Haloperidol

AVAILABILITY Tablet

ACTION & *THERAPEUTIC EFFECT*
Potent central dopamine antagonist
that alters release and turnover of
central dopamine stores. Blockade
of CNS dopaminergic receptors
results in suppression of the motor
and phonic tics that characterize
Tourette's disorder. *Effective in suppressing motor and phonic tics associated with Tourette's disorder.*

USES Tourette's syndrome resistant
to standard therapy.

UNLABELED USES Delusional
parasitosis.

CONTRAINDICATIONS Hypersensitivity to pimozide or any
component of the formulation;
treatment of simple tics other than
those associated with Tourette's
disorder; drug-induced tics; history of cardiac dysrhythmias and
conditions marked by prolonged
QT syndrome, patient taking drugs
that may prolong QT interval
(e.g., quinidine); congenital heart
defects; cardiac arrhythmias; torsade de pointes; electrolyte imbalance; Parkinson's disease; NMS;
severe toxic CNS depression or
coma states; lactation.

CAUTIOUS USE Kidney and
liver dysfunction; cardiac disease;
glaucoma; BPH; renal or hepatic
impairment; urinary retention;

low WBC; seizure disorders; older
adults; pregnancy (adverse effects
observed in some animal reproduction studies). Safe use in children
younger than 12 y is not known.

ROUTE & DOSAGE

Tourette's Disorder
Adult: **PO** 1–2 mg/day in divided
doses, gradually increase dose
every other day up to 0.2 mg/
kg/day or 10 mg/day in divided
doses (max: 0.2 mg/kg/day or
10 mg/day)
Adolescent: **PO** 0.05 mg/kg/day
at bedtime, gradually increase as
needed (max: 0.2 mg/kg/day or
10 mg, whichever is less)

**Pharmacogenetic dosage
adjustment**
CYP2D6 poor metabolizers
should be dose titrated in
≥14-day increments; max dose
4 mg/day

ADMINISTRATION
Oral
- May be taken with or without
  food; preferable to administer
  dose at bedtime.
- Increase drug dose gradually,
  usually over 1–3 wk, until maintenance dose is reached.
- Follow regimen prescribed by
  prescriber for withdrawal: Usually slow, gradual over
  a period of days or weeks (drug
  has a long half-life). Sudden withdrawal may cause reemergence
  of original symptoms (motor and
  phonic tics) and of neuromuscular adverse effects of the drug.

ADVERSE EFFECTS CNS: Headache, *sedation, drowsiness,*
insomnia, depression, akathisia,

---

behavioural changes, rigidity, nervousness. **HEENT:** Visual disturbances, photophobia, decreased accommodation, blurred vision, cataracts. **Skin:** Rash. **GI:** Increased thirst, increased salivation, diarrhea, dysgeusia, increased appetite, anorexia, *dry mouth, constipation.* **GU:** Impotence, nocturia. **Musculoskeletal:** Akinesia, weakness, muscle rigidity, stooped posture. **Other:** Speech disorder handwriting changes, tardive dyskinesia.

INTERACTIONS Drug: Alcohol and other CNS DEPRESSANTS increase CNS depression; CYP2D6 INHIBITORS increase concentration of pimozide; CYP3A4 INHIBITORS increase concentration of pimozide; ANTICHOLINERGIC AGENTS (e.g., TRICYCLIC ANTIDEPRESSANTS, **atropine**) increase anticholinergic effects; medications that increase QT interval, PHENOTHIAZINES, TRICYCLIC ANTIDEPRESSANTS, ANTIARRHYTHMICS, MACROLIDE ANTIBIOTICS, AZOLE ANTIFUNGALS, PROTEASE INHIBITORS, **nefazodone, sertraline, zileuton** increase risk of arrhythmias and heart block; pimozide antagonizes effects of ANTICONVULSANTS—there is loss of seizure control; increases risk of ulcer formation with potassium; SSRIS increase the risk of adverse effects. **Food: Grapefruit juice** (greater than 1 qt/day) may increase plasma concentrations and adverse effects.

PHARMACOKINETICS Absorption: Slowly and variably from GI tract (40–50% absorbed). **Peak:** 6–8 h. **Metabolism:** In liver (by CYP3A4, CYP2D6, CYP1A2). **Elimination:** 80–85% in urine, 15–20% in feces.

NURSING IMPLICATIONS

Note: See haloperidol for additional nursing implications.

Assessment & Drug Effects

- Obtain ECG baseline data at beginning of therapy and check periodically, especially during dosage adjustments.
- Notify prescriber immediately for widening or prolongation of the QT interval, which suggests developing cardiotoxicity.
- Risk of tardive dyskinesia appears to be greatest in women, older adults, and those on high-dose therapy.
- Be aware that extrapyramidal reactions often appear within the first few days of therapy, are dose-related, and usually occur when dose is high.
- Be aware that anticholinergic effects (dry mouth, constipation) may increase as dose is increased.
- Monitor mental status, vital signs, weight, height, BMI, waist circumference.
- Annual ocular examination.
- Monitor lab values: Baseline and periodic CBC, electrolytes, liver function fasting plasma glucose level/HbA1c, fasting lipid panel.

Patient & Family Education

- Adhere to established drug regimen (i.e., do not change dose or intervals and discontinue only with prescriber's guidance).
- Use measures to relieve dry mouth (frequent rinsing with water, saliva substitute, increased fluid intake) and constipation (increased dietary fiber, drink 6–8 glasses of water daily).
- Do not drive or engage in potentially hazardous activities because drug-caused hand tremors, drowsiness, and blurred vision may impair alertness and abilities.
- Pseudoparkinsonism symptoms are usually mild and reversible with dose adjustment.

- Be alert to the earliest symptom of tardive dyskinesia ("flycatching"—an involuntary movement of the tongue), and report promptly to the prescriber.
- Return to prescriber for periodic assessments of therapy benefit and cardiac status.
- Understand dangers of ingesting alcohol to prevent augmenting CNS depressant effects of pimozide.

PINDOLOL
(pin'doe-lole)

Classification:
BETA-ADRENERGIC RECEPTOR
ANTAGONIST; ANTIHYPERTENSIVE
Therapeutic: ANTIHYPERTENSIVE;
ANTIANGINAL
Prototype: Propranolol

AVAILABILITY Tablet

ACTION & *THERAPEUTIC EFFECT*
Competitively blocks beta-adrenergic receptors primarily in myocardium, and beta receptors within smooth muscle. *Lowers blood pressure by decreasing peripheral vascular resistance. Exerts vasodilation as well as hypotensive effects.*

USES Management of hypertension.

UNLABELED USES Angina, traumatic brain injury.

CONTRAINDICATIONS Bronchospastic diseases, asthma; cardiogenic shock, AV block, second and third degree heart block; severe bradycardia; overt cardiac failure; pulmonary failure; abrupt withdrawal; lactation.

CAUTIOUS USE Nonallergic bronchospasm; COPD; CHF; angina; history of cardiac failure that is well controlled; major surgery; DM; hyperthyroidism; MG; impaired liver and kidney function; pregnancy (category B). Safety and efficacy in children not established.

ROUTE & DOSAGE

Hypertension
Adult: **PO** 5 mg bid, may increase by 10 mg/day q3–4wk if needed up (max: 60 mg/day in 2–3 divided doses)
Geriatric: **PO** Start with 5 mg daily

ADMINISTRATION

Oral
- Give drug at same time of day each day with respect to time of food intake for most predictable results.
- Withdraw or discontinue treatment gradually over a period of 1–2 wk.

ADVERSE EFFECTS CV: *Bradycardia,* hypotension, CHF. **Respiratory:** Bronchospasm, pulmonary edema, dyspnea. **CNS:** *Fatigue,* dizziness, insomnia, drowsiness, confusion, fainting, decreased libido. **Endocrine:** Hypoglycemia (may mask symptoms of a hypoglycemic reaction). **GI:** Nausea, *diarrhea, constipation,* flatulence. **GU:** Impotence. **Hematologic:** Agranulocytosis. **Other:** Back or joint pain. Sensitivity reactions seen as antinuclear antibodies (ANA) (10–30% of patients).

INTERACTIONS Drug: DIURETICS and other HYPOTENSIVE AGENTS increase hypotensive effect; effects of **albuterol, metaproterenol, terbutaline, pirbuterol,** and **pindolol** antagonized; NSAIDS blunt hypotensive effect; decreases hypoglycemic effect of **glyburide; amiodarone** increases risk of bradycardia and sinus arrest.

PHARMACOKINETICS **Absorption:** Rapidly from GI tract; 50–95% reaches systemic circulation (first pass metabolism). **Onset:** 3 h. **Peak:** 1–2 h. **Duration:** 24 h. **Distribution:** Distributed into breast milk. **Metabolism:** 40–60% in liver. **Elimination:** In urine. **Half-Life:** 3–4 h.

NURSING IMPLICATIONS

Assessment & Drug Effects
- Monitor HR and BP. Report bradycardia and hypotension. Dosage adjustment may be indicated.
- Note: Hypotensive effect may begin within 7 days but is not at maximum therapeutically until about 2 wk after beginning of treatment.

Patient & Family Education
- Pindolol masks the dizziness and sweating symptoms of hypoglycemia. Monitor blood glucose for loss of glycemic control.
- Adhere to the prescribed drug regimen; if a change is desired, consult prescriber first. Abrupt withdrawal of drug might precipitate a thyroid crisis in a patient with hyperthyroidism, and angina in the patient with ischemic heart disease, leading to an MI.

PIOGLITAZONE HYDROCHLORIDE
(pi-o-glit'a-zone)
Actos
Classification: ANTIDIABETIC; THIAZOLIDINEDIONE (GLITAZONE)
Therapeutic: ANTIDIABETIC; INSULIN SENSITIZER
Prototype: Rosiglitazone maleate

AVAILABILITY Tablet

ACTION & *THERAPEUTIC EFFECT*
Decreases hepatic glucose output and increases insulin-dependent muscle glucose uptake in skeletal muscle and adipose tissue. Improves glycemic control in noninsulindependent diabetics (type 2) by enhancing insulin sensitivity of cells without stimulating pancreatic insulin secretion. *Improves glycemic control as indicated by improved blood glucose levels and decreased HbA1C.*

USES Adjunct to diet in the treatment of type 2 diabetes mellitus.

CONTRAINDICATIONS Hypersensitivity to pioglitazone, rosiglitazone; type 1 diabetes, or treatment of DKA; New York Heart Association (NYHA) Class III or IV heart failure; active liver disease or ALT levels greater than 2.5 × NL; jaundice; fracture risk factors; lactation.

CAUTIOUS USE Liver dysfunction; cardiovascular disease; hypertension, CHF, anemia, edema; osteoporosis; history of bladder cancer; older adults; pregnancy (category C). Safety and efficacy in children younger than 18 y not recommended.

ROUTE & DOSAGE

Type 2 Diabetes Mellitus

Adult: **PO** 15–30 mg once daily (max: 45 mg daily)

Disease State Dosage Adjustment

Patients with NHYA Class I or II heart failure: 15 mg once daily

Drug Interaction Dosage Adjustment

If used with gemfibrozil (max: 15 mg)

P

ADMINISTRATION

Oral

- Give without regard to food.
- Do not initiate therapy if baseline serum ALT greater than 2.5 × normal.
- Store at 15°–30° C (59°–86° F) in tightly closed container; protect from humidity and moisture.

ADVERSE EFFECTS CV: *Edema.* **Respiratory:** Upper respiratory infection. **CNS:** Headache. **Endocrine:** Hypoglycemia.

INTERACTIONS Drug: Pioglitazone may decrease serum levels of ORAL CONTRACEPTIVES; **ketoconazole, gemfibrozil, mifepristone** may increase serum levels of **pioglitazone.** Increased risk of hypoglycemia when used with insulin or ANTIDIABETIC medications. BILE ACID SEQUESTRANTS, **bosentan** may decrease effect. Serum concentrations may be increased by CYP2C8 inhibitors. **Herbal: Garlic, ginseng** may potentiate hypoglycemic effects.

PHARMACOKINETICS Absorption: Rapidly absorbed. **Peak:** 2 h; steady state concentrations within 7 days. **Duration:** 24 h. **Distribution:** Greater than 99% protein bound. **Metabolism:** In liver to active metabolites. **Elimination:** Primarily in bile and feces. **Half-Life:** 16–24 h.

NURSING IMPLICATIONS

Black Box Warning

Pioglitazone has been associated with exacerbation of CHF.

Assessment & Drug Effects

- Monitor for S&S hypoglycemia (possible when insulin/sulfonylureas are coadministered).

- Monitor closely for S&S of CHF or exacerbation of symptoms with preexisting CHF.
- Withhold drug and notify prescriber if ALT greater than 3 × ULN or patient has jaundice.
- Monitor weight and notify prescriber of development of edema.
- Monitor lab tests: Baseline and periodic LFTs; periodic fasting plasma glucose and HbA1C.

Patient & Family Education

- Be aware that resumed ovulation is possible in nonovulating premenopausal women.
- Use or add barrier contraceptive if using hormonal contraception.
- Report immediately to prescriber: Unexplained anorexia, nausea, vomiting, abdominal pain, fatigue, dark urine; or S&S of fluid retention such as weight gain, edema, or activity intolerance.
- Combination therapy: May need adjustment of other antidiabetic drugs to avoid hypoglycemia.
- Learn of and adhere strictly to guidelines for liver function tests. Be sure to have blood tests for liver function periodically.

PIPERACILLIN/ TAZOBACTAM ⓟ

(pi-per′a-cil-lin/taz-o-bac′tam)

Zosyn

Classification: ANTIBIOTIC; EXTENDED SPECTRUM PENICILLIN
Therapeutic: ANTIBIOTIC

AVAILABILITY Solution for injection

ACTION & THERAPEUTIC EFFECT
Tazobactam has little antibacterial activity itself; however, in combination with piperacillin, it extends the spectrum of bacteria that are susceptible to piperacillin. *Two-drug combination has antibiotic activity*

1352

Common adverse effects in *italic*; life-threatening effects underlined; generic names in **bold**; classifications in SMALL CAPS; ✦ Canadian drug name; ⓞ Prototype drug; ⚠ Alert

against an extremely broad spectrum of gram-positive, gram-negative, and anaerobic bacteria.

USES Treatment of moderate to severe appendicitis, uncomplicated and complicated skin and skin structure infections, endometritis, pelvic inflammatory disease, or nosocomial- or community-acquired pneumonia caused by beta-lactamase-producing bacteria.

CONTRAINDICATIONS Hypersensitivity to piperacillin, tazobactam, penicillins; coagulopathy.

CAUTIOUS USE Hypersensitivity to cephalosporins, carbapenem, or betalactamase inhibitors such as clavulanic acid and sulbactam; GI disease, colitis; CF; eczema; kidney failure; complicated urinary tract infections; pregnancy (category B); lactation.

ROUTE & DOSAGE

Moderate to Severe Infections

Adult: **IV** 3.375 g q6h, infused over 30 min, for 7–10 days
Child (younger than 6 mo):
IV 150–300 mg piperacillin/kg/day divided q6–8h; *6 mo or older:* 240 mg piperacillin component/kg/day divided q8h

Nosocomial Pneumonia

Adult: **IV** 4.5 g q6h, infused over 30 min, for 7–10 days

Renal Insufficiency Dosage Adjustment

CrCl 20–40 mL/min: 2.25 g q6h; *less than 20 mL/min:* 2.25 g q8h

Hemodialysis Dosage Adjustment

2.25 g q12h (for nosocomial pneumonia dose q8h); give additional 0.75 g after dialysis session

ADMINISTRATION

Note: Verify correct IV concentration and rate of infusion for administration to infants or children with prescriber.

Intravenous

PREPARE: **Intermittent:** Reconstitute powder with 5 mL of diluent (e.g., D5W, NS) for each 1 g or fraction thereof; shake well until dissolved. ▪ Further dilute to a total of 50 to 150 mL in selected diluent (e.g., NS, sterile water for injection, D5W, dextran 6% in NS, and LR only with solution containing EDTA).

ADMINISTER: **Intermittent:** Give over at least 30 min. ▪ **Do not** administer through a line with another infusion.

INCOMPATIBILITIES: Solution/additive: **Aminoglycosides, lactated Ringer's, albumin, blood products, solutions containing sodium bicarbonate. Y-site: Acyclovir, aminoglycosides, amiodarone, amphotericin B, amphotericin B cholesteryl complex, azithromycin, chlorpromazine, cisatracurium, cisplatin, dacarbazine, daunorubicin, dobutamine, doxorubicin, doxorubicin liposome, doxycycline, droperidol, famotidine, ganciclovir, gatifloxacin, gemcitabine, haloperidol, hydroxyzine, idarubicin, miconazole, minocycline, mitomycin, mitoxantrone, nalbuphine, prochlorperazine, promethazine, streptozocin, vancomycin.**

ADVERSE EFFECTS CNS: Headache, insomnia, fever. **Skin:** Rash, pruritus, hypersensitivity reactions. **GI:** Diarrhea, constipation, nausea, vomiting, dyspepsia, <u>pseudomembranous colitis</u>.

P

INTERACTIONS Drug: May increase risk of bleeding with ANTI-COAGULANTS; **probenecid** decreases elimination of piperacillin.

PHARMACOKINETICS Distribution: Distributes into many tissues, including lung, blister fluid, and bile; crosses placenta; distributed into breast milk. **Metabolism:** In liver. **Elimination:** In urine. **Half-Life:** 0.7–1.2 h.

NURSING IMPLICATIONS

Assessment & Drug Effects
- Obtain history of hypersensitivity to penicillins, cephalosporins, or other drugs prior to administration.
- Monitor patient carefully during the first 30 min after initiation of the infusion for signs of hypersensitivity (see Appendix E).
- Monitor lab tests: Baseline C&S; periodic renal function tests, CBC with differential, PT and PTT, serum electrolytes, and LFTs.

Patient & Family Education
- Report rash, itching, or other signs of hypersensitivity immediately.
- Report loose stools or diarrhea as these may indicate pseudomembranous colitis.

PIROXICAM
(peer-ox'i-kam)
Feldene
Classification: NONNARCOTIC ANALGESIC; NONSTEROIDAL ANTI-INFLAMMATORY DRUG (NSAID)
Therapeutic: ANALGESIC; NSAID; ANTIPYRETIC
Prototype: Ibuprofen

AVAILABILITY Capsule

ACTION & *THERAPEUTIC EFFECT*
Nonsteroidal anti-inflammatory agent that strongly inhibits enzyme cyclooxygenase, both COX1 and COX2, the catalyst of prostaglandin synthesis. Decreased prostaglandin results in anti-inflammatory properties, analgesic and antipyretic effects. *Decreases inflammatory processes in bone-joint disease as well as has analgesic and antipyretic effects.*

USES Acute and long-term relief of mild to moderate pain and for symptomatic treatment of osteoarthritis and rheumatoid arthritis; headache.

CONTRAINDICATIONS Hypersensitivity to NSAIDs or salicylates; hemophilia; active peptic ulcer, GI bleeding; CABG perioperative pain; ST-elevated MI; lactation.

CAUTIOUS USE History of upper GI disease including ulcerative colitis; SLE; kidney dysfunction; hepatic disease; CHF; acute MI; compromised cardiac function; hypertension or other conditions predisposing to fluid retention; renal disease; alcoholism; coagulation disorders; older adults; pregnancy (category C). Safe use in children not established.

ROUTE & DOSAGE

Arthritis, Pain
Adult: **PO** 20 mg daily

ADMINISTRATION
Oral
- Give at the same time every day.
- Give capsule with food or fluid to help reduce GI irritation.
- Dose adjustments should be made on basis of clinical response at

Common adverse effects in *italic;* life-threatening effects <u>underlined</u>; generic names in **bold**; classifications in SMALL CAPS; ♣ Canadian drug name; ◐ Prototype drug; ⚠ Alert

intervals of weeks rather than days in order to prevent over dosage.

- Store in tightly closed container at 15°–30° C (59°–86° F) unless otherwise directed.

ADVERSE EFFECTS CV: Edema.
CNS: Dizziness, headache. **HEENT:** Tinnitus. **Skin:** Pruritis, skin rash. **Hepatic/GI:** Increased liver enzymes, abdominal pain, anorexia, constipation, diarrhea, dyspepsia, gastrointestinal bleeding. **Hematologic:** Anemia, prolonged bleeding time.

DIAGNOSTIC TEST INTERFERENCE
May lead to false-positive *aldosterone/renin ratio.*

INTERACTIONS Drug: ORAL ANTICOAGULANTS, **heparin** may prolong bleeding time; may increase **lithium** toxicity; **alcohol,** NONSTEROIDAL ANTIINFLAMMATORIES increase risk of GI hemorrhage; enhances nephrotoxic effects of **cylcosporine**. Do not use with **cidofovir. Herbal:** Feverfew, garlic, ginger, ginkgo may increase bleeding potential.

PHARMACOKINETICS Absorption: Extensively from GI tract. **Onset:** 1 h analgesia; 7 days for rheumatoid arthritis. **Peak:** 3–5 h analgesia; 2–4 wk antirheumatic. **Duration:** 48–72 h analgesia. **Distribution:** Small amount distributed into breast milk. **Metabolism:** Extensively in liver by (CYP2C9). **Elimination:** Primarily in urine, some in bile (less than 5%). **Half-Life:** 50 h.

NURSING IMPLICATIONS

Black Box Warning

Piroxican has been associated with increased risk of serious, potentially fatal, GI bleeding and cardiovascular events (e.g., MI and CVA); risk may increase with duration of use and may be greater in the older adult and those with risk factors for CV disease.

Assessment & Drug Effects

- Clinical evidence of benefits from drug therapy include pain relief in motion and in rest, reduction in night pain, stiffness, and swelling; increased ROM (range of motion) in all joints.
- Monitor for and report promptly S&S of GI ulceration or bleeding. Significant GI bleeding may occur without prior warning.
- Monitor for and report promptly S&S of CV thrombotic events (i.e., angina, MI, TIA, or stroke).
- Monitor lab tests: Periodic renal function tests, LFTs, CBC, and electrolytes in the older adult and during long-term therapy.

Patient & Family Education

- Do not self-dose with aspirin or other OTC drug without prescriber's advice.
- Do not increase dosage beyond prescribed regimen. Higher than recommended doses are associated with increased incidence of GI irritation and peptic ulcer.
- Incidence of GI bleeding with this drug is relatively high. Report symptoms of GI bleeding (e.g., dark, tarry stools, coffee-colored emesis) or severe gastric pain promptly to prescriber.
- Stop taking drug and report promptly to prescriber if you experience chest pain, shortness of breath, weakness, slurring of speech, or other signs of a cardiac or neurologic problem.
- Be alert to symptoms of drug-induced anemia: Profound fatigue, skin and mucous membrane pallor, lethargy.

P

- Avoid alcohol since it may increase the risk of GI bleeding.
- Be alert to signs of hypoprothrombinemia including bruises, pinpoint rash, unexplained bleeding, nose bleed, blood in urine, when piroxicam is taken concomitantly with an anticoagulant.
- Do not drive or engage in potentially hazardous activities until response to drug is known.
- Drink at least 6–8 full glasses of water daily and report signs of renal insufficiency (see Appendix E) to prescriber because most of drug is excreted by kidneys and impaired kidney function increases danger of toxicity.

PITAVASTATIN CALCIUM

(pit-a-vah-stat'in)
Livalo, Zypitamag
Classification: ANTIHYPERLIPIDEMIC; LIPID-LOWERING AGENT; HMG-COA REDUCTASE INHIBITOR (STATIN)
Therapeutic: ANTILIPEMIC; LIPID-LOWERING AGENT; STATIN
Prototype: Lovastatin

P

AVAILABILITY Tablet

ACTION & *THERAPEUTIC EFFECT*

Pitavastatin is a HMG-CoA reductase inhibitor that reduces plasma cholesterol levels by interfering with the production of cholesterol in the liver. It also promotes removal of LDL and VLDL from plasma. *Effectiveness is measured by decrease in blood level of total cholesterol, LDL cholesterol, and triglycerides and an increase in HDL cholesterol.*

USES Treatment of primary hyperlipidemia and mixed dyslipidemia.

UNLABELED USES Regression of coronary atherosclerosis in patients with acute coronary syndrome (ACS).

CONTRAINDICATIONS Hypersensitivity to pitavastatin; myopathy and rhabdomyolysis; acute renal failure; ESRD not on hemodialysis; active liver disease; large amounts of alcohol; coadministration with cyclosporine; pregnancy (category X); lactation.

CAUTIOUS USE Renal impairment; hepatic impairment; DM; older adults. Safety and efficacy in children not established.

ROUTE & DOSAGE

Hypercholesterolemia, Hyperlipoproteinemia, and/or Hypertriglyceridemia

Adult: **PO** Initially 2 mg once daily; can be adjusted to 1–4 mg once daily

Renal Impairment Dosage Adjustment

CrCl 15 to less than 60 mL/min: Initially, 1 mg once daily; do not exceed 2 mg once daily

ADMINISTRATION

Oral
- May give without regard to meals any time of day.
- Store at 15°–30° C (59°–86° F).

ADVERSE EFFECTS Respiratory: Nasopharyngitis. **CNS:** Headache. **Hepatic/GI:** Increased liver enzymes, constipation. **Musculoskeletal:** Back pain.

INTERACTIONS Drug: Cyclosporine, erythromycin, HIV PROTEASE INHIBITORS, and **rifampin** increase pitavastatin levels. FIBRATES may increase the risk of myopathy and rhabdomyolysis. Combination use with **niacin** may increase the risk of skeletal muscle effects. Do not use with **fusidic acid**.

PHARMACOKINETICS
Absorption: 51% bioavailable. **Peak:** 1 h. **Distribution:** Greater than 99% plasma protein bound. **Metabolism:** In liver. **Elimination:** Primarily fecal (79%) with minor renal (15%) elimination. **Half-Life:** 12 h.

NURSING IMPLICATIONS

Assessment & Drug Effects
- Monitor for and report muscle pain, tenderness, or weakness.
- Withhold drug and notify prescriber for ALT/AST greater than 3 × ULN.
- Monitor lab tests: Lipid profile at baseline, at 4 wk, and periodically thereafter; LFTs at baseline, at 12 wk after initiation or elevation of dose, and periodically thereafter; creatine kinase levels if patient experiences muscle pain.

Patient & Family Education
- Report promptly unexplained muscle pain, tenderness, or weakness.
- Avoid or minimize alcohol consumption while on this drug.
- Use effective contraceptive measures to avoid pregnancy while taking this drug.

PLASMA PROTEIN FRACTION
(plas'ma)
Plasmanate
Classification: PLASMA VOLUME EXPANDER
Therapeutic: PLASMA VOLUME EXPANDER; ALBUMIN
Prototype: Normal serum albumin, human

AVAILABILITY Solution for injection

ACTION & *THERAPEUTIC EFFECT*
Provides plasma proteins that increase colloidal osmotic pressure within the intravascular compartment equal to human plasma. It shifts water from the extravascular tissues back into the intravascular space, thus expanding plasma volume. *Used to maintain cardiac output by expanding plasma volume in the treatment of shock due to various causes.*

USES
Emergency treatment of hypovolemic shock; temporary measure in treatment of blood loss when whole blood is not available.

CONTRAINDICATIONS
Hypersensitivity to albumin; severe anemia; cardiac failure; patients undergoing cardiopulmonary bypass surgery.

CAUTIOUS USE
Patients with low cardiac reserve; absence of albumin deficiency; liver or kidney failure; pregnancy (category C); children.

ROUTE & DOSAGE

Plasma Volume Expansion
Adult: IV 250–500 mL at a maximum rate of 10 mL/min

ADMINISTRATION

Intravenous
Do not use solutions that show a sediment or appear turbid. Do not use solutions that have been frozen.

PREPARE: **IV Infusion:** Give undiluted. ▪ Once container is opened, solution should be used within 4 h because it contains

P

no preservatives. ▪ Discard unused portions.

ADMINISTER: IV Infusion: Rate of infusion and volume of total dose will depend on patient's age, diagnosis, degree of venous and pulmonary congestion, Hct, and Hgb determinations. As with any oncotically active solution, infusion rate should be relatively slow. Range may vary from 1–10 mL/min.

INCOMPATIBILITIES: PROTEIN HYDRO-LYSATES or solutions containing alcohol.

ADVERSE EFFECTS GI: Nausea, vomiting, hypersalivation, headache. **Other:** Tingling, chills, fever, cyanosis, chest tightness, backache, urticaria, erythema, shock (systemic anaphylaxis), circulatory overload, pulmonary edema.

NURSING IMPLICATIONS

Assessment & Drug Effects

- Monitor vital signs (BP and pulse). Frequency depends on patient's condition. Flow rate adjustments are made according to clinical response and BP. Slow or stop infusion if patient suddenly becomes hypotensive.
- Report a widening pulse pressure (difference between systolic and diastolic); it correlates with increase in cardiac output.
- Report changes in I&O ratio and pattern.
- Observe patient closely during and after infusion for signs of hypervolemia or circulatory overload (see Appendix E). Report these symptoms immediately to prescriber.
- Make careful observations of patient who has had either injury or surgery in order to detect bleeding points that failed to bleed at lower BP.

PLAZOMICIN

(pla-zoe-mye'sin)

Zemdri

Classification: ANTIBIOTIC; AMINOGLYCOSIDE

Therapeutic: ANTIBIOTIC

Prototype: Gentamycin

AVAILABILITY Solution for injection

ACTION & *THERAPEUTIC EFFECT*
Broad-spectrum aminoglycoside antibiotic that binds to 30S subunit of bacterial ribosomes, resulting in cell death. *Active against microorganisms, specifically gram-negative bacilli and gram-positive cocci, which may be resistant to other treatment options.*

USES Treatment of complicated urinary tract infections including pyelonephritis.

CONTRAINDICATIONS History of hypersensitivity to other aminoglycosides; pregnancy.

CAUTIOUS USE Only to be used with proven or strongly suspected bacterial infection to prevent drug-resistance.

ROUTE & DOSAGE

Complicated Urinary Tract Infection

Adult: **IV** 15 mg/kg once a day for 4–7 days

Renal Impairment Dosage Adjustment

CrCL greater than or equal to 60 mL/min: **No dosage adjustment;** *30 to less than 60 mL/min:* 10 mg/kg every 24 h; *15 to less than 30 mL/min:* 10 mg/kg every 48 h

Obese Patient Dosage Adjustment

TBW greater than IBW by more than 25%: Utilize ABW for dosing weight

ADMINISTRATION

Intravenous

PREPARE: Dilute to volume of 50 mL with NS or LR; solution is stable for 24 h.
ADMINISTER: IV Infusion: Infuse over 30 min.
INCOMPATIBILITIES: Incompatibilities have yet to be established; the manufacturer recommends against simultaneous infusion with other medications

• Store solution at refrigerated temperatures 2°–8° C (35°–46° F).

ADVERSE EFFECTS CV: Hypotension or hypertension. **CNS:** Headache, dizziness. **HEENT:** Ototoxicity. **GU:** Diarrhea, nausea, vomiting, nephrotoxicity, increased serum creatinine. **Other:** Hypokalemia, hypersensitivity, (rash, pruritus, drug fever, anaphylaxis).

INTERACTIONS Drug: **Amphotericin B, capreomycin, cisplatin, methoxylurane, polymyxin B, vancomycin, ethacrynic acid** and **furosemide** increase risk of adverse effects. PENICILLINS may decrease effect of plazomicin. NEUROMUSCULAR BLOCKING AGENTS (e.g., **succinylcholine**) potentiate neuromuscular blockade.

PHARMACOKINETICS Absorption: Administered intravenously. **Peak:** Peaks quickly after infusion. **Distribution:** Distributed widely in body fluids; 20% protein bound. **Metabolism:** Not metabolized.

Elimination: Excreted primarily in the urine. **Half-Life:** 3.5 h.

NURSING IMPLICATIONS

Black Box Warning

Associated with nephrotoxicity, ototoxicity, and increased risk of adverse effect with neuromuscular blockade.

Assessment & Drug Effects
• Monitor urine output.
• Monitor for symptoms of ototoxicity or neuromuscular blockade.
• Monitor lab tests: Urinalysis, BUN, serum creatinine, plasma plazomicin trough.

Patient & Family Education
• Notify prescriber if experiencing any of the following symptoms: Unable to pass urine, change in urine amount, blood in the urine, or a significant weight gain.
• Notify prescriber of S&S of an allergic reaction such as hives; rash; itching; red, swollen, blistered, or peeling skin with or without fever; wheezing; tightness in the chest or throat; trouble breathing, swallowing, or talking; unusual hoarseness; or swelling of the mouth, face, lips, tongue, or throat.

PLECANATIDE
(ple-kan'a-tide)
Trulance
Classification: GUANYLATE CYCLASE-C AGONIST; ACCELERANT OF GI TRANSIT
Therapeutic: ACCELERANT OF GI TRANSIT

AVAILABILITY Tablet

ACTION & *THERAPEUTIC EFFECT*

Plecanatide increases the cyclic guanosine monophosphate (cGMP) levels by acting as an agonist of guanylate cyclase-C. This results in an increase of intestinal fluid and transit by stimulating chloride and bicarbonate excretion into the intestinal lumen. *Gastrointestinal time is accelerated which is helpful in combatting constipation.*

USES
Treatment of chronic idiopathic constipation.

CONTRAINDICATIONS
Known or suspected mechanical gastrointestinal obstruction. Patient currently has diarrhea; pediatric patients younger than 6 y.

CAUTIOUS USE
There are no adequate well-controlled studies of plecanatide used in pregnancy. Risk of birth defect or miscarriage cannot be determined. There are no data on the presence of plecanatide in animal or human milk, the effects on breast-feeding infants, or the effects of the milk production.

ROUTE & DOSAGE

Chronic Idiopathic Constipation
Adult: **PO** 3 mg daily

ADMINISTRATION

Gastric or Nasogastric
- Tablets may be mixed with water and administered through a gastric feeding tube.
- Mix 30 mL of room temperature water into a cup with the tablet and swirl for at least 15 sec, flush the feeding tube with 30 mL of water, draw up the mixture with a syringe and adminster the mixture via the feeding tube immediately.
- Add additional 30 mL of water to the cup if any part of the tablet remains, swirl for at least 15 sec, and use the same syringe to administer via the feeding tube.
- Flush the feeding tube with at least 10 mL of water after administration.

Oral
- Swallow tablets whole.
- Take with or without food.
- If patient has difficulty swallowing, tablets may be crushed and administered orally with water or applesauce.
- For administration with water, mix 30 mL of room temperature water into a cup with the tablet, swirl for at least 10 sec, and swallow entire amount immediately; add an additional 30 mL of water if any part of the tablet remains, swirl again, swallow immediately; do not store for later use.
- For administration with applesauce, crush the tablet into a powder and mix with 1 teaspoonful of applesauce at room temperature, consume the entire mixture immediately, do not store for later use.
- Store at 20°–25° C (68°–77° F); excursions permitted to 15°–30° C (59°–86° F). Do not subdivide or repackage; protect from moisture.

ADVERSE EFFECTS GI: Diarrhea.

PHARMACOKINETICS Absorption:
Minimal systemic absorption. **Metabolism:** Metabolized within GI tract to active metabolite; degraded in intestinal lumen to small peptides and amino acids.

NURSING IMPLICATIONS

Black Box Warning

Safety and efficacy of plecanaide not established in patients younger

---

Common adverse effects in *italic;* life-threatening effects <u>underlined;</u> generic names in **bold;** classifications in SMALL CAPS; ✚ Canadian drug name; ○ Prototype drug; ⚠ Alert

than 18 y. Diarrhea, sometimes severe, has been reported and dose interruption was required. Risk of serious dehydration in pediatric patients.

Assessment & Drug Effects

- Monitor the frequency and consistency of bowel movements.
- Monitor for S&S of dehydration.
- Improvement of constipation is indicative of efficacy.

Patient & Family Education

- Notify all health care providers that this drug is being taken. This includes doctors, nurses, pharmacists and dentists.
- If this drug is taken by accident, get help right away.
- Notify prescriber if you become pregnant or plan on getting pregnant while taking this drug.
- Notify prescriber if you are breast-feeding.
- Notify prescriber right away if very loose stools persist.
- If a dose is missed, skip the dose and go back to normal administration time. Do not take 2 doses at the same time or extra doses.
- Consult with prescriber before taking any other prescription drugs, over the counter drugs, natural products or vitamins.

PLERIXAFOR

(ple-rix'a-for)

Mozobil

Classification: BIOLOGICAL RESPONSE MODIFIER; INHIBITOR OF CXCR4 CHEMOKINE RECEPTOR

Therapeutic: CXCR4 CHEMOKINE RECEPTOR INHIBITOR; STEM CELL MOBILIZER

AVAILABILITY Solution for injection

ACTION & THERAPEUTIC EFFECT

A hematopoietic stem cell mobilizer that induces leukocytosis and increases the number of circulating hematopoietic progenitor cells. *Plerixafor enables collection of peripheral blood stem cell (PBSC) for autologous transplantation.*

USES In combination with granulocyte colony-stimulating factor (G-CSF), used to mobilize peripheral blood stem cell (PBSC) for collection and subsequent autologous transplantation in patients with non-Hodgkin's lymphoma and multiple myeloma.

CONTRAINDICATIONS Leukemia; pregnancy (category D); lactation.

CAUTIOUS USE Neutrophil count greater than 50,000/mm^3; thrombocytopenia; splenomegaly; moderate-to-severe renal impairment; concurrent drugs that reduce renal function. Safety and efficacy in children not established.

ROUTE & DOSAGE

Peripheral Blood Stem Cell Mobilization

Adult: **Subcutaneous** 0.24 mg/kg once daily (max: 0.40 mg/day), 11 h prior to initiation of apheresis; administer with filgrastim for up to 4 consecutive days.

Renal Impairment Dosage Adjustment

CrCl less than or equal to 50 mL/min: Reduce dose to 0.16 mg/kg (max: 27 mg/day)

Obesity Dosage Adjustment

Dose based on actual body weight up to 175% of IBW

P

ADMINISTRATION

Subcutaneous
- Give undiluted approximately 11 h prior to apheresis.
- Calculate the required dose as follows: 0.012 × actual weight in kg = mL to administer. Note that each vial contains 1.2 mL of 20 mg/mL solution. Discard unused solution.
- Store single-use vials at 15°–30° C (59°–86° F).

ADVERSE EFFECTS **CNS:** *Dizziness, fatigue, headache,* insomnia. **GI:** *Diarrhea,* flatulence, *nausea, vomiting.* **Other:** *Arthralgia, injection-site reactions.*

PHARMACOKINETICS **Peak:** 30–60 min. **Distribution:** 58% plasma protein bound. **Metabolism:** Not significantly metabolized. **Elimination:** Primarily in urine. **Half-Life:** 3–5 h.

NURSING IMPLICATIONS

Assessment & Drug Effects
- Monitor (during and for 1 h after administration) for and promptly report: Signs of a systemic reaction (e.g., urticaria, periorbital swelling, dyspnea, or hypoxia); signs of splenic enlargement (e.g., upper abdominal pain and/or scapular or shoulder pain).
- Monitor for orthostatic hypotension and syncope during or within 1 h of drug injection. Monitor ambulation or take other precautions as warranted.
- Monitor injection sites for skin reactions.
- Monitor lab tests: Baseline and periodic WBC with differential.

Patient & Family Education
- Report promptly any discomfort experienced during or shortly after drug injection.
- Exercise caution when changing position from lying or sitting to standing as rapid movement shortly after injection may trigger fainting.
- Report skin reactions at the injection site (e.g., itching, rash swelling, or pain).
- Females should use effective contraception while taking this drug.

PNEUMOCOCCAL 13-VALENT VACCINE, DIPHTHERIA
(noo-moe′кок-al)
Prevnar 13
See Appendix J.

PODOPHYLLUM RESIN (PODOPHYLLIN)
(pode-oh-fill′um)
Podoben, Podofin

PODOFILOX
Condylox
Classification: KERATOLYTIC
Therapeutic: CYTOTOXIC; KERATOLYTIC

AVAILABILITY **Podophyllum:** Liquid. **Podofilox:** Gel; solution

ACTION & *THERAPEUTIC EFFECT*
Directly affects epithelial cell metabolism by arresting mitosis through binding to protein subunits of microtubules; causes necrosis of visible wart tissue. *Slow disruption of cells and tissue erosion as a result of its caustic action. Selectively affects embryonic and tumor cells more than adult cells.*

USES Benign growths including external genital and perianal warts, papillomas, fibroids.

CONTRAINDICATIONS Birthmarks, moles, or warts with hair

growth from them; cervical, urethral, oral warts; normal skin and mucous membranes peripheral to treated areas; DM; patient with poor circulation; concurrent use of steroids; irritated, or bleeding skin; application of drug over large area.

CAUTIOUS USE Pregnancy (category C); lactation. Safe use in children is not known.

ROUTE & DOSAGE

Condylomata Acuminata

Adult: **Topical** Use 10% solution and repeat 1–2 × wk for up to 4 applications

Verruca Vulgaris (Common Wart)

Adult: **Topical** Apply 0.5% solution q12h for up to 4 wk

Genital/Perianal Warts

Adult: **Topical** Apply bid × 3 days then withhold treatment × 4 days, may repeat cycle up to 4 ×

ADMINISTRATION

Note: Use 10–25% solution for areas less than 10 cm² or 5% solution for areas of 10–20 cm², anal, or genital warts; apply drug to dry surface, allowing area to dry between drops, wash off after 1–4 h.

Topical

- Avoid podophyllum resin contact with eyes or similar mucosal surfaces; if it occurs, flush thoroughly with lukewarm water for 15 min and remove film precipitated by the water.
- Avoid application of drug to normal tissue. If it occurs, remove with alcohol. Protect surfaces surrounding area to be treated with

a layer of petrolatum or flexible collodion.
- Remove drug thoroughly with soap and water after each treatment of accessible tissue surface.
- Apply a protective coat of talcum powder after treatment and drying of anogenital area.
- Remove drug with alcohol, if application causes extreme pain, pruritus, or swelling.
- Store in a tight, light-resistant container; avoid exposure to excessive heat.

ADVERSE EFFECTS CNS: Localized burning, localized pain. **Skin:** *Skin erosion*, localized inflammation, localized pruritis. **Hematologic:** Localized hemorrhage.

NURSING IMPLICATIONS

Assessment & Drug Effects

- Warts become blanched, then necrotic within 24–48 h. Sloughing begins after about 72 h with no scarring. Frequently, a mild topical anti-infective agent, with or without a dressing, is applied until the healing is complete.
- Monitor neurologic status. Sensorimotor polyneuropathy, if it occurs, appears about 2 wk after application of drug, worsens for 3 mo, and may persist for up to 9 mo. Cerebral effects may persist for 7–10 days; ataxia, hypotonia, and areflexia improve more slowly than effects on sensorium.

Patient & Family Education

- Learn proper technique of treatment if self-administered as treatment of verruca vulgaris (common wart). Also be fully aware of the need to report treatment failure to prescriber.
- Be aware that as with any STD, the patient's sex partner should be examined.

P

- Systemic toxicity may be severe and serious and is associated with application of drug to large areas, to tissue that is friable, bleeding, or recently biopsied, or for prolonged time. Toxicity may occur within hours of application. There are significant dangers from overuse or misuse of this drug.
- Learn symptoms of toxicity and report any that appear promptly to prescriber (see ADVERSE EFFECTS).

POLYCARBOPHIL
(pol-i-kar'boe-fil)
FiberNorm, Fiber-LAX
Classification: BULK-PRODUCING LAXATIVE; ANTIDIARRHEAL
Therapeutic: BULK LAXATIVE; ANTI-DIARRHEAL
Prototype: Psyllium

AVAILABILITY Tablet; chewable tablet

ACTION & *THERAPEUTIC EFFECT*
Hydrophilic agent that absorbs free water in intestinal tract and opposes dehydrating forces of bowel by forming a gelatinous mass. *Restores more normal moisture level and motility in the lower GI tract; produces well-formed stool and reduces diarrhea.*

USES Constipation or diarrhea associated with acute bowel syndrome, diverticulosis, irritable bowel and in patients who should not strain during defecation. Also choleretic diarrhea, diarrhea caused by small-bowel surgery or vagotomy, and disease of terminal ileum.

CONTRAINDICATIONS Partial or complete GI obstruction; fecal impaction; dysphagia; acute abdominal pain; rectal bleeding; undiagnosed abdominal pain, or other symptoms symptomatic of appendicitis; poisonings; before radiologic bowel examination; bowel surgery.

CAUTIOUS USE Renal failure, renal impairment; pregnancy (category C); children younger than 3 y.

ROUTE & DOSAGE

Constipation or Diarrhea
Adult/Adolescent/Child (older than 6 y): **PO** 625 mg calcium polycarbophil 1–4 × day)

ADMINISTRATION
Oral
- Chewable tablets should be chewed well before swallowing.
- Give each dose with a full glass [240 mL (8 oz)] of water or other liquid.
- Store at 15°–30° C (59°–86° F) in tightly closed container unless otherwise directed.

ADVERSE EFFECTS GI: Abdominal fullness.

INTERACTIONS Drug: May decrease absorption and clinical effects of ANTIBIOTICS, **warfarin, digoxin, nitrofurantoin,** SALICYLATES. Do not use with CALCIUM SALTS.

PHARMACOKINETICS Absorption: Not absorbed from GI tract. **Onset:** 12–24 h. **Peak:** 1–3 days.

NURSING IMPLICATIONS
Assessment & Drug Effects
- Determine duration and severity of diarrhea in order to anticipate signs of fluid-electrolyte losses.

- Monitor and record number and consistency of stools/day, presence and location of abdominal discomfort (i.e., tenderness, distention), and bowel sounds.
- Monitor and record I&O ratio and pattern. Dehydration is indicated if output is less than 30 mL/h.

Patient & Family Education
- Consult prescriber if sudden changes in bowel habit persist more than 1 wk, action is minimal or ineffective for 1 wk, or if there is no antidiarrheal action within 2 days.
- Be aware that extended use of this drug may cause dependence for normal bowel function.
- Do not discontinue polycarbophil unless prescriber advises if also taking an oral anticoagulant, digoxin, salicylates, or nitrofurantoin.

POLYMYXIN B SULFATE

(pol-i-mix'in)
Classification: ANTIBIOTIC; POLYMYXIN
Therapeutic: ANTIBIOTIC

AVAILABILITY Solution for injection

ACTION & *THERAPEUTIC EFFECT*
Binds to lipid phosphates in bacterial membranes and changes permeability to permit leakage of cytoplasm from bacterial cells, resulting in cell death. *Bactericidal against susceptible gram-negative but not gram-positive organisms.*

USES Topically and in combination with other anti-infectives or corticosteroids for various superficial infections of eye, ear, mucous membrane, and skin. Concurrent systemic anti-infective therapy may be required for treatment of intraocular infection and severe progressive corneal ulcer. Used parenterally only in hospitalized patients for treatment of severe acute infections of urinary tract, bloodstream, and meninges; and in combination with Neosporin for continuous bladder irrigation to prevent bacteremia associated with use of indwelling catheter.

CONTRAINDICATIONS Hypersensitivity to polymyxin antibiotics; respiratory insufficiency; concurrent use of products that inhibit peristalsis, skeletal muscle relaxants, ether, or sodium citrate.

CAUTIOUS USE Impaired kidney function, renal failure; inflammatory bowel disease; myasthenia gravis; pulmonary disease. **IV/IM form:** Pregnancy (category C); lactation. **Topical form:** Pregnancy (category B). Safety and efficacy in children younger than 1 mo not established.

ROUTE & DOSAGE

Infections
Adult/Child: **IV** 15,000–25,000 units/kg/day divided q12h; **IM** 25,000–30,000 units/kg/day divided q4–6h; **Intrathecal** 50,000 units × 3–4 days then every other day × 2 wk; *younger than 2 y:* 20,000 units × 3–4 days, then 25,000 units every other day
Infant: **IV** Up to 40,000 units/kg/day

Renal Impairment Dosage Adjustment
Reduce, specific dose unknown

P

ADMINISTRATION

Intramuscular

- Routine administration by IM routes not recommended because it causes intense discomfort, along the peripheral nerve distribution, 40–60 min after IM injection.
- Make IM injection in adults deep into upper outer quadrant of buttock. Select IM site carefully to avoid injection into nerves or blood vessels. Rotate injection sites. Follow agency policy for IM site used in children.

Intravenous

PREPARE: **Intermittent:** Reconstitute by dissolving 500,000 units in 5 mL sterile water for injection or NS to yield 100,000 units/mL. Withdraw a single dose and then further dilute in 300–500 mL of D5W.

ADMINISTER: **Intermittent:** Infuse over period of 60–90 min.
- Inspect injection site for signs of phlebitis and irritation.

INCOMPATIBILITIES: **Solution/ additive: Amphotericin B, cefazolin, cephalothin, cephapirin, chloramphenicol, heparin, nitrofurantoin, prednisolone, tetracycline.**

- Protect unreconstituted product and reconstituted solution from light and freezing. Store in refrigerator at 2°–8° C (36°–46° F).
- Parenteral solutions are stable for 1 wk when refrigerated. Discard unused portion after 72 h.

ADVERSE EFFECTS CNS: Drowsiness, dizziness, vertigo, convulsions, coma; neuromuscular blockade (generalized muscle weakness, respiratory depression or arrest); meningeal irritation, increased protein and cell count in cerebrospinal fluid, fever, headache, stiff neck (intrathecal use). **HEENT:** Blurred vision, nystagmus, slurred speech, dysphagia, ototoxicity (vestibular and auditory) with high doses. **GI:** GI disturbances. **GU:** Albuminuria, cylindruria, azotemia, hematuria; nephrotoxicity. **Other:** Irritability, facial flushing, ataxia, circumoral, lingual, and peripheral paresthesias (stocking-glove distribution); severe pain (IM site), thrombophlebitis (IV site), superinfections, electrolyte disturbances (prolonged use; also reported in patients with acute leukemia); local irritation and burning (topical use), anaphylactoid reactions (rare).

INTERACTIONS Drug: ANESTHETICS and NEUROMUSCULAR BLOCKING AGENTS may prolong skeletal muscle relaxation. AMINOGLYCOSIDES, LOOP DIURETICS, and **amphotericin B** have additive nephrotoxic potential.

PHARMACOKINETICS Peak: 2 h IM. **Distribution:** Widely distributed except to CSF, synovial fluid, and eye; does not cross placenta. **Metabolism:** Unknown. **Elimination:** 60% excreted unchanged in urine. **Half-Life:** 4.3–6 h.

NURSING IMPLICATIONS

Black Box Warning

Polymixin B has been associated with nephrotoxicity and neurotoxicity.

Assessment & Drug Effects

- Review electrolyte results. Patients with low serum calcium are particularly prone to develop neuromuscular blockade.
- Inspect tongue every day. Assess for S&S of superinfection (see Appendix E). Polymyxin therapy

supports growth of opportunistic organisms. Report symptoms promptly.

- Monitor I&O. Maintain fluid intake sufficient to maintain daily urinary output of at least 1500 mL. Some degree of renal toxicity usually occurs within first 3 or 4 days of therapy even with therapeutic doses. Consult prescriber.

- Withhold drug and report findings to prescriber for any of the following: Decreases in urine output (change in I&O ratio), proteinuria, cellular casts, rising BUN, serum creatinine, or serum drug levels (not associated with dosage increase). All can be interpreted as signs of nephrotoxicity.

- Nephrotoxicity is generally reversible, but it may progress even after drug is discontinued. Therefore, close monitoring of kidney function is essential, even following termination of therapy.

- Be alert for respiratory arrest after the first dose and also as long as 45 days after initiation of therapy. It occurs most commonly in patients with kidney failure and high plasma drug levels and is often preceded by dyspnea and restlessness.

- Monitor lab tests: Baseline C&S and renal function tests; frequent serum drug levels during therapy.

Patient & Family Education

- Report to prescriber immediately any muscle weakness, shortness of breath, dyspnea, depressed respiration. These symptoms are rapidly reversible if drug is withdrawn.

- Report promptly to prescriber transient neurologic disturbances (burning or prickling sensations, numbness, dizziness). All occur commonly and usually respond to dosage reduction.

- Report promptly to prescriber the onset of stiff neck and headache (possible symptoms of neurotoxic reactions, including neuromuscular blockade). This response is usually associated with high serum drug levels or nephrotoxicity.

- Report promptly S&S of superinfection (see Appendix E).

- Report any S&S of colitis for up to 2 mo following discontinuation of drug.

PONATINIB

(poe-na'ti-nib)

Iclusig

Classification: ANTINEOPLASTIC; KINASE INHIBITOR

Therapeutic: ANTINEOPLASTIC

Prototype: Erlotinib

AVAILABILITY Tablet

ACTION & *THERAPEUTIC EFFECT*

Inhibits the action of certain tyrosine kinases (a family of enzymes needed for viability of leukemia cells). *Inhibits the growth and replication of mutant leukemic cells.*

USES Treatment of chronic phase, accelerated phase, or blast phase chronic myeloid leukemia (CML) and Philadelphia chromosome-positive acute lymphocytic leukemia (Ph+ALL) that is resistant or intolerant to prior tyrosine kinase inhibitor therapy.

CONTRAINDICATIONS Arterial thrombosis; stroke or MI, severe CHF, serious or severe hemorrhage induced by ponatinib; hepatotoxicity; tumor lysis syndrome; severe myelosuppression; compromised wound healing; GI perforation; pregnancy (category D); lactation.

CAUTIOUS USE CHF, hypertension, cardiac arrhythmias, myelosuppression, DVT; pancreatitis; fluid retention; moderate to severe hepatic impairment.

ROUTE & DOSAGE

Chronic Myeloid Leukemia (CML)/Acute Lymphocyte Leukemia (ALL)

Adult: PO 45 mg once daily

Toxicity Dosage Adjustment

See package insert

Strong CYP3A4 Inhibitors Dosage Adjustment

30 mg once daily

ADMINISTRATION

Oral

- May give without regard to food.
- Tablets must be swallowed whole. They must not be crushed or chewed.
- Avoid intake of grapefruit juice.
- Store at 15°–30° C (59°–86° F).

ADVERSE EFFECTS CV: *Hypertension, arterial ischemia, peripheral vascular disease, arterial embolism, cerebral ischemia, cerebrovascular accident, myocardial infarction,* peripheral edema, coronary occlusive disease, cardiac arrhythmia, cardiac failure, hypertensive crisis. **Respiratory:** Cough, dyspnea, pleural effusion, nasopharyngitis, pneumonia, upper respiratory tract infection. **CNS:** *Fatigue, headache,* peripheral neuropathy, pain, dizziness, insomnia, chills. **HEENT:** Conjunctival edema, conjunctival hemorrhage, conjunctivitis, dry eye syndrome, eye pain.

Endocrine: *Hyperglycemia, hypophosphatemia, fluid retention, hypocalcemia, hypoalbuminemia, hyponatremia,* decreased serum bicarbonate, hyperkalemia. **Skin:** *Skin rash, xeroderma,* pruritus, cellulitis, alopecia. **Hepatic/GI:** *Increased liver enzymes, hepatotoxicity, increased serum bilirubin, constipation, abdominal pain, increased serum lipase, nausea, decreased appetite,* vomiting, diarrhea, stomatitis, increased serum amylase. **GU:** UTI, increased serum creatinine. **Musculoskeletal:** *Arthralgia,* myalgia, limb pain, back pain, ostealgia, muscle spasm, muscle pain. **Hematologic:** *Leukopenia, bone marrow depression, neutropenia, anemia, thrombocytopenia, lymphocytopenia, hemorrhage,* febrile neutropenia.

INTERACTIONS Drug: Coadministration with strong CYP3A4 inducers (e.g., **carbamazepine, phenytoin, rifampin**) may decrease the levels of ponatinib. Coadministration with strong CYP3A4 inhibitors (e.g. **clarithromycin, conivaptan, indinavir, itraconazole, ketoconazole, lopinavir, nefazodone, nelfinavir, posaconazole, ritonavir, saquinavir, telaprenavir, telithromycin, voriconazole**) may increase the levels of ponatinib. Coadministration with drugs that elevate gastric pH (e.g., ANTACIDS, H₂ BLOCKERS, PROTON PUMP INHIBITORS) may decrease the levels of ponatinib. Studies have yet been done; however, since ponatinib inhibits the ABCG2 and P-gp transporter systems, it may alter the transport of drugs requiring either of these transporters. **Food:** Grapefruit juice may increase the levels of ponatinib. **Herbal: St. John's wort** may decrease the levels of ponatinib.

Common adverse effects in *italic;* life-threatening effects <u>underlined</u>; generic names in **bold;** classifications in SMALL CAPS; ♣ Canadian drug name; ◑ Prototype drug; ⚠ Alert

PHARMACOKINETICS Peak:
6 h. **Distribution:** Greater than
99% plasma protein bound.
Metabolism: Hepatic oxidation and hydrolysis. **Elimination:**
Fecal (87%) and renal (5%).
Half-Life: 24 h.

NURSING IMPLICATIONS

Black Box Warning

*Ponatinib has been associated
with cardiovascular, cerebrovascular, and peripheral vascular
thrombosis, including fatal MI
and stroke; and with hepatotoxicity and liver failure.*

Assessment & Drug Effects

- Monitor cardiovascular status
  closely.
- Report bradycardia, development
  of edema, and S&S of CHF.
- Monitor I&O and daily weight.
  Report rapid weight gain.
- Monitor BP frequently. Be alert
  for S&S of hypertensive crisis
  (e.g., confusion, headache, chest
  pain, or shortness of breath).
- Monitor for and promptly
  report S&S of hepatotoxicity or
  pancreatitis.
- Monitor lab tests: Baseline and
  monthly LFTs; serum lipase q2wk
  for first month, and monthly thereafter or more often as indicated;
  CBC with differential and platelet count q2wk for the first 3 mo;
  periodic serum electrolytes and
  uric acid.

Patient & Family Education

- Do not drink grapefruit juice
  while taking this drug.
- Report promptly signs of thrombosis (e.g., chest pain, shortness
  of breath, one-sided weakness,
  speech problems, leg pain or
  swelling).

- Report promptly signs of liver
  toxicity (e.g., jaundice, dark urine,
  clay-colored stool).
- Report promptly signs of heart
  failure (e.g., shortness of breath,
  chest pain, palpitations, dizziness, fainting, rapid weight gain,
  abdominal swelling).
- Women should use effective
  means of contraception to avoid
  pregnancy as ponatinib can cause
  severe fetal harm.

PORACTANT ALFA ⊙
(por-ac'tant)
Curosurf
Classification: LUNG SURFACTANT
Therapeutic: LUNG SURFACTANT

AVAILABILITY Suspension

ACTION & *THERAPEUTIC EFFECT*
Endogenous pulmonary surfactant lowers the surface tension on
alveoli surfaces during respiration,
and stabilizes the alveoli against
collapse at resting pressures. *Alle-
viates respiratory distress syndrome
(RDS) in premature infants caused
by deficiency of surfactant.*

USES Treatment (rescue) of respiratory distress syndrome in premature infants.

CONTRAINDICATIONS Hypersensitivity to porcine products or
poractant alpha.

CAUTIOUS USE Infants born
more than 3 wk after ruptured
membranes; intraventricular hemorrhage of grade III or IV; major
congenital malformations; nosocomial infection; pretreatment
of hypothermia or acidosis due
to increased risk of intracranial
hemorrhage.

ROUTE & DOSAGE

Respiratory Distress Syndrome
Neonate: **Intratracheal** 2.5 mL/kg birth weight, may repeat with 1.25 mL/kg q12h × 2 more doses if needed (max: 5 mL/kg)

ADMINISTRATION

Note: Correction of acidosis, hypotension, anemia, hypoglycemia, and hypothermia is recommended prior to administration of poractant alfa.

Intratracheal
- Warm vial slowly to room temperature; gently turn upside down to form uniform suspension, but do NOT shake.
- Withdraw slowly the entire contents of a vial (concentration equals 80 mg/mL) into a 3 or 5 mL syringe through a large gauge (greater than 20 gauge) needle.
- Attach a 5 French catheter, precut to 8 cm, to the syringe.
- Fill the catheter with poractant alfa and discard excess through the catheter so that only the total dose to be given remains in the syringe.
- Refer to specific instruction provided by manufacturer for proper dosing technique. Follow instructions carefully regarding installation of drug and ventilation of infant. Note that catheter tip should not extend beyond distal tip of endotracheal tube.
- Store refrigerated at 2°–8° C (36°–46° F) and protect from light. Do not shake vials. Do not warm to room temperature and return to refrigeration more than once.

ADVERSE EFFECTS CV: Bradycardia, hypotension. **Respiratory:** Intratracheal tube blockage, oxygen desaturation; pulmonary hemorrhage.

PHARMACOKINETICS Not studied.

NURSING IMPLICATIONS
Assessment & Drug Effects
- Stop administration of poractant alfa and take appropriate measures if any of the following occur: Transient episodes of bradycardia, decreased oxygen saturation, reflux of poractant alfa into endotracheal tube, or airway obstruction. Dosing may resume after stabilization.
- Do not suction airway for 1 h after poractant alfa instillation unless there is significant airway obstruction.

POSACONAZOLE
(pos-a-con'a-zole)
Noxafil
Classification: AZOLE ANTIFUNGAL
Therapeutic: ANTIFUNGAL
Prototype: Fluconazole

AVAILABILITY Oral suspension; delayed release tablets

ACTION & *THERAPEUTIC EFFECT*
Inhibits ergosterol synthesis, the principal sterol in the fungal cell membrane, thus interfering with the functions of fungal cell membrane. This results in increased membrane permeability causing leakage of cellular contents. *Has a broad spectrum of antifungal activity against common fungal pathogens.*

USES Prophylactic treatment of invasive *Aspergillus* and *Candida*, oropharyngeal candidiasis.

Common adverse effects in *italic*; life-threatening effects underlined; generic names in **bold**; classifications in SMALL CAPS; ✦ Canadian drug name; ☉ Prototype drug; ⚠ Alert

1370

UNLABELED USES Treatment of febrile neutropenia or refractory invasive fungal infection; treatment of periorbital cellulitis due to *Rhizopus* sp.; treatment of refractory histoplasmosis; treatment of refractory coccidioidomycosis; treatment of fungal necrotizing fasciitis.

CONTRAINDICATIONS Hypersensitivity to posaconazole or other azole antifungals; coadministration with sirolimus, ergot alkaloids, or CYP3A4 substrates; history of QT prolongation; abnormal levels of potassium, magnesium, or calcium; liver disease caused by posaconazole; lactation.

CAUTIOUS USE Hypersensitivity to other azole antifungal antibiotics; hepatic disease or hepatitis; cardiac arrhythmias, hypokalemia; history of proarrhythmic conditions; CHF, myocardial ischemia, atrial fibrillation; AIDS; obesity; severe renal impairment; pregnancy (category C); children younger than 13 y.

ROUTE & DOSAGE

Prophylactic Treatment of Invasive *Aspergillus* and *Candida* Infections

Adult/Adolescent: **PO** 200 mg tid

Thrush

Adult/Adolescent: **PO Oral Suspension** 100 mg bid × 1 day then 100 mg qd × 13 days; **PO Tablet** 300 mg bid for one day then 300 mg daily until recovery

ADMINISTRATION

Oral Suspension

- Shake well before use. Give with a full meal or liquid nutritional supplement.

Oral Tablet

- Swallow whole, do not crush. Administer with food.
- Store at 15°–30° C (59°–86° F).

ADVERSE EFFECTS CV: *Hypertension, hypotension, tachycardia.* **Respiratory:** *Cough, dyspnea, epistaxis, pharyngitis,* upper respiratory tract infection. **CNS:** QT/QT$_c$ prolongation, tremor. **HEENT:** Blurred vision, taste disturbances. **Endocrine:** *Bilirubinemia,* creatinine levels increased, elevated liver enzymes, hypocalcemia, *hyperglycemia, hypokalemia, hypomagnesemia.* **Skin:** *Pruritus, rash.* **GI:** *Abdominal pain, anorexia constipation, diarrhea, dyspepsia, mucositis, nausea,* vomiting. **GU:** *Vaginal hemorrhage.* **Musculoskeletal:** *Arthralgia, back pain, musculoskeletal pain.* **Hematologic:** *Anemia, febrile neutropenia, neutropenia, petechiae,* <u>thrombocytopenia</u>. **Other:** Anxiety, *bacteremia, dizziness, edema, fatigue, fever, headache, infection, insomnia, rigors,* weakness.

INTERACTIONS Drug: Posaconazole is known to increase the plasma levels of **cyclosporine, tacrolimus, rifabutin, midazolam,** and **phenytoin.** Coadministration with other drugs that cause QT prolongation (e.g., **quinidine**) can result in torsades de pointes. Posaconazole may increase the plasma levels of ERGOT ALKALOIDS, VINCA ALKALOIDS, HMG COA REDUCTASE INHIBITORS, and CALCIUM CHANNEL BLOCKERS. Avoid use with cimetidine, efavirenz, esomeprazole, phenytoin, due to decreases in efficacy. **Food:** Administration with food increases absorption of posaconazole.

PHARMACOKINETICS Peak: 3–5 h. **Distribution:** 98% protein bound.

Metabolism: Conjugated to inactive metabolites. **Elimination:** Primarily fecal elimination (71%) with minor renal elimination. **Half-Life:** 35 h.

NURSING IMPLICATIONS

Assessment & Drug Effects

- Monitor for and report S&S of breakthrough fungal infections, especially in those with severe renal impairment, or experiencing vomiting and diarrhea, or who cannot tolerate a full meal or supplement along with posaconazole.
- Monitor and report degree of improvement of oropharyngeal candidiasis.
- Monitor those with proarrhythmic conditions for development of arrhythmias.
- Withhold drug and notify prescriber of abnormal serum potassium, magnesium, or calcium levels.
- Monitor blood levels of phenytoin, cyclosporine, tacrolimus, and sirolimus with concurrent therapy. Monitor for adverse effects of concurrently administered statins or calcium channel blockers.
- Monitor lab tests: Baseline and periodic LFTs; periodic renal function tests, serum electrolytes, and CBC.

Patient & Family Education

- Do not take any prescription or nonprescription drugs without informing your prescriber.
- Know parameters for withholding drug (i.e., inability to take with a full meal or nutritional supplement).
- Report immediately any of the following to your health care provider: Vomiting, diarrhea, inability to eat, jaundice of skin, yellowing of eyes, itching, or skin rash.

POTASSIUM CHLORIDE ⚠

(poe-tass'ee-um)

Apo-K ✦, K-Dur, K-Long ✦, KCl 5% and 20%, Klor, Klor-10%, Klor-Con, Micro-K Extentabs, Slo-Pot ✦

POTASSIUM GLUCONATE

Classification: ELECTROLYTIC REPLACEMENT SOLUTION
Therapeutic: ELECTROLYTE REPLACEMENT

AVAILABILITY Chloride: Sustained release tablet; tablet; effervescent tablet; liquid; powder; solution for injection; vial. **Gluconate:** Liquid

ACTION & *THERAPEUTIC EFFECT*

Principal intracellular cation that is essential for maintenance of intracellular isotonicity, transmission of nerve impulses, contraction of cardiac, skeletal, and smooth muscles, maintenance of normal kidney function, and for enzyme activity. *Effectiveness in hypokalemia is measured by serum potassium concentration greater than 3.5 mEq/L.*

USES To prevent and treat potassium deficit; effective in the treatment of hypokalemic alkalosis (chloride, not the gluconate).

CONTRAINDICATIONS Severe renal impairment; severe hemolytic reactions; untreated Addison's disease; crush syndrome; early postoperative oliguria (except during GI drainage); adynamic ileus; acute dehydration; heat cramps, hyperkalemia, patients receiving potassium-sparing diuretics, digitalis intoxication with AV conduction disturbance.

CAUTIOUS USE Cardiac or kidney disease; systemic acidosis;

Common adverse effects in *italic*; life-threatening effects <u>underlined</u>; generic names in **bold**; classifications in SMALL CAPS; ✦ Canadian drug name; ◯ Prototype drug; ⚠ Alert

slow-release potassium preparations in presence of delayed GI transit or Meckel's diverticulum; extensive tissue breakdown (such as severe burns); pregnancy (category C); lactation.

ROUTE & DOSAGE

Hypokalemia

Adult: **PO** 40–100 mEq/day in divided doses; **IV** Dose per package insert dependent on current serum potassium concentration
Child: **PO** 2–5 mEq/kg/day in divided doses; sustained release tablets not recommended; **IV** 0.25–0.5 mEq/kg/dose (max: 40 mEq/day)

Prevention of Hypokalemia

Adult: **PO** 20 mEq/day in 1–2 doses
Child: **PO** 1–2 mEq/kg/day in 1–2 doses

ADMINISTRATION

Oral

- Give while patient is sitting up or standing (never in recumbent position) to prevent drug-induced esophagitis. Some patients find it difficult to swallow the large sized KCl tablet.
- Do not crush or allow to chew any potassium salt tablets. Observe to make sure patient does not suck tablet (oral ulcerations have been reported if tablet is allowed to dissolve in mouth).
- Swallow whole tablet with a large glass of water or fruit juice (if allowed) to wash drug down and to start esophageal peristalsis.
- Follow exactly directions for diluting various liquid forms of KCl.

In general, dilute each 20 mEq potassium in at least 90 mL water or juice and allow to dissolve completely before administration.
- Dilute liquid forms as directed before giving it through nasogastric tube.

Intravenous

PREPARE: **IV Infusion:** Add desired amount to 100–1000 mL IV solution (compatible with all standard solutions). ▪ Usual maximum is 80 mEq/1000 mL, however, 40 mEq/L is preferred to lessen irritation to veins. Note: **NEVER** add KCl to an IV bag/bottle which is hanging. ▪ After adding KCl invert bag/bottle several times to ensure even distribution.
ADMINISTER: **IV Infusion for Adult/ Child:** KCl is **never** given direct IV or in concentrated amounts by any route. ▪ Too rapid infusion may cause fatal hyperkalemia. **IV Infusion for Adult:** Infuse at rate not to exceed 10 mEq/h; in emergency situations, may infuse very cautiously up to 40 mEq/h with continuous cardiac monitoring. **IV Infusion for Child:** Infuse at a rate not to exceed 0.5–1.0 mEq/kg/h.
INCOMPATIBILITIES: **Solution/ additive: Amoxicillin/clavulanate furosemide, imipenem-cilastin pentobarbital, phenobarbital, succinylcholine. Y-site: Amphotericin B cholesteryl complex, azithromycin, dantrolene, diazepam, ergotamine, lansoprazole, methylprednisolone, phenytoin, sulfamethoxazole/ trimethoprim.**

- Take extreme care to prevent extravasation and infiltration. At first sign, discontinue infusion and select another site.

P

ADVERSE EFFECTS CV: <u>Asystole</u>, bradycardia, chest pain, thrombosis, ventricular fibrillation. **Respiratory:** Dyspnea. **Endocrine:** Hyperkalemia. **Skin:** Skin rash, burning at injection site, erythema at injection site, injection site phlebitis. **GI:** Abdominal pain, diarrhea, flatulence, gastrointestinal hemorrhage, gastrointestinal irritation, nausea, vomiting.

INTERACTIONS Drug: POTASSIUM-SPARING DIURETICS, ANGIOTENSIN-CONVERTING ENZYME (ACE) INHIBITORS, ANTICHOLINERGIC AGENTS may cause hyperkalemia. Use with CALCIUM SALTS can cause metabolic acidosis. **Food:** Salty foods could increase the risk of hyperkalemia.

PHARMACOKINETICS Absorption: Readily from upper GI tract. **Elimination:** 90% in urine, 10% in feces.

NURSING IMPLICATIONS

Assessment & Drug Effects
- Monitor I&O ratio and pattern in patients receiving the parenteral drug. If oliguria occurs, stop infusion promptly and notify prescriber.
- Monitor for and report signs of GI ulceration (esophageal or epigastric pain or hematemesis).
- Monitor cardiac status of patients receiving parenteral potassium. Irregular heartbeat is usually the earliest clinical indication of hyperkalemia.
- Be alert for potassium intoxication (hyperkalemia, see S&S, Appendix E); may result from any therapeutic dosage, and the patient may be asymptomatic.
- The risk of hyperkalemia with potassium supplement increases (1) in older adults because of decremental changes in kidney function associated with aging, (2) when dietary intake of potassium suddenly increases, and (3) when kidney function is significantly compromised.
- Monitor lab tests: Baseline and periodic serum potassium.

Patient & Family Education
- Do not be alarmed when the tablet carcass appears in your stool. The sustained release tablet (e.g., Slow-K) utilizes a wax matrix as carrier for KCl crystals that passes through the digestive system.
- Learn about sources of potassium with special reference to foods and OTC drugs.
- Do not use any salt substitute unless it is specifically ordered by the prescriber. These contain a substantial amount of potassium and electrolytes other than sodium.
- Do not self-prescribe laxatives. Chronic laxative use has been associated with diarrhea-induced potassium loss.
- Notify prescriber of persistent vomiting because losses of potassium can occur.
- Report continuing signs of potassium deficit to prescriber: Weakness, fatigue, polyuria, polydipsia.
- Advise dentist or new prescriber that a potassium drug has been prescribed as long-term maintenance therapy.
- Do not open foil-wrapped powders and tablets before use.

POTASSIUM IODIDE
(poe-tass'ee-um)
SSKI
Classification: ANTITHYROID; EXPECTORANT
Therapeutic: ANTITHYROID; EXPECTORANT

Common adverse effects in *italic*; life-threatening effects <u>underlined</u>; generic names in **bold**; classifications in SMALL CAPS; ♣ Canadian drug name; ○ Prototype drug; ⚠ Alert

AVAILABILITY oral solution; tablet

ACTION & *THERAPEUTIC EFFECT*
Appears to increase secretion of respiratory fluids by direct action on bronchial tissue, thereby decreasing mucus viscosity. When the thyroid gland is hyperplastic, excess iodide ions temporarily inhibit secretion of thyroid hormone, foster accumulation in thyroid follicles, and decrease vascularity of gland. *Administration for hyperthyroidism is limited to short-term therapy. As an expectorant, the iodine ion increases mucous secretion formation in bronchi, and decreases viscosity of mucus.*

USES Block thyroidal update of radioactive isotopes; expectorant for the symptomatic treatment of chronic pulmonary disease complicated by mucous.

CONTRAINDICATIONS Hypersensitivity to iodine; dermatitis herpetiformis; hypocomplementemic vasculitis; nodular thyroid condition with heart disease; pregnancy (may cause hypothyroidism in fetus/newborn); lactation.

CAUTIOUS USE Renal impairment; cardiac disease; pulmonary tuberculosis; Addison's disease.

ROUTE & DOSAGE

Expectorant

Adult: **PO** 300–600 mg 3–4 times per day

Thyroid Blocking in Radiation Emergency

Adult/Adolescent (over 68 kg): **PO** 130 mg/day for 10–14 days

Adolescent (less than 68 kg)/ Child 3–12 years **PO** 65 mg/day *Child/Infant (younger than 3 y):* **PO** 32.5 mg/day

ADMINISTRATION
Oral
- Give with meals in a full glass (240 mL) of water, milk, or fruit juice disguise salty taste and minimize gastric distress.
- Adhere strictly to schedule and accurate dose measurements when iodide is administered to prepare thyroid gland for surgery, particularly at end of treatment period when possibility of "escape" (from iodide) effect on thyroid gland increases.
- Store in airtight, light-resistant container.

ADVERSE EFFECTS CV: Cardiac arrhythmias, numbness, vasculitis. **Respiratory:** Dyspnea, rhinitis, wheezing. **CNS:** Confusion, fatigue, numbness, tingling sensation. **Endocrine:** Goiter, hypothyroidism, myxedema. **Skin:** Acne vulgaris, dermatitis, urticaria. **GI:** Diarrhea, nausea, vomiting, stomach pain, gastric distress, gastrointestinal haemorrhage, gingival pain, metallic taste, toothache. **Hematologic:** Eosinophilia, lymphedema, thyroid adenoma. **Musculoskeletal:** Arthralgia, weakness. **Other:** Hypersensitivity reaction. *Iodine poisoning (iodism):* Metallic taste, stomatitis, salivation, coryza, sneezing; swollen and tender salivary glands (sialadenitis), frontal headache, vomiting (blue vomitus if stomach contained starches, otherwise yellow vomitus), bloody diarrhea.

DIAGNOSTIC TEST INTERFERENCE
Potassium iodide may alter ***thyroid function*** test results.

P

INTERACTIONS Drug: ANTITHY-ROID DRUGS, **lithium** may potentiate hypothyroid and goitrogenic actions; POTASSIUM-SPARING DIURETICS, POTASSIUM SUPPLEMENTS, ACE INHIBITORS increase risk of hyperkalemia.

PHARMACOKINETICS Absorption: Adequately absorbed from GI tract. **Distribution:** Crosses placenta. **Elimination:** Cleared from plasma by renal excretion or thyroid uptake.

NURSING IMPLICATIONS

Assessment & Drug Effects
- Keep prescriber informed about characteristics of sputum: Quantity, consistency, color.
- Monitor lab tests: Baseline and periodic serum thyroid function tests, potassium.

Patient & Family Education
- Report to prescriber promptly the occurrence of abdominal pain, distension, nausea, or vomiting.
- Report clinical S&S of iodism (see ADVERSE EFFECTS). Usually, symptoms will subside with dose reduction and lengthened intervals between doses.
- Avoid foods rich in iodine if iodism develops: Seafood, fish liver oils, and iodized salt.
- Be aware that sudden withdrawal following prolonged use may precipitate thyroid storm.
- Do not use OTC drugs without consulting prescriber. Many preparations contain iodides and could augment prescribed dose [e.g., cough syrups, gargles, asthma medication, salt substitutes, cod liver oil, multiple vitamins (often suspended in iodide solutions)].
- Be aware that optimum hydration is the best expectorant when taking KI as an expectorant. Increase daily fluid intake.

PRALATREXATE
(pra-la-trex'ate)
Folotyn
Classification: ANTINEOPLASTIC; ANTIMETABOLITE, ANTIFOLATE
Therapeutic: ANTINEOPLASTIC
Prototype: Methotrexate

AVAILABILITY Solution for injection

ACTION & *THERAPEUTIC EFFECT*
Blocks folic acid participation in nucleic acid synthesis, thereby interfering with cell division (mitosis). Rapidly dividing cells, including cancer cells, are sensitive to this interference in the mitotic process. *Effective in treatment of relapsed or refractory peripheral T-cell lymphoma (PTCL).*

USES Treatment of relapsed or refractory peripheral T-cell lymphoma (PTCL) and non-Hodgkin's lymphoma.

CONTRAINDICATIONS Concomitant administration of hepatotoxity drugs; tumor lysis syndrome; pregnancy (category D); lactation.

CAUTIOUS USE Thrombocytopenia, neutropenia, anemia; moderate to severe renal function impairment; liver function impairment; pancreatic problems due to drug use; ulcerative colitis; poor nutritional status; older adults. Safety and efficacy in children not established.

ROUTE & DOSAGE

Peripheral T-Cell Lymphoma
Adult: **IV** 30 mg/m² over 3–5 min. Repeat weekly for 6 wk in 7-wk cycles.

Common adverse effects in *italic;* life-threatening effects <u>underlined</u>; generic names in **bold**; classifications in SMALL CAPS; ♣ Canadian drug name; ♦ Prototype drug; ⚠ Alert

Renal Impairment Dosage Adjustment

EGFR of 15–30 mL/min: Reduce dose to 15 mg/m^2

Toxicity and Organ Function Dosage Adjustments

See package insert

ADMINISTRATION

Intravenous

PREPARE: Direct: Withdraw from vial into syringe immediately before use. Do not dilute. Use gloves and other protective clothing during handling and preparation. ▪ Flush thoroughly if drug contacts skin or mucous membranes.

ADMINISTER: Direct: Give over 3–5 min via a side port of a free-flowing NS IV line. ▪ Withhold drug and notify prescriber for any of the following: Platelet count less than 100,000/mcL for first dose or less than 50,000/mcL for all subsequent doses, ANC less than 1000/mcL, or grade 2 or higher mucositis.

▪ Refrigerate at 2°–8° C (36°–46° F) until use and protect from light. ▪ Vials are stable at room temperature for up to 72 h if left in original carton.

ADVERSE EFFECTS CV: <u>Tachycardia</u>. **Respiratory:** *Cough, dyspnea, epistaxis,* pharyngolaryngeal pain, upper respiratory tract infection. **Endocrine:** Anorexia, elevated AST and ALT, hypokalemia. **Skin:** Pruritus, rash. **GI:** *Constipation, diarrhea, mucositis, nausea, vomiting,* stomatitis. **Musculoskeletal:** Back pain. **Hematologic:** *Anemia,* <u>leukopenia</u>, *neutropenia,* <u>thrombocytopenia</u>. **Other:** Abdominal pain, asthenia, *edema, fatigue,* night sweats, pain in extremity, *pyrexia,* <u>sepsis</u>.

INTERACTIONS Drug: **Probenecid** may increase pralatrexate levels. Drugs that are subject to substantial renal clearance (e.g., NSAIDS, **trimethoprim/sulfamethoxazole**) may delay the clearance of pralatrexate. Do not administer LIVE VACCINES.

PHARMACOKINETICS Distribution: 67% bound to plasma proteins. **Metabolism:** Not extensively metabolized. **Elimination:** Primarily excreted in the urine. **Half-Life:** 12–18 h.

NURSING IMPLICATIONS

Assessment & Drug Effects

▪ Monitor vitals signs. Report immediately S&S of infection, especially fever of 100.5° F or greater.
▪ Monitor status of mucus membranes because mucositis is a dose-limiting toxicity.
▪ Monitor lab tests: Prior to each dose, CBC with differential and platelet count; baseline and periodic LFTs and renal function tests.

Patient & Family Education

▪ Practice meticulous oral hygiene.
▪ Monitor for S&S of an infection. Contact the prescriber immediately if an infection is suspected or if your temperature is elevated.
▪ Report promptly unexplained bleeding or symptoms of anemia (e.g., excessive weakness, fatigue, intolerance to activity, pale skin).
▪ Folic acid and vitamin B$_{12}$ supplementation are recommended to reduce the risk of drug-related toxicities. Consult with prescriber.
▪ Use effective means of contraception to avoid pregnancy while taking this drug. If a pregnancy

P

does occur, notify prescriber immediately.
- Do not take aspirin or NSAIDs without consulting prescriber.

PRALIDOXIME CHLORIDE
(pra-li-dox′eem)
Protopam Chloride
Classification: CHOLINESTERASE RECEPTOR AGONIST;
DETOXIFICATION AGENT
Therapeutic: ANTIDOTE;
CHOLINESTERASE ENHANCER

AVAILABILITY Solution for injection

ACTION & THERAPEUTIC EFFECT
Reactivates cholinesterase by displacing the enzyme from its receptor sites; the free enzyme then can resume its function of degrading accumulated acetylcholine, thereby restoring normal neuromuscular transmission. *More active against effects of anticholinesterases at skeletal neuromuscular junction than at autonomic effector sites or in CNS respiratory center; therefore, atropine **must be** given concomitantly to block effects of acetylcholine and its accumulation in these sites.*

USES Antidote in treatment of poisoning by organophosphate insecticides and pesticides with anticholinesterase activity (e.g., parathion, TEPP, sarin) and to control overdosage by anticholinesterase drugs used in treatment of myasthenia gravis (cholinergic crisis).

UNLABELED USES To reverse toxicity of echothiophate ophthalmic solution.

CONTRAINDICATIONS Hypersensitivity to pralidoxime; use in

poisoning by insecticide of the carbonate class (Sevin), inorganic phosphates, or organophosphates having no anticholinesterase activity.

CAUTIOUS USE Myasthenia gravis; renal insufficiency; asthma; peptic ulcer; severe cardiac disease; pregnancy (category C); lactation.

ROUTE & DOSAGE

Organophosphate Poisoning
Adult/Adolescent (17 y or older):
IV 1–2 g in 100 mL NS infused over 15–30 min; or 1–2 g as 5% solution in sterile water over not less than 5 min, may repeat after 1 h if muscle weakness not relieved.; **IM** 600 mg, may repeat in 15 min to total dose of 1800 mg if IV route is not feasible.
Adolescent (younger than 17 y)/ Child/Infant: **IV** 20–50 mg/kg. May repeat in 1–2 h if needed (max dose: 2 g).

Anticholinesterase Overdose in Myasthenia Gravis
Adult: **IV** 1–2 g in 100 mL NS infused over 15–30 min, followed by increments of 250 mg q5min prn

ADMINISTRATION

Intramuscular
- Give only if unable to give IV; **not** preferred route.
- Reconstitute as for direct IV injection (see below).

Intravenous

PREPARE: Direct: Reconstitute 1-g vial by adding 20 mL sterile water for injection to yield 50 mg/mL (a 5% solution). ▪ If pulmonary edema is present,

---

give without further dilution. **IV Infusion (preferred):** Further dilute reconstituted solution in 100 mL NS.
ADMINISTER: **Direct:** In pulmonary edema, 1 g or fraction thereof over 5 min; do not exceed 200 mg/min. **IV Infusion (preferred):** Give over 15–30 min. ▪ Stop infusion or reduce rate if hypertension occurs.

ADVERSE EFFECTS CV: Tachycardia, hypertension (dose-related). **CNS:** Dizziness, headache, drowsiness. **HEENT:** Blurred vision, diplopia, impaired accommodation. **GI:** Nausea. **Other:** Hyperventilation, muscular weakness, <u>laryngospasm</u>, muscle rigidity.

INTERACTIONS Drug: May potentiate the effects of BARBITURATES.

PHARMACOKINETICS Peak: 5–15 min IV; 10–20 min IM. **Distribution:** Distributed throughout extracellular fluids; crosses blood–brain barrier slowly if at all. **Metabolism:** Probably in liver. **Elimination:** Rapidly in urine. **Half-Life:** 0.8–2.7 h.

NURSING IMPLICATIONS

Assessment & Drug Effects

▪ Monitor BP, vital signs, and I&O. Report oliguria or changes in I&O ratio.
▪ Monitor closely. It is difficult to differentiate toxic effects of organophosphates or atropine from toxic effects of pralidoxime.
▪ Be alert for and report immediately: Reduction in muscle strength, onset of muscle twitching, changes in respiratory pattern, altered level of consciousness, increases or changes in heart rate and rhythm.

▪ Observe necessary safety precautions with unconscious patient because excitement and manic behavior reportedly may occur following recovery of consciousness.
▪ Keep patient under close observation for 48–72 h, particularly when poison was ingested, because of likelihood of continued absorption of organophosphate from lower bowel.
▪ In patients with myasthenia gravis, overdosage with pralidoxime may convert cholinergic crisis into myasthenic crisis.

PRAMIPEXOLE DIHYDROCHLORIDE
(pra-mi-pex′ole)
Mirapex, Mirapex ER
Classification: NON-ERGOT DERIVATIVE DOPAMINE RECEPTOR AGONIST; ANTIPARKINSON
Therapeutic: ANTIPARKINSON
Prototype: Apomorphine

AVAILABILITY Tablet; extended release tablet

ACTION & *THERAPEUTIC EFFECT*
A dopamine agonist with specificity for the D_2 subfamily dopamine receptor; shown to bind to D_3 and D_4 receptors stimulating dopamine activity on the nerves of the striatum and substantia nigra. *Effectiveness is indicated by improved control of neuromuscular functioning. Improves ADLs.*

USES Treatment of idiopathic Parkinson disease and moderate to severe primary restless legs syndrome (RLS).

CONTRAINDICATIONS Hypersensitivity to pramipexole or ropinirole; abrupt withdrawal; lactation.

P

CAUTIOUS USE Renal impairment; impulse control/compulsive behavior symptoms; history of orthostatic hypotension; restless leg syndrome; older adults; pregnancy (insufficient information on the effect in pregnant women). Safety and efficacy in children not established.

ROUTE & DOSAGE

Parkinson Disease

Adult: **PO Immediate release** Start with 0.125 mg tid gradually increase every 5–7 days (max: 4.5 mg/day); **Extended release** 0.375 mg daily, may increase every 5–7 days (max: 4.5 mg/day)

Restless Legs Syndrome

Adult: **PO** 0.125 mg taken 2–3 h before bed; dose can be increased every 4–7 days (max: 0.75 mg/day)

Renal Impairment Dosage Adjustment

CrCl 35–59 mL/min: **PO Immediate release** Start with 0.125 mg bid; *CrCl 15–34 mL/min:* Start 0.125 mg once daily *CrCl 30–50 mL/min:* **PO Extended release** Start 0.375 mg every other day

ADMINISTRATION

Oral

- Ensure that extended release tablet is swallowed whole and not crushed, divided, or chewed.
- Administer with or without food to decrease nausea.
- For restless leg syndrome, administer 2 to 3 hours before bedtime.

ADVERSE EFFECTS CV: *Orthostatic hypotension,* peripheral edema. **Respiratory:** Dyspnea, nasal congestion. **CNS:** *Dizziness, insomnia, hallucinations, dyskinesia, extrapyramidal reaction,* drowsiness, headache, restless leg syndrome, confusion, fatigue, dystonia, abnormal gait, hypertonia, amnesia. **GI:** *Nausea, constipation,* anorexia, diarrhea, dry mouth, weight loss. **GU:** Urinary frequency. **Musculoskeletal:** Dyskinesia, asthenia, limb pain, muscle spasm. **Other:** Accidental injury, falls.

INTERACTIONS Drug: Cimetidine decreases clearance; BUTYROPHENONES, **metoclopramide**, PHENOTHIAZINES, ANTIPSYCHOTICS may antagonize effects. Closely monitor use with other CNS DEPRESSANTS; ANTIHYPERTENSIVES may have increased risk of hypotension.

PHARMACOKINETICS Absorption: Rapidly from GI tract, greater than 90% bioavailability. **Peak:** 2-6 h. **Distribution:** 15% protein bound. **Metabolism:** Minimally in the liver. **Elimination:** Primarily in urine. **Half-Life:** 8–12 h.

NURSING IMPLICATIONS

Assessment & Drug Effects

- Monitor Bp and Heart rate and for S&S of orthostatic hypotension, especially when the dosage is increased.
- Monitor cardiac status, especially in those with significant orthostatic hypotension.
- Monitor for and report signs of tardive dyskinesia (see Appendix E), CNS depression, and behaviour changes
- Periodic skin examinations.
- Monitor for body weight changes.

Common adverse effects in *italic*; life-threatening effects <u>underlined</u>; generic names in **bold**; classifications in SMALL CAPS; ✦ Canadian drug name; ◉ Prototype drug; ⚠ Alert

Patient & Family Education

- Do not abruptly stop taking this drug. It should be discontinued over a period of 1 wk.
- Hallucinations are an adverse effect of this drug and occur more often in older adults.
- Make position changes slowly especially from a lying or sitting to standing.
- Use caution with potentially dangerous activities until response to drug is known; drowsiness is a common adverse effect.
- Avoid alcohol and use extra caution if taking other prescribed CNS depressants; both may exaggerate drowsiness, dizziness, and orthostatic hypotension.

PRAMLINTIDE
Symlin
Classification: ANTIDIABETIC; AMYLIN ANALOG
Therapeutic: ANTIHYPERGLYCEMIC

AVAILABILITY Solution for injection

ACTION & *THERAPEUTIC EFFECT*
A synthetic analog of human amylin, a hormone secreted by pancreatic beta cells. Amylin reduces postmeal glucagon levels, thus lowering serum glucose level. *Pramlintide is an antihyperglycemic drug that controls postprandial blood glucose levels.*

USES Adjunct treatment of diabetes mellitus type 1 and type 2 in patients who use mealtime insulin therapy and who have failed to achieve desired glucose control despite optimal insulin therapy.

CONTRAINDICATIONS Hypersensitivity to pramlintide, metacresol; noncompliance with insulin regime or medical care; HbA1C greater than 9%; recurrent severe hypoglycemia; hypoglucemia unawareness; gastroparesis; dialysis.

CAUTIOUS USE Osteoporosis; alcohol; thyroid disease; older adults; pregnancy (category C); lactation. Safety and efficacy in children not established.

ROUTE & DOSAGE

Type 1 Diabetes Mellitus

Adult: **Subcutaneous** 15 mcg immediately before each major meal; may increase by 15 mcg increments if no clinically significant nausea for 3–7 days. If nausea or vomiting persists at 45 mcg or 60 mcg, reduce to 30 mcg.

Type 2 Diabetes Mellitus

Adult: **Subcutaneous** 60 mcg immediately before each major meal; may increase to 120 mcg if no clinically significant nausea for 3–7 days. If nausea or vomiting persists at 120 mcg, reduce to 60 mcg.

ADMINISTRATION

Subcutaneous

- Give subcutaneously into the abdomen or thigh (not the arm) immediately before each major meal. Rotate injection sites.
- Never mix pramlintide and insulin in the same syringe. Separate injection sites.
- Use a U100 insulin syringe to administer. One unit of pramlintide drawn from a 0.6 mg/mL vial contains 6 mcg of medication. Thus, a 30 mcg dose is equal to 5 units in a U100 syringe.

Common adverse effects in *italic*; life-threatening effects underlined; generic names in **bold**; classifications in SMALL CAPS; ♦ Canadian drug name; ○ Prototype drug; ⚠ Alert

- Do not administer to patients with HbA1C greater than 9% or those taking drugs to stimulate GI motility.
- Note: When initiating pramlintide therapy, insulin dose reduction is required.
- Store at 2°–8° C (36°–46° F), and protect from light. Do not freeze. Discard vials that have been frozen or overheated. Discard open vials after 30 days.

ADVERSE EFFECTS Respiratory:
Coughing, pharyngitis. **CNS:** Dizziness, fatigue, *headache.* **GI:** Abdominal pain, anorexia, *nausea, vomiting.* **Musculoskeletal:** Arthralgia. **Other:** *Allergic reaction, inflicted injury,* pancreatitis.

INTERACTIONS Drugs: Pramlintide can decrease rate and/or extent of GI absorption of other oral drugs. Significant slowing of gastric motility with ANTIMUSCARINICS.

PHARMACOKINETICS Absorption: 30–40% bioavailability. Peak: 20 min. Distribution: 60% protein bound. Metabolism: Extensive renal metabolism. Half-Life: 48 min.

NURSING IMPLICATIONS

Black Box Warning

Pramlintide use with insulin increases the risk of severe hypoglycemia, particularly in type 1 diabetics. When severe hypoglycemia occurs, it is seen within 3 h following a pramlintide injection. Serious injuries may occur.

Assessment & Drug Effects
- Monitor for severe hypoglycemia, which usually occurs within 3 h of injection. Hypoglycemia is worse in type 1 diabetics.

- Monitor diabetics for loss of glycemic control.
- Withhold drug and notify prescriber for clinically significant nausea or increased frequency or severity of hypoglycemia.
- Monitor for and report promptly S&S of pancreatitis (e.g., upper abdominal plain that radiates to back, nausea and vomiting).
- Monitor lab tests: Baseline and periodic HbA1C; frequent pre/postmeal plasma glucose levels.

Patient & Family Education
- Note: Patients should reduce a.c. rapid-acting or short-acting insulin dosages by 50% when pramlintide is initiated. Check with prescriber.
- Do not drive or engage in potentially hazardous activities until response to drug is known.
- Report any of the following to prescriber: Persistent, significant nausea; episodes of hypoglycemia (e.g., hunger, headache, sweating, tremor, irritability, or difficulty concentrating).

PRAMOXINE HYDROCHLORIDE
(pra-mox'een)
Pramox, ProctoFoam, Tronolane, Tronothane ✦
Classification: LOCAL ANESTHETIC (MUCOSAL); ANTIPRURITIC
Therapeutic: LOCAL ANESTHETIC; ANTIPRURITIC
Prototype: Procaine

AVAILABILITY Foam; gel; lotion; spray

ACTION & *THERAPEUTIC EFFECT*
Produces anesthesia by blocking conduction and propagation of sensory nerve impulses in skin and mucous membranes.

Common adverse effects in *italic;* life-threatening effects <u>underlined;</u> generic names in **bold;** classifications in SMALL CAPS; ✦ Canadian drug name; ○ Prototype drug; ⚠ Alert

1382

Provides temporary relief from pain and itching on skin or mucous membrane.

USES Temporary relief of pain/itching associated with hemorrhoids or burns/cuts/scrapes.

CONTRAINDICATIONS Application to large areas of skin; prolonged use; preparation for laryngopharyngeal examination, bronchoscopy, or gastroscopy.

CAUTIOUS USE Extensive skin disorders; pregnancy (insufficient information related to use in pregnant women); lactation. Safety in children younger than 2 y not established.

ROUTE & DOSAGE

Relief of Minor Pain and Itching

Adult/Child (2 y or older):
Topical Apply tid or qid

ADMINISTRATION

Topical
- Clean thoroughly and dry rectal area before use for temporary relief of hemorrhoidal pain and itching.
- Administer rectal preparations in the morning and evening and after bowel movement or as directed by prescriber. Avoid insertion into rectum.
- Apply lotion or cream to affected surfaces with a gloved hand. Wash hands thoroughly before and after treatment. Apply sparingly, use minimal effective dose.
- Do not apply in or around eyes or nasal membranes.

ADVERSE EFFECTS Skin: Burning, stinging, sensitization.

PHARMACOKINETICS Onset: 3–5 min. **Duration:** Up to 5 h.

NURSING IMPLICATIONS

Assessment & Drug Effects
- Monitor for and report promptly significant tissue irritation or sloughing.

Patient & Family Education
- Drug is usually discontinued if condition being treated does not improve within 2–3 wk or if it worsens, or if rash or condition not present before treatment appears, or if treated area becomes inflamed or infected.
- Discontinue and consult prescriber if rectal bleeding and pain occur during hemorrhoid treatment.

PRASUGREL

(pra-soo'grel)
Effient
Classification: ANTIPLATELET; PLATELET INHIBITOR; ADP RECEPTOR ANTAGONIST
Therapeutic: PLATELET INHIBITOR
Prototype: Clopidogrel

AVAILABILITY Tablet

ACTION & *THERAPEUTIC EFFECT*
An inhibitor of platelet activation and aggregation through irreversible binding to adenosine diphosphate (ADP) receptors on platelets. *Prasugrel prolongs bleeding time, thereby reducing atherosclerotic events in selected high risk patient managed with percutaneous coronary intervention (PCI).*

USES Prophylaxis of arterial thromboembolism in patients with acute coronary syndrome, including unstable angina, non–ST-elevation myocardial infarction (NSTEMI), or ST-elevation acute myocardial infarction (STEMI), who are being managed with percutaneous coronary intervention (PCI).

CONTRAINDICATIONS Active pathologic bleeding disorder; active bleeding; history of TIA or stroke; GI bleeding; within 7 days of CABG surgery or any surgery; adults over 75 y; concomitant use of NSAIDs or other drugs that increase risk of bleeding.

CAUTIOUS USE Severe hepatic impairment (Child-Pugh class C, total score greater than 10); end-stage renal disease; pts less than 60 kg; pregnancy (category B); lactation.

ROUTE & DOSAGE

Thromboembolism Prophylaxis

Adult (younger than 75 y, weight 60 kg or greater): **PO** 60 mg loading dose, then 10 mg once daily; *younger than 75 y, weight less than 60 kg:* 60 mg loading dose, then 5 mg once daily

ADMINISTRATION

Oral
- Give without regard to food.
- Daily aspirin is recommended with prasugrel.
- Do not administer to patient with active bleeding or who is likely to undergo urgent CABG.
- Store at 15°–30° C (59°–86° F).

ADVERSE EFFECTS CV: Hypertension. **Respiratory:** Epistaxis. **CNS:** Headache. **Endocrine:** Hypercholesterolemia, hyperlipidemia.

INTERACTIONS Drug: Warfarin or NSAIDs or ANTICOAGULANTS may increase the risk of bleeding. Do not use with PLATELET INHIBITOR or FIBRINOLYTICS.

PHARMACOKINETICS Absorption: 79% or higher. **Peak:** 30 min. **Metabolism:** Hydrolysis and oxidation to active metabolite. **Elimination:** Urine (68%) and feces (27%). **Half-Life:** 7 h.

NURSING IMPLICATIONS

Black Box Warning

Prasugrel has been associated with severe, sometimes fatal, bleeding (especially in patients with active pathological bleeding, history of TIA or stroke, or those age 75 and older).

Assessment & Drug Effects
- Monitor vital signs. Suspect bleeding if patient is hypotensive and has recently undergone an invasive or surgical procedure.
- Monitor for and report promptly any S&S of active bleeding.
- Monitor lab tests: Periodic Hct and Hgb.

Patient & Family Education
- Report promptly unexplained prolonged or excessive bleeding, or blood in urine or stool.
- Report immediately any of the following: Weakness, extremely pale skin, purple skin patches, jaundice, or fever.
- Inform all medical providers that you are taking prasugrel.
- Do not take OTC anti-inflammatory or pain medications without consulting prescriber.

PRAVASTATIN

(pra-vah-stat'in)

Pravachol

Classification: ANTIHYPERLIPEMIC; HMG-COA REDUCTASE INHIBITOR (STATIN)

Therapeutic: ANTILIPEMIC; STATIN
Prototype: Lovastatin

AVAILABILITY Tablet

ACTION & THERAPEUTIC EFFECT
Competitively inhibits HMG-CoA reductase, the enzyme that catalyzes cholesterol biosynthesis. HMG-CoA reductase inhibitors (statins) increase serum HDL cholesterol, decrease serum LDL cholesterol, VLDL cholesterol, and plasma triglyceride levels. *It is effective in reducing total and LDL cholesterol in various forms of hypercholesterolemia.*

USES Hypercholesterolemia (alone or in combination with bile acid sequestrants) and familial hypercholesterolemia; atherosclerosis.

CONTRAINDICATIONS Hypersensitivity to pravastatin; active liver disease or unexplained elevated serum transaminases; hepatic encephalopathy, hepatitis, jaundice, rhabdomyolysis; pregnancy (category X); lactation.

CAUTIOUS USE Alcoholics, history of liver disease; renal impairment; renal disease; women of child-bearing age who use contraceptive measures. Safe use in children younger than 8 y not established.

ROUTE & DOSAGE

Hyperlipidemia /Stroke Prophylaxis

Adult: **PO** Initially 40 mg daily then may increase up to 80 mg/day
Adult (also taking cylcosporine): **PO** 10 mg daily may titrate up to 20 mg

Adolescent: **PO** 40 mg daily
Child (8–13 y): **PO** 20 mg daily

ADMINISTRATION
Oral
- Give without regard to meals.

ADVERSE EFFECTS CV: Chest pain. CNS: Headache. Hepatic/GI: Increased liver enzymes, nausea, vomiting.

INTERACTIONS Drug: May increase PT when administered with **warfarin.** IMMUNOSPRESSANTS may increase risk of myopathy. **Clarithromycin** may increase risk of toxicity. **Herbal:** Do not use with red yeast rice.

PHARMACOKINETICS Absorption: Poorly from GI tract; 17% reaches systemic circulation. **Onset:** 2 wk. **Peak:** 4 wk. **Distribution:** 43–55% protein bound; does not cross blood–brain barrier; crosses placenta; distributed into breast milk. **Metabolism:** Extensive first-pass metabolism in liver; has no active metabolites. **Elimination:** 20% of dose excreted in urine, 71% in feces. **Half-Life:** 1.8–2.6 h.

NURSING IMPLICATIONS
Assessment & Drug Effects
- Monitor diabetics and prediabetics for loss of glycemic control.
- Monitor coagulation studies with patients receiving concurrent warfarin therapy. PT may be prolonged.
- Monitor lab tests: Baseline LFTs, repeat at 4–12 wk, then annually. LFTs and CPK if symptoms warrant testing.

Patient & Family Education
- Report unexplained muscle pain, tenderness, or weakness, especially

if accompanied by malaise or fever, to prescriber promptly.

- Report signs of bleeding to prescriber promptly when taking concomitant warfarin therapy.
- Monitor blood glucose for loss of glycemic control if diabetic or prediabetic.

PRAZIQUANTEL ©

(pray-zi-kwon'tel)
Biltricide
Classification: ANTHELMINTIC
Therapeutic: ANTHELMINTIC

AVAILABILITY Tablet

ACTION & *THERAPEUTIC EFFECT*

Increases permeability of parasite cell membrane to calcium. Leads to immobilization of their suckers and dislodgment from their residence in blood vessel walls. *Active against all developmental stages of schistosomes, including cercaria (free-swimming larvae). Also active against other trematodes (flukes) and cestodes (tapeworms).*

USES All stages of schistosomiasis (bilharziasis) caused by all *Schistosoma* species pathogenic to humans. Other trematode infections caused by Chinese liver fluke.

UNLABELED USES Lung, sheep liver, and intestinal flukes and tapeworm infections.

CONTRAINDICATIONS Hypersensitivity to praziquantel; ocular cysticercosis. Women should not breast-feed on day of praziquantel therapy or for 72 h after last dose of drug.

CAUTIOUS USE Hepatic disease; cardiac arrhythmias; pregnancy (category B); children younger than 4 y.

ROUTE & DOSAGE

Schistosomiasis
Adult/Child (4 y or older):
PO 60 mg/kg in 3 equally divided doses at 4–6 h intervals on the same day, may repeat in 2–3 mo after exposure

Other Trematodes
Adult/Child (4 y or older):
PO 75 mg/kg in 3 equally divided doses at 4–6 h intervals on the same day

Cestodiasis (Adult or Intestinal Stage)
Adult: **PO** 10–20 mg/kg as single dose

Cestodiasis (Larval or Tissue Stage)
Adult: **PO** 50 mg/kg in 3 divided doses/day for 14 days

ADMINISTRATION
Oral
- Give dose with food and fluids. Tablets can be broken into quarters but should **not** be chewed.
- Advise patient to take sufficient fluid to wash down the medication. Tablets are soluble in water; gagging or vomiting because of bitter taste may result if tablets are retained in the mouth.
- Store tablets in tight containers at less than 30° C (86° F).

ADVERSE EFFECTS CNS: *Dizziness, headache, malaise,* drowsiness, lassitude, <u>CSF reaction syndrome</u> (exacerbation of neurologic signs and symptoms such as seizures, increased CSF protein concentration, increased anticysticercal IgG levels, hyperthermia, intracranial hypertension) in patient treated for cerebral cysticercosis. **Skin:** Pruritus, urticaria. **Hepatic:** *Increased AST, ALT (slight).* **GI:** *Abdominal pain or discomfort with or without nausea;* vomiting, anorexia, diarrhea. **Other:** Fever, sweating, symptoms of host-mediated immunologic response to antigen release from worms (fever, eosinophilia).

DIAGNOSTIC TEST INTERFERENCE

Be mindful that selected drugs may interfere with stool studies for ova and parasites: ***Iron, bismuth, oil (mineral or castor), Metamucil*** (if ingested within 1 wk of test), ***barium, antibiotics, antiamebic*** and ***antimalarial drugs,*** and ***gallbladder dye*** (if administered within 3 wk of test).

INTERACTIONS Drug: Phenytoin

can lead to therapeutic failure. **Food: Grapefruit juice** (greater than 1 qt/day) may increase plasma concentrations and adverse effects.

PHARMACOKINETICS Absorption:

Rapidly, 80% reaches systemic circulation. **Peak:** 1–3 h. **Distribution:** Enters cerebrospinal fluid. **Metabolism:** Extensively to inactive metabolites. **Elimination:** Primarily in urine. **Half-Life:** 0.8–1.5 h.

NURSING IMPLICATIONS

Assessment & Drug Effects

- Patient is reexamined in 2 or 3 mo to ensure complete eradication of the infections.

Patient & Family Education

- Do not drive or operate other hazardous machinery on day of treatment or the following day because of potential drug-induced dizziness and drowsiness.
- Usually, all schistosomal worms are dead 7 days following treatment.
- Contact prescriber if you develop a sustained headache or high fever.

PRAZOSIN HYDROCHLORIDE ⊙

(pra′zoe-sin)

Minipress

Classification: ALPHA-ADRENERGIC RECEPTOR ANTAGONIST; ANTIHYPERTENSIVE

Therapeutic: ANTIHYPERTENSIVE

P

AVAILABILITY Capsule

ACTION & *THERAPEUTIC EFFECT*

Causes selective inhibition of alpha-adrenergic receptors that produces vasodilation in both venous and arteriole vessels with the result that both peripheral vascular resistance and blood pressure are reduced. *Lowers blood pressure in supine and standing positions with most pronounced effect on diastolic pressure.*

USES Treatment of hypertension.

UNLABELED USES Benign prostatic hypertrophy; PTSD related nightmares and sleep disorders; Raynaud phenomenon.

CONTRAINDICATIONS Hypersensitivity to prazosin; hypotension.

CAUTIOUS USE Renal impairment; chronic kidney failure; hypertensive patient with cerebral thrombosis; angina; men with sickle cell trait; older adults; pregnancy (use during pregnancy may increase risk of birth defects); lactation; children.

ROUTE & DOSAGE

Hypertension
Adult: **PO** 1 mg bid or tid, may titrate to 20 mg/day in divided doses (max: 40 mg/day)

ADMINISTRATION

Oral
- Administer with or without food at the same time each day.
- Store at 20°C to 25°C (68°F to 77°F). Protect from moisture and light.

ADVERSE EFFECTS CV: Edema, syncope, postural hypotension, *palpitations.* **Respiratory:** Dyspnea, epistaxis, nasal congestion. **CNS:** *Dizziness, headache, drowsiness,* fatigue, nervousness, vertigo, depression. **HEENT:** Blurred vision. **Skin:** Rash. **GI:** Dry mouth, *nausea,* vomiting, diarrhea, constipation. **GU:** Urinary frequency. **Musculoskeletal:** Weakness.

DIAGNOSTIC TEST INTERFERENCE False positives may occur in screening for *pheochromocytoma.*

INTERACTIONS Drug: DIURETICS, ANTIHYPERTENSIVE AGENTS and **alcohol** increase hypotensive effects. **Sildenafil, vardenafil,** and **tadalafil** may enhance hypotensive effects. Use with other ALPHA-BLOCKERS may increase adverse effects.

PHARMACOKINETICS Absorption: highly protein bound. **Onset:** 2 h. **Peak:** 2–4 h. **Duration:** 10–24 h. **Distribution:** Widely distributed, including into breast milk. **Metabolism:** Extensively in liver. **Elimination:** 6–10% in urine, rest in bile and feces. **Half-Life:** 2–3 h.

NURSING IMPLICATIONS

Assessmnt & Drug Effects
- Be alert for first-dose phenomenon (rare adverse effect: 0.15% of patients); characterized by a precipitous decline in BP, bradycardia, and consciousness disturbances (syncope) within 90–120 min after the initial dose of prazosin. Recovery is usually within several hours. Preexisting low plasma volume (from diuretic therapy or salt restriction), beta-adrenergic therapy, and recent stroke appear to increase the risk of this phenomenon.
- Monitor blood pressure, standing and sitting/supine. If it falls precipitously with first dose, notify prescriber promptly.
- Full therapeutic effect may not be achieved until 4–6 wk of therapy.

Patient & Family Education
- Avoid situations that would result in injury if you should faint, particularly during early phase of

Common adverse effects in *italic;* life-threatening effects <u>underlined</u>; generic names in **bold**; classifications in SMALL CAPS; ♣ Canadian drug name; ◑ Prototype drug; ⚠ Alert

treatment. In most cases, effect does not recur after initial period of therapy; however, it may occur during acute febrile episodes, when drug dose is increased, or when another antihypertensive drug is added to the medication regimen.

- Make position and direction changes slowly and in stages. Dangle legs and move ankles a minute or so before standing when arising in the morning or after a nap.
- Lie down immediately if you experience light-headedness, dizziness, a sense of impending loss of consciousness, or blurred vision. Attempting to stand or walk may result in a fall.
- Do not drive or engage in other potentially hazardous activities until response to drug is known.
- Take drug at same time(s) each day.
- Report priapism or impotence. A change in the drug regimen usually reverses these difficulties.
- Do not take OTC medications, especially remedies for coughs, colds, and allergy, without consulting prescriber.
- Be aware that adverse effects usually disappear with continuation of therapy, but dosage reduction may be necessary.

PREDNISOLONE

(pred-niss'oh-lone)
Prelone, Rayos

PREDNISOLONE ACETATE
Flo-Pred, Pred Forte, Pred Mild

PREDNISOLONE SODIUM PHOSPHATE
AK-Pred, Inflamase Forte, Inflamase Mild

Classification: ADRENAL CORTICOSTEROID
Therapeutic: ANTI-INFLAMMATORY; IMMUNOSUPPRESSANT
Prototype: Prednisone

AVAILABILITY Prednisolone: Tablet; delayed release tablet. **Acetate:** Ophthalmic suspension. **Sodium Phosphate:** Liquid; ophthalmic solution

ACTION & *THERAPEUTIC EFFECT*
Has glucocorticoid activity similar to the naturally occurring hormone. It prevents or suppresses inflammation and immune responses. Its actions include inhibition of leukocyte infiltration at the site of inflammation, interference in the function of inflammatory mediators, and suppression of humoral immune responses. *Effective as an anti-inflammatory agent.*

USES
Principally as an anti-inflammatory and immunosuppressant agent.

CONTRAINDICATIONS
Hypersensitivity to prednisolone; systemic fungal infections; coadministration with live or attenuated virus vaccines; Kaposi sarcoma.

CAUTIOUS USE
Cataracts; coagulopathy; elevated intraocular pressure; cataract; glaucoma; HF; hypertension; recent MI; TB; adrenal insufficiency; hyperthyroidism; DM; seizure disorders; hepatic impairment; renal impairment; psychosis; emotional instability; GI disorders/bleeding; osteoporosis; older adults; pregnancy (category C); children.

P

ROUTE & DOSAGE

Anti-Inflammatory

Adult: PO 5–60 mg/day in single or divided doses
Child: PO 0.1–2 mg/kg/day in divided doses
Ophthalmic See Appendix A-1

ADMINISTRATION

Oral

- Give with meals to reduce gastric irritation. If distress continues, consult prescriber about possible adjunctive antacid therapy.
- Ensure that delayed release tablets are swallowed whole and not crushed or chewed.

Alternate-Day Therapy (ADT) for Patient on Long-Term Therapy

- With ADT, the 48-h requirement for steroids is administered as a single dose every other morning.
- Be aware that ADT minimizes adverse effects associated with long-term treatment while maintaining the desired therapeutic effect.
- See PREDNISONE for numerous additional nursing implications.

ADVERSE EFFECTS CNS: Insomnia. HEENT: Perforation of cornea (with topical drug). Endocrine: Hirsutism (occasional), adverse effects on growth and development of the individual and on sperm; Cushing's syndrome. Skin: Ecchymotic skin lesions; vasomotor symptoms. Also see PREDNISONE. GI: Gastric irritation or ulceration. Other: Sensitivity to heat; fat embolism, hypotension and shock-like reactions.

INTERACTIONS Drug: BARBITURATES, **phenytoin, rifampin** increase steroid metabolism, therefore may need increased doses of prednisolone; **amphotericin B,** DIURETICS add to **potassium** loss; **neostigmine, pyridostigmine** may cause severe muscle weakness in patients with myasthenia gravis; VACCINES, TOXOIDS may inhibit antibody response. **Food: Licorice** may elevate plasma levels and adverse effects.

PHARMACOKINETICS Absorption: Readily from GI tract. Peak: 1–2 h. Duration: 1–1.5 days. Distribution: Crosses placenta; distributed into breast milk. Metabolism: In liver. Elimination: HPA suppression: 24–36 h; in urine. Half-Life: 3.5 h.

NURSING IMPLICATIONS

Assessment & Drug Effects

- Be alert to subclinical signs of lack of improvement such as continued drainage, low-grade fever, and interrupted healing. In diseases caused by microorganisms, infection may be masked, activated, or enhanced by corticosteroids. Observe and report exacerbation of symptoms after short period of therapeutic response.
- Be aware that temporary local discomfort may follow injection of prednisolone into bursa or joint.

Patient & Family Education

- Adhere to established dosage regimen (i.e., do not increase, decrease, or omit doses or change dose intervals).
- Report gastric distress or any sign of peptic ulcer.

PREDNISONE ⊙

(pred'ni-sone)
**Apo-Prednisone ♦,
Deltasone, Meticorten,
Orasone, Panasol, Prednicen-M,
Sterapred, Winpred ♦**

Common adverse effects in *italic*; life-threatening effects <u>underlined</u>; generic names in **bold;** classifications in SMALL CAPS; ♦ Canadian drug name; ⊙ Prototype drug; ⚠ Alert

1390

Classification: ADRENAL
CORTICOSTEROID
Therapeutic: IMMUNOSUPPRESSANT;
ANTI-INFLAMMATORY

AVAILABILITY Tablet; solution

ACTION & *THERAPEUTIC EFFECT*
Immediate-acting synthetic analog
of hydrocortisone with predominantly corticosteroid properties.
*Has anti-inflammatory and immu-
nosuppressant properties.*

USES May be used as a single agent
or conjunctively with antineoplastics in cancer therapy; also used
in treatment of myasthenia gravis
and inflammatory conditions as an
immunosuppressant; acute respiratory distress syndrome, Addison's
disease, adrenal hyperplasic, gout,
gouty arthritis, headache, hemolytic
anemia, sarcoidosis, Stevens–
Johnson syndrome.

UNLABELED USES Absence seizures. COPD exacerbation, Bells
palsy.

CONTRAINDICATIONS Known
hypersensitivity to prednisone;
systemic fungal infections; cerebral malaria; latent or active
amebiasis; viral infections; live
or attenuated vaccines; Kaposi
sarcoma.

CAUTIOUS USE Patients with
infections; nonspecific ulcerative
colitis; diverticulitis; active or latent
peptic ulcer; renal insufficiency;
coagulopathy; psychosis; seizure
disorders; adrenal insufficiency;
TB; thromboembolic disease; CHF;
hypertension; osteoporosis; MG;
older adults; pregnancy (category C);
lactation; children.

ROUTE & DOSAGE

Anti-Inflammatory
Doses are highly individualized
(ranges are provided)
Adult/Adolescent/Child: **PO**
5–60 mg/day in single or
divided doses

Acute Asthma
Child (younger than 12 y): **PO**
1–2 mg/kg/day for 3–10 days

ADMINISTRATION
Oral
- Crush tablet and give with fluid of
patient's choice if unable to swallow whole.
- Give at mealtimes or with a snack
to reduce gastric irritation.
- Dose adjustment may be required
if patient is subjected to severe
stress (serious infection, surgery,
or injury) or if a remission or disease exacerbation occurs.
- Do not abruptly stop drug.
Reduce dose gradually by scheduled decrements (various regimens) to prevent withdrawal
symptoms and permit adrenals to
recover from drug-induced partial
atrophy.

**Alternate-Day Therapy (ADT) for
Patient on Long-Term Therapy**
- With ADT, the 48-h requirement
for steroids is administered as a
single dose every other morning.
- Be aware that ADT minimizes
adverse effects associated with
long-term treatment while maintaining the desired therapeutic
effect.

ADVERSE EFFECTS CV: CHF,
edema. **CNS:** Euphoria, headache,
insomnia, confusion, psycho-
sis. **HEENT:** Cataracts. **Endocrine:**
Cushing's syndrome, growth

suppression in children, carbohydrate intolerance, hyperglycemia, hypokalemia. **GI:** Nausea, vomiting, peptic ulcer. **Musculoskeletal:** Muscle weakness, delayed wound healing, muscle wasting, osteoporosis, aseptic necrosis of bone, spontaneous fractures. **Hematologic:** Leukocytosis.

INTERACTIONS Drug: BARBITURATES, **phenytoin, rifampin** increase steroid metabolism—increased doses of prednisone may be needed; **amphotericin B,** DIURETICS increase **potassium** loss; **neostigmine, pyridostigmine** may cause severe muscle weakness in patients with myasthenia gravis; may inhibit antibody response to VACCINES, TOXOIDS.

PHARMACOKINETICS Absorption: Readily from GI tract. **Peak:** 1–2 h. **Duration:** 1–1.5 days. **Distribution:** Crosses placenta; distributed into breast milk. **Metabolism:** In liver. **Elimination:** Hypothalamus-pituitary axis suppression: 24–36 h; in urine. **Half-Life:** 3.5 h.

NURSING IMPLICATIONS

Assessment & Drug Effects

- Establish baseline and continuing data regarding BP, I&O ratio and pattern, weight, fasting blood glucose level, and sleep pattern. Start flow chart as reference for planning individualized pharmacotherapeutic patient care.
- Check and record BP during dose stabilization period at least 2 × daily. Report an ascending pattern.
- Monitor patient for evidence of HPA axis suppression during long-term therapy by determining plasma cortisol levels at weekly intervals.
- Be aware that older adult patients and patients with low serum albumin are especially susceptible to adverse effects because of excess circulating free glucocorticoids.
- Be alert to signs of hypocalcemia (see Appendix F). Patients with hypocalcemia have increased requirements for pyridoxine (vitamin B_6), vitamins C and D, and folates.
- Be alert to possibility of masked infection and delayed healing (anti-inflammatory and immunosuppressive actions). Prednisone suppresses early classic signs of inflammation. When patient is on an extended therapy regimen, incidence of oral *Candida* infection is high. Inspect mouth daily for symptoms: White patches, black furry tongue, painful membranes and tongue.
- Monitor bone density. Compression and spontaneous fractures of long bones and vertebrae present hazards, particularly in long-term corticosteroid treatment of rheumatoid arthritis or diabetes, in immobilized patients, and older adults.
- Be aware of previous history of psychotic tendencies. Watch for changes in mood and behavior, emotional stability, sleep pattern, or psychomotor activity, especially with long-term therapy, that may signal onset of recurrence. Report symptoms to prescriber.
- Monitor for withdrawal syndrome (e.g., myalgia, fever, arthralgia, malaise) and hypocorticism (e.g., anorexia, vomiting, nausea, fatigue, dizziness, hypotension, hypoglycemia, myalgia, arthralgia) with abrupt discontinuation of corticosteroids after long-term therapy.
- Monitor lab tests: Periodic fasting blood glucose and serum electrolytes during long-term use.

Common adverse effects in *italic*; life-threatening effects <u>underlined</u>; generic names in **bold**; classifications in SMALL CAPS; ✤ Canadian drug name; ✿ Prototype drug; ⚠ Alert

1392

Patient & Family Education

- Take drug as prescribed and do not alter dosing regimen or stop medication without consulting prescriber.
- Be aware that a slight weight gain with improved appetite is expected, but after dosage is stabilized, a sudden slow but steady weight increase [2 kg (5 lb)/wk] should be reported to prescriber.
- Avoid or minimize alcohol, which may contribute to steroid-ulcer development in long-term therapy.
- Report symptoms of GI distress to prescriber and do not self-medicate to find relief.
- Do not use aspirin or other OTC drugs unless they are prescribed specifically by the prescriber.
- Be fastidious about personal hygiene; give special attention to foot care, and be particularly cautious about bruising or abrading the skin.
- Report persistent backache or chest pain (possible symptoms of vertebral or rib fracture) that may occur with long-term therapy.
- Tell dentist or new prescriber about prednisone therapy.

PREGABALIN

Lyrica

Classification:
ANTICONVULSANT; GABA-ANALOG; ANALGESIC/MISCELLANEOUS; ANXIOLYTIC
Therapeutic: ANTICONVULSANT; ANALGESIC; ANTI-ANXIETY
Prototype: Gabapentin
Controlled Substance: Schedule V

AVAILABILITY Capsule; oral solution

ACTION & *THERAPEUTIC EFFECT*
An analog of gamma-aminobutyric acid (GABA) that increases neuronal GABA levels and reduces calcium currents in the calcium channels of neurons; this may account for its control of pain and anxiety. Its affinity for voltage-gated calcium channels may account for its antiseizure activity. *Has analgesic, anti-anxiety, and anticonvulsant properties.*

USES Management of neuropathic pain associated with diabetic peripheral neuropathy or spinal cord injury, adjunctive therapy for adult patients with partial-onset seizures, management of postherpetic neuralgia, fibromyalgia.

UNLABELED USES Treatment of generalized anxiety disorders, treatment of social anxiety disorder, treatment of moderate pain; myopathy related to drug use; restless leg syndrome, hot flashes.

CONTRAINDICATIONS Hypersensitivity to pregabalin or gabapentin.

CAUTIOUS USE History of angioedema; renal impairment or failure, hemodialysis; history of suicidal tendencies or depression; history of drug abuse or alcohol; history of PR interval prolongation; CHF, NYHA (Class III or IV) cardiac status; older adults; pregnancy (category C); lactation. Safe use in children younger than 18 y not established.

ROUTE & DOSAGE

Neuropathic Pain (Diabetic Peripheral Neuropathy)
Adult: **PO** 50–100 mg tid

Partial-Onset Seizures
Adult: **PO** Initial dose 75 mg or less bid or 50 mg tid; may increase to 300 mg bid or 200 mg tid

P

Neuropathic Pain (Spinal Cord Injury)

Adult: **PO** 75 mg bid may increase to 150–600 mg/day

Fibromyalgia

Adult: **PO** 75 mg bid may increase up to 150 bid within first week, then up to 300–450 mg daily (divided)

Postherpetic Neuralgia

Adult: **PO** Initial dose 75 mg bid or 50 mg tid; may increase to 150–300 mg bid or 100–200 mg tid

Renal Impairment Dosage Adjustment

CrCl 30–60 mL/min: 75–300 mg/day given in 2 or 3 divided doses;
15–30 mL/min: 25–150 mg/day given in 1 or 2 divided doses;
less than 15 mL/min: 25–75 mg once daily

Hemodialysis Dosage Adjustment

Dose based on renal function, give supplemental dose

ADMINISTRATION

Oral

- Dosage reduction is required with renal dysfunction.
- Drug should not be abruptly stopped; discontinue by tapering over a minimum of 1 wk.
- Give a supplemental dose immediately following dialysis.
- Store at 15°–30° C (59°– 86° F).

ADVERSE EFFECTS CV: Chest pain. **Respiratory:** Bronchitis, dyspnea. **CNS:** Abnormal gait, amnesia, *ataxia,* confusion, *dizziness,* euphoria, headache, incoordination, myoclonus, nervousness, neuropathy, *somnolence,* speech disorder, abnormal thinking, tremor, twitching, vertigo. **HEENT:** Abnormal vision, *blurry vision, diplopia.* **Endocrine:** Edema, facial edema, hypoglycemia, *peripheral edema, weight gain.* **GI:** Constipation, dry mouth, flatulence, increased appetite, vomiting. **GU:** Urinary incontinence. **Musculoskeletal:** Back pain, myasthenia. **Other:** *Accidental injury,* flu syndrome, pain.

INTERACTIONS Drug: Concomitant use with THIAZOLIDINEDIONES may exacerbate weight gain and fluid retention.

PHARMACOKINETICS Absorption: 90% bioavailability. **Peak:** 1.5 h. **Metabolism:** Negligible. **Elimination:** Primarily in the urine. **Half-Life:** 6 h.

NURSING IMPLICATIONS

Assessment & Drug Effects

- Monitor for and report promptly mental status or behavior changes (e.g., anxiety, panic attacks, restlessness, irritability, depression, suicidal thoughts).
- Monitor for weight gain, peripheral edema, and S&S of heart failure, especially with concurrent thiazolidinedione (e.g., rosiglitazone) therapy.
- Monitor diabetics for increased incidences of hypoglycemia.
- Supervise ambulation especially when other CNS drugs are used concurrently.
- Monitor lab tests: Baseline and periodic renal function tests; periodic platelet count.

Patient & Family Education

- Do not drive or engage in potentially hazardous activities until response to drug is known.

Common adverse effects in *italic;* life-threatening effects <u>underlined;</u> generic names in **bold;** classifications in SMALL CAPS; ♦ Canadian drug name; ○ Prototype drug; △ Alert

1394

- Report any of the following to a health care provider: Changes in vision (i.e., blurred vision); dizziness and incoordination; weight gain and swelling of the extremities, behavior or mood changes, especially suicidal thoughts.
- Avoid alcohol consumption while taking this drug.
- Inform your prescriber if you plan to become pregnant or father a child.

PRIMAQUINE PHOSPHATE

(prim'a-kween)

Classification: ANTIMALARIAL
Therapeutic: ANTIMALARIAL
Prototype: Chloroquine

AVAILABILITY Tablet

ACTION & *THERAPEUTIC EFFECT*
Acts on primary exoerythrocytic forms of *Plasmodium vivax* and *Plasmodium falciparum*. Destroys late tissue forms of *P. vivax* and thus effects radical cure (prevents relapse). *Gametocidal activity against all species of Plasmodia that infect humans; interrupts transmission of malaria.*

USES Malaria treatment

UNLABELED USES Treatment of *Pneumocystis carinii* pneumonia (PCP) in AIDS; malaria prophylaxis.

CONTRAINDICATIONS Hypersensitivity to primaquine or iodoquinol; rheumatoid arthritis; lupus erythematosus (SLE); hemolytic drugs, concomitant or recent use of agents capable of bone marrow depression (e.g., quinacrine; patients with G6PD deficiency), contraindicated in pregnancy; lactation—infant risk cannot be ruled out.

CAUTIOUS USE Bone marrow depression; hematologic disease; methemoglobin reductase deficiency; cardiac disease or hypertension, long QT syndrome, history of ventricular arrhythmia, bradycardia; hypokalemia, hypomagnesemia, children.

ROUTE & DOSAGE

Malaria Treatment

Screen for G6PD deficiency prior to initiating therapy
Adult: **PO** 30 mg daily for 14 days in combination with another appropriate agent

ADMINISTRATION

Oral

- Give drug at mealtime or with an antacid (prescribed); may prevent or relieve gastric irritation. Notify prescriber if GI symptoms persist.
- Do not administer to patients who have recently received quinacrine.
- Store at 25 degrees C (77 degrees F), with excursions permitted between 15 and 30 degrees C (59 and 86 degrees F).

ADVERSE EFFECTS GI: *Nausea, abdominal pain.* **Hematologic:** Hematologic reactions including granulocytopenia and acute hemolytic anemia in patients with G6PD deficiency, *leukopenia*, hemolytic anemia.

INTERACTIONS Drug: Avoid use with agents that prolong the QT interval (e.g., **dofetilide, dronedarone, pimozide, ziprasidone);** CYP2D6 INHIBITORS or CYP3A4 INDUCERS may decrease concentration of primaquine. **Food:** avoid grapefruit juice.

PHARMACOKINETICS Absorption: Readily from GI tract. **Peak:**

P

1–3 h. **Metabolism:** Rapidly in liver to active metabolites. **Elimination:** In urine. **Half-Life:** 3.7–9.6 h.

NURSING IMPLICATIONS

Assessment & Drug Effects

- Be aware drug may precipitate acute hemolytic anemia in patients with G6PD deficiency, an inherited error of metabolism carried on the X chromosome, present in about 10% of American black males and certain white ethnic groups: Sardinians, Sephardic Jews, Greeks, and Iranians. Whites manifest more intense expression of hemolytic reaction than do blacks. Screen for prior to initiation of therapy.
- Monitor ECG in patients with cardiac disease, long QT syndrome, a history of a ventricular arrhythmia, uncorrected hypokalemia or hypomagnesemia, bradycardia or if the person is taking a drug to prolong the QT interval.
- Monitor lab tests: Periodic CBC with differential, and Hct and Hgb, pregnancy test prior to initiation of treatment for sexually active females of reproductive potential.

Patient & Family Education

- Examine urine after each voiding and to report to prescriber darkening of urine, red-tinged urine, and decrease in urine volume. Also report chills, fever, precordial pain, cyanosis (all suggest a hemolytic reaction). Sudden reductions in hemoglobin or erythrocyte count suggest an impending hemolytic reaction. Patient needs to stay hydrated through therapy.
- Review adverse effects with patient and/or caregiver.
- Tell patient to take the drug with food to minimize gastric irritation.

PRIMIDONE
(pri′mi-done)

Mysoline

Classification: ANTICONVULSANT; BARBITURATE
Therapeutic: ANTICONVULSANT
Prototype: Phenobarbital

AVAILABILITY Tablet

ACTION & *THERAPEUTIC EFFECT*

Antiepileptic properties result from raising the seizure threshold and changing seizure patterns. *Effective as an anticonvulsant in all types of seizure disorders except absence seizures.*

USES Alone or concomitantly with other anticonvulsant agents in the prophylactic management of complex partial (psychomotor) and generalized tonic-clonic (grand mal) seizures.

UNLABELED USES Essential tremor.

CONTRAINDICATIONS Hypersensitivity to barbiturates, porphyria; suicidal ideation; pregnancy (category D).

CAUTIOUS USE Chronic lung disease, sleep apnea; liver or kidney disease, dialysis; hyperactive children; mental status changes, major depression, suicidal tendencies; lactation; children.

ROUTE & DOSAGE

Seizures

Adult/Child (8 y or older): **PO** 125–250 mg/day, increased by 125–250 mg/wk (max: 2 g in 2–4 divided doses)

Common adverse effects in *italic*; life-threatening effects underlined; generic names in **bold**; classifications in SMALL CAPS; ♣ Canadian drug name; ☯ Prototype drug; ⚠ Alert

1396

Child (younger than 8 y): **PO**
50–125 mg/day, increased by
50–125 mg/wk (max: 2 g/day
in 2–4 divided doses)
Neonates: **PO** 12–20 mg/kg/
day in 2–4 divided doses

ADMINISTRATION

Oral
- Give whole or crush with fluid of patient's choice.
- Give with food if drug causes GI distress.

ADVERSE EFFECTS CNS: *Drowsiness, sedation, vertigo, ataxia, headache,* excitement (children), confusion, unusual fatigue, hyperirritability, emotional disturbances, acute psychoses (usually patients with psychomotor epilepsy). **HEENT:** Diplopia, nystagmus, swelling of eyelids. **Skin:** Alopecia, maculopapular or morbilliform rash, edema, lupus erythematosus-like syndrome. **GI:** *Nausea, vomiting, anorexia.* **GU:** Impotence. **Hematologic:** *Leukopenia, thrombocytopenia,* eosinophilia, decreased serum folate levels, megaloblastic anemia (rare). **Other:** Lymphadenopathy, osteomalacia.

INTERACTIONS Drug: **Alcohol,** CNS DEPRESSANTS compound CNS depression; **phenobarbital** may decrease absorption and increase metabolism of ORAL ANTICOAGULANTS; increases metabolism of CORTICOSTEROIDS, ORAL CONTRACEPTIVES, ANTICONVULSANTS, **digitoxin,** possibly decreasing their effects; ANTIDEPRESSANTS potentiate adverse effects of primidone; **griseofulvin** decreases absorption of primidone. Do not use with **voriconazole. Herbal: Kava, valerian** may potentiate sedation.

PHARMACOKINETICS Absorption: Approximately 60–80% from GI tract. **Peak:** 4 h. **Distribution:** Distributed into breast milk. **Metabolism:** In liver to phenobarbital and PEMA. Affected cytochrome P450 isoenzymes and drug transporters: CYP2C9, CYP3A4, CYP1A2, CYP2C19, CYP2E1, UGT, and P-gp. **Elimination:** In urine. **Half-Life:** Primidone 3–24 h, PEMA 24–48 h; phenobarbital 72–144 h.

NURSING IMPLICATIONS

Assessment & Drug Effects
- Monitor primidone plasma levels (concentrations of primidone greater than 10 mcg/mL are usually associated with significant ataxia and lethargy). Therapeutic blood levels for primidone are 5–12 mcg/mL.
- Therapeutic response may not be evident for several weeks.
- Observe for S&S of folic acid deficiency: Mental dysfunction, psychiatric disorders, neuropathy, megaloblastic anemia. Determine serum folate levels if indicated.
- Monitor lab tests: Baseline CBC and complete metabolic panel, repeat q6mo; primidone blood level as needed.

Patient & Family Education
- Avoid driving and other potentially hazardous activities during beginning of treatment because drowsiness, dizziness, and ataxia may be severe. Symptoms tend to disappear with continued therapy; if they persist, dosage reduction or drug withdrawal may be necessary.
- Avoid alcohol and other CNS depressants unless otherwise directed by prescriber.
- Do not take OTC medications unless approved by prescriber.

Common adverse effects in *italic;* life-threatening effects <u>underlined;</u> generic names in **bold;** classifications in SMALL CAPS; ♣ Canadian drug name; ◎ Prototype drug; ⚠ Alert

- Pregnant women should receive prophylactic vitamin K therapy for 1 mo prior to and during delivery to prevent neonatal hemorrhage.
- Withdraw primidone gradually to avoid precipitating status epilepticus.

PROBENECID ⊙

(proe-ben'e-sid)
Benuryl ♣, Probalan
Classification: URICOSURIC; ANTIGOUT
Therapeutic: ANTIGOUT

AVAILABILITY Tablet

ACTION & *THERAPEUTIC EFFECT*
Competitively inhibits renal tubular reabsorption of uric acid, thereby promoting its excretion and reducing serum urate levels. *Prevents formation of new tophaceous deposits and uric acid build-up in the serum and tissues. As an additive to penicillin, it increases serum concentration of penicillins and prolongs their serum concentration.*

USES Hyperuricemia in chronic gouty arthritis and tophaceous gout.

UNLABELED USES Adjuvant to therapy with penicillin G and penicillin analogs to elevate and prolong plasma concentrations of these antibiotics; to promote uric acid excretion in hyperuricemia secondary to administration of thiazides and related diuretics, furosemide, ethacrynic acid, pyrazinamide.

CONTRAINDICATIONS Blood dyscrasias; uric acid kidney stones; during or within 2–3 wk of acute gouty attack; over excretion of uric acid (greater than 1000 mg/day); patients with creatinine clearance less than 50 mg/min; use with penicillin in presence of known renal impairment; use for hyperuricemia secondary to cancer chemotherapy.

CAUTIOUS USE History of peptic ulcer; pregnancy (category B); lactation; children older than 2 y.

ROUTE & DOSAGE

Gout
Adult: **PO** 250 mg bid for 1 wk, then 500 mg bid (max: 3 g/day)

Adjunct for Penicillin or Cephalosporin Therapy
Adult: **PO** 500 mg qid or 1 g with single dose therapy (e.g., gonorrhea)
Child (2–14 y or weight less than 50 kg): **PO** 25–40 mg/kg/day in 4 divided doses

ADMINISTRATION
Oral
- Therapy is usually not initiated during an acute gouty attack. Consult prescriber.
- Minimize GI adverse effects by giving after meals, with food, milk, or antacid (prescribed). If symptoms persist, dosage reduction may be required.
- Give with a full glass of water if not contraindicated.
- Be aware that prescriber may prescribe concurrent prophylactic doses of colchicine for first 3–6 mo of therapy because frequency of acute gouty attacks may increase during first 6–12 mo of therapy.

ADVERSE EFFECTS **Respiratory:** Respiratory depression.

Common adverse effects in *italic;* life-threatening effects underlined; generic names in **bold;** classifications in SMALL CAPS; ♣ Canadian drug name; ⊙ Prototype drug; ⚠ Alert

CNS: *Headache.* **Skin:** Dermatitis, pruritus. **GI:** *Nausea, vomiting, anorexia,* sore gums, hepatic necrosis (rare). **GU:** Urinary frequency. **Musculoskeletal:** Exacerbations of gout, uric acid kidney stones. **Hematologic:** Anemia, hemolytic anemia (possibly related to G6PD deficiency), aplastic anemia (rare).**Other:** Flushing, dizziness, fever, anaphylaxis.

DIAGNOSTIC TEST INTERFERENCE

False-positive *urine glucose* tests are possible with *Benedict's solution* or *Clinitest* [*glucose oxidase methods* not affected (e.g., *Clinistix, TesTape*)].

INTERACTIONS Drug: SALICYLATES

may decrease uricosuric activity; may decrease **methotrexate** elimination, causing increased toxicity; decreases **nitrofurantoin** efficacy and increases its toxicity. Decreases clearance of PENICILLINS, CEPHALOSPORINS, and NSAIDS.

PHARMACOKINETICS Absorption:

Readily from GI tract. **Onset:** 30 min. **Peak:** 2–4 h. **Duration:** 8 h. **Distribution:** Crosses placenta. **Metabolism:** In liver. **Elimination:** In urine. **Half-Life:** 4–17 h.

NURSING IMPLICATIONS

Assessment & Drug Effects

- Patients taking sulfonylureas may require dosage adjustment. Probenecid enhances hypoglycemic actions of these drugs (see DIAGNOSTIC TEST INTERFERENCES).
- Expect urate tophaceous deposits to decrease in size. Classic locations are in cartilage of ear pinna and big toe, but they can occur in bursae, tendons, skin, kidneys, and other tissues.
- Monitor lab tests: Periodic serum urate.

Patient & Family Education

- Drink fluid liberally (approximately 3000 mL/day) to maintain daily urinary output of at least 2000 mL or more. This is important because increased uric acid excretion promoted by drug predisposes to renal calculi.
- Prescriber may advise restriction of high-purine foods during early therapy until uric acid level stabilizes. Foods high in purine include organ meats (sweetbreads, liver, kidney), meat extracts, meat soups, gravy, anchovies, and sardines. Moderate amounts are present in other meats, fish, seafood, asparagus, spinach, peas, dried legumes, wild game.
- Avoid alcohol because it may increase serum urate levels.
- Do not stop taking drug without consulting prescriber. Irregular dosage schedule may sharply elevate serum urate level and precipitate acute gout.
- Report symptoms of hypersensitivity to prescriber. Discontinuation of drug is indicated.
- Do not take aspirin or other OTC medications without consulting prescriber. If a mild analgesic is required, acetaminophen is usually allowed.

PROCAINAMIDE HYDROCHLORIDE ⊙

(proe-kane-a'mide)

Classification: CLASS IA ANTIARRHYTHMIC
Therapeutic: CLASS IA ANTIARRHYTHMIC

AVAILABILITY Solution for injection

ACTION & *THERAPEUTIC EFFECT*

Potent class IA antiarrhythmic that depresses excitability of myocardium to electrical stimulation, reduces conduction velocity in atria, ventricles, and His-Purkinje system. Produces peripheral vasodilation and hypotension, especially with IV use. *Effectively used for atrial arrhythmias; suppresses automaticity of His-Purkinje ventricular muscle.*

USES Prophylactically to maintain normal sinus rhythm following conversion of atrial flutter or fibrillation by other methods; to prevent recurrence of paroxysmal atrial fibrillation and tachycardia, paroxysmal AV junctional rhythm, ventricular tachycardia, ventricular and atrial premature contractions. Also cardiac arrhythmias associated with surgery and anesthesia.

UNLABELED USES Malignant hyperthermia; atrial fibrillation.

CONTRAINDICATIONS Hypersensitivity to procainamide or procaine, yellow dye 5 (tartrazine); blood dyscrasias; bundle branch block; complete AV block, second and third degree AV block unassisted by pacemaker; QT prolongation, torsades de pointes; non-life-threatening ventricular arrhythmias; leukopenia or agranulocytosis; SLE; concurrent use with other antiarrhythmic agents; myasthenia gravis.

CAUTIOUS USE Patient who has undergone electrical conversion to sinus rhythm; first-degree heart block; bone marrow suppression or cytopenia; hypotension, cardiac enlargement, CHF, MI, ischemic heart disease; coronary occlusion, ventricular dysrhythmia from digitalis intoxication, ventricular arrhythmias; hepatic or renal insufficiency; electrolyte imbalance; bronchial asthma; aspirin

hypersensitivity; myasthenia gravis; cytopenia; pregnancy (category C); lactation.

ROUTE & DOSAGE

Arrhythmias

Adult: **IV** 100 mg q5min at a rate of 25–50 mg/min until arrhythmia is controlled or 1 g given, then 2–6 mg/min; **IV** ACLS recommendation is 20–50 mg/min until either the arrhythmia is suppressed, hypotension occurs, the QRS complex is widened by 50%, or the max dose of 17 mg/kg is given
Child: **IV** PALS recommendation is 15 mg/kg over 30–60 min

Renal Impairment Dosage Adjustment

CrCl 35–59 mL/min: Decrease initial maintenance dosage by approximately 30%.
CrCl 15–34 mL/min: Decrease initial maintenance dosage by 40–60%.
CrCl less than 15 mL/min: Individualize dosage

ADMINISTRATION

Intramuscular

- IM route should be used only when IV route is not feasible.

Intravenous

Use IV route for emergency situations.

PREPARE: Direct: Dilute each 100 mg with 5–10 mL of D5W or sterile water for injection. **IV Infusion:** Add 1 g of procainamide to 250–500 mL of D5W solution to yield 4 mg/mL in 250 mL or 2 mg/mL in 500 mL.
ADMINISTER: Direct: Usual rate is 20 mg/min. Faster rates (up to

Common adverse effects in *italic;* life-threatening effects <u>underlined</u>; generic names in **bold**; classifications in SMALL CAPS; ✦ Canadian drug name; ❍ Prototype drug; ⚠ Alert

50 mg/min) should be used with caution. **IV Infusion for Adult:** 2–6 mg/min. **IV Infusion for Child:** 20–80 mcg/kg/min. ▪ Control IV administration over several hours by assessment of procainamide plasma levels. ▪ Use an infusion pump with constant monitoring. ▪ Keep patient in supine position. ▪ Be alert to signs of too rapid administration of drug (speed shock: Irregular pulse, tight feeling in chest, flushed face, headache, loss of consciousness, shock, cardiac arrest).

INCOMPATIBILITIES: **Solution/ additive:** Bretylium, esmolol, ethacrynate, milrinone, phenytoin. **Y-site:** Acyclovir sodium, azathioprine sodium, carboplatin, carmustine, cefamandole, ceftizoxime, dantrolene sodium, diazepam, diazoxide, ganciclovir sodium, gemtuzumab ozogamicin, lansoprazole, metronidazole, milrinone acetate (amrinone), minocycline hydrochloride, phenytoin sodium, sulfamethoxazole-trimethoprim.

▪ Store solution for up to 24 h at room temperature and for 7 days under refrigeration at 2°–8° C (36°–46° F). ▪ Slight yellowing does not alter drug potency, but discard solution if it is markedly discolored or precipitated.

ADVERSE EFFECTS **CV:** Severe

hypotension, pericarditis, ventricular fibrillation, AV block, tachycardia, flushing. **CNS:** Dizziness, psychosis. **Skin:** Maculopapular rash, pruritus, erythema, skin rash. **GI:** Diarrhea, nausea, taste disorder, vomiting. **Hematologic:** Agranulocytosis with repeated use; *thrombocytopenia*. **Other:** Fever, muscle and joint pain, angioneurotic edema,

myalgia, *SLE-like syndrome (50% of patients on large doses for 1 y):* Polyarthralgias, pleuritic pain, pleural effusion.

INTERACTIONS **Drug:** Other

ANTIARRHYTHMICS add to therapeutic and toxic effects; ANTICHOLINERGIC AGENTS compound anticholinergic effects; ANTIHYPERTENSIVES add to hypotensive effects; **cimetidine** may increase levels with increase in toxicity; **fingolimod** increases antiarrhythmic effects.

PHARMACOKINETICS **Peak:**

15–60 min IM; **Duration:** 3 h; 8 h with sustained release. **Distribution:** Distributed to CSF, liver, spleen, kidney, brain, and heart; crosses placenta; distributed into breast milk. **Metabolism:** In liver to *N*-acetylprocainamide (NAPA), an active metabolite (30–60% metabolized to NAPA). **Elimination:** In urine. **Half-Life:** 3 h procainamide, 6 h NAPA.

NURSING IMPLICATIONS

Black Box Warning

Procainamide has been associated with bone marrow depression.

Assessment & Drug Effects

▪ Check apical radial pulses before each dose during period of adjustment to the oral route.

▪ Patients with severe heart, liver, or kidney disease and hypotension are at particular risk for adverse effects.

▪ Monitor the patient's ECG and BP continuously during IV drug administration.

▪ Discontinue IV drug temporarily when (1) arrhythmia is interrupted, (2) severe toxic effects are present, (3) QRS complex is excessively widened (greater than 50%), (4) PR interval is prolonged, or (5) BP drops 15 mm Hg or more. Obtain rhythm strip and notify prescriber.

- Ventricular dysrhythmias are usually abolished within a few minutes after IV dose and within an hour after IM administration.
- Report promptly complaints of chest pain, dyspnea, and anxiety. Digitalization may have preceded procainamide in patients with atrial arrhythmias. Cardiotonic glycosides may induce sufficient increase in atrial contraction to dislodge atrial mural emboli, with subsequent pulmonary embolism.

Patient & Family Education

- Report to prescriber signs of reduced procainamide control: Weakness, irregular pulse, unexplained fatigability, anxiety.

PROCAINE HYDROCHLORIDE ⊕

(proe'kane)

Novocain

Classification: LOCAL ANESTHETIC (ESTER-TYPE)

Therapeutic: LOCAL ANESTHETIC

AVAILABILITY Solution for injection

ACTION & *THERAPEUTIC EFFECT*

Decreases sodium flux into nerve cell, thus depressing initial depolarization and preventing propagation and conduction of the nerve impulse. *Local anesthetic action produces loss of sensation and motor activity in circumscribed areas that are treated.*

USES Spinal anesthesia and epidural and peripheral nerve block by injection and infiltration methods.

CONTRAINDICATIONS Known hypersensitivity to procaine or to other drugs of similar chemical structure, to PABA, and to parabens; generalized septicemia, inflammation, or sepsis at proposed injection site; cerebrospinal diseases (e.g., meningitis, syphilis); heart block, hypotension, hypertension; bowel pathology, GI hemorrhage; coagulopathy, anticoagulants, *thrombocytopenia*.

CAUTIOUS USE Debilitated, acutely ill patients; obstetric delivery; increased intra-abdominal pressure; known drug allergies and sensitivities; impaired cardiac function, dysrhythmias; shock; older adults; pregnancy (category C); lactation; children.

ROUTE & DOSAGE

Spinal Anesthesia

Adult: **Intrathecal** 2 mL of 10% solution diluted with NS

Infiltration Anesthesia/Peripheral Nerve Block

Adult/Adolescent/Child:
Regional Up to 200 mL of a 0.5% solution, up to 100 mL of a 1% solution

ADMINISTRATION

- **0.5% Solution Preparation:** To prepare 60 mL of a 0.5% solution (5 mg/mL), dilute 30 mL of 1% solution with 30 mL of NS. Add 0.5–1 mL epinephrine 1:1000/100 mL anesthetic solution for vasoconstrictive effect (1:200,000–1:100,000).
- **0.25% Solution Preparation:** To prepare 60 mL of a 0.25% solution (2.5 mg/mL), dilute 45 mL of 1% solution with 45 mL of NS.

Common adverse effects in *italic;* life-threatening effects <u>underlined</u>; generic names in **bold**; classifications in SMALL CAPS; ♣ Canadian drug name; ⊕ Prototype drug; ⚠ Alert

Add 0.5–1 mL epinephrine 1:1000/100 mL anesthetic solution for vasoconstrictive effect (1:200,000–1:100,000).

- Do not use solutions that are cloudy, discolored, or that contain crystals. Discard unused portion of solutions not containing a preservative. Avoid use of solution with preservative for spinal, epidural, or caudal block.

***INCOMPATIBILITIES:* Solution/ additive: Aminophylline, amobarbital, chlorothiazide, magnesium sulfate, phenobarbital, phenytoin, secobarbital, sodium bicarbonate.**

ADVERSE EFFECTS CV: Myocardial depression, arrhythmias including bradycardia (also fetal bradycardia); hypotension. **CNS:** Anxiety, nervousness, dizziness, circumoral paresthesia, tremors, drowsiness, sedation, convulsions, respiratory arrest. With spinal anesthesia: Postspinal headache, arachnoiditis, palsies, spinal nerve paralysis, meningism. **HEENT:** Tinnitus, blurred vision. **Skin:** Cutaneous lesions of delayed onset, urticaria, pruritus, angioneurotic edema, sweating, syncope, anaphylactoid reaction. **GI:** Nausea, vomiting. **GU:** Urinary retention, fecal or urinary incontinence, loss of perineal sensation and sexual function, slowing of labor and increased incidence of forceps delivery (all with caudal or epidural anesthesia).

INTERACTIONS Drug: May antagonize effects of SULFONAMIDES; increased risk of hypotension with MAOIS, ANTIHYPERTENSIVES.

PHARMACOKINETICS Absorption: Rapidly from injection site. **Onset:** 2–5 min. **Duration:** 1 h. **Metabolism:** Hydrolyzed by plasma pseudocholinesterases. **Elimination:** 80% of metabolites excreted in urine. **Half-Life:** 7.7 min.

NURSING IMPLICATIONS

Assessment & Drug Effects

- Be aware that reactions during dental procedure are usually mild, transient, and produced by epinephrine added to local anesthetic (e.g., headache, palpitation, tachycardia, hypertension, dizziness).
- Use procaine with epinephrine with caution in body areas with limited blood supply (e.g., fingers, toes, ears, nose). If used, inspect particular area for evidence of reduced perfusion (vasospasm): Pale, cold, sensitive skin.
- Hypotension is the most important complication of spinal anesthesia. Risk period is during first 30 min after induction and is intensified by changes in position that promote decreased venous return, or by preexisting hypertension, pregnancy, old age, or hypovolemia.

Patient & Family Education

- Understand that there will be temporary loss of sensation in the area of the injection.
- Do not consume hot liquids or foods until sensation returns when drug used for dental procedure.

PROCARBAZINE HYDROCHLORIDE

(proe-kar'ba-zeen)

Matulane

Classification: ANTINEOPLASTIC; ALKYLATING AGENT

Therapeutic: ANTINEOPLASTIC

Prototype: Cyclophosphamide

AVAILABILITY Capsule

ACTION & *THERAPEUTIC EFFECT*
Hydrazine derivative with anti-metabolite properties that is cell cycle–specific for the S phase of cell division. Suppresses mitosis at interphase and causes chromatin derangement. *Highly toxic to rapidly proliferating tissue.*

USES Treatment of stage III or IV Hodgkin lymphoma.

UNLABELED USES Solid CNS tumors.

CONTRAINDICATIONS Severe myelosuppression; pheochromocytoma; alcohol ingestion;foods high in tyramine content; diarrhea, sympathomimetic drugs. MAO inhibitors should be discontinued 14 days prior to therapy; tricyclic antidepressants discontinued 7 days before therapy; pregnancy — fetal risk cannot be ruled out; lactation—infant risk cannot be ruled out.

CAUTIOUS USE Hepatic or renal impairment; cardiac disease; bipolar disorder, mania, paranoid schizophrenia; G6PD deficiency; parkinsonism; following radiation or chemotherapy before at least 1 mo has elapsed; alcoholism; infection; children.

ROUTE & DOSAGE

Adjunct for Hodgkin Lymphoma
Adult: **PO** *as part of MOOP regimen* 100 mg/m² *daily days 1–14; repeat cycle q28 days*

ADMINISTRATION
Oral
- NIOSH recommends single gloves by anyone handling intact tablets or capsules or administering from a unit-dose package. Use double gloves and protective gown when cutting, crushing, or manipulating or handling of uncoated tablets. During administration uses single gloves and wear eye/face protection if the formulation is hard to swallow or if the patient may resist, vomit or spit up.
- Do not give if WBC count is less than 4000/mm³ or platelet count is less than 100,000/mm³. Consult prescriber.
- Avoid taking with high tyramine-containing foods.
- Store at 20 degrees C (68 degrees F). Protect from freezing, moisture, and light.

ADVERSE EFFECTS GI: *Severe nausea and vomiting.* **Hematologic:** *Bone marrow suppression (leukopenia*, anemia, *thrombocytopenia).*

INTERACTIONS Drug: Alcohol, PHENOTHIAZINES, and other CNS DEPRESSANTS add to CNS depression; TRICYCLIC ANTIDEPRESSANTS, MAO INHIBITORS, SYMPATHOMIMETICS, **ephedrine, phenylpropanolamine** may precipitate hypertensive crisis, hyperpyrexia; seizures or death. Procarbazine may enhance the effects of **CNS depressants.** Do not use with LIVE VACCINES; MYELOSUPPRESSIVE AGENTS AND IMMUNOSUPPRESSANTS increase risk of adverse effects. **Food: Tyramine**-containing foods may precipitate hypertensive crisis; alcohol may case disulfiram reaction. **Herbal:** Do not use with echinacea.

PHARMACOKINETICS Absorption: Readily from GI tract. **Peak:** 1 h. **Distribution:** Widely distributed with high concentrations in liver, kidneys, intestinal wall, and skin; crosses the blood-brain barrier.

Metabolism: In liver. **Elimination:** In urine. **Half-Life:** 1 h.

NURSING IMPLICATIONS

Black Box Warning

Procarbazine should be given only under supervision of or by a physician experienced in the use of potent antineoplastic drugs. Adequate clinical and laboratory facilities should be available to patients for proper monitoring of treatment.

Assessment & Drug Effects

- Monitor baseline and periodic BP, weight, temperature, pulse, and I&O ratio and pattern.
- Protect patient from exposure to infection and trauma when nadir of leukopenia is approached. Note and report changes in voiding pattern, hematuria, and dysuria (possible signs of urinary tract infection). Monitor I&O ratio and temperature closely.
- Withhold drug and notify prescriber of any of the following: CNS S&S (e.g., paresthesias, neuropathies, confusion); leukopenia [WBC count less than 4000/mm³; thrombocytopenia (platelet count less than 100,000/mm³)]; hypersensitivity reaction, the first small ulceration or persistent spot of soreness in oral cavity, diarrhea, and bleeding.
- Monitor for and report any of the following: Chills, fever, weakness, shortness of breath, productive cough. Drug will be discontinued.
- Assess for signs of liver dysfunction: Jaundice (yellow skin, sclerae, and soft palate), frothy or dark urine, clay-colored stools.
- Tolerance to nausea and vomiting (most common adverse effects) usually develops by end of first week of treatment. Doses are kept at a minimum during this time. If vomiting persists, therapy will be interrupted.
- Monitor lab tests: Baseline and q3–4days Hgb, Hct, CBC with differential every 3–4 days during therapy and for a minimum of two weeks after administration, reticulocyte, and platelet count; baseline and weekly LFTs and renal function tests.

Patient & Family Education

- Avoid OTC nose drops, cough medicines, and antiobesity preparations containing ephedrine, amphetamine, epinephrine, and tricyclic antidepressants because they may cause hypertensive crises. Do not use OTC preparations without prescriber's approval.
- Report to prescriber any sign of impending infection.
- Avoid vaccines during therapy.
- Do not eat foods high in tyramine content (e.g., aged cheese, beer, wine).
- Avoid alcohol; ingestion of any form of alcohol may precipitate a disulfiram-type reaction (see Appendix F).
- Report to prescriber immediately signs of hemorrhagic tendencies: Bleeding into skin and mucosa, easy bruising, nose bleeds, or blood in stool or urine. Bone marrow depression often occurs 2–8 wk after start of therapy.
- Report stomatitis, or diarrhea.
- Avoid excessive exposure to the sun because of potential photosensitivity reaction: Cover as much skin area as possible with clothing, and use sunscreen lotion (SPF higher than 12) on all exposed skin surfaces.
- Avoid smoking during therapy.
- Use caution while driving or performing hazardous tasks until

response to drug is known since drowsiness, dizziness, and blurred vision are possible adverse effects.

- Use contraceptive measures during procarbazine therapy. Drug may cause infertility in both men and women. Discuss family planning with healthcare provider before initiating therapy.

PROCHLORPERAZINE ⊙
(proe-klor-per′a-zeen)
Compro

PROCHLORPERAZINE EDISYLATE
Classification: ANTIPSYCHOTIC; PHENOTHIAZINE; ANTIEMETIC
Therapeutic: ANTIPSYCHOTIC; ANTIEMETIC

AVAILABILITY Tablet; rectal suppositories. **Edisylate:** Solution for injection

ACTION & *THERAPEUTIC EFFECT*
Strong antipsychotic effects thought to be due to blockade of postsynaptic dopamine receptors in the brain. Antiemetic effect is produced by suppression of the chemoreceptor trigger zone (CTZ). *Effective antipsychotic and antiemetic properties.*

USES To control severe nausea and vomiting.

UNLABELED USES Treatment of migraine; nausea/vomiting of pregnancy.

CONTRAINDICATIONS Hypersensitivity to prochlorperazine; blood dyscrasias, jaundice; comatose or severely depressed states; dementia-related psychosis in elderly; children weighing less than 9 kg (20 lb) or younger than 2 y of age; pediatric surgery; short-term vomiting in children or vomiting of unknown etiology; Reye's syndrome or other encephalopathies; pregnancy—fetal risk cannot be ruled out; lactation—infant risk cannot be ruled out.

CAUTIOUS USE Parkinson's disease; decreased GI motility; paralytic ileus; GI obstruction; CVD; cerebrovascular disease, history of cardiovascular impairment, hypovolemia;bone marrow depression, hepatic impairment; renal impairment; Alzheimer disease; narrow angle glaucoma; seizure disorders; urinary retention, BPH; children.

ROUTE & DOSAGE

Severe Nausea, Vomiting
Adult/Adolescent/Child (over 39 kg): **PO** 5–10 mg 3–4 × day (max: 40 mg/day); **IM** 5–10 mg 3–4 × day (max: 40 mg/day) **IV** 2.5–10 mg (max: 10 mg/dose or 40 mg/day); **PR** 25 mg bid
Child (2–12 y, weight 18–39 kg): **PO** 2.5 mg q8h or 5 mg q12h (max: 15 mg/day); *(weight 14–17 kg):* 2.5 mg q8–12h (max: 10 mg/day); *(weight 9–13 kg):* 2.5 mg q12–24h (max: 7.5 mg/day).

ADMINISTRATION
Oral
- Administer with food, milk, or a glass of water to decrease gastric irritation.
- Dosages for older adults, emaciated patients, and children should be increased slowly.
- Do not give oral concentrate to children.

Common adverse effects in *italic;* life-threatening effects <u>underlined</u>; generic names in **bold;** classifications in SMALL CAPS; ◆ Canadian drug name; ⊙ Prototype drug; ⚠ Alert

- Avoid skin contact with oral concentrate or injection solution because of possibility of contact dermatitis.
- Store at 20 to 25 degrees C (68 to 77degrees F). Protect from light.

Rectal
- Ensure that suppository is inserted beyond the anal sphincter.
- Do not unwrap suppository until ready for use.
- Store at 20 to 25 degrees C (68 to 77degrees F).

Intramuscular
- Do not inject drug subcutaneously.
- Make injection deep into the upper outer quadrant of the buttock in adults. Follow agency policy regarding IM injection site for children.
- Keep patient in recumbent position for at least 30 min following injection to minimize hypotensive effects.
- Store at 20 to 25 degrees C (68 to 77degrees F). Protect from light. Clear or slightly yellow solutions may be used.

Intravenous

PREPARE: **Direct:** May be given undiluted or diluted in small amounts of NS. **IV Infusion:** Dilute in 50–100 mL of D5W, NS, D5/0.45% NaCl, LR, or other compatible solution.
ADMINISTER: **Direct: Do not** give a bolus dose. Give at a maximum rate of 5 mg/min. **IV Infusion:** Give over 15–30 min. Do not exceed direct IV rate.
INCOMPATIBILITIES: Solution/additive: **Aminophylline, chloramphenicol, chlorothiazide, furosemide, hydrocortisone, thiopental.** Y-site: **Acyclovir, aldesleukin, allopurinol, amifostine, aminocaproic acid, aminophylline, amphotericin B cholesteryl complex, amphotericin B lipid, ampicillin, azathioprine, aztreonam, bivalirudin, bretylium, calcium chloride, cangrelor, cefamanadole, cefazolin, cefepime, cefoperazone, cefotaxime, cefotetan, cefoxitin, ceftazidime, ceftizoxime, ceftriaxone, cefuroxime, chloramphenicol, clindamycin, dantrolene, dexamethasone, diazepam, diazoxide, epoetin alfa, ertapenem, etoposide, fenoldopam, filgrastim, fludarabine, fluorouracil, folic acid, foscarnet, fosphenytoin, furosemide, gallium, ganciclovir, gemcitabine, gemtuzumab, imipenem-cilastatin, indomethacin, insulin, ketorolac, lansoprazole, levofloxacin, midazolam, minocycline, mitomycin, nitroprusside, pantoprazole, pemetrexed, pentamidine, pentobarbital, phenytoin, piperacillin-tazobactam, sodium bicarbonate, streptokinase, SMZ/TMP, urokinase.**

- Discard markedly discolored solutions; slight yellowing does not appear to alter potency.

ADVERSE EFFECTS CV: Hypotension, prolonged QT interval. **CNS:** *Extrapyramidal reactions (akathisia, dystonia, or parkinsonism),* persistent tardive dyskinesia.

DIAGNOSTIC TEST INTERFERENCE
Increased risk of false positives for phenylketouria and for pregnancy.

INTERACTIONS Drug: Alcohol,
CNS DEPRESSANTS increase CNS depression; **phenobarbital** increases metabolism of prochlorperazine; GENERAL ANESTHETICS increase excitation and hypotension; antagonizes antihypertensive action of **guanethidine; phenylpropanolamine**

---

poses possibility of sudden death; do not use with **amisulpride** due to increased risk of neuroleptic malignant syndrome; TRICYCLIC ANTIDEPRESSANTS intensify hypotensive and anticholinergic effects; decreases seizure threshold—ANTICONVULSANT dosage may need to be increased; increased adverse effects when used with ANTICHOLINERGIC AGENTS. Risk of decreased efficacy when used with ANTIPARKINSON AGENTS. **Herbal: Kava** may increase risk and severity of dystonic reactions.

PHARMACOKINETICS Absorption: Readily from GI tract. **Onset:** 30–40 min PO; 60 min PR; 10–20 min IM. **Duration:** 3–4 h PO/IM; PR 3–12 h. **Distribution:** Crosses placenta; distributed into breast milk. **Metabolism:** In liver. **Elimination:** In urine.

NURSING IMPLICATIONS

Black Box Warning

Prochlorperazine has been associated with increased mortality in older adults with dementia-related psychosis.

Assessment & Drug Effects

- Position carefully to prevent aspiration of vomitus; may have depressed cough reflex.
- Most older adult and emaciated patients and children, especially those with dehydration or acute illness, appear to be particularly susceptible to extrapyramidal effects. Be alert to onset of symptoms: Early in therapy watch for pseudoparkinson's and acute dyskinesia. After 1–2 mo, be alert to akathisia.
- Fall risk assessment.
- Monitor mental status and report significant changes in mood, behavior, or functional ability when used for long-term therapy.

- Be alert to signs of high core temperature: Red, dry, hot skin; full bounding pulse; dilated pupils; dyspnea; confusion; temperature over 40.6° C (105° F); elevated BP. Exposure to high environmental temperature places this patient at risk for heat stroke. Inform prescriber and institute measures to reduce body temperature rapidly.
- Monitor lab tests: Periodic CBC with differential baseline and every 6 months thereafter, every 3 weeks for high risk patients, LFTs.

Patient & Family Education

- Take drug only as prescribed and do not alter dose or schedule. Consult prescriber before stopping the medication.
- Avoid hazardous activities such as driving a car until response to drug is known because drug may impair mental and physical abilities, especially during first few days of therapy.
- Be aware that drug may color urine reddish brown. It also may cause the sun-exposed skin to turn gray-blue.
- Protect skin from direct sun's rays and use a sunscreen lotion (SPF higher than 12) to prevent photosensitivity reaction.
- Withhold dose and report to the prescriber if the following symptoms persist more than a few hours: Tremor, involuntary twitching, exaggerated restlessness. Other reportable symptoms include light-colored stools, changes in vision, sore throat, fever, rash.

PROGESTERONE ⊙

(proe-jess'ter-one)
Crinone Gel, Prometrium
Classification: PROGESTIN
Therapeutic: PROGESTIN

P

AVAILABILITY Capsule; solution for injection; gel; vaginal insert; vaginal suppository

ACTION & *THERAPEUTIC EFFECT*

Has estrogenic, anabolic, and androgenic activity. Transforms endometrium from proliferative to secretory state; suppresses pituitary gonadotropin secretion, thereby blocking follicular maturation and ovulation. *Relaxes estrogen-primed myometrium and prohibits spontaneous contraction of uterus. Sudden drop in blood levels of progestin (and estradiol) causes "withdrawal bleeding" from endometrium. Intrauterine placement of progesterone hypothetically inhibits sperm survival, and suppresses endometrial proliferation (antiestrogenic effect).*

USES Secondary amenorrhea, functional uterine bleeding, endometriosis, and premenstrual syndrome. Largely supplanted by new progestins, which have longer action and oral effectiveness. Treatment of infertile women with progesterone deficiency.

CONTRAINDICATIONS Hypersensitivity to progestins, known or suspected breast or genital malignancy; use as a pregnancy test; thrombophlebitis, thromboembolic disorders; ectopic pregnancy; cerebral apoplexy (or its history); severely impaired liver function or disease; undiagnosed vaginal bleeding, incomplete abortion; use during first 4 mo of pregnancy (category X); other than vaginal gel use for assisted reproductive technology (ART) in early pregnancy.

CAUTIOUS USE Anemia; diabetes mellitus; history of psychic depression; persons susceptible to acute intermittent porphyria or with conditions that may be aggravated by fluid retention (asthma, seizure disorders, cardiac or kidney function, migraine); impaired liver function; previous ectopic pregnancy; presence or history of salpingitis; venereal disease; unresolved abnormal Pap smear; genital bleeding of unknown etiology; previous pelvic surgery; lactation. **Vaginal gel:** In early first trimester (category B).

ROUTE & DOSAGE

Amenorrhea

Adult: **IM** 5–10 mg for 6–8 consecutive days; **PO** 400 mg at bedtime × 10 days; **Vaginal gel** 45 mg every other day (up to 6 doses)

Uterine Bleeding

Adult: **IM** 5–10 mg/day for 6 days

Premenstrual Syndrome

Adult: **PR** 200–400 mg/day

Assisted Reproductive Technology

Adult: **Vaginal** 90 mg gel daily or bid until placental autonomy OR 10–12 wk; 100 mg insert 2–3 × daily up to 10 wk

ADMINISTRATION

Oral

- Give at bedtime and advise caution with ambulation because drug may cause drowsiness or dizziness.
- Do not give oral capsules, which contain peanut oil, to patients allergic to peanuts.

Intramuscular

- Immerse vial in warm water momentarily to redissolve crystals (if present) and to facilitate aspiration of drug into syringe.

- Inject deeply IM. Injection site may be irritated. Inspect IM sites carefully and rotate areas systematically.

Rectal

- Ensure that suppository is inserted beyond the anal sphincter.

Vaginal

- A dosage increase from the 4% gel can only be accomplished by using the 8% gel. Increasing the volume of gel administered does not increase the amount of progesterone absorbed.
- Store drug at 15°–30° C (59°–86° F) unless otherwise specified by manufacturer. Protect from freezing and light.

ADVERSE EFFECTS CV: <u>Thromboembolic disorder, pulmonary embolism.</u> **CNS:** Migraine headache, *dizziness,* lethargy, mental depression, somnolence, insomnia. **HEENT:** Change in vision, proptosis, diplopia, papilledema, retinal vascular lesions. **Endocrine:** Hyperglycemia, decreased libido, transient increase in sodium and chloride excretion, pyrexia. Gynecomastia, galactorrhea. **Skin:** *Acne,* pruritus, allergic rash, photosensitivity, urticaria, hirsutism, alopecia. **GI:** Hepatic disease, cholestatic jaundice; *nausea,* vomiting, *abdominal cramps.* **GU:** Vaginal candidiasis, chloasma, cervical erosion and changes in secretions, *breakthrough bleeding,* dysmenorrhea, amenorrhea, pruritus vulvae. **Other:** *Edema, weight changes;* pain at injection site; fatigue.

DIAGNOSTIC TEST INTERFERENCE

PROGESTINS may decrease levels of *urinary pregnanediol* and increase levels of *serum alkaline phosphatase, plasma amino acids, urinary nitrogen,* and *coagulation factors VII, VIII, IX,* and *X.* They also decrease *glucose tolerance* (may cause false-positive *urine glucose tests*) and lower *HDL* (high-density lipoprotein) levels.

INTERACTIONS Drug: BARBITURATES, **carbamazepine, phenytoin, rifampin** may alter contraceptive effectiveness; **ketoconazole** may inhibit progesterone metabolism; may antagonize effects of **bromocriptine.**

PHARMACOKINETICS Absorption: Rapid from IM site; PO peaks at 3 h. **Metabolism:** Extensively in liver. **Elimination:** Primarily in urine; excreted in breast milk. **Half-Life:** 5 min.

NURSING IMPLICATIONS

Black Box Warning

Progesterone in combination with estrogen has been associated with increased risk of invasive breast cancer.

Assessment & Drug Effects

- Record baseline data for comparative value about patient's weight, BP, and pulse at onset of progestin therapy. Report deviations promptly.
- Monitor lab tests: Periodic LFTs, blood glucose, and serum electrolytes.
- Monitor for and report immediately S&S of thrombophlebitis or thromboembolic disease.

Patient & Family Education

- If other intravaginal therapy is being used concurrently, allow at least 6 h before/after progesterone vaginal gel insertion.

- Small, white globules may appear as a vaginal discharge, possibly caused by progesterone vaginal gel accumulation, even several days after usage.
- Inform prescriber promptly if any of the following occur: Sudden severe headache or vomiting, dizziness or fainting, numbness in an arm or leg, pain in calves accompanied by swelling, warmth, and redness; acute chest pain or dyspnea.
- Report to prescriber promptly unexplained sudden or gradual, partial or complete loss of vision, ptosis, or diplopia.
- Monitor for loss of glycemic control if diabetic.
- Notify prescriber if you become or suspect pregnancy. Learn the potential risk to the fetus from exposure to progestin.

PROMETHAZINE HYDROCHLORIDE ⚠

(proe-meth′a-zeen)

Histantil ✦, Phenergan, Promethagen

Classification: ANTIHISTAMINE; ANTIEMETIC; ANTIVERTIGO
Therapeutic: ANTIHISTAMINE; ANTIEMETIC; ANTIVERTIGO
Prototype: Prochlorperazine

AVAILABILITY Tablet; oral solution; rectal suppository; solution for injection

ACTION & *THERAPEUTIC EFFECT*
Exerts anti-serotonin, anticholinergic, and local anesthetic action. Antiemetic action thought to be due to depression of CTZ in medulla. *Long-acting derivative of phenothiazine with marked antihistamine activity and prominent sedative, amnesic, antiemetic, and anti-motion sickness actions.*

USES Motion sickness, nausea/vomiting, induction of sedation, treatment of allergic conditions.

UNLABELED USES hyperemesis gravidarum

CONTRAINDICATIONS Hypersensitivity to phenothiazines; acute MI; angina, atrial fibrillation, atrial flutter, cardiac arrhythmias, cardiomyopathy, uncontrolled hypertension; MAOI therapy; comatose or severely depressed states; lower respiratory tract symptoms, including history of asthma or sleep apnea; hepatic encephalopathy, hepatic diseases; acutely ill or dehydrated children; children with Reye's syndrome; pregnancy—fetal risk cannot be ruled out; lactation (infant risk cannot be ruled out); children younger than 2 y.

CAUTIOUS USE Impaired liver function; epilepsy; bone marrow depression; cardiovascular disease; peripheral vascular disease; acute or chronic respiratory impairment (particularly in children); narrow angle glaucoma; older adult or debilitated patients.

ROUTE & DOSAGE

Motion Sickness

Adult: **PO/PR** 25 mg 30–60 min before departure; repeat q8–12h prn
Child (2 y or older): **PO/PR** 0.5mg/kg 30–60 min before departure then q12h prn (max: 25 mg/dose)

Nausea

Adult: **PO/PR/IM/IV** 12.5–25 mg q4–6h prn
Child (2 y or older): **PO/PR/IM/IV** 1 mg/kg/dose q4–6h prn (max: 25 mg/dose)

Allergic Conditions

Adult: **PO/PR** 12.5 mg before meals and at bedtime or 25 mg at bedtime; **IM/IV** 25 mg, repeat in 2 h if necessary, switch to PO *Child (2 y or older):* **PO** 0.125 mg/kg/dose (max 12.5 mg/dose) q6h prn and 0.5 mg at bedtime.

Sedation

Adult: **PO/IM/IV** 25–50 mg/dose

ADMINISTRATION

Oral

- Give with food, milk, or a full glass of water may minimize GI distress.
- Tablets may be crushed and mixed with water or food before swallowing.
- Oral doses for allergy are generally prescribed before meals and on retiring or as single dose at bedtime.
- Store at controlled room temperature between 20 and 25 degrees C (68 and 77 degrees F). Protect from light.

Rectal

- Ensure that suppository is inserted beyond the rectal sphincter.
- Refrigerate between 2 and 8 degrees C (36 and 46 degrees F).

Intramuscular

- Give IM injection deep into large muscle mass. Aspirate carefully before injecting drug. Intra-arterial injection can cause arterial or arteriolar spasm, with resultant gangrene.

Intravenous

PREPARE: **Direct:** The 25 mg/mL concentration may be given undiluted. ▪ Dilute the 50 mg/mL concentration in NS to yield no more than 25 mg/mL (e.g., diluting the 50 mg/mL concentration in 4 mL yields 10 mg/mL) and at a rate no greater than 25 mg/minute.
▪ Inspect parenteral drug before preparation. Discard if it is darkened or contains precipitate. Preferred administration through a central venous catheter

ADMINISTER: **Direct:** Give each 25 mg or fraction thereof over at least 1 min.

INCOMPATIBILITIES: Solution/additive: **Aminophylline, cefotetan, chloramphenicol, chlorothiazide, floxacillin sodium, furosemide, heparin, hydrocortisone, methohexital, penicillin G sodium, phenobarbital, thiopental sodium. Y-site: Acyclovir, aldesleukin, allopurinol, aminophylline, amphotericin B, amphotericin B (lipid), ampicillin, asparaginase, azathioprine, bretylium, cangrelor, carmustine, cefamandole, cefepime, cefoperazone, cefotaxime, cefotetan, cefoxitin, ceftazidime, ceftobiprole, ceftriaxone, cefuroxime, chlorothiazide sodium, clindamycin, dantrolene, diazepam, diazoxide, dimenhydrinate, doxorubicin liposome, ertapenem, fluorescein, fluorouracil, folic acid, foscarnet, ganciclovir, gemtuzumab, inamrinone lactate, indomethacin, ketorolac, lansoprazole, methohexital sodium, methylprednisolone, minocycline, mitomycin, nafcillin, nitroprusside, oxacillin, pantoprazole, pentobarbital, phenobarbital, phenytoin, piperacillin/tazobactam, sodium bicarbonate, streptokinase, sulfamethoxazole-trimethoprim, ticarcillin disodium, urokinase**

Common adverse effects in *italic;* life-threatening effects underlined; generic names in **bold;** classifications in SMALL CAPS; ✦ Canadian drug name; ◑ Prototype drug; ⚠ Alert

- Injection and oral: Store at 20°–25° C (68°–77° F) in tight, light-resistant container unless otherwise directed.

ADVERSE EFFECTS (≥5%) CNS:
Delerium *dizziness, drowsiness*, Parkinsonian-like syndrome. **GI:** *Nausea, vomiting, dry mouth.*

DIAGNOSTIC TEST INTERFERENCE
May produce false results with *urinary pregnancy tests.* Promethazine can cause significant alterations of *flare response* in *intradermal allergen tests* if performed within 4 days of patient receiving promethazine. May cause false positive with *urine detection of amphetamine/methamphetamine;* increased serum glucose may be seen with glucose tolerance tests.

INTERACTIONS Drug: Alcohol
and other CNS DEPRESSANTS add to CNS depression and anticholinergic effects. ANTICHOLINERGIC AGENTS increase the risk of adverse effects. Do not use with **metoclopramide, levosulpiride**.

PHARMACOKINETICS Absorption:
Readily from GI tract. **Onset:** 20 min PO/PR/IM; 5 min IV. **Duration:** 4–6 h. **Distribution:** Crosses placenta. **Metabolism:** In liver (CYP2D6, 2B6). **Elimination:** Slowly in urine and feces.

NURSING IMPLICATIONS

Black Box Warning

Promethazine has been associated with severe respiratory depression and death in pediatric patients younger than 2 y.

Assessment & Drug Effects
- Monitor respiratory function in patients with respiratory problems, particularly children. Drug may suppress cough reflex and cause thickening of bronchial secretions.
- Supervise ambulation. Promethazine sometimes produces marked sedation and dizziness.
- Monitor blood pressure and mental status.
- Monitor for and report promptly S&S of neuroleptic malignant syndrome.
- Monitor for seizures in those with a history of seizure disorders.
- Patients in pain may develop involuntary (athetoid) movements of upper extremities following parenteral administration. These symptoms usually disappear after pain is controlled.

Patient & Family Education
- For motion sickness: Take initial dose 30–60 min before anticipated travel and repeat at 8–12 h intervals if necessary. For duration of journey, repeat dose on arising and again at evening meal.
- Do not drive or engage in other potentially hazardous activities requiring mental alertness and normal reaction time until response to drug is known.
- Supervise children to avoid potential harm during play activities.
- Avoid sunlamps or prolonged exposure to sunlight.
- Avoid alcohol and other CNS depressants.
- Patients with a history of seizures should report any increased seizure activity.

PROPAFENONE
(pro-pa'fen-one)
Rythmol, Rythmol SR
Classification: CLASS IC ANTIARRHYTHMIC
Therapeutic: CLASS IC ANTIARRHYTHMIC
Prototype: Flecainide

AVAILABILITY Tablet; sustained release capsule

ACTION & *THERAPEUTIC EFFECT*
Class IC antiarrhythmic drug with a direct stabilizing action on myocardial membranes. Reduces spontaneous automaticity. Exerts a negative inotropic effect on the myocardium. *Decreases rate of single and multiple PVCs and suppresses ventricular arrhythmias.*

USES Ventricular arrhythmias, atrial fibrillation, paroxysmal supraventricular tachycardia.

UNLABELED USES Wolff–Parkinson–White syndrome.

CONTRAINDICATIONS Hypersensitivity to propafenone; uncontrolled CHF, cardiogenic shock, sinoatrial, AV or intraventricular disorders (e.g., sick sinus node syndrome, AV block) without a pacemaker; cardiogenic shock; bradycardia, QT prolongation; marked hypotension; bronchospastic disorders; electrolyte imbalances; non-life-threatening arrhythmias.

CAUTIOUS USE CHF, COPD, chronic bronchitis; AV block; hepatic/renal impairment; older adult patients; pregnancy (category C); lactation. Safe use in children not established.

ROUTE & DOSAGE

Ventricular Arrhythmias
Adult: **PO Immediate release**
Initiate with 150 mg q8h, may be increased at 3–4 days intervals (max: 300 mg q8h)

Atrial Fibrillation
Adult: **PO Extended release**
225 mg q12h increase to response (max: 425 mg q12h).

ADMINISTRATION
Oral
- Dosage increments are usually made gradually with older adults or those with previous extensive myocardial damage.
- Significant dose reduction is warranted with severe liver dysfunction. Consult prescriber.
- Store at 15°–30° C (59°–86° F).

ADVERSE EFFECTS CV: Arrhythmias, ventricular tachycardia, hypotension, bundle branch block, AV block, complete heart block, sinus arrest, CHF. **CNS:** *Blurred vision, dizziness,* paresthesias, fatigue, somnolence, vertigo, headache. **Skin:** Rash. **GI:** Nausea, abdominal discomfort, constipation, vomiting, dry mouth, *taste alterations,* cholestatic hepatitis. **Hematologic:** Leukopenia, granulocytopenia (both rare).

INTERACTIONS Drug: Amiodarone, quinidine increases the levels and toxicity of propafenone. May increase levels and toxicity of TRICYCLIC ANTIDEPRESSANTS, **cyclosporine, digoxin,** BETA-BLOCKERS, **theophylline,** and **warfarin** may increase levels of both **propafenone** and **diltiazem. Phenobarbital** decreases levels of **propafenone.** Use with caution in drugs that prolong the QT interval.

PHARMACOKINETICS Absorption: Readily from GI tract. **Peak:** 3.5 h. **Distribution:** 97% protein bound, concentrates in the lung. Crosses placenta, distributed into breast milk. **Metabolism:** Hepatic via CY2D6, CYPD3A4, CYP1A2. **Elimination:** 18.5–38% of dose excreted in urine as metabolites. **Half-Life:** 2–10 h in extensive metabolizers and 10–32 h in slow metabolizers.

NURSING IMPLICATIONS

Assessment & Drug Effects

- Monitor cardiovascular status frequently (e.g., ECG, Holter monitor) to determine effectiveness of drug and development of new or worsened arrhythmias.
- Monitor closely patients with preexisting CHF for worsening of this condition. Monitor for digoxin toxicity with concurrent use, because drug may increase serum digoxin levels.
- Report development of second- or third-degree AV block or significant widening of the QRS complex. Dosage adjustment may be warranted.

Patient & Family Education

- Report to prescriber any of following: Chest pain, palpitations, blurred or abnormal vision, dyspnea, or signs and symptoms of infection.
- Be aware when taking concurrent warfarin of possible increase in plasma levels that increase bleeding risk. Report unusual bleeding or bruising.
- Monitor radial pulse daily and report decreased heart rate or development of an abnormal heartbeat.
- Be aware of possibility of dizziness and need for caution with walking, especially in older adult or debilitated patients.

PROPANTHELINE BROMIDE
(proe-pan'the-leen)

Propanthel ♦
Classification: ANTICHOLINERGIC; ANTIMUSCARINIC; ANTISPASMODIC
Therapeutic: ANTICHOLINERGIC
Prototype: Atropine

AVAILABILITY Tablet

ACTION & *THERAPEUTIC EFFECT*
Has potent postganglionic nicotinic receptor blocking action and diminishes gastric acid secretion. *Decreases motility (smooth muscle tone) resulting in antispasmodic action and decreases gastric acid secretion.*

USES Adjunct in treatment of peptic ulcer disease.

CONTRAINDICATIONS Narrow-angle glaucoma; tachycardia, MI; paralytic ileus, GI obstructive disease; hemorrhagic shock; myasthenia gravis.

CAUTIOUS USE CAD, CHF, cardiac arrhythmias; liver disease, ulcerative colitis, hiatus hernia, esophagitis; wkidney disease; BPH; glaucoma; debilitated patients; hyperthyroidism; autonomic neuropathy; brain damage; Down's syndrome; spastic disorders; pregnancy (category C); lactation. Safe use in children not established.

ROUTE & DOSAGE

Peptic Ulcer Disease
Adult: **PO** 15 mg before each meal and 30 mg at bedtime

ADMINISTRATION
Oral
- Give 30–60 min before meals and at bedtime. Advise not to chew tablet; drug is bitter.

- Give at least 1 h before or 1 h after an antacid (or antidiarrheal agent).
- Store dry powder and tablets at 20°–25° C (68°–77° F); protect from freezing and moisture.

ADVERSE EFFECTS CNS: Drowsiness, confusion, headache, insomnia, nervousness. **HEENT:** Blurred vision, mydriasis, increased intraocular pressure. **GI:** *Constipation, dry mouth.* **GU:** Decreased sexual activity, difficult urination. Neuromuscular and skeletal muscle weakness.

INTERACTIONS Drug: Decreased absorption of **ketoconazole;** ORAL POTASSIUM may increase risk of GI ulcers. Use with other ANTIMUSCARINIC agents can increase side effects. **Food:** Food significantly decreases absorption.

PHARMACOKINETICS Absorption: Incompletely from GI tract. **Onset:** 30–45 min. **Duration:** 4–6 h. **Metabolism:** 50% in GI tract before absorption; 50% in liver. **Elimination:** Primarily in urine; some in bile. **Half-Life:** 9 h.

NURSING IMPLICATIONS

Assessment & Drug Effects
- Assess bowel sounds, especially in presence of ulcerative colitis, since paralytic ileus may develop, predisposing to toxic megacolon.
- Be aware that older adult or debilitated patients may respond to a usual dose with agitation, excitement, confusion, drowsiness. Stop drug and report to prescriber if these symptoms are observed.
- Check BP, heart sounds and rhythm periodically in patients with cardiac disease.
- Monitor lab tests: Serum creatinine/BUN.

Patient & Family Education
- Void just prior to each dose to minimize risk of urinary hesitancy or retention. Record daily urinary volume and report problems to prescriber.
- Relieve dry mouth by rinsing with water frequently, chewing sugar-free gum, or sucking hard candy.
- Maintain adequate fluid and high-fiber food intake to prevent constipation.
- Make all position changes slowly and lie down immediately if faintness, weakness, or palpitations occur. Report symptoms to prescriber.
- Do not drive or engage in potentially hazardous activities until response to drug is known.

PROPOFOL
(pro'po-fol)

Diprivan

Classification: GENERAL ANESTHESIA; SEDATIVE-HYPNOTIC
Therapeutic: SEDATIVE-HYPNOTIC; GENERAL ANESTHESIA

AVAILABILITY Solution for injection

ACTION & *THERAPEUTIC EFFECT*
Sedative-hypnotic used in the induction and maintenance of anesthesia or sedation. Rapid onset (40 sec) and minimal excitation during induction of anesthesia. *Effectively used for conscious sedation and maintenance of anesthesia.*

USES Induction or maintenance of anesthesia as part of a balanced anesthesia technique; conscious sedation in mechanically ventilated patients.

CONTRAINDICATIONS Hypersensitivity to propofol or propofol emulsion, which contain soybean and soy products, and egg phosphatide; patients with increased intracranial pressure or impaired cerebral circulation; patients whom general anesthesia or sedation is contraindicated; obstetrical procedures; lactation. Do not use for induction of anesthesia in children younger than 3 y and for maintenance of anesthesia in infants younger than 2 mo.

CAUTIOUS USE Patients with severe cardiac or respiratory disorders, respiratory depression, hypoxemia, hypertension; history of epilepsy or seizures; hypovolemia; lipid metabolism disorders; older adults; pregnancy (category B).

ROUTE & DOSAGE

Induction of Anesthesia

Adult: **IV** 2–2.5 mg/kg as total dose; administered as approximately 40 mg q10 sec until onset of anesthesia
Adult (55 y or older): **IV** 1–1.5 mg/kg as total dose, administer approximately 20 mg q10sec until onset of anesthesia
Adolescent/Child (3 y or older): **IV** 2.5–3.5 mg/kg over 20–30 sec

Maintenance of Anesthesia

Adult: **IV** 50–200 mcg/kg/min for 10–15 min
Adult (55 y or older): **IV** 50–100 mcg/kg/min
Child/Infant (2 mo or older): **IV** 125–300 mcg/kg/min

ADMINISTRATION

- Use strict aseptic technique to prepare propofol for injection; drug emulsion supports rapid growth of microorganisms.

- Inspect for particulate matter and discoloration. Discard if either is noted.
- Shake well before use. Inspect for separation of the emulsion. Do not use if there is evidence of separation of phases of the emulsion.

Intravenous

PREPARE: **IV Infusion:** Give undiluted or diluted in D5W to a concentration not less than 2 mg/mL.Begin drug administration immediately after preparation and complete within 12 h.
ADMINISTER: **IV Infusion:** Use syringe or volumetric pump to control rate. ▪ Rate is determined by patient weight in kg. Depending on the form of the drug, indication, and patient's health status and age, drug may be given by variable rate infusion or intermittent IV bolus (usually over 3–5 min). ▪ Administer immediately after spiking the vial. Complete infusion within 12 h.
INCOMPATIBILITIES: **Y-site: Amikacin, amphotericin B, ascorbic acid, atracurium, atropine, bretylium, calcium chloride, ceftolozane-tazobactam, ciprofloxacin, cisatracurium, diazepam, digoxin, doripenem, doxorubicin, hydrochloric acid, hydroxocobalamin, isavuconazonium sulfate, gentamicin, levofloxacin, methotrexate, methylprednisolone, metoclopramide, metronidazole, minocycline, mitoxantrone, netilmicin, nimodipine, phenytoin, remifentanil, temocillin sodium, tobramycin, verapamil.**

- Store unopened between 4° C (40° F) and 22° C (72° F). Refrigeration is not recommended. Protect from light.

P

ADVERSE EFFECTS CV: *Hypotension*, bradycardia, ventricular asystole (rare). **Respiratory:** Cough, hiccups, apnea. **CNS:** Headache, dizziness, *twitching, bucking, jerking, thrashing, clonic/myoclonic movements*. **HEENT:** Decreased intraocular pressure. **GI:** Vomiting, abdominal cramping. **Other:** Pain at injection site.

DIAGNOSTIC TEST INTERFERENCE
Propofol produces a temporary reduction in *serum cortisol levels.* However, propofol does not seem to inhibit adrenal responsiveness to *ACTH.*

INTERACTIONS Drug:
Concurrent continuous infusions of propofol and **alfentanil** produce higher plasma levels of **alfentanil** than expected. CNS DEPRESSANTS cause additive CNS depression. **Amiodarone** use (current or recent) can increase risk of hypotension.

PHARMACOKINETICS Onset:
9–36 sec. **Duration:** 6–10 min. **Distribution:** Highly lipophilic, crosses placenta, excreted in breast milk. **Metabolism:** Extensively in the liver (CYP2B6, 2C9). **Elimination:** Approximately 88% of the dose is recovered in the urine as metabolites. **Half-Life:** 5–12 h.

NURSING IMPLICATIONS

Assessment & Drug Effects
- Monitor hemodynamic status and assess for dose-related hypotension.
- Monitor vital signs.
- Take seizure precautions. Tonic-clonic seizures have occurred following general anesthesia with propofol.

- Be alert to the potential for drug induced excitation (e.g., twitching, tremor, hyperclonus) and take appropriate safety measures.
- Provide comfort measures; pain at the injection site is quite common especially when small veins are used.
- Monitor lab tests: Urine zinc levels if administered for longer than 5 days or in patients experiencing burns, diarrhea, or major sepsis.

PROPRANOLOL HYDROCHLORIDE ℗
(proe-pran'oh-lole)

Apo-Propranolol ♦, Inderal, Inderal LA, InnoPran XL, Novopranol ♦
Classification: BETA-ADRENERGIC RECEPTOR ANTAGONIST; ANTIHYPERTENSIVE; CLASS II ANTIARRHYTHMIC
Therapeutic: ANTIHYPERTENSIVE; CLASS II ANTIARRHYTHMIC; ANTIANGINAL

AVAILABILITY Tablet; sustained release capsule; oral solution; solution for injection

ACTION & *THERAPEUTIC EFFECT*
Nonselective beta-blocker of both cardiac and bronchial adrenoreceptors that competes with epinephrine and norepinephrine for available beta receptor sites. In higher doses, it depresses cardiac function including contractility and arrhythmias. Lowers both supine and standing blood pressures in hypertensive patients. *Reduces heart rate, myocardial irritability (Class II antiarrhythmic), and force of contraction, depresses automaticity of sinus node and ectopic pacemaker, and*

decreases AV and intraventricular conduction velocity. Hypotensive effect is associated with decreased cardiac output. Has migraine prophylactic effects.

USES Management of cardiac arrhythmias, myocardial infarction, tachyarrhythmias associated with digitalis intoxication, anesthesia, and thyrotoxicosis, hypertrophic subaortic stenosis, angina pectoris due to coronary atherosclerosis, pheochromocytoma, hereditary essential tremor; also treatment of hypertension alone, but generally with a thiazide or other antihypertensives.

UNLABELED USES Anxiety states, migraine prophylaxis, essential tremors, schizophrenia, tardive dyskinesia, acute panic symptoms (e.g., stage fright), recurrent GI bleeding in cirrhotic patients, treatment of aggression and rage, drug induced tremors.

CONTRAINDICATIONS Hypersensitivity to propranolol; greater than first-degree heart block; right ventricular failure secondary to pulmonary hypertension; ventricular dysfunction; sinus bradycardia, cardiogenic shock, significant aortic or mitral valvular disease; bronchial asthma or bronchospasm, severe COPD, pulmonary edema; major depression; PVD, Raynaud's disease; abrupt discontinuation.

CAUTIOUS USE History of anaphylactic reaction; peripheral arterial insufficiency; compensated heart failure; history of systemic insect sting reaction; history of psychiatric illness; patients prone to nonallergenic bronchospasm; major surgery; cerebrovascular disease, stroke; renal or hepatic impairment; pheochromocytoma, vasospastic angina; DM; patients prone to hypoglycemia; hyperthyroidism, cardiac arrhythmias; surgery; MG and other skeletal muscular diseases; Wolff-Parkinson-White syndrome; older adults; pregnancy (category C); lactation.

ROUTE & DOSAGE

Hypertension

Adult: **PO Immediate release** 40 mg bid, usually need 160–480 mg/day in divided doses; **InnoPran XL** dose 80 mg each night, may increase to 120 mg at bedtime; **Other extended release forms:** 80 mg daily increase up to 120–160 mg

Angina

Adult: **PO Immediate release** 10–20 mg/day in divided doses (increase up to 160–320 mg/day); **Extended release** 80 mg QD (increase to 160–320 mg/day)

Arrhythmias

Adult: **PO** 10–30 mg q6–8h **IV** 1–3 mg q4h

Post MI

Adult: **PO** 180–240 mg/day in divided doses

Acute MI

Adult: **IV** Total dose of 0.1 mg/kg given in 3 divided doses at 2–3 min intervals **PO Immediate release:** 180–320 mg/day in divided doses

P

Migraine Prophylaxis

Adult: **PO Immediate release**
80 mg/day in divided
doses, may need 160–240
mg/day; **Extended release**
80 mg/day

Essential Tremor

Adult: **PO** 40 mg bid may
increase to 120–320 mg/day in
divided doses

ADMINISTRATION

- Take apical pulse and BP before
administering drug. Withhold
drug if heart rate less than
60 bpm or systolic BP less than
90 mm Hg. Consult prescriber for
parameters.

Oral

- Do not give within 2 wk of an
MAO inhibitor.
- Note that InnoPran XL should be
given at bedtime.
- Be consistent with regard to giving with food or on an empty
stomach to minimize variations in
absorption.
- Ensure that sustained release form
is not chewed or crushed. **Must
be** swallowed whole.
- Reduce dosage gradually
over a period of 1–2 wk and
monitor patient closely when
discontinued.

Intravenous

Note: Verify correct IV concentration and rate of infusion for
neonates with prescriber.

- Take apical pulse and BP
before administering drug. Withhold drug if heart rate less than
60 bpm or systolic BP less than
90 mm Hg. ▪ Consult prescriber
for parameters.

PREPARE: **Direct:** May be given
undiluted or dilute each 1 mg
in 10 mL of D5W. **Intermittent:**
Dilute a single dose in 50 mL
of NS.
ADMINISTER: **Direct:** Give each
1 mg or fraction thereof over 1 min.
Intermittent: Give each dose over
15–20 min.
INCOMPATIBILITIES: **Y-site:
Amphotericin B (conven-
tional and lipid), asparaginase, dantrolene, diazepam,
diazoxide, indomethacin,
insulin, lansoprazole, mitomycin, paclitaxel, pantoprazole,
phenytoin, piperacillin/tazo-
bactam, SMP/TMZ.**

- Store at 15°–30° C (59°–86° F)
in tightly closed, light-resistant
containers.

ADVERSE EFFECTS **CV:** Palpi-
tation, profound *bradycardia,*
AV heart block, cardiac stand-
still, hypotension, angina pectoris, tachyarrhythmia, acute CHF,
peripheral arterial insufficiency
resembling Raynaud's disease,
myotonia, paresthesia of *hands.*
Respiratory: Dyspnea, <u>laryn-
gospasm</u>, bronchospasm. **CNS:**
Drug-induced psychosis, *sleep
disturbances,* depression, *confusion,* agitation, giddiness, *light-
headedness, fatigue,* vertigo,
syncope, weakness, *drowsiness,*
insomnia, vivid dreams, visual hallucinations, delusions, reversible
organic brain syndrome. **HEENT:**
Dry eyes (gritty sensation), visual
disturbances, conjunctivitis, tinnitus, hearing loss, nasal stuffiness.
Endocrine: Hypoglycemia, hyperglycemia, hypocalcemia (patients
with hyperthyroidism). **Skin:** Erythematous, psoriasis-like eruptions; pruritus, <u>Stevens–Johnson
syndrome</u>, toxic

P

epidermal necrolysis, erythema multiforme, exfoliative dermatitis, urticaria. Reversible alopecia, hyperkeratoses of scalp, palms, feet; nail changes, dry skin. **GI:** Dry mouth, nausea, *vomiting*, heartburn, *diarrhea*, constipation, flatulence, abdominal cramps, mesenteric arterial thrombosis, ischemic colitis, pancreatitis. **GU:** Impotence or decreased libido. **Hematologic:** Transient eosinophilia, thrombocytopenic or nonthrombocytopenic purpura, agranulocytosis. **Other:** Fever; pharyngitis; respiratory distress, weight gain, LE-like reaction, cold extremities, *fatigue*, arthralgia, anaphylactic/anaphylactoid reactions.

DIAGNOSTIC TEST INTERFERENCE

BETA-ADRENERGIC BLOCKERS may produce false-negative test results in exercise tolerance ECG tests, and elevations in *serum potassium, peripheral platelet count, serum uric acid, serum transaminase, alkaline phosphatase, lactate dehydrogenase, serum creatinine, BUN,* and an increase or decrease in *blood glucose* levels in diabetic patients.

INTERACTIONS Drug: PHENOTHIAZINES have additive hypotensive effects. BETA-ADRENERGIC AGONISTS (e.g., **albuterol**) antagonize effects. **Atropine** and TRICYCLIC ANTIDEPRESSANTS block bradycardia. DIURETICS and other HYPOTENSIVE AGENTS increase hypotension. High doses of **tubocurarine** may potentiate neuromuscular blockade. **Cimetidine** decreases clearance, increases effects. ANTACIDS, **ascorbic acid** may decrease absorption.

PHARMACOKINETICS Absorption: Completely from GI tract; undergoes extensive first-pass

metabolism. **Peak:** 60–90 min immediate release; 6 h sustained release; 5 min IV. **Distribution:** Widely distributed including CNS, placenta, and breast milk. **Metabolism:** Almost completely in liver (CYP1A2, 2D6). **Elimination:** 90–95% in urine as metabolites; 1–4% in feces. **Half-Life:** 2.3 h.

NURSING IMPLICATIONS

Black Box Warning

Propranolol has been associated with exacerbation of angina and MI following abrupt discontinuance.

Assessment & Drug Effects

- Obtain careful medical history to rule out allergies, asthma, and obstructive pulmonary disease. Propranolol can cause bronchiolar constriction even in normal subjects.
- Monitor apical pulse, respiration, BP for 2 h after initiation or dosage adjustment. Consult prescriber for acceptable parameters.
- Evaluate adequate control or dosage interval for patients being treated for hypertension by checking blood pressure near end of dosage interval or before administration of next dose.
- Monitor I&O ratio and daily weight as significant indexes for detecting fluid retention and developing heart failure.
- Monitor diabetics for loss of glycemic control.

Patient & Family Education

- Do not discontinue abruptly; can precipitate withdrawal syndrome (e.g., tremulousness, sweating, severe headache, malaise, palpitation, rebound hypertension, MI, and life-threatening arrhythmias in patients with angina pectoris).

- Learn usual pulse rate and take radial pulse before each dose. Report to prescriber if pulse is below the established parameter or becomes irregular.
- Be aware that propranolol suppresses clinical signs of hypoglycemia (e.g., BP changes, increased pulse rate) and may prolong hypoglycemia.
- Understand importance of compliance. Do not alter established regimen (i.e., do not omit, increase, or decrease dosage or change dosage interval).
- Be aware that drug may cause mild hypotension (experienced as dizziness or light-headedness) in normotensive patients on prolonged therapy. Make position changes slowly and avoid prolonged standing. Notify prescriber if symptoms persist.
- Do not drive or engage in potentially hazardous activities until response to drug is known.
- Inform dentist, surgeon, or ophthalmologist that you are taking propranolol (drug lowers normal and elevated intraocular pressure).

PROPYLTHIOURACIL (PTU) ⊙₊

(proe-pill-thye-oh-yoor'a-sill)
Classification: ANTITHYROID
Therapeutic: ANTITHYROID

AVAILABILITY Tablet

ACTION & THERAPEUTIC EFFECT

Interferes with use of iodine and blocks synthesis of thyroxine (T_4) and triiodothyronine (T_3); blocks conversion of T_4 to T_3 in peripheral tissues and T_3 stores in circulating blood and the thyroid. *Effective as an antithyroid agent in various hyperthyroid conditions.*

USES Hyperthyroidism in patients with Graves' disease or toxic multinodular goiter; amelioration of hyperthyroid symptoms prior to surgery.

CONTRAINDICATIONS Hypersensitivity to propylthiouracil; acute liver failure; exfoliative dermatitis; unexplained fever; pregnancy (non teratogenic adverse effects, including fetal and neonatal hypothyroidism, goiter, and hyperthyroidism, have been reported following maternal).

CAUTIOUS USE Infection; bone marrow depression; impaired liver function; renal impairment; older adults; patients at risk for liver failure; lactation; children younger than 6 y.

ROUTE & DOSAGE

Hyperthyroidism
Adult: **PO** 300 mg/day divided q8h

ADMINISTRATION

Oral
- Give at the same time each day with relation to meals. Food may alter drug response by changing absorption rate.
- If drug is being used to improve thyroid state before radioactive iodine (RAI) treatment, discontinue 3 or 4 days before treatment to prevent uptake interference. PTU therapy may be resumed if necessary 3–5 days after the RAI administration.
- Store drug at 15°–30° C (59°–86° F) in light-resistant container.

ADVERSE EFFECTS Cardiovascular: Edema, periarteritis, vasculitis. **Respiratory:** Interstitial pneumonitis, pulmonary alveolar hemorrhage. **CNS:** Paresthesias, headache, vertigo, drowsiness, neuritis. **Endocrine:** Hypothyroidism (goitrogenic), enlarged thyroid, periorbital edema, puffy hands and feet, bradycardia, cool and pale skin, worsening of ophthalmopathy, sleepiness, fatigue, mental depression, sensitivity to cold, nocturnal muscle cramps, changes in menstrual periods, unusual weight gain. **Skin:** Skin rash, urticaria, pruritus, skin pigmentation, exfoliative dermatitis, alopecia, Stevens-Johnson Syndrome. **Hepatic/GI:** Nausea, vomiting, diarrhea, dyspepsia, loss of taste, stomach pain, hepatotoxicity, jaundice, hepatitis. **GU:** Acute renal failure, glomerulonephritis. **Hematologic:** Myelosuppression, lymphadenopathy, hypoprothrombinemia, *thrombocytopenia*, *leukopenia*, agranulocytosis, aplastic anemia, granulocytopenia, splenomegaly, hemorrhage. **Other:** Fever, lupus-like syndrome, arthralgia, myalgia.

INTERACTIONS Drug: May increase myleosuppression with MYELOSUPRESSIVE AGENTS. Do not use with LIVE VACCINES.

PHARMACOKINETICS Absorption: Rapidly from GI tract. **Peak:** 1–2 h. **Distribution:** Concentrates in thyroid gland; crosses placenta; some distribution into breast milk. **Metabolism:** Rapidly to inactive metabolites. **Elimination:** 35% in urine. **Half-Life:** 1–2 h.

NURSING IMPLICATIONS

Black Box Warning

Propylthiouracil has been associated with acute, sometimes fatal, liver injury.

Assessment & Drug Effects

- Be aware that about 10% of patients with hyperthyroidism have leukopenia less than 4000 cells/mm^3 and relative granulocytopenia.
- Observe for signs of clinical response to PTU (usually within 2 or 3 wk): Significant weight gain, reduced pulse rate, reduced serum T_4.
- Satisfactory euthyroid state may be delayed for several months when thyroid gland is greatly enlarged.
- Be alert to signs of hypoprothrombinemia: Ecchymoses, purpura, petechiae, unexplained bleeding. Warn ambulatory patients to report these signs promptly.
- Be alert for important diagnostic signs of excess dosage: Contraction of a muscle bundle when pricked, mental depression, hard and nonpitting edema, and need for high thermostat setting and extra blankets in winter (cold intolerance).
- Monitor for urticaria (occurs in 3–7% of patients during weeks 2–8 of treatment). Report severe rash.
- Monitor lab tests: Baseline and periodic T_3, T_4, and TSH; periodic LFTs and CBC with differential and platelet count.

Patient & Family Education

- Note that PTU treatment may be reinstituted if surgery fails to produce normal thyroid gland function.
- Report severe skin rash or swelling of cervical lymph nodes. Therapy may be discontinued.
- Report to prescriber sore throat, fever, and rash immediately (most apt to occur in first few months of treatment). Drug will be discontinued and hematologic studies initiated.

P

Common adverse effects in *italic;* life-threatening effects <u>underlined</u>; generic names in **bold;** classifications in SMALL CAPS; ✦ Canadian drug name; ○ Prototype drug; △ Alert

- Avoid use of OTC drugs for asthma, or cough treatment without checking with the prescriber. Iodides sometimes included in such preparations are contraindicated.
- Learn how to take pulse accurately and check daily. Report to prescriber continued tachycardia.
- Report diarrhea, fever, irritability, listlessness, vomiting, weakness; these are signs of inadequate therapy or thyrotoxicosis.
- Chart weight 2 or 3 × weekly; clinical response is monitored through changes in weight and pulse.
- Do not alter drug regimen (e.g., increase, decrease, omit doses, change dosage intervals).
- Check with prescriber about use of iodized salt and inclusion of seafood in the diet.

PROTAMINE SULFATE
(proe'ta-meen)
Classification: ANTIDOTE; HEPARIN ANTAGONIST
Therapeutic: ANTIHEMORRHAGIC

AVAILABILITY Solution for injection

ACTION & *THERAPEUTIC EFFECT*
Combines with heparin to produce a stable complex; thus it neutralizes the anticoagulant effect of heparin. *Effective antidote to heparin overdose.*

USES Antidote for heparin overdosage (after heparin has been discontinued).

UNLABELED USES Antidote for heparin administration during extracorporeal circulation.

CONTRAINDICATIONS Hemorrhage not induced by heparin overdosage; lactation.

CAUTIOUS USE Cardiovascular disease; history of allergy to fish; vasectomized or infertile males; diabetes mellitus; patients who have received protamine-containing insulin; pregnancy (category C); children.

ROUTE & DOSAGE

Antidote for Heparin Overdose
Adult/Child: **IV** 1 mg for every 100 units of heparin to be neutralized (max: 100 mg in a 2 h period), give the first 25–50 mg by slow direct IV and the rest over 2–3 h

ADMINISTRATION

Note: Titrate dose carefully to prevent excess anticoagulation because protamine has a longer half-life than heparin and also has some anticoagulant effect of its own.

Intravenous
Note: Verify correct IV concentration and rate of infusion for infants or children with prescriber.

***PREPARE:* Direct:** May be given as supplied direct IV. **Continuous:** Dilute in 50 mL or more of NS or D5W.
***ADMINISTER:* Direct** Give each 50 mg or fraction thereof slowly over 10–15 min. ▪ NEVER give more than 50 mg in any 10 min period or 100 mg in any 2 h period.
Continuous: Do not exceed direct rate. Give over 2–3 h or longer as determined by coagulation studies.
***INCOMPATIBILITIES:* Solution/additive:** RADIOCONTRAST MATERIALS, **furosemide.**

Common adverse effects in *italic;* life-threatening effects <u>underlined</u>; generic names in **bold;** classifications in SMALL CAPS; ◆ Canadian drug name; ● Prototype drug; ⚠ Alert

• Store protamine sulfate injection at 15°–30° C (59°–86° F).
• Solutions do not contain preservatives and should not be stored.

ADVERSE EFFECTS CV: *Abrupt drop in BP* (with rapid IV infusion), bradycardia. **GI:** Nausea, vomiting. **Hematologic:** Protamine overdose or "heparin rebound" (hyper-heparinemia). **Other:** Urticaria, angioedema, pulmonary edema, anaphylaxis, dyspnea, lassitude; transient flushing and feeling of warmth.

PHARMACOKINETICS Onset: 5 min. **Duration:** 2 h.

NURSING IMPLICATIONS

Black Box Warning

Protamine can cause severe hypotension, cardiovascular collapse, noncardiogenic pulmonary edema, catastrophic pulmonary vasoconstriction, and pulmonary hypertension.

Assessment & Drug Effects

• Monitor closely for a hypersensitivity reaction. Risk factors include high doses or overdose, repeated doses, and previous protamine administration (including protamine-containing drugs).
• Monitor BP, HR, and respiratory status q15–30min, or more often if indicated. Continue for at least 2–3 h after each dose, or longer as dictated by patient's condition.
• Observe closely patients who have had cardiac surgery for bleeding (heparin rebound). Even with apparent adequate neutralization of heparin by protamine, bleeding may occur 30 min to 18 h after surgery.

• Monitor lab tests: Activated clotting time or aPTT 5–15 min after administration of protamine, and again in 2–8 h if desirable.

PROTEIN C CONCENTRATE (HUMAN)

(pro'teen)
Ceprotin
Classification: HEMATOLOGIC; THROMBOLYTIC; PROTEIN SYNTHESIS INHIBITOR
Therapeutic: PROTEIN C REPLACEMENT THERAPY

AVAILABILITY Vial of lyophilized powder

ACTION & THERAPEUTIC EFFECT
Protein C is a critical element in a pathway that provides a natural mechanism for control of the coagulation system. It prevents excess procoagulant responses to activating stimuli. *Protein C is necessary to decrease thrombin generation and intravascular clot formation.*

USES Treatment of patients with severe congenital protein C deficiency; protein C replacement therapy for the prevention and treatment of venous thrombosis and purpura fulminans in children and adults.

CONTRAINDICATIONS Hypersensitivity to human protein C; concurrent administration with tissue plasminogen activator (tPA); hypernatremia; lactation.

CAUTIOUS USE Concurrent administration of anticoagulants; heparin induced thrombocytopenia (HIT); renal impairment; hepatic impairment; older adults; pregnancy (category C); children.

P

ROUTE & DOSAGE

Acute Episodes of Venous Thrombosis and Purpura Fulminans and Short-Term Prophylaxis

Adult/Adolescent/Child/Infant:
IV Initial dose 100–120 units/kg; then 60–80 units/kg q6h × 3; maintenance dose: 45–60 units/kg q6–12h.

ADMINISTRATION

Intravenous

PREPARE: **Direct/IV Infusion:** Bring powder and supplied diluent to room temperature. Insert supplied double-ended transfer needle into diluent vial, then invert and rapidly insert into protein C powder vial. (If vacuum does not draw diluent into vial, discard.) ▪ Remove transfer needle and gently swirl to dissolve. ▪ Resulting solution concentration is 100 units/mL and it should be colorless to slightly yellowish, clear to slightly opalescent and free from visible particles. ▪ Withdraw required dose with the supplied filter needle.

ADMINISTER: **Direct/IV Infusion:** Infuse at 2 mL/min. **Direct/IV Infusion for Child weighing greater than 10 kg:** Infuse at 0.2 mL/kg/min.
▪ Store at room temperature for no more than 3 h after reconstitution. ▪ Prior to reconstitution, protect from light.

ADVERSE EFFECTS CV: Hemothorax, hypotension. **CNS:** Lightheadedness. **Other:** Fever, hyperhidrosis, hypersensitivity reactions (rash, pruritus), restlessness.

INTERACTIONS Drug: Protein C concentrate can increase bleeding caused by **alteplase, reteplase,** or **tenecteplase.**

PHARMACOKINETICS Peak: 0.5–1 h. **Half-Life:** 9.9 h.

NURSING IMPLICATIONS

Assessment & Drug Effects

▪ Monitor for and promptly report S&S of bleeding or hypersensitivity reactions (see Appendix F).
▪ Monitor vital signs including BP and temperature.
▪ Monitor lab tests: Baseline and periodic protein C activity; periodic platelet count; frequent serum sodium with renal function impairment.

Patient & Family Education

▪ Report immediately early signs of hypersensitivity reactions including hives, generalized itching, tightness in chest, wheezing, difficulty breathing.
▪ Report immediately any signs of bleeding including black tarry stools, pink/red-tinged urine, unusual bruising.

PROTRIPTYLINE HYDROCHLORIDE

(proe-trip'te-leen)

Classification: TRICYCLIC ANTIDEPRESSANT
Therapeutic: ANTIDEPRESSANT
Prototype: Imipramine

AVAILABILITY Tablet

ACTION & *THERAPEUTIC EFFECT*

Believed to enhance actions of norepinephrine and serotonin by blocking their reuptake at the neuronal membrane. *Effective in the treatment of depressed individuals, particularly those who are withdrawn.*

USES Treatment of major depression.

UNLABELED USES Sleep apnea.

CONTRAINDICATIONS Hypersensitivity to TCAs; concurrent use of MAOIs; acute recovery phase following MI or within 14 days of use; QT prolongation, bundle branch block; cardiac conduction defects; suicidal ideation.

CAUTIOUS USE Hepatic, cardiovascular, or kidney dysfunction; DM; hyperthyroidism; history of alcoholism; patients with insomnia; asthma; bipolar disorder; suicidal tendencies; children and adolescents; pregnancy (category C); lactation.

ROUTE & DOSAGE

Depression

Adult: **PO** 15–40 mg/day in 3–4 divided doses (max: 60 mg/day)
Adolescent: **PO** 5 mg tid

ADMINISTRATION

Oral

- Give whole or crush and mix with fluid or food.
- Give dosage increases in the morning dose to prevent sleep interference and because this TCA has psychic energizing action.
- Give last dose of day no later than mid-afternoon; insomnia rather than drowsiness is a frequent adverse effect.
- Store at 15°–30° C (59°–86° F) in tightly closed container.

ADVERSE EFFECTS CV: Change in heat or cold tolerance; *orthostatic hypotension, tachycardia,* arrhythmia. **CNS:** Insomnia, headache, confusion, tremor. **HEENT:** Blurred vision. **GI:** *Xerostomia,*
constipation, paralytic ileus, dypepsia, nausea. **GU:** *Urinary retention,* ejaculation dysfunction. **Other:** Photosensitivity, edema (general or of face and tongue).

INTERACTIONS Drug: May decrease some response to ANTIHYPERTENSIVES; CNS DEPRESSANTS, **alcohol,** HYPNOTICS, BARBITURATES, SEDATIVES potentiate CNS depression; ORAL ANTICOAGULANTS may increase hypoprothrombinemic effects; **ethchlorvynol** causes transient delirium; **levodopa** SYMPATHOMIMETICS (e.g., **epinephrine, norepinephrine**) increases possibility of sympathetic hyperactivity with hypertension and hyperpyrexia; MAO INHIBITORS present possibility of severe reactions—toxic psychosis, cardiovascular instability; **methylphenidate** increases plasma TCA levels; THYROID DRUGS may increase possibility of arrhythmias; **cimetidine** may increase plasma TCA levels. Do not use with agents that prolong the QT interval (e.g., **dofetilide, dronedarone, ziprasidone**). **Herbal: Ginkgo** may decrease seizure threshold; **St. John's wort** may cause serotonin syndrome (headache, dizziness, sweating, agitation).

PHARMACOKINETICS Absorption: Rapidly from GI tract. **Peak levels:** 24–30 h. **Distribution:** Crosses placenta; distributed into breast milk. **Metabolism:** In liver. **Elimination:** Primarily in urine. **Half-Life:** 54–98 h.

NURSING IMPLICATIONS

Black Box Warning

Protriptyline has been associated with increased risk of suicidal thinking and behavior in children, adolescents, and young adults.

P

Assessment & Drug Effects

- Monitor therapeutic effectiveness. Onset of initial effect characterized by increased activity and energy is fairly rapid, usually within 1 wk after therapy is initiated. Maximum effect may not occur for 2 wk or more.
- Monitor adolescents as well as adults for changes in behavior that may indicate suicidality. Suicide is an inherent risk with any depressed patient and may remain until there is significant improvement.
- Monitor vital signs closely and CV system responses during early therapy, particularly in patients with cardiovascular disorders and older adults receiving daily doses in excess of 20 mg. Withhold drug and inform prescriber if BP falls more than 20 mm Hg or if there is a sudden increase in pulse rate.
- Monitor I&O ratio and bowel pattern during early therapy and when patient is on large doses.
- Assess and advise prescriber as indicated for prominent anticholinergic effects (xerostomia, blurred vision, constipation, paralytic ileus, urinary retention, delayed micturition).
- Assess condition of oral membranes frequently; institute symptomatic treatment if necessary. Xerostomia can interfere with appetite, fluid intake, and integrity of tooth surfaces.

Patient & Family Education

- Report promptly changes in mood or behavior indicative of suicidal thinking.
- Consult prescriber about safe amount of alcohol, if any, that can be taken. Actions of both alcohol and protriptyline are potentiated when used together for up to 2 wk after the TCA is discontinued.
- Consult prescriber before taking any OTC medications.
- Be aware that effects of barbiturates and other CNS depressants are enhanced by TCAs.
- Avoid potentially hazardous activities requiring alertness and skill until response to drug is known.
- Avoid exposure to the sun without protecting skin with sunscreen lotion (SPF higher than 12). Photosensitivity reactions may occur.

PRUCALOPRIDE

(proo-KAL-oh-pride)

Motegrity

Classifications: GI STIMULANT; PROKINETIC AGENT

Therapeutic: GI STIMULANT; ANTIEMETIC

Prototype: Metoclopramide

AVAILABILITY Oral tablet

ACTION & THERAPEUTIC EFFECT A selective, high affinity 5-HT_4 receptor agonist whose action at the receptor site promotes cholinergic and nonadrenergic, noncholinergic neurotransmission by enteric neurons. *Leads to stimulation of peristaltic reflex, intestinal secretions, and gastrointestinal motility.*

USES Treatment of Chronic Idiopathic Constipation (CIC).

CONTRAINDICATIONS Hypersensitivity to prucalopride or any component of the formulation; intestinal perforation or obstruction due to structural or functional disorder of the gut wall, obstructive ileus, or severe inflammatory conditions of the GI tract.

Common adverse effects in *italic;* life-threatening effects <u>underlined;</u> generic names in **bold;** classifications in SMALL CAPS; ✦ Canadian drug name; ☉ Prototype drug; ⚠ Alert

CAUTIOUS USE Renal impairment; elderly; pregnancy; lactation.

ROUTE & DOSAGE

Treatment of Chronic Idiopathic Constipation

Adult: **PO** 2 mg once daily

Renal Impairment Dosage Adjustment

CrCl less than 30 mL/min: 1 mg once daily
ESRD with dialysis: Avoid use

ADMINISTRATION

Oral

- Administer without regard to meals.
- Store at 20° to 25°C (68° to 77°F). Store in original container to protect from moisture.

ADVERSE EFFECTS CNS: Headache, dizziness. **GI:** Abdominal pain, nausea, diarrhea, abdominal distension.

INTERACTIONS No clinically relevant interactions reported.

PHARMACOKINETICS Absorption: 90% bioavailability. **Peak:** 2–3 h **Distribution:** 567 L (given IV); 30% protein bound. **Metabolism:** In the liver primarily by CYP3A4 (minor). **Elimination:** 84% in urine, 13% in feces. **Half-Life:** 24 h.

NURSING IMPLICATIONS

Assessment & Drug Effects

- Monitor frequency of bowel movements.
- Monitor for worsening of depression or emergence of suicidal thoughts or behavior.

- Assess for cardiovascular symptoms in patients with heart disease.
- Monitor lab tests: Baseline liver function tests, baseline renal function tests.

Patient & Family Education

- Notify health care provider if experiencing new or worse behavior or mood changes like depression or thoughts of suicide.
- Notify your doctor or get medical help right away if you have any of the following signs or symptoms of allergic reaction such as rash, hives, itching; red, swollen, blistered, or peeling skin with or without fever; wheezing; tightness in the chest or throat; trouble breathing, swallowing, or talking; unusual hoarseness; or swelling of the mouth, face, lips, tongue, or throat; or any dizziness or passing out.

PSEUDOEPHEDRINE HYDROCHLORIDE

(soo-doe-e-fed′rin)

Cenafed, Decongestant Syrup, Dorcol Children's Decongestant, Eltor ♣, Eltor 120 ♣, Halofed, Novafed, PediaCare, Pseudofrin ♣, Robidrine ♣, Sudafed, Sudrin

Classification: ALPHA- AND BETA-ADRENERGIC RECEPTOR AGONIST; DECONGESTANT
Therapeutic: NASAL DECONGESTANT
Prototype: Epinephrine

AVAILABILITY Tablet; sustained release tablet; liquid; drops

ACTION & *THERAPEUTIC EFFECT*

Sympathomimetic amine that produces decongestion of respiratory

P

tract mucosa by stimulating the sympathetic nerve endings including alpha-, beta$_1$-, and beta$_2$-receptors. *Effect is caused by vasoconstriction and thus increased nasal airway patency.*

USES Symptomatic relief of nasal congestion associated with rhinitis, coryza, and sinusitis and for eustachian tube congestion.

CONTRAINDICATIONS Hypersensitivity to sympathomimetic amines; severe hypertension; severe coronary artery disease; use within 14 days of MAOIS; hyperthyroidism; prostatic hypertrophy.

CAUTIOUS USE Hypertension, heart disease, renal impairment; acute MI, angina; closed-angle glaucoma; severe narrowing of bowel; concurrent use of ACE INHIBITOR; thryroid disease, DM, elevated IOP; PVD; BPH; pregnancy (category C); lactation. Safe use in children younger than 2 y **(PO)**, children younger than 12 y **(sustained release)** is not established.

ROUTE & DOSAGE

Nasal Congestion

Adult: **PO** 60 mg q4–6h or 120 mg sustained release q12h
Geriatric: **PO** 30–60 mg q6h prn
Child (2–6 y): **PO** 15 mg q4–6h (max: 60 mg/day); *6–11 y:* 30 mg q4–6h (max: 120 mg/day)

ADMINISTRATION

Oral

- Ensure that sustained release form is not chewed or crushed. **Must be** swallowed whole.

ADVERSE EFFECTS CV: Arrhythmias, palpitation, *tachycardia.* **CNS:** *Nervousness,* dizziness, headache, sleeplessness, numbness of extremities. **GI:** Anorexia, dry mouth, nausea, vomiting. **Other:** *Transient stimulation,* tremulousness, difficulty in voiding.

INTERACTIONS Drug: Other SYMPATHOMIMETICS increase pressor effects and toxicity; MAO INHIBITORS may precipitate hypertensive crisis; BETA-BLOCKERS may increase pressor effects; may decrease antihypertensive effects of **guanethidine, methyldopa, reserpine.**

PHARMACOKINETICS Absorption: Readily from GI tract. **Onset:** 15–30 min. **Duration:** 4–6 h (8–12 h sustained release). **Distribution:** Crosses placenta; distributed into breast milk. **Metabolism:** Partially metabolized in liver. **Elimination:** In urine.

NURSING IMPLICATIONS

Assessment & Drug Effects

- Monitor HR and BP, especially in those with a history of cardiac disease. Report tachycardia or hypertension.

Patient & Family Education

- Do not take drug within 2 h of bedtime because drug may act as a stimulant.
- Discontinue medication and consult prescriber if extreme restlessness or signs of sensitivity occur.
- Consult prescriber before concomitant use of OTC medications; many contain ephedrine or other sympathomimetic amines and might intensify action of pseudoephedrine.

PSYLLIUM HYDROPHILIC MUCILLOID ⊙

(sill'i-um)

Konsyl, Metamucil, Reguloid

Classification: BULK-PRODUCING LAXATIVE
Therapeutic: BULK LAXATIVE

AVAILABILITY Powder; granules

ACTION & *THERAPEUTIC EFFECT*
Bulk-producing laxative that absorbs liquid in the GI tract, facilitating peristalsis and bowel motility. *Bulk-producing laxative that promotes peristalsis and natural elimination.*

USES Chronic atonic or spastic constipation and constipation associated with rectal disorders or anorectal surgery.

CONTRAINDICATIONS Esophageal and intestinal obstruction, dysphagia; nausea, vomiting, fecal impaction, acute abdomen; undiagnosed abdominal pain, appendicitis.

CAUTIOUS USE Diabetics; pregnancy (category C); children younger than 6 y.

ROUTE & DOSAGE

Constipation or Diarrhea

Adult: **PO** 2.5 to 30 g per day in divided doses
Child (6–12 y): **PO** 1.25 to 15 g/day in 1 to 3 divided doses

ADMINISTRATION

Oral
- Fill an 8-oz (240-mL) water glass with cool water, milk, fruit juice, or other liquid; sprinkle powder into liquid; stir briskly; and give immediately (if effervescent form is used, add liquid to powder). Granules should not be chewed.
- Follow each dose with an additional glass of liquid to obtain best results.
- Exercise caution with older adult patient who may aspirate the drug.

ADVERSE EFFECTS GI: Nausea and vomiting, diarrhea (with excessive use); GI tract strictures when drug used in dry form, abdominal cramps. **Hematologic:** Eosinophilia.

INTERACTIONS Drug: Psyllium may decrease absorption and clinical effects of ANTIBIOTICS, **warfarin, digoxin, nitrofurantoin,** SALICYLATES.

PHARMACOKINETICS Absorption: Not absorbed from GI tract. **Onset:** 12–24 h. **Peak:** 1–3 days.

NURSING IMPLICATIONS

Assessment & Drug Effects
- Report promptly to prescriber if patient complains of retrosternal pain after taking the drug. Drug may be lodged as a gelatinous mass (because of poor mixing) in the esophagus.
- Monitor therapeutic effectiveness. When psyllium is used as either a bulk laxative or to treat diarrhea, the expected effect is formed stools. Laxative effect usually occurs within 12–24 h. Administration for 2 or 3 days may be needed to establish regularity.
- Assess for complaints of abdominal fullness. Smaller, more frequent doses spaced throughout the day may be indicated to relieve discomfort of abdominal fullness.

P

Common adverse effects in *italic*; life-threatening effects <u>underlined</u>; generic names in **bold**; classifications in SMALL CAPS; ✦ Canadian drug name; ⊙ Prototype drug; ⚠ Alert

- Monitor lab tests: Frequent warfarin and digoxin levels if either is given concurrently.

Patient & Family Education
- Note sugar and sodium content of preparation if on low-sodium or low-calorie diet. Some preparations contain natural sugars, whereas others contain artificial sweeteners.
- Understand that drug works to relieve both diarrhea and constipation by restoring a more normal moisture level to stool.
- Be aware that drug may reduce appetite if it is taken before meals.

PYRANTEL PAMOATE
(pi-ran'tel)
Pin-X
Classification: ANTHELMINTIC
Therapeutic: ANTHELMINTIC
Prototype: Praziquantel

AVAILABILITY Capsule; oral suspension

ACTION & *THERAPEUTIC EFFECT*
Exerts selective depolarizing neuromuscular blocking action that results in spastic paralysis of worm. *Causes evacuation of worms from intestines.*

USES *Enterobius vermicularis* (pinworm) and *Ascaris lumbricoides* (roundworm) infestations.

UNLABELED USES Hookworm infestations; trichostrongylosis.

CONTRAINDICATIONS Hypersensitivity to pyrantel.

CAUTIOUS USE Liver dysfunction; malnutrition; dehydration; anemia; pregnancy (category C).

ROUTE & DOSAGE

Pinworm or Roundworm
Adult/Child: **PO** 11 mg/kg as a single dose (max: 1 g)

ADMINISTRATION
Oral
- Shake suspension well before pouring it to ensure accurate dosage.
- Give with milk or fruit juices and without regard to prior ingestion of food or time of day.
- Store below 30° C (86° F). Protect from light.

ADVERSE EFFECTS CNS: Dizziness, headache, drowsiness, insomnia. **Skin:** Skin rashes. **GI:** Anorexia, *nausea,* vomiting, abdominal distention, diarrhea, *tenesmus,* transient elevation of AST.

INTERACTIONS Drug: Piperazine and pyrantel may be mutually antagonistic.

PHARMACOKINETICS Absorption: Poorly from GI tract. **Peak:** 1–3 h. **Metabolism:** In liver. **Elimination:** Greater than 50% in feces, 7% in urine.

NURSING IMPLICATIONS
Assessment & Drug Effects
- Monitor stool for presence of eggs, worms, and occult blood.

Patient & Family Education
- Do not drive or engage in other potentially hazardous activities until response to drug is known.

CAUTIOUS USE History of gout or diabetes mellitus; impaired kidney function; alcoholism; history of peptic ulcer; acute intermittent porphyria; pregnancy (category C); lactation; children.

ROUTE & DOSAGE

Tuberculosis

Adult/Child: **PO** 15–30 mg/kg/day (max: 3 g/day)

Renal Impairment Dosage Adjustment

CrCl 10–50 mL/min: Extend interval to q48–72 hours; *CrCl less than 10 mL/min:* Extend interval to q72h

ADMINISTRATION

Oral

- Discontinue drug if hepatic reactions (jaundice, pruritus, icteric sclerae, yellow skin) or hyperuricemia with acute gout (severe pain in great toe and other joints) occurs.
- Store at 15°–30° C (59°–86° F) in tightly closed container.

ADVERSE EFFECTS CNS: Headache. **Endocrine:** *Rise in serum uric acid.* **Skin:** Urticaria. **GI:** Splenomegaly, <u>fatal hemoptysis</u>, aggravation of peptic ulcer, *hepatotoxicity, abnormal liver function tests.* **GU:** Difficulty in urination. **Hematologic:** Hemolytic anemia, decreased plasma prothrombin. **Other:** *Active gout,* arthralgia, lymphadenopathy.

DIAGNOSTIC TEST INTERFERENCE Pyrazinamide may produce a temporary decrease in *17-ketosteroids* and an increase in *protein-bound iodine.*

INTERACTIONS Drug: Increase in liver toxicity (including fatal hepatoxicity in when treating latent TB) with **rifampin.**

PHARMACOKINETICS Absorption: Readily from GI tract. **Peak:** 2 h. **Distribution:** Crosses blood-brain barrier. **Metabolism:** In liver. **Elimination:** Slowly in urine. **Half-Life:** 9–10 h.

NURSING IMPLICATIONS

Assessment & Drug Effects

- Observe and supervise closely. Patients should receive at least one other effective antituberculosis agent concurrently.
- Examine patients at regular intervals and question about possible signs of toxicity: Liver enlargement or tenderness, jaundice, fever, anorexia, malaise, impaired vascular integrity (ecchymoses, petechiae, abnormal bleeding).
- Hepatic reactions appear to occur more frequently in patients receiving high doses.
- Monitor lab tests: Baseline and periodic LFTs and uric acid level.

Patient & Family Education

- Report to prescriber onset of difficulty in voiding. Keep fluid intake at 2000 mL/day if possible.
- Monitor blood glucose (diabetics) for possible loss of glycemic control.

PYRETHRINS

(peer′e-thrins)

A-200 Pyrinate, Barc, Blue, Pyrinate, Pyrinyl, R&C, RID, TISIT, Triple X

Classification: ANTIPARASITIC; PEDICULICIDE
Therapeutic: SCABICIDE
Prototype: Permethrin

AVAILABILITY Liquid; gel; shampoo

ACTION & *THERAPEUTIC EFFECT*

Acts as a contact poison affecting the parasite's nervous system, causing paralysis and death. *Controls head lice, pubic (crab) lice, and body lice and their eggs (nits).*

USES External treatment of *Pediculus humanus* infestations.

CONTRAINDICATIONS Sensitivity to solution components; skin infections and abrasions.

CAUTIOUS USE Ragweed-sensitized patient; asthma; pregnancy (category C); lactation; infants; children.

ROUTE & DOSAGE

Pediculus humanus Infestations

Adult: **Topical** See ADMINISTRATION for appropriate application

ADMINISTRATION

Topical
- Apply enough solution to completely wet infested area, including hair. Allow to remain on area for 10 min.
- Wash and rinse with large amounts of warm water.
- Use fine-toothed comb to remove lice and eggs from hair.
- Shampoo hair to restore body and luster.
- Repeat treatment once in 24 h if necessary.
- Repeat treatment in 7–10 days to kill newly hatched lice.
- Do not apply to eyebrows or eyelashes without consulting prescriber.
- Flush eyes with copious amounts of warm water if accidental contact occurs.

ADVERSE EFFECTS Other: Irritation with repeated use.

NURSING IMPLICATIONS

Patient & Family Education
- Do not swallow, inhale, or allow pyrethrins to contact mucosal surfaces or the eyes.
- Discontinue use and consult prescriber if treated area becomes irritated.
- Examine each family member carefully; if infested, treat immediately to prevent spread or reinfestation of previously treated patient.
- Dry clean, boil, or otherwise treat contaminated clothing. Sterilize (soak in pyrethrins) combs and brushes used by patient.
- Do not share combs, brushes, or other headgear with another person.

PYRIDOSTIGMINE BROMIDE

(peer-id-oh-stig′meen)
Mestinon, Regonol
Classification: CHOLINERGIC MUSCLE STIMULANT; ANTICHOLINESTERASE
Therapeutic: CHOLINESTERASE INHIBITOR; MUSCLE STIMULANT
Prototype: Neostigmine

AVAILABILITY Syrup; tablet; extended release tablet; solution for injection

ACTION & *THERAPEUTIC EFFECT*

Indirect-acting cholinergic agent that inhibits cholinesterase activity. Facilitates transmission of impulses across myoneural junctions by blocking destruction of acetylcholine. *Has direct stimulant action on voluntary muscle fibers and possibly on autonomic ganglia and CNS neurons. Produces increased tone in skeletal muscles.*

Common adverse effects in *italic*; life-threatening effects underlined; generic names in **bold;** classifications in SMALL CAPS; ♣ Canadian drug name; ✺ Prototype drug; ⚠ Alert

USES Myasthenia gravis and as an antagonist to nondepolarizing skeletal muscle relaxants (e.g., curariform drugs).

CONTRAINDICATIONS Hypersensitivity to anticholinesterase agents; mechanical obstruction of urinary or intestinal tract; hypotension; lactation.

CAUTIOUS USE Hypersensitivity to bromides; bronchial asthma; epilepsy; recent cardiac occlusion; renal impairment; vagotonia; hyperthyroidism; peptic ulcer; cardiac dysrhythmias; bradycardia; pregnancy (category C).

ROUTE & DOSAGE

Myasthenia Gravis

Adult: **PO** 60 mg–1.5 g/day spaced according to response of individual patient; **Sustained release** 180–540 mg 1–2 × day at intervals of at least 6 h; **IM/IV** Approximately $1/30$ of PO dose
Child: **PO** 7 mg/kg/day divided into 5–6 doses
Neonates: **PO** 5 mg q4–6h; **IM/IV** 0.05–0.15 mg/kg q4–6h

Reversal of Muscle Relaxants

Adult: **IV** 10–20 mg immediately preceded by IV atropine

ADMINISTRATION

Oral

- Give with food or fluid.
- Ensure that sustained release form is not chewed or crushed. **Must be** swallowed whole.
- Note: A syrup is available. Some patients may not like it because it is sweet; try to make it more palatable by giving it over ice chips.

The syrup formulation contains 5% alcohol.

Intramuscular

- Note: Parenteral dose is about $1/30$ the oral adult dose.
- Give deep IM into a large muscle.

Intravenous

PREPARE: Direct: Give undiluted. **Do not** add to IV solutions. **ADMINISTER: Direct:** Give at a rate of 0.5 mg over 1 min for myasthenia gravis; 5 mg over 1 min for reversal of muscle relaxants.

- Store at 15°–30° C (59°–86° F). Protect from light and moisture.

ADVERSE EFFECTS CV: Bradycardia, hypotension. **Respiratory:** Increased bronchial secretion, bronchoconstriction. **HEENT:** *Miosis.* **Skin:** Acneiform rash. **GI:** *Nausea, vomiting, diarrhea.* **Hematologic:** Thrombophlebitis (following IV administration). **Other:** *Excessive salivation and sweating,* weakness, fasciculation.

INTERACTIONS Drug: Atropine NONDEPOLARIZING MUSCLE RELAXANTS antagonize effects of pyridostigmine.

PHARMACOKINETICS Absorption: Poorly from GI tract. **Onset:** 30–45 min PO; 15 min IM; 2–5 min IV. **Duration:** 3–6 h. **Distribution:** Crosses placenta. **Metabolism:** In liver and in serum and tissue by cholinesterases. **Elimination:** In urine.

NURSING IMPLICATIONS

Assessment & Drug Effects

- Report increasing muscular weakness, cramps, or fasciculations. Failure of patient to show improvement may reflect either underdosage or overdosage.

- Observe patient closely if atropine is used to abolish GI adverse effects or other muscarinic adverse effects because it may mask signs of overdosage (cholinergic crisis): Increasing muscle weakness, which through involvement of respiratory muscles can lead to death.
- Monitor vital signs frequently, especially respiratory rate.
- Observe for signs of cholinergic reactions (see Appendix F), particularly when drug is administered IV.
- Observe neonates of myasthenic mothers, who have received pyridostigmine, closely for difficulty in breathing, swallowing, or sucking.
- Observe patient continuously when used as muscle relaxant antagonist. Airway and respiratory assistance **must be** maintained until full recovery of voluntary respiration and neuromuscular transmission is assured. Complete recovery usually occurs within 30 min.

Patient & Family Education

- Be aware that duration of drug action may vary with physical and emotional stress, as well as with severity of disease.
- Report onset of rash to prescriber. Drug may be discontinued.
- Sustained release tablets may become mottled in appearance; this does not affect their potency.

PYRIDOXINE HYDROCHLORIDE (VITAMIN B₆)

(peer-i-dox'een)

Classification: VITAMIN
Therapeutic: VITAMIN B₆
REPLACEMENT

AVAILABILITY Tablet; solution for injection

ACTION & *THERAPEUTIC EFFECT*

Water-soluble complex of three closely related compounds with B₆ activity. Converted in body to pyridoxal, a coenzyme that functions in protein, fat, and carbohydrate metabolism and in facilitating release of glycogen from liver and muscle. In protein metabolism, participates in enzymatic transformations of amino acids and conversion of tryptophan to niacin and serotonin. Aids in energy transformation in brain and nerve cells, and is thought to stimulate heme production. *Effectiveness is evaluated by improvement of B₆ deficiency manifestations: Nausea, vomiting, skin lesions resembling those of riboflavin and niacin deficiency, edema, CNS symptoms, hypochromic microcytic anemia.*

USES Prophylaxis and treatment of pyridoxine deficiency, as seen with inadequate dietary intake, drug-induced deficiency (e.g., isoniazid, oral contraceptives), and inborn errors of metabolism (vitamin B₆-dependent convulsions or anemia). Also to prevent chloramphenicol-induced optic neuritis, to treat acute toxicity caused by overdosage of cycloserine, hydralazine, isoniazid (INH); alcoholic polyneuritis; sideroblastic anemia associated with high serum iron concentration. Has been used for management of many other conditions ranging from nausea and vomiting in radiation sickness and pregnancy to suppression of postpartum lactation.

CONTRAINDICATIONS IV: Cardiac disease.

CAUTIOUS USE Renal impairment; neonatal prematurity with renal impairment; cardiac disease; pregnancy [category A or (C if greater than RDA)].

Common adverse effects in *italic*; life-threatening effects underlined; generic names in **bold**; classifications in SMALL CAPS; ♣ Canadian drug name; ○ Prototype drug; △ Alert

1436

ROUTE & DOSAGE

Dietary Deficiency

Adult: **PO/IM/IV** 10–20 mg/day × 2–3 wk
Child: **PO** 5–25 mg/day × 3 wk, then 1.5–2.5 mg/day

Pyridoxine Deficiency Syndrome

Adult: **PO/IM/IV** Initial dose up to 600 mg/day may be required; then up to 50 mg/day

Isoniazid-Induced Deficiency

Adult: **PO/IM/IV** 100 mg/day × 3 wk, then 30 mg/day
Child: **PO** 10–50 mg/day × 3 wk, then 1–2 mg/kg/day

Pyridoxine-Dependent Seizures

Neonate/Infant: **PO/IM/IV** 50–100 mg/day

ADMINISTRATION

Oral

▪ Ensure that sustained release and enteric forms are not chewed or crushed. **Must be** swallowed whole.

Intramuscular

▪ Give deep IM into a large muscle.

Intravenous

PREPARE: Direct: Give undiluted. **Continuous:** May be added to most standard IV solutions. **ADMINISTER: Direct:** Give at a rate of 50 mg or fraction thereof over 60 sec. **Continuous:** Give according to ordered rate for infusion.

▪ Store at 15°–30° C (59°–86° F) in tight, light-resistant containers. Avoid freezing.

ADVERSE EFFECTS CNS: Somno-
lence seizures (particularly following large parenteral doses). **Endocrine:** Low folic acid levels. **Other:** Paresthesias, slight flushing or feeling of warmth, temporary burning or stinging pain in injection site.

INTERACTIONS Drug: Isonia-
zid, cycloserine, penicillamine, hydralazine, and ORAL CONTRACEPTIVES may increase pyridoxine requirements; may reverse or antagonize therapeutic effects of levodopa.

PHARMACOKINETICS Absorp-
tion: Readily from GI tract. **Distribution:** Stored in liver; crosses placenta. **Metabolism:** In liver. **Elimination:** In urine.

NURSING IMPLICATIONS

Assessment & Drug Effects

▪ Monitor neurologic status to determine therapeutic effect in deficiency states.
▪ Record a complete dietary history so poor eating habits can be identified and corrected (a single vitamin deficiency is rare; patient can be expected to have multiple vitamin deficiencies).

Patient & Family Education

▪ Learn rich dietary sources of vitamin B₆: Yeast, wheat germ, whole grain cereals, muscle and glandular meats (especially liver), legumes, green vegetables, bananas.
▪ Do not self-medicate with vitamin combinations (OTC) without first consulting prescriber.

PYRIMETHAMINE

(peer-i-meth′a-meen)
Daraprim
Classification: FOLIC ACID ANTAGONIST
Therapeutic: ANTIMALARIAL
Prototype: Chloroquine

AVAILABILITY Tablet

ACTION & *THERAPEUTIC EFFECT*
Selectively inhibits action of dehydrofolic reductase in parasites with resulting blockade of folic acid metabolism. *Prevents development of fertilized gametes in the mosquito and thus helps to prevent transmission of malaria.*

USES Treatment of toxoplasmosis (with a sulfonamide).

UNLABELED USES Cystoisosporiasis, pneumocystis pneumonia in patients with HIV.

CONTRAINDICATIONS Chloroguanide-resistant malaria; hypersensitivity to pyrimethamine or any component of the formulation; megaloblastic anemia caused by folate deficiency; lactation.

CAUTIOUS USE Convulsive disorders; asthma; bone marrow suppression; folate deficiency; hepatic disease; renal disease; seizure disorder; pregnancy (use with caution in patients with possible folate deficiency, including pregnant women); children.

ROUTE & DOSAGE

Toxoplasmosis
Adult: **PO** 50–75 mg/day for 1–3 wk, then decrease dose by half and continue for 4–5 weeks
Child: varies based on age, weight, concurrent medications and concurrent disease states, see package insert.

ADMINISTRATION

Oral
- Minimize GI distress by giving with meals.

- Give on same day each week for malaria prophylaxis. Begin when individual enters malarious area and continue for 10 wk after leaving the area.

ADVERSE EFFECTS Cardiovascular: Cardiac arrhythmia. **Respiratory:** Eosinophilic pneumonitis. **Skin:** Skin rashes, erythema multiforme, Stevens-Johnson Syndrome, toxic epidermal necrolysis. **GI:** Anorexia, vomiting, atrophic glossitis. **Hematologic:** *Folic acid deficiency (megaloblastic anemia, leukopenia, thrombocytopenia, pancytopenia).*

INTERACTIONS Drug: Folic acid may decrease effectiveness against toxoplasmosis. Do not use with **artemether, dapsone, lumefantrine** due to increased risk of adverse effects.

PHARMACOKINETICS Absorption: Readily from GI tract. **Peak:** 2 h. **Distribution:** Concentrates in kidneys, lungs, liver, and spleen; distributed into breast milk. **Elimination:** Slowly in urine. **Half-Life:** 80–95 h.

NURSING IMPLICATIONS

Assessment & Drug Effects
- Monitor patient response closely. Dosages required for treatment of toxoplasmosis approach toxic levels.
- Withhold drug and notify prescriber if hematologic abnormalities appear.
- Monitor lab tests: Twice weekly CBC, including platelets; LFTs and renal function tests.

Patient & Family Education
- Be aware that folic acid deficiency may occur with long-term use of pyrimethamine. Report to

prescriber weakness, and pallor (from anemia), ulcerations of oral mucosa, superinfections, glossitis; GI disturbances such as diarrhea and poor fat absorption, fever. Folate (folinic acid) replacement may be prescribed. Increase food sources of folates (if allowed) in diet.

QUAZEPAM

(qua′ze-pam)
Doral
Classification:
SEDATIVE-HYPNOTIC,
NONBARBITUATE; BENZODIAZEPINE
Therapeutic: SEDATIVE
Prototype: Triazolam
Controlled Substance: Schedule IV

AVAILABILITY Tablet

ACTION & *THERAPEUTIC EFFECT*
Believed to potentiate gamma-aminobutyric acid (GABA) neuronal inhibition in the limbic, neocortical, and mesencephalic reticular systems. *Significantly decreases total wake time and significantly increases sleep time. REM sleep is essentially unchanged.*

USES Insomnia characterized by difficulty in falling asleep, frequent nocturnal awakenings, or early morning awakenings.

CONTRAINDICATIONS Hypersensitivity to quazepam or benzodiazepines; sleep apnea; respiratory depression or insufficiency; suicidal ideation; pregnancy (category X); lactation.

CAUTIOUS USE Impaired liver and kidney function; history of seizures; depression; older adults; debilitated clients. Safety and efficacy in children younger than 18 y not established.

ROUTE & DOSAGE

Insomnia
Adult: **PO** 7.5–15 mg at bedtime

ADMINISTRATION
Oral
- Initial dose is usually 15 mg but can often be effectively reduced after several nights of therapy.
- Use lowest effective dose in older adults as soon as possible.

ADVERSE EFFECTS CNS: *Drowsiness, headache,* fatigue, dizziness, dry mouth. **GI:** Dyspepsia. **Other:** Physiological or psychological dependence.

INTERACTIONS Drug: Alcohol, CNS DEPRESSANTS, ANTICONVULSANTS potentiate CNS depression; **cimetidine** increases quazepam plasma levels, increasing its toxicity; may decrease antiparkinsonism effects of **levodopa;** may increase **phenytoin** levels; **smoking** decreases sedative effects of quazepam. **Sodium oxybate** is contraindicated with quazepam. **Herbal: Kava, valerian** may potentiate sedation.

PHARMACOKINETICS Absorption: Readily from GI tract. **Onset:** 30 min. **Peak:** 2 h. **Distribution:** Crosses placenta; distributed into breast milk. **Metabolism:** In liver to active metabolites. **Elimination:** In urine and feces. **Half-Life:** 39 h.

NURSING IMPLICATIONS
Assessment & Drug Effects
- Monitor for respiratory depression in patients with chronic respiratory insufficiency.

Q

- Monitor for suicidal tendencies in previously depressed clients.
- Daytime drowsiness is more likely to occur in older adult clients.
- For inpatient use, institute safety measures to prevent falls.

Patient & Family Education

- Inform prescriber about any alcohol consumption and prescription or nonprescription medication that you take. Avoid alcohol use since it potentiates CNS depressant effects.
- Inform prescriber immediately if you become pregnant. This drug causes birth defects.
- Do not drive or engage in potentially hazardous activities until response to drug is known.
- Do not increase the dose of this drug; inform prescriber if the drug no longer works.
- This drug may cause daytime sedation, even for several days after drug is discontinued.

QUETIAPINE FUMARATE

(ke-ti-a'peen)
Seroquel, Seroquel XR
Classification: ATYPICAL ANTIPSYCHOTIC
Therapeutic: ANTIPSYCHOTIC
Prototype: Clozapine

AVAILABILITY Tablet; extended release tablet

ACTION & *THERAPEUTIC EFFECT*

Antagonizes multiple neurotransmitter receptors in the brain including serotonin ($5-HT_{1A}$ and $5-HT_2$) as well as dopamine D_1 and D_2 receptors. *Effectiveness indicated by a reduction in psychotic behavior.*

USES Management of schizophrenia, maintenance of acute bipolar disorder, and add-on therapy for major depressive disorder.

UNLABELED USES Management of agitation with dementia; generalized anxiety disorder; PTSD, psychosis in Parkinson disease.

CONTRAINDICATIONS Hypersensitivity to quetiapine; alcohol use; suicidal ideation; dementia-related psychosis in older adults; NMS; lactation.

CAUTIOUS USE Liver function impairment; history of seizures or suicidical thoughts; or hepatic impairment; cardiovascular disease (history of MI or ischemic heart disease, heart failure, arrhythmias, congenital QT prolongation; CVA, hypotension, dehydration, treatment with antihypertensives); MDD; risk factors for diabetes; DM; abnormal lipid profile; breast cancer; Alzheimer disease, Parkinson disease; patient at risk for aspiration pneumonia; debilitated patients; BPH; decreased GI motility; cerebrovascular disease; hypothyroidism; older adults; pregnancy (antipsychotic use during the third trimester of pregnancy has a risk for abnormal muscle movements and/or withdrawal symptoms in newborns following delivery). Safe use in children younger than 10 y not established.

ROUTE & DOSAGE

Bipolar Disorder/Bipolar Depression

Adult/Adolescent: **PO Immediate release** 100–200 mg daily at bedtime on day 1; then increase by 100 mg/day in divided doses as tolerated to 400 mg/day on day 4 (max dose: 800 mg/day) or **Extended release** 300 mg daily at bedtime, increase to

600 mg on day 2 (max dose: 800 mg/day)

Child (older than 10 y): **PO Immediate release** 25 mg bid on day 1, 50 mg bid on day 2, 100 mg bid on day 3, 150 mg bid on day 4, and 200 mg bid beginning day 5, may increase as needed (max 600 mg/day) **Extended release** 50 mg daily on day 1, 100 mg daily on day 3, increase by 100 mg/day each day until target dose of 400 mg daily is reached.

Schizophrenia

Adult: **PO Immediate release** Start 25 mg bid, may increase by 25–50 mg bid to tid on the second or third day as tolerated to a target dose of 300–400 mg/day divided bid to tid, may adjust dose by 25–50 mg bid daily as needed (max: 800 mg/day); **Extended release** 300 mg daily at bedtime, titrate up to 400–800 mg daily (max: 800 mg/day) *Adolescent:* **PO Immediate release** 25 mg bid then taper up by 50 mg each day to 200 mg bid **Extended release** 50 mg daily, then 100 mg daily on day 2 then increase in 100 mg/day increments to target dose of 400 mg daily.

Major Depressive Disorder (Adjunct)

Adult: **PO Extended release** 50 mg once daily × day 1 and day 2, then increase to 150 mg daily

Hepatic Impairment Dosage Adjustment

PO Immediate release Start with 25 mg dose and increase by 25–50 mg/day; **Extended release** Start with 50 mg on day 1, then increase by 50 mg/day to the lowest effective and tolerable dose

ADMINISTRATION

Oral

- Dose is usually retitrated over a period of several days when patient has been off the drug for longer than 1 wk.
- Follow recommended lower doses and slower titration for the older adults, the debilitated, and those with hepatic impairment or a predisposition to hypotension.
- May be administered with or without food. Swallow extended release tablets whole.
- Store at 25° C (77° F).

ADVERSE EFFECTS CV: *Increased diastolic Bp, increased systolic Bp, orthostatic hypotension, tachycardia.* **Respiratory:** Nasal congestion. **CNS:** *Dizziness, headache, somnolence,* agitation, extrapyramidal reaction, fatigue, withdrawal syndrome, irritability. **Endocrine:** Decreased HDL cholesterol, increased serum cholesterol, increased serum triglycerides, increased LDL cholesterol, weight gain. **Hepatic/GI:** *Dry mouth,* dyspepsia, nausea, constipation, *increased appetite,* increased liver enzymes. **Hematologic:** <u>Leukopenia,</u> decreased hemoglobin. **Other:** <u>Increased risk of suicidal thinking.</u>

DIAGNOSTIC TEST INTERFERENCE:

May cause false positive TCA (serum) or methadone (urine) screen.

INTERACTIONS Drug: CYP3A4 inducers **carbamazepine,**

phenytoin, rifampin, thio-ridazine may increase clearance of quetiapine. Quetiapine may potentiate the cognitive and motor effects of **alcohol,** enhance the effects of ANTIHYPERTENSIVE AGENTS. May decrease the effect of ANTI-PARKINSON AGENTS. CYP3A4 inhibitors, **ketoconazole, itraconazole, fluconazole, erythromycin** may increase serum concentration of quetiapine and increase risk of adverse effects. There is potential for additive adverse effects with CNS DEPRESSANTS, OPIOIDS. Drugs that increase the QT interval (e.g., **amiodarone, clarithromycin,** ANTIARRHYTHMICS, **haloperidol, ziprasodone**) increase risk of cardiac effects. Other ANTIPSYCHOTICS increase the risk of adverse effects; increased risk of adverse effects with ANTICHOLINERGICS Do not use with **metoclopramide. Herbal: St. John's wort** may cause **serotonin** syndrome (see Appendix F).

PHARMACOKINETICS Absorption: Rapidly and completely absorbed from GI tract. **Peak:** 1.5 h. **Distribution:** 83% protein bound. **Metabolism:** In liver (CYP3A4). **Elimination:** 73% in urine, 20% in feces. **Half-Life:** 6 h.

NURSING IMPLICATIONS

Black Box Warning

Quetiapine has been associated with increased mortality in older adults with dementia-related psychosis, and with increased risk of suicidical thoughts and behavior in children, adolescents, and young adults.

Assessment & Drug Effects

- Monitor diabetics for loss of glycemic control.

- Monitor for changes in behavior that may indicate suicidality.
- Reassess need for continued treatment periodically.
- Withhold the drug and immediately report S&S of tardive dyskinesia or neuroleptic malignant syndrome (see Appendix F).
- Monitor Bp and ECG periodically, especially in those with known cardiovascular disease.
- Baseline cataract exam is recommended when therapy is started and at 6 mo intervals thereafter.
- Monitor patients with a history of seizures for lowering of the seizure threshold.
- Monitor lab tests: Periodic LFTs, lipid profile, thyroid function, HbA1C, CBC with differential.

Patient & Family Education

- Carefully monitor blood glucose levels if diabetic.
- Exercise caution with potentially dangerous activities requiring alertness, especially during the first week of drug therapy or during dose increments.
- Make position changes slowly, especially when changing from lying or sitting to standing to avoid dizziness, palpitations, and fainting.
- Avoid alcohol consumption and activities that may cause overheating and dehydration.

QUINAPRIL HYDROCHLORIDE

(quin'a-pril)

Accupril

Classification: ANGIOTENSIN-CONVERTING ENZYME (ACE) INHIBITOR; ANTIHYPERTENSIVE
Therapeutic: ANTIHYPERTENSIVE
Prototype: Enalapril

AVAILABILITY Tablet

ACTION & *THERAPEUTIC EFFECT*

Potent, long-acting ACE inhibitor that lowers BP by interrupting the conversion sequences initiated by renin to form angiotensin II, a vasoconstrictor. Also decreases circulating aldosterone. Reduces PCWP, systemic vascular resistance, and mean arterial pressure, with concurrent increases in cardiac output, cardiac index, and stroke volume. *Lowers BP by producing vasodilation. Effective in the treatment of CHF since it improves cardiac indicators.*

USES
Management of hypertension, heart failure.

UNLABELED USES:
Non-ST elevation acute coronary syndrome, stable coronary artery disease, ST-elevation acute coronary syndrome.

CONTRAINDICATIONS
Hypersensitivity to quinapril or other ACE inhibitors (angioedema specifically); cholestatic jaundice; concomitant use with aliskiren in diabetic patients; concomitant use with neprilysin inhibitor; pregnancy (exposure to an ACE inhibitor during the first trimester of pregnancy may be associated with an increased risk of fetal malformation).

CAUTIOUS USE
History of angioedema; renal insufficiency; autoimmune disease, volume-depleted patients, aortic stenosis, hypertrophic cardiomyopathy; HF; renal artery stenosis, neutropenia; older adults; lactation. Safety and efficacy in children not established.

ROUTE & DOSAGE

Hypertension
Adult: **PO** 10–20 mg daily, may increase up to 80 mg/day in 1–2 divided doses

Geriatric: **PO** Start with 10 mg daily

Heart Failure
Adult: **PO** 5 mg bid may increase to 10–20 mg bid

Renal Impairment Dosage Adjustment
CrCl 30–60 mL/min: Start at 5 mg daily initially; *less than 10–30 mL/min:* 2.5 mg/day initially

ADMINISTRATION
Oral
- May be administered without regard to food.
- Store at 15°–30° C (59°–86° F) and protect from moisture.

ADVERSE EFFECTS
CV: Hypotension, chest pain. **Respiratory:** *Cough.* **CNS:** *Dizziness,* fatigue, headache. **Endocrine:** *Hyperkalemia.* **GI:** Nausea, vomiting, diarrhea, <u>intestinal angioedema.</u> **Other:** <u>Angioedema.</u>

DIAGNOSTIC TEST INTERFERENCE
May lead to false negative aldosterone/renin ratio.

INTERACTIONS
Drug: POTASSIUM-SPARING DIURETICS, **aliskiren** may increase risk of hyperkalemia. May elevate serum **lithium** levels, resulting in **lithium** toxicity. May increase risk of hypotension with ANTIHYPERTENSIVES.

PHARMACOKINETICS
Absorption: Rapidly from GI tract. **Onset:** 1 h. **Peak:** 2–4 h. **Duration:** Up to 24 h. **Distribution:** 97% bound to plasma proteins; crosses placenta; distributes into breast milk. **Metabolism:** Extensively metabolized in liver to its active metabolite, quinaprilat. **Elimination:** 50–60% in

Q

urine, primarily as quinaprilat; 30% in feces. **Half-Life:** 2 h.

NURSING IMPLICATIONS

Black Box Warning

Quinapril has been associated with fetal toxicity and death.

Assessment & Drug Effects

- Following initial dose, monitor for several hours for first-dose hypotension, especially in salt- or volume-depleted patients (e.g., those pretreated with a diuretic).
- Monitor BP at time of peak effectiveness, 2–4 h after dosing, and at end of dosing interval just before next dose.
- Report diminished antihypertensive effect toward end of dosing interval. Inadequate trough response may indicate need to divide daily dose.
- Observe for S&S of hyperkalemia (see Appendix F).
- Monitor lab tests: Baseline and periodic BUN, serum creatinine, and potassium; periodic CBC with differential.

Patient & Family Education

- Discontinue quinapril and report S&S of angioedema (e.g., swelling of face or extremities, difficulty breathing or swallowing) to prescriber.
- Notify prescriber immediately if you become or suspect you are pregnant.
- Maintain adequate fluid intake and avoid potassium supplements or salt substitutes unless specifically prescribed by prescriber.
- Light-headedness and dizziness may occur, especially during the

initial days of therapy. If fainting occurs, stop taking quinapril until the prescriber has been consulted.

QUINIDINE SULFATE

(kwin'i-deen sul-fate)
Classification: CLASS IA ANTIARRHYTHMIC
Therapeutic: CLASS IA ANTIARRHYTHMIC
Prototype: Procainamide

AVAILABILITY Tablet.

ACTION & *THERAPEUTIC EFFECT*

Depresses myocardial excitability, contractility, automaticity, and conduction velocity as well as prolongs refractory period. *Depresses myocardial excitability, conduction velocity, and irregularity of nerve impulse conduction.*

USES Premature atrial, AV junctional, and ventricular contraction; paroxysmal atrial tachycardia, chronic ventricular tachycardia (when not associated with complete heart block); maintenance therapy after electrical conversion of atrial fibrillation or flutter; life-threatening malaria; Wolff-Parkinson-White syndrome.

CONTRAINDICATIONS Hypersensitivity to quinine or quinidine; thrombocytopenic purpura resulting from prior use of quinidine or quinine; myasthenia gravis; intraventricular conduction defects, complete AV block, AV conduction disorders; bundle branch block; marked QRS widening; thyrotoxicosis; extensive myocardial damage, frank CHF, hypotensive states;

Common adverse effects in *italic;* life-threatening effects underlined; generic names in **bold;** classifications in SMALL CAPS; ♦ Canadian drug name; ○ Prototype drug; ▲ Alert

1444

history of drug-induced torsades de pointes.

CAUTIOUS USE Incomplete heart block; impaired kidney or liver function; sick sinus syndrome; bronchial asthma or other respiratory disorders; potassium imbalance; pregnancy (crosses the placenta and can be detected in the amniotic fluid and neonatal serum); lactation. Safe use for children as an antiarrhymthic agent is not known.

ROUTE & DOSAGE

Conversion to and/or Maintenance of Sinus Rhythm Sulfate Immediate Release
Adult: **PO** 200–300 mg q6–8h until sinus rhythm restored or toxicity occurs (max: 3–4 g)

Sulfate Extended Release
Adult: **PO** 300–600 mg q8–12h

ADMINISTRATION
Oral
- Give with a full glass of water on an empty stomach for optimum absorption (i.e., 1 h before or 2 h after meals). Administer drug with food if GI symptoms occur (nausea, vomiting, diarrhea are most common). Do not administer with grapefruit juice.
- Ensure that extended release tablets are swallowed whole. They should not be crushed or chewed.
- Store in tight, light-resistant containers away from excessive heat.

ADVERSE EFFECTS CV: Palpitations, angina pectoris, cardiac arrhythmia. **CNS:** Headache, fatigue, dizziness. **Skin:** Skin rash. **GI:** Diarrhea, upper gastrointestinal distress. **Other:** Weakness, fever.

INTERACTIONS Drug: Do not use with agents metabolized by CYP2D6. May increase **digoxin** levels by 50%; **amiodarone** may increase quinidine levels, increasing its risk of heart block; other ANTIARRHYTHMICS, PHENOTHIAZINES, **reserpine** add to cardiac depressant effects; ANTICHOLINERGIC AGENTS add to vagolytic effects; CHOLINERGIC AGENTS may antagonize cardiac effects; ANTICONVULSANTS, BARBITURATES, **rifampin** increase the metabolism of quinidine, thus decreasing its efficacy; CARBONIC ANHYDRASE INHIBITORS, **sodium bicarbonate,** CHRONIC ANTACIDS decrease renal elimination of quinidine, thus increasing its toxicity; **verapamil** causes significant hypotension; may increase hypoprothrombinemic effects of **warfarin.** Coadministration of other drug that prolongs the QT interval (e.g., **disopyramide, procainamide, amiodarone, bretylium, clarithromycin, levofloxacin**) may cause additive effects. **Diltiazem** may increase levels and decrease elimination of quinidine. **Food: Grapefruit juice** (greater than 1 qt/day) may decrease absorption.

PHARMACOKINETICS Absorption: Almost completely from GI tract. **Onset:** 1–3 h. **Peak:** 0.5–1 h. **Duration:** 6–8 h. **Distribution:** Widely distributed to most body tissues except the brain; crosses placenta; distributed into breast milk. **Metabolism:** In liver (CYP3A4, P-gp).

Q

Elimination: Greater than 95% in urine, less than 5% in feces. **Half-Life:** 6–8 h.

NURSING IMPLICATIONS

Black Box Warning

Quinidine as been associated with increased mortality (especially in those with structural heart disease) when used to treat non-life-threatening arrhythmias.

Assessment & Drug Effects

- Observe cardiac monitor and report immediately the following indications for stopping quinidine: (1) Sinus rhythm, (2) widening QRS complex in excess of 25% (i.e., longer than 0.12 sec), (3) changes in QT interval or refractory period, (4) disappearance of P waves, (5) sudden onset of or increase in ectopic ventricular beats (extrasystoles, PVCs), (6) decrease in heart rate to 120 bpm. Also report immediately any worsening of minor side effects.
- Monitor vital signs q1–2h or more often as needed during acute treatment. Count apical pulse for a full minute. Report any change in pulse rate, rhythm, or quality or any fall in BP.
- Severe hypotension is most likely to occur in patients receiving high oral doses.
- Monitor I&O. Diarrhea occurs commonly during early therapy; most patients become tolerant to this side effect. Evaluate serum electrolytes, acid-base, and fluid balance when symptoms become severe; dosage adjustment may be required.
- Monitor lab tests: Routine CBC and liver and renal function tests.

Patient & Family Education

- Report feeling of faintness to prescriber. "Quinidine syncope" is caused by quinidine-induced changes in ventricular rhythm resulting in decreased cardiac output and syncope.
- Do not self-medicate with OTC drugs without advice from prescriber.
- Do not increase, decrease, skip, or discontinue doses without consulting prescriber.
- Notify prescriber immediately of disturbances in vision, ringing in ears, sense of breathlessness, onset of palpitations, and unpleasant sensation in chest. Be sure to note the time of occurrence and duration of chest symptoms.

QUININE SULFATE

(kwye'nine)

Qualaquin, Novoquinine ✦

Classification: ANTIMALARIAL

Therapeutic: ANTIMALARIAL

Prototype: Chloroquine

AVAILABILITY Capsule

ACTION & *THERAPEUTIC EFFECT*

Decreases oxygen uptake and carbohydrate metabolism; intercalates into DNA, disrupting the parasite's replication and transcription; cardiovascular effects similar to quinidine. *Effective against Plasmodium vivax and Plasmodium malariae but not Plasmodium falciparum.*

USES Treatment of malaria

UNLABELED USES Babesiosis.

CONTRAINDICATIONS Hypersensitivity to quinine or quinidine especially thrombocytopenia; prolonged QT interval; tinnitus, optic neuritis; myasthenia gravis; G6PD deficiency; severe hepatic impairment (Child-Pugh class C).

CAUTIOUS USE Cardiac arrhythmias; restless leg syndrome. Same precautions as for quinidine sulfate when used in patients with cardiovascular conditions; chronic renal impairment; mild or moderate hepatic impairment; pregnancy (may cause significant maternal hypoglycemia and an increased risk of other adverse maternal events); lactation.

ROUTE & DOSAGE

Malaria Treatment

Adult: **PO** 648 mg q8h for 3–7 days
Child: **PO** 10 mg/kg/day q8h for 3–7 days

Renal Impairment Dosage Adjustment

GFR 10–50 mL/min administer q8–12h; GFR less than 10 mL/min administer q24h

ADMINISTRATION

Oral

- Give with or after meals or a snack to minimize gastric irritation. Swallow dose whole to avoid bitter taste.
- Avoid use of aluminium- or magnesium-containing antacids because of drug absorption problems.
- Store in tight, light-resistant containers.

ADVERSE EFFECTS CV: Angina, hypotension, tachycardia, <u>cardiovascular collapse,</u> appearance of u-wave on ECG. **Respiratory:** Asthma, dyspnea, pulmonary edema. **CNS:** Confusion, excitement, apprehension, syncope, delirium, convulsions, blackwater fever (extensive intravascular hemolysis with renal failure), <u>death.</u> **Hematologic:** <u>Leukopenia, thrombocytopenia, agranulocytosis,</u> hypoprothrombinemia, hemolytic anemia. **Other:** Cinchonism (tinnitus, decreased auditory acuity, dizziness, vertigo, headache, visual impairment, *nausea, vomiting, diarrhea*, fever); hypersensitivity (cutaneous flushing, visual impairment, pruritus, skin rash, gastric distress, dyspnea, tinnitus); <u>hypothermia, coma.</u>

DIAGNOSTIC TEST INTERFERENCE Quinine may interfere with quantitative urine dipstick protein assays and ***urinary steroids*** (via ***Zimmerman*** method); may cause false positive for OPIOIDS.

INTERACTIONS Drug: May increase **digoxin** levels; ANTICHOLINERGIC AGENTS add to vagolytic effects; CHOLINERGIC AGENTS may antagonize cardiac effects; ANTICONVULSANTS, BARBITURATES, CYP3A4 INDUCERS, **rifampin** increase the metabolism of quinine, thus decreasing its efficacy; CYP3A4 INHIBITORS decrease metabolism CARBONIC ANHYDRASE INHIBITORS, **sodium bicarbonate,** ANTACIDS decrease renal elimination of quinine, thus increasing its toxicity; **warfarin** may increase hypoprothrombinemic effects; may increase adverse effects of

Q

ANTIMALARIAL agents. **Amantadine, carbamazepine, phenobarbital** levels may be increased; use with QT Prolonging agents increase risk of cardiac adverse effects; ANTIHEPACIVIRAL COMBINATION PRODUCTS may increase serum concentrations; can increase adverse effects of drugs metabolized by P-glycoprotein (ex **betrixaban**). Avoid use with **ritonavir**. **Food: Grapefruit juice** (greater than 1 qt/day) may increase plasma concentrations and adverse effects.

PHARMACOKINETICS Absorption: Well from GI tract. **Peak:** 1–3 h. **Duration:** 6–8 h. **Distribution:** Widely distributed to most body tissues except the brain; crosses placenta; distributed into breast milk. **Metabolism:** In liver. **Elimination:** Greater than 95% in urine, less than 5% in feces. **Half-Life:** 8–21 h.

NURSING IMPLICATIONS

Black Box Warning

Quinine use for treatment or prevention of nocturnal leg cramps has been associated with serious and life-threatening hematologic reactions and renal impairment.

Assessment & Drug Effects

- Be alert for S&S of rising plasma concentration of quinine marked by tinnitus and hearing impairment, which usually do not occur until concentration is 10 mcg/mL or more.
- Follow the same precautions with quinine as are used with quinidine in patients with atrial fibrillation; quinine may produce cardiotoxicity in these patients.

- Baseline and periodic ECG.
- Baseline and periodic ophthalmologic examination.
- Monitor lab values: CBC with platelet count, LFTs, blood glucose.

Patient & Family Education

- Learn possible adverse reactions and report onset of any unusual symptom promptly to prescriber.

QUINUPRISTIN/ DALFOPRISTIN

(quin-u-pris'tin/dal'fo-pris-tin)

Synercid

Classification: STREPTOGRAMIN ANTIBIOTIC; CYCLIC MACROLIDE

Therapeutic: ANTIBIOTIC

AVAILABILITY Injection, powder for reconstitution

ACTION & *THERAPEUTIC EFFECT*

Inhibits bacterial protein synthesis by binding to different sites on the 50S bacterial ribosomal subunit leading to cell death. *Effectiveness indicated by clinical improvement in S&S of life-threatening bacteremia. Active against gram-positive pathogens including vancomycin-resistant Enterococcus faecium (VREF), as well as some gram-negative anaerobes.*

USES complicated skin and skin structure infections caused by *Staphylococcus aureus* or *Streptococcus pyogenes.*

UNLABELED USES MRSA bacteremia, infective endocarditis (multidrug resistant), VREF meningitis.

CONTRAINDICATIONS Hypersensitivity to quinupristin/dalfopristin, pristinamycin, other streptogramins.

Common adverse effects in *italic*; life-threatening effects <u>underlined</u>; generic names in **bold**; classifications in SMALL CAPS; ✦ Canadian drug name; ⊙ Prototype drug; ⚠ Alert

CAUTIOUS USE Renal or hepatic dysfunction; IBD; GI disease; pregnancy (adverse effects have not been observed in animal reproduction studies); lactation. Safe use in children younger than 16 y not established.

ROUTE & DOSAGE

Complicated Skin and Skin Structure Infections

Adult: **IV** 7.5 mg/kg infused over 60 min q12h × 7 days

ADMINISTRATION

Intravenous

PREPARE: **Intermittent:** Reconstitute a single 500 mg vial by slowly adding 5 mL D5W or sterile water for injection to yield 100 mg/mL. ▪ Gently swirl to dissolve but **do not** shake. Allow solution to clear. ▪ Withdraw the required dose and further dilute by adding to 100 mL (central line) or 250–500 mL (peripheral site) of D5W.

ADMINISTER: **Intermittent:** Flush line before and after with D5W. **Do not** use saline. ▪ Administer over 1 h.

INCOMPATIBILITIES: **Solution/additive: Saline** (flush lines with **D5W** before infusing other drugs). **Y-site: Acyclovir, amifostine, aminocaproic acid, aminophylline, amphotericin B (conventional), amphotericin B (lipid), ampicillin, atenolol, azithromycin, bivalirudin, bumetanide, calcium chloride, calcium gluconate, cangrelor, cefazolin, cefepime, cefoperazone, cefotaxime, cefotetan, cefoxitin, ceftazidime, ceftizoxime, ceftriaxone, cefuroxime, clindamycin, dexamethasone, diazepam, digoxin, ertapenem, fludarabine, fluorouracil, foscarnet, fosphenytoin, furosemide, ganciclovir, gemtuzumab, heparin, hydrocortisone, imipenem/cilastatin, insulin, ketorolac, lepirudin, leucovorin, meropenem, mesna, methotrexate, methylprednisolone, metronidazole, nitroprusside, pantoprazole, pemetrexed, pentobarbital, phenobarbital, phenytoin, piperacillin, potassium salts, rituximab, sodium acetate, sodium bicarbonate, sulfamethoxazole/trimethoprim, thiopental, ticarcillin, tigecycline.**

▪ Refrigerate unopened vials. After reconstitution solution is stable for 5 h at room temperature and 54 h refrigerated.

ADVERSE EFFECTS

Skin: Rash. **Hepatic/GI:** Hyperbilirubinemia, nausea, vomiting. **Other:** Myalgia, arthralgia. *Inflammation, pain, or edema at infusion site, other infusion site reactions.*

INTERACTIONS

Drug: Inhibits CYP3A4 metabolism of **cyclosporine, midazolam, nifedipine,** PROTEASE INHIBITORS, **vincristine, vinblastine, docetaxel, paclitaxel, diazepam, tacrolimus, carbamazepine, quinidine, lidocaine, disopyramide.**

PHARMACOKINETICS

Distribution: Moderately protein bound. **Metabolism:** Metabolized to several active metabolites. **Elimination:** Primarily in feces (75–77%). **Half-Life:** 3 h quinupristin, 1 h dalfopristin.

Q

NURSING IMPLICATIONS

Assessment & Drug Effects

- Monitor for S&S of infusion site irritation; change infusion site if irritation is apparent.
- Monitor for cutaneous reaction (e.g., pruritus/erythema of neck, face, upper body).
- Monitor lab tests: Baseline C&S; conjugated bilirubin if indicated.

Patient & Family Education

- Report burning, itching, or pain at infusion site to prescriber.
- Report any sensation of swelling of face and tongue; difficulty swallowing.

RABEPRAZOLE SODIUM

(rab-e-pra'zole)

AcipHex

Classification: GASTRIC PROTON PUMP INHIBITOR

Therapeutic: ANTIULCER

Prototype: Omeprazole

AVAILABILITY Delayed release tablet; delayed release capsule

ACTION & *THERAPEUTIC EFFECT*

Suppresses gastric acid secretion by inhibiting the parietal cell $H+/K+$ ATP pump in the parietal cells of the stomach. Produces an antisecretory effect on the hydrogen ion (H^+) in the parietal cells. *Effectiveness indicated by a negative for H. pylori with preexisting gastric ulcer; also by elimination of S&S of GERD or peptic ulcers.*

USES Healing and maintenance of healing of erosive or ulcerative gastroesophageal reflux disease (GERD); healing of duodenal ulcers; treatment of hypersecretory conditions; eradication of h. pylori.

CONTRAINDICATIONS Hypersensitivity to rabeprazole, or proton pump inhibitors (PPIs); concomitant use with rilpivirine-containing products; lactation.

CAUTIOUS USE Severe hepatic impairment; mild to moderate hepatic disease; Japanese heritage; older adults; pregnancy (category B); children.

ROUTE & DOSAGE

Healing of Erosive GERD

Adult: **PO** 20 mg daily × 4–8 wk, may continue up to 16 wk if needed

Symptomatic Therapy for GERD

Adult/Adolescent: **PO** 20 mg daily × 4–8 w
Child (weight greater than 15 kg): 10 mg daily × 12 wk; *weight less than 15 kg:* 5 mg daily × 12 wk

Healing Duodenal Ulcer

Adult: **PO** 20 mg daily × 4 wk

Hypersecretory Disease

Adult: **PO** 60 mg daily in 1–2 divided doses (max: 100 mg daily or 60 mg bid)

ADMINISTRATION

Oral

- Ensure that the tablet is swallowed whole. It should not be crushed or chewed. Capsule should be opened and sprinkled on a small amount of soft food 30 min before a meal. Do not chew or crush. May be administered with an antacid.
- Store at 15°–30° C (59°–86° F).

ADVERSE EFFECTS CNS: Headache. **GI:** *Diarrhea, abdominal pain, vomiting, nausea.*

INTERACTIONS Drug: Contraindicated with **atazanavir** or **rilpivirine.** May decrease concentration of **cefuroxime, ketoconazole, delaviridine, erlotinib, gefinitinib, itraconazole, neratinib, pazopanib, rilpivirine, nelfinavir, velpatasvir;** may increase **digoxin** levels. May decrease effect of **risendronate. Herbal: Ginkgo** may decrease plasma levels.

DIAGNOSTIC TEST INTERFERENCE

Falsely elevate serum chromogranin A (CgA) levels. Hyperresponse in gastrin secretion in adults in response to secretin stimulation test. False positive urine screening tests for tetrahydrocannabinol (THC) have been reported

PHARMACOKINETICS Absorption: 52% bioavailability. **Distribution:** 96% protein bound. **Metabolism:** In liver by (CYP3A4, 2C19). **Elimination:** Primarily in urine. **Half-Life:** 1–2 h.

NURSING IMPLICATIONS

Assessment & Drug Effects

- Coadministered drugs: Monitor for changes in digoxin blood level.
- Monitor lab tests: Periodic magnesium level in patients on long-term treatment or those taking drugs that cause hypomagnesemia (e.g., digoxin, diuretics).

Patient & Family Education

- Report diarrhea, skin rash, other bothersome adverse effects to prescriber.

RALOXIFENE HYDROCHLORIDE

(ra-lox'i-feen)

Evista

Classification: SELECTIVE ESTROGEN RECEPTOR ANTAGONIST/ AGONIST

Therapeutic: OSTEOPOROSIS PROPHYLACTIC
Prototype: Tamoxifen

AVAILABILITY Tablet

ACTION & THERAPEUTIC EFFECT

Exhibits selective estrogen receptor antagonist activity on uterus and breast tissue. Prevents tissue proliferation in both sites. Decreases bone resorption and increases bone density. *Effectiveness indicated by increased bone mineral density. Reduces the risk of invasive breast cancer in high risk postmenopausal women (e.g., breast cancer in situ, or atypical hyperplasia).*

USES Prevention and treatment of osteoporosis in postmenopausal women; breast cancer prophylaxis.

CONTRAINDICATIONS Active or past history of a thromboembolic event; drug induced venous thrombosis; hypersensitivity to raloxifene; severe hepatic impairment; pregnancy (category X); lactation.

CAUTIOUS USE Concurrent use of raloxifene and estrogen hormone replacement therapy and lipid-lowering agents; hyperlipidemia; hepatic impairment; moderate or severe renal impairment.

ROUTE & DOSAGE

Prevention/Treatment of Osteoporosis

Adult: **PO** 60 mg daily

Breast Cancer Prophylaxis

Postmenopausal Adult: **PO** 60 mg daily

R

ADMINISTRATION

Oral

- Calcium and vitamin D supplementation are recommended with raloxifene: 1500 mg/day of elemental calcium and 400–800 units/day of vitamin D.
- Store at 15°–30° C (59°–86° F) in a tightly closed container and protect from light.

ADVERSE EFFECTS CV: *Hot flashes*, chest pain, peripheral edema, decreased serum cholesterol. **Respiratory:** Sinusitis, pharyngitis, cough, pneumonia, laryngitis. **CNS:** Migraine headache, depression, insomnia. **Skin:** Rash, sweating. **GI:** Nausea, dyspepsia, vomiting, flatulence, GI disorder, gastroenteritis, weight gain. **GU:** Vaginitis, UTI, cystitis, leukorrhea, endometrial disorder, breast pain, vaginal bleeding. **Other:** Infection, flu-like syndrome, leg cramps, fever, arthralgia, myalgia, arthritis.

INTERACTIONS Drug: Use of ESTROGENS not recommended; absorption reduced by **cholestyramine;** use with **warfarin** may result in changes in prothrombin time (PT). **Herbal: Soy isoflavones** should be used with caution.

PHARMACOKINETICS Absorption: 60% absorbed, absolute bioavailability 2%. **Metabolism:** Extensive first-pass metabolism in liver. **Elimination:** Primarily in feces. **Half-Life:** 27.7–32.5 h.

NURSING IMPLICATIONS

Black Box Warning

Raloxifene has been associated with increased risk of venous thromboembolism and death from stroke.

Assessment & Drug Effects

- Monitor carefully for and immediately report S&S of thromboembolic events.
- Do not give drug concurrently with cholestyramine; however, if unavoidable, space the two drugs as widely as possible.
- Monitor lab tests: Periodic LFTs.

Patient & Family Education

- Contact prescriber immediately if unexplained calf pain or tenderness occurs.
- Avoid prolonged restriction of movement during travel.
- Drug does not prevent and may induce hot flashes.
- Do not take drug with other estrogen-containing drugs.
- Raloxifene is normally discontinued 72 h prior to prolonged immobilization (e.g., postsurgical recovery, prolonged bedrest). Consult prescriber.

RALTEGRAVIR ●

(ral-te-gra'vir)

Isentress

Classification: ANTIRETROVIRAL; INTEGRASE INHIBITOR
Therapeutic: ANTIRETROVIRAL

AVAILABILITY Tablet; chewable tablet, oral suspension

ACTION & *THERAPEUTIC EFFECT*

Inhibits HIV-1 integrase, an enzyme required for integration of proviral DNA into the helper T-cell genome, thus preventing formation of the HIV-1 provirus. *Inhibiting integration prevents replication and proliferation of the HIV-1 virus.*

USES In combination with other antiretroviral agents for the treatment of HIV-1 infection.

Common adverse effects in *italic;* life-threatening effects underlined; generic names in **bold;** classifications in SMALL CAPS; ♣ Canadian drug name; ● Prototype drug; ⚠ Alert

CONTRAINDICATIONS Lactation.

CAUTIOUS USE Hepatitis; mild to moderate hepatic impairment; individuals at increased risk of myopathy or rhabdomyolysis; lactase deficiency; PKU; history of psychiatric disease or suicidal ideation; older adults; pregnancy (no increased risk of overall birth defects observed following first trimester exposure to raltegravir; use with caution during pregnancy); children younger than 2 y. Safety and efficacy in patients with severe hepatic impairment not established.

ROUTE & DOSAGE

HIV-1 Infection

Adult/Adolescent (over 25 kg):
PO (treatment naïve) 400 mg bid or 1200 mg once daily **(treatment experienced)** 400 mg bid
Child (over 11 kg): **PO** 6 mg/kg bid (max: 300 mg/dose)
Child /infant (under 20 kg): **PO** 6 mg/kg bid (max: 100 mg/dose)

ADMINISTRATION

Oral

- May be given without regard to food.
- Film-coated tablets must be swallowed whole (400 mg). Chewable tablets (25 or 100 mg) may be chewed or swallowed whole.
- Give before dialysis.
- Store at 15–30° C (59–86° F).

ADVERSE EFFECTS CNS: Dizziness, headache, insomnia. **Hepatic/ GI:** Increased serum ALT/AST/ALP, hyperbilirubinemia, abdominal pain, *diarrhea*, nausea, vomiting. **Hematologic:** Anemia, neutropenia.

INTERACTIONS Drug: Aluminum, calcium carbonate, fosamprenavir, magnesium, rifampin and tipranavir/ritonavir may decrease plasma levels of raltegravir.

PHARMACOKINETICS Peak: 3 h. **Distribution:** 83% protein bound. **Metabolism:** In the liver via UGT1A1. **Elimination:** Feces and urine. **Half-Life:** 9 h.

NURSING IMPLICATIONS

Assessment & Drug Effects

- Monitor for and report S&S of immune reconstitution syndrome (inflammatory response to residual opportunistic infections such as MAC, CMV, PCP, or reactivation of varicella zoster).
- Monitor diabetics for loss of glycemic control.
- Monitor for suicidal ideation.
- Monitor lab tests: Baseline and periodic CD4+ cell count and HIV RNA viral load; periodic CBC with differential, LFTs.

Patient & Family Education

- Inform prescriber immediately if you plan to become or become pregnant during therapy.
- Report promptly unexplained leg pain or muscle cramping.

R

RAMELTEON ⦿

(ra-mel'tee-on)

Rozerem
Classification: MELATONIN RECEPTOR AGONIST; SEDATIVE-HYPNOTIC
Therapeutic: SEDATIVE

AVAILABILITY Tablet

ACTION & *THERAPEUTIC EFFECT*

A melatonin receptor agonist with

high affinity for melatonin receptors in the brain. This activity is believed to promote sleep, as these receptors, in response to endogenous melatonin, are thought to be involved in maintaining the circadian rhythm underlying the normal sleep-wake cycle. *Effective in promoting onset of sleep.*

USES Treatment of insomnia characterized by difficulty with sleep onset.

CONTRAINDICATIONS Hypersensitivity to ramelteon; severe hepatic function impairment (Child-Pugh class C); severe sleep apnea or severe COPD; severe depression; suicidal ideation; lactation.

CAUTIOUS USE Moderate hepatic function impairment (Child-Pugh class B); depression with suicidal tendencies; older adults; pregnancy (category C). Safety and efficacy in children younger than 18 y not established.

ROUTE & DOSAGE

Insomnia
Adult: **PO** 8 mg within 30 min of bedtime

ADMINISTRATION

Oral
- Give within 30 min of bedtime.
- Do not administer to anyone on concurrent fluvoxamine therapy without alerting prescriber. This combination causes a dramatic increase in ramelteon blood level.
- Store at 15°–30° C (59°– 86° F).

ADVERSE EFFECTS Respiratory: Upper respiratory tract infection. **CNS:** Depression, dizziness, fatigue, headache, insomnia, somnolence. **GI:** Diarrhea, unpleasant taste, nausea. **Musculoskeletal:** Arthralgia, myalgia.

INTERACTIONS Drug: Concurrent use with **ethanol** produces additive CNS depressant effects; **ketoconazole, itraconazole,** and **fluvoxamine** increase ramelteon levels; other CYP1A2 INHIBITORS (e.g., **ciprofloxacin, enoxacin, mexiletine, norfloxacin**) may also increase ramelteon levels; **rifampin** decreases ramelteon levels. **Food:** High-fat meal, **grapefruit** or **grapefruit juice** increase ramelteon levels.

PHARMACOKINETICS Absorption: 84%. **Peak:** 45 min. **Distribution:** 82% protein bound. **Metabolism:** Rapid and extensive first pass hepatic metabolism; one metabolite, M-II, is active. **Elimination:** Primarily renal. **Half-Life:** 1–2.5 h.

NURSING IMPLICATIONS

Assessment & Drug Effects
- Monitor for and report worsening insomnia and cognitive or behavioral changes.
- Monitor for S&S of decreased testosterone levels (e.g., loss of libido) or increased prolactin levels (galactorrhea).
- Lab test: Baseline LFTs.

Patient & Family Education
- Do not take with or immediately after a high fat meal.
- Do not drive or engage in potentially hazardous activities until response to drug is known.
- Do not consume alcohol while taking this drug.
- Report any of the following to prescriber: Worsening insomnia, cognitive or behavioral changes, problem with reproductive function.

Common adverse effects in *italic*; life-threatening effects <u>underlined</u>; generic names in **bold**; classifications in SMALL CAPS; ✦ Canadian drug name; ⊙ Prototype drug; ⚠ Alert

RAMIPRIL
(ram'i-pril)

Altace

Classification: ANGIOTENSIN-CONVERTING ENZYME (ACE) INHIBITOR; ANTIHYPERTENSIVE

Therapeutic: ANTIHYPERTENSIVE

Prototype: Enalapril

AVAILABILITY Capsule

ACTION & THERAPEUTIC EFFECT
Reduces peripheral vascular resistance by inhibiting the formation of angiotensin II, a potent vasoconstrictor. This also decreases serum aldosterone levels and reduces peripheral arterial resistance (afterload) as well as improves cardiac output and exercise tolerance. *Lowers BP, and improves cardiac output as well as exercise tolerance.*

USES
hypertension, heart failure post myocardial infarction, reduction in risk of MI, stroke, and death from CV causes.

UNLABELED USES
Stable coronary artery disease, heart failure with reduced ejection fraction.

CONTRAINDICATIONS
Hypersensitivity to ramipril or any other ACE inhibitor, history of angioneurotic edema; intestinal angioedema; jaundice; elevated hepatic enzymes; hyperkalemia; concurrent use of aliskiren in diabetic patients; concomitant use with neprilysin inhibitor; oliguria, or progressive azotemia; pregnancy (exposure to ACE inhibitor during first trimester of pregnancy may be associated with increased risk of fetal malformations); lactation.

CAUTIOUS USE
Impaired kidney or liver function, surgery or anesthesia; CHF; SLE, scleroderma. Safety and efficacy in children not established.

ROUTE & DOSAGE

Hypertension
Adult: **PO** 2.5 mg daily, may titrate after 2–4 weeks up to 20 mg/day in 1–2 divided doses

Stroke/MI Risk Reduction
Adult: **PO** 2.5 mg daily × 1wk then 5 mg daily × 3wk, may increase up to 10 mg/day

Heart Failure Post Myocardial Infarction
Adult: **PO** 2.5 mg bid × 1 week then may titrate up every 3 weeks as needed (up to 5 mg bid)

Renal Impairment Dosage Adjustment
CrCl less than 40 mL/min: administer 25% of normal dose

ADMINISTRATION

Oral
- Swallow capsule whole; may open the capsule and mix contents with 120 mL of water, apple juice, or applesauce.
- Store at 15°–30° C (59°–86° F) and protect from moisture.

ADVERSE EFFECTS
CV: *Hypotension.* **Respiratory:** *Cough.* **CNS:** Dizziness, fatigue, headache. **Endocrine:** Hyperkalemia, hyponatremia. **Skin:** Stevens–Johnson syndrome. **Other:** Angioedema.

DIAGNOSTIC TEST INTERFERENCE
may cause false negative aldosterone/renin ratio; may cause false positive results in urine acetone

R

determination using **sodium nitro-prusside** reagent; positive direct **Coombs' test**.

INTERACTIONS Drug: POTASSIUM-SPARING DIURETICS may increase risk of hyperkalemia. May elevate serum **lithium** levels, resulting in lithium toxicity. Use with **azathioprine** increases risk of hematologic side effects. **Pregabalin** use increases the risk of angioedema. Use with ANGIOTENSION II RECEPTOR ANTAGONISTS does not offer additional benefit. ANTIHYPERTENSIVES, **obinutuzumab** increase the risk of hypotension. May increase the risk of adverse effects with **iron**. Do not use with **lanthanum, telmisartan**.

PHARMACOKINETICS Absorption: 60% from GI tract. **Onset:** 2 h. **Peak:** 6–8 h. **Duration:** Up to 24 h. **Distribution:** Crosses placenta; not known if distributed into breast milk. **Metabolism:** Rapidly metabolized in liver to active metabolite, ramiprilat. **Elimination:** 60% in urine, 40% in feces. **Half-Life:** 2–3 h.

NURSING IMPLICATIONS

Black Box Warning

Ramipril has been associated with fetal injury and death.

Assessment & Drug Effects

- Monitor BP at time of peak effectiveness, 3–6 h after dosing and at end of dosing interval just before next dose.
- Report diminished antihypertensive effect.
- Monitor for first-dose hypotension, especially in salt- or volume-depleted persons.
- Observe for S&S of hyperkalemia (see Appendix F).

- Monitor lab tests: Periodic BUN, serum creatinine, serum potassium, and CBC with differential

Patient & Family Education

- Notify prescriber immediately if you become or suspect you are pregnant.
- Discontinue drug and report S&S of angioedema to prescriber (e.g., swelling of face or extremities, difficulty breathing or swallowing).
- Maintain adequate fluid intake and avoid potassium supplements or salt substitutes unless specifically prescribed by the prescriber.
- Light-headedness and dizziness may occur, especially during the initial days of therapy. If fainting occurs, stop taking ramipril until the prescriber has been consulted.

RAMUCIRUMAB

(ram-u-cir'u-mab)

Cyramza

Classification: IMMUNOMODULATOR; MONOCLONAL ANTIBODY; VASCULAR ENDOTHELIAL GROWTH FACTOR RECEPTOR 2 (VEGFR2) ANTAGONIST

Therapeutic: IMMUNOMODULATOR

AVAILABILITY Solution for injection

ACTION & THERAPEUTIC EFFECT Inhibits vascular endothelial growth factor receptor 2 (VEGFR2) by binding to it and blocking its activation, thereby inhibiting proliferation and migration of endothelial cells. *VEGFR2 inhibition results in reduced tumor vascularity and growth.*

USES Treatment of advanced gastric cancer or gastroesophageal junction adenocarcinoma, as a single-agent after prior fluoropyrimidine- or platinum-containing chemotherapy.

CONTRAINDICATIONS Uncontrolled severe hypertension; Grade 3–4 infusion-related reactions; urine protein greater than 3 mg/24 h; nephrotic syndrome; arterial thromboembolic events; GI perforation; Grade 3 or 4 bleeding; severe arterial thromboembolic event; Posterior Leukoencephalopathy Syndrome; lactation.

CAUTIOUS USE Hypertension; protein urea; infusion related reactions; concurrent NSAIDs or drug that increase bleeding risk; impaired wound healing; hepatic impairment; pregnancy (category C). Safety and efficacy in children younger than 18 y not established.

ROUTE & DOSAGE

Gastric Cancer

Adult: **IV** 8 mg/kg every 2 wk

Toxicity Dosage Adjustment

Infusion related reactions:
Grade 1–2, decrease IV rate by 50%; Grade 3–4, permanently discontinue
Severe hypertension: Interrupt therapy until BP managed; permanently discontinue if BP cannot be controlled
Proteinuria: Urine protein levels 2g/24h or greater, interrupt therapy until levels are less than 2g/24h then reinitiate at 6 mg/kg q2wk (or 5 mg/kg q2wk in a recurrence); protein level is greater than 3mg/24h or nephrotic syndrome, permanently discontinue
Arterial Thromboembolic Events, GI Perforation, or Grade 3 or 4 Bleeding: Permanently discontinue

ADMINISTRATION

Intravenous

This drug is a cytotoxic agent and caution should be used to prevent any contact with the drug. Follow institutional or standard guidelines for preparation, handling, and disposal of cytotoxic agents.
***PREPARE:* IV Infusion:** Dilute required dose in NS to a final volume of 250 mL. Invert gently to mix but do not shake. Discard unused portion of the vial.
***ADMINISTER:* IV Infusion:** Give over 60 min through a 0.22 micron protein-sparing filter. **Do not** give IV push or bolus. Flush the line after infusion with NS. Reduce infusion rate (by 50%) for Grade 1 or 2 infusion reaction. Stop infusion for Grade 3 or 4 infusion reaction.
INCOMPATIBILITIES: Do not mix or infuse with any other drugs or solutions.

▪ Store diluted solutions at 2°–8° C (36°–46° F) for no longer than 24 h (do not freeze) or may store for 4 h at room temperature [below 25° C (77° F)].

ADVERSE EFFECTS CV: *Hypertension.* **CNS:** Headache. **Endocrine:** Hyponatremia, proteinuria. **Skin:** Rash. **GI:** *Diarrhea,* intestinal obstruction. **Hematological:** <u>Arterial thromboembolic events, hemorrhage,</u> neutropenia. **Other:** Infusion related reactions, epistaxis.

PHARMACOKINETICS Half-Life: Dose related (200–300 h).

NURSING IMPLICATIONS

Black Box Warning

Ramucirumab has been associated with increased risk of

hemorrhage, including severe and sometimes fatal hemorrhagic events. Permanently discontinue if severe bleeding occurs.

Assessment & Drug Effects

- Monitor closely for infusion related reactions.
- Monitor BP throughout therapy. Withhold drug and notify prescriber if severe hypertension occurs. Resume drug only after hypertension is medically controlled.
- If unexplained bleeding occurs, withhold drug and notify prescriber.
- Monitor for and report promptly S&S of liver dysfunction.
- Inspect wounds closely. If poor wound healing is suspected, withhold drug and notify prescriber.
- Monitor lab tests: Periodic LFTs, thyroid function, and urine protein.

Patient & Family Education

- Report promptly to prescriber if blood pressure is elevated or if symptoms of hypertension occur including severe headache, lightheadedness, or neurologic symptoms.
- Contact prescriber for bleeding or symptoms of bleeding including lightheadedness.
- Notify prescriber for severe diarrhea, vomiting, or severe abdominal pain.
- Monitor any wounds and report slow wound healing.
- Do not undergo surgery without first discussing the risk of poor wound healing with prescriber.

RANOLAZINE

(ra-no'la-zeen)

Ranexa

Classification: ANTIANGINAL; PARTIAL FATTY ACID OXIDATION (PFOX) INHIBITOR

Therapeutic: ANTIANGINAL

AVAILABILITY Extended release tablet

ACTION & *THERAPEUTIC EFFECT*
A partial fatty-acid oxidation inhibitor that shifts myocardial metabolism away from fatty acids to glucose. This shift requires less oxygen for oxidation and results in decreased oxygen demand. *Improves exercise tolerance and angina symptoms.*

USES Treatment of chronic stable angina in combination with calcium channel blockers, beta-blockers, or nitrates.

CONTRAINDICATIONS Severe hepatic impairment; severe renal impairment, renal failure, hypokalemia, hypomagnesemia; history of acute MI; lactation.

CAUTIOUS USE History of QT prolongation or torsades de pointes; renal impairment; older adult; pregnancy (category C); children.

ROUTE & DOSAGE

Chronic Stable Angina

Adult: **PO** 500 mg bid (max: 1000 mg bid) (patients taking concurrent CYP3A4 inhibitors have a max dose of 500 mg bid)

ADMINISTRATION

Oral

- **Must be** swallowed whole. Should not be crushed, broken, or chewed.
- Store at 15°–30° C (59°–86° F).

Common adverse effects in *italic*; life-threatening effects underlined; generic names in **bold;** classifications in SMALL CAPS; ◆ Canadian drug name; ● Prototype drug; ⚠ Alert

1458

ADVERSE EFFECTS CV: Palpitations. **Respiratory:** Dyspnea. **CNS:** *Dizziness,* headache. **HEENT:** Tinnitus, vertigo. **GI:** Abdominal pain, *constipation,* dry mouth, nausea, vomiting. **Other:** Peripheral edema.

DIAGNOSTIC TEST INTERFERENCE
Ranolazine is not known to interfere with any diagnostic laboratory test.

INTERACTIONS Drug: INHIBITORS OF P-GLYCOPROTEIN (e.g., **ritonavir, cyclosporine**) may increase ranolazine absorption. Ranolazine increases the plasma concentrations of **digoxin** and **simvastatin.** INHIBITORS OF CYP3A4 [e.g., **diltiazem, erythromycin, grapefruit juice,** HIV PROTEASE INHIBITORS, **ketoconazole,** MACROLIDE ANTIBIOTICS (especially **ketoconazole**), **verapamil**] can increase plasma levels and QT$_c$ elevation. **Paroxetine,** a CYP2D6 INHIBITOR, increases the plasma levels of ranolazine. CLASS I or III ANTIARRHYTHMICS (e.g., **quinidine, dofetilide, sotalol**), **thioridazine,** and **ziprasidone** can cause additive increases in QT$_c$ elevation. **Food: Grapefruit juice.**

PHARMACOKINETICS Absorption: 73% of PO dose absorbed. **Peak:** 2–5 h. **Distribution:** 62% protein bound. **Metabolism:** Extensive hepatic metabolism. **Elimination:** 75% in urine; 25% in feces. **Half-Life:** 7 h.

NURSING IMPLICATIONS
Assessment & Drug Effects
▪ Monitor ECG at baseline and periodically for prolongation of the QT$_c$ interval.
▪ Monitor blood levels of digoxin with concurrent therapy.
▪ When coadministered with simvastatin, monitor for and report unexplained muscle weakness or pain.
▪ Monitor lab tests: Baseline and periodic renal function tests with moderate-to-severe renal impairment.

Patient & Family Education
▪ Do not engage in hazardous activities until response to drug is known.
▪ Contact prescriber if you experience fainting while taking ranolazine.
▪ Do not drink grapefruit juice or eat grapefruit while taking this drug.

RASAGILINE
(ras-a-gi'leen)
Azilect
Classification: MONOAMINE OXIDASE-B (MAO-B) INHIBITOR; ANTIPARKINSON
Therapeutic: ANTIPARKINSON

AVAILABILITY Tablet

ACTION & *THERAPEUTIC EFFECT*
A potent monoamine oxidase B (MAO-B) inhibitor that prevents the enzyme monoamine oxidase B from breaking down dopamine in the brain. Rasagiline also interferes with dopamine reuptake at synapses in the brain. *Rasagiline helps to overcome dopaminergic motor dysfunction in Parkinson's disease.*

USES Treatment of Parkinson disease (monotherapy or adjunct).

CONTRAINDICATIONS Moderate to severe hepatic impairment; alcoholism; biliary cirrhosis; major psychotic disorders; uncontrolled hypertension; within 14 days of use of other MAOIs; concomitant use with cyclobenzaprine, dextromethorphan, or St. John's wort.

CAUTIOUS USE Mild hepatic dysfunction; cardiovascular disease; DM; asthma, bronchitis, hyperthyroidism; postural or orthostatic hypotension; migraine headaches; moderate to severe renal impairment, anuria; epilepsy or preexisting seizure disorders; pregnancy (Adverse effects have been observed in animal reproduction studies.); lactation. Safety and efficacy in children not established.

ROUTE & DOSAGE

Parkinson Disease

Adult: **PO** 1 mg/day as monotherapy; 0.5–1 mg/day if used with levodopa as adjunctive therapy

Hepatic Impairment Dosage Adjustment

Mild Impairment: 0.5 mg/day

Concomitant Use of CYP1A2 Inhibitors Dosage Adjustment

Max dose: 0.5 mg once daily

ADMINISTRATION

Oral
- May be given without regard to food.
- Avoid foods containing high amounts of tyramine (> 150 mg) such as aged cheeses, cured meats, tap/draft beer, fava or broad bean pods, sauerkraut, soy sauce.
- Store at 25° C (77° F).

ADVERSE EFFECTS Respiratory: Flu-like symptoms. **CNS:** *Depression, fall, headache.* **HEENT:** Conjunctivitis. **GI:** Dyspepsia. **Musculoskeletal:** Arthralgia.

INTERACTIONS Drug: There are extensive drug interactions, consult a drug information database for a complete list, some significant interactions are highlighted below. INHIBITORS OF CYP1A2 (e.g., **atazanavir, ciprofloxacin, mexiletine**) may increase rasagiline plasma levels. Rasagiline increases the plasma levels of ANESTHETICS; thus it must be discontinued 14 days prior to elective surgery. Rasagiline can cause severe CNS toxicity, including hyperpyrexia and death, with ANTIDEPRESSANTS, SELECTIVE SEROTONIN REUPTAKE INHIBITORS (SSRI), SEROTONIN-NOREPINEPHRINE REUPTAKE INHIBITORS (SNRI), NONSELECTIVE MAO INHIBITORS, or SELECTIVE MAO-B INHIBITORS. Rasagiline can increase the plasma levels of **cyclobenzaprine** and SYMPATHOMIMETIC AMINES. Rasagiline and **dextromethorphan** can cause brief episodes of psychosis and bizarre behavior. Use with ALPHA OR BETA AGONISTS, AMPHETAMINES can cause hypertension. Rasagiline can potentiate the dopaminergic effects of **levodopa.** Rasagiline can increase the plasma levels of **meperidine, methadone, propoxyphene,** and **tramadol, acetaminophen,** resulting in coma, severe hypertension or hypotension, severe respiratory depression, convulsions, and death. **Food:** Caffeine or ethanol can cause significant side effects and caution should be used. Foods rich in tyramine can cause severe high blood pressure. **Herbal:** Rasagiline increases the plasma levels of **St. John's wort.**

PHARMACOKINETICS Absorption: Rapidly absorbed with 36% bioavailability. **Peak:** 1 h. **Distribution:** 88–94% protein bound. **Metabolism:** Extensive hepatic metabolism (CYP1A2, CYP2C8/9).

R

Elimination: Primarily renal (62%) with minor fecal elimination. **Half-Life:** 3 h.

NURSING IMPLICATIONS

Assessment & Drug Effects

- Monitor BP for new onset hypertension or hypertension not adequately controlled.
- Monitor for orthostatic hypotension especially in combination with levodopa.
- Monitor for and report to prescriber any of the following: Symptoms of parkinsonism; new or worsening mental status and behavioral changes; somnolence and falling asleep during activities of daily living.
- Perform baseline and periodic skin examination for presence of melanoma.
- Monitor lab values: Baseline and periodic liver and renal function tests.

Patient & Family Education

- Do not take any prescription or nonprescription drug without consulting prescriber.
- Periodic skin examinations should be scheduled with a dermatologist. If you notice changes in a skin mole or new skin lesion, contact the dermatologist.
- Avoid foods and beverages containing tyramine (e.g., aged cheeses and meats, tap beer, red wine, soybean products).
- Make position changes slowly, especially when standing from a lying or sitting position.
- Do not drive or engage in potentially hazardous activities until response to drug is known.
- Report immediately any of the following to a health care provider: Palpitations, severe headache, blurred vision, difficulty thinking, seizures, chest pain, unexplained nausea or vomiting, or any sudden weakness or paralysis.

RASBURICASE
(ras-bur'i-case)
Elitek, Fasturtec ♦
Classification: ANTIGOUT;
ANTIMETABOLITE
Therapeutic: ANTIGOUT

AVAILABILITY Powder for injection

ACTION & *THERAPEUTIC EFFECT* A recombinant urate-oxidase enzyme produced by DNA technology. In humans, uric acid is the final step in the catabolic pathway of purines. Rasburicase catalyzes enzymatic oxidation of uric acid; thus it is only active at the end of the purine catabolic pathway. *Used to manage plasma uric acid levels in pediatric patients with leukemia, lymphoma, and solid tumor malignancies who are receiving anticancer therapy that results in tumor lysis, and therefore elevates plasma uric acid.*

USES Initial management of increased uric acid levels secondary to tumor lysis.

CONTRAINDICATIONS Severe hypersensitivity to rasburicase; deficiency in glucose-6-phosphate de-hydrogenase (G6PD); history of anaphylaxis; hemolytic reactions or methemoglobinemia reactions to rasburicase; lactation.

CAUTIOUS USE Patients at risk for G6PD deficiency (e.g., African or Mediterranean ancestry); asthma; bone marrow suppression; pregnancy (category C); children younger than 1 mo.

R

ROUTE & DOSAGE

Hyperuricemia
Adult/Child (1 mo or older): **IV** 0.2 mg/kg/day for up to 5 days

ADMINISTRATION

Intravenous

PREPARE: IV Infusion: Reconstitute each 1.5 mg vial or 7.5 mg vial with 1 or 5 mL, respectively, of the provided diluent and mix by swirling very gently. **Do not shake.** Discard if particulate matter is visible or if product is discolored after reconstitution. ▪ Remove the predetermined dose from the reconstituted vials and inject into enough NS in an infusion bag to achieve a final total volume of 50 mL.

ADMINISTER: IV Infusion: Give over 30 min. **Do not give bolus dose.** Infuse through an **unfiltered** line used for no other medications. ▪ If a separate line is not possible, flush the line with at least 15 mL of saline solution before/after infusion of rasburicase. ▪ Immediately discontinue IV infusion and institute emergency measures for S&S of anaphylaxis including chest pain, dyspnea, hypotension, and/or urticaria.

INCOMPATIBILITIES: Do not mix or infuse with other drugs.

ADVERSE EFFECTS CNS: *Headache,* anxiety. **Skin:** *Rash.* **GI:** *Mucositis, vomiting, nausea, diarrhea, abdominal pain.* **Hematologic:** Neutro-penia. **Other:** *Fever,* sepsis, severe hypersensitivity reactions including anaphylaxis at any time during treatment.

DIAGNOSTIC TEST INTERFERENCE

May give false elevations for *uric acid* if blood sample is left at room temperature.

PHARMACOKINETICS Half-Life: 18 h.

NURSING IMPLICATIONS

Black Box Warning

Rasburicase has been associated with severe hypersensitivity reactions and with development of methemoglobinemia.

Assessment & Drug Effects

▪ Patients at higher risk for G6PD deficiency (e.g., patients of African or Mediterranean ancestry) should be screened prior to starting therapy as this deficiency is a contraindication for this drug.
▪ Monitor closely for S&S of hypersensitivity and be prepared to institute emergency measures for anaphylaxis.
▪ Monitor cardiovascular, respiratory, neurologic, and renal status throughout therapy.
▪ Monitor lab tests: Plasma uric acid levels (4 h after rasburicase administration and q6–8h until tumor lysis syndrome resolution); CBC as needed; baseline G6PD deficiency screening (in patients at high risk for deficiency).

Patient & Family Education

▪ Report immediately any distressing S&S to prescriber.

REGORAFENIB

(re-gor'a-fe-nib)
Stivarga
Classification: ANTINEOPLASTIC; KINASE INHIBITOR; MULTIKINASE INHIBITOR
Therapeutic: ANTINEOPLASTIC
Prototype: Erlotinib

AVAILABILITY Tablet

Common adverse effects in *italic;* life-threatening effects <u>underlined</u>; generic names in **bold**; classifications in SMALL CAPS; ✦ Canadian drug name; ⊙ Prototype drug; ⚠ Alert

ACTION & *THERAPEUTIC EFFECT*

Inhibits multiple kinase enzymes systems involved in normal cellular functions and in pathologic processes such as tumor development (oncogenesis), tumor angiogenesis, and maintenance of the tumor microenvironment. *Inhibits colorectal cancer tumor growth and metastasis.*

USES Metastatic colorectal cancer (CRC) in those previously treated with fluoropyrimidine-, oxaliplatin-, and irinotecan-based chemotherapy, an antivascular endothelial growth factor (VEGF) therapy, and, if cancer is a KRAS gene wild type, an anti-epidermal growth factor receptor (EGFR) therapy. Treatment of locally advanced, unresectable or metastatic gastrointestinal stromal tumors (GIST) in patients who have previously received imatinib and sunitinib; hepatocellular carcinoma.

CONTRAINDICATIONS Severe hepatic impairment (Child-Pugh class C); severe or life-threatening hemorrhage; severe or uncontrolled hypertension; posterior reversible encephalopathy syndrome; 2 wk before surgery; pregnancy (may cause fetal harm if administered during pregnancy); lactation.

CAUTIOUS USE Mild to moderate hepatic impairment; moderate-to-severe renal impairment; hypertension; history of myocardial ischemia. Safety and efficacy in children younger than 18 y not established.

ROUTE & DOSAGE

Colorectal Cancer, GIST, Hepatocellular Cancer

Adult: PO 160 mg once daily for the first 21 days of a 28 day cycle; repeat until disease progression or unacceptable toxicity

Dosing Modifications

Withhold drug and consult prescriber for any Grade 2 or higher reaction according to the National Cancer Institute (NCI) Common Terminology Criteria for Adverse Events (CTCAE). See package insert for more specific details.

Permanently discontinue if:

- Unable to tolerate 80 mg dose
- AST or ALT levels greater than 20 × ULN
- Reversible posterior leukoencephalopathy syndrome occurs
- AST or ALT levels greater than 3 × ULN with concurrent bilirubin greater than 2 × ULN
- Previously elevated AST or ALT levels return to greater than 5 × ULN despite dose reduction to 120 mg
- Any Grade 4 adverse reaction occurs (resume only if the potential benefit outweighs the risks)
- Severe hemorrhage

ADMINISTRATION

Oral

- Give at same time each day.
- Swallow tablet whole with water after a low-fat meal containing < 600 calories and < 30% fat.
- Avoid grapefruit juice.
- Store at 25° C (77° F). Keep tightly closed in original bottle and do not remove desiccant. Discard unused tablets 28 days after opening bottle.

ADVERSE EFFECTS CV: *Hypertension.* **Respiratory:** Nasopharyngitis.

R

CNS: Headache, fatigue, pain. **HEENT:** Voice disorder. **Endocrine:** Hypocalcemia, hypokalemia, hyponatremia, hypophosphatemia, hypothyroidism, increased INR, increased lipase, *weight loss*. **Skin:** *Palmar-plantar erythrodysesthesia*, rash, alopecia. **Hepatic/ GI:** *Diarrhea*, decreased appetite, *stomatitis*, nausea, vomiting, gastrointestinal pain, hepatotoxicity, increased liver enzymes, hyperbilirubinemia, increased serum amylase/lipase. **GU:** Proteinuria, urinary tract infection. **Musculoskeletal:** Asthenia, muscle spasms. **Hematological:** Anemia, lymphopenia, increased INR, haemorrhage, <u>neutropenia</u>, thrombocytopenia. **Other:** Fever, *infection*.

INTERACTIONS Drug: Coadministration of strong CYP3A4 inhibitors (e.g., **clarithromycin, itraconazole, ketoconazole, posaconazole, telithromycin, voriconazole**) increases the levels of regorafenib and decreases the levels of its active metabolites. Coadministration of strong CYP3A4 inducers (e.g., **carbamazepine, phenobarbital, phenytoin, rifampin**) decreases the levels of regorafenib and increases the levels of one of its active metabolites. May increase the concentration of drugs metabolized by CVRP/ABCG2 (ex **ozanimod, pazopanib, topotecan** etc). **Food:** Grapefruit juice can increase the levels of regorafenib and decrease the levels of its active metabolites. **Herbal: St. John's wort** can decrease the levels of regorafenib and increase the levels of one of its active metabolites.

PHARMACOKINETICS Absorption: 69–83% bioavailable. **Peak:** 4 h. **Distribution:** Greater than 99% plasma protein bound. **Metabolism:** In liver to active metabolites. (CYP3A4 and UGT1A9). Also affects CYP2C9, CYP2B6, CYP2D6, UGT1A1, breast cancer resistance protein (BCRP). **Elimination:** Fecal (71%) and renal (19%). **Half-Life:** 28 h for parent drug, 25 h for one active metabolite, and 5 h for a second active metabolite.

NURSING IMPLICATIONS

Black Box Warning

Regorafenib has been associated with severe and sometimes fatal hepatotoxicity.

Assessment & Drug Effects

- Monitor BP weekly for first 6 wk then once every cycle or more often as needed. Notify prescriber for recurrent or persistently elevated BP (e.g., greater than 150/100).
- Monitor cardiac status and assess for S&S of myocardial ischemia.
- Monitor for and report promptly S&S dermatological toxicity (i.e., hand–foot skin reaction) or hepatotoxicity (see Appendix F).
- Add for 2 wk prior to surgery to allow for proper wound healing.
- Monitor lab tests: Baseline and biweekly LFTs first 2 mo and monthly (or more frequently) thereafter; baseline and periodic CBC with differential, platelet count, and serum electrolytes, frequent INR with concurrent warfarin therapy.

Patient & Family Education

- Seek medical attention immediately if you experience any of the following: Chest pain, shortness of breath, dizziness, fainting, severe abdominal pain, persistent abdominal swelling, high fever, chills, nausea, vomiting, severe diarrhea, or dehydration.

Common adverse effects in *italic*; life-threatening effects <u>underlined</u>; generic names in **bold;** classifications in SMALL CAPS; ♣ Canadian drug name; ☉ Prototype drug; ⚠ Alert

- Report promptly any of the following: Redness, pain, blisters, bleeding, or swelling on the palms of hands or soles of feet; signs of bleeding; signs of high BP including severe headaches, lightheadedness, or changes in vision.
- Women and men should use effective means of birth control during therapy and for at least 2 mo following completion of therapy.
- Contact your prescriber immediately if you become pregnant during treatment.
- Do not breast-feed while receiving this drug.

REMIFENTANIL HYDROCHLORIDE

(rem-i-fent'a-nil)

Ultiva

Classification: ANALGESIC, NARCOTIC (OPIATE AGONIST); GENERAL ANESTHESIA

Therapeutic: NARCOTIC ANALGESIC; GENERAL ANESTHESIA

Prototype: Morphine

Controlled Substance: Schedule II

AVAILABILITY Solution for injection

ACTION & *THERAPEUTIC EFFECT*
Synthetic, potent narcotic agonist analgesic that is rapidly metabolized; therefore respiratory depression is of shorter duration when discontinued. *Used as the analgesic component of an anesthesia regime.*

USES Analgesic during induction and maintenance of general anesthesia, as the analgesic component of monitored anesthesia care.

CONTRAINDICATIONS Hypersensitivity to fentanyl analogs, epidural or intrathecal administration.

CAUTIOUS USE Head injuries, increased intracranial pressure; debilitated, morbid obesity, poor-risk patients; COPD, other respiratory problems, bradyarrhythmia; older adults; pregnancy (category C); lactation. Safety in labor and delivery not established.

ROUTE & DOSAGE

Adjunct to Anesthesia

Adult: **IV** 0.5–1 mcg/kg/min or 1 mcg/kg bolus
Child (birth–2 mo): **IV** 0.4–1 mcg/kg/min; *1–12 y:* 0.5–1 mcg/kg/min or 1 mcg/kg bolus

Obesity Dosage Adjustment

Dose based on IBW

ADMINISTRATION

Intravenous

IV administration to infants and children: Verify correct IV concentration and rate of infusion with prescriber.

PREPARE: **Direct/Continuous Infusion** Reconstitute by adding 1 mL of sterile water for injection, D5W, NS, D5NS, 1/2NS, or D5LR to each 1 mg of remifentanil to yield 1 mg/mL. Shake well to dissolve. ▪ Further dilute to a final concentration of 20, 25, 50, or 250 mcg/mL by adding the required dose to the appropriate amount of IV solution.

ADMINISTER: **Direct/Continuous Infusion** Give at the ordered rate according to patient's weight.

▪ Note that bolus doses should **not** be given during a continuous infusion of remifentanil.
▪ Flush IV tubing thoroughly following infusion.

R

INCOMPATIBILITIES: Solution/ additive: Unknown. Y-site: **Ampho-tericin B, amphoteri-cin B cholesteryl, chlorprom-azine, diazepam.**

▪ Clear IV tubing completely of the drug following discontinuation of remifentanil infusion to ensure that inadvertent administration of the drug will not occur at a later time. ▪ Reconstituted solution is stable for 24 h at room temperature. Store vials of powder at 2°–25° C (36°–77° F).

ADVERSE EFFECTS CV: Hypotension, hypertension, bradycardia. **Respiratory:** Respiratory depression, apnea. **CNS:** Dizziness, headache. **Skin:** Pruritus. **GI:** *Nausea,* vomiting. **Other:** Muscle rigidity, shivering.

INTERACTIONS Drug: Alcohol and other CNS DEPRESSANTS potentiate effects; MAO INHIBITORS may precipitate hypertensive crisis.

PHARMACOKINETICS Duration: 12 min. **Distribution:** 70% protein bound. **Metabolism:** Hydrolyzed by nonspecific esterases in the blood and tissues. **Elimination:** In urine. **Half-Life:** 3–10 min.

NURSING IMPLICATIONS
Assessment & Drug Effects
▪ Monitor vital signs during postoperative period; observe for and immediately report any S&S of respiratory distress or respiratory depression, or skeletal and thoracic muscle rigidity and weakness.
▪ Monitor for adequate postoperative analgesia.

REPAGLINIDE ℗

(rep-a-gli'nide)
Prandin, GlucoNorm ♦
Classification: ANTIDIABETIC; MEGLITINIDE
Therapeutic: ANTIHYPERGLYCEMIC

AVAILABILITY Tablet

ACTION & *THERAPEUTIC EFFECT*
Hypoglycemic agent that lowers blood glucose levels by stimulating release of insulin from the pancreatic islets. *Significantly reduces postprandial blood glucose in type 2 diabetes. Minimal effects on fasting blood glucose.*

USES Adjunct to diet and exercise in type 2 diabetes.

CONTRAINDICATIONS Hypersensitivity to repaglinide; insulin-dependent diabetes, diabetic ketoacidosis; lactation.

CAUTIOUS USE Hypoglycemia; loss of glycemic control due to secondary failure; hepatic impairment; severe renal impairment; older adults, surgery, fever, systemic infection, trauma; pregnancy (category C); Safety and efficacy in children not established.

ROUTE & DOSAGE

Type 2 Diabetes
Adult (initial dose): **PO** 0.5 mg 15–30 min a.c.; *initial dose for patients previously using glucose-lowering agents:* 1–2 mg 15–30 min a.c. (2–4 doses/day depending on meal pattern; max: 16 mg/day); *dosage range:* 0.5–4 mg 15–30 min a.c.

Common adverse effects in *italic;* life-threatening effects <u>underlined</u>; generic names in **bold**; classifications in SMALL CAPS; ♦ Canadian drug name; ℗ Prototype drug; ⚠ Alert

ADMINISTRATION

Oral

- Give within 30 min of beginning a meal.
- Store at 15°–30° C (59°–86° F) in a tightly closed container and protect from moisture.

ADVERSE EFFECTS CV: Chest pain, angina. **Respiratory:** URI, sinusitis, rhinitis, bronchitis. **CNS:** Headache. **Endocrine:** *Hypoglycemia.* **GI:** Nausea, diarrhea, constipation, vomiting, dyspepsia. **Other:** Arthralgia, back pain, paresthesia, allergy.

INTERACTIONS Drug: Erythromycin, ketoconazole may inhibit metabolism and potentiate hypoglycemia; BARBITURATES, **carbamazepine, rifabutin, rifampin, rifapentine, pioglitazone** may induce metabolism and cause hyperglycemia; **gemfibrozil** may increase risk of hypoglycemia and duration of action. Use with **deferasirox** requires a repaglinide dose reduction. **Herbal: Ginseng, garlic** may increase hypoglycemic effects. **Food: Grapefruit juice** (greater than 1 qt/day) may increase plasma concentrations and adverse effects.

PHARMACOKINETICS Absorption: Rapidly from GI tract, 56% bioavailability. **Peak:** 1 h. **Distribution:** 98% protein bound. **Metabolism:** In liver (CYP3A4). **Elimination:** 90% in feces. **Half-Life:** 1 h.

NURSING IMPLICATIONS

Assessment & Drug Effects

- Monitor carefully for S&S of hypoglycemia especially during the 1-wk period following transfer from a longer-acting sulfonylurea.
- Monitor lab tests: Frequent FBS, postprandial blood glucose, and HbA1C q3mo.

Patient & Family Education

- Take only with meals to lessen the chance of hypoglycemia. If a meal is skipped, skip a dose; if a meal is added, add a dose.
- Start repaglinide the morning after the other agent is stopped when changing from another oral hypoglycemia drug.
- Be alert for S&S of hyperglycemia or hypoglycemia (see Appendix F); report poor blood glucose control to prescriber.

RESLIZUMAB

(res-liz'ue-mab)
Cinqair
Classification: INTERLEUKIN-5 ANTAGONIST; ANTIINFLAMMATORY; MONOCLONAL ANTIBODY
Therapeutic: ANTIINFLAMMATORY; ANTIASTHMATIC
Prototype: Basiliximab

AVAILABILITY Solution for injection

ACTION & *THERAPEUTIC EFFECT*

An antibody that acts as an interleukin-5 antagonist (IgG1 kappa). IL-5 is the major cytokine responsible for the growth and differentiation, recruitment, activation, and survival of eosinophils. Eosinophils are involved in the inflammation associated with the pathogenesis of asthma. *The inhibition of IL-5 signaling by reslizumab, reduces the production and survival of eosinophils.*

USES Treatment of patients with severe asthma 18 y and older with an eosinophilic phenotype; reslizumab should not be used for treatment of other eosinophilic conditions or for the relief of acute bronchospasm or status asthmaticus.

CONTRAINDICATIONS Hypersensitivity to reslizumab. Should not be used to treat acute asthma symptoms.

CAUTIOUS USE Use cautiously in patients with history of systemic neoplastic disease and in patients with a high risk of malignancy. Treat patients with pre-existing helminth infections prior to initiating treatment with reslizumab. Do not discontinue systemic or corticosteroids abruptly upon initiation of reslizumab. Pregnancy and lactation data are insufficient to determine risk. Safety and efficacy in children and adolescents younger than 18 y not established.

ROUTE & DOSAGE

Severe Asthma
Adult: IV 3 mg/kg once every 4 wk

ADMINISTRATION

Intravenous

PREPARE: **IV Infusion:** Solution is clear to slightly hazy/opalescent, colorless to slightly yellow. Small particles may be translucent to white. Discard and do not use if discolored or other foreign particulate matter. ▪ Dilute in 50 mL of 0.9% sodium chloride. ▪ Reslizumab is compatible with polyvinylchloride (PVC) or polyolefin infusion bags. Gently invert the bag to mix. Do not shake.
ADMINISTER: **IV Infusion:** ▪ **Do not** administer IV push or bolus. Administer immediately after preparation. ▪ Use an infusion set with an in-line, low protein-binding filter (pore size of 0.2 micron). Compatible with polyethersulfone, polyvinylidene fluoride, nylon, cellulose acetate in-line filters. ▪ Infuse intravenously over 20–50 min. ▪ Do not infuse any other medication in the tubing. ▪ Stop infusion immediately if patient exhibits any signs of anaphylaxis and treat appropriately. ▪ Flush the intravenous administration set with 0.9% sodium chloride injection to ensure complete administration.
INCOMPATIBILITIES: **Solution/ additive:** None listed (should be mixed with NS).

▪ Store intact vials in refrigerator at 2°–8° C (36°–46° F). Do not freeze or shake. Protect from light. If not used immediately, store in the refrigerator at 2°–8° C (36°–46° F) or at room temperature up to 25° C (77° F), protected from light for up to 16 h max. If refrigerated, warm to room temperature before administering. Single use vials; discard any unused portion.

ADVERSE EFFECTS Respiratory: Oropharyngeal pain. **Musculoskeletal:** Myalgia. **Other:** Elevated creatine phosphokinase, immunogenicity.

PHARMACOKINETICS Metabolism: Proteolytic degradation. **Half-Life:** 24 days.

NURSING IMPLICATIONS

Assessment & Drug Effects

▪ Assess for anaphylaxis has been noted to occur on the second dose, within 20 min after infusion is complete.
▪ Signs of anaphylaxis include dyspnea, decreased oxygen saturation, wheezing, and vomiting. If any symptoms occur, stop administration and notify prescriber.
▪ Assess respiratory status including pulse oximetry.

Common adverse effects in *italic;* life-threatening effects underlined; generic names in **bold;** classifications in SMALL CAPS; ♥ Canadian drug name; ○ Prototype drug; △ Alert

- Patients should be treated for parasitic helminth infections prior to administration of drug.

Patient & Family Education
- Women should use contraceptive measures.
- This is not a rescue drug and should not be used in an acute asthma attack.
- May experience sore throat and muscle pain.

RETAPAMULIN
(re-te-pam'ue-lin)
Altabax
Classification: ANTIBIOTIC; PLEUROMUTILIN
Therapeutic: TOPICAL ANTIBIOTIC

AVAILABILITY Topical ointment

ACTION & *THERAPEUTIC EFFECT*
Selectively inhibits bacterial protein synthesis at a site on the 50S subunit of the bacterial ribosome. *Effective against* Staphylococcus *(MRSA) and* Streptococcus *organisms.*

USES Treatment of impetigo due to susceptible stains of *Staphylococcus aureus* (methicillin-sensitive strains only) or *Streptococcus pyogenes.*

CONTRAINDICATIONS Severe hypersensitivity to retapamulin.

CAUTIOUS USE Pregnancy (category B); lactation; children less than 9 mo.

ROUTE & DOSAGE

Impetigo Infection
Adult/Child/Infant (9 mo or older): Apply in thin layer bid × 5 days

ADMINISTRATION
Topical
- Apply a thin layer to infected region. May cover with gauze dressing.
- Store at 15°–30° C (59°–86° F).

ADVERSE EFFECTS Respiratory: Nasopharyngitis. **CNS:** Headache. **Endocrine:** Creatinine phosphokinase increased. **Skin:** Eczema, pruritus. **GI:** Diarrhea, nausea. **Other:** Application-site irritation, pyrexia.

PHARMACOKINETICS Absorption: Minimal systemic absorption. **Metabolism:** In liver.

NURSING IMPLICATIONS
Assessment & Drug Effects
- Monitor for excessive skin irritation. Report swelling, blistering, or oozing.

Patient & Family Education
- Report any of the following at application site: Redness, itching, burning, swelling, blistering, or oozing.

RETEPLASE RECOMBINANT
(re'te-plase)
Retavase
Classification: THROMBOLYTIC ENZYME, TISSUE PLASMINOGEN ACTIVATOR (T-PA)
Therapeutic: THROMBOLYTIC
Prototype: Alteplase

AVAILABILITY 10.4 international unit vials

ACTION & *THERAPEUTIC EFFECT*
DNA recombinant human tissue-type plasminogen activator (t-PA) that acts as a catalyst in the cleavage of plasminogen to plasmin.

R

Responsible for degrading the fibrin matrix of a clot. *Has antithrombolytic properties.*

USES Thrombolysis management of acute MI to reduce the incidence of CHF and mortality.

CONTRAINDICATIONS Active internal bleeding, history of CVA, recent neurologic surgery or trauma, intercranial neoplasm, or aneurysm, bleeding disorders, severe uncontrolled hypertension.

CAUTIOUS USE Any condition in which bleeding constitutes a significant hazard (i.e., severe hepatic or renal disease, CVA, hypertension, acute pancreatitis, septic thrombophlebitis); pregnancy (category C); lactation. Safety and efficacy in children not established.

ROUTE & DOSAGE

Thrombolysis during Acute MI

Adult: **IV** 10 units injected over 2 min. Repeat dose in 30 min (20 units total).

ADMINISTRATION

Intravenous

PREPARE: **Direct:** Reconstitute using only the diluent, syringe, needle, and dispensing pin provided with reteplase. ▪ Withdraw diluent with syringe provided. Remove needle from syringe, replace with dispensing pin and transfer diluent to vial of reteplase. Leave pin and syringe in place in vial and swirl to dissolve. **Do not** shake. ▪ When completely dissolved, remove 10 mL solution, replace dispensing pin with a 20-gauge needle.

ADMINISTER: **Direct:** Flush IV line before and after with 30 mL NS or D5W and **do not** give any other drug simultaneously through the same IV line. ▪ Give a single dose evenly over 2 min. *INCOMPATIBILITIES:* **Solution/ additive: Heparin. Y-site: Bivali-rudin, heparin.**

▪ Store drug kit unopened at 2°–25° C (36°–77° F).

ADVERSE EFFECTS CV: Reperfusion arrhythmias. **Hematologic:** *Hemorrhage* (including *intracranial*, GI, genitourinary), anemia.

DIAGNOSTIC TEST INTERFERENCE Causes decreases in plasminogen and fibrinogen, making *coagulation* and *fibrinolytic* tests unreliable.

INTERACTIONS Drug: Aspirin, abciximab, dipyridamole, heparin may increase risk of bleeding.

PHARMACOKINETICS Elimination: In urine. **Half-Life:** 13–16 min.

NURSING IMPLICATIONS

Assessment & Drug Effects

▪ Discontinue concomitant heparin immediately if serious bleeding not controllable by local pressure occurs and, if not already given, withhold the second reteplase bolus.
▪ Monitor carefully all potential bleeding sites; monitor for S&S of internal hemorrhage (e.g., GI, GU, intracranial, retroperitoneal, pulmonary).
▪ Monitor carefully cardiac status for arrhythmias associated with reperfusion.
▪ Avoid invasive procedures, arterial and venous punctures, IM injections, and nonessential

handling of the patient during reteplase therapy.

Patient & Family Education
- Report changes in consciousness or signs of bleeding to prescriber immediately.

RH$_0$(D) IMMUNE GLOBULIN
(row)

RhoGAM, Rhophylac, WinRho SDF

RH$_0$(D) IMMUNE GLOBULIN MICRO-DOSE

BayRho-D Mini Dose, MICRho-GAM

Classification: BIOLOGICAL RESPONSE MODIFIER; IMMUNOGLOBULIN (IgG)
Therapeutic: IMMUNOGLOBULIN
Prototype: Immune globulin

AVAILABILITY RhoGAM, MICRho-GAM: Solution in prefilled syringe. **Rhophylac:** Prefilled syringe; **WinRho SDF:** Vial

ACTION & *THERAPEUTIC EFFECT*
Provides passive immunity by suppressing active antibody response and formation of anti-Rh$_0$(D) in Rh-negative [Rh$_0$(D)-negative] individuals previously exposed to Rh-positive [Rh$_0$(D)-positive, D^u-positive] blood. *Effective against exposure to Rh-positivie blood in Rh-negative individuals.*

USES To prevent isoimmunization in Rh-negative individuals exposed to Rh-positive RBC (see above). Rh$_0$(D) immune globulin microdose is for use only after spontaneous or induced abortion or termination of ectopic pregnancy up to and including 12 wk of gestation. Treatment of idiopathic thrombocytopenia purpura.

CONTRAINDICATIONS Rh$_0$(D)-positive patient; person previously immunized against Rh$_0$(D) factor, severe immune globulin hypersensitivity, bleeding disorders.

CAUTIOUS USE IgA deficiency; pregnancy (category C); neonates.

ROUTE & DOSAGE

Note: Only **WinRho SDF** and **Rhophylac** can be given IV. **BayRho-D** and **RhoGAM** are available in regular and mini-dose vials.

Antepartum Prophylaxis
Adult: **IM/IV** 300 mcg at approximately 28-wk gestation; followed by 1 vial of mini-dose or 120 mcg within 72 h of delivery if infant is Rh-positive

Postpartum Prophylaxis
Adult: **IM/IV** 300 mcg preferably within 72 h of delivery if infant is Rh-positive

Following Amniocentesis, Miscarriage, Abortion, Ectopic Pregnancy
Adult: **IM** If over 13-wk gestation, 300 mcg, preferably within 3 h but at least within 72 h; if less than 13 wk, give 50 mcg

Transfusion Accident
Adult: **IM/IV** 300 mcg for each volume of RBCs infused divided by 15, given within at least 72 h of accident
Child: **IV** Administer 600 mcg q8h until total dose given. Exposure to positive whole blood 9 mcg/mL, exposure to positive RBCs 18 mcg/mL. **IM** Administer 1200 mcg q12h until

R

total dose given. Exposure to positive whole blood 12 mcg/mL, exposure to positive RBCs 24 mcg/mL.

Idiopathic Thrombocytopenia Purpura

Adult/Child: **IV** 50 mcg/kg, then 25–60 mcg/kg depending on response

ADMINISTRATION

- BayRho-D (HyperRHO S/D), MIC-RhoGam, and RhoGAM are administered by IM route only. NEVER give IV.
- WinRho SDF and Rhophylac may be given IM or IV depending on the indication.

Intramuscular

- Use the deltoid muscle. Give in divided doses at different sites, all at once or at intervals, as long as the entire dose is given within 72 h after delivery or termination of pregnancy.
- Observe patient closely for at least 20 min after administration. Keep epinephrine immediately available; systemic allergic reactions sometimes occur.

Intravenous

PREPARE: Direct: No dilution is required for products supplied in liquid form. ■ **WinRho SDF:** Remove entire contents of vial to obtain the labeled dosage. If partial vial is needed for dosage calculation, withdraw the entire contents to ensure accurate calculation of dosage requirement. ■ **Rhophylac:** Bring to room temperature before use.

ADMINISTER: Direct: Rhophylac: Give at a rate of 2 mL/15–60 sec for ITP. ■ **WinRho SDF:** Give over 3–5 min.

- Refrigerate commercially prepared solutions, although it may remain stable up to 30 days at room temperature according to manufacturer. ■ Discard solutions that have been frozen. ■ Store powder at 2°–8° C (36°–46° F) unless otherwise directed; avoid freezing.

ADVERSE EFFECTS Other: Injection site irritation, slight fever, myalgia, lethargy.

INTERACTIONS Drug: May interfere with immune response to LIVE VIRUS VACCINE; should delay use of LIVE VIRUS VACCINES for 3 mo after administration of Rh₀(D) immune globulin.

PHARMACOKINETICS Peak: 2 h IV, 5–10 days IM. **Half-Life:** 25 days.

NURSING IMPLICATIONS

Black Box Warning

Rh₀(D) immune globulin has been associated with severe anemia, acute renal insufficiency, renal failure, DIC, and intravascular hemolysis leading to death.

Assessment & Drug Effects

- Obtain history of systemic allergic reactions to human immune globulin preparations prior to drug administration in patients with ITP.
- Monitor closely patients with ITP for at least 8 h after administration.
- Monitor for S&S of intravascular hemolysis, including back pain, shaking chills, fever, and discolored urine or hematuria.
- Monitor lab test: Dipstick urinalysis at baseline, 2 and 4 h after administration, and prior to the end of the monitoring period; periodic CBC, renal function tests, LFTs.

Patient & Family Education

- Report promptly early signs of allergic or hypersensitivity reactions to Rh₀(D) immune globulin, including anaphylaxis, chest tightness, generalized urticaria, hives, and wheezing.
- When treated for ITP, immediately report symptoms of intravascular hemolysis (i.e., back pain, decreased urine output, discolored urine, fluid retention/edema, fever, shaking chills, shortness of breath, and/or sudden weight gain).
- Be aware that administration of Rh₀(D) immune globulin (antibody) prevents hemolytic disease of the newborn in a subsequent pregnancy.

RIBAVIRIN

(rye-ba-vye'rin)

Rebetol, Virazole

Classification: ANTIHEPACIVIRIAL, NUCLEOSIDE

Therapeutic: ANTIVIRAL

Prototype: Acyclovir

AVAILABILITY Inhalation solution; tablet; capsule; oral solution

ACTION & *THERAPEUTIC EFFECT*

Inhibits replication of DNA and RNA viruses; inhibits influenza virus RNA polymerase activity and inhibits the initiation and elongation of RNA fragments resulting in inhibition of viral protein synthesis. *Active against many RNA and DNA viruses.*

USES Aerosol product used for selected infants and young children with respiratory syncytial virus (RSV). Oral product used in combination with direct-acting antivirals to treat chronic hepatitis C infection.

UNLABELED USES viral hemorrhagic fever.

CONTRAINDICATIONS Mild RSV infections of lower respiratory tract; infants requiring simultaneous assisted ventilation; unstable cardiac disease; pancreatitis; autoimmune hepatitis; HCV infection; renal failure; suicidal ideations; hemoglobinopathy; hepatic decompensation; hypersensitivity to ribavirin or any component of the formulation; concomitant use with didanosine; women who are of child bearing age; pregnancy (significant teratogenic and embryocidal effects; avoid pregnancy during therapy and for 6 months after completion of treatment in both female patients and female partners of male patients who are taking ribavirin therapy); lactation.

CAUTIOUS USE COPD, asthma; risk for severe anemia; history of MI, cardiac arrhythmias, cardiac disease; decreased renal, hepatic, or cardiac function; respiratory depression; severe anemia; history of depression or suicidal tendencies; older adults; children younger than 3 y.

ROUTE & DOSAGE

RSV

Child: **Inhalation** 6g continuous aerosolization administered over 12–18 h/day for 3–7 days **Inhalation** 2000 mg over 2 hours tid inn non mechanically ventilated patients for 3–7 days

Hepatitis C *adjust per genotype

Adult/Adolescent/Child (weight greater than 80 kg): **PO** 1.2 g daily in 2 divided doses;

---

weight less than 75 kg: 1 g daily in 2 divided doses
Child/Adolescent (weight 66–80 kg): **PO** 1000 mg/day in 2 divided doses; *weight 50–65 kg:* 800 mg/day in 2 divided doses; *weight 47–49 kg:* 600 mg/day in 2 divided doses; *3 y or older, weight less than 47 kg:* 15 mg/kg/day in divided doses

Renal Impairment Dosage Adjustment

CrCl less than 50 mL/min: varies per dosage form confirm with package insert.

ADMINISTRATION

Oral

- Give tablets/solution with food. Ensure that tablets and capsules are swallowed whole. Do not open, crush, or chew capsules.

Inhalation

- Administer only by SPAG-2 aerosol generator, following manufacturer's directions.
- Caution: Ribavirin has demonstrated teratogenicity in animals. Advise pregnant health care personnel of the potential teratogenic risks associated with exposure during ribavirin administration to patients.
- Do not give other aerosol medication concomitantly with ribavirin.
- Discard solution in the SPAG-2 reservoir at least q24h and whenever liquid level is low before fresh reconstituted solution is added.
- Store unopened vial in a dry place at 15°–25° C (59°–78° F) unless otherwise directed.
- Following reconstitution, store solution at 20°–30° C (68°–86° F) for 24 h.

ADVERSE EFFECTS CV: Chest pain. **Respiratory:** Cough, dyspnea, dyspnea on exertion, flu-like symptoms, pharyngitis, sinusitis, rhinitis, upper respiratory tract infection. **CNS:** Anxiety, depression, emotional lability, irritability, lack of concentration, nervousness, RUQ pain, rigors, malaise, memory impairment, mood changes, *dizziness, headache, insomnia, fatigue,* back pain. **HEENT:** Conjunctivitis, blurred vision. **Endocrine:** *Weight loss,* growth retardation, hyperuricemia, hypothyroidism, menstrual disease. **Hepatic/GI:** *Diarrhea, nausea, vomiting,* abdominal pain, anorexia, dyspepsia, xerostomia, decreased appetite, hyperbilirubinemia, constipation. **Skin:** Alopecia, dermatitis, diaphoresis, skin rash, xeroderma, eczema. **Hematologic:** *Neutropenia,* lymphocytopenia, <u>hemolytic anemia</u> (especially in combination with interferon alpha), leukopenia, thrombocytopenia. **Musculoskeletal:** Arthralgia, asthenia, musculoskeletal pain, myalgia, back pain. **Other:** Viral infection, bacterial infection, chills, fever, injection site reaction (erythema, inflammation).

INTERACTIONS Drug: Ribavirin may antagonize the antiviral effects of **zidovudine** against HIV; increased risk of fetal defects with **peginterferon.** Do not administer with LIVE VIRUS VACCINES. Increases risk of adverse effects with **azathioprine, cladribine, didanosine.**

PHARMACOKINETICS Absorption: Rapidly absorbed orally (44%) and systemically from lungs. **Peak:** Inhaled 60–90 min. PO 1.7–3 h. **Distribution:** Crosses placenta; distributed into breast milk. **Metabolism:** In cells to an active metabolite. **Elimination:** 85% in urine, 15% in feces.

Half-Life: 24 h in plasma, 16–40 days in RBCs.

NURSING IMPLICATIONS

Black Box Warning

Ribavirin has been associated with hemolytic anemia which may worsen cardiac disease and cause MI, and with fetal toxicity.

Assessment & Drug Effects

- Monitor respiratory function and fluid status closely during therapy. Note baseline rate and character of respirations and pulse. Observe for signs of labored breathing: Dyspnea, apnea; rapid, shallow respirations, intercostal and substernal retraction, nasal flaring, limited excursion of lungs, cyanosis. Auscultate lungs for abnormal breath sounds.
- Monitor cardiac status, including ECG, especially in those with pre-exisiting cardiac dysfunction.
- Monitor lab tests: Baseline CBC with differential and platelet count, repeat at 2 and 4 wk, and periodically thereafter; baseline and periodic serum electrolytes, LFTs, renal function tests, CD4+ cell count, TSH and T4. Perform baseline pregnancy test.

Patient & Family Education

- Both male and female patients should take every precaution to prevent pregnancy during treatment and for 6 mo following the end of therapy.
- Inform prescriber immediately if a pregnancy occurs within 6 mo of completing therapy.
- Drink fluids liberally unless otherwise advised by prescriber.
- Use caution with hazardous activities until response to drug is known.

RIBOFLAVIN (VITAMIN B₂)

(rye′bo-flay-vin)

Classification: VITAMIN
Therapeutic: VITAMIN REPLACEMENT

AVAILABILITY Tablet

ACTION & *THERAPEUTIC EFFECT*

Works with a wide variety of proteins to catalyze many cellular respiratory reactions by which the body derives its energy. *Evaluated by improvement of clinical manifestations of deficiency: Digestive disturbances, headache, burning sensation of skin (especially "burning" feet), cracking at corners of mouth (cheilosis), glossitis, seborrheic dermatitis (and other skin lesions), mental depression, corneal vascularization (with photophobia, burning and itchy eyes, lacrimation, roughness of eyelids), anemia, neuropathy.*

USES To prevent and treat riboflavin deficiency, also to treat microcytic anemia.

CAUTIOUS USE Pregnancy (category A; category C if greater than RDA); lactation.

ROUTE & DOSAGE

R

Nutritional Deficiency Treatment

Adult: **PO** 5–30 mg/day in divided doses
Child: **PO** 3–10 mg/day

Microcytic Anemia

Adult: **PO** 10 mg/day × 10 days

ADMINISTRATION

Oral

- Give with food to enhance absorption.

Common adverse effects in *italic;* life-threatening effects <u>underlined;</u> generic names in **bold;** classifications in SMALL CAPS; ♣ Canadian drug name; ○ Prototype drug; △ Alert

■ Store in airtight containers protected from light.

ADVERSE EFFECTS GU: May discolor urine bright yellow.

DIAGNOSTIC TEST INTERFERENCE
In large doses, riboflavin may produce yellow-green fluorescence in *urine* and thus cause false elevations in certain *fluorometric determinations* of *urinary catecholamines.*

PHARMACOKINETICS Absorption: Readily absorbed from GI tract. **Distribution:** Little is stored; excess amounts are excreted in urine. **Elimination:** In urine. **Half-Life:** 66–84 min.

NURSING IMPLICATIONS
Assessment & Drug Effects
■ Collaborate with prescriber, dietitian, patient, and responsible family member in planning for diet. A complete dietary history is an essential part of vitamin replacement so that poor eating habits can be identified and corrected. Deficiency in one vitamin is usually associated with other vitamin deficiencies.

Patient & Family Education
■ Be aware that large doses may cause an intense yellow discoloration of urine.
■ Note: Rich dietary sources of riboflavin are found in liver, kidney, beef, pork, heart, eggs, milk and milk products, yeast, wholegrain cereals, vitamin B–enriched breakfast cereals, green vegetables, and mushrooms.

RIFABUTIN
(rif-a-bu'tin)
Mycobutin

Classification: ANTIBIOTIC; ANTITUBERCULOSIS
Therapeutic: ANTITUBERCULOSIS
Prototype: Rifampin

AVAILABILITY Capsule

ACTION & *THERAPEUTIC EFFECT*
Semisynthetic bacteriostatic antibiotic. Inhibits DNA-dependent RNA polymerase in susceptible bacterial cells but not in human cells. *Effective against* Mycobacterium avium *complex (MAC) (or* M. avium-intra-cellulare*) and many strains of* M. tuberculosis.

USES The prevention of disseminated *Mycobacterium avium* complex (MAC) disease in patients with advanced HIV infection.

CONTRAINDICATIONS Hypersensitivity to rifabutin or any other rifamycins; lactation.

CAUTIOUS USE Older adults, pregnancy (rifabutin crosses the placenta; use with caution); children.

ROUTE & DOSAGE

Prevention of MAC
Adult/Adolescent: **PO** 300 mg daily
Infant/Child: **PO** 10–20 mg/kg/dose daily (max 300 mg)

ADMINISTRATION
Oral
■ Give the usual dose of 300 mg/day or in two divided doses of 150 mg with food if needed to reduce GI upset.
■ Store at room temperature, 25° C (77° F).

R

Common adverse effects in *italic;* life-threatening effects <u>underlined;</u> generic names in **bold;** classifications in SMALL CAPS; ♣ Canadian drug name; ۞ Prototype drug; ⚠ Alert

ADVERSE EFFECTS CNS: *Headache.* **Skin:** *Rash.* **GI:** *Abdominal pain, nausea.* **Hematologic:** Thrombocytopenia, leukopenia, neutropenia. **Other:** *Turns urine, feces, saliva, sputum, perspiration, and tears orange. Soft contact lenses may be permanently discolored.*

INTERACTIONS Drug: Extensive drug interactions for complete list consult drug interaction database. May decrease levels of BENZODIAZEPINES, BETA-BLOCKERS, **clofibrate, dapsone, delavirdine, doravirine,** NARCOTICS, ANTICOAGULANTS, CORTICOSTEROIDS, HMG–COA REDUCTASE INHIBITORS, **cyclosporine, quinidine,** ORAL CONTRACEPTIVES, PROGESTINS, SULFONYLUREAS, **ketoconazole, fluconazole,** BARBITURATES, **theophylline,** ANTICONVULSANTS, and other medications metabolized by CYP3A4 or UGT1A4 resulting in therapeutic failure. ANTIFUNGALS, **atazanavir, darunavir, fosamprenavir,** may increase adverse effects. Do not use with LIVE VIRUS VACCINES. Efavirenz may decrease levels of rifabutin.

PHARMACOKINETICS Absorption: 12–20% of oral dose reaches the systemic circulation. **Peak:** 2–3 h. **Distribution:** 85% protein bound. Widely distributed, high concentrations in the lungs, liver, spleen, eyes, and kidney. Crosses placenta, distributed into breast milk. **Metabolism:** In the liver. Causes induction of hepatic enzymes. **Elimination:** Urine (53% as metabolites), 30% in feces. **Half-Life:** 16–96 h (average 45 h).

NURSING IMPLICATIONS

Assessment & Drug Effects

- Monitor patients for S&S of active TB. Report immediately.

- Evaluate patients on concurrent oral hypoglycemic therapy for loss of glycemic control.
- Review patient's complete drug regimen because dosage adjustment of a significant number of drugs may be needed when rifabutin is added to regimen.
- Monitor lab tests: Periodic LFTs, CBC with differential and platelet count.

Patient & Family Education

- Learn S&S of TB and MAC (e.g., persistent fever, progressive weight loss, anorexia, night sweats, diarrhea) and notify prescriber if any of these develop.
- Notify prescriber of following: Muscle or joint pain, eye pain or other discomfort, chest pain with dyspnea, rash, or a flu-like syndrome.
- Be aware that urine, feces, saliva, sputum, perspiration, tears, and skin may be colored brown-orange. Soft contact lens may be permanently discolored.
- Rifabutin may reduce the activity of a wide variety of drugs. Provide a complete and accurate list of concurrent drugs to the prescriber for evaluation.

RIFAMPIN ⊙

(rif'am-pin)

Rifadin, Rofact ◆

Classification: ANTIBIOTIC; ANTITUBERCULOSIS

Therapeutic: ANTITUBERCULOSIS

AVAILABILITY Capsule; solution for injection

ACTION & THERAPEUTIC EFFECT
Inhibits DNA-dependent RNA polymerase activity in susceptible bacterial cells, thereby suppressing RNA synthesis. *Active against*

Mycobacterium tuberculosis, M. leprae, Neisseria meningitidis, *and a wide range of gram-negative and gram-positive organisms.*

USES Initial treatment and retreatment of tuberculosis; as short-term therapy to prevent meningococcal infection.

UNLABELED USES Chemoprophylaxis in contacts of patients with *Haemophilus influenzae* type B infection; leprosy (especially dapsone-resistant leprosy); endocarditis, pruritus.

CONTRAINDICATIONS Hypersensitivity to rifampin; obstructive biliary disease; meningococcal disease; intermittent rifampin therapy.

CAUTIOUS USE Hepatic disease; history of alcoholism; IBD. Concomitant use of other hepatotoxic agents; pregnancy (postnatal hemorrhages have been observed in the infant and mother with administration during the last weeks of pregnancy).

ROUTE & DOSAGE

Pulmonary Tuberculosis

Adults: **PO/IV** 10 mg/kg (max: 600 mg) daily for 2 mo with other agents
Child: **PO** 15–20 mg/kg/day (max: 600 mg/day) with other agents
Infant/Child (with HIV): **PO** 10–20 mg/kg once daily (max: 600 mg) daily for 2 mo with other agents

Meningococcal Prophylaxis

Adult: **PO** 600 mg q12h for 2 consecutive days

Adolescent/Child/Infant: **PO** 20 mg/kg/day in divided doses × 2 consecutive days (max: 600 mg/day)

ADMINISTRATION

Oral
- Give 1 h before or 2 h after a meal on an empty stomach with a glass of water. Peak serum levels are delayed and may be slightly lower when given with food; capsule contents may be emptied into fluid or mixed with food.
- Note: An oral suspension can be prepared from capsules for use with pediatric patients. Shake oral suspension well before using. May mix capsule contents with applesauce or jelly.
- Keep a desiccant in bottle containing capsules to prevent moisture causing instability.

Intravenous

PREPARE: IV Infusion: Reconstitute vial by adding 10 mL of sterile water for injection to each 600-mg to yield 60 mg/mL. Swirl to dissolve. ▪ Withdraw the ordered dose and further dilute in 500 mL of D5W (preferred) or NS. ▪ If absolutely necessary, 100 mL of D5W or NS may be used.
ADMINISTER: IV Infusion: Infuse 500 mL solution over 3 h and 100 mL solution over 30 min. ▪ Note: A less concentrated solution infused over a longer period is preferred. Avoid extravasation.
INCOMPATIBILITIES: Solution/additive: ethambutol, isoniazid, minocycline. Y-site: diltiazem, tramadol.

- Use NS solutions within 24 h and D5W solutions within 4 h of preparation.

Common adverse effects in *italic*; life-threatening effects underlined; generic names in **bold**; classifications in SMALL CAPS; ✦ Canadian drug name; ◯ Prototype drug; ⚠ Alert

1478

ADVERSE EFFECTS **Cardiovascular:** Decreased Bp, flushing, shock, vasculitis. **Respiratory:** Dyspnea, flu-like symptoms, wheezing. **CNS:** Fatigue, drowsiness, headache, ataxia, confusion, dizziness, inability to concentrate, generalized numbness, peripheral pain, muscular weakness, behavioural changes. **HEENT:** Visual disturbances. **Endocrine:** Adrenocortical insufficiency, menstrual disease. **Skin:** Erythema multiforme, pemphigoid reaction, pruritis, skin rash, urticarial. **GI:** *Epigastric distress, nausea, vomiting, anorexia, flatulence, cramps, diarrhea,* staining of teeth, *elevated liver function tests* (bilirubin, BSP, alkaline phosphatase, ALT, AST), jaundice. **GU:** Acute renal failure, renal insufficiency, renal tubular necrosis, interstitial nephritis. **Hematologic:** Thrombocytopenia, transient leukopenia, anemia, including hemolytic anemia. **Musculoskeletal:** Myopathy. **Other:** Hypersensitivity (fever, pruritus, urticaria, skin eruptions, soreness of mouth and tongue, eosinophilia, hemolysis), flu-like syndrome. Increasing lethargy, liver enlargement and tenderness, jaundice, brownish-red or orange discoloration of skin, sweat, saliva, tears, and feces.

DIAGNOSTIC TEST INTERFERENCE

Rifampin interferes with contrast media used for *gallbladder study;* therefore, test should precede daily dose of rifampin. Inhibits standard assays for *serum folate* and *vitamin B₁₂,* may cause false positive opiate urine screen.

INTERACTIONS **Drug:** Extensive drug interactions, for complete list consult drug interaction database. Do not use with PROTEASE INHIBITORS and **nevirapine** as it may increase treatment failure rate. **Alcohol, isoniazid, pyrazinamide, ritonavir,** saquinavir increase risk of drug-induced hepatotoxicity. decreases concentrations of **alfentanil, alosetron, alprazolam, amprenavir,** BARBITURATES, BENZODIAZEPINES, **carbamazepine, atovaquone, cevimeline, chloramphenicol, clofibrate,** CORTICOSTEROIDS, **cyclosporine, dapsone, delavirdine, diazepam, digoxin, diltiazem, disopyramide, estazolam, estramustine, fentanyl, fosphenytoin, fluconazole galantamine, indinavir, itraconazole, ketoconazole, lamotrigine, levobupivacaine, lopinavir, methadone, metoprolol, mexiletine, midazolam, nelfinavir,** ORAL SULFONYLUREAS, ORAL CONTRACEPTIVES, **phenytoin,** PROGESTINS, **propafenone, propranolol, quinidine, quinine, ritonavir, siro-limus, the-ophylline,** THYROID HORMONES, **tocainide, tramadol, verapamil, warfarin, zaleplon,** and **zonisamide,** drugs metabolized by CYP3A4 leading to potential therapeutic failure. Do not use with **simvastatin.**

PHARMACOKINETICS **Absorption:** Readily from GI tract. **Peak:** 2–4 h. **Distribution:** Widely distributed, including CSF; crosses placenta; distributed into breast milk; 80% protein bound. **Metabolism:** In liver to active and inactive metabolites; is enterohepatically cycled. **Elimination:** Up to 30% in urine, 60–65% in feces. **Half-Life:** 3 h.

NURSING IMPLICATIONS

Assessment & Drug Effects

- Monitor for extravasation during injection; local irritation and inflammation due to infiltration of

the infusion may occur. If so, DC infusion and restart at another site.
- Check prothrombin time daily or as necessary to establish and maintain required anticoagulant activity when patient is also receiving an anticoagulant.
- Monitor lab tests: Periodic LFTs, serum creatinine, CBC, and platelet count.

Patient & Family Education
- Do not interrupt prescribed dosage regimen. Hepatorenal reaction with flu-like syndrome has occurred when therapy has been resumed following interruption.
- Be aware that drug may impart a harmless red-orange color to urine, feces, sputum, sweat, and tears. Soft contact lenses may be permanently stained.
- Report onset of jaundice, hypersensitivity reactions, and persistence of GI adverse effects to prescriber.
- Use or add barrier contraceptive if using hormonal contraception. Concomitant use of rifampin and oral contraceptives leads to decreased effectiveness of the contraceptive and to menstrual disturbances (spotting, breakthrough bleeding).
- Keep drug out of reach of children.

RIFAMYCIN
(rif-a-mye-sin)
Aemcolo
Classifications: ANTIDIARRHEAL; ANTIBIOTIC
Therapeutic: ANTIDIARRHEAL
Prototype: Rifampin

AVAILABILITY Oral tablet

ACTION & *THERAPEUTIC EFFECT*
Inhibits bacterial synthesis by inhibiting the beta-subunit of the bacterial DNA-dependent RNA polymerase. *Used to treat travelers' diarrhea caused by noninvasive strains of Escherichia coli in adults.*

USES Treatment of traveler's diarrhea.

CONTRAINDICATIONS Hypersensitivity to rifamycin class antimicrobial agents or any component of the formulation.

CAUTIOUS USE Prolonged use may cause superinfection. Use with caution in the elderly, during pregnancy, and with lactation.

ROUTE & DOSAGE

Traveler's Diarrhea
Adult: **PO** 388 mg (two tablets) twice a day for three days

ADMINISTRATION

Oral
- Administer each dose with 6 to 8 ounces of non-alcoholic liquid, with or without food.
- Swallow tablets whole; do not crush, break, or chew.
- Store at 20° to 25° C (68° to 77° F).

ADVERSE EFFECTS CNS: Headache. **GI:** Constipation, abdominal pain.

INTERACTIONS Do not use with LIVE VACCINES.

PHARMACOKINETICS Absorption: <0.1% bioavailability. **Distribution:** 80% protein bound. **Elimination:** 86% excreted in the feces.

Common adverse effects in *italic;* life-threatening effects underlined; generic names in **bold;** classifications in SMALL CAPS; ♣ Canadian drug name; ◐ Prototype drug; ⚠ Alert

NURSING IMPLICATIONS

Assessment & Drug Effects

- Monitor for bloody stools as well as the frequency of diarrhea.

Patient & Family Education

- Notify your doctor or get medical help right away if you have any of the following signs or symptoms of allergic reaction such as rash, hives, itching; red, swollen, blistered, or peeling skin with or without fever; wheezing; tightness in the chest or throat; trouble breathing, swallowing, or talking; unusual hoarseness; or swelling of the mouth, face, lips, tongue, or throat; or any dizziness or passing out.

RIFAPENTINE

(rif'a-pen-teen)

Priftin

Classification: ANTIBIOTIC; ANTITUBERCULOSIS; MYCOBACTERIUM

Therapeutic: ANTITUBERCULOSIS

Prototype: Rifampin

AVAILABILITY Tablet

ACTION & THERAPEUTIC EFFECT

Inhibits DNA-dependent RNA polymerase activity in susceptible bacterial cells, thereby suppressing RNA synthesis. *Effective against* Mycobacterium tuberculosis.

USES Active or latent pulmonary tuberculosis in conjunction with at least one other agent.

CONTRAINDICATIONS Hypersensitivity to any rifamycins (e.g., rifampin, rifabutin, rifapentine); porphyria; continuation phase of treatment in HIV-seropositive patients; soft contact lens; lactation.

CAUTIOUS USE Patients with abnormal liver function tests or hepatic disease; HIV disease; cavitary pulmonary lesions, bilateral pulmonary disease; older adults; pregnancy (limited information related to use in pregnant women); children.

ROUTE & DOSAGE

Active Tuberculosis

Adult/Adolescent: **PO** 600 mg twice weekly (at least 72 h apart) × 2 mo, then 600 mg once weekly × 4 mo

Latent Tuberculosis

Adult/Adolescent/Child (weight greater than 50 kg): **PO** 900 mg once weekly; *weight 32.1–50 kg:* 750 mg once weekly; *weight 25.1–32 kg:* 600 mg once weekly

ADMINISTRATION

Oral

- Give with an interval of NO LESS than 72 h between doses.
- Give with food to minimize GI upset. For patients who cannot swallow tablets, tablets may be crushed and added to small amount of semi-solid food and consumed immediately.
- Store at 25° C (77° F) in a tightly closed container and protect from excess moisture.

ADVERSE EFFECTS CV: Chest pain, edema. **Respiratory:** Hemoptysis, cough. **CNS:** Headache, pain. **Endocrine:** Hypoglycemia.

R

Skin: Rash, diaphoresis. **GI:** Increased liver function tests (ALT, AST). **GU:** *Hyperuricemia*, pyuria, urinary tract infection, hematuria, urinary casts. **Hematologic:** Neutropenia, lymphocytopenia, anemia, leukopenia, thrombocytosis. **Musculoskeletal:** Back pain, arthralgia. **Other:** Hypersensitivity reaction, influenza, accidental injury.

INTERACTIONS Drug: There are extensive drug interactions, consult a drug information database for a complete list. Decreased activity of ORAL CONTRACEPTIVES, **phenytoin, disopyramide, mexiletine, quinidine, tocainide, warfarin, fluconazole, itraconazole, ketoconazole, diazepam,** BETA-BLOCKERS, CALCIUM CHANNEL BLOCKERS, CORTICOSTEROIDS, **haloperidol,** SULFONYLUREAS, **cyclosporine, tacrolimus, levothyroxine,** NARCOTIC ANALGESICS, **quinine,** REVERSE TRANSCRIPTASE INHIBITORS, TRICYCLIC ANTIDEPRESSANTS, ANTIHEPACIVIRAL **sildenafil, theophylline,** drugs metabolized by CYP3A4. ANTIFUNGAL AGENTS may increase the concentration of rifapentine

PHARMACOKINETICS Absorption: 70% absorbed. **Peak:** 5–6 h. **Distribution:** 97.7% protein bound. **Metabolism:** Hydrolyzed by esterase enzyme to active metabolite in liver; inducer of cytochromes P450 3A4 and 2C8/9. **Elimination:** 70% in feces, 17% in urine. **Half-Life:** 13.3 h.

NURSING IMPLICATIONS

Assessment & Drug Effects

- Monitor carefully for S&S of toxicity with concurrent use of oral anticoagulants, digitalis preparations, or anticonvulsants.
- Monitor lab tests: Sputum smear and culture, baseline LFTs and repeat q4–6wk in those with pre-existing hepatic impairment.

Patient & Family Education

- Follow strict adherence to the prescribed dosing schedule to prevent emergence of resistant strains of tuberculosis.
- Be aware that food may be useful in preventing GI upset.
- Report immediately any of the following to the prescriber: Fever, weakness, nausea or vomiting, loss of appetite, dark urine or yellowing of eyes or skin, pain or swelling of the joints, severe or persistent diarrhea.
- Use or add barrier contraceptive if using hormonal contraception.

RIFAXIMIN

(ri-fax′i-min)

Xifaxan

Classification: RIFAMYCIN ANTIBIOTIC; MYCOBACTERIUM

Therapeutic: MYCOBACTERIUM

Prototype: Rifampin

AVAILABILITY Tablet

ACTION & *THERAPEUTIC EFFECT*
Inhibits bacterial RNA synthesis by binding to DNA-dependent RNA polymerase, thereby blocking RNA transcription. *Its spectrum of activity includes gram-positive and gram-negative aerobes and anaerobes.*

USES Treatment of traveler's diarrhea, hepatic encephalopathy.

UNLABELED USES Crohn's disease, diverticulitis, irritable bowel syndrome.

CONTRAINDICATIONS Hypersensitivity to rifaximin, other rifamycin antimicrobial agents or to any of its components; dysentery; lactation.

Common adverse effects in *italic*; life-threatening effects <u>underlined</u>; generic names in **bold**; classifications in SMALL CAPS; ♦ Canadian drug name; ● Prototype drug; ⚠ Alert

CAUTIOUS USE Diarrhea with fever and/or blood in the stool, or diarrhea due to organisms other than *E. coli;* IBD, worsening diarrhea or diarrhea persisting for longer than 24–48 h; pregnancy (category C); children younger than 12 y.

ROUTE & DOSAGE

Traveler's Diarrhea
Adult/Adolescent: PO 200 mg tid for 3 days

Reduce Risk of Hepatic Encephalopathy Recurrence
Adult: PO 550 mg bid

ADMINISTRATION
Oral
- May be given without regard to food.
- Store at 15°–30° C (59°–86° F).

ADVERSE EFFECTS CNS: Headache. GI: *Flatulence,* abdominal pain, rectal tenesmus, defecation urgency, nausea, constipation, vomiting. Other: Fever.

PHARMACOKINETICS Absorption: Less than 0.4% absorbed orally. Peak: 1.21 h. Elimination: In feces. Half-Life: 5.85 h.

NURSING IMPLICATIONS
Assessment & Drug Effects
- Withhold drug and notify prescriber if diarrhea worsens or lasts longer than 48 h after starting drug; an alternative treatment should be considered.
- Report promptly the appearance of blood in the stool.

Patient & Family Education
- Report promptly any of the following: Fever; difficulty breathing; skin rash, itching, or hives; worsening diarrhea during or after treatment or blood in the stool.

RILPIVIRINE
(ril-pi'vi-reen)
Edurant
Classification: ANTIRETROVIRAL; NONNUCLEOSIDE REVERSE TRANSCRIPTASE INHIBITOR (NNRTI)
Therapeutic: ANTIRETROVIRAL; NNRTI
Prototype: Efavirenz

AVAILABILITY Tablet

ACTION & *THERAPEUTIC EFFECT*
A nonnucleoside reverse transcriptase inhibitor (NNRTI) of human immunodeficiency virus type 1 (HIV-1). *Inhibits HIV-1 replication and slows/prevents disease progression.*

USES Treatment of HIV-1 infection in combination with other antiretroviral agents in adult patients who are treatment-naïve.

CONTRAINDICATIONS Concurrent drugs that significantly decrease rilpivirine plasma level such as anticonvulsants, antimycobacterials, proton pump inhibitors, systemic dexamethasone, St. John's wort; lactation.

CAUTIOUS USE Congenital prolonged QT interval or concurrent drugs that prolong the QT interval; depressive disorders or suicidal ideation; older adult; severe renal impairment; hepatic impairment; pregnancy (category B). Safety and efficacy in children not established.

ROUTE & DOSAGE

HIV-1 Infection (with Other Agents)
Adult: PO 25 mg once daily

R

ADMINISTRATION

Oral

- Give with a full meal.
- Swallow tablet whole with water.
- If antacids are prescribed, they must be given at least 2 h before or 4 h after rilpivirine.
- Store at 15–30° C (59–86° F) and protect from light.

ADVERSE EFFECTS CNS: Depression, headache, drowsiness, <u>suicidal thoughts</u>. **Endocrine:** Decreased plasma cortisol, increased serum cholesterol. **Hepatic:** Increased serum ALT, increased serum AST.

INTERACTIONS Drug: Strong CYP3A4 inhibitors (e.g., **atazanavir, clarithromycin, delaviridine, indinavir, itraconazole, ketoconazole, nefazodone, nelfinavir, ritonavir, saquinavir,** and **telithromycin**) **voriconazole,** can increase rilpivirine levels, while strong CYP3A4 inducers (e.g., **rifampin, dexamethasone, phenytoin, carbamazepine, efavirenz,** and **phenobarbital**) can decrease rilpivirine levels. Antacids, GLUCOCORTICOIDS, H$_2$ RECEPTOR ANTAGONISTS, **methadone** can decrease rilpivirine. Rilpivirine can decrease the levels of **methadone.** Rilpivirine has been associated with QT prolongation. Coadministration of other drug that prolongs the QT interval (e.g., **disopyramide, procainamide, amiodarone, bretylium, clarithromycin, levofloxacin**) may cause additive effects. **Food:** Administration with a meal enhances absorption. **Herbal: St. John's wort** may decrease the levels of rilpivirine.

PHARMACOKINETICS Peak: 4–5 h. **Distribution:** 99.7% plasma protein bound. **Metabolism:** In liver (CYP3A4). **Elimination:** Fecal (85%) and renal (6%). **Half-Life:** 50 h.

NURSING IMPLICATIONS

Assessment & Drug Effects

- Monitor closely for adverse effects in those with severe renal impairment.
- Monitor for and report promptly signs of depression or suicidal ideation.
- Monitor lab tests: Periodic plasma HIV RNA; baseline and periodic LFTs, cholesterol, and triglycerides.

Patient & Family Education

- Drug absorption is improved when taken with a full meal.
- Seek immediate medical assistance if you experience depression or thoughts of suicide.
- Do not self-treat depression with St. John's wort.
- Report to prescriber all prescription and nonprescription drugs and herbal products you use.
- Do not use over-the-counter stomach medications without consent of your health care provider.
- If you use an antacid, take it at least 2 h before or 4 h after taking rilpivirine.

RILUZOLE
(ri-lu′zole)

Rilutek

Classification: AMYOTROPHIC LATERAL SCLEROSIS (ALS) AGENT; GLUTAMATE ANTAGONIST

Therapeutic: ALS AGENT

AVAILABILITY Tablet

ACTION & *THERAPEUTIC EFFECT*

Inhibits the presynaptic release of glutamic acid in the CNS. Effectiveness based on theory that pathogenesis of amyotrophic lateral sclerosis (ALS) is related to injury of motor neurons by glutamate. *Believed to reduce the degeneration of neurons in ALS.*

Common adverse effects in *italic*; life-threatening effects <u>underlined</u>; generic names in **bold**; classifications in SMALL CAPS; ♣ Canadian drug name; ☺ Prototype drug; ⚠ Alert

1484

USES Treatment of ALS.

CONTRAINDICATIONS Hypersensitivity to riluzole; ALT levels are 5 × ULN or if clinical jaundice develops; lactation.

CAUTIOUS USE Hepatic dysfunction, renal impairment; hypertension, history of other CNS disorders; older adults; pregnancy (category C). Safe use in children younger than 12 y is not established.

ROUTE & DOSAGE

ALS
Adult: **PO** 50 mg q12h

ADMINISTRATION

Oral
- Give at same time daily and at least 1 h before or 2 h after a meal. Do not give before/after a high-fat meal.
- Store at room temperature; protect from bright light.

ADVERSE EFFECTS CV: Hypertension, tachycardia, phlebitis, palpitation. **Respiratory:** *Decreased lung function,* rhinitis, increased cough, apnea, bronchitis, dysphagia, dyspnea. **CNS:** Hypertonia, depression, dizziness, dry mouth, insomnia, somnolence, circumoral paresthesia. **Skin:** Pruritus, eczema, alopecia, exfoliative dermatitis (rare). **GI:** Abdominal pain, *nausea,* vomiting, dyspepsia, anorexia, diarrhea, flatulence, stomatitis. **GU:** UTI. **Other:** *Asthenia,* headache, back pain, malaise, arthralgia, weight loss, peripheral edema, flu-like syn-drome.

INTERACTIONS Drug: BARBITURATES, **carbamazepine** may increase risk of hepatotoxicity.

PHARMACOKINETICS Absorption: Well absorbed from GI tract, 60% reaches systemic circulation. **Peak:** Steady-state levels by day 5. **Distribution:** 96% protein bound. **Metabolism:** In liver by CYP1A2. **Elimination:** 90% in urine. **Half-Life:** 12 h.

NURSING IMPLICATIONS

Assessment & Drug Effects
- Withhold drug and notify prescriber if liver enzymes are elevated.
- Monitor lab tests: Baseline LFTs, then monthly for 3 mo, then q3mo for remainder of first year, and periodically thereafter.

Patient & Family Education
- Report any febrile illness to prescriber.
- Do not engage in potentially hazardous activities until response to drug is known.
- Learn common adverse effects and possible adverse interaction with alcohol.

RIMANTADINE
(ri-man'ta-deen)
Classification: ANTIVIRAL; ADMANTANE
Therapeutic: ANTIVIRAL
Prototype: Amantadine

AVAILABILITY Tablet

ACTION & *THERAPEUTIC EFFECT*
Exerts an inhibitory effect early in the viral replication cycle, probably by interfering with the viral uncoating procedure of the influenza A virus. Inhibits synthesis of both viral RNA and viral protein, thus causing viral destruction. *Prevents or interrupts influenza A infections.*

USES Prophylaxis and treatment of influenza A.

R

CONTRAINDICATIONS Hypersensitivity to rimantadine and amantadine; lactation; children younger than 1 y for prophylaxis treatment.

CAUTIOUS USE History of seizures; renal or hepatic impairment; older adults; pregnancy (adverse effects have been observed in animal reproduction studies). Safe use in children younger than 17 y for treatment of Influenza A is not known.

ROUTE & DOSAGE

Prophylaxis of Influenza A

Adult/Child (10 y or older): **PO** 100 mg bid × 7 days; *Child (1–9 y):* **PO** 5 mg/kg daily (max: 150 mg/day) in divided doses *Geriatric:* **PO** 100 mg daily

Treatment of Influenza A

Adult/Adolescent (17 y or older): **PO** 100 mg bid started within 48 h of symptoms and continued for 5–7 days from initial symptoms; *Child (over 10 y):* **PO** 5 mg/kg daily in divided doses (max: 200 mg/day) *(1–9 y):* 6.6 mg/kg daily in divided doses (max: 150 mg/day)

Hepatic Impairment Dosage Adjustment

100 mg daily with severe liver disease

Renal Impairment Dosage Adjustment

CrCl 10–30 mL/min: 100 mg daily

ADMINISTRATION

Oral

- May administer with food.
- Store at 25° C (77° F).

ADVERSE EFFECTS CNS: Insomnia, lack of concentration. **GI:** Nausea, anorexia.

INTERACTIONS Drug: Intranasal influenza vaccine should not be used within 48 h.

PHARMACOKINETICS Absorption: Readily absorbed from GI tract. **Peak:** Serum levels 3.2–4.3 h. **Distribution:** Concentrates in respiratory secretions. **Metabolism:** Extensively in liver. **Elimination:** By kidneys. **Half-Life:** 20–36 h.

NURSING IMPLICATIONS

Assessment & Drug Effects

- Monitor carefully for seizure activity in patients with a history of seizures. Seizures are an indication to discontinue the drug.
- Monitor for adverse GI or CNS effects.

Patient & Family Education

- Report bothersome adverse effects to prescriber; especially hallucinations, palpitations, difficulty breathing, and swelling of legs.
- Use caution with hazardous activities until reaction to drug is known.

RIMEXOLONE

(rim-ex'o-lone)

Vexol

See Appendix A-1.

RISANKIZUMAB-RZA

(ris-an-kiz-ue-mab)

Skyrizi

Classifications: ANTIPSORIATIC AGENT; IL-23 INHIBITOR
Therapeutic: ANTIPSORIATIC
Prototype: Guselkumab

Common adverse effects in *italic*; life-threatening effects <u>underlined</u>; generic names in **bold**; classifications in SMALL CAPS; ♣ Canadian drug name; ☼ Prototype drug; ⚠ Alert

AVAILABILITY Subcutaneous Injection

ACTION & THERAPEUTIC EFFECT A human IgG1 monoclonal antibody which selectively binds to the p19 subunit of interleukin (IL)-23 resulting in inhibition of the release of proinflammatory cytokines and chemokines. *Used to treat moderate-to-severe plaque psoriasis in adults who are candidates for systemic therapy or phototherapy.*

USES Treatment of moderate to severe plaque psoriasis in patients who are candidates for systemic therapy or phototherapy

CAUTIOUS USE Tuberculosis; infection; pregnancy; lactation.

ROUTE & DOSAGE

Plaque psoriasis
Adult: **Subcutaneous** Two injections of 75 mg (total 150 mg) at weeks 0, 4, and then every 12 weeks thereafter

ADMINISTRATION

Subcutaneous
- Administer the two consecutive injections subcutaneously at different sites such as thighs, abdomen, or back of upper arms. Do not inject into tissue that is tender, bruised, or hard, or affected by psoriasis. Self injection may occur after proper training.
- Store at 2° to 8° C (36° to 46° F) in the original carton; do not freeze. Protect from light. Do not shake.

ADVERSE EFFECTS Respiratory: Upper respiratory infection. **CNS:** Headache, fatigue. **Other:** Antibody development, infection.

INTERACTIONS Drug: Avoid the use of live vaccines in patients being treated with risankizumab. Do not use with IMMUNOSUPPRESANTS.

PHARMACOKINETICS Absorption: 89% bioavailability. **Peak:** 3–14 days. **Distribution:** 11.2 L. **Metabolism:** Similar to endogenous IgG; degraded into small peptides and amino acids through catabolic pathways. **Half-Life:** 28 days.

NURSING IMPLICATIONS

Assessment & Drug Effects
- Perform baseline and ongoing screening for tuberculosis or signs and symptoms of infection. Do not initiate therapy if active infection present.
- Monitor lab tests: Tuberculin skin testing.

Patient & Family Education
- Notify your health care provider if you currently have or experience any symptoms of infection including tuberculosis or if you have had a recent live vaccine.
- Talk with your provider before getting any vaccines or if you are pregnant, planning on getting pregnant, or are breastfeeding.
- Notify your doctor or get medical help right away if you have any of the following signs or symptoms of allergic reaction such as rash, hives, itching; red, swollen, blistered, or peeling skin with or without fever; wheezing; tightness in the chest or throat; trouble breathing, swallowing, or talking; unusual hoarseness; or swelling

R

---

of the mouth, face, lips, tongue, or throat; or any dizziness or passing out.

RISEDRONATE SODIUM

(ri-se-dron'ate)

Actonel, Atelvia

Classification: BISPHOSPHONATE; BONE METABOLISM REGULATOR
Therapeutic: BONE RESORPTION INHIBITOR; OSTEOPOROSIS TREATMENT
Prototype: Etidronate disodium

AVAILABILITY Tablet; delayed release tablet

ACTION & *THERAPEUTIC EFFECT*
Inhibits bone resorption via action on osteoclasts or osteoclast precursors; decreases the rate of bone resorption leading to an indirect increase in bone mineral density. *Effectiveness indicated by decreased bone and joint pain and improved bone density.*

USES Paget's disease, prevention and treatment of osteoporosis.

UNLABELED USES Osteolytic metastases.

CONTRAINDICATIONS Hypersensitivity to risedronate or other bisphosphonates; hypocalcemia, vitamin D deficiency; severe renal impairment (CrCl less than 30 mL/min); esophageal stricture; lactation.

CAUTIOUS USE Renal impairment; CHF; hyperphosphatemia or vitamin D deficiency; hepatic disease; UGI disease; fever related to infection or other causes; pregnancy (category C). Safety and efficacy in children younger than 18 y not established.

ROUTE & DOSAGE

Paget's Disease
Adult: **PO** 30 mg daily for 2 mo, may repeat after 2 mo rest if necessary

Prevention and Treatment of Osteoporosis (post menopausal)
Adult (female): **PO** 5 mg daily OR 35 mg once weekly OR 150 mg once monthly; **Delayed release** 35 mg weekly
Adult (male): **PO** 35 mg weekly
Adult (with chronic systemic glucocorticoid): **PO** 5 mg daily

Osteoporosis (glucocorticoid-induced) Prevention
Adult: **PO** 5 mg daily

Renal Impairment Dosage Adjustment
CrCl less than 30 mL/min: Use not recommended

ADMINISTRATION
Oral
- Give on an empty stomach (at least 30 min before first food or drink of the day) with at least 6–8 oz plain water. Ensure that tablet is swallowed whole. It should not be crushed or chewed.
- Note: Patient should be upright. Maintain upright position and empty stomach for at least 30 min after administration.
- Space calcium supplements and antacids as far as possible from risedronate.
- Store at 15°–30° C (59°–86° F) in a tightly closed container and protect from light.

Common adverse effects in *italic;* life-threatening effects <u>underlined</u>; generic names in **bold**; classifications in SMALL CAPS; ♣ Canadian drug name; ☺ Prototype drug; ⚠ Alert

ADVERSE EFFECTS CV: Hypertension. **CNS:** Headache. **Skin:** Skin rash. **GI:** Gastrointestinal perforation, ulcers, or bleeding, diarrhea, nausea, abdominal pain. **GU:** Urinary tract infection.

DIAGNOSTIC TEST INTERFERENCE
May interfere with the use of *bone-imaging agents*.

INTERACTIONS Drug: Calcium, ANTACIDS significantly decrease absorption, use with NONSTEROIDAL ANTI-INFLAMMATORIES may increase risk of gastric ulcer. Do not use with ANTIHISTAMINES. Use caution with PPIs due to changes in bioavailability. **Food:** Any food will decrease bioavailability. Take at least 30 min before first food or drink of the day.

PHARMACOKINETICS Absorption: Minimally absorbed from GI tract, bioavailability 0.63%. **Peak:** 1 h. **Distribution:** Approximately 60% of dose is distributed to bone. **Metabolism:** Not metabolized. **Elimination:** In urine; unabsorbed drug excreted in feces. **Half-Life:** 220 h.

NURSING IMPLICATIONS

Assessment & Drug Effects
- Monitor carefully for and immediately report S&S of GI bleeding and hypocalcemia.
- Monitor lab tests: Baseline and periodic electrolytes including serum calcium, phosphorus, and alkaline phosphatase.

Patient & Family Education
- Administration guidelines regarding upright position, empty stomach, and spacing relative to calcium supplements and antacids **must be** strictly followed.
- Report any of the following to prescriber: Eye irritation, significant GI upset, or flu-like symptoms.

- Preventive dental care important for at-risk populations.

RISPERIDONE
(ris-per'i-done)
Risperdal, Risperdal M-TAB, Risperdal Consta
Classification: ATYPICAL ANTIPSYCHOTIC
Therapeutic: ANTIPSYCHOTIC
Prototype: Clozapine

AVAILABILITY Tablet; oral disintegrating tablet; oral solution; solution for injection; suspension for injection

ACTION & *THERAPEUTIC EFFECT*
Interferes with binding of dopamine to D_2-interlimbic region of the brain, serotonin (5-HT$_2$) receptors, and alpha-adrenergic receptors in the occipital cortex. It has low to moderate affinity for the other serotonin (5-HT) receptors. *Effective in controlling symptoms of schizophrenia as well as other psychotic symptoms.*

USES Treatment of schizophrenia; treatment of bipolar disorder; irritability associated with autism.

UNLABELED USES Insomnia in elderly patient, obsessive-compulsive disorder, stuttering, tardive dyskinesia, Tourette syndrome.

CONTRAINDICATIONS Hypersensitivity to risperidone; older adults with dementia-related psychosis; drug induced narcoleptic malignant syndrome (NMS); severe CNS depression, head trauma; lactation. **Risperdal Consta:** Lactation during use and for 12 wk after last injection.

R

CAUTIOUS USE Arrhythmias, hypotension, breast cancer, blood dyscrasia, cardiac disorders, cerebrovascular disease, hypotension, dehydration, DM; diabetic ketoacidosis, hyperglycemia, MI, obesity, orthostatic hypotension, mild or moderate CNS depression; GI obstruction, dysphagia; electrolyte imbalance, drug and alcohol abuse; heart failure, MI, ischemia; arrhythmias; renal or hepatic impairment; seizure disorder, suicidal tendencies; stroke, Parkinson's disease; Alzheimer dementia; risks for aspiration pneumonia; PKU; older adults; pregnancy (may cause hyperprolactemia which may cause decrease in reproductive function in females). Safe use in children younger than 13 y for schizophrenia; children younger than 10 y for bipolar disease and children younger than 5 y for autism not established.

ROUTE & DOSAGE

Schizophrenia

Adult: **PO** 1–2 mg/day in 1 or 2 doses, may titrate in 24 hour increments (max: 16 mg/day); *Adult/Geriatric:* **IM** 25 mg once q2wk (max: 50 mg) **Subcutaneous:** 90–120 mg monthly *Geriatric:* **PO** Start 0.5 mg bid and increase by 0.5 mg bid daily to an initial target of 1.5 mg bid (max: 4 mg/day)

Bipolar Disorder

Adult: **PO** 1–3 mg once daily in divided doses for up to 3 wk (max: 6 mg/day); **IM** Initiate Risperdal Consta with 25 mg every 2 wk; may increase to 37.5–50 mg every 2 wk *Geriatric:* **PO** Start with 0.5 mg bid and increase by 0.5 mg bid daily to an initial target of 1.5 mg bid (max: 6 mg/day). May convert to once daily dosing after stabilized.
Adolescent (10 y or older): **PO** 0.5 mg once daily titrate to recommended target dose range of 1–2.5 mg/day

Irritability Associated with Autism

Adolescent/Child (5 y or older, weight 20 kg or greater): **PO** 0.5 mg daily; after 4 days, increase to 1 mg daily; can increase by 0.5 mg q2wk; *Child 5 y or older; weight 15–20 kg:* 0.25 mg daily; after 4 days, increase to 0.5 mg daily; can increase by 0.25 mg q2wk

Renal Impairment Doasage Adjustment

CrCl less than 30 mL/min: Start with 0.5 mg bid, increase by 0.5 mg bid daily to an initial target of 1.5 mg bid, may increase by 0.5 mg bid at weekly intervals (max: 6 mg/day) **IM** Initial with oral dosing; then begin 25 mg IM q2weeks.

Hepatic Impairment Dosage Adjustment

Child Pugh Class C **PO** start with dose of 0.5 mg bid; **IM** Initial with oral dosing; then begin 25 mg IM q2weeks.

Enzyme Inducer or CYP2D6 Inhibitor Dosage Adjustment

See package insert

ADMINISTRATION

Oral

- The oral solution may be mixed with water, orange juice, low-fat

Common adverse effects in *italic;* life-threatening effects <u>underlined;</u> generic names in **bold;** classifications in SMALL CAPS; ♣ Canadian drug name; ○ Prototype drug; ⚠ Alert

milk, or coffee. It is not compatible with cola or tea.

- Orally disintegrating tablets should not be removed from the blister until immediately before administration. Tablets disintegrate immediately and may be swallowed with/without liquid.
- Store at 15°–30° C (59°–86° F).

Subcutaneous

- Administer SC into the abdomen only. Rotate injection sites. Do not rub injection site. Be aware of placement of any belts or clothing waistbands.

Intramuscular

- Reconstitute using only in the diluent supplied in the dose pack. Shake vigorously for at least 10 sec to produce a uniform, thick, milky suspension. If 2 min or more pass before injection, shake vial again.
- Give deep IM into the upper-outer quadrant of the gluteal muscle with the supplied needle; do not substitute. Follow the manufacturer's instructions for use of the SmartSite Needle-Free Vial Access Device and Needle-Pro device.
- Store unopened vials at 2°–8° C (36°–46° F). Protect from light.

ADVERSE EFFECTS

CV: Prolonged QTc interval, tachycardia, orthostatic hypotension with initial doses. **Respiratory:** Rhinitis, *cough,* dyspnea, nasopharyngitis. **CNS:** *Sedation, drowsiness, headache,* transient blurred vision, *insomnia,* disinhibition, *agitation,* anxiety, increased dream activity, *dizziness,* catatonia, *extrapyramidal symptoms* (akathisia, dystonia, parkinsonism), especially with doses greater than 10 mg/day, neuroleptic malignant syndrome (rare), increased risk of stroke in elderly.

Endocrine: Galactorrhea; Hyperglycemia, diabetes mellitus, *hyperprolactinemia, weight gain,* decrease in HDL cholesterol, increased serum cholesterol. **Skin:** Photosensitivity, sweating, skin rash. **GI:** *Dry mouth,* dyspepsia, nausea, *vomiting, diarrhea, constipation,* elevated liver function tests (AST, ALT). **GU:** Urinary retention, menorrhagia, incontinence, decreased sexual desire, erectile dysfunction, sexual dysfunction male and female. **Hematologic:** Anemia, neutropenia. **Musculoskeletal:** Tremor.

INTERACTIONS

Drug: Risperidone may enhance the effects of certain ANTIHYPERTENSIVE AGENTS. May antagonize the antiparkinson effects of **bromocriptine, cabergoline, levodopa, pergolide, pramipexole, ropinirole, carbamazepine, phenytoin, phenobarbital, rifampin** may decrease risperidone levels. Monitor closely when used with CYP3A4 substrates. CYP2D6 inhibitors may increase the concentration of risperidone **Clozapine** may increase risperidone levels. Do not use with nasal **azelastine, metoclopramide, orphenadrine, sulpiride, thalidomide, tiotropium.** Do not use with agents that prolong the QT interval (e.g., **dofetilide, dronedarone, procaine, ziprasidone**).

PHARMACOKINETICS

Absorption: Rapidly; not affected by food. **Onset:** Therapeutic effect 1–2 wk. **Peak:** 1–2 h. **Distribution:** 0.7 L/kg; in animal studies, risperidone has been found in breast milk. **Metabolism:** Primarily in liver [CYP2D6, CYP3A4, P-glycoprotein (P-gp)]. **Elimination:** 70% in urine; 14% in feces. **Half-Life:** 20 h for slow metabolizers, 30 h for fast metabolizers.

R

NURSING IMPLICATIONS

Black Box Warning

Risperidone has been associated with increased mortality in older adults with dementia-related psychosis.

Assessment & Drug Effects

- Monitor diabetics for loss of glycemic control.
- Reassess patients periodically and maintain on the lowest effective drug dose.
- Monitor closely neurologic status of older adults.
- Monitor cardiovascular status closely; assess for orthostatic hypotension, especially during initial dosage titration.
- Monitor closely those at risk for seizures.
- Assess degree of cognitive and motor impairment and assess for environmental hazards.
- Monitor lab tests: Periodic CBC, electrolytes, renal function tests, LFTs, HbA1c, fasting lipid panel.

Patient & Family Education

- Carefully monitor blood glucose levels if diabetic.
- Do not engage in potentially hazardous activities until the response to drug is known.
- Be aware of the risk of orthostatic hypotension.
- Avoid alcohol while taking this drug.

RITONAVIR
(ri-ton′a-vir)
Norvir
Classification: PROTEASE INHIBITOR
Therapeutic: PROTEASE INHIBITOR
Prototype: Saquinavir

AVAILABILITY Tablet; capsule; oral solution; powder packets

ACTION & *THERAPEUTIC EFFECT*
HIV protease inhibitor that renders the enzyme incapable of processing the polyprotein precursor necessary for the production of mature HIV-1 particles. *Protease inhibitor of both HIV-1 and HIV-2 resulting in the formation of noninfectious viral particles.*

USES Alone or in combination with other agents for treatment of HIV infection. Often used to increase the effect of other antiretrovirals.

CONTRAINDICATIONS Hypersensitivity to ritonavir; severe hepatic impairment; concurrent use of saquinavir and ritonavir in patients with conditions that affect cardiac electrical activity; coadministration with sedative hypnotics, alpha 1 adrenoreceptor antagonists, anitanginal, antiarrhythmics, anti fungals, anti gout medications, GI motility agents, St. John's wort, HMG-CoA reductase inhibitors, phosphodiesterase type-5 inhibitor; ergot alkaloids; antimicrobial resistance to protease inhibitors; pancreatitis; toxic epidermal necrolysis, lactation for HIV patients.

CAUTIOUS USE Mild to moderate hepatic diseases, liver enzyme abnormalities, or hepatitis, jaundice; cardiac myopathy, ischemic heart disease or structural heart disease; diabetes mellitus, diabetic ketoacidosis, hyperlipidemia, hypertriglyceridemia; pancreatitis; hemophilia A or B, renal insufficiency; Graves' disease; Guillain-Barre syndrome; pregnancy—fetal risk cannot be ruled out; lactation—infant risk cannot be ruled out.

Common adverse effects in *italic*; life-threatening effects underlined; generic names in **bold**; classifications in SMALL CAPS; ◆ Canadian drug name; ☺ Prototype drug; ⚠ Alert

Safe use in children younger than 1 mo not established.

ROUTE & DOSAGE

HIV

Adult: **PO** 600 mg bid
Child (1 mo or older): **PO** start with 250 mg/m² bid, increase by 50 mg/m² q2–3days up to 350–400 mg/m² bid (max: 600 mg bid)

ADMINISTRATION

Oral

- Give preferably with food; oral solution may be mixed with chocolate milk or nutritional therapy liquids within 1 h of dosing to improve taste.
- Capsules should be stored refrigerated at 2°–8° C (36°–46° F). Protect from light in tightly closed container. May be left at room temperature: Less than 25° C (77° F) if used within 30 days.
- Tablets should be stored at less than 30° C (86° F). May store at greater than 50° C (122° F) for up to 7 days.
- Store oral powder at less than 30° C (86° F).
- Store solution at 20°–25° C (68°–77° F).

ADVERSE EFFECTS CV: Edema, peripheral edema. **Respiratory:** Cough, throat pain. **CNS:** *Weakness, fatigue,* dizziness, *altered sensation like "pins and needles",* peripheral neuropathy, headache. **HEENT:** Blurred vision. **Endocrine:** *Hypercholesterolemia,* increased triglycerides. **Skin:** Flushing, pruritus, *rash.* **Hepatic:** Increased gammaglutamyl transferase, increased serum AST, increased serum ALT, hepatitis. **GI:** *Abdominal pain, diarrhea, nausea, vomiting,* altered taste, dyspepsia. **Musculoskeletal:** Joint pain, muscle pain, back pain. **Other:** Fever.

INTERACTIONS Drug: Carbamazepine, dexamethasone, phenobarbital, phenytoin, rifabutin, rifampin, smoking can decrease ritonavir levels. **Ritonavir** may increase serum levels and toxicity of **clarithromycin,** especially in patients with renal insufficiency (reduce **clarithromycin** dose in patients with CrCl less than 60 mL/min); **alfuzosin, amiodarone, bepridil, bupropion, clozapine, desipramine; dihydroergotamine, flecainide, fluticasone, meperidine, pimozide, piroxicam, propoxyphene, quinidine, rifabutin, saquinavir, trazodone.** Ritonavir decreases levels of ORAL CONTRACEPTIVES, **theophylline;** may increase **ergotamine** toxicity with **dihydroergotamine, ergotamine;** may increase systemic steroid exposure with **fluticasone.** Liquid formulation may cause disulfiram-like reaction with **alcohol** or **metronidazole.** Can not be used with **lovastatin.** Concurrent use of **dasatinib** requires dose reduction. Use with **darunavir** may increase risk of hepatoxicity. Use with lowest possible dose of **atorvastatin.** See the complete prescribing information for a comprehensive table of potential, but not studied, drug interactions. **Herbal: St. John's wort, garlic, red yeast rice,** may decrease antiretroviral activity.

PHARMACOKINETICS Absorption: Rapidly from GI tract. **Peak:** 2–4 h. **Distribution:** 98–99% protein bound. **Metabolism:** In liver (CYP3A4 and 2D6). **Elimination:** Primarily in feces (greater than 80%).

R

NURSING IMPLICATIONS

Black Box Warning

Coadministration of ritonavir with sedative hypnotics, antiarrhythmics, or ergot alkaloids has been associated with potentially serious and/or life-threatening adverse reactions.

Assessment & Drug Effects

- Withhold drug and notify prescriber in the presence of abnormal liver function.
- Assess for S&S of GI distress, peripheral neuropathy, and other potential adverse effects.
- Monitor lab tests: Periodic LFTs, uric acid, lipid profile, CPK, blood glucose, urinalysis, hepatitis C antibody levels, electrolytes, CBC with differential, and HbA1C.

Patient & Family Education

- Learn potential adverse reactions and drug interactions; report to prescriber use of any OTC or prescription drugs.
- Take this drug exactly as prescribed. Do not skip doses. Take at same time each day.
- Do not take ritonavir with any of the following drugs as fatal reactions may occur: **Amiodarone, astemizole, alfuzosin, bepridil, dihydroergotamine, ergotamine, flecainide, methylergonovine, midazolam, pimozide, propafenone, quinidine, triazolam, voriconazole.**

RITUXIMAB

(ri-tux'i-mab)

Rituxan

Classification: DISEASE-MODIFYING- ANTIRHEUMATIC DRUG (DMARD)

Therapeutic: ANTINEOPLASTIC; ANTIRHEUMATIC; DMARD

AVAILABILITY Solution for injection

ACTION & *THERAPEUTIC EFFECT*

A monoclonal antibody against the protein CD20, which is primarily found on the surface of immune system B cells. It destroys B cells by attaching to CD20 and is therefore used to treat diseases which are characterized by excessive numbers of B cells, overactive B cells, or dysfunctional B cells. CD20 antigen is expressed in more than 90% of B-cell non-Hodgkin lymphomas. B cells are also believed to play a role in the pathogenesis of RA and associated chronic synovitis as they may be acting at multiple sites in the autoimmune/inflammatory process. *Rituximab effectiveness in both rheumatoid arthritis and non-Hodgkin's lymphoma is measured by induced depletion of peripheral B-lymphocytes.*

USES Rheumatoid arthritis, CLL, non-Hodgkin lymphoma, granulomatosis, microscopic polyangiitis.

UNLABELED USES Acute lymphocytic leukemia, idiopathic thrombocytopenic purpura, multiple sclerosis, hemolytic anemia, mantle cell lymphoma.

CONTRAINDICATIONS Hypersensitivity to murine proteins, rituximab, or abciximab; serious infection; life-threatening cardiac arrhythmias; severe infusion reactions to rituximab; drug-induced activation of hepatitis B virus (HBV); drug-induced progressive multifocal leukoencephalopathy (PML); tumor lysis syndrome; severe mucocutaneous reaction to rituximab; oliguria, rising serum creatinine; live vaccines; lactation (infant risk cannot be ruled out).

CAUTIOUS USE Prior exposure to murine-based monoclonal antibodies; history of allergies; asthma and other pulmonary disease (increased risk of bronchospasm); respiratory insufficiency; CAD; thrombocytopenia; history of cardiac arrhythmias; hypertension, renal impairment; older adults; pregnancy (fetal risk cannot be ruled out). Safety and efficacy in children not established.

ROUTE & DOSAGE

Non-Hodgkin Lymphoma

Adult: **IV** Varies based on disease-specific parameters, consult package insert

Rheumatoid Arthritis

Adult: **IV** 1000 mg on days 1 and 15 (with methotrexate); repeat every 24 wk

CLL

Adult: **IV** 375 mg/m^2 on day 1 of cycle 1 then 500 mg/m^2 (in combination with fludarabine/cyclophosphamide) on day 1 of cycles 2–6.

Granulomatosis/Microscopic Polyangiitis (Induction Therapy)

Adult: **IV** 375 mg/m^2 weekly × 4 wk

ADMINISTRATION

Intravenous ONLY

Premedicate before each infusion with acetaminophen and an antihistamine.

PREPARE: **IV Infusion:** Dilute ordered dose to 1–4 mg/mL by adding to an infusion bag of NS or D5W. ▪ Examples: 500 mg in 400 mL yields 1 mg/mL; 500 mg in 75 mL yields 4 mg/mL. ▪ Gently invert bag to mix. Discard unused portion left in vial.

ADMINISTER: **IV Infusion:** Infuse first dose at a rate of 50 mg/h; may increase rate at 50 mg/h increments q30min to maximum rate of 400 mg/h. ▪ For subsequent doses, infuse at a rate of 100 mg/h and increase by 100 mg/h increments q30min up to maximum rate of 400 mg/h. ▪ Slow or stop infusion if S&S of hypersensitivity appear (see Appendix F).

INCOMPATIBILITES: **Y-site: aldesleukin, amphotericin B colloidal, ciprofloxacin, cyclosporine, daunorubicin, doxorubicin, furosemide, levofloxacin, minocycline, ofloxacin, ondansetron, quinupristin/dalfopristin, sodium bicarbonate, topotecan, vancomycin.**

▪ Store unopened vials at 2°–8° C (36°–46° F) and protect from light. Solutions for infusion can be kept at room temperature for 24 h and an additional 24 h if refrigerated.

ADVERSE EFFECTS
CV: Hypotension, hypertension, tachycardia, peripheral edema, *hypertension*. **Respiratory:** Bronchospasm, dyspnea, rhinitis, epistaxis, cough. **CNS:** Headache, dizziness, depression, insomnia. **Skin:** Pruritus, rash, urticaria. **GI:** *Nausea,* diarrhea, vomiting, throat irritation, anorexia, abdominal pain, hepatitis B reactivation with fulminant hepatitis, hepatic failure, and death. **Musculoskeletal:** Arthralgia, asthenia. **Hematologic:** Leukopenia, thrombocytopenia, anemia, neutropenia. **Infusion-related reactions:** *Fever, chills, rigors, pruritus, urticaria, pain, flushing,* chest pain, hypotension, hypertension, dyspnea; fatal infusion-related reactions have

been reported. **Other:** Angioedema, *fatigue,* night sweats, *fever, chills,* myalgia.

INTERACTIONS Drug: Do not use with MONOCLONAL ANTIBODIES, DMARDS or TNF INHIBITORS. Avoid LIVE VACCINES. **Herbal:** Do not use with echinacea due to effect on immune system.

PHARMACOKINETICS Duration: 6–12 mo. **Half-Life:** 60–174 h (increases with multiple infusions).

NURSING IMPLICATIONS

Black Box Warning

Rituximab has been associated with severe and sometimes fatal infusion reactions, severe mucocutaneous reactions, hepatitis B reactivation, and progressive multifocal leukoencephalopathy.

Assessment & Drug Effects
- Monitor carefully BP and ECG status during infusion and immediately report S&S of hypersensitivity (e.g., fever, chills, urticaria, pruritus, hypotension, bronchospasms; see Appendix F for others).
- Monitor for and report promptly S&S of progressive multifocal leukoencephalopathy (PML) (e.g., hemiparesis, visual field deficits, cognitive impairment, aphasia, ataxia, and/or cranial nerve deficits).
- Monitor lab tests: Baseline and periodic CBC with differential and platelet count, peripheral CD20+ B lymphocytes, LFTs, renal function tests, and serum uric acid.

Patient & Family Education
- Do not take antihypertensive medication within 12 h of rituximab infusions.

- Note: Use effective contraception during and for up to 12 mo following rituximab therapy.
- Report any of the following experienced during infusion: Itching, difficulty breathing, tightness in throat, dizziness, headache, or nausea.

RIVAROXABAN ●

(riv'a-rox'a-ban)
Xarelto
Classification: ANTICOAGULANT; ANTITHROMBOTIC; SELECTIVE FACTOR XA INHIBITOR
Therapeutic: ANTICOAGULANT; ANTITHROMBOTIC

AVAILABILITY Tablet

ACTION & *THERAPEUTIC EFFECT*
A factor Xa inhibitor that selectively blocks the active site of factor Xa thus blocking activation of factor X to factor Xa (FXa) via the intrinsic and extrinsic pathways. *Inhibits the coagulation cascade thus preventing thrombosis formation.*

USES Prevention or treatment of deep venous thrombosis (DVT); nonvalvular atrial fibrillation; treatment or prevention of venous thromboembolism; coronary artery disease (stable).

UNLABELED USE: heparin-induced thrombocytopenia, superficial vein thrombosis.

CONTRAINDICATIONS Hypersensitivity to rivaroxaban; major active bleeding; severe renal impairment (CrCl less than 30 mL/min); elderly with CrCl less than 50 mL/min. moderate-to-severe hepatic impairment (Child-Pugh class B or C); patients with triple-positive antiphospholipid syndrome (APS); patients with prosthetic heart valves or who have had transcatheter aortic valve replacement; pregnancy—fetal risk cannot be ruled out; lactation—infant risk cannot be ruled out.

CAUTIOUS USE Spinal/epidural anesthesia or spinal puncture; concurrent platelet aggregation inhibitors, other antithrombotic agents, fibrinolytic therapy, thienopyridines and chronic use of NSAIDs; mild hepatic impairment (Child-Pugh class A); moderate renal impairment (CrCl 49–30 mL/min); elderly; surgical patientsSafety and efficacy in children younger than 18 y not established.

ROUTE & DOSAGE

Nonvalvular Atrial Fibrillation
Adult: **PO** 20 mg daily

Coronary Artery Disease
Adult: **PO** 2.5 mg daily with low dose aspirin and clopidogrel

Venous Thromboembolism Prophylaxis
Adult: **PO** 10 mg once daily × 31–39 days

Venous Thromboembolism Treatment
Adult: **PO** 15 mg bid × 21 days followed by 20 mg daily

Indefinite Anticoagulation
Adult: **PO** 10 mg qd

Hepatic Impairment Dosage Adjustment
Child-Pugh class B or C and hepatic disease with coagulopathy: Avoid use

Renal Impairment Dosage Adjustment
Varies based on indication; see package insert for details

ADMINISTRATION
Oral
- 2.5 mg and 10 mg tablets may be given without regard to food; 15 and 20 mg tablets should be taken with food at approximately the same time each day; food should immediately follow swallowing of medication.
- If unable to swallow whole tablets, may crush any strength table and mix with applesauce immediately prior to use; crushed tablets are stable in applesauce for up to 4 hours.
- *Following spinal/epidural anesthesia or spinal puncture:* Wait at least 18 h after the last dose of rivaroxaban to remove an epidural catheter. Do not give the next rivaroxaban dose earlier than 6 h after the removal of catheter. If traumatic puncture occurs, wait 24 h before giving rivaroxaban.
- Store at controlled room temperature at 25 degrees C (77 degrees F); with excursions permitted between 15°–30° C (59°–86° F).

ADVERSE EFFECTS (≥5%) Hematologic: *Bleeding complications, hemorrhage.*

DIAGNOSTIC TEST INTERFERENCE
Use prolongs aPTT, **HepTest** and Russell viper venom time.

INTERACTIONS Drug: Concomitant use with drugs that are combined P-gp and CYP3A4 inhibitors (**ketoconazole, ritonavir, clarithromycin, erythromycin, itraconazole, lopinavir, indinavir, conivaptan, azithromycin,**

R

diltiazem, verapamil, quinidine, ranolazine, dronedarone, amiodarone, felodipine) may increase rivaroxaban exposure and increase bleeding risk. Concomitant use with drugs that are combined P-gp and CYP3A4 inducers (e.g., rifampin, carbamazepine, phenytoin) may decrease rivaroxaban levels. Concomitant use with ANTICOAGULANTS, ANTIPLATELTS, NSAIDS increase bleeding time and tendencies. Estrogens or PROGESTINS may decrease anticoagulant effects. **Herbal: St. John's wort** may decrease rivaroxaban levels.

PHARMACOKINETICS **Absorption:** 80–100% bioavailable. **Peak:** 2–4 h. **Distribution:** 92–95% plasma protein bound. **Metabolism:** Hepatic via CYP3A4/5 and CYP2J2. **Elimination:** Renal (66%) and fecal (28%). **Half-Life:** 5–9 h.

NURSING IMPLICATIONS

Black Box Warning

Rivaroxaban has been associated with epidural or spinal hematomas in those receiving neuraxial anesthesia or undergoing spinal puncture which may result in long-term or permanent paralysis.

Assessment & Drug Effects

- Monitor vital signs closely and report immediately S&S of bleeding and internal hemorrhage (e.g., intracranial and epidural hematoma, retinal hemorrhage, GI bleeding).
- Monitor frequently and report immediately S&S of neurologic impairment such as tingling, numbness (especially in the lower limbs), and muscular weakness.
- Report immediately neurologic impairment or an unexplained drop in BP or falling Hgb & Hct values.

- Monitor lab tests: Baseline renal and hepatic function tests; chromogenic anti-FXa assay; peak drug levels; CBC at initiation and at regular intervals; baseline and periodic Hgb & Hct.

Patient & Family Education

- Report promptly any of the following: Unusual bleeding or bruising; blood in urine or tarry stools; tingling or numbness (especially in the lower limbs); and muscular weakness.
- Notify prescriber immediately if you become pregnant or intend to become pregnant, or if you are breast-feeding or intend to breast-feed.
- Do not discontinue the drug without notifying the prescriber.
- Confer with prescriber before using a nonsteroidal anti-inflammatory drug (NSAID), aspirin, or herbal products as these may increase risk of bleeding.
- A missed dose should be taken as soon as possible on the same day. For the 15 mg twice daily schedule, 2 tablets can be taken together if necessary.

RIVASTIGMINE TARTRATE

(ri-vas'tig-meen)

Exelon

Classification: CHOLINESTERASE INHIBITOR; ANTIDEMENTIA
Therapeutic: ANTIALZHEIMER

AVAILABILITY Capsule; transdermal patch

ACTION & *THERAPEUTIC EFFECT*

Inhibits acetylcholinesterase G_1 form of this enzyme in the cerebral cortex and the hippocampus. The G_1 form of acetylcholinesterase is found in higher levels in the brains of patients with Alzheimer disease.

Inhibits acetylcholinesterase more specifically in the brain (hippocampus and cortex) than in the heart or skeletal muscle in Alzheimer disease.

USES Alzheimer dementia, Parkinson disease-related dementia.

CONTRAINDICATIONS Hypersensitivity to rivastigmine or carbamate derivatives; safety and efficacy has not been established in children; pregnancy—fetal risk cannot be ruled; lactation—infant risk cannot be ruled out.

CAUTIOUS USE History of toxicity to cholinesterase inhibitors; DM; sick sinus syndrome, bradycardia, or other supraventricular cardiac conduction conditions; asthma or obstructive pulmonary disease; GI disorders including intestinal obstruction; history of or at risk for PUD or GI bleeding; urogenital tract obstruction, BPH; history of seizures; smokers; hepatic or renal impairment; low body weight; elderly.

ROUTE & DOSAGE

Alzheimer/Parkinson Related Dementia

Adult/Geriatric: **PO** Start with 1.5 mg bid may increase by 1.5 mg/dose q2wk if tolerated, (max recommended: 6 mg bid)

Transdermal

Adult: Apply 4.6 mg patch daily, after 4 wk, can increase to 9.5 mg patch if tolerated, then 13.3 mg patch (max dose)

Hepatic Impairment Dosage Adjustment

Child-Pugh Class A and B: PO dose of 1.5 mg daily with slow titration up; Transdermal dose max 4.6 mg/24 hours

ADMINISTRATION

Oral

- Give capsules with food.
- For solution, use dosing syringe supplied. May swallow directly from the syringe or mix with water, cold fruit juice, or soda (do not mix with any other liquids). Stir well before drinking.
- Withhold drug and notify prescriber if significant anorexia, nausea, or vomiting occur.
- Store capsules below 25° C (77° F). Store solution in upright position and protect from freezing.

Transdermal

- Apply patch at same time each day to dry, hairless, healthy skin on the back, upper arm, or chest. Preferred site of application is the upper or lower back.
- Remove old patch before applying the new one.
- Rotate application sites and do not reapply to same site for at least 14 days.
- Do not tape or otherwise cover the patch.
- If a patch falls off, do not reapply. Replace with a new patch and remove it following the original schedule for replacement.
- Bathing and hot weather are acceptable when using the patch, but avoid long exposure to external heat sources.
- Store patch at controlled room temperature, 25 degrees C (77 degrees F); with excursions permitted to 15°–30° C (59°–86° F) in sealed pouch until ready to use.

ADVERSE EFFECTS (≥5%) CNS:

Dizziness, asthenia, headache, tremor. **Endocrine:** *Weight loss.*

R

Common adverse effects in *italic;* life-threatening effects <u>underlined</u>; generic names in **bold;** classifications in SMALL CAPS; ✦ Canadian drug name; ◎ Prototype drug; ⚠ Alert

GI: *Nausea, vomiting, anorexia, dyspepsia, diarrhea, abdominal pain.*

INTERACTIONS Drug: May exaggerate muscle relations with **succinylcholine** and other NEUROMUSCULAR BLOCKING AGENTS, may attenuate effects of ANTICHOLINERGIC AGENTS. Do not use with BETA BLOCKING AGENTS due to increased bradycardia; use caution with other medications (**bromopride, ceritinib**) that cause bradycardia

PHARMACOKINETICS Absorption: Well absorbed. **Peak:** 1 h. **Duration:** 10 h. **Distribution:** Crosses blood–brain barrier with CSF peak concentrations in 1.4–2.6 h. **Metabolism:** By cholinesterase-mediated hydrolysis. **Elimination:** In urine. **Half-Life:** 1.5 h.

NURSING IMPLICATIONS

Assessment & Drug Effects

- Monitor cognitive function and ability to perform ADLs prior to driving and operating machinery.
- Monitor for and report S&S of GI distress or GI bleeding: Anorexia, weight loss, nausea, and vomiting.
- Monitor ambulation as dizziness is a common adverse effect.
- Monitor diabetics for loss of glycemic control.

Patient & Family Education

- Review instruction sheet provided with liquid form of the drug.
- Caution driving and operating machinery until effects of the drug are known.
- Monitor weight at least weekly.
- Report any of the following to the prescriber: Loss of appetite, weight loss, significant nausea and/or vomiting.

- Supervise activity since there is a high potential for dizziness.
- Contact healthcare professional if dose is missed for several days in a row; the drug may need to be restarted at a lower dose.

RIZATRIPTAN BENZOATE

(ri-za-trip'tan ben'zo-ate)
Maxalt, Maxalt-MLT
Classification: 5-HT$_1$ RECEPTOR AGONIST (TRIPTANS)
Therapeutic: ANTIMIGRAINE
Prototype: Sumatriptan

AVAILABILITY Tablet; disintegrating tablets

ACTION & *THERAPEUTIC EFFECT*
Selective (5-HT$_{1B/1D}$) receptor agonist that reverses the vasodilation of cranial blood vessels associated with a migraine. *Activation of the 5-HT$_{1B/1D}$ receptors reduces the pain pathways associated with the migraine headache as well as reversing vasodilation of cranial blood vessels.*

USES Acute migraine headaches with or without aura.

CONTRAINDICATIONS Hypersensitivity to rizatriptan; CAD; Prinzmetal's angina (potential for vasospasm); ischemic heart disease; risk factors for CAD such as hypertension, hypercholesterolemia, obesity, diabetes, smoking, and strong family history; hemiplegia; concurrent administration with ergotamine drugs or sumatriptan; concurrent administration with MAOIS; or within 14 days of use; stroke or TIA or history basilar or hemiplegic migraine.

CAUTIOUS USE Hypersensitivity to sumatriptan; renal or hepatic impairment; hypertension; asthmatic patients; pregnancy (category C); lactation (infant risk cannot be ruled out). Safety and efficacy in children younger than 18 y not established.

ROUTE & DOSAGE

Acute Migraine

Adult/Adolescent/Child (older than 6 y and weight greater than 40 kg): **PO** 5–10 mg, may repeat in 2 h if necessary (max: 30 mg/24 h); 5 mg with concurrent propranolol (max: 15 mg/24 h)

ADMINISTRATION

Oral

- Give any time after symptoms of migraine appear. If symptoms return, a second tablet may be given but no sooner than 2 h after the first.
- Do not exceed 30 mg (three doses) in any 24 h period.
- Do not give within 24 h of an ergot-containing drug or another 5-HT$_1$ agonist.
- Store at 15°–30° C (59°–86° F) and protect from light and moisture.

ADVERSE EFFECTS CV: Chest pain. **CNS:** Dizziness, weakness, sleepy. **GI:** Nausea. **Other:** Fatigue.

INTERACTIONS Drug: Propranolol may increase concentrations of rizatriptan, use smaller rizatriptan doses; **dihydroergotamine, methysergide,** MAOIs, other 5-HT$_1$ AGONISTS may cause prolonged vasospastic reactions; SSRIs have rarely caused weakness, hyperreflexia, and incoordination; MAOIS should not be used with 5-HT$_1$ AGONISTS or **dapoxetine. Herbal: St. John's wort** may increase triptan toxicity.

PHARMACOKINETICS Absorption: 45% of oral dose reaches systemic circulation. **Peak:** 1–1.5 h for oral tabs; 1.6–2.5 h for orally disintegrating tablets. **Metabolism:** Via oxidative deamination by monoamine oxidase A. **Elimination:** Primarily in urine (82%). **Half-Life:** 2–3 h.

NURSING IMPLICATIONS

Assessment & Drug Effects

- Monitor cardiovascular status carefully following first dose in patients at risk for CAD (e.g., postmenopausal women, men older than 40 y, persons with known CAD risk factors) or coronary artery vasospasms.
- ECG is recommended following first administration of rizatriptan to someone with known CAD risk factors.
- Report immediately to prescriber: Chest pain or tightness in chest or throat that is severe or does not quickly resolve.
- Monitor periodically cardiovascular status with continued rizatriptan use.

Patient & Family Education

- Do not exceed 30 mg (three doses) in 24 h.
- Allow orally disintegrating tablets to dissolve on tongue; no liquid is needed.
- Contact prescriber immediately if any of the following develop following rizatriptan use: Symptoms of angina (e.g., severe and/or persistent pain or tightness in chest or throat), hypersensitivity (e.g., wheezing, facial swelling, skin rash, or hives), abdominal pain.
- Report any other adverse effects (e.g., tingling, flushing, dizziness) at next prescriber visit.

R

ROFLUMILAST

(ro-flu′mi-last)

Daliresp

Classification: RESPIRATORY AGENT; ANTI-INFLAMMATORY; PHOSPHODIESTERASE 4 (PDE4) INHIBITOR

Therapeutic: ANTI-INFLAMMATORY; PDE4 INHIBITOR

AVAILABILITY Tablet

ACTION & *THERAPEUTIC EFFECT*

Selectively inhibits phosphodiesterase 4 (PDE4), a major enzyme found in inflammatory and immune cells, thus indirectly suppressing the release of cytokines and other products of inflammation. *Has an anti-inflammatory effect in pulmonary diseases.*

USES Reduction of the prevalence of chronic obstructive pulmonary disease (COPD) exacerbations.

CONTRAINDICATIONS Moderate-to-severe liver impairment (Child-Pugh class B or C); suicidal ideation; lactation.

CAUTIOUS USE Mild hepatic impairment (Child-Pugh class A); history of psychiatric illness including anxiety, depression, or suicidal thoughts; clinically significant weight loss; pregnancy (category C). Safety and efficacy in children not established.

ROUTE & DOSAGE

Chronic Obstructive Pulmonary Disease
Adult: **PO** 500 mcg once daily

ADMINISTRATION

Oral
- May be given with or without food.
- Store at 15°–30° C (59°–86° F).

ADVERSE EFFECTS **Respiratory:** Rhinitis, sinusitis. **CNS:** Anxiety, depression, dizziness, headache, insomnia, tremor. **GI:** Abdominal pain, decreased appetite, *diarrhea*, dyspepsia, gastritis, nausea, vomiting, *weight loss*. **GU:** Urinary tract infection, acute renal failure. **Musculoskeletal:** Back pain, muscle spasms. **Other:** Influenza.

INTERACTIONS **Drug:** Coadministration with strong CYP3A4 or CYP3A4/CYP1A2 inhibitors (e.g., **cimetidine, ketoconazole, ritonavir, erythromycin, fluvoxamine**) may increase the levels of roflumilast. Coadministration with strong CYP3A4 inducers (i.e., **carbamazepine, phenobarbital, phenytoin,** RIFAMYCINS) may decrease the levels of roflumilast. Coadministration **gestodene** may increase the levels of roflumilast. **Food:** None listed. **Herbal: St. John's wort** may decrease the levels of roflumilast.

PHARMACOKINETICS **Absorption:** 80% Bioavailable. **Peak:** 1 h. **Distribution:** 99% plasma protein bound. **Metabolism:** In liver to active and inactive metabolites. **Elimination:** Primarily renal. **Half-Life:** 17 h (30 h for active metabolite).

NURSING IMPLICATIONS

Assessment & Drug Effects
- Monitor for and report promptly new onset or worsening insomnia, anxiety, depression, suicidal thoughts, or other significant mood changes.

- Monitor weight at regular intervals. Report significant weight loss to prescriber.

Patient & Family Education
- Roflumilast is not a bronchodilator and does not provide relief of acute bronchospasm.
- Report to prescriber any of the following: Disturbing mood changes such as anxiety or depression; difficulty sleeping; suicidal thoughts; persistent nausea and/or diarrhea.
- Monitor your weight and report unexplained weight loss.
- Do not self-treat depression with St. John's wort.

ROLAPITANT
(ro-la′pi-tant)
Varubi
Classification: CENTRALLY ACTING ANTIEMETIC; SUBSTANCE P/NEUROKININ 1 (NK1) ANTAGONIST
Therapeutic: ANTIEMETIC
Prototype Aprepitant

AVAILABILITY Tablets

ACTION & *THERAPEUTIC EFFECT*
Acts at neurokinin-1 (NK-1) receptors in vomiting centers within the CNS to block their activation by substance P which is released as an unwanted consequence of chemotherapy. *Prevents both acute and delayed chemotherapy-induced nausea and vomiting.*

USES Prevention of chemotherapy-induced nausea and vomiting.

CONTRAINDICATIONS Hypersensitivity to rolapitant; concurrent use of thioridazine or CYP2D6 substrates with a narrow therapeutic window; severe hepatic impairment (Child-Pugh class C); children

less than 2 y; safety and efficacy have not been established in pediatric patients; pregnancy – fetal risk cannot be ruled out; lactation—infant risk cannot be ruled out.

CAUTIOUS USE mild or moderate hepatic impairment (Child-Pugh class A or B; prolonged QT interval;

ROUTE & DOSAGE

Chemotherapy-Induced Nausea/ Vomiting Prophylaxis
Adult: **PO** 180 mg single dose 1–2 h prior to chemotherapy;

Hepatic Impairment Dosage Adjustment
Severe impairment (Child-Pugh class C): Avoid use

ADMINISTRATION
Oral
- May give without regard to meals 1–2 h prior to chemotherapy.
- Capsule should be swallowed whole.
- Store at controlled room temperature between 20 and 25 degrees C (68 and 77 degrees F), with excursions permitted between 15°–30° C (59°–86° F).

ADVERSE EFFECTS (≥5%) Respiratory: *Hiccoughs.* **CNS:** *Dizziness.* **GI:** *Anorexia.* **Hematologic:** Neutropenia.

INTERACTIONS Drug: There are extensive drug interactions, consult a drug interaction database for a complete list. Rolapitant may increase the levels of coadministered drugs that require CYP2D6 for metabolism (e.g., **dextromethorphan, pimozide, thioridazine**),

are BCRP substrates (e.g., **irinotecan, methotrexate, topotecan**). Strong CYP3A4 inducers (e.g., **rifampin**) reduce the levels of rolapitant. Inhibits P-glycoprotein/ABCB1 so may increase concentration of drugs metabolized by that route.

PHARMACOKINETICS Peak: 4 h. **Distribution:** Highly plasma protein bound (>99.8%). **Metabolism:** In liver; primarily by CYP3A4. **Elimination:** Fecal (73%) and renal (14%). **Half-Life:** Approx. 7 d.

NURSING IMPLICATIONS

Assessment & Drug Effects
- Monitor for degree of emetic control.
- Monitor for sensitivity and anaphylaxis.

Patient & Family Education
- Report to prescriber if nausea and vomiting are not well controlled.
- Review adverse effects with patient and/or caregiver.
- Do not take rolapitant if taking thioridazine as the combination can cause serious or life-threatening heart rhythm changes.
- Do not take rolapitant more than once every 14 days.
- Inform prescriber when starting or stopping any concomitant medications.

ROMIDEPSIN
(rom-i-dep'sin)
Istodax
Classification: ANTINEOPLASTIC; HISTONE DEACETYLASE (HDAC) INHIBITOR
Therapeutic: ANTINEOPLASTIC

AVAILABILITY Powder for reconstitution for injection

ACTION & *THERAPEUTIC EFFECT*
Inhibits histone deacetylase, an enzyme required for completion of the cell cycle in certain cancers, thus inducing cell cycle arrest and apoptosis in these cancer cells. The mechanism of antineoplastic effect has not been fully characterized. *Effective as a cytotoxic agent against cutaneous T-cell lymphoma.*

USES Treatment of cutaneous or peripheral T-cell lymphoma.

CONTRAINDICATIONS Severe bone marrow depression; pregnancy (category D); lactation.

CAUTIOUS USE Risk factors for potassium or magnesium imbalance, thrombocytopenia, or leukopenia; congenital long QT syndrome, history of significant CV disease; moderate-to-severe hepatic impairment; end-stage renal disease. Safe use in children not established.

ROUTE & DOSAGE

Cutaneous or Peripheral T-Cell Lymphoma (CTCL)
Adult: **IV** 14 mg/m^2 over 4 h on days 1, 8, and 15, repeat every 28 days. Repeat cycle until disease progression has been treated or unacceptable toxicity occurs.

Toxicity Dosage Adjustment (National Cancer Institute Common Toxicity Criteria, CTC)
For CTC grade 3 or 4 neutropenia or thrombocytopenia: Hold romidepsin until ANC is 1,500/mm^3 or higher and/or platelet count is 75,000/mm^3 or higher, or parameters return to baseline values. Then, resume romidepsin 14 mg/m^2.

For CTC grade 4 febrile neutropenia or thrombocytopenia requiring platelet transfusion: Hold romidepsin until cytopenia is no greater than grade 1 and permanently reduce dose to 10 mg/m^2.

For CTC grade 2 or 3 nonhematological toxicity: Hold romidepsin until toxicity is no greater than grade 1 or returns to baseline. Resume romidepsin 14 mg/m^2.

For recurrent CTC grade 3 nonhematological toxicity: Hold romidepsin until toxicity is no greater than grade 1 or returns to baseline and permanently reduce dose to 10 mg/m^2.

For CTC grade 4 nonhematological toxicity: Hold romidepsin until toxicity is no greater than grade 1 or returns to baseline and permanently reduce dose to 10 mg/m^2.

For recurrent CTC grade 3 or 4 nonhematological toxicity after dose reduction: Discontinue therapy.

ADMINISTRATION

Intravenous ONLY

This drug is a cytotoxic agent and caution should be used to prevent any contact with the drug. Follow institutional or standard guidelines for preparation, handling, and disposal of cytotoxic agents.

PREPARE: **IV Infusion:** Withdraw 2 mL of supplied diluent and inject slowly into the 10 mL powder vial to yield 5 mg/mL. Swirl to dissolve. ▪ Withdraw the required dose of reconstituted solution and add to 500 mL NS and invert container to dissolve. ▪ Should be administered as soon as possible after dilution.

ADMINISTER: **IV Infusion:** Give over 4 h. Note: Ensure that potassium and magnesium are within normal range before administration.

INCOMPATIBILITIES: **Solution/additive:** Do not mix with another drug. **Y-site:** Do not mix with another drug.

▪ Reconstituted vials are stable for 8 h and IV solutions are stable for 24 h at room temperature. Store unopened vials at 15°–30° C (59°–86° F).

ADVERSE EFFECTS **CV:** ECG ST-T wave changes, hypotension. **Endocrine:** Elevated ALT, elevated AST, hypermagnesemia, hyperuricemia, hypoalbuminemia, hypocalcemia, hypokalemia, hypomagnesemia, hyponatremia, hypophosphatemia. **Skin:** Pruritus, dermatitis, exfoliative dermatitis. **GI:** *Anorexia, constipation, diarrhea, dysgeusia, nausea, vomiting.* **Hematologic:** *Anemia, neutropenia,* leukopenia, *lymphopenia,* <u>*thrombocytopenia*</u>. **Other:** *Asthenia,* fatigue, hyperglycemia, *infections,* fever.

INTERACTIONS **Drug:** Coadministration of CYP3A4 inducers (e.g., **carbamazepine, phenobarbital, phenytoin, rifampin**) can decrease the levels of romidepsin. Coadministration of strong CYP3A4 inhibitors (e.g., **atazanavir, indinavir, itraconazole, ketoconazole, nefazodone, nelfinavir, ritonavir, saquinavir, telithromycin, voriconazole**) can increase the levels of romidepsin. Coadministration of drugs that prolong the QT interval (e.g., **amiodarone, bretylium, disopyramide, dofetilide, procainamide, quinidine, sotalol**), **arsenic trioxide, chlorpromazine, cisapride,**

dolasetron, droperidol, mefloquine, mesoridazine, moxifloxacin, pentamidine, pimozide, tacrolimus, thioridazine, and ziprasidone) may produce life-threatening arrhythmias. **Food:** Grapefruit juice can increase the levels of romidepsin. **Herbal: St. John's wort** can decrease the levels of romidepsin.

PHARMACOKINETICS Distribution: 92–94% plasma protein bound. **Metabolism:** Extensive hepatic metabolism by CYP3A4. **Elimination:** Primarily biliary excretion. **Half-Life:** 3 h.

NURSING IMPLICATIONS

Assessment & Drug Effects

- Monitor ECG at baseline and periodically throughout treatment.
- Report immediately electrolyte imbalances or QT prolongation.
- Monitor lab tests: Baseline and prior to each dose: Serum electrolytes, CBC with differential including platelet count, LFTs and serum albumin.

Patient & Family Education

- Report promptly any of the following: Excessive nausea, chest pain, shortness of breath, or abnormal heart beat.
- Seek medical attention if unusual bleeding occurs.
- Women of childbearing age who use an estrogen-containing contraceptive should add a barrier contraceptive to prevent pregnancy.

ROPINIROLE HYDROCHLORIDE

(re-pin'i-role)

Requip XL

Classification: NON-ERGOT DERIVATIVE DOPAMINE AGONIST; ANTIPARKINSON

Therapeutic: ANTIPARKINSON
Prototype: Apomorphine

AVAILABILITY Tablet; extended release tablet

ACTION & *THERAPEUTIC EFFECT*
Precise mechanism of action is unknown, but believed to be due to stimulation of postsynaptic dopamine D_2-type receptors within the caudate putamen in the brain. *Effectiveness indicated by improvement in idiopathic Parkinson disease.*

USES Parkinson disease, restless legs syndrome.

CONTRAINDICATIONS Hypersensitivity to ropinirole or any component of the product; major psychotic disorder; pregnancy—fetal risk cannot be ruled out; lactation—infant risk cannot be ruled out.

CAUTIOUS USE Hepatic impairment; severe renal impairment; mental instability; concomitant use of CNS depressants; history of cardiovascular disease; elderly;. Safety and efficacy in children not established.

ROUTE & DOSAGE

Parkinson Disease

Adult: **PO Immediate release** Start with 0.25 mg tid, titrate daily based on response; usual dose 12–16 mg/day. (max: 24 mg/day); **Extended release** 2 mg daily for 1–2 wk then increase by 2 mg/day at one week intervals; usual dose 12–16 mg/day (max: 24 mg/day)

Restless Legs Syndrome

Adult: **PO** Take 0.25 mg 1–3 h before bed × 2 days, increase to 0.5 mg for the first wk, then increase by 0.5 mg qwk to a maximum of 4 mg

ADMINISTRATION

Oral

- Give with food to reduce occurrence of nausea.
- Do not crush extended release tablets. Ensure that they are swallowed whole.
- Drug should not be abruptly discontinued. Dose should be tapered over a period of days.
- Store tablet in a tightly closed container at a controlled room temperature between 20 and 25 degrees C (68 and 77 degrees F), with excursions permitted between at 15°–30° C (59°–86° F). Protect from light and moisture. Extended release tablets store at controlled room temperature of 25 degrees C (77 degrees F), with excursions permitted between 15 and 30 degrees C (59 and 86 degrees F).

ADVERSE EFFECTS (≥5%) CV:
Hypertension, *orthostatic hypotension*. **CNS:** *Dizziness, somnolence, sudden sleep attacks,* hallucinations, *dyskinesia.* **GI:** *Nausea, vomiting, abdominal pain.* **Other:** *fatigue.*

INTERACTIONS Drug:
Ropinirole levels may be increased by CYP 1A2 inhibitors; ESTROGENS, **diltiazem, erythromycin, fluvoxamine, mexiletine;** effects may be antagonized by PHENOTHIAZINES, BUTYROPHENONES, **metoclopramide** may increase ropinirole levels; may increase hypotensive effects of ANTIHYPERTENSIVES; may decrease the effect of ANTIPSYCHOTIC AGENTS.

PHARMACOKINETICS
Absorption: Rapidly from GI tract; 55% bioavailability. **Peak:** 1–2 h. **Distribution:** 30–40% protein bound. **Metabolism:** In liver (CYP1A2). **Elimination:** Primarily in urine. **Half-Life:** 6 h.

NURSING IMPLICATIONS

Assessment & Drug Effects

- Monitor cardiac status. Report increases in BP and HR to prescriber.
- Monitor carefully for orthostatic hypotension, especially during dose escalation.
- Monitor level of alertness. Institute appropriate precautions to prevent injury due to dizziness or drowsiness.
- Monitor lab test: Periodic BUN and creatinine, and LFTs.

Patient & Family Education

- Be aware that hallucinations are a possible adverse effect and occur more often in older adults.
- Make position changes slowly, especially after long periods of lying or sitting. Postural hypotension is common, especially during early treatment.
- Reports of falling asleep during activities of daily living have been reported and if this occurs, contact healthcare provider. Effects are additive with alcohol or other CNS depressants.
- Avoid driving and other activities requiring mental alertness or coordination until the drug effects are realized.
- Avoid sudden discontinuation of the drug.
- Notify provider if patient starts or stops taking estrogen-containing drugs such as birth control pills during drug therapy.
- Report behavioral changes (e.g., impulsive behavior) to prescriber.

R

ROPIVACAINE HYDROCHLORIDE
(ro-piv'i-cane)

Naropin

Classification: LOCAL ANESTHETIC (ESTER-TYPE)

Therapeutic: LOCAL ANESTHETIC

Prototype: Procaine HCl

AVAILABILITY Solution for injection

ACTION & THERAPEUTIC EFFECT
Blocks the generation and conduction of nerve impulses, probably by increasing the threshold for electrical excitability. *Local anesthetic action produces loss of sensation and motor activity in areas of the body close to the injection site.*

USES Local and regional anesthesia, postoperative pain management, anesthesia/pain management for obstetric procedures.

CONTRAINDICATIONS Hypersensitivity to ropivacaine or any local anesthetic of the amide type; generalized septicemia, inflammation or sepsis at the proposed injection site; cerebral spinal diseases (e.g., meningitis); heart block, hypotension, hypertension, GI hemorrhage.

CAUTIOUS USE Debilitated, older adult, or acutely ill patients; arrhythmias, shock; pregnancy (category B); lactation.

ROUTE & DOSAGE

Surgical Anesthesia
Adult: **Epidural** 25–200 mg (0.5–1% solution); **Nerve block** 5–250 mg (0.5%, 0.75% solution)

Labor Pain
Adult: **Epidural** 20–40 mg (0.2% solution) then 12–28 mg/h

Postoperative Pain Management
Adult: **Epidural** 12–28 mg/h (0.2% solution); **Infiltration** 2–200 mg (0.2–0.5% solution)

ADMINISTRATION

Intrathecal
- Avoid rapid injection of large volumes of ropivacaine. Incremental doses should always be used to achieve the smallest effective dose and concentration.
- Use an infusion concentration of 2 mg/mL (0.2%) for postoperative analgesia.
- Do not use disinfecting agents containing heavy metal ions (e.g., mercury, copper, zinc, etc.) on skin insertion site or to clean the ropivacaine container top.
- Discard continuous infusions solution after 24 h; it contains no preservatives.
- Store unopened at 20°–25° C (68°–77° F).

ADVERSE EFFECTS CV: *Hypotension,* bradycardia, hypertension, tachycardia, chest pain, fetal bradycardia. **CNS:** Paresthesia, headache, dizziness, anxiety. **Skin:** Pruritus. **GI:** Nausea. **GU:** Urinary retention, oliguria. **Hematologic:** Anemia. **Other:** Pain, fever, rigors, hypoesthesia.

INTERACTIONS Drug: Additive adverse effects with other LOCAL ANESTHETICS.

PHARMACOKINETICS Onset: 1–30 min (average 10–20 min) depending on dose/route of administration. **Duration:** 0.5–8 h depending on dose/route of

R

administration. **Distribution:** 94% protein bound. **Metabolism:** In the liver by CYP1A. **Elimination:** In urine. **Half-Life:** 1.8–4.2 h.

NURSING IMPLICATIONS

Assessment & Drug Effects

▪ Monitor carefully cardiovascular and respiratory status throughout treatment period. Assess for hypotension and bradycardia.
▪ Report immediately S&S of CNS stimulation or CNS depression.

Patient & Family Education

▪ Report any of the following to prescriber immediately: Restlessness, anxiety, tinnitus, blurred vision, tremors.

ROSIGLITAZONE MALEATE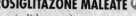

(ros-i-glit′a-zone)

Avandia

Classification: THIAZOLIDINEDIONE (GLITAZONE)

Therapeutic: ANTIHYPERGLYCEMIC

AVAILABILITY Tablet

ACTION & *THERAPEUTIC EFFECT*

Lowers blood sugar levels by improving target cell response to insulin in Type 2 diabetics. It reduces cellular insulin resistance and decreases hepatic glucose output (gluconeogenesis). *Reduces hyperglycemia and hyperlipidemia, thus improving hyperinsulinemia without stimulating pancreatic insulin secretion. Effectiveness indicated by decreased HbA1C.*

USES Type 2 diabetes.

UNLABELED USES Polycystic ovary syndrome.

CONTRAINDICATIONS Hypersensitivity to rosiglitazone; patients with New York Heart Association Class III and IV cardiac status (e.g., CHF); symptomatic heart failure; initiation in patients with ischemic heart disease; active hepatic disease; ALT enzyme greater than 2.5 × ULN; high risk for bone fractures; Type I DM; lactation (infant risk cannot be ruled out).

CAUTIOUS USE CHF or risk for CHF; angina; patients with ongoing edema; anemia; hepatic impairment; older adults; pregnancy (category C). Safety and efficacy in children younger than 18 y not established.

ROUTE & DOSAGE

Type 2 Diabetes Mellitus

Adult: **PO** Start at 4 mg daily or 2 mg bid, may increase after 8–12 wk (max: 8 mg/day in 1–2 divided doses)

Hepatic Impairment Dosage Adjustment

If ALT is greater than 2.5 × ULN: Do not use

ADMINISTRATION

Oral

▪ May be given without regard to meals.
▪ Store at 15°–30° C (59°–86° F) in tight, light-resistant container.

ADVERSE EFFECTS CV: Edema. **Respiratory:** URI, nasopharyngitis. **CNS:** Headache. **Endocrine:** Weight gain, increased HDL cholesterol, increased LDL cholesterol. **Musculoskeletal:** Bone fracture.

INTERACTIONS Drug: **Insulin** may increase risk of heart failure or edema; enhance hypoglycemia with ORAL ANTIDIABETIC AGENTS,

R

ketoconazole, gemfibrozil may increase effect. **Bosentan, dabrafenib, rifampin** may reduce effect. **Cholestyramine** may decrease concentration of rosiglitazone. **Herbal: Garlic, ginseng, green tea** may potentiate hypoglycemic effects.

PHARMACOKINETICS Absorption: 99% from GI tract. Peak: 1 h, food delays time to peak by 1.75 h. **Duration:** Greater than 24 h. **Distribution:** Greater than 99% protein bound. **Metabolism:** In liver (CYP2C8) to inactive metabolites. **Elimination:** 64% urine, 23% feces. **Half-Life:** 3–4 h. Liver disease increases serum concentrations and increases half-life by 2 h.

NURSING IMPLICATIONS

Assessment & Drug Effects
- Monitor for S&S of hypoglycemia (possible when insulin/sulfonylureas are coadministered).
- Monitor for S&S of CHF or exacerbation of symptoms with preexisting CHF.
- Withhold drug and notify prescriber if ALT greater than 2.5 × normal or patient jaundiced.
- Monitor weight and notify prescriber of development of edema.
- Monitor lab tests: Baseline LFTs, and periodically thereafter or more often when elevated; periodic fasting serum glucose and HbA1C.

Patient & Family Education
- Report promptly any of the following: Rapid weight gain, edema, shortness of breath, or exercise intolerance.
- Be aware that resumed ovulation is possible in non ovulating premenopausal women.
- Use or add barrier contraceptive if using hormonal contraception.

- Report immediately to prescriber: S&S of liver dysfunction such as unexplained anorexia, nausea, vomiting, abdominal pain, fatigue, dark urine; or S&S of fluid retention such as weight gain, edema, or activity intolerance.
- Combination therapy: May need adjustment of other antidiabetic drugs to avoid hypoglycemia.

ROSUVASTATIN
(ro-su-va-sta′ten)
Crestor
Classification: STATIN
Therapeutic: ANTILIPEMIC; STATIN
Prototype: Lovastatin

AVAILABILITY Tablet

ACTION & *THERAPEUTIC EFFECT*
A potent inhibitor of HMG-CoA reductase, an enzyme that catalyzes the conversion of HMG-CoA to mevalonic acid, an early and rate-limiting step in cholesterol biosynthesis. This results in reducing the amount of mevalonic acid, a precursor of cholesterol. It increases the number of hepatic HDL receptors on the cell surface to enhance uptake and catabolism of LDL. It also inhibits hepatic synthesis of very low density lipoprotein (VLDL). *Reduces total cholesterol and LDL cholesterol; additionally, lowers plasma triglycerides and VLDL while increasing HDL.*

USES Adjunct to diet for the reduction of LDL cholesterol and triglycerides in patients with primary hypercholesterolemia, hypertriglyceridemia, and mixed dyslipidemia; prevention of cardiovascular disease.

CONTRAINDICATIONS Hypersensitivity to any component of

the product, active liver disease or unexplained persistent elevations of serum transaminases; rhabdomyolysis; pregnancy (fetal risk has been demonstrated), women of childbearing potential not using appropriate contraceptive measures; lactation—infant risk has been demonstrated.

CAUTIOUS USE Concomitant use of cyclosporine and gemfibrozil; Asian descent; DM; excessive alcohol use or history of liver disease; renal impairment; older adults; hypothyroidism. Safe use in children younger than 6 y not established.

ROUTE & DOSAGE

Hyperlipidemia/Slowing Atherosclerosis Progression

Adult/Adolescent/Child (10 y or older): **PO** 10–20 mg once daily (max: 40 mg/day)
Conservative Dosing: Initial dose of 5 mg/day

Homozygous Familial Hypercholesterolemia

Adult: **PO** 20 mg daily (max: 40 mg/day)

Prevention of Cardiovascular Disease

Adult: **PO** 5–40 mg daily

Renal Impairment Dosage Adjustment

CrCl less than 30 mL/min: 5 mg once daily (max: 10 mg/day)

Concurrent Medication Dosage Adjustment

If taking cyclosporine, gemfibrozil, lopinavir/ritonavir, start with 5 mg/day

ADMINISTRATION

Oral

- Persons of Asian descent may be slow metabolizers and may require half the normal dose.
- May give any time of day without regard to food.
- Do not give within 2 h of an antacid.
- Store between 20°–25° C (68°–77° F). Protect from light.

ADVERSE EFFECTS CNS: Headache. **GI:** Nausea, constipation. **Musculoskeletal:** Muscle pain, joint pain, weakness.

INTERACTIONS Drug: Atazanavir, cyclosporine, gemfibrozil, niacin may increase risk of rhabdomyolysis; ANTACIDS may decrease rosuvastatin absorption; may cause increase in INR with **warfarin.** **Herbal: Red yeast rice** increases rhabdomyolysis risk.

PHARMACOKINETICS Absorption: Well absorbed. **Peak:** 3–5 h. **Metabolism:** Limited metabolism in the liver (not CYP3A4). **Elimination:** Primarily in feces (90%). **Half-Life:** 20 h.

NURSING IMPLICATIONS

Assessment & Drug Effects

- Monitor for and report promptly S&S of myopathy (e.g., skeletal muscle pain, tenderness or weakness).
- Withhold drug and notify prescriber if CPK levels are markedly elevated (10 or more × ULN) or if myopathy is diagnosed or suspected.
- Monitor CV status, especially with a known history of hypertension or heart disease.
- Monitor diabetics for loss of glycemic control.

R

- Monitor lab tests: Baseline CPK and repeat with S&S of myopathy; periodic LFTs.

Patient & Family Education
- Do not take antacids within 2 h of taking this drug.
- Women should use reliable means of contraception to prevent pregnancy while taking this drug.

ROTIGOTINE
(roe TIG oh teen)

Neupro

Classifications: ANTIPARKINSON AGENT; DOPAMINE AGONIST

Therapeutic: ANTIPARKINSON AGENT

Prototype: Apomorphine

AVAILABILITY Transdermal patch

ACTION & *THERAPEUTIC EFFECT*

A non-ergoline dopamine receptor agonist. The precise mechanism of action in treatment of Parkinson disease and restless legs syndrome is unknown, but thought to be related to the drug's ability to stimulate dopamine receptors. In Parkinson disease, it is thought to specifically stimulate dopamine receptors within the caudate-putamen in the brain. Used to improve symptoms of Parkinson disease (tremors, stiffness, slowed movements, and unsteadiness) and restless legs syndrome.

USES Parkinson disease; restless leg syndrome

CONTRAINDICATIONS Hypersensitivity to rotigotine or any component of the product; major psychotic disorder; pregnancy—fetal risk cannot be ruled out; lactaion—milk effects are possible; safety and efficacy in chidren has not been established.

CAUTIOUS USE History of cardiac impairment, hypertension, CHF, renal insufficiency, patients with psychosis.

ROUTE & DOSAGE

Early stage Parkinson Disease

Adult: **Transdermal** 2 mg daily, increase by 2 mg/24 hours weekly (max dose: 6 mg/24hrs)

Advanced stage Parkinson Disease

Adult: **Transdermal** 4 mg daily, increase by 2 mg/24 hours weekly (max dose: 16 mg/24hrs)

ADMINISTRATION

Transdermal
- Apply the patch to clean, dry, intact, healthy, hairless skin (shaved at least 3 days prior) on front of the abdomen, thigh, hip, flank, shoulder, or upper arm that will not be rubbed by tight clothes. Avoid oily, irritated or damaged skin.
- Apply to a new site every day rotating from side to side and from upper to lower body; do not apply to the same site more than once every 14 days.
- After removing from protective liner, apply immediately by pressing in place for 30 seconds.
- Wear continually for 24 hours and apply a new patch at approximately the same time every day.
- If replacement patch is forgotton, or existing patch becomes dislodged, apply anoher patch for the remainder of the day then replace at the next regular time.
- Store unopened pouch between 20 and 25 degrees C (68 and

Common adverse effects in *italic;* life-threatening effects <u>underlined</u>; generic names in **bold;** classifications in SMALL CAPS; ✦ Canadian drug name; ⊙ Prototype drug; ⚠ Alert

77 degrees F), with excursions permitted between 15 and 30 degrees C (59 and 86 degrees F). Use immediately after opening.

ADVERSE EFFECTS (≥5%) CV:
Orthostatic hypotension. **CNS:** *Dizziness, dyskinesia, headache, sleep disorder, somnolence.* **Skin:** *Application site reaction,* diaphoresis. **GI:** Anorexia, *nausea, vomiting,* xerostomia **Other:** Compulsive behavior and hallucinations.

INTERACTIONS ANTIHYPERTENSIVES
may have increased hypotensive effects. DOPAMINE AGONISTS, ANTIPSYHOTICS may decrease effectiveness.

PHARMACOKINETICS Distribution: ~90% protein bound Metabolism: Hepatic via CYP isoenzymes Elimination: Urine Half-Life: 5-7 hours

NURSING IMPLICATIONS

Assessment & Drug Effects
- Monitor for improved symptoms of tremor, stiffness, movement and steadiness
- Patient at risk for falls related to adverse affect of somnolence.
- Monitor blood pressure. Patient at risk for orthostatic hypotensive event.
- Monitor weight, and intake and output
- Perform a thorough skin assessment
- Monitor lab tests: renal function tests in patients with renal insufficiency

Patient & Family Education
- Avoid activities that require mental alertness or coordination until the effects of the drug are known. May cause somnolence up to 1 year after initiation.

- Advise patient that the patch contains aluminum and should be removed prior to a MRI or cardioversion.
- Avoid exposing the patch to direct heat as it may cause an increased drug absorption.
- Report signs of a site reaction: nausea, vomiting, dizziness, heaadache, insomnia, syncope, hallucinations, racing heart beat, swelling of extremities.
- Report any changes in moles and routinely inspect skin.
- Report any compulsive behavior: gambling, sexual urges, or binge eating.
- Review proper patch placement.
- Importance of not discontinuing the drug without consulting with the healthcare provider.
- Use extreme caution when taking alcohol, sedating medications or other CNS depressants when taking this drug.

SACUBITRIL AND VALSARTAN
(sac'u-bi-tril and val-sar-tan)
Entresto
Classification: CARDIOVASCULAR AGENT; NEPRILYSIN INHIBITOR; ANGIOTENSIN II RECEPTOR BLOCKER
Therapeutic: HEART FAILURE AGENT

AVAILABILITY Tablet

ACTIONS & *THERAPEUTIC EFFECT*
Sacubitril is a prodrug that, when converted to an active metabolite (LBQ657), inhibits the enzyme, neprilysin, leading to increased levels of natriuretic peptides. Valsartan is an angiotensin receptor antagonist that selectively blocks the vasoconstriction and aldosterone-secreting effects of angiotensin II. *Decreases afterload thus facilitating increased cardiac output.*

USES Indicated for risk reduction of cardiovascular death and hospitalization from heart failure (HF) in patients with chronic HF (NYHA Class II-IV) and reduced ejection fraction.

CONTRAINDICATIONS Hypersensitivity to any component; history of angioedema related to previous ACE inhibitor or ARB therapy; concomitant use with ACE inhibitors; concomitant use with aliskiren in patients with diabetes; severe hepatic impairment; pregnancy; lactation.

CAUTIOUS USE Prior history of angioedema; African American ancestry; concomitant use of potassium-sparing diuretics, NSAIDs, or lithium; hypotension; renal impairment; mild to moderate hepatic impairment; potassium imbalance; risk factors for hyperkalemia including diabetes, hypoaldosteronism, or high potassium diet; older adults. Safety and efficacy in children 18 y or younger not established.

ROUTE & DOSAGE

Heart Failure

Adult: **PO** (Treatment naive or previous low dose ACE/ARB) Initial dose of 24/26 mg (sacubitril/valsartan) or (previously taking moderate/high dose ACE or ARB) 49/51 mg bid

Hepatic Impairment Dosage Adjustment

Moderate impairment (Child-Pugh class B): Initial dose of 24/26 mg bid
Severe impairment (Child-Pugh class C): Not recommended

Renal Impairment Dosage Adjustment

Severe impairment: Initial dose of 24/26 mg bid

ADMINISTRATION

Oral

- Correct volume or salt depletion prior to administration.
- May be given without regard to food.
- Store at 15°–30° C (59°–86° F). Protect from moisture.

ADVERSE EFFECTS **CV:** *Hypotension,* orthostatic hypotension. **Respiratory:** Cough. **CNS:** Dizziness. **Endocrine:** *Hyperkalemia.* **Hematologic:** Decreased hemoglobin and hematocrit, increased serum creatinine. **Other:** Falls, renal failure.

INTERACTIONS **Drug:** Concomitant use with an ANGIOTENSION CONVERTING ENZYME INHIBITOR increases the risk of angioedema. Concomitant use of POTASSIUM SPARING DIURETICS (e.g., **amiloride, spironolactone, triamterene**) may lead to increased potassium levels. Concomitant use with NSAIDs in older adults, patients who are volume-depleted, or patients with compromised renal function may result in worsening of renal function. Sacubitril/valsartan may increase the levels of **lithium.**

PHARMACOKINETICS **Absorption:** **Sacubitril** is greater than 60% bioavailable. **Peak:** Sacubitril 0.5 h.; LBQ657 2h.; valsartan 1.5 h. **Distribution:** Highly plasma protein bound (94–97%). **Metabolism:** Sacubitril is metabolized to an active metabolite, LBQ657; Valsartan minimal metabolism. **Elimination:** Sacubitril, 52–68% renal and 37–48% fecal; valsartan, 13% renal and 86% fecal. **Half-Life:** Sacubitril 1.4 h.; LBQ657 11.5 h.; valsartan 9.9 h.

S

NURSING IMPLICATIONS

Black Box Warning

The valsartan component of the drug has been associated with fetal toxicity.

Assessment & Drug Effects

- Monitor cardiac status and BP frequently. Risk of hypotension increases with salt and/or volume depletion.
- Monitor activity tolerance and S&S of heart failure.
- Monitor for angioedema; if suspected, take measures necessary to ensure maintenance of a patent airway.
- Monitor for S&S of hyperkalemia (see Appendix F).
- Monitor for S&S of lithium toxicity with concurrent use.
- Monitor lab tests: Baseline and periodic LFTs and renal function tests; periodic serum potassium and Hct & Hgb.

Patient & Family Education

- Seek medical care immediately if experiencing swelling of face, lips, tongue, and throat (angioedema). Persons of African heritage are at greater risk for angioedema.
- Make position changes slowly, especially when standing from a lying or sitting position.
- Do not use potassium supplements, salt substitutes, or OTC nonsteroidal anti-inflammatory drugs (NSAIDs) without consulting prescriber.
- Women should use effective means of contraception while taking this drug. If pregnancy is suspected, stop taking this drug and report immediately to prescriber.
- Do not breast-feed while taking this drug.

SAFINAMIDE
(sa-fin′a-mide)
Xadago
Classification: MONOAMINE OXIDASE (MAO) B INHIBITOR
Therapeutic: ANTI-PARKINSON AGENT

AVAILABILITY Tablet

ACTION & *THERAPEUTIC EFFECT*
Decreases dopamine catabolism via inhibition of type-B MAO which increases dopamine levels in the brain and subsequently increases dopaminergic activity. *Helpful adjunctive therapy in improving "off" episodes of Parkinson's disease.*

CONTRAINDICATIONS Hypersensitivity to safinamide or any component of the formulation; severe hepatic impairment (Child-Pugh class C); concomitant use of other monamine oxidase inhibitors (MAOIs) or other drugs that are potent inhibitors of monoamine oxidase, opioids, serotonin-norepinephrine reuptake inhibitors (SNRIs) tricyclic or triazolopyridine antidepressants, cyclobenzaprine, methylphenidate, amphetamines, and their derivatives, St. John's wort, dextromethorphan; lactation.

CAUTIOUS USE Hepatic impairment; ophthalmic disorders; psychotic disorders; pregnancy (category C).

ROUTE & DOSAGE

Parkinson's Disease

Adult: **Initial PO** 50 mg daily; after 2 wk titrate to 100 mg daily

Hepatic Impairment Dosage Adjustment

Moderate impairment (Child-Pugh class B): Max: 50 mg daily

Severe impairment (Child-Pugh class C): Do not use

ADMINISTRATION

Oral

- Administer without regard to meals at the same time every day. Always administer in association with levodopa/carbidopa.
- At doses 100 mg/day or less, interaction with tyramine-containing foods and beverages is unlikely, however, patients should avoid foods and beverages with very high (greater than 150 mg) tyramine concentrations. Food's freshness is also a consideration; improperly stored or spoiled food can create an environment where tyramine concentrations may increase.
- Store at 25° C (77° F); excursions permitted between 15°–30° C (59°–86° F).

ADVERSE EFFECTS CV: <u>Hypertension</u>. CNS: *Dyskinesia*, insomnia. GI: *Nausea*. Other: Falls, hallucinations, impulse control disorder, serotonin syndrome.

INTERACTIONS Drug: MAO-INHIBITORS or similar acting drugs (e.g., **linezolid**) may increase risk of nonselective MAO inhibition, which may lead to a hypertensive crisis; 14 days washout is appropriate between discontinuing safinamide and initiating another MAOI. SYMPATHOMIMETIC medications utilized with safinamide increases risk of hypertensive crisis (e.g., **methylphenidate, amphetamine,** and nasal or oral decongestants). Safinamide and **dextromethorphan** can cause brief episodes of psychosis and bizarre behavior. DOPAMINE ANTAGONISTS may decrease effectiveness of safinamide. Safinamide can increase the plasma levels of **cyclobenzaprine** and other serotonergic medications increasing the risk of serotonin syndrome; therefore the combination should be avoided [e.g., SELECTIVE SEROTONIN REUPTAKE INHIBITORS (SSRI), SEROTONIN-NOREPINEPHRINE REUPTAKE INHIBITORS (SNRI)]. Selective OPIOIDS such as **tramadol** and **methadone** may also increase risk of serotonin syndrome when taken with safinamide, so the combination is contraindicated. Safinamide and its major metabolite may inhibit the breast cancer resistance protein, increasing concentrations of BCRP substrates; monitor use with substrates of BCRP (e.g., **methotrexate, irinotecan, topotecan**). Food: Tyramine containing foods (e.g., aged, fermented, cured, smoked, or pickled foods) may cause a release of norepinephrine resulting in a rise of blood pressure, and therefore should be avoided while on safinamide. Herbal: **St. John's wort** should be avoided.

PHARMACOKINETICS Absorption: 95% bioavailability. Distribution: 88% protein binding, volume of distribution 165 L. Onset: Time to peak 2–3 h. Metabolism: Primarily by cytosolic amidases and MAOA. Elimination: 76% in urine. Half-Life: 20–26 h.

NURSING IMPLICATIONS

Assessment & Drug Effects

- Monitor for an increase of daily "on" time without troublesome dyskinesia associated with Parkinson's disease may indicate efficacy.
- Monitor blood pressure.
- Monitor for new or increased impulse control or compulsive behaviors such as gambling, sexual, or spending urges, which may be unrecognizable by the patient.

S

- Monitor for visual changes in patients with a history of retinal or macular degeneration, uveitis, inherited retinal conditions, family history of hereditary retinal disease, albinism, retinitis pigmentosa, or any active retinopathy (diabetic retinopathy).

Patient & Family Education

- Notify all health care providers that this drug is being taken. This includes prescribers, doctors, nurses, pharmacists, and dentists.
- Avoid driving and doing other tasks or actions that require alertness until drug affects are known; some people have fallen asleep during activities.
- Monitor blood pressure at home as directed by prescriber; this drug may cause high blood pressure.
- Avoid foods high in tyramine (e.g., cheese, and red wine).
- Do not stop this drug without calling prescriber.
- Notify prescriber before drinking alcohol or using drugs and natural products that may slow actions.
- Notify prescriber if pregnant or have plans to get pregnant to discuss drug risks during pregnancy.
- Notify prescriber right away with S&S of an allergic reaction: Rash, hives, wheezing, chest tightness, trouble breathing, swelling in the mouth, face or lips
- Notify prescriber if experiencing symptoms of high blood pressure: Very bad headache, dizziness, passing out, or change in eyesight.
- Notify prescriber regarding the following: Movement control difficulty, hallucinations, confused or agitated feelings, strong urges that are hard to control, or experiencing falls.
- If this drug is taken along with drugs for depression, notify prescriber right away if experiencing

the following: Agitation, change in balance, confusion, hallucinations, fast heart beat, muscle twitching or stiffness, seizure, shivering or shaking, profuse sweating, very bad diarrhea, upset stomach, vomiting or very bad headache.

SALMETEROL XINAFOATE

(sal-me'ter-ol xin'a-fo-ate)

Serevent

Classification: BETA$_2$-ADRENERGIC RECEPTOR AGONIST
Therapeutic: BRONCHODILATOR
Prototype: Albuterol

AVAILABILITY Powder diskus for inhalation

ACTION & *THERAPEUTIC EFFECT*
Long-acting beta$_2$-adrenoreceptor agonist that stimulates beta$_2$-adrenoreceptors, relaxes bronchospasm, and increases ciliary motility, thus facilitating expectoration. *Relaxes bronchospasm and increases ciliary motility, thus facilitating expectoration of pulmonary secretions.*

USES Maintenance therapy for asthma or bronchospasm associated with COPD. Prevention of exercise-induced bronchospasm.

CONTRAINDICATIONS Hypersensitivity to salmeterol or milk proteins; primary treatment of status asthmaticus; acute asthma; acute bronchospasm; acutely deteriorating COPD; MAOI therapy.

CAUTIOUS USE Cardiovascular disorders; cardiac arrhythmias, hypertension, QT prolongation, hypokalemia; history of seizures or thyrotoxicosis; hyperthyroidism;

Common adverse effects in *italic*; life-threatening effects <u>underlined</u>; generic names in **bold**; classifications in SMALL CAPS; ♣ Canadian drug name; ✪ Prototype drug; ⚠ Alert

pheochromocytoma; liver and renal impairment; COPD; DM, sensitivity to other beta-adrenergic agonists; older adults; women in labor; pregnancy (category- C); lactation (infant risk cannot be ruled out). Safe use in children younger than 4 y not established.

ROUTE & DOSAGE

Asthma or Bronchospasm (COPD associated)

Adult/Child (4 y or older): Inhalation 1 powder diskus (50 mcg) bid approximately 12 h apart

Prevention of Exercise-Induced Bronchospasm

Adult/Child (4 y or older): Inhalation 1 powder diskus (50 mcg) 30–60 min before exercise

ADMINISTRATION

Inhalation

- Do not use to relieve symptoms of acute asthma.
- Activate diskus by moving lever until it clicks. Patient should exhale fully (not into diskus), place diskus in mouth, and inhale quickly and deeply through the diskus. Diskus should be removed and breath held for 10 sec.
- Store at room temperature, 15°–30° C (59°–86° F).

ADVERSE EFFECTS Respiratory:
Congestion, bronchitis, throat irritation, cough, sinusitis, rhinitis. **CNS:** Headache, pain. **Musculoskeletal:** Muscle pain.

INTERACTIONS Drug: Effects
antagonized by BETA-BLOCKERS, MAOIS. Avoid use of strong CYP3A4 inhibitors. Do not use with **cobicistat** or **telaprevir**. Do not use with other BETA 2 AGONISTS.

PHARMACOKINETICS Onset:
10–20 min. **Peak:** Effect 2 h. **Duration:** Up to 12 h. **Distribution:** 94–95% protein bound, excreted in breast milk. **Metabolism:** Salmeterol is extensively metabolized by hydroxylation. **Elimination:** Primarily in feces. **Half-Life:** 3–4 h.

NURSING IMPLICATIONS

Black Box Warning

Salmeterol has been associated with increased risk of asthma-related hospitalization and death.

Assessment & Drug Effects

- Withhold drug and notify prescriber immediately if bronchospasms occur following its use.
- Monitor cardiovascular status; report tachycardia.
- Monitor lab tests: Periodic serum glucose and serum potassium.

Patient & Family Education

- Never use a spacer device with the drug.
- Do not use this drug to treat an acute asthma attack.
- Notify prescriber immediately of worsening asthma or failure to respond to the usual dose of salmeterol.
- Do not use an additional dose prior to exercise if taking twice-daily doses of salmeterol.
- Take the preexercise dose 30–60 min before exercise and wait 12 h before an additional dose.

SALSALATE
(sal'sa-late)

Classification: NONSTEROIDAL ANTI-INFLAMMATORY DRUG (NSAID)

Therapeutic: NONNARCOTIC ANALGESIC, NSAID

Prototype: Aspirin

Common adverse effects in *italic*; life-threatening effects <u>underlined</u>; generic names in **bold;** classifications in SMALL CAPS; ✦ Canadian drug name; ◎ Prototype drug; ⚠ Alert

1518

AVAILABILITY Tablet

ACTION & *THERAPEUTIC EFFECT*

Anti-inflammatory and analgesic activity of salsalate may be mediated through inhibition of the prostaglandin synthetase enzyme complex. *Has analgesic, anti-inflammatory, and antirheumatic effects.*

USES Symptomatic treatment, rheumatoid arthritis, osteoarthritis, and related rheumatic disorders.

CONTRAINDICATIONS Hypersensitivity to salicylates or NSAIDs; chronic renal insufficiency; peptic ulcer; children younger than 12 y; hemophilia; chickenpox, influenza, tinnitus.

CAUTIOUS USE Liver function impairment; older adults; pregnancy (category C); lactation (infant risk cannot be ruled out). Safety and efficacy in children not established.

ROUTE & DOSAGE

Rheumatic Disorders

Adult: **PO** 3 g /day in 2 to 3 divided doses

ADMINISTRATION

Oral

- Give with a full glass of water or food or milk to reduce GI adverse effects.
- Store at controlled room temperature 15°–30° C (59°–86° F).

ADVERSE EFFECTS CV: Hypotension. **Respiratory:** Bronchospasm. **CNS:** Dizziness. **HEENT:** Auditory impairment, tinnitus. **Skin:** Rash, Stevens-Johnson syndrome, toxic epidermal necrolysis, urticaria.

Hepatic: Increased liver function tests, hepatitis. **GI:** Abdominal pain, diarrhea, gastrointestinal hemorrhage, gastrointestinal perforation, gastrointestinal ulcer, nausea. **GU:** Decreased creatinine clearance, nephritis. **Hematologic:** Anemia.

DIAGNOSTIC TEST INTERFERENCE

False-negative results for *Clinistix;* false-positives for *Clinitest;* false results for plasma T4.

INTERACTIONS Drug: Aminosalicylic acid increases risk of salicylate toxicity. ACIDIFYING AGENTS decrease renal elimination and increase risk of salicylate toxicity. ANTICOAGULANTS increase risk of bleeding. Do not use with NSAIDS. ORAL HYPOGLYCEMIC AGENTS increase hypoglycemic activity with salsalate doses greater than 2 g/day. CARBONIC ANHYDRASE INHIBITORS enhance salicylate toxicity. CORTICOSTEROIDS add to ulcerogenic effects. **Methotrexate** toxicity is increased. Low doses of salicylates may antagonize uricosuric effects of **probenecid** and **sulfinpyrazone. Herbal: Feverfew, garlic, ginger, ginkgo** may increase bleeding potential.

PHARMACOKINETICS Absorption: Readily absorbed from small intestine. **Peak:** 1.5–4 h. **Metabolism:** Hydrolyzed in liver, GI mucosa, plasma, whole blood, and other tissues. **Elimination:** In urine. **Half-Life:** 1 h.

NURSING IMPLICATIONS

Black Box Warning

NSAIDS may cause increased risk of serious cardiovascular thrombotic events, myocardial infarction, and stroke, which can be fatal.

S

Assessment & Drug Effects
- Symptom relief is gradual (may require 3–4 days to establish steady-state salicylate level).
- Monitor for adverse GI effects, especially in patient with a history of peptic ulcer disease.
- Monitor labs: CBC, fecal occult blood test, LFTs, BUN, creatinine, plasma salicylic acid.

Patient & Family Education
- Do not take another salicylate (e.g., aspirin) while on salsalate therapy.
- Monitor blood glucose for loss of glycemic control in diabetes; drug may induce hypoglycemia when used with sulfonylureas.
- Report tinnitus, hearing loss, vertigo, rash, or nausea.

SAQUINAVIR MESYLATE ⊘
(sa-quin'a-vir mes'y-late)
Invirase
Classification: PROTEASE INHIBITOR
Therapeutic: PROTEASE INHIBITOR

AVAILABILITY Gelatin capsule; tablet

ACTION & *THERAPEUTIC EFFECT*
Inhibits the activity of HIV protease and prevents the cleavage of viral polyproteins essential for the maturation of HIV. *Effectiveness indicated by reduced viral load (decreased number of RNA copies), and increased number of T helper CD4 cells.*

USES HIV infection (used with other antiretroviral agents).

CONTRAINDICATIONS Significant hypersensitivity to saquinavir; congenital long QT syndrome; severe hepatic impairment; AV block; hypokalemia, or

hypomagnesia; antimicrobial resistance to other protease inhibitors; monotherapy; lactation (infant risk cannot be ruled out).

CAUTIOUS USE Hepatic insufficiency; severe renal impairment; hepatitis B or C; DM, diabetic ketoacidosis; CHF, bradyarrhythmias, electrolyte imbalances; hemophilia A or B; older adults; pregnancy (category B). Safety and efficacy in HIV-infected children younger than 16 y not established.

ROUTE & DOSAGE

HIV
Adult/Adolescent: **PO** 1000 mg bid with ritonavir 100 mg bid

ADMINISTRATION
Oral
- Give with or up to 2 h after a full meal to ensure adequate absorption and bioavailability. Give with ritonavir.
- If patient is unable to swallow capsule, contents may be added to 3 tsps of jam or 15 mL of sugar syrup (sorbitol syrup for diabetic or glucose-intolerant patients); mix for 30–60 seconds.
- Do not administer to anyone taking rifampin or rifabutin because these drugs significantly decrease the plasma level of saquinavir.
- Store at 15°–30° C (59°–86° F) in a tightly closed bottle.

ADVERSE EFFECTS CV: Atrioventricular block, prolonged QT interval, prolonged PR interval. **CNS:** Fatigue. **Endocrine:** Lipodystrophy. **GI:** Abdominal pain, diarrhea, nausea, vomiting.

INTERACTIONS Drug: Do not use with sildenafil, alfuzosin, or

Common adverse effects in *italic*; life-threatening effects underlined; generic names
in **bold;** classifications in SMALL CAPS; ♣ Canadian drug name; ⊘ Prototype drug; ⚠ Alert
1520

salmeterol. Rifampin, **rifabutin** significantly decrease saquinavir levels. **Phenobarbital, phenytoin, dexamethasone, carbamazepine** may also reduce saquinavir levels. Saquinavir levels may be increased by **delavirdine, ketoconazole, ritonavir, clarithromycin, indinavir.** May increase serum levels of **triazolam, midazolam,** ERGOT DERIVATIVES, **nelfinavir, simvastatin.** PHENOTHIAZINES may increase arrhythmogenic effect of saquinavir. May increase risk of **ergotamine** toxicity of **dihydroergotamine, ergotamine.** Dosage adjustments are needed when used with **bosentan, tadalafil,** or **colchicine. Herbal: St. John's wort, garlic** may decrease antiretroviral activity. **Food: Grapefruit juice** (greater than 1 qt/day) may increase plasma concentrations and adverse effects.

PHARMACOKINETICS Absorption: Rapidly from GI tract; food significantly increases bioavailability. **Distribution:** 98% protein bound. **Metabolism:** In liver (CYP3A4), first-pass metabolism. **Elimination:** Primarily in feces (greater than 80%). **Half-Life:** 13 h.

NURSING IMPLICATIONS

Assessment & Drug Effects
- Assess for buccal mucosa ulceration or other distressing GI S&S.
- Monitor weight periodically.
- Monitor for toxicity if any of the following drugs is used concomitantly: Calcium channel blockers, clindamycin, dapsone, quinidine, triazolam, or simvastatin.
- Monitor for and report S&S of peripheral neuropathy.
- Monitor lab tests: Baseline and periodic CD_4 count, serum electrolytes, hepatitis screening, LFTs, CBC with differential, fasting blood glucose, urinalysis, for women of child bearing potential base line pregnancy test, fasting blood glucose or HgbA1c at baseline and with modification, and lipid profile.

Patient & Family Education
- Take drug within 2 h of a full meal.
- Be aware of all drugs which should not be taken concurrently with saquinavir.
- Be aware that saquinavir is not a cure for HIV infection and that its long-term effects are unknown.
- Report any distressing adverse effects to prescriber.

SARECYCLINE
(sar e SYE kleen)
Seysara
Classifications: TETRACYCLINE ANTIBIOTIC
Therapeutic: ANTIBIOTIC
Prototype: TETRACYCLINE

AVAILABILITY Oral tablet

ACTION & *THERAPEUTIC EFFECT*
Bacteriostatic action that appears to be a result of reversible binding to ribosomal units of susceptible bacteria and inhibition of bacterial protein synthesis. *Effective against gram-positive and gram negative bacteria, but direct influence on acne vulgaris is unknown.*

USES Treatment of inflammatory acne vulgaris.

CONTRAINDICATIONS Known hypersensitivity to any of the tetraclines; pregnancy – fetal risk cannot be ruled out; lactation – infant risk cannot be ruled out.

CAUTIOUS USE Obese women of childbearing age, premature infants, approved for children 9 years or older.

ROUTE & DOSAGE

Acne vulgaris

Adult/Adolescent/Child (9 y or older, weight 33 to <55kg): **PO** 60 mg once daily
(weight 55 to <85kg): **PO** 100 mg once daily
(weight 85 to 136kg): **PO** 150 mg once daily

ADMINISTRATION

Oral

- Administer once daily with or without food; give with an adequate amount of fluid to prevent esophageal irritation and ulceration.
- Store at a controlled room temperature between 20 and 25 degrees of C (68 and 77 degrees F), with excursions permitted between 15 and 30 degrees C (59 and 86 degrees F). Protect from moisture and excessive heat.

ADVERSE EFFECTS CNS: Psuedotumor cerebri **GI:** Nausea, Clostridium difficile diarrhea, staining of teeth **Musculoskeletal:** delayed bone development and/or growth

INTERACTIONS Drug: ANTACIDS, **calcium, magnesium,** and iron containing products bind sarecycline in gut and decrease absorption; may enhance effects of ANTICOAGULANTS (eg. warfarin); increases **digoxin** absorption, thus increasing risk of **digoxin** toxicity. Do not use with **acitretin** or **isotretinoin.**

PHARMACOKINETICS Peak: 1.5–2h **Distribution:** 91.4–97 L, 62.5–74.7% protein bound **Metabolism:** Minimal metabolism **Elimination:** 42.6% and 44.1% excreted in feces and urine respectively **Half-Life:** 21–22h

NURSING IMPLICATIONS

Assessment & Drug Effects

- Monitor for improvement in acne vulgaris lesion count.
- Assess for diarrhea. Risk for Clostridium difficile related diarrhea may occur 2 months after administration.
- Evaluate for visual disturbances, may indicate intracranial hypertension.

Patient & Family Education

- Report severe diarrhea.
- Review adverse effects.
- Avoid activities requiring mental alertness or coordination until drug effects are realized.
- Instruct patient to use sunscreen, wear protective clothing, and avoid tanning beds due to potential for photosensitivity.
- Report blurred vision or headaches, nausea, or vomiting as it may be indicative of intracranial hypertension.
- Make sure to take drug with adequate amounts of fluid to reduce the risk of esophageal irritation and ulceration.

SARGRAMOSTIM (GM-CSF)

(sar-gra'mos-tim)

Leukine

Classification: GRANULOCYTE MACROPHAGE COLONY STIMULATING FACTOR (GM-CSF)

Therapeutic: HEMAPOIETIC GROWTH FACTOR; GM-CSF

Prototype: Filgrastim

AVAILABILITY Solution for injection

ACTION & *THERAPEUTIC EFFECT*

GM-CSF is a hematopoietic growth factor that stimulates proliferation and differentiation of progenitor cells in the granulocyte-macrophage pathways. *Effectiveness is measured by an increase in the number of mature white blood cells (i.e., neutrophil count).*

USES

Febrile neutropenia, neutropenia caused by chemotherapy, peripheral blood stem cell (PBSC) mobilization.

UNLABELED USES

Neutropenia secondary to other diseases; aplastic anemia, Crohn's disease, malignant melanoma.

CONTRAINDICATIONS

Hypersensitivity to GM-CSF, yeast-derived products; excessive leukemic myeloid blasts in bone marrow or blood greater than or equal to 10%; within 24 h of chemotherapy or radiation treatment; if ANC exceeds 20,000 cells/mm^3 discontinue drug or use half the dose; increased growth of tumor size; pregnancy (fetal risk cannot be ruled out); lactation (infant risk cannot be ruled out).

CAUTIOUS USE

Hypersensitivity to benzyl alcohol; history of cardiac arrhythmias, preexisting cardiac disease, renal or hepatic dysfunction, CHF, hypoxia, myelodysplastic syndromes; pulmonary infiltrates; fluid retention; kidney and liver dysfunction; use in AML for adults younger than 55 y. Safety and efficacy in children younger than 2 y not established.

ROUTE & DOSAGE

Neutropenia following Stem Cell Transplantation

Adult: **IV** 250 mcg/m^2/day infused over 2 h for 21 days, begin 2–4 h after bone marrow transfusion and not less than 24 h after last dose of chemotherapy or 12 h after last radiation therapy

Following PBSC

Adult: **IV/Subcutaneous** 250 mg/m^2/day

Neutropenia following Chemotherapy/Febrile Neutropenia

Adult: **IV/Subcutaneous** 250 mcg/m^2/day starting ~day 11 or 4 days following induction chemotherapy

ADMINISTRATION

- Note: Do not give within 24 h preceding or following chemotherapy or within 12 h preceding or following radiotherapy.

Subcutaneous

- Reconstitute each 250 mcg powder vial with 1 mL of sterile water for injection (without preservative). Direct sterile water against side of vial and swirl gently. Avoid excessive or vigorous agitation. Do not shake. Use without further dilution for subcutaneous injection.

Intravenous

PREPARE: **IV Infusion:** Reconstitute powder vial as for subcutaneous, then further dilute reconstituted solution with NS. If the final concentration is less than 1 mcg/mL, add albumin (human) to NS before addition of sargramostim. ▪ Use 1 mg albumin/1 mL of NS to give a final concentration of 0.1% albumin. ▪ Administer as soon as possible and within 6 h of reconstitution or dilution for IV infusion. ▪ Discard after 6 h. ▪ Sargramostim

vials are single-dose vials, do not re-enter or reuse. Discard unused portion.
ADMINISTER: **IV Infusion:** Give over 2, 4, or 24 h as ordered. ▪ Do not use an in-line membrane filter. ▪ Interrupt administration and reduce the dose by 50% if absolute neutrophil count exceeds 20,000/mm^3 or if platelet count exceeds 500,000/mm^3. Notify prescriber. ▪ Reduce the IV rate 50% if patient experiences dyspnea during administration. ▪ Discontinue infusion if respiratory symptoms worsen. Notify prescriber.
INCOMPATIBILITIES: **Y-site: Acyclovir, ampicillin, ampicillin/sulbactam, cefoperazone, chlorpromazine, ganciclovir, haloperidol, hydrocortisone, hydromorphone, hydroxyzine, imipenem/cilastatin, lorazepam, methylprednisolone, mitomycin, morphine, nalbuphine, ondansetron, piperacillin, sodium bicarbonate, tobramycin, vancomycin hydrochloride.**

▪ Refrigerate the sterile powder, the reconstituted solution, and store diluted solution at 2°–8° C (36°–46° F). ▪ Do not freeze or shake.

ADVERSE EFFECTS CV: *Hypertension, edema, pericardial effusion,* chest pain, peripheral edema, tachycardia. **Respiratory:** Pharyngitis, epistaxis, dyspnea. **CNS:** Weakness, joint pain, muscle pain, bone pain. **HEENT:** Retinal hemorrhage. **Endocrine:** *Weight loss, hyperglycemia,* hypercholesterolemia, hypomagnesemia. **Skin:** *Rash,* pruritis. **Hepatic:** *Hyperbilirubinemia.* **GI:** *Diarrhea, nausea, vomiting, abdominal pain,* anorexia, hematemesis, dysphagia, <u>gastrointestinal hemorrhage</u>. **GU:** UTI. **Musculoskeletal:** *Weakness,* bone pain, joint pain, muscle pain. **Other:** Fever.

INTERACTIONS Drug: CORTICOSTEROIDS and **lithium** should be used with caution because it may potentiate the myeloproliferative effects.

PHARMACOKINETICS Absorption: Readily from subcutaneous site. **Onset:** 3–6 h. **Peak:** 1–2 h. **Duration:** 5–10 days subcutaneous. **Elimination:** Probably in urine. **Half-Life:** 80–150 min.

NURSING IMPLICATIONS

Assessment & Drug Effects

▪ Discontinue treatment and notify prescriber if WBC 50,000/mm^3.
▪ Monitor cardiac status. Occasional transient supraventricular arrhythmias have occurred during administration, particularly in those with a history of cardiac arrhythmias. Arrhythmias are reversed with discontinuation of drug.
▪ Give special attention to respiratory symptoms (dyspnea) during and immediately following IV infusion, especially in patients with preexisting pulmonary disease.
▪ Use drug with caution in patients with preexisting fluid retention, pulmonary infiltrates, or CHF. Peripheral edema, pleural or pericardial effusion has occurred after administration. It is reversible with dose reduction.
▪ Notify prescriber of any severe adverse reaction immediately.
▪ Monitor lab tests: Baseline and biweekly CBC with differential and platelet count; biweekly LFTs and renal function tests in patients with established kidney or liver dysfunction.

Common adverse effects in *italic;* life-threatening effects <u>underlined;</u> generic names in **bold;** classifications in SMALL CAPS; ♥ Canadian drug name; ⊙ Prototype drug; ⚠ Alert

Patient & Family Education

- Notify nurse or prescriber immediately of any adverse effect (e.g., dyspnea, palpitations, peripheral edema, bone or muscle pain) during or after drug administration.

SARILUMAB

(sar-il'ue-mab)

Kevzara

Classification: DISEASE MODIFYING ANTIRHEUMATIC (DMARD); INTERLEUKIN-6 RECEPTOR ANTAGONIST; MONOCLONAL ANTIBODY

Therapeutic: DISEASE-MODIFYING ANTIRHEUMATIC (DMARD)

AVAILABILITY Subcutaneous injection

ACTION & THERAPEUTIC EFFECT

Inhibits interleukin-6 (IL-6)-mediated signaling by binding to IL-6 receptors that are both soluble and membrane-bound. *Inhibition of the IL-6 receptors by sarilumab leads to a reduction in CRP levels, which can improve inflammatory processes such as rheumatoid arthritis.*

USES Treatment of rheumatoid arthritis that has failed or had insufficient response to other disease-modifying medications.

CONTRAINDICATIONS Hypersensitivity to sarilumab or excipients, live vaccines. Limited available data to determine if sarilumab during pregnancy is associated with risk for major birth defects or miscarriage. Monoclonal antibodies, like sarilumab, are transported across the placenta. There is no current data available on the presence of sarilumab in human milk or its effects on the breast-fed infant or milk production.

CAUTIOUS USE History of diverticulitis or concomitant use of NSAIDS or corticosteroid use, active hepatic disease, or impairment.

ROUTE & DOSAGE

Rheumatoid Arthritis

Adult: **Subcutaneous** 200 mg every 2 wk

Hepatic Impairment Dosage Adjustment

ALT/AST greater than 3–5 × ULN: Hold therapy until ALT/ALT is less than 3 × ULN, then restart medication at 150 mg every 2 wk; increase to original dose as appropriate

ALT/AST greater than 5 × ULN: Discontinue therapy

ADMINISTRATION

Subcutaneous

- Allow to sit at room temperature for 30 min prior to administration; do not warm any other way.
- Solution should be clear and colorless to pale yellow.
- Do not shake.
- Not for IV administration.
- Rotate injection sites; do not inject where skin is tender, damaged, bruised, or scarred.
- Inject full amount of the prefilled syringe.
- If 3 days or less since missed dose, take as soon as possible; take next dose at regularly scheduled time.
- Store at 2°–8° C (36°–46° F) in the original carton to protect from light. Do not freeze or shake. May store at 25° C (77° F) or cooler for up to 14 days. After removal from the refrigerator, use within 14 days.

S

ADVERSE EFFECTS Endocrine: *Increased LFTs*. **Skin:** Injection site pruritis and erythema. **GU:** UTI. **Hematologic:** Neutropenia, leukopenia.

INTERACTIONS Do not give live virus vaccines to patients on sarilumab; not studied with the use of JAK inhibitors or other biological DMARD agents (such as TNF antagonists). Potential interaction with CYP450 substrates, specifically those with narrow therapeutic index or specific desired effectiveness (e.g., **warfarin**, **theophylline**, oral contraceptives).

PHARMACOKINETICS Absorption: 34% bioavailability. **Onset:** Peak effect in 2–4 days. **Metabolism:** Similar to endogenous IgG, undergoes catabolic metabolism to small peptides and amino acids. **Elimination:** Through proteolytic pathway. **Half-Life:** 8–10 days, dependent on dose.

NURSING IMPLICATIONS

Black Box Warning

Serious infections (e.g., bacterial, mycobacterial, invasive fungal, viral and opportunistic infections) which have led to hospitalization or death. Do not administer during active infections. Monitor patients for infection during use. Use caution in patients with TB exposure or history of serious opportunistic, chronic, or recurrent infection. Stop sarilumab if serious opportunistic infection develops.

Assessment & Drug Effects

- Monitor for improvement of signs or symptoms of rheumatoid arthritis.
- Monitor neutrophils and platelets: 4–8 wk after treatment initiation

and approximately every 3 mo thereafter.
- Monitor for latent TB prior to initiation.
- Monitor for active TB in all patients, even if initial latent TB was negative.
- Monitor for S&S of infection during and after therapy.
- Monitor for gastrointestinal perforation.
- Monitor lab tests: ALT and AST levels 4–8 wk after treatment initiation and approximately every 3 mo thereafter. Other LFTs may be ordered if clinically indicated.

Patient & Family Education

- Do not take this drug if infection is present.
- TB has been seen in patients that take this drug.
- Notify health care provider right away of signs of infection such as fever, flu-like symptoms, chills, very bad sore throat, ear or sinus pain, cough, pain while urinating, mouth sores or sores that will not heal.
- Notify all health care providers that this drug is being taken. This includes prescribers, doctors, nurses, pharmacists, and dentists.
- Talk to prescriber before getting any vaccines.
- Birth control pills and other hormone-based birth control may not work to prevent pregnancy. Use another effective method for birth control while taking this drug.
- Notify prescriber if pregnant or plan to get pregnant.
- If pregnancy occurs while using this drug, notify your prescriber right away.
- Discuss possible breast-feeding risks with prescriber.
- Notify prescriber right away with S&S of an allergic reaction: Rash, hives, blistered skin, wheezing, chest tightness, unusual

Common adverse effects in *italic*; life-threatening effects <u>underlined</u>; generic names in **bold**; classifications in SMALL CAPS; ✦ Canadian drug name; ○ Prototype drug; ⚠ Alert

1526

hoarseness, swelling of the mouth, face, lips, tongue or throat; very bad belly pain; vomiting dark brown coffee ground emesis, black tarry stools, shortness of breath, chest pain, dizziness, muscle pain or weakness, coughing up blood.

SAXAGLIPTIN
(sax-a-glip'tin)

Onglyza

Classification: DIPEPTIDYL PEPTIDASE-4 (DPP-4) INHIBITOR
Therapeutic: ANTIDIABETIC; HORMONE MODIFIER; DDP-4 INHIBITOR
Prototype: Sitagliptin

AVAILABILITY Tablet

ACTION & THERAPEUTIC EFFECT
Slows inactivation of incretin hormones [e.g., glucagon-like peptide-1 (GLP-1) and glucose-dependent insulinotropic polypeptide (GIP)]. As plasma glucose rises, incretin hormones stimulate release of insulin from the pancreas and GLP-1 also lowers glucagon secretion, resulting in reduced hepatic glucose production. *In type 2 diabetics, saxagliptin elevates the level of incretin hormones, thus increasing insulin secretion and reducing glucagon secretion. It lowers both fasting and postprandial plasma glucose levels.*

USES Treatment of type 2 diabetes mellitus.

CONTRAINDICATIONS Hypersensitivity to saxagliptin; exfoliative skin condition; type 1 DM, concurrent administration with insulin.

CAUTIOUS USE Moderate to severe renal impairment; acute

pancreatitis; history of angioedema with use of another DDP4 inhibitor; HF; lactose intolerance; older adults; pregnancy (category B) (fetal risk cannot be ruled out); lactation (infant risk cannot be ruled out). Safe use in children younger than 18 y not established.

ROUTE & DOSAGE

Type 2 Diabetes Mellitus
Adult: **PO** 2.5–5 mg daily. Limited to 2.5 mg daily when used with a strong CYP3A4/5 inhibitor.

Renal Impairment Dosage Adjustment
eGFR less than 45 mL/min/ 1.73 m^2: **2.5 mg once daily**

ADMINISTRATION
Oral
- May be taken without regard to meals.
- Ensure that tablets are taken whole; they must not be cut or split.
- Dosing in the older adults should be based on creatinine clearance.
- Store at 15°–30° C (59°–86° F).

ADVERSE EFFECTS CV: Peripheral edema. **Respiratory:** URI. **CNS:** Headache. **Endocrine:** Hypoglycemia. **GU:** UTI.

INTERACTIONS Drug: **Rifampin** and other inducers of CYP3A4/5 enzymes decrease saxagliptin levels. Moderate (e.g., **amprenavir, aprepitant, erythromycin, fluconazole, fosamprenavir, verapamil**) and strong (e.g., **atazanavir, clarithromycin, indinavir, itraconazole, ketoconazole, nefazodone, nelfinavir, ritonavir, saquinavir, telithromycin**)

S

inhibitors of CYP3A4/5 increase saxagliptin levels. Decrease saxagliptin dose when used with INSULIN or ANTIDIABETIC drug to minimize risk of hypoglycemia. **Food: Grapefruit juice** increases saxagliptin levels.

PHARMACOKINETICS Peak: 2 h. **Distribution:** Negligible plasma protein binding. **Metabolism:** Hepatic metabolism to active and inactive compounds. **Elimination:** Renal (75%) and fecal (22%). **Half-Life:** 2.5–3.1 h.

NURSING IMPLICATIONS

Assessment & Drug Effects

- Monitor for and report S&S of significant GI distress including NV&D.
- Monitor for S&S of hypoglycemia when used in combination with a sulfonylurea or insulin.
- Monitor lab tests: Baseline and periodic creatinine clearance; periodic fasting and postprandial plasma glucose and HbA1C.

Patient & Family Education

- Carry out blood glucose monitoring as directed by prescriber.
- Consult prescriber during periods of stress and illness as dosage adjustments may be required.
- When taken alone to control diabetes, saxagliptin is unlikely to cause hypoglycemia because it only works when the blood sugar is rising after food intake.
- Stop taking drug immediately if you experience symptoms of a serious allergic reaction such as swelling about the face or throat, or difficulty breathing or swallowing.

SCOPOLAMINE

(skoe-pol′a-meen)

Transderm Scop

SCOPOLAMINE HYDROBROMIDE

Classification: ANTICHOLINERGIC; ANTIMUSCARINIC; ANTISPASMODIC; ANTIVERTIGO
Therapeutic: ANTISPASMODIC; ANTI-EMETIC; ANTIVERTIGO
Prototype: Atropine

AVAILABILITY Scopolamine: Transdermal patch.

ACTION & *THERAPEUTIC EFFECT*
Inhibits the action on acetylcholine (ACh) on postganglionic cholinergic nerves as well as on smooth muscles that lack cholinergic innervation. *Produces CNS depression with marked sedative and tranquilizing effects for use in anesthesia. Effective as a preanesthetic agent to control bronchial, nasal, pharyngeal, and salivary secretions. Additionally, it prevents nausea and vomiting associated with motion sickness.*

USES Prevention of nausea/vomiting associated with motion sickness and recovery from anesthesia.

CONTRAINDICATIONS Hypersensitivity to anticholinergic drugs; narrow angle glaucoma; severe ulcerative colitis, GI obstruction; urinary tract obstruction diseases; renal impairment; hepatic impairment; chronic lung disease; prostatic hypertrophy; infants under 6 months of age; toxemia of pregnancy; pregnancy—fetal risk cannot be ruled out; lactation—infant risk cannot be ruled out.

CAUTIOUS USE Remove patch before undergoing MRI to prevent burns at the patch site. Hypertension; patients older than 40 y, pyloric obstruction, autonomic

Common adverse effects in *italic*; life-threatening effects underlined; generic names in **bold;** classifications in SMALL CAPS; ♣ Canadian drug name; ● Prototype drug; ▲ Alert

neuropathy, myasthenia gravis; thyrotoxicosis, liver disease; CAD; CHF; tachycardia, or other tachyarrhythmias; paralytic ileus; hiatal hernia, mild or moderate ulcerative colitis, gastric ulcer, GERD; renal impairment; parkinsonism; COPD, asthma or allergies; hyperthyroidism; brain damage, psychosis; spastic paralysis; Down syndrome; older adults; children, infants.

ROUTE & DOSAGE

Motion Sickness

Adult: **Topical** 1 patch at least 4 h before anticipated travel and q3days as needed

ADMINISTRATION

Transdermal

- Apply transdermal disc system (Transderm Scōp, a controlled-release system) to dry hairless surface behind the ear. Wear gloves or wash hands thoroughly before and after application.
- Replace with another disc on another site behind the ear if disc system becomes dislodged.
- Upon removal, fold the used transdermal system in half with sticky sides together and discard in the household trash in a manner that prevents accidental contact or ingestion by children, pets or others.
- Store patch in an upright position at a controlled room temperature between 20 and 25 degrees C (68 and 77 degrees F). Do not bend or roll the pouch.

ADVERSE EFFECTS **CV:** Tachycardia. **CNS:** Amnesia (injection), somnolence (injection). **HEENT:**

Dilated pupils. **Skin:** Local irritation from patch adhesive, rash, diminished sweating. **GI:** *Dry mouth and throat* (injection). **Other:** Local irritation.

INTERACTIONS **Drug: Amantadine,** ANTICHOLINERGIC AGENTS, ANTIHISTAMINES, TRICYCLIC ANTIDEPRESSANTS, **quinidine, disopyramide, procainamide** add to anticholinergic effects; decreases **levodopa** effects; **methotrimeprazine** may precipitate extrapyramidal effects; decreases antipsychotic effects (decreased absorption) of PHENOTHIAZINES; CNS DEPRESSANTS add to CNS related side effects; **clozapine** may have increased adverse effects. **Food: Grapefruit juice** (greater than 1 qt/day) may increase plasma concentrations and adverse effects.

DIAGNOSTIC TEST INTERFERENCE

Interferes with *gastric secretion test.*

PHARMACOKINETICS **Absorption:** Readily from GI tract and percutaneously. **Peak:** 24 hours. **Duration:** 72 hours. **Distribution:** Crosses placenta; distributed to CNS. **Metabolism:** In liver. **Elimination:** In urine.

NURSING IMPLICATIONS

Assessment & Drug Effects

- Observe patient closely; some patients manifest excitement, delirium, and disorientation shortly after drug is administered until sedative effect takes hold.
- Monitor I and Os and watch for improvement in nausea/vomiting.
- Use of side rails is advisable, particularly for older adults, because of amnesic effect of scopolamine.

- Monitor blood pressure.
- In the presence of pain, scopolamine may cause delirium, restlessness, and excitement unless given with an analgesic.
- Be aware that tolerance may develop with prolonged use.
- Terminate ophthalmic use if local irritation, edema, or conjunctivitis occur.

Patient & Family Education

- Vision may blur when used as mydriatic or cycloplegic; do not drive or engage in potentially hazardous activities until vision clears.
- Opthalmic and injectable forms may cause photophobia. Wear sunglasses outside and avoid bright lights
- Injectable form may impair heat regulation. Use caution with activities leading to an increased core temperature such as strenuous exercise, exposure to extreme heat, or dehydration.
- Review proper administration of ophthalmic drops.
- Place disc on skin site the night before an expected trip or anticipated motion for best therapeutic effect.
- Wash hands carefully after handling scopolamine. Anisocoria (unequal size of pupils, blurred vision can develop by rubbing eye with drug-contaminated finger).
- Avoid alcohol and any other drugs that affect the central nervous system.

SECNIDAZOLE

(sek-nik′a-zole)
Solosec
Classification: ANTIBACTERIAL;
NITROIMIDAZOLE

Therapeutic: ANTIBACTERIAL;
ANTIPROTOZOAL
Prototype: Metronidazole

AVAILABILITY Oral granules

ACTION & *THERAPEUTIC EFFECT*

As a 5-nitroimidazole antimicrobial, produces radical anions within bacterial cells which interfere with bacterial DNA synthesis. *Secnidazole targets microorganisms often responsible for bacterial vaginosis in adult women.*

USES Bacterial vaginosis treatment.

CONTRAINDICATIONS Previous hypersensitivity to secnidazole or other nitroimidazole like medications.

CAUTIOUS USE May increase the incidence of vulvo-vaginal candidiasis, patients should be monitored for symptoms; chronic treatment with nitroimidazole derivatives has shown carcinogenicity in animal studies; the use of secnidazole in the absence of a suspected bacterial infection may increase the risk of drug-resistant microorganisms.

ROUTE & DOSAGE

Ailment

Adult: **PO** 2 grams as a single dose

ADMINISTRATION

Oral

- Administer with or without food.
- Granules should not be crushed or chewed.
- Packet contents can be sprinkled onto food such as applesauce; granules are not intended to be dissolved in liquid.

Common adverse effects in *italic;* life-threatening effects underlined; generic names in **bold;** classifications in SMALL CAPS; ♣ Canadian drug name; ○ Prototype drug; ⚠ Alert

S

- Granules should be consumed within 30 min of use.
- Store granule packet at 20°–25° C (68°–77° F) protected from moisture.

ADVERSE EFFECTS CNS: Headache. **HEENT:** Taste disturbances. **Skin:** Vulvovaginal pruritus. **GU:** Vulvo-vaginal candidiasis, nausea, diarrhea, abdominal pain, vomiting.

PHARMACOKINETICS Peak: 4 h. **Distribution:** Less than 5% protein bound. **Metabolism:** Hepatic via CYP450. **Elimination:** Urine 15% (unchanged). **Half-Life:** 17 h.

NURSING IMPLICATIONS

Assessment & Drug Effects
- Monitor for vaginal discharge or allergic reaction.

Patient & Family Education
- Administer without regard to timing of meals. Sprinkle entire contents of one packet onto applesauce, yogurt, or pudding; granules will not dissolve; do not chew or crunch granules.

SECOBARBITAL SODIUM
(see-koe-bar′bi-tal)

Seconal
Classification: SEDATIVE-HYPNOTIC; BARBITURATE; ANXIOLYTIC
Therapeutic: SEDATIVE-HYPNOTIC
Controlled Substance: Schedule II

AVAILABILITY Capsule

ACTION & THERAPEUTIC EFFECT
Short-acting barbiturate with CNS depressant effects as well as mood alteration from excitation to mild sedation, hypnosis, and deep coma. Depresses the sensory cortex,
decreases motor activity, alters cerebellar function and produces drowsiness, sedation, and hypnosis. *Alters cerebellar function and produces drowsiness, sedation, and hypnosis.*

USES Preoperatively to provide basal hypnosis for general, spinal, or regional anesthesia; management of insomnia.

CONTRAINDICATIONS History of sensitivity to barbiturates; porphyria; hepatic coma; severe respiratory disease; parturition, fetal immaturity; uncontrolled pain; pregnancy (category D).

CAUTIOUS USE Pregnant women with toxemia or history of bleeding; labor and delivery; seizure disorders; aspirin hypersensitivity; liver function impairment; renal impairment; hyperthyroidism; diabetes mellitus; depression; history of suicidal tendencies or drug abuse; acute or chronic pain; severe anemia; older adults (short term use only), debilitated individuals; lactation; children younger than 6 y.

ROUTE & DOSAGE

Preoperative Sedative
Adult: **PO** 200–300 mg 1–2 h before surgery
Child: **PO** 2–6 mg/kg 1–2 h before surgery

Insomnia
Adult: **PO** 100 mg at bedtime

ADMINISTRATION
Oral
- Give hypnotic dose only after patient retires for the evening.
- Crush and mix with a fluid or with food if patient cannot swallow pill.

ADVERSE EFFECTS Respiratory: Respiratory depression, laryngospasm. **CNS:** Drowsiness, lethargy, hangover, paradoxical excitement in older adults.

INTERACTIONS Drug: Phenmetrazine antagonizes effects of secobarbital; CNS DEPRESSANTS, **alcohol,** SEDATIVES compound CNS depression; MAO INHIBITORS cause excessive CNS depression; **methoxyflurane** increases risk of nephrotoxicity. Do not use **nifedipine** concurrently. **Herbal: Kava, valerian** may potentiate sedation.

PHARMACOKINETICS Absorption: 90% from GI tract. **Onset:** 15–30 min. **Duration:** 1–4 h. **Distribution:** Crosses placenta; distributed into breast milk. **Metabolism:** In liver (CYP2C9, CYP2C19, CYP2E1, CYP3A, CYP1A2, UGT). **Elimination:** In urine. **Half-Life:** 30 h.

NURSING IMPLICATIONS

Assessment & Drug Effects

- Be alert to unexpected responses and report promptly. Older adults or debilitated patients and children sometimes have paradoxical response to barbiturate therapy (i.e., irritability, marked excitement as inappropriate tearfulness and aggression in children, depression, and confusion).
- Be aware that barbiturates do not have analgesic action, and may produce restlessness when given to patients in pain.
- Be alert for acute toxicity (intoxication) characterized by profound CNS depression, respiratory depression, hypoventilation, cyanosis, cold clammy skin, hypothermia, constricted pupils (but may be dilated in severe intoxication), shock, oliguria, tachycardia,

hypotension, respiration arrest, circulatory collapse, and death.

- Monitor lab tests: Periodic LFTs, renal function tests and hematology tests during prolonged therapy.

Patient & Family Education

- Instances of sleep driving and sleep walking with no memory of the occurrence have been reported. Do not drive or engage in potentially hazardous activities until response to drug is established.
- Store barbiturates in a safe place; not on the bedside table or other readily accessible places. It is possible to forget having taken the drug, and in half-wakened conditions take more and accidentally overdose.
- Do not become pregnant. Use or add barrier contraception if using hormonal contraceptives.
- Report onset of fever, sore throat or mouth, malaise, easy bruising or bleeding, petechiae, or jaundice, rash to prescriber during prolonged therapy.
- Do not consume alcohol in any amount when taking a barbiturate. It may severely impair judgment and abilities.

SECUKINUMAB
(se-cu-kin'u-mab)

Cosentyx
Classification: MONOCLONAL ANTIBODY; INTERLEUKIN INHIBITOR; ANTIPSORIATIC
Therapeutic: ANTIPSORIATIC
Prototype: Basilixumab

AVAILABILITY Solution for injection

ACTION & THERAPEUTIC EFFECT Selectively binds to interleukin-17A (IL-17A) and inhibits its interaction with the IL-17 receptor. IL-17A is a naturally occurring cytokine

Common adverse effects in *italic*; life-threatening effects <u>underlined</u>; generic names in **bold**; classifications in SMALL CAPS; ♣ Canadian drug name; ● Prototype drug; ⚠ Alert

1532

involved in normal inflammatory and immune responses. *Inhibits the release of proinflammatory cytokines and chemokines, thus reducing psoriatic skin inflammation.*

USES Treatment of moderate to severe plaque psoriasis in adult patients who are candidates for systemic therapy or phototherapy; ankylosing spondylitis; psoriatic arthritis.

CONTRAINDICATIONS Serious hypersensitivity to secukinumab or any component of the formulation; active TB. Avoid live virus vaccines and understand that non-live vaccines may not elicit sufficient immune response. Pregnancy—fetal risk cannot be ruled out; lactation—infant risk cannot be ruled out.

CAUTIOUS USE Concurrent infectious disease; history of chronic or recurrent infection; Crohn's disease; latex allergy when using *Sensoready*® pen or prefilled syringe. Safety and efficacy in children younger than 18 y not established.

ROUTE & DOSAGE

Plaque Psoriasis

Adult: **Subcutaneous** 300 mg at wk 0, 1, 2, 3, and 4; then 300 mg q4wk

Ankylosing Spondylitis/Psoriatic arthritis

Adult: **Subcutaneous** 150 mg at wk 0, 1, 2, 3, and 4; then 150 mg q4wk

ADMINISTRATION

Subcutaneous ONLY

- Remove *Sensoready*® pen, prefilled syringe, or vial from refrigerator and allow to stand for 15–30 min to reach room temperature.

Administer within 1 hour of removing from refrigerator.
- Vial reconstitution: Slowly inject 1 mL of SW onto the powder. Tilt vial 45° and gently rotate for about 1 min; do not shake or invert. Let vial stand at room temperature for approx. 10 min for powder to dissolve. Once again, tilt vial 45° and gently rotate for about 1 min; do not shake or invert. Allow vial to stand undisturbed at room temperature for about 5 min. Use immediately or store refrigerated for up to 24 h.
- Inject into outer thigh, lower abdomen (2 inches or greater away from the navel) or outer upper arm; rotate injection sites and avoid areas where the skin is tender, bruised, erythematous, indurated, or affected by psoriasis.
- Store intact vials, *Sensoready*® pens, and prefilled syringes refrigerated at 2°–8° C (36°–46° F). Store in original carton until administering and protect from light.

ADVERSE EFFECTS (≥5%) Respiratory: *Nasopharyngitis.*

INTERACTIONS Drug: Do not give LIVE VACCINES; IMMUNOSUPPRESSANTS may have additive effects. **Herbal:** Do not use with echinacea.

PHARMACOKINETICS Absorption: 55–77% bioavailable. **Peak:** 6 days. **Metabolism:** Peptide degradation. **Half-Life:** 22–31 days.

NURSING IMPLICATIONS

Assessment & Drug Effects

- Monitor for and report development of infection (e.g., nasopharyngitis, upper respiratory tract infection, and mucocutaneous candida infection).
- Monitor patients with Crohn's disease for exacerbations.

Patient & Family Education

- Minimize exposure to persons with known, active infections as this drug may lower the ability of your immune system to fight infections.
- Immediately report to prescriber if you develop S&S of an infection.
- Do not accept immunizations/vaccines while receiving this drug.
- Do not breast-feed while taking this drug without consulting prescriber.
- Avoid live vaccinations during therapy.

SELEGILINE HYDROCHLORIDE (L-DEPRENYL)
(se-leg'i-leen)
Emsam, Zelapar
Classification: ANTIPARKINSON; ANTIDEPRESSANT (MAOI)
Therapeutic: ANTIPARKINSON; ANTI-DEPRESSANT

AVAILABILITY Tablet, capsule; orally disintegrating tablet; transdermal patch

ACTION & *THERAPEUTIC EFFECT*
Effectiveness in parkinsonism is thought to be due to increased dopaminergic activity. It interferes with dopamine reuptake at the synapse of neurons as well as its inhibition of MAO type B dopaminergic activity in the brain. Interference with dopamine reuptake at the MAO type A dopaminergic receptors in the brain is thought to be the mechanism for antidepression. *Effectiveness is measured in decreased tremors, reduced akinesia, improved speech and motor abilities as well as improved walking. At slightly higher doses it is an effective antidepressant.*

USES Adjunctive therapy of Parkinson disease for patients being treated with levodopa and carbidopa who exhibit deterioration in the quality of their response to therapy, major depressive disorder.

UNLABELED USES Attention deficit/hyperactivity disorder.

CONTRAINDICATIONS Hypersensitivity to selegiline; uncontrolled hypertension; use with dextromethorphan, other MAO inhibitors (MAOIs), meperidine, methadone, propoxyphene, and tramadol; suicidal ideation; pregnancy—fetal risk cannot be ruled out; lactation infant risk cannot be ruled out.

CAUTIOUS USE Hypertension; hepatic or renal impairment; history of suicidal tendencies, bipolar disorder; restless leg disorder; impulse control disorder; psychosis; older adults. Safety and efficacy not established in pediatric patients.

ROUTE & DOSAGE

Parkinson Disease
Adult: **PO Tablet/Capsule** 5 mg bid with breakfast and lunch (max: 10 mg/day); **PO Orally disintegrating tablet** 1.25 mg daily × 6 wk (max: 2.5 mg daily)

Depression
Adult: **Transdermal** 6 mg/day, may increase by 3 mg/day q2wk up to 12 mg/day

Hepatic Impairment Dosage Adjustment
Child Pugh A and B: **Orally disintegrating tablet:** 1.25 mg once daily.

ADMINISTRATION

Oral

- Give orally disintegrating tablets before breakfast and lunch, without liquid. Do not push tablets through the foil backing; peel back the backing of blister with dry hands and gently remove tablet. Immediately place tablet on top of the tongue. Neither food nor liquids should be ingested for 5 min before/after administration.
- Store tablet and capsule at controlled room temperature between 20 and 25 degrees C (68 to 77 degrees F). Store disintegrating tablet at controlled room temperature of 25 degrees C (77 degrees F), with excursions permitted between at 15°–30° C (59°–86° F).

Transdermal

- Do not cut or trim patch.
- Apply only one patch at approximately the same time every day.
- Before application wash the area with soap and warm water. Dry thoroughly.
- Apply to upper torso, upper thigh, or outer surface of upper arm. Do not apply to hairy, oily, irritated, broken, or calloused skin.
- Rotate sites.
- Avoid dermal contact with sticky side of the patch. Wash hands after application.
- Avoid exposure of application site to direct heat (eg, heating pads, blankets, lamps, saunas, heated water beds, direct sunlight).

ADVERSE EFFECTS Respiratory:
Rhinitis. **CNS:** *Sleep disturbances* dyskinesia, dizziness, *headache.* **GI:** *nausea, indigestion xerostomia.* **Musculoskeletal:** Backache.

INTERACTIONS Drug: There
are extensive drug interactions, consult a drug interaction database for complete listing, some interactions of significance are listed here. TRICYCLIC ANTIDEPRESSANTS may cause hyperpyrexia, seizures; SSRIS may cause serotonin syndrome or hyperthermia, diaphoresis, tremors, seizures, delirium; SYMPATHO-MIMETIC AGENTS, ALPHA AGONISTS, BETA AGONISTS (e.g., **amphetamine, phenylephrine, phenylpropanolamine**), **guanethidine,** may cause hypertensive crisis; CNS DEPRESSANTS have additive CNS depressive effects; OPIATE ANALGESICS (especially **meperidine**) may cause hypertensive crisis and circulatory collapse; **buspirone,** hypertension; GENERAL ANESTHETICS: Prolonged hypotensive and CNS depressant effects; hypertension, headache, hyperexcitability reported with **dopamine, methyldopa, levodopa, tryptophan;** HYPOTENSIVE AGENTS and DIURETICS have additive hypotensive effects. **Food:** Aged meats or aged cheeses, protein extracts, sour cream, alcohol, anchovies, liver, sausages, overripe figs, bananas, avocados, chocolate, soy sauce, bean curd, natural yogurt, fava beans—**tyramine**-containing foods—may precipitate hypertensive crisis (less frequent with usual doses of **selegiline** than with other MAOIS). **Herbal: Ginseng, ephedra, ma huang, St. John's wort** may cause hypertensive crisis.

PHARMACOKINETICS Absorption:
Rapid; 73% reaches systemic circulation. **Onset:** 1–2 weeks (antidepressant). **Duration:** 1–3 days. **Distribution:** Crosses placenta; not known if distributed into breast milk. **Metabolism:** In liver to *N*-desmethyldeprenyl-amphetamine and methamphetamine. **Elimination:** In urine. **Half-Life:** 10 h.

S

NURSING IMPLICATIONS

Black Box Warning

Selegiline transdermal patch for depression has been associated with increased risk of suicidal thinking and behavior in children, adolescents, and young adults.

Assessment & Drug Effects

- Monitor vital signs, particularly during period of dosage adjustment. Report alterations in BP or pulse. Indications for discontinuation of the drug include orthostatic hypotension, hypertension, and arrhythmias.
- Monitor for changes in behavior that may indicate increased suicidality, especially in adolescents or children being treated for depression.
- Monitor all patients closely for behavior changes (e.g., hallucinations, confusion, depression, delusions).

Patient & Family Education

- Do not exceed the prescribed drug dose.
- Report symptoms of MAO inhibitor-induced hypertension (e.g., severe headache, palpitations, neck stiffness, nausea, vomiting) immediately to prescriber.
- Do not drive or engage in potentially hazardous activities until response to drug is known.
- Make positional changes slowly and in stages. Orthostatic hypotension is possible as well as dizziness, light-headedness, and fainting.
- If the transdermal patch falls off, apply a new patch to a new area, and resume previous schedule.
- Only one should be worn at a given time. Remove the old transdermal patch.
- Routine screening by dermatologist for melanoma.

SELEXIPAG

(se-lex'i-pag)

Uptravi

Classification: PROSTAGLANDIN; PULMONARY ANTIHYPERTENSIVE

Therapeutic: PULMONARY ANTIHYPERTENSIVE

Prototype: Epoprostenol

AVAILABILITY Tablets

ACTION & *THERAPEUTIC EFFECT*

Hydrolyzed in vivo to produce an active metabolite that acts as an agonist at the prostacyclin IP receptor. *Agonist action at the IP receptor produces inhibition of platelet function, a reduction in pulmonary vascular resistance, and relaxation of pulmonary vascular smooth muscle.*

USES Treatment of pulmonary arterial hypertension (PAH) in order to delay disease progression and reduce the risk of hospitalization.

CONTRAINDICATIONS Concomitant use with strong CYP2C8 inhibitors.

CAUTIOUS USE Avoid use in patients with severe hepatic impairment or pulmonary veno-occlusive disease (PVOD). There are no adequate and well-controlled studies in pregnancy or lactation.

ROUTE & DOSAGE

Pulmonary Arterial Hypertension

Adult: **PO** 200 mcg bid; may increase weekly in 200 mcg increments (max dose: 1600 mcg)

Common adverse effects in *italic*; life-threatening effects underlined; generic names in **bold**; classifications in SMALL CAPS; ♣ Canadian drug name; ❍ Prototype drug; ⚠ Alert

Hepatic Impairment Dosage Adjustment

Moderate impairment (Child-Pugh class B): Reduce dosing interval to once daily
Severe impairment (Child-Pugh class C): Avoid use

ADMINISTRATION

Oral

- Administer without regard to food. Administering with food may improve tolerability.
- Do not split, crush, or chew tablets.
- Store at 15°–30° C (59°–86° F).

ADVERSE EFFECTS CNS: *Headache.* **Endocrine:** Hyperthyroidism; Decreased hemoglobin. **Skin:** Rash. **GI:** *Diarrhea, nausea,* anorexia, vomiting. **Musculoskeletal:** Arthralgia, jaw pain, limb pain, *myalgia.* **Other:** Anemia, decreased appetite, flushing, *jaw pain,* pain in extremity, rash.

DIAGNOSTIC TEST INTERFERENCE

Causes a reduction in thyroid function test results.

INTERACTIONS Drug: Do not use with strong CYP2C8 inhibitors (e.g., **gemfibrozil**), may increase the levels of selexipag and its active metabolite. **Rifampin** may decrease serum concentrations.

PHARMACOKINETICS Peak: 3–4 h. **Distribution:** 99% plasma protein bound. **Metabolism:** Hydrolyzed to active metabolite; hepatic metabolism to inactive metabolites. Metabolized via CYP3A4, CYP2C8, UGT1A3. **Elimination:** Primarily fecal (93%). **Half-Life:** 6.2–13.5 h (active metabolite).

NURSING IMPLICATIONS

Assessment & Drug Effects

- Skin assessment for flushing and rash.
- Respiratory assessment, including pulse oximetry.
- Complaint of jaw, limb, muscle, or joint pain.
- Monitor lab tests: Thyroid function tests, LFTs.

Patient & Family Education

- Women need to use appropriate contraceptive measures.
- Report any signs of significant reaction: Wheezing, chest tightness, fever, itching, swelling of face, lips, tongue, or throat.
- Patients may have decreased appetite.
- Report any shortness of breath, severe loss of strength or energy.

SEMAGLUTIDE

(sem-a-gloo'tide)
Ozempic
Classification: ANTIDIABETIC; GLUCAGON-LIKE PEPTIDE-1 RECEPTOR AGONIST; INCRETIN MIMETICS
Therapeutic: ANTIDIABETIC
Prototype: Exenatide

AVAILABILITY Solution for injection; peninjector

ACTION & *THERAPEUTIC EFFECT*

Semaglutide is a glucagon-like peptide-1 (GLP-1) receptor agonist that causes increased insulin release and decreased glucagon release in the presence of elevated blood glucose, and delays the rate of gastric emptying. *Semaglutide lowers postprandial blood glucose levels and helps normalize HbA1C.*

USES Treatment of type 2 diabetes mellitus in combination with diet and exercise

CONTRAINDICATIONS Family or personal history of medullary thyroid carcinoma (MTC); history of multiple endocrine neoplasia syndrome 2 (MEN 2); serious hypersensitivity reaction to semaglutide; Type 1 DM; pancreatitis.

CAUTIOUS USE History of pancreatitis; alcohol abuse; history of cholethiasis; history of severe hypoglycemia; gastroparesis; history of angioedema; renal or hepatic impairment; concurrent use with insulin secretagogues (e.g., sulfonylureas); older adults; pregnancy category C. Safety and efficacy in children younger than 18 y not established.

ROUTE & DOSAGE

Type 2 Diabetes Mellitus
Adult: **Subcutaneous** Initial dose 0.25 mg once a wk for 4 wk (max: 1mg once a wk)

ADMINISTRATION

Subcutaneous
- Inject into abdomen, thigh, or upper arm without regard to meals.
- Rotate injection sites weekly.
- Solution should be clear; do not use if particulate matter or color are seen.
- Do not mix with other injections in same syringe.
- Store in refrigeration until first use, then either continue refrigeration or store at 15°–30 °C (59°–86° F) for up to 56 days.

ADVERSE EFFECTS CV: Tachycardia. **CNS:** Dizziness, fatigue. **Endocrine:** Increased amylase and lipase, pancreatitis, hypoglycemia. **GI:** Nausea, vomiting, diarrhea, dyspepsia abdominal pain, constipation, flatulence, gastroesophageal reflux disease, cholelithiasis, gastritis. **Other:** Discomfort at injection site.

INTERACTIONS Drug: Due to its ability to slow gastric emptying, semaglutide can decrease absorption rate and plasma levels of oral medications; with other INSULIN SECRETAGOGUE (e.g., **sulfonylurea**) semaglutide may increase the risk of hypoglycemia.

PHARMACOKINETICS Absorption: 89% bioavailability. **Peak:** 1–3 days after single dose. **Distribution:** greater than 99% protein bound. **Metabolism:** Metabolized by endogenous proteolytic enzymes. **Elimination:** Urine, feces; 3% unchanged. **Half-Life:** 1 wk.

NURSING IMPLICATIONS

Black Box Warning

Semaglutide has been shown to cause thyroid C-cell tumors in animals. Clinical relevance in humans has not been established.

Assessment & Drug Effects
- Monitor for S&S of gall bladder disease.
- Monitor lab tests: Plasma glucose (HbA1C) at least twice yearly, renal function tests, triglycerides.

Patient & Family Education
- Wear medical alert ID bracelet.
- Check blood sugar as instructed by prescriber.
- Do not drive if blood sugar has been low.
- Have bloodwork checked as ordered by prescriber.
- Talk with prescriber before drinking alcohol.

SENNA (SENNOSIDES)
(sen'na)

Black-Draught, Gentlax B, Senexon, Senokot, Senolax
Classification: STIMULANT LAXATIVE
Therapeutic: STIMULANT LAXATIVE
Prototype: Bisacodyl

AVAILABILITY Tablet; syrup

ACTION & *THERAPEUTIC EFFECT*
Senna glycosides are converted in colon to active aglycone, which stimulates peristalsis. Concentrate is purified and standardized for uniform action and is claimed to produce less colic than crude form. *Peristalsis stimulated by conversion of drug to active chemical resulting in a softening of the stool and relief from constipation.*

USES Acute constipation and preoperative and preradiographic bowel evacuation.

CONTRAINDICATIONS Hypersensitivity; appendicitis, fecal impaction; fluid and electrolyte imbalances; irritable colon, nausea, vomiting, undiagnosed abdominal pain, intestinal obstruction.

CAUTIOUS USE Diabetes mellitus; fluid and electrolyte imbalances; pregnancy; lactation (infant risk is minimal). Safe use in children younger than 2 y not established.

ROUTE & DOSAGE

Constipation
Adult: **PO** 1–2 tablets (max: 4 tablets); **Syrup, Liquid** 10–15 mL at bedtime

Child (6–11 y): **PO** 5–7.5mL at bedtime (max: 7.5 mL bid);
2–5 y: 2.5–3.75mL at bedtime (max: 3.75 mL bid)

ADMINISTRATION

Oral
- Give at bedtime, generally.
- Avoid exposing drug to excessive heat; protect fluid extracts from light.
- Store between 15°–30° C (59°–86° F).

ADVERSE EFFECTS **Endocrine:**
Electrolyte imbalance. **GI:** Abdominal pain, cramps, diarrhea, nausea, and vomiting. **GU:** Nephritis.

PHARMACOKINETICS **Onset:**
6–10 h; may take up to 24 h. **Metabolism:** In liver. **Elimination:** In feces.

NURSING IMPLICATIONS

Assessment & Drug Effects
- Reduce dose in patients who experience considerable abdominal cramping.

Patient & Family Education
- Be aware that drug may alter urine and feces color; yellowish brown (acid), reddish brown (alkaline).
- Continued use may lead to dependence. Consult prescriber if constipation persists beyond one week.
- See bisacodyl for additional nursing implications.

SERTACONAZOLE NITRATE
(ser-ta-con'a-zole)

Ertaczo
Classification: ANTIBIOTIC; AZOLE ANTIFUNGAL
Therapeutic: ANTIFUNGAL
Prototype: Fluconazole

S

AVAILABILITY Cream

ACTION & *THERAPEUTIC EFFECT*
Believed to act primarily by inhibiting cytochrome P450–dependent synthesis of ergosterol, a key component of the cell membrane of fungi resulting in fungal cell injury. *Has a broad spectrum of activity against common fungal pathogens.*

USES Treatment of tinea pedis in immunocompetent patients.

CONTRAINDICATIONS Hypersensitivity to imidazoles.

CAUTIOUS USE History of hypersensitivity to azole antifungals; pregnancy (category C); lactation; children younger than 12 y.

ROUTE & DOSAGE

Tinea Pedis
Adult/Child (12 y or older):
Topical Apply thin layer to affected area twice daily for 4 wk

ADMINISTRATION
Topical
- Cleanse the affected area and dry thoroughly before application.
- Apply a thin layer of the cream to affected area between the toes and the immediately surrounding healthy skin. Gently rub into the skin.
- Store at 15°–30° C (57°–86° F).

ADVERSE EFFECTS Skin: Contact dermatitis, dry skin, burning, application site reaction, skin tenderness.

PHARMACOKINETICS Absorption: Negligible through intact skin.

NURSING IMPLICATIONS
Assessment & Drug Effects
- Monitor for clinical improvement, which should be seen about 2 wk after initiating treatment.

Patient & Family Education
- Report any of the following: Severe skin irritation, redness, burning, blistering, or itching.
- Do not stop using this medication prematurely. Athlete's foot takes about 4 wk to clear completely.
- Nursing mothers should ensure that this topical cream does not accidentally get on the breast.

SERTRALINE HYDROCHLORIDE
(ser'tra-leen)
Zoloft
Classification: ANTIDEPRESSANT; SELECTIVE SEROTONIN REUPTAKE INHIBITOR (SSRI)
Therapeutic: ANTIDEPRESSANT; SSRI
Prototype: Fluoxetine

AVAILABILITY Tablet; oral solution

ACTION & *THERAPEUTIC EFFECT*
Potent inhibitor of serotonin (5-HT) reuptake in the brain. Chronic administration results in downregulation of norepinephrine, a reaction found with other effective antidepressants. *Effective in controlling depression, obsessive-compulsive disorder, anxiety, and panic disorder.*

USES Major depression, obsessive-compulsive disorder, panic disorder, social anxiety disorder, premenstrual dysphoric disorder, post-traumatic stress disorder.

UNLABELED USES Eating disorders, generalized anxiety disorder.

CONTRAINDICATIONS Patients taking MAO inhibitors or within

14 days of discontinuing MAO inhibitor; concurrent use of Antabuse; suicidal ideation, hyponatremia; mania or hypomania; children with MDD.

CAUTIOUS USE Seizure disorders, major affective disorders, bipolar disorder, history of suicide; liver dysfunction, renal impairment; abrupt discontinuation; anorexia nervosa, recent history of MI or unstable cardiac disease, dehydration; DM; risk factor for QT prolongation; ECT therapy, older adults; pregnancy (category C); lactation. Safe use for OCD in children younger than 6 y is not established.

ROUTE & DOSAGE

Depression, Panic Disorder, PTSD

Adult: **PO** Begin with 50 mg/day, gradually increase every few weeks according to response (range: 50–200 mg)
Geriatric: **PO** Start with 25 mg/day

Premenstrual Dysphoric Disorder

Adult: **PO** Begin with 50 mg/day for first cycle, may titrate up to 150 mg/day

Obsessive-Compulsive Disorder

Adult /Adolescent: **PO** Begin with 50 mg/day, may titrate at weekly intervals up to 200 mg/day
Child (6–12 y): **PO** Begin with 25 mg/day, may increase by 50 mg/wk, as tolerated and needed, up to 200 mg/day

ADMINISTRATION

Oral

- Give in the morning or evening.
- Do not give concurrently with an MAO inhibitor or within 14 days of discontinuing an MAO inhibitor.

- Oral solution: Dilute concentrate before use with 4 oz of water, ginger ale, lemon/lime soda, lemonade, or orange juice ONLY. Give immediately after mixing. Caution with latex sensitivity, as the dropper contains dry natural rubber.

ADVERSE EFFECTS CV: Palpitations, chest pain, hypertension, hypotension, edema, syncope, tachycardia. **Respiratory:** Rhinitis, pharyngitis, cough, dyspnea, bronchospasm. **CNS:** *Agitation, insomnia, headache, dizziness, somnolence, fatigue,* ataxia, incoordination, vertigo, abnormal dreams, aggressive behavior, delusions, hallucinations, emotional lability, paranoia, suicidal ideation, seizure, depersonalization. **HEENT:** Exophthalmos, blurred vision, dry eyes, diplopia, photophobia, tearing, conjunctivitis, mydriasis, tinnitus. **Endocrine:** Gynecomastia, *male sexual dysfunction*; Hyponatremia in older adults. **Skin:** Rash, urticaria, acne, alopecia. **GI:** *Nausea, vomiting, diarrhea, constipation,* indigestion, anorexia, flatulence, abdominal pain, dry mouth. **Other:** Myalgia, arthralgia, muscle weakness, bone fracture (older adults).

DIAGNOSTIC TEST INTERFERENCE

May cause asymptomatic elevations in *liver function tests.* Slight decrease in *uric acid.*

INTERACTIONS Drug: MAOIS (e.g., **selegiline, phenelzine**) should be stopped 14 days before sertraline is started because of serious problems with other SEROTONIN REUPTAKE INHIBITORS (shivering, nausea, diplopia, confusion, anxiety). **Sertraline** may increase levels and toxicity of **diazepam, pimozide, tolbutamide.** Use cautiously with other centrally acting CNS drugs; increase risk of **ergotamine** toxicity with **dihydroergotamine, ergotamine.** Avoid with agents that prolong the QT interval (e.g., **bepridil, dronedarone, ziprasidone**). Concentrate interacts with **disulfiram. Herbal: St. John's wort** may cause **serotonin** syndrome (headache, dizziness, sweating, agitation). **Food: Grapefruit juice** (greater than 1 qt/day) may increase plasma concentrations and adverse effects.

PHARMACOKINETICS Absorption:
Slowly from GI tract. **Onset:** 2–4 wk. **Distribution:** 99% protein bound; distribution into breast milk unknown. **Metabolism:** Extensive first-pass metabolism in liver to inactive metabolites (substrate of CYP2B6, CYP2C9, CYP2D6, CYP3A4, and CYP2C19). **Elimination:** 40–45% in urine, 40–45% in feces. **Half-Life:** 24 h.

NURSING IMPLICATIONS

Black Box Warning

Sertraline has been associated with increased risk of suicidal thinking and behavior in children, adolescents, and young adults.

Assessment & Drug Effects
- Supervise patients at risk for suicide closely during initial therapy.
- Monitor for worsening of depression or emergence of suicidal ideation.
- Monitor older adults for fluid and sodium imbalances.
- Monitor patients with a history of a seizure disorder closely.
- Monitor lab tests: Thyroid function tests.

Patient & Family Education
- Report diarrhea, nausea, dyspepsia, insomnia, drowsiness, dizziness, or persistent headache to prescriber.

- Report emergence of agitation, irritability, hostility or aggression, mania.
- Report signs of bleeding promptly to prescriber when taking concomitant warfarin.

SEVELAMER HYDROCHLORIDE ⬤

(se-vel'a-mer)
Renagel, Renvela
Classification: ELECTROLYTE AND WATER BALANCE AGENT; PHOSPHATE BINDER
Therapeutic: PHOSPHATE BINDER

AVAILABILITY
Tablet; oral powder for suspension

ACTION & *THERAPEUTIC EFFECT*
Polymer that binds intestinal phosphate; interacts with phosphate by way of ion exchange and hydrogen binding. *Effectiveness indicated by a serum phosphate level 6.0 mg/dL or less.*

USES
Hyperphosphatemia.

CONTRAINDICATIONS
Hypersensitivity to sevelamer HCl; hypophosphatemia; fecal impaction; bowel obstruction; appendicitis; dysphagia, GI bleeding, major GI surgery; lactation.

CAUTIOUS USE
GI motility disorders; vitamin deficiencies (especially vitamins D, E, and K and folic acid); pregnancy (category C); children younger than 18 y.

ROUTE & DOSAGE

Hyperphosphatemia
Adult: **PO** 800–1600 mg tid based on severity of hyperphosphatemia

Common adverse effects in *italic*; life-threatening effects <u>underlined</u>; generic names in **bold**; classifications in SMALL CAPS; ♣ Canadian drug name; ⬤ Prototype drug; ⚠ Alert

1542

S

ADMINISTRATION

Oral

- Give with meals.
- Give other oral medications 1 h before or 3 h after Renagel.
- Store at 15°–30° C (59°–86° F); protect from moisture.

ADVERSE EFFECTS CV: Hypertension, hypotension, thrombosis. **Respiratory:** Increased cough. **GI:** Diarrhea, dyspepsia, vomiting, nausea, constipation, flatulence. **Other:** Headache, infection, pain.

NURSING IMPLICATIONS

Assessment & Drug Effects

- Monitor lab tests: Periodic 24-hour urinary calcium and phosphorus, and serum magnesium; alkaline phosphatase q12mo or more often with elevated PTH; iPTH q3–12 mo depending on CKD severity.

Patient & Family Education

- Take daily multivitamin supplement approved by prescriber.

SILDENAFIL CITRATE ⊙

(sil-den'a-fil ci'trate)
Revatio, Viagra
Classification: PHOSPHODIESTERASE (PDE) INHIBITOR; IMPOTENCE; PULMONARY ANTIHYPERTENSIVE
Therapeutic: PULMONARY ANTIHYPERTENSIVE; IMPOTENCE

AVAILABILITY Tablet; solution for injection; powder for oral suspension

ACTION & *THERAPEUTIC EFFECT*

Enhances vasodilation effect of nitric oxide in the corpus cavernosus of the penis, thus sustaining an erection. PDE-5 inhibitors increase pulmonary vasodilation by sustaining levels of cyclic guanosine monophosphate (cGMP). Additionally, sildenafil produces a reduction in the pulmonary to systemic vascular resistance ratio. *Effective for treatment of erectile dysfunction, whether organic or psychogenic in origin. Sildenafil produces a significant improvement in arterial oxygenation in pulmonary arterial hypertension (PAH).*

USES Erectile dysfunction, pulmonary arterial hypertension.

UNLABELED USES Altitude sickness, Raynaud's phenomenon, sexual dysfunction, anorgasmy.

CONTRAINDICATIONS Hypersensitivity to sildenafil. Patients with pulmonary veno-occlusive disease (PVOD) and patients taking nitrate/nitrite therapy.

CAUTIOUS USE CAD with unstable angina, heart failure, MI, cardiac arrhythmias, stroke within 6 mo of starting drug; hypotension and hypertension; risk factors for CVA; aortic stenosis; anatomic deformity of the penis; sickle cell anemia, polycythemia; multiple myeloma; leukemia; active bleeding or a peptic ulcer, GERD, hiatal hernia; coagulopathy; retinitis pigmentosa; visual disturbances; hepatic disease, hepatitis, cirrhosis; severe renal impairment; older adults; pregnancy (category B); lactation; children and infants.

ROUTE & DOSAGE

Erectile Dysfunction

Adult: **PO** 50 mg 0.5–4 h before sexual activity (dose range: 25 to 100 mg once/day)

Geriatric: **PO** 25 mg approximately 1 h before sexual activity

Pulmonary Arterial Hypertension

Adult: **PO** 5 mg or 20 mg tid (4–6 h apart); **IV** 2.5 mg or 10 mg tid

Hepatic Impairment Dosage Adjustment

Child-Pugh class A or B: Starting dose of 25 mg

Renal Impairment Dosage Adjustment

CrCl less than 30 mL/min: Starting dose of 25 mg

ADMINISTRATION

Oral

- For erectile dysfunction: Dose 1 h prior to sexual activity (effective range is 0.5–4 h).

Intravenous

PREPARE: **Direct:** Give undiluted. *ADMINISTER:* **Direct:** Give as a bolus dose.

- Store at 15°–30° C (59°–86° F) in a tightly closed container; protect from light.

ADVERSE EFFECTS

CV: Flushing, chest pain, <u>MI</u>, angina, AV block, tachycardia, palpitation, hypotension, postural hypotension, <u>cardiac arrest</u>, <u>sudden cardiac death</u>, heart failure, cardiomyopathy, abnormal ECG, edema. **Respiratory:** Nasal congestion, asthma, dyspnea, epistaxis, laryngitis, pharyngitis, sinusitis, bronchitis, cough. **CNS:** *Headache,* dizziness, migraine, syncope, cerebral thrombosis, ataxia, neuralgia, paresthesias, tremor, vertigo, depression, insomnia, somnolence, abnormal dreams. **HEENT:** Abnormal vision (color changes, photosensitivity, blurred vision, sudden vision loss). **Endocrine:** Gout, hyperglycemia, hyperuricemia, hypoglycemia, hypernatremia. **Skin:** Rash, urticaria, pruritus, sweating, <u>exfoliative dermatitis</u>. **GI:** Dyspepsia, diarrhea, abdominal pain, vomiting, colitis, dysphagia, gastritis, gastroenteritis, esophagitis, stomatitis, dry mouth, abnormal liver function tests, thirst. **GU:** UTI. **Hematologic:** Anemia, <u>leukopenia</u>. **Other:** Face edema, photosensitivity, shock, asthenia, pain, chills, fall, allergic reaction, arthritis, myalgia.

INTERACTIONS

Drug: NITRATES increase risk of serious hypotension; if used within 4 h of **doxazosin, prazosin, terazosin, tamsulosin;** cimetidine, erythromycin, ketoconazole, itraconazole, PROTEASE INHIBITORS increase sildenafil levels; **rifampin** can decrease sildenafil levels. Do not use with **telaprevir. Food: Grapefruit juice** (greater than 1 qt/day) may increase plasma concentrations and adverse effects.

PHARMACOKINETICS

Absorption: Rapidly from GI tract. **Peak:** 30–120 min. **Distribution:** 96% protein bound. **Metabolism:** In liver (CYP3A4 and 2C9). **Elimination:** 80% in feces, 12% in urine. **Half-Life:** 4 h.

NURSING IMPLICATIONS

Assessment & Drug Effects

- Monitor carefully for and immediately report S&S of cardiac distress.

Patient & Family Education

- Do not take sildenafil within 4 h of taking doxazosin, prazosin, terazosin, or tamsulosin.

S

Common adverse effects in *italic;* life-threatening effects <u>underlined;</u> generic names in **bold;** classifications in SMALL CAPS; ✤ Canadian drug name; ❖ Prototype drug; ⚠ Alert

- Consuming a high-fat meal before taking drug may cause delay in drug action.
- Report to prescriber: Headaches, flushing, chest pain, indigestion, blurred vision, sensitivity to light, changes in color vision.
- Seek medical attention if erection lasts for more than 4 h.

SILODOSIN
(sil'o-do-sin)
Rapaflo
Classification: ALPHA-1 ADRENERGIC RECEPTOR ANTAGONIST; GENITOURINARY SMOOTH MUSCLE RELAXANT
Therapeutic: GENITOURINARY SMOOTH MUSCLE RELAXANT
Prototype: Tamsulosin

AVAILABILITY Capsule

ACTION & *THERAPEUTIC EFFECT*
Selective antagonist of post-synaptic alpha-1 adrenoreceptors located in the prostate, bladder base, bladder neck, prostatic capsule, and prostatic urethra. *Blockade of these alpha-1 adrenoreceptors causes the smooth muscle in these tissues to relax, resulting in improvement in urine flow and reduction in signs and symptoms of benign prostatic hyperplasia (BPH).*

USES Treatment of the signs and symptoms of BPH.

CONTRAINDICATIONS Severe renal impairment (CrCl less than 30 mL/min); severe hepatic impairment (Child-Pugh score greater than or equal to 10); hypersensitivity to silodosin or any other ingredients in the product; pregnancy—fetal risk cannot be ruled out; lactation—infant risk cannot be ruled out.

CAUTIOUS USE Moderate renal impairment; history of hypotension; cataract surgery; older adults. Safe use in children not established.

ROUTE & DOSAGE

Benign Prostatic Hyperplasia
Adult: **PO** 8 mg once daily with a meal

Renal Impairment Dosage Adjustment
CrCl 30–49 mL/min: 4 mg once daily; *less than 30 mL/min:* Contraindicated

ADMINISTRATION
Oral
- Give with meals.
- If unable to swallow whole, may sprinkle capsule contents on 1 Tablespoon of applesauce and swallow without chewing within 5 minutes; follow with 8 oz. of cool water.
- Store at controlled room temperature of 25 degrees C (77 degrees F), with excursions permitted between 15°–30° C (59°–86° F). Protect from light and moisture.

ADVERSE EFFECTS (≥ 5%) GU: *Retrograde ejaculation.*

DIAGNOSTIC TEST INTERFERENCE
Increased ***prostate specific antigen (PSA).***

INTERACTIONS Drug: Strong CYP3A4 inhibitors (e.g., **idelalisib, itraconazole, ritonavir**) or strong P-GLYCOPROTEIN INHIBITORS (e.g., **ketoconazole**) greatly increases silodosin levels. Moderate CYP3A4 inhibitors (e.g., **clarithromycin, diltiazem, erythromycin,**

verapamil) may increase silodosin levels. Other ALPHA-BLOCKERS can cause additive hypotensive effects. INHIBITORS OF UDP-GLUCURONOSYLTRANSFERASE 2B7 (e.g., **probenecid, valproic acid, fluconazole**) may increase silodosin levels.

PHARMACOKINETICS Absorption:
32% bioavailable. **Distribution:** Approximately 97% plasma protein bound. **Metabolism:** By CYP3A4 hepatic enzymes and is a P-glycoprotein (P-gp) substrate. **Elimination:** Feces and urine. **Half-Life:** 13.3 h.

NURSING IMPLICATIONS

Assessment & Drug Effects
- Monitor I&O and ease of voiding.
- Monitor orthostatic vital signs (lying and then standing) at the beginning of therapy. Report a systolic pressure drop of 15 mm Hg or greater and HR increase of 15 beats or greater upon standing.
- Monitor for orthostatic hypotension, especially at the beginning of therapy and in those taking concurrent antihypertensive drugs.

Patient & Family Education
- Make position changes slowly and in stages to minimize risk of dizziness and fainting.
- Take the drug once daily with a meal.
- Avoid hazardous activities until reaction to drug is known.
- Review adverse effects with patient and/or caregiver.
- Report unexplained skin eruptions or purple skin patches.
- If cataract surgery is planned, inform ophthalmologist that you are taking silodosin.
- Contact provider before taking any other medication or herbal supplement.

SILVER SULFADIAZINE ⊙
(sul-fa-dye'a-zeen)
Silvadene, SSD
Classification: SULFONAMIDE
Therapeutic: TOPICAL
ANTI-INFECTIVE

AVAILABILITY Cream

ACTION & *THERAPEUTIC EFFECT*
Silver salt is released slowly and exerts bactericidal effect only on bacterial cell membrane and wall. *Broad antimicrobial activity including many gram-negative and gram-positive bacteria and yeast.*

USES Prevention and treatment of sepsis in second- and third-degree burns.

CONTRAINDICATIONS Hypersensitivity to other sulfonamides; pregnant women at term.

CAUTIOUS USE Impaired kidney or liver function; porphyria; impaired respiratory function; G6PD deficiency; thrombocytopenia, leukopenia, hematological disease; pregnancy (category B); lactation; preterm infants; neonates younger than 2 mo.

ROUTE & DOSAGE

Burn Wound Treatment
Adult/Child: **Topical** Apply 1% cream 1–2 × day to thickness of approximately 1.5 mm ($^1/_{16}$ in.)

ADMINISTRATION
Topical
- Do not use if cream darkens; it is water soluble and white.

Common adverse effects in *italic*; life-threatening effects <u>underlined</u>; generic names in **bold**; classifications in SMALL CAPS; ♣ Canadian drug name; ⊙ Prototype drug; ⚠ Alert

1546

- Apply with sterile, gloved hands to cleansed, debrided burned areas. Reapply cream to areas where it has been removed by patient activity; cover burn wounds with medication at all times.
- Bathe patient daily (in whirlpool or shower or in bed) as aid to debridement. Reapply drug.
- Note: Dressings are not required but may be used if necessary. Drug does not stain clothing.
- Store at room temperature away from heat.

ADVERSE EFFECTS Other: Pain
(occasionally), burning, itching, rash, reversible leukopenia. Potential for toxicity as for other SULFONAMIDES if applied to extensive areas of the body surface.

INTERACTIONS Drug: PROTEOLYTIC
ENZYMES are inactivated by silver in cream.

PHARMACOKINETICS Absorption: Not absorbed through intact
skin, however, approximately 10% could be absorbed when applied to second- or third-degree burns. **Distribution:** Distributed into most body tissues. **Metabolism:** In the liver. **Elimination:** In urine.

NURSING IMPLICATIONS
Assessment & Drug Effects
- Observe for and report hypersensitivity reaction: Rash, itching, or burning sensation in unburned areas.
- Observe patient for reactions attributed to sulfonamides.
- Note: Analgesic may be required. Occasionally, pain is experienced on application; intensity and duration depend on depth of burn.
- Continue treatment until satisfactory healing or burn site is ready for grafting, unless adverse reactions occur.

SIMEPREVIR
(sim-e-pre'vir)
Olysio
Classification: ANTIVIRAL; VIRAL PROTEIN INHIBITOR; DIRECT-ACTING ANTI-VIRUS; ANTIHEPATITIS
Therapeutic: ANTIHEPATITIS

AVAILABILITY Capsules

ACTION & THERAPEUTIC EFFECT
A direct-acting antiviral agent (DAA) that inhibits viral enzymes needed for critical steps in HCV replication; *prevents HCV replication.*

USES Treatment of chronic hepatitis
C (CHC) infection in combination with other agents, in HCV genotype 1 infection.

CONTRAINDICATIONS Severe
hepatic impairment (Child-Pugh class C); autoimmune hepatitis; decompensated liver disease; lactation.

CAUTIOUS USE Renal impair-
ment; mild or moderate hepatic impairment; sulfa allergy; individuals of eastern Asian ancestry; older adults; pregnancy (category C). Safety and efficacy in children younger than 18 y not established.

ROUTE & DOSAGE

Hepatitis C Infection
Adult: **PO** 150 mg once a day for 12 wk in combination with other agents

Discontinuation Based on Inadequate Virologic Response
If HCV RNA 25 IU/mL or greater at wk 4: Discontinue all therapy

---

ADMINISTRATION

Oral

- Give with food and concurrently with peginterferon alfa and ribavirin.
- Capsules **must be** swallowed whole. They should not be cut or chewed.
- If peginterferon alfa or ribavirin is discontinued for any reason, simeprevir also **must be** discontinued.
- The dose of simeprevir **must not be** reduced or interrupted. If discontinued because of adverse reactions or inadequate response, treatment **must not be** reinitiated.
- Store at room temperature below 30° C (86° F). Protect from light.

ADVERSE EFFECTS Respiratory:

Dyspnea. **CNS:** Dizziness, fatigue, headache, insomnia. **Skin:** Grade 3 photosensitivity, pruritus, *rash* (includes: Cutaneous vasculitis, dermatitis exfoliative, eczema, erythema, maculopapular rash, photosensitivity reaction, toxic skin eruption, urticaria). **GI:** *Nausea.* **Musculoskeletal:** *Myalgia.* **Hematologic:** *Increased serum bilirubin,* increased serum alkaline phosphatase. **Other:** *Pruritus.*

INTERACTIONS Drug: Simeprevir

may increase the levels of drugs that are substrates for OATP1B1/3 and P-gp transport (e.g., **digoxin,** HMG COA REDUCTASE INHIBITORS). Simeprevir may increase the levels of drugs requiring intestinal CYP3A4 for metabolism (e.g., CALCIUM CHANNEL BLOCKERS, **cisapride, midazolam, sildenafil, tadalafil, triazolam, vardenafil**). Co-administration of simeprevir with moderate or strong inhibitors of CYP3A4 (e.g., AZOLE ANTIFUNGALS, HIV PROTEASE INHIBITORS, MACROLIDES), may increase the levels of simeprevir. Co-administration with moderate or strong inducers of CYP3A4 (e.g., **carbamazepine, dexamethasone, efavirenz, phenobarbital, phenytoin**) may decrease the levels of simeprevir. **Food: Grapefruit** and **grapefruit juice** may increase the levels of simeprevir. **Herbal: Milk thistle** may increase the levels of simeprevir. **St. John's wort** may decrease the levels of simeprevir.

PHARMACOKINETICS Absorption:

Orally bioavailable. **Peak:** 4–6 h. **Distribution:** 99.9% plasma protein bound, extensively distributed to gut and liver. **Metabolism:** In liver. **Elimination:** Primarily unchanged in feces. **Half-Life:** 10–13 h.

NURSING IMPLICATIONS

Assessment & Drug Effects

- Monitor for adverse dermatologic effects (e.g., including erythema, eczema, maculopapular rash, urticaria, toxic skin eruption, exfoliative dermatitis) and follow for progression and/or development of mucosal signs (e.g., oral lesions, conjunctivitis) or systemic symptoms. If rash becomes severe, report promptly to prescriber.
- Monitor lab tests: Baseline and periodic LFTs, uric acid; serum HCV-RNA at baseline and at wk 4, 12, 24, and end of treatment, and during treatment follow-up; pretreatment and monthly pregnancy tests and up to 6 mo after therapy is discontinued.

Patient & Family Education

- **Do not** reduce or interrupt the dose of simeprevir.
- Avoid excessive sunlight and tanning devices, and take precautions to limit exposure as drug (e.g., sunscreen) may cause moderate to severe phototoxicity reaction.

Common adverse effects in *italic;* life-threatening effects <u>underlined</u>; generic names in **bold;** classifications in SMALL CAPS; ♣ Canadian drug name; ⊙ Prototype drug; ⚠ Alert

1548

S

• Women of childbearing potential and male partners of pregnant women should use effective means of contraception while taking this drug and for at least 6 mo following discontinuation of therapy.

SIMVASTATIN
(sim-vah-sta'tin)
Zocor
Classification: HMG-COA REDUC-TASE INHIBITOR (STATIN)
Therapeutic: ANTILIPEMIC; STATIN
Prototype: Lovastatin

AVAILABILITY Tablet

ACTION & *THERAPEUTIC EFFECT*
Inhibitor of HMG-CoA reductase. HMG-CoA reductase inhibitors increase HDL cholesterol, and decrease LDL cholesterol, and total cholesterol synthesis. *Effectiveness indicated by decreased serum triglycerides, decreased LDL, cholesterol, and modest increases in HDL cholesterol.*

USES Hypercholesterolemia (alone or in combination with other agents), familial hypercholesterolemia. Reduces risk of CHD death and nonfatal MI and stroke.

CONTRAINDICATIONS Hypersensitivity to simvastatin; active liver disease or unexplained elevation of serum transaminase, hepatic encephalopathy, hepatitis, jaundice, AST or ALT of 3 × ULN; rhabdomyolysis, acute renal failure; cholestasis; myopathy; MS; pregnancy (may cause fetal harm); lactation (harm to infant).

CAUTIOUS USE Homozygous familial hypercholesterolemia, history of liver disease, alcoholics; renal disease, renal impairment; DM; ALS patients; seizure disorder; children younger than 10 y.

ROUTE & DOSAGE

Hypercholesterolemia, Hyperlipidemia, CV Prevention
Adult: **PO** 10–20 mg each evening; range 5–40 mg daily (max: 80 mg daily).
Adolescent/Child (10 y or older): **PO** 10 mg each night (may increase to 40 mg each day)

Homozygous Familial Hypercholesterolemia
Adult: **PO** 40 mg each evening

Renal Impairment Dosage Adjustment
CrCl less than 20 mL/min: Start with 5 mg each night

ADMINISTRATION
Oral
• Adjust dosage usually at 4-wk intervals.
• Shake suspension at least 20 sec prior to use and suspension should be taken on an empty stomach.
• Give in the evening.
• Store tablet at 5°–30° C (41°–86° F).
• Store suspension between 20°–25° C (68°–77° F). Do not freeze or refrigerate and protect from heat. Discard bottle 1 mo after first use.

ADVERSE EFFECTS CV: <u>Atrial fibrillation</u>. **Respiratory:** URI, bronchitis. **CNS:** Headache, vertigo. **Skin:** Eczema. **GI:** Abdominal pain, constipation, nausea. **Musculoskeletal:** Increased CPK levels.

INTERACTIONS Drug: Avoid use with **itraconazole, ketoconazole,**

erythromycin, clarithromycin, telithromycin, PROTEASE INHIBITORS, nefazodone. Simvastatin dose will need to be decreased when given with **gemfibrozil, cyclosporine, danazole, amiodarone, verapamil, diltiazem.** May increase PT when administered with **warfarin. Cyclosporine, gemfibrozil, fenofibrate, clofibrate,** antilipemic doses of **niacin, fluconazole, miconazole, sildenafil, tacrolimus, amlodipine** may increase serum levels and increase risk of myopathy, rhabdomyolysis and acute kidney failure. Avoid use with **rifampin. Food: Grapefruit juice** (greater than 1 qt/day) may increase risk of myopathy, rhabdomyolysis. **Herbal: St. John's wort** may decrease efficacy.

PHARMACOKINETICS
Absorption: Rapidly from GI tract. **Onset:** 2 wk. **Peak:** 4–6 wk. **Distribution:** 95% protein bound; achieves high liver concentrations; crosses placenta. **Metabolism:** Extensive first-pass metabolism to its active metabolite. **Elimination:** 60% in bile and feces.

NURSING IMPLICATIONS

Assessment & Drug Effects
- Assess for and report unexplained muscle pain. Determine CPK level at onset of muscle pain.
- Monitor coagulation studies with patients receiving concurrent warfarin therapy. PT may be prolonged.
- Monitor lab tests: Baseline and periodic lipid profile, LFTs, creatinine kinase.

Patient & Family Education
- Report unexplained muscle pain, tenderness, or weakness, especially if accompanied by malaise or fever, to prescriber.
- Report signs of bleeding to prescriber promptly when taking concurrent warfarin.
- Moderate intake of grapefruit juice while taking this medication.

SIPULEUCEL-T
(sip-u-lew'cel)
Provenge
Classification: BIOLOGIC RESPONSE MODIFIER; ACTIVE CELL IMMUNOTHERAPEUTIC; ANTINEO-PLASTIC
Therapeutic: ANTINEOPLASTIC

AVAILABILITY Intravenous suspension

ACTION & *THERAPEUTIC EFFECT*
While the mechanism of action is unknown, sipuleucel-T is designed to induce an immune response against prostatic acid phosphatase (PAP), an antigen expressed on most prostate cancer cells. *Stimulation of humoral and T-cell mediated responses are thought to slow tumor progression and improve survival.*

USES Prostate cancer.

CONTRAINDICATIONS Pregnancy category undetermined; not for use in women.

CAUTIOUS USE Concomitant use of chemotherapy; history of infusion reactions.

ROUTE & DOSAGE

Prostate Cancer
Adult: **IV** 250 mL infusion q2wk for a total of 3 doses

Common adverse effects in *italic*; life-threatening effects underlined; generic names in **bold**; classifications in SMALL CAPS; ♣ Canadian drug name; ◯ Prototype drug; ⚠ Alert

ADMINISTRATION

Intravenous

- Use universal precautions when handling sipuleucel-T. ▪ Note: Pre-medication is recommended with oral acetaminophen and an anti-histamine (e.g., diphenhydramine) approximately 30 min prior to administration.

PREPARE: **IV Infusion:** ▪ Product is intended only for autologous use (i.e., patient donates to self). ▪ Open the outer cardboard shipping box to verify the product and patient-specific labels located on the top of the insulated container. ▪ **Do not** remove the insulated container from the shipping box, or open the lid of the insulated container, until the patient is ready for infusion. Inspect for leakage. ▪ Contents of bag will be slightly cloudy, with a cream-to-pink color. Gently tilt bag to resuspend contents; inspect for clumps and clots that should disperse with gentle manual mixing. ▪ Do not administer if the bag leaks during handling or if clumps remain in the bag.

ADMINISTER: **IV Infusion:** ▪ Infusion must be started prior to the expiration date and time on *Cell Product Disposition Form* and label. Give over 60 min. ▪ Administer through a dedicated line and **do not** use a cell filter. Ensure that entire contents of bag are infused. ▪ Monitor closely during and for 1 h after infusion for an infusion reaction (e.g., dyspnea, hypertension, tachycardia, chills, fever, nausea). Infusion may be stopped or slowed depending on severity of reaction. ▪ Do not reinitiate infusion with a bag held at room temperature for more than 3 h.

INCOMPATIBILITIES: **Solution/additive:** Do not mix with another drug. **Y-site:** Do not mix with another drug.

ADVERSE EFFECTS

Respiratory: Cough, dyspnea, upper respiratory infection. **CNS:** *Asthenia, dizziness, fatigue, headache,* insomnia, *paresthesia,* tremor. **Skin:** Rash, sweating. **GI:** Anorexia, *constipation,* diarrhea, *nausea, vomiting,* weight loss. **GU:** Hematuria, urinary tract infection. **Musculoskeletal:** *Back pain,* bone pain, *joint ache,* neck pain, *muscle ache,* muscle spasms, musculoskeletal chest pain, musculoskeletal pain, *pain in extremity.* **Hematologic:** *Anemia.* **Other:** *Chills, citrate toxicity, fever,* hot flush, influenza-like illness, *pain,* peripheral edema.

INTERACTIONS

Drug: Due to the ability of sipuleucel-T to stimulate the immune system, concomitant use of immunosuppressive agents (e.g., **cortico-steroids**) may alter the efficacy and/or safety of sipuleucel-T.

NURSING IMPLICATIONS

Assessment & Drug Effects

- Observe closely during infusion and for at least 1 h following for an infusion reaction (see Administration). Monitor vital signs throughout observation period. Note that an acute infusion reaction is more likely after the second infusion.
- Report immediately to prescriber if an infusion reaction occurs.

Patient & Family Education

- Report immediately any of the following: Fever, chills, fatigue, breathing problems, dizziness, high blood pressure, palpitations, nausea, vomiting, headache, or muscle aches.

S

SIROLIMUS
(sir-o-li'mus)
Rapamune
Classification: IMMUNOMODULATOR;
IMMUNOSUPPRESSANT
Therapeutic: IMMUNOSUPPRESSANT
Prototype: Cyclosporine

AVAILABILITY Tablet; oral solution

ACTION & *THERAPEUTIC EFFECT*
Active in reducing a transplant rejection by inhibiting the response of helper T-lymphocytes and B-lymphocytes to cytokines [(interleukin) IL-2, IL-4, and IL-5]. *Inhibits antibody production and acute transplant rejection reaction in autoimmune disorders [e.g., systemic lupus erythematosus (SLE)]. Indicated by non rejection of transplanted organ.*

USES Prophylaxis of kidney transplant rejection; treatment of lymphangioleiomyomatosis.

CONTRAINDICATIONS Hypersensitivity to sirolimus; lung or liver transplant patients; soya lecithin (soy fatty acids) hypersensitivity; PML; lactation.

CAUTIOUS USE Hypersensitivity to tacrolimus; impaired renal function; renal transplant patients; dialysis patients; hepatic impairment; UV exposure, retransplant patients, multiorgan transplant recipients; African American transplant patients; interstitial lung disease; viral or bacterial infection; hyperlipidemia, DM, atrial fibrillation, CHF, hypervolemia, palpitations; hepatic disease; CAD; myelosuppression; older adults; pregnancy (category C); children younger than 13 y.

ROUTE & DOSAGE

Kidney Transplant
Adult/Adolescent (over 40 kg):
PO 6 mg loading dose immediately after transplant, then 2 mg/day. Doses will need to be much higher if using cyclosporine or corticosteroids.
Adolescent (13 y or older, weight less than 40 kg): **PO** 3 mg/m^2 loading dose immediately after transplant, then 1 mg/m^2/day.

Lymphangioleiomyomatosis
Adult: **PO** 2 mg daily, then adjust to target concentration of 5–15 mg/mL

Hepatic Impairment Dosage Adjustment
Loading dose does not need to be modified.
Mild to moderate: Reduce maintenance does by 33% *Severe impairment:* Reduce maintenance by 50%

ADMINISTRATION
Oral
- Give 4 h after oral cyclosporine.
- Tablets should be swallowed whole. They should not be crushed or chewed.
- Add prescribed amount of sirolimus oral solution to a glass containing 2 oz (60 mL) or more of water or orange juice (do not use any other type of liquid). Stir vigorously and administer immediately. Refill glass with 4 oz (120 mL) or more of water or orange juice. Stir vigorously and administer immediately.
- Give consistently with respect to amount and type of food.
- Refrigerate; protect from light; use multidose bottles within 1 mo of opening.

Common adverse effects in *italic*; life-threatening effects <u>underlined</u>; generic names in **bold**; classifications in SMALL CAPS; ♥ Canadian drug name; ❂ Prototype drug; ⚠ Alert

1552

ADVERSE EFFECTS CV: *Hypertension,* atrial fibrillation, CHF, hypervolemia, hypotension, palpitation, peripheral vascular disorder, postural hypotension, syncope, tachycardia, thrombophlebitis, thrombosis, vasodilation. **Respiratory:** *Dyspnea, pharyngitis, upper respiratory tract infection,* asthma, atelectasis, bronchitis, cough, epistaxis, hypoxia, lung edema, pleural effusion, pneumonia, rhinitis, sinusitis. **CNS:** *Insomnia, tremor, headache,* anxiety, confusion, depression, dizziness, emotional lability, hypertonia, hyperesthesia, hypotonia, neuropathy, paresthesia, somnolence. **HEENT:** Abnormal vision, cataract, conjunctivitis, deafness, ear pain, otitis media, tinnitus. **Endocrine:** *Edema, hypercholesterolemia, hyperkalemia, hyperlipidemia, hypokalemia, hypophosphatemia, peripheral edema, weight gain,* Cushing's syndrome, diabetes, acidosis, hypercalcemia, hyperglycemia, hyperphosphatemia, hypomagnesemia, hypoglycemia, hypomagnesemia, hyponatremia; increased LDH, alkaline phosphatase, BUN, creatine phosphokinase, ALT, or AST; weight loss. **Skin:** *Acne, rash,* fungal dermatitis, hirsutism, pruritus, skin hypertrophy, skin ulcer, sweating. **GI:** *Constipation, diarrhea, dyspepsia, nausea, vomiting, abdominal pain,* anorexia, dysphagia, eructation, esophagitis, flatulence, gastritis, gastroenteritis, gingivitis, gum hyperplasia, ileus, mouth ulceration, oral moniliasis, stomatitis, abnormal liver function tests. **GU:** *UTI,* albuminuria, bladder pain, dysuria, hematuria, hydronephrosis, impotence, kidney pain, nocturia, renal tubular necrosis, oliguria, pyuria, scrotal edema, incontinence, urinary retention, glycosuria. **Hematologic:** *Anemia,* thrombocytopenia, leukopenia, hemorrhage, ecchymosis, leukocytosis, lymphadenopathy, polycythemia, thrombotic, thrombocytopenic purpura. **Other:** *Asthenia, back pain, chest pain, fever, pain, arthralgia;* flu-like syndrome; generalized edema; infection; lymphocele; malaise; sepsis, arthrosis, bone necrosis, leg cramps, myalgia, osteoporosis, tetany, abscess, ascites, cellulitis, chills, face edema, hernia, pelvic pain, peritonitis.

INTERACTIONS Drug: Sirolimus concentrations increased by **clarithromycin, cyclosporine, diltiazem, erythromycin, ketoconazole, itraconazole, telithromycin;** sirolimus concentrations decreased by **rifabutin, rifampin;** VACCINES may be less effective with sirolimus; **tacrolimus** increases mortality, hepatic artery thrombosis, and graft loss. **Food: Grapefruit juice** significantly increases plasma levels. High fat meals increase levels. **Herbal: St. John's wort** decreases efficacy.

PHARMACOKINETICS Absorption: Rapidly with 14% bioavailability. **Peak:** 2 h. **Distribution:** 92% protein bound, distributes in high concentrations to heart, intestines, kidneys, liver, lungs, muscle, spleen, and testes. **Metabolism:** In liver (CYP3A4). **Elimination:** 91% in feces, 2.2% in urine. **Half-Life:** 62 h.

NURSING IMPLICATIONS

Black Box Warning

Sirolimus has been associated with increased susceptibility to infection and development of lymphoma.

Assessment & Drug Effects

- Monitor for S&S of graft rejection.
- Control hyperlipidemia prior to initiating drug.

- Monitor for and report promptly S&S of infection.
- Draw trough whole-blood sirolimus levels 1 h before a scheduled dose.
- Monitor lab tests: Periodic lipid profile, CBC with differential, LFTs, urinary protein, and creatinine, and serum sirolimus as indicated.

Patient & Family Education

- Avoid grapefruit juice within 2 h of taking sirolimus.
- Limit exposure to sunlight (UV exposure).
- Note: Decreased effectiveness possible for vaccines during therapy.
- Use or add barrier contraceptive before, during, and for 12 wk after discontinuing therapy.

SITAGLIPTIN ○

(sit-a-glip'tin)
Januvia
Classification: DIPEPTIDYL PEPTIDASE-4 (DPP-4) INHIBITOR
Therapeutic: ANTIDIABETIC; INCRETIN MODIFIER; DDP-4 INHIBITOR

AVAILABILITY Tablet

ACTION & *THERAPEUTIC EFFECT*

Slows inactivation of incretin hormones [e.g., glucagon-like peptide-1 (GLP-1) and glucose-dependent insulinotropic polypeptide (GIP)] that are released by the intestine. As plasma glucose rises following food intake, incretin hormones stimulate release of insulin from the pancreas, and GLP-1 also lowers glucagon secretion, resulting in reduced hepatic glucose production. *Sitagliptin lowers both fasting and postprandial plasma glucose levels.*

USES Adjunct treatment of type 2 diabetes mellitus.

CONTRAINDICATIONS Serious hypersensitivity to sitagliptin; type I DM; diabetic ketoacidosis.

CAUTIOUS USE Moderate to severe renal impairment, renal failure, hemodialysis; heart failure, older adults; history of pancreatitis; pregnancy (fetal risk cannot be ruled out); lactation (infant risk cannot be ruled out). Safe use in children younger than 18 y not established.

ROUTE & DOSAGE

Type 2 Diabetes Mellitus

Adult: **PO** 100 mg/day

Renal Impairment Dosage Adjustment

CrCl between 30 mL/min and 50 mL/min: **50 mg/day**; *less than 30 mL/min:* **25 mg/day**

ADMINISTRATION

Oral

- May be given without regard to meals.
- Note that dosage adjustment is recommended for moderate to severe renal impairment.
- Store at 20°–25° C (68°–77° F).

ADVERSE EFFECTS Respiratory: Nasopharyngitis, URI. **CNS:** Headache. **Endocrine:** Hypoglycemia.

INTERACTIONS Drug: Sitagliptin may increase **digoxin** levels. QUINOLONES may increase blood glucose. Monitor closely with **insulin** or SULFONYLUREAS.

PHARMACOKINETICS Absorption: 87% absorbed. **Peak:** 1–4 h. **Distribution:** 38% protein bound. **Metabolism:** 20% metabolized in the liver.

Common adverse effects in *italic*; life-threatening effects <u>underlined</u>; generic names in **bold**; classifications in SMALL CAPS; ✦ Canadian drug name; ○ Prototype drug; ⚠ Alert

1554

Elimination: Primarily renal (87%) with minor elimination in the kidneys. **Half-Life:** 12.4 h.

NURSING IMPLICATIONS

Assessment & Drug Effects

- Monitor for and report S&S of significant GI distress, including NV&D.
- Monitor for S&S of hypoglycemia when used in combination with a sulfonylurea drug or insulin.
- Monitor blood levels of digoxin with concurrent therapy.
- Monitor lab tests: Baseline and periodic CrCl; periodic fasting and postprandial plasma glucose and HbA1C.

Patient & Family Education

- Taking this drug with another drug that can lower your blood sugar, such as a sulfonylurea or insulin, increases your risk of hypoglycemia.
- Stop taking this drug and notify prescriber immediately if you have an allergic reaction (e.g., swelling of your face, lips, throat; difficulty swallowing or breathing; raised, red areas on your skin (hives); skin rash, itching, flaking or peeling.
- Contact prescriber if you experience unexplained symptoms of liver problems (e.g., nausea or vomiting, abdominal pain, unusual tiredness, loss of appetite, dark urine, yellowing of your skin or the whites of your eyes) or if swelling is noted in lower extremities.

SODIUM BICARBONATE NA(HCO₃)

(sod'i-um bi-car'bon-ate)

Sodium Bicarbonate

Classification: FLUID AND ELECTROLYTE BALANCE AGENT; ANTACID
Therapeutic: ANTACID

AVAILABILITY Tablet; solution for injection

ACTION & *THERAPEUTIC EFFECT*

Rapidly neutralizes gastric acid to form sodium chloride, carbon dioxide, and water. After absorption of sodium bicarbonate, plasma alkali reserve is increased and excess sodium and bicarbonate ions are excreted in urine, thus rendering urine less acid. *Short-acting, potent systemic antacid; rapidly neutralizes gastric acid or systemic acidosis.*

USES Systemic alkalinizer to correct metabolic acidosis (as occurs in diabetes mellitus, shock, cardiac arrest, or vascular collapse), to minimize uric acid crystallization associated with uricosuric agents, to increase the solubility of sulfonamides, and to enhance renal excretion of barbiturate and salicylate overdosage. Commonly used as home remedy for relief of occasional heartburn, indigestion, or sour stomach. Used topically as paste, bath, or soak to relieve itching and minor skin irritations such as sunburn, insect bites, prickly heat, poison ivy, sumac, or oak. Sterile solutions are used to buffer acidic parenteral solutions to prevent acidosis. Also as a buffering agent in many commercial products (e.g., mouthwashes, douches, enemas, ophthalmic solutions).

CONTRAINDICATIONS Prolonged therapy with sodium bicarbonate; patients losing chloride (as from vomiting, GI suction, diuresis); hypocalcemia; metabolic alkalosis; respiratory alkalosis; peptic ulcer.

CAUTIOUS USE Edema, sodium retaining disorders; heart disease, hypertension; preexisting respiratory acidosis; renal disease, renal

S

SODIUM BICARBONATE NA(HCO₃)

insufficiency; hyperkalemia, hypokalemia; older adults; pregnancy (category C); children.

ROUTE & DOSAGE

Antacid
Adult: **PO** 0.3–2 g 1–4 × day or ½ tsp of powder in glass of water

Urinary Alkalinizer
Adult: **PO** 4 g initially, then 1–2 g q4h
Child: **PO** 84–840 mg/kg/day in divided doses

Cardiac Arrest
Adult: **IV** 1 mEq/kg initially, then 0.5 mEq/kg q10min depending on arterial blood gas determinations (8.4% solutions contain 50 mEq/50 mL), give over 1–2 min
Child: **IV** 0.5–1 mEq/kg q10min depending on arterial blood gas determinations, give over 1–2 min

Metabolic Acidosis
Adult/Child: **IV** Dose adjusted according to pH, base deficit, PaCO₂, fluid limits, and patient response

ADMINISTRATION

Oral
▪ Do not add oral preparation to calcium-containing solutions.

Intravenous

PREPARE: Direct/IV Infusion May give 4.2% (0.5 mEq/mL) and 5% (0.595 mEq/mL) NaHCO₃ solutions undiluted. ▪ Dilute 7.5% (0.892 mEq/mL) and 8.4% (1 mEq/mL) solutions with compatible IV solutions to a maximum concentration of 0.5 mEq/mL.

▪ For infants and children, dilute to at least 4.2%.
ADMINISTER: Direct: Give a bolus dose over 1–2 min only in emergency situations. ▪ For neonates or infants younger than 2 y, use only 4.2% solution for direct IV injection. **IV Infusion:** Usual rate is 2–5 mEq/kg over 4–8 h; do not exceed 50 mEq/h. ▪ Flush line before/after with NS. ▪ Stop infusion immediately if extravasation occurs. Severe tissue damage has followed tissue infiltration.

INCOMPATIBILITIES: Solution/additive: Alcohol 5%, lactated Ringer's, amoxicillin, ascorbic acid, bupivacaine, carboplatin, carmustine, ciprofloxacin, cisplatin, codeine, corticotropin, dobutamine, dopamine, epinephrine, glycopyrrolate, hydromorphone, imipenem/cilastatin, insulin, isoproterenol, labetalol, levorphanol, magnesium sulfate, meperidine, meropenem, methadone, metoclopramide, morphine, norepinephrine, oxytetracycline, penicillin G, pentazocine, pentobarbital, phenobarbital, procaine, promazine, streptomycin, succinylcholine, tetracycline, vancomycin, vitamin B complex with C. **Y-site:** Allopurinol, amiodarone, amphotericin B cholesteryl complex, calcium chloride, ciprofloxacin, cisatracurium, diltiazem, doxorubicin liposome, fenoldopam, hetastarch, idarubicin, imipenem/cilastatin, leucovorin, lidocaine, midazolam, milrinone acetate, nalbuphine, ondansetron, oxacillin, sargramostim, verapamil, vincristine, vindesine, vinorelbine.

▪ Store in airtight containers. ▪ Note expiration date.

ADVERSE EFFECTS Endocrine: Metabolic alkalosis; electrolyte imbalance: Sodium overload (pulmonary edema), hypocalcemia (tetany), hypokalemia, milk-alkali syndrome, dehydration. **Skin:** Severe tissue damage following extravasation of IV solution. **GI:** *Belching, gastric distention,* flatulence. **GU:** Renal calculi or crystals, impaired kidney function. **Other:** Rapid IV in neonates (hypernatremia, reduction in CSF pressure, intracranial hemorrhage).

DIAGNOSTIC TEST INTERFERENCE Small increase in *blood lactate* levels (following IV infusion of sodium bicarbonate); false-positive *urinary protein* determinations (using *Ames reagent, sulfacetic acid,* heat and *acetic acid* or *nitric acid ring method*); elevated *urinary urobi-linogen* levels (*urobilinogen* excretion increases in alkaline urine).

INTERACTIONS Drug: May decrease absorption of **ketoconazole;** may decrease elimination of **dextroamphetamine, ephedrine, pseudoephedrine, quinidine;** may increase elimination of **chlorpropamide, lithium,** SALICYLATES, TETRACYCLINES.

PHARMACOKINETICS Absorption: Readily from GI tract. **Onset:** 15 min. **Duration:** 1–2 h. **Elimination:** In urine within 3–4 h.

NURSING IMPLICATIONS

Assessment & Drug Effects
- Be aware that long-term use of oral preparation with milk or calcium can cause milk-alkali syndrome: Anorexia, nausea, vomiting, headache, mental confusion, hypercalcemia, hypophosphatemia, soft tissue calcification, renal and ureteral calculi, renal insufficiency, metabolic alkalosis.
- Observe for and report S&S of improvement or reversal of metabolic acidosis (see Appendix F).
- Monitor lab tests: Periodic measurements of acid-base status (blood pH, Po_2, Pco_2, HCO_3^-, and other electrolytes), usually several times daily during acute period.

Patient & Family Education
- Do not use sodium bicarbonate as antacid. A nonabsorbable OTC alternative for repeated use is safer.
- Do not take antacids longer than 2 wk except under advice and supervision of a prescriber. Self-medication with routine doses of sodium bicarbonate or soda mints may cause sodium retention and alkalosis, especially when kidney function is impaired.
- Be aware that commonly used OTC antacid products contain sodium bicarbonate (e.g., Alka Seltzer).

SODIUM FERRIC GLUCONATE COMPLEX

(so'di-um fer'ric glu'co-nate)

Ferrlecit

Classification: NUTRITIONAL SUPPLEMENT; IRON PREPARATION

Therapeutic: ANTIANEMIC; IRON REPLACEMENT

Prototype: Ferrous sulfate

AVAILABILITY Intravenous solution

ACTION & *THERAPEUTIC EFFECT* Stable iron complex used to restore iron loss in chronic kidney failure patients. The use of erythropoietin therapy and blood loss through hemodialysis require iron replacement. The ferric ion combines with transferrin and is transported to bone marrow where it is incorporated into hemoglobin. *Effectiveness indicated by improved Hgb and Hct, iron saturation, and serum ferritin levels.*

USES Treatment of iron deficiency anemia.

CONTRAINDICATIONS Any anemia not related to iron deficiency; hypersensitivity to sodium ferric gluconate complex; hemochromatosis, hemosiderosis; hemolytic anemia; thalassemia; neonates.

CAUTIOUS USE Hypersensitivity to benzyl alcohol; active or suspected infection; cardiac disease; hepatic disease; older adults; pregnancy (category B); lactation. Safety and efficacy in children younger than 6 y not established.

ROUTE & DOSAGE

Iron Deficiency in Dialysis Patients

Adult/Adolescent: **IV** 125 mg infused over 1 h
Child (6–15 y): **IV** 1.5 mg/kg infused over 1 h (max:125 mg/dose)

ADMINISTRATION

Intravenous ONLY

PREPARE: Direct for Adult: May be given undiluted. **Direct for Child:** Dilute required doses in 25 mL NS. **IV Infusion for Adult/Child:** Dilute 125 mg in 100 mL of NS.

▪ Use immediately after dilution. **ADMINISTER: Direct for Adult:** Give no faster than 12.5 mg/min. **IV Infusion for Adult/Child:** Give over **not** less than 60 min. **INCOMPATIBILITIES: Solution/additive:** Do not mix with any other medications or add to parenteral nutrition solutions.

▪ Store unopened ampules at 20°–25° C (68°–77° F).

ADVERSE EFFECTS CV: Flushing, hypotension, hypertension, tachycardia. **Respiratory:** Dyspnea. **GI:** Vomiting, nausea, diarrhea. **Musculoskeletal:** Muscle cramps. **Other:** Hypersensitivity reaction (cardiovascular collapse, cardiac arrest, bronchospasm, oral/pharyngeal edema, dyspnea, angioedema, urticaria, pruritus).

PHARMACOKINETICS Half-life Elimination: 1 h (bound iron).

NURSING IMPLICATIONS

Assessment & Drug Effects
▪ Monitor closely for S&S of severe hypersensitivity (see Appendix F) during IV administration.
▪ Monitor vital signs periodically during IV administration (transient hypotension possible especially during dialysis).
▪ Stop infusion immediately and notify prescriber if hypersensitivity is suspected.
▪ Monitor lab tests: Periodic Hgb, Hct, Fe saturation, and serum ferritin.

Patient & Family Education
▪ Report to prescriber immediately: Difficulty breathing, itching, flushing, rash, weakness, lightheadedness, pain, or any other discomfort during infusion.

SODIUM POLYSTYRENE SULFONATE

(pol-ee-stye'reen)
Kayexalate, SPS
Suspension
Classification: ELECTROLYTE AND WATER BALANCE; CATION EXCHANGE
Therapeutic: CATION EXCHANGE

AVAILABILITY Suspension; powder

ACTION & *THERAPEUTIC EFFECT*
Sulfonic cation-exchange resin that removes potassium by exchanging sodium ion for potassium, particularly in large intestine; potassium containing resin is then excreted through the bowel. *Removes potassium by exchanging sodium ion for potassium through the large intestine.*

USES Hyperkalemia.

CONTRAINDICATIONS Hypersensitivity to Kayexalate; GI obstruction; hypokalemia; lactation.

CAUTIOUS USE Acute or chronic kidney failure; low birth weight infants; neonates with reduced gut; patients receiving digitalis preparations; patients who cannot tolerate even a small increase in sodium load (e.g., CHF, severe hypertension, and marked edema); patients with constipation or bowel obstruction; renal insufficiency, older adults; pregnancy (category C); children.

ROUTE & DOSAGE

Hyperkalemia

Adult: **PO** 15 g 1–4 × per day **Rectal** 30–50 g q6h as warm emulsion high into sigmoid colon
Child: **PO** 1 g/kg q6h; **Rectal** 1 g/kg q2–6h

ADMINISTRATION

Oral
- Give as a suspension in a small quantity of water or in syrup. Usual amount of fluid ranges from 20–100 mL or approximately 3–4 mL/g of drug.

Rectal
- Use warm fluid (as prescribed) to prepare the emulsion for enema.
- Administer a cleansing enema (non-sodium-containing fluid) before and after rectal administration.
- Administer at body temperature and introduce by gravity, keeping suspension particles in solution by stirring. Flush suspension with 50–100 mL of fluid; then clamp tube and leave it in place.
- Urge patient to retain enema at least 30–60 min but as long as several hours if possible.
- Irrigate colon (after enema solution has been expelled) with 1 or 2 qt flushing solution (non-sodium containing). Drain returns constantly through a Y-tube connection.
- Store remainder of prepared solution for 24 h; then discard.

ADVERSE EFFECTS Respiratory: Bronchitis, bronchopneumonia. **Endocrine:** Sodium retention, hypocalcemia, hypokalemia, hypomagnesemia, hypervolemia. **GI:** *Constipation, fecal impaction (in older adults);* anorexia, gastric irritation, nausea, vomiting, diarrhea (with sorbitol emulsions), <u>gastrointestinal hemorrhage</u>.

INTERACTIONS Drug: ANTACIDS, LAXATIVES containing **calcium** or **magnesium** may decrease potassium exchange capability of the resin. Do not use with products containing sorbitol.

Common adverse effects in *italic;* life-threatening effects <u>underlined</u>; generic names in **bold;** classifications in SMALL CAPS; ✦ Canadian drug name; ○ Prototype drug; ⚠ Alert

PHARMACOKINETICS Absorption: Not absorbed systemically. **Onset:** Several hours to days. **Metabolism:** Not metabolized. **Elimination:** In feces.

NURSING IMPLICATIONS

Assessment & Drug Effects

- Serum potassium levels do not always reflect intracellular potassium deficiency. Observe patient closely for early clinical signs of severe hypokalemia (see Appendix F). ECGs are also recommended.
- Consult prescriber about restricting sodium content from dietary and other sources since drug contains approximately 100 mg (4.1 mEq) of sodium/g (1 tsp, 15 mEq sodium).
- Monitor lab tests: Daily serum potassium; periodic acid–base balance, and serum electrolytes.

Patient & Family Education

- Check bowel function daily. Usually, a mild laxative is prescribed to prevent constipation (common adverse effect). Older adult patients are particularly prone to fecal impaction.

SODIUM ZIRCONIUM CYCLOSILICATE

(sow'dee-um zir-koe'nee-um sye'kloe-sil'i-kate)

Lokelma

Classification: ELECTROLYTE AND WATER BALANCE; CATION EXCHANGE
Therapeutic: CATION EXCHANGE

AVAILABILITY Oral packet for suspension

ACTION & *THERAPEUTIC EFFECT*
Sodium zirconium cyclosilicate is a nonabsorbed substance which has a high affinity for potassium ions, binding and increasing fecal elimination of free potassium. *Will lower potassium in nonemergent treatment of of hyperkalemia.*

USES Treatment of hyperkalemia.

CONTRAINDICATIONS Previous hypersensitivity to tildrakizumab or components of the formulation.

CAUTIOUS USE Avoid use in patients with gastroparesis, or motility disorders such as bowel obstruction or severe constipation. Contents may increase patient's risk of edema due to high sodium content. Should not be used for life-threatening hyperkalemia due to delayed onset of action. History of CHF or renal disease.

ROUTE & DOSAGE

Hyperkalemia

Adult: **Oral** 10 g 3 × day; titrated to serum potassium (max: 15 g/day)

ADMINISTRATION

Oral

- Empty entire contents of a packet into 3 or more tablespoons of water; stir contents and drink entire contents immediately.
- Administer other oral medications 2 h before or 2 h after this medication.
- Store packets at 15°–30° C (59°–86° F) in a dry place.

ADVERSE EFFECTS CV: Edema, peripheral edema. **Endocrine:** Hypokalemia.

INTERACTIONS Potential for sodium zirconium cyclosilicate to increase gastric pH, which may alter the absorption of medications with pH dependent solubility. Administering medications 2 h before or after may avoid this interaction.

PHARMACOKINETICS **Absorption:** Not systemically absorbed. **Metabolism:** Not subject to metabolism, due to lack of absorption. **Elimination:** Exclusively eliminated through feces.

NURSING IMPLICATIONS

Assessment & Drug Effects
- Assess for edema.
- Monitor lab tests: Serum potassium levels.

Patient & Family Education
- Review proper mixing instructions with patient and family.
- Any other oral medications should be taken 2 h before or 2 hs after sodium zirconium cyclosilicate.
- Follow low sodium diet since medication contains 400 mg of sodium in each 5-g dose.

SOFOSBUVIR
(so-fos'bu-vir)
Sovaldi
Classification: ANTIVIRAL; NUCLEOTIDE ANALOG; VIRAL POLYMERASE INHIBITOR
Therapeutic: ANTIHEPATITIS

AVAILABILITY Film-coated tablets

ACTION & *THERAPEUTIC EFFECT*
A direct acting antiviral agent against HCV; is a prodrug converted to its active form via intracellular metabolism. *It inhibits HCV NS5B RNA-dependent RNA polymerase thus inhibiting viral replication.*

USES Treatment of chronic hepatitis C (CHC) infection as part of a combination treatment.

CONTRAINDICATIONS Inability to take concurrent peginterferon alfa/ribavirin or ribavirin alone; concomitant potent P-gp inducers (e.g., rifampin and St. John's wort); suicidal ideation; hepatic decompensation; pregnancy—fetal risk cannot be ruled out; lactation—infant risk cannot be ruled out.

CAUTIOUS USE Concomitant drugs that are P-gp inducers, anticonvulsants, antimycobacterials and amiodarone; post-liver transplant; chronic depression; history of suicide; severe renal impairment; ESRD; liver transplant. Safety and efficacy in children younger than 3 y not established.

ROUTE & DOSAGE

Hepatitis C Infection
Adult: **PO** (see manufacturer's guidelines for dosing by genotype)

ADMINISTRATION

Oral
- Give without regard to food.
- Do not chew pellets. If administered with food, sprinkle on one or more spoonful of non-acidic soft food or below room temperature pudding, chocolate syrup, mashed potatoes or ice cream. Take within 30 minutes of mixing.
- Do not use as monotherapy; use only in combination with ribavirin (with or without peginterferon alfa).
- If the other agents used in combination with sofosbuvir are permanently discontinued, sofosbuvir should also be discontinued.
- Store at room temperature below 30° C (86° F).

ADVERSE EFFECTS CNS: *Fatigue, headache, insomnia.* **Skin:** *Pruritus.* **GI:** *Diarrhea.* **Hematologic:** *Anemia.*

INTERACTIONS Drug: Co-administration with drugs that are potent P-gp inducers in the intestine (e.g., RIFAMYCINS) may decrease the levels of sofosbuvir. Co-administration with drugs that inhibit P-gp may increase the levels of sofosbuvir. Co-administration of sofosbuvir with **carbamazepine, phenytoin, phenobarbital,** or **oxcarbazepine** may decrease the levels of sofosbuvir. Do not use with **amiodarone,** may increase bradycardic effect. **Herbal: St. John's wort must not** be used with sofosbuvir because it is a potent P-gp inducer.

PHARMACOKINETICS Peak: 0.5–2 h. **Distribution:** 61–65% plasma protein bound. **Metabolism:** Converted to active metabolite. **Elimination:** Primarily renal. **Half-Life:** 27 h (active metabolite).

NURSING IMPLICATIONS

Assessment & Drug Effects

- Monitor for and report promptly changes in mental status such as depression or suicidal ideation.
- Monitor for S&S of infection or anemia.
- Monitor lab tests: Baseline and periodic LFTs; serum creatinine; serum HCV-RNA at baseline during treatment, end of treatment, and during treatment follow-up; pretreatment and monthly pregnancy tests and up to 6 mo after therapy discontinued; periodic CBC with differential.

Patient & Family Education

- Report immediately to prescriber if patient experiences mental status changes such as depression, thoughts of suicide, anxiety, emotional instability, or illogical thinking.
- Review adverse effects with patient and/or caregiver.
- Women of childbearing potential and male partners of pregnant women should use effective means of contraception while taking this drug and for at least 6 mo following discontinuation of therapy when medication is combined with ribavirin and with peginterferon and ribavirin.
- Avoid taking St. John's Wort during therapy.

SOFOSBUVIR AND VELPATASVIR

(soe-fos'bue-vir and vel-pat'as-vir)

Epclusa

Classification: ANTIVIRAL; VIRAL POLYMERASE INHIBITOR; ANTIHEPATITIS

Therapeutic: ANTIHEPATITIS

AVAILABILITY Tablets

ACTION & *THERAPEUTIC EFFECT*

Sofosbuvir is a prodrug that is metabolized to its active form (GS-461203) which then inhibits hepatitis C viral (HCV) NS5B RNA-dependent RNA polymerase, an enzyme required for viral replication. Velpatasvir inhibits HCV NS5A protein which is required for viral replication. *Inhibits replication of the HCV virus.*

USES Treatment of chronic hepatitis C virus (HCV) genotype 1, 2, 3, 4, 5, or 6 infection in adult patients without cirrhosis, with compensated cirrhosis, or in combination with ribavirin, with decompensated cirrhosis.

Common adverse effects in *italic;* life-threatening effects underlined; generic names in **bold;** classifications in SMALL CAPS; ♦ Canadian drug name; ○ Prototype drug; ⚠ Alert

CONTRAINDICATIONS Combination with ribavirin is contraindicated in patients for whom ribavirin is contraindicated.

CAUTIOUS USE No adequate human-controlled trials have been done to determine safety in pregnancy or lactation. No data is available to establish safety and efficacy in patients with severe renal impairment or end stage renal disease. Use with caution with patients previously infected with hepatitis B virus (HBV).

ROUTE & DOSAGE

Hepatitis C Viral Infection

Adult: **PO** One tablet (400 mg sofosbuvir and 100 mg velpatasvir) once daily for 12 wk

Hepatic Impairment Dosage Adjustment

Patients with decompensated cirrhosis (Child-Pugh class B or C): Add ribavirin, maintain dose and duration

Renal Impairment Dosage Adjustment

Severe impairment (eGFR less than 30 mL/min/1.73 m^2) or with end stage renal disease: Safety and efficacy not established

ADMINISTRATION

Oral

- Take without regard to food.
- If administered with ribavirin, take ribavirin with food.
- Store below 30° C (86° F). Dispense only in original container.

ADVERSE EFFECTS CNS: Depression, *headache.* **Skin:** Rash. **GI:** Diarrhea, *nausea.* **Hematologic:** *Anemia, decreased hemoglobin,* elevated lipase enzymes, elevated serum creatinine levels. **Other:** Asthenia, *fatigue,* insomnia.

INTERACTIONS Drug: Coadministration of inducers of P-gp and/or CYP2B6, CYP2C8, or CYP3A4 (e.g., **carbamazepine, phenobarbital, phenytoin, rifabutin, rifampin, rifapentine**) may decrease the levels of sofosbuvir and/or velpatasvir. ACID REDUCING AGENTS (e.g., ANTACIDS, **famotidine, omeprazole**) may decrease the levels of velpatasvir. Coadministration of **amiodarone** may result in serious symptomatic bradycardia. Sofosbuvir and/or velpatasvir may increase the levels of **digoxin, topotecan,** HMG-COA REDUCTASE INHIBITORS, and **tenofovir disoproxil fumarate.** Efavirenz, **ritonavir,** and **tipranavir** can decrease the levels of of sofosbuvir and/or velpatasvir. **Herbal: St. John's wort** may decrease the levels of sofosbuvir and/or velpatasvir.

PHARMACOKINETICS Peak: Sofosbuvir, 0.5–1 h; velpatasvir, 3 h. **Distribution:** Sofosbuvir, 61–65% plasma protein bound; velpatsavir, greater than 99.5% plasma protein bound. **Metabolism:** Hydrolytic and oxidative metabolism. **Elimination:** Sofosbuvir, renal (80%) and fecal (14%); velpatasvir, primarily fecal (95%). **Half-Life:** Sofosbuvir, 0.5 h; GS-r61203, 25 h; velpatasvir, 15 h.

NURSING IMPLICATIONS

Assessment & Drug Effects

- Monitor vital signs, as bradycardia and arrhythmias have been reported.
- Monitor cognition: Irritability, insomnia, and depression have been reported.

Common adverse effects in *italic;* life-threatening effects <u>underlined</u>; generic names in **bold;** classifications in SMALL CAPS; ♣ Canadian drug name; ⊘ Prototype drug; ⚠ Alert

- Monitor lab tests: LFTs, plasma hepatitis, pregnancy testing, serum creatinine/BUN.

Patient & Family Education
- Seek medical attention immediately if fainting or near fainting, fatigue, dizziness, shortness of breath, chest pain, and confusion or memory problems.
- Make sure to keep a list of all medications that the patient is taking and share that information with all prescribers.
- Do not take any other over-the-counter medications, herbals, vitamins, or other prescription drugs without first checking with your health care provider.

SOLRIAMFETOL
(sol-ri-am-fe-tol)
Sunosi
Classifications: ANALEPTIC; DOPAMINE AND NOREPINEPHRINE REUPTAKE INHIBITOR (DNRI)
Therapeutic: ANTINARCOLEPTIC
Controlled Substance: Schedule IV

AVAILABILITY Oral tablet

ACTION & THERAPEUTIC EFFECT
Acts as a doapamine and norepinephrine reuptake inhibitor, although specific activity is unknown. *Solriamfetol causes wakefulness.*

USES Improve wakefulness in patients with narcoplepsy or excessive sleepiness associated with obstructive sleep apnea.

CONTRAINDICATIONS Pregnancy—fetal risk cannot be ruled out; lactation—infant risk cannot be ruled out.

CAUTIOUS USE Patients with risk factors for major adverse cardiovascular events and those with moderate to severe renal impairment, history of psychosis or bipolar disorders, patient with ESRD and estimated glomerular filtration rate less than 15 mL/minute/1.73 m(2). Elderly; Safety and efficacy not established in children.

ROUTE & DOSAGE

Narcolepsy
Adult: **PO** 75 mg once daily

Obstructive Sleep Apnea
Adult: **PO** 37.5 mg once daily

Renal Impairment Dosage Adjustment
eGFR 30–59 mL/min: maximum dose 75 mg a day
eGFR 15–29 mL/min: maximum dose 37.5 mg a day
eGFR <15 mL/min: Avoid use

ADMINISTRATION

Oral
- Take upon awakening with or without food. Avoid taking within 9 hours of planned bedtime due to potential for interfering with sleep if taken too late in the day.
- Store at a controlled room temperature between 20 and 25 degrees C (68 and 77 degrees F), with excursions permitted between 15 and 30 degrees F).

ADVERSE EFFECTS CNS: *Headache, insomnia.* **GI:** *Decrease in appetite, nausea and vomiting.* **Other:** Psychiatric symptoms.

Common adverse effects in *italic;* life-threatening effects <u>underlined;</u> generic names in **bold;** classifications in SMALL CAPS; ✦ Canadian drug name; ◐ Prototype drug; △ Alert

1564

INTERACTIONS Drug: MAO
INHIBITORS (eg. **selegiline**) can
precipitate hypertensive crisis (fatalities reported), do not administer solriamfetol during or within 14 days of
these drugs; SYMPATHOMIMETIC
medications utilized with solriametol increase risk of hypertensive
crisis (eg. **methylphenidate**,
amphetamine, and nasal or oral
decongestants). DOPAMINE AGONISTS (eg. pramipexole, ropinirole)
may have increase toxic effects; Solriamfetol may precipitate effects of
medications which increase blood
pressure of heart rate

PHARMACOKINETICS Absorption: 95% bioavailability. **Peak:**
2 h. **Distribution:** 199 L, 13.3–19.4%
protein bound. **Elimination:** 95%
excreted unchained in urine. **Half-
Life:** 7.1 h

NURSING IMPLICATIONS

Assessment & Drug Effects
- Monitor for improved wakefulness and reduction in daytime
sleepiness.
- Monitor pulse and blood pressure
prior to initiating therapy and
periodically throughout treatment,
especially in patiet with known
cardiovascular and cerebrovascular disease, preexisting hypertension, and advanced age.
- Monitor for the development of
psychiatric symptoms during
treatment.
- Monitor elderly patients closely,
particularly those with likelihood
of decreased renal function
- Monitor for signs of misuse or abuse.
- Monitor lab tests: Renal function
tests.

Patient & Family Education
- Teach patient and/or caregiver
how to take blood pressure and

have them report any elevations
of blood pressure or pulse.
- Review side effects.
- Report psychiatric symptoms,
symptoms of psychosis or bipolar
disorder.

SOLIFENACIN SUCCINATE

(sol-i-fen′a-sin)
VESIcare
Classification: ANTICHOLINERGIC;
ANTIMUSCARINIC; ANTISPASMODIC
Therapeutic: URINARY
ANTISPASMODIC
Prototype: Oxybutynin

AVAILABILITY Tablet

ACTION & THERAPEUTIC EFFECT
A selective muscarinic antagonist
that depresses both voluntary and
involuntary bladder contractions
caused by detrusor overactivity.
*Solifenacin improves the volume
of urine/void and reduces the frequency of incontinent and urgency
episodes.*

USES Treatment of overactive bladder (OAB); neurogenic detrusor
overactivity.

CONTRAINDICATIONS Hypersensitivity to solifenacin; severe
hepatic impairment (Child-Pugh
class C); gastric retention; uncontrolled narrow-angle glaucoma; urinary retention; toxic megacolon; GI
obstruction; ileus; pregnancy—fetal
risk cannot be ruled out; lactation—
infant risk cannot be ruled out.

CAUTIOUS USE Bladder outflow obstruction; concurrent use
of ketoconazole or other potent
CYP3A4 inhibitors; obstructive disorders; decreased GI motility; history of QT prolongation; controlled

narrow-angle glaucoma; renal impairment; renal disease; mild to moderate hepatic impairment; older adults; myasthenia gravis. Safety and efficacy in children under the age of 2 y not established.

ROUTE & DOSAGE

Overactive Bladder

Adult: **PO** 5 mg once daily; may be increased to 10 mg once daily if tolerated (max: 5 mg/day if taking drugs that inhibit CYP3A4—see INTERACTIONS, Drug)

Hepatic Impairment Dosage Adjustment

Child-Pugh class B: Do not exceed 5 mg/day. *Child-Pugh class C:* Do not use

Renal Impairment Dosage Adjustment

CrCl less than 30 mL/min: Max dose 5 mg/day

ADMINISTRATION

Oral

- Tablets should be swallowed whole and followed by liquid (water). Without regard to food.
- Suspension: Any missed dose should be taken as soon as remembered, unless more than 12 hours have passed. If more than 12 ours have passed, the dose should be skipped and the next dose taken at the usual time.
- Store suspension at a controlled room temperature between 20 and 25 degrees C (68 and 77 degrees F), with excursions permitted between 15°–30° C (59°–86° F). Store in original bottle to protect from degradation. discard any unused product 28 days after opening the original bottle.

Tablets should be stored at 25 degrees C (77 degrees C), with excursions permitted between 15°–30° C (59°–86° F).

ADVERSE EFFECTS (≥5%) GI: *Dry mouth, constipation.*

INTERACTIONS Drug: There are extensive drug interactions, consult a drug interaction database for complete listing, some interactions of significance are listed here. CYP3A4 inhibitors (e.g., **clarithromycin, delavirdine, diltiazem, efavirenz, erythromycin, fluconazole, fluvoxamine, itraconazole, nefazodone, norfloxacin, omeprazole,** PROTEASE INHIBITORS, **quinine, verapamil, voriconazole, zafirlukast**) may increase levels and toxicity (max: 5 mg/day); **amantadine, amoxapine, bupropion, clozapine, cyclobenzaprine, diphenhydramine, disopyramide, maprotiline, olanzapine, orphenadrine,** PHENOTHIAZINES, TRICYCLIC ANTIDEPRESSANTS have additive anticholinergic adverse effects. Do not use with agents that increase QT interval (e.g., **dofetilide, dronedarone, posaconazole, ziprasidone**). May increase ulcerogenic risk with **potassium. Food: Grapefruit juice** may increase solifenacin levels and toxicity.

PHARMACOKINETICS Absorption: 90% absorbed from GI tract.; 98% protein bound **Peak:** 3–8 h. **Metabolism:** Extensively metabolized in the liver by CYP3A4. **Elimination:** Primarily in urine, 22% in feces. **Half-Life:** 45–68 h.

NURSING IMPLICATIONS

Assessment & Drug Effects

- Monitor bladder function and report promptly urinary retention.

Common adverse effects in *italic;* life-threatening effects <u>underlined;</u> generic names in **bold;** classifications in SMALL CAPS; ♣ Canadian drug name; ☉ Prototype drug; ⚠ Alert

- Review adverse effects with patient and/or caregiver.
- Monitor ECG in patients with a known history of QT prolongation or patients taking medications that prolong the QT interval.

Patient & Family Education
- Stop taking this drug and report to prescriber if urinary retention occurs.
- Remind patient to take with water or milk, other liquids may cause a bitter taste.
- Report severe abdominal pain or constipation for more than 3 days.
- Avoid activities requiring mental alertness or coordination until drug effects are realized.
- Report promptly any of the following: Blurred vision or difficulty focusing vision, palpitations, confusion, or severe dizziness.
- Report to prescriber problems with bowel elimination, especially constipation lasting 3 days or longer.
- Exercise caution in hot environments, as the risk of heat prostration and impaired heat regulation increases with this drug.
- Review directions for missed dose with patient and/or caregiver described under administration.

SOMATROPIN ✪
(soe-ma-troe'pin)
Genotropin, Genotropin MiniQuick, Humatrope, Norditropin, NuSpin, Omnitrope, Saizen, Serostim, Zomacton, Zorbtive
Classification: GROWTH HORMONE
Therapeutic: GROWTH HORMONE

AVAILABILITY Solution for injection

ACTION & THERAPEUTIC EFFECT
Recombinant growth hormone with the natural sequence of 191 amino acids characteristic of endogenous growth hormone (GH), of pituitary origin. *Induces growth responses in children.*

USES Growth failure due to GH deficiency; replacement therapy prior to epiphyseal closure in patients with idiopathic GH deficiency; GH deficiency secondary to intracranial tumors or panhypopituitarism; inadequate GH secretion; short stature in girls with Turner's syndrome; AIDS wasting syndrome; short bowel syndrome; small for gestational age.

UNLABELED USES Growth deficiency in children with rheumatoid arthritis.

CONTRAINDICATIONS Hypersensitivity to somatropin or any ingredient; pediatric patient with closed epiphyses; underlying intracranial lesion or growing cranial tumor; acute critical illness caused by complications following open heart surgery or abdominal surgery, acute respiratory failure; acute diabetic retinopathy; during chemotherapy, radiation therapy, active neoplastic disease; selective cases of Prader-Willi syndrome who are severely obese or have severe respiratory impairment; children with an intracranial tumor; drug-induced acute pancreatitis.

CAUTIOUS USE Diabetes mellitus or family history of the disease, history of glucose intolerance; Prader-Willi syndrome with a diagnosis of growth hormone deficiency (GHD); skeletal abnormalities; Turner syndrome; HIV patients; history of upper airway obstruction, sleep apnea, or unidentified URI; concomitant or prior use of thyroid or androgens in prepubertal male; hypothyroidism; chronic renal failure; obesity; older adults; pregnancy (category B or category C depending on the brand); lactation; children.

ROUTE & DOSAGE

Note: Dosing will vary based on specific brand of product

Growth Hormone Deficiency (GHD)

Adult: **Subcutaneous Humatrope** Not more than 0.006 mg/kg once daily; dose may be increased (max: 0.0125 mg/kg/day); **Genotropin, Omnitrope** 0.04 mg/kg qwk divided into daily doses (max: 0.08 mg/kg/wk); **Norditropin** Initially 0.004 mg/kg/day (max: 0.016 mg/kg/day)
Child: **Subcutaneous Genotropin** 0.16–0.24 mg/kg/wk divided into 6–7 daily doses; **Humatrope** 0.18–0.3 mg/kg/wk (0.54 international unit/kg/wk) divided into equal doses given on either 3 alternate days or 6 × wk; **Norditropin** 0.024–0.034 mg/kg/day 6–7 × wk; **Omnitrope** 0.16–0.24 mg/kg/week divided into 6–7 injections

Small for Gestational Age

Child: **Subcutaneous Genotropin/Omnitrope** 0.48 mg/kg/week in divided doses; **Humatrope** 0.47 mg/kg divided into daily doses

AIDS Wasting or Cachexia

Adult (weight greater than 55 kg): **Subcutaneous Serostim** 6 mg each night; *weight 45–55 kg:* 5 mg each night; *weight 35–45 kg:* 4 mg each night; *weight less than 35 kg:* 0.1 mg/kg each night

Short Bowel Syndrome

Adult: **Subcutaneous Zorbtive** 0.1 mg/kg once daily for 4 wk (max: 8 mg/day)

ADMINISTRATION

Subcutaneous

- Reconstitute each brand following its manufacturer's instructions (vary from brand to brand).
- Read and carefully follow directions for use supplied with the Nutropin AQ Pen™ cartridge if this is the product being used.
- Rotate injection sites; abdomen and thighs are preferred sites. Do not use buttocks until the child has been walking for a year or more and the muscle is adequately developed.
- Store lyophilized powder at 2°–8° C (36°–46° F). After reconstitution, most preparations are stable for at least 14 days under refrigeration. **Do not freeze.**

ADVERSE EFFECTS

CV: Chest pain, edema. **CNS:** Pain, headache, malaise, paresthesia, dizziness. **Endocrine:** *Hypercalciuria;* oversaturation of bile with cholesterol, hyperglycemia, ketosis; High circulating GH antibodies with resulting treatment failure, accelerated growth of intracranial tumor, pancreatitis. **GI:** Nausea, flatulence, abdominal pain, vomiting. **Musculoskeletal:** Arthralgia, limb pain, myalgia. **Other:** Pain, swelling at injection site; peripheral edema, myalgia. <u>Fatalities reported in patients with Prader-Willi syndrome and one or more of the following: Severe obesity, history of</u>

respiratory impairment or sleep apnea, or unidentified respiratory infection, especially male patients.

INTERACTIONS Drug: ANABOLIC STEROIDS, **thyroid hormone,** ANDROGENS, ESTROGENS may accelerate epiphyseal closure; **ACTH,** CORTICOSTEROIDS may inhibit growth response to somatropin.

PHARMACOKINETICS Metabolism: In liver. **Elimination:** In urine. **Half-Life:** 15–50 min.

NURSING IMPLICATIONS

Assessment & Drug Effects

- Monitor growth at designated intervals.
- Hypercalciuria, a frequent adverse effect in the first 2–3 mo of therapy, may be symptomless; however, it may be accompanied by renal calculi, with these reportable symptoms: Flank pain and colic, GI symptoms, urinary frequency, chills, fever, and hematuria.
- Observe diabetics or those with family history of diabetes closely. Obtain regular fasting blood glucose and HbA1C.
- Examine patients with GH deficiency secondary to intracranial lesion frequently for progression or recurrence of underlying disease.
- Monitor lab test: Periodic serum and urine calcium and plasma glucose. Test for circulating GH antibodies (antisomatropin antibodies) in patients who respond initially but later fail to respond to therapy, thyroid function tests.

Patient & Family Education

- Be aware that during first 6 mo of successful treatment, linear growth rates may be increased 8–16 cm or more/year (average

about 7 cm/y or approximately 3 in.). Additionally, subcutaneous fat diminishes but returns to pretreatment value later.

- Record accurate height measurements at regular intervals and report to prescriber if rate is less than expected.
- In general, growth response to somatropin is inversely proportional to duration of treatment.
- Bone age is typically assessed annually in all patients and especially those also receiving concurrent thyroid or androgen treatment, since these drugs may precipitate early epiphyseal closure. Take child for bone age assessment on appointed annual dates.

SONIDEGIB

(son-i-de'gib)

Odomzo

Classification: ANTINEOPLASTIC; BIOLOGICAL RESPONSE MODIFIER; SIGNAL TRANSDUCTION INHIBITOR; HEDGEHOG PATHWAY INHIBITOR

Therapeutic: ANTINEOPLASTIC

Prototype: Vismodegib

AVAILABILITY Capsules

ACTION & THERAPEUTIC EFFECT

Hedgehog mutations associated with basal cell cancer can activate cell growth pathways resulting in unrestricted proliferation of skin basal cells. Sonidegib inhibits the Hedgehog pathway by binding to smoothened homologue (SMO), a transmembrane protein involved in Hedgehog signal transduction. Hedgehog regulates cell growth and differentiation in embryogenesis but is generally not active in adult tissue. Hedgehog regulates cell growth and differentiation in embryogenesis, but is generally not

S

active in adult tissue. Hedgehog mutations associated with basal cell cancer can activate the pathway resulting in unrestricted proliferation of skin basal cells. *Inhibits the growth and differential of basal carcinoma cells.*

USES Treatment of adult patients with locally advanced basal cell carcinoma (BCC) that has recurred following surgery or radiation therapy, or those who are not candidates for surgery or radiation therapy.

CONTRAINDICATIONS Active TB infection; recurrent serum CK greater than 5 × ULN; recurrent severe musculoskeletal reactions.

CAUTIOUS USE History of rhabdomyolysis with other drugs which inhibit the Hedgehog pathway; Crohn's disease. Concomitant use of CYP3A4 inhibitors; grapefruit consumption; pregnancy (category B); lactation. Safety and efficacy in children not established.

ROUTE & DOSAGE

Advanced BCC
Adult: **PO** 200 mg once daily

Toxicity Dosage Adjustment

Severe musculoskeletal reactions, first occurrence of serum CK 2.5–10 × ULN, or recurrent serum CK 2.5–5 × ULN: Temporarily discontinue, then resume at 200 mg upon resolution
Serum CK greater than 2.5 × ULN with worsening renal function: Permanently discontinue
Serum CK greater than 10 × ULN: Permanently discontinue
Recurrent serum CK greater than 5 × ULN: Permanently discontinue

Recurrent severe musculoskeletal reactions: Permanently discontinue

ADMINISTRATION

Oral
- Give on an empty stomach at least 1 h before or 2 h after a meal.
- Capsules should be swallowed whole.

ADVERSE EFFECTS CNS: *Dysgeusia, headache.* **Endocrine:** *Decreased appetite,* hyperglycemia, increased ALT/AST, increased amylase, increased lipase, increased serum creatinine, increased serum creatine kinase (CK), *weight loss.* **Skin:** *Alopecia, pruritus.* **GI:** *Abdominal pain, diarrhea, nausea, vomiting.* **Musculoskeletal:** *Muscle spasm, musculoskeletal pain, myalgia.* **Hematologic:** Anemia, lymphopenia. **Other:** *Fatigue, pain.*

INTERACTIONS Drug: Concomitant use with strong CYP3A4 inhibitors (e.g., **itraconazole, ketoconazole, nefazodone, posaconazole, saquinavir, telithromycin, voriconazole**) or moderate CYP3A4 inhibitors (e.g., **atanzavir, diltiazem, fluconazole**) increases the levels of sonidegib. Concomitant use with strong and moderate inhibitors (e.g., **carbamazepine, efavirenz, modafinil, phenobarbital, phenytoin, rifabutin, rifampin**) decreases the levels of sonidegib. **Food: Grapefruit** or **grapefruit juice** may increase the levels of sonidegib. **Herbal: St. John's wort** decreases the levels of sonidegib.

PHARMACOKINETICS Absorption: Less than 10% absorbed. **Peak:** 2–4 h. **Distribution:** Greater than 97% plasma protein binding.

Metabolism: In liver by CYP450 enzymes. **Elimination:** Fecal (70%) and renal (30%). **Half-Life:** 28 days.

NURSING IMPLICATIONS

Black Box Warning

Sonidegib can cause embryo-fetal death or severe birth defects. Pregnancy status must be verified prior to initiating therapy. (See Patient & Family Education.)

Assessment & Drug Effects

- Monitor for and report to prescriber development of musculoskeletal pain, myalgia, dark urine, decreased urine output, or the inability to urinate.
- Monitor lab tests: Baseline pregnancy test; baseline and periodic serum creatine kinase (CK) and creatinine levels.

Patient & Family Education

- Women of childbearing age should discuss potential risks of this drug to fetal development.
- Women should use effective means of contraception while taking this drug and for at least 20 mo after the last dose.
- Women taking this drug or partners of males taking this drug should immediately report to prescriber if a pregnancy is suspected.
- Do not breast-feed while taking this drug.
- Males should use condoms (even after a vasectomy) during treatment and for at least 8 mo after the last dose to prevent exposure of females of childbearing age to this drug.
- Males should not donate semen during treatment and for at least 8 mo after the last dose.
- Report promptly any new unexplained muscle pain, tenderness or weakness occurring during treatment or that persists after discontinuing this drug.
- Report promptly dark urine, decreased urine output, or the inability to urinate.
- Avoid grapefruit products while taking this drug.

SORAFENIB

(sor-a-fe'nib)

Nexavar

Classification: ANTINEOPLASTIC; KINASE INHIBITOR; KINASE INHIBITOR

Therapeutic: ANTINEOPLASTIC

Prototype: Erlotinib

AVAILABILITY Tablet

ACTION & *THERAPEUTIC EFFECT*

A multi-kinase inhibitor targeting enzyme systems in both tumor cells and tumor vasculature. It appears to be cytostatic, requiring continued drug exposure for tumor growth inhibition. *Sorafenib inhibits enzymes responsible for uncontrolled tumor cellular proliferation and angiogenesis.*

USES Treatment of advanced renal cell cancer; hepatocellular cancer; differentiated thyroid carcinoma.

UNLABELED USES Gastrointestinal stromal tumor.

CONTRAINDICATIONS Active infection; severe hypersensitivity to sorafenib or any other component of the product. severe renal impairment (less than 30 mL/min), or hemodialysis; concurrent use of gemcitabine and cisplatin in patients with squamous cell lung cancer; pregnancy – fetal risk cannot be ruled out. lactation – infant risk cannot be ruled out.

CAUTIOUS USE Previous myelo-suppressive therapy, either radiation or chemotherapy; mild or moderate renal disease; hepatic disease; heart failure, ventricular dysfunction, cardiac disease, peripheral edema; females of child-bearing age. Safe use in children younger than 18 y not established.

ROUTE & DOSAGE

Renal Cell Cancer/Hepatocellular Cancer/Differentiated Thyroid Carcinoma
Adult: **PO** 400 mg bid

Renal Impairment Dosage Adjustment
CrCl 20–39 mL/min: 200 mg bid; CrCl less than 20 mL/min dose not defined

Dosage Adjustments Toxicity
Varies by indication and specific level of toxicity; see package insert

ADMINISTRATION

Oral
- NIOSH: Use of single gloves by anyone handling intact tablets or capsules or administering from a unit-dose package is recommended. In preparation of tablets or capsules, including cutting, crushing or manipulating, or the handling of uncoated tablets, use double gloves and a protective gown. During administration, wear gloves, and wear single gloves and eye/face protection if the formulation is hard to swallow or if the patient may resist, vomit or spit up.
- Tablets **must be** swallowed whole. They should not be crushed, broken, or chewed.
- Give on an empty stomach 1 h before or 2 h after eating.
- Store at 25 degrees C (77 degrees F), excursions permitted between 15°–30° C (59°–86° F). Protect from moisture.

ADVERSE EFFECTS (≥5%) CV:
Hypertension. **Endocrine:** *Amylase elevation, hypoalbuminemia, hypocalcemia, elevated TSH, hypophosphatemia, lipase elevation, weight loss.* **Skin:** Acne, *alopecia, desquamation, dry skin,* erythema, exfoliative dermatitis, flushing, *hand-foot skin reaction, rash.* **Hepatic:** ALT/SGPT elevation, elevated aminotransferase serum level. **GI:** *Abdominal pain, anorexia, diarrhea, nausea,* gastrointestinal hemorrhage. **Hematologic:** Hemorrhage, *Lymphocytopenia,* thrombocytopenia. *fatigue* pain.

INTERACTIONS Drug: There are extensive drug interactions, consult a drug interaction database for complete listing, some interactions of significance are listed here. Sorafenib may increase levels of drugs requiring glucuronidation by the UGT1A1 and UGT1A9 pathways (e.g., **irinotecan**). Due to thrombocytopenic effects, sorafenib can contribute to increased bleeding from NON-STEROIDAL ANTI-INFLAMMATORY DRUGS, PLATELET INHIBITORS (e.g., **aspirin, clopidogrel**), THROMBOLYTIC AGENTS, and **warfarin.** Inducers of CYP3A4 (e.g., **carbamazepine, phenobarbital, phenytoin, rifampin**) may decrease the levels of sorafenib. Do not use with LIVE VACCINES. May increase adverse effects with MYELO-SUPRESSIVE AGENTS **Food:** Food, especially high fat food, decreases the absorption of sorafenib. **Herbal: St. John's wort** may decrease the levels of sorafenib.

PHARMACOKINETICS Absorption: 38–49% absorbed. **Peak:** 3 h. **Distribution:** 99.5% protein bound. **Metabolism:** In the liver (CYP3A4 and UGT1A9). **Elimination:** Primarily fecal (77%) with minor elimination in the urine (19%). **Half-Life:** 25–48 h.

NURSING IMPLICATIONS

Assessment & Drug Effects

- Monitor for and report S&S of skin toxicity (e.g., rash, erythema, dermatitis, paresthesia, swelling, or pain in hands or feet). Severe reactions may require temporary suspension of therapy or dose reduction.
- Monitor for S&S of bleeding, especially in those on anticoagulation therapy.
- Monitor BP weekly for the first 6 wk of therapy and periodically thereafter. New-onset hypertension has been associated with sorafenib.
- Monitor blood levels of warfarin with concurrent therapy.
- ECG for QT interval prolongation in patients with CHF, bradyarrhythmia, or concurrent drug therapy known to prolong the QT interval.
- Monitor lab tests: Periodic CBC with differential and platelet count, serum electrolytes, TSH, LFTs, lipase, amylase, and alkaline phosphatase.

Patient & Family Education

- Report any of the following to a health care provider: Skin rash; redness, blisters, pain, or swelling of the palms or hands or soles of feet; signs of bleeding; unexplained chest, shoulder, neck and jaw, or back pain.
- Review adverse effects with patient and/or caregiver.

- Review administration guidelines discussed under administration.
- Do not take any prescription or nonprescription drugs without consulting the prescriber.
- Notify prescriber prior to any major surgical procedure as the drug may need to be temporarily discontinued.
- Female patients should use effective birth control during treatment and for at least 6 months following completion of treatment. Male patient with a female partner of reproductive potential to use effective contraception during therapy and for 3 months after the last dose.

SOTALOL

(so-ta'lol)

Betapace, Betapace AF, Sorine, Sotylize

Classification: BETA-ADRENERGIC ANTAGONIST; CLASS II AND III ANTIARRHYTHMIC

Therapeutic: CLASS II AND III ANTIARRHYTHMIC

Prototype: Amiodarone

AVAILABILITY Tablet; solution for injection

ACTION & *THERAPEUTIC EFFECT*

Has both class II and class III antiar-rhythmic properties. Slows heart rate, decreases AV nodal conduction, and increases AV nodal refractoriness. Produces significant reduction in both systolic and diastolic blood pressure. *Antiarrhythmic properties are effective in controlling ventricular arrhythmias as well as atrial fibrillation/flutter.*

USES Treatment of life-threatening ventricular arrhythmias (sustained ventricular tachycardia)

S

and maintenance of normal sinus rhythm in patients with atrial fibrillation/flutter.

CONTRAINDICATIONS Hypersensitivity to sotalol; bronchial asthma, acute bronchospasm; sinus bradycardia, second and third degree AV block without a functioning pacemaker, uncontrolled HF; cardiogenic shock; emphysema; major disease; congenital or acquired long QT prolongation; hypokalemia less than 4 mEq/L creatinine clearance of less than 40 mL/min; lactation.

CAUTIOUS USE CHF, electrolyte disturbances, within 14 days of MI, DM; sick sinus rhythm, PVD; untreated pheochromocytoma; MG; thyroid disease; history of psychiatric disease; hyperthyroidism; renal impairment; excessive diarrhea, or profuse sweating; older adults; pregnancy (category B).

ROUTE & DOSAGE

Ventricular Arrhythmias (Betapace, Sorine, Sotylize)

Adult: **PO** Initial dose of 80 mg bid or 160 mg daily taken prior to meals, may increase every 3–4 days (most patients respond to 240–320 mg/day in 2 or 3 divided doses, doses greater than 640 mg/day have not been studied)

Renal Impairment Dosage Adjustment

CrCl greater than 60 mL/min: q12h; 30–60 mL/min: q24h; 10–30 mL/min: q36–48h; less than 10 mL/min: Individualize carefully

Atrial Fibrillation/Flutter (Betapace AF, Sotylize)

Adult: **PO** Initial dose of 80 mg bid, may increase every 3–4 days (max: 240 mg/day in 1–2 divided doses); **IV** 75 mg bid may increase after 3 days depending on patient response

Renal Impairment Dosage Adjustment

CrCl 40–60 mL/min: Dose q24h; less than 40 mL/min contraindicated

ADMINISTRATION

Oral

- Sotalol and sotalol AF are **not** interchangeable because of significant differences in labeling (i.e., patient package insert, dosing administration, safety information).
- Give without regard to meals.
- Drug should be initiated and doses increased only under close supervision, preferably in a hospital with cardiac rhythm monitoring and frequent assessment.
- Use smallest effective dose for patients with nonallergic bronchospasms.
- Do not discontinue drug abruptly. Gradually reduce dose over 1–2 wk.
- Store at room temperature, 15°–30° C (59°–86° F).

Intravenous

PREPARE: **IV Infusion: Sotalol** infusion must be prepared to compensate for dead space in the infusion set. The directions that follow will yield 120 mL of prepared volume, but only 100 mL will be infused when using a volumetric infusion pump.

Possible diluents include NS, D5W, and LR. For a target dose of 75 mg, use 6 mL sotalol injection and 114 mL diluent; for a target dose of 112.5 mg, use 9 mL sotalol injection and 111 mL diluent; for a target dose of 150 mg, use 12 mL sotalol injection and 108 mL diluent.
ADMINISTER: IV Infusion: Give at a constant rate over 5 h.
INCOMPATIBILITIES: Do not infuse with any other drugs or solutions.

ADVERSE EFFECTS CV: AV block, hypotension, aggravation of CHF, although the incidence of heart failure may be lower than for other beta-blockers, <u>life-threatening ventricular arrhythmias, including polymorphous ventricular tachycardia or torsades de pointes,</u> *bradycardia, dyspnea, chest pain, palpitation,* bleeding (less than 2%). **Respiratory:** Respiratory complaints. **CNS:** Headache, *fatigue, dizziness,* weakness, lethargy, depression, lassitude. **HEENT:** Visual disturbances. **Endocrine:** Hyperglycemia. **Skin:** Rash. Hyperglycemia. **GI:** Nausea, vomiting, diarrhea, dyspepsia, dry mouth. **GU:** Impotence, decreased libido.

INTERACTIONS Drug: Antagonizes the effects of BETA AGONISTS. **Amiodarone** may lead to symptomatic bradycardia and sinus arrest. The hypoglycemic effects of ORAL HYPOGLYCEMIC AGENTS may be potentiated. May cause resistance to **epinephrine** in anaphylactic reactions. Should be used with caution with other ANTIARRHYTHMIC AGENTS, withhold Class I (e.g., **disopyramide, procainamide, quinidine**) or Class III ANTIARRHYTHMICS (e.g., **amiodarone, dofetilide**)

for at least three half-lives prior to initiating sotalol. **Food:** Absorption may be reduced by food, especially **milk** and MILK PRODUCTS.

PHARMACOKINETICS Absorption: Slowly and completely from GI tract. Negligible first-pass metabolism. Reduced by food, especially milk and milk products. **Peak:** 2–3 h. **Duration:** 24 h. **Distribution:** Drug is hydrophilic and will enter the CSF slowly (about 10%). Crosses placental barrier. Distributed in breast milk. Not appreciably protein bound. **Metabolism:** Does not undergo significant hepatic enzyme metabolism and no active metabolites have been identified. **Elimination:** In urine with 75% of the drug excreted unchanged within 72 h. **Half-Life:** 7–18 h.

NURSING IMPLICATIONS

Black Box Warning

Sotalol initiation, reinitiation, and dosage adjustment have been associated with serious, life-threatening arrhythmias; thus patients should be in a facility that can provide continuous ECG monitoring, calculation of creatinine clearance, and cardiac resuscitation.

Assessment & Drug Effects

- Monitor ECG at baseline and periodically thereafter (especially when doses are increased) because proarrhythmic events most often occur within 7 days of initiating therapy or increasing dose.
- Monitor cardiac status throughout therapy. Exercise special caution when sotalol is used concurrently with other antiarrhythmics, digoxin, or calcium channel blockers.

- Monitor patients with broncho-spastic disease (e.g., bronchitis, emphysema) carefully for inhibition of bronchodilation.
- Monitor diabetics for loss of glycemic control. Beta blockage reduces the release of endogenous insulin in response to hyperglycemia and may blunt symptoms of acute hypoglycemia (e.g., tachycardia, BP changes).
- Monitor lab test: Baseline and periodic creatinine clearance, and serum electrolytes. Correct electrolyte imbalances of hypokalemia or hypomagnesemia prior to initiating therapy.

Patient & Family Education
- Be aware of risk for hypotension and syncope, especially with concurrent treatment with cate-cholamine-depleting drugs (e.g., guanethidine).
- Take radial pulse daily and report marked bradycardia (pulse below 60 or other established parameter) hold the dose and notify the prescriber.
- Type 2 diabetics are at increased risk for hyperglycemia. All diabetics are at risk of possible masking of symptoms of hypoglycemia.
- Do not abruptly discontinue drug because of the risk of exacerbation of angina, arrhythmias, and possible myocardial infarction.

SPINOSAD
(spin'oh-sad)
Natroba
Classification: SCABICIDE; PEDICULICIDE
Therapeutic: SCABICIDE; PEDICULICIDE
Prototype: Permethrin

AVAILABILITY Topical suspension

ACTION & THERAPEUTIC EFFECT
Kills lice directly without measurable absorption into the human body. *Eliminates lice infestation in humans.*

USES Topical treatment of head lice infestations caused by *Pediculus capitis* in patients 4 y or older.

CONTRAINDICATIONS Contains benzyl alcohol and is not recommended for use in neonates and infants below the age of 6 months.

CAUTIOUS USE Inflammatory skin conditions (e.g., psoriasis, eczema); pregnancy (category B); lactation; children 4 y or older.

ROUTE & DOSAGE

Head Lice Infestation
Adult/Child (4 y or older): **Topical** May apply up to 120 mL to cover scalp/hair; may repeat in 7 d if necessary.

ADMINISTRATION
Topical
- Shake well immediately prior to use.
- Apply sufficient amount (up to one bottle) to cover dry scalp, then apply to dry hair; leave on 10 min, then rinse hair and scalp thoroughly with warm water.
- Store at 15°–30° C (59°–86° F).

ADVERSE EFFECTS HEENT: Ocular erythema. **Other:** Application-site erythema and irritation.

NURSING IMPLICATIONS
Assessment & Drug Effects
- Assess hair and scalp for presence of lice. If still present after 7 days

Common adverse effects in *italic;* life-threatening effects <u>underlined</u>; generic names in **bold;** classifications in SMALL CAPS; ♣ Canadian drug name; ◐ Prototype drug; ⚠ Alert

of treatment, a second treatment should be applied.

Patient & Family Education
- Avoid contact with eyes. If spinosad gets in or near the eyes, rinse thoroughly with water.
- Wash hands after applying spinosad.
- Use on children only under direct supervision of an adult.

SPIRONOLACTONE ⊙
(speer-on-oh-lak′tone)
Aldactone, CaroSpir
Classification: POTASSIUM-SPARING DIURETIC
Therapeutic: POTASSIUM-SPARING DIURETIC; ANTIHYPERTENSIVE

AVAILABILITY Tablet; suspension

ACTION & *THERAPEUTIC EFFECT*
Competes with aldosterone for cellular receptor sites in distal renal tubules. Promotes sodium and chloride excretion without loss of potassium. *A diuretic agent that promotes sodium and chloride excretion without concomitant loss of potassium. Lowers systolic and diastolic pressures in hypertensive patients. Effective in treatment of primary aldosteronism.*

USES Management of edema, heart failure, hypertension unresponsive to other therapies, primary hyperaldosteronism (tablet only).

UNLABELED USES Hirsutism in women with polycystic ovary syndrome or idiopathic hirsutism; hormone therapy for transgender females (male-to-female).

CONTRAINDICATIONS Anuria, acute renal insufficiency; renal failure; diabetic nephropathy; progressive impairment of kidney function, or worsening of liver disease; hyperkalemia; lactic acidosis; Addison disease; Concomitant eplerenone; pregnancy (fetal risk cannot be ruled out).

CAUTIOUS USE BUN of 40 mg/dL or greater, mild renal impairment; fluid and electrolyte imbalance; liver disease; severe heart failure; natremia; older adults; lactation (infant risk is minimal); children.

ROUTE & DOSAGE

Edema

Note: Tablet and suspension are not interchangeable

Adult: **PO Tablet** 100 mg daily in single or divided dose; titrate as needed (range 25–200 mg/day) **Suspension** 75 mg daily in single or divided dose

Hypertension

Adult: **PO Tablet** 25–50 mg/day in single or divided doses, may titrate at 2 wk intervals; **Suspension** 20–100 mg daily may titrate at 2 wk intervals

Primary Aldosteronism

Adult: **PO Tablet** 100–400 mg/day

Severe Heart Failure

Adult: **PO Tablet** 12.5–25 mg qd; may increase dose to 50 mg qd if needed

Renal Impairment Dosage Adjustment

eGFR 30–50 mL/min/1.73 m²: 25 mg/day (tablet); 10 mg/day (suspension)

S

Common adverse effects in *italic;* life-threatening effects <u>underlined;</u> generic names in **bold;** classifications in SMALL CAPS; ✦ Canadian drug name; ⊙ Prototype drug; ⚠ Alert   1577

ADMINISTRATION

Oral

- NIOSH recommends using single gloves when handling intact tablets or capsules or administering from unit package. If cutting or crushing or handling uncoated tablets, use double gloves and a protective gown. During administration, wear single gloves, and wear eye/face protection if the formulation is hard to swallow or if the patient may resist, vomit, or spit up.
- Give with food to enhance absorption. Avoid taking with potassium supplements and foods that are high in potassium (e.g., salt substitutes).
- Crush tablets and give with fluid of patient's choice if unable to swallow whole.
- Store in tight, light-resistant containers. Store suspension at 20°–25° C (68°–77° F). Store tablets below 25° C (77° F).

ADVERSE EFFECTS CV: Vasculitis.
CNS: Ataxia, confusion, dizziness, drowsiness, headache, lethargy, nipple pain. **Endocrine:** Amenorrhea, decreased libido, electrolyte disturbance, hyperkalemia, hyponatremia, hypovolemia. **Skin:** Alopecia, chloasma, rash, Stevens-Johnson syndrome, toxic epidermal necrolysis, urticaria. **Hepatic:** Hepatotoxicity. **GI:** Abdominal cramps, diarrhea, gastritis, gastrointestinal hemorrhage, gastrointestinal ulcer, nausea, vomiting. **GU:** Erectile dysfunction, impotence, irregular menses, mastalgia, postmenopausal bleeding, Increased BUN, renal failure, renal insufficiency. **Musculoskeletal:** Leg cramps. **Hematologic:** Agranulocytosis, leukopenia, breast malignancy, thrombocytopenia. **Other:** Fever.

DIAGNOSTIC TEST INTERFERENCE
May produce marked increases in **plasma cortisol** determinations by **Mattingly fluorometric** method; these may persist for several days after termination of drug (spironolactone metabolite produces fluorescence). There is the possibility of false elevations in measurements of **digoxin serum levels** by **RIA** procedures; may lead to false negative aldosterone/renin ratio.

INTERACTIONS Drug: Diuretic effect of spironolactone may be antagonized by **aspirin** and other SALICYLATES. **Digoxin** should be monitored for decreased effect of CARDIAC GLYCOSIDES. Hyperkalemia may result with **amiloride, cyclosporine, tacrolimus,** POTASSIUM SUPPLEMENTS, ACE INHIBITORS, ARBS, **heparin;** may decrease **lithium** clearance resulting in increased tenacity; may alter anticoagulant response in **warfarin.** Do not use with **eplerenone, darifenacin,** or **tranylcypromine. Food:** Salt substitutes may increase risk of hyperkalemia.

PHARMACOKINETICS Absorption: ~73% from GI tract. **Onset:** Gradual. **Peak:** 2–3 days; maximum effect may take up to 2 wk. **Duration:** 2–3 days or longer. **Distribution:** Crosses placenta, distributed into breast milk. **Metabolism:** In liver and kidneys to active metabolites; potent inhibitor of P-gp. **Elimination:** 40–57% in urine, 35–40% in bile. **Half-Life:** 1.4 hours (tablet) 1–2 hours (suspension).

NURSING IMPLICATIONS

Black Box Warning

Spironolactone has been associated with tumor development in laboratory animals. Unnecessary use of this drug should be avoided.

Common adverse effects in *italic*; life-threatening effects underlined; generic names in **bold**; classifications in SMALL CAPS; ♣ Canadian drug name; ○ Prototype drug; ⚠ Alert

Assessment & Drug Effects

- Check blood pressure before initiation of therapy and at regular intervals throughout therapy.
- Assess for signs of fluid and electrolyte imbalance, and signs of digoxin toxicity.
- Monitor daily I&O and check for edema. Report lack of diuretic response or development of edema; both may indicate tolerance to drug.
- Weigh patient under standard conditions before therapy begins and daily throughout therapy. Weight is a useful index of need for dosage adjustment. For patients with ascites, prescriber may want measurements of abdominal girth.
- Observe for and report immediately the onset of mental changes, lethargy, or stupor in patients with liver disease.
- Adverse reactions are generally reversible with discontinuation of drug. Gynecomastia appears to be related to dosage level and duration of therapy; it may persist in some after drug is stopped.
- Monitor lab tests: Periodic serum electrolytes especially during early therapy, blood glucose, BUN/creatinine, uric acid.

Patient & Family Education

- Be aware that the maximal diuretic effect may not occur until third day of therapy and that diuresis may continue for 2–3 days after drug is withdrawn.
- Report signs of hyponatremia or hyperkalemia (see Appendix F), most likely to occur in patients with severe cirrhosis.
- Avoid replacing fluid losses with large amounts of free water (can result in dilutional hyponatremia).
- Weigh 2–3 × each wk. Report gains/loss of 5 lb or more.
- Do not drive or engage in potentially hazardous activities until response to the drug is known.

- Avoid excessive intake of high potassium foods and salt substitutes.

STAVUDINE (D4T)
(sta'vu-deen)

Classification: ANTIRETRO-VIRAL; NUCLEOSIDE REVERSE TRANSCRIPTASE INHIBITOR (NRTI)
Therapeutic: ANTIRETROVIRAL; NRTI
Prototype: Lamivudine

AVAILABILITY Capsule

ACTION & *THERAPEUTIC EFFECT*
Appears to act by being incorporated into growing DNA chains by viral transcriptase, thus terminating viral replication. *Inhibits the replication of HIV in human cells and decreases viral load.*

USES HIV treatment. (not recommended in current treatment guidelines)

CONTRAINDICATIONS Hypersensitivity to stavudine; patient concurrently taking zidovudine or didanosine; lactic acidosis; pregnancy—fetal risk cannot be ruled out; lactation—infant risk cannot be ruled out.

CAUTIOUS USE Previous hypersensitivity to zidovudine, didanosine, or zalcitabine; folic acid or B_{12} deficiency; liver and renal insufficiency; alcoholism; peripheral neuropathy; history of pancreatitis or hepatitis C.

ROUTE & DOSAGE

HIV Infection

Adult/Adolescent (weight less than 60 kg): **PO** 30 mg q12h; *weight 60 kg or greater:* 40 mg q12h

S

Renal Impairment Dosage Adjustment

CrCl 25–50 mL/min: Reduce dose by 50%; less than 25 mL/min: Reduce dose by 50% and extend interval to q24h

ADMINISTRATION

Oral

- Adhere strictly to 12-h interval between doses.
- Take with or without food.
- Capsules may be stored at a controlled room temperature of 25° C (77° F), excursions permitted between 15 and 30 degrees C (59 to 86 degrees F). Protect powder from excessive moisture.

ADVERSE EFFECTS (≥5%) CNS:
Peripheral neuropathy, headache. **Skin:** Rash. **Hepatic:** Abnormal liver function tests. **GI:** Nausea, vomiting, diarrhea, increased pancreatic enzyme levels. **Hematologic:** Macrocytosis.

INTERACTIONS Drug: Didanosine, hydroxyurea may increase risk of pancreatitis and hepatotoxicity; **zidovudine** may impact metabolism, avoid concurrent use. Use INTERFERONS, **ribavirin** cautiously. **Herbal:** Avoid use with echinacea.

PHARMACOKINETICS Absorption: Readily absorbed from GI tract; 82% reaches systemic circulation. **Peak:** 1 hour. **Distribution:** Distributes into CSF; excreted in breast milk of animals. **Metabolism:** intracellularly to active form. **Elimination:** In urine. **Half-Life:** 1–1.6 h.

NURSING IMPLICATIONS

Black Box Warning

Stavudine has been associated with lactic acidosis and severe, sometimes fatal, hepatomegaly with steatosis. Fatal lactic acidosis has been reported in pregnant females who received the combination of stavudine an didanosine with other antiretroviral agents. Fatal and nonfatal pancreatitis has occurred with patients when taking stavudine with didanosine.

Assessment & Drug Effects

- Monitor for peripheral neuropathy and report numbness, tingling, or pain, which may indicate a need to interrupt stavudine.
- Monitor for development of opportunistic infection.
- Monitor lab tests: Periodic measurement of acid–base balance, electrolytes, LFTs, renal function tests, urinalysis. CBC with differential and serum lipid profile at baseline and with modifications, fasting blood glucose and HbA1C at baseline and with modifications, viral loads, CD4 counts, at baseline and with modification of antiretroviral treatment.

Patient & Family Education

- Take drug exactly as prescribed.
- Educate patient on safe sex practice.
- Report to provider if pregnancy occurs.
- Report to prescriber any adverse drug effects that are bothersome.
- Report symptoms of peripheral neuropathy to prescriber immediately.
- The medication has several drug-drug interactions. Consult

Common adverse effects in *italic*; life-threatening effects underlined; generic names in **bold**; classifications in SMALL CAPS; ✤ Canadian drug name; ✪ Prototype drug; ⚠ Alert healthcare provider before taking any new medications (including over-the-counter and herbal supplements).

STREPTOMYCIN SULFATE

(strep-toe-mye'sin)

Classification: AMINO-GLYCOSIDE ANTIBIOTIC; ANTITUBERCULOSIS
Therapeutic: ANTIBIOTIC; ANTITUBERCULOSIS
Prototype: Gentamicin

AVAILABILITY Reconstituted solution for injection

ACTION & *THERAPEUTIC EFFECT*
Inhibits bacterial protein synthesis through irreversible binding to the 30S ribosomal subunit of susceptible bacteria. *Active against a variety of gram-positive, gram-negative, and acid-fast organisms.*

USES Treatment of tuberculosis;. Used for tularemia, plague, and brucellosis, subacute bacterial endocarditis and in treatment of peritonitis, respiratory tract infections, granuloma inguinale, and chancroid when other drugs have failed.

UNLABELED USE: Mycobacterium avium complex infection.

CONTRAINDICATIONS History of toxic reaction or severe hypersensitivity to streptomycin; clinically significant reaction to other aminoglycosides; labyrinthine disease; concurrent or sequential use of neurotoxic and/or nephrotoxic drugs; myasthenia gravis; pregnancy – fetal risk cannot be ruled out.

CAUTIOUS USE Impaired renal function; prerenal azotemia; auditory dysfunction; older adults; lactation – infant risk is minimal; children.

ROUTE & DOSAGE

Endocarditis
Adult: **IM** 7.5 mg/kg q12h × 4 wk

Tuberculosis
Adult: **IM** 15 mg/kg daily or 25 mg/kg 3 times per week

Tularemia
Adult: **IM** 1 g bid for at least 10 days

Plague
Adult: **IM** 15 mg/kg (max 1 g) q12h × 10 days

Renal Impairment Dosage Adjustment
CrCl 10–50 mL/min: administer q24–72 h; *CrCl less than 10 mL/min:* administer q72–96 h

ADMINISTRATION

Intramuscular
- Give IM deep into large muscle mass to minimize possibility of irritation. Injections are painful. Preferred sites for the adult are upper outer quadrant of the buttock, or the midlateral thigh.
- Avoid direct contact with drug; sensitization can occur. Use gloves during preparation of drug.
- Use commercially prepared IM solution undiluted; intended only for IM injection (contains a preservative, and therefore is not suitable for other routes). Reconstituted solution may be stored for

S

1 week at room temperature and protected from light.

- Store dry powder at controlled room temperature between 20 and 25 degrees C (68 and 77 degrees F). Protect from light; exposure to light may slightly darken solution, with no apparent loss of potency.

ADVERSE EFFECTS Respiratory:
<u>Respiratory depression</u>. **CNS:** Paresthesias (peripheral, facial). **Skin:** Skin rashes, pruritus. **Hematologic:** Increased eosinophil count. *Fever.*

INTERACTIONS Drug: May potentiate anticoagulant effects of **warfarin;** additive nephrotoxicity with **acyclovir, amphotericin B,** AMINOGLYCOSIDES, **carboplatin, cidofovir, cisplatin, cyclosporine, foscarnet, ganciclovir,** SALICYLATES, **tacrolimus, vancomycin.** Do not use with LIVE VACCINES.

PHARMACOKINETICS Peak:
1–2 h. **Distribution:** Diffuses into most body tissues and extracellular fluids; crosses placenta; distributed into breast milk; 34% protein bound. **Elimination:** In urine. **Half-Life:** 2–3 h adults, 4–10 h newborns.

NURSING IMPLICATIONS

Black Box Warning

Streptomycin has been associated with increased risk of severe neurotoxic reactions, especially in those with impaired renal function.

Assessment & Drug Effects

- Be alert for and report immediately symptoms of ototoxicity (see Appendix F). Symptoms are most likely to occur in patients with impaired kidney function, patients receiving high doses

(1.8–2 g/day) or other ototoxic or neurotoxic drugs, and older adults. Irreversible damage may occur if drug is not discontinued promptly.

- Early damage to vestibular portion of eighth cranial nerve (higher incidence than auditory toxicity) is initially manifested by moderately severe headache, nausea, vomiting, vertigo in upright position, difficulty in reading, unsteadiness, and positive Romberg sign.

- Be aware that auditory nerve damage is usually preceded by vestibular symptoms and high-pitched tinnitus, roaring noises, impaired hearing (especially to high-pitched sounds), sense of fullness in ears. Audiometric test should be done if these symptoms appear, and drug should be discontinued. Hearing loss can be permanent if damage is extensive. Tinnitus may persist several days to weeks after drug is stopped.

- Monitor I&O. Report oliguria or changes in I&O ratio (possible signs of diminishing kidney function). Sufficient fluids to maintain urinary output of 1500 mL/24 h are generally advised. Consult prescriber.

- Monitor lab tests: Baseline C&S; periodic BUN and creatinine; serum drug concentration as indicated.

Patient & Family Education

- Report any unusual symptoms. Review adverse reactions with prescriber periodically, especially with prolonged therapy.

- Report if the infection does not improve or worsens while taking the drug.

- Be aware of possibility of ototoxicity and its symptoms (see Appendix F).

- Report to prescriber immediately any of the following: Nausea,

Common adverse effects in *italic*; life-threatening effects <u>underlined</u>; generic names in **bold;** classifications in SMALL CAPS; ✦ Canadian drug name; ◗ Prototype drug; ⚠ Alert

1582

S

vomiting, vertigo, incoordination, tinnitus, fullness in ears, impaired hearing.
- Avoid taking any muscle relaxants while taking this drug.

STREPTOZOCIN
(strep-toe-zoe′sin)
Zanosar
Classification: ANTINEOPLASTIC, ALKYLATING; NITROSOUREA
Therapeutic: ANTINEOPLASTIC
Prototype: Cyclophosphamide

AVAILABILITY Solution for injection

ACTION & *THERAPEUTIC EFFECT*
Inhibits DNA synthesis in cells and prevents progression of cells into mitosis, affecting all phases of the cell cycle (cell-cycle nonspecific). *Successful therapy with streptozocin (alone or in combination) produces a biochemical response evidenced by decreased secretion of hormones as well as measurable tumor regression. Thus, serial fasting insulin levels during treatment indicate response to this drug.*

USES Pancreatic cancer.

UNLABELED USES palliative treatment of metastatic carcinoid tumor.

CONTRAINDICATIONS Concurrent use with nephrotoxic drugs; pregnancy – fetal risk cannot be ruled out; lactation – infant risk cannot be ruled out; safety and efficacy in pediatrics are not approved by the FDA.

CAUTIOUS USE Renal impairment; hepatic disease, hepatic impairment; patients with history of hypoglycemia; DM.

ROUTE & DOSAGE

Islet Cell Carcinoma of Pancreas
Adult/Adolescent/Child: **IV** 500 mg/m^2/day on days 1–5 q6w or 1 g/m^2/wk for 2 wk, then increase to 1.5 g/m^2/wk × 4–6 wk

Renal Impairment Dosage Adjustment
CrCl 10–50 mL/min: Give 75% of dose; *CrCl less than 10 mL/min:* Give 50% of dose

ADMINISTRATION

Intravenous

This drug is a cytotoxic agent and caution should be used to prevent any contact with the drug. Follow institutional or standard guidelines for preparation, handling, and disposal of cytotoxic agents.

Use only under constant supervision by prescriber experienced in therapy with cytotoxic agents and only when the benefit to risk ratio is fully and thoroughly understood by patient and family.

***PREPARE:* IV Infusion:** Reconstitute with 9.5 mL D5W or NS, to yield 100 mg/mL. Solution will be pale gold. ▪ May be further diluted with up to 250 mL of the original diluent. ▪ Protect reconstituted solution and vials of drug from light.
ADMINISTER: NIOSH recommends the use of gloves when handling the preparation of the powder and solution. Use double gloves and protective gown during administration. eye/face protection may be needed. If there is a potential that the substance

could splash or if the patient may resist, use eye/face protection. Use a closed system drug transfer device. **IV Infusion:** Give over 15–60 min. ▪ Inspect injection site frequently for signs of extravasation (patient complaints of stinging or burning at site, swelling around site, no blood return or questionable blood return). ▪ If extravasation occurs, area requires immediate attention to prevent necrosis. Remove needle, apply ice, and contact prescriber regarding further treatment to infiltrated tissue. Total storage time once the drug is in solution should not exceed 12 hours. Unopened vials should be refrigerated between 2 and 8 degrees C (35 to 46 degrees F) and protected from light.
INCOMPATIBILITIES: **Y-site: Acyclovir, allopurinol, amphotericin, aztreonam, cefepime, daptomycin, garenoxacin, levofloxacin, pantoprazole, piperacillin/tazobactam, trastuzumab.**

▪ Note: An antiemetic given routinely every 4 or 6 h and prophylactically 30 min before a treatment may provide sufficient control to maintain the treatment regimen (even if it reduces but does not completely eliminate nausea and vomiting).
▪ Discard reconstituted solutions after 12 h (contains no preservative and not intended for multidose use).

ADVERSE EFFECTS CNS: *Confusion, lethargy.* GI: *Nausea.* Other: *Psychological depression.*

INTERACTIONS Drug: MYELOSUPPRESSIVE AGENTS add to hematologic toxicity; nephrotoxic agents (e.g., AMINOGLYCOSIDES, **vancomycin,** **amphotericin B, cisplatin**) increase risk of nephrotoxicity; deferiprone may have increased risk of neutropenia. Do not administer LIVE VACCINES.

PHARMACOKINETICS Absorption: Undetectable in plasma within 3 h. Distribution: Metabolite enters CSF. Metabolism: In liver and kidneys. Elimination: 70–80% of dose in urine. Half-Life: 35–40 min.

NURSING IMPLICATIONS

Black Box Warning

Streptozocin has been associated with severe, sometimes fatal, renal toxicity, and with severe GI, hepatic, and hematologic toxicities.

Assessment & Drug Effects

▪ Ensure that repeat courses of streptozocin treatment are not given until patient's liver, kidney, and hematologic functions are within acceptable limits.
▪ Be alert to and report promptly early laboratory evidence of kidney dysfunction: Hypophosphatemia, mild proteinuria, and changes in I&O ratio and pattern.
▪ Mild adverse renal effects may be reversible following discontinuation of streptozocin, but nephrotoxicity may be irreversible, severe, or fatal.
▪ Be alert to symptoms of sepsis and superinfections or increased tendency to bleed (thrombocytopenia). Myelosuppression is severe in 10–20% of patients and may be cumulative and more severe if patient has had prior exposure to radiation or to other antineoplastics.
▪ Monitor and record temperature pattern to promptly recognize impending sepsis.

Common adverse effects in *italic;* life-threatening effects <u>underlined;</u> generic names in **bold;** classifications in SMALL CAPS; ✦ Canadian drug name; ⊙ Prototype drug; ⚠ Alert

- Monitor lab tests: Weekly CBC; LFTs prior to each course of therapy; serial urinalyses, urine protein and kidney function tests; baseline and weekly serum electrolytes, then for 4 wk after termination of therapy.

Patient & Family Education

- Inspect site at weekly intervals and report changes in tissue appearance if extravasation occurred during IV infusion.
- Report symptoms of hypoglycemia (see Appendix F) even though this drug has minimal, if any, diabetogenic action.
- Drink fluids liberally (2000–3000 mL/day). Hydration may protect against drug toxicity effects.
- Report S&S of nephrotoxicity (see Appendix F).
- Do not take aspirin or NSAIDs without consulting prescriber.
- Avoid vaccines during therapy.
- Report to prescriber promptly any signs of bleeding: Hematuria, epistaxis, ecchymoses, petechiae.
- Report symptoms that suggest anemia: Shortness of breath, pale mucous membranes and nail beds, exhaustion, rapid pulse.
- Avoid alcohol, aspirin or ibuprofen during therapy.

SUCCINYLCHOLINE CHLORIDE ⊙

(suk-sin-ill-koe'leen)

Anectine, Quelicin

Classification: DEPOLARIZING SKELETAL MUSCLE RELAXANT

Therapeutic: SKELETAL MUSCLE RELAXANT

AVAILABILITY Solution for injection

ACTION & *THERAPEUTIC EFFECT*

Synthetic, ultrashortacting depolarizing neuromuscular blocking agent with high affinity for acetylcholine (ACh) receptor sites. *Initial transient contractions and fasciculations are followed by sustained flaccid skeletal muscle paralysis produced by state of accommodation that develops in adjacent excitable muscle membranes.*

USES To produce skeletal muscle relaxation as adjunct to anesthesia; to facilitate intubation and endoscopy, to increase pulmonary compliance in assisted or controlled respiration, and to reduce intensity of muscle contractions in pharmacologically induced or electroshock convulsions.

CONTRAINDICATIONS Hypersensitivity to succinylcholine; family history of malignant hyperthermia; burns; trauma.

CAUTIOUS USE Kidney, liver, pulmonary, metabolic, or cardiovascular disorders; myasthenia gravis; dehydration, electrolyte imbalance, patients taking digitalis, severe burns or trauma, fractures, spinal cord injuries, degenerative or dystrophic neuromuscular diseases, low plasma pseudocholinesterase levels (recessive genetic trait, but often associated with severe liver disease, severe anemia, dehydration, marked changes in body temperature, exposure to neurotoxic insecticides, certain drugs); collagen diseases, porphyria, intraocular surgery, glaucoma; during delivery with cesarean section; pregnancy (category C); lactation; children.

ROUTE & DOSAGE

Surgical and Anesthetic Procedures

Adult: **IV** 0.3–1.1 mg/kg administered over 10–30 sec, may give additional doses prn; **IM** 2.5–4 mg/kg up to 150 mg

---

Common adverse effects in *italic;* life-threatening effects <u>underlined</u>; generic names in **bold;** classifications in SMALL CAPS; ✦ Canadian drug name; ⊙ Prototype drug; ⚠ Alert

Child: **IV** 1–2 mg/kg administered over 10–30 sec, may give additional doses prn; **IM** 2.5–4 mg/kg up to 150 mg

Prolonged Muscle Relaxation

Adult: **IV** 0.5–10 mg/min by continuous infusion

Obesity Dosage Adjustment

Dose based on IBW

ADMINISTRATION

Intramuscular

- Give IM injections deeply, preferably high into deltoid muscle.

Intravenous

Use only freshly prepared solutions; succinylcholine hydrolyzes rapidly with consequent loss of potency.

- Give initial small test dose (0.1 mg/kg) to determine individual drug sensitivity and recovery time.

PREPARE: **Direct:** Give undiluted. **Intermittent/Continuous:** Dilute 1 g in 500–1000 mL of D5W or NS. *ADMINISTER:* **Direct:** Give a bolus dose over 10–30 sec. **Intermittent/Continuous (Preferred):** Give at a rate of 0.5–10 mg/min. Do not exceed 10 mg/min.

INCOMPATIBILITIES: **Solution/additive: Pentobarbital, sodium bicarbonate. Y-site: Amphotericin B conventional, azathioprine, dantrolene, diazepam, diazoxide, ganciclovir, gemtuzumab, indomethacin, mitomycin, nafcillin,** PENICILLINS, **pentobarbital, phenobarbital, phenytoin, sodium bicarbonate.**

- Note: Expiration date and storage before and after reconstitution; varies with the manufacturer.

ADVERSE EFFECTS CV: *Bradycardia,* tachycardia, hypotension, hypertension, arrhythmias, sinus arrest. **Respiratory:** <u>Respiratory depression</u>, bronchospasm, hypoxia, <u>apnea</u>. **CNS:** *Muscle fasciculations,* profound and prolonged muscle relaxation, muscle pain. **Endocrine:** Myoglobinemia, hyperkalemia. **GI:** Decreased tone and motility of GI tract (large doses). **Other:** <u>Malignant hyperthermia</u>, increased IOP, excessive salivation, enlarged salivary glands.

INTERACTIONS Drug: **Aminoglycosides, colistin, cyclophosphamide, cyclopropane, echothiophate iodide, halothane, lidocaine,** MAGNESIUM SALTS, **methotrimeprazine,** NARCOTIC ANALGESICS, ORGANOPHOSPHAMIDE INSECTICIDES, MAO INHIBITORS, PHENOTHIAZINES, **procaine, procainamide, quinidine, quinine, propranolol** may prolong neuromuscular blockade; DIGITALIS GLYCOSIDES may increase risk of cardiac arrhythmias.

PHARMACOKINETICS Onset: 0.5–1 min IV; 2–3 min IM. **Duration:** 2–3 min IV; 10–30 min IM. **Distribution:** Crosses placenta in small amounts. **Metabolism:** In plasma by pseudocholinesterases. **Elimination:** In urine.

NURSING IMPLICATIONS

Black Box Warning

Succinylcholine has been associated with rare cases of acute rhabdomyolysis with hyperkalemia followed by ventricular arrhythmias, cardiac arrest, and death in children and adolescents.

Assessment & Drug Effects

- Be aware that transient apnea usually occurs at time of maximal drug effect (1–2 min); spontaneous respiration should return in a few seconds or, at most, 3 or 4 min.

- Have immediately available: Facilities for emergency endotracheal intubation, artificial respiration, and assisted or controlled respiration with oxygen.
- Monitor vital signs and keep airway clear of secretions.

Patient & Family Education
- Patient may experience postprocedural muscle stiffness and pain (caused by initial fasciculations following injection) for as long as 24–30 h.
- Be aware that hoarseness and sore throat are common even when pharyngeal airway has not been used.
- Report residual muscle weakness to prescriber.

SUCRALFATE
(soo-kral'fate)
Carafate, Sulcrate ♦
Classification: ANTIULCER; GASTROADHESIVE
Therapeutic: ANTIULCER; GASTRO-PROTECTANT

AVAILABILITY Tablet; suspension

ACTION & *THERAPEUTIC EFFECT*
Sucralfate and gastric acid react to form a viscous, adhesive, paste-like substance that resists further reaction with gastric acid. This "paste" adheres to the GI mucosa with a major portion binding electrostatically to the positively charged protein molecules in the damaged mucosa of an ulcer crater or an acute gastric erosion. *Absorbs bile, inhibits the enzyme pepsin, and blocks back diffusion of H^+ ions. These actions plus adherence of the* paste-like complex protect damaged mucosa against further destruction from ulcerogenic secretions and drugs.

USES Duodenal ulcer.

UNLABELED USES Aspirin induced erosions, stress ulcer prophylaxis, suspension for chemotherapy-induced mucositis.

CONTRAINDICATIONS Hypersensitivity to sucralfate.

CAUTIOUS USE Chronic kidney failure or dialysis due to aluminum accumulation; pregnancy (category B); lactation. Safe use in children not established.

ROUTE & DOSAGE

Duodenal Ulcer (Active disease)
Adult: **PO** 1 g qid × 4–8 wk
Duodenal Ulcer (Maintenance)
Adult: **PO** 1g bid

ADMINISTRATION
Oral
- Use drug solubilized in an appropriate diluent by a pharmacist when given through nasogastric tube.
- Administer antacids prescribed for pain relief 30 min before or after sucralfate.
- Separate administration of quinolones, digoxin, phenytoin, tetracycline from that of sucralfate by 2 h to prevent sucralfate from binding to these compounds in the intestinal tract and reducing their bioavailability.
- Store in tight container at room temperature, 15°–30° C (59°–86° F). Stable for 2 y after manufacture.

ADVERSE EFFECTS GI: Nausea, gastric discomfort, *constipation,* diarrhea.

INTERACTIONS Drug: May decrease absorption of QUINO-LONES (e.g., **ciprofloxacin, norfloxacin**), **digoxin, phenytoin, tetracycline.**

PHARMACOKINETICS Absorption: Minimally absorbed from GI tract (less than 5%). **Duration:** Up to 6 h (depends on contact time with ulcer crater). **Elimination:** 90% in feces.

NURSING IMPLICATIONS

Assessment & Drug Effects
• Be aware of drug interactions and schedule other medications accordingly.

Patient & Family Education
• Although healing has occurred within the first 2 wk of therapy, treatment is usually continued 4–8 wk.
• Be aware that constipation is a drug-related problem. Follow these measures unless contraindicated: Increase water intake to 8–10 glasses/day; increase physical exercise, increase dietary bulk. Consult prescriber: A suppository or bulk laxative (e.g., Metamucil) may be prescribed.

SULFACETAMIDE SODIUM
(sul-fa-see'ta-mide)
Bleph 10, Cetamide, Ophthacet, Ovace, Sebizon, Sodium Sulamyd, Sulf-10

SULFACETAMIDE SODIUM/ SULFUR
Sulfacet, Rosula
Classification: SULFONAMIDE ANTIBIOTIC

Therapeutic: ANTIBIOTIC
Prototype: Silver sulfadiazine

AVAILABILITY Sulfacetamide: Lotion; solution; ointment; **Sulfacetamide/Sulfur:** Gel, lotion

ACTION & *THERAPEUTIC EFFECT*
Exerts bacteriostatic effect by interfering with bacterial utilization of PABA, thereby inhibiting folic acid biosynthesis required for bacterial growth. *Effective against a wide range of gram-positive and gram-negative microorganisms.*

USES Ophthalmic preparations are used for conjunctivitis, corneal ulcers, and other superficial ocular infections and as adjunct to systemic sulfonamide therapy for trachoma. The topical lotion is used for scaly dermatoses, seborrheic dermatitis, seborrhea sicca, and other bacterial skin infections.

CONTRAINDICATIONS Hypersensitivity to sulfonamides; neonates, pregnancy (category D near term).

CAUTIOUS USE Application of lotion to denuded or debrided skin; pregnancy (category C except near term); lactation. Safe use in children is not established.

ROUTE & DOSAGE

Conjunctivitis

Adult: **Ophthalmic** 1–3 drops of 10%, 15%, or 30% solution into lower conjunctival sac q2–3h, may increase interval as patient responds or use 1.5–2.5 cm (½–1 in.) of 10% ointment q6h and at bedtime

Seborrhea, Rosacea

Adult: **Topical** Apply thin film to affected area 1–3 × day

Common adverse effects in *italic;* life-threatening effects underlined; generic names in **bold;** classifications in SMALL CAPS; ♣ Canadian drug name; ☺ Prototype drug; ⚠ Alert

ADMINISTRATION

Instillation

- Be aware that ophthalmic preparations and skin lotion are not interchangeable.
- Check strength of medication prescribed.
- See patient instructions for instilling eye drops.
- Discard darkened solutions; results when left standing for a long time.
- Store at 8°–15° C (46°–59° F) in tightly closed containers unless otherwise directed.

ADVERSE EFFECTS HEENT: *Temporary stinging or burning sensation,* retardation of corneal healing associated with long-term use of ophthalmic ointment. **Other:** Hypersensitivity reactions (Stevens–Johnson syndrome, lupus-like syndrome), superinfections with nonsusceptible organisms.

INTERACTIONS Drug: Tetracaine and other LOCAL ANESTHETICS DERIVED FROM PABA may antagonize the antibacterial effects of SULFONAMIDES; SILVER PREPARATIONS may precipitate sulfacetamide from solution.

PHARMACOKINETICS Absorption: Minimal systemic absorption, but may be enough to cause sensitization. **Metabolism:** In liver to inactive metabolites. **Elimination:** In urine.

NURSING IMPLICATIONS

Assessment & Drug Effects

- Discontinue if symptoms of hypersensitivity appear (erythema, skin rash, pruritus, urticaria).

Patient & Family Education

- Wash hands thoroughly with soap and running water (before and after instillation).

- Examine eye medication; discard if cloudy or dark in color.
- Avoid contaminating any part of eye dropper that is inserted in bottle.
- Tilt head back, pull down lower lid. At the same time, look up while drop is being instilled into conjunctival sac. Immediately apply gentle pressure just below the eyelid and next to nose for 1 min. Close eyes gently, so as not to squeeze out medication.
- Report purulent eye discharge to prescriber. Sulfacetamide sodium is inactivated by purulent exudates.

SULFADIAZINE

(sul-fa-dye'a-zeen)
Classification: SULFONAMIDE ANTIBIOTIC
Therapeutic: ANTIBIOTIC
Prototype: Silver sulfadiazine

AVAILABILITY Tablet

ACTION & *THERAPEUTIC EFFECT*
Exerts bacteriostatic effect by interfering with bacterial utilization of PABA, thereby inhibiting folic acid biosynthesis required for bacterial growth. *Effective against a wide range of gram-positive and gram-negative microorganisms.*

USES Used in combination with pyrimethamine for treatment of cerebral toxoplasmosis and chloroquine-resistant malaria.

CONTRAINDICATIONS Hypersensitivity to sulfonamides or to any ingredients in the formulation; porphyria; pregnancy (category D near term); lactation.

CAUTIOUS USE Application of lotion to denuded or debrided

S

skin; dehydration; hepatic disease; impaired renal function; pregnancy (category C except near term).

ROUTE & DOSAGE

Mild to Moderate Infections

Adult: **PO Loading Dose** 2–4 g loading dose; **PO Maintenance Dose** 2–4 g/day in 4–6 divided doses
Child (2 mo or older): **PO Loading Dose** 75 mg/kg; **PO Maintenance Dose** 150 mg/kg/day in 4–6 divided doses (max: 6 g/day)

Rheumatic Fever Prophylaxis

Adult (weight less than 30 kg): **PO** 500 mg/day; *weight greater than 30 kg:* 1 g/day

Toxoplasmosis

Adult: **PO** 2–8 g/day divided q6h
Child (2 mo or older): **PO** 100–200 mg/kg/day divided q6h
Neonate: **PO** 50 mg/kg q12h × 12 mo

ADMINISTRATION

Oral

- Maintain sufficient fluid intake to produce urinary output of at least 1500 mL/24 h for children between 3000 and 4000 mL/24 h for adults. Concomitant administration of urinary alkalinizer may be prescribed to reduce possibility of crystalluria and stone formation.
- Store in tight, light-resistant containers.

ADVERSE EFFECTS CNS: Headache, peripheral neuritis, peripheral neuropathy, tinnitus, hearing loss, vertigo, insomnia, drowsiness, mental depression, acute psychosis, ataxia, convulsions, kernicterus (newborns). **HEENT:** Conjunctivitis, conjunctival or scleral infection, retardation of corneal healing (ophthalmic ointment). **Endocrine:** Goiter, hypoglycemia. **Skin:** Pruritus, urticaria, rash, erythema multiforme including *Stevens–Johnson syndrome, exfoliative dermatitis,* alopecia, photosensitivity, vascular lesions. **GI:** *Nausea, vomiting, diarrhea,* abdominal pains, hepatitis, jaundice, pancreatitis, stomatitis. **GU:** *Crystalluria,* hematuria, proteinuria, anuria, toxic nephrosis, reduction in sperm count. **Hematologic:** Acute hemolytic anemia (especially in patients with G6PD deficiency), aplastic anemia, methemoglobinemia, agranulocytosis, thrombocytopenia, leukopenia, eosinophilia, hypoprothrombinemia. **Other:** Headache, *fever,* chills, arthralgia, malaise, allergic myocarditis, serum sickness, anaphylactoid reactions, lymphadenopathy, local reaction following IM injection, fixed drug eruptions, diuresis, overgrowth of nonsusceptible organisms, LE phenomenon.

INTERACTIONS Drug: PABA-CONTAIN-ING LOCAL ANESTHETICS may antagonize sulfa's effects; ORAL ANTICOAGULANTS potentiate hypoprothrombinemia; may potentiate SULFONYLUREA-induced hypoglycemia. May decrease concentrations of **cyclosporine;** may increase levels of **phenytoin.**

PHARMACOKINETICS Absorption: Readily absorbed from GI tract. **Peak:** 3–6 h. **Distribution:** Distributed to most tissues, including CSF; crosses placenta. **Metabolism:** In liver. **Elimination:** In urine.

S

NURSING IMPLICATIONS

Assessment & Drug Effects

- Monitor hydration status.
- Monitor lab tests: Baseline and periodic urine C&S; frequent CBC and urinalysis; sulfadiazone blood levels with serious infections.

Patient & Family Education

- Take drug exactly as prescribed. Do not alter schedule or dose; take total amount prescribed unless prescriber changes the regimen.
- Drink fluids liberally unless otherwise directed.
- Report early signs of blood dyscrasias (sore throat, pallor, fever) promptly to the prescriber.

SULFAMETHOXAZOLE-TRIMETHOPRIM (SMZ-TMP)

(sul-fa-meth'ox-a-zole-tri-meth'o-prim)

Bactrim, Bactrim DS, Septra, Septra DS

Classification: URINARY TRACT ANTI-INFECTIVE; SULFONAMIDE
Therapeutic: URINARY TRACT ANTI-INFECTIVE
Prototype: Trimethoprim

AVAILABILITY Tablet; suspension; solution for injection

ACTION & *THERAPEUTIC EFFECT*

Both components of the combination are synthetic folate antagonist anti-infectives. Principal action is by enzyme inhibition that prevents bacterial synthesis of essential nucleic acids and proteins. *Effective against Pneumocystis jiroveci pneumonitis (formerly PCP), Shigellosis enteritis, and severely complicated UTIs due to most strains of the Enterobacteriaceae.*

USES *Pneumocystis jiroveci* pneumonitis (formerly PCP), shigellosis enteritis, and severe complicated UTIs. Also children with acute otitis media due to susceptible strains of *Haemophilus influenzae,* and acute episodes of chronic bronchitis or traveler's diarrhea in adults.

UNLABELED USES Isosporiasis; cholera; genital ulcers caused by *Haemophilus ducreyi;* prophylaxis for *P. jiroveci* pneumonia (formerly PCP) in neutropenic patients.

CONTRAINDICATIONS Hypersensitivity to SMZ, TMP, sulfonamides, or bisulfites, carbonic anhydrase inhibitors; group A beta-hemolytic streptococcal pharyngitis; megaloblastic anemia due to folate deficiency; G6PD deficiency; hyperkalemia; porphyria; pregnancy (category D near term); lactation.

CAUTIOUS USE Impaired kidney or liver function; bone marrow depression; possible folate deficiency; severe allergy or bronchial asthma; hypersensitivity to sulfonamide derivative drugs (e.g., acetazolamide, thiazides, tolbutamide); pregnancy (category C except near term). Safe use in infants younger than 2 mo not established.

ROUTE & DOSAGE

(Weight-based doses are calculated on TMP component) Systemic Infections

Adult: **PO** 160 mg TMP/800 mg SMZ q12h; **IV** 8–10 mg/kg/day TMP divided q6–12h
Child (2 mo or older, weight less than 40 kg): **PO** 4 mg/kg/day TMP q12h; *weight greater than*

40 kg: 160 mg TMP/800 mg SMZ q12h
Child/Infant (2 mo or older): **IV** 6–10 mg/kg/day TMP divided q6–12h

Pneumocystis jiroveci Pneumonia (formerly PCP)

Adult: **PO** 15–20 mg/kg/day TMP divided q6h
Adult/Adolescent/Child: **IV** 15–20 mg/kg/day TMP divided q6h

Prophylaxis for *Pneumocystis jiroveci* Pneumonia (formerly PCP)

Adult: **PO** 160 mg TMP/800 mg SMZ q24h
Child: **PO** 150 mg/m^2 TMP/ 750 mg/m^2 SMZ bid 3 consecutive days/wk (max: 320 mg TMP/day)

Renal Impairment Dosage Adjustment

CrCl 10–30 mL/min: Reduce dose by 50%; *less than 10 mL/ min:* Reduce dose by 50–75%

ADMINISTRATION

Oral

- Give with a full glass of desired fluid.
- Maintain adequate fluid intake (at least 1500 mL/day) during therapy.
- Store at 15°–30° C (59°–86° F) in dry place protected from light. Avoid freezing.

Intravenous

***PREPARE:* Intermittent:** Add contents of the 5 mL vial to 125 mL D5W. ▪ Use within 6 h. ▪ If less fluid is desired, dilute in 75 of 100 mL and use within 2 or 4 h, respectively.

***ADMINISTER:* Intermittent:** Infuse over 60–90 min. ▪ Avoid rapid infusion.

***INCOMPATIBILITIES:* Solution/ additive:** Stability in **dextrose** and **normal saline** is concentration dependent, **fluconazole, linezolid, verapamil. Y-site: Alfentanil, amikacin, aminophylline, amphotericin B, ampicillin, ampicillin/sulbactam, atropine, azathioprine, benztropine, bumetanide, buprenorphine, butorphanol, calcium, caspofungin, cefamandole, cefazolin, cefmetazole, cefonicid, cefotaxime, cefotetan, cefoxitin, ceftazidime, ceftizoxime, ceftriaxone, cefuroxime, cephalothin, chloramphenicol, chlorpromazine, cimetidine, cisatracurium, clindamycin, codeine, cyanocobalamine, cyclosporine, dantrolene, dexamethasone, dexmedetomidine, diazepam, diazoxide, digoxin, diphenhydramine, dobutamine, dopamine, doxorubicin, doxycycline, ephedrine, epinephrine, epirubicin, epoetin alfa, erythromycin, famotidine, fentanyl, fluconazole, foscarnet, furosemide, ganciclovir, gentamicin, haloperidol, heparin, hydralazine, hydrocortisone, hydroxyzine, idarubicin, imipenem/cilastain, indomethacin, isoproterenol, ketorolac, lidocaine, mannitol, metaraminol, methicillin, methylprednisolone, metoclopramide, mezlocillin, miconazole, milrinone acetate, minocycline, midazolam, nafcillin, nalbuphine, naloxone, netilmicin, nitroglycerin, nitroprusside, norepinephrine, ondansetron, oxacillin, oxytocin,**

papaverine, penicillin, pentamidine, pentazocine, pentobarbital, phenobarbital,
phentolamine, phenyleph-
rine, phenytoin, phytonadione, piperacillin, potassium,
prochlorperazine, promethazine, propranolol, protamine,
pyridoxine, quinupristin/
dalfopristin, ritodrine, succinylcholine, sufentanil,
theophylline, ticarcillin,
tobramycin, tolazoline, vancomycin, verapamil, vinorelbine.

- Store unopened ampule at 15°–30° C
(50°–86° F).

ADVERSE EFFECTS Skin: *Mild to
moderate rashes (including fixed
drug eruptions),* toxic epidermal
necrolysis. GI: *Nausea, vomiting,*
diarrhea, *anorexia,* hepatitis, pseudomembranous enterocolitis, stomatitis, glossitis, abdominal pain.
GU: Kidney failure, oliguria, anuria,
crystalluria. Hematologic: Agranulocytosis (rare), aplastic anemia
(rare), megaloblastic anemia,
hypoprothrombinemia, thrombocytopenia (rare). Other: Weakness,
arthralgia, myalgia, photosensitivity, allergic myocarditis.

DIAGNOSTIC TEST INTERFERENCE
May elevate levels of ***serum creatinine, transaminase, bilirubin, alkaline phosphatase.***

INTERACTIONS Drug: May
enhance hypoprothrombinemic
effects of ORAL ANTICOAGULANTS;
may increase **methotrexate** toxicity. **Alcohol** may cause disulfiram
reaction.

PHARMACOKINETICS Absorp-
tion: Readily from GI tract. Peak:
1–4 h (oral). Distribution: Widely distributed, including CNS; crosses placenta; distributed into breast milk.

Metabolism: In liver. Elimination: In
urine. Half-Life: 8–10 h TMP, 10–13
h SMZ.

NURSING IMPLICATIONS
Assessment & Drug Effects
- Be aware that IV forms of the
drug may contain sodium metabi-
sulfite, which produces allergic
type reactions in susceptible
patients: Hives, itching, wheezing,
anaphylaxis. Susceptibility (low in
general population) is seen most
frequently in asthmatics or atopic
nonasthmatic persons.
- Monitor coagulation tests and
prothrombin times in patient also
receiving warfarin. Change in
warfarin dosage may be indicated.
- Monitor I&O volume and pattern.
Report significant changes to fore-
stall renal calculi formation. Also
report failure of treatment (i.e.,
continued UTI symptoms).
- Older adult patients are at risk for
severe adverse reactions, especially if liver or kidney function is
compromised or if certain other
drugs are given. Most frequently
observed: Thrombocytopenia
(with concurrent thiazide diuretics); severe decrease in platelets
(with or without purpura); bone
marrow suppression; severe skin
reactions.
- Be alert for overdose symptoms
(no extensive experience has
been reported): Nausea, vomiting,
anorexia, headache, dizziness,
mental depression, confusion,
and bone marrow depression.
- Monitor lab tests: Baseline and
periodic urinalysis; CBC with differential, platelet count, BUN and
creatinine clearance with prolonged therapy.

Patient & Family Education
- Report immediately to prescriber
if rash appears. Other reportable

symptoms are sore throat, fever, purpura, jaundice; all are early signs of serious reactions.

- Monitor for and report fixed eruptions to prescriber. This drug can cause fixed eruptions at the same sites each time the drug is administered. Every contact with drug may not result in eruptions; therefore, patient may overlook the relationship.
- Drink 2.5–3 L (1 L is approximately equal to 1 qt) daily, unless otherwise directed.

SULFASALAZINE

(sul-fa-sal'a-zeen)
Azulfidine, PMS Sulfasalazine ♦, PMS Sulfasalazine E.C. ♦, Salazopyrin ♦, SAS Enteric-500 ♦, S.A.S.-500 ♦
Classification: ANTI-INFLAMMATORY; SULFONAMIDE
Therapeutic: GI ANTI-INFLAMMATORY; IMMUNOMODULATOR; DISEASE-MODIFYING ANTIRHEUMATIC DRUG (DMARD)
Prototype: Mesalamine

AVAILABILITY Tablet; sustained release tablet

ACTION & *THERAPEUTIC EFFECT*
Exerts antibacterial and anti-inflammatory effects. Inhibits prostaglandins known to cause diarrhea and affect mucosal transport as well as interference with absorption of fluids and electrolytes from colon. Reduces *Clostridium* and *Escherichia coli* in the stools. *Anti-inflammatory and immunomodulatory properties are effective in controlling the S&S of ulcerative colitis and rheumatoid arthritis.*

USES Ulcerative colitis and relatively mild regional enteritis; rheumatoid arthritis.

UNLABELED USES Granulomatous colitis, Crohn's disease, scleroderma.

CONTRAINDICATIONS Sensitivity to sulfasalazine, other sulfonamides and salicylates, trimethoprim; folate deficiency; megaloblastic anemia; renal failure, renal impairment; agranulocytosis; intestinal and urinary tract obstruction; porphyria; pregnancy (category D near term); lactation.

CAUTIOUS USE Severe allergy, or bronchial asthma; blood dyscrasias; hepatic or renal impairment; G6PD deficiency; older adults; pregnancy (category C except near term). Safe use in children younger than 6 y not established.

ROUTE & DOSAGE

Ulcerative Colitis, Rheumatoid Arthritis
Adult: **PO** 1–2 g/day in 4 divided doses, may increase up to 8 g/day if needed
Child: **PO** 40–50 mg/kg/day in 4 divided doses (max: 75 mg/kg/day)

Juvenile Rheumatoid Arthritis
Child: **PO** 10 mg/kg/day, increase weekly by 10 mg/kg/day [usual dose: 15–25 mg/kg q12h (max: 2 g/day)]

ADMINISTRATION
Oral
- Give after eating to provide longer intestine transit time.
- Do not crush or chew sustained release tablets; **must be** swallowed whole.
- Use evenly divided doses over each 24-h period; do not exceed 8-h intervals between doses.

Common adverse effects in *italic*; life-threatening effects underlined; generic names in **bold**; classifications in SMALL CAPS; ♦ Canadian drug name; ○ Prototype drug; △ Alert

- Consult prescriber if GI intolerance occurs after first few doses. Symptoms are probably due to irritation of stomach mucosa and may be relieved by spacing total daily dose more evenly over 24 h or by administration of enteric-coated tablets.
- Store at 15°–30° C (59°–86° F) in tight, light-resistant containers.

ADVERSE EFFECTS Other: *Nausea, vomiting, bloody diarrhea; anorexia,* arthralgia, rash, anemia, oligospermia (reversible), blood dyscrasias, liver injury, infectious mononucleosis–like reaction, *allergic reactions.*

INTERACTIONS Drug: Iron, ANTIBIOTICS may alter absorption of sulfasalazine.

PHARMACOKINETICS Absorption: 10–15% from GI tract unchanged; remaining drug is hydrolyzed in colon to sulfapyridine (most of which is absorbed) and 5-aminosalicylic acid (30% of which is absorbed). Peak: 1.5–6 h sulfasalazine; 6–24 h sulfapyridine. Distribution: Crosses placenta; distributed into breast milk. Metabolism: In intestines and liver. Elimination: All metabolites are excreted in urine. Half-Life: 5–10 h.

NURSING IMPLICATIONS
Assessment & Drug Effects
- Monitor for GI distress. GI symptoms that develop after a few days of therapy may indicate need for dosage adjustment. If symptoms persist, prescriber may withhold drug for 5–7 days and restart it at a lower dosage level.
- Be aware that adverse reactions generally occur within a few days to 12 wk after start of therapy; most likely to occur in patients

receiving high doses (4 g or more).
- Monitor lab tests: Periodic RBC and folate in patients on high doses (more than 2 g/day).

Patient & Family Education
- Examine stools and report to prescriber if enteric-coated tablets have passed intact in feces. Some patients lack enzymes capable of dissolving coating; conventional tablet will be ordered.
- Be aware that drug may color alkaline urine and skin orange-yellow.
- Remain under close medical supervision. Relapses occur in about 40% of patients after initial satisfactory response. Response to therapy and duration of treatment are governed by endoscopic examinations.

SULINDAC
(sul-in′dak)

Classification: NONSTEROIDAL ANTI-INFLAMMATORY DRUG (NSAID)
Therapeutic: NONNARCOTIC ANALGESIC; NSAID
Prototype: Ibuprofen

AVAILABILITY Tablet

ACTION & *THERAPEUTIC EFFECT*
Anti-inflammatory action thought to result from inhibition of prostaglandin synthesis. *Exhibits anti-inflammatory, analgesic, and antipyretic properties.*

USES Acute and long-term symptomatic treatment of osteoarthritis, rheumatoid arthritis, ankylosing spondylitis; acute painful shoulder (acute subacromial bursitis or supraspinatus tendinitis); acute gouty arthritis.

S

CONTRAINDICATIONS Hypersensitivity to sulindac; hypersensitivity to aspirin (patients with "aspirin triad": Acute asthma, rhinitis, nasal polyps), other NSAIDs, or salicylates; significant kidney or liver dysfunction; CABG perioperative pain; GI bleeding; drug-induced CV event; pancreatitis; pregnancy (fetal risk of birth defects is known); lactation (infant risk cannot be ruled out).

CAUTIOUS USE History of upper GI tract disorders; anticoagulant therapy; CHF; moderate or mild renal impairment; hepatic impairment; infection; preexisting asthma; SLE; older adults, compromised cardiac function, hypertension. Safety and efficacy in children not established.

ROUTE & DOSAGE

Arthritis, Ankylosing Spondylitis, Acute Gouty Arthritis
Adult: **PO** 150–200 mg bid (max: 400 mg/day)

ADMINISTRATION

Oral
- Crush and give mixed with liquid or food if patient cannot swallow tablet.
- Administer with food, milk, or antacid (if prescribed) to reduce possibility of GI upset. Note: Food retards absorption and delays and lowers peak concentrations.

ADVERSE EFFECTS CNS: Dizziness, headache, feeling nervous. **Skin:** Rash. **GI:** Abdominal pain, constipation, diarrhea, indigestion, nausea.

DIAGNOSTIC TEST INTERFERENCE May lead to false-positive aldosterone/renin ratio.

INTERACTIONS Drug: Do not use with **ketorolac, acemetacin, aminolevulinic acid,** or **cidofovir. Heparin,** ORAL ANTICOAGULANTS may prolong bleeding time; may increase **lithium** or **methotrexate** toxicity; **aspirin,** other NSAIDs add to ulcerogenic effects; **dimethylsulfoxide (DMSO)** may decrease effects of sulindac; **altretamine** may cause hypoprothrombinemia. **Herbal:** **Feverfew, garlic, ginger, ginkgo** may increase bleeding potential.

PHARMACOKINETICS Absorption: 90% from GI tract. **Peak:** 3–4 h with food. **Duration:** 10–12 h. **Distribution:** Minimal passage across placenta; distributed into breast milk. **Metabolism:** In liver to active metabolite. **Elimination:** 75% in urine, 25% in feces. **Half-Life:** 7.8 h sulindac, 16.4 h sulfide metabolite.

NURSING IMPLICATIONS

Black Box Warning

Sulindac has been associated with increased risk of serious, potentially fatal, GI bleeding and cardiovascular events (e.g., MI and CVA); risk may increase with duration of use and may be greater in the older adult and those with risk factors for CV disease.

Assessment & Drug Effects
- Assess for and report promptly unexplained GI distress.
- Monitor for and report promptly S&S of CV thrombotic events (i.e., angina, MI, TIA, or stroke).
- Schedule auditory and ophthalmic examinations in patients receiving prolonged or high-dose therapy.
- Monitor lab tests: Baseline and periodic CBC and metabolic panel, fecal occult blood test, LFTs.

Patient & Family Education

- Do not drive or engage in potentially hazardous activities until response to drug is known.
- Report any incidence of unexplained bleeding or bruising immediately to prescriber (e.g., bleeding gums, black and tarry stools, coffee-colored emesis).
- Report onset of skin rash, itching, hives, jaundice, swelling of feet or hands, sore throat or mouth, shortness of breath, or night cough to prescriber.
- Be aware that adverse GI effects are relatively common. Report abdominal pain, nausea, dyspepsia, diarrhea, or constipation.
- Avoid alcohol and aspirin as they may increase risk of GI ulceration and bleeding tendencies.
- Monitor for and report promptly S&S of CV thrombotic events (i.e., angina, MI, TIA, or stroke).

SUMATRIPTAN ⊙

(sum-a-trip'tan)

Imitrex, Sumavel DosePro, Zembrace SymTouch

Classification: SEROTONIN 5-HT$_1$ RECEPTOR AGONIST

Therapeutic: ANTIMIGRAINE

AVAILABILITY Tablet; solution for injection; nasal spray.

ACTION & THERAPEUTIC EFFECT

Selective agonist for a serotonin receptor (probably 5-HT$_{1D}$) that causes vasoconstriction of cranial blood vessels and reduces neurogenic inflammation. *Relieves migraine headache. Also relieves photophobia, phonophobia, nausea and vomiting associated with migraine attacks.*

USES Treatment of acute migraine attacks with or without aura, cluster headache.

CONTRAINDICATIONS Hypersensitivity to sumatriptan; ischemic CAD; acute MI, angina, arteriosclerosis; cerebrovascular disease; colitis; concurrent use with MAO inhibitors; uncontrolled hypertension; intracranial bleeding; PVD; Raynaud's disease; stroke; severe hepatic disease; Wolff-Parkinson-White syndrome; basilar or hemiplegic migraine.

CAUTIOUS USE Impaired liver or kidney function; MAO inhibitors; older adults; pregnancy (category C). Safety and efficacy in children not established.

ROUTE & DOSAGE

Migraine

Adult: **Subcutaneous** 6 mg any time after onset of migraine, if headache returns, may repeat with 6 mg subcutaneously at least 1 h after first injection (max: 12 mg/24 h); **PO** 50–100 mg once, if headache returns may repeat once after 2 h (max: 200 mg/24 hours); **Intranasal** 20 mg in one nostril, if headache returns, may repeat once after 2 h (max: 40 mg/24 h);

Cluster Headache

Adult: **Subcutaneous:** 6 mg once, pay repeat if headache recur after 1 hour. (max 12 mg in 24 hours).

ADMINISTRATION

Note: Do not give within 24 h of an ergot-containing drug.

Oral

- Give any time after symptoms of migraine appear.

- A second tablet may be given if symptoms return but no sooner than 2 h after the first tablet.
- Do not exceed 100 mg in a single oral dose or 300 mg/day.

Intranasal

- Note: A single dose is one spray into ONE nostril.

Subcutaneous

- A second injection may be given 1 h or longer following first injection if initial relief is not obtained or if migraine returns.
- Be aware that if adverse effects are dose limiting, a lower dose may be effective.
- Store all forms at room temperature, 15°–30° C (59°–86° F). Protect from light.

ADVERSE EFFECTS CV: Flushing. **CNS:** Tingling sensation, dizziness, vertigo, "hot" feeling. **Skin:** Injection site reaction, warm sensation at injection site.

INTERACTIONS Drug: Dihydroergotamine, ERGOT ALKALOIDS may cause vasospasm and a slight elevation in blood pressure. MAO INHIBITORS increase sumatriptan levels and toxicity (especially the oral form); do not use concurrently or within 2 wk of stopping MAO INHIBITORS; use with other serotonin altering drugs increases risk of serotonin syndrome (see Appendix F). **Herbal: St. John's wort** may increase triptan toxicity.

PHARMACOKINETICS Onset: 10–30 min after subcutaneous administration. **Duration:** 1–2 h. **Distribution:** Widely distributed, 10–20% protein bound. May be excreted in breast milk. **Metabolism:** Hepatically to inactive metabolite. **Elimination:** 57% in urine, 38% in feces. **Half-Life:** 2 h.

NURSING IMPLICATIONS

Black Box Warning

Sumatriptan has been associated with increased risk of serious, sometimes fatal, cardiovascular thrombotic reactions, MI, and CVA.

Assessment & Drug Effects

- Monitor cardiovascular status carefully following first dose in patients at relatively high risk for coronary artery disease (e.g., postmenopausal women, men over 40 years old, persons with known CAD risk factors) or who have coronary artery vasospasms.
- Report to prescriber immediately chest pain or tightness in chest or throat that is severe or does not quickly resolve following a dose of sumatriptan.
- Monitor therapeutic effectiveness. Pain relief usually begins within 10 min of injection, with complete relief in approximately 65% of all patients within 2 h.

Patient & Family Education

- Review patient information leaflet provided by the manufacturer carefully.
- Learn correct use of autoinjector for self-administration of subcutaneous dose.
- Pain or redness at injection site is common but usually disappears in less than 1 h.
- Notify prescriber immediately if symptoms of severe angina (e.g., severe or persistent pain or tightness in chest, back, neck, or throat) or hypersensitivity (e.g., wheezing, facial swelling, skin rash, or hives) occur.
- Do not take any other serotonin receptor agonist (Axert, Maxalt, Zomig, Amerge) within 24 h of taking sumatriptan.

Common adverse effects in *italic;* life-threatening effects <u>underlined</u>; generic names in **bold;** classifications in SMALL CAPS; ✤ Canadian drug name; ◗ Prototype drug; ⚠ Alert

- Check with prescriber before taking any new OTC or prescription drugs.
- Report any other adverse effects (e.g., tingling, flushing, dizziness) at next prescriber visit.

SUNITINIB

(sun-i-ti′nib)

Sutent

Classification: ANTINEOPLASTIC; KINASE INHIBITOR

Therapeutic: ANTINEOPLASTIC

Prototype: Erlotinib

AVAILABILITY Capsule

ACTION & *THERAPEUTIC EFFECT*

An antineoplastic agent that is a selective inhibitor of receptors for tyrosine kinases (RTKs) in solid tumors. Carcinogenic activity within these tumors is a result of tumor angiogenesis and proliferation. *Sunitinib causes tumor regression and decreased tumor growth.*

USES Treatment of advanced renal cell cancer; treatment of gastrointestinal stromal tumors (GIST), pancreatic neuroendocrine tumor.

CONTRAINDICATIONS Hypersensitivity to sunitinib; acute MI; fever, hepatotoxicity; tumor lysis syndrome; pancreatitis; urine protein of at least 3 g per 24 h; RPLS; pregnancy (category D); lactation.

CAUTIOUS USE Cardiac dysfunction, CHF, poorly controlled hypertension, history of MI; history of QT_c prolongation; thyroid dysfunction; DM; CVA; hepatic impairment; renal insufficiency (CrCl of 60 mL/min or less); females of childbearing age; children.

ROUTE & DOSAGE

Advanced Renal Cell Cancer/GIST Tumor

Adult: **PO** 50 mg/day for 4 wk, followed by 2 wk off treatment.

Pancreatic Neuroendocrine Tumor

Adult: **PO** 37.5 mg daily

Dosage Adjustments with Concurrent Hepatic CYP3A4 Modifiers

CYP3A4 Inducers: Increase to maximum of 87.5 mg/day (GIST, RCC) or 62.5 mg/day (PNET)

CYP3A4 Inhibitors: Decrease to minimum of 37.5 mg/day (GIST, RCC) or 25 mg/day (PNET)

ADMINISTRATION

Oral

- Incremental dosage changes of 12.5 mg are recommended.
- May be administered with or without food.
- Store at 15°–30° C (59°–86° F).

ADVERSE EFFECTS CV: Hypertension, decreased left ventricular ejection fraction, peripheral edema, chest pain. **Respiratory:** Cough, dyspnea, epistaxis, nasopharyngitis, oropharyngeal pain, upper respiratory tract infection. **CNS:** Fatigue, glossalgia, headache, insomnia, chills, depression, dizziness. **Endocrine:** Increased uric acid, abnormal serum calcium, decreased serum albumin, decreased serum phosphate, increased serum glucose, abnormal serum potassium, abnormal serum sodium, decreased serum magnesium. **Skin:** Skin discoloration, hair discoloration, palmar-plantar erythrodysesthesia, xeroderma, skin rash, alopecia, erythema, pruritus. **Hepatic:**

S

Increased serum AST, increased serum ALT, increased serum ALP, increased serum bilirubin. **GI:** Diarrhea, nausea, increased serum lipase, anorexia, mucositis, dysgeusia, vomiting, abdominal pain, increased serum amylase, constipation, weight loss, flatulence, xerostomia, GERD. **GU:** Increased serum creatinine. **Musculoskeletal:** Increased creatine phosphokinase, limb pain, weakness, arthralgia, back pain, myalgia. **Hematologic:** Decreased hemoglobin, decreased neutrophils, abnormal absolute lymphocyte count, decreased platelet count, hemorrhage. **Other:** Fever.

INTERACTIONS Drug: Coadministration of CYP3A4 INDUCERS (e.g., **carbamazepine, dexamethasone, phenobarbital, phenytoin, rifabutin, rifampin, rifapentine**) may decrease plasma levels of sunitinib. Coadministration of CYP3A4 INHIBITORS (e.g., **atazanavir, clarithromycin, erythromycin, indinavir, itraconazole, ketoconazole, nefazodone, nelfinavir, ritonavir, saquinavir, telithromycin, voriconazole**) may increase plasma levels of sunitinib. Do not use with LIVE VACCINES, **bevacizumab, pimecrolimus, topical tacrolimus. Food:** Grapefruit and **grapefruit juice** may increase the plasma levels of sunitinib. **Herbal:** St. John's wort may decrease the plasma levels of sunitinib.

PHARMACOKINETICS Peak: 6–12 h. **Distribution:** 95–98% protein bound. **Metabolism:** Extensive hepatic metabolism (CYPE 3A4 substrate). **Elimination:** Primarily fecal (61%). **Half-Life:** 40–60 h.

NURSING IMPLICATIONS

Black Box Warning

Sunitinib has been associated with severe, sometimes fatal, hepatotoxicity.

Assessment & Drug Effects
- Monitor for and report S&S of bleeding (e.g., GI, GU, gingival).
- Monitor BP regularly and assess regularly for S&S of congestive heart failure. Withhold drug and notify prescriber if severe hypertension or signs of heart failure develop.
- Monitor for and report S&S of hepatotoxicity (see Appendix F).
- Monitor lab tests: At the beginning of each treatment cycle, urinalysis for proteinuria, CBC with differential and platelet count; periodic LFTs and serum electrolytes; thyroid function tests as indicated.

Patient & Family Education
- Do not use any prescription or nonprescription drugs without consulting a prescriber.
- Skin discoloration (yellow color) and/or loss of skin and hair pigmentation may occur with this drug.
- Report any of the following to a health care provider: Painful redness of palms and soles of feet; severe abdominal pain, vomiting, and diarrhea; signs of bleeding; chest pain or discomfort; shortness of breath; swelling of feet, legs, or hands; rapid weight gain.
- Women of childbearing age are advised not to become pregnant while taking sunitinib.

SUVOREXANT
(su-vor′ex-ant)

Common adverse effects in *italic*; life-threatening effects underlined; generic names in **bold**; classifications in SMALL CAPS; ♣ Canadian drug name; ◐ Prototype drug; ⚠ Alert

Belsomra
Classification:
SEDATIVE-HYPNOTIC; OXERIN
RECEPTOR ANTAGONIST
Therapeutic: SEDATIVE-HYPNOTIC

AVAILABILITY Tablets

ACTIONS & *THERAPEUTIC EFFECT*

Promotes the natural transition from wakefulness to sleep by inhibiting the wakefulness-promoting orexin neurons of the arousal system. *Suvorexant improves sleep onset and sleep maintenance.*

USES Treatment of insomnia characterized by difficulties with sleep onset and/or sleep maintenance.

CONTRAINDICATIONS Narcolepsy; severe hepatic impairment; suicidal ideation.

CAUTIOUS USE Daytime somnolence; persistent insomnia after 7–10 days of treatment; complex nighttime behaviors while out of bed and not fully awake; concurrent CNS depressants or CYP3A4 inhibitors; alcohol use; history of drug abuse; depression; history of suicidal thoughts; behavioral changes; compromised respiratory function; obese individuals especially females; pregnancy (category C); lactation. Safety and efficacy in children younger than 18 y not established.

ROUTE & DOSAGE

Insomnia

Adult: **PO** 10 mg no more than once per night and within 30 min of bedtime; dose can be increased to 20 mg if tolerated

CYP3A4 Inhibitors Dosage Adjustment

Moderate inhibitors: Decrease dose to 5 mg (max: 10 mg)
Strong inhibitors: Not recommended

Hepatic Impairment Dosage Adjustment

Severe impairment: Not recommended

ADMINISTRATION

Oral

- Give within 30 min of bedtime, with at least 7 h before the planned time of awakening.
- Effect may be delayed if taken with or soon after a meal.
- Store at 20°–25° C (66°–77° F).

ADVERSE EFFECTS Respiratory: Cough, upper respiratory tract infection. **CNS:** Abnormal dreams, dizziness, headache, somnolence. **GI:** Diarrhea, dry mouth.

INTERACTIONS Drug: Concomitant use with strong CYP3A4 inhibitors (e.g., **clarithromycin, conivaptan, indinavir, itraconazole, ketoconazole, nefazodone, nelfinavir, posaconazole, ritonavir, saquinavir, telaprevir, telithromycin**) or moderate CYP3A4 inhibitors (e.g., **amprenavir, aprepitant, atazanavir, ciprofloxacin, diltiazem, erythromycin, fluconazole, fosamprenavir, imatinib, verapamil**) will increase the levels of suvorexant. Concomitant use with strong CYP3A4 inducers (e.g., **carbamazepine, phenytoin, rifampin**) will decrease the levels of suvorexant. **Food: Grapefruit juice** will increase the levels of suvorexant.

S

Herbal: St. John's wort may decrease the levels of suvorexant.

PHARMACOKINETICS Absorption: 82% bioavailable. **Peak:** 2 h. **Distribution:** Greater than 99% plasma protein bound. **Metabolism:** In liver by CYP3A4. **Elimination:** Fecal (66%) and renal (23%). **Half-Life:** 12 h.

NURSING IMPLICATIONS

Assessment & Drug Effects

- Monitor for adverse effects. Note that dose reduction may be required in obese women due to adverse effects, and in those using other CNS depressant drugs due to potential additive effects.
- Monitor respiratory status and level of daytime alertness.
- Monitor for and report promptly signs of abnormal thinking, worsening of depression, suicidal thoughts, or other abnormal behaviors.

Patient & Family Education

- Do not take this drug if a full night of sleep is not anticipated.
- Report to prescriber if insomnia does not improve within 7–10 days.
- Avoid alcohol while taking this drug.
- Do not engage in potentially dangerous activities (e.g., driving) until response to drug is known.
- Report immediately to prescriber if experiencing any of the following: More outgoing or aggressive behavior than normal, confusion, agitation, memory loss, hallucinations, worsening depression or suicidal thoughts.
- Contact prescriber immediately if experiencing "sleep-walking" or doing other activities when asleep (e.g., eating, talking, driving a car).

TACROLIMUS
(tac-rol'i-mus)
Astagraf XL, Hecoria, Prograf, Protopic
Classification: BIOLOGIC RESPONSE MODIFIER; IMMUNOSUPPRESSANT
Therapeutic: IMMUNOSUPPRESSANT
Prototype: Cyclosporine

AVAILABILITY Capsule; injection; ointment; extended release capsule

ACTION & *THERAPEUTIC EFFECT*
Inhibits helper T-lymphocytes by selectively inhibiting secretion of in-terleukin-2, interleukin-3, and interleukin-gamma, thus reducing transplant rejection. *Inhibits antibody production (thus subduing immune response) by creating an imbalance in favor of suppressor T-lymphocytes.*

USES Prophylaxis for organ transplant rejection, moderate to severe atopic dermatitis (e.g., eczema).

UNLABELED USES Acute organ transplant rejection, severe plaque-type psoriasis, ulcerative colitis, nephrotic syndrome.

CONTRAINDICATIONS Hypersensitivity to tacrolimus or castor oil; postoperative oliguria or renal failure with CrCl greater than or equal to 4 mg/dL; potassium sparing diretics; lactation.

CAUTIOUS USE Renal or hepatic insufficiency, liver transplants; hyperkalemia, QT prolongation; CHF; serious infections; polyoma virus infections; CMV disease diabetes mellitus, gout, history of seizures, hypertension; cardiomyopathy, left ventricular dysfunction (e.g., heart failure); neoplastic disease, especially lymphoproliferative disorders; pregnancy (category C). **Ointment:** Children younger than 2 y.

ROUTE & DOSAGE

Rejection Prophylaxis (Dose Varies Based on Concurrent Meds)

Adult: **PO** 0.075–0.2 mg/kg/day in divided doses q12h, start no sooner than 6 h after transplant; give first oral dose 8–12 h after discontinuing IV therapy; **IV** 0.01–0.05 mg/kg/day as continuous IV infusion, start no sooner than 6 h after transplant, continue until patient can take oral therapy
Child: **PO** 0.15–0.2 mg/kg/day **IV** 0.03–0.05 mg/kg/day

Atopic Dermatitis

Adult: **Topical** Apply thin layer to affected area bid, continue until clearing of symptoms
Child (2–15 y): **Topical** Apply thin layer of 0.03% ointment to affected area bid, continue until clearing of symptoms

Renal Impairment Dosage Adjustment

Start with lower dose

Hemodialysis Dosage Adjustment

Supplementation not necessary

ADMINISTRATION

Oral

- Patient should be converted from IV to oral therapy as soon as possible.
- Give first oral dose 8–12 h after discontinuing IV infusion.

Topical

- Ensure that skin is clean and completely dry before application.

- Apply a thin layer to the affected area and rub in gently and completely.
- Do not apply occlusive dressing over the site.

Intravenous

PREPARE: **IV Infusion:** Dilute 5 mg/mL ampules with NS or D5W to a concentration of 0.004–0.02 mg/mL (4–20 mcg/mL). ▪ Lower concentrations are preferred for children.
ADMINISTER: **IV Infusion:** Give as continuous IV. ▪ PVC-free tubing is recommended, especially at lower concentrations.
INCOMPATIBILITIES: **Y-site: Acyclovir, allopurinol, azathioprine, cefepime, dantrolene, diazepam, diazoxide, esomeprazole, ganciclovir, gemtuzumab, iron sucrose, lansoprazole, levothyroxine, omeprazole, phenytoin.**

- Store ampules at 5°–25° C (41°–77° F); store capsules at room temperature, 15°–30° C (59°–86° F). ▪ Store the diluted infusion in glass or polyethylene containers and discard after 24 h.

ADVERSE EFFECTS **CV:** *Mild to moderate hypertension.* **Respiratory:** *Pleural effusion, atelectasis, dyspnea.* **CNS:** *Headache, tremors, insomnia, paresthesia, hyperesthesia* and/or sensations of warmth, circumoral numbness. **HEENT:** Blurred vision, photophobia. **Endocrine:** Hirsutism, *hyperglycemia, hyperkalemia, hypokalemia, hypomagnesemia,* hyperuricemia, decreased serum cholesterol. **Skin:** *Flushing, rash, pruritus, skin irritation,* alopecia, erythema, folliculitis, hyperesthesia, <u>exfoliative dermatitis</u>, hirsutism, photosensitivity, skin discoloration, skin ulcer, sweating. **GI:** *Nausea, abdominal pain, gas,* appetite changes,

vomiting, anorexia, constipation, diarrhea, ascites. **GU:** UTI, oliguria, nephrotoxicity, nephropathy. **Hematologic:** *Anemia, leukocytosis,* thrombocytopenic *purpura.* **Other:** *Pain, fever, peripheral edema, increased risk of cancer.*

INTERACTIONS Drug: Use with **cyclosporine** increases risk of nephrotoxicity. **Metoclopramide, lansoprazole,** CALCIUM CHANNEL BLOCKER, ANTIFUNGAL AGENTS, MACROLIDE ANTIBIOTICS, **bromocriptine, cimetidine, cyclosporine, methylprednisolone, omeprazole** may increase levels; **caspofungin, rifampin** may decrease levels. NSAIDS may lead to oliguria or anuria. **Herbal: St. John's wort** decreases efficacy. **Food: Grapefruit juice** (greater than 1 qt/day) may increase plasma concentrations and adverse effects.

PHARMACOKINETICS Absorption: Erratic and incompletely from GI tract; absolute bioavailability approximately 14–25%; absorption reduced by food. **Peak:** PO 1–4 h. **Duration:** IV 12 h. **Distribution:** Within plasma, tacrolimus is found primarily in lipoprotein-deficient fraction; 75–97% protein bound; distributed into red blood cells; blood:plasma ratio reported greater than 4; animal studies have demonstrated high concentrations of tacrolimus in lung, kidney, heart, and spleen; distributed into breast milk. **Metabolism:** Extensively in liver (CYP3A4). **Elimination:** Metabolites primarily in bile. **Half-Life:** 8.7–11.3 h.

NURSING IMPLICATIONS

Black Box Warning

Tacrolimus has been associated with increased susceptibility to bacterial, viral, fungal, and protozoal infections and possible development of lymphoma and skin cancer.

Assessment & Drug Effects
- Monitor for and promptly report S&S of infection.
- Monitor kidney function closely; report elevated serum creatinine or decreased urinary output.
- Monitor for neurotoxicity, and report tremors, changes in mental status, or other signs of toxicity.
- Monitor cardiovascular status and report hypertension.
- Monitor for ECG for QT prolongation especially in those with renal or hepatic impairment.
- Monitor lab tests: Periodic serum tacrolimus, serum electrolytes, blood glucose, LFTs, and renal function tests.

Patient & Family Education
- Do not eat grapefruit or drink grapefruit juice while taking this drug.
- Report promptly unexplained hunger, thirst, and frequent urination.
- Be aware of potential adverse effects including increased risk for infection.
- Minimize exposure to natural or artificial sunlight while using the ointment.
- Notify prescriber of S&S of neurotoxicity.

TADALAFIL
(ta-dal'a-fil)
Adcirca, Cialis
Classification: IMPOTENCE; PHOSPHODIESTERASE (PDE) INHIBITOR; VASODILATOR
Therapeutic: IMPOTENCE; PULMONARY ANTIHYPERTENSIVE
Prototype: Sildenafil

Common adverse effects in *italic;* life-threatening effects underlined; generic names in **bold;** classifications in SMALL CAPS; ♣ Canadian drug name; ☾ Prototype drug; ⚠ Alert

AVAILABILITY Tablet

ACTION & *THERAPEUTIC EFFECT*

PDE is responsible for degradation of cyclic GMP in the corpus cavernosum of the penis. Cyclic GMP causes smooth muscle relaxation in lung tissue and the corpus cavernosum, thereby allowing inflow of blood into the penis. PDE-5 inhibitors reduce pulmonary vasodilation by sustaining levels of cyclic guanosine monophosphate (cGMP). Additionally, tadalafil produces a reduction in the pulmonary-to-systemic vascular resistance ratio. *Tadalafil promotes sustained erection only in the presence of sexual stimulation. It also produces a significant improvement in arterial oxygenation in pulmonary hypertension.*

USES Treatment of erectile dysfunction, BPH, pulmonary hypertension.

CONTRAINDICATIONS Hypersensitivity to tadalafil, vardenafil, or sildenafil; MI within last 90 days; Class 2 or greater heart failure within last 6 mo; unstable angina or angina during intercourse; uncontrolled cardiac arrhythmias; nitrate/nitrite therapy; hypotension, uncontrolled hypertension; retinitis pigmentosa; CVA within last 6 mo; left ventricular outflow obstruction, aortic stenosis; severe (Child-Pugh class C) hepatic cirrhosis; women; lactation.

CAUTIOUS USE CAD, risk factors for CVA; renal insufficiency; mild to moderate (Child-Pugh class A or B) hepatic disease; anatomic deformity of the penis; sickle cell anemia; multiple myeloma; leukemia; active bleeding or a peptic ulcer; hiatal hernia, GERD; sickle cell disease; retinitis pigmentosa; severe renal impairment; concurrent use with other medicines for penile dysfunction; older adults; pregnancy (category B). Safety and efficacy for PAH in children younger than 18 y not established.

ROUTE & DOSAGE

Erectile Dysfunction

Adult: **PO** 2.5 mg daily OR 10 mg prior to anticipated sexual activity. May increase (max: 20 mg/day or reduce to 5 mg/day if needed)

Pulmonary Hypertension

Adult: **PO** 40 mg daily

BPH

Adult: **PO** 5 mg daily

Hepatic Impairment Dosage Adjustment

Mild to moderate impairment (Child-Pugh class A and B): Max 10 mg/day; not recommended with severe hepatic impairment *Severe hepatic impairment (Child-Pugh class C):* Not recommended

Renal Impairment Dosage Adjustment

CrCl 30–50 mL/min: Start at half normal dose; *less than 30 mL/min:* Max dose 5 mg and once daily dosing is not recommended

ADMINISTRATION

Oral

- If not on the daily dose regimen, tadalafil is taken approximately 30 min before expected intercourse, but preferably not after a heavy or high-fat meal.
- Store at 15°–30° C (59°–86° F).

Common adverse effects in *italic;* life-threatening effects <u>underlined;</u> generic names in **bold;** classifications in SMALL CAPS; ♣ Canadian drug name; ○ Prototype drug; ⚠ Alert

ADVERSE EFFECTS CV: Angina, chest pain, hyper-tension, hypotension, MI, orthostatic hypotension, palpitations, syncope, sinus tachycardia. **Respiratory:** Nasal congestion, dyspnea, epistaxis, pharyngitis. **CNS:** *Head-ache,* dizziness, insomnia, somnolence, vertigo, hypesthesia, paresthesia. **HEENT:** Blurred vision, changes in color vision, conjunctivitis, eye pain, lacrimation, swelling of eyelids, sudden vision loss. **Endocrine:** Increased GGTP. **Skin:** Rash, pruritus, sweating. **GI:** Dyspepsia, nausea, vomiting, abdominal pain, abnormal liver function tests, diarrhea, loose stools, dysphagia, esophagitis, gastritis, GERD, xerostomia. **GU:** Spontaneous penile erection. **Musculoskeletal:** Arthralgia, myalgia, neck pain. **Other:** Flushing, back pain, asthenia, facial edema, fatigue, pain, transient global amnesia.

INTERACTIONS Drug: Do not use with any form of NITRATES or **riociguat** due to increased risk of hypotension. Do not use with **telaprevir.** May potentiate hypotensive effects of ETHANOL, **alfuzosin, doxazosin, prazosin, tamsulosin** (doses greater than 0.4 mg/day), **terazosin; erythromycin** (and other MACROLIDES), **indinavir,** PROTEASE INHIBITORS, **saquinavir,** may increase levels and toxicity of tadalafil; **barbiturates, bosentan, carbamazepine, dexamethasone, fosphenytoin, nevirapine, phenytoin, rifabutin, rifampin, troglitazone** may reduce level and effectiveness of tadalafil. If taking **ritonavir, itraconazole, ketoconazole,** or **voriconazole** (max dose: 10 mg q72h). **Food: Grapefruit juice** may increase levels and toxicity of tadalafil.

PHARMACOKINETICS Absorption: Rapidly absorbed, 15% reaches systemic circulation. **Onset:** 30–45 min. **Peak:** 2 h. **Duration:** Up to 36 h. **Metabolism:** In liver by CYP3A4. **Elimination:** In feces (61%) and urine (39%). **Half-Life:** 17.5 h.

NURSING IMPLICATIONS

Assessment & Drug Effects
- Monitor CV status and report angina or other S&S of cardiac dysfunction.
- Monitor for orthostatic hypotension.
- Monitor lab tests: Baseline and periodic PSA.

Patient & Family Education
- Do not take more than once/day.
- Note: With moderate renal insufficiency, the maximum recommended dose is 10 mg not more than once in every 48 h.
- Moderate use of alcohol when taking this drug.
- Do not take this drug without consulting prescriber if you are taking drugs called "alpha-blockers" or "nitrates" or any other drugs for high blood pressure, chest pain, or enlarged prostate.
- Report promptly any of the following: Palpitations, chest pain, back pain, difficulty breathing, or shortness of breath; dizziness or fainting; changes in vision; swollen eyelids; muscle aches; painful or prolonged erection (lasting longer than 4 h); skin rash, or itching.

TAMOXIFEN CITRATE ℗

(ta-mox'i-fen)

Soltamox

Classification: ANTINEOPLASTIC; SELECTIVE ESTROGEN RECEPTOR MODIFIER (SERM)

Therapeutic: ANTINEOPLASTIC; ANTIESTROGEN

Common adverse effects in *italic*; life-threatening effects underlined; generic names in **bold**; classifications in SMALL CAPS; ♣ Canadian drug name; ℗ Prototype drug; ⚠ Alert

1606

T

AVAILABILITY Tablet

ACTION & *THERAPEUTIC EFFECT*

Competes with estradiol at estrogen receptor (ER-positive) sites in target tissues such as breast, uterus, vagina, anterior pituitary. Estrogen is thought to increase breast cancer cell proliferation in ER-positive tumors. *Has effects on tumor with high concentration of estrogen receptors. Tamoxifen-receptor complexes move into the cell nucleus, decreasing DNA synthesis and estrogen responses.*

USES Palliative treatment of metastatic estrogen receptors (ER)-positive breast cancer in postmenopausal women, adjunctively with surgery in the treatment of breast carcinoma with positive lymph nodes; reduce incidence of breast cancer in high risk patient.

UNLABELED USES Gynecomastia, idiopathic male infertility.

CONTRAINDICATIONS Hypersensitivity to tamoxifen or any component of the formulation; concurrent warfarin therapy; history of DVT or pulmonary embolism; preexisting endometrial hyperplasia; intramuscular injections if platelets less than 50,000/mm^3; history of thromboembolic disease; pregnancy (in utero exposure to tamoxifen may cause fetal harm), especially during first trimester; lactation; children.

CAUTIOUS USE Vision disturbances; cataracts, visual disturbance; leukopenia, bone marrow suppression; thrombocytopenia; hypercalcemia; hypercholesterolemia, lipid protein abnormalities; women with ductal carcinoma in situ (DCIS).

ROUTE & DOSAGE

Breast Cancer Treatment

Adult: **PO** 20 mg daily for initial duration of 5 years; possibly up to 10 years

Breast Cancer Prophylaxis

Adult: **PO** 20 mg daily × 5 y

ADMINISTRATION

Oral

- Administer tablets or oral solution with or without food. Use supplied dosing cup for oral solution.
- Store at 20°–25° C (68°–77° F); protect from light. Oral solution should be used within 3 mo of opening.

ADVERSE EFFECTS CV: Flushing, hypertension, peripheral edema, vasodilation, chest pain. **Respiratory:** Pharyngitis, bronchitis, cough, dyspnea, flu-like symptoms, sinusitis, throat irritation (oral solution). **CNS:** Depression, fatigue, mood changes, pain, anxiety, dizziness, headache, insomnia, paresthesia. **HEENT:** Cataract. **Endocrine:** Amenorrhea, fluid retention, hot flash, weight loss, weight gain, infrequent uterine bleeding, menstrual disease. **Skin:** Skin rash, skin changes, alopecia, diaphoresis. **Hepatic/GI:** *Nausea, vomiting,* abdominal pain, constipation, diarrhea, dyspepsia, increased AST. **GU:** Irregular menses, vaginal discharge, vaginal hemorrhage, leukorrhea, mastalgia, urinary tract infection, vaginitis, vulvovaginitis. **Hematologic:** Lymphedema, anemia, neoplasm, thrombocytopenia. **Musculoskeletal:** Arthralgia, arthritis, asthenia, arthropathy, back pain, bone fracture, myalgia, ostealgia, osteoporosis. **Other:** Infection, sepsis, cyst.

T

Common adverse effects in *italic;* life-threatening effects <u>underlined</u>; generic names in **bold;** classifications in SMALL CAPS; ♣ Canadian drug name; ✪ Prototype drug; ⚠ Alert

DIAGNOSTIC TEST INTERFERENCE

Tamoxifen may produce elevation of T4.

INTERACTIONS Drug:

May enhance hypoprothrombinemic effects of **warfarin**; may increase risk of thromboembolic events with CYTOTOXIC AGENTS; SSRI ANTIDEPRESSANTS may decrease effectiveness of tamoxifen; do not use with **anastrozole, ospermifene**. CYP 3A4 INHIBITORS may increase concentration of tamoxifen; CYP 3A4 INDUCERS may decrease concentration of tamoxifen; CYP 2D6 INHIBITORS may decrease concentration of tamoxifen.

PHARMACOKINETICS Absorption:

Slowly from GI tract. **Distribution**: widely distributed; highly protein bound. **Peak:** 3–6 h. **Metabolism:** In liver (CYP2D6), enterohepatically cycled. **Elimination:** Primarily in feces. **Half-Life:** 7 days.

NURSING IMPLICATIONS

Black Box Warning

Tamoxifen has been associated with increased risk of uterine malignancies, stroke, and pulmonary embolism.

Assessment & Drug Effects

- Be aware that local swelling and marked erythema over preexisting lesions or the development of new lesions may signal soft-tissue disease response to tamoxifen. These symptoms rapidly subside.
- Monitor for signs and symptoms of DVT or PE.
- Baseline ophthalmic exam if vision problem.
- Monitor lab tests: Periodic CBC with platelet count, serum calcium, LFTs, lipid profile, INR, PT, pregnancy test, and bone mineral density test (premenopausal women).

Patient & Family Education

- Do not change established dose schedule.
- Report to prescriber any of the following: Marked weakness or numbness in face or leg, especially on one side of the body; difficulty walking or loss of balance; unexplained sleepiness or mental confusion; edema; shortness of breath; or blurred vision.
- Report promptly any unexpected vaginal discharge or pain or pressure in your pelvis.
- Avoid OTC drugs unless specifically prescribed by the prescriber; particularly OTC pain medicines.
- Report onset of tenderness or redness in an extremity.

TAMSULOSIN HYDROCHLORIDE ○

(tam'su-lo-sin)

Flomax
Classification: ALPHA-ADRENERGIC RECEPTOR ANTAGONIST
Therapeutic: SMOOTH MUSCLE RELAXANT OF BLADDER OUTLET & PROSTATE GLAND

AVAILABILITY Capsule

ACTION & *THERAPEUTIC EFFECT*

Antagonist of the alpha$_{1A}$-adrenergic receptors located in the prostate. This blockage can cause smooth muscles in the bladder outlet and the prostate gland to relax, resulting in improvement in urinary flow and a reduction in symptoms of BPH. *Improves symptoms related to benign prostatic hypertrophy (BPH) related to bladder outlet obstruction.*

1608

Common adverse effects in *italic*; life-threatening effects underlined; generic names in **bold**; classifications in SMALL CAPS; ♣ Canadian drug name; ○ Prototype drug; ▲ Alert

USES Benign prostatic hypertrophy.

CONTRAINDICATIONS Hypersensitivity to tamsulosin; women; lactation; children.

CAUTIOUS USE History of syncope, hypersensitivity to sulfonamides; hypotension; renal impairment, renal failure, renal disease; older adults; pregnancy (limited information related to use during pregnancy; use with caution).

ROUTE & DOSAGE

Benign Prostatic Hypertrophy

Adult: **PO** 0.4 mg daily 30 min after a meal, may increase up to 0.8 mg daily

ADMINISTRATION

Oral
- Give 30 min after the same meal each day.
- Instruct to swallow capsules whole; do not crush, chew, or open.
- If dose is interrupted for several days, reinitiate at the lowest dose, 0.4 mg.
- Store at 25° C (77° F).

ADVERSE EFFECTS CV: *Orthostatic hypotension (especially with first dose).* **Respiratory:** *Rhinitis,* dyspnea, epistaxis, increased cough, pharyngitis. **CNS:** *Headache, dizziness.* **HEENT:** Amblyopia. **GI:** Diarrhea, nausea. **GU:** *Abnormal ejaculation,* priapism. **Other:** Asthenia, back pain, infection.

INTERACTIONS Drug: Cimetidine may decrease clearance of tamsulosin. **Sildenafil, vardenafil,** and **tadalafil,** and alcohol may enhance hypotensive effects. CYP 3A4 INHIBITORS may increase concentration of tamsulosin; CYP 3A4 INDUCERS may decrease concentration of tamsulosin; may increase hypotensive effect with ANTIHYPERTENSIVES.

PHARMACOKINETICS Absorption: Rapidly from GI tract. Greater than 90% bioavailability. **Peak:** 4–5 h fasting, 6–7 h fed. **Distribution:** Widely distributed in body tissues, including kidney and prostate. **Metabolism:** In the liver via CYP3A4 and 2D6. **Elimination:** 76% in urine. **Half-Life:** 14–15 h.

NURSING IMPLICATIONS

Assessment & Drug Effects
- Monitor for signs of orthostatic hypotension; take BP lying down, then upon standing. Report a systolic pressure drop of 15 mm Hg or more or a HR 15 beats or more upon standing.
- Monitor patients on warfarin therapy closely.
- Monitor urinary symptoms.

Patient & Family Education
- Make position changes slowly to minimize orthostatic hypotension.
- Report dizziness, vertigo, or fainting to prescriber. Exercise caution with hazardous activities until response to drug is known.
- Be aware that concurrent use of cimetidine may increase the orthostatic hypotension adverse effect.

TAPENTADOL

(ta-pent'a-dol)

Nucynta, Nucynta ER
Classification: CENTRALLY ACTING NARCOTIC ANALGESIC; MU-OPIOID RECEPTOR AGONIST; INHIBITOR OF NOREPINEPHRINE REUPTAKE
Therapeutic: CENTRALLY ACTING NARCOTIC ANALGESIC
Controlled Substance: Schedule II

T

AVAILABILITY Tablet; extended release tablet

ACTION & *THERAPEUTIC EFFECT*

Tapentadol is a centrally acting synthetic analgesic that is a mu-opioid agonist and also thought to inhibit norepinephrine reuptake. There is potential for opioid agonist abuse or addiction. *Effective in treatment of moderate to severe acute pain.*

USES Relief of acute moderate to severe pain, chronic pain (ER form only).

CONTRAINDICATIONS Hypersensitivity to tapentadol (e.g., anaphylaxis, angioedema); impaired pulmonary function (e.g., significant respiratory depression, acute or severe bronchial asthma, hypercapnia without monitoring or the absence of resuscitation equipment); known or suspected paralytic ileus; concomitant use of MAOI or use within 14 days; head injury, intracranial pressure (ICP); severe hepatic or renal impairment (CrCl less than 30 mL/min); alcohol consumption especially with tapentadol ER; labor and delivery; lactation.

CAUTIOUS USE Debilitated patients; upper airway obstruction; COPD; cor pulmonale; patients with decreased respiratory reserve; history of low blood pressure; cranial lesions without increased ICP; history of drug or alcohol abuse; history of seizures; mild or moderate renal or hepatic impairment; older adults; pregnancy (category C). Safe use in children younger than 18 y not established.

ROUTE & DOSAGE

Acute Moderate to Severe Pain

Adult: **PO** 50–100 mg q 4–6 h. On first day of dosing a second dose may be given 1 h later if initial dose ineffective (may titrate to max total daily dose: 700 mg day 1 and 600 mg thereafter).

Chronic Pain (ER Form Only)

Adult: **PO** 100–250 mg bid

Hepatic Impairment Dosage Adjustment

Moderate impairment: Reduce initial dose to 50 mg q 8 h. *Severe impairment (Child-Pugh class C):* Not recommended for use.

ADMINISTRATION

Oral

- Extended release (ER) tablets must be swallowed whole. They must not be cut, chewed, dissolved, or crushed due to risk of rapid release of a potentially fatal dose.
- On day 1 of therapy, a second dose may be given as soon as 1 h after the initial dose if pain relief is inadequate. All subsequent doses should be at 4–6 h intervals.
- Do not exceed a total daily dose of 700 mg on day 1 or 600 mg on subsequent days.
- When extended-release (ER) tablets are discontinued, a gradual downward titration of the dose should be used to prevent S&S of drug withdrawal.
- Do not administer if a paralytic ileus is suspected.
- Do not give within 14 days of an MAOI.
- Store at 15°–30° C (59°–86° F).

ADVERSE EFFECTS CV: Hot flush. **Respiratory:** Nasopharyngitis, <u>respiratory depression</u>, upper respiratory tract infection. **CNS:**

Common adverse effects in *italic*; life-threatening effects <u>underlined</u>; generic names in **bold**; classifications in SMALL CAPS; ♦ Canadian drug name; ☺ Prototype drug; ⚠ Alert

Headache, abnormal dreams, anxiety, confusional state, *dizziness,* insomnia, lethargy, *somnolence,* tremor. **Endocrine:** Decreased appetite. **Skin:** Hyperhidrosis, pruritus, rash. **GI:** *Constipation,* dry mouth, dyspepsia, *nausea, vomiting.* **GU:** Urinary tract infection. **Musculoskeletal:** Arthralgia. **Other:** Fatigue.

INTERACTIONS Drug: Other OPIOID AGONISTS, GENERAL ANESTHETICS, PHENOTHIAZINES, ANTIEMETICS, other TRANQUILIZERS, SEDATIVES, HYPNOTICS, or other CNS DEPRESSANTS may cause additive CNS depression. MAO INHIBITORS can raise **norepinephrine** levels resulting in adverse cardiovascular events.

PHARMACOKINETICS Absorption: 32% bioavailability. **Peak:** 1.25 h. **Metabolism:** In liver. **Elimination:** Primarily renal. **Half-Life:** 4 h.

NURSING IMPLICATIONS

Black Box Warning

Tapentadol ER has been associated with serious, sometimes fatal, respiratory depression and with neonatal withdrawal syndrome.

Assessment & Drug Effects
- Monitor degree of pain relief, mental status, and level of alertness.
- Monitor vital signs. Withhold drug and notify prescriber for a respiratory rate of 12/min or less.
- If an opioid antagonist is required to reverse the action of tapentadol, continue to monitor respiratory status since respiratory depression may outlast duration of action of the opioid antagonists.
- Monitor for signs of misuse, abuse, and addiction.

- Withhold drug and report promptly S&S of serotonin syndrome (see Appendix F).
- Monitor ambulation. Fall precautions may be warranted.

Patient & Family Education
- Avoid engaging in hazardous activities until reaction to drug is known.
- Avoid alcohol while taking the extended release (ER) form of this drug.
- Consult prescriber before taking OTC drugs.

TASIMELTEON
(tas-i-mel'tee-on)
Hetlioz
Classification:
SEDATIVE-HYPNOTIC; MELATONIN RECEPTOR AGONIST
Therapeutic: SEDATIVE
Prototype: Ramelteon

AVAILABILITY Gelatin capsules

ACTION & THERAPEUTIC EFFECT Agonist of melatonin receptors MT1 and MT2. Activation of MT1 is thought to induce sleepiness, and MT2 activation is thought to help regulate circadian rhythms. *Improves insomnia or excessive sleepiness related to abnormal synchronization between the 24-h light–dark cycle and endogenous circadian rhythms.*

USES Treatment of non-24 h sleep–wake disorder (non-24).

CONTRAINDICATIONS Severe hepatic impairment.

CAUTIOUS USE Concomitant drugs (including alcohol) that cause CNS depression; mild-to-moderate hepatic impairment;

| T |

older adults; pregnancy (category C); lactation. Safety and efficacy in children younger than 18 y not established.

ROUTE & DOSAGE

Sleep-Wake Disorder (Non-24)
Adult: **PO** 20 mg once daily at the same time before bedtime

ADMINISTRATION

- Give with food at approximately same time every night before bedtime.
- Capsules **must be** swallowed whole. They should not be opened or chewed.
- Store at 15°–30° C (59°–86° F). Protect from light and moisture.

ADVERSE EFFECTS Respiratory:
Upper respiratory tract infection. **CNS:** Headache, nightmare/abnormal dreams. **Endocrine:** Increased ALT. **GU:** Urinary tract infection.

INTERACTIONS Drug: Tasimelteon
may enhance the effects of other CNS depressants. Co-administration with strong CYP1A2 inhibitors (e.g., **fluvoxamine**) or strong CYP3A4 inhibitors (e.g., **ketoconazole**) may increase the levels of tasimelteon. Co-administration with strong CYP3A4 inducers (e.g., **carbamazepine, phenytoin, rifampin**) may decrease the levels of tasimelteon. **Food: Grapefruit** and **grapefruit juice** may increase the levels of tasimelteon. **Herbal: St. John's wort** decreases the levels of tasimelteon.

PHARMACOKINETICS Peak:
0.5–3 h. **Distribution:** 90% plasma protein bound. **Metabolism:** Extensive metabolism in liver. **Elimination:** Primarily renal. **Half-Life:** 1.3 h.

NURSING IMPLICATIONS
Assessment & Drug Effects
- Monitor for and report worsening insomnia and cognitive or behavioral changes.
- Monitor urinary output and report immediately dysuria or difficulty urinating.
- Assess risk for falls in older adults and otherwise frail persons.
- Monitor lab test: Baseline LFTs.

Patient & Family Education
- If drug cannot be taken at approximately the same time on a given night, that dose should be skipped.
- Do not drive or engage in potentially hazardous activities until response to drug is known.
- Do not consume alcohol while taking this drug.
- Report any of the following to prescriber: Worsening insomnia, cognitive or behavioral changes, difficulty with urination.

TAZAROTENE
(ta-zar'o-teen)
Avage, Tazorac
Classification: RETINOID; ANTIACNE
Therapeutic: ANTIACNE
Prototype: Isotretinoin

AVAILABILITY Gel; cream

ACTION & THERAPEUTIC EFFECT
Retinoid prodrug that blocks epidermal cell proliferation and hyperplasia. Suppresses inflammation present in the epidermis of psoriasis. *Effectiveness indicated by improvement in acne or psoriasis.*

USES Topical treatment of plaque
psoriasis on up to 20% of the body, mild to moderate acne, facial fine

wrinkling, mottled hypo- and hyper-pigmentation (blotchy skin discoloration), and benign facial lentigines.

CONTRAINDICATIONS Hypersensitivity to tazarotene; pregnancy (category X), women who are or may become pregnant; lactation.

CAUTIOUS USE Concurrent administration with drugs that are photosensitizers (e.g., thiazide diuretics, tetracyclines); retinoid hypersensitivity. Safety and efficacy in children younger than 12 y not established.

ROUTE & DOSAGE

Plaque Psoriasis

Adult: **Topical** Apply thin film to affected area once daily in evening

Acne

Adult: **Topical** After cleansing and drying face, apply thin film to acne lesions once daily in evening

Fine Wrinkles

Adult: **Topical** Apply thin film of cream to affected area once daily

ADMINISTRATION

Topical

- Dry skin completely before application of a thin film of medication.
- Apply medication to no more than 20% of body surface in those with psoriasis.
- Apply only to affected areas; avoid contact with eyes and mucous membranes.

ADVERSE EFFECTS Skin: *Pruritus, burning/stinging, erythema, worsening of psoriasis, irritation, skin pain,* rash, desquamation of skin, irritant contact dermatitis, inflammation, fissuring, bleeding, dry skin, sunburn.

INTERACTIONS Drug: Increased risk of photosensitivity reactions with QUINOLONES (especially **sparfloxacin**), PHENOTHIAZINES, SULFONAMIDES, SULFONYLUREAS, TETRACYCLINES, THIAZIDE DIURETICS.

PHARMACOKINETICS Absorption: Rapidly absorbed through skin. **Distribution:** Active metabolite greater than 99% protein bound; crosses placenta, distributed into breast milk. **Metabolism:** Undergoes esterase hydrolysis to active metabolite AGN 190299. **Elimination:** In both urine and feces. **Half-Life:** 18 h.

NURSING IMPLICATIONS

Assessment & Drug Effects

- Monitor for photosensitivity in those concurrently using any of the following: Thiazides, tetracyclines, fluoroquinolones, phenothiazines, sulfonamides.

Patient & Family Education

- Understand fully the risk of serious fetal harm. Use reliable forms of effective contraception. Discontinue treatment and notify prescriber if pregnancy occurs.
- Alert: Immediately rinse thoroughly with water if contact with eyes occurs.
- Avoid all unnecessary exposure to sunlight or artificial UV light. If brief exposure is necessary, cover as much skin surface as possible and use sunscreens (minimum SPF 15).
- Do not apply to sunburned skin.
- Discontinue medication and notify prescriber if any of the following occur: Pruritus, burning, skin redness, excessive peeling, worsening of psoriasis.

T

Common adverse effects in *italic;* life-threatening effects <u>underlined;</u> generic names in **bold;** classifications in SMALL CAPS; ♣ Canadian drug name; ○ Prototype drug; ⚠ Alert

- Limit application of topicals with strong skin-drying effects to skin areas being treated with tazarotene.

TEDIZOLID PHOSPHATE
(ted-i-zo'lid)
Sivextro
Classification: OXAZOLIDINONE ANTIBIOTIC
Therapeutic: ANTIBIOTIC
Prototype: Linezolid

AVAILABILITY Tablets, lyophilized power for injection

ACTION & THERAPEUTIC EFFECT
Prevents formation of a functional 70S essential for the bacterial translation process, thus inhibiting protein synthesis and cell proliferation. *Bacteriostatic against enterococci, staphylococci, and streptococci.*

USES Treatment of acute bacterial skin and skin structure infections (ABSSSI) caused by designated susceptible bacteria.

CONTRAINDICATIONS
Clostridium difficile-associated diarrhea, except of treatment thereof; neutrophil counts less than 1,000 cells/mm^3.

CAUTIOUS USE Colitis; cardiac arrhythmia; history of anemia; pregnancy (category C); lactation. Safety and efficacy in children younger than 18 y not established.

ROUTE & DOSAGE

Skin and Skin Structure Infection
Adult: **PO or IV** 200 mg once daily for 6 days

ADMINISTRATION
Oral
- Give without regard to food.
- Store at 15°–30° C (59°–86° F).

Intravenous

PREPARE: **IV Infusion:** Reconstitute vial with 4 mL SW. **Do not** shake. Swirl gently and let stand until dissolved and foam disperses. If needed, invert vial to completely dissolve and swirl gently to prevent foaming. Place vial upright, tilt, and insert a syringe into bottom corner to remove 4 mL. **Do not** invert the vial during extraction. Further dilute in 250 mL of NS. Invert bag gently to mix but do not shake.
ADMINISTER: **IV Infusion:** Give over 1 h. **Do not** give IV push or bolus. Flush line before/after with NS if used for other drugs or solutions.
INCOMPATIBILITIES: **Solution/additive:** Solutions containing divalent cations (e.g., Ca^{+2}, Mg^{+2}), Lactated Ringer's, Hartmann's Solution.

- Store reconstituted solution for up to 24 h at room temperature or under refrigeration at 2°–8° C (36°–46° F).

ADVERSE EFFECTS CV: Hypertension, palpitations, <u>tachycardia</u>. **CNS:** Dizziness, headache, hypoesthesia, insomnia, paresthesia, nerve paralysis, peripheral neuropathy. **HEENT:** Asthenopia, blurred vision, visual impairment, vitreous floaters. **Endocrine:** Decreased hemoglobin, decreased white blood cell count, increased ALT and AST, decreased platelet count, thrombocytopenia. **Skin:** Dermatitis, pruritus, urticarial. **GI:** *Clostridium difficile* colitis, diarrhea, nausea, vomiting. **GU:**

Common adverse effects in *italic*; life-threatening effects <u>underlined</u>; generic names in **bold**; classifications in SMALL CAPS; ♣ Canadian drug name; ○ Prototype drug; △ Alert

1614

Vulvovaginal mycotic infection. **Hematological:** Anemia. **Other:** Flushing, hypersensitivity reactions, phlebitis, oral candidiasis.

INTERACTIONS Drug: Tedizolid may increase the levels of other drugs (e.g., **aproclonidine, benzafibrate, bupropion, carbamazepine, levodopa,** SEROTONIN 5-HT1D RECEPTOR AGONISTS) that require MAO for metabolism. Do not use with LIVE VACCINES. Use with **fentanyl** or other OPIOIDS could cause serotonin syndrome.

PHARMACOKINETICS Absorption: 91% Bioavailable. **Peak:** 3 h. **Distribution:** 70–90% plasma protein bound; distributes into adipose and skeletal muscle tissue. **Elimination:** Fecal (82%) and renal (18%). **Half-Life:** 12 h.

NURSING IMPLICATIONS

Assessment & Drug Effects

- Monitor for S&S of superinfection, including *C. difficile*-associated diarrhea (CDAD) and pseudomembranous colitis that may develop months after treatment.
- Monitor lab tests: Baseline CBC with differential.

Patient & Family Education

- Report promptly to prescriber if you develop frequent watery or bloody diarrhea even 2 mo or more after last dose of antibiotic.
- Consult with prescriber if you are a female who is or plans to become pregnant.
- Do not breast-feed without consulting prescriber.

TELAVANCIN HYDROCHLORIDE

(tel-a-van'sin)
Vibativ

Classification: ANTIBIOTIC; GLYCOPROTEIN
Therapeutic: ANTIBIOTIC
Prototype: Vancomycin

AVAILABILITY Powder for reconstitution and injection

ACTION & *THERAPEUTIC EFFECT*

Inhibits cell wall synthesis of bacteria. It binds to the bacterial membrane and disrupts the barrier function of the cell membrane of gram-positive bacteria. *Effective against a broad range of gram-positive bacteria.*

USES Treatment of complicated skin and skin structure infections hospital-acquired and ventilator-associated pneumonia.

CONTRAINDICATIONS End-stage renal disease or hemodialysis; uncompensated heart failure; QT prolongation.

CAUTIOUS USE Moderate or severe renal impairment; renal disease; elderly; ulcerative colitis; severe hepatic impairment; women of childbearing potential; pregnancy (category C); lactation. Safe use in children younger than 18 y has not been established.

ROUTE & DOSAGE

Complicated Skin and Skin Structure Infections

Adult: **IV** 10 mg/kg q24h for 7–14 days

Hospital-Acquired and Ventilator-Associated Bacterial Pneumonia

Adult: **IV** 10 mg/kg q24h × 7–21 days

Renal Impairment Dosage Adjustment

CrCl 30–50 mL/min: Decrease to 7.5 mg/kg q 24 h; *10–29 mL/min:* Decrease to 10 mg/kg q 48 h

ADMINISTRATION

Intravenous

PREPARE: Infusion: Reconstitute each 250 mg with 15 mL or each 750 mg vial with 45 mL of D5W or NS to yield 15 mg/mL. Mix thoroughly to dissolve. For doses of 150–800 mg, must further dilute in 100–250 mL of IV solution. For doses less than 100 mg or greater than 800 mg, should be further diluted in D5W, NS, or LR to a final concentration in the range of 0.6–8 mg/mL.
ADMINISTER: Infusion: Infuse over 60 min or longer to minimize infusion-related reactions. ▪ Do not infuse through the same line with any other drugs or additives.

▪ Storage: Reconstituted vials or infusion solution should be used within 4 h if at room temperature or 72 h if refrigerated. **Important note:** The total time holding time for reconstituted vials plus infusion solution cannot exceed 4 h at room temperature or 72 h refrigerated.

ADVERSE EFFECTS CNS: Dizziness, *taste disturbance.* **Endocrine:** Decreased appetite, *increased serum creatinine.* **Skin:** Pruritus, rash. **GI:** Abdominal pain, *Clostridium difficile*-associated diarrhea, diarrhea, *nausea, vomiting.* **GU:** *Foamy urine.* **Other:** Generalized pruritus, rigors, infusion site erythema and pain.

DIAGNOSTIC TEST INTERFERENCE
Telavancin may cause increases in *PT, INR, aPTT,* and *ACT.* Telavancin interferes with **urine qualitative dipstick protein assays,** as well as quantitative **dye methods** (e.g., **pyrogallol red-molybdate**).

PHARMACOKINETICS Distribution: 93% bound to albumin. **Metabolism:** Metabolized to 3-hydroxylated metabolites. **Elimination:** Primarily via the urine. **Half-Life:** 8–9 h.

NURSING IMPLICATIONS

Black Box Warning

Telavancin has been associated with new-onset or worsening renal impairment and fetal toxicity.

Assessment & Drug Effects
▪ Monitor for red man syndrome (i.e., flushing of upper body, urticaria, pruritus, or rash) during infusion. If syndrome develops, slow infusion immediately. If reaction does not cease, stop infusion and notify prescriber.
▪ Withhold drug and notify prescriber for CrCl of 50 mL/min or less.
▪ Monitor for and report promptly the onset of watery diarrhea with or without fever, passage of tarry or bloody stools, pus, or mucus.
▪ Monitor ECG with concurrent use of drugs known to prolong the QT interval.
▪ Monitor lab tests: Baseline C&S. Baseline and frequent (q48–72h) renal function tests throughout therapy.

Patient & Family Education
▪ Report promptly appearance of rash or itching during drug infusion.

Common adverse effects in *italic*; life-threatening effects underlined; generic names in **bold**; classifications in SMALL CAPS; ♣ Canadian drug name; ☉ Prototype drug; ⚠ Alert

- Report promptly loose stools or diarrhea even after completion of drug.
- Women should use effective means of contraception while on this drug. Notify prescriber if pregnancy occurs during treatment.

TELBIVUDINE
(tel-bi'vu-deen)
Classification:
ANTIRETROVIRAL; NUCLEOSIDE REVERSE TRANSCRIPTASE INHIBITOR (NRTI)
Therapeutic: ANTIRETROVIRAL; NRTI
Prototype: Lamivudine

AVAILABILITY Tablet

ACTION & THERAPEUTIC EFFECT
Its metabolite inhibits HBV DNA polymerase (reverse transcriptase) by competing with the natural nucleoside substrate. Incorporation into HBV viral DNA causes DNA chain termination, resulting in inhibition of HBV replication. *Effectiveness is measured by reducing the viral load and preventing infection of new hepatocytes.*

USES Chronic hepatitis B infection.

CONTRAINDICATIONS Hypersensitivity to telbivudine; concurrent use with peginterferon alfa-2a; lactic acidosis; severe hepatomegaly with steatosis; peripheral neuropathy; lactation.

CAUTIOUS USE Moderate to severe renal impairment, hemodialysis; alcoholism; obesity in females; risk of hepatic disease; individuals with organ transplants; older adults; pregnancy (in hepatitis B-infected women (not coinfected by HIV),

treatment guidelines suggest antiviral therapy to reduce the risk of perinatal transmission of hepatitis B in HBsAg-positive pregnant women). Safe use in children younger than 16 y has not been established.

ROUTE & DOSAGE

Chronic Hepatitis B

Adults/Adolescents (16 y or older): **PO** 600 mg/day; duration is variable based on HBeAg status, duration of HBV suppression, presence of cirrhosis

Renal Impairment Dosage Adjustment

CrCl 30–49 mL/min: 600 mg q48h; *CrCl less than 30 mL/min (not requiring dialysis):* 600 mg q72h; *CrCl less than 5–10 mL/min (ESRD):* 600 mg q96h

ADMINISTRATION
Oral
- May be given without regard to food.
- Store at 25° C (77° F).

ADVERSE EFFECTS Respiratory: *Cough,* pharyngolaryngeal pain. **CNS:** Fatigue, headache, dizziness, insomnia. **Endocrine:** *Increased CPK levels,* increased serum ALT and AST. **Skin:** Rash. **GI:** *Abdominal pain, diarrhea.* **Musculoskeletal:** Arthralgia, back pain, myalgia. **Other:** Neutropenia.

INTERACTIONS Drug: Coadministration with drugs that alter renal function may alter plasma concentrations of telbivudine. Do not use with **pegylated interferon alfa-2a** or **interferon alfa-2b** because of increased risk of peripheral neuropathy.

T

PHARMACOKINETICS Peak: 1–4 h.
Distribution: Minimal protein binding; widely distributed in tissues.
Elimination: in urine. **Half-Life:** 40–49 h.

NURSING IMPLICATIONS

Black Box Warning

Telbivudine has been associated with lactic acidosis and severe hepatomegaly with steatosis.

Assessment & Drug Effects

- Monitor for and report S&S of lactic acidosis (e.g., anorexia, nausea, vomiting, bloating, abdominal pain, malaise, tachycardia or other arrhythmia, and difficulty in breathing).
- Monitor for signs and symptoms of peripheral neuropathy
- Monitor lab tests: Periodic LFTs during and for several months after discontinuation of telbivudine; periodic renal function tests, serum creatine kinase.

Patient & Family Education

- Notify your provider if you are pregnant or breastfeeding.
- Report any of the following to a health care provider: Loss of appetite, nausea and vomiting, abdominal pain, palpitations, or difficulty breathing.

TELITHROMYCIN

(tel-i-thro-my'sin)
Ketek
Classification: ANTIBIOTIC; KETOLIDE
Therapeutic: ANTIBIOTIC
Prototype: Erythromycin

AVAILABILITY Tablet

ACTION & *THERAPEUTIC EFFECT*

Results in inhibition of RNA-dependent protein synthesis of bacteria, thus resulting in cell death. Telithromycin concentrates in phagocytes where it works against intracellular respiratory pathogens. *Its broad spectrum of activity is effective against respiratory pathogens, including erythromycin- and penicillin-resistant pneumococci.*

USES Treatment of community-acquired pneumonia.

UNLABELED USES Sinusitis.

CONTRAINDICATIONS Macrolide antibiotic hypersensitivity; QT prolongation; ongoing proarrhythmic conditions such as hypokalemia, hypomagnesemia, significant bradycardia, myasthenia gravis; severe renal impairment or renal failure; viral infections.

CAUTIOUS USE History of GI disease; hepatic disease; history of hepatitis or jaundice; pregnancy (category C); lactation. Safety and efficacy in children not established.

ROUTE & DOSAGE

Community-Acquired Pneumonia

Adult: **PO** 800 mg daily for 7–10 days

Renal Impairment Dosage Adjustment

CrCl less than 30 mL/min: 600 mg daily (400 mg daily with concomitant hepatic impairment)

ADMINISTRATION

Oral

- May be administered with or without food.

Common adverse effects in *italic*; life-threatening effects <u>underlined</u>; generic names in **bold**; classifications in SMALL CAPS; ♦ Canadian drug name; ○ Prototype drug; ▲ Alert

- Do not administer concurrently with simvastatin, lovastatin, atorvastatin, Class 1A (e.g., quinidine, procainamide) or Class III (e.g., dofetilide) antiarrhythmic agents.
- Store at 15°–30° C (59°–86° F). Keep container tightly closed. Protect from light.

ADVERSE EFFECTS CV: Potential to cause QT_c prolongation. **CNS:** Headache, dizziness. **HEENT:** Blurred vision, diplopia, difficulty focusing. **Endocrine:** Elevated LFTs, liver failure. **GI:** *Diarrhea,* nausea, vomiting, loose stools, dysgeusia. **Musculoskeletal:** May exacerbate myasthenia gravis.

INTERACTIONS Drug: Pimozide or CLASS IA or CLASS III ANTIARRHYTHMICS may cause life-threatening arrhythmias; may increase concentrations of **atorvastatin, lovastatin, sim-vastatin,** BENZODIAZEPINES; **rifampin** decreases telithromycin levels; ERGOT DERIVATIVES (**ergotamine, dihydroergotamine**) may cause severe peripheral vasospasm; **theophylline** may exacerbate adverse GI effects. **Food: Grapefruit juice** (greater than 1 qt/day) may increase plasma concentrations and adverse effects.

PHARMACOKINETICS Absorption: 57% bioavailable. **Peak:** 1 h. **Metabolism:** 50% in liver (CYP3A4), 50% by CYP-independent mechanisms. **Elimination:** In urine and feces. **Half-Life:** 10 h.

NURSING IMPLICATIONS

Black Box Warning

Telithromycin has been associated with fatal respiratory failure in patients with myasthenia gravis and is contraindicated in these patients.

Assessment & Drug Effects
- Monitor ECG in patients at risk for QT_c interval prolongation (i.e., bradycardia).
- Withhold drug and notify prescriber for S&S of QT_c interval prolongation such as dizziness or fainting.
- Monitor for and report promptly S&S of liver dysfunction: Fatigue, anorexia, nausea, clay-colored stools, etc.
- Monitor lab tests: Baseline and periodic LFTs.

Patient & Family Education
- Stop taking drug and notify prescriber for episodes of dizziness or fainting; report signs of jaundice (yellow color of the skin and/or eyes), unexplained fatigue, loss of appetite, nausea, dark urine, or clay-colored stool.
- Exercise caution when engaging in potentially hazardous activities; visual disturbances (e.g., blurred vision, difficulty focusing, double vision) are potential side effects of this drug. If visual problems occur, avoid quick changes in viewing between close and distant objects.

TELMISARTAN
(tel-mi-sar'tan)
Micardis
Classification: ANGIOTENSIN II RECEPTOR ANTAGONIST; ANTIHYPERTENSIVE
Therapeutic: ANTIHYPERTENSIVE
Prototype: Losartan potassium

AVAILABILITY Tablet

ACTION & THERAPEUTIC EFFECT
Selectively blocks the binding of angiotensin II to the AT_1 receptors in many tissues (e.g., vascular smooth muscles, adrenal glands).

T

Blocks the vasoconstricting and aldosterone-secreting effects of angiotensin II, thus resulting in an antihypertensive effect. *Effectiveness is indicated by a reduction in BP.*

USES Treatment of hypertension, cardiovascular risk reduction.

CONTRAINDICATIONS Hypersensitivity to telmisartan; development of angioedema due to use of telmisartan; women of child bearing age; concurrent use of aliskiren in diabetics; pregnancy (category D); lactation.

CAUTIOUS USE CAD; hypertropic cardiomyopathy; CHF; oliguria; hypotension in volume depleted patients; renal artery stenosis; advanced renal impairment; biliary obstruction; liver dysfunction; renal impairment; older adults; pregnancy (category C first trimester, discontinue use as soon as detected). Safety and efficacy in children younger than 18 y not established.

ROUTE & DOSAGE

Hypertension
Adult: **PO** 20–40 mg daily, may increase to 80 mg/day

CV Risk Reduction
Adult: **PO** 80 mg/day

ADMINISTRATION
Oral
- Do not remove tablets from blister pack until immediately before administration.
- May be administered without regard to meals.
- Store at 15°–30° C (59°–86° F).

ADVERSE EFFECTS CV: Intermittent claudication. **Respiratory:** Upper respiratory tract infection. **CNS:** Dizziness, fatigue.

DIAGNOSTIC TEST INTERFERENCE
May lead to false-negative aldosterone/renin ratio

INTERACTIONS Drug: Telmisartan may increase **digoxin** or **lithium** levels. Increased risk of hyptension with ACE INHIBITORS or other ANTIHYPERTENSIVES.

PHARMACOKINETICS Absorption: Dose dependent, 42% of 40 mg dose is absorbed. **Peak:** 0.5–1 h. **Distribution:** Greater than 99% protein bound. **Metabolism:** Minimally metabolized. **Elimination:** Primarily in feces. **Half-Life:** 24 h.

NURSING IMPLICATIONS

Black Box Warning

Telmisartan has been associated with fetal toxicity and death.

Assessment & Drug Effects
- Monitor BP carefully after initial dose; and periodically thereafter. Monitor more frequently with preexisting biliary obstructive disorders or hepatic insufficiency.
- Monitor dialysis patients closely for orthostatic hypotension.
- Monitor concomitant digoxin levels throughout therapy.
- Monitor lab tests: Periodic serum electrolytes, creatinine clearance, and BUN.

Patient & Family Education
- Report pregnancy to prescriber immediately.
- Allow between 2 and 4 wk for maximum therapeutic response.

Common adverse effects in *italic*; life-threatening effects <u>underlined</u>; generic names in **bold**; classifications in SMALL CAPS; ♣ Canadian drug name; ◐ Prototype drug; ⚠ Alert

TEMAZEPAM
(te-maz'e-pam)
Restoril
Classification: BENZODIAZEPINE; SEDATIVE-HYPNOTIC
Therapeutic: SEDATIVE
Prototype: Triazolam
Controlled Substance: Schedule IV

AVAILABILITY Capsule

ACTION & *THERAPEUTIC EFFECT*
Beleived to potentiate gamma-aminobutyric acid (GABA) neuronal inhibition. The sedative and anticonvulsant actions involve GABA receptors located in the limbic, neocortical, and mesencephalic reticular systems. *Reduces night awakenings and early morning awakenings; increases total sleep times, absence of rebound effects*.

USES To relieve insomnia.

CONTRAINDICATIONS Hypersensitivity reaction including angioedema; ethanol intoxication; drug abuse; narrow-angle glaucoma; psychoses; women of child-bearing age; abrupt discontinuation of temazepam; pregnancy (category X); lactation.

CAUTIOUS USE Severely depressed patient or one with suicidal thinking; history of drug abuse or dependence, acute intoxication; alcoholism; chronic pulmonary insufficiency; COPD; liver or kidney dysfunction; sleep apnea; debilitated individuals; older adults. Safe use in children younger than 18 y not established.

ROUTE & DOSAGE

Insomnia
Adult: **PO** 15–30 mg at bedtime
Geriatric: **PO** 7.5 mg at bedtime

ADMINISTRATION
Oral
▪ Give 20–30 min before bedtime.
▪ Store at 15°–30° C (59°–86° F) in tight container unless otherwise specified by manufacturer.

ADVERSE EFFECTS CV: Palpitations, *hypotension*. CNS: *Drowsiness,* dizziness, lethargy, confusion, headache, euphoria, relaxed feeling, weakness. GI: Anorexia, diarrhea. Other: Physiological and psychological dependence.

INTERACTIONS Drug: **Alcohol,** CNS DEPRESSANTS, ANTICONVULSANTS potentiate CNS depression; **cimetidine** increases temazepam plasma levels, thus increasing its toxicity; may decrease antiparkinsonism effects of **levodopa;** may increase **phenytoin** levels; smoking decreases sedative effects. Do not use with **sodium oxybate.** Herbal: **Kava, valerian** may potentiate sedation.

PHARMACOKINETICS Absorption: Readily from GI tract; 98% protein bound. Onset: 30–50 min. Peak: 2–3 h. Duration: 10–12 h. Distribution: Crosses placenta; distributed into breast milk. Metabolism: In liver to oxazepam. Elimination: In urine. Half-Life: 8–24 h.

NURSING IMPLICATIONS
Assessment & Drug Effects
▪ Be alert to signs of paradoxical reaction (excitement,

hyperactivity, and disorientation) in older adults. Psychoactive drugs are the most frequent cause of acute confusion in this age group.

- CNS adverse effects are more apt to occur in the patient with hypo-albuminemia, liver disease, and in older adults. Report promptly incidence of bradycardia, drowsi-ness, dizziness, clumsiness, lack of coordination. Supervise ambu-lation, especially at night.
- Be alert to S&S of overdose: Weakness, bradycardia, somno-lence, confusion, slurred speech, ataxia, coma with reduced or absent reflexes, hypertension, and respiratory depression.

Patient & Family Education

- Be aware that improvement in sleep will not occur until after 2–3 doses of drug.
- Notify prescriber if dreams or nightmares interfere with rest. An alternate drug or reduced dose may be prescribed.
- Be aware that difficulty getting to sleep may continue. Drug effect is evidenced by the increased amount of rest once asleep.
- Consult prescriber if insomnia continues in spite of medication.
- Do not smoke after medication is taken.
- Do not use OTC drugs (especially for insomnia) without advice of prescriber.
- Consult prescriber before discon-tinuing drug especially after long-term use. Gradual reduction of dose may be necessary to avoid withdrawal symptoms.
- Avoid use of alcohol and other CNS depressants.
- Do not drive or engage in other potentially hazardous activities until response to drug is known. This drug may depress psycho-motor skills and cause sedation.

TEMOZOLOMIDE

(tem-o-zol'o-mide)

Temodar

Classification: ANTINEOPLASTIC; IMIDAZOTETRAZINE DERIVATIVE

Therapeutic: ANTINEOPLASTIC

AVAILABILITY Capsule; solution for injection

ACTION & THERAPEUTIC EFFECT

Cytotoxic agent with alkylating properties that are cell cycle non-specific. Interferes with purine (e.g., guanine) metabolism and thus pro-tein synthesis in rapidly proliferat-ing cells. *Effectiveness is indicated by objective evidence of tumor regression.*

USES Adult patients with refractory anaplastic astrocytoma, glioblas-toma multiforme with radiotherapy.

UNLABELED USES Malignant melanoma.

CONTRAINDICATIONS Hyper-sensitivity to temozolomide, or dacarbazine; severe bone marrow suppression; pregnancy (category D); lactation.

CAUTIOUS USE Bacterial or viral infection; severe hepatic or renal impairment; myelosuppression; prior radiotherapy or chemother-apy; older adults; children younger than 3 y.

ROUTE & DOSAGE

Astrocytoma

Adult: **PO/IV** 150 mg/m² daily days 1–5/28-day treatment cycle (may increase to 200 mg/m²/day); subsequent doses are based

Common adverse effects in *italic*; life-threatening effects underlined; generic names in **bold**; classifications in SMALL CAPS; ♣ Canadian drug name; ◐ Prototype drug; ⚠ Alert

1622

on absolute neutrophil count on day 21 or at least 48 h before next scheduled cycle (see prescribing information for dosage adjustments based on neutrophil count)

Glioblastoma Multiforme

Adult: **PO** 75 mg/m² daily for 42 days with focal radiotherapy; after 4 wk, maintenance phase of 150–200 mg/m² on days 1–5 of 28-day cycle

ADMINISTRATION

Oral

- Give consistently with regard to food.
- Do not administer unless absolute neutrophil count greater than 1500/microliter and platelet count greater than 100,000/microliter.
- Do not open capsules. Avoid inhalation or contact with skin or mucous membranes, if accidentally opened/damaged.
- Store at room temperature, 15°–30° C (59°–86° F).

Intravenous

PREPARE: Infusion: Bring the 100 mg vial to room temperature, then reconstitute with 41 mL sterile water to yield 2.5 mg/mL. Gently swirl to dissolve but do not shake, and do not further dilute. Must use within 14 h of reconstitution, including infusion time. **ADMINISTER: Infusion:** Infuse over 90 min. Flush line before and after with NS. Note: May be administered in the same line with NS but not with any other IV solution.

ADVERSE EFFECTS CV: *Peripheral edema.* **Respiratory:** Upper respiratory tract infection, pharyngitis, sinusitis, cough. **CNS:** *Convulsions, hemiparesis, dizziness, abnormal coordination, amnesia, insomnia,* paresthesia, somnolence, paresis, ataxia, dysphasia, abnormal gait, confusion, anxiety, depression. **HEENT:** Diplopia, abnormal vision. **Endocrine:** Adrenal hypercorticism. **Skin:** Rash, pruritus. **GI:** *Nausea, vomiting, constipation, diarrhea,* abdominal pain, anorexia. **GU:** Urinary incontinence. **Hematologic:** Anemia, <u>neutropenia, thrombocytopenia</u>, <u>leukopenia</u>, lymphopenia. **Other:** *Headache, fatigue, asthenia, fever,* back pain, myalgia, weight gain; viral infection.

INTERACTIONS Drug: **Valproic acid** may decrease **temozolomide** levels.

PHARMACOKINETICS Absorption: Rapidly. **Peak:** 1 h. **Metabolism:** Spontaneously metabolized to active metabolite MTIC. **Elimination:** Primarily in urine. **Half-Life:** 1.8 h.

NURSING IMPLICATIONS

Assessment & Drug Effects

- Monitor for S&S of toxicity: Infection, bleeding episodes, jaundice, rash, CNS disturbances.
- Monitor lab tests: Periodic CBC with differential and platelet count; periodic LFTs and routine serum chemistry, including serum calcium.

Patient & Family Education

- Take consistently with respect to meals.
- Report to prescriber signs of infection, bleeding, discoloration of skin or skin rash, dizziness, lack of balance, or other bothersome side effects promptly.
- Exercise caution with hazardous activities until response to drug is known.
- Use effective methods of contraception; avoid pregnancy.

T

TEMSIROLIMUS
(tem-si-ro-li′mus)
Torisel
Classification: BIOLOGIC
RESPONSE MODIFIER;
ANTINEO-PLASTIC; KINASE
INHIBITOR; mTOR INHIBITOR
Therapeutic: ANTINEOPLASTIC
Prototype: Erlotinib

AVAILABILITY Injectable

ACTION & *THERAPEUTIC EFFECT*
Inhibits an intracellular protein that
controls cell division in renal carcinoma and other tumor cells. *Results
in arrest of growth in tumor cells.*

USES Treatment of advanced renal
cell carcinoma.

UNLABELED USES Astrocytoma,
mantle cell lymphoma (MCL).

CONTRAINDICATIONS Hyper-
sensitivity reaction including anaphylaxis; live vaccines; intracranial
bleeding; bilirubin greater than
1.5 X ULN; interstitial lung disease;
bowel perforation; acute renal
failure; pregnancy (category D);
lactation.

CAUTIOUS USE Hypersensitivity
to temsirolimus, sirolimus, or poly-
sorbate 80, renal impairment; DM;
hyperlipemia; respiratory disorders;
perioperative period due to potential for abnormal wound healing;
CNS tumors (primary or by metastasis); hepatic impairment; older
adults; children.

ROUTE & DOSAGE

Renal Cell Carcinoma
Adult: **IV** 25 mg qwk

Dosage Adjustment
*Regimen with a strong CYP3A4
inhibitor:* 12.5 mg/wk
*Regimen with a strong CYP3A4
inducer:* 50 mg based on
tolerability

Hepatic Impairment Adjustment
Dose reduction req1uired

ADMINISTRATION
Intravenous

Patients should receive prophylactic IV diphenhydramine
25–50 mg (or similar antihistamine)
30 min before each dose.

PREPARE: **IV Infusion:** Inject 1.8 mL
of supplied diluent into the
25 mg/mL vial to yield 10 mg/mL.
▪ Withdraw the required dose
and inject rapidly into a 250 mL
DEHP-free container of NS.
Invert to mix.

ADMINISTER: **IV Infusion:** Use
DEHP-free infusion line with a
5 micron or less in-line filter. ▪
Infuse over 30–60 min. ▪ Complete infusion within 6 h of
preparation.

INCOMPATIBILITIES: **Solution/
additive:** Do not add other
drugs or agents to temsirolimus
IV solutions.

▪ Store at 2°–8° C (36°–46° F). Protect from light. The 10 mg/mL drug
solution is stable for up to 24 h at
15°–30° C (59°–86° F).

ADVERSE EFFECTS CV: Hyper-
tension, thrombophlebitis, venous
thromboembolism. **Respiratory:**
Cough, dyspnea, epistaxis, interstitial lung disease, pharyngitis, pneumonia, rhinitis, upper respiratory
tract infection. **CNS:** Depression,
dysgeusia, headache, insomnia.

HEENT: Conjunctivitis. **Endocrine:** *Elevated alkaline phosphatase, elevated AST, elevated serum creatinine,* hypokalemia, *hypophosphatemia,* hyperbilirubinemia, hypercholesterolemia, *hyperglycemia, hypertriglyceridemia,* weight loss. **Skin:** Acne, dry skin, nail disorder, pruritus, *rash.* **GI:** Abdominal pain, *anorexia,* constipation, diarrhea, fatal bowel perforation, *mucositis, nausea,* vomiting. **GU:** Urinary tract infection. **Musculoskeletal:** Arthralgia, back pain, myalgia. **Hematologic:** Decrease hemoglobin, *leukocytopenia, lymphopenia,* neutropenia, thrombocytopenia. **Other:** Allergic/hypersensitivity reactions, *asthenia,* chest pain, chills, *edema,* impaired wound healing, infections, pain, pyrexia.

INTERACTIONS Drug: AZOLE ANTIFUNGAL AGENTS **(fluconazole, itraconazole, ketoconazole, posaconazole, voriconazole), cyclosporine,** INHIBITORS OF CYP3A4 (HIV PROTEASE INHIBITORS, **clarithromycin, diltiazem**), **mycophenolate mofetil,** and **sunitinib** increase the plasma levels of **temsirolimus.** INDUCERS OF CYP3A4 (**dexamethasone, rifampin, rifabutin, phenytoin**) decrease the plasma level of temsirolimus. **Food:** Grapefruit and grapefruit juice increase the plasma level of temsirolimus. **Herbal:** St. John's wort decreases the plasma level of temsirolimus.

PHARMACOKINETICS Peak: 0.5–2 h. **Metabolism:** In liver. **Elimination:** Primarily in stool. **Half-Life:** 17.3 h.

NURSING IMPLICATIONS

Assessment & Drug Effects
- Withhold drug and notify prescriber for absolute neutrophil count less than 1000/mm^3 or platelet count less than 75,000/mm^3.
- Monitor for infusion-related reactions during and for at least 1 h after completion of infusion.
- Slow or stop infusion for infusion-related reactions. If infusion is restarted after 30–60 min of observation, slow rate to up to 60 min and continue observation.
- Monitor respiratory status and report promptly dyspnea, cough, S&S of hypoxia, fever.
- Monitor diabetics for loss of glycemic control.
- Monitor lab tests: Baseline and periodic CBC with differential and platelet count, lipid profile, LFTs, alkaline phosphatase, renal function tests, serum electrolytes, plasma glucose, and ABGs.

Patient & Family Education
- Avoid live vaccines and close contact with those who have received live vaccines.
- Use effective contraceptive measures to prevent pregnancy.
- Men with partners of childbearing age should use reliable contraception throughout treatment and for 3 mo after the last dose of temsirolimus.
- Report promptly any of the following: S&S of infection, difficulty breathing, abdominal pain, blood in stools, abnormal wound healing, S&S of hypersensitivity (see Appendix F).

T

TENAPANOR
(ten-A-pa-nor)
Ibsrela
Classifications: SODIUM/ HYDROGEN EXCHANGER 3 (NHE3) INHIBITOR
Therapeutic: SODIUM/HYDROGEN EXCHANGER 3 (NHE3) INHIBITOR

AVAILABILITY Oral tablet

ACTION & *THERAPEUTIC EFFECT*
A sodium/hydrogen exchange inhibitor which acts locally to reduce sodium absorption from the small intestine and colon. *Reduced sodium absorption results in increased intestinal lumen water secretion, accelerated intestinal transit time, and softening of stool consistency.*

USES Treatment of irritable bowel syndrome with constipation (IBS-C) in adults.

CONTRAINDICATIONS Patients < 6 years of age; known or suspected mechanical GI obstruction.

CAUTIOUS USE Use with caution if patient experiencing diarrhea or has existing renal impairment, is pregnant, or lactating.

ROUTE & DOSAGE

Irritable Bowel Syndrome with constipation (IBS-C)
Adult: **PO** 50 mg twice a day

ADMINISTRATION
Oral
- Administer immediately prior to breakfast or the first meal of the day and immediately before dinner.
- Store at 20° to 25° C (68° to 77° F). Store in original container to protect from moisture.

ADVERSE EFFECTS GI: Diarrhea, flatulence, abdominal distension.

INTERACTIONS No reported drug interactions

PHARMACOKINETICS Distribution: 99% protein bound. **Metabolism:** In the liver primarily by CYP3A4/5. **Elimination:** 65% in feces (unchanged drug).

NURSING IMPLICATIONS
Assessment & Drug Effects
- Monitor frequency of bowel movements and for signs and symptoms of dehydration in patients with diarrhea.
- Monitor lab tests: Serum potassium in patients with renal impairment.

Patient & Family Education
- Notify your doctor or get medical help right away if you have any of the following signs or symptoms of allergic reaction such as rash, hives, itching; red, swollen, blistered, or peeling skin with or without fever; wheezing; tightness in the chest or throat; trouble breathing, swallowing, or talking; unusual hoarseness; or swelling of the mouth, face, lips, tongue, or throat; or any dizziness or passing out.

TENECTEPLASE RECOMBINANT
(ten-ect′e-plase)
TNKase
Classification: THROMBOLYTIC ENZYME, TISSUE PLASMINOGEN ACTIVATOR (t-PA)
Therapeutic: THROMBOLYTIC ENZYME
Prototype: Alteplase

AVAILABILITY Vial

ACTION & *THERAPEUTIC EFFECT*
Activates plasminogen, a substance created by endothelial cells in

Common adverse effects in *italic*; life-threatening effects <u>underlined</u>; generic names in **bold;** classifications in SMALL CAPS; ✦ Canadian drug name; ◯ Prototype drug; ⚠ Alert

1626

response to arterial wall injury that contributes to clot formation. Plasminogen is converted to plasmin which breaks down the fibrin mesh that binds the clot together, thus dissolving the clot. *Effective in producing thrombolysis of a clot involved in a myocardial infarction.*

USES Reduction of mortality associated with acute myocardial infarction (AMI).

CONTRAINDICATIONS Active internal bleeding; history of CVA; intracranial or intraspinal surgery with 2 mo; intracranial neoplasm; arteriovenous malformation, or aneurysm; known bleeding diathesis; brain tumor; increased intracranial pressure; coagulopathy; head trauma; stroke; surgery; severe uncontrolled hypertension; lactation.

CAUTIOUS USE Recent major surgery, previous puncture of compressible vessels, CVA, recent GI or GU bleeding, recent trauma; hypertension, mitral valve stenosis, acute pericarditis, bacterial endocarditis; severe liver or kidney disease; hemorrhagic ophthalmic conditions; septic thrombophlebitis or occluded, infected AV cannula; advanced age; pregnancy (category C). Safety and efficacy in children not established.

ROUTE & DOSAGE

Acute Myocardial Infarction

Adult (weight less than 60 kg):
IV Infuse dose over 5 sec 30 mg; *weight 60–70 kg:* 35 mg; *weight 70–80 kg:* 40 mg; *weight 80–90 kg:* 45 mg; *weight greater than 90 kg:* 50 mg

ADMINISTRATION
Intravenous

PREPARE: **Direct:** Read and follow instructions supplied with TwinPak™ Dual Cannula Device. ▪ Withdraw 10 mL of sterile water for injection from the supplied vial; inject entire contents into the TNKase vial directing the diluent stream into the powder. ▪ Gently swirl until dissolved but do not shake. The resulting solution contains 5 mg/mL. ▪ Withdraw the appropriate dose and discard any unused solution. ▪ Follow directions supplied with TwinPak™ for proper handling of syringe.
ADMINISTER: **Direct:** Dextrose-containing IV line **must be** flushed before and after bolus with NS. ▪ Give as a single bolus dose over 5 sec. ▪ The total dose given should not exceed 50 mg.
INCOMPATIBILITIES: **Solution/additive: Dextrose** solutions.

▪ Store unopened TwinPak™ at or below 30° C (86° F) or under refrigeration at 2°–8° C (36°–46° F).

ADVERSE EFFECTS Hematologic: Major bleeding, *hematoma,* GI bleed, bleeding at puncture site, hematuria, pharyngeal, epistaxis.

DIAGNOSTIC TEST INTERFERENCE Unreliable results for *coagulation test I* and measures of *fibrinolytic activity.*

PHARMACOKINETICS Metabolism: In liver. **Half-Life:** 90–130 min.

NURSING IMPLICATIONS
Assessment & Drug Effects
▪ Avoid IM injections and unnecessary handling or invasive

procedures for the first few hours after treatment.

- Monitor for S&S of bleeding. Should bleeding occur, withhold concomitant heparin and antiplatelet therapy; notify prescriber.
- Monitor cardiovascular and neurologic status closely. Persons at increased risk for life-threatening cardiac events include those with: A high potential for bleeding, recent surgery, severe hypertension, mitral stenosis and atrial fibrillation, anticoagulant therapy, and advanced age.
- Coagulation parameters may not predict bleeding episodes.

Patient & Family Education

- Notify prescriber of the following immediately: A sudden, severe headache; any sign of bleeding; signs or symptoms of hypersensitivity (see Appendix F).
- Stay as still as possible and do not attempt to get out of bed until directed to do so.

TENOFOVIR DISOPROXIL FUMARATE

(ten-o-fo'vir dy-so-prox'il fum'a-rate)

Viread

Classification: ANTIRETROVIRAL; NUCLEOTIDE REVERSE TRANSCRIPTASE INHIBITOR (NRTI)

Therapeutic: ANTIRETROVIRAL; NRTI

Prototype: Lamivudine

AVAILABILITY Tablet; oral powder

ACTION & *THERAPEUTIC EFFECT*
A potent inhibitor of retroviruses, including HIV-1. The active form of tenofovir persists in HIV-infected cells for prolonged periods, thus, it results in sustained inhibition of HIV replication. *It reduces the viral load (plasma HIV-RNA), and CD4 counts.*

USES In combination with other antiretrovirals for the treatment of HIV; chronic hepatitis B infection.

CONTRAINDICATIONS Hypersensitivity to tenofovir.

CAUTIOUS USE Hepatic dysfunction, alcoholism; renal impairment; obesity; low body weight; pathologic bone fractures; lactic acidosis, severe hepatomegaly, concurrent administration of nephrotoxic agents, acute renal failure; immune reconstitution syndrome; lactation; older adults; pregnancy (no increased risk of overall birth defects has been observed following first trimester exposure); children.

ROUTE & DOSAGE

HIV Infection

Adult: **PO** 300 mg once daily with meal

Adolescent/ Child: **PO** See package insert for weight based dose (approx. 8 mg/kg daily)

Chronic Hepatitis B

Adult/Child (12 y or older, weight 35 kg): **PO** 300 mg daily duration is variable based on HBeAg status, duration of HBV suppression, presence of cirrhosis

Child (2 y or older, weight at least 10 kg): **PO** 8 mg/kg once daily (max dose 300 mg/day)

Renal Impairment Dosage Adjustment

CrCl 30–49 mL/min: Dose q48h; 10–29 mL/min: Dose q72–96 hours

Hemodialysis Dosage Adjustment

Dose weekly or after 12 h of dialysis

Common adverse effects in *italic*; life-threatening effects <u>underlined</u>; generic names in **bold**; classifications in SMALL CAPS; ♣ Canadian drug name; ⊙ Prototype drug; ⚠ Alert

ADMINISTRATION

Oral

- Give at the same time each day with a meal.
- Measure powder form only with supplied dosing scoop. One level scoop contains 40 mg of tenofovir. Mix powder in 2–4 oz of soft food such as applesauce or yogurt (do not mix with liquid) and swallow immediately after mixing to avoid bitter taste.
- Store at room temperature; excursions to 25° C (77° F) are permitted.

ADVERSE EFFECTS **Respiratory:**
Sinusitis, upper respiratory tract infection, nasopharyngitis, pneumonia. **CNS:** Headache, insomnia, pain, dizziness, depression, fatigue, anxiety, peripheral neuropathy. **Endocrine:** Increased *creatine kinase*, AST, ALT, serum amylase, cholesterol, triglycerides, serum glucose. **Skin:** Skin rash, pruritis. **GI:** *Nausea,* vomiting, diarrhea, flatulence, abdominal pain, anorexia. **GU:** Increased serum creatinine, renal failure. **Hematologic:** Neutropenia. **Musculoskeletal:** Decreased bone mineral density, increased CPK, weakness, back pain, arthralgia. **Other:** Fever.

INTERACTIONS **Drug:** May increase **didanosine** toxicity; **acyclovir, amphotericin B, cidofovir, foscarnet, ganciclovir, probenecid, valacyclovir, valganciclovir,** NSAIDs may increase tenofovir toxicity by decreasing its renal elimination. Do not use with **adefovir, diclofenac, ledipasvir. Food:** Food increases absorption.

PHARMACOKINETICS **Absorption:** Bioavailability 25% fasting, 40% with high fat meal. **Peak:** 1 h. **Distribution:** Less than 7% protein bound. **Metabolism:** Not metabolized by CYP450 enzyme system. **Elimination:** Renally eliminated. **Half-Life:** 11–14 h.

NURSING IMPLICATIONS

Black Box Warning

Tenofovir has been associated with lactic acidosis and severe, sometimes fatal, hepatomegaly with steatosis, and with posttreatment exacerbation of hepatitis.

Assessment & Drug Effects

- Withhold drug and notify prescriber if patient develops clinical or lab findings suggestive of lactic acidosis or pronounced hepatotoxicity (e.g., hepatomegaly and steatosis even in the absence of marked transaminase elevations).
- Monitor for S&S of bone abnormalities (e.g., bone pain, stress fractures).
- Monitor closely patients receiving other nephrotoxic agents for changes in serum creatinine and phosphorus. Withhold drug and notify prescriber for creatinine clearance less than 60 mL/min.
- Monitor lab tests: Baseline and periodic CBC with differential, reticulocyte count, creatine kinase, CD4 count, HIV RNA plasma levels, serum phosphorus, renal function tests, LFTs, urine protein, bone density, and HBV (prior to first treatment).

Patient & Family Education

- Take this drug exactly as prescribed. Do not miss any doses. If you miss a dose, take it as soon as possible and then take your next dose at its regular time. If it is almost time for your next dose, do not take the missed dose. Wait and take the next dose at the regular time. Do not double the next dose.

- Report any of the following to prescriber: Unexplained anorexia, nausea, vomiting, abdominal pain, fatigue, dark urine.

TERAZOSIN

(ter-ay'zoe-sin)

Classification: ALPHA-ADRENERGIC RECEPTOR ANTAGONIST; ANTIHYPERTENSIVE
Therapeutic: ANTIHYPERTENSIVE; BPH AGENT
Prototype: Prazosin

AVAILABILITY Capsule

ACTION & *THERAPEUTIC EFFECT*

Selectively blocks alpha$_1$-adrenergic receptors in vascular smooth muscle in many tissues, including the bladder neck and the prostate. Promotes vasodilation, thus producing relaxation that leads to reduction of peripheral vascular resistance and lowered BP as well as increased urine flow. *Effectiveness is measured in lowering of blood pressure values and controlling the symptoms of benign prostate hypertrophy.*

USES Management of hypertension; to treat symptoms of benign prostatic hypertrophy (BPH).

CONTRAINDICATIONS Hypersensitivity to terazosin.

CAUTIOUS USE Prostate cancer; history of hypotensive episodes; angina; renal impairment, renal disease, renal failure; older adults; pregnancy (adverse effects have been noted in animal reproduction studies); lactation. Safe use in children is not established.

ROUTE & DOSAGE

Hypertension

Adult: **PO** Start with 1 mg daily, titrate based on response up to 20 mg daily (single or divided doses)

Benign Prostatic Hypertrophy

Adult: **PO** Start with 1 mg at bedtime, then titrate up as needed, most patients require 10 mg/day (max: 20 mg/day)

ADMINISTRATION

Oral

- Give initial dose at bedtime to reduce the potential for severe hypotensive effect. Administer at the same time each day.
- Store at 20°–25° C (68°–77° F) in tightly closed container away from heat and strong light. Do not freeze.

ADVERSE EFFECTS CV: Orthostatic hypotension, peripheral edema. **Respiratory:** *Nasal congestion.* **CNS:** Myasthenia, *dizziness,* drowsiness. **GI:** *Nausea.*

INTERACTIONS Drug: Antihypertensive effects may be attenuated by NSAIDS. **Sildenafil, vardenafil, tadalafil, obintuzumab,** and ANTIHYPERTENSIVES may enhance hypotensive effects. Avoid use of **alfuzosin** or **tranylcypromine** due to increased hypotension risk.

PHARMACOKINETICS Absorption: Readily from GI tract (90–94% protein bound). **Peak:** 1–2 h. **Metabolism:** In liver. **Elimination:** 60% in feces, 40% in urine. **Half-Life:** 9–12 h.

NURSING IMPLICATIONS

Assessment & Drug Effects

- Be alert for possible first-dose phenomenon (precipitous decline in BP with consciousness disturbance). This is rare; occurs within 90–120 min of initial dose.
- Monitor BP at end of dosing interval (just before next dose) to determine level of antihypertensive control.
- Be aware that drug-induced decrease in BP appears to be more position dependent (i.e., greater in the erect position) during the first few hours after dosing than at end of 24 h.
- A greatly diminished hypotensive response at end of 24 h indicates need for change in dosage (increased dose or twice daily regimen). Report to prescriber.

Patient & Family Education

- Avoid situations that would result in injury should syncope (loss of consciousness) occur after first dose. If faintness develops, lie down promptly.
- Make position changes slowly (i.e., change in direction or from recumbent to upright posture). Dangle legs and move ankles a minute or so before standing when arising. Orthostatic hypotension (greatest shortly after dosing) can pose a problem with ambulation.
- Do not drive or engage in potentially hazardous activities for at least 12 h after first dose, after dosage increase, or when treatment is resumed after interruption of therapy.
- Do not alter established drug regimen. Consult prescriber if drug is omitted for several days. Drug will be started with the initial dosing regimen.
- Keep scheduled appointments for assessment of BP control and other clinically significant tests.

TERBINAFINE HYDROCHLORIDE ○

(ter-bin′a-feen)

Lamisil, Lamisil DermaGel

Classification: ANTIBIOTIC; ANTIFUNGAL

Therapeutic: ANTIFUNGAL

AVAILABILITY Tablet; cream; gel

ACTION & THERAPEUTIC EFFECT
Synthetic antifungal agent that inhibits sterol biosynthesis in fungi and ultimately causes fungal cell death. *Effective as an antifungal.*

USES Topical treatment of superficial mycoses such as interdigital tinea pedis, tinea cruris, and tinea corporis; oral treatment of onychomycosis due to tinea unguium.

CONTRAINDICATIONS Hypersensitivity to terbinafine; alcoholism; hepatic disease; hepatitis; jaundice; renal impairment; renal failure; lactation.

CAUTIOUS USE History of depression; pregnancy (category B). Safety and efficacy in children younger than 12 y not established.

ROUTE & DOSAGE

Tinea Pedis, Tinea Cruris, or Tinea Corporis

Adult: **Topical** Apply daily or bid to affected and immediately surrounding areas until clinical signs and symptoms are significantly improved (1–7 wk)

Onychomycosis

Adult: **PO** 250 mg daily × 6 wk for fingernails or × 12 wk for toenails

ADMINISTRATION

Oral
- Give tablets without regard to meals.
- Granules should be given with food. Sprinkle on a spoonful of soft, nonacidic food; do not mix granules with applesauce or other fruit-based foods. Entire spoonful should be swallowed without chewing.

Topical
- Apply externally. Avoid application to mucous membranes and avoid contact with eyes.
- Do not use occlusive dressings unless specifically directed to do so by prescriber.
- Store at 15°–30° C (59°–86° F).

ADVERSE EFFECTS CNS: *Headache.* **HEENT:** Taste disturbances, vision impairment. **Skin:** Pruritus, local burning, dryness, rash, vesiculation, redness, contact dermatitis at application site. **GI:** Diarrhea, dyspepsia, abdominal pain, liver test abnormalities, liver failure (rare). **Hematologic:** Neutropenia (rare).

INTERACTIONS Drug: May increase **theophylline** levels; may decrease **cyclosporine** levels; **rifampin** may decrease **terbinafine** levels.

PHARMACOKINETICS Absorption: 70% PO; approximately 3.5% of topical dose is absorbed systemically. **Elimination:** In urine. **Half-Life:** 36 h.

NURSING IMPLICATIONS

Assessment & Drug Effects
- Monitor for and report increased skin irritation.

Patient & Family Education
- Learn correct technique for application of cream.
- Notify prescriber if drug causes increased skin irritation or sensitivity.
- Be aware that medication **must be** used for full treatment time to be effective.

TERBUTALINE SULFATE
(ter-byoo′te-leen)

Classification: BETA-ADRENERGIC RECEPTOR AGONIST; BRONCHODILATOR
Therapeutic: RESPIRATORY SMOOTH MUSCLE RELAXANT; BRONCHODILATOR
Prototype: Albuterol

AVAILABILITY Tablet; solution for injection

ACTION & *THERAPEUTIC EFFECT*
Synthetic adrenergic stimulant with selective beta$_2$-receptor activity in bronchial smooth muscles, inhibits histamine release from mast cells, and increases ciliary motility. *Relieves bronchospasm in chronic obstructive pulmonary disease (COPD) and significantly increases vital capacity. Increases uterine relaxation (thereby preventing or abolishing high intrauterine pressure).*

USES Asthma, prevention and reversal of bronchospasm.

UNLABELED USES To delay delivery in preterm labor.

Common adverse effects in *italic;* life-threatening effects underlined; generic names in **bold;** classifications in SMALL CAPS; ♦ Canadian drug name; ○ Prototype drug; △ Alert

CONTRAINDICATIONS Known hypersensitivity to sympathomimetic amines; severe hypertension and coronary artery disease; tachycardia with digitalis intoxication; within 14 days of MAO inhibitor therapy; angle-closure glaucoma; acute or maintenance tocolysis; prolonged use during preterm labor.

CAUTIOUS USE Angina, stroke, hypertension; DM; thyrotoxicosis; history of seizure disorders; MAOI therapy; cardiac arrhythmias; QT prolongation; thyroid disease; older adults; kidney and liver dysfunction; pregnancy (category C). Use caution in second and third trimester (may inhibit uterine contractions and labor). Children younger than 12 y.

ROUTE & DOSAGE

Bronchodilator

Adult/Adolescent (15 y or older):
PO 5 mg tid at 6 h intervals (max: 15 mg/day); **Subcutaneous** 0.25 mg q20min for 3 doses
Adolescent (12–15 y): **PO** 2.5 mg tid at 6 h intervals (max: 7.5 mg/day); **Subcutaneous** 0.25 mg q15–30min up to 0.5 mg in 4 h

ADMINISTRATION

Oral

- Give with fluid of patient's choice; tablets may be crushed.
- Be certain about recommended doses: PO preparation, 2.5 mg; subcutaneous, 0.25 mg. A decimal point error can be fatal.
- Give with food if GI symptoms occur.
- Administer around-the-clock to promote less variation in peak and trough serum levels.

Subcutaneous

- Give subcutaneous injection into lateral deltoid area.
- Store all forms at 15°–30° C (59°–86° F); protect from light. Do not freeze.

ADVERSE EFFECTS CNS: Nervousness, restlessness. **Endocrine:** Decreased serum potassium, increased serum glucose. **Musculoskeletal:** Tremor.

DIAGNOSTIC TEST INTERFERENCE Terbutaline may increase *blood glucose* and free *fatty acids.*

INTERACTIONS Drug: Epinephrine, other SYMPATHOMIMETIC BRONCHODILATORS may add to effects; MAO INHIBITORS, TRICYCLIC ANTIDEPRESSANTS potentiate action on vascular system; effects of both BETA-ADRENERGIC BLOCKERS and terbutaline antagonized.

PHARMACOKINETICS Absorption: 33–50% from GI tract. **Onset:** 30 min PO; less than 15 min subcutaneous; 5–30 min inhaled. **Peak:** 2–3 h PO; 30–60 min subcutaneous; 1–2 h inhaled. **Duration:** 4–8 h PO; 1.5–4 h subcutaneous; 3–4 h inhaled. **Distribution:** Into breast milk. **Metabolism:** In liver. **Elimination:** Primarily in urine, 3% in feces. **Half-Life:** 3–4 h.

NURSING IMPLICATIONS

Black Box Warning

Terbutaline has been associated with serious, sometimes fatal, adverse reactions in pregnant women including cardiac arrhythmias, myocardial ischemia, hypokalemia, and pulmonary edema.

Assessment & Drug Effects

- Assess vital signs: Baseline pulse and BP and before each dose. If significantly altered from baseline level, consult prescriber. Cardiovascular adverse effects are more apt to occur when drug is given by subcutaneous route or it is used by a patient with cardiac arrhythmia.
- Most adverse effects are transient, however, rapid heart rate may persist for a relatively long time.
- Aerosolized drug produces minimal cardiac stimulation or tremors.
- Be aware that muscle tremor is a fairly common adverse effect that appears to subside with continued use.
- Monitor patient being treated for premature labor for CV S&S for 12 h after drug is discontinued. Report tachycardia promptly.
- Monitor I&O ratio. Fluid restriction may be necessary. Consult prescriber.
- Monitor serum potassium, glucose.

Patient & Family Education

- Inhalator therapy: Review instructions for use of inhalator (included in the package).
- Learn how to take your own pulse and the limits of change that indicate need to notify the prescriber.
- Consult prescriber if breathing difficulty is not relieved or if it becomes worse within 30 min after an oral dose.
- Consult prescriber if symptomatic relief wanes; tolerance can develop with chronic use.
- Do not self-dose this drug, particularly during long-term therapy. In the face of waning response, increasing the dose will not improve the clinical condition and may cause overdosage. Understand that decreasing relief with continued treatment indicates need for another bronchodilator, not an increase in dose.
- Do not puncture container, use or store it near heat or open flame, or expose to temperatures above 49° C (120° F), which may cause bursting. Contents of the aerosol (inhalator) are under pressure.
- Do not use any other aerosol bronchodilator while being treated with aerosol terbutaline. Do not self-medicate with an OTC aerosol.
- Do not use OTC drugs without prescriber approval. Many cold and allergy remedies, for example, contain a sympathomimetic agent that when combined with terbutaline may cause harmful adverse effects.

TERCONAZOLE

(ter-con′a-zole)
Terazol 7, Terazol 3
Classification: AZOLE ANTIFUNGAL
Therapeutic: VAGINAL ANTIFUNGAL
Prototype: Fluconazole

AVAILABILITY Vaginal cream; vaginal suppository

ACTION & *THERAPEUTIC EFFECT* Thought to exert antifungal activity by disruption of normal fungal cell membrane permeability. *Exhibits fungicidal activity against Candida albicans.*

USES Local treatment of vulvovaginal candidiasis.

CONTRAINDICATIONS Hypersensitivity to terconazole or azole antifungals; use of tampons; lactation.

CAUTIOUS USE Pregnancy (category C). Safety and efficacy in children younger than 18 y not established.

ROUTE & DOSAGE

Candidiasis

Adult: **Intravaginal** One suppository (2.5 g) each night × 3 days; one applicator full of 0.4% cream each night × 7 days; one applicator full of 0.8% cream each night × 3 days

ADMINISTRATION

Intravaginal

- Insert applicator high into the vagina (except during pregnancy).
- Wash applicator before and after each use.
- Store away from direct heat and light.

ADVERSE EFFECTS CNS: *Headache.* GU: Vaginal itching, burning, irritation. Other: Rash, flu-like syndrome (fever, chills, headache, hypotension).

INTERACTIONS Drug: May inactivate **nonoxynol-9** spermicides.

PHARMACOKINETICS Absorption: Slow minimal absorption from vagina. Onset: Within 3 days. Metabolism: In liver. Elimination: Half in urine, half in feces. Half-Life: 4–11 h.

NURSING IMPLICATIONS

Assessment & Drug Effects

- Do not use if patient has a history of allergic reaction to other antifungal agents, such as miconazole.
- Monitor for sensitization and irritation; these may indicate need to discontinue drug.

Patient & Family Education

- Use correct application technique.
- Do not use tampons concurrently with terconazole.
- Learn potential adverse reactions, including sensitization and allergic response.
- Be aware that terconazole may interact with diaphragms and latex condoms; avoid concurrent use within 72 h.
- Refrain from sexual intercourse while using terconazole.
- Wear only cotton underwear; change daily.

TERIFLUNOMIDE

(ter-i-flu′no-mide)

Aubagio

Classification: IMMUNOMODULATOR; PYRIMIDINE SYNTHESIS INHIBITOR; ANTI-INFLAMMATORY
Therapeutic: IMMUNOMODULATOR; ANTI-INFLAMMATORY

AVAILABILITY Tablet

ACTION & *THERAPEUTIC EFFECT*

An immunomodulatory agent with anti-inflammatory properties; exact mechanism of action unknown, but may involve a reduction in the number of activated lymphocytes in the CNS. *Reduces the number of MS relapses.*

USES Treatment of patients with relapsing forms of multiple sclerosis.

CONTRAINDICATIONS Severe liver impairment; coadministration with leflunomide; acute renal failure; pregnancy (category X); lactation.

CAUTIOUS USE Pre-existing liver disease; myelosuppression; serious

T

infections; DM; history of peripheral neuropathy; hypertension. Safety and efficacy in children younger than 18 y not established.

ROUTE & DOSAGE

Multiple Sclerosis
Adult: PO 7 or 14 mg once daily

ADMINISTRATION

Oral
- May give with or without food.
- Store at 15°–30° C (59°–86° F).

ADVERSE EFFECTS CV: Palpitations. **Respiratory:** Bronchitis, sinusitis, upper respiratory tract infection. **CNS:** Anxiety, burning sensation, carpal tunnel syndrome, headache, *paraesthesia*, sciatica. **HEENT:** Blurred vision, conjunctivitis. **Endocrine:** ALT and AST increased, gamma-glutamyltransferase increased, hypophosphatemia, neutrophil count decreased, white blood cell count decreased hepatotoxicity. **Skin:** Acne, *alopecia*, pruritus. **GI:** Abdominal distension, *diarrhea, nausea,* toothache, upper abdominal pain, viral gastroenteritis. **GU:** Cystitis. **Musculoskeletal:** Musculoskeletal pain, myalgia. **Hematological:** Leukopenia, neutropenia. **Other:** *Influenza*, oral herpes, seasonal allergy.

INTERACTIONS Drug: Teriflunomide may increase the levels of other drugs requiring CYP2C8 for metabolism (e.g., **paclitaxel, pioglitazone, repaglinide, rosiglitazone**) and may decrease the levels of other drugs requiring CYP1A2 for metabolism (e.g., **alosetron, duloxetine, theophylline, tizanidine**). Teriflunomide may decrease the effectiveness of **warfarin.** Teriflunomide can increase the levels of **ethinylestradiol** and **levonorgestrel.**

PHARMACOKINETICS Peak: 1–4 h. **Distribution:** Greater than 99% plasma protein bound. **Metabolism:** Primarily unchanged in liver. **Elimination:** Fecal (61%) and renal (23%). **Half-Life:** 18–19 d.

NURSING IMPLICATIONS

Black Box Warning

Teriflunomide has been associated with severe liver injury, including fatal liver failure; it has also been associated with major birth defects.

Assessment & Drug Effects

- Monitor BP especially in those with a history of hypertension.
- Monitor for and report promptly S&S of hepatotoxicity (see Appendix F). Withhold drug until prescriber consulted if hepatotoxicity suspected.
- Assess for peripheral neuropathy (e.g., bilateral numbness or tingling of hands or feet) and S&S of hypokalemia (see Appendix F).
- Monitor lab tests: Baseline (within last 6 mo before beginning therapy) CBC with differential and LFTs; monthly LFTs for next 6 mo or more often when given with other potentially hepatotoxic drugs.

Patient & Family Education

- Report promptly any of the following: Numbness or tingling of hands or feet; unexplained nausea, vomiting, or abdominal pain; fatigue; anorexia; jaundice and/or dark urine; fever.
- Consult with prescriber before accepting a vaccination during

Common adverse effects in *italic*; life-threatening effects <u>underlined</u>; generic names in **bold**; classifications in SMALL CAPS; ♣ Canadian drug name; ⊙ Prototype drug; ⚠ Alert

and for 6 mo following termination of therapy.

- Women should use effective contraception during treatment and until completion of an accelerated, drug-elimination procedure.
- Men should instruct their female partners to use reliable contraception. Those who wish to father a child should discontinue the drug and request an accelerated drug-elimination procedure.

TERIPARATIDE

(ter-i-par′a-tide)

Forteo

Classification: PARATHYROID HORMONE AGONIST

Therapeutic: PARATHYROID HORMONE AGONIST

AVAILABILITY Solution for injection

ACTION & *THERAPEUTIC EFFECT*

Parathyroid hormone (PTH) is the primary regulator of calcium and phosphate metabolism in bone and kidney. Biological actions of PTH and teriparatide are similar in bone and kidneys. *Stimulates new bone formation by preferential stimulation of osteoblastic activity over osteoclastic activity; improves bone microarchitecture, and increases bone mass and strength by stimulating new bone formation.*

USES Treatment of osteoporosis.

CONTRAINDICATIONS Hypersensitivity to teriparatide; osteosarcoma; Paget's disease; unexplained elevations of alkaline phosphatase; bone metastases or a history of skeletal malignancies; metabolic bone diseases other than osteoporosis; preexisting hypercalcemia; prior history of radiation therapy

involving the skeleton; pediatric patients or young adults with open epiphyses; lactation.

CAUTIOUS USE Active or recent urolithiasis, hypercalciuria; hypotension; concurrent use of digitalis; hepatic, renal, and cardiac disease; pregnancy (category C); children younger than 18 y.

ROUTE & DOSAGE

Osteoporosis

Adult: **Subcutaneous** 20 mcg daily

ADMINISTRATION

Subcutaneous

- Do not administer to anyone with hypercalcemia. Consult prescriber.
- Rotate subcutaneous injection sites.

ADVERSE EFFECTS CV: Hypertension, angina, syncope. **Respiratory:** Rhinitis, cough, pharyngitis, dyspnea, pneumonia. **CNS:** Headache, dizziness, depression, insomnia, vertigo. **Endocrine:** *Transient increase in calcium levels,* increase in serum uric acid, antibodies to teriparatide after 12 mo therapy. **Skin:** Rash, sweating. **GI:** Nausea, constipation, dyspepsia, vomiting. **Musculoskeletal:** *Arthralgia,* leg cramps. **Other:** *Pain,* asthenia, neck pain.

INTERACTIONS Drug: May increase risk of **digoxin** toxicity.

PHARMACOKINETICS Absorption: Extensively absorbed from subcutaneous site. **Onset:** 2 h for calcium concentration increase. **Peak:** Max calcium concentrations 4–6 h. **Duration:** 16–24 h. **Metabolism:** Parathyroid hormone

T

is metabolized by nonspecific enzymes. **Elimination:** Primarily in urine. **Half-Life:** 1 h subcutaneous.

NURSING IMPLICATIONS

Black Box Warning

Teriparatide has been associated with development of osteosarcoma in laboratory animals, and it should not be prescribed for those at increased baseline risk for osteosarcoma.

Assessment & Drug Effects
- Monitor cardiovascular status including BP and subjective reports of angina.
- Concurrent drugs: Monitor closely for digoxin toxicity with concurrent use.
- Monitor lab tests: Periodic serum calcium, alkaline phosphatase, and uric acid.

Patient & Family Education
- Report unexplained leg cramps and bone pain.
- Learn correct technique for subcutaneous injection.

TESAMORELIN ACETATE

(tes′a-moe-rel′in as′e-tate)

Egrifta

Classification: GROWTH HORMONE RELEASING FACTOR ANALOG; GROWTH HORMONE MODIFIER

Therapeutic: GROWTH HORMONE MODIFIER

AVAILABILITY Powder for reconstitution and injection

ACTION & *THERAPEUTIC EFFECT*

Binds to pituitary growth hormone-releasing factor receptors and stimulates the secretion of endogenous growth hormone which has anabolic and lipolytic properties. *Reduces fat deposition in those with HIV-associated lipodystrophy.*

USES Reduction of excess abdominal fat in HIV-infected patients with lipodystrophy.

CONTRAINDICATIONS Active malignancy; hypersensitivity to tesamorelin and/or mannitol; suppression of the hypothalamic-pituitary from hypophysectomy, hypopituitarism, pituitary tumor/surgery, head irradiation or trauma; pregnancy (category X); lactation.

CAUTIOUS USE Acute illness or trauma; injection site reactions; nonmalignant neoplasms; renal or hepatic impairment; conditions resulting in or associated with fluid retention (e.g., edema, carpal tunnel syndrome); glucose intolerance or diabetes; retinopathy; age 65 y and older. Safety and efficacy in children not established.

ROUTE & DOSAGE

Lipodystrophy in HIV Patients
Adult: **Subcutaneous** 2 mg once daily

ADMINISTRATION

Subcutaneous
- Use provided diluent only.
- Reconstitute 2 mg vial with 2.1 mL diluent; gently roll vial for 30 sec to mix; do not shake.
- When using 1 mg vials, to produce a 2 mg dose, reconstitute the first 1 mg vial with 2.2 mL diluent; gently roll vial (do not shake) for 30 sec to mix; reconstitute the second 1 mg vial with the entire solution from first vial; gently roll

T

vial (do not shake) for 30 sec to mix.

- Use immediately after prepreparation. Rotate injection sites.
- Store dry vials at 2°–8° C (36°–46° F). Protect from light. Reconstituted solution should be discarded if not used immediately.

ADVERSE EFFECTS CV: Hypertension, palpitations. **CNS:** Depression, hypesthesia, insomnia, pareshesia, peripheral neuropathy. **Endocrine:** Increased blood creatine phosphate. **Skin:** Hot flush, night sweats, pruritus, rash, urticarial. Erythema, hemorrhage, irritation, pain, pruritus, rash reaction, swelling, urticaria at injection site. **GI:** Dyspepsia, nausea, upper abdominal pain, vomiting. **Musculoskeletal:** *Arthralgia*, carpal tunnel syndrome, joint stiffness and swelling, muscle spasm, muscle pain, musculoskeletal pain, musculoskeletal stiffness, *myalgia, pain in extremity.* **Other:** Chest pain, pain, peripheral edema.

INTERACTIONS Drug: Tesamorelin may decrease the enzymatic activation of **cortisone** and **prednisone**. Tesamorelin may alter the metabolism of compounds requiring CYP450 enzymes; careful monitoring is suggested.

PHARMACOKINETICS Peak: 15 min. **Half-Life:** 26–38 min.

NURSING IMPLICATIONS

Assessment & Drug Effects

- Evaluate abdominal girth with periodic measurements at the level of the umbilicus.
- Assess for injections site reactions (i.e., erythema, pruritus, pain, irritation, and bruising).
- Monitor prediabetics and diabetics for loss of glycemic control.

- Monitor lab tests: Baseline and frequent IGF-1 level baseline and periodic FBG and HbA1C.

Patient & Family Education

- Seek immediate medical attention for any of the following: Rash or hives; swelling of face or throat; shortness of breath or trouble breathing; rapid heartbeat; feeling of faintness or fainting.
- Notify your prescriber if you experience swelling, an increase in joint pain, or pain or numbness in your hands or wrist (carpal tunnel syndrome).
- Women should discontinue tesamorelin and notify prescriber if pregnancy occurs.
- If diabetic, monitor fasting and postprandial blood glucose as directed.

TESTOSTERONE ⊕

(tess-toss′ter-one)

Androderm, AndroGel, Axiron, Foresta, Natesto, STRIANT, Testim, Testopel, Vogelxo

TESTOSTERONE CYPIONATE

Depo-Testosterone

TESTOSTERONE ENANTHATE

Delatestryl, Malogex ✦

Classification: ANDROGEN/ ANABOLIC STEROID; ANTINEOPLASTIC
Therapeutic: ANTINEOPLASTIC; ANABOLIC STEROID
Controlled Substance: Schedule III

AVAILABILITY Testosterone: Implantable pellet; transdermal patch; transdermal gel; intranasal gel; buccal tablet. **Testosterone Cypionate:** IM injection. **Testosterone Enanthate:** IM injection

ACTION & *THERAPEUTIC EFFECT*

Synthetic steroid compound with

both androgenic and anabolic activity. Controls development and maintenance of secondary sexual characteristics. **Androgenic activity:** Responsible for the growth spurt of the adolescent, onset of puberty, and for growth termination by epiphyseal closure. **Anabolic activity:** Increases protein metabolism and decreases its catabolism. Large doses suppress spermatogenesis, thereby causing testicular atrophy. *Antagonizes effects of estrogen excess on female breast and endometrium. Responsible for the growth spurt of the adolescent male and onset of puberty.*

USES Androgen replacement therapy, delayed puberty (male), hypogonadism, palliation of female mammary cancer (1–5 y postmenopausal), palliative treatment of breast cancer, and to treat postpartum breast engorgement. Available in fixed combination with estrogens in many preparations.

CONTRAINDICATIONS Hypersensitivity or toxic reactions to androgens; benzoic acid or benzyl alcohol hypersensitvity; serious cardiac, liver, or kidney disease; hypercalcemia; known or suspected prostatic or breast cancer in male; BPH with obstruction; asthenic males who may react adversely to androgenic overstimulation; conditions aggravated by fluid retention; hypertension; DVT; hepatic dysfunction as a result of use of testosterone; older adults; pregnancy (category X); possibility of virilization of external genitalia of female fetus; lactation.

CAUTIOUS USE Cardiac, liver, and kidney disease; prepubertal males; DM; history of MI; CAD; BPH; older adults; acute intermittent porphyria.

ROUTE & DOSAGE

Male Hypogonadism

Adult: **IM Cypionate, Enanthate** 50–400 mg q2–4wk; **IM Propionate** 10–25 mg 2–3/wk; **Topical** Start with 6 mg/day system applied daily, if scrotal area inadequate, use 4 mg/day system; **Androderm** Apply to torso; **AndroGel** Apply one packet to upper arms, shoulders, or abdomen once daily; **Striant** Apply one patch to the gum region just above the incisor tooth q12h

Delayed Puberty

Adult: **IM Cypionate, Enanthate** 50–200 mg q2–4wk; **Subcutaneous** 2–6 pellets inserted q3–6mo; **IM Propionate** up to 100 mg per mo

Metastatic Breast Cancer

Adult: **IM Cypionate, Enanthate** 200–400 mg q2–4wk; **IM Propionate** 50–100 mg 3 × wk

ADMINISTRATION

Buccal

- Apply buccal patch to gum just above the incisor tooth.

Nasal

- Instruct not to blow nose or sniff for 1 h after receiving Natesto.

Transdermal

- Apply transdermal system on clean, dry scrotal skin. Dry shave scrotal hair for optimal skin contact. Do not use chemical depilatories. Wear patch for 22–24 h.
- Topical gel preparations may be applied to shoulders and upper arms.
- Store at 15°–30° C (59°–86° F).

T

Intramuscular

- Give IM injections deep into gluteal musculature.
- Store IM formulations prepared in oil at room temperature. Warming and shaking vial will redisperse precipitated crystals.

ADVERSE EFFECTS

CV: Skin flushing and vascularization. **CNS:** Excitation, insomnia. **Endocrine:** Hypercalcemia, hypercholesterolemia, *sodium and water retention (especially in older adults) with edema.* Renal calculi (especially in the immobilized patient); bladder irritability; female—suppression of ovulation, lactation, or menstruation; hoarseness or deepening of voice (often irreversible); hirsutism; oily skin; clitoral enlargement; regression of breasts; male-pattern baldness (in disseminated breast cancer); flushing, sweating, vaginitis with pruritus, drying, bleeding; menstrual irregularities. Male—prepubertal-premature epiphyseal closure, phallic enlargement, priapism. Postpubertal—testicular atrophy, decreased ejaculatory volume, azoospermia, oligospermia (after prolonged administration or excessive dosage), impotence, epididymitis, priapism, *gynecomastia.* **Skin:** *Acne,* injection site irritation and sloughing, pruritus. **GI:** Nausea, vomiting, anorexia, diarrhea, gastric pain, jaundice. **GU:** *Increased libido.* **Hematologic:** <u>Leukopenia</u>. Precipitation of acute intermittent porphyria. **Other:** Hypersensitivity to testosterone, <u>anaphylactoid reactions</u> (rare).

DIAGNOSTIC TEST INTERFERENCE

Testosterone alters *glucose tolerance* tests; decreases *thyroxine-binding globulin concentration* (resulting in decreased *total T_4* serum levels and increased *resin of T_3* and *T_4*). Increases *creatinine* and *creatinine* excretion (lasting up to 2 wk after therapy is discontinued) and alters response to *metyrapone test.* It suppresses *clotting factors II, V, VII, X* and decreases excretion of *17-ketosteroids.* May increase or decrease *serum cholesterol.*

INTERACTIONS

Drug: ORAL ANTICOAGULANTS may potentiate hypoprothrombinemia. May decrease **insulin** requirements. May have increased concentration if used with **ceritinib, conivaptan, topotecan.**

PHARMACOKINETICS

Absorption: Cypionate and **enanthate** are slowly absorbed from lipid tissue. **Duration:** 2–4 wk **cypionate** and **enanthate. Distribution:** 98% bound to sex hormone-binding globulin. **Metabolism:** Primarily in liver. **Elimination:** 90% in urine, 6% in feces. **Half-Life:** 10–100 min.

NURSING IMPLICATIONS

Assessment & Drug Effects

- Check I&O and weigh patient daily during dose adjustment period. Weight gain (due to sodium and water retention) suggests need for decreased dosage. When dosage is stabilized, urge patient to check weight at least twice weekly and to report increases, particularly if accompanied by edema in dependent areas. Dose adjustment and diuretic therapy may be started.
- Monitor serum calcium closely. Androgenic therapy is usually terminated if serum calcium rises above 14 mg/dL.
- Report S&S of hypercalcemia (see Appendix F) promptly. The immobilized patient is particularly prone to develop hypercalcemia,

T

which indicates progression of bone metastasis in patients with metastatic breast cancer. Treatment includes withdrawing testosterone and checking calcium, phosphate, and BUN levels daily.

- Instruct diabetic to report sweating, tremor, anxiety, vertigo. Testosterone-induced anabolic action enhances hypoglycemia (hyperinsulinism). Dosage adjustment of antidiabetic agent may be required.

- Observe patients on concomitant anticoagulant treatment for signs of overdosage (e.g., ecchymoses, petechiae). Report promptly to prescriber; anticoagulant dose may need to be reduced.

- Monitor prepubertal or adolescent males throughout therapy to avoid precocious sexual development and premature epiphyseal closure. Skeletal stimulation may continue 6 mo beyond termination of therapy.

- Monitor lab tests: Periodic serum cholesterol, serum electrolytes, and LFTs.

Patient & Family Education

- Review directions for application of transdermal patches.

- Report soreness at injection site, because a postinjection site boil may be an associated adverse reaction.

- Report priapism (sustained and often painful erections occurring especially in early replacement therapy), reduced ejaculatory volume, and gynecomastia to prescriber. Symptoms indicate necessity for temporary withdrawal or discontinuation of testosterone therapy.

- Notify prescriber promptly if pregnancy is suspected or planned. Masculinization of the fetus is most likely to occur if testosterone (androgen) therapy is provided during first trimester of pregnancy.

- Androgens may cause virilism in women at dosage required to treat carcinoma. Report increase in libido (early sign of toxicity), growth of facial hair, deepening of voice, male-pattern baldness. The onset of hoarseness can easily be overlooked unless its significance as an early and possibly irreversible sign of virilism is appreciated. Reevaluation of treatment plan is indicated.

TETRACAINE HYDROCHLORIDE

(tet′ra-kane)

Pontocaine

Classification: LOCAL ANESTHETIC (ESTER TYPE)

Therapeutic: LOCAL ANESTHETIC

Prototype: Procaine HCl

AVAILABILITY Solution for injection; powder; solution; cream; gel; ointment; ophthalmic solution

ACTION & *THERAPEUTIC EFFECT*

A potent and toxic local anesthetic that depresses initial depolarization phase of the action potential, thus preventing propagation and conduction of the nerve impulse. *Effectiveness indicated by loss of sensation and motor activity in circumscribed body areas close to injection or application site.*

USES Spinal anesthesia (high, low, saddle block) and topically to produce surface anesthesia. **Eye:** To anesthetize conjunctiva and cornea prior to superficial procedures (including tonometry, gonioscopy, removal of foreign bodies or sutures, corneal scraping). **Nose and Throat:** To abolish laryngeal and esophageal reflexes prior to bronchoscopy, esophagoscopy. **Skin:** To relieve pruritus, pain, burning.

CONTRAINDICATIONS Debilitated patients; prolonged use of ophthalmic preparations; known hypersensitivity to tetracaine or other local anesthetics of ester type (e.g., procaine, chloroprocaine, cocaine), sulfite, or to PABA or its derivatives; coagulopathy; anticoagulant therapy; thrombocytopenia; increased bleeding time; infection at application or injection site.

CAUTIOUS USE Shock; cachexia, cardiac decompensation; QT prolongation; older adults; pregnancy (category C); lactation; children younger than 16 y.

ROUTE & DOSAGE

Local Anesthesia

Adult: **Topical** Before procedure, 1–2 drops of 0.5% solution or 1.25–2.5 cm of ointment in lower conjunctival fornix or 0.5% solution or ointment to nose or throat; **Spinal** 1% solution diluted with equal volume of 10% dextrose injected in subarachnoid space

ADMINISTRATION

Topical
- Avoid use of solutions that are cloudy, discolored, or crystallized.
- When tetracaine is used on mucosa of larynx, trachea, or esophagus, the manufacturer recommends adding 0.06 mL of a 0.1% epinephrine solution to each mL tetracaine solution to slow absorption of the anesthetic.
- Store ophthalmic solution and ointment at 15°–30° C (59°–86° F); refrigerate topical. Avoid freezing. Use tight, light-resistant containers.

ADVERSE EFFECTS CV: Bradycardia, arrhythmias, hypotension.

CNS: Postspinal headache, headache, spinal nerve paralysis, anxiety, nervousness, seizures. **HEENT:** Stinging; corneal erosion, retardation or prevention of healing of corneal abrasion, transient pitting and sloughing of corneal surface, dry corneal epithelium; dry mucous membranes, prolonged depression of cough reflex. **Other:** Anaphylactic reactions, convulsions, faintness, syncope.

INTERACTIONS Drug: May antagonize effects of SULFONAMIDES.

PHARMACOKINETICS Onset: 1 min eye; 3 min mucosal surface; 3 min spinal. **Duration:** Up to 15 min eye; 30–60 min mucosal surface; 1.5–3 h spinal. **Metabolism:** In liver and plasma. **Elimination:** In urine.

NURSING IMPLICATIONS

Assessment & Drug Effects
- Recovery from anesthesia to the pharyngeal area is complete when patient has feeling in the hard and soft palates and when muscles in the faucial (tonsillar) pillars contract with stimulation.
- Do not give food or liquids until these normal pharyngeal responses are present (usually about 1 h after anesthetic administration). The first small amount of liquid (water) should be given under supervision of care provider.
- Be aware that increased blood concentration of the drug may result from excess application of tetracaine to the skin (to relieve pruritus or burning), application to debrided or infected skin surfaces, or too rapid injection rate.
- High blood concentrations of tetracaine can lead to adverse systemic effects involving CNS and CV systems: Convulsions, respiratory arrest, dysrhythmias, cardiac arrest.

Patient & Family Education

- Do not use ophthalmic drug longer than prescribed period. Prolonged use to eye surface may cause corneal epithelial erosions and retard healing of corneal surface.
- Natural barriers to eye infection and injury are removed by the anesthesia. Do not rub eye after drug instillation until anesthetic effect has dissipated (evidenced by return of blink reflex). Patching for temporary protection of the corneal epithelium may be ordered.
- Wash or disinfect hands before and after self-administration of solutions or ointment.

TETRACYCLINE HYDROCHLORIDE ℗

(tet-ra-sye′kleen)

Novotetra ✦, Sumycin

Classification: ANTIBIOTIC; TETRACYCLINE

Therapeutic: ANTIBIOTIC

AVAILABILITY Capsule; suspension

ACTION & THERAPEUTIC EFFECT Tetracyclines exert antiacne action by suppressing growth of *Propionibacterium acnes* within sebaceous follicles. *Effective against a variety of gram-positive and gram-negative bacteria and against most chlamydiae, mycoplasmas, rickettsiae, and certain protozoa (e.g., amebae). Exerts antiacne action against* Propionibacterium acnes.

USES Chlamydial infections (e.g., lymphogranuloma venereum, psittacosis, trachoma, inclusion conjunctivitis, nongonococcal urethritis); mycoplasmal infections (e.g., *Mycoplasma pneumoniae*); rickettsial infections (e.g., Q fever, Rocky Mountain spotted fever, typhus); spirochetal infections: Relapsing fever *(Borrelia)*, leptospirosis, syphilis (penicillin-hypersensitive patients); amebiases; uncommon gram-negative bacterial infections [e.g., brucellosis, shigellosis, cholera, gonorrhea (penicillin-hypersensitive patients), granuloma inguinale, tularemia]; gram-positive infections (e.g., tetanus). Also used orally (solution) for inflammatory acne vulgaris.

UNLABELED USES Actinomycosis, acute exacerbations of chronic bronchitis; Lyme disease; pericardial effusion (metastatic); acute PID; sexually transmitted epididymo orchitis; with quinine for multi-drug-resistant strains of *Plasmodium falciparum* malaria; anti-infective prophylaxis for rape victims; recurrent cystic thyroid nodules; melioidosis; and as fluorescence test for malignancy.

CONTRAINDICATIONS Hypersensitivity to tetracyclines; severe renal or hepatic impairment, common bile duct obstruction; UV exposure; pregnancy (category D); lactation.

CAUTIOUS USE History of kidney or liver dysfunction; myasthenia gravis; history of allergy, asthma, hay fever, urticaria; undernourished patients; infants, children younger than 8 y.

ROUTE & DOSAGE

Systemic Infection

Adult: **PO** 250–500 mg bid–qid (1–2 g/day)

Child (8 y or older): **PO** 25–50 mg/kg/day in 2–4 divided doses

Acne

Adult/Child (8 y or older): **PO** 500–1000 mg/day in 4 divided doses

ADMINISTRATION

Oral

- Give with a full glass of water on an empty stomach at least 1 h before or 2 h after meals (food, milk, and milk products can reduce absorption by 50% or more).
- Do not give immediately before bed.
- Give with food if patient is having GI symptoms (e.g., nausea, vomiting, anorexia); do not give with foods high in calcium such as milk or milk products.
- Shake suspension well before pouring to ensure uniform distribution of drug. Use calibrated liquid measure to dispense.
- Check expiration date for all tetracyclines. Fanconi-like syndrome (renal tubular dysfunction) and also an LE-like syndrome have been attributed to outdated tetracycline preparations.
- Tetracycline decomposes with age, exposure to light, and when improperly stored under conditions of extreme humidity, heat, or cold. The resultant product may be toxic.
- Store at 15°–30° C (59°–86° F) in tightly covered container in dry place. Protect from light.

ADVERSE EFFECTS

CNS: Headache, intracranial hypertension (rare). **HEENT:** Pigmentation of conjunctiva due to drug deposit. **Skin:** Dermatitis, *phototoxicity:* Discoloration of nails, onycholysis (loosening of nails); cheilosis; fixed drug eruptions particularly on genitalia; thrombocytopenic purpura; urticaria, rash, exfoliative dermatitis; with topical applications: Skin irritation, dry scaly skin, transient stinging or burning sensation, slight yellowing of skin at application site, acute contact dermatitis. **GI:** Reported mostly for oral administration, but also may occur with parenteral tetracycline (*nausea, vomiting,* epigastric distress, heartburn, *diarrhea,* bulky loose stools, steatorrhea, *abdominal discomfort, flatulence,* dry mouth); dysphagia, retrosternal pain, esophagitis, esophageal ulceration with oral administration, abnormally high liver function test values, decrease in serum cholesterol, fatty degeneration of liver [jaundice, increasing nitrogen retention (azotemia), hyperphosphatemia, acidosis, irreversible shock]; foul-smelling stools or vaginal discharge, stomatitis, glossitis; black hairy tongue (lingua nigra), diarrhea: Staphylococcal enterocolitis. **GU:** Particularly in patients with kidney disease; increase in BUN/serum creatinine, renal impairment even with therapeutic doses; Fanconi-like syndrome (outdated tetracycline) (characterized by polyuria, polydipsia, nausea, vomiting, glycosuria, proteinuria acidosis, aminoaciduria); vulvovaginitis, pruritus vulvae or ani (possibly hypersensitivity). **Other:** Drug fever, angioedema, serum sickness, anaphylaxis. Pancreatitis, local reactions: Pain and irritation (IM site), Jarisch-Herxheimer reaction.

DIAGNOSTIC TEST INTERFERENCE

TETRACYCLINES may cause false increases in **urinary catecholamines** (by **fluorometric methods**), and false decreases in **urinary urobilinogen.** Parenteral TETRACYCLINES containing **ascorbic acid** reportedly may produce false-positive **urinary glucose** determinations by **copper reduction methods** (e.g., **Benedict's reagent, Clinitest**); TETRACYCLINES may cause false-negative results with **glucose oxidase methods** (e.g., **Clinistix, TesTape**).

T

INTERACTIONS Drug: ANTACIDS, **calcium**, and **magnesium** bind tetracycline in gut and decrease absorption. ORAL ANTICOAGULANTS potentiate hypoprothrombinemia. ANTIDIARRHEAL AGENTS with **kaolin** and pectin may decrease absorption. Effectiveness of ORAL CONTRACEPTIVES decreased. **Methoxyflurane** may produce fatal nephrotoxicity. **Food:** Dairy products and **iron, zinc** supplements decrease tetracycline absorption.

PHARMACOKINETICS Absorption: 75–80% of dose absorbed. **Peak:** 2–4 h. **Distribution:** Widely distributed, preferentially binds to rapid growing tissues; crosses placenta; enters breast milk. **Metabolism:** Not metabolized; enterohepatic cycling. **Elimination:** 50–60% in urine within 72 h. **Half-Life:** 6–12 h.

NURSING IMPLICATIONS

Assessment & Drug Effects

- Report GI symptoms (e.g., nausea, vomiting, diarrhea) to prescriber. These are generally mostly dose-dependent, occurring mostly in patients receiving 2 g/day or more and during prolonged therapy. Frequently, symptoms are controlled by reducing dosage or administering with compatible foods.
- Be alert to evidence of superinfections (see Appendix F). Regularly inspect tongue and mucous membrane of mouth for candidiasis (thrush). Suspect superinfection if patient complains of irritation or soreness of mouth, tongue, throat, vagina, or anus, or persistent itching of any area, diarrhea, or foul-smelling excreta or discharge.
- Withhold drug and notify prescriber if superinfection develops. Superinfections occur most frequently in patients receiving prolonged therapy, the debilitated, or those who have diabetes.
- Monitor I&O in patients receiving parenteral tetracycline. Report oliguria or any changes in appearance of urine or in I&O.
- Monitor lab tests: Periodic renal function tests, LFTs, and hematopoietic function tests, particularly during high-dose, long-term therapy.

Patient & Family Education

- Report onset of diarrhea to prescriber. It is important to determine whether diarrhea is due to irritating drug effect or superinfections or pseudomembranous colitis (caused by overgrowth of toxin-producing bacteria: *Clostridium difficile*) (see Appendix F). The latter two conditions can be life threatening and require immediate withdrawal of tetracycline and prompt initiation of symptomatic and supportive therapy.
- Reduce incidence of superinfection (see Appendix F) by meticulous care of mouth, skin, and perineal area. Rinse mouth of food debris after eating; floss daily and use a soft-bristled toothbrush.
- Avoid direct exposure to sunlight during and for several days after therapy is terminated to reduce possibility of photosensitivity reaction (appearing like an exaggerated sunburn).
- Exercise caution with potentially hazardous activities until reaction to drug is known.
- Report immediately sudden onset of painful or difficult swallowing (dysphagia) to prescriber. Esophagitis and esophageal ulceration have been associated with bedtime administration of tetracycline capsules or tablets with insufficient fluid, particularly to patients with hiatal hernia or esophageal problems.

- Response to acne therapy usually requires 2–8 wk, maximal results may not be apparent for up to 12 wk.

TETRAHYDROZOLINE HYDROCHLORIDE

(tet-ra-hye-drozz'a-leen)

Mallazine, Murine Plus, Optigene, Soothe, Tyzine, Visine

Classification: EYE AND NOSE PREPARATION; VASOCONSTRICTOR; DECONGESTANT

Therapeutic: NASAL DECONGESTANT; OCULAR VASOCONSTRICTOR

Prototype: Naphazoline

AVAILABILITY Ophthalmic solution; nasal solution

ACTION & *THERAPEUTIC EFFECT*
Alpha-adrenergic agonist that causes intense vasoconstriction when applied topically to mucous membranes, and when applied as eyedrops. *Ophthalmic solution is effective for allergic reactions of the eye; nasal solution is anti-inflammatory and also decreases allergic congestion.*

USES Symptomatic relief of minor eye irritation and allergies and for nasopharyngeal congestion of allergic or inflammatory origin.

CONTRAINDICATIONS Hypersensitivity to tetrahydrozoline; use of ophthalmic preparation in glaucoma or other serious eye diseases; use within 14 days of MAO inhibitor therapy.

CAUTIOUS USE Hypertension; cardiovascular disease; hyperthyroidism; DM; pregnancy (category C); lactation. Use in children younger than 2 y; use of 0.1% or higher strengths in children younger than 6 y.

ROUTE & DOSAGE

Decongestant

Adult: **Ophthalmic** See Appendix A-1; **Nasal** 2–4 drops of 0.1% solution or spray in each nostril q3h prn
Child (2–6 y): **Nasal** 2–4 drops of 0.05% solution or spray in each nostril q3h prn; *6 y or older:* Same as adult

ADMINISTRATION

Instillation

- Make sure interval between doses is at least 4–6 h since drug action lasts 4–8 h.
- Place patient in upright position when using nasal spray. (If patient is reclining, a stream rather than a spray may be ejected, with consequent overdosage.)
- Use lateral, head-low position to administer nasal drops.

ADVERSE EFFECTS HEENT: *Transient stinging*, irritation, *sneezing*, dryness, headache, tremors, drowsiness, light-headedness, insomnia, palpitation. **Other:** With overdose: Marked drowsiness, sweating, <u>coma</u>, hypotension, <u>shock</u>, bradycardia.

PHARMACOKINETICS Absorption: May be absorbed from nasal mucosa. **Duration:** 4–8 h.

NURSING IMPLICATIONS

Patient & Family Education

- Discontinue medication and consult prescriber if relief is not obtained within 48 h or if symptoms persist or increase.

- Do not exceed recommended dosage. Rebound congestion and rhinitis may occur with frequent or prolonged use of nasal preparation.

THEOPHYLLINE ⊙
(thee-off'i-lin)
Elixophyllin, Pulmophylline ◆, Theo-24, Theochron, Uniphyl ◆
Classification: BRONCHODILATOR (RESPIRATORY SMOOTH MUSCLE RELAXANT); XANTHINE
Therapeutic: BRONCHODILATOR

AVAILABILITY Liquid; sustained release tablet; sustained release capsule; solution for injection

ACTION & THERAPEUTIC EFFECT Xanthine derivative that relaxes smooth muscle by direct action, particularly of bronchi and pulmonary vessels, and stimulates medullary respiratory center with resulting increase in vital capacity. *Effective for relief of bronchospasm in asthmatics, chronic bronchitis, and emphysema.*

USES Reversible airflow obstruction. Note: This is not a preferred agent for COPD nor is it recommended for use in asthma management in children 5 y or younger.

UNLABELED USES Treatment of apnea and bradycardia of premature infants and to reduce severe bronchospasm associated with cystic fibrosis and acute descending respiratory infection.

CONTRAINDICATIONS Hypersensitivity to theophylline; CAD or angina pectoris when myocardial stimulation might be harmful; severe renal or hepatic impairment.

CAUTIOUS USE Compromised cardiac or circulatory function, cardiac arrhythmias; hypertension; acute pulmonary edema; multiple organ failure; CHF; seizure disorders; hyperthyroidism; active peptic ulcer; prostatic hypertrophy; glaucoma; DM; older adults; pregnancy (category C); lactation; children; and neonates.

ROUTE & DOSAGE

Note: Dose individualized by steady state serum concentrations

Reversible Airflow Obstruction
Adult: **Immediate release** 300 mg/day in divided doses q6–8h; **Extended release** 12 h formulation 150 mg bid; **Extended release** 24 h formulation 300–400 mg daily

Obesity Dosage Adjustment
Dose based on IBW

ADMINISTRATION

Note: All doses based on ideal body weight.

Oral
- Wait 4–6 h after the last IV dose, when switching from IV to oral dosing.
- Give with a full glass of water and after meals to minimize gastric irritation.
- Give sustained release forms and enteric-coated tablets whole. Chewable tablets **must be** chewed thoroughly before swallowing. Sustained release granules from capsules can be taken on an empty stomach

T

or mixed with applesauce or water.

- Note: Timing of dose is critical. Be certain patient understands necessity to adhere to the correct intervals between doses.

Intravenous

PREPARE: Use as supplied with no further preparation.
ADMINISTER: IV Infusion: Infuse at a rate based on patient's weight.
INCOMPATIBILITIES: Solution/ additive: Ascorbic acid, ceftriaxone, cimetidine, hetastarch. Y-site: Hetastarch, phenytoin.

ADVERSE EFFECTS CV: Cardiac flutter, tachycardia. **CNS:** Headache, insomnia, restlessness. **Endocrine:** Hypercalcemia. **GI:** GERD, gastrointestinal ulcer, nausea, vomiting. **GU:** Dysuria, diuresis. **Musculoskeletal:** Tremor.

DIAGNOSTIC TEST INTERFERENCE
Plasma glucose, uric acid, free fatty acids, total cholesterol, HDL, HDL/LDL ratio, and *urinary free cortisol excretion* may be increased by **theophylline. Probenecid** may cause false high *serum theophylline* readings, and spectrophotometric methods of determining *serum theophylline* are affected by a furosemide, sulfathiazole, phenylbutazone, probenecid, theobromine.

INTERACTIONS Drug: Increases **lithium** excretion, lowering lithium levels; **cimetidine,** high-dose **allopurinol** (600 mg/day), QUINOLONES, MACROLIDE ANTIBIOTICS, and **zileuton** can significantly increase theophylline levels; **tobacco** use significantly decreases levels. **Herbal: St. John's wort** may decrease theophylline efficacy.

Daidzein (in soy), **black pepper** increase serum concentrations and adverse effects.

PHARMACOKINETICS Absorption: Most products are 100% absorbed from GI tract. **Peak:** IV 30 min; uncoated tablet 1 h; sustained release 4–6 h. **Duration:** 4–8 h; varies with age, smoking, and liver function. **Distribution:** Crosses placenta. **Metabolism:** Extensively in liver. **Elimination:** Parent drug and metabolites excreted by kidneys; excreted in breast milk.

NURSING IMPLICATIONS
Assessment & Drug Effects
- Monitor vital signs. Improvement in respiratory status is the expected outcome.
- Observe and report early signs of possible toxicity: Anorexia, nausea, vomiting, dizziness, shakiness, restlessness, abdominal discomfort, irritability, palpitation, tachycardia, marked hypotension, cardiac arrhythmias, seizures.
- Monitor for tachycardia, which may be worse in patients with severe cardiac disease. Conversely, theophylline toxicity may be masked in patients with tachycardia.
- Monitor drug levels closely in heavy smokers. Cigarette smoking induces hepatic microsomal enzyme activity, decreasing serum half-life and increasing body clearance of theophylline. An increase of dosage from 50–100% is usual in heavy smokers.
- Monitor plasma drug level closely in patients with heart failure, kidney or liver dysfunction, alcoholism, high fever. Plasma clearance of xanthines may be reduced.
- Take necessary safety precautions and forewarn older adult patients

T

of possible dizziness during early therapy.

- Monitor patients on sustained release preparations for S&S of overdosage. Continued slow absorption leads to high plasma concentrations for a prolonged period.
- Note: Neonates of mothers using this drug have exhibited slight tachycardia, jitteriness, and apnea.
- Monitor **closely** for adverse effects in infants younger than 6 mo and prematures; theophylline metabolism is prolonged as is the half-life in this age group.
- Monitor lab tests: Theophylline plasma level when initiating therapy and with dosage increases.

Patient & Family Education

- Take medication at the same time every day.
- Avoid charcoal-broiled foods (high in polycyclic carbon content); may increase theophylline elimination and reduce the half-life as much as 50%.
- Limit caffeine intake because it may increase incidence of adverse effects.
- Cigarette smoking may significantly lower theophylline plasma concentration.
- Be aware that a low-carbohydrate, high-protein diet increases theophylline elimination, and a high-carbohydrate, low-protein diet decreases it.
- Drink fluids liberally (2000–3000 mL/day) if not contraindicated to decrease viscosity of airway secretions.
- Avoid self-dosing with OTC medications, especially cough suppressants, which may cause retention of secretions and CNS depression.

THIAMINE HYDROCHLORIDE (VITAMIN B$_1$)

(thye'a-min)

Classification: VITAMIN B$_1$
Therapeutic: VITAMIN B$_1$ REPLACEMENT THERAPY

AVAILABILITY Tablet; capsule; solution for injection

ACTION & *THERAPEUTIC EFFECT*

Water-soluble B$_1$ vitamin and member of B-complex group used for thiamine replacement therapy. Functions as an essential coenzyme in carbohydrate metabolism and has a role in conversion of tryptophan to nicotinamide. *Effectiveness is evidenced by improvement of clinical manifestations of thiamine deficiency (e.g., anorexia, depression, loss of memory).*

USES Treatment and prophylaxis of thiamine deficiency.

CONTRAINDICATION Hypersensitivity to thiamine.

CAUTIOUS USE Pregnancy (category A; category C if above RDA).

ROUTE & DOSAGE

Thiamine Deficiency

Adult: **IV/IM/PO** 30–50 mg daily
Child: **IV/IM/PO** 10–25 mg daily × 2 wk then 5–10 **PO** × 1 mo

Wernicke's Encephalopathy

Adult: **IV/IM** 100 mg/day then 50–100 mg/day until on normal diet

T

Common adverse effects in *italic*; life-threatening effects <u>underlined</u>; generic names in **bold**; classifications in SMALL CAPS; ♣ Canadian drug name; ⊙ Prototype drug; ⚠ Alert

Dietary Supplement
Adult: **PO** 15–30 mg/day
Child: **PO** 10–50 mg/day

ADMINISTRATION

Oral

- Do not crush or chew enteric-coated tablets. These **must be** swallowed whole.

Intramuscular

- Give deep IM into a large muscle; may be painful. Rotate sites and apply cold compresses to area if necessary for relief of discomfort.

Intravenous

Note: Intradermal test dose is recommended prior to administration in suspected thiamine sensitivity. Deaths have occurred following IV use.
PREPARE: **Direct:** Give undiluted. **IV Infusion:** Diluted in 1000 mL of most IV solutions.
ADMINISTER: **Direct:** Give at a rate of 100 mg over 5 min. **IV Infusion:** Give at the ordered rate.
INCOMPATIBILITIES: **Y-site: aminophylline, amphotericin B, azathioprine, cefoperazone, ceftazidime, ceftizoxime, chloramphenicol, dantrolene, diazepam, diazoxide, folic acid, furosemide, ganciclovir, hydrocortisone, imipenem/cilastatin, iamrinone, indomethacin, methylprednisolone, pentobarbital, phenobarbital, phenytoin, sodium bicarbonate, SMZ/TMP.**

- Preserve in tight, light-resistant, nonmetallic containers. Thiamine is unstable in alkaline solutions (e.g., solutions of acetates, barbiturates, bicarbonates, carbonates, citrates) and neutral solutions.

ADVERSE EFFECTS **CV:** <u>Cardiovascular collapse</u>, slight fall in BP following rapid IV administration. **Respiratory:** Cyanosis, pulmonary edema. **Skin:** Urticaria, pruritus. **GI:** GI hemorrhage, nausea. **Other:** Feeling of warmth, weakness, sweating, restlessness, tightness of throat, angioneurotic edema, <u>anaphylaxis</u>.

INTERACTIONS **Drug:** No clinically significant interactions established.

PHARMACOKINETICS **Absorption:** Limited from GI tract. **Distribution:** Widely distributed, including into breast milk. **Elimination:** In urine.

NURSING IMPLICATIONS

Assessment & Drug Effects

- Record patient's dietary history carefully as an essential part of vitamin replacement therapy. Collaborate with prescriber, dietitian, patient, and responsible family member in developing a diet teaching plan that can be sustained by patient.

Patient & Family Education

- Food–drug relationships: Learn about rich dietary sources of thiamine (e.g., yeast, pork, beef, liver, wheat and other whole grains, nutrient-added breakfast cereals, fresh vegetables, especially peas and dried beans).
- Body requirement of thiamine is directly proportional to

T

carbohydrate intake and metabolic rate; requirement increases when diet consists predominantly of carbohydrates.

THIOGUANINE (TG, 6-THIOGUANINE)

(thye-oh-gwah'neen)
Lanvis ✦, Tabloid
Classification: ANTINEOPLASTIC; ANTIMETABOLITE; PURINE ANTAGONIST
Therapeutic: ANTINEOPLASTIC
Prototype: Mercaptopurine

AVAILABILITY Tablet

ACTION & *THERAPEUTIC EFFECT*
Tumor inhibitory properties may be caused by a sequential blockade of the synthesis and utilization of the purine nucleotides in DNA and DNA. *Interferes with nucleic acid biosynthesis, and has been found active against selected human neoplastic diseases.*

USES In combination with other antineoplastics for remission induction in acute myelogenous leukemia and as treatment of chronic myelogenous leukemia.

CONTRAINDICATIONS Patients with prior resistance to this drug; severe bone marrow depression; liver toxicity caused by drug; pregnancy (category D); lactation.

CAUTIOUS USE Resistance to mercaptopurine; hepatic disease; children.

ROUTE & DOSAGE

Leukemia
Adult: **PO** 2 mg/kg/day, may increase to 3 mg/kg/day if no response after 4 wk

ADMINISTRATION

Oral
- Withhold drug and notify prescriber if toxicity develops. There is no known antagonist; prompt discontinuation of the drug is essential to avoid irreversible myelosuppression from toxicity.
- Store at 15°–30° C (59°–86° F) in airtight container.

ADVERSE EFFECTS CV: Esophogeal varices, portal hypertension. **Endocrine:** Fluid retention, hyperuricemia, weight gain. **Hepatic:** Ascites, hepatomegaly, hepatotoxicity, hyperbilirubinemia, increased liver enzymes, jaundice, periportal fibrosis. **GI:** Anorexia, intestinal perforation, nausea, vomiting, stomatitis. **Musculoskeletal:** Bone hypoplasia. **Hematologic:** Anemia, bone marrow depression, granulocytopenia, hemorrhage, leukopenia, pancytopenia, splemomegaly, thrombocytopenia. **Other:** Infection.

INTERACTIONS Drug: Severe hepatotoxicity with **busulfan;** may decrease immune response to VACCINES; increase risk of bleeding with ANTICOAGULANTS; NSAIDS, SALICYLATES; PLATELET INHIBITORS, THROMBOLYTIC AGENTS; effects may be reversed by **filgrastim, sargramostim.** Do not use with **deferoprone, dipyrone,**

natalizumab, pimecrolimus, tacrolimus.

PHARMACOKINETICS
Absorption: Variable and incomplete absorption from GI tract. **Peak:** 8 h. **Distribution:** Crosses placenta. **Metabolism:** In liver. **Elimination:** In urine. **Half-Life:** 5–9 h.

NURSING IMPLICATIONS

Assessment & Drug Effects
- Determine hematologic parameters for withholding drug.
- Monitor I&O ratio and report oliguria.
- Observe patient's skin and sclera for jaundice. It should be reported promptly as a symptom of toxicity; drug will be discontinued promptly.
- Expect that the drop in leukocyte count may be slow over a period of 2–4 wk. Treatment is interrupted if there is a rapid fall within a few days.
- Monitor lab tests: Frequent CBC with differential and platelet count; weekly LFTs early in therapy and monthly thereafter.

Patient & Family Education
- Report promptly to prescriber any of the following: Fever, sore throat, jaundice, nausea, vomiting, signs of infection, bleeding from any site, or symptoms of anemia.
- Women should use effective means of contraception while taking this drug.

THIORIDAZINE HYDROCHLORIDE
(thye-o-rid′a-zeen)

Classification: ANTIPSY-CHOTIC; PHENOTHIAZINE
Therapeutic: ANTIPSYCHOTIC
Prototype: Chlorpromazine

AVAILABILITY
Tablet

ACTION & THERAPEUTIC EFFECT
Blocks postsynaptic dopamine receptors in the mesolimbic system of the brain. The decrease in dopamine neurotransmission has been found to correlate to antipsychotic effects. *Effective in reducing excitement, hypermotility, abnormal initiative, affective tension, and agitation by inhibiting psychomotor functions. Also effective as an antipsychotic agent, and for behavioral disorders in children.*

USES
Treatment of schizophrenia in patients who fail to respond adequately to treatment with other antipsychotics.

CONTRAINDICATIONS
Hypersensitivity to phenothiazines; severe CNS depression; severe hyper-/hypotensive heart disease; family history of QT prolongation or cardiac arrhythmias; coadministration of drug that is known to prolong the QTc interval; suicidal ideation; older adults with dementia related psychosis; lactation.

CAUTIOUS USE
Premature ventricular contractions; previously diagnosed breast cancer; patients exposed to extremes in heat or to organophosphorus insecticides; history of suicidal tendencies; Parkinson's disease; seizure disorders; closed-angle glaucoma; respiratory disorders; pregnancy (maternal antipsychotic use during the third trimester of pregnancy has a risk for abnormal muscle movements

T

---

and withdrawal symptoms in newborns). Safe use in children younger than 2 y not established.

ROUTE & DOSAGE

Schizophrenia

Adult: **PO** 50–100 mg tid, may increase up to 800 mg/day as needed or tolerated
Child (2 y or older): **PO** 0.5 mg/kg/day in divided doses; (max: 3 mg/kg/day)

Pharmacogenetic Dosage Adjustment

Poor CYP2D6 metabolizers: reduce initial dose

ADMINISTRATION

Oral

- Administer with water, food, or milk to decrease GI upset.
- Schedule phenothiazine at least 1 h before or 1 h after an antacid or antidiarrheal medication.
- Add increases in dose to the first dose of the day to prevent sleep disturbance.
- Store at 20°–25° C (68°–77° F) in tightly covered, light-resistant containers unless otherwise indicated.

ADVERSE EFFECTS **CV:** ECG changes, hypotension, orthostatic hypotension, peripheral edema, prolonged QT$_c$ interval. **CNS:** *Sedation,* dizziness, drowsiness, lethargy, extrapyramidal syndrome, nocturnal confusion, hyperactivity, headache, restlessness. **HEENT:** Nasal congestion, blurred vision, corneal opacity. **GI:** Xerostomia, *constipation,* weight gain. **GU:** Amenorrhea, breast engorgement, galactorrhea, sexual difficulty. **Hematologic:** Agranulocytosis, leukopenia.

DIAGNOSTIC TEST INTERFERENCE
Possible false positive with urine detection of methadone and phencyclidine.

INTERACTIONS **Drug: Alcohol,** ANXIOLYTICS, SEDATIVE-HYPNOTICS, other CNS DEPRESSANTS add to CNS depression; additive adverse effects with other PHENOTHIAZINES. Use with other agents affecting QT interval can prolong QT$_c$ interval resulting in arrhythmias. Use with ANTIPARKINSON AGENTS, ANTICHOLINERGIC AGENTS, ANTIPSYCHOTIC AGENTS results in increased adverse effects. Do not use with **aminolevulinic acid, amisulpride, asunaprevir, dapoxetine, eliglustat, glycopyrrolate. Herbal: Kava** may increase risk and severity of dystonic reactions.

PHARMACOKINETICS **Absorption:** Well absorbed from GI tract. **Onset:** Days to weeks. **Distribution:** Crosses placenta; distributed into breast milk. **Metabolism:** In liver (CYP2D6). **Elimination:** In urine. **Half-Life:** 5-27 h.

NURSING IMPLICATIONS

Black Box Warning

Thioridazine has been associated with prolongation of the QTc interval, development of torsades de pointes–type arrhythmias and sudden death; and with increased mortality in older adults with dementia-related psychosis.

Assessment & Drug Effects

- Monitor for changes in behavior that may indicate increased possibility of suicide ideation.
- Orthostatic hypotension may occur in early therapy. Monitor ambulation.
- Monitor ECG periodically throughout therapy, especially during a period of dose adjustment.
- Report promptly S&S of torsades de pointes (e.g., dizziness, palpitations, syncope).
- Monitor I&O ratio and bowel elimination pattern. Check for abdominal distention and pain. Encourage adequate fluid intake as prophylaxis for constipation and xerostomia. The depressed patient may not seek help for either symptom or for urinary retention.
- Obtain baseline and periodic ophthalmic exam.
- Monitor lab tests: Periodic CBC, serum electrolytes, lipid profile, fasting plasma glucose level, HbA1C, and LFTs.

Patient & Family Education

- Avoid alcohol during phenothiazine therapy. Concomitant use enhances CNS depression effects.
- Be aware that marked drowsiness generally subsides with continued therapy or reduction in dosage.
- Do not drive or engage in potentially hazardous activities until response to drug is known.
- Make position changes slowly, particularly from lying down to upright posture; dangle legs a few minutes before standing.
- Vasodilation produced by hot showers or baths or by long exposure to environmental heat may accentuate hypotensive effect.
- Do not use any OTC drugs unless approved by the prescriber.

THIOTEPA
(thye-oh-tep′a)
Tepadina
Classification: ANTINEOPLASTIC; ALKYLATING AGENT
Therapeutic: ANTINEOPLASTIC
Prototype: Cyclophosphamide

AVAILABILITY Solution for injection

ACTION & THERAPEUTIC EFFECT
Cell-cycle nonspecific alkylating agent that selectively reacts with DNA phosphate groups to produce chromosome cross-linkage and consequent blocking of nucleoprotein synthesis. Highly toxic hematopoietic agent. *Myelosuppression is cumulative and unpredictable and may be delayed.*

USES
To reduce the risk of graft rejection when with other agents as a preparative regimen for allogeneic hematopoietic progenitor (stem) cell transplantation in pediatric patients with class 3 beta-thalassemia.

UNLABELED USES
Hematopoietic stem cell transplant, malignant meningeal neoplasms.

CONTRAINDICATIONS
Hypersensitivity to thiotepa; acute leukemia; acute infection; concomitant use with live or attenuated vaccines; pregnancy (in utero exposure to thiotepa may cause fetal harm); lactation.

CAUTIOUS USE
Chronic lymphocytic leukemia; myelosuppression produced by radiation; bone marrow invasion by tumor cells; impaired kidney or liver function; children.

T

ROUTE & DOSAGE

Hematopoietic stem cell transplant

Child/Adolescent: **IV**
300 mg/m² daily ×3 days beginning 8 days before transplant

ADMINISTRATION

Intravenous

Use only under constant supervision by prescribers experienced in therapy with cytotoxic agents.
▪ Avoid exposure of skin and respiratory tract to particles of thiotepa during solution preparation.
▪ Antiemetics may be recommended to prevent nausea and vomiting.
PREPARE: Direct: Reconstitute each 15 mg vial with 1.5 mL sterile water for infusion. Reconstituted concentration is 10 mg/mL. Solutions for IV infusion should be further diluted in NS. ▪ Filter solution through a 0.2 micron filter.
ADMINISTER: Direct: Administer over 3 hours via a central line. Infusion times may vary by protocol or dose for off-label uses; refer to specific protocols. Flush with 5 mL NS before and after infusion.
INCOMPATIBILITIES: Solution/additive: Cisplatin. Y-site: Alemtuzumab, amiodarone, busulfan, cisplatin, dantrolene, diazepam, **filgrastim,** gemtuzumab, **minocycline,** naloxone, nicardipine, nitroprusside, pantoprazole, phenytoin, **verapamil.**

▪ Store powder for injection and reconstituted solutions at 2°–8° C (35°–46° F); protect from light.
▪ Solutions reconstituted with sterile water only are stable for 8 h under refrigeration.

ADVERSE EFFECTS CNS: Intracranial hemorrhage, seizure, dizziness, fatigue, headache. **Respiratory:** Pneumonia. **Skin:** Alopecia, contact dermatitis, skin depigmentation, rash, urticaria. **Hepatic/GI:** Anorexia, nausea, vomiting, stomatitis, abdominal pain, elevated liver enzymes, increased serum bilirubin. **GU:** Amenorrhea, interference with spermatogenesis. **Hematologic:** Neutropenia, thrombocytopenia, anemia, pancytopenia. **Other:** Cytomegalovirus disease, febrile reactions.

INTERACTIONS Drug: May prolong muscle paralysis with **mivacurium;** ANTICOAGULANTS, NSAIDS, SALICYLATES, ANTIPLATELET AGENTS may increase risk of bleeding. Increased risk of adverse effects when used with IMMUNOSUPPRESSANT or MYELOSUPPRESSIVE AGENTS. Do not administer with LIVE VACCINES. CYP 3A4 INHIBITORS may decrease concentration of thiotepa. **Herbal:** Avoid use of echinacea.

PHARMACOKINETICS Absorption: Rapidly cleared from plasma. **Onset:** Gradual response over several weeks. **Metabolism:** In liver. **Elimination:** 60% in urine within 24–72 h.

NURSING IMPLICATIONS

Assessment & Drug Effects

▪ Monitor closely for symptoms of dermatologic or CNS toxicity.
▪ Be aware that because of cumulative effects, maximum myelosuppression may be delayed 3–4 wk after termination of therapy.

Common adverse effects in *italic*; life-threatening effects underlined; generic names in **bold**; classifications in SMALL CAPS; ♣ Canadian drug name; ◯ Prototype drug; ⚠ Alert

1656

T

- Withhold drug and notify prescriber if leukocyte count falls to 3000/mm^3 or below or if platelet count falls below 150,000/mm^3.
- Monitor lab tests: CBC with differential, LFTs, renal function tests, and platelet count at least weekly during therapy and for at least 3 wk after therapy is discontinued.

Patient & Family Education
- Be aware of possibility of amenorrhea (usually reversible in 6–8 mo).
- Report onset of fever, bleeding, a cold or illness, no matter how mild to prescriber; medical supervision may be necessary.

THIOTHIXENE HYDROCHLORIDE

(thye-oh-thix′een)
Navane ♦
Classification: ANTIPSYCHOTIC; PHENOTHIAZINE
Therapeutic: ANTIPSYCHOTIC
Prototype: Chlorpromazine

AVAILABILITY Capsule

ACTION & *THERAPEUTIC EFFECT*
Mechanism of action is related to blockade of postsynaptic dopamine receptors in the mesolimbic region of the brain. Additionally, blockade of alpha$_1$-adrenergic receptors in the CNS produces sedation and muscle relaxation. *Possesses antipsychotic, sedative, adrenolytic, and antiemetic activity.*

USES Management of schizophrenia.

CONTRAINDICATIONS Hypersensitivity to thiothixene; CNS depression; coma; older adults with dementia related psychosis; circulatory collapse; blood dyscrasias; NMS; lactation.

CAUTIOUS USE History of convulsive disorders; alcohol withdrawal; glaucoma; prostatic hypertrophy; cardiovascular disease; older adults; patients who might be exposed to organophosphorus insecticides or to extreme heat; previously diagnosed breast cancer; pregnancy (adverse effects were observed in some animal reproduction studies). Safe use in children younger than 12 y not established.

ROUTE & DOSAGE

Schizophrenia
Adult/Adolescent: **PO** 2 mg tid, may increase up to 15 mg/day as needed or tolerated (max: 60 mg/day)

ADMINISTRATION
Oral
- Capsules may be opened and mixed with food or water for ease of administration.

ADVERSE EFFECTS CV: Tachycardia, *orthostatic hypotension,* cardiac arrest, ECG changes, peripheral edema, syncope. **Respiratory:** Asphyxia, nasal congestion. **CNS:** *Drowsiness,* insomnia, dizziness, cerebral edema, convulsions, *extrapyramidal symptoms (dose related),* paradoxical exaggeration of psychotic symptoms; sudden death, neuroleptic malignant syndrome, tardive dyskinesia, seizure, restlessness. **HEENT:** Blurred vision, pigmentary retinopathy. **Skin:** Rash,

---

photosensitivity, contact dermatitis, diaphoresis, pruritis, skin discoloration (blue-gray). **Hepatic/GI:** Xerostomia, constipation, anorexia, nausea, stomach pain, elevated liver enzymes. **GU:** Impotence, gynecomastia, galactorrhea, amenorrhea, breast hypertrophy, difficult micturition, ejaculatory disorder. **Hematologic:** Leukocytosis, leukopenia. **Other:** Fever.

DIAGNOSTIC TEST INTERFERENCE

may cause false positive pregnancy test

INTERACTIONS Drug: Alcohol,

ANXIOLYTICS, SEDATIVE-HYPNOTICS, other CNS DEPRESSANTS add to CNS depression; additive adverse effects with other PHENOTHIAZINES; Use with ANTIPARKINSON AGENTS, ANTICHOLINERGIC AGENTS, ANTIPSYCHOTIC AGENTS results in increased adverse effects. Do not use with, **amisulpride, glycopyrrolate. Herbal: Kava** may increase risk and severity of dystonic reactions.

PHARMACOKINETICS Absorption: Slowly absorbed from GI tract. **Duration:** Up to 12 h. **Distribution:** May remain in body for several weeks; crosses placenta. **Metabolism:** In liver, substrate of CYP1A2. **Elimination:** In bile and feces. **Half-Life:** 34 h.

NURSING IMPLICATIONS

Black Box Warning

Thiothixene has been associated with increased mortality in older adults with dementia-related psychosis.

Assessment & Drug Effects

- Monitor BP for excessive hypotensive response when thiothixene is added to drug regimen of patient on hypertensive treatment until therapy is stabilized.
- Report extrapyramidal effects (pseudoparkinsonism, akathisia, dystonia) to prescriber; dose adjustment or short-term therapy with an antiparkinsonism agent may provide relief.
- Be alert to first symptoms of tardive dyskinesia (see Appendix F). Withhold drug and notify prescriber.
- Monitor lab tests: Periodic electrolytes, lipid profile, LFTs, HbA1c, plasma fasting glucose.

Patient & Family Education

- Make position changes slowly, particularly from lying down to upright because of danger of light-headedness; sit a few minutes before walking.
- Do not drive or engage in potentially hazardous activities until response to drug is known.
- Avoid alcohol and other depressants during therapy.
- Take drug as prescribed; do not alter dosing regimen or stop medication without consulting prescriber. Abrupt discontinuation can cause delirium.
- Do not use any OTC drugs without approval of prescriber.
- Avoid excessive exposure to sunlight to prevent a photosensitivity reaction. If sun exposure is expected, protect skin with sunscreen lotion (SPF 12 or above).

- Schedule periodic eye exams and report blurred vision to prescriber.

THROMBIN
(throm'bin)
Recothrom, Thrombinar, Thrombostat
Classification: COAGULATOR; TOPICAL HEMOSTATIC
Therapeutic: COAGULATOR; HEMOSTATIC

AVAILABILITY Topical application

ACTION & *THERAPEUTIC EFFECT*
Plasma protein prepared from prothrombin of bovine origin. Induces clotting of whole blood or fibrinogen solution without addition of other substances. *Facilitates conversion of fibrinogen to fibrin resulting in clotting of whole blood.*

USES Hemostasis aid.

CONTRAINDICATIONS Known hypersensitivity to any of thrombin components or to material of bovine origin; parenteral use; entry or infiltration into large blood vessels.

CAUTIOUS USE Older adults; pregnancy (category C). Safety and efficacy in children and infants not established.

ROUTE & DOSAGE

Hemostasis
Adult: **Topical** 100–2000 NIH units/mL, depending on extent of bleeding, may be used as solution, in dry form, by mixing thrombin with blood plasma to form a fibrin "glue," or in conjunction with absorbable gelatin sponge

ADMINISTRATION
Topical
- Ensure that sponge recipient area is free of blood before applying thrombin.
- Prepare solutions in sterile distilled water or isotonic saline.
- Use solutions within a few hours of preparation. If several hours are to elapse between time of preparation and use, solution should be refrigerated, or preferably frozen, and used within 48 h.
- Store lyophilized preparation at 2°–8° C (36°–46° F).

ADVERSE EFFECTS Other: Sensitivity, allergic and febrile reactions, intravascular clotting and death when thrombin is allowed to enter large blood vessels.

THYROID DESSICATED
(thye'roid)
Armour Thyroid, Nature-Thyroid, NP Thyroid, Westhroid, WP Thyroid
Classification: THYROID REPLACEMENT
Therapeutic: THYROID HORMONE REPLACEMENT
Prototype: Levothyroxine sodium

AVAILABILITY Tablet

ACTION & *THERAPEUTIC EFFECT*
The mechanisms by which thyroid hormones exert their effects are not well understood. They enhance oxygen consumption, increase the basal metabolic rate and the metabolism of carbohydrates, lipids, and proteins. They exert a profound

T

influence on every organ system and are of particular importance in the development of the CNS. *Effectiveness indicated by diuresis, followed by sense of well-being, increased pulse rate, increased pulse pressure, increased appetite, increased psychomotor activity, loss of constipation, normalization of skin texture and hair, and increased T_3 and T_4 serum levels.*

USES Treatment of hypothyroidism of any etiology, and for the treatment or prevention of various types of euthyroid (non-toxic) goiter.

CONTRAINDICATIONS Thyrotoxicosis; acute MI not associated with hypothyroidism, cardiovascular disease; morphologic hypogonadism; nephrosis; uncorrected hypoadrenalism.

CAUTIOUS USE Angina pectoris, hypertension, older adults who may have occult cardiac disease; renal insufficiency; DM; history of hyperthyroidism; malabsorption states; pregnancy (category A); lactation (infant risk cannot be ruled out).

ROUTE & DOSAGE

Hypothyroidism

Adult/Adolescent: **PO** 30 mg/day, may increase by 15 mg q2–3 wk to 60–180mg/day
Infant/Child: See package insert for weight-based dosing.

ADMINISTRATION

Oral
- Give preferably on an empty stomach.
- Initiate dosage generally at low level and systematically increase in small increments to desired maintenance dose.
- Store in dark bottle to minimize spontaneous deiodination. Keep desiccated thyroid dry. Store at temperatures between 15°–30° C (59°–86° F).

ADVERSE EFFECTS CV: Palpitations and tachycardia (with excessive doses). **CNS:** Insomnia, tremor and restlessness (with excessive doses). **GI:** Diarrhea, nausea and vomiting (with excessive doses).

DIAGNOSTIC TEST INTERFERENCE Thyroid increases *basal metabolic rate;* may increase *blood glucose levels, creatine phosphokinase, AST, LDH, PBI.* It may decrease *serum uric acid, cholesterol, thyroid-stimulating hormone (TSH), iodine 131* uptake. Many medications may produce false results in *thyroid function tests.*

INTERACTIONS Drug: ORAL ANTICOAGULANTS potentiate hypoprothrombinemia; may increase requirements for **insulin,** SULFONYLUREAS; **epinephrine** may precipitate coronary insufficiency; **cholestyramine,** aluminum, or calcium-containing products may decrease thyroid absorption. **Food:** Certain foods, beverages, and enteral feedings can inhibit the absorption of thyroid hormones.

PHARMACOKINETICS Absorption: Variably absorbed from GI tract. **Peak:** 1–3 wk. **Distribution:** Does not readily cross placenta; minimal amounts in breast milk. **Metabolism:** Deiodination in thyroid gland. **Elimination:** In urine and feces. **Half-Life:** T_3, 1–2 days; T_4, 6–7 days.

T

NURSING IMPLICATIONS

Assessment & Drug Effects

- Observe patient carefully during initial treatment for untoward reactions such as angina, palpitations, cardiac pain.
- Be alert for symptoms of overdosage (see ADVERSE EFFECTS) that may occur 1–3 wk after therapy is started.
- Monitor response until regimen is stabilized to prevent iatrogenic hyperthyroidism. In drug-induced hyperthyroidism, there may also be increased bone loss. Such a patient is vulnerable to pathologic fractures.
- Monitor vital signs: Assess pulse before each dose during period of dosage adjustment. Consult prescriber if rate is 100 or more or if there has been a marked change in rate or rhythm.
- TSH 4–8 wk after initiation or dose change, repeat at 6 mo, then q12 mo thereafter.

Patient & Family Education

- Be aware that replacement therapy for hypothyroidism is life-long; continued follow-up care is important.
- Monitor pulse rate and report increases greater than parameter set by prescriber.
- Report to prescriber onset of chest pain or other signs of aggravated CV disease (dyspnea, tachycardia).
- Report evidence of any unexplained bleeding to prescriber when taking concomitant anticoagulant.
- Use monthly height and weight measurement to monitor growth in juvenile undergoing treatment.

TIAGABINE HYDROCHLORIDE

(ti-a′ga-been)

Gabitril

Classification: ANTICONVULSANT; GABA INHIBITOR

Therapeutic: ANTICONVULSANT

Prototype: Valproic acid sodium (sodium valproate)

AVAILABILITY Tablet

ACTION & THERAPEUTIC EFFECT

Potent and selective inhibitor of GABA uptake into presynaptic neurons; allows more GABA to bind to the surfaces of postsynaptic neurons in the CNS. *Effectiveness indicated by reduction in seizure activity.*

USES Adjunctive therapy for partial seizures.

CONTRAINDICATIONS Hypersensitivity to tiagabine; lactation.

CAUTIOUS USE Liver function impairment; history of spike and wave discharge on EEG; status epilepticus; pregnancy (category C). Safe use in children younger than 12 y not established.

ROUTE & DOSAGE

Seizures

Adult: **PO** Start with 4 mg daily, may increase dose by 4–8 mg/day qwk (max: 56 mg/day in 2–4 divided doses)

Adolescent (12–18 y): **PO** Start with 4 mg daily, after 2 wk may increase dose by 4–8 mg/day qwk (max: 32 mg/day in 2–4 divided doses)

ADMINISTRATION

Oral

- Give with food.
- Make dosage increases, when needed, at weekly intervals.

- Store at 20°–25° C (68°–77° F) in a tightly closed container and protect from light.

ADVERSE EFFECTS CV: Vasodilation, hypertension, palpitations, tachycardia, syncope, edema, peripheral edema. **Respiratory:** Pharyngitis, cough, bronchitis, dyspnea, epistaxis, pneumonia. **CNS:** *Dizziness, asthenia, tremor, somnolence, nervousness,* difficulty concentrating, ataxia, depression, insomnia, abnormal gait, hostility, confusion, speech disorder, difficulty with memory, paresthesias, emotional lability, agitation, dysarthria, euphoria, hallucinations, paranoia, hyperkinesia, hypertonia, hypotonia, myoclonus, twitching, vertigo. Risk of new-onset seizures. **HEENT:** Amblyopia, nystagmus, tinnitus. **Skin:** Rash, pruritus, alopecia, dry skin, sweating, ecchymoses. **GI:** Abdominal pain, diarrhea, nausea, vomiting, increased appetite, mouth ulcers. **GU:** Dysmenorrhea, dysuria, metrorrhagia, incontinence, vaginitis, UTI. **Other:** Infection, flu-like syndrome, pain, myasthenia, allergic reactions, chills, malaise, arthralgia.

INTERACTIONS Drug: Carbamazepine, mitotane, phenytoin, phenobarbital decrease levels of tiagabine. Use with ANTIDEPRESSANTS, ANTIPSYCHOTICS, STIMULANTS, AMPHETAMINES, and NARCOTICS may increase seizure risk. Avoid use of **ceritinib, idelalisib, posaconazole,** as it may increase toxicity risk. **Herbal: Ginkgo, kava** may decrease anticonvulsant effectiveness. **Evening primrose oil** may affect seizure threshold. **Food:** Use of ethanol regularly may require lower tiagabine dose.

PHARMACOKINETICS Absorption: Rapidly absorbed; 90% bioavailability.

Peak: 45 min. **Distribution:** 96% protein bound. **Metabolism:** In liver (CYP3A4). **Elimination:** 25% in urine, 63% in feces. **Half-Life:** 7–9 h (4–7 h with other enzyme-inducing drugs).

NURSING IMPLICATIONS

Assessment & Drug Effects

- Be aware that concurrent use of other anticonvulsants may decrease effectiveness of tiagabine or increase the potential for adverse effects.
- Monitor carefully for S&S of CNS depression and suicidal ideation.
- Monitor lab tests: Plasma tiagabine before and after changes are made in the drug regimen, LFTs.

Patient & Family Education

- Do not stop taking drug abruptly; may cause sudden onset of seizures.
- Exercise caution while engaging in potentially hazardous activities because drug may cause dizziness.
- Use caution when taking other prescription or OTC drugs that can cause drowsiness.
- Report any of the following to the prescriber: Rash or hives; red, peeling skin; dizziness; drowsiness; depression; GI distress; nervousness or tremors; difficulty concentrating or talking.

TICAGRELOR

(tye'ka-gre-lor)

Brilinta

Classification: ANTIPLATELET INHIBITOR; ANTITHROMBOTIC

Therapeutic: PLATELET AGGREGATION INHIBITOR; ANTITHROMBOTIC

Prototype: Clopidogrel

AVAILABILITY Tablet

ACTION & *THERAPEUTIC EFFECT*

Ticagrelor and its major metabolite reversibly interact with the platelet ADP receptor to prevent signal transduction and platelet activation. *Prevents platelet activation and clot formation.*

USES Prophylaxis to prevent arterial thromboembolism in patients with acute coronary syndrome (ACS).

UNLABELED USES Unstable angina/non-ST elevation MI.

CONTRAINDICATIONS Hypersensitivity (e.g., angioedema) to ticagrelor; severe hepatic impairment; history of intracranial hemorrhage; active bleeding (e.g., peptic ulcer); use within 24 h.

CAUTIOUS USE Mild-to-moderate hepatic impairment; second or third AV block, sick sinus syndrome; history of bleeding disorders, percutaneous invasive procedures, and use of drugs that increase risk of bleeding (e.g., anticoagulant and fibrinolytic therapy, high dose aspirin, long-term NSAIDs); older adults; pregnancy (category C); lactation (infant risk cannot be ruled out). Safety and efficacy in children not established.

ROUTE & DOSAGE

Arterial Thromboembolism Prophylaxis

Adult: **PO** 180 mg loading dose (plus aspirin) followed by 90 mg bid (with 75–100 mg aspirin once daily) for 1 y; after 1 y 60 mg bid

ADMINISTRATION

Oral

- May be given without regard to food.
- Tablets may be crushed and mixed with water for oral or NG administration.
- Store at 15°–30° C (59°–86° F) and protect from moisture.

ADVERSE EFFECTS CV: Bradyarrhythmia. **Respiratory:** Dyspnea, pulmonary hemorrhage. **CNS:** Dizziness. **GU:** Increased serum creatinine.

INTERACTIONS Drug: Strong CYP3A4 inhibitors (e.g., **ketoconazole, itraconazole, voriconazole, clarithromycin, nefazodone, ritonavir, saquinavir, nelfinavir, indinavir, atazanavir,** and **telithromycin**) can increase ticagrelor levels, while potent CYP3A4 inducers (e.g., **rifampin, dexamethasone, phenytoin, carbamazepine,** and **phenobarbital**) can decrease ticagrelor levels. Ticagrelor can increase the levels of **simvastatin** and **lovastatin.** Avoid use with ANTIPLATELETS or ANTICOAGULANTS. Do not use with **avanafil, defibrotide. Herbal:** Do not use with **St. John's wort.**

PHARMACOKINETICS Absorption: 30–42% Bioavailable. **Onset:** 1.5–5 h. **Distribution:** Greater than 99% plasma protein bound. **Metabolism:** CYP3A4, CYP3A5, P-gp metabolism to active compound. **Elimination:** Fecal (58%) and renal (26%). **Half-Life:** 7 h (ticagrelor); 9 h (active metabolite).

NURSING IMPLICATIONS

Black Box Warning

Ticagrelor has been associated with serious, sometimes fatal, bleeding.

Assessment & Drug Effects

- Monitor cardiac status with ECG and frequent BP measurements. Report immediately development of hypotension in any one who has recently undergone coronary angiography, PCI, CABG, or other surgical procedures.
- Monitor for and report promptly S&S of bleeding or dyspnea. Monitor lab tests: CBC hemoglobin, hematocrit, renal functions, uric acid levels, and LFTs.

Patient & Family Education

- Report promptly to prescriber any of the following: Unexplained, prolonged, or excessive bleeding; blood in stool or urine; shortness of breath.
- Daily doses of aspirin **should not** exceed 100 mg. Do not take any other drugs that contain aspirin. Consult prescriber if taking a nonsteroidal anti-inflammatory drug (NSAID).
- Inform all health care providers that you are taking ticagrelor.

TICARCILLIN DISODIUM/ CLAVULANATE POTASSIUM

(tye-kar-sill'in/clav-yoo'la-nate)

Timentin

Classification: ANTIBIOTIC; EXTENDED-SPECTRUM PENICILLIN

Therapeutic: ANTIBIOTIC

Prototype: Piperacillin/ tazobactam

AVAILABILITY Solution for injection

ACTION & THERAPEUTIC EFFECT

Used alone, clavulanic acid antibacterial activity is weak, but in combination with ticarcillin prevents degradation by beta-lactamase and extends ticarcillin spectrum of activity. *Combination drug extends ticarcillin spectrum of activity against many strains of beta-lactamase-producing bacteria (synergistic effect).*

USES Infections of lower respiratory tract and urinary tract and skin and skin structures, infections of bone and joint, and septicemia caused by susceptible organisms. Also mixed infections and as presumptive therapy before identification of causative organism.

CONTRAINDICATIONS Hypersensitivity to ticarcillin/clavulanate or penicillins or to cephalosporins, coagulopathy.

CAUTIOUS USE DM; GI disease; asthma; history of allergies; renal impairment; pregnancy (category B); lactation.

ROUTE & DOSAGE

Moderate to Severe Infections

Adult/Adolescent/Child (weight greater than 60 kg): **IV** 3.1 g q4–6h
Child/Infant (3 mo or older and weight less than 60 kg): **IV** 200–300 mg/kg/day divided q4–6h (based on ticarcillin)
Infant (younger than 3 mo and weight less than 60 kg): **IV** 200–300 mg/kg/day divided q6–8h (based on ticarcillin)

Renal Impairment Dosage Adjustment

CrCl 30–60 mL/min: Give 2 g q4h; *10–30 mL/min:* Give 2 g q8h; *less than 10 mL/min:* Give 2 g q12h

Hemodialysis Dosage Adjustment

2 g q12h, supplement with 3.1 g after dialysis

ADMINISTRATION

Intravenous

Note: Verify correct IV concentration and rate of infusion for administration to infants and children with prescriber.

PREPARE: **Intermittent:** Reconstitute by adding 13 mL sterile water for injection or NS injection to the 3.1 g vial to yield 200 mg/mL ticarcillin with 6.7 mg/mL clavulanic acid. Shake until dissolved. ▪ Further dilute the required does in NS, D5W, or LR to concentrations between 10–100 mg/mL. ▪ **Do not** use if discoloration or particulate matter is present.

ADMINISTER: **Intermittent:** Give over 30 min.

INCOMPATIBILITIES: **Solution/additive:** AMINOGLYCOSIDES, **sodium bicarbonate.** **Y-site:** **acyclovir, alatrofloxacin, amphotericin B cholesteryl complex, azathioprine, azithromycin, caspofungin, cefamandole, chlorpromazine, dantrolene, daunorubicin, diazepam, diazoxide, dobutamine, dolasetron, alfa, epirubicin, erythromycin, ganciclovir, gemtuzumab, haloperidol, hydroxyzine, idarubicin, inamrinone, lansoprazole, minocycline, mitomycin, mitoxantrone, mycophenolate, papaverine, pentamidine, pentazocine, phenytoin, promethazine, protamine, quinupristin/dalfopristin, SMZ/TMP, vancomycin.**

▪ Store vial with sterile powder at 21°–24° C (69°–75° F) or colder. ▪ If exposed to higher temperature, powder will darken, indicating degradation of clavulanate potassium and loss of potency. Discard vial. ▪ See package insert for information about storage and stability of reconstituted and diluted IV solutions of drug.

ADVERSE EFFECTS **CNS:** Headache, blurred vision, mental deterioration, convulsions, hallucinations, seizures, giddiness, neuromuscular hyperirritability. **Endocrine:** Hypernatremia, transient increases in serum AST, ALT, BUN, and alkaline phosphatase; increases in serum LDH, bilirubin, and creatinine and decreased serum uric acid. **GI:** *Diarrhea, nausea,* vomiting, disturbances of taste or smell, stomatitis, flatulence. **Hematologic:** Eosinophilia, thrombocytopenia, leukopenia, neutropenia, hemolytic anemia. **Other:** Hypersensitivity reactions, pain, burning, swelling at injection site; phlebitis, thrombophlebitis; superinfections.

DIAGNOSTIC TEST INTERFERENCE

May interfere with test methods used to determine **urinary proteins** except for tests for urinary protein that use **bromphenol blue. Positive direct antiglobulin (Coombs') test** results, apparently caused by clavulanic acid, have been reported. This test may interfere with **transfusion cross-matching procedures.**

INTERACTIONS **Drugs:** May increase risk of bleeding with ANTI-COAGULANTS; **probenecid** decreases elimination of ticarcillin.

PHARMACOKINETICS **Distribution:** Widely distributed with highest concentrations in urine and bile; crosses placenta; distributed into breast milk. **Metabolism:** In liver. **Elimination:** In urine. **Half-Life:** 1.1–1.2 h ticarcillin, 1.1–1.5 h clavulanate.

NURSING IMPLICATIONS

Assessment & Drug Effects

- Be aware that serious and sometimes fatal anaphylactoid reactions have been reported in patients with penicillin hypersensitivity or history of sensitivity to multiple allergens. Reported incidence is low with this combination drug.
- Monitor cardiac status because of high sodium content of drug.
- Overdose symptoms: This drug may cause neuromuscular hyperirritability or seizures.
- Monitor lab tests: Baseline C&S; periodic LFTs and renal function tests, CBC, platelet count, and serum electrolytes.

Patient & Family Education

- Report urticaria, rashes, or pruritus to prescriber immediately.
- Report frequent loose stools, diarrhea, or other possible signs of pseudomembranous colitis (see Appendix F) to prescriber.

TICLOPIDINE HYDROCHLORIDE

(ti-clo′pi-deen)

Classification: ANTICOAGULANT; PLATELET AGGREGATION INHIBITOR; ADP RECEPTOR ANTAGONIST
Therapeutic: PLATELET AGGREGATION INHIBITOR
Prototype: Clopidogrel

AVAILABILITY Tablet

ACTION & *THERAPEUTIC EFFECT*

Platelet aggregation inhibitor that interferes with platelet membrane functioning and therefore platelet interactions. Ticlopidine interferes with ADP-induced binding of fibrinogen to the platelet membrane at specific receptor sites. *Platelet adhesion and platelet aggregation are inhibited and prolong bleeding time.*

USES Reduction of the risk of thrombotic stroke; adjunctive therapy for stent thrombosis prophylaxis.

UNLABELED USES Prevention of venous thromboembolic disorders; maintenance of bypass graft patency and of vascular access sites in hemodialysis patients; improvement of exercise performance in patients with ischemic heart disease and intermittent claudication; prevention of postoperative deep venous thrombosis (DVT).

CONTRAINDICATIONS Hypersensitivity to ticlopidine; hematopoietic disease, coagulopathy; neutropenia thrombotic thrombocytopenic purpura (TTP) leukemia; pathologic bleeding; severe liver impairment; lactation.

CAUTIOUS USE Hepatic function impairment, renal impairment; patients at risk for bleeding from trauma, surgery, or a bleeding disorder; GI bleeding in patients with history of thienopyridine hypersensitivity; allergic cross-reactivity; pregnancy (category B). Safe use in children younger than 18 y not established.

ROUTE & DOSAGE

Prevention of Stroke/Stent Thrombosis

Adult: **PO** 250 mg bid with food

ADMINISTRATION

Oral

- Hold medication and notify provider if neutrophil count falls below 1200/mm^3.

Common adverse effects in *italic;* life-threatening effects <u>underlined</u>; generic names in **bold**; classifications in SMALL CAPS; ✚ Canadian drug name; ◐ Prototype drug; ⚠ Alert

1666

- Give with food or just after eating to minimize GI irritation.
- Do not give within 2 h of an antacid.
- Store at 15°–30° C (59°–86° F).

ADVERSE EFFECTS CNS: Dizziness. **Endocrine:** Hypercholesterolemia. **Skin:** Urticaria, maculopapular rash, erythema nodosum (generally occur within the first 3 mo of therapy, with most occurring within the first 3–6 wk). **GI:** Nausea, vomiting, diarrhea, abdominal cramps; dyspepsia, flatulence, anorexia; hypercholesterolemia, abnormal liver function tests (few cases of hepatotoxicity reported). **Hematologic:** Neutropenia (resolves in 1–3 wk), thrombocytopenia, leukopenia, agranulocytosis (usually within first 3 mo), and pancytopenia; hemorrhage (ecchymosis, epistaxis, menorrhagia, GI bleeding), thrombotic thrombocytopenic purpura (usually within first month).

DIAGNOSTIC TEST INTERFERENCE
Increases *total serum cholesterol* by 8–10% within 4 wk of beginning therapy. *Lipoprotein ratios* remain unchanged. Elevates *alkaline phosphatase* and *serum transaminases.*

INTERACTIONS Drug: ANTACIDS decrease bioavailability of ticlopidine. ANTICOAGULANTS increase risk of bleeding. **Cimetidine** decreases clearance of ticlopidine. CORTICOSTEROIDS counteract increased bleeding time associated with ticlopidine. May decrease **cyclosporine** levels. Increases **theophylline** serum levels. May increase levels of **citalopram, metoprolol, pimozide, phenytoin, tizanidine.** Can decrease levels of **clopidogrel.** Do not use with **defibrotide.**

Food: Food may increase bioavailability of **ticlopidine. Herbal: Evening primrose oil** increases bleeding risk.

PHARMACOKINETICS Absorption: 90% from GI tract; increased absorption when taken with food. **Onset:** Antiplatelet activity, 6 h; maximal effect at 3–5 days. **Peak:** Peak serum levels at 2h. **Duration:** Bleeding times return to baseline within 4–10 days. **Distribution:** 90% bound to plasma proteins. **Metabolism:** Rapidly and extensively metabolized in liver (CYP1A2, CYP2B6, CYP2C19). **Elimination:** 60% of metabolites excreted in urine, 23% in feces. **Half-Life:** 12.6 h; terminal half-life is 4–5 days with repeated dosing.

NURSING IMPLICATIONS

Black Box Warning

Ticlopidine has been associated with life-threatening neutropenia, agranulocytosis, thrombotic thrombocytopenic purpura (TTP), and aplastic anemia.

Assessment & Drug Effects
- Report promptly laboratory values indicative of neutropenia, thrombocytopenia, or agranulocytosis.
- Monitor for signs of bleeding (e.g., ecchymosis, epistaxis, hematuria, GI bleeding).
- Monitor lab tests: Baseline CBC with differentials and platelet count, repeat q2wk from second week to end of third month of therapy, repeat as indicated thereafter if S&S of infection develop, and LFTs.

Patient & Family Education
- Stop taking this drug and report promptly to prescriber any of

the following: Nausea, diarrhea, rash, sore throat, or other signs of infection, signs of bleeding, or signs of liver damage (e.g., yellow skin or sclera, dark urine or clay-colored stools).

- Understand risk of GI bleeding; do not take aspirin along with ticlopidine.
- Do not take antacids within 2 h of ticlopidine.
- Keep appointments for regularly scheduled blood tests.

TIGECYCLINE

(ti-ge-cy'cline)

Tygacil
Classification: ANTIBIOTIC;
GLYCYLCYCLINE
Therapeutic: ANTIBIOTIC
Prototype: Tetracycline

AVAILABILITY Solution for injection

ACTION & *THERAPEUTIC EFFECT*

Inhibits protein production in bacteria by binding to the 30S ribosomal subunit and blocking entry of transfer RNA molecules into ribosome of bacteria. This prevents formation of peptide chains within bacteria, thus interfering with their growth. *Tigecycline is active against a broad spectrum of bacterial pathogens and is bacteriostatic.*

USES Treatment of complicated skin and skin structure infections, community acquired pneumonia, and complicated intra-abdominal infections.

CONTRAINDICATIONS Hypersensitivity to tigecycline; viral infections; pregnancy (category D); and during tooth development of the fetus.

CAUTIOUS USE Severe hepatic impairment (Child-Pugh class C); hypersensitivity to tetracycline, intestinal perforations, intra-abdominal infections; GI disorders; lactation. Safe use in children younger than 8 y not established.

ROUTE & DOSAGE

Community Acquired Pneumonia, Complicated Skin/ Intra-abdominal Infections

Adult: **IV** 100 mg initially, followed by 50 mg q12h over 30–60 min × 5–14 days

Hepatic Impairment Dosage Adjustment

Child-Pugh class C: Initial dose 100 mg, followed by 25 mg q12h

ADMINISTRATION

- Note that dosage adjustment is required with severe hepatic impairment.

Intravenous

PREPARE: **Intermittent:** Reconstitute each 50 mg with 5.3 mL of NS or D5W to yield 10 mg/mL. ▪ Swirl gently to dissolve; reconstituted solution should be yellow to orange in color. ▪ After reconstitution, immediately withdraw exactly 5 mL from each vial and add to 100 mL of NS or D5W for infusion. ▪ The maximum concentration in the IV bag should be 1 mg/mL (two 50 mg doses). *ADMINISTER:* **Intermittent:** Give over 30–60 min through a dedicated line or Y-site; when using Y-site, flush IV line with NS or D5W before/after infusion.

INCOMPATIBILITIES: Y-site: **Amiodarone, amphotericin B, bleomycin, chloramphenicol, chlorpromazine, dantrolene, daunorubicin, diazepam, epirubicin, esomeprazole, idarubicin, methylprednisolone, nicardipine, omeprazole, phenytoin, quinuprustin/dalfopristin, verapamil, voriconazole.**

▪ Store in the IV bag at room temperature for up to 6 h, or refrigerated at 2°–8° C (36°–46° F) for up to 24 h.

ADVERSE EFFECTS CV: Hypertension, hypotension, peripheral edema, phlebitis. **Respiratory:** Dyspnea, increased cough, pulmonary physical findings. **CNS:** Asthenia, dizziness, headache, insomnia. **Endocrine:** Alkaline phosphatase increased, ALT increased, amylase increased, AST increased, bilirubinemia, BUN increased, hyperglycemia, hypokalemia, hypoproteinemia, lactic dehydrogenase increased. **Skin:** Pruritus, rash, sweating. **GI:** Abdominal pain, constipation, diarrhea, dyspepsia, *nausea, vomiting.* **Musculoskeletal:** Back pain. **Hematologic:** Abnormal healing, anemia, infection, leukocytosis, thrombocythemia. **Other:** Abscess, fever, local reaction to injection, pain.

INTERACTIONS Drug: Increased concentrations of **warfarin** required close monitoring of INR. Efficacy of ORAL CONTRACEPTIVES may be decreased when used in combination with tigecycline.

PHARMACOKINETICS Distribution: 71–89% protein bound. **Metabolism:** Negligible. **Elimination:** Fecal (major) and renal.

Half-Life: 27 h (single dose); 42 h (multiple doses).

NURSING IMPLICATIONS

Black Box Warning

Tigecycline has been associated with increased mortality, thus its use should be reserved for situations where alternative treatments are not suitable.

Assessment & Drug Effects
▪ Monitor for hypersensitivity reaction in those with reported tetracycline allergy.
▪ Monitor for and report S&S of superinfection (see Appendix F) or pseudomembranous enterocolitis (see Appendix F).
▪ Monitor diabetics for loss of glycemic control.
▪ Monitor lab tests: Baseline C&S, and periodic LFTs.

Patient & Family Education
▪ Avoid direct exposure to sunlight during and for several days after therapy is terminated to reduce risk of photosensitivity reaction.
▪ Report to prescriber loose stools or diarrhea either during or shortly after termination of therapy.
▪ Use a barrier contraceptive in addition to oral contraceptives if trying to avoid pregnancy.

TILDRAKIZUMAB
(til-dra-kiz′ue-mab)
Ilumya
Classification: ANTIPSORIATIC AGENT; IL-23 INHIBITOR; MONOCLONAL ANTIBODY
Therapeutic: ANTIPSORIATIC

AVAILABILITY Subcutaneous injection, prefilled syringe

T

ACTION & *THERAPEUTIC EFFECT*

Human monoclonal IgG1/k antibody that selectively binds with interleukin-23 receptor to inhibit the release of proinflammatory cytokines and chemokines. *Reduces inflammatory response in adults with moderate to severe plaque psoriasis.*

USES Treatment of moderate to severe plaque psoriasis in patients who are candidates for systemic therapy or phototherapy.

CONTRAINDICATIONS Previous hypersensitivity to tildrakizumab or components of the formulation.

CAUTIOUS USE Pregnancy and lactation. Use of tildrakizumab increases the risk of serious infections. Patients should be evaluated for tuberculosis infection prior to use of tildrakizumab. Safety in children younger than 18 y not established.

ROUTE & DOSAGE

Psoriasis

Adult: **Subcutaneous** 100 mg at wk 0 and 4, and then every 12 wk thereafter

ADMINISTRATION

Subcutaneous
- To be administered by a healthcare provider.
- Remove prefilled syringe from the refrigerator and allow to warm at room temperature for 30 min.
- Inspect solution for any particulate matter or discoloration; solution should be slightly opalescent, colorless, to lightly yellow.
- Injection should be given in abdomen, thighs, or upper arm.

- Store original carton at 2°–8° C (36°–46° F); do not freeze and protect from light. Solution may be stored in original carton at room temperature not exceeding 25° C (77° F) for up to 30 days. Discard if not used within 30 days.

ADVERSE EFFECTS HEENT:

Upper respiratory infections. **Skin:** Localized injection site reactions, pruritus, erythema, inflammation, swelling, bruising. **GI:** Diarrhea. **Other:** Infection, antibody development.

INTERACTIONS Drug: Avoid the use of LIVE VACCINES in patients being treated with tildrakizumab.

PHARMACOKINETICS Absorption: 73–80% bioavailability. **Peak:** 6 days. **Distribution:** 73–80% bioavailability. **Metabolism:** Similar to endogenous IgG; degraded into small peptides and amino acids through catabolic pathways. **Half-Life:** 23 days.

NURSING IMPLICATIONS

Assessment & Drug Effects
- Assess skin for improvement of plaque psoriasis.
- Respiratory assessment for S&S of upper respiratory infection and TB (bad cough that lasts for at least 3 wk, coughing up blood or sputum, chest pain, weakness, fatigue, and weight loss).
- Monitor lab tests: TB screening prior to beginning treatment.

Patient & Family Education
- Report to prescriber any symptoms of itching, redness, soreness, difficulty breathing which may indicate an infection.
- Report to provider any signs of a respiratory infection (cough, fever,

Common adverse effects in *italic*; life-threatening effects <u>underlined</u>; generic names in **bold**; classifications in SMALL CAPS; ♣ Canadian drug name; ✪ Prototype drug; ⚠ Alert

runny nose, congestion, coughing up blood, etc.). Local redness, swelling, soreness or itching at injection site or diarrhea.
- Avoid live vaccines during treatment.

TIMOLOL MALEATE
(tye'moe-lole)
Betimol, Istalol, Timoptic, Timoptic XE
Classification: BETA-ADRENERGIC ANTAGONIST; EYE PREPARATION; MIOTIC; ANTIHYPERTENSIVE; ANTIANGINAL
Therapeutic: ANTIGLAUCOMA; ANTIHYPERTENSIVE; ANTIANGINAL
Prototype: Propranolol

AVAILABILITY Tablet; ophthalmic solution; opthalmic gel

ACTION & THERAPEUTIC EFFECT
Exhibits antihypertensive, antiarrhythmic, and antianginal properties, and suppresses plasma renin activity. When applied topically, lowers elevated and normal intraocular pressure (IOP) by reducing formation of aqueous humor and possibly by increasing outflow. *Topically, lowers elevated and normal intraocular pressure (IOP). Orally, useful for mild hypertension, angina, and migraine headaches.*

USES Topically (ophthalmic solution) to reduce elevated IOP in chronic, open-angle glaucoma, aphakic glaucoma, secondary glaucoma, and ocular hypertension. Oral product is used as monotherapy or in combination with a thiazide diuretic to prevent reinfarction after MI and to treat mild hypertension; migraine prophylaxis.

UNLABELED USES Prophylactic management of stable, uncomplicated angina pectoris.

CONTRAINDICATIONS Bronchospasm; severe COPD; bronchial asthma or history there of; HF; abrupt discontinuation, acute bronchospasm, second and third degree AV block, sinus bradycardia, cardiogenic shock, acute pulmonary edema, Raynaud's disease.

CAUTIOUS USE Bronchitis, patients subject to bronchospasm, asthma; first-degree heart block, HF; renal impairment; hepatic disease; vasospastic angina; PVD; pheochromocytoma; thyrotoxicosis, hyperthyroidism; COPD; cerebrovascular insufficiency; stroke, CVD; depression; psoriasis; MG, DM, history of spontaneous hypoglycemia; older adults; pregnancy (category C). Safe use in children not established.

ROUTE & DOSAGE

Glaucoma
See Appendix A-1.

Hypertension
Adult: **PO** 10 mg bid (may increase to 20 mg bid)

Post-MI Reinfarction
Adult: **PO** 10 mg bid

Migraine Prophylaxis
Adult: **PO** 10 mg bid or up to 30 mg daily

ADMINISTRATION
Oral
- Give with fluid of patient's choice; tablet may be crushed.
- Dosage increases for hypertension should be made at weekly intervals.

ADVERSE EFFECTS CV: Palpitation, *bradycardia, hypotension*, syncope, <u>AV conduction disturbances</u>, CHF, aggravation of peripheral vascular insufficiency. **Respiratory:** Difficulty in breathing, bronchospasm. **CNS:** *Fatigue*, lethargy, weakness, somnolence, anxiety, *headache*, dizziness, *confusion*, psychic dissociation, *depression*. **HEENT:** *Eye irritation* including conjunctivitis, blepharitis, keratitis, superficial punctate keratopathy. **Endocrine:** Hypoglycemia, hypokalemia. **Skin:** Rash, urticaria. **GI:** Anorexia, *dyspepsia, nausea*. **Other:** Fever.

INTERACTIONS Drug: ANTIHYPERTENSIVE AGENTS, DIURETICS, SELECTIVE SEROTONIN REUPTAKE INHIBITORS potentiate hypotensive effects; NSAIDS may antagonize hypotensive effects.

PHARMACOKINETICS Absorption: 90% from GI tract; some systemic absorption from topical application. **Peak:** 1–2 h PO; 1–5 h topical. **Distribution:** Distributed into breast milk. **Metabolism:** 80% metabolized in liver to inactive metabolites. **Elimination:** In urine.

NURSING IMPLICATIONS

Black Box Warning

Timolol has been associated with exacerbation of angina and MI when abruptly discontinued following chronic administration.

Assessment & Drug Effects

- Check pulse before administering timolol, topical or oral. If there are extremes (rate or rhythm), withhold medication and notify prescriber.

- Assess pulse rate and BP at regular intervals and more often in patients with severe heart disease.
- Note: Some patients develop tolerance during long-term therapy.

Patient & Family Education

- Be aware that drug may cause slight reduction in resting heart rate. Learn how to assess pulse rate and report significant changes. Consult prescriber for parameters.
- Do not stop drug abruptly; angina may be exacerbated. Dosage is reduced over a period of 1–2 wk.
- Report promptly to prescriber difficulty breathing. Drug withdrawal may be indicated.

TINIDAZOLE
(tin′i-da-zole)
Classification:
ANTIPROTOZOAL
Therapeutic: ANTIBIOTIC;
ANTIPROTOZOAL; AMEBICIDE
Prototype: Metronidazole

AVAILABILITY Tablet

ACTION & *THERAPEUTIC EFFECT*
Effective against dividing and nondividing cells of targeted bacteria and protozoa. It inhibits formation of their DNA helix and thus inhibits DNA synthesis of these organisms. This leads to bacterial and protozoal cell death. *Demonstrates activity against infections caused by protozoa and anaerobic bacteria.*

USES Treatment of trichomoniasis, giardiasis, amebiasis, bacterial vaginosis, and amebic liver abscess.

CONTRAINDICATIONS Hypersensitivity to tinidazole or other azole antibiotics; pregnancy

Common adverse effects in *italic*; life-threatening effects <u>underlined</u>; generic names in **bold;** classifications in SMALL CAPS; ♣ Canadian drug name; ◑ Prototype drug; ⚠ Alert

(first trimester); lactation within 72 h of tinidazole use.

CAUTIOUS USE CNS diseases, liver dysfunction, alcoholism, ethanol intoxication; hematologic disease; neurologic disease; bone marrow depression; dialysis; candidiasis; pregnancy (second and third trimester); children younger than 3 y.

ROUTE & DOSAGE

Giardiasis

Adult: **PO** 2 g as single dose
Child (3 y or older): **PO** 50 mg/kg (up to 2 g) as single dose

Intestinal Amebiasis

Adult: **PO** 2 g once daily for 3 days
Child (3 y or older): **PO** 50 mg/kg/day (up to 2 g/day) once daily for 3 days

Amebic Liver Abscess

Adult: **PO** 2 g once daily for 3–5 days
Child (3 y or older): **PO** 50 mg/kg/day (up to 2 g/day) once daily for 3–5 days

Trichomoniasis

Adult/Adolescent: **PO** 2 g as single dose
Child (older than 3 y): **PO** 50 mg/kg as a single dose; (max: 2000 mg)

Bacterial Vaginosis

Adult/Adolescent: **PO** 2 g daily × 2 days OR 1 g daily × 5 days

Hemodialysis Dosage Adjustment

If dose given on dialysis day, give supplemental dose (½ regular dose) post-dialysis

ADMINISTRATION

Oral

- Give with food to minimize GI distress; may be crushed in artificial cherry syrup if tablets cannot be swallowed whole (suspension is stable for 7 days at room temperature).
- If given on a dialysis day, add a 50% dose of tinidazole at the end of hemodialysis.
- Separate the dosing of cholestyramine and tinidazole by 2–4 h when used concurrently.
- Do not give within 2 wk of the last dose of disulfiram.
- Store at 15°–30° C (59°–86° F). Protect from light.

ADVERSE EFFECTS GI: Altered taste, nausea. **GU:** Vulvovaginal candidiasis.

DIAGNOSTIC TEST INTERFERENCE May interfere with *AST, ALT, triglycerides, glucose,* and *LDH* testing.

INTERACTIONS Drug: May increase INR with **warfarin; alcohol** may cause **disulfiram**-like reaction; may increase the half-life of **fosphenytoin, phenytoin;** may increase levels and toxicity of **lithium, fluorouracil, cyclosporine, tacrolimus; cholestyramine** may decrease absorption of tinidazole; **cimetidine** or **ketoconazole** may increase levels.

PHARMACOKINETICS Peak: 2 h. **Distribution:** Crosses blood–brain barrier and placenta and is excreted in breast milk. **Metabolism:** In the liver by CYP3A4. **Elimination:** Primarily in urine. **Half-Life:** 12–14 h.

NURSING IMPLICATIONS

Black Box Warning

Carcinogenicity has been seen in animal studies with another agent

T

in the nitroimidazole class. Unnecessary use of tinidazole should be avoided.

Assessment & Drug Effects

- Withhold drug and notify prescriber for S&S of CNS dysfunction (e.g., seizures, numbness or paresthesia of extremities). Drug should be discontinued if abnormal neurologic signs appear.
- Monitor INR/PT frequently with concomitant oral anticoagulants. Continue monitoring for at least 8 days after discontinuation of tinidazole.
- Monitor serum lithium levels with concurrent use.
- Monitor for phenytoin toxicity with concurrent IV phenytoin.
- Monitor lab tests: CBC with differential if retreatment is required.

Patient & Family Education

- Stop taking the drug and report promptly: Convulsions, numbness, tingling, pain, or weakness in the hands or feet; dizziness or unsteadiness; fever.
- Harmless urine discoloration may occur while taking this drug.

TIOCONAZOLE

(ti-o-con′a-zole)
Vagistat-1
Classification: AZOLE
ANTIFUNGAL
Therapeutic: ANTIFUNGAL
Prototype: Fluconazole

AVAILABILITY Vaginal ointment

ACTION & *THERAPEUTIC EFFECT*

Broad-spectrum antifungal agent that inhibits growth of human pathogenic yeasts by disrupting normal fungal cell membrane permeability. *Effective against* Candida

albicans, *other species of* Candida, *and* Torulopsis glabrata.

USES Local treatment of vulvovaginal candidiasis.

CONTRAINDICATIONS Hypersensitivity to tioconazole or other imidazole antifungal agents; lactation.

CAUTIOUS USE Diabetes mellitus; HIV infections; immunosuppression; pregnancy (category C); children younger than 12 y.

ROUTE & DOSAGE

Candidiasis

Adult: **Intravaginal** One applicator full at bedtime × 1 day

ADMINISTRATION

Instillation

- Insert applicator high into the vagina (except during pregnancy).
- Wash applicator before and after each use.
- Store away from direct heat and light.

ADVERSE EFFECTS GU: Mild erythema, burning, discomfort, rash, itching.

INTERACTIONS Drug: May inactivate spermicidal effects of **nonoxynol-9**.

PHARMACOKINETICS Absorption: Minimal absorption from vagina.

NURSING IMPLICATIONS

Assessment & Drug Effects

- Do not use for patient with a history of allergic reaction to other antifungal agents, such as miconazole.

- Monitor for sensitization and irritation; these may be an indication to discontinue drug.

Patient & Family Education
- Learn correct application technique.
- Understand potential adverse reactions, including sensitization and allergic response.
- Tioconazole may interact with diaphragms and latex condoms; avoid concurrent use within 72 h.
- Refrain from sexual intercourse while using tioconazole.
- Wear only cotton underwear; change daily.

TIOTROPIUM BROMIDE
(ti-o-tro'pi-um)
Spiriva HandiHaler, Spiriva Respimat
Classification: RESPIRATORY SMOOTH MUSCLE RELAXANT
Therapeutic: BRONCHODILATOR; ANTISPASMODIC
Prototype: Atropine

AVAILABILITY Capsule with powder for inhalation; respiratory spray

ACTION & *THERAPEUTIC EFFECT*
A long-acting, antispasmodic agent. In the bronchial airways, it exhibits inhibition of muscarinic receptors of the smooth muscle resulting in bronchodilation. *Bronchodilation after inhalation of tiotropium is predominantly a site-specific effect.*

USES Maintenance treatment of bronchospasm associated with chronic obstructive pulmonary disease (COPD); reducing COPD exacerbations; long-term maintenance treatment of asthma.

CONTRAINDICATIONS Hypersensitivity to tiotropium, atropine, or ipratropium; acute bronchospasm.

CAUTIOUS USE Decreased renal function; BPH, urinary bladder neck obstruction; narrow-angle glaucoma; older adults; pregnancy (fetal risk cannot be ruled out); lactation (infant risk cannot be ruled out). Safe use in children younger than 6 y not established.

ROUTE & DOSAGE

COPD
Adult: **Inhaled Spiriva HandiHaler 18 mcg OR Spiriva Respimat 2 inhalations once daily using inhaler device provided**

Asthma
Adult: **Inhaled Spiriva Respimat 2.5 mcg daily**

ADMINISTRATION
Inhalation ONLY
- Place capsule in HandiHaler® and press button to puncture. Instruct patient to exhale deeply, then put the mouthpiece to the lips and breathe in the dose deeply and slowly; remove HandiHaler® and hold breath for at least 10 sec, and then exhale slowly; rinse mouth with water to minimize dry mouth.
- Ensure that drug does not contact the eyes.
- Store at 15°–30° C (59°–86° F). Do not expose to extreme temperature or moisture. Do not store in HandiHaler device.

ADVERSE EFFECTS CV: Chest pain, edema. **Respiratory:** Cough, pharyngitis, rhinitis, *URI.* **GI:** Dry mouth, abdominal pain, indigestion. **GU:** UTI.

T

INTERACTIONS Drug: May cause additive anticholinergic effects with other ANTICHOLINERGIC AGENTS. Do not use with inhaled form of **loxapine**.

PHARMACOKINETICS **Absorption:** 19.5% absorbed from the lungs. **Peak:** 5 min. **Metabolism:** Less than 25% of dose is metabolized in liver by CYP2D6 and 3A4. **Elimination:** 14% of dose excreted in urine; remaining is excreted in feces as nonabsorbed drug. **Half-Life:** 5–6 days.

NURSING IMPLICATIONS

Assessment & Drug Effects
- Withhold drug and notify prescriber if S&S of angioedema occurs.
- Monitor for anticholinergic effects (e.g., tachycardia, urinary retention).
- Monitor lab tests: Pulmonary function tests.

Patient & Family Education
- Do not allow powdered medication to contact the eyes, as this may cause blurring of vision and pupil dilation.
- Tiotropium bromide is intended as a once-daily maintenance treatment. It is not useful for treatment of acute episodes of bronchospasm (i.e., rescue therapy).
- Withhold drug and notify prescriber if swelling around the face, mouth, or neck occurs.
- Report any of the following: Constipation, increased heart rate, blurred vision, urinary difficulty.

TIPRANAVIR
(ti-pra′na-vir)
Aptivus
Classification: PROTEASE INHIBITOR
Therapeutic: ANTIRETROVIRAL
Prototype: Saquinavir

AVAILABILITY Capsule; oral solution

ACTION & *THERAPEUTIC EFFECT*
Inhibits virus-specific processing of the viral polyproteins in HIV-1 infected cells, thus preventing the formation of mature viral particles. *Helps decrease viral load of HIV-1 strains resistant to other protease inhibitors.*

USES Treatment of HIV-1 infection in combination with other agents.

CONTRAINDICATIONS Known hypersensitivity to tipranavir; moderate to severe (Child-Pugh class B and C, respectively) hepatic impairment; drug induced hepatic decomposition or intracranial hemorrhage; pancreatitis; lactation (infant risk cannot be ruled out).

CAUTIOUS USE Hypersensitivity to sulfonamides; patients with chronic hepatitis B or hepatitis C coinfection; hepatic impairment, surgery and trauma patients; hemophilia; coagulopathy; elevated liver enzymes; diabetes mellitus or hyperglycemia; hyperlipidemia; autoimmune disorders, including Graves disease, polymyositis, & Guillain-Barr syndrome; pregnancy (fetal risk cannot be ruled out); children younger than 2 y.

ROUTE & DOSAGE

HIV-1 Infection
Adult: **PO** 500 mg (with 200 mg ritonavir) bid
Adolescent/Child (older than 2 y): **PO** 14 mg/kg bid OR 375 mg/m^2 bid (with ritonavir)

ADMINISTRATION

Oral

- Coadminister with ritonavir. Give with food.
- Store solution at 15°–30° C (59°–86° F). Once opened, use contents of bottle within 60 days.
- Store capsules prior to opening bottle at 2°–8° C (36°–46° F). After bottle is opened, may be stored at 25° C (77° F) for up to 60 days.

ADVERSE EFFECTS CNS: Headache, dizziness. Endocrine: *Hypertriglyceridemia*, hypercholesterolemia, increased amylase. Skin: Rash. Hepatic: Increased ALT/SGPT, increased AST/SGOT, *increased liver aminotransferase*. GI: Diarrhea, nausea, vomiting. Other: Fatigue, fever.

INTERACTIONS Drug: Do not use with sildenafil, alfuzosin, salmeterol. Do not use with ERGOT ALKALOIDS. Do not use with other PROTEASE INHIBITORS. Adjust tipranavir dosing when used with bosentan, tadalafil, colchicine. Aluminum- and magnesium-based ANTACIDS may decrease tipranavir absorption. AZOLE ANTIFUNGAL AGENTS, clarithromycin, erythromycin, and other inhibitors of CYP3A4 may increase tipranavir levels. Efavirenz, loperamide, NRTIS, and RIFAMYCINS (e.g., rifampin) may decrease tipranavir levels. Tipranavir increases rifabutin levels. Coadministration of tipranavir and tenofovir decreases the levels of both compounds. Tipranavir increases the concentration of BENZODIAZEPINES, desipramine, and numerous ANTIARRHYTHMIC AGENTS (amiodarone, flecainide, propafenone, quinidine). Combination use of tipranavir and HMG COA REDUCTASE INHIBITORS increases the risk of myopathy. Tipranavir capsules contain alcohol that can produce disulfiram-like reactions with metronidazole and disulfiram. Adjust midazolam dose. Food: Food enhances the bioavailability of tipranavir, avoid large doses of vitamin E. Herbal: St. John's wort decreases the levels of tipranavir.

PHARMACOKINETICS Peak: 3 h. Distribution: Greater than 99.9% protein bound. Metabolism: Extensive hepatic oxidation (CYP 3A4) to inactive metabolites (when given alone); minimal metabolism (when given with ritonavir). Elimination: Fecal (primary) and renal (minimal). Half-Life: 6 h.

NURSING IMPLICATIONS

Black Box Warning

Tipranavir has been associated with hepatitis, hepatic decompensation, and intracranial hemorrhage.

Assessment & Drug Effects

- Monitor for and report immediately S&S of liver toxicity (see Appendix F).
- Monitor for S&S of adverse drug reactions and toxicity from concurrently administered drugs. Many drugs interact with tipranavir.
- Monitor diabetics for loss of glycemic control: Hyperglycemia.
- Use barrier contraceptive if using hormonal contraceptive.
- Monitor blood levels of anticoagulants with concurrent therapy.
- Monitor lab tests: Baseline and frequent LFTs and lipid profile; CBC with differential, urinalysis, electrolytes, for women of childbearing potential (pregnancy test before starting therapy), viral

T

load, CD4 count, and fasting plasma glucose as indicated.

Patient & Family Education

- If a dose is missed, take it as soon as possible and then return to the normal schedule. Never double a dose.
- Inform prescriber of all medications and herbal products you are taking.
- Protect against sunlight exposure to minimize risk of photosensitivity.
- Report any of the following to prescriber: Fatigue, weakness, loss of appetite, nausea, jaundice, dark urine, or clay colored stools.

TIROFIBAN HYDROCHLORIDE

(tir-o-fi'ban)

Aggrastat

Classification: ANTICOAGULANT; ANTIPLATELET; GLYCOPROTEIN (GP) IIB/IIIA RECEPTOR INHIBITOR

Therapeutic: ANTIPLATELET

Prototype: Abciximab

AVAILABILITY Solution for injection

ACTION & *THERAPEUTIC EFFECT*

Binds to the glycoprotein IIb/IIIa receptor on platelets thus inhibiting platelet aggregation. *Effectiveness indicated by minimizing thrombotic events during treatment of acute coronary syndrome.*

USES Acute coronary syndromes (unstable angina, non ST elevation MI).

CONTRAINDICATIONS Hypersensitivity to tirofiban; active internal bleeding within 30 days; acute pericarditis; aortic dissection; intracranial aneurysm, intracranial mass, coagulopathy; history of aneurysm

or AV malformation; history of intracranial hemorrhage or neoplasm; active abnormal bleeding; retinal bleeding; hemorrhagic retinopathy; major surgery or trauma within 3 days; stroke within 30 days; history of hemorrhagic stroke; thrombocytopenia following administration of tirofiban; history of thrombopenia due to prior exposure to tirofiban; severe rash during use of tirofiban; within 4 h of PCI; pregnancy—fetal risk cannot be ruled out; lactation infant risk cannot be ruled out.

CAUTIOUS USE Platelet count less than 150,000 mm^3; severe renal insufficiency. Safety and efficacy in children younger than 18 y not established.

ROUTE & DOSAGE

Unstable Angina, non ST-elevation MI

Adult: **IV** *25 mcg/kg over 5 min and then 0.15 mcg/kg/min for up to 18 h*

Renal Impairment Dosage Adjustment

CrCl less than or equal to 60 mL/min: Give 25 mcg/kg over less than 5 min and then 0.075 mcg/kg/min

ADMINISTRATION

Intravenous Only

PREPARE: **IV Infusion:** Use as supplied with no further preparation.
ADMINISTER: **IV Infusion:** Give an initial loading dose of 25 mcg/kg over 3 min and then 0.15 mcg/kg/min for up to 18 h.
INCOMPATIBILITIES: **Y-site: Amphotericin B, dantrolene, diazepam, lansoprazole, phenytoin.**

T

- Discard unused IV solution 24 h following start of infusion. ▪ Store unopened containers at 25 degrees C (77 degrees F), occasional excursions between 15°–30° C (59°–86° F) are permissible. ▪ Do not freeze and protect from light.

ADVERSE EFFECTS (≥5%) CV: Coronary artery dissection. **Hematologic:** *Bleeding (minor)*, **GU:** Pelvic pain.

INTERACTIONS Drug: Increased risk of bleeding with ANTICOAGULANTS, NSAIDS, SALICYLATES, ANTIPLATELET AGENTS. **Herbal: Feverfew, garlic, ginger, ginkgo, horse chestnut** may increase risk of bleeding.

PHARMACOKINETICS Duration: 4–8 h after stopping infusion. **Distribution:** 65% protein bound. **Metabolism:** Minimally metabolized. **Elimination:** 65% in urine, 25% in feces. **Half-Life:** 2 h.

NURSING IMPLICATIONS

Assessment & Drug Effects
- Withhold drug and notify prescriber if thrombocytopenia (platelets less than 100,000) is confirmed.
- Monitor carefully for and immediately report S&S of internal or external bleeding.
- Minimize unnecessary invasive procedures and devices to reduce the risk of bleeding.
- Monitor lab tests: Platelet count, Hgb and Hct before treatment, (within 6 h of infusing loading dose), and frequently throughout treatment; periodic APTT and ACT.

Patient & Family Education
- Report unexplained pelvic, leg or abdominal pain, dizziness, sweating, edema/swelling.

- Report episodes of bleeding or bruising. Review instructions that coffee ground emesis and black tarry stools are also a sign of bleeding as well as bright red blood.
- There are many drug-drug interactions. Consult healthcare provider before taking any new drug, over-the-counter, or herbal drugs.

TIZANIDINE HYDROCHLORIDE
(ti-zan'i-deen)
Zanaflex
Classification: CENTRAL ACTING SKELETAL MUSCLE RELAXANT; ALPHA 2 ADRENERGIC AGONIST
Therapeutic: SKELETAL MUSCLE RELAXANT; ANTISPASMODIC
Prototype: Cyclobenzaprine

AVAILABILITY Tablet; capsule

ACTION & *THERAPEUTIC EFFECT*
Reduces spasticity by increasing presynaptic inhibition of motor neurons. Greatest effect on polysynaptic afferent reflex activity at the spinal cord level. *Site of action is the spinal cord; reduces skeletal muscle spasms. Effectiveness indicated by decreased muscle tone.*

USES Acute and intermittent management of spasticity.

CONTRAINDICATIONS Hypersensitivity to tizanidine; concomitant therapy with **ciprofloxacin** or **fluvoxamine** (potent CYP1A2 inhibitors); pregnancy—fetal risk cannot be ruled out; lactation infant risk cannot be ruled out. Effect of tizanidine on labor and delivery is unknown.

CAUTIOUS USE Patients with hepatic impairment, hepatic

T

disease; renal insufficiency (CrCl less than 25 mL/min), or renal failure; history of hypotension; psychosis; women taking oral contraceptives; history of QT prolongation; history of narcotic abuse; older adults because of renal impairment and orthostatic hypotension. Safety and efficacy in children not established.

ROUTE & DOSAGE

Spasticity

Adult: PO Start with 2 mg can be increased by 2–4 mg per day (max: 36 mg/day)

Renal Impairment Dosage Adjustment

CrCl less than 25 mL/min: If dose increases are needed increase dose not dosing frequency

ADMINISTRATION

Oral

- Can be given without regard to food, but patient should choose with food or without food and administer medication consistently.
- Dose increases are usually made gradually in 2- to 4-mg increments.
- Store at 25 degrees C (77 degrees F), excursions permitted from 15°–30° C (59°–86° F).

ADVERSE EFFECTS CV: *Hypotension.* **CNS:** *Somnolence, dizziness, asthenia.* **GI:** *Dry mouth.*

INTERACTIONS Drug: Alcohol, OPIOIDS and other CNS DEPRESSANTS increase CNS depression. **Ciprofloxacin** increase tizanidine levels and toxicity. Avoid use of agents

that can prolong the QT interval (e.g., **dofetilide, dronedarone, pimozide, thioridazine, ziprasidone**); agents that cause bradycardia can have an additive adverse effect. CYP 1A2 INHIBITORS may increase concentration of tizanidine and increase adverse effects. **Herbal: Kava, valerian** may potentiate sedation.

PHARMACOKINETICS Absorption: Rapidly from GI tract; 40% bioavailability; tablets and capsules are bioequivalent in fasting conditions but not in nonfasting conditions. **Peak:** 1–2 h. **Duration:** 3–6 h. **Distribution:** Crosses placenta, distributed into breast milk. **Metabolism:** In the liver (CYP1A2). **Elimination:** 60% in urine, 20% in feces. **Half-Life:** 2.5 h.

NURSING IMPLICATIONS

Assessment & Drug Effects

- Monitor cardiovascular status and report orthostatic hypotension or bradycardia.
- Monitor closely older adults, those with renal impairment, and women taking oral contraceptives for adverse effects because drug clearance is reduced.
- Monitor lab tests: Baseline LFTs and 1 mo after max dose is achieved or if hepatic injury suspected, renal function tests.

Patient & Family Education

- Exercise caution with potentially hazardous activities requiring alertness since sedation is a common adverse effect. Effects are additive with alcohol or other CNS depressants.
- Make position changes slowly because of the risk of orthostatic hypotension.
- Report unusual sensory experiences; hallucinations and

T

delusions have occurred with tizanidine use.

- Do not suddenly discontinue the drug.
- Drug has multiple drug-drug interactions. Consult healthcare provider prior to taking any new drug, over-the-counter drug or herbal supplement.

TOBRAMYCIN SULFATE

(toe-bra-mye'sin)

AKTob, Bethkis,TobraDex, Tobrex, Tobi Podhaler, Tobrasol

Classification: AMINOGLYCOSIDE ANTIBIOTIC
Therapeutic: ANTIBIOTIC
Prototype: Gentamicin sulfate

AVAILABILITY Solution for injection; nebulizer solution; capsule for inhalation; ophthalmic solution; ophthalmic ointment

ACTION & *THERAPEUTIC EFFECT*
Binds irreversibly to one of two aminoglycoside binding sites on the 30S ribosomal subunit of the bacteria, thus inhibiting protein synthesis, resulting in bacterial cell death. *Effective in treatment of gram-negative bacteria. Exhibits greater antibiotic activity against* Pseudomonas aeruginosa *than other aminoglycosides.*

USES Treatment of severe infections caused by susceptible organisms.

CONTRAINDICATIONS History of hypersensitivity to tobramycin and other aminoglycoside; pregnancy (category D).

CAUTIOUS USE Impaired kidney function; renal disease; dehydration; hearing impairment; myasthenia gravis; parkinsonism; older adults; lactation; premature, neonatal infants.

ROUTE & DOSAGE

Moderate to Severe Infections

Adult: **IV/IM** 3–6 mg/kg/day in 2–3 divided doses OR 4–7 mg/kg/day single dose
Adolescent/Child/Infant: **IM/IV** 2.5 mg/kg/dose q8h
Neonate: **IM/IV** 2.5 mg/kg q12–24h
Premature Neonate: **IV/IM** See package insert for dosage by weight and gestational age

Cystic Fibrosis

Adult: Child: **IM/IV** 10 mg/kg/dose q24h; **Nebulized** 300 mg inhaled bid × 28 days, may repeat after 28-day drug-free period
Podhaler: 112 mg (4 caps) q12h × 28 days may repeat after 28 drug-free days

Ocular Infection

Adults/Adolescents/Children/Infants 2 mo or older: **Topical** Apply a thin strip to the conjunctiva (about 1 cm) q8–12h; **Drops** 1–2 drops into the infected eye q4h

Renal Impairment Dosage Adjustment

Increase interval

Hemodialysis Dosage Adjustment

Administer dose after dialysis and monitor levels

Obesity Dosage Adjustment

Dose based on IBW; in morbid obesity, use dosing weight of IBW + 0.4 (Weight − IBW)

ADMINISTRATION

Note: Doses should be based on ideal body weight.

Inhalation

- Administer over 10–15 min using a handheld reusable nebulizer with a compressor (use only those supplied). Patient should sit upright and breathe normally through the nebulizer mouthpiece.

Intramuscular

- Give deep IM into a large muscle. Rotate injection sites.

Intravenous

Note: Verify correct IV concentration and rate of infusion to neonates, infants, or children with prescriber.

PREPARE: Intermittent ▪ Dilute each dose in 50–100 mL or more of D5W, NS or D5/NS. ▪ Final concentration should not exceed 5 mg/mL.

ADMINISTER: Intermittent: Infuse diluted solution over 20–60 min. ▪ Avoid rapid infusion.

INCOMPATIBILITIES: Solution/ additive: Alcohol 5% in dextrose, cefamandole, cefepime. **Y-site:** Allopurinol, amphotericin B cholesteryl complex, azathioprine sodium, azathioprine, azithromycin, cangrelor, cefazolin, cefoperazone, cefotetan, ceftobiprole, ceftriaxone, cloxacillin sodium, dacarbazine, dantrolene, defibrotide, dexamethasone, diazepam, diazoxide, folic acid, ganciclovir, garenoxacin mesylate, gemtuzumab, heparin, hetastarch, indomethacin, lansoprazole, oxacillin, pemetrexed, pentamidine, pentobarbital, phenytoin, piperacillin/ tazobactam, propofol, sargramostim, SMZ/TMP.

- Store at 15°–30° C (59°–86° F) prior to reconstitution. After reconstitution, solution may be refrigerated and used within 96 h.
- If kept at room temperature, use within 24 h.

ADVERSE EFFECTS CNS: Neurotoxicity (including ototoxicity), *nephrotoxicity,* increased AST, ALT, LDH, serum bilirubin; anemia, fever, rash, pruritus, urticaria, nausea, vomiting, headache, lethargy, superinfections; hypersensitivity. **HEENT:** *Burning, stinging of eye after drug instillation;* eyelid itching and edema. **GU:** Oliguria, proteinuria.

INTERACTIONS Drug: ANESTHETICS, SKELETAL MUSCLE RELAXANTS add to neuromuscular blocking effects; **acyclovir, amphotericin B, capreomycin,** CEPHALOSPORINS, **colistin, cisplatin, carboplatin, foscarnet, methoxyflurane, polymyxin B, vancomycin, furosemide, ethacrynic acid** increase risk of ototoxicity, nephrotoxicity. Do not use with **cidofovir** or **gallium.**

PHARMACOKINETICS Peak: 30–90 min IM. **Duration:** Up to 8 h. **Distribution:** Crosses placenta; accumulates in renal cortex. **Elimination:** In urine. **Half-Life:** 2–3 h in adults.

NURSING IMPLICATIONS

Black Box Warning

Tobramycin has been associated with ototoxicity and nephrotoxicity.

Assessment & Drug Effects

- Weigh patient before treatment for calculation of dosage.

- Observe patient receiving tobramycin closely because of the high potential for toxicity, even in conventional doses.
- Monitor auditory, and vestibular functions closely, particularly in patients with known or suspected renal impairment and patients receiving high doses.
- Be aware that drug-induced auditory changes are irreversible (partial or total); usually bilateral. Partial or bilateral deafness may continue to develop even after therapy discontinued.
- Monitor I&O. Report oliguria, changes in I&O ratio, and cloudy or frothy urine (may indicate proteinuria). Keep patient well hydrated to prevent chemical irritation in renal tubules; older adults are especially susceptible to renal toxicity.
- Be aware that prolonged use of ophthalmic solution may encourage superinfection with nonsusceptible organisms including fungi.
- Report overdose symptoms for eye medication: Increased lacrimation, keratitis, edema and itching of eyelids.
- Monitor lab tests: Baseline C&S; baseline and periodic renal function tests; periodic peak and trough drug levels.

Patient & Family Education

- Report symptoms of superinfections (see Appendix F) to prescriber. Prompt treatment with an antibiotic or antifungal medication may be necessary.
- Report S&S of hearing loss, tinnitus, or vertigo to prescriber.

TOCILIZUMAB

(to-si-ly'zu-mab)

Actemra

Classification: DISEASE-MODIFYING ANTIRHEUMATIC DRUG (DMARD)

Therapeutic: DISEASE-MODIFYING ANTIRHEUMATIC DRUG (DMARD)

AVAILABILITY Solution for injection

ACTION & THERAPEUTIC EFFECT
Binds to interleukin 6 (IL-6) receptors inhibiting IL-6 mediated signaling and suppressing systemic inflammatory responses; also reduces IL-6 production in joints affected by inflammatory processes such as rheumatoid arthritis. *Reduction of joint inflammation reduces joint pain and improves joint function.*

USES Treatment of moderate to severe rheumatoid arthritis or juvenile idiopathic arthritis; cytokine release syndrome.

CONTRAINDICATIONS History of anaphylaxis reaction with tocilizumab; severe neutropenia, severe thrombocytopenia; live vaccines; severe hepatic impairment; positive hepatitis B or hepatitis C virus serology; active hepatic disease.

CAUTIOUS USE History of chronic or recurring infections; history of hypersensitivity; mild hepatic impairment; thrombocytopenia or neutropenia; risk for GI perforation; demyelinating disorders; preexisting or recent-onset demyelinating disorders; history of hyperlipidemia; older adults; pregnancy (fetal risk cannot be ruled out); lactation (infant risk cannot be ruled out). Safety and efficacy in children younger than 2 y not established.

ROUTE & DOSAGE

Rheumatoid Arthritis

Adult: **IV** 4 mg/kg q4wk. May increase up to 8 mg/kg q4wk
Adult (weight greater than 100 kg): **Subcutaneous** 162 mg every wk
Adult (weight less than 100 kg): **Subcutaneous** 162 mg every other wk

Polyarticular Juvenile Idiopathic Arthritis

Child/Adolescent (older than 2 y and weight greater than 30 kg): **IV** 8 mg/kg q4wk; *older than 2 y and weight less than 30 kg:* **IV** 10 mg/kg q4wk

Systematic Juvenile Idiopathic Arthritis

Child/Adolescent (older than 2 y and weight greater than 30 kg): **IV** 8 mg/kg q2wk; **Subcutaneous** 162 mg/dose every 2 wk; *older than 2 y and weight less than 30 kg:* **IV** 12 mg/kg q2wks; **Subcutaneous** 162 mg/dose every 3 wk

Cytokine Release Syndrome

Adult (30 kg or more): **IV** 12 mg/kg (max: 800 mg/dose), may repeat for 3 additional doses (at least 8 h apart)
Adult/Adolescent/Child (weight less than 30 kg) **IV** 8 mg/kg (max: 800 mg/dose), may repeat for 3 additional doses (at least 8 h apart)

Giant Cell Arteritis

Adult: **Subcutaneous** 162 mg every other wk

Absolute Neutrophil Count (ANC) Adjustment

ANC = 500–1000/mm^3: Stop tocilizumab and restart at 4 mg/kg with an increase to 8 mg/kg as appropriate when ANC is greater than 1000 cells/mm^3. *ANC less than 500/mm^3:* Discontinue tocilizumab.

Platelet Count Dosage Adjustment

Platelet count 50,000–100,000/mm^3: Stop tocilizumab and restart at 4 mg/kg with an increase to 8 mg/kg as appropriate when platelet count is greater than 100,000/mm^3. *Platelet count less than 50,000/mm^3:* Discontinue tocilizumab.

Hepatic Impairment Dosage Adjustment

Do not initiate tocilizumab if AST/ALT is greater than 1.5 × ULN. Mild impairment (AST and/or ALT 1–3 × ULN): Modify dose of concomitant DMARDs, if appropriate. For persistent increases in this range, reduce tocilizumab dose to 4 mg/kg or interrupt tocilizumab until AST/ALT have normalized. *Moderate impairment (AST and/or ALT greater than 3–5 × ULN confirmed by repeat testing):* Interrupt tocilizumab until AST/ALT is less than 3 × ULN, then follow recommendations for 1–3 × ULN. *For persistent increases greater than 3 × ULN:* Discontinue tocilizumab. *Severe impairment (AST and/or ALT greater than 5 × ULN):* Discontinue tocilizumab.

Common adverse effects in *italic;* life-threatening effects <u>underlined;</u> generic names in **bold;** classifications in SMALL CAPS; ✦ Canadian drug name; ◯ Prototype drug; ⚠ Alert

ADMINISTRATION

Subcutaneous

- When transitioning from IV to subcutaneous route, give the first subcutaneous dose at the time of the next scheduled IV dose. Administer the full amount in the prefilled syringe. Allow to reach room temperature prior to use (30–45 min).

Intravenous

PREPARE: **IV Infusion:** For children weighing less than 30 kg, start with 50 mL of NS. For adults or children weighing 30 kg or more, start with 100 mL NS. From the bag of NS remove a volume of solution equal to the volume of tocilizumab necessary to deliver the required dose. Slowly add the required dose of tocilizumab to the IV bag, then gently invert to mix. Solution should reach room temperature prior to infusion. Discard unused drug remaining in vial.
ADMINISTER: **IV Infusion:** Give over 60 min. **Do not** give IV push or a bolus dose.
INCOMPATIBILITIES: **Solution/additive:** Do not mix with another drug. **Y-site:** Do not infuse tocilizumab concurrently with any drug in the same IV line.

- Store IV solution refrigerated for up to 24 h or at room temperature for up to 4 h. Protect from light. Store unopened vials refrigerated in original packaging to protect from light.

ADVERSE EFFECTS **CV:** Hypertension. **Respiratory:** Nasopharyngitis. **CNS:** Headache. **Endocrine:** Increased cholesterol. **Skin:** Injection site reaction, *polyarticular*

juvenile idiopathic arthritis, systemic juvenile idiopathic arthritis. **Hepatic:** *Increased ALT/SGPT, increased AST/SGOT.* **GI:** *Diarrhea.* **Hematologic:** Neutropenia. **Other:** Infusion-related reaction.

INTERACTIONS **Drug:** Do not use with other biological DMARDs. Caution should be used when tocilizumab is combined with CYP3A4 substrate drugs (like **cyclosporine**) that have a narrow therapeutic index. Use with other IMMUNE MODULATORS can increase risk of infection. Do not administer LIVE VACCINES.

PHARMACOKINETICS **Half-Life:** 14–16 days.

NURSING IMPLICATIONS

Black Box Warning

Tocilizumab has been associated with increased risk of serious infections that may lead to hospitalization or death.

Assessment & Drug Effects

- Monitor for signs of serious allergic reactions during and shortly following each infusion.
- Monitor for and promptly report S&S of infection, including TB or hepatitis B infection in carriers of HBV.
- Monitor for S&S of polyneuropathy.
- Monitor lab tests: Baseline latent TB screening; baseline and frequent (q4–8wk) WBC with differential and platelet count; baseline and periodic LFTs; periodic lipid profile.

Patient & Family Education

- Do not accept vaccinations with live vaccines while taking this drug.

T

- You should be tested for TB prior to taking this drug.
- Promptly report S&S of infection including: Chills, fever, cough, shortness of breath, diarrhea, stomach or abdominal pain, burning on urination, sores anywhere on your body, unexplained or excessive fatigue.
- Carriers of hepatitis B should report promptly signs of activation of the virus (e.g., clay-colored stools, dark urine, jaundice, unexplained fatigue).
- Report promptly if you become pregnant.

TOFACITINIB
(toe'fa-sye'ti-nib)
Xeljanz
Classification: DISEASE-MODIFYING ANTIRHEUMATIC DRUG (DMARD)
Therapeutic: DISEASE-MODIFYING ANTIRHEUMATIC DRUG (DMARD)

AVAILABILITY Tablet, extended release tablet

ACTION & THERAPEUTIC EFFECT
Inhibits a specific tyrosine kinase enzyme and interferes with a signaling pathway that transmits extracellular information to the cell nucleus, influencing DNA transcription. *It improves rheumatoid arthritis by inhibiting the production of inflammatory mediators.*

USES Treatment of moderately to severely active rheumatoid arthritis in patients who have had an inadequate response or intolerance to methotrexate. It may be used as monotherapy or in combination with methotrexate or other nonbiologic disease-modifying antirheumatic drugs (DMARDs). Treatment of active psoriatic arthritis. Treatment of moderately to severely active ulcerative colitis.

CONTRAINDICATIONS Serious uncontrolled infection, opportunistic infection or sepsis; live vaccines; severe hepatic impairment; hepatitis B or C; lactation (infant risk cannot be ruled out).

CAUTIOUS USE Renal transplant patients; active TB or history of latent or active TB; history of herpes virus infection; history of chronic or recurrent infections; history or risk of GI perforation; DM; patients with history of melanoma, bradycardia, prolonged PR interval, conduction abnormalities; ischemic heart disease; patients at risk for interstitial lung disease; moderate or severe renal impairment; moderate hepatic impairment; Asian patients; malignancy; older adults; pregnancy (fetal risk cannot be ruled out). Safety and efficacy in children not established.

ROUTE & DOSAGE

Rheumatoid Arthritis, Psoriatic Arthritis

Adult: PO Immediate release 5 mg bid; Extended release 11 mg daily

Ulcerative Colitis

Adult: PO Immediate release 10 mg bid × 8 wk then 5–10 mg bid

Hepatic Impairment Dosage Adjustment

Moderate impairment (Child-Pugh class B): 5 mg once daily
Severe impairment (Child-Pugh class C): Not recommended

Renal Impairment Dosage Adjustment

Moderate to severe impairment:
5 mg once daily

Lymphopenia Dosage Adjustment

If less than 500 cells/m³:
Discontinue

Neutropenia Dosage Adjustment

If ANC = 500–1000 cells/m³:
Withhold until ANC is greater than 1000 cells/m³ then resume at normal dose
If ANC less than 500–1000 cells/m³: Discontinue

Anemia Dosage Adjustment

If hemoglobin is less than 8 g/dL or if decreased by greater than 2 g/dL: Withhold until hemoglobin levels normalize

ADMINISTRATION

Oral

- NIOSH recommends use of single gloves when handling intact tablets or capsules or administering from a unit-dosed package. Use double gloves if cutting or crushing the medication. During administration, use single gloves and wear eye/face protection if the formulation is hard to swallow or if the patient may resist, vomit or spit up.
- May be given without regard to food.
- Store at 20°–25° C (68°–77° F).

ADVERSE EFFECTS **Respiratory:** Nasopharyngitis, URI. **CNS:** Headache. **Endocrine:** Increased HDL, increased LDL. **Other:** Infection.

INTERACTIONS **Drug:** Coadministration with potent inhibitors of CYP3A4 (e.g., **ketoconazole**) may increase the levels of tofacitinib. Coadministration with drugs that are moderate inhibitors of CYP3A4 and potent inhibitors of CYP2C19 (e.g., **fluconazole**) may increase the levels of tofacitinib. Coadministration with potent CYP3A4 inducers (e.g., **phenobarbital, phenytoin, rifampin**) may decrease the levels of tofacitinib. Coadministration with other potent immunosuppressive drugs (e.g., **azathioprine, tacrolimus, cyclosporine**) increases the risk of added immunosuppression. Do not use with LIVE VACCINES **Food: Grapefruit juice** may increase the levels of tofacitinib. **Herbal: St. John's wort** may decrease the levels of tofacitinib, use caution with **echinacea**.

PHARMACOKINETICS **Absorption:** 74% bioavailable. **Peak:** 0.5–1 h. **Distribution:** 40% plasma protein bound. **Metabolism:** Hepatic oxidation (substrate of CYP219 and CYP 3A4). **Elimination:** Hepatic (70%) and renal (30%). **Half-Life:** 3 h.

NURSING IMPLICATIONS

Black Box Warning

Tofacitinib has been associated with increased risk of developing serious infections that may lead to hospitalization or death.

Assessment & Drug Effects

- Evaluate for latent or active infection prior to administration of tofacitinib.
- Monitor closely for S&S of TB, including those who tested negative for latent TB prior to initiating therapy.
- Monitor for reactivation of viral infection (herpes zoster).

T

- Monitor closely for S&S of other infections during and after treatment. Withhold therapy and notify prescriber if an infection is suspected.
- Monitor lab tests: Baseline lymphocyte count and q3mo thereafter; baseline neutrophil count and Hgb, then q3mo after 4–8 wk of treatment; periodic LFTs; lipid profile 4–8 wk after initiation of therapy.

Patient & Family Education
- Report promptly to prescriber any new-onset abdominal symptoms, S&S of respiratory tract infection or any other type of infection.

TOLAZAMIDE
(tole-az′a-mide)

Classification: SULFONYLUREA
Therapeutic: ANTIDIABETIC
Prototype: Glyburide

AVAILABILITY Tablet

ACTION & *THERAPEUTIC EFFECT*
Lowers blood glucose primarily by stimulating pancreatic beta cells to secrete insulin. Antidiabetic action is a result of stimulation of the pancreas to secrete more insulin in the presence of blood sugar; it requires functioning beta cells. *Effectiveness is measured in decreasing the serum blood level to within normal limits and decreasing HbA1C value to 6.5 or lower.*

USES Type 2 diabetes mellitus

CONTRAINDICATIONS Known
sensitivity to sulfonylureas and to sulfonamides; type 1 diabetes complicated by ketoacidosis; infection; trauma; lactation (infant risk cannot be ruled out).

CAUTIOUS USE Renal disease;
renal failure, renal impairment; adrenal or pituitary insufficiency; debilitated or malnourished patients; hemolytic anemia; hepatic insufficiency; stress from infection, fever, trauma or surgery; older adults; pregnancy (category C). Safety in children not established.

ROUTE & DOSAGE

Type 2 Diabetes Mellitus
Adult: **PO** 100 mg–250 mg daily, may adjust dose by 100–250 mg/day at weekly intervals (max: 1 g/day)

ADMINISTRATION
Oral
- Give in the morning with or before first main meal of the day.
- Divide dose of more than 500 mg and give bid
- Store at 20°–25° C (68°–77° F) in a tightly closed container unless otherwise directed. Protect from light. Keep drug out of the reach of children.

ADVERSE EFFECTS CNS: Dizziness, fatigue, headache, malaise, vertigo. **Endocrine:** Hypoglycemia, hyponatremia, SIADH. **Skin:** Rash, pruritis, photosensitivity, uritcaria. **Hepatic:** Jaundice. **GI:** Epigastric fullness, indigestion, nausea, anorexia, constipation, diarrhea, vomiting. **GU:** Diuretic effect. **Musculoskeletal:** Weakness. **Hematologic:** Agranulocytosis, aplastic anemia, hemolytic anemia, leukopenia, pancytopenia, thrombocytopenia.

INTERACTIONS Drug: **Alcohol** elicits disulfiram-type reaction in

some patients; ORAL ANTICOAGU-
LANTS, **chloramphenicol, clofibrate, phenylbutazone,** MAO
INHIBITORS, SALICYLATES, **probenecid,**
SULFONAMIDES may potentiate hypoglycemic actions; THIAZIDES may
antagonize hypoglycemic effects;
cimetidine may increase tolazamide levels, causing hypoglycemia; **aminolevulinic acid** may
increase photosensitivity. **Herbal:
Ginseng** may potentiate hypoglycemic effects.

PHARMACOKINETICS Absorp-
tion: Slowly from GI tract. **Onset:**
60 min. **Peak:** 4–6 h. **Duration:**
10–15 h (up to 20 h in some
patients). **Distribution:** Distributed
in highest concentrations in liver,
kidneys, and intestines; crosses placenta; distributed into breast milk.
Metabolism: Extensively in liver.
Elimination: 85% in urine, 15% in
feces. **Half-Life:** 7 h.

NURSING IMPLICATIONS

Assessment & Drug Effects
- Monitor closely for daytime and
  nighttime hypoglycemia since
  tolazamide is long acting.
- Monitor for and report signs of an
  allergic reaction (e.g., rash, urticaria, pruritus).
- Monitor lab tests: Periodic HbA1C
  and frequent FBS; periodic CBC;
  renal function tests.

Patient & Family Education
- Check blood glucose daily or as
  ordered by prescriber. Important
  to continue close medical supervision for first 6 wk of treatment.
- Learn the S&S of hypoglycemia
  and hyperglycemia and check
  blood glucose level when either
  is suspected.
- Report to prescriber if you experience frequent and/or severe episodes of hypoglycemia.

- Do not take OTC preparations
  unless approved or prescribed by
  prescriber.
- Understand that alcohol can precipitate a disulfiram-type reaction.
- Many drugs interact with tolazamide. Monitor blood glucose
  more frequently whenever a new
  drug is added to your regimen.

TOLBUTAMIDE
(tole-byoo′ta-mide)

TOLBUTAMIDE SODIUM
Classification: SULFONYLUREA
Therapeutic: ANTIDIABETIC
Prototype: Glyburide

AVAILABILITY Tablet

ACTION & *THERAPEUTIC EFFECT*
Lowers blood glucose concentration by stimulating pancreatic beta
cells to synthesize and release
insulin. No action demonstrated
if functional beta cells are absent.
*Lowers blood glucose concentration
by stimulating pancreatic beta cells
to synthesize and release insulin.*

USES Management of mild to mod-
erately severe, stable type 2 diabetes that is not controlled by diet
and weight reduction alone.

CONTRAINDICATIONS Hyper-
sensitivity to sulfonylureas or to
sulfonamides; history of repeated
episodes of diabetic ketoacidosis;
type 1 diabetes as sole therapy; diabetic coma; severe stress, infection,
trauma, or major surgery; severe
renal insufficiency, liver or endocrine disease; lactation (infant risk
cannot be ruled out).

CAUTIOUS USE Cardiac, thy-
roid, pituitary, or adrenal dysfunction; severe hepatic disease, renal

T

disease, renal impairment, renal failure; history of peptic ulcer; alcoholism; infection; debilitated, malnourished, or uncooperative patient, older adults; stress caused by fever, infection, surgery, or trauma; pregnancy (category C). Safe use in children not established.

ROUTE & DOSAGE

Type 2 Diabetes

Adult: **PO** 1–2 g/day as a single dose in the morning or in divided doses

ADMINISTRATION

Oral

- Tablets may be crushed and given with full glass of water if patient desires.
- Do not give at bedtime because of danger of nocturnal hypoglycemia, unless specifically prescribed.
- Store at 20°–25° C (68°–77° F) in well-closed container. Protect from light.

ADVERSE EFFECTS CNS:
Disulfiram-like reaction, headache. **Endocrine:** Hypoglycemia, hyponatremia, SIADH, build up of porphyrins. **Skin:** Rash, pruritis, photosensitivity, urticaria. **Hepatic:** Jaundice. **GI:** Altered sense of taste, epigastric fullness, heartburn, nausea. **Hematologic:** Agranulocytosis, aplastic anemia, hemolytic anemia, leukopenia, pancytopenia, thrombocytopenia.

DIAGNOSTIC TEST INTERFERENCE
The SULFONYLUREAS may produce abnormal *thyroid function test* results and reduced *RAI uptake* (after long-term administration).

INTERACTIONS Drug: Phenylbutazone increases hypoglycemic effects; THIAZIDE DIURETICS may attenuate hypoglycemic effects; **alcohol** may produce disulfiram reaction; BETA-BLOCKERS may mask symptoms of a hypoglycemic reaction. **Herbal: Ginseng,** may potentiate hypoglycemic effects.

PHARMACOKINETICS Absorption: Readily from GI tract. **Peak:** 3–5 h. **Distribution:** Into extracellular fluids. **Metabolism:** Principally in liver. **Elimination:** 75–85% in urine; some in feces. **Half-Life:** 7 h.

NURSING IMPLICATIONS

Assessment & Drug Effects

- Supervise closely during initial period of therapy until dosage is established. One or 2 wk of therapy may be required before full therapeutic effect is achieved.
- Monitor closely during adjustment period, watching for S&S of impending hypoglycemia (see Appendix F). Detection of a hypoglycemic reaction in a diabetic patient also receiving a beta-blocker, especially older adults, is difficult.
- Evaluate nondefinitive vague complaints; hypoglycemic symptoms may be especially vague in older adults. Observe patient carefully, especially 2–3 h after eating, check urine for sugar and ketone bodies and capillary blood glucose.
- Report repetitive complaints of headache and weakness a few hours after eating; may signal incipient hypoglycemia.
- Be aware that pruritus and rash, frequently reported adverse

Common adverse effects in *italic;* life-threatening effects <u>underlined;</u> generic names in **bold;** classifications in SMALL CAPS; ✦ Canadian drug name; ⊙ Prototype drug; ⚠ Alert

effects, may clear spontaneously; if these persist, drug will be discontinued.

- Monitor lab tests: Periodic HbA1C, fasting serum glucose and urine glucose.

Patient & Family Education

- Learn the S&S of hyperglycemia (see Appendix A) and check blood glucose level when hyperglycemia is suspected.
- Hypoglycemia is frequently caused by overdosage of hypoglycemic drug, inadequate or irregular food intake, nausea, vomiting, diarrhea, and added exercise without caloric supplement or dose adjustment. Learn the S&S of hypoglycemia (see Appendix F) and check blood glucose level whenever hypoglycemia is suspected.
- Report any illness promptly. Prescriber may want to evaluate need for insulin.
- Do not self-medicate with OTC drugs unless approved or prescribed by prescriber.
- Be aware that alcohol, even in moderate amounts, can precipitate a disulfiram-type reaction (see Appendix F). A hypoglycemic response after ingesting alcohol requires emergency treatment.
- Protect exposed skin areas from the sun with a sunscreen lotion (SPF 12–15) because of potential photosensitivity (especially in the alcoholic).
- Monitor blood glucose daily or as directed by prescriber.
- Be alert to added danger of loss of control (hyperglycemia) when a drug that affects the hypoglycemic action of sulfonylureas (see DRUG INTERACTIONS) is withdrawn or added to the tolbutamide regimen. Monitor blood glucose carefully.

- Use or add barrier contraceptive if using hormonal contraceptives.

TOLCAPONE ⊙
(tol′ca-pone)

Tasmar

Classification: ANTICHOLINERGIC; CATECHOLAMINE-O-METHYLTRANSFERASE (COMT) INHIBITOR

Therapeutic: ANTIPARKINSON

AVAILABILITY Tablet

ACTION & *THERAPEUTIC EFFECT*
Selective and reversible inhibitor of catecholamine-O-methyltransferase (COMT). COMT is the enzyme responsible for metabolizing catecholamines and, therefore, levodopa. *Concurrent administration of tolcapone and levodopa increases the amount of levodopa available to control Parkinson's disease by increasing dopaminergic brain stimulation.*

USES Idiopathic Parkinson disease as adjunct to levodopa/carbidopa.

CONTRAINDICATIONS Hypersensitivity to tolcapone; liver disease; drug-induced signs of liver decompensation; history of nontraumatic rhabdomyolysis, history of hyperpyrexia and confusion related to a medication, MAOI therapy; history of major psychiatric disorder; pregnancy—fetal risk cannot be ruled out; lactation—infant risk cannot be ruled out.

CAUTIOUS USE History of hypersensitivity to other COMT inhibitors (e.g., entacapone, nitecapone); anorexia nervosa; hematuria; hypotension; syncope; renal disease; renal impairment; history of dyskinesias, elderly.

T

ROUTE & DOSAGE

Parkinson Disease
Adult: **PO** 100 mg tid (max: 200 mg tid)

ADMINISTRATION

Oral
- Give with food if GI upset occurs.
- Give only in conjunction with levodopa/carbidopa therapy.
- Therapy with tolcapone **should not** be initiated if patient has ALT/AST greater than 2 × ULN or has known liver disease.
- Store at 20°–25° C (68°–77° F) in a tightly closed container.

ADVERSE EFFECTS (≥5%) CV:
Orthostatic hypotension, syncope. **Respiratory:** URI. **CNS:** *Dyskinesia, dystonia, somnolence, confusion, dizziness,* headache, hallucination, syncope, paresthesias. **Skin:** Sweating. **GI:** *Nausea, anorexia, diarrhea, vomiting.* **GU:** Hematuria. **Musculoskeletal:** Cramps. **Other:** Dream disorder, sleep disorder, compulsive behavior, drug-induced psychosis, hallucinations.

INTERACTIONS Drug:
Will increase **levodopa** levels when taken simultaneously; CNS DEPRESSANTS may cause additive sedation; may have increased risk of hypotension when used with ANTIHYPERTENSIVES; do not give with non-selective MAOIS **(isocarboxazid, phenelzine, or tranylcypromine furazolidone, linezolid, procarbazine). Food:** Decreases levels. **Herbal:** Avoid use of valerian, **St. John's wort,** kava.

PHARMACOKINETICS Absorption:
Rapidly from GI tract, bioavailability 65%. **Peak:** 2 h. **Distribution:** Over 99% protein bound. **Metabolism:** Extensively metabolized by COMT and glucuronidation. **Elimination:** 60% in urine, 40% in feces; clearance reduced by 50% in patients with liver disease. **Half-Life:** 2–3 h.

NURSING IMPLICATIONS

Black Box Warning

Tolcapone has been associated with risk of potentially fatal, acute fulminant liver failure.

Assessment & Drug Effects
- More frequent PT and INR when given concurrently with warfarin.
- Withhold drug and notify prescriber if liver dysfunction is suspected.
- Monitor carefully for and immediately report S&S of hepatic impairment (e.g., jaundice, dark urine).
- Monitor level of consciousness.
- Monitor lab tests: Monthly LFTs for first 3 mo, every 6 wk for the next 3 mo, and periodically thereafter.

Patient & Family Education
- Notify prescriber promptly about any of following: Increased loss of muscle control, fainting, yellowing of skin or eyes, darkening of urine, severe diarrhea, hallucinations.
- Do not engage in hazardous activities until response to drug is known. Avoid use of alcohol or sedative drugs while on tolcapone.
- Rise slowly from a sitting or lying position to avoid a rapid drop in BP with possible weakness or fainting.
- Dermatological exams will be needed periodically to monitor

for melanoma. Report any skin changes suggestive of melanoma.
- Report any intense urges or compulsive behavior such as gambling, sexual urges or binge eating.
- Nausea is a common possible adverse effect especially at the beginning of therapy.
- Do not suddenly stop taking this drug. Doses **must be** gradually reduced over time.

TOLMETIN SODIUM
(tole′met-in)

Classification: NONSTEROIDAL ANTI-INFLAMMATORY (NSAID)
Therapeutic: NONNARCOTIC ANALGESIC, NSAID; DISEASE-MODIFYING ANTIRHEUMATIC DRUG (DMARD)
Prototype: Ibuprofen

AVAILABILITY Tablet; capsule

ACTION & THERAPEUTIC EFFECT Competitively inhibits both cyclooxygenase (COX) isoenzymes, COX-1 and COX-2, by blocking arachidonate binding to prostaglandin sites, and thus inhibits prostaglandin synthesis. *Possesses analgesic, antiinflammatory, antipyretic, and antirheumatic activity.*

USES In treatment of rheumatoid arthritis, juvenile rheumatoid arthritis, juvenile idiopathic arthritis.

CONTRAINDICATIONS History of intolerance or hypersensitivity to tolmetin, aspirin, and other NSAIDs; active peptic ulcer, CABG perioperative pain; in patients with active GI disease including peptic ulcer and ulcerative colitis; in patients with functional class IV rheumatoid arthritis (severely incapacitated, bedridden, or confined to a wheelchair). Safety during pregnancy (fetal risk cannot be ruled out); lactation (infant risk cannot be ruled out).

CAUTIOUS USE History of PUD or GI bleeding; impaired kidney function; SLE; hypertension; patients with fluid retention; CHF; compromised cardiac function; liver dysfunction; coagulation disorders; asthma; older adults. Safe use in children younger than 2 y not established.

ROUTE & DOSAGE

Arthritis
Adult: **PO** 400 mg tid (max: 2 g/day)

Juvenile Rheumatoid Arthritis
Child (2 y or older): **PO** 20 mg/kg/day in 3–4 divided doses (max: 30 mg/kg/day)

ADMINISTRATION
Oral
- Schedule to include a morning dose (on arising) and a bedtime dose.
- May be administered with magnesium or aluminum hydroxide containing antacids to minimize GI irritation. Administration with food or milk reduces bioavailability of the drug by 16%.
- Give with fluid of patient's choice; crush tablet or empty capsule to mix with water or food if patient cannot swallow tablet/capsule.
- Store at 20°–25° C (68°–77° F) in tightly capped and light-resistant container unless otherwise instructed.

ADVERSE EFFECTS

CV: Hypertension, edema. **Respiratory:** Bronchospasm. **CNS:** Stroke, dizziness, headache. **Endocrine:** Weight changes. **Hepatic:** Hepatitis, increased LFTs, jaundice. **GI:** Nausea, abdominal pain, diarrhea, indigestion, flatulence, vomiting, constipation. **Musculoskeletal:** Weakness.

DIAGNOSTIC TEST INTERFERENCE

Tolmetin prolongs *bleeding time*, inhibits *platelet aggregation*, elevates *BUN, alkaline phosphatase,* and *AST* levels. Metabolites may produce false-positive results for *proteinuria* [with tests that rely on acid precipitation (e.g., *sulfosalicylic acid*)]. May interfere with urine detection of *cannabinoids* (false-positive); may lead to false-positive aldosterone/renin ratio.

INTERACTIONS

Drug: ORAL ANTICOAGULANTS, **heparin** may prolong bleeding time; may increase **lithium** toxicity; **aspirin,** other NSAIDS add to ulcerogenic effects; may increase **methotrexate** toxicity. Do not use with **ketorolac** due to increased risk of toxicities. **Herbal: Feverfew,** cat's claw, **garlic, ginger, ginkgo** may increase bleeding potential.

PHARMACOKINETICS

Absorption: Rapidly from GI tract. **Peak:** 30–60 min; therapeutic effect in 3–7 days. **Distribution:** Crosses blood–brain barrier and placenta; distributed into breast milk. **Metabolism:** In liver. **Elimination:** In urine. **Half-Life:** 60–90 min.

NURSING IMPLICATIONS

Black Box Warning

Tolmetin sodium has been associated with increased risk of serious, potentially fatal, GI bleeding and cardiovascular events (e.g., MI and CVA); risk may increase with duration of use and may be greater in the older adult and those with risk factors for CV disease.

Assessment & Drug Effects

- Monitor for and report promptly S&S of GI ulceration or bleeding. Significant GI bleeding may occur without prior warning.
- Monitor for and report promptly S&S of CV thrombotic events (i.e., angina, MI, TIA, or stroke).
- Monitor BP throughout the course of therapy.
- Monitor patients with kidney damage closely. Evaluate I&O ratio and encourage patient to increase fluid intake to at least 8 full glasses/day.
- Monitor lab tests: Periodic renal function tests with long-term therapy; CBC; Hct & Hgb if symptoms of anemia appear; C-reactive protein levels, erythrocyte sedimentation rate, LFTs, serum creatinine/BUN, and stool guaiac.

Patient & Family Education

- Stop taking drug and report promptly to prescriber if you experience S&S of GI ulceration: Stomach pain, frequent indigestion and nausea, bloody or tarry stools, vomit with blood or coffee-ground appearance.
- Monitor weight and report an increase greater than 2 kg (4 lb)/wk with impaired kidney or cardiac function; check for swelling in ankles, shins, hands, and feet.
- Report promptly signs of abnormal bleeding (ecchymosis, epistaxis, melena, petechiae bruising, bloody nose, black tarry stools, tiny, circular patches on skin), itching, skin rash, persistent headache, edema.

Common adverse effects in *italic;* life-threatening effects <u>underlined;</u> generic names in **bold;** classifications in SMALL CAPS; ♣ Canadian drug name; ⊙ Prototype drug; ⚠ Alert

- Stop taking drug and report promptly to prescriber if you experience chest pain, shortness of breath, weakness, slurring of speech, or other signs of a cardiac or neurologic problem.
- Avoid potentially hazardous activities until response to drug is known because dizziness and drowsiness are common adverse effects.

TOLNAFTATE
(tole-naf'tate)
Pitrex ✦, Tinactin
Classification: ANTIFUNGAL ANTIBIOTIC
Therapeutic: ANTIFUNGAL

AVAILABILITY Cream; solution; gel; powder; spray

ACTION & *THERAPEUTIC EFFECT*
Distorts hyphae and stunts mycelial growth on susceptible fungi. *Fungistatic or fungicidal as well as anti-infective against bacteria, protozoa, and viruses.*

USES Tinea pedis (athlete's foot), tinea cruris (jock itch), tinea corporis (body ringworm); prevention of tinea pedis.

CONTRAINDICATIONS Skin irritations prior to therapy, previous hypersensitivity to tolnaftate, nail and scalp infections; immunosuppressed patients, diabetes mellitus, peripheral vascular disease; pregnancy—fetal risk cannot be ruled out; lactation—infant risk cannot be ruled out.

CAUTIOUS USE Safe use in children younger than 2 y is not established.

ROUTE & DOSAGE

Tinea Infestations
Adult/Child: **Topical** Apply bid in morning and evening

ADMINISTRATION
Topical
- Cleanse site thoroughly with water and dry completely before applying. Massage thin layer gently into skin. Make sure area is not wet from excess drug after application.
- Shake aerosol powder or aerosol liquid container well before use. Apply powder or liquid aerosol liberally to affected areas from a distance of 6 to 10 inches.
- Apply powder to affected areas; can be applied to socks and shoes when treating foot infections.
- Note: Cream and powder are not recommended for nail or scalp infection.
- Use liquids (solutions) for scalp infection or to treat hairy areas.
- Store cream, gel, powder, and topical solution in light-resistant containers at 15°–30° C (59°–86° F); store aerosol container at 2°–30° C (38°–86° F). Avoid freezing.

ADVERSE EFFECTS **Skin:** Local irritation, *pruritus.*

NURSING IMPLICATIONS
Assessment and Drug effects
- Monitor for symptomatic improvement and for local reactions (burning, itching, irritation).

Patient & Family Education
- Expect relief from pruritus, soreness, and burning within 24–72 h after start of treatment.

T

- Continue treatment for 2–3 wk after disappearance of all symptoms to prevent recurrence.
- Review application instructions with patient and/or caregiver.
- Instruct patient to not apply any other medicines or creams to affected skin area unless prescribed by a healthcare provider.
- Do not apply cosmetics or other skin products to affected areas.
- Return to prescriber in absence of improvement within 1 wk or if condition worsens.
- Note: If skin has thickened as a result of the infection, desired clinical response may be delayed for 4–6 wk.
- Avoid contact with eyes of all drug forms.
- Place container in warm water to liquify contents if solution solidifies. Potency is unaffected.

TOLTERODINE TARTRATE

(tol-ter'o-deen tar'trate)
Detrol, Detrol LA
Classification: ANTICHOLINERGIC; MUSCARINIC RECEPTOR ANTAGONIST
Therapeutic: ANTIMUSCARINIC; BLADDER ANTISPASMODIC
Prototype: Oxybutynin

AVAILABILITY Tablet; sustained release capsule

ACTION & *THERAPEUTIC EFFECT*
Selective muscarinic urinary bladder receptor antagonist. Reduces urinary incontinence, urgency, and frequency. *Controls urinary bladder incontinence by controlling contractions.*

USES Overactive bladder.

CONTRAINDICATIONS Hypersensitivity to tolterodine or fesoterodine; uncontrolled narrow-angle glaucoma; gastric retention, obstruction, or pyloric stenosis; urinary retention; older patients with delirium or high risk for delirium; pregnancy—fetal risk cannot be ruled out; lactation—infant risk cannot be ruled out. **Extended release:** Severe hepatic impairment (Child-Pugh class C); if CrCl less than 10 mL/min.

CAUTIOUS USE Cardiovascular disease; liver disease; controlled narrow-angle glaucoma; significant urinary retention; severe hepatic impairment; obstructive GI disease; obstructive uropathy; myasthenia gravis; history of QT prolongation; paralytic ileus or intestinal atony; renal impairment; CrCl 10–30 mL/min; ulcerative colitis; older adults. Safety and efficacy in children not established.

ROUTE & DOSAGE

Overactive Bladder
Adult: **PO** 2 mg bid or **Sustained release:** 4 mg daily

Hepatic Impairment Dosage Adjustment
Reduce dose by 50%

Renal Impairment Dosage Adjustment
CrCl less than 30 mL/min: Reduce dose 50%

Medication Dosage Adjustment
Concurrent CYP3A4 inhibiting drugs: Reduce dose by 50%

ADMINISTRATION

Oral
- Do not crush or chew sustained release tablets. These **must be** swallowed whole.

- Doses greater than 1 mg bid are not recommended for those with significantly reduced liver function or kidney function or concurrently receiving macrolide antibiotics, azole antifungal agents, or other cytochrome P450 3A4 inhibitors.
- Store at 15°–30° C (59°–86° F) in a tightly closed container.

ADVERSE EFFECTS (≥5%) CNS:
Headache. GI: *Dry mouth,* constipation, abdominal pain.

INTERACTIONS Drug: Additive anticholinergic effects with **amantadine, clozapine,** SEDATING H₁-BLOCKERS, PHENOTHIAZINES, TRICYCLIC ANTIDEPRESSANTS. Increased effects with CYP3A4 inhibitors (e.g., **clarithromycin, cyclosporine, erythromycin, itraconazole,** or **ketoconazole**). Food: **Grapefruit juice** may increase **tolterodine** levels in some patients.

PHARMACOKINETICS Absorption: 77% absorbed, decreased with food. **Peak:** 1–2 h. **Distribution:** 96% protein bound. **Metabolism:** In liver by CYP2D6 and CYP3A4. **Elimination:** 77% in urine, 17% in feces. **Half-Life:** 2–10 h (immediate release); 7–18 h (extended release)

NURSING IMPLICATIONS
Assessment & Drug Effects
- Monitor voiding pattern and report promptly urinary retention.
- Monitor vital signs carefully (HR and BP), especially in those with cardiovascular disease.
- Monitor lab tests: LFTs and renal function tests.

Patient & Family Education
- Notify prescriber promptly if you experience eye pain, rapid heartbeat, difficulty breathing, skin rash or hives, confusion, or incoordination.
- Avoid activities requiring mental alertness or coordination until drug effects are realized, as drug may cause blurred vision, dizziness and drowsiness.
- Report blurred vision, sensitivity to light, and dry mouth (all common adverse effects) to prescriber if bothersome.
- Avoid the use of alcohol or OTC antihistamines.

TOLVAPTAN
(tol-vap'tan)
Samsca
Classification: ELECTROLYTE & WATER BALANCE AGENT; DIURETIC; VASOPRESSIN ANTAGONIST
Therapeutic: VASOPRESSIN ANTAGONIST; DIURETIC
Prototype: Conivaptan

AVAILABILITY Tablet

ACTION & THERAPEUTIC EFFECT
Selective vasopressin V_2-receptor antagonist; antagonizes the effect of vasopressin and causes an increase in urine water excretion, decrease in urine osmolality, and increase in serum sodium concentrations. *Effectiveness is measured by increase in serum sodium level toward lower limit of normal, and/ or decrease in sign and symptoms of hyponatremia.*

USES Treatment of hypervolemic and euvolemic hyponatremia.

CONTRAINDICATIONS Rapid correction of serum sodium (e.g., greater than 12 mEq/L/24 h); cognitively impaired; serious neurologic symptoms; hypovolemic hyponatremia; hypertonic saline;

concurrent administration with strong CYP3A inhibitors; lactation.

CAUTIOUS USE Must be initiated or reinitiated in a hospital setting; cirrhosis; pregnancy (category C). Safe use in children younger than 18 y not established.

ROUTE & DOSAGE

Hyponatremia

Adult: **PO** Initially 15 mg once daily; may be adjusted up to 60 mg once daily

ADMINISTRATION

Oral

- Administer ONLY in setting where serum sodium can be closely monitored.
- Doses may be increased at 24 h intervals or greater.
- Do not administer if patient is unable to sense or respond to thirst.
- Store at 15°–30°C (59°–86°F).

ADVERSE EFFECTS Endocrine: Anorexia, *hyperglycemia*. **GI:** *Constipation, dry mouth, nausea*. **GU:** *Pollakiuria, polyuria*. **Other:** *Asthenia*, pyrexia, *thirst*.

INTERACTIONS Drug: Strong CYP3A4 INHIBITORS (e.g., **clarithromycin, ketoconazole, itraconazole, telithromycin, saquinavir, nelfinavir, ritonavir, nefazodone**) may increase tolvaptan levels. Moderate CYP3A INHIBITORS (e.g., **erythromycin, fluconazole, aprepitant, diltiazem, verapamil**) may increase tolvaptan levels. P-GLYCOPROTEIN INHIBITORS (e.g., **cyclosporine**) may require tolvaptan dosage reduction. CYP3A INDUCERS (e.g.,

rifabutin, rifapentine, rifampin, barbiturates, phenytoin, carbamazepine) decrease the levels of tolvaptan. Tolvaptan increases the levels of **digoxin.** BETA-BLOCKERS, ANGIOTENSIN RECEPTOR BLOCKERS, ANGIOTENSIN-CONVERTING ENZYME INHIBITORS and POTASSIUM-SPARING DIURETICS may cause hyperkalemia. **Food:** Administration with **grapefruit juice** may increase tolvaptan levels. **Herbal: St. John's wort** may decrease the levels of tolvaptan.

PHARMACOKINETICS Absorption: Approximately 40% absorbed. **Peak:** 2–4 h. **Distribution:** 99% plasma protein bound. **Metabolism:** In liver through CYP3A4. **Elimination:** Eliminated entirely by nonrenal routes. **Half-Life:** 12 h.

NURSING IMPLICATIONS

Black Box Warning

Tolvaptan has been associated with serious, sometime fatal, adverse events when hyponatremia is corrected too rapidly (e.g., more than 12 mEq/L per 24 h).

Assessment & Drug Effects

- Monitor vital signs frequently throughout therapy. Monitor ECG as warranted.
- Monitor weight and I&O closely as copious diuresis is expected.
- Fluid restriction should be avoided during the first 24 h of therapy.
- Monitor mental status throughout treatment. Report promptly changes in mental status (e.g., lethargy, confusion, disorientation, hallucinations, seizures).
- Report promptly symptoms of osmotic demyelination syndrome (ODS): Dysarthria, mutism, dysphagia, lethargy, affective

Common adverse effects in *italic*; life-threatening effects <u>underlined</u>; generic names in **bold**; classifications in SMALL CAPS; ♣ Canadian drug name; ◐ Prototype drug; ⚠ Alert

changes, spasticity, seizures, or coma.
- Monitor digoxin levels closely with concurrent administration.
- Monitor lab tests: Baseline and frequent serum electrolytes; frequent serum sodium during initiation and titration.

Patient & Family Education
- Continue to drink fluid in response to thirst until otherwise directed. Fluid restrictions are usually required after the first 24 h of therapy.
- Report promptly any of the following: Trouble speaking or swallowing, drowsiness, mood changes, confusion, involuntary body movements, or muscle weakness in arms or legs.

TOPIRAMATE
(to-pir'a-mate)
Topamax, Qudexy XR, Trokendi XR
Classification: ANTICONVULSANT; GAMMA-AMINOBUTYRATE (GABA) ENHANCER
Therapeutic: ANTICONVULSANT; ANTIEPILEPTIC

AVAILABILITY Tablet; extended release capsule; sprinkle capsule

ACTION & *THERAPEUTIC EFFECT*
Exhibits sodium channel-blocking action, as well as enhances the ability of GABA to induce a flux of chloride ions into the neurons, thus potentiating the activity of this inhibitory neurotransmitter (GABA). *Effectiveness indicated by a decrease in seizure activity.*

USES Adjunctive therapy for partial-onset seizures; generalized tonic-clonic seizures; migraine prophylaxis.

UNLABELED USES Cluster headache, bulimia nervosa, neuropathic pain, infantile spasms, bipolar disorder, obesity.

CONTRAINDICATIONS Hypersensitivity to topiramate; suicidal ideation; visual field defects, or persistent or severe metabolic acidosis due to drug; abrupt withdrawal; pregnancy (category D); lactation. Effect on labor and delivery is unknown. **Extended release:** Recent alcohol use (i.e., within 6 h prior to and 6 h after administration).

CAUTIOUS USE Moderate and severe renal impairment, hepatic impairment; COPD; chronic acidosis; history of suicidal thoughts or psychiatric disturbances; severe pulmonary disease; older adults. **Immediate release:** Children younger than 2 y.

ROUTE & DOSAGE

Partial-Onset Seizures (Monotherapy)
Adult/Adolescent/Child (older than 10 y): **PO Immediate release** Initiate with 25 mg bid, increase by 25 mg/wk to efficacy; **PO Maintenance dose** 200–400 mg/day divided bid (max: 1600 mg/day); **PO Extended release** 50 mg daily then increase by 50 mg/wk to reach 400 mg daily
Child (2–16 y): **PO** Initiate with 1–3 mg/kg at bedtime × 1 wk, then increase by 1–3 mg/kg/day in 2 divided doses q1–2wk to a target range of 5–9 mg/kg/day

Epilepsy (Adjunctive Therapy)
Adult: **PO Immediate release** Start at 25 mg daily then titrate

---

to 100–200 mg bid; **Extended release** Start with 25 mg daily then titrate to 200–400 mg daily

Generalized Tonic-Clonic Monotherapy

Adults/Adolescents/Children (older than 10 y): **PO Immediate release** 50 mg/day in 2 daily divided doses, taper up dose by 50 mg per wk up to 400 mg/day *Child (2–10 y):* **PO** Weight-based dosing in package insert

Migraine Prophylaxis

Adult: **PO Immediate release** Initiate with 25 mg bid, increase by 25 mg/wk to 100 mg/day or max tolerated dose

Renal Impairment Dosage Adjustment

CrCl less than 70 mL/min: Decrease dose by 50%

ADMINISTRATION

Oral

- Make dosage increments of 50 mg at weekly intervals to the recommended dose, usually 400 mg/day.
- Do not break tablets unless absolutely necessary because of bitter taste.
- Store at 15°–30° C (59°–86° F) in a tightly closed container. Protect from light and moisture.

ADVERSE EFFECTS CNS: *Somnolence, dizziness, ataxia, psychomotor slowing, confusion, nystagmus, paresthesia, memory difficulty, difficulty concentrating, nervousness,* depression, anxiety, tremor. **HEENT:** Angle closure glaucoma (rare). **Endocrine:** *Abnormal bicarbonate level.* **GI:** *Anorexia,* nausea. **Other:** *Fatigue, speech problems, weight loss;* decreased sweating and hyperthermia in children; metabolic acidosis, upper respiratory infection.

INTERACTIONS Drug: Increased CNS depression with **alcohol** and other CNS DEPRESSANTS; may increase **phenytoin** concentrations; may decrease ORAL CONTRACEPTIVE, **valproate** concentrations; may increase risk of kidney stone formation with other CARBONIC ANHYDRASE INHIBITORS. **Carbamazepine, phenytoin, valproate** may decrease topiramate concentrations. Use cautiously with **metformin. Herbal:** Ginkgo may decrease anticonvulsant effectiveness.

PHARMACOKINETICS Absorption: Rapidly absorbed from GI tract; 80% bioavailability. **Peak:** 2 h. **Distribution:** 13–17% protein bound. **Metabolism:** Minimally metabolized in the liver. **Elimination:** Primarily in urine. **Half-Life:** 21 h.

NURSING IMPLICATIONS

Assessment & Drug Effects

- Monitor mental status and report significant cognitive impairment.
- Monitor lab tests: Periodic electrolytes and serum creatinine.

Patient & Family Education

- Do not stop drug abruptly; discontinue gradually to minimize seizures.
- To minimize risk of kidney stones, drink at least 6–8 full glasses of water each day.
- Exercise caution with potentially hazardous activities. Sedation is common, especially with concurrent use of alcohol or other CNS depressants.
- Use or add barrier contraceptive if using hormonal contraceptives.
- Be aware that psychomotor slowing and speech/language problems may develop while on topiramate therapy.
- Report adverse effects that interfere with activities of daily living.

TOPOTECAN HYDROCHLORIDE ○

(toe-po-tee'can)

Hycamtin

Classification: ANTINEOPLASTIC; CAMPTOTHECIN; DNA TOPOISOMERASE I INHIBITOR

Therapeutic: ANTINEOPLASTIC

AVAILABILITY Solution for injection; oral capsule

ACTION & *THERAPEUTIC EFFECT*
Antitumor mechanism is related to inhibition of the activity of topoisomerase I, an enzyme required for DNA replication. Topoisomerase I is essential for the relaxation of supercoiled double-stranded DNA that enables replication and transcription to proceed. *Topotecan permits uncoiling of DNA strands but prevents recoiling of the two strands of DNA, resulting in a permanent break in the DNA strands.*

USES Metastatic ovarian cancer, cervical cancer, small cell lung cancer.

CONTRAINDICATIONS Previous hypersensitivity to topotecan, irinotecan, or other camptothecin analogs; acute infection; severe bone marrow depression; severe thrombocytopenia; neutropenic colitis; interstitial lung disease; pregnancy (category D); lactation.

CAUTIOUS USE Myelosuppression; mild to moderate renal impairment; history of bleeding disorders; previous cytotoxic or radiation therapy; older adults.

ROUTE & DOSAGE

Metastatic Ovarian Cancer and Small Cell Lung Cancer

Adult: **IV** 1.5 mg/m^2 daily for 5 days starting on day 1 of a 21-day course. Four courses of therapy recommended. Subsequent doses can be adjusted by 0.25 mg/m^2 depending on toxicity. **PO** 2.3 mg/m^2 × 5 days, repeat q21days

Cervial Cancer

Adult: 0.75 mg/m^2 days 1–3 every 3 weeks

Renal Impairment Dosage Adjustment

CrCl 20–39 mL/min: **IV** Use 0.75 mg/m^2 **PO** Reduce to 1.8 mg/m^2

Toxicity Dosage Adjustment

In severe neutropenia reduce dose by 0.4 mg/m^2 for subsequent courses

ADMINISTRATION

Oral

- Capsules must be swallowed whole. They must not be crushed, chewed, or opened.
- Avoid direct contact of the capsule contents with the skin or mucous membranes. If contact occurs, wash thoroughly with soap and water or wash eyes immediately with gently flowing water for at least 15 min.

Intravenous

- Initiate therapy only if baseline neutrophil count 1500/mm^3 or higher and platelet count 100,000/mm^3 or higher. ■ Do not give subsequent doses until neutrophils 1000/mm^3 or higher, platelets 100,000/mm^3 or higher, and Hgb greater than 9.0 mg/dL.

This drug is a cytotoxic agent and caution should be used to prevent any contact with the drug. Follow institutional or standard guidelines for preparation, handling, and disposal of cytotoxic agents.

PREPARE: IV Infusion: Reconstitute each 4-mg vial with 4 mL sterile water for injection to yield 1 mg/mL. ▪ Withdraw the required dose and inject into 50–100 mL of NS or D5W.

ADMINISTER: IV Infusion: Give over 30 min immediately after preparation.

INCOMPATIBILITIES: Y-site: Acyclovir, allopurinol, amifostine, aminophylline, amphotericin B, ampicillin/sulbactam, atenolol, bumetanide, calcium gluconate, cefepime, ceftazidime, clindamycin, dantrolene, dexamethasone, diazepam, digoxin, ertapenem, fluorouracil, foscarnet, fosphenytoin, ganciclovir, hydrocortisone, imipenem/cilastatin, ketorolac, meropenem, methohexital, mitomycin, nafcillin, pantoprazole, pemetrexed, pentobarbital, phenobarbital, phenytoin, piperacillin, piperacillin/tazobactam, potassium acetate, potassium phosphate, rituximab, sodium bicarbonate, sodium phosphate, SMZ/TMP, thiopental, ticarcillin, trastuzumab.

▪ Store vials at 20°–25° C (68°–77° F); protect from light. Reconstituted vials are stable for 24 h.

ADVERSE EFFECTS Respiratory: *Dyspnea,* cough. **CNS:** *Headache, asthenia, pain.* **Skin:** *Alopecia, rash.* **GI:** *Nausea, vomiting, diarrhea, constipation, abdominal pain, stomatitis, anorexia,* transient elevations in liver function tests. **Hematologic:** <u>Leukopenia, neutropenia, anemia, thrombocytopenia</u>. **Other:** *Asthenia, fever, fatigue.*

INTERACTIONS Drug: Increased risk of bleeding with ANTICOAGULANTS, NSAIDS, SALICYLATES, ANTIPLATELET AGENTS. Avoid use with **clozapine, filgrastim, phenytoin, leflunomide, natalizumab, pimecrolimus, tacrolimus, tofacitinib,** and LIVE VACCINES.

PHARMACOKINETICS Distribution: 35% bound to plasma proteins. **Metabolism:** Undergoes pH-dependent hydrolysis. **Elimination:** ~30% in urine. **Half-Life:** 2–3 h.

NURSING IMPLICATIONS

Black Box Warning

Topotecan has been associated with severe bone marrow suppression.

Assessment & Drug Effects

▪ Assess for GI distress, respiratory distress, neurosensory symptoms, and S&S of infection throughout therapy.
▪ Monitor lab tests: Baseline and periodic CBC with differential; periodic renal function tests and LFTs.

Patient & Family Education

▪ Learn common adverse effects and measures to control or minimize when possible. Immediately report any distressing adverse effects to prescriber.
▪ Avoid pregnancy during therapy.

TORSEMIDE
(tor'se-mide)
Demadex
Classification: LOOP DIURETIC
Therapeutic: DIURETIC; ANTIHYPERTENSIVE
Prototype: Furosemide

AVAILABILITY Tablet

ACTION & THERAPEUTIC EFFECT
Inhibits reabsorption of sodium and

chloride primarily in the loop of Henle and renal tubules. Binds to the sodium/potassium/chloride carrier in the loop of Henle and in the renal tubules. *Long-acting potent "loop" diuretic and antihypertensive agent.*

USES Management of edema, hypertension.

CONTRAINDICATIONS Hypersensitivity to torsemide or sulfonamides; anuria; hepatic coma.

CAUTIOUS USE Renal impairment; CVD; ventricular arrhythmias; gout or hyperuricemia; DM or history of pancreatitis; liver disease with cirrhosis and ascites; fluid and electrolyte depletion; hyperuricemia; hyperglycemia; hearing impairment; older adults; pregnancy (fetal risk cannot be ruled out); lactation (infant risk cannot be ruled out). Safety and efficacy in children not established.

ROUTE & DOSAGE

Edema of HF or Chronic Renal Failure

Adult: **PO** 10–20 mg once daily, may increase up to 200 mg/day as needed

Edema with Hepatic Cirrhosis

Adult: **PO** 5–10 mg once daily, may increase by doubling dose (max: dose 40 mg) administered with an aldosterone antagonist or potassium-sparing diuretic

Hypertension

Adult: **PO** 5 mg once daily, may increase to 10 mg/day if no response after 4–6 wk

ADMINISTRATION

- Note: With hepatic cirrhosis, use an aldosterone antagonist

concomitantly to prevent hypokalemia and metabolic alkalosis.
- Store tablet at 15°–30° C (59°–86° F).

ADVERSE EFFECTS **GU:** Polyuria.

DIAGNOSTIC TEST INTERFERENCE
May lead to false-negative aldosterone/renin ratio.

INTERACTIONS **Drug:** NSAIDS may reduce diuretic effects. Also see furosemide for potential drug interactions such as increased risk of **digoxin** toxicity due to hypokalemia, prolonged neuromuscular blockade with NEUROMUSCULAR BLOCKING AGENTS, and decreased **lithium** elimination with increased toxicity. Do not use with **desmopressin, foscarnet, levosulpiride, promazine. Herbal: Ginseng** may decrease efficacy.

PHARMACOKINETICS **Absorption:** Readily from GI tract. **Onset:** 60 min. **Peak:** 60–120 min. **Duration:** 6–8 h. **Metabolism:** In liver (CYP system). **Elimination:** 80% in bile; 20% in urine. **Half-Life:** 210 min.

NURSING IMPLICATIONS

Assessment & Drug Effects

- Monitor BP often and assess for orthostatic hypotension; assess respiratory status for S&S of pulmonary edema.
- Monitor ECG, as electrolyte imbalances predispose to cardiac arrhythmias.
- Monitor I&O with daily weights. Assess for improvement in edema.
- Monitor diabetics for loss of glycemic control.
- Monitor coagulation parameters and lithium levels in patients on concurrent anticoagulant and/or lithium therapy.
- Monitor lab tests: Periodic serum electrolytes, blood glucose.

T

Patient & Family Education
- Check weight at least weekly and report abrupt gains or losses to prescriber.
- Understand the risk of orthostatic hypotension.
- Report symptoms of hypokalemia (see Appendix F) or hearing loss immediately to prescriber.
- Monitor blood glucose for loss of glycemic control if diabetic.

TRAMADOL HYDROCHLORIDE
(tra′mad-ol)

ConZip, Rybix, Ryzolt, Ultram, Ultram ER, Zydol ◆
Classification: ANALGESIC; NARCOTIC (OPIATE AGONIST)
Therapeutic: NARCOTIC ANALGESIC
Prototype: Morphine sulfate
Controlled Substance: Schedule IV

AVAILABILITY Tablet; orally disintegrating tablet; extended release tablet; extended release capsule

ACTION & THERAPEUTIC EFFECT Centrally acting opiate receptor agonist that inhibits the uptake of norepinephrine and serotonin, suggesting both opioid and nonopioid mechanisms of pain relief. May produce opioid-like effects, but causes less respiratory depression than morphine. *Effective agent for control of moderate to moderately severe pain.*

USES Management of moderate or moderately severe pain.

CONTRAINDICATIONS Hypersensitivity to tramadol or other opioid analgesics including anaphylactoid reaction; severe respiratory depression; severe or acute asthmas; patients on MAO Inhibitors; substance abuse; suicidal; alcohol intoxication; lactation. **Extended release:** Do not administer to patients with severe hepatic impairment.

CAUTIOUS USE Debilitated patients; chronic respiratory disorders; respiratory depression; liver disease; renal impairment; myxedema, hypothyroidism, or hypoadrenalism; GI disease; acute abdominal conditions; increased ICP or head injury, increased intracranial pressure; history of seizures; older adults: pregnancy (category C); children younger than 16 y. **Extended release:** Do not use in children younger than 18 y.

ROUTE & DOSAGE

Pain

Adult: **PO Immediate release** 25 mg daily, titrated up to dose of 100 mg/day (max: 400 mg/day); **PO Extended release** 100 mg qd may titrate up q5d (max dose: 300 mg/day) **PO Disintegrating tablet** 50 mg q4–6h may increase q3d to 200 mg/day

Renal Impairment Dosage Adjustment

CrCl less than 30 mL/min: Decrease to 50–100 mg q12h

Hepatic Impairment Dosage Adjustment

Cirrhosis: Decrease to 50–100 mg q12h

ADMINISTRATION

Oral
- Extended release tablets should be swallowed whole. They should not be crushed or chewed.
- Store at 15°–30° C (59°–86° F).

ADVERSE EFFECTS CV: Palpitations, vasodilation, orthostatic hypotension. **CNS:** Drowsiness, *dizziness, vertigo, fatigue, headache, somnolence,* restlessness,

Common adverse effects in *italic;* life-threatening effects underlined; generic names in **bold;** classifications in SMALL CAPS; ◆ Canadian drug name; ◑ Prototype drug; ⚠ Alert

euphoria, confusion, anxiety, coordination disturbance, sleep disturbances, seizures. **HEENT:** Visual disturbances. **Skin:** Rash. **GI:** *Nausea, constipation,* vomiting, xerostomia, dyspepsia, diarrhea, abdominal pain, anorexia, flatulence. **GU:** Urinary retention/ frequency, menopausal symptoms. **Other:** Sweating, anaphylactic reaction (even with first dose), withdrawal syndrome (anxiety, sweating, nausea, tremors, diarrhea, piloerection, panic attacks, paresthesia, hallucinations) with abrupt discontinuation, flushing.

DIAGNOSTIC TEST INTERFERENCE

Increased ***creatinine, liver enzymes;*** decreased ***hemoglobin; proteinuria.***

INTERACTIONS **Drug: Carbamazepine** significantly decreases tramadol levels (may need up to twice usual dose). Tramadol may increase adverse effects of MAO INHIBITORS. TRICYCLIC ANTIDEPRESSANTS, **cyclobenzaprine,** PHENOTHIAZINES, SELECTIVE SEROTONIN-REUPTAKE INHIBITORS (SSRIS), MAO INHIBITORS may enhance seizure risk with tramadol. May increase CNS adverse effects when used with other CNS DEPRESSANTS. **Herbal: St. John's wort** may increase sedation.

PHARMACOKINETICS **Absorption:** Rapidly absorbed from GI tract; 75% reaches systemic circulation. **Onset:** 30–60 min. **Peak:** 2 h. **Duration:** 3–7 h. **Distribution:** Approximately 20% bound to plasma proteins; probably crosses blood–brain barrier; crosses placenta; 0.1% excreted into breast milk. **Metabolism:** Extensively in liver by cytochrome P450 system. **Elimination:** Primarily in urine. **Half-Life:** 6–7 h.

NURSING IMPLICATIONS

Assessment & Drug Effects

- Assess for level of pain relief and administer prn dose as needed but not to exceed the recommended total daily dose.
- Monitor vital signs and assess for orthostatic hypotension or signs of CNS depression.
- Withhold drug and notify prescriber if S&S of hypersensitivity occur.
- Assess bowel and bladder function; report urinary frequency or retention.
- Use seizure precautions for patients who have a history of seizures or who are concurrently using drugs that lower the seizure threshold.
- Monitor ambulation and take appropriate safety precautions.

Patient & Family Education

- Exercise caution with potentially hazardous activities until response to drug is known.
- Do not exceed the total number of mg prescribed for a 24 h period.
- Understand potential adverse effects and report problems with bowel and bladder function, CNS impairment, and any other bothersome adverse effects to prescriber.

TRAMETINIB

(tra-me′ti-nib)

Mekinist

Classification: ANTINEOPLASTIC; MITOGEN-ACTIVATED EXTRACELLULAR KINASE (MEK) INHIBITOR
Therapeutic: ANTINEOPLASTIC
Prototype: Erlotinib

AVAILABILITY Tablet

ACTION & *THERAPEUTIC EFFECT*

A reversible inhibitor of certain kinases that transmit signals and promote cellular proliferation and cancer growth. *Trametinib inhibits BRAF*

V600 mutation-positive melanoma cell growth in vitro and in vivo.

USES Treatment of unresectable or metastatic melanoma in patients with BRAF V600E or V600K mutations, as detected by an FDA-approved test.

CONTRAINDICATIONS Symptomatic cardiomyopathy or LVEF decreases by 10% below pre-treatment level and less than the LLN; drug-related loss of vision or other visual disturbances; drug-induced interstitial lung disease or pneumonitis; pregnancy (category D); lactation.

CAUTIOUS USE Severe renal impairment; moderate or severe hepatic impairment; cardiac disorders; CHF; respiratory disorders; ocular disorders; hypertension. Safety and efficacy in children not established.

ROUTE & DOSAGE

Malignant Melanoma
Adult: **PO** 2 mg once daily

Toxicity Dosage Adjustment
For specific toxicities see manufacturer guidelines.

ADMINISTRATION

Oral
- Give at least 1 h before or 2 h after a meal.
- Store at 2°–8° C (36°–46° F) and protect from moisture and light. Keep in original bottle and do not remove desiccant.

ADVERSE EFFECTS CV: Bradycardia, *cardiomyopathy*, hypertension. **CNS:** Dizziness, dysgeusia. **HEENT:** Dry eye, blurred vision. **Endocrine:** Anemia, *hypoalbuminemia, increased alkaline phosphatase,*

increased ALT/AST. **Skin:** *Dermatitis acneiform,* cellulitis, dry skin, folliculitis, paronychia, pruritus, *rash.* **GI:** Abdominal pain and tenderness, aphthous stomatitis, *diarrhea,* mouth ulceration, mucosal inflammation, and stomatitis. **Musculoskeletal:** Rhabdomyolysis. **Hematologic:** Conjunctival hemorrhage, *edema,* epistaxis, gingival bleeding, hematochezia, hematuria, hemorrhoidal hemorrhage, *lymphedema,* melena, *peripheral edema,* rectal hemorrhage, and vaginal hemorrhage.

PHARMACOKINETICS Absorption: 72% bioavailable. **Peak:** 1.5 h. **Distribution:** 97.4% plasma protein bound. **Metabolism:** In liver. **Elimination:** Fecal (80%) and renal (20%). **Half-Life:** 3.9–4.8 d.

NURSING IMPLICATIONS

Assessment & Drug Effects
- Monitor cardiovascular status throughout therapy. Report promptly new-onset or worsening hypertension and S&S of heart failure.
- Monitor pulmonary status throughout therapy. Report promptly signs of interstitial lung disease including cough, dyspnea, and signs of hypoxia or pleural effusion.
- Monitor for and report promptly S&S of retinal detachment.
- Evaluate for signs of skin toxicity. Report to prescriber development of progressive rash or signs of skin infection.
- Monitor lab tests: Prior to therapy the presence of BRAF V600E or V600K mutation in tumor specimens must be confirmed.

Patient & Family Education
- Report to prescriber if you experience any of the following S&S of heart failure or lung problems:

Rapid heart rate, shortness of breath, unproductive cough, swelling of ankles and feet, excessive fatigue.
- Report to prescriber if you experience blurred vision, see colored dots or halo around objects.
- Report promptly signs of skin toxicity such as skin rash, acne, redness, swelling, peeling, or tenderness of hands or feet.
- Women should use highly effective contraception during treatment due to potential for serious fetal harm.
- Contact prescriber immediately if a pregnancy is suspected.

TRANDOLAPRIL
(tran-do'la-pril)
Classification: ANGIOTENSIN-CONVERTING ENZYME (ACE) INHIBITOR; ANTIHYPERTENSIVE
Therapeutic: ANTIHYPERTENSIVE; ACE INHIBITOR
Prototype: Enalapril

AVAILABILITY Tablet

ACTION & THERAPEUTIC EFFECT
Inhibits ACE and interrupts conversion by renin which leads to the formation of angiotensin II from angiotensin I. Inhibition of ACE leads to vasodilation as well as to decreased aldosterone. Decreased aldosterone leads to diuresis and a slight increase in serum potassium. *Lowers blood pressure by specific inhibition of ACE. Unlike other ACE inhibitors, all racial groups respond to trandolapril, including low-renin hypertensives.*

USES Treatment of hypertension

UNLABELED USES: reduction of CV morbidity/mortality post MI in patients with heart failure; non ST elevation acute coronary syndrome.

CONTRAINDICATIONS Hypersensitivity to trandolapril or ACE inhibitors; history of angioedema related to previous treatment with an ACE inhibitor; history of idiopathic or hereditary angioedema; jaundice due to trandolapril; concomitant use of aliskiren in patients with diabetes, pregnancy—fetal risk cannot be ruled out and fetal injury and death have been reported; lactation—infant risk cannot be ruled out.

CAUTIOUS USE Renal impairment, hepatic insufficiency; patients prone to hypotension (e.g., CHF, ischemic heart disease, aortic stenosis, CVA, dehydration); systemic lupus erythematosus, scleroderma; patients being treated with hymenoptera venom. Safety and efficacy in children younger than 18 y not established.

ROUTE & DOSAGE

Hypertension
Adult: **PO** 1 mg once daily, may increase weekly to 2–4 mg once daily (max: 8 mg/day).

Renal Impairment Dosage Adjustment
CrCl less than 30 mL/min: Start with 0.5 mg once daily

Hepatic Impairment Dosage Adjustment
Hepatic cirrhosis: Start with 0.5 mg once daily

ADMINISTRATION
Oral
- Note: If concurrently ordered diuretic cannot be discontinued 2–3 days before beginning

trandolapril therapy, initial dose is usually reduced to 0.5 mg.

- Dosage adjustments are typically made at intervals of at least 1 wk.
- Store at controlled room temperatures between 20 and 25 degrees C (59 to 77 degrees F). Capsules are stable for 2 years.

ADVERSE EFFECTS (≥5%)

CV: *Hypotension*, syncope. **Respiratory:** *Cough*. **CNS:** *Dizziness*. **Endocrine:** Hyperkalemia. **GI:** Dyspepsia. **GU:** elevated serum BUN.

DIAGNOSTIC TEST INTERFERENCE

may lead to false negative aldosterone/renin ratio.

INTERACTIONS Drug: DIURETICS, ANTIHYPERTENSIVES, **rituximab** may enhance hypotensive effects. POTASSIUM-SPARING DIURETICS (**amiloride, spironolactone, triamterene**), POTASSIUM SUPPLEMENTS, POTASSIUM-CONTAINING SALT SUBSTITUTES, **aliskiren,** may increase risk of hyperkalemia. May increase serum levels and toxicity of **lithium.** NSAIDs may reduce the therapeutic response. Avoid use with **cyclosporine.** Increases adverse effects of **iron dextran, sodium phosphate.**

PHARMACOKINETICS Absorption: Rapidly absorbed from GI tract and converted to active form, trandolaprilat, in liver; 70% of dose reaches systemic circulation as trandolaprilat. **Peak:** 4–10 h. **Distribution:** 80% protein bound; crosses placenta, secreted into breast milk of animals (human secretion unknown). **Metabolism:** In liver to trandolaprilat. **Elimination:** 33% in urine, 66% in feces. **Half-Life:** 6 h trandolapril, 22.5 h trandolaprilat.

NURSING IMPLICATIONS

Black Box Warning

Trandolapril has been associated with fetal toxicity.

Assessment & Drug Effects

- Monitor BP carefully for 1–3 h following initial dose, especially in patients using concurrent diuretics, on salt restriction, or volume depleted.
- Monitor serum lithium levels frequently with concurrent lithium therapy and assess for S&S of lithium toxicity; increase caution when diuretic therapy is also used.
- Monitor lab tests: Baseline LFTs and renal function tests; periodic serum potassium and sodium, fasting blood glucose, comprehensive metabolic panel, urinalysis, uric acid.

Patient & Family Education

- Discontinue drug and immediately report S&S of angioedema of face or extremities to prescriber. Seek emergency help for swelling of the tongue or any other sign of potential airway obstruction.
- Women with reproduction potential should be counseled on importance of birth control while taking this drug and if pregnancy occurs, notify provider right away. This medication is known to cause fetal harm.
- Review adverse effects with patient and/or caregiver.
- Be aware that lightheadedness can occur, especially during early therapy. Excess fluid loss of any kind will increase risk of hypotension and syncope.
- Patient should avoid activities requiring coordination until drug effects are realized as drug may cause dizziness.

- Report promptly if you are or suspect you are pregnant.

TRANYLCYPROMINE SULFATE
(tran-ill-sip'roe-meen)

Parnate

Classification: ANTIDEPRESSANT; MONOAMINE OXIDASE INHIBITOR (MAOI)

Therapeutic: ANTIDEPRESSANT; MAOI

Prototype: Phenelzine

AVAILABILITY Tablet

ACTION & *THERAPEUTIC EFFECT*

Potent MAO with a antidepressant activity that arises from the increased availability of monoamines resulting from the inhibition of the enzyme MAO. This leads to increased concentration of neurotransmitters, such as epinephrine, norepinephrine, and dopamine in the CNS. *Drug of last choice for severe depression unresponsive to other MAO inhibitors.*

USES Major depression.

UNLABELED USES Orthostatic hypotension, panic disorder, social anxiety disorder.

CONTRAINDICATIONS Confirmed or suspected cerebrovascular defect, cardiovascular disease; hepatic disease or abnormal LFT; hypertension, pheochromocytoma history of severe or recurrent headaches; recent acute MI; angina; renal failure; suicidal ideation; anuria; lactation.

CAUTIOUS USE Bipolar disorder; Parkinson's disease; psychosis; schizophrenia, anxiety/agitation; CHF; DM; seizure disorders; hyperthyroidism; history of suicidal attempts; renal impairment; older adults; pregnancy (category C); children and adolescents with major depressive disorder or other psychiatric disorders.

ROUTE & DOSAGE

Major Depression
Adult: **PO** 30 mg/day in 2 divided doses, may increase by 10 mg/day at 2–3 wk intervals (max: 60 mg/day)

ADMINISTRATION

Oral
- Contraindicated drugs should be discontinued 1–2 wk before starting therapy.
- Crush tablet and give with fluid or mix with food if patient cannot swallow pill.
- Note: Doses given in the late evening may cause insomnia.

ADVERSE EFFECTS CV: *Orthostatic hypotension*, arrhythmias, hypertensive crisis. **CNS:** Vertigo, dizziness, tremors, muscle twitching, headache, blurred vision suicidality. **Skin:** Rash. **GI:** Dry mouth, anorexia, constipation, diarrhea, abdominal discomfort. **GU:** Impotence. **Other:** Peripheral edema, sweating.

INTERACTIONS Drug: TRICYCLIC ANTIDEPRESSANTS, SSRIS, AMPHETAMINES, **ephedrine, guanethidine, buspirone, methyldopa, dopamine, levodopa, tryptophan** may precipitate hypertensive crisis, and must be discontinued before **tranylcypromine** treatment. **Alcohol** and other CNS DEPRESSANTS add to CNS depressant effects; **meperidine** can cause fatal cardiovascular collapse; ANESTHETICS exaggerate hypotensive and CNS depressant effects;

metrizamide increases risk of seizures; DIURETICS and other ANTIHYPERTENSIVE AGENTS add to hypotensive effects. **Food: Tyramine**-containing foods may precipitate hypertensive crisis (e.g., aged or matured cheese, air-dried or cured meats including sausages and salamis; fava or broad bean pods, tap/draft beers, sauerkraut, soy sauce, and other soybean condiments). **Herbal: Ginseng, ephedra, ma huang, St. John's wort** may lead to hypertensive crisis; **ginseng** may lead to manic episodes.

PHARMACOKINETICS Absorption: Completely from GI tract. **Onset:** 10 days. **Metabolism:** Rapidly in liver to active metabolite. **Elimination:** Primarily in urine. **Half-Life:** 90–190 min.

NURSING IMPLICATIONS

Black Box Warning

Tranylcypromine sulfate has been associated with suicidal thinking and behavior in children, adolescents, and young adults.

Assessment & Drug Effects

- Monitor BP closely. Severe hypertensive reactions are known to occur with MAO inhibitors.
- Report immediately to prescriber signs of worsening mental status such as suicidal ideation, aggressiveness, agitation, anxiety, hostility, impulsivity, insomnia, irritability, panic attacks, and worsening of depression.
- Expect therapeutic response within 3 days, but full antidepressant effects may not be obtained until 2–3 wk of drug therapy.

Patient & Family Education

- Do not eat tyramine-containing foods (see FOOD–DRUG INTERACTIONS).

- Be aware that excessive use of caffeine-containing beverages (chocolate, coffee, tea, cola) can contribute to development of rapid heartbeat, arrhythmias, and hypertension.
- Report promptly emergence of anxiety, agitation, panic attacks, insomnia, irritability, hostility, aggressiveness, impulsivity, mania, worsening depression, suicidal ideation, or other unusual changes in behavior.
- Make position changes slowly, particularly from recumbent to upright posture.
- Avoid potentially hazardous activities until response to drug is known.
- Avoid alcohol or other CNS depressants because of their possible additive effects.

TRASTUZUMAB ⊙

(tra-stu′zu-mab)

Herceptin

Classification: IMMUNOMODULATOR; MONOCLONAL ANTIBODY; ANTINEOPLASTIC; ANTI-HUMAN EPIDERMAL GROWTH FACTOR (ANTI-HER)

Therapeutic: ANTINEOPLASTIC; IMMUNOMODULATOR; ANTI-HER

AVAILABILITY Solution for injection

ACTION & *THERAPEUTIC EFFECT*

Recombinant DNA monoclonal antibody (IgG_1 kappa) that selectively binds to the human epidermal growth factor receptor-2 protein (HER_2). *Inhibits growth of human tumor cells that overexpress HER_2 proteins.*

USES Metastatic breast cancer in those whose tumors overexpress the HER_2 protein. HER_2-positive breast cancer after surgery.

T

CONTRAINDICATIONS Concurrent administration of anthracycline or radiation; anaphylaxis; angioedema; interstitial pneumonitis; acute respiratory distress syndrome; drug induced nephrotic syndrome; pregnancy (category D); lactation during and for 6 mo following administration of trastuzumab.

CAUTIOUS USE Preexisting cardiac dysfunction; pulmonary disease; previous administration of cardiotoxic therapy (e.g., anthracycline or radiation); hypersensitivity to benzyl alcohol; older adults.

ROUTE & DOSAGE

Metastatic Breast Cancer
Adult: **IV** 4 mg/kg, then 2 mg/kg qwk

ADMINISTRATION

Note: Trastuzumab and ado-trastuzumab emtansine are different products and are **not** interchangeable.

Intravenous

PREPARE: **IV Infusion:** Reconstitute each vial with 20 mL of supplied diluent (bacteriostatic water) to produce a multidose vial containing 21 mg/mL. ▪ Note: For patients with a hypersensitivity to benzyl alcohol, reconstitute with sterile water for injection; this solution **must be** used immediately with any unused portion discarded. ▪ Withdraw the ordered dose and add to a 250 mL of NS and invert bag to mix. ▪ Do not give or mix with dextrose solutions.
ADMINISTER: **IV Infusion:** Infuse loading dose (4 mg/kg) over 90 min; infuse subsequent doses (2 mg/kg) over 30 min. ▪ Do not give IV push or as a bolus dose. *INCOMPATIBILITIES:* **Solution/additive: Dextrose** solution; do not mix or coadminister with other drugs. **Y-site: Aldesleukin, amikacin, amphotericin B, aztreonam, cefoperazone, cefotaxime, cefotetan, cefoxitin, chlorpromazine, clindamycin, cyclosporine, fludarabine, furosemide, idarubicin, irinotecan, levofloxacin, levorphanol, morphine, nalbuphine, netilmicin, ofloxacin, ondansetron, piperacillin, piperacillin/tazobactam, streptozocin, ticarcillin, topotecan.**

▪ Store unopened vials and reconstituted vials at 2°–8° C (36°–46° F). ▪ Discard reconstituted vials 28 days after reconstitution.

ADVERSE EFFECTS CV: <u>CHF</u>, cardiac dysfunction (dyspnea, cough, paroxysmal nocturnal dyspnea, peripheral edema, S3 gallop, reduced ejection fraction), tachycardia, *edema*, cardiotoxicity. **Respiratory:** *Cough, dyspnea*, rhinitis, pharyngitis, sinusitis. **CNS:** *Headache, insomnia, dizziness, paresthesias*, depression, peripheral neuritis, neuropathy myalgia. **Skin:** *Rash*, herpes simplex, acne. **GI:** *Diarrhea, abdominal pain, nausea, vomiting*, anorexia. **Hematologic:** *Anemia*, <u>leukopenia</u>, *thrombocytopenia, neutropenia*. **Other:** *Pain, asthenia, fever, chills*, flu syndrome, allergic reaction, *fatigue* bone pain, *arthralgia*, <u>hypersensitivity (anaphylaxis, urticaria, bronchospasm, angioedema, or hypotension)</u>, *increased incidence of infections*, infusion reaction (*chills, fever*, nausea, vomiting, pain, rigors, headache, dizziness, dyspnea, hypotension, rash).

T

INTERACTIONS Drug: Paclitaxel may increase trastuzumab levels and toxicity.

PHARMACOKINETICS Half-Life: 5.8 days.

NURSING IMPLICATIONS

Black Box Warning

Trastuzumab has been associated with cardiomyopathy, infusion reactions, pulmonary toxicity, and embryo-fetal toxicity.

Assessment & Drug Effects

- Monitor for infusion reactions within 24 h of infusion. Stop infusion and notify prescriber if patients develop dyspnea, significant hypotension, or any other sign of infusion reaction. Monitor closely until symptoms resolve. chills and fever during the first IV infusion; these adverse events usually respond to prompt treatment without the need to discontinue the infusion. Notify prescriber immediately.
- Monitor carefully cardiovascular status at baseline and throughout course of therapy, assessing for S&S of heart failure (e.g., dyspnea, increased cough, PND, edema, S3 gallop). Those with preexisting cardiac dysfunction are at high risk for cardiotoxicity.
- Monitor lab tests: Periodic CBC with differential, platelet count, and Hgb and Hct.

Patient & Family Education

- Report promptly any unusual symptoms (e.g., chills, nausea, fever) during infusion.
- Report promptly any of the following: Shortness of breath, swelling of feet or legs, persistent cough, difficulty sleeping, loss of appetite, abdominal bloating.

TRAVOPROST

(tra'vo-prost)

Travatan
See Appendix A-1.

TRAZODONE HYDROCHLORIDE

(tray'zoe-done)

Oleptro
Classification: ANTIDEPRESSANT
Therapeutic: ANTIDEPRESSANT
Prototype: Imipramine

AVAILABILITY Tablet; extended release tablet

ACTION & *THERAPEUTIC EFFECT* Potentiates serotonin effects by selectively blocking its reuptake at presynaptic membranes in CNS. Produces varying degrees of sedation in normal and mentally depressed patients. *Increases total sleep time, decreases number and duration of awakenings in depressed patient, and decreases REM sleep. Has antianxiety effect in severely depressed patient.*

USES Major depressive disorder.

UNLABELED USES Adjunctive treatment of alcohol dependence, anxiety, panic disorder, insomnia.

CONTRAINDICATIONS Initial recovery phase of MI; ventricular ectopy; electroshock therapy; within 14 days of MAOIs use; initiation in patients treated with linezolid or methylene blue IV; suicidal ideation.

CAUTIOUS USE Bipolar disorder, MDD; older adults; history of suicidal tendencies; cardiac

Common adverse effects in *italic*; life-threatening effects <u>underlined</u>; generic names in **bold**; classifications in SMALL CAPS; ♣ Canadian drug name; ○ Prototype drug; ⚠ Alert

arrhythmias or disease; patients at risk for QT prolongation; volume depleted individuals; hepatic disease, renal impairment; history of GI bleeding; older adults; pregnancy (category C); lactation. Safe use in children not established.

ROUTE & DOSAGE

Depression

Adult: **PO Immediate release** 150 mg/day in divided doses, may increase by 50 mg/day q3–4days (max: 400–600 mg/day); **PO Extended release** 150 mg daily may increase by 75 mg/day at 3 day intervals (max: 375 mg/day)

Pharmacogenetic Dosage Adjustment

Poor CYP2D6 metabolizer: Start with 80% of normal dose

ADMINISTRATION

Oral

- Ensure that extended release tablets are swallowed whole. They should not be crushed or chewed.
- Give drug with food; increases amount of absorption by 20% and appears to decrease incidence of dizziness or light-headedness. Maintain the same schedule for food-drug intake throughout treatment period to prevent variations in serum concentration.
- Store in tightly closed, light-resistant container at 15°–30° C (59°–86° F).

ADVERSE EFFECTS **CV:** Hypotension (including orthostatic hypotension), hypertension, syncope, shortness of breath, chest pain, tachycardia, palpitations, bradycardia, PVCs, ventricular tachycardia (short episodes of 3–4 beats). **CNS:** *Drowsiness*, light-headedness, tiredness, dizziness, insomnia, *nervousness*, headache, agitation, impaired memory and speech, disorientation. **HEENT:** Nasal and sinus congestion, blurred vision, eye irritation, sweating or clamminess, tinnitus. **Skin:** Skin eruptions, rash, pruritus, acne, photosensitivity. **GI:** *Dry mouth*, anorexia, constipation, abdominal distress, nausea, vomiting, dysgeusia, flatulence, diarrhea. **GU:** Hematuria, increased frequency, delayed urine flow, male priapism, ejaculation inhibition. **Musculoskeletal:** Skeletal aches and pains, muscle twitches. **Hematologic:** Anemia. **Other:** Weight change.

INTERACTIONS **Drug:** ANTIHYPERTENSIVE AGENTS may potentiate hypotensive effects; **alcohol** and other CNS DEPRESSANTS add to depressant effects; may increase **digoxin** or **phenytoin** levels; MAO INHIBITORS may precipitate hypertensive crisis; **ketoconazole, indinavir, ritonavir, saquinavir** may increase levels and toxicity. Use of other serotonergic agents may increase risk of serotonin syndrome. Do not use with **conivaptan, ivabradine, linezolid, mifepristone, saquinavir. Herbal: Ginkgo** may increase sedation.

PHARMACOKINETICS **Absorption:** Readily from GI tract. **Onset:** 1–2 wk. **Peak:** 1–2 h. **Distribution:** Distributed into breast milk. **Metabolism:** In liver (CYP2D6). **Elimination:** 75% in urine, 25% in feces. **Half-Life:** 5–9 h.

NURSING IMPLICATIONS

Black Box Warning

Trazodone hydrochloride has been associated with suicidal thinking and behavior in children, adolescents, and young adults.

Assessment & Drug Effects

- Monitor BP and heart rate and rhythm. Report to prescriber development of tachycardia, bradycardia, or palpitations.
- Monitor for orthostatic hypotension, especially in the elderly or those taking concurrent antihypertensive drugs.
- Monitor children and adolescents for changes in behavior that indicate increased suicidality.
- Observe patient's level of activity. If it appears to be increasing toward sleeplessness and agitation with changes in reality orientation, report to prescriber. Manic episodes have been reported.
- Be aware that overdose is characterized by an extension of common adverse effects: Vomiting, lethargy, drowsiness, and exaggerated anticholinergic effects.

Patient & Family Education

- Report immediately to prescriber signs of worsening mental status such as suicidal ideation, aggressiveness, agitation, anxiety, hostility, impulsivity, insomnia, irritability, panic attacks, and worsening of depression.
- Consult prescriber if drowsiness becomes a distressing adverse effect. Dose regimen may be changed so that largest dose is at bedtime.
- Limit or abstain from alcohol use. The depressant effects of CNS depressants and alcohol may be potentiated by this drug.
- Do not self-medicate with OTC drugs for colds, allergy, or insomnia treatment without advice of prescriber. Many of these drugs contain CNS depressants.
- Male patient should report inappropriate or prolonged penile erections. The drug may be discontinued.

TRETINOIN
(tret′i-noyn)
Atralin, Avita, Refissa, Renova, Retin-A, Retin-A Micro, Retinoic Acid, Tretin-X, Vesanoid
Classification: ANTINEOPLASTIC; ANTIACNE (RETINOID); ANTIPSORIATIC
Therapeutic: ANTINEOPLASTIC; ANTIACNE; ANTIPSORIATIC
Prototype: Isotretinoin

AVAILABILITY Cream; gel; capsule

ACTION & THERAPEUTIC EFFECT

Antiacne activity: Reverses retention hyperkeratosis and micro comedo formation in acne pathology. **Antineoplastic activity:** Induces cellular differentiation in malignant cells. Its exact mechanism of action is unknown. *Effective in early treatment and control of acne vulgaris grades I–III. Effective in treatment of (Acute Promyelocytic Leukemia) APL.*

USES Topical treatment of acne vulgaris grades I–III, especially during early stages when number of comedones is greatest; adjunctively in management of associated comedones and in treatment of flat warts; oral for remission induction treatment of acute promyelocytic leukemia; cream as adjunctive therapy for mitigation of fine wrinkles; palliation of fine wrinkles, mottled hyperpigmentation and facial skin roughness.

UNLABELED USES Psoriasis, senile keratosis, ichthyosis vulgaris, keratosis palmaris and plantaris, basal cell carcinoma, photodamaged skin (photoaging), and other skin conditions. **Orphan drug:** For squamous metaplasia of conjunctiva or cornea with mucous deficiency and keratinization.

Common adverse effects in *italic*; life-threatening effects <u>underlined</u>; generic names in **bold**; classifications in SMALL CAPS; ♦ Canadian drug name; ○ Prototype drug; ⚠ Alert

CONTRAINDICATIONS Hypersensitivity to tretinoin or other retinoids; eczema; exposure to sunlight or ultraviolet rays, sunburn; pregnancy (high risk that a severely deformed infant will result if tretinoin capsules are administered during pregnancy).

CAUTIOUS USE Patient in an occupation necessitating considerable sun exposure or weather extremes; hepatic disease; lactation; children younger than 18 y.

ROUTE & DOSAGE

Acne
Adult: **Topical** Apply once/day at bedtime

Acute Promyelocytic Leukemia
Adult: **PO** 45 mg/m^2/day

Antiwrinkle Cream
Adult: **Topical** (0.05% cream) Apply to face once daily at bedtime

ADMINISTRATION

Oral
- Administer with a meal.
- Capsules must be swallowed whole; they cannot be opened, crushed, or chewed. Tretinoin has also been administered sublingually by squeezing the capsule contents beneath the tongue.

Topical
- Cleanse using a mild bland soap, and thoroughly dry areas being treated before applying drug. Avoid use of medicated, drying, or abrasive soaps and cleansers.
- Wash hands before and after treatment. Apply lightly over affected areas. Do not apply to nonaffected skin area.
- Avoid contact of drug with eyes, mouth, angles of nose, open wounds, mucous membranes.
- Store gel and liquid formulations below 30° C (86° F) and solution below 27° C (80° F).

ADVERSE EFFECTS CV: *Arrhythmias, flushing, hypotension, hypertension,* CHF, peripheral edema, chest discomfort, facial edema. **Respiratory:** *Dyspnea,* upper and/or lower respiratory complaint, pleural effusion, pulmonary infiltrates, pneumonia, rales, wheezing. **CNS:** *Dizziness, paresthesias, anxiety, insomnia, depression, headache,* cerebral hemorrhage, intracranial hypertension, hallucinations, malaise, shivering, pain, confusion, agitation. **HEENT:** Visual disturbances, eye disease, ear fullness, hearing loss. **Endocrine:** Hypercholesterolemia, hypertriglyceridemia, weight gain, weight loss. **Skin:** Cellulitis, pallor, diaphoresis, skin rash, xeroderma, pruritis, alopecia. **Hepatic/GI:** *Dry mucus membranes, nausea, vomiting, abdominal pain,* flank pain, *diarrhea, constipation, dyspepsia, GI hemorrhage,* mucositis, anorexia, dyspepsia, increased liver enzymes, hepatomegaly, splenomegaly. **GU:** Renal insufficiency, fluid imbalance, dysuria. **Musculoskeletal:** Ostealgia, myalgia. **Hematologic:** Hemorrhage, leucocytosis, DIC, lymphatic disease. **Other:** Infection, *fever.*

INTERACTIONS Drug: TOPICAL ACNE MEDICATIONS (including **sulfur, resorcinol, benzoyl peroxide,** and **salicylic acid**) may increase inflammation and peeling; topical products containing **alcohol** or **menthol** may cause stinging. PHOTOSENSITIZING AGENTS increase the risk of adverse effects. Do not use

T

with **vitamin A** or multivitamins containing vitamin A due to risk of adverse effects. **Oral product:** PHOTOSENSITIZING AGENTS increase the risk of adverse effects. Do not use with **vitamin A** or multivitamins containing vitamin A due to risk of adverse effect

PHARMACOKINETICS Absorption: Minimally absorbed from intact skin, topical; 60% absorbed, PO. **Elimination:** About 0.1% of topical dose is excreted in urine within 24 h; 63% excreted in urine and 31% in feces, PO. **Half-Life:** 45 min, topical; 2–2.5 h, PO.

NURSING IMPLICATIONS

Assessment & Drug Effects

Topical

- Be aware that topical treatment to dark-skinned individuals may cause postinflammatory hyperpigmentation; reversible with termination of drug treatment.
- Clinical response to topical treatment should be evident in 2–3 wk; complete and satisfactory response (in 75% of the patients) may require 3–4 mo.
- Be aware that erythema and desquamation during the first 1–3 wk of topical treatment do not represent exacerbation of the skin problem but a probable response to the drug from deep previously unseen lesions.
- Monitor lab values: CBC with differential, coagulation profile, LFTs, triglyceride, and cholesterol.

Patient & Family Education

Topical

- As treatment is continued, lesions gradually disappear, leaving an inflammatory background; scaling and redness decrease after 8–10 wk of therapy.

- Wash face no more often than 2–3 × daily.
- Be aware that drug is not curative; relapses commonly occur within 3–6 wk after treatment has been discontinued.
- Avoid exposure to sun; when cannot be avoided, use a SPF 15 or higher sunscreen.
- Do not self-medicate with additional acne treatment because of danger of drug interactions.

TRIAMCINOLONE

(trye-am-sin'oh-lone)

Atolone, Kenacort, Kenalog-E

TRIAMCINOLONE ACETONIDE

Azmacort, Cenocort A$_2$, Kenalog, Nasacort HFA, Triam-A, Triamonide, Trikort, Trilog, Tri-Nasal

TRIAMCINOLONE DIACETATE

Kenacort

TRIAMCINOLONE HEXACETONIDE

Aristospan

Classification: ADRENAL CORTICOSTEROID; GLUCOCORTICOID **Therapeutic:** ANTI-INFLAMMATORY; IMMUNOSUPPRESSANT **Prototype:** Prednisone

AVAILABILITY Triamcinolone: Tablet; syrup. **Triamcinolone acetonide:** Solution for injection; aerosol; inhaler; spray; nasal spray; cream, ointment, lotion; topical spray. **Triamcinolone diacetate:** Tablet. **Triamcinolone hexacetonide:** Solution for injection

ACTION & *THERAPEUTIC EFFECT* Immediate-acting synthetic fluorinated adrenal corticosteroid with

T

glucocorticoid properties. Possesses minimal sodium and water retention properties in therapeutic doses. *Anti-inflammatory and immunosuppressant drug that is effective in the treatment of bronchial asthma.*

USES An anti-inflammatory or immunosuppressant agent. Orally inhaled: Bronchial asthma in patient who has not responded to conventional inhalation treatment. Therapeutic doses do not appear to suppress HPA (hypothalamic-pituitary-adrenal) axis.

CONTRAINDICATIONS Hypersensitivity to corticosteroids or benzyl alcohol; kidney dysfunction; glaucoma; acute bronchospasm; fungal infection.

CAUTIOUS USE Coagulopathy, hemophilia, diabetes mellitus, GI disease; CHF; herpes infection; infection; IBD; myasthenia gravis; MI; ocular exposure, ocular infection; osteoporosis; peptic ulcer disease; PVD; skin abrasion; pregnancy (category C); lactation. Safe use in children younger than 6 y not established.

ROUTE & DOSAGE

Inflammation, Immunosuppression

Adult: **IM/Subcutaneous** 4–48 mg/day in divided doses; **Intra-articular/Intradermal** 4–48 mg/day; **Inhaled** 2–4 inhalations qid. **Topical** See Appendix A
Child: **IM/Subcutaneous** 3.3–50 mg/m^2/day in divided doses; **Intra-articular/Intradermal** 3.3–50 mg/m^2/day

Acetonide

Adult: **IM** 60 mg, may repeat with 20–100 mg q6wk; **Intradermal** 1 mg/injection site (max: 30 mg total); **Intra-articular** 2.5–4.0 mg; **Inhalation** See Appendix A
Child (6–12 y): **IM** 0.03–0.2 mg q1–7days; **Inhalation** See Appendix A

Hexacetonide

Adult: **Intralesional** Up to 0.5 mg/in^2 of skin; **Intra-articular** 2–20 mg q3–4wk

ADMINISTRATION

Inhalation

- Follow manufacturer's directions for specific oral or nasal inhaler and instruct patient on proper administration technique.

Subcutaneous/Intramuscular

- Do not give triamcinolone injection IV.
- IM injections should only be given into a large, well developed muscle such as the gluteal muscle.
- Store at 15°–30° C (59°–86° F). Protect from light.

ADVERSE EFFECTS CV: CHF, edema. **CNS:** Euphoria, headache, insomnia, confusion, psychosis. **HEENT:** Cataracts. **Endocrine:** Cushingoid features, growth suppression in children, carbohydrate intolerance, hyperglycemia, hypokalemia. **Skin:** Burning, itching, folliculitis, hypertrichosis, hypopigmentation. **GI:** Nausea, vomiting, peptic ulcer. **Musculoskeletal:** Muscle weakness, delayed wound healing, muscle wasting, osteoporosis, aseptic necrosis of bone, spontaneous fractures. **Hematologic:** Leukocytosis.

Common adverse effects in *italic;* life-threatening effects <u>underlined</u>; generic names in **bold;** classifications in SMALL CAPS; ♣ Canadian drug name; ○ Prototype drug; ⚠ Alert

INTERACTIONS Drug: BARBI-
TURATES, **phenytoin, rifampin**
increase steroid metabolism—may
need increased doses of triamcinolone; **amphotericin B**, DIURETICS
add to potassium loss; **neostigmine, pyridostigmine** may cause
severe muscle weakness in patients
with myasthenia gravis; may inhibit
antibody response to VACCINES,
TOXOIDS.

PHARMACOKINETICS Absorp-
tion: Readily absorbed from all
routes. **Onset:** 24–48 h PO, IM.
Peak: 1–2 h PO; 8–10 h IM. **Duration:** 2.25 days PO; 1–6 wk IM.
Metabolism: In liver. **Elimination:**
In urine. **Half-Life:** 2–5 h; HPA suppression, 18–36 h.

NURSING IMPLICATIONS

Assessment & Drug Effects

- Notify prescriber if wheezing
  occurs immediately following a
  dose of inhaled triamcinolone.
- Do not use occlusive dressing
  over topical application unless
  specifically ordered to do so.
- Monitor growth in children
  receiving prolonged, systemic triamcinolone therapy.
- Monitor for signs of negative
  nitrogen balance (e.g., muscle
  atrophy), especially in older or
  debilitated patients receiving prolonged therapy.
- Report to prescriber immediately
  if a local infection develops at site
  of topical application.
- Report symptoms of hypercor-
  tisolism or Cushing's syndrome
  (see Appendix F), hyperglycemia
  (see Appendix F), and glucosuria
  (e.g., polyuria). These may arise
  from systemic absorption after
  topical application, especially in
  children and if used over extensive areas for prolonged periods
  or if occlusive dressings are used.

Patient & Family Education

- Report promptly any of the following: Sore throat, fever, swelling of feet or ankles, or muscle
  weakness.
- Adhere to drug regimen; do not
  increase or decrease established
  regimen and do not discontinue
  abruptly.
- Asthmatics should report promptly
  worsening of asthma symptoms
  following oral inhalation.

TRIAMTERENE
(trye-am'ter-een)
Dyrenium
Classification: POTASSIUM-
SPARING DIURETIC
Therapeutic: POTASSIUM-SPARING
DIURETIC
Prototype: Spironolactone

AVAILABILITY Capsule

ACTION & *THERAPEUTIC EFFECT*
Blocks epithelial sodium channels
in the late distal convoluted tubule
and collecting duct which inhibits sodium reabsorption from the
lumen effectively reducing intracellular sodium; leads to potassium
retention and decreased calcium,
magnesium, and hydrogen excretion. *Has a diuretic action and a
potassium-sparing effect.*

USES Treatment of edema.

CONTRAINDICATIONS Hyper-
sensitivity to triamterene; anuria,
severe or progressive kidney disease or dysfunction with possible
exception of nephrosis; severe
liver disease; diabetic neuropathy;
elevated serum potassium; severe
electrolyte or acid-base imbalance;
coadministration of other potassium-sparing agents.

Common adverse effects in *italic;* life-threatening effects underlined; generic names
in **bold;** classifications in SMALL CAPS; ♣ Canadian drug name; ☉ Prototype drug; ⚠ Alert

CAUTIOUS USE Impaired kidney or liver function; gout; history of gouty arthritis; CHF; arrhythmias; DM; history of kidney stones; older adults; pregnancy (category C). Safety and efficacy in children not established.

ROUTE & DOSAGE

Edema

Adult: **PO** 100 mg bid (max: 300 mg/day)

Renal Impairment Dosage Adjustment

CrCl less than 10 mL/min: Avoid use

ADMINISTRATION

Oral

- Empty capsule and give with fluid or mix with food, if patient cannot swallow capsule.
- Give drug with or after meals to prevent or minimize nausea.
- Schedule doses to prevent interruption of sleep from diuresis (e.g., with or after breakfast if a single dose is taken, or no later than 6 p.m. if more than one dose is prescribed). Consult prescriber.
- Withdraw drug gradually in patients on prolonged or high-dose therapy in order to prevent rebound increased urinary excretion of potassium.
- Store in tight, light-resistant containers at 15°–30° C (59°–86° F) unless otherwise directed.

ADVERSE EFFECTS **CNS:** Dizziness, fatigue, headache. **Endocrine:** Hyperkalemia, increased uric acid, metabolic acidosis. **Skin:** Photosensitivity, rash. **Hepatic/GI:** Jaundice, diarrhea, nausea, vomiting, xerostomia. **GU:** Azotemia, increased BUN, increased serum creatinine, nephrolithiasis. **Musculoskeletal:** Weakness. **Hematologic:** Anemia, thrombocytopenia. **Other:** Anaphylaxis.

DIAGNOSTIC TEST INTERFERENCE

Pale blue fluorescence in urine interferes with *fluorometric assay* of *quinidine* and *lactic dehydrogenase activity*. May lead to false-negative aldosterone/renin ratio.

INTERACTIONS **Drug:** May increase **lithium** levels, thus increasing its toxicity; **indomethacin** may decrease renal elimination of triamterene; ANGIOTENSIN-CONVERTING ENZYME (ACE) INHIBITORS, other POTASSIUM-SPARING DIURETICS may cause hyperkalemia. Do not use with **cyclosporine. Food: High potassium foods** may increase risk of hyperkalemia.

PHARMACOKINETICS **Absorption:** Rapidly but variably from GI tract. **Onset:** 2–4 h. **Duration:** 7–9 h. **Metabolism:** In liver to active and inactive metabolites. **Elimination:** In urine. **Half-Life:** 100–150 min.

NURSING IMPLICATIONS

Black Box Warning

Triamterene has been associated with increased risk of hyperkalemia.

Assessment & Drug Effects

- Monitor BP during periods of dosage adjustment. Hypotensive reactions, although rare, have been reported. Take care with ambulation, particularly for older adults.
- Weigh patient under standard conditions, prior to drug initiation and daily during therapy.

Common adverse effects in *italic;* life-threatening effects underlined; generic names in **bold;** classifications in SMALL CAPS; ♣ Canadian drug name; ☉ Prototype drug; △ Alert   **1719**

- Diuretic response usually occurs on first day of therapy; maximum effect may not occur for several days.
- Monitor and report oliguria and unusual changes in I&O ratio. Consult prescriber regarding allowable fluid intake.
- Be alert for S&S of kidney stone formation; reported in patients taking high doses or who have low urine volume and increased urine acidity.
- Observe for S&S of hyperkalemia (see Appendix F), particularly in patients with renal insufficiency, on high-dose or prolonged therapy, older adults, and those with diabetes.
- Monitor diabetics closely for loss of glycemic control.
- Monitor lab tests: Baseline and periodic serum potassium; periodic renal function tests with known or suspected renal insufficiency.

Patient & Family Education
- Do not use salt substitutes; unlike most diuretics, triamterene promotes potassium retention.
- Do not restrict salt; there is a possibility of low-salt syndrome (hyponatremia). Consult prescriber.
- Report significant fatigue or weakness, malaise, fever, sore throat, or mouth and unusual bleeding or bruising to prescriber.
- Be aware that drug may cause photosensitivity; avoid exposure to sun and sunlamps.
- Drug may impart a harmless pale blue fluorescence to urine.

TRIAZOLAM ⊙
(trye-ay'zoe-lam)
Halcion
Classification: SEDATIVE-HYPNOTIC; BENZODIAZEPINE
Therapeutic: SEDATIVE
Controlled Substance: Schedule IV

AVAILABILITY Tablet

ACTION & *THERAPEUTIC EFFECT*
Blockade of cortical and limbic arousal results in hypnotic activity. *Decreases sleep latency and number of nocturnal awakenings, decreases total nocturnal wake time, and increases duration of sleep.*

USES Short-term management of insomnia.

CONTRAINDICATIONS Hypersensitivity to triazolam and benzodiazepines; ethanol intoxication; suicidal ideations; pregnancy (category X); lactation.

CAUTIOUS USE Depression; bipolar disorder; dementia; psychosis; myasthenia gravis; Parkinson's disease; debilitated patients; patients with suicidal tendency; impaired kidney or liver function; chronic pulmonary insufficiency; sleep apnea; older adults.

ROUTE & DOSAGE

Insomnia
Adult: **PO** 0.25 mg at bedtime (max: 0.5 mg/day)
Geriatric: **PO** 0.125 mg at bedtime

ADMINISTRATION
Oral
- Give immediately before bed; onset of drug action is rapid.
- Do not exceed recommended doses.
- Store at 15°–30° C (59°–86° F).

ADVERSE EFFECTS CNS: *Drowsiness*, lightheadedness, headache, dizziness, ataxia, visual disturbances, confusional states, *memory impairment, "rebound insomnia,"* *anterograde amnesia*, paradoxical reactions, minor changes in EEG patterns. **GI:** Nausea, vomiting, constipation. **Other:** Physiological dependence, psychological dependence, tolerance, withdrawal.

INTERACTIONS Drug: Alcohol, CNS DEPRESSANTS, ANTICONVULSANTS, **nefazodone**, BENZODIAZEPINES potentiate CNS depression; **cimetidine** increases triazolam plasma levels, thus increasing its toxicity; may decrease antiparkinsonism effects of **levodopa**. Contraindicated with **cobicistat, delavirdine**, systemic AZOLE ANTIFUNGALS, PROTEASE INHIBITORS. **Herbal: Kava, valerian** may potentiate sedation. **St. John's wort** may decrease efficacy. **Food: Grapefruit juice** (greater than 1 qt/day) may increase plasma concentrations and adverse effects.

PHARMACOKINETICS Absorption: Readily from GI tract. **Onset:** 15–30 min. **Peak:** 1–2 h. **Duration:** 6–8 h. **Distribution:** Crosses placenta; distributed into breast milk. **Metabolism:** In liver via CYP3A4. **Elimination:** In urine. **Half-Life:** 2–3 h.

NURSING IMPLICATIONS

Assessment & Drug Effects
- Be aware that signs of developing tolerance or adaptation (with long-term use) include increased daytime anxiety, increased wakefulness during last one third of the night.
- Evaluate smoking habit. As with other benzodiazepines, smoking may decrease hypnotic effects.
- Monitor for symptoms of overdosage: Slurred speech, somnolence, confusion, impaired coordination, and coma.

Patient & Family Education
- Do not drive or engage in potentially hazardous activities until response to drug is known.
- Avoid use of alcohol or other CNS depressants while on this drug; they may increase sedative effects.
- Do not stop taking drug suddenly, especially if you are subject to seizures. Withdrawal symptoms may occur and range from mild dysphoria to more serious symptoms (e.g., tremors, abdominal and muscle cramps, convulsions). Consult prescriber for schedule to discontinue therapy.
- Do not increase dose without prescriber's advice because of toxic potential of drug.

TRIFLUOPERAZINE HYDROCHLORIDE
(trye-floo-oh-per′a-zeen)

Classification: ANTIPSYCHOTIC; PHENOTHIAZINE
Therapeutic: ANTIPSYCHOTIC
Prototype: Chlorpromazine

AVAILABILITY Tablet

ACTION & *THERAPEUTIC EFFECT*
Phenothiazine with antipsychotic effects thought to be related to blockade of postsynaptic dopamine receptors in the brain. *Effectiveness indicated by increase in mental and physical activity.*

USES Management of schizophrenia.

CONTRAINDICATIONS Hypersensitivity to trifluoperazine, phenothiazines or any component of the formulation; comatose states; CNS depression; ethanol intoxication; blood dyscrasias; hematologic disease, bone marrow suppression; dementia related psychosis in older adults; hepatic disease; lactation.

CAUTIOUS USE Previously detected breast cancer; history of QT

T

prolongation; significant cardiac disease or pulmonary disease; compromised respiratory function; seizure disorders; impaired liver function; pregnancy (nonpharmacologic interventions should be considered first due to unknown maternal and fetal risk); children younger than 6 y.

ROUTE & DOSAGE

Schizophrenia

Adult: **PO** 2–5 mg once daily or bid, may increase up to 15–20 mg/day
Child (6–12 y): **PO** 1 mg 1–2 × day, may increase up to 15 mg/day

ADMINISTRATION

Oral

- May be taken with food to decrease GI upset; do not take within 2 hours of any antacids.
- Store in light-resistant container at 20°–25° C (68°–77° F) unless otherwise directed.

ADVERSE EFFECTS CV: Orthostatic hypotension, *hypotension.* **Respiratory:** Nasal congestion. **CNS:** Dizziness, *extrapyramidal effects,* neuroleptic malignant syndrome, decreased seizure threshold, disruption of body temperature regulation, headache, tremor. **HEENT:** Corneal changes, lens disease, retinitis pigmentosa. **Endocrine:** Gynecomastia, galactorrhea, change in libido, change in menstrual flow, hyperglycemia, hypoglycemia, weight gain. **Skin:** Photosensitivity, skin rash, skin discoloration (blue-gray). **Hepatic/GI:** Constipation, nausea, stomach pain, vomiting, xerostomia, jaundice, hepatotoxicity. **GU:** Difficulty in micturition, ejaculatory disorder, lactation, mastalgia, priapism,

urinary retention. **Hematologic:** Agranulocytosis, aplastic anemia, eosinophilia, haemolytic anemia, immune thrombocytopenia, leukopenia, pancytopenia.

DIAGNOSTIC TEST INTERFERENCE may produce a false positive for phenylketonuria.

INTERACTIONS Drug: Alcohol and other CNS DEPRESSANTS add to CNS depression. Do not use with agents that prolong QT interval (e.g., **bepridil, dofetilide, dronedarone, procaine, ziprasidone** **metoclopramide,** or **piribedil.** ANTICHOLINERGIC AGENTS and ANTIPARKINSON AGENTS may decrease effect. **Herbal: Kava** may increase risk and severity of dystonic reactions.

PHARMACOKINETICS Absorption: Well absorbed from GI tract. **Onset:** Rapid onset. **Peak:** 2–3 h. **Duration:** Up to 12 h. **Metabolism:** In liver. **Elimination:** In bile and feces.

NURSING IMPLICATIONS

Black Box Warning

Trifluoperazine has been associated with increased risk of mortality in older adults with dementia-related psychosis.

Assessment & Drug Effects

- Monitor HR and BP. Hypotension is a common adverse effect.
- Hypotension and extrapyramidal effects (especially akathisia and dystonia) are most likely to occur in patients receiving high doses or in older adults. Withhold drug and notify prescriber if patient has dysphagia, neck muscle spasm, or if tongue protrusion occurs.
- Monitor I&O ratio and bowel elimination pattern. Check for

Common adverse effects in *italic;* life-threatening effects <u>underlined</u>; generic names in **bold;** classifications in SMALL CAPS; ♣ Canadian drug name; ⊙ Prototype drug; ⚠ Alert

1722

abdominal distention and pain. Encourage adequate fluid intake as prophylaxis for constipation and xerostomia.

- Expect maximum therapeutic response within 2–3 wk after initiation of therapy.
- Annual ocular examination.
- Monitor lab tests: Periodic CBC, serum electrolytes, LFTs, lipid profile, plasma glucose, and HbA1C.

Patient & Family Education

- Take drug as prescribed; do not alter dosing regimen or stop medication without consulting prescriber.
- Consult prescriber about use of any OTC drugs during therapy.
- Do not take alcohol and other depressants during therapy.
- Avoid potentially hazardous activities such as driving or operating machinery, until response to drug is known.
- Cover as much skin surface as possible with clothing when you **must be** in direct sunlight. Use an SPF higher than 12 sunscreen on exposed skin.

TRIFLURIDINE

(trye-flure'i-deen)

Classification: ANTIVIRAL
Therapeutic: ANTIVIRAL

AVAILABILITY Ophthalmic solution

ACTION & THERAPEUTIC EFFECT Interferes with viral replication. *Active against herpes simplex virus (HSV) types 1 and 2, vaccinia virus, and certain strains of adenovirus.*

USES Topically to eyes for treatment of primary keratoconjunctivitis and recurring epithelial keratitis caused by herpes simplex virus types 1 and 2.

CONTRAINDICATIONS Known sensitivity to trifluridine or any component of the formulation; lactation.

CAUTIOUS USE Dry eye syndrome; pregnancy (adverse effects have not been observed in animal reproduction studies); children younger than 6 y.

ROUTE & DOSAGE

Viral Infections of Eye

Adult: **Ophthalmic** 1 drop 1% ophthalmic solution into affected eye q2h during waking hours (max: 9 drops/day); when healing appears to be complete, dosage reduced to 1 drop q4h during waking hours for an additional 7 days (max: 5 drops/day); continuous administration beyond 21 days not recommended

ADMINISTRATION

Instillation

- Wash hands before and after instillation.
- Wait several minutes between applications when used concurrently with other eye drops. Remove contact lenses prior to use.
- Store refrigerated at 2°–8° C (36°–46° F) unless otherwise directed.

ADVERSE EFFECTS HEENT: Burning or stinging sensation in the eyes, epithelial keratopathy, eye irritation, hyperemia, increased ocular pressure, stromal edema, keratitis sicca, hyperemia, increased intraocular pressure.

PHARMACOKINETICS Absorption: penetrates cornea and aqueous humor (inflammation enhances

T

penetration). Systemic absorption does not appear to be significant.

NURSING IMPLICATIONS

Assessment & Drug Effects

- Expect epithelial eye infections to respond to therapy within 2–7 days, with complete healing occurring in 1–2 wk; not for long term use.

Patient & Family Education

- Inform prescriber of progress and keep follow-up appointments. Herpetic eye infections have a tendency to recur and can lead to corneal damage if not adequately treated.

TRIHEXYPHENIDYL HYDROCHLORIDE

(trye-hex-ee-fen′i-dill)

Classification: CENTRALLY ACTING CHOLINERGIC RECEPTOR ANTAGONIST; ANTIPARKINSON; ANTISPASMODIC
Therapeutic: ANTIPARKINSON; ANTISPASMODIC
Prototype: Benztropine

AVAILABILITY Tablet; oral solution

ACTION & THERAPEUTIC EFFECT
Thought to act by blocking excess of acetylcholine at certain cerebral synaptic sites. Relaxes smooth muscle directly and has an indirect inhibitory effect on the parasympathetic nervous system. *Diminishes the characteristic tremor of Parkinson disease.*

USES Symptomatic treatment of all forms of parkinsonism (arteriosclerotic, idiopathic, postencephalitic). Also to treat drug-induced extrapyramidal disorders.

UNLABELED USES Huntington's chorea, spasmodic torticollis.

CONTRAINDICATIONS Hypersensitivity to trihexyphenidyl; narrow angle glaucoma.

CAUTIOUS USE Tardive dyskinesia; history of drug hypersensitivities; glaucoma; arteriosclerosis; hypertension; cardiac disease, kidney or liver disorders; MG; alcoholism; CNS diseases; obstructive diseases of GI or genitourinary tracts; BPH; older adults; pregnancy (animal reproduction studies have not been conducted); lactation. Safe use in children not established.

ROUTE & DOSAGE

Parkinsonism
Adult: **PO** 1 mg/day, increase by 2 mg increments at intervals of 3–5 days, up to 6–10 mg/day in divided doses.

Extrapyramidal Effects
Adult: **PO** 1 mg/day then increase as needed; usual dose 5–15 mg/day in 3–4 divided doses

ADMINISTRATION

Oral
- May be given before or after meals, depending on how patient reacts. Older adults and patients prone to excessive salivation (e.g., postencephalitic parkinsonism) may prefer to take drug after meals. If drug causes excessive mouth dryness, it may be better given before meals, unless it causes nausea.
- Store at 20°–25° C (68°–77°F) in tight container unless otherwise directed.

ADVERSE EFFECTS CV: Tachycardia. **CNS:** *Dizziness, nervousness,* insomnia, drowsiness, confusion,

Common adverse effects in *italic;* life-threatening effects <u>underlined</u>; generic names in **bold;** classifications in SMALL CAPS; ♣ Canadian drug name; ● Prototype drug; ⚠ Alert

agitation, delirium, delusions, hallucinations, headache, paranoia, psychotic manifestations, euphoria. **HEENT:** *Blurred vision*, mydriasis, increased ocular pressure, glaucoma. **Skin:** Skin rash. **GI:** *Dry mouth, nausea*, constipation, intestinal obstruction, parotitis, toxic megacolon. **GU:** Urinary retention. **Other:** Weakness.

INTERACTIONS Drug: Reduces therapeutic effects of **chlorpromazine, haloperidol,** PHENOTHIAZINES; increases bioavailability of **digoxin**; MAO INHIBITORS potentiate actions of trihexyphenidyl. ANTICHOLINERGIC AGENTS and ANTIPARKINSON AGENTS, PROKINETIC AGENTS may decrease effect. **Herbal: Betel nut** may increase risk of extrapyramidal symptoms.

PHARMACOKINETICS Absorption: Readily from GI tract. **Onset:** Within 1 h. **Peak:** 2–3 h. **Duration:** 6–12 h. **Elimination:** In urine and bile.

NURSING IMPLICATIONS

Assessment & Drug Effects

- Be aware that incidence and severity of adverse effects are usually dose related and may be minimized by dosage reduction. Older adults appear more sensitive to usual adult doses.
- Monitor vital signs. Pulse is a particularly sensitive indicator of response to drug. Report tachycardia, palpitations, paradoxical bradycardia, or fall in BP.
- Assess for and report severe CNS stimulation (see ADVERSE EFFECTS) that occurs with high doses, and in patients with arteriosclerosis, or those with history of hypersensitivity to other drugs.
- In patients with severe rigidity, tremors may appear to be accentuated during therapy as rigidity diminishes.

- Monitor daily I&O if patient develops urinary hesitancy or retention. Voiding before taking drug may relieve problem.
- Check for abdominal distention and bowel sounds if constipation is a problem.
- Baseline and periodic gonioscopic and intraocular pressure exams.

Patient & Family Education

- Learn measures to relieve drug-induced dry mouth; rinse mouth frequently with water and suck ice chips, sugarless gum, or hard candy. Maintain adequate total daily fluid intake.
- Do not to engage in potentially hazardous activities requiring alertness and skill. Drug causes dizziness, drowsiness, and blurred vision. Help walking may be indicated.

TRIMETHOBENZAMIDE HYDROCHLORIDE

(trye-meth-oh-ben′za-mide)

Tigan

Classification: ANTIEMETIC
Therapeutic: ANTIEMETIC
Prototype: Prochlorperazine

AVAILABILITY Capsule; solution for injection

ACTION & *THERAPEUTIC EFFECT*

Acts centrally to inhibit the medullary chemoreceptor trigger zone by blocking emetic impulses to the vomiting center. *Less effective than phenothiazine antiemetics but produces fewer adverse effects.*

USES Control of nausea and vomiting.

CONTRAINDICATIONS Parenteral use in children or infants; rectal administration in prematures and newborns; hypersensitivity to trimethobenzamide or any component of the formulation.

CAUTIOUS USE Presence of high fever, dehydration, electrolyte imbalance; pregnancy (use of other agents during pregnancy is preferred); lactation; children.

ROUTE & DOSAGE

Nausea and Vomiting
Adult: **PO** 300 mg tid or qid; **IM** 200 mg tid or qid prn

ADMINISTRATION

Oral
- Empty capsule and give with water or mix with food if patient cannot swallow capsule.

Intramuscular
- Give IM deep into upper outer quadrant of gluteal muscle.
- Minimize possibility of irritation and pain by avoiding escape of solution along needle track. Use Z-track technique. Rotate injection sites.
- Injection not for use in children or infants.

ADVERSE EFFECTS CV: Hypotension. **CNS:** Pseudoparkinsonism, coma, depression, disorientation, dizziness, drowsiness, extrapyramidal reaction, headache, opisthotonos, seizure. **HEENT:** Blurred vision. **Hepatic/GI:** Diarrhea, jaundice. **Musculoskeletal:** Muscle cramps. **Other:** Hypersensitivity reactions (including allergic skin reaction); pain, stinging, burning, redness, irritation at IM site.

INTERACTIONS Drug: Alcohol and other CNS DEPRESSANTS add to depressant activity; PHENOTHIAZINES, ANTICHOLINERGIC AGENTS may precipitate extrapyramidal syndrome. Do not use with **sodium oxybate.**

PHARMACOKINETICS Onset: 10–40 min PO; 15–35 min IM. **Duration:** 3–4 h PO; 2–3 h IM. **Elimination:** 30–50% of dose excreted unchanged in urine within 48–72 h.

NURSING IMPLICATIONS

Assessment & Drug Effects
- Monitor BP. Hypotension may occur particularly in surgical patients receiving drug parenterally.
- Report promptly and stop drug therapy if an acute febrile illness accompanies or begins during therapy.
- Antiemetic effect of drug may obscure diagnoses of GI or other pathologic conditions or signs of toxicity from other drugs. Avoid use in older adults.
- Monitor lab results: Renal function tests (in the elderly and patients with reduced renal function).

Patient & Family Education
- Report promptly to prescriber onset of rash or other signs of hypersensitivity (see Appendix F). Discontinue drug immediately.
- Do not drive or engage in potentially hazardous activities until response to drug is known.
- Do not drink alcohol or alcoholic beverages during therapy with this drug.

TRIMETHOPRIM ⊙

(trye-meth'oh-prim)

Primsol
Classification: URINARY TRACT ANTI-INFECTIVE
Therapeutic: URINARY TRACT ANTI-INFECTIVE

AVAILABILITY Tablet; oral solution

ACTION & *THERAPEUTIC EFFECT*
Anti-infective and folic acid antagonist with slow bactericidal action. Binds and interferes with bacterial cell growth. *Effective against most common UTI pathogens. Most pathogens causing UTI are in normal vaginal and fecal flora. Effective in treatment of acute otitis media.*

USES Initial episodes of acute uncomplicated UTIs, acute otitis media in children.

UNLABELED USES Treatment and prophylaxis of chronic and recurrent UTI in both men and women; treatment in conjunction with dapsone of initial episodes of *Pneumocystis carinii* pneumonia; treatment of travelers' diarrhea; acne; otitis media.

CONTRAINDICATIONS Hypersensitivity to trimethoprim; megaloblastic anemia secondary to folate deficiency; creatinine clearance less than 15 mL/min, impaired kidney or liver function; possible folate deficiency; children with fragile X chromosome associated with mental retardation.

CAUTIOUS USE Possible folate deficiency; risk factors for hyperkalemia; renal disease; mild or moderate renal impairment; hepatic impairment; older adults; pregnancy (category C); lactation; children younger than 12 y.

ROUTE & DOSAGE

Urinary Tract Infection
Adult/Adolescent: **PO** 100 mg bid or 200 mg once/day

ADMINISTRATION

Oral
- Give with 240 mL (8 oz) of fluid if not contraindicated.
- Store at 15°–30° C (59°–86° F) in dry, light-protected place.

ADVERSE EFFECTS Endocrine: Increased serum transaminases (ALT, AST), bilirubin, creatinine, BUN. **Skin:** *Rash, pruritus,* exfoliative dermatitis, photosensitivity. **GI:** Epigastric discomfort, nausea, vomiting, glossitis, abnormal taste sensation. **Hematologic:** Neutropenia, *megaloblastic anemia,* methemoglobinemia, leukopenia, thrombocytopenia (rare). **Other:** Fever.

DIAGNOSTIC TEST INTERFERENCE Interferes with serum ***methotrexate assays*** that use a competitive binding protein technique with a bacterial dihydrofolate reductase as the binding protein. May cause falsely elevated ***creatinine*** values when ***Jaffe reaction*** is used.

INTERACTIONS Drug: May inhibit **phenytoin** metabolism causing increased levels. Do not use with **dofetilide.**

PHARMACOKINETICS Absorption: Almost completely from GI tract. **Peak:** 1–4 h. **Distribution:** Widely distributed, including lung, saliva, middle ear fluid, bile, bone, CSF; crosses placenta; appears in breast milk. **Metabolism:** In liver. **Elimination:** 80% in urine unchanged. **Half-Life:** 8–11 h.

NURSING IMPLICATIONS

Assessment & Drug Effects
- Reinforce necessity to adhere to established drug regimen.

Recurrent infection after terminating prophylactic treatment of UTI may occur even after 6 mo of therapy.

- Assess urinary pattern during treatment. Altered pattern (frequency, urgency, nocturia, retention, polyuria) may reflect emerging drug resistance, necessitating change of drug regimen. Periodically check for bladder distention.
- Be alert for toxic effects on bone marrow, particularly in older adults, malnourished, alcoholic, pregnant, or debilitated patients. Recognize and report signs of infection or anemia.
- Drug-induced rash, a common adverse effect, is usually maculopapular, pruritic, or morbilliform and appears 7–14 days after start of therapy with daily doses of 200 mg or less.
- Monitor lab tests: Baseline C&S.

Patient & Family Education

- Drink fluids liberally (2000–3000 mL/day, if not contraindicated) to help flush out urinary bacteria.
- Report pain and hematuria to prescriber immediately.
- Do not postpone voiding even though increases in fluid intake may cause more frequent urination.
- Do not use douches or sprays during treatment periods; practice careful perineal hygiene to prevent reinfection.
- Report to prescriber promptly any symptoms of a blood disorder (fever, sore throat, pallor, purpura, ecchymosis).
- Consult prescriber if severe traveler's diarrhea does not respond to 3–5 days therapy (i.e., persistence of symptoms of severe nausea, abdominal pain, diarrhea with mucus or blood, and dehydration).

- Drug-induced rash, a common adverse effect, may appear 7–14 days after start of therapy. Report rash to prescriber for evaluation.

TRIMIPRAMINE MALEATE

(tri-mip'ra-meen)

Surmontil

Classification: TRICYCLIC ANTIDEPRESSANT

Therapeutic: TRICYCLIC ANTIDEPRESSANT (TCA)

Prototype: Imipramine

AVAILABILITY Capsule

ACTION & *THERAPEUTIC EFFECT*
Antidepressant effects are thought to result from postsynaptic sensitization to serotonin. *More effective in alleviation of endogenous depression than other depressive states.*

USES Treatment of depression.

CONTRAINDICATIONS Hypersensitivity to tricyclic antidepressants; prostatic hypertrophy; during recovery period after MI; AV block; QT prolongation; bundle-branch block; ileus; MAOI therapy; suicide ideation; concurrent use with linezolid or IV methylene blue.

CAUTIOUS USE Schizophrenia, electroshock therapy, psychosis, bipolar disease; Parkinson's disease; seizure disorders; increased intraocular pressure; history of urinary retention; history of narrow-angle glaucoma; hyperthyroidism, suicidal tendency; cardiovascular, liver, thyroid, kidney disease; pregnancy (category C); lactation. Safe use in children younger than 12 y not established.

Common adverse effects in *italic;* life-threatening effects underlined; generic names in **bold;** classifications in SMALL CAPS; ◆ Canadian drug name; ○ Prototype drug; ▲ Alert

ROUTE & DOSAGE

Depression

Adult: **PO** 25–50 mg daily in divided doses, may increase gradually up to 150 mg/day if needed (max dose: 300 mg/day)
Geriatric/Adolescent: **PO** 50 mg/day with gradual increases up to 100 mg/day

Pharmacogenetic Dosage Adjustment

Poor CYP2D6 metabolizer: Start with 30% of dose

ADMINISTRATION
Oral

- Give with food to decrease gastric distress. Administer maintenance doses as a single dose at bedtime.
- Store in tightly closed container at 15°–30° C (59°–86° F) unless otherwise specified.

ADVERSE EFFECTS CV: Tachycardia, *orthostatic hypotension*, hypertension. **CNS:** Seizures, tremor, confusion, *sedation*, suicidality, dizziness, drowsiness, headache. **HEENT:** Blurred vision. **Skin:** Photosensitivity, sweating. **GI:** *Xerostomia, constipation*, paralytic ileus, appetite stimulation, dyspepsia. **GU:** *Urinary retention*, ejaculation dysfunction.

INTERACTIONS Drug: CNS DEPRESSANTS, **alcohol**, HYPNOTICS, BARBITURATES, SEDATIVES potentiate CNS depression; may increase hypoprothrombinemic effect of ORAL ANTICOAGULANTS; **levodopa**, SYMPATHOMIMETICS (e.g., **epinephrine, norepinephrine**) increase possibility of sympathetic hyperactivity with hypertension and hyperpyrexia; do not use with MAO INHIBITORS; **methylphenidate** increases plasma TCA levels; **cimetidine** may increase plasma TCA levels. **Herbal: Ginkgo** may decrease seizure threshold; **St. John's wort** may cause **serotonin** syndrome.

PHARMACOKINETICS Absorption: Rapidly absorbed from GI tract. **Peak:** 2 h. **Metabolism:** In liver (CYP2D6). **Elimination:** In urine and feces. **Half-Life:** 9.1 h.

NURSING IMPLICATIONS

Black Box Warning

Trimipramine maleate has been associated with increased risk of suicidal thinking and behavior in children, adolescents, and young adults.

Assessment & Drug Effects

- Monitor for changes in behavior that may indicate increased incidence of suicidality.
- Assess vital signs (BP and pulse rate) during adjustment period of tricyclic antidepressant (TCA) therapy. If BP falls more than 20 mm Hg or if there is a sudden increase in pulse rate, withhold medication and notify prescriber.
- Orthostatic hypotension may be sufficiently severe to require protective assistance when patient is ambulating. Instruct patient to change position from recumbency to standing slowly and in stages.
- Report fine tremors, a distressing extrapyramidal adverse effect, to prescriber.
- Monitor bowel elimination pattern and I&O ratio. Severe constipation and urinary retention are potential problems, especially in older adults. Advise increased fluid intake to at least 1500 mL/day (if allowed).

- Inspect oral membranes daily with high-dose therapy. Urge outpatient to report symptoms of stomatitis or xerostomia.
- Regulate environmental temperature and patient's clothing carefully; drug may cause intolerance to heat or cold.

Patient & Family Education
- Report immediately to prescriber signs of worsening mental status such as suicidal ideation, aggressiveness, agitation, anxiety, hostility, impulsivity, insomnia, irritability, panic attacks, and worsening of depression.
- Be aware that your ability to perform tasks requiring alertness and skill may be impaired.
- Do not use OTC drugs unless approved by prescriber.
- Understand that the actions of both alcohol and trimipramine are increased when used together during therapy and for up to 2 wk after the TCA is discontinued. Consult prescriber about safe amounts of alcohol, if any, that can be taken.
- Be aware that the effects of barbiturates and other CNS depressants may also be enhanced by trimipramine.

TRIPTORELIN PAMOATE
(trip-tor'e-lyn)
Trelstar Depot, Trelstar LA, Triptodur
Classification: GONADOTROPIN RELEASING HORMONE (GNRH) AGONIST ANALOG
Therapeutic: GNRH AGONIST ANALOG
Prototype: Leuprolide acetate

AVAILABILITY Solution for injection

ACTION & *THERAPEUTIC EFFECT*
An agonist analog of GnRH that causes suppression of ovarian and testicular hormone production due to decreased levels of LH and FSH with subsequent decrease in testosterone and estrogen levels. *In men, the level of serum testosterone is equivalent to a surgically castrated man.*

USES Palliative treatment of advanced prostate cancer; central percocious puberty.

UNLABELED USES Breast cancer hypersexuality, endometriosis, infertility, hirsutism.

CONTRAINDICATIONS Hypersensitivity to triptorelin, other LHRH agonists, or LHRH; dysfunctional uterine bleeding; pregnancy; lactation.

CAUTIOUS USE Prostatic carcinoma; hepatic or renal dysfunction; patients with impending spinal cord compression or severe urogenital disorder; premenstrual syndrome; renal insufficiency. Safety and efficacy in children not established.

ROUTE & DOSAGE

Prostate Cancer
Adult: IM 3.75 mg q4w OR 11.25 mg q12w or 22.5 mg q24w

Central Percocious Puberty (Triptodur)
Adolescent/Child (older than 2 y): IM 22.5 mg q24wk

ADMINISTRATION

Intramuscular
- Give deep into a large muscle.
- Alternate injection sites. Administer immediately after reconstitution.

ADVERSE EFFECTS CV: Hypertension, lower extremity edema. **CNS:** Headache, dizziness, insomnia, impotence, emotional lability. **Skin:** Pruritus, skin rash. **GI:** Diarrhea, vomiting, nausea, anorexia. **GU:** Urinary retention, UTI. **Musculoskeletal:** Musculoskeletal pain. **Hematologic:** Anemia. **Other:** *Hot flushes*, pain, leg pain, fatigue. Pain at injection site, hyperglycemia, increased serum testosterone, increased ALT/AST, increased BUN, decreased libido, gynecomastia.

DIAGNOSTIC TEST INTERFERENCE May interfere with tests for *pituitary-gonadal function*.

INTERACTIONS Drug: Do not use with **corifollitropin alfa**. Use with QT prolonging agents (e.g., **amiodarone, citalopram, dofetilide**) should be avoided.

PHARMACOKINETICS Peak: 1–3 h. **Duration:** 1 mo. **Metabolism:** Unknown. **Elimination:** Eliminated by liver and kidneys. **Half-Life:** 3 h.

NURSING IMPLICATIONS
Assessment & Drug Effects
- Monitor for S&S of disease flare, especially during the first 1–2 wk of therapy: Increased bone pain, blood in urine, urinary obstruction, or symptoms of spinal compression.
- Monitor for S&S of emerging CV disease.
- Monitor lab tests: Periodic serum testosterone and HbA1C.

Patient & Family Education
- Disease flare (see ASSESSMENT & DRUG EFFECTS) is a common, temporary adverse effect of therapy; however, symptoms may become serious enough to report to the prescriber.

- Notify prescriber promptly of the following: S&S of an allergic reaction (itching, hives, swelling of face, arms, or legs; tingling in mouth or throat, tightness in chest or trouble breathing); weakness or loss of muscle control; rapid weight gain.

TROPICAMIDE
(troe-pik′a-mide)
See Appendix A-1.

TROSPIUM CHLORIDE
(tro-spi′um)
Classification: ANTICHOLINERGIC; ANTIMUSCARINIC; ANTISPASMODIC
Therapeutic: URINARY SMOOTH MUSCLE RELAXANT
Prototype: Oxybutynin

AVAILABILITY Tablet; extended release capsule

ACTION & THERAPEUTIC EFFECT Antagonizes the effect of acetylcholine on muscarinic receptors in smooth muscle. Its parasympatholytic action reduces smooth muscle tone of the bladder. *Decreases urinary frequency, urgency, and urge incontinence in patients with overactive bladders.*

USES Treatment of overactive (neurogenic) bladder, urinary incontinence.

CONTRAINDICATIONS Hypersensitivity to trospium; patients with or at risk for urinary retention; uncontrolled narrow-angle glaucoma; gastroparesis; GI obstruction, ileus, pyloric stenosis, toxic megacolon, severe ulcerative colitis.

CAUTIOUS USE Significant bladder obstruction, closed-angle glaucoma; BPH; ulcerative colitis, GERD, intestinal atony; myasthenia gravis, autonomic neuropathy; moderate or severe hepatic dysfunction; severe renal insufficiency, renal failure; older adults; pregnancy (category C); lactation. Safety in children not established.

ROUTE & DOSAGE

Overactive Bladder
Adult: **PO** 20 mg twice daily OR **Extended release** 60 mg daily
Geriatric (75 y or older): **PO Immediate release** 20 mg once daily

Renal Impairment Dosage Adjustment
CrCl less than 30 mL/min: **Immediate release** 20 mg once daily at bedtime

ADMINISTRATION
Oral
- Give at least 1 h before meals or on an empty stomach.
- Store at 20°–25° C (66°–77° F).

ADVERSE EFFECTS CV: Tachycardia. **Respiratory:** Nasopharyngitis, dry nose. **CNS:** Headache. **HEENT:** Dry eyes, blurred vision, skin rash. **GI:** *Dry mouth, constipation*, abdominal pain, dyspepsia, flatulence, vomiting. **GU:** Urinary retention, urinary tract infection. **Other:** Fatigue, dry skin.

INTERACTIONS Drug: Increased anticholinergic adverse effects with ANTICHOLINERGIC AGENTS. Do not use with **potassium citrate** due to increased ulerogenic effect.

PHARMACOKINETICS Absorption: Less than 10% absorbed orally. **Peak:** 5–6 h. **Metabolism:** In liver via CYP2D6. **Elimination:** Primarily in feces. **Half-Life:** 20 h.

NURSING IMPLICATIONS
Assessment & Drug Effects
- Monitor bowel and bladder function. Report urinary hesitancy or significant constipation.
- Withhold drug and notify prescriber if urinary retention develops.
- Monitor for and report worsening of GI symptoms in those with GERD.

Patient & Family Education
- Report promptly any of the following: Signs of an allergic reaction (e.g., itching or hives), blurred vision or difficulty focusing, confusion, dizziness, difficulty passing urine.
- Moderate intake of tea, coffee, caffeinated sodas, and alcohol to minimize side effects of this drug.
- Avoid situations in which overheating is likely, as drug may impair sweating, which is a normal cooling mechanism.
- Do not engage in hazardous activities until response to the drug is known.

ULIPRISTAL
(u-li-pris'tal)
Ella
Classification: PROGESTERONE AGONIST/ANTAGONIST; POSTCOITAL CONTRACEPTIVE
Therapeutic: POSTCOITAL CONTRACEPTIVE

AVAILABILITY Tablet

ACTION & THERAPEUTIC EFFECT
A selective progesterone receptor modulator with antagonistic and

partial agonistic effects. It binds to the progesterone receptor preventing the binding of progesterone. *If taken immediately before ovulation, it delays follicular rupture and inhibits ovulation. It may also alter the endometrium and interfere with implantation of a fertilized ovum.*

USES Postcoital contraception after unprotected intercourse or a known or suspected contraceptive failure.

CONTRAINDICATIONS Known or suspected pregnancy (category X); lactation.

ROUTE & DOSAGE

Postcoital Contraception

Adult: **PO** 30 mg within 120 h of unprotected intercourse or known or suspected contraceptive failure; may repeat within 3 h if patient vomits initial dose

ADMINISTRATION

Oral
▪ Give within 120 h of unprotected intercourse.
▪ Store at controlled room temperature 20°–25° C (68°–77° F).

ADVERSE EFFECTS CNS: Fatigue, dizziness, *headache*. **GI:** *Nausea*. **GU:** Dysmenorrhea. **Other:** *Abdominal and upper abdominal pain.*

INTERACTIONS Drug: Coadministration of CYP3A4 inducers (e.g., **carbamazepine, phenobarbital, phenytoin, rifampin, topiramate**) can decrease the levels of ulipristal. Coadministration of strong CYP3A4 INHIBITORS (e.g., **itraconazole, ketoconazole**) can increase the levels of ulipristal. **Food: Grapefruit juice** can increase the levels of ulipristal. **Herbal: St. John's wort** can decrease the levels of ulipristal.

PHARMACOKINETICS Peak: 1 h. **Distribution:** 94% plasma protein bound. **Metabolism:** Hepatic oxidation by CYP3A4 to active metabolite. **Half-Life:** 32.4 h.

NURSING IMPLICATIONS

Assessment & Drug Effects
▪ Monitor for vomiting. Drug may be re-administered if patient vomits within 3 h of initial dose.

Patient & Family Education
▪ Ulipristal is not intended for repeated use. It should not replace conventional means of contraception.
▪ Certain concurrently taken drugs may interfere with the contraceptive effects of ulipristal. Consult prescriber.
▪ Ulipristal may interfere with the length of the next menstrual cycle (i.e., cycle may occur sooner or later than expected).
▪ Ulipristal does not protect against sexually transmitted diseases.

UPADACITINIB
(ue-pad-a-sye-ti-nib)
Rinvoq
Classification: BIOLOGICAL RESPONSE MODIFIER; JANUS KINASE (JAK) INHIBITOR; DISEASE-MODIFYING ANTIRHEUMATIC DRUG (DMARD)
Therapeutic: DISEASE-MODIFYING ANTIRHEUMATIC DRUG (DMARD)
Prototype: Tofacitinib

AVAILABILITY Oral tablet

ACTION & *THERAPEUTIC EFFECT*
Inhibits Janus kinase (JAK) enzymes which stimulate hematopoiesis and

U

immune cell function through a signaling pathway. JAK enzymes activate signal transducers and activators of transciption (STATs) which regulate gene expression and intracellular activity. Treats moderate to severe rheumatoid arthritis by inhibiting JAKs thereby preventing activation of STATs.

USES Treatment of moderately to severely active rheumatoid arthritis in patients who have had an inadequate response or intolerance to methotrexate. It may be used as monotherapy or in combination with methotrexate or other nonbiologic disease-modifying antirheumatic drugs (DMARDs).

CAUTIOUS USE GI perforation; hematologic toxicity; impaired liver function; infection; malignancy; thrombosis; tuberculosis; pregnancy; lactation.

ROUTE & DOSAGE

Rheumatoid Arthritis

Adult: **PO** 15 mg once a day

Hepatic Impairment Dosage Adjustment

Severe impairment (Child-Pugh class C): Use not recommended

ADMINISTRATION

Oral

- Administer with or without food. Swallow tablet whole; do not crush, split, or chew.
- Store at 2° to 25° C (36° to 77° F). Store in the original bottle to protect from moisture.

ADVERSE EFFECTS **Respiratory:** Upper respiratory tract infection. **GI:** Nausea.

INTERACTIONS Drug: Coadministration with potent inhibitors of CYP3A4 (e.g., **ketoconazole**) may increase the levels of upadacitinib. Coadministration with potent CYP3A4 inducers (e.g., **phenobarbital, phenytoin, rifampin**) may decrease the levels of tofacitinib. Coadministration with other potent immunosuppressive drugs (e.g., azathioprine, tacrolimus, cyclosporine) increases the risk of added immunosuppression. **Food:** Grapefruit juice may increase the levels of upadacitinib. **Herbal:** St. John's wort may decrease the levels of upadacitinib.

PHARMACOKINETICS Peak: 2—4 h. **Distribution:** 52% protein bound. **Metabolism:** In the liver, through CYP3A4 (major) and CYP2D6 (minor). **Elimination:** 24% in urine, 38% in feces. **Half-Life:** 8–14 h.

NURSING IMPLICATIONS

Assessment & Drug Effects

- Monitor for signs and symptoms of infection, skin cancer, and thrombosis.
- Monitor lab tests: Baseline and periodic lymphocyte count, neutrophil count, hemoglobin, and LFTs; lipid levels 12 weeks after initiating therapy and periodically thereafter; baseline tuberculosis (TB) screen; baseline and periodic viral hepatitis screen.

Patient & Family Education

- Notify your health care provider if you experience swollen glands, night sweats, shortness of breath, stomach pain that is new or worse, change in bowel habits, or weight loss without trying.
- Notify your doctor or get medical help right away if you have any of the following signs or symptoms of allergic reaction such as rash, hives,

U

itching; red, swollen, blistered, or peeling skin with or without fever; wheezing; tightness in the chest or throat; trouble breathing, swallowing, or talking; unusual hoarseness; or swelling of the mouth, face, lips, tongue, or throat; or any dizziness or passing out.

USTEKINUMAB

(us-te-kin'u-mab)

Stelara

Classification: IMMUNOMODULATOR; MONOCLONAL ANTIBODY; INTERLEUKIN-12 AND INTERLEUKIN-23 RECEPTOR ANTAGONIST
Therapeutic: IMMUNOSUPPRESSANT
Prototype: Basiliximab

AVAILABILITY Solution for injection

ACTION & *THERAPEUTIC EFFECT*
A human monoclonal antibody that disrupts IL-12 and IL-23 mediated signaling and cytokine cascades. *Inhibits inflammatory and immune responses associated with plaque psoriasis thereby improving psoriasis.*

USES Treatment of moderate to severe plaque psoriasis; psoriatic arthritis.

CONTRAINDICATIONS Clinically significant hypersensitivity to ustekinumab; active infection (e.g., active TB); live vaccines; BCG vaccines within 1 y prior to, during, or 1 y following drug treatment; reversible posterior leukoencephalopathy syndrome (RPLS).

CAUTIOUS USE Chronic infection or history of recurrent infection (e.g., latent TB); prior malignancy; phototherapy; older

adults; pregnancy (category B); lactation. Safety and efficacy in children younger than 18 y not established.

ROUTE & DOSAGE

Psoriasis

Adult 100 kg or less: **Subcutaneous** 45 mg initially and 4 wk later, followed by 45 mg q12wk
Adult over 100 kg: **Subcutaneous** 90 mg initially and 4 wk later, followed by 90 mg q12wk

Psoriatic Arthritis

Adult: **Subcutaneous** 45 mg initially and 4 wk later then 45 mg q12w

ADMINISTRATION

Subcutaneous
- Solution may contain a few small translucent or white particles. **Do not** shake.
- Note: Needle cover on prefilled syringe is natural rubber and should not be handled by latex sensitive persons.
- When using a single-use vial, withdraw dose using a 27 gauge syringe with a one-half inch needle.
- Rotate injection sites and do not inject into an area that is tender, bruised, red, or irritated.
- Store unopened vials upright in refrigerator. Discard unused portions in single-use vials.

ADVERSE EFFECTS Respiratory:
Nasopharyngitis, upper respiratory tract infection. **CNS:** Depression, dizziness, fatigue, headache. **Skin:** Injection-site erythema, pruritus. **GI:** Diarrhea. **Musculoskeletal:** Back pain, myalgia. **Other:** *Infection.*

U

Common adverse effects in *italic;* life-threatening effects underlined; generic names in **bold;** classifications in SMALL CAPS; ◆ Canadian drug name; ○ Prototype drug; ⚠ Alert

INTERACTIONS Drug: LIVE VAC-CINES should not be administered concurrently with ustekinumab therapy. Do not use with IMMUNOSUPPRESANTS. Closely monitor use with narrow therapeutic index drugs (e.g., **warfarin**, **cyclosporine**).

PHARMACOKINETICS Peak: 7–13.5 days. **Metabolism:** Degraded to smaller proteins. **Half-Life:** 14.9–45.6 days.

NURSING IMPLICATIONS

Assessment & Drug Effects

- Monitor for and promptly report S&S of TB or other infection.
- Monitor neurologic status and report promptly: Seizures, problems with vision, headaches, or confusion.
- Note: BCG vaccines should not be given during treatment, for one year prior to initiating treatment, or one year following discontinuation of treatment.
- Monitor lab tests: Prior to initiation of therapy, test for latent TB.

Patient & Family Education

- Do not accept vaccinations with live vaccines while taking this drug. Note that non-live vaccines may not be effective if given during a course of ustekinumab.
- You should be tested for TB prior to taking this drug.
- Report promptly S&S of infection including: Chills, fever, cough, shortness of breath, diarrhea, stomach or abdominal pain, burning on urination, sores anywhere on your body, unexplained or excessive fatigue.
- Report immediately seizures, problems with vision, headaches, or confusion.

VACCINIA IMMUNE GLOBULIN (VIG-IV)
(vac-cin′i-a)

Classification: BIOLOGIC RESPONSE MODIFIER; IMMUNOGLOBULIN
Therapeutic: IMMUNOGLOBULIN
Prototype: Immune globulin

AVAILABILITY Solution for injection

ACTION & THERAPEUTIC EFFECT

Vaccinia immune globulin, VIG (VIG-IV) is a purified human immunoglobulin G (IgG). VIG (VIG-IV) contains high titers of antivaccinia antibodies. *VIG is effective in the treatment of smallpox vaccine adverse reactions secondary to continued vaccinia virus replication after vaccination.*

USES Prevention of serious complications of smallpox vaccine; treatment of progressive vaccinia; severe generalized vaccinia; eczema vaccinatum; vaccinia infection in patients with skin conditions (e.g., burns, impetigo, varicella-zoster, poison ivy, or eczematous skin lesions); treatment or modification of aberrant infections induced by vaccinia virus.

CONTRAINDICATIONS Predisposition to acute renal failure (i.e., preexisting renal insufficiency, DM, volume depletion, sepsis proteinemia, patients older than 65 y); AIDS; chronic skin conditions; bone marrow suppression; chemotherapy; radiation therapy; corticosteroid therapy, eczema; hematologic disease, thrombosis; hypotension; herpes infection; postvaccinal encephalitis; aseptic meningitis syndrome (AMS); pulmonary edema; lactation.

V

CAUTIOUS USE Renal impairment; autoimmune disease; cardiomyopathy, impaired cardiac output, cardiac disease, history of hypercoagulation; pregnancy (category C). Safe use in children not established.

ROUTE & DOSAGE

Vaccinia

Adults: **IV** 100–500 mg/kg

Renal Impairment Dosage Adjustment

Max dose: 400 mg/kg

ADMINISTRATION

Intravenous

PREPARE: **IV Infusion:** No dilution required. Use solution as supplied. Do not shake. Avoid foaming.
ADMINISTER: **IV Infusion:** Begin infusion within 6 h of entering the vial. Complete infusion within 12 h of entering the vial. ▪ Use inline filter (0.22 microns), infusion pump, and dedicated IV line [may infuse into a preexisting catheter if it contains NS, D2.5W, D5W, D10W, or D20W (or any combination of these)]. ▪ Infuse at 1 mL/kg/h the first 30 min, increase to 2 mL/kg/h the next 30 min, and then increase to 3 mL/kg/h until infused.

ADVERSE EFFECTS Respiratory: Upper respiratory infection. **CNS:** Dizziness, *headache.* **Skin:** Erythema, flushing. **GI:** Abdominal pain, nausea, vomiting. **Musculoskeletal:** Arthralgia, back pain. **Other:** Injection site reaction.

INTERACTIONS Drug: May interfere with the immune response to LIVE VIRUS VACCINES. Vaccination with LIVE VIRUS VACCINES should be deferred until approximately 6 mo after administration of VIG-IV.

PHARMACOKINETICS Half-Life: 22 days.

NURSING IMPLICATIONS

Black Box Warning

Vaccinia immune globulin IV has been associated with serious renal dysfunction, acute renal failure, and death.

Assessment & Drug Effects
- Monitor vital signs continuously during infusion, especially after infusion rate changes.
- Slow infusion rate for any of the following: Flushing, chills, muscle cramps, back pain, fever, nausea, vomiting, arthralgia, and wheezing.
- Discontinue infusion, institute supportive measures, and notify prescriber for any of the following: Increase in heart rate, increase in respiratory rate, shortness of breath, rales or other signs of anaphylaxis.
- Have loop diuretic available for management of fluid overload.

Patient & Family Education
- Promptly report any discomfort that develops while drug is being infused.

VALACYCLOVIR HYDROCHLORIDE
(val-a-cy'clo-vir)
Valtrex
Classification: ANTIVIRAL; ANTIHERPES
Therapeutic: ANTIVIRAL; ANTIHERPES
Prototype: Acyclovir

V

AVAILABILITY Tablet

ACTION & *THERAPEUTIC EFFECT*
An antiviral agent hydrolyzed in the intestinal wall or liver to acyclovir, which interferes with viral DNA synthesis. *Active against herpes simplex virus types 1 (HSV-1) and 2 (HSV-2), varicella zoster virus, and cytomegalovirus. Inhibits viral replication.*

USES Herpes zoster (shingles) in immunocompetent adults. Treatment and suppression of recurrent genital herpes; suppression of recurrent herpes in HIV-positive patients; treatment of cold sores; treatment of varicella infection.

CONTRAINDICATIONS Hypersensitivity to valacyclovir, acyclovir, or any component of the formulation.

CAUTIOUS USE Renal impairment, patients receiving nephrotoxic drugs, advanced HIV disease, allogeneic bone marrow transplant and renal transplant recipients, treatment of disseminated herpes zoster, immunocompromised patients, pregnancy (studies show no increased rate of birth defects related to maternal exposure to valacyclovir); lactation; children younger than 2 y for chicken pox.

ROUTE & DOSAGE

Herpes Zoster
Adult/Adolescent: **PO** 1 g tid for 7 days, start within 48 h of onset of zoster rash

Renal Impairment Dosage Adjustment
CrCl 30–49 mL/min: 1 g q12h; *10–29 mL/min:* 1 g q24h; *less than 10 mL/min:* 500 mg q24h

Treatment of Recurrent Genital Herpes
Adult/Adolescent: **PO** 500 mg bid × 3 days

Renal Impairment Dosage Adjustment
CrCl 10 mL/min or less: 500 mg daily

Treatment of Cold Sores
Adult/Adolescent: **PO** 2 g 12 h × 1 day

Chickenpox Prophylaxis in immunocompromised patients
Adolescent/Child (2 y or older): **PO** 15–30 mg/kg tid (max: 1 g tid)

ADMINISTRATION

Oral
- If GI upset occurs, administer with meals.
- Give valacyclovir after hemodialysis.
- Store at 15°–25° C (59°–77° F).

ADVERSE EFFECTS Respiratory: Nasopharyngitis. **CNS:** *Headache,* dizziness, fatigue, depression. **Skin:** Rash. **Hepatic/GI:** *Nausea, vomiting, diarrhea,* abdominal pain, elevated liver enzymes. **GU:** Dysmenorrhea. **Musculoskeletal:** Arthralgia.

INTERACTIONS Drug: Zidovudine may cause increased drowsiness and lethargy. Do not use with **cladribine, foscarnet**, or LIVE VACCINES.

PHARMACOKINETICS Absorption: Rapidly absorbed from GI tract; 54% reaches systemic circulation as acyclovir. **Peak:** 1.5 h. **Distribution:** 14–18% bound to plasma proteins; distributes into plasma, cerebrospinal fluid, saliva, and major body

Common adverse effects in *italic;* life-threatening effects <u>underlined</u>; generic names in **bold**; classifications in SMALL CAPS; ✦ Canadian drug name; ◑ Prototype drug; ⚠ Alert

1738

V

organs; crosses placenta; excreted in breast milk. **Metabolism:** Rapidly converted to acyclovir during first pass through intestine and liver. **Elimination:** 40–50% in urine. **Half-Life:** 2.5–3.3 h.

NURSING IMPLICATIONS

Assessment & Drug Effects

- Monitor kidney function in patients with kidney impairment or those receiving potentially nephrotoxic drugs.
- Monitor for S&S of hypersensitivity; if present, withhold drug and notify prescriber.
- Monitor lab tests: Urinalysis, BUN, serum creatinine, liver enzymes, and CBC.

Patient & Family Education

- Be aware of potential adverse effects; do not discontinue drug until full course is completed.
- Note: Post-herpes pain is likely to be present for several months after completion of therapy.

VALBENAZINE

(val-ben′a-zeen)

Ingrezza

Classification: CENTRAL MONOAMINE-DEPLETING AGENT; VMAT2-INHIBITOR
Therapeutic: CENTRAL NERVOUS SYSTEM AGENT

AVAILABILITY Capsule

ACTION & THERAPEUTIC EFFECT

Thought to reversibly inhibit the vesicular monoamine transporter 2 (VMAT2) transporter, affecting the uptake of monoamines to the synaptic vesicle from the cytoplasm. *Improves stiff and jerky involuntary musculoskeletal movement.*

USES Treatment of tardive dyskinesia.

CONTRAINDICATIONS Avoid in patients with congenital long QT syndrome or cardiac arrhythmias associated with prolonged QT interval; patients with severe renal impairment or renal failure; patients taking monoamine oxidase inhibitor therapy (MAOI therapy). Data regarding valbenazine use in human pregnancy is insufficient to provide information on drug-associated risks; lactation.

CAUTIOUS USE History of hepatic disease. Safety in children not established.

ROUTE & DOSAGE

Tardive Dyskinesia

Adult: **PO** 40 mg daily; after 1 wk titrate to 80 mg daily

Renal Impairment Dosage Adjustment

CrCL less than 30 mL/min: Use is not recommended

Hepatic Impairment Dosage Adjustment

Moderate to Severe impairment (Child-Pugh class B or C): 40 mg daily

Concomitant CYP3A4 Inhibitor/ Inducer

Strong CYP3A4 inducer: Do not use
Strong CYP3A4 inhibitor: Max dose: 40 mg daily

ADMINISTRATION

Oral

- May be administered with or without food.
- Store at 20°–25° C (68°–77° F); excursions permitted to 15°–30° C (59°–86° F).

V

Common adverse effects in *italic;* life-threatening effects underlined; generic names in **bold;** classifications in SMALL CAPS; ♣ Canadian drug name; ⊙ Prototype drug; ⚠ Alert

ADVERSE EFFECTS Respiratory:
Infection. **CNS:** Drowsiness, sedation, dizziness, falling, drooling, insomnia. **Endocrine:** Hyperglycemia, weight gain. **GI:** Vomiting. **Musculoskeletal:** Joint pain, involuntary movement.

INTERACTIONS CYP3A4 substrate; avoid use with strong CYP3A4 inducers (e.g., **carbamazepine**, **phenytoin**, **rifampin**); 40 mg daily max dose with CYP3A4 inhibitors (e.g., clarithyromycin, itraconazole, ketoconazole) **Herbal: St. John's wort** should not be combined with valbenazine.

PHARMACOKINETICS Absorption: 49% bioavailability, AUC and C_{max} decreased with high fat meals. **Distribution:** 99% protein bound. **Onset:** Peak effect in 0.5–1 h. **Metabolism:** Hepatic hydrolysis to an active metabolite, primarily by CYP3A4/5. **Elimination:** 30% in feces, 60% in urine. **Half-Life:** 15–22 h.

NURSING IMPLICATIONS

Assessment & Drug Effects
- Monitor for decrease in severity of tardive dyskinesia (abnormal involuntary movement) symptoms as indicative of efficacy.
- Monitor QT interval for patients at risk, prior to increasing the dose.
- EKG in patients at risk for QT prolongation.
- Monitor lab tests: Baseline LFTs.

Patient & Family Education
- Notify all health care providers that you this drug is being taken. This includes prescribers, doctors, nurses, pharmacists, and dentists.
- Avoid driving or other tasks that require alertness until drug affects are known.
- Notify prescriber if taking digoxin. Blood work will need to be monitored more closely.
- Notify prescriber of pregnancy or plan to get pregnant.
- Do not breast-feed while taking this drug or at least 5 days after final dose. Milk should be pumped and dumped during this time.
- Notify prescriber right away with S&S of an allergic reaction: Rash, hives, itching, blistered skin, fever, wheezing, chest or throat tightness, trouble breathing, unusual hoarseness, swelling of the mouth, face, lips, tongue, or throat.
- Notify prescriber right away with difficulties in focusing, blurred vision, difficulty urinating, a fast heartbeat that does not feel normal, or fainting.

VALGANCICLOVIR HYDROCHLORIDE
(val-gan-ci′clo-vir)
Valcyte
Classification: ANTIVIRAL
Therapeutic: ANTIVIRAL
Prototype: Acyclovir

AVAILABILITY Tablet; powder for oral solution

ACTION & *THERAPEUTIC EFFECT*
Rapidly converted to ganciclovir by intestinal and hepatic enzymes. In cells infected with cytomegalovirus (CMV), ganciclovir is converted to ganciclovir triphosphate that inhibits viral DNA synthesis. *Effective antiviral that prevents replication of viral CMV DNA.*

USES Treatment or prevention of CMV retinitis; prevention of CMV disease in high-risk kidney, kidney-pancreas, and heart transplant patients (not effective in liver transplants).

UNLABELED USES CMV in solid organ transplant.

Common adverse effects in *italic;* life-threatening effects <u>underlined</u>; generic names in **bold;** classifications in SMALL CAPS; ✤ Canadian drug name; ⊙ Prototype drug; ⚠ Alert

V

CONTRAINDICATIONS Hypersensitivity to valganciclovir, ganciclovir, or acyclovir; females of childbearing age; lactation.

CAUTIOUS USE Renal impairment; blood dyscrasias; older adults; pregnancy (based on animal reproduction studies, has the potential to cause birth defects in humans). Safe use in infants younger than 4 mo not established.

ROUTE & DOSAGE

Cytomegalovirus Prophylaxis

Adult/Adolescent: **PO** 900 mg once daily, duration depends on type of transplant, donor and recipient CMV serostatus
Child/Infant (older than 4 mo): See package insert for dose calculation formula (max: 900 mg)

Cytomegalovirus Retinitis Treatment

Adult: **PO** 900 mg bid × 14–21 days then 900 mg daily

Renal Impairment Dosage Adjustment

CrCl 40–59 mL/min: 450 mg bid (induction) or daily (maintenance); *25–39 mL/min:* 450 mg daily (induction) or q2days (maintenance); *10–24 mL/min:* 450 mg q2days (induction) or twice weekly (maintenance)

ADMINISTRATION

Oral

- Exercise caution in handling tablets, powder for oral solution, and the oral solution. Do not crush or break tablets. Avoid direct contact of any form of the drug with skin or mucous membranes. Note that adults should receive tablets, not the oral solution.
- Give with food.
- Store tablets at 20°–25° C (68°–77° F). Store oral solution at 2°–8° C (36°–46° F) for no longer than 49 days.

ADVERSE EFFECTS Cardiovascular: Hypertension, hypotension, peripheral edema, cardiac arrhythmia. **Respiratory:** Cough, dyspnea, pharyngitis, URI. **CNS:** *Headache, insomnia*, peripheral neuropathy, paresthesia, seizure, psychosis, confusion, hallucinations, agitation, anxiety, chills, depression, dizziness, fatigue, malaise, pain, tremor. **HEENT:** *Retinal detachment*, eye pain, macular edema, deafness. **Endocrine:** Hyperkalemia, hypophosphatemia, weight loss. **Skin:** Dermatitis, increased wound secretion, night sweats, pruritis, cellulitis. **Hepatic/GI:** *Diarrhea, nausea, vomiting, abdominal pain*, abdominal distension, constipation, decreased appetite, dyspepsia, oral mucosa ulceration, dysgeusia, pancreatitis, increased serum ALT and AST. **GU:** Increased serum creatinine, hematuria, decreased creatinine clearance, renal impairment, renal failure. UTI. **Hematologic:** *Neutropenia, anemia*, thrombocytopenia, pancytopenia, bone marrow suppression, aplastic anemia, hemorrhage. **Musculoskeletal:** Arthralgia, back pain, muscle spasm, myalgia, weakness, limb pain. **Other:** *Fever*, graft rejection, organ transplant rejection, local and systemic infections, hypersensitivity reactions.

INTERACTIONS Drug: ANTINEOPLASTIC AGENTS, **amphotericin B, didanosine, dapsone, probenecid, zidovudine** may increase bone marrow suppression and other toxic effects of valganciclovir;

may increase risk of nephrotoxicity from **cyclosporine**; ANTIRETROVIRAL AGENTS may decrease valganciclovir levels; valganciclovir may increase levels and toxicity of ANTIRETROVIRAL AGENTS; do not use with **cladribine**; may increase risk of seizures due to **imipenem-cilastatin**.

PHARMACOKINETICS **Absorption:** 60% reaches systemic circulation as ganciclovir. **Onset:** 3–8 days. **Peak:** 1–3 h. **Duration:** Clinical relapse can occur 14 days to 3.5 mo after stopping therapy; positive blood and urine cultures recur 12–60 days after therapy. **Distribution:** Distributes throughout body including CSF, eye, lungs, liver, and kidneys; crosses placenta in animals; not known if distributed into breast milk. **Metabolism:** Metabolized in intestinal wall to ganciclovir, ganciclovir is not metabolized. **Elimination:** 94–99% of dose is excreted unchanged in urine. **Half-Life:** 4 h (in adults).

NURSING IMPLICATIONS

Black Box Warning

Valganciclovir has been associated with granulocytopenia, anemia, and thrombocytopenia.

Assessment & Drug Effects

- Withhold drug and notify prescriber for any of the following: Absolute neutrophil count less than 500 cells/mm^3, platelet count less than 25,000/mm^3, hemoglobin less than 8 g/dL, declining creatinine clearance.
- Monitor for S&S of bronchospasm in asthma patients; notify prescriber immediately.
- Monitor lab tests: Baseline and frequent serum creatinine or creatinine clearance, CBC with

differential, platelet count; pregnancy test prior to initiation in females of reproductive potential.

Patient & Family Education

- Schedule ophthalmologic follow-up examinations at least every 4–6 wk while being treated with valganciclovir.
- Keep all scheduled appointments for laboratory tests.
- Do not drive or engage in potentially hazardous activities until response to drug is known.
- Report any of the following immediately: Unexpected bleeding, infection.
- Use effective methods of contraception (barrier and other types) during and for at least 90 days following treatment.
- Discontinue drug and notify prescriber immediately in the event of pregnancy.

VALPROIC ACID (DIVALPROEX SODIUM, SODIUM VALPROATE) 🅟
(val-proe'ic)

Depacon, Depakene, Depakote, Depakote ER, Depakote Sprinkle, Epival ♦
Classification: ANTICONVULSANT; GAMMA-AMINOBUTYRIC ACID (GABA) INHIBITOR
Therapeutic: ANTICONVULSANT

AVAILABILITY Capsule; sprinkle capsule; delayed release tablet; syrup; solution for injection

ACTION & *THERAPEUTIC EFFECT*
The mechanisms of action is unknown. Its activity in epilepsy may be related to increased brain concentrations of gamma-aminobutyric acid (GABA). *Depresses abnormal neuron discharges in the CNS, thus decreasing seizure activity.*

V

USES Alone or with other anti-convulsants in management of absence (petit mal) and mixed seizures; mania; migraine headache prophylaxis.

UNLABELED USES Status epilepticus refractory to IV diazepam, petit mal variant seizures, febrile seizures in children, other types of seizures including psychomotor (temporal lobe), myoclonic, akinetic and tonic-clonic seizures, photosensitivity seizures, and those refractory to other anticonvulsants.

CONTRAINDICATIONS Hypersensitivity to valproate sodium; significant hepatic function impairment; known urea cycle disorders; hyperammonemia, encephalopathy; suicidal ideations; thrombocytopenia, patient with bleeding disorders or liver dysfunction or disease, drug induced pancreatitis; congenital metabolic disorders, mitochondrial disorders caused by mutations in mitochondrial DNA and children younger than 2 y who are suspected of having a mitochondial DNA polemerase related disorder; pancreatitis; pregnancy (category D); lactation.

CAUTIOUS USE History of suicidal tendencies; history of kidney disease, renal impairment or failure; history of mild or moderate liver impairment; congenital metabolic disorders, those with severe epilepsy; HIV; CMV-infected patients; hypoalbuminemia; organic brain syndrome or mental retardation; use as sore agent; older adults. Safe use in children with partial seizures younger than 10 y not established. Safe use for migraine use in children younger than 12 y not established.

ROUTE & DOSAGE

Note: May need to increase dose when converting from immediate release to extended release products

Management of Seizures

Adult/Child (10 y or older): **PO/IV** 10–15 mg/kg/day in divided doses when total daily dose greater than 250 mg, increase at 1 wk intervals by 5–10 mg/kg/day until seizures are controlled or adverse effects develop (max: 60 mg/kg/day)
Conversion of PO to IV: Give normal dose in divided doses q6h

Migraine Headache Prophylaxis

Adult: **PO** 250 mg bid (max: 1000 mg/day) or **Depakote ER** 500 mg daily × 1 wk, may increase to 1000 mg daily

Mania

Adult: **PO** 750 mg/day administered in divided doses OR **Extended release** 25 mg/kg/day

Hepatic Impairment Dosage Adjustment

Dose reduction recommended

Renal Impairment Dosage Adjustment

Severe impairment may require close monitoring

ADMINISTRATION
Oral

- Give tablets and capsules whole; instruct patient to swallow whole and not to chew. Instruct to swallow sprinkle capsules whole or sprinkle entire contents on teaspoonful of soft food, and instruct to not chew food.

- Avoid using a carbonated drink as diluent for the syrup because it will release drug from delivery vehicle; free drug painfully irritates oral and pharyngeal membranes.
- Reduce gastric irritation by administering drug with food.

Intravenous

PREPARE: IV Infusion: Dilute each dose in 50 mL or more of D5W, NS, or LR.
ADMINISTER: IV Infusion: Give a single dose over at least 60 min (20 mg/min or less). ▪ Avoid rapid infusion.
INCOMPATIBILITIES: Solution/additive: Should avoid mixing with other drugs. Y-site: **Vancomycin**.

ADVERSE EFFECTS Respiratory: Pulmonary edema (with overdose). CNS: Breakthrough seizures, *sedation, drowsiness, headache, tremor, muscle weakness*, dizziness, increased alertness, hallucinations, emotional upset, aggression; deep coma, death (with overdose). Endocrine: Irregular menses, secondary amenorrhea. Hyperammonemia (usually asymptomatic), hyperammonemic encephalopathy in patients with urea cycle disorders, pancreatitis. Skin: Skin rash, photosensitivity, transient hair loss, curliness or waviness of hair, alopecia. GI: *Nausea, vomiting, indigestion (transient)*, hypersalivation, anorexia with weight loss, increased appetite with weight gain, abdominal cramps, diarrhea, constipation, liver failure, pancreatitis. Hematologic: *Prolonged bleeding time*, leukopenia, lymphocytosis, thrombocytopenia, hypofibrinogenemia, bone marrow depression, anemia.

DIAGNOSTIC TEST INTERFERENCE
Valproic acid produces false-positive results for **urine ketones**, elevated **AST**, **ALT**, **LDH**, and **serum alkaline phosphatase**, prolonged **bleeding time**, altered **thyroid function tests**.

INTERACTIONS Drug: Alcohol and other CNS DEPRESSANTS potentiate depressant effects; other ANTICONVULSANTS, BARBITURATES increase or decrease anticonvulsant and BARBITURATE levels; **haloperidol, loxapine, maprotiline**, MAOIS, PHENOTHIAZINES, THIOXANTHENES, TRICYCLIC ANTIDEPRESSANTS can increase CNS depression or lower seizure threshold; **aspirin, dipyridamole, warfarin** increase risk of spontaneous bleeding; **clonazepam** may precipitate absence seizures; SALICYLATES, **cimetidine, isoniazid** may increase valproic acid levels and toxicity. **Mefloquine** can decrease valproic acid levels; **meropenem** may decrease valproic acid levels; **cholestyramine** may decrease absorption. Herbal: **Ginkgo** may decrease anticonvulsant effectiveness.

PHARMACOKINETICS Absorption: Readily from GI tract. Peak: 1–4 h valproic acid; 3–5 h divalproex. Therapeutic Range: 50–100 mcg/mL. Distribution: Crosses placenta; distributed into breast milk. Metabolism: In liver. Elimination: Primarily in urine; small amount in feces and expired air. Half-Life: 5–20 h.

NURSING IMPLICATIONS

Black Box Warning

Valproic acid, sodium valproate, and divalproex sodium have been associated with severe hepatotoxicity, life-threatening pancreatitis, and fetal harm.

V

Assessment & Drug Effects

- Monitor patient alertness especially with multiple drug therapy for seizure control.
- Monitor patient carefully during dose adjustments and promptly report presence of adverse effects. Increased dosage is associated with frequency of adverse effects.
- Monitor for and report promptly S&S of pancreatitis (e.g., abdominal pain, nausea, vomiting, and/or anorexia).
- Multiple drugs for seizure control increase the risk of hyperammonemia, marked by lethargy, anorexia, asterixis, increased seizure frequency, and vomiting. Report such symptoms promptly to prescriber. If they persist with decreased dosage, the drug will be discontinued.
- Monitor lab tests: Baseline LFTs, platelet count, bleeding time, coagulation parameters, and serum ammonia; then repeat at least q2mo, especially during the first 6 mo of therapy.

Patient & Family Education

- Women of childbearing age should be aware of the potential for birth defects should a pregnancy occur while taking this drug.
- Do not discontinue therapy abruptly; such action could result in loss of seizure control. Consult prescriber before you stop or alter dosage regimen.
- Notify prescriber promptly if spontaneous bleeding or bruising occurs (e.g., petechiae, ecchymotic areas, otorrhagia, epistaxis, melena).
- Withhold dose and notify prescriber for following symptoms: Visual disturbances, rash, jaundice, light-colored stools, protracted vomiting, diarrhea. Fatal liver failure has occurred in patients receiving this drug.
- Avoid alcohol and self-medication with other depressants during therapy.
- Consult prescriber before using any OTC drugs during anticonvulsant therapy, especially drugs containing aspirin or sedatives and medications for hay fever or other allergies.
- Do not drive or engage in potentially hazardous activities until response to drug is known.

VALRUBICIN

(val-roo'bi-sin)

Valstar

Classification: ANTINEOPLASTIC; (ANTIBIOTIC) ANTHRACYCLINE
Therapeutic: ANTINEOPLASTIC
Prototype: Doxorubicin hydrochloride

AVAILABILITY Solution

ACTION & THERAPEUTIC EFFECT

A cytotoxic agent that inhibits the incorporation of nucleosides in DNA and RNA, resulting in extensive chromosomal damage. It arrests the cell cycle of the HIV virus in the G2 phase by interfering with normal DNA action of topoisomerase II, which is responsible for separating DNA strands and resealing them. *Valrubicin has higher antitumor efficacy and lower toxicity than doxorubicin.*

USES Intravesical therapy of BCG-refractory carcinoma *in situ* of the urinary bladder.

CONTRAINDICATIONS Hypersensitivity to valrubicin, doxorubicin, anthracyclines, or castor oil; patients with a perforated bladder, concurrent UTI, active infection; severe irritable bladder symptoms; severe myelosuppression; lactation.

CAUTIOUS USE Within 2 wk of a transureteral resection; compromised bladder mucosa; mild to moderate myelosuppression; history of bleeding disorders; GI disorders, renal impairment; pregnancy (category C).

ROUTE & DOSAGE

BCG-Refractory Bladder Carcinoma *in situ*
Adult: **Intravesically** 800 mg once/wk × 6 wk

ADMINISTRATION

Instillation
Avoid skin reactions by using gloves during preparation/administration.
▪ Use only glass, polypropylene, or polyolefin containers and tubing.

Intravenous
PREPARE: Slowly warm 4 vials (5 mL each) to room temperature. ▪ When a precipitate is initially present, warm vials in hands until solution clears. ▪ Add contents of 4 vials to 55 mL of 0.9% NaCl injection to yield 75 mL of diluted solution.
ADMINISTER: Aseptically insert a urethral catheter and drain the bladder. ▪ Use gravity drainage to instill valrubicin slowly over several min. ▪ Withdraw catheter; instruct patient not to void for 2 h. ▪ Note: Do not leave a clamped catheter in place.

▪ Store vials in refrigerator. Do not freeze.

ADVERSE EFFECTS **CV:** Vasodilation. **Respiratory:** Pneumonia. **CNS:** Dizziness. **Skin:** Rash. **GI:** Diarrhea, flatulence, nausea, vomiting. **GU:** *Urinary frequency, urgency, dysuria, bladder spasm, hematuria, bladder pain, incontinence, cystitis, UTI,* nocturia, local burning, urethral pain, pelvic pain, gross hematuria, urinary retention. **Other:** Abdominal pain, asthenia, back pain, fever, headache, malaise, myalgia. Anemia, hyperglycemia, peripheral edema.

PHARMACOKINETICS **Absorption:** Not absorbed. **Distribution:** Penetrates bladder wall. **Metabolism:** Not metabolized. **Elimination:** Almost completely excreted by voiding the instillate.

NURSING IMPLICATIONS

Assessment & Drug Effects
▪ Therapeutic effectiveness: Indicated by regression of the bladder tumor.
▪ Notify prescriber if bladder spasms with spontaneous discharge of valrubicin occur during/shortly after instillation.

Patient & Family Education
▪ Expect red-tinged urine during the first 24 h after administration.
▪ Report prolonged passage of red-colored urine or prolonged bladder irritation.
▪ Drink plenty of fluids during 48 h period following administration.
▪ Use reliable contraception during therapy period (approximately 6 wk).

VALSARTAN
(val-sar'tan)
Diovan, Prexxartan
Classification: RENIN ANGIOTENSIN SYSTEM ANTAGONIST; ANTIHYPERTENSIVE
Therapeutic ANTIHYPERTENSIVE; ANGIOTENSIN II RECEPTOR (AT_1) ANTAGONIST
Prototype: Losartan

AVAILABILITY Capsule; oral solution

ACTION & *THERAPEUTIC EFFECT*
An angiotensin II receptor antagonist that blocks the angiotensin converting enzyme (ACE). It inhibits the binding of angiotensin II to the AT_1 subtype receptors found in many tissues (e.g., vascular smooth muscle, adrenal glands). Angiotensin II is a potent vasoconstrictor and primary vasoactive hormone of the renin–angiotensin–aldosterone system (RAAS). *Blocking angiotensin II receptors results in vasodilation as well as decreasing the aldosterone-secreting effects of angiotensin II. These actions result in the antihypertensive effect of valsartan.*

USES Treatment of hypertension, heart failure; reduction of cardiovascular mortality in stable patients with left ventricular failure or left ventricular dysfunction (LVD) following acute myocardial infarction.

CONTRAINDICATIONS Hypersensitivity to valsartan or losartan; severe heart failure with compromised renal function; volume depletion; history of ACE inhibitor–induced angioedema concomitant use with aliskiren in patients with diabetes mellitus; children with CrCl of 30 mL/min/1.73 mm³; pregnancy (category D); lactation.

CAUTIOUS USE Severe renal impairment; hyperuricemia; hyperglycemia; increases in cholesterol and triglycerides; acute angle-closure glaucoma; SLE; history of allergy or bronchial asthma; mild to moderate hepatic impairment; biliary stenosis; renal artery stenosis; hypovolemia; hyperkalemia; transient hypotension; use prior to surgery; history of angioedema; congestive heart failure; older adults; children younger than 6 y.

ROUTE & DOSAGE

Hypertension
Adult: **PO** 80 or 160 mg daily (max: 320 mg daily) **Oral solution** 40–80 mg bid
Adolescent/Child (6–16 y): **PO** 1.3 mg/kg (max: 40 mg/day); **Oral solution** 0.65 mg/kg/dose bid may titrate up (max dose: 160 mg/day)

Heart Failure
Adult: **PO** 20–40 mg bid and titrate up to 160 mg bid

Left Ventricular Dysfunction Post MI
Adult: **PO** 20 mg bid titrate to dose of 160 mg bid if tolerated

Hemodialysis Dosage Adjustment
Adjustment not needed

ADMINISTRATION
Oral
- May be given with or without food.
- Reduce dosage with severe hepatic or renal impairment.
- Note: Daily dose may be titrated up to 320 mg.
- Store at 15°–30° C (59°–86° F).

ADVERSE EFFECTS CV: Hypotension, orthostatic hypotension. **Respiratory:** Dry cough. **CNS:** Dizziness. Renal: Increased blood urea nitrogen.

DIAGNOSTIC TEST INTERFERENCE May lead to false-negative aldosterone/renin ratio.

INTERACTIONS Do not use with **tranylcypromine**. Do not use within 12 h of **rituximab** administration. Use cautiously with **amifostine** due to increased risk of hypotension.

V

PHARMACOKINETICS Absorption: Rapidly from GI tract, 25% bioavailability. **Onset:** Blood pressure decreased in 2 wk. **Peak:** Plasma levels, 2–4 h; blood pressure effect 4 wk. **Distribution:** 99% protein bound. **Metabolism:** In the liver (CYP2C9). **Elimination:** Primarily in feces. **Half-Life:** 6 h.

NURSING IMPLICATIONS

Black Box Warning

Valsartan has been associated with fetal toxicity.

Assessment & Drug Effects

- Monitor BP periodically; take trough readings, just prior to the next scheduled dose, when possible.
- Monitor lab tests: Periodic electrolyte panel and renal function tests.

Patient & Family Education

- Inform prescriber immediately if you become pregnant.
- Note: Maximum pressure lowering effect is usually evident between 2 and 4 wk after initiation of therapy. Use precaution when changing positions.
- Notify prescriber of episodes of dizziness, especially those that occur when making position changes.
- Do not use potassium supplements or salt substitutes containing potassium without consulting the prescribing prescriber.

VANCOMYCIN HYDROCHLORIDE ◐

(van-koe-mye′sin)
Vancocin
Classification: ANTIBIOTIC; GLYCOPEPTIDE
Therapeutic: ANTIBIOTIC

AVAILABILITY Capsule; solution for injection

ACTION & *THERAPEUTIC EFFECT*

Bactericidal action is due to inhibition of cell-wall biosynthesis and alteration of bacterial cell-membrane permeability and ribonucleic acid (RNA) synthesis. *Active against many gram-positive organisms.*

USES Parenterally for potentially life-threatening infections in patients allergic, nonsensitive, or resistant to other less toxic antimicrobial drugs. Used orally only in *Clostridium difficile* colitis and staphylococcccal enterocolitis (not effective by oral route for treatment of systemic infections).

UNLABELED USES Rectal administration for complicated *C. difficile* infection.

CONTRAINDICATIONS Hypersensitivity to vancomycin.

CAUTIOUS USE Impaired kidney function, renal failure, renal impairment, hearing impairment; colitis, inflammatory disorders of the intestine; older adults; pregnancy (category B), children, neonates.

ROUTE & DOSAGE

Systemic Infections

Adult/Adolescent: **IV** 500 mg q6h or 1 g q12h or 15 mg/kg q12h
Child/Infant (1 mo or older): **IV** 30–40 mg/kg/day divided q6–8h
Neonate: **IV** 10–15 mg/kg q8–24h

Clostridium difficile Colitis

Adult: **PO** 125 mg qid × 10 days
Child: **PO** 40 mg/kg/day divided q6h (max: 2 g/day)

Staphylococcal Enterocolitis

Adult: **PO** 500 mg–2g in 3–4 divided doses × 7–10 days
Child: **PO** 40 mg/kg/day divided q6h (max: 2 g/day)

Surgical Prophylaxis (in Patients Allergic to Beta-Lactams)

Adult/Adolescent/Child (weight at least 27 kg): **IV** 10–15 mg/kg starting 1 h before surgery
Child (weight less than 27 kg): **IV** 20 mg/kg starting 1 h before surgery

Endocarditis

Adult: **IV** 500 mg q6h or 1 g q12h *Infant older than 1 mo:* **IV** 10 mg/kg/dose q6h
Neonate: **IV** 15 mg/kg initial dose then 10 mg/kg q12h for first wk then q8h up to 1 mo old

Renal Impairment Dosage Adjustment

CrCl 40–60 mL/min: Dose q24h; *less than 40 mL/min:* Extend interval based on monitoring levels

Hemodialysis Dosage Adjustment

Not dialyzed

ADMINISTRATION

Oral

- May be given with or without food.
- Note: Some parenteral products may be administered orally; check manufacturer's package insert.

Intravenous

PREPARE: **Intermittent:** Reconstitute 500 mg vial, 750 mg vial, or 1 g vial with 10 mL, 15 mL, or 20 mL, respectively, of sterile water for injection to yield 50 mg/mL. ▪ Further dilute each 500 mg with at least 100 mL, each 750 mg with at least 150 mL, and each 1 g with at least 200 mL of D5W, NS, or LR.

ADMINISTER: **Intermittent:** Give a single dose at a rate of 10 mg/min or over **not less** than 60 min (whichever is longer). ▪ Avoid rapid infusion, which may cause sudden hypotension. ▪ Monitor IV site closely; necrosis and tissue sloughing will result from extravasation.

INCOMPATIBILITIES: **Solution/additive: Aminophylline,** BARBITURATES, **aztreonam** (high concentration), **calcium chloride, chloramphenicol, chlorothiazide, ciprofloxacin, dexamethasone, heparin, methicillin, pentobarbital, phenobarbital, sodium bicarbonate, sodium fusidate, warfarin. Y-site: Albumin, aminophylline, amphotericin B cholesteryl, azathioprine, aztreonam, bivalirudin, cefazolin, cefepime, cefoperazone, cefotaxime, cefotetan, cefoxitin, ceftazidime, ceftriaxone, cefuroxime, chloramphenicol, clorazepate, dantrolene, daptomycin, defibrotide, diazepam, diazoxide, dimenhydrinate, epoetin, fluorouracil, foscarnet, furosemide, ganciclovir, gemtuzumab, heparin, ibuprofen, idarubicin, indomethacin, ketorolac, lansoprazole, leucovorin, mitomycin, moxifloxacin, nafcillin, omeprazole,**

V

phenytoin, piperacillin/ tazobactam, rituximab, sargramostim, streptokinase, SMZ/TMP, temocillin, ticarcillin, ticarcillin/clavulanate, valproate sodium, warfarin.

• Store oral and parenteral solutions in refrigerator for up to 14 days; after further dilution, parenteral solution is stable 24 h at room temperature.

ADVERSE EFFECTS HEENT: Ototoxicity (auditory portion of eighth cranial nerve). **GI:** Nausea, warmth. **GU:** <u>Nephrotoxicity leading to uremia</u>. **Hematologic:** Transient <u>leukopenia</u>, eosinophilia. **Other:** Hypersensitivity reactions (chills, fever, skin rash, urticaria, <u>shock-like state</u>), <u>anaphylactoid reaction with vascular collapse</u>, superinfections, severe pain, thrombophlebitis at injection site, generalized tingling following rapid IV infusion. Injection reaction that includes *hypotension accompanied by flushing and erythematous rash on face and upper body* ("red-neck syndrome") following rapid IV infusion.

INTERACTIONS Drug: Adds to toxicity of ototoxic and nephrotoxic drugs (AMINOGLYCOSIDES), **amphotericin B, colistin, capreomycin; cidofovir; cisplatin; cyclosporine; foscarnet; ganciclovir; IV pentamidine; polymyxin B; streptozocin; tacrolimus**). **Cholestyramine, colestipol** can decrease absorption of oral vancomycin; may increase risk of lactic acidosis with **metformin**.

PHARMACOKINETICS Absorption: Not absorbed. **Peak:** 30 min after end of infusion. **Distribution:** Diffuses into pleural, ascitic, pericardial, and synovial fluids; small amount penetrates CSF if meninges are inflamed; crosses placenta. **Elimination:** 80–90% of IV dose in urine within 24 h; PO dose excreted in feces. **Half-Life:** 4–8 h.

NURSING IMPLICATIONS
Assessment & Drug Effects
• Monitor BP and heart rate continuously through period of drug administration.
• Assess hearing. Drug may cause damage to auditory branch (not vestibular branch) of eighth cranial nerve, with consequent deafness, which may be permanent.
• Be aware that serum levels of 60–80 mcg/mL are associated with ototoxicity. Tinnitus and high-tone hearing loss may precede deafness, which may progress even after drug is withdrawn. Older adults and those on high doses are especially susceptible.
• Monitor I&O: Report changes in I&O ratio and pattern. Oliguria or cloudy or pink urine may be a sign of nephrotoxicity (also manifested by transient elevations in BUN, albumin, and hyaline and granular casts in urine).
• Monitor lab tests: Periodic renal function tests, urinalysis, and WBC count; serial vancomycin blood levels (peak and trough) in patients with borderline kidney function, in infants and neonates, and in patients older than 60 y.

Patient & Family Education
• Notify prescriber promptly of ringing in ears.
• Adhere to drug regimen (i.e., do not increase, decrease, or interrupt dosage. The full course of prescribed drug therapy **must be** completed).

VARDENAFIL HYDROCHLORIDE

(var-den'a-fil hy-dro-chlo'ride)

Levitra, Staxyn

Classification: IMPOTENCE AGENT; PHOSPHODIESTERASE (PDE) INHIBITOR; VASODILATOR

Therapeutic: IMPOTENCE; PDE TYPE 5 INHIBITOR

Prototype: Sildenafil

AVAILABILITY Tablet; orally disintegrating tablet

ACTION & *THERAPEUTIC EFFECT*

Phosphodiesterases-5 (PDE5) is an enzyme that speeds up the degradation of cyclic guanosine monophosphate (cGMP), an enzyme needed to cause and maintain increased blood flow into the penis necessary for an erection. Vardenafil is a PDE5 inhibitor. *It enhances erectile function by increasing the amount of cGMP in the penis.*

USES Treatment of erectile dysfunction.

CONTRAINDICATIONS Hypersensitivity to vardenafil or sildenafil; coadministration of nitrates; QT prolongation, renal failure, severe renal impairment; retinitis pigmentosa. **Levitra:** Severe hepatic impairment (Child-Pugh class C); **Staxyn:** Moderate or severe hepatic impairment (Child-Pugh class B and C); lactation.

CAUTIOUS USE CAD, MI, or stroke within 6 mo; hypotension, or hypertension; risk factors for CVA; anatomic deformity of the penis; subaortic stenosis; sickle cell anemia, leukemia; multiple myeloma; leukemia; coagulopathy; active bleeding or a peptic ulcer; coagulopathy; GERD; hepatitis, cirrhosis; older adults; pregnancy (category B).

ROUTE & DOSAGE

Erectile Dysfunction

Adult: **PO** 10 mg approximately 60 min before sexual activity. May increase to max 20 mg/day (**Levitra** only) if needed.
Geriatric: **PO** Start with 5 mg 60 min before sexual activity (max: 20 mg/day)

Hepatic Impairment Dosage Adjustment

Moderate impairment: For **Levitra** reduce dose to 5 mg (max: 10 mg/day). For **Staxyn** dosing do not use in patients with moderate or severe (class B or C) hepatic impairment.

Drug Interaction Dosage Adjustment

If taking **Ritonavir**, max dose: 2.5 mg/72 h; if taking **erythromycin, indinavir, itraconazole, ketoconazole,** max dose: 2.5–5 mg/24 h

ADMINISTRATION

Oral

- Take approximately 1 h before expected intercourse, but preferably not after a heavy or high-fat meal.
- Store at 15°–30° C (59°–86° F).

ADVERSE EFFECTS CV: Angina, hypertension, hypotension, MI, orthostatic hypotension, palpitations, syncope, sinus tachycardia. **Respiratory:** Rhinitis, sinusitis, dyspnea, epistaxis, pharyngitis. **CNS:** *Headache*, dizziness, insomnia, somnolence, vertigo. **HEENT:** Tinnitus, sudden vision loss, blurred vision, changes in color vision. **Endocrine:** Increased creatine kinase. **Skin:** Photosensitivity, rash,

V

pruritus, sweating. **GI:** Dyspepsia, nausea, vomiting, abdominal pain, abnormal liver function tests, diarrhea, dysphagia, esophagitis, gastritis, GERD, xerostomia. **GU:** Ejaculation dysfunction. **Musculoskeletal:** Arthralgia, myalgia, hypertonia, hyperesthesia. **Other:** *Flushing*, flu-like syndrome, back pain, anaphylactoid reactions, asthenia, facial edema, pain, paresthesias.

INTERACTIONS Drug: May potentiate hypotensive effects of NITRATES, ALPHA-BLOCKERS, **alfuzosin, doxazosin, prazosin, tamsulosin, terazosin; amiodarone, dofetilide, procainamide, quinidine, sotalol** may increase QT_c interval leading to arrhythmias; dosage adjustment required with potent CYP3A4 inhibitors (**atazanavir, erythromycin, idinavir, itraconazole, ketaconazole**, etc.). If taking ritonavir, max dose is 2.5 mg/72 h. If taking erythromycin, indinavir, itraconazole, ketoconazole, max dose is 2.5–5 mg/24 h.

PHARMACOKINETICS Absorption: Rapidly absorbed, 15% reaches systemic circulation; 95% protein bound. **Onset:** Within 1 h. **Peak:** 0.5–2 h. **Metabolism:** In liver by CYP3A4, CYP3A5, and CYP2C. **Elimination:** Primarily in feces (90–95%). **Half-Life:** 4–5 h.

NURSING IMPLICATIONS

Assessment & Drug Effects
- Monitor CV status and report angina or other S&S of cardiac dysfunction.

Patient & Family Education
- Do not take more than once a day and never take more than the prescribed dose.
- Do not take this drug without consulting prescriber if you are taking drugs called "alpha-blockers" or

"nitrates" or any other drugs for high blood pressure, chest pain, or enlarged prostate.
- Report promptly any of the following: Palpitations, chest pain, back pain, difficulty breathing, or shortness of breath; dizziness or fainting; changes in vision; dizziness; swollen eyelids; muscle aches; painful or prolonged erection (lasting longer than 4 h); skin rash, or itching.

VARENICLINE
(var-en'i-cline)
Chantix
Classification: SMOKING DETERRENT; NICOTINIC RECEPTOR AGONIST
Therapeutic: SMOKING CESSATION
Prototype: Nicotine

AVAILABILITY Tablet

ACTION & *THERAPEUTIC EFFECT*
Nicotine increases dopamine release in the brain and cravings for nicotine are stimulated by low levels of dopamine during periods of abstinence. Varenicline is a partial agonist at nicotinic acetylcholine receptors (nAChRs), the sites responsible for the dopamine effects of nicotine. It partially stimulates these receptors to produce a modest level of dopamine but blocks nicotine from binding to many of the nicotinic receptor sites. *By blocking nicotinic receptors, it reduces effects of nicotine in cases where patient relapses and uses tobacco.*

USES Adjunct for smoking cessation in patients experiencing nicotine withdrawal.

CONTRAINDICATIONS Suicidal ideation; chronic depression; serious psychiatric disease; lactation.

Common adverse effects in *italic*; life-threatening effects underlined; generic names in **bold**; classifications in SMALL CAPS; ✦ Canadian drug name; ○ Prototype drug; ⚠ Alert

V

CAUTIOUS USE History of suicidal tendencies, depression; renal impairment, older adults; pregnancy (category C). Safe use in children younger than 18 y not known.

ROUTE & DOSAGE

Smoking Cessation

Adult: PO Begin with 0.5 mg/day for 3 days, increase to 0.5 mg bid for 4 days, then increase to 1 mg bid on day 8. Treat for 12 wk and may repeat an additional 12 wk.

Renal Impairment Dosage Adjustment

CrCl 50 mL/min or less: Titrate to 0.5 mg bid (max)

ADMINISTRATION

Oral

▪ Give after a meal with a full glass of water.
▪ Dose titration over 8 days (from 0.5 to 2 mg daily) is recommended to minimize adverse effects.
▪ Store at 15°–30° C (59°–86° F).

ADVERSE EFFECTS CV: Chest pain, hypertension. **Respiratory:** Dyspnea, epistaxis, respiratory disorder, rhinorrhea. **CNS:** *Abnormal dreams,* anorexia, anxiety, asthenia, disturbance in attention, depression, dizziness, drowsiness, emotional lability, *insomnia,* irritability, *nightmares,* restlessness, sensory disturbance, *sleep disorder,* suicidality. **HEENT:** Dysgeusia, xerostomia. **Endocrine:** Abnormal liver function test, appetite stimulation, weight gain. **Skin:** Hyperhidrosis, pruritus, rash. **GI:** Abdominal pain, *constipation,* diarrhea, dyspepsia, *flatulence,* gastroesophageal reflux, *nausea, vomiting.* **GU:** Menstrual irregularity, polyuria. **Musculoskeletal:** Arthralgia, back pain, muscle cramps, musculoskeletal pain, myalgia. **Other:** Fatigue, flushing, gingivitis, headache, influenza-like symptoms, lethargy, malaise, thirst.

INTERACTIONS Drug: Cimetidine increases systemic exposure to varenicline by 29%.

PHARMACOKINETICS Absorption: Complete absorption from GI tract. **Peak:** 3–4 h. **Distribution:** Less than 20% protein bound. **Metabolism:** Minimal. **Elimination:** Primarily eliminated unchanged in the urine. **Half-Life:** 24 h.

NURSING IMPLICATIONS

Black Box Warning

Varenicline has been associated with increased risk of depression, suicidal ideation, and suicide attempt.

Assessment & Drug Effects

▪ Monitor smoking cessation behavior and adverse effects.
▪ Monitor BP for new-onset hypertension.
▪ Monitor diabetics for loss of glycemic control.
▪ Monitor for increased suicidality, or increase in agitation or aggression.

Patient & Family Education

▪ Report persistent nausea, vomiting, or insomnia to a health care provider.
▪ Report new-onset of depressed mood, suicidal ideation, or changes in emotion and behavior resulting from the use of varenicline.

VARICELLA VACCINE

(var-i-cel′la)

Varivax

See Appendix J.

VASOPRESSIN INJECTION ○ ◆

(vay-soe-press′in)

Vasostrict

Classification: PITUITARY HORMONE; ANTIDIURETIC HORMONE (ADH)

Therapeutic: ADH REPLACEMENT

AVAILABILITY Solution for injection

ACTION & THERAPEUTIC EFFECT Produces concentrated urine by increasing tubular reabsorption of water (ADH activity), thus reabsorbing up to 90% of water in renal tubules. Causes contraction of smooth muscles of the GI tract as well as the vascular system, especially capillaries, arterioles, and venules. *Effective in reversing diuresis caused by diabetes insipidus. When given intravenously, it is effective as an adjunct in treating massive GI bleeding.*

USES Antidiuretic to treat diabetes insipidus, vasodilatory shock (Vasostrict only).

UNLABELED USES Test for differential diagnosis of nephrogenic, psychogenic, and neurohypophyseal diabetes insipidus; test to elevate ability of kidney to concentrate urine, and provocative test for pituitary release of corticotropin and growth hormone; emergency and adjunct pressor agent in the control of massive GI hemorrhage (e.g., esophageal varices).

CONTRAINDICATIONS Hypersensitivity to vasopression or any of the components in formulation; uncorrected nephritis accompanied by nitrogen retention; ischemic heart disease, PVCs, advanced arteriosclerosis; lactation.

CAUTIOUS USE Epilepsy; migraine; asthma; heart failure, angina pectoris; any state in which rapid addition to extracellular fluid may be hazardous; vascular disease; older adults; labor and delivery; pregnancy (category C); children.

ROUTE & DOSAGE

Diabetes Insipidus

Adult: **IM/Subcutaneous** 5–10 units aqueous solution 2–4 × day (5–60 units/day) or 1.25–2.5 units in oil q2–3days; **Intranasal** Apply to cotton pledget or intranasal spray

Child: **IM/Subcutaneous** 2.5–10 units aqueous solution 2–4 × day

Vasodilatory Shock

Adult: **IV** 0.03 units/min can titrate up by 0.005 units/min at 10–15 min intervals (max: 0.1 unit/min)

GI Hemorrhage

Adult: **IV** 20 units bolus then 0.2–0.4 units/min up to 0.9 units/min

Septic Shock

Adult: **IV** 0.01 units/min then can titrate up by 0.005 units/min (max: 0.07 units/min)

ADMINISTRATION

Intramuscular/Subcutaneous

- Give 1–2 glasses of water with vasopressin to reduce adverse effects such as skin blanching, abdominal cramps and nausea.

- Give IM injection deeply into a large muscle.
- With subcutaneous injection, exercise caution not to inject intradermally.

Intravenous

PREPARE: **Direct/IV Infusion:** Dilute with NS or D5W to a concentration of 0.1–1 units/mL.
ADMINISTER: **Direct:** Give rapid bolus dose. **IV Infusion:** Titrate dose and rate to patient's response.
- Ensure patency prior to injection or infusion as extravasation may cause severe vasoconstriction with tissue necrosis and gangrene.

ADVERSE EFFECTS CV: Angina pectoris, atrial fibrillation, bradycardia, cardiac arrhythmia, peripheral vasoconstriction. **Respiratory:** Bronchoconstriction. **CNS:** Headache, vertigo. **Endocrine:** Hyponatremia, hypovolemic shock. **Skin:** Circumoral pallor, diaphoresis, urticaria. **Hepatic/GI:** Increased serum bilirubin, abdominal cramps, flatulence, nausea, vomiting. **GU:** Renal insufficiency. **Musculoskeletal:** Tremor. **Hematologic:** Decreased platelet count, hemorrhage. **Other:** Anaphylaxis.

DIAGNOSTIC TEST INTERFERENCE Vasopressin increases *plasma cortisol* levels.

INTERACTIONS Drug: Alcohol, demeclocycline, epinephrine, heparin, lithium, phenytoin may decrease antidiuretic effects of vasopressin; **guanethidine, neostigmine** increase vasopressor actions; **chlorpropamide, clofibrate, carbamazepine,** THIAZIDE DIURETICS may increase antidiuretic activity.

PHARMACOKINETICS Duration: 2–8 h in aqueous solution, 48–72 h in oil, 30–60 min IV infusion. **Distribution:** Extracellular fluid. **Metabolism:** In liver and kidneys. **Elimination:** In urine. **Half-Life:** 10–20 min.

NURSING IMPLICATIONS
Assessment & Drug Effects

- Monitor infants and children closely. They are more susceptible to volume disturbances (such as sudden reversal of polyuria) than adults.
- Establish baseline data of BP, weight, I&O pattern and ratio. Monitor BP and weight throughout therapy. (Dose used to stimulate diuresis has little effect on BP.) Report sudden changes in pattern to prescriber.
- Be alert to the fact that even small doses of vasopressin may precipitate MI or coronary insufficiency, especially in older adult patients. Keep emergency equipment and drugs (antiarrhythmics) readily available.
- Check patient's alertness and orientation frequently during therapy. Lethargy and confusion associated with headache may signal onset of water intoxication, which, although insidious in rate of development, can lead to convulsions and terminal coma.
- Monitor urine output, specific gravity, and serum osmolality while patient is hospitalized.
- Withhold vasopressin, restrict fluid intake, and notify prescriber if urine-specific gravity is less than 1.015.

Patient & Family Education

- Be prepared for possibility of anginal attack and have coronary vasodilator available (e.g., nitroglycerin) if there is a history of coronary artery disease. Report to prescriber.
- With diabetes insipidus, measure and record data related to

V

polydipsia and polyuria. Keep an accurate record of output. Understand that treatment should diminish intense thirst and restore undisturbed normal sleep.

- Avoid concentrated fluids (e.g., undiluted syrups), since these increase urine volume.

VECURONIUM BROMIDE

(vek-yoo-roe'nee-um)

Classification: NONDEPOLARIZING SKELETAL MUSCLE RELAXANT; ACETYLCHOLINE RECEPTOR ANTAGONIST
Therapeutic: SKELETAL MUSCLE RELAXANT
Prototype: Atracurium

AVAILABILITY Intravenous solution

ACTION & THERAPEUTIC EFFECT
Intermediate-acting nondepolarizing skeletal muscle relaxant that inhibits neuromuscular transmission by competitively binding with acetylcholine at receptors located on motor endplate receptors. *Effective as a skeletal muscle relaxant.*

USES Adjunct for general anesthesia to produce skeletal muscle relaxation during surgery.

CONTRAINDICATIONS Hypersensitivity to vecuronium.

CAUTIOUS USE Severe liver disease; impaired acid–base, fluid and electrolyte balance; long-term use; severe obesity; adrenal or neuromuscular disease (myasthenia gravis, Eaton–Lambert syndrome); patients with slow circulation time (cardiovascular disease, old age, edematous states); obesity, pregnancy (category C); lactation; children younger than 1 y and older than 7 wk.

ROUTE & DOSAGE

Skeletal Muscle Relaxation

Adult/Child (10 y or older): **IV** 0.08–0.1 mg/kg initially, then after 25–40 min, 0.01–0.15 mg/kg q12–15min or 0.001 mg/kg/min by continuous infusion for prolonged procedures
Child (1–10 y)/Infant: **IV** Varies greatly; may require higher initial dose

Obesity Dosage Adjustment

Dose based on IBW

ADMINISTRATION

Note: Vecuronium is administered only by qualified clinicians.

Intravenous

PREPARE: Direct: Reconstitute the 10 or 20 mg vial with 10 or 20 mL, respectively, of sterile water for injection (supplied). **Continuous:** Further dilute the reconsituted solution in up to 100 mL D5W, NS, or LR to yield 0.1–0.2 mg/mL.
ADMINISTER: Direct: Give a bolus dose over 30 sec. **Continuous:** Give at the required rate.
INCOMPATIBILITIES: Y-site: Amphotericin B cholesteryl complex, diazepam, etomidate, furosemide.

- Refrigerate after reconstitution below 30° C (86° F), unless otherwise directed. Discard solution after 24 h.

ADVERSE EFFECTS Respiratory: <u>Respiratory depression.</u> **Other:** Skeletal muscle weakness, <u>malignant hyperthermia.</u>

INTERACTIONS Drug: GENERAL ANESTHETICS increase neuromuscular

V

blockade and duration of action; AMINOGLYCOSIDES, **polymyxin B, clindamycin, lidocaine, parenteral magnesium, quinidine, quinine, trimethaphan, verapamil** increase neuromuscular blockade; DIURETICS may increase or decrease neuromuscular blockade; **lithium** prolongs duration of neuromuscular blockade; NARCOTIC ANALGESICS increase possibility of additive respiratory depression; **succinylcholine** increases onset and depth of neuromuscular blockade; **phenytoin** may cause resistance to or reversal of neuromuscular blockade.

PHARMACOKINETICS Onset: Less than 1 min. **Peak:** 3–5 min. **Duration:** 25–40 min. **Distribution:** Well distributed to tissues and extracellular fluids; crosses placenta; distribution into breast milk unknown. **Metabolism:** Rapid nonenzymatic degradation in bloodstream. **Elimination:** 30–35% in urine, 30–35% in bile. **Half-Life:** 30–80 min.

NURSING IMPLICATIONS

Assessment & Drug Effects

- Use peripheral nerve stimulator during and following drug administration to avoid risk of overdosage and to identify residual paralysis during recovery period. This is especially indicated when cautious use of drug is specified.
- Monitor vital signs at least q15min until stable, then q30min for the next 2 h. Also monitor airway patency until assured that patient has fully recovered from drug effects. Note rate, depth, and pattern of respirations. Obese patients and patients with myasthenia gravis or other neuromuscular disease may have ventilation problems.

- Evaluate patients for recovery from neuromuscular blocking (curare-like) effects as evidenced by ability to breathe naturally or take deep breaths and cough, to keep eyes open, and to lift head keeping mouth closed and by adequacy of hand grip strength. Notify prescriber if recovery is delayed.
- Note: Recovery time may be delayed in patients with cardiovascular disease, edematous states, and in older adults.
- Monitor lab tests: Baseline serum electrolytes, acid–base balance, LFTs, and renal function tests.

VEDOLIZUMAB
(ve-dol'i-zu-mab)
Entyvio
Classification: BIOLOGICAL RESPONSE MODIFIER; MONOCLONAL ANTIBODY; INTEGRIN INHIBITOR
Therapeutic: IMMUNOSUPPRESSANT
Prototype: Basiliximab

AVAILABILITY Lyophilized powder for reconstitution and injection

ACTION & *THERAPEUTIC EFFECT* Inhibits the migration of memory T-lymphocytes, which promote inflammation, across the endothelium into inflamed GI tissue. *Decreases inflammation and other responses.*

USES Treatment of moderate-to-severe ulcerative colitis (UC) and Crohn's disease (CD) in adults who have had inadequate response to a tumor necrosis factor (TNF) blocker or immunomodulator, or were unable to achieve corticosteroid-free remission.

CONTRAINDICATIONS Known serious or severe hypersensitivity to vedolizumab or any component

V

of the formulation; dyspnea, bronchospasm; progressive multifocal leukoencephalopathy (PML); active serious infection; jaundice or liver injury due to vedolizumab.

CAUTIOUS USE History of recurrent mild or moderate infection; liver impairment. Safety and efficacy in children younger than 18 y not established.

ROUTE & DOSAGE

Ulcerative Colitis or Crohn's Disease

Adult: **IV** 300 mg infusion, again at wk 2 and wk 6, then 300 mg every 8 wk; discontinue if no benefit after wk 14

ADMINISTRATION

Intravenous

PREPARE: **IV Infusion:** Reconstitute vial with 4.8 mL of SW. Swirl gently for at least 15 sec but do not vigorously shake or invert. Allow vial sit up to 20 min at room temperature to allow foam to settle; vial can be swirled during this time. If not fully dissolved after 20 min, allow another 10 min for dissolution. Do not use the vial if the drug is not dissolved in 30 min. Prior to withdrawing the reconstituted solution from the vial for dilution, gently invert vial 3 times. Withdraw 5 mL (300 mg) of reconstituted solution and add to 250 mL of NS and gently mix the infusion bag. Use as soon as possible.
ADMINISTER: **IV Infusion:** Give over 30 min. **Do not** give IV push or bolus. Flush line after infusion with 30 mL of NS. Observe closely during infusion (until complete) and monitor for hypersensitivity reactions; stop infusion if a reaction occurs.
INCOMPATIBILITIES: Do not add any other drugs or solutions to the IV line.

▪ Store up to 4 h at 2°–8° C (36°–46° F). Do not freeze.

ADVERSE EFFECTS Respiratory: Nasopharyngitis. **CNS:** Headache, fatigue. **Musculoskeletal:** Arthralgia. **Other:** Antibody development.

INTERACTIONS Drug: TUMOR NECROSIS FACTOR BLOCKERS may increase the risk of progressive multifocal leukoencephalopathy and other infections if given with vedolizumab. Concomitant use of vedolizumab with ANTINEOPLASTIC AGENTS, IMMUNOSUPPRESSIVES, IMMUNOMODULATING AGENTS, or **natalizumab** may enhance the risk of opportunistic infections.

PHARMACOKINETICS Half-Life: 25 d (300 mg dose).

NURSING IMPLICATIONS

Assessment & Drug Effects

▪ Monitor closely for S&S of a hypersensitivity reaction (see Appendix F). Interrupt infusion and notify prescriber if hypersensitivity is suspected.
▪ Monitor for and report promptly S&S of an infection, especially in the upper respiratory tract.
▪ Monitor for signs of hepatotoxicity (see Appendix F).
▪ Monitor lab test: Baseline TB screening; periodic LFTs.

Patient & Family Education

▪ Report immediately if you experience S&S of a hypersensitivity reaction (e.g., itching, rash, swelling about the mouth and face,

Common adverse effects in *italic*; life-threatening effects <u>underlined</u>; generic names in **bold**; classifications in SMALL CAPS; ♣ Canadian drug name; ◑ Prototype drug; ⚠ Alert

V

difficulty breathing, dizziness, feeling hot, or palpitations).

- Needed immunizations should be brought up to date before beginning therapy with vedolizumab.
- Report promptly to prescriber S&S of an infection (e.g., sinus infection, fever, cough, bronchitis, flu-like symptoms).
- Report to prescriber if you develop S&S of liver damage (e.g., tiredness, loss of appetite, pain on the right side of abdomen, dark urine, or yellowing of the skin and eyes).
- If you are pregnant or plan to become pregnant, immediately consult prescriber.
- Do not breast-feed while taking this drug without consulting prescriber.

VENLAFAXINE ⊕

(ven-la-fax′een)

Effexor, Effexor XR

DESVENLAFAXINE

Khedezla, Pristiq

Classification: ANTIDEPRESSANT; SEROTONIN NOREPINEPHRINE REUPTAKE INHIBITOR (SNRI)

Therapeutic: ANTIDEPRESSANT; SNRI

AVAILABILITY Tablet; sustained release capsule; extended release tablet. **Desvenlafaxine:** Extended release tablet

ACTION & *THERAPEUTIC EFFECT*

Potent inhibitor of neuronal serotonin and norepinephrine reuptake. *Antidepressant effect presumed to be due to potentiation of neurotransmitter activity in the CNS.*

USES Depression, generalized anxiety disorder; premenstrual dysphoric disorder; social anxiety disorder.

UNLABELED USES Diabetic neuropathy, migraine prevention, obsessive-compulsive disorder, hot flashes.

CONTRAINDICATIONS Hypersensitivity to venlafaxine, desvenlafaxine, or other SNRI drugs; concurrent administration with MAO inhibitors or within 14 days of last dose; initiation in patients receiving linezolid or IV methylene blue; abrupt discontinuation; treatment for bipolar depression; serotonin syndrome symptoms; hyponatremia; suicidal ideation; lactation.

CAUTIOUS USE Renal and hepatic impairment, renal failure; anorexia nervosa, history of mania or other psychiatric disorders, history of suicidal tendencies or increase in suicidality especially in individuals younger than 24 y; elevated intraocular pressure, acute closed-angle glaucoma; cardiac disorders, recent MI, heart failure; hypertension; hyperthyroidism; CNS depression; history of seizures or seizure disorders; volume depleted individuals; hypertriglycerides; risk factors for interstitial lung disease; older adults; pregnancy (category C). Safety in children younger than 18 y not established.

ROUTE & DOSAGE

Depression

Adult: **PO Immediate release** 75 mg/day in 2–3 divided doses; **Extended release** 75 mg daily; **Desvenlafaxine:** 50 mg daily, may increase dose (max: 400 mg/day)

Anxiety

Adult: **PO Sustained release** Start with 75 mg daily and increase q4days (max: 225 mg/day)

Social Anxiety Disorder

Adult: PO 75 mg daily

Renal Impairment Dosage Adjustment

Venlafaxine: *CrCl 10–70 mL/ min:* Reduce total daily dose by 25–50%; *less than 10 mL/min:* Reduce total daily dose by 50%; **Desvenlafaxine:** *CrCl 3–50 mL/ min:* Max dose: 50 mg/day; *less than 30 mL/min:* Max dose: 50 mg every other day

Pharmacogenetic Dosage Adjustment

Poor CYP2D6 metabolizer: Start with 70% of dose

ADMINISTRATION

Oral

- Give with food. Extended-release *capsules* **must be** swallowed whole or carefully opened and sprinkled on a spoonful of applesauce. The applesauce mixture should be swallowed without chewing and followed with a glass of water. Extended release *tablets* should be swallowed whole and not divided, crushed, or chewed.
- Dosage increments of up to 75 mg/day are usually made at 4 days or longer intervals.
- Allow 14 days interval after discontinuing an MAO inhibitor before starting venlafaxine or desvenlafaxine.
- Do not abruptly withdraw drug after 1 wk or more of therapy.
- Store at room temperature, 15°–30° C (59°–86° F).

ADVERSE EFFECTS CV: *Increased blood pressure and heart rate*, palpitations. **CNS:** *Dizziness,* fatigue, headache, anxiety, *insomnia, somnolence,* suicidality. **HEENT:** Blurred vision. **Endocrine:** Small but statistically significant increase in serum cholesterol, weight loss (approximately 3 lb). **GI:** *Nausea, vomiting, dry mouth,* constipation, anorexia. **GU:** Sexual dysfunction, erectile failure, delayed orgasm, anorgasmia, impotence, abnormal ejaculation. **Other:** *Sweating,* asthenia, Stevens–Johnson syndrome.

DIAGNOSTIC TEST INTERFERENCE

False positive *urine drug screen* may occur for amphetamine or phencyclidine; use alternative tests to confirm results.

INTERACTIONS Drug: **Cimetidine**, MAO INHIBITORS, **desipramine, haloperidol** may increase levels and toxicity. Should not use in combination with MAO INHIBITORS: Do not start until greater than 14 days after stopping MAO INHIBITOR; do not start MAO INHIBITOR until 7 days after stopping venlafaxine/desvenlafaxine. **Trazodone** may lead to **serotonin** syndrome. Avoid use with agents that increase QT interval (e.g., **dofetilide, dronedarone, posaconazole, voriconazole, ziprasidone**). Herbal: **St. John's wort, sour date nut** may cause **serotonin** syndrome.

PHARMACOKINETICS Absorption: Well absorbed from GI tract. **Onset:** 2 wk. **Peak:** Venlafaxine 1–2 h; metabolite 3–4 h. **Duration:** Extensively tissue bound. **Metabolism:** Undergoes substantial first-pass metabolism to its major active metabolite (CYP2D6, CYP3A4). **Elimination:** ~60% in urine as parent compound and metabolites. **Half-Life:** Venlafaxine 3–4 h, desvenlafaxine ~11 h.

Common adverse effects in *italic;* life-threatening effects <u>underlined</u>; generic names in **bold;** classifications in SMALL CAPS; ♣ Canadian drug name; ○ Prototype drug; △ Alert

1760

V

NURSING IMPLICATIONS

Black Box Warning

Venlafaxine has been associated with increased risk of suicidal thinking and behavior.

Assessment & Drug Effects

- Monitor for worsening of depression or emergence of suicidal ideation.
- Monitor cardiovascular status periodically with measurements of HR and BP.
- Monitor neurologic status and report excessive anxiety, nervousness, and insomnia.
- Monitor weight periodically and report excess weight loss.
- Assess safety, as dizziness and sedation are common.
- Monitor lab tests: Periodic lipid profile.

Patient & Family Education

- Be aware of potential adverse effects and notify prescriber of those that are bothersome.
- Report promptly worsening mental status, especially thoughts of suicide.
- Do not drive or engage in potentially hazardous activities until response to drug is known.
- Avoid using alcohol while on venlafaxine.
- Do not use herbal medications without consulting prescriber.

VERAPAMIL HYDROCHLORIDE ⊙

(ver-ap'a-mill)

Calan, Calan SR, Covera-HS, Isoptin SR, Verelan, Verelan PM

Classification: CALCIUM CHANNEL BLOCKER; ANTIHYPERTENSIVE; CLASS IV ANTIARRHYTHMIC

Therapeutic CLASS IV ANTIARRHYTHMIC; ANTIHYPERTENSIVE; ANTIANGINAL

AVAILABILITY Tablet; sustained release tablet; sustained release capsule; solution for injection

ACTION & THERAPEUTIC EFFECT Inhibits calcium ion influx through slow channels into cells of myocardial and arterial smooth muscle. Dilates coronary arteries and arterioles and inhibits coronary artery spasm. Decreases and slows SA and AV node conduction without affecting normal arterial action potential or intraventricular conduction. Dilates peripheral arterioles, causing decreased total peripheral resistance, and this results in lowering the BP. *Decreases angina attacks by dilating coronary arteries and inhibiting coronary vasospasms. Decreases nodal conduction, resulting in an antiarrhythmic effect. Decreased total peripheral vascular resistance; and therefore, reduction in BP.*

USES Supraventricular tachyarrhythmias; Prinzmetal's (variant) angina, chronic stable angina; unstable, crescendo or preinfarctive angina and essential hypertension.

UNLABELED USES Paroxysmal supraventricular tachycardia, atrial fibrillation; prophylaxis of migraine headache; and as alternate therapy in manic depression.

CONTRAINDICATIONS Severe hypotension (systolic less than 90 mm Hg), cardiogenic shock, cardiomegaly, digitalis toxicity, second- or third-degree AV block; Wolff–Parkinson–White syndrome including atrial flutter and fibrillation; accessory AV pathway, severe

V

left ventricular dysfunction, severe CHF, sinus node disease, sick sinus syndrome (except in patients with functioning ventricular pacemaker); lactation.

CAUTIOUS USE Duchenne's muscular dystrophy; hepatic and renal impairment; mild to moderate left ventricular heart failure; MI followed by coronary occlusion, aortic stenosis; MG; Duchenne muscular dystrophy; GI obstruction, GERD, hiatal hernia, ileus; older adults; pregnancy (category C). **Extended release:** Safe use in children younger than 18 y not established.

ROUTE & DOSAGE

Angina

Adult: **PO** 80 mg q6–8h, may increase up to 320–480 mg/day in divided doses (Note: **Covera-HS must be** given once daily at bedtime)

Hypertension

Adult: **PO Immediate release** 80 mg tid; **Sustained release tablet** 180 mg daily may increase to 240 mg daily (Note: Covera-HS **must be** given once daily at bedtime); **Sustained release capsule** 240 mg daily may adjust to response

Supraventricular Tachycardia, Atrial Fibrillation

Adult/Adolescent (15 y or older): **IV** 5–10 mg after 30 min may give 10 mg (max total dose: 20 mg)
Child/Adolescent (younger than 15 y): **IV** 0.1–0.3 mg/kg (do not exceed 5 mg)
Infant: **IV** 0.1–0.2 mg/kg may repeat after 30 min

Renal Impairment Dosage Adjustment

CrCl less than 10 mL/min: Give 50–75% of dose

Hemodialysis Dosage Adjustment

Supplemental dose not necessary

Hepatic Impairment Dosage Adjustment

Cirrhosis: Use 20–50% of normal dose

ADMINISTRATION

Oral

- Give with food to reduce gastric irritation.
- Capsules can be opened and contents sprinkled on food. **Do not** dissolve or chew capsule contents.
- Do not withdraw abruptly; may increase and extend duration of pain in the angina patient.

Intravenous

PREPARE: IV Direct: Given undiluted or diluted in 5 mL of sterile water for injection. ▪ Inspect parenteral drug preparation before administration. Make sure solution is clear and colorless.
ADMINISTER: Direct: Give a single dose over 2–3 min.
INCOMPATIBILITIES: Solution/additive: Albumin, aminophylline, amphotericin B, hydralazine, trimethoprim/sulfamethoxazole. **Y-site:** Acyclovir, albumin, amphotericin B cholesteryl complex, ampicillin, azathioprine, cefperazone, ceftazidime, chloramphenicol, dantrolene, diazepam, diazoxide, ertapenem, fluorouracil, folic acid, foscarnet, ganciclovir, indomethacin, lansoprazole, nafcillin, oxacillin, pantoprazole,

V

Common adverse effects in *italic;* life-threatening effects <u>underlined;</u> generic names in **bold;** classifications in SMALL CAPS; ✦ Canadian drug name; ⊙ Prototype drug; ⚠ Alert

pentobarbital, phenobarbital, phenytoin, piperacillin/tazobactam, propofol, sodium bicarbonate, SMZ/TMP, thiotepa, tigecycline.

▪ Store at 15°–30° C (59°–86° F) and protect from light.

ADVERSE EFFECTS CV: *Hypotension*, congestive heart failure, bradycardia, severe tachycardia, peripheral edema, AV block. **Respiratory:** Pharyngitis, sinusitis. **CNS:** Dizziness, vertigo, *headache*, fatigue, sleep disturbances, depression, syncope. **Skin:** Pruritus. **GI:** Nausea, abdominal discomfort, *constipation*, elevated liver enzymes. **Other:** Flushing, pulmonary edema, muscle fatigue, diaphoresis.

DIAGNOSTIC TEST INTERFERENCE
May cause false positive for *urine screen* detection of **methadone**.

INTERACTIONS Drug: BETA-BLOCKERS increase risk of CHF, bradycardia, or heart block; significantly increased levels of **digoxin** and **carbamazepine** and toxicity; potentiates hypotensive effects of HYPOTENSIVE AGENTS; levels of **lithium** and **cyclosporine** may be increased, increasing their toxicity; **calcium salts** (IV) may antagonize verapamil effects. **Food: Grapefruit juice** may increase verapamil levels. **Herbal: Hawthorne** may have additive hypotensive effects. **St. John's wort** may decrease efficacy.

PHARMACOKINETICS Absorption: 90% absorbed, but only 25–30% reaches systemic circulation (first pass metabolism). **Peak:** 1–2 h PO; 4–8 h sustained release; 5 min IV. **Distribution:** Widely distributed, including CNS; crosses placenta; present in breast milk. **Metabolism:** In liver (CYP3A4). **Elimination:** 70% in urine; 16% in feces. **Half-Life:** 2–8 h.

NURSING IMPLICATIONS
Assessment & Drug Effects
▪ Establish baseline data and periodically monitor BP and pulse with oral administration.
▪ Following IV infusion, instruct patient to remain in recumbent position for at least 1 h after dose is given to diminish subjective effects of transient asymptomatic hypotension that may accompany infusion.
▪ Monitor for AV block or excessive bradycardia when IV infusion is given concurrently with digitalis.
▪ Monitor I&O ratio during IV and early oral maintenance therapy. Renal impairment prolongs duration of action, increasing potential for toxicity and incidence of adverse effects. Advise patient to report gradual weight gain and evidence of edema.
▪ Monitor ECG continuously during IV administration. Essential because drug action may be prolonged and incidence of adverse reactions is highest during IV administration in older adults, patients with impaired kidney function, and patients of small stature.
▪ Check BP shortly before administration of next dose to evaluate degree of control during early treatment for hypertension.
▪ Monitor lab tests: Baseline and periodic LFTs and renal function tests.

Patient & Family Education
▪ Monitor radial pulse before each dose, notify prescriber of an irregular pulse or one slower than established guideline.

V

- Do not drive or engage in potentially hazardous activities until response to drug is known.
- Decrease intake of caffeinecontaining beverage (i.e., coffee, tea, chocolate).
- Change positions slowly from lying down to standing to prevent falls because of drug-related vertigo until tolerance to reduced BP is established.
- Notify prescriber of easy bruising, petechiae, unexplained bleeding.
- Do not use OTC drugs, especially aspirin, unless they are specifically prescribed by prescriber.

VILAZODONE
(vil-az'oh-done)
Vibryd
Classification: SELECTIVE
SEROTONIN REUPTAKE INHIBITOR
(SSRI); PSYCHOTHERAPEUTIC AGENT;
ANTIDEPRESSANT
Therapeutic: ANTIDEPRESSANT;
SSRI
Prototype: Fluoxetine

AVAILABILITY Tablet

ACTION & *THERAPEUTIC EFFECT*
A selective serotonin reuptake inhibitor (SSRI). Antidepressant effect is presumed to be linked to inhibition of CNS neuronal uptake of the neurotransmitter, serotonin. *Improves mood in those with major depressive disorder.*

USES Treatment of major depressive disorder.

CONTRAINDICATIONS Concomitant use of MAOIs or MAOIs within the preceding 14 days; suicidal ideation.

CAUTIOUS USE History of suicidal thoughts; potential precursors to suicidal impulses (e.g., anxiety, agitation, panic attacks, insomnia, irritability, hostility, aggressiveness, impulsivity, psychomotor restlessness, hypomania, mania); history of seizure disorder; concurrent use of NSAIDs, aspirin, or other drugs that affect coagulation or bleeding; pregnancy (category C); lactation. Safety and efficacy in children younger than 18 y not established.

ROUTE & DOSAGE

Major Depressive Disorder
Adult: **PO** Initial dose of 10 mg once daily for 7 days, increase to 20 mg once daily for 7 days, then to 40 mg once daily

ADMINISTRATION

Oral
- Give with food to enhance absorption.
- Store at 15°–30° C (59°–86° F).

ADVERSE EFFECTS **CV:** Palpitations. **CNS:** Abnormal dreams, akathisia, *dizziness*, fatigue, insomnia, libido decreased, migraine, abnormal orgasm, paresthesia, restless leg syndrome, restlessness, sedation, somnolence, tremor, suicidality. **HEENT:** Blurred vision, dry eye. **Skin:** Hyperhidrosis, night sweats. **GI:** *Diarrhea*, dry mouth, dyspepsia, flatulence, gastroenteritis, *nausea*, vomiting. **GU:** Delayed ejaculation, erectile dysfunction. **Other:** Arthralgia, decreased appetite, feeling jittery, increased appetite.

INTERACTIONS **Drug:** Inducers of CYP3A4 (e.g., **phenytoin**) may reduce the levels of vilazodone. Coadministration or moderate (e.g., **erythromycin**) and strong (e.g., **ketoconazole**) increase the

V

levels of vilazodone and require a dosage reduction to 20 mg once daily. MONOAMINE OXIDASE INHIBITORS increase the levels of vilazodone and should not be used in combination with vilazodone. Coadministration of serotonergic agents (e.g, **busipirone, tramadol, thyptophan,** SELECTIVE SEROTONIN REUPTAKE INHIBITORS, SEROTONIN-NOREPINEPHRINE REUPTAKE INHIBITORS, TRIPTANS) increase the risk of serotonin syndrome. Vilazodone can increase the risk of bleeding if used in combination with **aspirin** or NSAIDs. **Food:** Ingestion of food enhances the absorption of vilazodone.

PHARMACOKINETICS Absorption: Bioavailability 72%. **Peak:** 4–5 h. **Distribution:** 96–99% plasma protein bound. **Metabolism:** Hepatic oxidative metabolism (CYP3A4). **Elimination:** Renal and fecal. **Half-Life:** 25 h.

NURSING IMPLICATIONS

Black Box Warning

Vilazodone has been associated with increased risk of suicidal thinking and behavior.

Assessment & Drug Effects

- Monitor closely and report promptly any of the following: Worsening of clinical symptoms; emergence of suicidal ideation; agitation, irritability, or unusual changes in behavior; signs of serotonin syndrome or neuroleptic malignant syndrome (see Appendix F).
- Supervise patients closely who are high suicide risks; be especially vigilant for changes in behavior and suicidal ideation in children and adolescents.
- Monitor those at risk for volume depletion (e.g., diuretics use) for S&S of hyponatremia.

- Monitor lab tests: Periodic serum sodium.

Patient & Family Education

- Report promptly worsening of condition, suicidal thoughts or thoughts of self-harm.
- Do not abruptly stop taking this drug without consulting prescriber.
- Notify prescriber if you become pregnant or intend to breast-feed.
- Do not drive or engage in other hazardous activities until response to drug is known.
- Consult prescriber prior to using nonsteroidal anti-inflammatory drugs (NSAIDs), aspirin, or other drugs that affect coagulation.

VINBLASTINE SULFATE
(vin-blast'een)

Classification: ANTINEOPLASTIC; MITOTIC INHIBITOR; VINCA ALKALOID
Therapeutic: ANTINEOPLASTIC
Prototype: Vincristine

AVAILABILITY Solution for injection

ACTION & *THERAPEUTIC EFFECT*

Cell cycle–specific drug that binds to tubulin and inhibits microtubule formation by disrupting the mitotic spindle during metaphase. Has an effect on cell energy production needed for mitosis and interferes with nucleic acid synthesis. *Interrupts the cell cycle in metaphase, thus preventing cell replication and cancer cell proliferation.*

USES treatment of Hodgkin lymphoma. Kaposi sarcoma, Langerhans cell histiocytosis, testicular cancer and non-Hodgkin lymphomas. Used singly or in combination with other chemotherapeutic drugs.

V

UNLABELED USES treatment of bladder cancer, non small cell lung cancer.

CONTRAINDICATIONS Severe bone marrow suppression, significant granulocytopenia; bacterial infection; older adult patients with cachexia or skin ulcers; men and women of childbearing potential; pregnancy (females of reproductive potential should avoid becoming pregnant during vinblastine treatment); lactation.

CAUTIOUS USE Malignant cell infiltration of bone marrow; leukopenia; stomatitis; obstructive jaundice, hepatic impairment; history of gout; use of small amount of drug for long periods; use in eyes; children.

ROUTE & DOSAGE

Antineoplastic

Adult: IV dose varies based on protocol; usual range 5.5–7.4 mg/m^2 q7 days; (max dose: 18.5 mg/m^2)

Hodgkin Lymphoma

Child: IV 6 mg/m^2 on days 1 and 15 or days 1 and 8 (depends on protocol) of a 28 day cycle.

Hepatic Impairment Dosage Adjustment

bilirubin over 3 mg/dL: Administer 50% of dose

ADMINISTRATION

Intravenous

This drug is a cytotoxic agent and caution should be used to prevent any contact with the drug. Follow institutional or standard guidelines for preparation, handling, and disposal of cytotoxic agents.

PREPARE: Direct: Add 10 mL NS to 10 mg of drug to yield 1 mg/mL. Do not use other diluents. • Avoid contact with eyes. Severe irritation and persisting corneal changes may occur. Flush immediately and thoroughly with copious amounts of water. Wash both eyes; do not assume one eye escaped contamination.
ADMINISTER: Direct: Drug is usually injected into tubing of running IV infusion of NS or D5W over period of 1 min. Prolonged administration over > 30–60 minutes may increase the risk of vein irritation and extravasation. • Stop injection promptly if extravasation occurs. Use applications of moderate heat and local injection of hyaluronidase to help disperse extravasated drug. • Observe injection site for sloughing. • Restart infusion in another vein.
INCOMPATIBILITIES: Y-site: Amphotericin B, cefepime, dantrolene, diazepam, furosemide, gemtuzumab, lansoprazole, pantoprazole, phenytoin.

• Refrigerate reconstituted solution in tight, light-resistant containers up to 30 days without loss of potency.

ADVERSE EFFECTS Cardiovascular: Angina pectoris, ECG abnormality, hypertension, Raynaud's phenomenon, limb ischemia, myocardial infarction. **Respiratory:** Bronchospasm, dyspnea, pharyngitis. **CNS:** Mental depression, peripheral neuritis, numbness and paresthesias of tongue and extremities, loss of deep tendon reflexes, headache, convulsions. **HEENT:** Nystagmus, auditory disturbance, deafness, vestibular

Common adverse effects in *italic;* life-threatening effects underlined; generic names in **bold;** classifications in SMALL CAPS; ✦ Canadian drug name; ⊙ Prototype drug; ⚠ Alert

disturbance. **Endocrine:** SIADH. **Skin:** *Alopecia (reversible)*, dermatitis, photosensitivity, skin blister; phlebitis, cellulitis, and sloughing following extravasation (at injection site). **GI:** Vesiculation of mouth, stomatitis, pharyngitis, anorexia, *nausea, vomiting*, diarrhea, ileus, abdominal pain, constipation, rectal bleeding, hemorrhagic enterocolitis. **GU:** Urinary retention, *hyperuricemia*, azoospermia. **Hematologic:** Leukopenia, thrombocytopenia, *bone marrow depression, granulocytopenia*, thrombocytopenic purpura, anemia. **Musculoskeletal:** *Jaw pain*, myalgia, ostealgia, weakness.

INTERACTIONS Drug: Mitomycin may cause acute shortness of breath and severe bronchospasm; ALFA INTERFERONS, **erythromycin, itraconazole** may increase vinblastine toxicity. Increased risk of neutropenia when used with **deferiprone**. CYP 3A4 INHIBITORS (ex ketoconazole, clarithromycin, ritonavir) may increase concentration of vinblasine; CYP 3A4 INDUCERS may decrease concentration of vinblastine. Use with IMMUNOSUPPRESSANTS may have additive immunosuppressant effects. Do not administer LIVE VACCINES.

PHARMACOKINETICS Distribution: Concentrates in liver, platelets, and leukocytes; poor penetration of blood–brain barrier. **Metabolism:** Partially in liver (via CYP 3A4) **Elimination:** In feces and urine. **Half-Life:** 24 h.

NURSING IMPLICATIONS

Black Box Warning

Vinblastine extravasation has been associated with severe tissue irritation. Vinblastine is fatal if given intrathecally.

Assessment & Drug Effects

- Monitor for and report promptly unexplained bruising or bleeding.
- Adverse reactions seldom persist beyond 24 h with exception of leukopenia, and neurological adverse effects.
- Monitor GI adverse effects which may range from nausea and vomiting to severe constipation.
- Report promptly if oral mucosa tissue breakdown is noted.
- Monitor lab tests: Baseline and periodic CBC with differential, platelet count, serum uric acid, LFTs.

Patient & Family Education

- Be aware that temporary mental depression sometimes occurs on second or third day after treatment begins.
- Avoid exposure to infection, injury to skin or mucous membranes, and excessive physical stress.
- Report immediately to prescriber development of sore mouth, sore throat, fever, or chills.
- Notify prescriber promptly about onset of symptoms of agranulocytosis (see Appendix F). Do not delay seeking appropriate treatment.

VINCRISTINE SULFATE

(vin-kris'teen)

Classification: ANTINEOPLASTIC; MITOTIC INHIBITOR; VINCA ALKALOID
Therapeutic: ANTINEOPLASTIC

AVAILABILITY solution for injection

ACTION & *THERAPEUTIC EFFECT*

Cell cycle–specific vinca alkaloid arrests mitosis at metaphase by inhibition of mitotic spindle function, thereby inhibiting cell division. *Induction of metaphase arrest in 50% of cells results in inhibition of cancer cell proliferation.*

USES Acute lymphoblastic leukemia, Hodgkin lymphoma, lymphosarcoma, neuroblastoma, Wilms tumor, rhabdomyosarcoma.

UNLABELED USES Central nervous system tumors, Ewing sarcoma, multiple myeloma.

CONTRAINDICATIONS Obstructive jaundice; active infection; adynamic ileus; radiation of the liver; patient with demyelinating form of Charcot–Marie–Tooth syndrome; men and women of childbearing potential; pregnancy (in utero exposure to vincristine may cause fetal harm); lactation.

CAUTIOUS USE Leukopenia; preexisting neuromuscular or neurologic disease; hypertension; hepatic or biliary tract disease; older adults; children.

ROUTE & DOSAGE

ALL
Adult: **IV** Varies based on concurrent medications usually 1.5 or 2 mg/m² *Child (weight greater than 10 kg):* **IV** Varies based on concurrent medications usually 1.5 mg/m² (max: 2 mg/m²)

Hodgkin Lymphoma
Adult/Adolescent/Child: **IV** 1.4 mg/m² frequency varies based on concurrent medications

Non-Hodgkin Lymphoma
Adult/Adolescent/Child: **IV** usually 1.5 or 2 mg/m² frequency varies based on concurrent medications

Hepatic Impairment Dosage Adjustment
Bilirubin 1.5–3 mg/dL: Use 50% of dose

ADMINISTRATION
Intravenous

This drug is a cytotoxic agent and caution should be used to prevent any contact with the drug. Follow institutional or standard guidelines for preparation, handling, and disposal of cytotoxic agents.

PREPARE: **Direct:** No dilution is required. Administer as supplied. ▪ Avoid contact with eyes. Severe irritation and persisting corneal changes may occur. Flush immediately and thoroughly with copious amounts of water. Wash both eyes; do not assume one eye escaped contamination.

ADMINISTER: **Direct:** Administer minibag (25 to 50 mL bag) over 5 to 15 minutes. ▪ Stop injection promptly if extravasation occurs. Use applications of moderate heat and local injection of hyaluronidase to help disperse extravasated drug. ▪ Restart infusion in another vein. Observe injection site for sloughing.

INCOMPATIBILITIES: **Y-site: Amphotericin B colloidal, cefepime, diazepam, gemtuzumab, idarubicin, lansoprazole, nafcillin, pantoprazole, phenytoin.**

▪ Store solution in the refrigerator.

ADVERSE EFFECTS CV: Hypertension, hypotension, edema, ischemic heart disease, myocardial infarction, phlebitis. **Respiratory:** Bronchospasm, dyspnea. **CNS:** *Peripheral neuropathy,* neuritic pain, *paresthesias, especially of hands and feet;* foot and hand drop, sensory loss, athetosis, ataxia, loss of deep tendon reflexes, muscle atrophy, dysphagia, weakness in larynx and extrinsic eye muscles, ptosis, diplopia, mental depression, abnormal gait.

Common adverse effects in *italic;* life-threatening effects <u>underlined;</u> generic names in **bold;** classifications in SMALL CAPS; ♣ Canadian drug name; ○ Prototype drug; ⚠ Alert

HEENT: Optic atrophy with blindness; transient cortical blindness, ptosis, diplopia, photophobia, deafness. **Endocrine:** Hyperuricemia, hyperkalemia. **Skin:** Urticaria, rash, *alopecia*, cellulitis and phlebitis following extravasation (at injection site). **GI:** Stomatitis, pharyngitis, anorexia, nausea, vomiting, diarrhea, abdominal cramps, *severe constipation (upper-colon impaction), paralytic ileus (especially in children)*, rectal bleeding; hepatotoxicity. **GU:** Urinary retention, polyuria, dysuria, SIADH (high urinary sodium excretion, hyponatremia, dehydration, hypotension); uric acid nephropathy. **Other:** Convulsions with hypertension, malaise, fever, headache, pain in parotid gland area, weight loss.

INTERACTIONS Drug: Mitomycin may cause acute shortness of breath and severe bronchospasm; CYP 3A4 INHIBITORS (ex **ketoconazole, clarithromycin, ritonavir**) may increase concentration of vincristine; CYP 3A4 INDUCERS may decrease concentration of vincristine.

PHARMACOKINETICS Distribution: Concentrates in liver, platelets, and leukocytes; poor penetration of blood–brain barrier. **Metabolism:** Partially in liver (CYP3A4). **Elimination:** Primarily in feces. **Half-Life:** 10–155 h.

NURSING IMPLICATIONS

Black Box Warning

Vincristine extravasation has been associated with severe tissue irritation. Vincristine is fatal if given intrathecally.

Assessment & Drug Effects

- Monitor I&O ratio and pattern, BP, and temperature daily.

- Monitor respiratory status. Report promptly shortness of breath (bronchospasms) which may occur within minutes or hours of drug infusion.
- Be aware that neuromuscular adverse effects, most apt to appear in the patient with preexisting neuromuscular disease, usually disappear after 6 wk of treatment. Children are especially susceptible to neuromuscular adverse effects.
- Assess for hand muscular weakness, and check deep tendon reflexes (depression of Achilles reflex is the earliest sign of neuropathy). Also observe for and report promptly: Mental depression, ptosis, double vision, hoarseness, paresthesias, neuritic pain, and motor difficulties.
- Provide special protection against infection or injury during leukopenic days.
- Avoid use of rectal thermometer or intrusive tubing to prevent injury to rectal mucosa.
- Monitor ability to ambulate and supply support as needed.
- Start a prophylactic bowel regimen against constipation and paralytic ileus at beginning of treatment (paralytic ileus is most likely to occur in young children).
- Monitor for signs/symptoms of peripheral neuropathy.
- Monitor lab tests: Baseline and periodic CBC with differential; electrolytes; LFTs; and serum uric acid levels.

Patient & Family Education

- Notify prescriber promptly of stomach, bone, or joint pain, and swelling of lower legs and ankles.
- Report changes in bowel habit as soon as manifested.
- Report a steady gain or sudden weight change to prescriber.
- Women should use effective means of contraception during treatment.

V

VINORELBINE TARTRATE

(vin-o-rel'been)

Navelbine

Classification: ANTINEOPLASTIC;
MITOTIC INHIBITOR; VINCA
ALKALOID

Therapeutic: ANTINEOPLASTIC

Prototype: Vincristine

AVAILABILITY Solution for injection

ACTION & *THERAPEUTIC EFFECT*

A semisynthetic vinca alkaloid
with antineoplastic activity. Inhibits polymerization of tubules into
microtubules, which disrupts mitotic
spindle formation. *Arrests mitosis at
metaphase, thereby inhibiting cell
division in cancer cells.*

USES Non–small-cell lung cancer.

UNLABELED USES Breast cancer, ovarian cancer, Hodgkin
lymphoma.

CONTRAINDICATIONS Hypersensitivity to vinorelbine, infection;
severe bone marrow suppression;
granylocyte counts greater than or
equal to 1000 cells/mm³; pulmonary toxicity to drug; constipation,
ileus; pregnancy (may cause fetal
harm if administered to a pregnant
female); lactation.

CAUTIOUS USE Hypersensitivity to vincristine or vinblastine;
leukopenia or other indicator(s)
of bone marrow suppression;
chickenpox or herpes zoster infection; hepatic insufficiency, severe
liver disease; pulmonary disease;
preexisting neurologic or neuromuscular disorders; older adults.
Safety and efficacy in children not
established.

ROUTE & DOSAGE

Non–Small-Cell Lung Cancer

Adult: **IV** 25–30 mg/m² weekly;
may require toxicity adjustment

Hepatic Impairment Dosage Adjustment

Bilirubin 2.1–3 mg/dL: Use 50%
of dose; *greater than 3 mg/dL:*
Use 25% of dose

ADMINISTRATION

Intravenous

This drug is a cytotoxic agent
and caution should be used to
prevent any contact with the
drug. Follow institutional or standard guidelines for preparation,
handling, and disposal of cytotoxic agents.

PREPARE: **IV Infusion:** *Method
One:* Dilute each 10 mg in a
syringe with either 2 or 5 mL of
D5W or NS to yield 3 mg/mL or
1.5 mg/L, respectively. *Method
Two:* Dilute the required dose in
an IV bag with D5W, NS, or LR to
a final concentration of 0.5–2 mg/
mL (e.g., 10 mg diluted in 19 mL
yields 0.5 mg/mL).
ADMINISTER: **IV Infusion:** Give
diluted solution over 6–10 min
into the side port closest to an IV
bag with free-flowing IV solution;
follow by flushing with at least
75–125 mL of IV solution over
10 min. ▪ Take every precaution
to avoid extravasation. If suspected, discontinue IV immediately and begin in a different site.
INCOMPATIBILITIES: **Y-site: Acyclovir, allopurinol, aminophylline,
amphotericin B, amphotericin
B cholesteryl complex, ampicillin, cefazolin, cefepime,
cefoperazone, cefotetan, cefoxitin, ceftriaxone, cefuroxime,**

V

chloramphenicol, dantrolene, diazepam, fluorouracil, foscarnet, furosemide, ganciclovir, ketorolac, lansoprazole, methohexital, methylprednisolone, mitomycin, nafcillin, nitroprusside, pantoprazole, phenobarbital, phenytoin, piperacillin, sodium bicarbonate, SMZ/TMP, thiotepa.

■ Store at 2°–8° C (36°–46° F).

ADVERSE EFFECTS
Cardiac: Chest pain. **CNS:** *Neurotoxicity, peripheral neuropathy.* **Skin:** Alopecia. **Hepatic/GI:** Paralytic ileus, *constipation, nausea, vomiting, diarrhea,* stomatitis, mucositis, hepatotoxicity *(elevated LFT),* increased serum bilirubin. **GU:** Increased serum creatinine. **Hematologic:** *Anemia, febrile neutropenia, granulocytopenia,* thrombocytopenia, leukopenia. **Musculoskeletal:** Asthenia. **Other:** *Injection site reaction,* sepsis.

INTERACTIONS
Drug: Increased severity of granulocytopenia in combination with **cisplatin**; increased risk of acute pulmonary reactions in combination with **mitomycin; paclitaxel** may increase neuropathy. CYP 3A4 INHIBITORS (ex **ketoconazole, clarithromycin, ritonavir**) may increase concentration of vinorelbine; CYP 3A4 INDUCERS may decrease concentration of vinorelbine; do not administer LIVE VACCINES. Use with IMMUNOSUPPRESSANTS may have additive adverse effects.

PHARMACOKINETICS
Distribution: 60–80% bound to plasma proteins (including platelets and lymphocytes); sequestered in tissues, especially lung, spleen, liver, and kidney, and released slowly. **Metabolism:** In liver (CYP3A4). **Elimination:** Primarily in bile and feces (50%), 10% in urine. **Half-Life:** 42–45 h.

NURSING IMPLICATIONS

Black Box Warning

Vinorelbine has been associated with severe granulocytopenia and increased risk of infection, and extravasation has been associated with severe local tissue necrosis.

Assessment & Drug Effects
■ Withhold drug and notify prescriber if the granulocyte count is less than 1000 cells/mm^3.
■ Monitor for neurologic dysfunction including paresthesia, decreased deep tendon reflexes, weakness, constipation, and paralytic ileus.
■ Monitor for S&S of infection, especially during period of granulocyte nadir 7–10 days after dosing.
■ Monitor lab results: CBC with differential (prior to each dose and after treatment); Periodic LFTs, kidney functions, and serum electrolytes. Verify pregnancy status prior to initiation of therapy.

Patient & Family Education
■ Be aware of potential and inevitable adverse effects.
■ Women should use reliable forms of contraception to prevent pregnancy.
■ Notify prescriber of distressing adverse effects, especially symptoms of leukopenia (e.g., chills, fever, cough) and peripheral neuropathy (e.g., pain, numbness, tingling in extremities).
■ Report changes in bowel habits as soon as manifested.

V

VISMODEGIB ⊙
(vis-mo-de′gib)
Erivedge
Classification: ANTINEOPLASTIC;
BIOLOGICAL RESPONSE MODIFIER;
SIGNAL TRANSDUCTION INHIBITOR;
HEDGEHOG PATHWAY INHIBITOR
Therapeutic: ANTINEOPLASTIC

AVAILABILITY Capsule

ACTION & *THERAPEUTIC EFFECT*
Inhibits the Hedgehog pathway
which is needed to produce angio-
genic factors and decrease activity
of apoptotic genes that allow for
tumor expansion. *Slow basal cell
tumor growth and development.*

USES Treatment of adults with
metastatic basal cell carcinoma,
or locally advanced basal cell
carcinoma.

CONTRAINDICATIONS Preg-
nancy (category D); lactation.

CAUTIOUS USE Renal and hepatic
impairment; females of reproductive age. Safety and efficacy in
children younger than 18 y not
established.

ROUTE & DOSAGE

Basal Cell Carcinoma
Adult: **PO** 150 mg once daily

ADMINISTRATION
Oral
- May be given without regard to
food.
- Ensure that capsules are swal-
lowed whole. They should not
be opened or crushed.
- Store at 15°–30° C (59°–86° F).

ADVERSE EFFECTS Endocrine:
Azotemia, decreased appetite,
hypokalemia, hyponatremia, *weight
loss.* **GI:** Ageusia, constipation, diarrhea, *dysgeusia, nausea,* vomiting.
Musculoskeletal: Arthralgias, *muscle spasms.* **Other:** *Alopecia,* fatigue.

INTERACTIONS Drug: Coadmin-
istration with drugs that inhibit
P-glycoprotein (e.g., **clarithromycin, erythromycin, azithromycin**) may increase the levels of
vismodegib. Drugs that alter the pH
of the upper GI tract (e.g., PROTON
PUMP INHIBITORS, H₂-RECEPTOR ANTAG-
ONISTS, and ANTACIDS) may decrease
the bioavailability of vismodegib.

PHARMACOKINETICS Absorp-
tion: 32% bioavailability. **Distribution:** Greater than 99% plasma
protein bound. **Metabolism:** In the
liver. **Elimination:** Primarily fecal
(82%). **Half-Life:** 4 days.

NURSING IMPLICATIONS

Black Box Warning

*Vismodegib has been associ-
ated with embryo-fetal death and
severe birth defects.*

Assessment & Drug Effects
- Ensure that women and men
understand the risks associated
with fetal exposure to this drug
during a pregnancy. Advise males
of the potential risk of vismodegib exposure through semen.
- Monitor lab tests: Baseline pregnancy test within 7 d before start
of therapy; repeat pregnancy test
anytime the possibility of a pregnancy arises.

Patient & Family Education
- If a dose is missed, skip the dose
and wait for the next scheduled
dose.

V

- Women should use a highly effective means of birth control during therapy and for at least 7 mo following completion of therapy. Contact your prescriber immediately if you become pregnant during treatment.
- Men (even those with a vasectomy) should always use a condom with a spermicide during sex with female partners during treatment and for 2 mo following completion of therapy. Report to prescriber immediately if your partner becomes pregnant or thinks she is pregnant while you are taking this drug.
- Do not breast-feed while receiving this drug.

VITAMIN A

(vye'ta-min A)
Aquasol A, Del-Vi-A
Classification: VITAMIN SUPPLEMENT
Therapeutic: VITAMIN A REPLACEMENT

AVAILABILITY Tablet; capsule; solution for injection

ACTION & *THERAPEUTIC EFFECT*
Acts as a cofactor in mucopolysaccharide synthesis, cholesterol synthesis, and the metabolism of hydroxysteroids. *Essential for normal growth and development of bones and teeth, for integrity of epithelial and mucosal surfaces, and for synthesis of visual purple necessary for visual adaptation to the dark. Has antioxidant properties.*

USES Vitamin A deficiency and as dietary supplement during periods of increased requirements, such as pregnancy, lactation, infancy, and infections. Used during fat malabsorption diagnosis, ichthyosis, keratosis follicularis, measles.

CONTRAINDICATIONS History of sensitivity to vitamin A, hypervitaminosis A, oral administration to patients with malabsorption syndrome. Safe use in amounts exceeding 6000 international units during pregnancy (category X if greater than RDA) is not established.

CAUTIOUS USE Women on oral contraceptives, hepatic disease, hepatic dysfunction, hepatitis; renal disease; pregnancy (category A within RDA limit); lactation; children, low-birth weight infants.

ROUTE & DOSAGE

Severe Deficiency

Adult/Child (8 y or older): **PO** 500,000 international units/day for 3 days followed by 50,000 international units/day for 2 wk, then 10,000–20,000 international units/day for 2 mo; **IM** 100,000 international units/day for 3 days followed by 50,000 international units/day for 2 wk
Child (younger than 1 y): **PO/ IM** 7500–15,000 international units/day for 10 days; *1–8 y:* 17,000–35,000 international units/day for 2 wk

Dietary Supplement

Child (younger than 4 y): **PO** 300 mcg/day; *4–8 y:* 400 mcg/day

ADMINISTRATION

Oral
- Give on an empty stomach or following food or milk if GI upset occurs.
- Store in tight, light-resistant containers.

V

Intramuscular
- Use IM route only if oral route not feasible.
- Inject deeply into a large muscle.

ADVERSE EFFECTS CNS: Irritability, headache, intracranial hypertension (pseudotumor cerebri), increased intracranial pressure, bulging fontanelles, papilledema, exophthalmos, miosis, nystagmus. **Endocrine:** Hypervitaminosis A syndrome (malaise, lethargy, abdominal discomfort, anorexia, vomiting), hypercalcemia. Polydipsia, polyurea. **Skin:** Gingivitis, lip fissures, excessive sweating, drying or cracking of skin, pruritus, increase in skin pigmentation, massive desquamation, brittle nails, alopecia. **GI:** Hepatosplenomegaly, jaundice. **GU:** Hypomenorrhea. **Musculoskeletal:** Slow growth; deep, tender, hard lumps (subperiosteal thickening) over radius, tibia, occiput; migratory arthralgia; retarded growth; premature closure of epiphyses. **Hematologic:** Leukopenia, hypoplastic anemias, vitamin A plasma levels greater than 1200 international units/dL, elevations of sedimentation rate and prothrombin time. **Other:** Anaphylaxis, death (after IV use).

DIAGNOSTIC TEST INTERFERENCE
Vitamin A may falsely increase *serum cholesterol* determinations *(Zlatkis-Zak reaction)*; may falsely elevate *bilirubin* determination (with *Ehrlich's reagent*).

INTERACTIONS Drug: Mineral oil, cholestyramine, orlistat may decrease absorption of vitamin A.

PHARMACOKINETICS Absorption: Readily from GI tract in presence of bile salts, pancreatic lipase, and dietary fat. **Distribution:** Stored mainly in liver; small amounts also found in kidney and body fat; distributed into breast milk. **Metabolism:** In liver. **Elimination:** In feces and urine.

NURSING IMPLICATIONS

Assessment & Drug Effects
- Take dietary and drug history (e.g., intake of fortified foods, dietary supplements, self-administration or prescription drug sources). Women taking oral contraceptives tend to have significantly higher plasma vitamin A levels.
- Monitor therapeutic effectiveness. Vitamin A deficiency is often associated with protein malnutrition as well as other vitamin deficiencies. It may manifest as night blindness, restriction of growth and development, epithelial alterations, susceptibility to infection, abnormal dryness of skin, mouth, and eyes (xerophthalmia) progressing to keratomalacia (ulceration and necrosis of cornea and conjunctiva), and urinary tract calculi.

Patient & Family Education
- Avoid use of mineral oil while on vitamin A therapy.
- Notify prescriber of symptoms of overdosage (e.g., nausea, vomiting, anorexia, drying and cracking of skin or lips, headache, loss of hair).

VITAMIN B₁
See Thiamine HCl.

VITAMIN B₂
See Riboflavin.

VITAMIN B₃
See Niacin.

VITAMIN B₆
See Pyridoxine.

1774

Common adverse effects in *italic;* life-threatening effects <u>underlined</u>; generic names in **bold;** classifications in SMALL CAPS; ✦ Canadian drug name; ⊙ Prototype drug; ⚠ Alert

VITAMIN B₉
See Folic acid.

VITAMIN B₁₂
See Cyanocobalamin.

VITAMIN B₁₂A
See Hydroxocobalamin.

VITAMIN C
See Ascorbic acid.

VITAMIN D
See Calcitriol, Ergocalciferol.

VITAMIN E (TOCOPHEROL)
(vit'a-min E)
Aquasol E, Vita-Plus E, Vitec
Classification: VITAMIN SUPPLEMENT
Therapeutic: VITAMIN E SUPPLEMENT

AVAILABILITY Tablet; capsule; liquid

ACTION & *THERAPEUTIC EFFECT*
An antioxidant, it prevents peroxidation, a process that gives rise to free radicals (highly reactive chemical structures that damage cell membranes and alter nuclear proteins). *Prevents cell membrane and protein damage, protects against blood clot formation by decreasing platelet aggregation, enhances vitamin A utilization, and promotes normal growth, development, and tone of muscles.*

USES To treat and prevent hemolytic vitamin E deficiency; for the treatment of familial hypocholesterolemia. Also used topically for dry or chapped skin and minor skin disorders.

UNLABELED USES Muscular dystrophy and a number of other conditions with no conclusive evidence of value. A component of many multivitamin formulations and of topical deodorant preparations as an antioxidant.

CONTRAINDICATIONS Bleeding disorders; thrombocytopenia.

CAUTIOUS USE Large doses may exacerbate iron deficiency anemia; pregnancy (category A within RDA); children.

ROUTE & DOSAGE

Vitamin E Deficiency
Adult: **PO** 60–75 international units/day
Child: **PO** 1 international unit/kg/day

Prophylaxis for Vitamin E Deficiency
Adult: **PO** 12–15 international units/day
Child: **PO** 7–10 international units/day
Neonate: **PO** 5 international units/day

Familial Hypocholesterolemia
Child/Infant: **PO** 50 international units/kg/day

ADMINISTRATION
Oral
- Give on an empty stomach or following food or milk if GI upset occurs.
- Ensure that capsules are swallowed whole. They should not be crushed or chewed.

V

- Store in tight containers protected from light.

ADVERSE EFFECTS HEENT: Blurred vision. **Endocrine:** Increased serum creatine kinase, cholesterol, triglycerides; decreased serum thyroxine and triiodothyronine; increased urinary estrogens, androgens; creatinuria. **Skin:** Sterile abscess, thrombophlebitis, contact dermatitis. **GI:** Nausea, diarrhea, intestinal cramps. **GU:** Gonadal dysfunction. **Other:** Skeletal muscle weakness, headache, fatigue (with excessive doses).

INTERACTIONS Drug: Mineral oil, cholestyramine may decrease absorption of vitamin E; may enhance anticoagulant activity of **warfarin**. Avoid use with **amprenavir, tipranavir** due to increased risk of bleeding.

PHARMACOKINETICS Absorption: 20–60% absorbed from GI tract if fat absorption is normal; enters blood via lymph. **Distribution:** Stored mainly in adipose tissue; crosses placenta. **Metabolism:** In liver. **Elimination:** Primarily in bile.

NURSING IMPLICATIONS

Patient & Family Education
- Natural sources of vitamin E are found in wheat germ (the richest source) as well as in vegetable oils (sunflower, corn, soybean, cottonseed), green leafy vegetables, nuts, dairy products, eggs, cereals, meat, and liver.

VORAPAXAR

(vor-a-pax′ar)
Zontivity
Classification: ANTIPLATELET; PROTEASE-ACTIVATED RECEPTOR-1 (PAR-1) ANTAGONIST

Therapeutic: PLATELET AGGREGATION INHIBITOR; ANTITHROMBOTIC

AVAILABILITY Tablet

ACTION & *THERAPEUTIC EFFECT*
A reversible antagonist of the protease-activated receptor 1 (PAR-1) expressed on platelets; inhibits platelet aggregation induced by thrombin and thrombin receptor agonist peptide (TRAP). *Reduces the incidence of thrombus formation in those with preexisting risk factors.*

USES Reduction of thrombotic cardiovascular events in patients with a history of myocardial infarction (MI) or with peripheral arterial disease (PAD).

CONTRAINDICATIONS History of stroke, TIA, or intracranial hemorrhage (ICH); active pathological bleeding (e.g., hemorrhage, peptic ulcer bleeding); severe hepatic impairment; lactation.

CAUTIOUS USE Bleeding disorder; concomitant use of drugs that increase the risk for bleeding (e.g., anticoagulants, NSAIDs, SSRIs, SNRIs); depression; mild to moderate hepatic impairment; renal impairment; older adults; pregnancy (discontinue use if pregnancy detected due to potential for serious adverse effect of bleeding. Safety and efficacy in children younger than 18 y not established.

ROUTE & DOSAGE

Thromboembolism Prophylaxis
Adult: **PO** 2.08 mg once daily with aspirin and/or clopidogrel

Common adverse effects in *italic*; life-threatening effects <u>underlined</u>; generic names in **bold**; classifications in SMALL CAPS; ✦ Canadian drug name; ◯ Prototype drug; ⚠ Alert

ADMINISTRATION

Oral
- Give without regard to food.
- Store at 20°–25° C (68°–77° F) and protect from moisture.

ADVERSE EFFECTS Hematologic: Hemorrhage, bleeding. **GI:** GI hemorrhage. **Hematologic:** Anemia.

INTERACTIONS Drug: Strong inhibitors of CYP3A (e.g., **clarithromycin, conivaptan, indinavir, itraconazole, ketoconazole, nefazodone, nelfinavir, posaconazole, ritonavir, saquinavir, telaprevir, telithromycin**) can increase the levels of vorapaxar and can increase the risk of bleeding if used in combination. Strong inducers of CYP3A (e.g., **carbamazepine, phenytoin, rifampin**) can decrease the levels of vorapaxar. Use with ANTICOAGULANTS or ANTIPLATELETS may have additive adverse effects. **Herbal: St. John's wort** can decrease the levels of vorapaxar.

PHARMACOKINETICS Absorption: 100% bioavailable. **Peak:** 1 h. **Distribution:** Greater than 99% plasma protein bound. **Metabolism:** In liver to active and inactive metabolites. Substrate of CYP2J2 and CYP3A4. **Elimination:** Fecal (58%) and renal (25%). **Half-Life:** 8 days (range 5–13 days).

NURSING IMPLICATIONS

Black Box Warning

Vorapaxar has been associated with an increased risk of bleeding, including fatal bleeding events especially in those with a history of stroke, transient ischemic attack (TIA), or intracranial hemorrhage (ICH).

Assessment & Drug Effects
- Monitor for and report immediately S&S of bleeding. There is no antidote for vorapaxar-induced bleeding.
- Monitor closely those with risk factors for bleeding (e.g., older age, low body weight, reduced renal or hepatic function, history of bleeding disorders, and concomitant use of anticoagulants, NSAIDs, SSRIs, and SNRIs).
- Monitor lab test: Periodic Hct and Hgb.

Patient & Family Education
- Immediately report to prescriber if you experience any of the following: Bleeding that is severe or that you cannot control; pink, red, or brown urine; vomiting blood or your vomit looks like coffee grounds; red or black tarry stools; coughing up blood or blood clots.
- Consult prescriber before taking any new prescription or OTC drugs to determine possible interaction the vorapaxar.
- Be careful to avoid injury. Use a soft toothbrush and an electric razor.

VORICONAZOLE
(vor-i-con'a-zole)
Vfend
Classification: ANTIBIOTIC; AZOLE ANTIFUNGAL
Therapeutic: ANTIFUNGAL
Prototype: Fluconazole

AVAILABILITY Solution for injection; oral suspension

ACTION & *THERAPEUTIC EFFECT* Inhibits fungal cytochrome P450 enzymes used for an essential step in fungal ergosterol biosynthesis. The subsequent loss of ergosterol in the fungal cell wall is thought to be responsible for the antifungal

V

activity. *Voriconazole is active against Aspergillus and* Candida.

USES Treatment of invasive aspergillosis, esophageal candidiasis, candidemia in nonneutropenic patients and disseminated skin infections, and abdomen, kidney, bladder wall, and wound infections due to *Candida*.

CONTRAINDICATIONS Known hypersensitivity to voriconazole; should be avoided in moderate or severe renal impairment (CrCl less than 50 mL/min) and severe Child-Pugh class C hepatic impairment; development of S&S of hepatic disease in response to voriconazole; history of galactose intolerance; Lapp lactase deficiency or glucose-galactose malabsorption; development of exfoliative cutaneous reaction; sunlight (UV) exposure; pregnancy (category D); lactation.

CAUTIOUS USE Mild to moderate hepatic cirrhosis, hepatitis, Child-Pugh class A and B hepatic disease; proarrhythmic conditions; renal disease; mild or moderate renal impairment; ocular disease; hypersensitivity to other azole antifungal agents such as fluconazole. Safety and efficacy in children younger than 12 y not established.

ROUTE & DOSAGE

Invasive Aspergillosis

Adult/Adolescent: **IV** 6 mg/kg q12h × 2 doses then 4 mg/kg q12h. Treatment continues until 7–14 days after symptom resolution; *weight greater than 40 kg:* **PO** 200 mg q12h; *weight less than 40 kg:* **PO** 100 mg q12h

Candidemia

Adult: **IV** 6 mg/kg q12h × 2 doses then 3–4 mg/kg q12h; *weight greater than 40 kg:* **PO** 200 mg q12h may titrate dose; *weight less than 40 kg:* 100 mg q12h, may titrate dose

Esophageal Candidiasis

Adult (weight greater than 40 kg): **PO** 200 mg q12h for a minimum of 14 days and for at least 7 days after resolution of symptoms (max: 600 mg daily); *weight less than 40 kg:* 100 mg q12h for a minimum of 14 days and for at least 7 days after resolution of symptoms (max: 300 mg daily)

Drug Interaction Dosage Adjustment

Needed for concomitant CYP 450 enzyme inducers/substrates. See package insert for specific efavirenz and phenytoin adjustments.

Renal Impairment Dosage Adjustment

CrCl less than 50 mL/min: Switch to PO therapy after loading dose; hemodialysis does not require supplemental dose

Hepatic Impairment Dosage Adjustment

Child-Pugh class A or B: Reduce maintenance dose by 50%; *Child-Pugh class C:* Avoid drug use

ADMINISTRATION

Oral

- Give at least 1 h before or 1 h following a meal.
- Store tablets at 15°–30° C (59°–86° F).

Intravenous

PREPARE: **Intermittent:** Use a 20-mL syringe to reconstitute each 200 mg powder vial with exactly 19 mL of sterile water for injection to yield 10 mg/mL. Discard vial if a vacuum does not pull the diluent into vial. Shake until completely dissolved. ▪ Calculate the required dose of voriconazole based on patient's weight. ▪ From an IV infusion bag of NS, D5W, D5/NS, D5/.45NS, LR or other suitable solution, withdraw and discard a volume of IV solution equal to the required dose. ▪ Inject the required dose of voriconazole into the IV bag. The IV solution should have a final voriconazole concentration of 0.5–5 mg/mL. ▪ Infuse immediately.

ADMINISTER: **Intermittent:** Infuse over 1–2 h at a maximum rate of 3 mg/kg/h. ▪ **Do not** give a bolus dose.

INCOMPATIBILITIES: **Solution/additive:** Do not dilute with **sodium bicarbonate**; do not mix with any other drugs. **Y-site:** Do not infuse with other drugs.

▪ Store unreconstituted vials at 15°–30° C (59°–86° F).

ADVERSE EFFECTS

CV: Tachycardia, hypotension, hypertension, vasodilation. **CNS:** Headache, *hallucinations,* dizziness, chills. **HEENT:** *Abnormal vision (enhanced brightness, blurred vision, or color vision changes),* photophobia. **Endocrine:** Increased alkaline phosphatase, AST, ALT, hypokalemia, hypomagnesemia, increased serum creatinine. **Skin:** *Rash,* pruritus. **GI:** *Nausea,* vomiting, abdominal pain, abnormal LFTs, diarrhea, cholestatic jaundice, dry mouth. **Other:** Peripheral edema, *fever,* chills.

INTERACTIONS

Drug: Due to significant increased toxicity or decreased activity, the following drugs are <u>contraindicated</u> with voriconazole: BARBITURATES, **carbamazepine, efavirenz,** ERGOT ALKALOIDS, **pimozide, quinidine, rifabutin, sirolimus; fosphenytoin, phenytoin, rifampin,** Avoid use with CYP3A4 inhibitors (e.g., **atazanavir, itraconazole, ketoconazole, ritonavir**). PROTEASE INHIBITORS (except **indinavir**) may increase voriconazole toxicity; voriconazole may increase the toxicity of BENZODIAZEPINES, **cyclosporine,** NONNUCLEOSIDE REVERSE TRANSCRIPTASE INHIBITORS, **omeprazole, tacrolimus, vinblastine, vincristine, warfarin, fentanyl, oxycodone,** NSAIDS; **Food:** Absorption reduced with high-fat meals. **Herbal: St. John's wort** may decrease efficacy.

PHARMACOKINETICS

Absorption: 96% absorbed. Has a nonlinear pharmacokinetic profile, a small change in dose may cause a large change in serum levels. Steady state not achieved until day 5–6 if no loading dose is given. **Peak:** 1–2 h. **Metabolism:** In liver by (and inhibits) CYP3A4, 2C9, and 2C19. **Elimination:** Primarily in urine. **Half-Life:** 6 h–6 days depending on dose.

NURSING IMPLICATIONS

Assessment & Drug Effects

▪ Visual acuity, visual field, and color perception should be monitored if treatment continues beyond 28 days.
▪ Withhold drug and notify prescriber if skin rash develops.
▪ Monitor cardiovascular status especially with preexisting CV disease.
▪ Concurrent drugs: Monitor PT/INR closely with warfarin as dose adjustments of warfarin may be needed. Monitor frequently blood glucose levels with sulfonylurea

V

drugs as reduction in the sulfo-nylurea dosage may be needed. Monitor for and report any of the following: S&S of rhabdomyolysis in patient receiving a statin drug; prolonged sedation in patient receiving a benzodiazepine; S&S of heart block, bradycardia, or CHF in patient receiving a calcium channel blocker.

- Monitor lab tests: Baseline and periodic LFTs; frequent renal function tests; trough serum drug concentrations on day 5 and weekly thereafter for 4–6 wk; periodic CBC with platelet count, Hct and Hgb, serum electrolytes, blood glucose, and lipid profile.

Patient & Family Education

- Use reliable means of birth control to prevent pregnancy. If you suspect you are pregnant, contact prescriber immediately.
- Do not drive at night while taking voriconazole as the drug may cause blurred vision and photophobia.
- Do not drive or engage in other potentially hazardous activities until reaction to drug is known.
- Avoid strong, direct sunlight while taking voriconazole.

VORTIOXETINE

(vor-ti-ox'e-teen)
Trintellix
Classification: ANTIDEPRESSANT; SEROTONIN MODULATOR
Therapeutic: ANTIDEPRESSANT

AVAILABILITY Tablet

ACTION & *THERAPEUTIC EFFECT*
Mechanism of action unknown but thought to be through inhibition of the reuptake of serotonin (5-HT), 5-HT3 receptor antagonism, and 5-HT1A receptor agonism.

Enhanced serotonergic activity in the CNS is believed to produce an antidepressant effect.

USES Treatment of major depressive disorder (MDD).

CONTRAINDICATIONS Hypersensitivity to vortioxetine including angioedema; suicidal ideation; MAOIs within 14 days of starting vortioxetine or 21 days of stopping vortioxetine; serotonin syndrome; symptomatic hyponatremia; severe hepatic impairment; lactation.

CAUTIOUS USE History of suicidal thoughts; history of or family history of bipolar disorder, mania, or hypomania; history of bleeding disorders; history of GI bleeding; mild to moderate hepatic impairment; older adults; pregnancy (category C). Safety and efficacy in children not established.

ROUTE & DOSAGE

Major Depressive Disorder
Adult: PO 10 mg once daily; may increase to 20 mg or decrease to 5 mg as needed or tolerated

Metabolism Dosage Adjustment
Use with a strong CYP2D6 inhibitor: Decrease dose by 50%
Use with a strong CYP2D6 inducer: Increase dose up to 3 × normal
Use in patients who are poor CYP2D6 metabolizers: Maximum dose is 10 mg once daily

ADMINISTRATION

Oral
- May give without regard to food.
- To avoid adverse reactions, it is recommended that doses of

V

15–20 mg/day be decreased to 10 mg/day for 1 wk before discontinuation.
- Store at 15°–30° C (59°–86° F).

ADVERSE EFFECTS CNS: Abnormal abnomal dreams, *dizziness*. **Endocrine:** Hyponatremia. **Skin:** Pruritus. **GI:** Constipation, *diarrhea, dry mouth*, flatulence, *nausea*, vomiting. **GU:** Sexual dysfunction.

INTERACTIONS Drug: Coadministration of other drugs that affect serotonin transmission (e.g., SSRIS, SNRIS, MAOIS, TRIPTANS, **buspirone, linezolid, tramadol**) may increase the risk of serotonin syndrome. Strong CYP2D6 inhibitors (e.g., **bupropion, fluoxetine, paroxetine, quinidine**) may increase the levels of vortioxetine. Strong CYP2D6 inducers (e.g., **carbamazepine, phenytoin, rifampin**) may decrease the levels of vortioxetine. **Food: Tryptophan** containing foods may increase the risk of serotonin syndrome.

PHARMACOKINETICS Absorption: 75% bioavailable. **Peak:** 7–11 h. **Distribution:** 98% plasma protein bound. **Metabolism:** Hepatic oxidation via CYP2D6, CYP3A4/5, CYP2C19, CYP2C9, CYP2A6, CYP2C8, and CYP2B6. **Elimination:** Renal (59%) and fecal (26%). **Half-Life:** 66 h.

NURSING IMPLICATIONS

Black Box Warning

Vortioxetine has been associated with suicidal thinking and behavior in children, adolescents, and young adults.

Assessment & Drug Effects
- Report immediately to prescriber signs of worsening mental status

such as suicidal ideation, aggressiveness, agitation, anxiety, hostility, impulsivity, insomnia, irritability, panic attacks, and worsening of depression.
- Monitor for S&S of serotonin syndrome (see Appendix F). If serotonin syndrome is suspected withhold drug, notify prescriber and initiate supportive treatment.
- Monitor for and report promptly S&S of hyponatremia (see Appendix F) and any signs of abnormal bleeding.
- Monitor lab tests: Baseline LFTs and periodic serum sodium.

Patient & Family Education
- Report promptly to prescribe suicidal ideation or behavior, aggressive or impulsive behavior, worsening depression or anxiety, mania or unusual changes in behavior or mood.
- Do not take OTC supplements such as tryptophan or St. John's wort without consulting prescriber.
- Inform prescriber if you are taking OTC nonsteroidal anti-inflammatory drugs (NSAIDs) or aspirin for pain relief.
- Report promptly any of the following: S&S of serotonin syndrome (see Appendix F); abnormal bleeding; S&S of low serum sodium (see hyponatremia Appendix F).
- Notify prescriber immediately if you are or suspect you are pregnant.
- Do not breast-feed while taking this drug.

VOXELOTOR
(vox-el-oh-tor)

Oxbryta
Classifications: HEMOGLOBIN S (HBS) POLYMERIZATION INHIBITOR
Therapeutic: HEMOGLOBINS (HbS) POLYMERIZATION INHIBITOR

V

AVAILABILITY Oral tablet

ACTION & THERAPEUTIC EFFECT
An HbS polymerization inhibitor that reversibly binds to Hb and stabilizes the oxygenated Hb state. *Used to inhibit RBC sickling, improve RBC deformability, and reduce whole blood; may also extend RBC half-life and reduce anemia and hemolysis.*

USES Treatment of sickle cell disease in adults and pediatric patients older than 12 years old.

CONTRAINDICATIONS Hypersensitivity to voxelotor or any component of the formulation.

CAUTIOUS USE Hepatic impairment; pregnancy (no adverse effects observed in animal reproduction studies); lactation.

ROUTE & DOSAGE

Sickle Cell Disease
Adult: **PO** 1,500 mg once daily
Hepatic Impairment Dosage Adjustment
Severe impairment (Child-Pugh class C): **PO** 1,000 mg once daily

ADMINISTRATION
Oral
- Can be given with or without food.
- Swallow tablets whole; do not cut, crush, or chew tablets.
- Store at ≤30° C (86° F).

ADVERSE EFFECTS CNS: Headache, fatigue. **Skin:** Rash. **GI:** Diarrhea, abdominal pain, nausea. **Other:** Fever, hypersensitivity reaction.

INTERACTIONS Drug: Coadministration with potent inhibitors of CYP3A4 (e.g., **ketoconazole, fluconazole**) may increase the levels of voxelotor, increasing risk of toxicity; dose should be adjusted to 1,000 mg when interaction unavoidable. Coadministration with potent or moderate CYP3A4 inducers (e.g. **phenobarbital, phenytoin, rifampin**) may decrease the levels of voxelotor, dose should be adjusted to 2,500 mg when interaction unavoidable.

PHARMACOKINETICS Absorption: Plasma Cmax and AUC increased by 42% and 95% respectively, when administered with high-fat, high-calorie meal. **Peak:** 2 h. **Distribution:** 388 L, 99% protein-bound. **Metabolism:** In the liver, primarily through CYP3A4 oxidation (major). **Elimination:** 36% in urine, 63% in feces. **Half-Life:** 35.5 h

NURSING IMPLICATIONS

Assessment & Drug Effects
- Assess for signs/symptoms of hypersensitivity reaction.
- Monitor lab tests: Liver function tests.

Patient & Family Education
- Notify your doctor or get medical help right away if you have any of the following signs or symptoms of allergic reaction such as rash, hives, itching; red, swollen, blistered, or peeling skin with or without fever; wheezing; tightness in the chest or throat; trouble breathing, swallowing, or talking; unusual hoarsenses; or swelling of the mouth, face, lips, tongue, or throat; or any dizziness or passing out.

WARFARIN SODIUM

(war'far-in)

Coumadin, Jantoven, Warfilone ✦

Classification: ANTICOAGULANT
Therapeutic: ANTICOAGULANT

AVAILABILITY Tablet

ACTION & *THERAPEUTIC EFFECT*

Indirectly interferes with blood clotting by depressing hepatic synthesis of vitamin K-dependent coagulation factors: II, VII, IX, and X. *Deters further extension of existing thrombi and prevents new clots from forming.*

USES Prophylaxis and treatment of deep vein thrombosis and its extension, pulmonary embolism; treatment of atrial fibrillation with embolization. Also used as adjunct in treatment of coronary occlusion, cerebral transient ischemic attacks (TIAs), and as a prophylactic in patients with prosthetic cardiac valves; reduce the risk of death, recurrent MI, and thromboembolic events, post MI.

CONTRAINDICATIONS Hemorrhagic tendencies, hemophilia, coagulation factor deficiencies, dyscrasias; active bleeding; open wounds, active peptic ulcer, visceral carcinoma, esophageal varices, malabsorption syndrome; uncontrolled hypertension, cerebral vascular disease; heparin-induced thrombocytopenia (HIT); pericarditis; severe hepatic or renal disease; continuous tube drainage of any orifice; subacute bacterial endocarditis; recent surgery of brain, spinal cord, or eye; regional or lumbar block anesthesia; threatened abortion; unreliable patients; pregnancy (category X).

CAUTIOUS USE Alcoholism, allergic disorders, during menstruation, senility, psychosis; debilitated patients; CVD; renal impairment; hepatic impairment. Endogenous factors that may increase prothrombin time response (enhance anticoagulant effect): Carcinoma, CHF, collagen diseases, hepatic and renal insufficiency, diarrhea, fever, pancreatic disorders, malnutrition, vitamin K deficiency. Endogenous factors that may decrease prothrombin time response (decrease anticoagulant response): Edema, hypothyroidism, hyperlipidemia, hypercholesterolemia, chronic alcoholism, hereditary resistance to coumarin therapy; older adults; children.

ROUTE & DOSAGE

Anticoagulant

Adult: **PO** Usual dose 2–5 mg daily with dose adjusted to maintain a PT 1.2–2 × control or INR of 2–3 (target varies per disease state)

Pharmacogenetic Dosage Adjustment

Variations in CYP2C9 or VKORC1 may require dose adjustments (see package insert for tables)

ADMINISTRATION

Note: Antidote for bleeding—anticoagulant effect usually is reversed by omitting 1 or more doses of warfarin and by administration of specific antidote phytonadione (vitamin K_1) 2.5–10 mg orally. Prescriber may advise patient to carry vitamin K_1 at all times, but not to take it until after consultation. If bleeding persists or progresses to a severe level, vitamin K 10 mg IV is given, or a fresh whole blood transfusion may be necessary.

W

Oral

- Give tablet whole or crushed with fluid of patient's choice.

ADVERSE EFFECTS GI: Anorexia, nausea, vomiting, abdominal cramps, diarrhea, steatorrhea, stomatitis. **Other:** Major or minor hemorrhage from any tissue or organ; hypersensitivity (dermatitis, urticaria, pruritus, fever). Increased serum transaminase levels, hepatitis, jaundice, burning sensation of feet, transient hair loss, internal or external bleeding, paralytic ileus; skin necrosis of toes (purple toes syndrome), tip of nose, buttocks, thighs, calves, female breast, abdomen, and other fat-rich areas.

DIAGNOSTIC TEST INTERFERENCE Warfarin (coumarins) may cause alkaline urine to be red-orange; may enhance *uric acid* excretion, cause elevation of *serum transaminases*, and may increase *lactic dehydrogenase* activity.

INTERACTIONS Drug: In addition to the drugs listed below, many other drugs have been reported to alter the expected response to warfarin; however, clinical importance of these reports has not been substantiated. The addition or withdrawal of any drug to an established drug regimen should be made cautiously, with more frequent *INR* determinations than usual and with careful observation of the patient and dose adjustment as indicated. The following may enhance the anticoagulant effects of warfarin: **Acetohexamide, acetaminophen**, ALKYLATING AGENTS, **allopurinol**, AMINOGLYCOSIDES, **aminosalicylic acid, amiodarone**, ANABOLIC STEROIDS, ANTIBIOTICS (ORAL), ANTIMETABOLITES, ANTIPLATELET DRUGS, **aspirin, asparaginase,** **capecitabine, celecoxib, chloramphenicol, chlorpropamide, chymotrypsin, cimetidine, clofibrate, cotrimoxazole, danazol, dextran, dextrothyroxine, diazoxide, disulfiram, erythromycin, ethacrynic acid, fluconazole, glucagons, guanethidine**, HEPATOTOXIC DRUGS, **influenza vaccine, isoniazid, itraconazole, ketoconazole**, MAO INHIBITORS, **meclofenamate, mefenamic acid, methyldopa, methylphenidate, metronidazole, miconazole, mineral oil, nalidixic acid, neomycin (oral)**, NONSTEROIDAL ANTI-INFLAMMATORY DRUGS, **oxandrolone, plicamycin**, POTASSIUM PRODUCTS, **propoxyphene, propylthiouracil, quinidine, quinine, rofecoxib, salicylates, streptokinase, sulindac**, SULFONAMIDES, SULFONYLUREAS, TETRACYCLINES, THIAZIDES, THYROID DRUGS, **tolbutamide**, TRICYCLIC ANTIDEPRESSANTS, **urokinase, vitamin E, zileuton**. The following may increase or decrease the anticoagulant effects of warfarin: **Alcohol** (acute intoxication may increase, chronic alcoholism may decrease effects), DIURETICS. The following may decrease the anticoagulant effects of warfarin: BARBITURATES, **carbamazepine, cholestyramine**, CORTICOSTEROIDS, **corticotropin, glutethimide, griseofulvin**, LAXATIVES, **mercaptopurine**, ORAL CONTRACEPTIVES, **rifampin, spironolactone, vitamin C, vitamin K. Herbal:** Boldo, capsicum, celery, chamomile, chondroitin, clove, coenzyme Q10, danshen, devil's claw, dong quai, echinacea, evening primrose oil, fenugreek, feverfew, fish oil, garlic, ginger, ginkgo, glucosamine, horse chestnut, licorice root, passionflower herb, turmeric, willow bark may increase risk of bleeding;

W

ginseng, green tea, seaweed, soy, St. John's wort may decrease effectiveness of warfarin. **Food: Cranberry juice** may increase **INR. Green leafy vegetables** may affect efficacy. **Avocado** may decrease effectiveness of warfarin.

PHARMACOKINETICS Absorption: Well absorbed from GI tract. **Onset:** 2–7 days. **Peak:** 0.5–3 days. **Distribution:** 97% protein bound; crosses placenta. **Metabolism:** In liver (CYP2C9). **Elimination:** In urine and bile. **Half-Life:** 0.5–3 days.

NURSING IMPLICATIONS

Black Box Warning

Warfarin has been associated with serious, sometimes fatal, bleeding events.

Assessment & Drug Effects

- Determine INP prior to initiation of therapy and then daily until maintenance dosage is established.
- Obtain a COMPLETE medication history prior to start of therapy and whenever altered responses to therapy require interpretation; extremely IMPORTANT since many drugs interfere with the activity of anticoagulant drugs (see INTERACTIONS).
- Dose is typically adjusted to maintain an INR of 2–4 depending on diagnosis.
- Note: Patients at greatest risk of hemorrhage include those whose INR is difficult to regulate, who have an aortic valve prosthesis, who are receiving long-term anticoagulant therapy, and older adult and debilitated patients.
- Monitor lab tests: INR prior to initiation of therapy and then daily until maintenance dosage

is established. For maintenance dosage, INR determinations at 1–4-wk intervals depending on patient's response; periodic urinalyses, stool guaiac, and LFTs.

Patient & Family Education

- Understand that bleeding can occur even though INR are within therapeutic range. Stop drug and notify prescriber immediately if bleeding or signs of bleeding appear: Blood in urine, bright red or black tarry stools, vomiting of blood, bleeding with tooth brushing, blue or purple spots on skin or mucous membrane, round pinpoint purplish red spots (often occur in ankle areas), nosebleed, bloody sputum; chest pain; abdominal or lumbar pain or swelling, profuse menstrual bleeding, pelvic pain; severe or continuous headache, faintness or dizziness; prolonged oozing from any minor injury (e.g., nicks from shaving).
- Stop drug and report immediately any symptoms of hepatitis (dark urine, itchy skin, jaundice, abdominal pain, light stools) or hypersensitivity reaction (see Appendix F).
- Take drug at same time each day, and **do not** alter dose.
- Risk of bleeding is increased for up to 1 mo after receiving the influenza vaccine.
- Fever, prolonged hot weather, malnutrition, and diarrhea lengthen INR (enhanced anticoagulant effect).
- A high-fat diet, sudden increase in vitamin K–rich foods (cabbage, cauliflower, broccoli, asparagus, lettuce, turnip greens, onions, spinach, kale, fish, liver), coffee or green tea (caffeine), or by tube feedings with high vitamin K content shorten INR.
- Avoid excess intake of alcohol.

W

- Use a soft toothbrush and floss teeth gently with waxed floss.
- Use barrier contraceptive measures; if you become pregnant while on anticoagulant therapy the fetus is at great potential risk of congenital malformations.
- Do not take any other prescription or OTC drug unless specifically approved by prescriber or pharmacist.

XYLOMETAZOLINE HYDROCHLORIDE

(zye-loe-met-az'oh-leen)

Otrivin

Classification: NASAL DECONGESTANT; VASOCONSTRICTOR

Therapeutic: NASAL DECONGESTANT

Prototype: Naphazoline

AVAILABILITY Nasal solution

ACTION & *THERAPEUTIC EFFECT*
Markedly constricts dilated arterioles of nasal membrane. *Decreases fluid exudate and mucosal engorgement associated with rhinitis and may open up obstructed eustachian tubes.*

USES Temporary relief of nasal congestion associated with common cold, sinusitis, acute and chronic rhinitis, and hay fever and other allergies.

CONTRAINDICATIONS Sensitivity to adrenergic substances; angle-closure glaucoma; concurrent therapy with MAO inhibitors or tricyclic antidepressants; pregnancy (category C); lactation.

CAUTIOUS USE Hypertension; hyperthyroidism; heart disease, including angina; advanced

arteriosclerosis, older adults, pregnancy (category C); children younger than 2 y and infants.

ROUTE & DOSAGE

Nasal Congestion

Adult/Child (12 y or older):
Nasal 1–2 sprays or 1–2 drops of 0.1% solution in each nostril q8–10h (max: 3 doses/day)
Child (2 –12 y): **Nasal** 1 spray or 2–3 drops of 0.05% solution in each nostril q8–10h (max: 3 doses/day)

ADMINISTRATION

Instillation

- Have patient clear each nostril gently before administering spray or drops.
- Store at 15°–30° C (59°–86° F) in a tight, light-resistant container.

ADVERSE EFFECTS With Excessive Use: *Rebound nasal congestion* and vasodilation, tremulousness, hypertension, palpitations, tachycardia, arrhythmia, somnolence, sedation, coma. **Other:** Usually mild and infrequent; local stinging, burning, dryness and ulceration, sneezing, headache, insomnia, drowsiness.

INTERACTIONS Drug: May cause increase BP with **guanethidine, methyldopa,** MAO INHIBITORS; PHENOTHIAZINES may decrease effectiveness of nasal decongestant.

PHARMACOKINETICS Onset: 5–10 min. **Duration:** 5–6 h.

NURSING IMPLICATIONS

Assessment & Drug Effects

- Evaluate for development of rebound congestion (see ADVERSE EFFECTS).

X

Common adverse effects in *italic;* life-threatening effects <u>underlined</u>; generic names in **bold;** classifications in SMALL CAPS; ◆ Canadian drug name; ☉ Prototype drug; ⚠ Alert

Patient & Family Education

- Prevent contamination of nasal solution and spread of infection by rinsing dropper and tip of nasal spray in hot water after each use; restrict use to the individual patient.
- Note: Prolonged use can cause rebound congestion and chemical rhinitis. **Do not** exceed prescribed dosage and report to prescriber if drug fails to provide relief within 3–4 days.
- **Do not** self-medicate with OTC drugs, sprays, or drops without prescriber's approval.
- Note: Excessive use by a child may lead to CNS depression.

ZAFIRLUKAST ⊙

(za-fir-lu'kast)

Accolate

Classification: RESPIRATORY SMOOTH MUSCLE RELAXANT; LEUKOTRIENE RECEPTOR ANTAGONIST (LTRA); BRONCHODILATOR

Therapeutic: BRONCHODILATOR; LTRA

AVAILABILITY Tablet

ACTION & *THERAPEUTIC EFFECT*

Selective leukotriene receptor antagonist (LTRA) that inhibits binding of leukotriene D_4 and E_4, thus inhibiting inflammation and bronchoconstriction. Leukotriene production and receptor affinity have been correlated with the pathogenesis of asthma. *Zafirlukast helps to prevent the signs and symptoms of asthma, including airway edema, smooth muscle constriction, and altered cellular activity due to inflammation.*

USES Prophylaxis and chronic treatment of asthma in adults and children older than 5 y (not for acute bronchospasm).

UNLABELED USES Chronic urticaria.

CONTRAINDICATIONS Hypersensitivity to zafirlukast; acute asthma attacks, including status asthmaticus, acute bronchospasm; hepatic impairment including cirrhosis; lactation.

CAUTIOUS USE Patients 65 y or older, pregnancy (category B); children younger than 5 y.

ROUTE & DOSAGE

Asthma

Adult/Child (12 y or older): **PO** 20 mg bid
Child (5 y or older): **PO** 10 mg bid

ADMINISTRATION

Oral

- Give 1 h before or 2 h after meals.
- Store at 20°–25° C (68°–77° F); protect from light and moisture.

ADVERSE EFFECTS CNS: Headache, dizziness.

INTERACTIONS Drug: May increase *prothrombin time (PT)* in patients on **warfarin. Erythromycin** decreases bioavailability of zafirlukast. Avoid use with CYP2C8 inhibitors and strong CYP2C9 inhibitors/inducers. Do not use with **loxapine**.

PHARMACOKINETICS Absorption: Rapidly from GI tract, bioavailability significantly reduced by food. **Onset:** 1 wk. **Peak:** 3 h. **Distribution:** Greater than 99% protein bound; secreted into breast milk. **Metabolism:** In liver (CYP2C9). **Elimination:** 90% in feces, 10% in urine. **Half-Life:** 10 h.

NURSING IMPLICATIONS

Assessment & Drug Effects

- Assess respiratory status and airway function regularly.

Common adverse effects in *italic;* life-threatening effects underlined; generic names in **bold;** classifications in SMALL CAPS; ♣ Canadian drug name; ⊙ Prototype drug; ⚠ Alert

Z 1787

- Monitor closely phenytoin level with concurrent phenytoin therapy.
- Monitor lab tests: Periodic LFTs, and INR with concurrent warfarin therapy.

Patient & Family Education

- Taking medication regularly, even during symptom-free periods.
- Note: Drug is not intended to treat acute episodes of asthma.
- Report S&S of hepatic toxicity (see Appendix F) or flu-like symptoms to prescriber. Follow-up lab work is very important.
- Notify prescriber immediately if condition worsens while using prescribed doses of all antiasthmatic medications.

ZALEPLON

(zal′ep-lon)
Sonata
Classification: SEDATIVE-HYPNOTIC; NONBARBITUATE
Therapeutic: SEDATIVE-HYPNOTIC
Prototype: Zolpidem
Controlled Substance: Schedule IV

AVAILABILITY Capsule

ACTION & *THERAPEUTIC EFFECT*
Short-acting nonbenzodiazepine with sedative-hypnotic, muscle relaxant. *Reduces difficulty in initially falling asleep. Preserves deep sleep (stages 3 through 4) at hypnotic dose with minimal-to-absent rebound insomnia when discontinued.*

USES Short-term treatment of insomnia.

CONTRAINDICATIONS Hypersensitivity to zaleplon, or tartrazine dye (Yellow 5); severe hepatic impairment; suicidal ideation.

CAUTIOUS USE Hypersensitivity to salicylates; chronic depression;

history of suicidal thoughts; history of drug abuse; COPD; respiratory insufficiency; hepatic impairment; pulmonary disease; older adults; pregnancy (category C); lactation. Safe use in children not established.

ROUTE & DOSAGE

Insomnia

Adult: **PO** 10 mg at bedtime (max: 20 mg at bedtime)
Geriatric: **PO** 5 mg at bedtime (max: 10 mg at bedtime)

ADMINISTRATION

Oral

- Give immediately before bedtime; not while patient is still ambulating.
- Ensure that extended release tablets are swallowed whole and are not crushed or chewed.
- Sublingual tablets should not be given with water and should not be swallowed.
- Oral spray container must be primed before first use. Ensure that a full dose (5 mg) is sprayed directly into the mouth over the tongue. For a 10 mg dose, administer a second spray.
- Store at 20°–25° C (68°–77° F).

ADVERSE EFFECTS Respiratory:
Bronchitis. **CNS:** Amnesia, dizziness, paresthesia, somnolence, tremor, vertigo, depression, hypertonia, nervousness, difficulty concentrating. **HEENT:** Eye pain, hyperacusis, conjunctivitis. **Skin:** Pruritus, rash. **GI:** Abdominal pain, dyspepsia, nausea, constipation, dry mouth. **GU:** Dysmenorrhea. **Other:** Asthenia, fever, *headache*, migraine, myalgia, back pain.

INTERACTIONS Drug: Alcohol, imipramine, thioridazine,

Common adverse effects in *italic*; life-threatening effects underlined; generic names in **bold;** classifications in SMALL CAPS; ♣ Canadian drug name; ◑ Prototype drug; ⚠ Alert

Z

1788

topiramate, BARBITURATES, may cause additive CNS impairment; **rifampin** increases metabolism of **zaleplon**; **cimetidine** increases serum levels of **zaleplon**. Do not use with **sodium oxybate**. **Herbal: Valerian, melatonin** may produce additive sedative effects. **Food: High-fat meals** may delay absorption.

PHARMACOKINETICS Absorption: Rapidly and completely absorbed, 30% reaches systemic circulation. **Onset:** 15–20 min. **Peak:** 1 h. **Duration:** 3–4 h. **Distribution:** 60% protein bound. **Metabolism:** Extensively in liver (CYP3A4) to inactive metabolites. **Elimination:** 70% in urine, 17% in feces. **Half-Life:** 1 h.

NURSING IMPLICATIONS

Assessment & Drug Effects

- Monitor behavior and notify prescriber for significant changes. Use extra caution with preexisting clinical depression.
- Provide safe environment and monitor ambulation after drug is ingested.
- Monitor respiratory status with preexisting compromised pulmonary function.

Patient & Family Education

- Exercise caution when walking; avoid all hazardous activities after taking zaleplon.
- Do not take in combination with alcohol or any other sleep medication.
- Note: Exhibits altered effectiveness if taken with/immediately after high-fat meal.
- Do not use longer than 2–3 wk.
- Expect possible mild/brief rebound insomnia after discontinuing regimen.
- Report use of OTC medications to prescriber (e.g., cimetidine).
- Report pregnancy to prescriber immediately.

ZANAMIVIR

(zan′a-mi-vir)

Relenza

Classification: ANTIVIRAL; NEURAMINIDASE INHIBITOR
Therapeutic: ANTIINFLUENZA
Prototype: Oseltamivir

AVAILABILITY Powder for inhalation

ACTION & THERAPEUTIC EFFECT

Inhibitor of influenza A and B viral enzyme; does not permit the release of newly formed viruses from the surface of the infected cells. *Prevents viral spread across the mucus lining of the respiratory tract, and inhibits the replication of influenza A and B virus. Relieves flu-like symptoms.*

USES Treatment of uncomplicated acute influenza in patients symptomatic less than 2 days; prophylaxis for influenza.

CONTRAINDICATIONS Hypersensitivity to zanamivir or milk protein; severe renal impairment, renal failure; COPD; severe asthma.

CAUTIOUS USE Renal impairment; cardiac disease; severe metabolic disease; older adults; pregnancy (an increased risk of adverse neonatal or maternal outcomes has not been observed following use of zanamivir during pregnancy); lactation. **Acute influenza:** Safety and efficacy in children younger than 7 y not established. **Influenza prophylaxis:** Safe use in children younger than 5 y not established.

ROUTE & DOSAGE

Influenza Treatment

Adult/Child (7 y or older):
Inhaled 2 inhalations (one 5 mg blister/inhalation) bid × 5 days

---

Influenza Prophylaxis

Adult/Child (5 y or older):
Inhaled 2 inhalations daily for 10 days (household prophylaxis) or for 28 days (community outbreak)

ADMINISTRATION

Inhalation

- Most effective if initiated within 48 h of onset of flu-like symptoms. Administer at approximately the same time each day (with the exception of the first dose).
- Give any scheduled inhaled bronchodilator before zanamivir.
- Store at 25° C (77° F).

ADVERSE EFFECTS Respiratory:
Nasal symptoms, bronchitis, cough, sinusitis. **CNS:** Dizziness. **Skin:** Urticaria. **GI:** Abdominal pain.

INTERACTIONS Drug: Do not use
with LIVE VACCINES.

PHARMACOKINETICS Absorption: 4–17% of inhaled dose is systemically absorbed. **Peak:** 1–2 h. **Distribution:** Less than 10% protein bound. **Metabolism:** Not metabolized. **Elimination:** In urine. **Half-Life:** 2.5–5.1 h.

NURSING IMPLICATIONS

Patient & Family Education

- Start within 48 h of onset of flu-like symptoms for most effective response.
- Use any scheduled inhaled bronchodilator first; then use zanamivir.
- Monitor for any change in behaviour.

ZICONOTIDE

(zi-con'o-tide)

Prialt
Classification: MISCELLANEOUS ANALGESIC; N-TYPE CALCIUM CHANNEL ANTAGONIST
Therapeutic: MISCELLANEOUS ANALGESIC

AVAILABILITY Solution for injection

ACTION & *THERAPEUTIC EFFECT*
Ziconotide binds to N-type calcium channels located on the afferent nerves in the dorsal horn in the spinal cord. It is thought that these binding blocks of N-type calcium channels lead to a blockade of excitatory neurotransmitter release in the afferent nerve endings. *Ziconotide is effective in controlling severe chronic pain that is intractable to other analgesics.*

USES Management of severe chronic pain in patients for whom intrathecal (IT) therapy is warranted.

CONTRAINDICATIONS Hypersensitivity to ziconotide; preexisting history of psychosis; epidural or intravenous administration; sepsis; depression with suicidal ideation; cognitive impairment; bipolar disorder; schizophrenia; dementia; presence of infection at the injection site, uncontrolled bleeding, or spinal canal obstruction that impairs circulation of CSF; coagulopathy; seizures; lactation.

CAUTIOUS USE Renal, hepatic, and cardiac impairment; older adults; pregnancy (adverse events and maternal toxicity were observed in animal reproduction studies). Safe use in children and infants not established.

ROUTE & DOSAGE

Severe Chronic Pain

Adult: **Intrathecal** Initial dose up to 0.1 mcg/h; may titrate up 0.1 mcg/h q2–3days to 0.8 mcg/h (19.2 mcg/day)

ADMINISTRATION

Intrathecal

- May be administered undiluted (25 mcg/mL in 20 mL vial) or diluted using the 100 mcg/mL vials. Diluted ziconotide is prepared with NS without preservatives.
- Administer using an implanted variable-rate microinfusion device or an external microinfusion device and catheter.
- Note: Due to serious adverse events, 19.2 mcg/day (0.8 mcg/h) is the maximum recommended dose.
- Doses should normally be titrated upward by no more than 2.4 mcg/day (0.1 mcg/h) at intervals of 2–3 × wk.
- Refrigerate all ziconotide solutions after preparation and begin infusion within 24 h. Discard any unused portion left in a vial.

ADVERSE EFFECTS CV: Hypotension, orthostatic hypotension, peripheral edema. **Respiratory:** Sinusitis. **CNS:** *Dizziness*, confusion, memory impairment, drowsiness abnormal gait, ataxia, speech disorder, headache, aphasia, hallucination, abnormal thinking, amnesia, anxiety, dysarthria, paresthesia, rigors, vertigo, insomnia. **HEENT:** Blurred vision, nystagmus. **Skin:** Pruritis, diaphoresis. **GI:** *Nausea*, vomiting, diarrhea, anorexia, dysgeusia. **GU:.** Urinary retention. **Musculoskeletal:** *Increased CPK*, weakness, tremor, muscle spasm, limb pain. **Hematologic:** Anemia, ecchymosis. **Other:** Fever.

INTERACTIONS Drug: **Ethanol** and other CNS DEPRESSANTS may increase drowsiness, dizziness, and confusion.

PHARMACOKINETICS Distribution: 50% protein bound. **Metabolism:** Hydrolyzed by peptidases. **Half-Life:** 4.6 h.

NURSING IMPLICATIONS

Black Box Warning

Ziconotide has been associated with severe psychiatric symptoms and neurologic impairment.

Assessment & Drug Effects

- Monitor for and report S&S of meningitis, cognitive impairment, hallucinations, changes in mood or consciousness, or other psychiatric symptoms.
- Monitor lab values: Serum CPK (every other week for first month then monthly).

Patient & Family Education

- Report any of the following to prescriber: Muscle pain, soreness, or weakness, confusion, unusual behavior, symptoms of depression or suicidal thoughts, fever, headache, stiff neck, nausea or vomiting, seizures.
- Note: Taking this drug with other depressants (e.g., alcohol, sedatives, tranquilizers) will increase the risk of side effects.

ZIDOVUDINE (ZDV) (FORMERLY AZIDOTHYMIDINE, AZT)

(zye-doe'vyoo-deen)

Retrovir

Classification: ANTIVIRAL; NUCLEOSIDE REVERSE TRANSCRIPTASE INHIBITOR

Therapeutic: ANTIVIRAL; NRTI

Prototype: Lamivudine

Common adverse effects in *italic;* life-threatening effects underlined; generic names in **bold;** classifications in SMALL CAPS; ◆ Canadian drug name; ○ Prototype drug; △ Alert 1791

Z

AVAILABILITY Tablet; capsule; syrup; solution for injection

ACTION & *THERAPEUTIC EFFECT* A thymidine analog which interferes with the HIV viral RNA-dependent DNA polymerase resulting in inhibition of viral replication. *Zidovudine has antiviral action against HIV, LAV (lymphadenopathy-associated virus), and ARV (AIDS-associated retrovirus).*

USES Treatment of HIV (along with other antiretroviral agents), prevention of perinatal transfer of HIV during pregnancy.

UNLABELED USES Postexposure chemoprophylaxis, thrombocytopenia.

CONTRAINDICATIONS Life-threatening allergic reactions to any of the components of the drug; drug induced lactic acidosis; pronounced hepatotoxicity; lactation.

CAUTIOUS USE Severe renal impairment; or impaired hepatic function, alcoholism; anemia; chemotherapy; radiation therapy; bone marrow depression; older adults; pregnancy (high level of transfer across the placenta; in general, ART is recommended for pregnant females living with HIV); children.

ROUTE & DOSAGE

HIV Infection

Adult/Adolescent/Child (weight 30 kg or greater): **PO** 300 mg bid; **IV** 1 mg/kg given q4h around the clock *Adolescent/Child/Infant (older than 4 wk, weight 9–30 kg):* 9 mg/kg/dose bid; *weight less than 9 kg:* 12 mg/kg/dose bid

Prevention of Maternal-Fetal Transmission

Maternal: **IV** (preferred route) During labor, 2 mg/kg loading dose, then 1 mg/kg/h until clamping umbilical cord

Toxicity Dosage Adjustment

Hemoglobin falls below 7.5 g/dL or falls 25% from baseline: Interrupt therapy. *ANC falls below 750 cells/mm³ or decreases 50% from baseline:* Interrupt therapy.

Renal Impairment Adjustment (Adult)

CrCl less than 15 mL/min: 100 mg tid (oral) or 1 mg/kg q6–8h (IV)

ADMINISTRATION

Oral

- May be given with or without food.

Intravenous

PREPARE: **Intermittent:** Withdraw required dose from vial and dilute with D5W to a concentration not to exceed 4 mg/mL.
ADMINISTER: **Intermittent for HIV infection:** Give calculated dose at a constant rate over 60 min; avoid rapid infusion or bolus injection. **IV Infusions for Prevention of Maternal-Fetal Transmission:** Give maternal loading dose over 1 h, then continuous infusion at 1 mg/kg/h. **Intermittent Infusion for Prevention of Maternal Transmission of HIV to Neonate:** Give calculated dose at a constant rate over 30 min.
INCOMPATIBILITIES: Y-site: **Dexrazoxane, gemtuzumab, lansoprazole.**

- Store at 15°–25° C (59°–77° F) and protect from light. Store diluted IV solutions refrigerated for 24 h.

ADVERSE EFFECTS Cardiac: Cardiac failure, ECG abnormality, edema, left ventricular dilation. **Respiratory:** *Cough, wheezing,* nasal congestion, rhinorrhea, abnormal breath sounds. **CNS:** *Headache,* insomnia, anxiety, restlessness, agitation, hyporeflexia, irritability, nervousness, chills, fatigue, neuropathy. **Endocrine:** Lactic acidosis, weight loss, increased amylase. **Skin:** *Rash,* itching, diaphoresis. **Hepatic/GI:** *Nausea,* diarrhea, *vomiting, anorexia,* GI pain, constipation, stomatitis, abdominal pain/cramps, dyspepsia, hepatomegaly, elevated liver enzymes. **GU:** Hematuria. **Hematologic:** Bone marrow depression, granulocytopenia, anemia, macrocytosis, lymphadenopathy, neutropenia, splenomegaly, thrombocytopenia. **Musculoskeletal:** Asthenia, arthralgia, musculoskeletal, myalgia. **Other:** *Fever,* injection site reaction.

INTERACTIONS Drug: Acetaminophen, ganciclovir, interferon-alfa may enhance bone marrow suppression; **aspirin, dapsone, doxorubicin, fluconazole, flucytosine, methadone, pentamidine, vincristine, valproic acid** may increase risk of **AZT** toxicity; **probenecid** will decrease **AZT** elimination, resulting in increased serum levels and thus toxicity. **Nelfinavir, rifampin, ritonavir** may decrease zidovudine (**AZT**) concentrations; other ANTIRETROVIRAL AGENTS may cause lactic acidosis and severe hepatomegaly with steatosis; **stavudine, doxorubicin** may antagonize **AZT** effects. Do not administer LIVE VACCINES; use with MYELOSUPPRESSIVE AGENTS may have additive adverse effects.

PHARMACOKINETICS Absorption: Readily from GI tract; 60–70% reaches systemic circulation (first-pass metabolism). **Peak:** 0.5–1.5 h. **Distribution:** Crosses blood–brain barrier and placenta. **Metabolism:** In liver. **Elimination:** 63–95% in urine. **Half-Life:** 1 h.

NURSING IMPLICATIONS

Black Box Warning

Zidovudine has been associated with hematologic toxicity (including neutropenia and severe anemia), myopathy, lactic acidosis, and severe hepatomegaly with steatosis.

Assessment & Drug Effects

- Evaluate patient at least weekly during the first month of therapy.
- Myelosuppression results in anemia, which commonly occurs after 4–6 wk of therapy, and granulocytopenia in 6–8 wk.
- Monitor for common adverse effects, especially severe headache, nausea, insomnia, and myalgia.
- Monitor lab tests: Baseline and periodic CBC with differential; LFTs; serum creatinine; HIV viral load and CD4 count.

Patient & Family Education

- Contact prescriber promptly if health status worsens or any unusual symptoms develop.
- Report to prescriber any of the following: Muscle weakness, shortness of breath, symptoms of hepatitis or pancreatitis, or any other unexpected adverse reaction.
- Understand that this drug is not a cure for HIV infection; you will continue to be at risk for opportunistic infections.
- Do not share drug with others; take drug exactly as prescribed.
- Drug does **not** reduce the risk of transmission of HIV infection through body fluids.

ZILEUTON
(zi-leu'ton)
Zyflo, Zyflo CR
Classification: RESPIRATORY
SMOOTH MUSCLE RELAXANT; BRON-
CHODILATOR; LEUKOTRIENE RECEPTOR
ANTAGONIST (LTRA)
Therapeutic: BRONCHODILATOR; LTRA
Prototype: Zafirlukast

AVAILABILITY Immediate release
tablet; controlled release tablet

ACTION & *THERAPEUTIC EFFECT*
Inhibits 5-lipoxygenase, the enzyme
needed to start the conversion of
arachidonic acid to leukotrienes,
which are important inflammatory
agents that induce bronchoconstriction and mucus production.
*Zileuton helps to prevent the signs
and symptoms of asthma including airway edema, smooth muscle
constriction, and altered cellular
activity due to inflammation.*

USES Prophylaxis and chronic
treatment of asthma in adults and
children older than 12 y.

CONTRAINDICATIONS Hypersensitivity to zileuton or zafirlukast,
active liver disease, status asthmaticus; QT prolongation; lactation.

CAUTIOUS USE Hepatic insufficiency; alcoholism; fever; infection;
history of QT prolongation; older
females; older adults; pregnancy (category C). Safety and efficacy in children
younger than 12 y not established.

ROUTE & DOSAGE

Asthma

Adult/Child (12 y or older): **PO**
Controlled release 1200 mg bid
OR **Immediate release** 600 mg qid

ADMINISTRATION
Oral
- Ensure that controlled release tablets are swallowed whole. Do not
crush or chew.
- Give without regard to meals.
- Store at room temperature, 15°–
30° C (59°–86° F); protect from
light.

ADVERSE EFFECTS CV: Chest
pain. **Respiratory:** Upper respiratory tract infection, sinusitis. **CNS:**
Headache, pain.

INTERACTIONS Drug: May double
theophylline levels and increase
toxicity. Increases hypoprothrombinemic effects of **warfarin**. May
increase levels of BETA-BLOCKERS
(especially **propranolol**), leading
to hypotension and bradycardia. Do
not use with **loxapine, pimozide**.

**PHARMACOKINETICS Absorp-
tion:** Rapidly from GI tract. **Peak:**
1.7 h. **Duration:** 5–8 h. **Distribution:**
93% protein bound; secreted in the
breast milk of rats. **Metabolism:**
In liver primarily via glucuronide
conjugation. Substrate of CYP1A2,
CYPD2C9, CYP3A4. **Elimination:**
Primarily in urine (94%). **Half-Life:**
2.5 h.

NURSING IMPLICATIONS
Assessment & Drug Effects
- Assess respiratory status and airway function regularly.
- Monitor closely each of the following with concurrent drug
therapy: With theophylline, theophylline levels; with warfarin,
PT and INR; with phenytoin,
phenytoin level; with propranolol, HR and BP for excessive beta
blockade.
- Monitor lab tests: Baseline and
periodic LFTs.

Patient & Family Education

- Take medication regularly even during symptom-free periods.
- Drug is not intended to treat acute episodes of asthma.
- Report to prescriber promptly S&S of hepatic toxicity (see Appendix F) or flu-like symptoms. Follow-up lab work is very important.
- Notify prescriber if condition worsens while using prescribed doses of all antiasthmatic medications.

ZIPRASIDONE HYDROCHLORIDE

(zip-ra-si'done)

Geodon

Classification: ATYPICAL ANTIPSYCHOTIC

Therapeutic: ANTIPSYCHOTIC

Prototype: Clozapine

AVAILABILITY Capsule; solution for injection

ACTION & *THERAPEUTIC EFFECT*
Exerts antischizophrenic effects through dopamine (D_2) and serotonin ($5-HT_{2A}$) receptor antagonism. Exerts antidepressant effects through $5-HT_{1A}$ agonism, $5-HT_{1D}$ antagonism, and serotonin/norepinephrine reuptake inhibition. *Improves signs and symptoms of schizophrenia, schizoaffective disorder, and psychotic depression.*

USES Treatment of schizophrenia, bipolar disorder, agitation associated with psychiatric disorder.

UNLABELED USES Psychosis associated with dementia, major depressive disorder.

CONTRAINDICATIONS Hypersensitivity to ziprasidone; history of QT prolongation including congenital long QT syndrome or with other drugs known to prolong the QT interval; recent MI or uncompensated heart failure; NMS; older adults with dementia-related psychosis; lactation.

CAUTIOUS USE History of seizures, CVA, dementia, Parkinson's disease, or Alzheimer disease; known cardiovascular disease, conduction abnormalities, cerebrovascular disease; hepatic impairment; seizure disorder, seizures; breast cancer; risk factors for elevated core body temperature; esophageal motility disorders and risk of aspiration pneumonia; schizophrenia; suicide potential; DM; pregnancy (antipsychotic use during third trimester of pregnancy may cause increased risk for abnormal muscle movements and/or withdrawal symptoms in newborns); children older than 7 y for use in Tourette's syndrome only. Safety and efficacy in children or adolescents (except for treatment of Tourette's syndrome) not established.

ROUTE & DOSAGE

Schizophrenia

Adult: **PO** Start with 20 mg bid with food, may increase slowly as needed (normal dose 40–80 mg bid)

Acute Episodes of Agitation/ Acute Psychosis

Adult: **IM** 10 mg q2h or 20 mg q4h up to max of 40 mg/day

Acute Mania/Bipolar Disorder

Adult: **PO** Start with 40 mg bid with food; may increase q2days up to 80 mg bid if needed

---

Common adverse effects in *italic;* life-threatening effects <u>underlined;</u> generic names in **bold;** classifications in SMALL CAPS; ✦ Canadian drug name; ◯ Prototype drug; ⚠ Alert

ADMINISTRATION

Oral
- Administer with a meal containing at least 500 calories.
- Store at 25° C (77° F).

Intramuscular
- Give deep IM into a large muscle.
- Store at 25° C (77° F).

ADVERSE EFFECTS CV: Orthostatic hypotension, prolonged QT_c interval. **Respiratory:** Rhinitis, respiratory tract infection. **CNS:** *Drowsiness*, dizziness, extrapyramidal effects, headache, anxiety, akathisia. **HEENT:** Visual disturbances. **Endocrine:** Weight gain. **Skin:** Rash. **GI:** *Nausea*, constipation, dyspepsia, diarrhea, dry mouth, vomiting. **Musculoskeletal:** Weakness, myalgia. **Other:** Pain at injection site.

INTERACTIONS Drug: Carbamazepine may decrease **ziprasidone** levels; **ketoconazole** may increase **ziprasidone** levels; increased risk of arrhythmias and heart block due to prolonged QT_c interval with agents that affect QT interval (ex ANTIARRHYTHMIC AGENTS, **amoxapine, arsenic trioxide, chlorpromazine, clarithromycin, citalopram, daunorubicin, diltiazem, dolasetron, doxorubicin, droperidol, erythromycin, halofantrine, indapamide, levomethadyl,** LOCAL ANESTHETICS, **maprotiline, mefloquine, mesoridazine, octreotide, pentamidine, pimozide, levofloxacin, moxifloxacin, sparfloxacin,** TRICYCLIC ANTIDEPRESSANTS, **tacrolimus, thioridazine, troleandomycin**); additive CNS depression with SEDATIVE-HYPNOTICS, ANXIOLYTICS, **ethanol,** OPIATE AGONISTS.

PHARMACOKINETICS Absorption: Well absorbed with 60% reaching systemic circulation. **Peak:** 6–8 h. **Metabolism:** In liver (CYP3A4). **Elimination:** Feces and urine. **Half-Life:** 7 h.

NURSING IMPLICATIONS

Black Box Warning

Ziprasidone has been associated with increased mortality in older adults with dementia-related psychosis.

Assessment & Drug Effects
- Monitor diabetics for loss of glycemic control.
- Monitor for S&S of torsade de pointes (e.g., dizziness, palpitations, syncope), tardive dyskinesia (see Appendix F) especially in older adult women and with prolonged therapy, and the appearance of an unexplained rash. Withhold drug and report to prescriber immediately if any of these develop.
- Monitor for signs and symptoms of suicidality.
- Monitor I&O ratio and pattern: Notify prescriber if diarrhea, vomiting or any other conditions develops which may cause electrolyte imbalance.
- Monitor BP lying, sitting, and standing. Report orthostatic hypotension to prescriber.
- Monitor cognitive status and take appropriate precautions.
- Monitor for loss of seizure control, especially with a history of seizures or dementia.
- Baseline and annual ocular examination.
- Monitor lab tests: Baseline and periodic CBC with differential; electrolytes; fasting blood glucose; lipid panel; LFTs.

Patient & Family Education
- Carefully monitor blood glucose levels if diabetic.
- Be aware that therapeutic effect may not be evident for several weeks.

Z

1796   Common adverse effects in *italic;* life-threatening effects underlined; generic names in **bold;** classifications in SMALL CAPS; ✦ Canadian drug name; ⚫ Prototype drug; ⚠ Alert

- Report any of the following to a health care provider immediately: Palpitations, faintness or loss of consciousness, rash, abnormal muscle movements, vomiting or diarrhea.
- Do not drive or engage in potentially hazardous activities until response to drug is known.
- Make position changes slowly and in stages to prevent dizziness upon arising.
- Avoid strenuous exercise, exposure to extreme heat, or other activities that may cause dehydration.

ZIV-AFLIBERCEPT
(ziv-a-fli'ber-cept)

Zaltrap

Classification: BIOLOGICAL RESPONSE MODIFIER; GROWTH FACTOR INHIBITOR; SIGNAL TRANSDUCTION INHIBITOR; RECOMBINANT FUSION PROTEIN; ANTINEOPLASTIC

Therapeutic: ANTINEOPLASTIC

AVAILABILITY Solution

ACTION & THERAPEUTIC EFFECT
Binds to certain vascular growth factors thus inhibiting their binding to and activation of receptors that stimulate neovascularization (new blood vessel growth) and increased vascular permeability. *Decreased neovascularization in tumors slows growth of metastatic colorectal tumors.*

USES Treatment of metastatic colorectal cancer in combination chemotherapy with 5-flurouracil, leucovorin, and irinotecan in patients whose condition has progressed or is resistant to an oxaliplatin-containing combination

CONTRAINDICATIONS Severe hemorrhage; GI perforation; compromised wound healing; fistula

development; 4 wk before or after elective surgery; hypertensive crisis or hypertensive encephalopathy; drug induced arterial thromboembolic event or nephrotic syndrome; reversible posterior leukoencephalopathy syndrome (RPLS); lactation.

CAUTIOUS USE Hypersensitivity to ziv-aflibercept; hemorrhage; history of GI perforation; poor wound healing; severe hypertension or hypertension; thromboembolic events; proteinuria; infection; diarrhea and dehydration; older adults; pregnancy (category C). Safety and efficacy in children younger than 18 y not established.

ROUTE & DOSAGE

Colorectal Cancer
Adult: **IV** 4 mg/kg q2wk; administer prior to 5-flurouracil, leucovorin, and irinotecan

Toxicity Dosage Adjustments
Recurrent of severe hypertension: Hold therapy until hypertension is controlled; permanently reduce dose to 2 mg/kg for subsequent cycles
Proteinuria: Hold therapy until proteinuria is less than 2 g/24 h; permanently reduce dose to 2 mg/kg for subsequent cycles

ADMINISTRATION

Intravenous

PREPARE: IV Infusion: Withdraw required dose of ziv-aflibercept and dilute to a final concentration of 0.6–8 mg/mL in NS or D5W (enter vial only once to withdraw dose). Dilute in PVC infusion bags containing bis (2-ethylhexyl) phthalate (DEHP) or polyolefin.

Common adverse effects in *italic;* life-threatening effects <u>underlined;</u> generic names in **bold;** classifications in SMALL CAPS; ♣ Canadian drug name; ○ Prototype drug; ⚠ Alert **1797**

Z

ADMINISTER: **IV Infusion:** Infuse over 1 h through a 0.2 micron polyethersulfone filter. Do not use filters made of polyvinylidene fluoride or nylon. **Do not** give IV push or as bolus dose. Use an infusion set made of PVC containing DEHP or one of the other materials approved by manufacturer.

INCOMPATIBILITIES: Solution/additive: Do not combine ziv-aflibercept with other drugs in the same IV solution. Y-site: Do not administer ziv-aflibercept in the same IV line with other drugs

▪ Store diluted solution at 2°–8° C (36°–46° F) for up to 4 h.

ADVERSE EFFECTS **CV:** Deep venous thrombosis, pulmonary embolism, hypertension. **Respiratory:** Dysphonia, dyspnea, epistaxis, nasopharyngitis, oropharyngeal pain, pulmonary embolism, rhinorrhea, upper respiratory tract infection. **CNS:** Headache. **HEENT:** Blurred vision, cataract, *conjunctival hemorrhage*, conjunctival hyperemia, corneal edema, corneal erosion, detachment of the retinal pigment epithelium, *eye pain*, eyelid edema, foreign body sensation in the eyes, increased intraocular pressure, increased lacrimation, retinal pigment epithelium tear, tooth infection, vitreous detachment, vitreous floaters. **Endocrine:** *Decreased appetite*, dehydration, *increased ALT and AST, weight decreased*. **Skin:** Palmar-plantar erythrodysesthesia syndrome, skin hyperpigmentation. **GI:** *Abdominal pain, diarrhea*, hemorrhoids, proctalgia, rectal hemorrhage, *stomatitis*, GI perforation. **GU:** *Proteinuria, serum creatinine increased*, urinary tract infections. **Hematologic:** Leukopenia, neutropenia, thrombocytopenia, hemorrhage.

Other: Asthenia, *fatigue*, catheter site infection, hypersensitivity, injection site hemorrhage, injection site pain, pneumonia.

PHARMACOKINETICS **Peak:** 1–3 d. **Metabolism:** Via proteolysis. **Half-Life:** 5–6 d.

NURSING IMPLICATIONS

Black Box Warning

Ziv-aflibercept has been associated with severe, sometimes fatal hemorrhage, GI perforation, and seriously compromised wound healing.

Assessment & Drug Effects
▪ Monitor vital signs, especially BP for exacerbation of hypertension.
▪ Monitor for and report immediately S&S of bleeding and GI perforation.
▪ Monitor for diarrhea and dehydration, especially in the older adult.
▪ Monitor lab tests: Baseline and prior to each cycle, CBC with differential; periodic LFTs, renal function tests, and urinalysis for proteinuria; 24 h urine when urinary protein creatinine ratio is greater than 1.

Patient & Family Education
▪ Report promptly any of the following: S&S of bleeding including light-headedness; S&S of hypertension including severe headache, or dizziness; severe diarrhea, vomiting, or abdominal pain.
▪ Frequent monitoring of BP is advised. Contact prescriber if BP is elevated beyond usual parameters.
▪ Men and women should use effective means of birth control during therapy and for at least 3 mo following completion of therapy.

Common adverse effects in *italic*; life-threatening effects underlined; generic names in **bold;** classifications in SMALL CAPS; ✦ Canadian drug name; ◯ Prototype drug; ⚠ Alert

- Contact your prescriber immediately if you or your partner becomes pregnant during treatment with ziv-aflibercept.
- Do not breast-feed while receiving this drug without consultation with prescriber.

ZOLEDRONIC ACID

(zo-le-dron'ic)

Aclasta ♦, Reclast

Classification: BISPHOSPHONATE; BONE METABOLISM REGULATOR

Therapeutic: BONE METABOLISM REGULATOR

Prototype: Etidronate disodium

AVAILABILITY Solution for injection

ACTION & *THERAPEUTIC EFFECT* Zoledronic acid inhibits various stimulatory factors of osteoclastic activity produced by bone tumors. It also induces osteoclast apoptosis. *Zoledronic acid blocks osteoclastic resorption of bone, thus reducing the amount of calcium released from bone.*

USES Treatment of hypercalcemia of malignancy, multiple myeloma, and bony metastases from solid tumors, Paget's disease (Reclast), postmenopausal or glucocorticoid-induced osteoporosis (Reclast).

CONTRAINDICATIONS Hypersensitivity to zoledronic acid preexisting hypocalcemia (**Reclast** only); serum creatinine less than 35 mL/min; pregnancy (category D); lactation.

CAUTIOUS USE Aspirin-sensitive asthma; cancer chemotherapy; renal and/or hepatic impairment; dental work; multiple myeloma; Paget disease; hypoparathyroidism, malabsorption syndrome; QT prolongation, cardiac arrhythmias; neurologic events; older adults. Safety and efficacy in children not established.

ROUTE & DOSAGE

Hypercalcemia of Malignancy

Adult: **IV** 4 mg over a minimum of 15 min. May consider retreatment if serum calcium has not returned to normal, may repeat after 7 days

Multiple Myeloma and Bone Metastases from Solid Tumors

Adult: **IV** 4 mg q3–4wk

Osteoporosis (Reclast)

Adult: **IV** 5 mg infusion once/year

Osteoporosis Prophylaxis in Postmenopausal Women (Reclast)

Adult: **IV** 5 mg every other year

Paget's Disease (Reclast)

Adult: **IV** 5 mg dose, retreatment may be necessary

Renal Impairment Dosage Adjustment (for Oncology Uses)

CrCl 50–60 mL/min: 3.5 mg; *40–49 mL/min:* 3.3 mg; *30–39 mL/min:* 3 mg; *less than 30 mL/min:* Do not use

Renal Impairment Dosage Adjustment (Reclast)

CrCl less than 35 mL/min: Do not use

ADMINISTRATION

Intravenous

Do not administer to anyone who is dehydrated or suspected of being dehydrated. Consult prescriber.

• Do not administer until serum creatinine values have been evaluated by the prescriber.

PREPARE: IV Infusion: *Reclast:* No further preparation is necessary. *Zometa concentrate:* Further dilute in 100 mL NS or D5W. *Powder for injection:* Reconstitute with 5 mL of sterile water for injection (provided) to yield 0.8 mg/mL. Further dilute in 100 mL NS or D5W prior to administration. • If not used immediately, refrigerate. The total time between reconstitution and end of infusion must not exceed 24 h.

ADMINISTER: IV Infusion: Infuse a single dose over NO LESS than 15 min. Flush line with 10 mL NS following infusion.

INCOMPATIBILITIES: Solution/ additive and Y-site: Do not mix or infuse with **calcium**-containing solutions (e.g., **lactated Ringer's**). **Alemtuzumab, dantrolene, dauorubicin, diazepam, gemtuzumab, pheytoin**.

• Store at 2°–8° C (36°–46° F) following dilution. • **Must be** completely infused within 24 h of reconstitution.

ADVERSE EFFECTS CV: Lower extremity edema, hypotension. **Respiratory:** Dyspnea, cough. **CNS:** *Fatigue*, headache, dizziness, insomnia, depression, anxiety, agitation, confusion, hypoesthesia, rigors. **Endocrine:** Dehydration, hypophosphotemia, hypokalemia, hypomagnesemia. **Skin:** Alopecia, dermatitis. **GI:** *Nausea*, vomiting, *constipation*, diarrhea, anorexia, weight loss, abdominal pain, dyspepsia, decreased appetite. **GU:** Urinary tract infection, renal insufficiency. **Musculoskeletal:** *Osteolgia*, weakness, myalgia, arthralgia, back pain, paresthesia, limb pain. **Hematologic:** Anemia, progression of cancer, neutropenia. **Other:** *Fever*, candidiasis.

INTERACTIONS Drug: NSAIDS may increase the risk of GI toxicity. **Thalidomide** and other NEPHROTOXIC DRUGS may increase risk of renal toxicity.

PHARMACOKINETICS Onset: 4–10 days. **Duration:** 3–4 wk. **Metabolism:** Not metabolized. **Elimination:** In urine. **Half-Life:** 146 h.

NURSING IMPLICATIONS

Assessment & Drug Effects

• Notify prescriber immediately of deteriorating renal function as indicated by rising serum creatinine levels over baseline value.

• Withhold zoledronic acid and notify prescriber if serum creatinine is not within 10% of the baseline value.

• Monitor closely patient's hydration status. Note that loop diuretics should be used with caution due to the risk of hypocalcemia.

• Monitor for S&S of *bronchospasm* in aspirin-sensitive asthma patients; notify prescriber immediately.

• Baseline dental exam prior to initiation of therapy for patients at risk for osteonecrosis including all cancer patients.

• Monitor lab tests: Baseline renal function tests prior to each dose and periodically thereafter; periodic ionized calcium or corrected serum calcium levels, serum phosphate and magnesium, electrolytes, CBC with differential, Hct and Hgb.

Patient & Family Education

- Maintain adequate daily fluid intake. Consult with prescriber for guidelines.
- Report unexplained weakness, tiredness, irritation, muscle pain, insomnia, or flu-like symptoms.
- Use reliable means of birth control to prevent pregnancy. If you suspect you are pregnant, contact prescriber immediately.

ZOLMITRIPTAN

(zol-mi-trip'tan)

Zomig, Zomig ZMT

Classification: SEROTONIN 5-HT$_1$ RECEPTOR AGONIST

Therapeutic: ANTIMIGRAINE

Prototype: Sumatriptan

AVAILABILITY Tablet; orally disintegrating tablet; nasal spray

ACTION & THERAPEUTIC EFFECT Selective serotonin (5-HT$_{1B/1D}$) receptor agonist. The agonist effects at 5-HT$_{1B/1D}$ reverse the vasodilation of cranial blood vessels and inhibit release of proinflammatory neuropeptides. *Vasoconstricts dilated cranial blood vessels and decreased neuropeptide release relieve the pain of a migraine headache.*

USES Acute migraine headaches with or without aura.

CONTRAINDICATIONS Hypersensitivity to zolmitriptan; history of stroke or TIA; ischemic heart disease (angina, arteriosclerosis, ECG changes, history of MI or Prinzmetal's angina); cardiac arrhythmias associated with cardiac accessory conduction pathway disorders; symptomatic Wolff–Parkinson–White syndrome, uncontrolled hypertension; patients with other cardiac risk factors, such as diabetes, obesity, cigarette smoking, high cholesterol levels; hemiplegia or basilar migraine; concurrent administration of ergotamine or sumatriptan; concurrent use of MAOIs or within 14 days of use; vasospasm-related events; lactation.

CAUTIOUS USE Men older than 40 y; postmenopausal women; strong family history of CAD; GI disease, PVD, ischemic colitis, Raynaud's disease, hepatic impairment; adults older than 65 y; pregnancy (category C); children younger than 12 y.

ROUTE & DOSAGE

Acute Migraine

Adult: **PO** 1.25–2.5 mg, may repeat in 2 h if necessary (max: 10 mg/24 h); **Orally disintegrating tablet** 2.5 mg

Adult/Adolescent: **Nasal Spray** One spray into one nostril

Hepatic Impairment Dosage Adjustment

Moderate to severe: 1.25 mg tablet (max: 5 mg)

ADMINISTRATION

Oral

- Give any time after symptoms of migraine appear. Give 2.5 mg or less by breaking a 5 mg tablet in half. If headache returns, may repeat q2h up to 10 mg in 24 h.

Common adverse effects in *italic;* life-threatening effects <u>underlined</u>; generic names in **bold;** classifications in SMALL CAPS; ✦ Canadian drug name; ◑ Prototype drug; ⚠ Alert 1801

Z

- **Do not** give zolmitriptan within 24 h of an ergot-containing drug or other 5-HT₁ agonist.
- Discard unused tablets that have been removed from the packaging.

Intranasal

- Unit-dose spray device delivers a 5 mg dose. Do not exceed the maximum dose of 10 mg in 24 h.
- Store at 2°–25° C (36°–77° F) and protect from light.

ADVERSE EFFECTS **CNS:** Dizziness, paresthesia, drowsiness. **GI:** Unpleasant taste, nausea.

INTERACTIONS **Drug: Dihydroergotamine, methysergide**, ERGOT ALKALOIDS, other 5-HT₁ AGONISTS may cause prolonged vasospastic reactions; SSRIS have rarely caused weakness, hyperreflexia, and incoordination; MAOIS should not be used with 5-HT₁ AGONISTS; **cimetidine** increases half-life of zolmitriptan. **Herbal: St. John's wort** may increase TRIPTAN toxicity.

PHARMACOKINETICS **Absorption:** Rapidly absorbed, 40% bioavailability. **Peak:** 2–3 h. **Distribution:** 25% protein bound. **Metabolism:** In liver to active metabolite. **Elimination:** Primarily in urine (65%), 30% in feces. **Half-Life:** 3 h.

NURSING IMPLICATIONS

Assessment & Drug Effects

- Monitor for therapeutic effectiveness: Relief or reduction of migraine pain within 1–4 h.
- Monitor cardiovascular status carefully following first dose in patients at risk for CAD (e.g., postmenopausal women, men older than 40 y, persons with known CAD risk factors) or coronary artery vasospasms.
- Periodic cardiovascular evaluation is recommended with long-term use.
- Report to prescriber immediately chest pain, nausea, or tightness in chest or throat that is severe or does not quickly resolve.

Patient & Family Education

- Carefully review patient information insert and guidelines for taking drug.
- **Do not** take zolmitriptan during the aura phase, but as early as possible after onset of migraine.
- Do not remove orally disintegrating tablet from blister until just prior to dosing.
- Concurrent oral contraceptive use may increase incidence of adverse effects.
- Contact prescriber immediately if any of the following occur after zolmitriptan use: Symptoms of angina (e.g., severe or persistent pain or tightness in chest or throat, sudden nausea), hypersensitivity (e.g., wheezing, facial swelling, skin rash, hives), fainting, or abdominal pain.
- Report any other adverse effects (e.g., tingling, flushing, dizziness) at next prescriber visit.

ZOLPIDEM ⓟ

(zol'pi-dem)

Ambien, Ambien CR, Edluar, Intermezzo, Zolpimist

Classification: SEDATIVE-HYPNOTIC, NONBARBITUATE
Therapeutic: SEDATIVE-HYPNOTIC
Controlled Substance: Schedule IV

AVAILABILITY Tablet; extended release tablet; sublingual tablet

ACTION & *THERAPEUTIC EFFECT*

An agonist that binds the gamma-aminobutyric acid (GABA)-A receptor chloride channel, thus inhibiting its action potential in the cortical region of the brain. *Effective as a sedative.*

USES Short-term treatment of insomnia.

CONTRAINDICATIONS Hypersensitivity of zolpidem including angioedema; suicidal ideation, worsening of depression; labor or obstetric delivery.

CAUTIOUS USE Depressed patients, psychiatric disorders; history of suical tendencies; hepatic/renal impairment, alcohol or drug abuse; patients with compromised respiratory status, COPD, sleep apnea; chronic depression; older adults; pregnancy (category C). Safe use in children younger than 18 y not established.

ROUTE & DOSAGE

Short-Term Treatment of Insomnia

Adult: **PO Immediate release/sublingual** 5–10 mg OR **Extended release** 12.5 mg at bedtime; **Spray** 1–2 sprays before bedtime

Insomnia (Intermezzo Only)

Adult: **PO** 1.75 mg (women) or 3.5 mg (men) once/night if needed
Geriatric: **PO Immediate release/sublingual** 5 mg OR **Extended release** 6.25 mg at bedtime; **Spray** 1 spray before bedtime (max: 2 sprays)

Hepatic Impairment Dosage Adjustment

Immediate release 5 mg OR **Extended release** 6.25 mg at bedtime

ADMINISTRATION

Oral

- Give immediately before bedtime; for more rapid sleep onset, **do not** give with or immediately after a meal.
- Ensure that sublingual tablets are not swallowed.
- Extended release tablets should be swallowed whole. Ensure that they are not crushed or chewed.
- Store at room temperature, 15°–30° C (59°–86° F).

ADVERSE EFFECTS **CNS:** *Headache on awakening, drowsiness, fatigue, lethargy,* drugged feeling, depression, anxiety, irritability, dizziness, double vision. Doses greater than 10 mg may be associated with anterograde amnesia or memory impairment. **GI:** Dyspepsia, nausea, vomiting, diarrhea. **Other:** Myalgia.

INTERACTIONS Drug: CNS DEPRESSANTS, **alcohol**, PHENOTHIAZINES by augmenting CNS depression. **Food:** Extent and rate of absorption of zolpidem are significantly decreased.

PHARMACOKINETICS Absorption: Readily from GI tract. 70% reaches systemic circulation. **Onset:** 7–27 min. **Peak:** 0.5–2.3 h. **Duration:** 6–8 h. **Distribution:** Highly protein bound. Lowest concentrations in CNS, highest concentrations in glandular tissue and fat. Crosses placenta. **Metabolism:** In the liver to 3 inactive metabolites. **Elimination:** 79–96% in the bile, urine, and feces. **Half-Life:** 1.7–2.5 h.

Common adverse effects in *italic;* life-threatening effects <u>underlined</u>; generic names in **bold;** classifications in SMALL CAPS; ♣ Canadian drug name; ○ Prototype drug; ▲ Alert   1803

Z

NURSING IMPLICATIONS

Assessment & Drug Effects

- Assess respiratory function in patients with compromised respiratory status. Report immediately to prescriber significantly depressed respiratory rate (less than 12/min).
- Monitor patients for S&S of depression (see Appendix F); zolpidem may increase level of depression.
- Monitor closely older adult or debilitated patients for impaired cognitive or motor function and unusual sensitivity to the drug's effects.

Patient & Family Education

- Avoid taking alcohol or other CNS depressants while on zolpidem.
- Do not drive or engage in other potentially hazardous activities until response to drug is known.
- Report vision changes to prescriber.
- Note: Onset of drug is more rapid when taken on an empty stomach.

ZONISAMIDE ●

(zon-i'sa-mide)

Zonegran

Classification: ANTICONVULSANT; SULFONAMIDE

Therapeutic: ANTICONVULSANT

AVAILABILITY Capsule

ACTION & *THERAPEUTIC EFFECT*

A broad-spectrum anticonvulsant that facilitates dopaminergic and serotonergic neurotransmission but does not potentiate the activity of gamma-aminobutyric acid (GABA) in the synapses of the CNS neurons. *Suppresses focal spike discharges and electroshock seizures. Effective against a variety of seizure types.*

USES Adjunctive therapy for partial seizures.

UNLABELED USES Antipsychotic-induced weight gain.

CONTRAINDICATIONS Hypersensitivity to sulfonamides or zonisamide; suicidal ideation; worsening of depression; severe metabolic acidosis; abrupt discontinuation; lactation.

CAUTIOUS USE Depressive individuals; CNS effects; history of suicidal tendencies; renal or hepatic insufficiency, dehydration, hypovolemia; renal impairment; older adults; pregnancy (category C). Safety and efficacy in children younger than 16 y not established.

ROUTE & DOSAGE

Partial Seizures

Adult/Child (16 y or older):
PO Start at 100 mg daily; may increase after 2 wk to 200 mg/day, may then increase q2wk, if necessary (max: 400 mg/day in 1–2 divided doses)

ADMINISTRATION

Oral

- Do not crush or break capsules; ensure capsules are swallowed whole with adequate fluid.

Z

- Withdraw drug gradually when discontinued to minimize seizure potential.
- Store at 25° C (77° F); room temperature permitted. Protect from light and moisture.

ADVERSE EFFECTS Respiratory:
Rhinitis, pharyngitis, cough. **CNS:** Agitation, irritability, anxiety, ataxia, confusion, depression, difficulty concentrating, difficulty with memory, *dizziness*, fatigue, *headache*, insomnia, mental slowing, nervousness, nystagmus, paresthesia, schizophrenic behavior, *somnolence*, tiredness, tremor, convulsion, abnormal gait, hyperesthesia, incoordination. **HEENT:** Difficulties in verbal expression, diplopia, speech abnormalities, taste perversion, amblyopia, tinnitus. **Endocrine:** Oligohidrosis, sometimes resulting in heat stroke and hyperthermia in children. **Skin:** Ecchymosis, rash, pruritus. **GI:** Abdominal pain, *anorexia*, constipation, diarrhea, dyspepsia, nausea, dry mouth, flatulence, gingivitis, gum hyperplasia, gastritis, stomatitis, cholelithiasis, glossitis, melena, rectal hemorrhage, ulcerative stomatitis, ulcer, dysphagia. **GU:** Kidney stones. **Other:** Flu-like syndrome, weight loss.

INTERACTIONS Drug: **Phenytoin, carbamazepine, phenobarbital, valproic acid** may decrease half-life of zonisamide.

PHARMACOKINETICS Peak: 2–6 h.
Distribution: 40% protein bound, extensively binds to erythrocytes. **Metabolism:** Acetylated in liver by CYP3A4. **Elimination:** Primarily in urine. **Half-Life:** 63–105 h.

NURSING IMPLICATIONS
Assessment & Drug Effects
- Withhold drug and notify prescriber if an unexplained rash or S&S of hypersensitivity appear (see Appendix F).
- Monitor for and report S&S of CNS impairment (somnolence, excessive fatigue, cognitive deficits, speech or language problems, incoordination, gait disturbances); oligohidrosis (lack of sweating) and hyperthermia in pediatric patients.
- Monitor lab tests: Periodic BUN and serum creatinine, and CBC with differential.

Patient & Family Education
- Do not abruptly stop taking this medication.
- Increase daily fluid intake to minimize risk of renal stones. Notify prescriber immediately of S&S of renal stones: Sudden back or abdominal pain, and blood in urine.
- Report any of the following: Dizziness, excess drowsiness, frequent headaches, malaise, double vision, lack of coordination, persistent nausea, sore throat, fever, mouth ulcers, or easy bruising.
- Exercise special caution with concurrent use of alcohol or CNS depressants.
- Do not drive or engage in other potentially hazardous activities until response to drug is known.

ZOSTER VACCINE ☉
(zos'ter)
Zostavax
See Appendix J.

Common adverse effects in *italic;* life-threatening effects <u>underlined</u>; generic names in **bold;** classifications in SMALL CAPS; ♣ Canadian drug name; ☉ Prototype drug; ⚠ Alert   1805

Z

APPENDICES

◆ APPENDIX A

(Generic names are in **bold**)

APPENDIX A-1

OCULAR MEDICATIONS

BETA-ADRENERGIC BLOCKERS **Prototype for classification: Betaxolol**
Use: Intraocular hypertension and chronic open-angle glaucoma.

Betaxolol HCl Betoptic S, 0.25% suspension, 0.5% solution	*Adult:* Topical 1 drop in affected eye bid for 0.25% suspension; 1–2 drops in affected eye for 0.5% solution.
Carteolol HCl Ocupress, 1% solution	*Adult:* Topical 1 drop bid
Levobunolol Betagan, 0.25%, 0.5% solution	*Adult:* Topical 1–2 drops of 0.25% solution bid or 1–2 drops of 0.5% solution daily.
Metipranolol HCl 0.3% solution	*Adult:* Topical 1 drop bid
Timolol maleate Betimol, Istalol, Timoptic, Timoptic XE, 0.25%, 0.5% solution	*Adult:* Topical 1 drop of 0.25–0.5% solution bid; may decrease to daily. Apply gel daily. Apply Istalol solution once daily.

ADVERSE EFFECTS/CLINICAL IMPLICATIONS May cause *mild ocular stinging* and discomfort; tearing; may also have the adverse effects of systemic beta-blockers. May precipitate thyroid storm in patients with hyperthyroidism. Patients with impaired cardiac function and the elderly should report to prescriber signs and symptoms of heart failure. Monitor BP for hypotension and heart rate for bradycardia.

MIOTICS **Prototype for classification: Pilocarpine HCl Use:** Open-angle and angle-closure glaucomas; to reduce IOP and to protect the lens during surgery and laser iridotomy; to counteract effects of mydriatics and cycloplegics following surgery or ophthalmoscopic examination.

Apraclonidine HCl Iopidine, 0.5%, 1% solution	**Intraoperative and Postsurgical Increase in IOP:** *Adult:* **Topical** 1 drop of 1% solution in affected eye 1 h before surgery and 1 drop in same eye immediately after surgery. **Open-Angle Glaucoma:** *Adult:* **Topical** 1 drop of 0.5% solution in affected eye tid
Brimonidine tartrate Alphagan P,0.1%, 0.15%, 0.2% solution	**Glaucoma:** *Adult:* **Topical** 1 drop in affected eye(s) tid approximately 8 h apart. *Child (2 y or older):* **Topical** 1 drop in affected eye tid approximatively 8 h apart.

Brinzolamide
Azopt,
1% suspension

Ocular Hypertension or Open-Angle Glaucoma:
Adult: **Topical** 1 drop in affected eye(s) tid

Carbachol
Miostat 1.5%,
3% solution

Glaucoma: *Adult:* **Topical** 2 drops in affected eye(s) up to 3 × daily.

Dorzolamide
Trusopt,
2% solution

Ocular Hypertension or Open-Angle Glaucoma:
Adult, Child: **Topical** 1 drop in affected eye(s) tid

Echothiophate
0.125% solution

Ocular Hypertension: *Adult:* **Topical** 1 drop in affected eye(s) bid

Pilocarpine HCl
Isopto Carpine,
1%, 2%,
4% solution

Acute Glaucoma: *Adult:* **Topical** 1 drop of 1–2% solution in affected eye q5–10min for 3–6 doses, then 1 drop q1–3h until IOP is reduced. **Chronic Glaucoma:** *Adult:* **Topical** 1 drop of 0.5–4% solution in affected eye q4–12h or 1 ocular system (Ocusert) q7days. **Miotic:** *Adult:* **Topical** 1 drop of 1% solution in affected eye.

ADVERSE EFFECTS/CLINICAL IMPLICATIONS Ocular: Ciliary spasm with brow ache, twitching of eyelids, eye pain with change in eye focus, miosis, *diminished vision in poorly illuminated areas,* blurred vision, reduced visual acuity, sensitivity, contact allergy, lacrimation, follicular conjunctivitis, conjunctival irritation, cataract, retinal detachment. **CNS:** *Headache, drowsiness,* depression, syncope. **GI:** Abnormal taste, dry mouth. **Clinical Implications:** Wait 15 min after instillation before inserting soft contact lenses to avoid staining lenses. Use with MAO inhibitors may increase risk of hypertensive emergency. May increase the effects of beta-blockers and other antihypertensives on blood pressure and heart rate. TCAs may reduce the effects of **brimonidine. Brinzolamide** is a carbonic anhydrase inhibitor (prototype: Acetazolamide) and is a sulfonamide. It should not be used by patients with sulfa allergies. Reconstituted solutions of **echothiophate** remain stable for 1 mo at room temperature. Expiration date should appear on label. The length of time solutions remain stable under refrigeration varies with manufacturer. **Echothiophate** therapy is generally discontinued 2–6 wk before surgery. If necessary, alternate therapy is substituted. Medication should be given in the evening. Give at least 5 min apart from other topical ophthalmic drugs.

PROSTAGLANDINS Prototype for classification: Latanoprost

Use: Open-angle glaucoma and intraocular hypertension.

Bimatoprost
Lumigan, 0.01%,
0.03% solution

Adult: **Topical** 1 drop in affected eye(s) once daily in the evening.

Latanoprost
Xalatan, 0.005%
solution

Adult: **Topical** 1 drop (1.5 mcg) in affected eye(s) once daily in the evening.

Trafluprost
Zioptan 0.015 mg/Ml

Adult: **Topical** 1 drop in the conjunctival sac of the affected eye(s) once daily in the evening.

Travoprost
Travatan, 0.004% solution

Adult: **Topical** 1 drop in affected eye(s) once daily in the evening.

ADVERSE EFFECTS Ocular: *Conjunctival hyperemia, growth of eyelashes, ocular pruritus,* ocular dryness, visual disturbance, ocular burning, foreign body sensation, eye pain, pigmentation of the periocular skin, blepharitis, cataract, superficial punctate keratitis, eyelid erythema, ocular irritation, eyelash darkening, eye discharge, tearing, photophobia, allergic conjunctivitis, increases in iris pigmentation (brown pigment), conjunctival edema. **Body as a Whole:** Headaches, abnormal liver function tests, asthenia, and hirsutism. **Clinical Implications:** Should instill in the evening. Wait 15 min after instillation before inserting soft contact lenses to avoid staining the lenses. Give at least 5 min apart from other topical ophthalmic drugs.

MYDRIATIC Prototype for classification: Homatropine HBr
Use: Mydriatic for ocular examination and as cycloplegic to measure errors of refraction. Also inflammatory conditions of uveal tract, ciliary spasm, as a cycloplegic and mydriatic in preoperative and postoperative conditions, and as an optical aid in select patients with axial lens opacities.

Cyclopentolate HCl
Cyclogyl, 0.5%, 1%, 2% solution

Cycloplegic Refraction: *Adult:* **Topical** 1 drop of 1% solution in eye 40–50 min before procedure, followed by 1 drop in 5 min; may need 2% solution in patients with darkly pigmented eyes. *Child:* **Topical** 1 drop of 0.5–1% solution in eye 40–50 min before procedure, followed by 1 drop in 5 min; may need 2% solution in patients with darkly pigmented eyes.

Homatropine HBr
Homatropaire, Isopto Homatropine, 2%, 5% solution

Cycloplegic Refraction: *Adult:* **Topical** 1–2 drops of 2% or 5% solution in eye repeated in 5–10 min if necessary. **Ocular Inflammation:** *Adult:* **Topical** 1–2 drops of 2% or 5% solution in eye up to q3–4h.

Phenylephrine HCl
AK-Dilate Ophthalmic, Mydfrin, 0.12%, 2.5%, 10% solution

Ophthalmoscopy: *Adult:* **Topical** 1 drop of 2.5% or 10% solution before examination. *Child:* **Topical** 1 drop of 2.5% solution before examination. **Vasoconstrictor:** *Adult:* **Topical** 2 drops of 0.12% solution q3–4h as necessary.

Tropicamide
Mydriacyl, Tropicacyl, 0.5%, 1% solution

Refraction: *Adult:* **Topical** 1–2 drops of 1% solution in each eye, repeat in 5 min; if patient is not seen within 20–30 min, an additional drop may be instilled. **Examination of Fundus:** *Adult:* **Topical** 1–2 drops of 0.5% solution in each eye 15–20 min prior to examination; may repeat q30min if necessary.

CONTRAINDICATED IN Primary (narrow-angle) glaucoma or pre-disposition to glaucoma; children younger than 6 y. **Cautious Use in:** Increased IOP, infants, children, pregnancy (category C), the elderly or debilitated; hypertension; hyperthyroidism; diabetes; cardiac disease. **Adverse Effects:** Increased IOP, *blurred vision, photophobia.* **Prolonged Use:** Local irritation, congestion, edema, eczema, follicular conjunctivitis. **Excessive Dosage/Systemic Absorption:** Symptoms of atropine poisoning (flushing, dry skin, mouth, nose; decreased sweating; fever, rash, rapid/irregular pulse; abdominal and bladder distention; hallucinations, confusion). **CNS:** Psychotic reaction, behavior disturbances, ataxia, incoherent speech, restlessness, hallucinations, somnolence, disorientation, failure to recognize people, grand mal seizures. **Clinical Implications:** Carefully monitor **cyclopentolate** patients with seizure disorders, since systemic absorption may precipitate a seizure. Photophobia associated with mydriasis may require patient to wear dark glasses. Since drug causes blurred vision, supervision of activity may be indicated.

VASOCONSTRICTOR; DECONGESTANT Prototype for classification: **Naphazoline HCl** Use: Ocular vasoconstrictor.

Naphazoline HCl 0.012%, 0.02%, 0.1% solution	*Adult:* **Topical** 1–3 drops of 0.1% solution q3–4h prn or 1–2 drops of a 0.012–0.03% solution q4h prn.
Tetrahydrozoline HCl Opti-Clear, Visine Original, 0.05% solution	*Adult:* **Topical** 1–2 drops of 0.05% solution in eye bid or tid

CONTRAINDICATED IN Narrow-angle glaucoma; concomitant use with MAO INHIBITORS or TRICYCLIC ANTIDEPRESSANTS **Cautious Use in:** Hypertension, cardiac irregularities, advanced arteriosclerosis; diabetes; hyperthyroidism; elderly patients. **Adverse Effects:** Pupillary dilation, increased intraocular pressure, rebound redness of the eye, headache, hypertension, nausea, weakness, sweating. **Overdosage:** Drowsiness, hypothermia, bradycardia, shocklike hypotension, coma.

CORTICOSTEROID, ANTI-INFLAMMATORY Prototype for classification: **Hydrocortisone** Use: Inflammation. **Unlabeled Use:** Anterior uveitis.

Difluprednate Durezol, 0.05% suspension	*Adult:* **Topical** 1 drop in conjunctival sac qid for the first 24 h; qid for 2 wk; then bid for 2 wk.
Fluorometholone Flarex, FML Forte, FML Liquifilm, 0.1%, 0.25% suspension; 0.1% ointment	*Adult/Child (2 y or older):* **Topical** 1–2 drops of suspension in conjunctival sac q.h. for the first 24–48 h; then bid to qid; or a thin strip of ointment q4h for the first 24–48 h; then 1–3 × day.

Loteprednol etabonate
Alrex, Lotemax, 0.2%, 0.5% suspension

Adult: **Topical** 1–2 drops in conjunctival sac qid during initial treatment, may increase to q1h if necessary.

Prednisolone sodium phosphate
Inflamase Mild, Pred Mild, Prednisol, Inflamase Forte, 0.11%, 0.12%, 0.9% suspension

Adult: **Topical** 1–2 drops in conjunctival sac q.h. during the day; then q2h at night; may decrease to 1 drop tid or qid

Rimexolone
Vexol, 1% solution

Postoperative Ocular Inflammation: *Adult:* **Topical** 1–2 drops qid beginning 24 h after surgery, continue through first 2 wk postoperatively. **Anterior Uveitis:** *Adult:* **Topical** 1–2 drops in affected eye every hour while awake for first wk, then q2h for second wk, then taper frequency until uveitis resolves.

CONTRAINDICATED IN Ocular fungal diseases, *herpes simplex* keratitis, ocular infections, ocular mycobacterial infections, viral disease of cornea or conjunctiva such as vaccinia, varicella. **Adverse Effects: Ocular:** Blurred vision, photophobia, conjunctival edema, corneal edema, erosion, eye discharge, dryness, irritation, pain. **Prolonged Use:** Glaucoma, ocular hypertension, damage to optic nerve, defects in visual acuity and visual fields, posterior subcapsular cataract formation, secondary ocular infections. **Other:** Headache, taste perversion. **Clinical Implications:** Shake all products well before use.

OCULAR ANTIHISTAMINES **Prototype for classification: Emedastine Use:** Relief of signs and symptoms of allergic conjunctivitis.

Azelastine HCl
OPTIVAR, 0.05% solution

Adult/Child (3 y or older): **Topical** 1 drop in affected eye(s) bid

Bepotastine
Bepreve, 1.5% solution

Adult: **Topical** 1 drop in affected eye(s) bid

Cetirizine
Zerviate, 0.24% solution

Adult: **Topical** 1 drop in each eye bid

Cromolyn sodium
Crolom, Opticrom, 4% solution

Adult: **Topical** 1–2 drops in each eye 4–6 × day.

Emedastine difumarate
0.05% solution

Adult/Child (3 y or older): **Topical** 1 drop in affected eye(s) up to qid

Epinastine hydrochloride
Elestat, 0.05% solution

Adult/Child (3 y or older): **Topical** 1 drop in affected eye(s) up to bid

Ketotifen fumarate
Zaditor, 0.025% solution

Adult: **Topical** 1 drop in affected eye(s) q8–12h.

Lodoxamide
Alomide, 0.1% solution

Adult/Child (2 mo or older): **Topical** 1–2 drop in affected eye(s) qid for up to 3 mo.

Nedocromil sodium
Alocril, 2% solution

Adult/Child (3 y or older): **Topical** 1–2 drops in affected eye(s) bid

Olopatadine HCl
Patanol, 0.1% solution;
Pataday, 0.2% solution;
Pazeo, 0.7% solution

Adult/Child (3 y or older): **Topical** 1–2 drops in affected eye(s) bid at least 6–8 h apart.

ADVERSE EFFECTS Ocular: Allergic reactions, *burning, stinging,* discharge, dry eyes, eye pain, eyelid disorder, itching, keratitis, lacrimation disorder, mydriasis, photophobia, rash. **CNS:** Drowsiness, fatigue, headache. **Other:** Dry mouth, cold syndrome, pharyngitis, rhinitis, sinusitis, taste perversion. **Clinical Implications:** Wait 10 min after instilling drops before inserting soft contact lenses.

OCULAR NONSTEROIDAL ANTI-INFLAMMATORY DRUGS Prototype for classification: Ibuprofen Use: Treatment of ocular pain and inflammation associated with cataract surgery.

Bromfenac
Xibrom, 0.09% solution

Adult: **Topical** 1 drop into affected eye(s) bid beginning 24 h after cataract surgery and continuing for 14 days.

Diclofenac
0.1% solution

Adult: **Topical** 1–2 drops in affected eye(s) within 1 h prior to surgery then 1–2 drops 15 min after surgery, then daily beginning 4–6 h after surgery, continue up to 3 days.

Flurbiprofen
Ocufen, 0.03% solution

Adult: **Topical** 1 drop q30min beginning 2 h prior to surgery for total of 4 drops.

Ketorolac
Acular, Acular LS, Acuvail, 0.4% 0.45%, 0.5% solution

Adult: **Topical** 1 drop to affected eye(s) 4 × day beginning 24 h after surgery and continuing for 14 days.

Nepafenac
Nevanac, 0.1% suspension

Adult/Child (10 y or older): **Topical** 1 drop into affected eye(s) tid beginning 24 h after cataract surgery and continuing for 14 days.

ADVERSE EFFECTS Ocular: Conjunctival hyperemia, ocular hypertension, foreign body sensation, decreased visual acuity, headache, iritis, ocular inflammation (e.g., edema, erythema), ocular irritation (burning/stinging), ocular pruritus, ocular pain, photophobia, lacrimation, abnormal sensation in the eye, delayed wound healing, keratitis, lid margin crusting, corneal erosion, corneal perforation, corneal thinning, and epithelial breakdown. Continued use can lead to ulceration or perforation. **Clinical Implications: Nepafenac** suspension **must be** shaken well prior to use.

OCULAR ANTIBIOTIC, QUINOLONE Prototype for classification: Ciprofloxacin Use: Treatment of ocular infection.

Besifloxacin
Besivance, 0.6% suspension

Adult/Adolescent/Child (1 y or older):
Topical 1 drop in affected eye(s) tid × 7 days

Ciprofloxacin
Ciloxin, 0.3% solution

Adult/Adolescent/Child (1 y or older):
Topical 1–2 drops in affected eye(s) q2h × 2 days then q4h × 5 days.

Levofloxacin
0.5% solution

Adult/Adolescent/Child (6 y or older):
Topical 1–2 drops in affected eye(s) q2h (up to 8 × day) on days 1 and 2 then q4h (up to 4 × day)

Moxifloxacin
Vigamox, 0.5% solution
Moxeza, 0.5% solution

Adult/Child (1 y or older): **Topical** (Vigamox) 1 drop in affected eye(s) tid × 7 days. (Moxeza) 1 drop in affected eye(s) bid × 7 days

Ofloxacin
Ocuflox 0.3% solution

Adult/Adolescent/Child: **Ophthalmic** Instill 1–2 drops q2–4h for first 2 days, then qid × 5 additional days

ADVERSE EFFECTS Ocular: Conjunctival redness, blurred vision, irritation, pain, pruritus. **CNS:** Headache.

APPENDIX A-2

LOW MOLECULAR WEIGHT HEPARINS

ANTICOAGULANT, LOW MOLECULAR WEIGHT HEPARIN Prototype for classification: Enoxaparin Use: Prevention and treatment of DVT following hip or knee replacement or abdominal surgery, unstable angina, acute coronary syndromes.

Dalteparin sodium
Fragmin, 10,000 international units/mL, 25,000 international units/mL

DVT Prophylaxis, Abdominal Surgery: *Adult:* **Subcutaneous** 2500 international units daily starting 1–2 h prior to surgery and continuing for 5–10 days postoperatively. DVT Prophylaxis, Total Hip Arthroplasty: *Adult:* **Subcutaneous** 2500–5000 international units daily starting 1–2 h prior to surgery and continuing for 5–14 days postoperatively. Acute Thromboembolism:

Adult: **Subcutaneous** 120 international units/kg bid for at least 5 days. Recurrent Thromboembolism: *Adult:* **Subcutaneous** 5000 international units bid for 3–6 mo. Unstable Angina/Non–Q-Wave MI: *Adult:* **Subcutaneous** 120 international units/kg (max: 10,000 international units) q12h.

DVT Prophylaxis with risk of PE: *Adult:* **Subcutaneous** 5000 international units once daily for 12–14 days. **Extended Treatment of VTE or Proximal DVT:** *Adult:* **Subcutaneous** 200 international units/kg daily for 1 mo, then 150 international units/kg daily for 2–6 mo.

Enoxaparin
Lovenox,
100 mg/mL

Prevention of DVT after Hip or Knee Surgery: *Adult:* **Subcutaneous** 30 mg subcutaneously bid for 10–14 days starting 12–24 h post-surgery. **Prevention of DVT after Abdominal Surgery:** *Adult:* **Subcutaneous** 40 mg daily starting 2 h before surgery and continuing for 7–10 days (max: 12 days). **Treatment of DVT and Pulmonary Embolus:** *Adult:* **Subcutaneous** 1 mg/kg bid; monitor anti-Xa activity to determine appropriate dose. **Acute Coronary Syndrome:** *Adult:* **Subcutaneous** 1 mg/kg q12h × 2–8 days. Give concurrently with aspirin 100–325 mg/day.

CONTRAINDICATED IN Hypersensitivity to ardeparin, other low molecular weight heparins, pork products, or parabens; active major bleeding, thrombocytopenia that is positive for antiplatelet antibodies with ardeparin; uncontrolled hypertension; nursing mothers. **Tizaparin** contraindicated in patients over 90 years old with CrCl less than 60 mL/min. **Cautious Use in:** Hypersensitivity to heparin; history of heparin-induced thrombocytopenia; bacterial endocarditis; severe and uncontrolled hypertension, cerebral aneurysm or hemorrhagic stroke, bleeding disorders, recent GI bleeding or associated GI disorders (e.g., ulcerative colitis), thrombocytopenia, or platelet disorders; severe liver or renal disease, diabetic retinopathy, hypertensive retinopathy, invasive procedures; pregnancy (category C). **Adverse Effects: Body as a Whole:** Allergic reactions (rash, urticaria), arthralgia, pain and inflammation at injection site, peripheral edema, fever. **CNS:** *CVA*, dizziness, headache, insomnia. **CV:** Chest pain. **GI:** Nausea, vomiting. **Hematologic:** *Hemorrhage*, thrombocytopenia, ecchymoses, anemia. **Respiratory:** Dyspnea. **Skin:** Rash, pruritus. **Drug Interactions: Aspirin,** NSAIDS, **warfarin** can increase risk of hemorrhage **Clinical Implications:** Alternate injection sites using the abdomen, anterior thigh, or outer aspect of upper arms. **Lab Tests:** CBC with platelet count, urinalysis, and stool for occult blood should be tested throughout therapy. Routine coagulation tests are not required. Carefully monitor for and immediately report S&S of excessive anticoagulation (e.g., bleeding at venipuncture sites or surgical site) or hemorrhage (e.g., drop in BP or Hct). Patients on oral anticoagulants, platelet inhibitors, or with impaired renal function **must be** very carefully monitored for hemorrhage. Patient should be sitting or lying supine for injection. Inject deep subcutaneously with entire length of needle inserted into skin fold. Hold skin fold gently throughout injection and do not rub site after injection.

APPENDIX A-3

INHALED CORTICOSTEROIDS (ORAL AND NASAL INHALATIONS)

CORTICOSTEROID, ANTIINFLAMMATORY Prototype for classification: Hydrocortisone Use: Oral inhalation to treat steroid-dependent asthma, nasal inhalation for the management of the symptoms of seasonal or perennial rhinitis.

Beclomethasone dipropionate Beconase AQ, Qnasl, QVAR	**Asthma:** *Adult:* **Oral Inhaler** 40–80 mcg bid may try to reduce systemic steroids after 1 wk of concomitant therapy; (max: 320 mcg/day). *Child (5–11 y):* **Oral Inhaler QVAR** 40 mcg bid (max: 160 mcg/day). *Child (4-5 y):* **Oral Inhaler Qvar Redihaler** 40 mcg bid **Allergic Rhinitis:** *Adult:* **Nasal Inhaler** 1 spray/nostril bid to qid Child (older than 6 y): 1–2 sprays daily.
Budesonide Pulmicort, Rhinocort Aqua	**Asthma, Maintenance Therapy:** *Adult:* **Oral Inhalation** 360 mcg bid (max: 800 mcg bid). *Child (6 y or older):* **Oral Inhalation** 180 mcg bid (max: 400 mcg bid). *Child (12 mo–8 y):* **Nebulization** 0.5 mg/day in 1–2 divided doses. **Rhinitis:** *Adult/Child (6 y or older):* **Intranasal** 2 sprays/nostril in the morning and evening or 4 sprays/nostril in the morning.
Ciclesonide Alvesco, Omnaris, Zetonna	**Rhinitis:** *Adult/Child (6 y or older):* **Intranasal** 1–2 sprays/nostril once daily (depends on product used). **Asthma:** *Adult/Child (12 y and older):* **Inhaled** 80 mcg bid; may increase to 160 mcg bid
Flunisolide 0.025% solution	**Allergic Rhinitis:** *Adult:* **Intranasal** 2 sprays intranasally/nostril, bid; may increase to tid, if needed. *Child:* **Intranasal** 6–14 y, 1 spray intranasally/nostril tid or 2 sprays bid
Fluticasone ArmonAir RespiClick, Flonase, Flovent, Flovent HFA, 44 mcg, 110 mcg, 220 mcg aerosol, **Veramyst,** 27.5 mcg/ actuation	**Seasonal Allergic Rhinitis:** *Adult:* **Intranasal** 100 mcg (1 inhalation)/nostril 1–2 × daily (max: 4 × daily). **Inhalation** 1–2 inhalations daily. *Child (4 y or older):* **Intranasal** 1 spray/nostril once daily. May increase to 2 sprays/nostril once daily if inadequate response, then decrease to 1 spray/ nostril once daily. when control is achieved. *Adult/ Adolescent/Child (12 y or older):* **Intranasal (Veramyst)** 2 sprays/nostril daily then reduce to 1 spray daily. *Child (2–11 y):* **Intranasal (Veramyst)** 1 spray/nostril daily, may increase to 2 sprays/ nostril daily if necessary. *Adult/Adolescent:* **Inhaled (Advair)** 1–2 inhalations q12h.

Fluticasone/ Vilanterol Breo Ellipta, 100 mcg/25 mcg powder for inhalation	*Adult:* **Inhalation** 1 inhalation every 24 h.
Mometasone furoate Asmanex, Nasonex, 220 mcg/ inhalation, 50 mcg/inhalation	**Allergic Rhinitis:** *Adult/Child (12 y or older):* **Intranasal** 2 sprays (50 mcg each) in each nostril once daily. *Child (2 y –11 y):* **Intranasal** 1 spray in each nostril once daily. *Adult/Child (12 y or older):* **Powder for Inhalation** 1 inhalation (220 mcg) once or twice daily (max: 1 inhalation bid). *Child (4–11 y):* **Powder for Inhalation** 200 mcg (may increase to 400 mcg) bid
Triamcinolone acetonide Nasacort, 100 mcg/ inhalation	*Adult:* **Inhalation** 2 puffs 3–4 × day (max: 16 puffs/ day) or 4 puffs bid **Nasal Spray** 2 sprays/nostril once daily (max: 8 sprays/day). *Child (6–12 y):* **Inhalation** 1–2 sprays tid or qid (max: 12 sprays/ day) or 2–4 sprays bid **Intranasal** 1 spray in each nostril daily.

CONTRAINDICATED IN Nonasthmatic bronchitis, primary treatment of status asthmaticus, acute attack of asthma. **Cautious Use in:** Patients receiving systemic corticosteroids; use with extreme caution if at all in respiratory tuberculosis, untreated fungal, bacterial, or viral infections, and ocular herpes simplex; nasal inhalation therapy for nasal septal ulcers, nasal trauma, or surgery. **Adverse Effects: Oral Inhalation:** *Candidal infection of oropharynx* and occasionally larynx, hoarseness, dry mouth, sore throat, sore mouth. **Nasal (Inhaler):** *Transient nasal irritation, burning,sneezing,* epistaxis, bloody mucus, nasopharyngeal itching, dryness, crusting, and ulceration; headache, nausea, vomiting. **Other:** With excessive doses, symptoms of hypercorticism. Increased risk of adverse effects if Advair is used with other long-acting beta-agonists. **Clinical Implications:** Note that oral inhalation and nasal inhalation products are not to be used interchangeably. **Oral Inhaler:** Emphasize the following: (1) Shake inhaler well before using. (2) After exhaling fully, place mouthpiece well into mouth with lips closed firmly around it. (3) Inhale slowly through mouth while activating the inhaler. (4) Hold breath 5–10 sec, if possible, then exhale slowly. (5) Wait 1 min between puffs. Clean inhaler daily. Separate parts as directed in package insert, rinse them with warm water, and dry them thoroughly. Rinsing mouth and gargling with warm water after each oral inhalation removes residual medication from oropharyngeal area. Mouth care may also delay or prevent onset of oral dryness, hoarseness, and candidiasis. **Nasal Inhaler:** Directions for use of nasal inhaler provided by manufacturer should be carefully reviewed with patient. Emphasize the following points: (1) Gently blow nose to clear nostrils. (2) Shake inhaler well before using. (3) If 2 sprays in each nostril are prescribed, direct one spray toward upper, and the other toward lower part of nostril. (4) Wash cap and plastic nosepiece daily with warm water; dry thoroughly. Inhaled steroids do not provide immediate symptomatic relief and are not prescribed for this purpose.

APPENDIX A-4

TOPICAL CORTICOSTEROIDS

CORTICOSTEROID, ANTI-INFLAMMATORY Prototype for classification: Hydrocortisone Use: As a topical corticosteroid, the drug is used for the relief of the inflammatory and pruritic manifestations of corticosteroid-responsive dermatoses.

Hydrocortisone
Aeroseb-HC, Alphaderm, Cetacort, Cortaid, Cortenema, Dermolate, Hytone, Rectacort, Synacort, Caldecort, 0.5%, 1%, 2.5% cream, lotion, ointment, spray

Adult: **Topical** Apply a small amount to the affected area 1–4 × day. **PR** Insert 1% cream, 10% foam, 10–25 mg suppository, or 100 mg enema nightly.

Hydrocortisone acetate
Anusol HC, Carmol HC, Colifoam, Cortaid, Cort-Dome, Corticaine, Cortifoam, Epifoam, 0.5%, 1% ointment, cream

Alclometasone dipropionate
Aclovate, 0.05% cream, ointment

Adult: **Topical** 0.05% cream or ointment applied sparingly bid or tid; may use occlusive dressing for resistant dermatoses.

Amcinonide
Cyclocort, 0.1% cream, lotion, ointment

Adult: **Topical** Apply thin film bid or tid

Betamethasone dipropionate
Diprolene, Diprolene AF, Diprosone, Maxivate, 0.05% cream, gel, lotion, ointment

Adult: **Topical** Apply thin film bid

Betamethasone valerate
Luxiq, Valisone, Psorion, Beta-Val, 0.1% cream, ointment, lotion; 0.12% aerosol foam

Adult: **Topical** Apply sparingly bid

Clobetasol propionate
Clobex, Cormax, Embeline, Olux, Temovate, 0.05% cream, gel, ointment, lotion, aerosol foam

Adult: **Topical** Apply sparingly bid (max: 50 g/wk), or bid 3 day/wk or 1–2 × wk for up to 6 mo.

Clocortolone pivalate
Cloderm, 0.1% cream

Adult: **Topical** Apply thin layer 1–4 × day.

Desonide
DesOwen, Tridesilon, 0.05% cream, ointment, lotion

Adult: **Topical** Apply thin layer bid to qid

Desoximetasone
Topicort, 0.05%, 0.25% cream, ointment; 0.25% topical spray

Adult: **Topical** Apply thin layer bid

Diclofenac
Flector, Pennsaid, 1.3% topical patch; 1% topical gel

Adult: **Topical** Up to 4 g 4 × day on affected joint (max: 16 g).

Diflorasone diacetate
Florone, Florone E, Maxiflor, Psorcon E, Psorcon, 0.05% cream, ointment

Adult: **Topical** Apply thin layer of ointment 1–3 × day or cream 2–4 × day.

Fluocinolone acetonide
Fluoderm, Synalar, 0.025% ointment, cream; 0.2% cream; 0.01% cream, solution, shampoo, oil; 0.59 mg ophthalmic insert

Adult: **Topical** Apply thin layer bid to qid

Fluocinonide
Vanos, 0.05% cream, ointment, solution, gel; 0.1% cream

Adult: **Topical** Apply thin layer bid to qid

Flurandrenolide
Cordran, Cordran SP, 0.05% cream, lotion; 4 mcg/sq cm tape

Adult: **Topical** Apply thin layer bid or tid; apply tape 1–2 × day at 12 h intervals. *Child:* **Topical** Apply thin layer 1–2 × day; apply tape once/day.

Fluticasone
Cutivate, 0.005%, 0.05% cream; 0.005% ointment

Adult/Child (3 mo or older): **Topical** Apply a thin film of cream or ointment to affected area once or twice daily.

Halcinonide
Halog, 0.1% cream, ointment, solution

Adult: **Topical** Apply thin layer bid or tid *Child:* **Topical** Apply thin layer once/day.

Halobetasol
Ultravate, 0.05% cream, ointment

Adult: **Topical** Apply sparingly bid

Mometasone furoate
Elocon, 0.1% cream, lotion, ointment

Adult: **Topical** Apply a thin film of cream or ointment or a few drops of lotion to affected area once/day.

Triamcinolone
Kenalog, Triderm,
0.025%, 0.5%, 0.1%
cream, ointment; 0.025%,
0.1% lotion

Adult: **Topical** Apply sparingly bid or tid

CONTRAINDICATED IN Topical steroids contraindicated in presence of varicella, vaccinia, on surfaces with compromised circulation, and in children younger than 2 y. **Cautious Use in:** Children; diabetes mellitus; stromal *herpes simplex;* glaucoma, tuberculosis of eye; osteoporosis; untreated fungal, bacterial, or viral infections **Adverse Effects: Skin:** Skin thinning and atrophy, *acne, impaired wound healing;* petechiae, ecchymosis, easy bruising; suppression of skin test reaction; hypopigmentation or hyperpigmentation, hirsutism, acneiform eruptions, subcutaneous fat atrophy; allergic dermatitis, urticaria, angioneurotic edema, increased sweating. **Clinical Implications:** Administer retention enema preferably after a bowel movement. The enema should be retained at least w1 h or all night if possible. If an occlusive dressing is to be used, apply medication sparingly, rub until it disappears, and then reapply, leaving a thin coat over lesion. Completely cover area with transparent plastic or other occlusive device or vehicle. Avoid covering a weeping or exudative lesion. Usually, occlusive dressings are not applied to face, scalp, scrotum, axilla, and groin. Inspect skin carefully between applications for ecchymotic, petechial, and purpuric signs, maceration, secondary infection, skin atrophy, striae or miliaria; if present, stop medication and notify prescriber. Warn patient not to self-dose with OTC topical preparations of a corticosteroid more than 7 days. They should not be used for children younger than 2 y. If symptoms do not abate, consult prescriber. Usually, topical preparations are applied after a shower or bath when skin is damp or wet. Cleansing and application of prescribed preparation should be done with extreme gentleness because of fragility, easy bruisability, and poor-healing skin. Hazard of systemic toxicity is higher in small children because of the greater ratio of skin surface area to body weight. Apply sparingly. Urge patient on long-term therapy with topical corticosterone to check expiration date.

APPENDIX A-5

TOPICAL ANTIFUNGAL AGENTS

USES Treatment of fungal infections managed by topical agents. This could include: Tinea (pityriasis) versicolor due to *M. furfur* (formerly *P. orbiculare*), interdigital tinea pedis (athlete's foot), tinea corporis (ringworm) and tinea cruris (jock itch) due to *E. floccosum, T. mentagrophytes, T. rubrum,* and *T. tonsurans.* Shampoo for treatment of seborrheic dermatitis.

Butenafine
Lotrimin Ultra, Mentax, 1% cream

Adult: **Topical** Apply 1–2 × daily for 2–4 wk.

Ciclopirox
Ciclodan, Loprox,
Penlac, 8% solution,
1% shampoo, 0.77% gel

Adult: **Topical** Apply twice daily (morning and evening). Nail lacquer solution should be applied once daily.

Econazole
Ecoza, 1% cream, 1% foam

Adult: **Topical** Apply once daily × 2–4 wk (depending on area).

Efinaconazole
Jublia, 10% solution

Adult: **Topical** Apply daily to affected toenail × 48 wk.

Ketoconazole
2% cream

Adult: **Topical** Apply to affected area daily × 2 wk.

Luliconazole
Luzu, 1% cream

Adult: **Topical** Apply to affected area daily × 1–2 wk.

Miconazole
2% cream

Adult: **Topical** Apply to affected area bid × 2–4 weeks

Naftifine
Naftin, 1%, 2% cream; 1%, 2% gel

Adult: **Topical** Apply cream once daily or gel twice daily to affected areas × 2–4 wk.

Oxiconazole
Oxistat, 1% cream

Adult: **Topical** Apply to affected area 1–2 times daily × 2–4 wk.

Sertaconazole
Eratczo, 2% cream

Adult: **Topical** Apply to affected area bid × 4 wk.

Sulconazole
Exelderm, 1% cream; 1% solution

Adult: **Topical** Apply to affected area 1–2 times daily × 3–4 wk.

Tavaborole
Kerydin 5% solution

Adult: **Topical** Apply to affected toenails daily × 48 wk.

Terbinafine
Lamisil, 1% cream

Adult: **Topical** Apply to affected area 1–2 times daily for at least 1 week

Tolnaftate
Fungi-Guard, Fongoid-D, Lamisil AF Defense, Mycocide Clinical NS, Tinactin, Tinaspore, 1% solution, 1% powder, 1% cream, 1% aerosol, 1% aerosol powder

Adult/Adolescent/Child (2 y or older): **Topical** Apply to affected area 1–2 times daily × 4 wk.

CONTRAINDICATED IN Patients with known or suspected sensitivity to agent.

CAUTIOUS USE Pregnancy or lactation, cautious use in children (except tolnaftate), avoid use with occlusive dressing.

ADVERSE EFFECTS Skin: Stinging/burning at application site, contact dermatitis, erythema, irritation, itching. **Dermatologic:** Ingrown toenail.

CLINICAL IMPLICATIONS If symptoms not resolving within recommended therapy duration patient needs to be re-evaluated. Patients using a nail product should avoid pedicures, or use of nail polish during treatment.

◆ APPENDIX B U.S. SCHEDULES OF CONTROLLED SUBSTANCES

Schedule I

High potential for abuse and of no currently accepted medical use. Examples: heroin, LSD, ecstasy peyote. Not obtainable by prescription but may be legally procured for research, study, or instructional use.

Schedule II

High abuse potential and high liability for severe psychological or physical dependence. Prescription required and cannot be renewed.[a] Includes opium derivatives, other opioids, and short-acting barbiturates. Examples: Amphetamine, cocaine, meperidine, morphine, fentanyl.

Schedule III

Potential for abuse is less than that for drugs in Schedules I and II. Moderate to low physical dependence and high psychological dependence. Includes certain stimulants and depressants not included in the above schedules and preparations containing limited quantities of certain opioids. Examples: Ketamine, anabolic steroids, testosterone. Prescription required.[a,b]

Schedule IV

Lower potential for abuse than Schedule III drugs. Examples: Certain psychotropics (tranquilizers), chlordiazepoxide, diazepam, meprobamate, phenobarbital. Prescription required.[a,b]

Schedule V

Abuse potential less than that for Schedule IV drugs. Preparations contain limited quantities of certain narcotic drugs; generally intended for antitussive and antidiarrheal purposes and may be distributed without a prescription provided that:

1. Such distribution is made only by a pharmacist.
2. Not more than 240 mL or not more than 48 solid dosage units of any substance containing opium, nor more than 120 mL or not more than 24 solid dosage units of any other controlled substance may be distributed at retail to the same purchaser in any given 48-hour period without a valid prescription order.
3. The purchaser is at least 18 years old.

4. The pharmacist knows the purchaser or requests suitable identification.
5. The pharmacist keeps an official written record of: name and address of purchaser, name and quantity of controlled substance purchased, date of sale, initials of dispensing pharmacist. This record is to be made available for inspection and copying by U.S. officers authorized by the Attorney General.
6. Other federal, state, or local law does not require a prescription order.

Under jurisdiction of the Federal Controlled Substances Act:
°Except when dispensed directly by a practitioner, other than a pharmacist, to an ultimate user, no controlled substance in Schedule II may be dispensed without a *written* prescription, except that in emergency situations such drug may be dispensed upon oral prescription and a written prescription must be obtained within the time frame prescribed by law. No prescription for a controlled substance in Schedule II may be refilled.
ᵇRefillable up to 5 × within 6 mo, but only if so indicated by prescriber.

In December 2014 the FDA released a final rule replacing the historic *letter categories* (listed below) with new detailed subsections describing the risk of medication exposure in the real-world context of caring for pregnant patients. The final rule requires the use of three subsections in the labeling titled, *Pregnancy, Lactation,* and *Females and Males of Reproductive Potential* that provide details about use of the drug or biological product. The historic categories described by the FDA are as follows:

Category A

Controlled studies in women fail to demonstrate a risk to the fetus in the first trimester (and there is no evidence of risk in later trimesters), and the possibility of fetal harm appears remote.

Category B

Either animal-reproduction studies have not demonstrated a fetal risk but there are no controlled studies in pregnant women, or animal-reproduction studies have shown an adverse effect (other than a decrease in fertility) that was not confirmed in controlled studies in women in the first trimester (and there is no evidence of a risk in later trimesters).

Category C

Either studies in animals have revealed adverse effects on the fetus (teratogenic or embryocidal effects or other) and there are no controlled studies in women, or studies in women and animals are not available. Drugs should be given only if the potential benefit justifies the potential risk to the fetus.

Category D

There is positive evidence of human fetal risk, but the benefits from use in pregnant women may be acceptable despite the risk (e.g., if the drug is needed in a life-threatening situation or for a serious disease for which safer drugs cannot be used or are ineffective). There will be an appropriate statement in the "warnings" section of the labeling.

Category X

Studies in animals or human beings have demonstrated fetal abnormalities or there is evidence of fetal risk based on human experience, or both, and the risk of the use of the drug in pregnant women clearly outweighs any possible benefit. The drug is contraindicated in women who are or may become pregnant. There will be an appropriate statement in the "contraindications" section of the labeling.

Drugs approved after June 2015 will not have a *pregnancy category* but will instead include the categories of *Pregnancy, Lactation,* and *Females and Males of Reproductive Potential.*

Acanya (ANTIACNE) *gel:* benzoyl peroxide 2.5%/clindamycin (see p. 380) 1.2%.

Accuretic (ANTIHYPERTENSIVE) *tablet:* quinapril (see p. 1442) 10 mg/ hydrochlorothiazide (see p. 809) 12.5 mg; 20 mg quinapril (see p. 1442)/12.5 mg hydrochlorothiazide; 20 mg quinapril/25 mg hydrochlorothiazide.

Activella (HORMONE REPLACEMENT THERAPY) *tablet:* estradiol (see p. 650) 1 mg/norethindrone acetate (see p. 1194) 0.5 mg.

Actonel with Calcium (BISPHOSPHONATE) *tablet:* risedronate (see p. 1448) 35 mg/1250 calcium carbonate (see p. 249).

ACTOplus Met (ANTIDIABETIC) *tablet:* pioglitazone (see p. 1351) 15 mg/metformin (see p. 1051) 500 mg; pioglitazone 15 mg/metformin 850 mg.

Advair Diskus (BRONCHODILATOR) *Inhalation powder:* fluticasone propionate (see p. 737) 100 mcg/ salmeterol (see p. 1517) 50 mcg; fluticasone propionate 250 mcg/salmeterol 50 mcg; fluticasone propionate 115 mcg/ salmeterol 21 mcg; fluticasone propionate 230 mcg/salmeterol 21 mcg; fluticasone propionate 45 mcg/salmeterol 21 mcg.

Advicor (ANTILIPEMIC) *tablets, sustained release:* niacin (see p. 1164) 500 mg/lovastatin (see p. 1001) 20 mg; niacin 1000 mg/ lovastatin 20 mg.

Aggrenox (ANTIPLATELET) *extended release capsule:* dipyridamole (see p. 529) 200 mg/aspirin (see p. 126) 25 mg.

AirDuo RespiClick (BRONCHODILATOR) *inhalation powder:* fluticasone (see p. 737) 113 mcg/ salmeterol (see p. 1517) 14 mcg; fluticasone 232 mcg/salmeterol 14 mcg; fluticasone 55 mcg/salmeterol 14 mcg.

Akynzeo (ANTIEMETIC) *solution:* reconsituted fosnetupitant 235 mg/plonosetron 0.25 mg.

Aldactazide 25/25 (DIURETIC) *tablet:* spironolactone (see p. 1577) 25 mg/hydrochlorothiazide (see p. 809) 25 mg.

Aldactazide 50/50 (DIURETIC) *tablet:* spironolactone (see p. 1577) 50 mg/hydrochlorothiazide (see p. 809) 50 mg.

Allegra D 12 hour (ANTIHISTAMINE, DECONGESTANT) *tablet, extended release:* fexofenadine (see p. 708) 60 mg/pseudoephedrine (see p. 1429) 120 mg.

Allegra D 24 hour (ANTIHISTAMINE, DECONGESTANT) *tablet, extended release:* fexofenadine (see p. 708) 180 mg/pseudoephedrine (see p. 1429) 240 mg.

Anexsia 5/325 (NARCOTIC ANALGESIC [schedule III]) *tablet:* hydrocodone (see p. 811) 5 mg/acetaminophen (see p. 13) 325 mg.

Anexsia 7.5/325 (NARCOTIC ANALGESIC [schedule III]) *tablet:* hydrocodone (see p. 811) 7.5 mg/ acetaminophen (see p. 13) 325 mg.

Angeliq (HORMONE) *tablet:* drospirenone 0.5 mg/estradiol (see p. 650) 1 mg.

Apresazide 25/25 (ANTIHYPERTENSIVE) *capsule:* hydralazine hydrochloride (see p. 807) 25 mg/hydrochlorothiazide (see p. 809) 25 mg.

Apresazide 50/50 (ANTIHYPERTENSIVE) *capsule:* hydralazine hydrochloride (see p. 807) 50 mg/hydrochlorothiazide (see p. 809) 50 mg.

Apresodex (ANTIHYPERTENSIVE) *tablet:* hydralazine hydrochloride (see p. 807) 25 mg/hydrochlorothiazide (see p. 809) 15 mg.

Aralen Phosphate with Primaquine Phosphate (ANTIMALARIAL) *tablet:* chloroquine phosphate (see p. 340) 500 mg (300 mg base)/primaquine phosphate (see p. 1395) 79 mg (45 mg base).

Arthrotec 50 (NSAID) *tablet:* diclofenac sodium (see p. 499) 50 mg/misoprostol (see p. 1108) 200 mcg.

Arthrotec 75 (NSAID) *tablet:* diclofenac sodium (see p. 499) 75 mg/misoprostol (see p. 1108) 200 mcg.

Atacand HCT (ANTIHYPERTENSIVE) *tablet:* candesartan (see p. 258) 32 mg/hydrochlorothiazide (see p. 809) 12.5 mg; candesartan 16 mg/hydrochlorothiazide 12.5 mg.

Atripla (ANTIRETROVIRAL) *tablet:* 600 mg efavirenz (see p. 581)/200 mg emtricitabine (see p. 594)/300 mg tenofovir (see p. 1628).

Augmentin (ANTIBIOTIC) *tablet:* amoxicillin (see p. 86) 250 mg/clavulanic acid 125 mg; amoxicillin 500 mg/clavulanic acid 125 mg; amoxicillin 875 mg/clavulanic acid 125 mg; amoxicillin 1000 mg/clavulanic acid 125 mg; *chewable tablet:* amoxicillin 125 mg/clavulanic acid 31.25 mg; amoxicillin 200 mg/clavulanic acid 28.5 mg; amoxicillin 250 mg/clavulanic acid 62.5 mg; amoxicillin 400 mg/clavulanic acid 57 mg; *suspension (per 5 mL):* amoxicillin 125 mg/clavulanic acid 31.25 mg; amoxicillin 200 mg/clavulanic acid 28.5 mg; amoxicillin 250 mg/clavulanic acid 62.5 mg; amoxicillin 400 mg/clavulanic acid 57 mg; amoxicillin 600 mg/clavulanic acid 42.9 mg.

Auralgan Otic (OTIC PREPARATION: DECONGESTANT, ANALGESIC) *solution:* acetic acid 0.1%, antipyrine 5.4%, benzocaine (see p. 180) 1.4%, u-polycosanol 410 0.01%.

Avalide (ANTIHYPERTENSIVE) *tablet:* irbesartan (see p. 886) 150 mg/hydrochlorothiazide (see p. 809) 12.5 mg; irbesartan 300 mg/hydrochlorothiazide 12.5 mg; irbesartan 300 mg/hydrochlorothiazide 25 mg.

Avandamet (HYPOGLYCEMIC AGENT) *tablet:* 1 mg rosiglitazone maleate (see p. 1509)/500 mg metformin HCl (see p. 1051); 2 mg rosiglitazone/500 mg metformin; 4 mg rosiglitazone/500 mg metformin; 2 mg rosiglitazone/1000 mg metformin; 4 mg rosiglitazone/1000 mg metformin.

Avandaryl (HYPOGLYCEMIC AGENT) *tablet:* rosiglitazone (see p. 1509) 4 mg/glimepiride (see p. 776) 1 mg; rosiglitazone 4 mg/glimepiride 2 mg; rosiglitazone 4 mg/glimepiride 4 mg.

Azo Gantanol (URINARY ANTI-INFECTIVE, ANALGESIC) *tablet:* sulfamethoxazole (see p. 1591) 500 mg, phenazopyridine hydrochloride (see p. 1325) 100 mg.

Azo Gantrisin (URINARY ANTI-INFECTIVE, ANALGESIC) *tablet:* sulfisoxazole (see p. 1008) 500 mg/phenazopyridine hydrochloride (see p. 1325) 50 mg.

Azor (ANTIHYPERTENSIVE) *tablet:* amlodipine (see p. 84) 5 mg/olmesartan (see p. 1210) 20 mg; amlodipine 5 mg/olmesartan 40 mg; amlodipine 10 mg/olmesartan 20 mg; amlodipine 10 mg/olmesartan 40 mg.

B-A-C (ANALGESIC) acetaminophen (see p. 13) 650 mg/caffeine (see p. 243) 40 mg/butalbital 50 mg.

Bacticort Ophthalmic (ANTI-INFLAM-MATORY) *suspension:* hydrocortisone (see p. 812) 1%/neomycin sulfate (see p. 1157) 0.35%/polymyxin B (see p. 1365) 10,000 units.

Bactrim (URINARY TRACT AGENT) *tablet:* sulfamethoxazole (see p. 1591) 400 mg/trimethoprim (see p. 1591) 80 mg.

Bactrim DS (URINARY TRACT AGENT) *tablet:* sulfamethoxazole (see p. 1591) 800 mg/trimethoprim (see p. 1726) 160 mg.

Benicar HCT (ANTIHYPERTENSIVE) *tablet:* 20 mg olmesartan medoxomil (see p. 1210)/12.5 mg hydrochlorothiazide (see p. 809); 40 mg olmesartan medoxomil/12.5 mg hydrochlorothiazide; 40 mg olmesartan medoxomil/25 mg hydrochlorothiazide.

Betoptic Pilo Suspension (ANTI-GLAUCOMA) *suspension:* betaxolol (see p. 188) 0.25%/pilocarpine (see p. 1343) 1.75%.

Bevespi   Aerosphere (ANTICHOLINERGIC/BETA AGONIST) inhaler: glycopyrrolate 9 mcg/formoterol fum 4.8 mcg.

Beyaz (ORAL CONTRACEPTIVE) *tablet:* drosperinone 3 mg/ethinyl estradiol 0.02 mg/levomefolate calcium 0.451 mg.

BiDil (ANTIHYPERTENSIVE) *tablet:* isosorbide dinitrate (see p. 901) 20 mg/hydralazine (see p. 807) 37.5 mg.

Breo Ellipta (BRONCHODIALATOR) *powder for inhalation:* fluticasone (see p. 737) 100 mcg/vilanterol 25 mcg.

Blephamide (OPHTHALMIC STEROID, SULFONAMIDE) *suspension:* prednisolone acetate (see p. 1389) 0.2%/sulfacetamide sodium (see p. 1588) 10%.

Blephamide S.O.P. (OPHTHALMIC STEROID, SULFONAMIDE) *ointment:* prednisolone acetate (see p. 1389) 0.2%/sulfacetamide sodium (see p. 1588) 10%.

Brevicon (MONOPHASIC ORAL CONTRACEPTIVE [ESTROGEN, PROGESTIN]) *tablet:* ethinyl estradiol 35 mcg/norethindrone (see p. 1194) 0.5 mg.

Bromfed (DECONGESTANT, ANTIHISTAMINE) *sustained release capsule:* pseudoephedrine hydrochloride (see p. 1194) 120 mg/brompheniramine maleate (see p. 220) 12 mg.

Bromfed-PD (DECONGESTANT, ANTIHISTAMINE) *sustained release capsule:* pseudoephedrine hydrochloride (see p. 1429) 60 mg/brompheniramine maleate (see p. 220) 6 mg.

Bronchial Capsules (ANTIASTHMATIC) *capsule:* theophylline (see p. 1648) 150 mg/guaifenesin (see p. 793) 90 mg.

Byvalson (ANTIHYPERTENSIVE) tablet: nebivolol 5 mg/valsartan 80 mg.

Caduet (ANTIHYPERTENSIVE/ANTILIPEMIC) *tablet:* 2.5 mg amlodipine (see p. 84)/10 mg atorvastatin (see p. 135); 2.5 mg amlodipine/20 mg atorvastatin; 2.5 mg amlodipine/40 mg atorvastatin; 5 mg amlodipine/10 mg atorvastatin; 10 mg amlodipine/10 mg atorvastatin; 5 mg amlodipine/20 mg atorvastatin; 10 mg amlodipine/20 mg atorvastatin; 5 mg amlodipine/40 mg atorvastatin; 10 mg amlodipine/40 mg atorvastatin; 5 mg amlodipine/80 mg atorvastatin; 10 mg amlodipine/80 mg atorvastatin.

Cafergot Suppositories (ANTIMIGRAINE) *suppository:* ergotamine tartrate (see p. 627) 2 mg/caffeine (see p. 243) 100 mg.

Cam-ap-es (ANTIHYPERTENSIVE) suspension, *tablet:* hydrochlorothiazide (see p. 809) 15 mg/hydralazine hydrochloride (see p. 807) 25 mg.

Carisoprodol Compound (SKELETAL MUSCLE RELAXANT, ANALGESIC) *tablet:* carisoprodol (see p. 281) 200 mg/aspirin (see p. 126) 325 mg.

Carmol HC (ANTI-INFLAMMATORY) *cream:* hydrocortisone acetate (see p. 812) 1%/urea 10%.

Celestone-Soluspan (GLUCOCORTICOID) *injection (suspension) (per mL):* betamethasone acetate (see p. 185) 3 mg/betamethasone sodium phosphate (see p. 185) 3 mg.

Cetacaine (TOPICAL ANESTHETIC) *gel, liquid, ointment, aerosol:* benzocaine (see p. 180) 14%/tetracaine hydrochloride (see p. 1642) 2%/butamben 2%/benzalkonium chloride (see p. 179) 0.5%.

Cheracol Syrup (NARCOTIC ANTITUSSIVE, EXPECTORANT [schedule V]) *syrup (per 5 mL):* codeine phosphate (see p. 400) 10 mg/guaifenesin (see p. 793) 100 mg/alcohol 4.75%.

Cipro HC Otic (ANTI-INFECTIVE/ANTI-INFLAMMATORY) *topical:* ciprofloxacin (see p. 365) 2 mg/dexamethasone (see p. 481) 10 mg otic suspension.

Ciprodex Otic (ANTI-INFECTIVE/ANTI-INFLAMMATORY) *topical:* ciprofloxacin (see p. 365) 0.3%/dexamethasone (see p. 481) 0.1% otic suspension.

Claritin D (ANTIHISTAMINE, DECONGESTANT) loratadine (see p. 995), 5 mg/pseudoephedrine (see p. 1429) 120 mg; loratadine 10 mg/pseudoephedrine 240 mg.

Clarinex D 24 hr (ANTIHISTAMINE, DECONGESTANT) *tablet:* desloratadine (see p. 477) 5 mg/pseudoephedrine (see p. 1429) 240 mg.

Climara Pro (HORMONE REPLACEMENT THERAPY) *transdermal patch:* estradiol (see p. 650) 0.045 mg/levonorgestrel acetate 0.015 mg.

Codiclear DH Syrup (ANTITUSSIVE [schedule III]) *syrup (per 5 mL):* hydrocodone (see p. 811) 5 mg/guaifenesin (see p. 793) 100 mg/alcohol 10%.

Codimal DH (ANTITUSSIVE [schedule III]) *syrup (per 5 mL):* phenylephrine hydrochloride (see p. 1334) 5 mg/pyrilamine maleate 8.33 mg/hydrocodone bitartrate (see p. 811) 1.66 mg.

Codimal PH (ANTITUSSIVE [schedule III]) *syrup (per 5 mL):* codeine (see p. 400) 10 mg/pyrilamine maleate 8.33 mg/phenylephrine (see p. 1334) 5 mg.

Coly-Mycin S Otic (OTIC: STEROID, ANTIBIOTIC) *suspension (per mL):* hydrocortisone acetate (see p. 812) 1%/neomycin sulfate (see p. 1157) 3.3 mg/colistin sulfate 3 mg/thonzonium bromide 0.05%.

Combigan (GLAUCOMA) *ophthalmic solution:* brimonidine (see p. 215) 0.2%/timolol (see p. 1671) 0.5%.

CombiPatch (HORMONE REPLACEMENT THERAPY) *transdermal patch:* estradiol (see p. 650) 0.05 mg/norethindrone acetate (see p. 1194) 0.14 mg; estradiol 0.05 mg/norethindrone acetate 0.25 mg.

Combivent Respimat (BETA-AGONIST/ANTICHOLINERGIC BRONCHODILATOR) *inhalation solution:* 100 mcg albuterol sulfate/20 mcg ipratropium

Combivir (ANTIVIRAL) *tablet:* zidovudine (see p. 1791) 300 mg/lamivudine (see p. 931) 150 mg.

Complera (ANTIRETROVIRAL) *tablet:* rilpivirine 25 mg/emtricitabine 200 mg/tenofovir 300 mg.

Cortisporin (OPHTHALMIC STEROID, ANTIBIOTIC) *suspension (per mL):* hydrocortisone (see p. 812) 1%/neomycin sulfate (see p. 1157) (equivalent to 0.35% neomycin base)/polymyxin B sulfate (see p. 1324) 10,000 units.

Cortisporin Ointment (OPHTHALMIC STEROID, ANTIBIOTIC) *ointment:* hydrocortisone (see p. 812) 1%/neomycin sulfate (see p. 1157) (equivalent to 0.35% neomycin base)/bacitracin zinc (see p. 160) 400 units, polymyxin B sulfate (see p. 1365) 10,000 units/g.

Corzide (ANTIHYPERTENSIVE) *tablet:* nadolol (see p. 1128) 40 mg/bendroflumethiazide 5 mg; nadolol 80 mg/bendoflumethiazide 5 mg.

Cosopt (OPHTHALMIC, GLAUCOMA) *ophthalmic solution:* dorzolamide (see p. 550) 2%/timolol (see p. 1671) 0.5%.

Cyclomydril (OPHTHALMIC DECONGESTANT) *ophthalmic solution:* atropine hydrochloride 0.2%/phenylephrine hydrochloride (see p. 1334) 1%.

Decadron with Xylocaine (GLUCOCORTICOID) *injection (per mL):* dexamethasone sodium phosphate (see p. 481) 4 mg/lidocaine hydrochloride (see p. 966) 10 mg.

Deconamine (DECONGESTANT, ANTIHISTAMINE) *syrup (per 5 mL):* pseudoephedrine hydrochloride (see p. 1429) 30 mg/chlorpheniramine maleate (see p. 344) 2 mg; *tablet:* pseudoephedrine hydrochloride 60 mg/chlorpheniramine maleate 4 mg.

Deconamine SR (DECONGESTANT, ANTIHISTAMINE) *sustained release capsule:* pseudoephedrine hydrochloride (see p. 1429) 120 mg/chlorpheniramine maleate (see p. 344) 8 mg.

Depo-Testadiol (ESTROGEN, ANDROGEN) *injection (per mL):* estradiol cypionate (see p. 650) 2 mg/testosterone cypionate (see p. 1639) 50 mg.

Descovy (REVERSE TRANSCRIPTASE INHIBITOR) *tablet:* emtricitabine 200 mg/tenofovir alafenamide 25 mg.

Diclegis (ANTIEMETIC) *tablet:* doxylamine 10 mg/pyridoxine (see p. 1436) 10 mg.

Diovan HCT (ANTIHYPERTENSIVE) *tablet:* hydrochlorothiazide (see p. 809) 12.5 mg/valsartan (see p. 1513) 80 mg; hydrochlorothiazide 12.5 mg/valsartan 160 mg; hydrochlorothiazide 25 mg/valsartan 160 mg; hydrochlorothiazide 12.5 mg/valsartan 320 mg; hydrochlorothiazide 25 mg/valsartan 320 mg.

Donnatal (GASTROINTESTINAL ANTICHOLINERGIC, SEDATIVE) *tablet, elixir:* atropine sulfate (see p. 141) 0.0194 mg/scopolamine hydrobromide (see p. 1528) 0.0065 mg/hyoscyamine hydrobromide or sulfate (see p. 826) 0.1037 mg/phenobarbital (see p. 1329) 16.2 mg. The elixir contains alcohol 23%/5 mL.

Donnatal Extentab (GASTROINTESTINAL ANTICHOLINERGIC, SEDATIVE) *tablet:* atropine sulfate (see p. 141) 0.0582 mg/scopolamine hydrobromide (see p. 1528) 0.0195 mg/hyoscyamine sulfate (see p. 826) 0.3111 mg/phenobarbital (see p. 1329) 48.6 mg.

Duac (ANTIACNE) *gel:* clindamycin (see p. 380) 1%/benzoyl peroxide 5%.

Duavee (HORMONE REPLACEMENT) tablet conjugated estrogen 0.45 mg/bazedoxifene 20 mg.

Duetact (ANTIDIABETIC) *tablet:* pioglitazone (see p. 1351) 30 mg/glimepiride (see p. 776) 2 mg; pioglitazone 30 mg/glimepiride 4 mg.

Duexis (ANTIULCERATIVE) *tablet:* ibuprofen 800 mg/famotidine 26.6 mg.

Dulera (CORTICOSTEROID/BETA-AGONIST) *inhaler:* mometasone 100 mcg/fomoterol 5 mcg; mometasone 200 mcg/fomoterol 5 mcg.

DuoNeb (BETA-AGONIST/ANTICHOLINERGIC BRONCHODILATOR) *inhalation solution:* 2.5 mg albuterol sulfate (see p. 39)/0.5 mg ipratropium bromide (see p. 885) per 3 mL.

Duzallo (ANTIGOUT) *tablet:* lesinurad (see p. 946) 200 mg/allopurinol (see p. 48) 200 mg; lesinurad 200 mg/allopurinol 300 mg.

Dyazide (DIURETIC) *capsule:* triamterene (see p. 809) 37.5 mg/hydrochlorothiazide (see p. 809) 25 mg.

Dymista (ANTIHISTAMINE) *Nasal spray:* azelastine 137 mcg/fluticasone 50 mcg.

Edarbyclor (ANTIHYPERTENSIVE) *tablet:* azilsartan 40 mg/chlorthalidone 12.5 mg; azilsartan 40 mg/chlorthalidone 25 mg.

EluRyng (CONTRACEPTIVE) *vaginal ring:* ethinyl estradiol 0.015 mg/etonogestrel 0.12 mg.

Embeda (ANALGESIC [schedule II]) *tablet:* morphine (see p. 1119) 20 mg/naltrexone (see p. 1139) 0.8 mg; morphine 30 mg/naltrexone 1.2 mg; morphine 50 mg/naltrexone 2 mg; morphine 60 mg/naltrexone 2.4 mg; morphine 80 mg/naltrexone 3.2 mg; morphine 100 mg/naltrexone 4 mg.

Endocet (NARCOTIC ANALGESIC [schedule II]) *tablet:* oxycodone (see p. 1249) 7.5 mg/acetaminophen (see p. 13) 325 mg; oxycodone 7.5 mg/acetaminophen 500 mg; oxycodone 10 mg/acetaminophen 325 mg; oxycodone 10 mg/acetaminophen 650 mg.

Enlon Plus (ANTICHOLINESTERASE) *solution:* edrophonium 10 mg/atropine 0.14 mg.

Entresto (NAPRILYSIN INHIBITOR/ANGIOTENSION II BLOCKER) *tablet:* sacubitril 24 mg/valsartan 26 mg; sacubitril 49 mg/valsartan 51 mg; sacubitril 97 mg/valsartan 103 mg.

Epiduo (ANTIACNE) *gel:* adapalene (see p. 28) 0.1%/benzoyl peroxide 2.5%.

Epclusa (ANTIVIRAL) *tablet:* sofosbuvir 400 mg/velpatasvir 100 mg.

Epzicom (ANTIRETROVIRAL AGENT) *tablet:* abacavir (see p. 1) 600 mg/lamivudine (see p. 931) 300 mg.

Estratest (ESTROGEN, ANDROGEN) *tablet:* esterified estrogens (see p. 658) 1.25 mg/methyltestosterone (see p. 1078) 2.5 mg.

Estratest H.S. (ESTROGEN, ANDROGEN) *tablet:* esterified estrogens (see p. 658) 0.625 mg/methyltestosterone (see p. 1078) 1.25 mg.

Evotaz (ANTIVIRAL/PROTEASE INHIBITOR) *tablet:* atazanavir (see p. 129) 300/cobicistat 150.

Exforge (ANTIHYPERTENSIVE) *tablet:* amlodipine (see p. 84) 5 mg/valsartan (see p. 1513) 160 mg; amlodipine 10 mg/valsartan 160 mg; amlodipine 5 mg/valsartan 320 mg; amlodipine 10 mg/valsartan 320 mg.

Exforge HCT (ANTIHYPERTENSIVE) *tablet:* amlodipine (see p. 84) 5 mg/valsartan (see p. 1513) 160 mg/hydrochlorothiazide (see p. 809) 12.5 mg; amlodipine 5 mg/valsartan 160 mg/hydrochlorothiazide 25 mg; amlodipine 10 mg/valsartan 160 mg/hydrochlorothiazide 12.5 mg; amlodipine 10 mg/valsartan 160 mg/hydrochlorothiazide 25 mg.

Fioricet with Codeine (NONNARCOTIC AGONIST ANALGESIC) *capsule:* acetaminophen (see p. 13) 300 mg/ butalbital 50 mg/caffeine (see p. 243) 40 mg/codeine (30 mg).

Fiorinal (NONNARCOTIC AGONIST ANALGESIC [schedule III]) *capsule,* aspirin (see p. 126) 325 mg/butalbital 50 mg/caffeine (see p. 243) 40 mg.

Fiorinal with Codeine (NARCOTIC AGONIST ANALGESIC [schedule III]) *capsule:* codeine phosphate (see p. 395) 30 mg/aspirin (see p. 126) 325 mg/caffeine (see p. 243) 40 mg/ butalbital 50 mg.

Fosamax Plus D (BISPHOSPHONATE) *tablet:* alendronate (see p. 41) 70 mg/vitamin D (see p. 1775) 2800 international units.

Glucovance (ANTIDIABETIC) *tablet:* glyburide (see p. 780) 1.25 mg/metformin (see p. 1051) 250 mg; glyburide 2.5 mg/metformin 500 mg; glyburide 5 mg/metformin 500 mg.

Harvoni (ANTIVIRAL) *tablet:* ledipasvir (see p. 942) 90 mg/sofosbuvir (see p. 942) 400 mg.

Helidac (ANTIULCER, ANTIBIOTIC) *tablet:* bismuth subsalicylate (see p. 198) 262.4 mg/metronidazole (see p. 1086) 250 mg/tetracycline (see p. 1644) 500 mg.

Herceptin Hylecta (ANTINEOPLASTIC) *solution for injection:* trastuzumab 600 mg/hyaluronidase 10,000 units/5 mL

Hycodan (ANTITUSSIVE [schedule III]) *tablet, syrup:* hydrocodone bitartrate (see p. 811) 5 mg/homatropine methylbromide 1.5 mg.

Hycotuss Expectorant (ANTITUSSIVE [schedule III]) guaifenesin (see p. 793) 100 mg/hydrocodone (see p. 811) 5 mg.

Hyzaar (ANTIHYPERTENSIVE) *tablet:* losartan (see p. 1000) 50 mg/hydrochlorothiazide (see p. 809) 12.5 mg/losartan 100 mg/hydrochlorothiazide 12.5 mg/losartan 100 mg/hydrochlorothiazide 25 mg.

Inderide 40/25 (ANTIHYPERTENSIVE) *tablet:* propranolol hydrochloride (see p. 1418) 40 mg/hydrochlorothiazide (see p. 809) 25 mg.

Invokamet (ANTIDIABETIC) *tablet:* canagliflozin (see p. 257) 150/metformin (see p. 1051) 1000 mg; canagliflozin 50/metformin 500 mg.

Jalyn (BPH AGENT) *capsule:* dutasteride 0.5 mg/tamsulosin 0.4 mg.

Janumet (ANTIDIABETIC) *tablet:* sitagliptin (see p. 1554) 50 mg/metformin (see p. 1051) 500 mg; sitagliptin 50 mg/metformin 1000 mg.

Janumet XR (ANTIDIABETIC) *extended release tablet:* sitagliptin 100 mg/metformin 1000 mg; sitagliptin 50 mg/metformin 1000 mg; sitagliptin 50 mg/metformin 500 mg.

Jentadueto (ANTIDIABETIC) *tablet:* linagliptan 2.5 mg/metformin 1000 mg; linagliptan 2.5 mg/metformin 500; mglinagliptan 2.5 mg/metformin 850 mg.

Jusvisync (ANTIDIABETIC) *tablet:* sitagliptin 100 mg/simvastatin 10 mg; sitagliptin 100 mg/simvastatin 20 mg; sitagliptin 100 mg/simvastatin 40 mg.

Kazano (ANTIDIABETIC) *tablet:* alogliptin (see p. 52) 12.5 mg/metformin (see p. 1051) 500 mg alogliptin 12.5 mg/metformin 1000 mg.

Kisqali Femara (ANTINEOPLASTIC) *tablet:* letrozole (see p. 949) 2.5 mg/ribociclib 200 mg; letrozole 2.5 mg/ribociclib 400 mg; letrozole 2.5 mg/ribociclib 600 mg.

Kombiglyze XR (ANTIDIABETIC) *extended release tablet:* saxagliptin 5 mg/metformin 500 mg; saxagliptin 2.5 mg/metformin 1000 mg; saxagliptin 5 mg/metformin 1000 mg.

LidoSite (LOCAL ANESTHETIC) *transdermal patch:* lidocaine (see p. 966) 100 mg/epinephrine (see p. 609) 1.05 mg.

Limbitrol (PSYCHOTHERAPEUTIC [schedule IV]) *tablet:* chlordiazepoxide (see p. 338) 5 mg/amitriptyline (see p. 80) 12.5 mg; chlordiazepoxide 10 mg/amitriptyline 25 mg.

Limbitrol DS (PSYCHOTHERAPEUTIC [schedule IV]) *tablet:* chlordiazepoxide (see p. 338) 10 mg/amitriptyline (see p. 82) 25 mg.

Liptruzet (LIPID-LOWERING AGENT) *tablet:* atorvastatin (see p. 135) 10 mg/ezetimibe (see p. 686) 10 mg atorvastatin 20 mg/ezetimibe 10 mg atorvastatin 40 mg/ezetimibe 10 mg atorvastatin 80mg/ezetimibe 10 mg.

Loestrin 1/20 (ORAL CONTRACEPTIVE) *tablet:* ethinyl estradiol 20 mcg/norethindrone acetate (see p. 1194) 1 mg.

Loestrin 1/20 Fe (ORAL CONTRACEPTIVE) *tablet:* ethinyl estradiol 20 mcg/norethindrone acetate (see p. 1194) 1 mg/ferrous fumarate 75 mg in last 7 tablets.

Loestrin 1.5/30 (ORAL CONTRACEPTIVE) *tablet:* ethinyl estradiol 30 mcg/norethindrone acetate (see p. 1161) 1.5 mg.

Loestrin 1.5/30 Fe (ORAL CONTRACEPTIVE) *tablet:* ethinyl estradiol 30 mcg/norethindrone acetate (see p. 1194) 1.5 mg/ferrous fumarate 75 mg in last 7 tablets.

Lomotil (ANTIDIARRHEAL) *tablet:* diphenoxylate (see p. 527) 2.5 mg/atropine (see p. 141) 0.025 mg.

Lo/Ovral 28 (ORAL CONTRACEPTIVE) tablet: ethinyl estradiol 30 mcg/norgestrel 0.3 mg.

Lopressor HCT (ANTIHYPERTENSIVE) *tablet:* metoprolol tartrate (see p. 1083) 50 mg/hydrochlorothiazide (see p. 809) 25 mg; meto-prolol tartrate 100 mg/hydrochlorothiazide 25 mg; metoprolol tartrate 100 mg/hydrochlorothiazide 50 mg.

LoSeasonique (ORAL CONTRACEPTIVE) *tablet:* ethinyl estradiol 0.01 mg/ethinyl estradiol 0.02 mg/levonorgestrel (see p. 962) 0.1 mg.

Lotensin HCT (ANTIHYPERTENSIVE) *tablet:* hydrochlorothiazide (see p. 809) 25 mg/benazepril (see p. 176) 20 mg; hydrochlorothiazide 12.5/benazepril 20 mg; hydrochlorothiazide 12.5 mg/benazepril 10 mg.

Lotrel (ANTIHYPERTENSIVE) *tablet:* amlodipine (see p. 84) 2.5 mg/benazepril (see p. 176) 10 mg; amlodipine 5 mg/benazepril 10 mg; amlodipine 5 mg/benazepril 20 mg; amlodipine 10 mg/benazepril 20 mg; amlodipine 10 mg/benazepril 40 mg.

Lotrisone (CORTICOSTEROID, ANTIFUNGAL) *cream:* betamethasone (see p. 185) (as dipropionate) 0.05%/clotrimazole (see p. 397) 1%.

Malarone (ANTIMALARIAL) *tablet:* atovaquone (see p. 136) 250 mg/proguanil HCl 100 mg; atovaquone 62.5 mg/proguanil HCl 25 mg.

Maxitrol (OPHTHALMIC STEROID, ANTIBIOTIC) *ophthalmic ointment, ophthalmic suspension:* dexamethasone (see p. 481) 0.1%/neomycin sulfate (see p. 1157) (equivalent to 0.35% neomycin base)/polymyxin B sulfate (see p. 1365) 10,000 units.

Maxzide (DIURETIC) *tablet:* triamterene (see p. 1718) 75 mg/hydrochlorothiazide (see p. 809) 50 mg.

Maxzide 25 (DIURETIC) *tablet:* triamterene (see p. 1718) 37.5 mg/hydrochlorothiazide (see p. 809) 25 mg.

Metaglip (HYPOGLYCEMIC AGENT) *tablet:* glipizide (see p. 777) 2.5 mg/metformin HCl (see p. 1051) 250 mg; glipizide 2.5 mg/metformin 500 mg; glipizide 5 mg/metformin 500 mg.

Micardis HCT (ANTIHYPERTENSIVE) *tablet:* telmisartan (see p. 1619) 40 mg/hydrochlorothiazide (see p. 809) 12.5 mg; telmisartan 80 mg/hydrochlorothiazide 12.5 mg; telmisartan 80 mg/hydrochlorothiazide 25 mg.

Minizide (ANTIHYPERTENSIVE) *capsule:* polythiazide 0.5 mg/prazosin hydrochloride (see p. 1387) 1 mg; polythiazide 0.5 mg/prazosin hydrochloride 2 mg; polythiazide 0.5 mg/prazosin hydrochloride 5 mg.

Modicon 28 (ORAL CONTRACEPTIVE) *tablet:* ethinyl estradiol 35 mcg/norethindrone (see p. 1194) 0.5 mg.

Moduretic (DIURETIC) *tablet:* amiloride hydrochloride (see p. 70) 5 mg/hydrochlorothiazide (see p. 809) 50 mg.

Mycitracin (OPHTHALMIC ANTIBIOTIC) *ophthalmic ointment:* polymyxin B sulfate (see p. 1365) 10,000 units/neomycin sulfate (see p. 1157) 3.5 mg/bacitracin (see p. 160) 500 units/g.

Mycolog II (CORTICOSTEROID, ANTI-FUNGAL) *cream, ointment:* triamcinolone acetonide (see p. 1716) 0.1%/nystatin (see p. 1198) 100,000 units/g.

Mydayis (ATTENTION DEFICIT DISORDER AGENT [schedule II]) *extended release capsule:* amphetamine aspartate 3.125 mg, amphetamine sulfate (see p. 89) 3.125 mg, dextroamphetamine saccharate 3.125 mg, dextroamphetamine sulfate (see p. 491) 3.125 mg.

Neo-Cortef (CORTICOSTEROID ANTIBIOTIC) *water-soluble cream, topical ointment:* hydrocortisone acetate (see p. 812) 1%/neomycin sulfate (see p. 1157) 0.5%.

Neosporin (OPHTHALMIC ANTIBIOTIC) *ophthalmic drops:* polymyxin B sulfate (see p. 1365) 10,000 units/neomycin sulfate (see p. 1157) 1.75 mg/gramicidin 0.025 mg/mL; *ophthalmic ointment:* polymyxin B sulfate 10,000 units/neomycin sulfate 3.5 mg/bacitracin zinc (see p. 160) 400 units/g.

Neosporin G.U. Irrigant (ANTIBIOTIC) *solution:* neomycin sulfate (see p. 1157) 40 mg/polymyxin B sulfate (see p. 1365) 200,000 units/mL.

Neutra-Phos (PHOSPHORUS REPLACEMENT) *capsule, powder:* phosphorus 250 mg/potassium (see p. 1372) 231 mg/sodium (see p. 1555) 167 mg/combination of monobasic, dibasic, sodium, and potassium phosphate.

Nexlizet (ANTILIPEMIC AGENT) *tablet:* bempedoic acid 180 mg/ezetimibe 10 mg

Norco (NARCOTIC AGONIST ANALGESIC [schedule III]) *tablet:* hydrocodone bitartrate (see p. 811) 10 mg/acetaminophen (see p. 13) 325 mg; hydrocodone bitartrate 7.5 mg/acetaminophen 325 mg.

Nordette 28 (ORAL CONTRACEPTIVE) *tablet:* ethinyl estradiol 30 mcg/levonorgestrel (see p. 962) 0.15 mg.

Norgesic (SKELETAL MUSCLE RELAXANT) *tablet:* orphenadrine citrate (see p. 1230) 25 mg/aspirin (see p. 126) 385 mg/caffeine (see p. 243) 30 mg.

Norgesic Forte (SKELETAL MUSCLE RELAXANT, ANALGESIC) *tablet:* orphenadrine citrate (see p. 1230) 50 mg/aspirin (see p. 126) 770 mg/caffeine (see p. 243) 60 mg.

Norinyl 1+35 (ORAL CONTRACEPTIVE) *tablet:* ethinyl estradiol 35 mcg/norethindrone (see p. 1194) 1 mg.

Norinyl 1+50 (ORAL CONTRACEPTIVE) *tablet:* mestranol 50 mcg/norethindrone (see p. 1194) 1 mg.

NuvaRing (CONTRACEPTIVE) *vaginal ring:* ethinyl estradiol (see p. 650) 0.015 mg/etonogestrel 0.12 mg.

Odefsey (NUCLEOSIDE REVERSE TRANSCRIPTASE INHIBITOR/NONNUCLEOSIDE REVERSE TRANSCRIPTASE INHIBITOR) *tablet:* emtricitabine (see p. 594) 200 mg/rilpivirine (see p. 1483) 25 mg/tenofovir alafenamide (see p. 1628) 25 mg.

Oriahnn (ESTROGEN/PROGESTIN) *capsule:* elagolix 300 mg/ estradiol 1 mg/norethindrone 0.5 mg

Ortho Evra (CONTRACEPTIVE) *transdermal patch:* norelgestromin 0.15 mg/ethinyl estradiol 0.02 mg.

Osensi (ANTIDIABETIC) *tablet:* alogliptin 25 mg/pioglitazone (see p. 1351) 15 mg; alogliptin 25 mg/pioglitazone 30 mg; alogliptin 25 mg/pioglitazone 45 mg; alogliptin 12.5 mg/pioglitazone 15 mg; alogliptin 12.5 mg/pioglitazone 30 mg; alogliptin 12.5 mg/pioglitazone 45 mg

Oxycet (NARCOTIC ANALGESIC [schedule II]) *tablet:* acetaminophen (see p. 13) 325 mg/ oxycodone (see p. 1249) 5 mg.

Paremyd (MYDRIATIC) ophthalmic *solution:* 1% hydroxyamphetamine hydrobromide, 0.25% tropicamide (see p. 1731).

Percocet (NARCOTIC ANALGESIC [schedule II]) *tablet:* oxycodone (see p. 1249) 2.5 mg/acetaminophen (see p. 13) 325 mg; oxycodone 7.5 mg/acetaminophen 325 mg; oxycodone 10 mg/acetaminophen 325 mg; oxycodone 10 mg/acetaminophen 650 mg.

Percodan (NARCOTIC ANALGESIC [schedule II]) *tablet:* oxycodone hydrochloride (see p. 1249) 4.5 mg/oxycodone terephthalate 0.38 mg/aspirin (see p. 126) 325 mg.

Phesgo (ANTINEOPLASTIC) *solution for injection:* pertuzumab 60 mg/ trastuzumab 60 mg/hyaluronidase 2000units/mL; pertuzumab 80 mg/trastuzumab 40 mg/hyaluronidase 2000units/mL

Polysporin Ointment (ANTI-INFECTIVE [OPHTHALMIC]) *ophthalmic ointment:* polymyxin B sulfate (see p. 1365) 10,000 units/bacitracin zinc (see p. 160) 500 units/g.

Prandimet (HYPOGLYCEMIC AGENT) *tablet:* repaglinide (see p. 1466) 1 mg/metformin (see p. 1051) 500 mg; repaglinide 2 mg/metformin 500 mg.

Premphase (ESTROGEN, PROGESTERONE) *tablet:* conjugated estrogens (see p. 658) 0.625 mg/medroxyprogesterone acetate (see p. 1026) 5 mg.

Prempro (ESTROGEN, PROGESTIN) *tablet:* conjugated estrogens (see p. 658) 0.3 mg/medroxyprogesterone (see p. 1026) 1.5 mg; conjugated estrogen 0.45 mg/ medroxyprogesterone 1.5 mg; conjugated estrogen 0.625 mg/ medroxyprogesterone 2.5 mg; conjugated estrogen 0.625 mg/ medroxyprogesterone 5 mg.

Prestalia (ACE INHIBITOR/CALCIUM CHANNEL BLOCKER) *tablets:* perindopril 14 mg/amlodipine besylate 10 mg; perindopril 3.5 mg/amlodipine besylate 2.5 mg; perindopril 7 mg/amlodipine besylate 5 mg.

Prevacid NapraPAC (PROTON PUMP INHIBITOR/ANTI-INFLAMMATORY) capsules and *tablets:* lansoprazole (see p. 935) 15 mg capsule/naproxen sodium (see p. 1142) 375 mg table; lansoprazole 15 mg capsule/naproxen sodium 500 mg tablet.

Prevpac (ANTIBIOTIC/ANTISECRETORY) capsules and *tablets:* amoxicillin (see p. 86) 500 mg capsules, clarithromycin (see p. 375) 500 mg tablets, lansoprazole (see p. 935) 30 mg capsules.

Prinzide (ANTIHYPERTENSIVE) *tablet:* hydrochlorothiazide (see p. 809) 12.5 mg/lisinopril (see p. 983) 10 mg; hydrochlorothiazide 12.5 mg/lisinopril 20 mg; hydrochlorothiazide 25 mg/lisinopril 20 mg.

Probenecid and Colchicine (ANTIGOUT) *tablet:* probenecid (see p. 1398) 500 mg/colchicine (see p. 402) 0.5 mg.

Pyridium Plus (ANALGESIC) *tablet:* phenazopyridine hydrochloride (see p. 1325) 150 mg/hyoscyamine hydrobromide (see p. 826) 0.3 mg/butalbital 15 mg.

Qsymia (ANTIOBESITY) *extended release capsule:* phentermine 3.75/topiramate 23 mg; phentermine 7.5 mg/topiramate 46 mg; phentermine 11.25 mg/topiramate 69 mg phentermine 15 mg/ topiramate 92 mg.

Qtren (ANTIDIABETIC) *tablet:* dapagliflozin (see p. 448) 10 mg/saxagliptin (see p. 1527) 5 mg.

Quartette (ORAL CONTRACEPTIVE) *tablet:* various combinations of levonorgestrel and ethinyl estradiol.

Rebetron (INTERFERON, ANTIVIRAL) ribavirin (see p. 1473) tablet polythiazide 2 mg.

Recarbrio (ANTIBIOTIC) *solution for injection:* imipenem (see p. 845) 500 mg/cilastatin 500 mg/relebactam 250 mg

Rifamate (ANTITUBERCULOSIS) *capsule:* isoniazid (see p. 898) 150 mg/rifampin (see p. 1477) 300 mg.

Rifater (ANTITUBERCULOSIS) *tablet:* rifampin (see p. 1477) 120 mg/isoniazid (see p. 898) 50 mg/pyrazinamide 300 mg.

Rimactane/INH Dual Pack (ANTITUBERCULOSIS) *pack:* thirty isoniazid (see p. 898) 300 mg tablets, sixty rifampin (see p. 1477) 300 mg capsules.

Rondec (DECONGESTANT, ANTIHISTAMINE) *tablet:* pseudoephedrine hydrochloride (see p. 1429) 60 mg/carbinoxamine maleate 4 mg; *drops (per mL):* pseudoephedrine hydrochloride 25 mg/carbinoxamine maleate 2 mg; *syrup (per mL):* pseudoephedrine hydrochloride 60 mg/carbinoxamine maleate 4 mg.

Roxicet (NARCOTIC ANALGESIC [schedule II]) *tablet:* oxycodone (see p. 1249) 5 mg/acetaminophen (see p. 13) 325 mg.

Ryzodeg 70/30 (INSULIN); *injection:* insulin degludec 70/insulin aspart 30.

Simcor (ANTILIPIDEMIC) extended release *tablet:* niacin (see p. 1164) 1000 mg/simvastatin (see p. 1549) 20 mg; niacin 1000 mg/simvastatin 40 mg, niacin 500 mg/simvastatin 20 mg; niacin 500 mg/simvastatin 40 mg, niacin 750 mg/simvastatin 20 mg.

Soliqua (ANTIDIABETIC) *injection:* insulin glargine (see p. 869) 100 units/lixisenatide (see p. 987) 33 mg.

Soma Compound (SKELETAL MUSCLE RELAXANT) *tablet:* carisoprodol (see p. 281) 200 mg/aspirin (see p. 126) 325 mg.

Soma Compound with Codeine (SKELETAL MUSCLE RELAXANT [schedule III]) *tablet:* carisoprodol (see p. 281) 200 mg, aspirin (see p. 126) 325 mg/codeine phosphate 16 mg.

Stalevo (ANTIPARKINSON AGENT) *tablet:* carbidopa (see p. 270) 12.5 mg/levodopa (see p. 957) 50 mg/entacapone (see p. 603) 200 mg; carbidopa 18.75 mg/levodopa 75 mg/entacapone 200 mg; carbidopa 25 mg/levodopa 100 mg/entacapone 200 mg; carbidopa 31.25 mg/levodopa 125 mg/entacapone 200 mg; carbidopa 37.5 mg/levodopa 150 mg/entacapone 200 mg.

Stiolto (BRONCHODIALATOR) *powder for inhalation:* tiotropium 2.5 mcg/ olodaterol 2.5 mcg.

Suboxone (ANALGESIC) sublingual *tablet:* buprenorphine (see p. 225) 2 mg/naloxone (see p. 1138) 0.5 mg; buprenorphine 8 mg/naloxone 2 mg.

Symbicort (MINERALOCORTICOID/BRONCHODILATOR) *inhaler:* budesonide (see p. 221) 0.08 mg/formoterol (see p. 743) 0.045 mg; budesonide 0.16 mg/formoterol 0.045 mg.

Symbyax (ATYPICAL ANTIPSYCHOTIC/SSRI) *capsule:* olanzapine (see p. 1208) 6 mg/fluoxetine (see p. 729) 25 mg; olanzapine 6 mg/fluoxetine 50 mg; olanzapine 12 mg/fluoxetine 25 mg; olanzapine 12 mg/fluoxetine 50 mg.

Synera (LOCAL ANESTHETIC) *transdermal patch:* lidocaine (see p. 966) 70 mg/tetracycline (see p. 1644) 70 mg.

Syntest D.S. (ESTROGEN, ANDROGEN) *tablet:* esterified estrogens (see p. 658) 1.25 mg/methyltestosterone (see p. 1078) 2.5 mg.

Syntest H.S. (ESTROGEN, ANDROGEN) *tablet:* esterified estrogens (see p. 658) 0.625 mg/methyltestosterone (see p. 1078) 1.25 mg.

Taclonex Scalp (NSAID) *topical suspension:* betamethasone (see p. 185) 0.064%/calcipotriene (see p. 245) 0.005%.

Tanafed DP (DECONGESTANT, ANTIHISTAMINE) *suspension:* pseudoephedrine (see p. 1429) 75 mg/chlorpheniramine tannate 4.5 mg.

Tarka (ANTIHYPERTENSIVE) *tablet:* trandolapril (see p. 1707) 2 mg/verapamil HCl (see p. 1761) 180 mg; trandolapril 4 mg/verapamil HCl 240 mg; trandolapril 1 mg/verapamil HCl 240 mg, trandolapril 2 mg/verapamil HCl 240 mg.

Technivie (ANTIVIRAL) *tablet:* ombitasvir 12.5 mg/paritaprevir 75 mg/ritonavir 50 mg.

Tekamlo (ANTIHYPERTENSIVE) *tablet:* aliskiren 150 mg/amlodipine 10 mg; aliskiren 150 mg/amlodipine 5 mg: aliskiren 300 mg/amlodipine 10 mg; aliskiren 300 mg/amlodipine 5 mg.

Tekurna HCT (ANTIHYPERTENSIVE) *tablet:* aliskiren (see p. 46) 150 mg/hydrochlorothiazide (see p. 809) 12.5 mg.

Tenoretic 50 (ANTIHYPERTENSIVE) *tablet:* chlorthalidone (see p. 351) 25 mg/atenolol (see p. 131) 50 mg.

Tenoretic 100 (ANTIHYPERTENSIVE) *tablet:* chlorthalidone (see p. 351) 25 mg/atenolol (see p. 131) 100 mg.

Terra-Cortril Suspension (OCULAR STEROID AND ANTIBIOTIC) *suspension:* hydrocortisone acetate (see p. 812) 1.5%/oxytetracycline 0.5%.

Teveten HCT (ANTIHYPERTENSIVE) *tablet:* eprosartan mesylate (see p. 620) 600 mg/hydrochlorothiazide (see p. 809) 12.5 mg; eprosartan 600 mg/hydrochlorothiazide 25 mg.

Timolide (ANTIHYPERTENSIVE) *tablet:* hydrochlorothiazide (see p. 809) 25 mg/timolol maleate (see p. 1671) 10 mg.

Tobradex (ANTI-INFECTIVE) *ophthalmic suspension:* dexamethasone (see p. 481) 0.1%/tobramycin (see p. 1681) 0.3%; ophthalmic ointment: dexamethasone 0.1%/tobramycin 0.3%.

Treximet (ANALGESIC) *tablet:* naproxen (see p. 1142) 500 mg/sumatriptan (see p. 1597) 85 mg.

Triacin-C Cough Syrup (ANTITUSSIVE [schedule V]) *syrup:* pseudoephedrine (see p. 1429) 30 mg/triprolidine 1.25 mg/codeine (see p. 400) 10 mg.

Tribenzor (ANTIHYPERTENSIVE) *tablet:* olmesartan 20 mg/amlodipine 5 mg/hydrochlorothiazide 12.5 mg; olmesartan 40 mg/amlodipine 10 mg/hydrochlorothiazide 12.5 mg; olmesartan40 mg/amlodipine 10 mg/hydrochlorothiazide 25 mg; ol-mesartan 40 mg/amlodipine 5 mg/hydrochlorothiazide 12.5 mg; olmesartan 40 mg/amlodipine 5 mg/hydrochlorothiazide 25 mg.

Trijardy XR (ANTIDIABETIC) *tablet:* empagliflozin (see p. 592) 10 mg/linagliptin (see p. 970) 5 mg/metformin (see p. 1051) 1000 mg; empagliflozin 25 mg/linagliptin 5 mg/ metformin (see p. 1051) 1000 mg; empagliflozin 5 mg/linagliptin 2.5 mg/ metformin 1000 mg; empagliflozin 12.5 mg/linagliptin 2.5 mg/ metformin 1000 mg

Tri-Hydroserpine (ANTIHYPERTENSIVE) *tablet:* hydrochlorothiazide (see p. 809) 15 mg/hydralazine hydrochloride (see p. 807) 25 mg.

Tri-Luma Cream (STEROID) *cream:* 4% hydroquinone (see p. 818)/0.05% tretinoin (see p. 1043)/0.01% fluocinolone acetonide (see p. 726).

Tri-Norinyl 28 (ORAL CONTRACEPTIVE) *tablet:* ethinyl estradiol (see p. 650) 35 mcg/norethindrone (see p. 1194) 0.5 mg × 7 d, ethinyl estradiol 35 mcg/norethindrone 1 mg × 9 d, ethinyl estradiol 35 mcg/norethindrone 0.5 mg × 5 d.

Triple Antibiotic (OPHTHALMIC ANTIBIOTIC) *ophthalmic ointment:* hydrocortisone (see p. 812) 1%/neomycin sulfate (see p. 1157) 0.5%/bacitracin zinc (see p. 160) 400 units/polymyxin B sulfate (see p. 1365) 10,000 units/g.

Triumeq (ANTIRETROVIRAL) *tablet:* abacavir (see p. 1) 600 mg/dolutegravir (see p. 542) 50 mg/lamivudine (see p. 931) 300 mg.

Trizivir (REVERSE TRANSCRIPTASE INHIBITOR) *tablet:* abacavir (see p. 1) 300 mg/lamivudine (see p. 931) 150 mg/zidovudine (see p. 1791) 300 mg.

Truvada (NUCLEOSIDE REVERSE TRANSCRIPTASE INHIBITOR) *tablet:* emtricitabine (see p. 588) 200 mg/tenofovir disoproxil fumarate (see p. 1628) 300 mg.

Tussicap (ANTITUSSIVE [schedule III]) *extended release capsule:* chlorpheniramine (see p. 344) 8 mg/hydrocodone (see p. 811) 10 mg.

Tussigon (ANTITUSSIVE [schedule III]) *tablet:* homatropine methylbromide 1.5 mg/hydrocodone (see p. 811) 5 mg.

Tussionex (ANTITUSSIVE [schedule III]) *tablet:* chlorpheniramine (see p. 344) 8 mg/hydrocodone (see p. 811) 10 mg.

Twinrix (VACCINE) *injection:* hepatitis A vaccine (see p. 804) 720 ELU/hepatitis B recombinant vaccine (see p. 804) 20 mcg per single dose vial.

Twynsta (ANTIHYPERTENSIVE) *tablet:* telmisartan 40 mg/amlodipine 5 mg; telmisartan 40 mg/amlodipine 10 mg; telmisartan 80 mg/amlodipine 5 mg; telmisartan 80 mg/amlodipine 10 mg.

Tylenol with Codeine No. 3 (NARCOTIC AGONIST ANALGESIC [schedule III]) *tablet:* acetaminophen (see p. 13) 300 mg/codeine phosphate 30 mg.

Tylenol with Codeine No. 4 (NARCOTIC AGONIST ANALGESIC [schedule III]) *tablet:* acetaminophen (see p. 13) 300 mg/codeine phosphate 60 mg.

Ultracet (ANALGESIC/ANTIPYRETIC) *tablet:* tramadol (see p. 1704) 37.5 mg/acetaminophen (see p. 13) 325 mg.

Uniretic (ANTIHYPERTENSIVE) *tablet:* moexipril (see p. 1116) 7.5 mg/hydrochlorothiazide (see p. 809) 12.5 mg; moexipril 15 mg/hydrochlorothiazide 12.5 mg, moexipril 15 mg/hydrochlorothiazide 25 mg.

Urised (URINARY ANTI-INFECTIVE) *tablet:* methenamine (see p. 1058) 40.8 mg/phenyl salicylate 18.1 mg/atropine sulfate (see p. 141) 0.03 mg/hyoscyamine (see p. 826) 0.03 mg/benzoic acid 4.5 mg/methylene blue 5.4 mg.

Vabomere (ANTI-INFECTIVE) *solution for injection:* meropenem (see p. 1045) 1 g/vaborbactam 1 g.

Valturna (ANTIHYPERTENSIVE) *tablet:* aliskiren (see p. 46) 150 mg/valsartan (see p. 1513) 160 mg; aliskiren 300 mg/valsartan 320 mg.

Vaseretic (ANTIHYPERTENSIVE) *tablet:* enalapril maleate (see p. 595) 10 mg/hydrochlorothiazide (see p. 809) 25 mg.

Vasocidin (OPHTHALMIC CORTICOSTEROID, ANTI-INFECTIVE) *ophthalmic solution:* prednisolone sodium phosphate (see p. 1389) 0.23%/sulfacetamide sodium (see p. 1588) 10%.

Vasocon-A (OPHTHALMIC DECONGESTANT) *ophthalmic solution:* naphazoline hydrochloride (see p. 1141) 0.05%/antazoline phosphate 0.5%.

Veltin (ANTIACNE) *gel:* clindamycin 1/2%/tretinoin 0.025%.

Viekira XR (ANTIVIRAL) *tablet:* ombitasvir 8.33 mg/paritaprevir 50 mg/ritonavir 33.33 mg/dasabuvir 200 mg.

Vimovo (ANALGESIC) *tablet:* naproxen 375 mg/esomeprazole 20 mg; naproxen 500 mg/esomeprazole 20 mg.

Vosevi (ANTIVIRAL) *tablet:* sofosbuvir (see p. 1561) 400 mg/velpatasvir 100 mg/voxilaprevir 100 mg.

Vytorin (ANTILIPEMIC AGENT) *tablet:* ezetimibe (see p. 686) 10 mg/simvastatin (see p. 1549) 10 mg; ezetimibe 10 mg/simvastatin 20 mg; ezetimibe 10 mg/simvastatin 40 mg; ezetimibe 10 mg/simvastatin 80 mg.

Vyxeos (ANTINEOPLASTIC) *powder for injection:* daunorubicin (see p. 461) 44 mg/cytarabine (see p. 429) 100 mg.

Xerese (TOPICAL ANTIINFECTIVE) *cream:* acyclovir 5%/hydrocortisone 1%.

Yasmin (ORAL CONTRACEPTIVE) *tablet:* ethinyl estradiol 30 mcg/drospirenone 3 mg.

Yosprala (ANTIPLATELET/ANTIULCERATIVE) *tablet:* aspirin 81 mg/omeprazole 40 mg; aspirin 325 mg/omeprazole 40 mg.

Zepatier (ANTIVIRAL/PROTEASE INHIBITOR) *tablet:* elbasvir 50 mg/grazoprevir 100 mg.

Zestoretic (ANTIHYPERTENSIVE) *tablet:* hydrochlorothiazide (see p. 809) 12.5 mg/lisinopril (see p. 983) 10 mg; hydrochlorothiazide 12.5 mg/lisinopril 20 mg; hydrochlorothiazide 25 mg/lisinopril 20 mg.

Ziac (ANTIHYPERTENSIVE) *tablet:* bisoprolol (see p. 199) 2.5 mg/hydrochlorothiazide (see p. 809) 6.25 mg; bisoprolol 5 mg/hydrochlorothiazide 6.25 mg; bisoprolol 10 mg/hydrochlorothiazide 6.25 mg.

Ziana (ANTIACNE) *gel:* clindamycin 0.5%/tretinoin 0.025%.

Zubsolv (ANALGESIC) *sublingual tablet:* buprenorphine 1.4 mg/naloxone 0.36 mg; buprenorphine 2.9 mg/naloxone 0.71 mg; buprenorphine 5.7 mg/naloxone 1.4 mg; buprenorphine 8.6 mg naloxone 2.1 mg; buprenorphine 11.4 mg/naloxone 2.9 mg.

Zylet (OPHTHALMIC ANTIBIOTIC) *solution:* loteprednol etabonate (see p. 1001) 0.5%/tobramycin (see p. 1681) 0.3%.

Zyrtec-D (ANTIHISTAMINE/DECONGESTANT) *sustained release tablet:* cetirizine (see p. 328) 5 mg/pseudoephedrine (see p. 1429) 120 mg.

acute coronary syndrome an acute ischemic event with or without marked ST segment elevation.

acute dystonia extrapyramidal symptom manifested by abnormal posturing, grimacing, spastic torticollis (neck torsion), and oculogyric (eyeball movement) crisis.

adverse effect unintended, unpredictable, and nontherapeutic response to drug action. Adverse effects occur at doses used therapeutically or for prophylaxis or diagnosis. They generally result from drug toxicity, idiosyncrasies, or hypersensitivity reactions caused by the drug itself or by ingredients added during manufacture (e.g., preservatives, dyes, or vehicles).

afterload resistance that ventricles must work against to eject blood into the aorta during systole.

agranulocytosis sudden drop in leukocyte count; often followed by a severe infection manifested by high fever, chills, prostration, and ulcerations of mucous membrane such as in the mouth, rectum, or vagina.

akathisia extrapyramidal symptom manifested by a compelling need to move or pace, without specific pattern, and an inability to be still.

analeptic restorative medication that enhances excitation of the CNS without affecting inhibitory impulses.

anaphylactoid reaction excessive allergic response manifested by wheezing, chills, generalized pruritic urticaria, diaphoresis, sense of uneasiness, agitation, flushing, palpitations, coughing, difficulty breathing, and cardiovascular collapse.

anticholinergic actions inhibition of parasympathetic response manifested by dry mouth, decreased peristalsis, constipation, blurred vision, and urinary retention.

bioavailability fraction of active drug that reaches its action sites after administration by any route. Following an IV dose, bioavailability is 100%; however, such factors as first-pass effect, enterohepatic cycling, and biotransformation reduce bioavailability of an orally administered drug.

blood dyscrasia pathological condition manifested by fever, sore mouth or throat, unexplained fatigue, easy bruising, or bleeding.

cardiotoxicity impairment of cardiac function manifested by one or more of the following: hypotension, arrhythmias, precordial pain, dyspnea, electrocardiogram (ECG) abnormalities, cardiac dilation, congestive failure.

cholinergic response stimulation of the parasympathetic response manifested by lacrimation, diaphoresis, salivation, abdominal cramps, diarrhea, nausea, and vomiting.

circulatory overload excessive vascular volume manifested by increased central venous pressure (CVP), elevated blood pressure, tachycardia, distended neckveins, peripheral edema, dyspnea, cough, and pulmonary rales.

CNS stimulation excitement of the CNS manifested by hyperactivity, excitement, nervousness, insomnia, and tachycardia.

CNS toxicity impairment of CNS function manifested by ataxia, tremor, incoordination, paresthesias, numbness, impairment of pain or touch sensation, drowsiness, confusion, headache, anxiety, tremors, and behavior changes.

congestive heart failure (CHF) impaired pumping ability of the heart manifested by paroxysmal nocturnal dyspnea, cough, fatigue or dyspnea on exertion, tachycardia, peripheral or pulmonary edema, and weight gain.

Cushing's syndrome fatty swellings in the interscapular area (buffalo hump) and in the facial area (moon face), distention of the abdomen, ecchymoses following even minor trauma, impotence, amenorrhea, high blood pressure, general weakness, loss of muscle mass, osteoporosis, and psychosis.

dehydration decreased intracellular or extracellular fluid manifested by elevated temperature, dry skin and mucous membranes, decreased tissue turgor, sunken eyes, furrowed tongue, low blood pressure, diminished or irregular pulse, muscle or abdominal cramps, thick secretions, hard feces and impaction, scant urinary output, urine specific gravity above 1.030, an elevated hemoglobin.

disulfiram-type reaction Antabuse-type reaction manifested by facial flushing, pounding headache, sweating, slurred speech, abdominal cramps, nausea, vomiting, tachycardia, fever, palpitations, drop in blood pressure, dyspnea, and sense of chest constriction. Symptoms may last up to 24 hours.

enzyme induction stimulation of microsomal enzymes by a drug resulting in its accelerated metabolism and decreased activity. If reactive intermediates are formed, drug-mediated toxicity may be exacerbated.

extravasation escape of fluids or drugs into the subcutaneous tissue; a complication of intravenous infusion.

first-pass effect reduced bioavailability of an orally administered drug due to metabolism in GI epithelial cells and liver or to biliary excretion. Effect may be avoided by use of sublingual tablets or rectal suppositories.

fixed drug eruption drug-induced circumscribed skin lesion that persists or recurs in the same site. Residual pigmentation may remain following drug withdrawal.

gamma-glutamyl transpeptidase screening test for possible liver damage and/or suspected alcohol abuse.

half-life ($t_{1/2}$) time required for concentration of a drug in the body to decrease by 50%. Half-life also represents the time necessary to reach steady state or to decline from steady state after a change (i.e., starting or stopping) in the dosing regimen. Half-life may be affected by a disease state and age of the drug user.

heart failure left- and/or right-sided failure associated with systolic and/or diastolic dysfunction.

heat stroke a life-threatening condition manifested by absence of sweating; red, dry, hot skin; dilated pupils; dyspnea; full bounding pulse; temperature above 40° C (105° F); and mental confusion.

hepatotoxicity impairment of liver function manifested by jaundice, dark urine, pruritus, light-colored stools, eosinophilia, itchy skin or rash, and persistently high elevations of alanine aminotransferase (ALT) and aspartate aminotransferase (AST).

hyperammonemia elevated level of ammonia or ammonium in the blood manifested by lethargy, decreased appetite, vomiting, asterixis (flapping tremor), weak pulse, irritability, decreased responsiveness, and seizures.

hypercalcemia elevated serum calcium manifested by deep bone and flank pain, renal calculi, anorexia, nausea, vomiting, thirst, constipation, muscle hypotonicity, pathologic fracture, bradycardia, lethargy, and psychosis.

hyperglycemia elevated blood glucose manifested by flushed, dry skin, low blood pressure and elevated pulse, tachypnea, Kussmaul's respirations, polyuria, polydipsia; polyphagia, lethargy, and drowsiness.

hyperkalemia excessive potassium in blood, which may produce life-threatening cardiac arrhythmias, including bradycardia and heart block, unusual fatigue, weakness or heaviness of limbs, general muscle weakness, muscle cramps, paresthesias, flaccid paralysis of extremities, shortness of breath, nervousness, confusion, diarrhea, and GI distress.

hypermagnesemia excessive magnesium in blood, which may produce cathartic effect, profound thirst, flushing, sedation, confusion, depressed deep tendon reflexes (DTRs), muscle weakness, hypotension, and depressed respirations.

hypernatremia excessive sodium in blood, which may produce confusion, neuromuscular excitability, muscle weakness, seizures, thirst, dry and flushed skin, dry mucous membranes, pyrexia, agitation, and oliguria or anuria.

hypersensitivity reactions excessive and abnormal sensitivity to given agent manifested by urticaria, pruritus, wheezing, edema, redness, and anaphylaxis.

hyperthyroidism excessive secretion by the thyroid glands, which increases basal metabolic rate, resulting in warm, flushed, moist skin; tachycardia, exophthalmos; infrequent lid blinking; lid edema; weight loss despite increased appetite; frequent urination; menstrual irregularity; breathlessness; hypoventilation; congestive heart failure; excessive sweating.

hyperuricemia excessive uric acid in blood, resulting in pain in flank; stomach, or joints, and changes in intake and output ratio and pattern.

hypocalcemia abnormally low calcium level in blood, which may result in depression; psychosis; hyperreflexia; diarrhea; cardiac arrhythmias; hypotension; muscle spasms; paresthesias of feet, fingers, tongue; positive Chvostek's sign. Severe deficiency (tetany) may result in carpopedal spasms, spasms of face muscle, laryngospasm, and generalized convulsions.

hypoglycemia abnormally low glucose level in the blood, which may result in acute fatigue, restlessness, malaise, marked irritability and weakness, cold sweats, excessive hunger, headache, dizziness, confusion, slurred speech, loss of consciousness, and death.

hypokalemia abnormally low level of potassium in blood, which may result in malaise, fatigue, paresthesias, depressed reflexes, muscle weakness and cramps, rapid, irregular pulse, arrhythmias, hypotension, vomiting, paralytic ileus, mental confusion, depression, delayed thought process, abdominal distention, polyuria, shallow breathing, and shortness of breath.

hypomagnesemia abnormally low level of magnesium in blood, resulting in nausea, vomiting, cardiac arrhythmias, and neuromuscular symptoms (tetany, positive Chvostek's and Trousseau's signs, seizures, tremors, ataxia, vertigo, nystagmus, muscular fasciculations).

hyponatremia a decreased serum concentration (less than 125 mEq) of sodium that results in intracellular swelling. The resulting signs and symptoms include nausea, malaise, headache, lethargy, obtundation, seizures, and coma. There is significant variability in the symptomatology of hyponatremia manifested in patients.

hypophosphatemia abnormally low level of phosphates in blood, resulting in muscle weakness, anorexia, malaise, absent deep tendon reflexes, bone pain, paresthesias, tremors, negative calcium balance, osteomalacia, osteoporosis.

hypothyroidism condition caused by thyroid hormone deficiency that lowers basal metabolic rate and may result in periorbital edema, lethargy, puffy hands and feet, cool, pale skin, vertigo, nocturnal cramps, decreased GI motility, constipation, hypotension, slow pulse, depressed muscular activity, and enlarged thyroid gland.

hypoxia insufficient oxygenationin the blood manifested by dyspnea, tachypnea, headache, restlessness, cyanosis, tachycardia, dysrhythmias, confusion, decreased level of consciousness, and euphoria or delirium.

immune reconstitution inflammatory syndrome (IRIS) describes a collection of inflammatory disorders associated with worsening of preexisting infectious processes following initiation of highly active antiretroviral therapy in HIV-infected individuals. Usually the inflammatory reaction is self-limiting but long-term sequelae and fatal outcomes may occur, particularly when neurologic structures are involved.

international normalizing ratio measurement that normalizes for the differences obtained from various laboratory readings in the value for thromboplastin blood level.

ischemic colitis blood flow to part of the colon is reduced due to narrowing or blocked arteries resulting in insufficient oxygen to those cells. Signs and symptoms can include pain, tenderness, or cramping in the abdomen which can occur suddenly or gradually, bright red or maroon-colored blood in stool, or passage of blood alone from the rectum, a feeling of urgency to defecate, and diarrhea.

lactic acidosis is characterized by low pH (pH less than 7.35) in body tissues and blood (acidosis) accompanied by buildup of lactate. Lactate buildup results from metabolizing glucose anaerobically (low oxygen). Signs and symptoms include nausea, vomiting, hyperventilation, abdominal pain, lethargy, anxiety, hypotension, irregular heart rate, tachycardia, and severe anemia.

leukopenia abnormal decrease in number of white blood cells, usually below 5000 per cubic millimeter, resulting in fever, chills, sore mouth or throat, and unexplained fatigue.

liver toxicity manifested by anorexia, nausea, fatigue, lethargy, itching, jaundice, abdominal pain, dark-colored urine, and flu-like symptoms.

metabolic acidosis decrease in pH value of the extracellular fluid caused by either an increase in hydrogen ions or a decrease in bicarbonate ions. It may result in one or more of the following: lethargy, headache, weakness, abdominal pain, nausea, vomiting, dyspnea, hyperpnea progressing to Kussmaul breathing, dehydration, thirst, weakness, flushed face, full bounding pulse, progressive drowsiness, mental confusion, combativeness.

metabolic alkalosis increase in pH value of the extracellular fluid caused by either a loss of acid from the body (e.g., through vomiting) or an increased level of bicarbonate ions (e.g., through ingestion of sodium bicarbonate). It may result in muscle weakness, irritability, confusion, muscle twitching, slow and shallow respirations, and convulsive seizures.

microsomal enzymes drug-metabolizing enzymes located in the endoplasmic reticulum of the liver and other tissues chiefly responsible for oxidative drug metabolism (e.g., cytochrome P450).

myopathy any disease or abnormal condition of striated muscles manifested by muscle weakness, myalgia, diaphoresis, fever, and reddish-brown urine (myoglobinuria) or oliguria.

nephrotoxicity impairment of the nephrons of the kidney manifested by one or more of the following: oliguria, urinary frequency, hematuria, cloudy urine, rising BUN and serum creatinine, fever, graft tenderness or enlargement.

neuroleptic malignant syndrome (NMS) potentially fatal complication associated with antipsychotic drugs manifested by hyperpyrexia, altered mental status, muscle rigidity, irregular pulse, fluctuating BP, diaphoresis, and tachycardia.

orphan drug (as defined by the Orphan Drug Act, an amendment of the Federal Food, Drug, and Cosmetic Act which took effect in January 1983): drug or biological product used in the treatment, diagnosis, or prevention of a rare disease. A rare disease or condition is one that affects fewer than 200,000 persons in the United States, or affects more than 200,000 persons but for which there is no reasonable expectation that drug research and development costs can be recovered from sales within the United States.

ototoxicity impairment of the ear manifested by one or more of the following: headache, dizziness or vertigo, nausea and vomiting with motion, ataxia, nystagmus.

pharmacogenetic genetic variation affecting response to different drugs.

post-transplant lymphoproliferative disorder (PTLD) of B-cell proliferation that is a life-threatening complication after hematopoietic stem cell or organ transplant due to therapeutic immunosuppression after transplant. The majority of cases are associated with Epstein-Barr virus (EBV), while other causes are endogenous anti-T cell cytokine and anti-T cell antibodies, or production of interleukin-10. Some of the B cell mutations can result in lymphoma.

prodrug inactive drug form that becomes pharmacologically active through biotransformation.

protein binding reversible interaction between protein and drug resulting in a drug-protein complex (bound drug) which is in equilibrium with free (active) drug in plasma and tissues. Since only free drug can diffuse to action sites, factors that influence drug-binding (e.g., displacement of bound drug by another drug, or decreased albumin concentration) may potentiate pharmacologic effect.

pseudomembranous enterocolitis life-threatening superinfection characterized by severe diarrhea and fever.

pseudoparkinsonism extrapyramidal symptom manifested by slowing of volitional movement (akinesia), mask facies, rigidity and tremor at rest (especially of upper extremities); and pill rolling motion.

pulmonary edema excessive fluid in the lung tissue manifested by one or more of the following: shortness of breath, cyanosis, persistent productive cough (frothy sputum may be blood tinged), expiratory rales, restlessness, anxiety, increased heart rate, sense of chest pressure.

QT prolongation longer than normal time interval from the Q wave (QRS complex) to the end of the T wave; may be congenital or drug-induced.

renal insufficiency reduced capacity of the kidney to perform its functions as manifested by one or more of the following: dysuria, oliguria, hematuria, swelling of lower legs and feet.

serotonin syndrome may include several of the following: Confusion, agitation or restlessness, dilated pupils, headache, status changes, nausea and/or vomiting, diarrhea, rapid heart rate, tremor, loss of muscle coordination, twitching muscles, shivering, or diaphoresis.

somogyi effect rebound phenomenon clinically manifested by fasting hyperglycemia and worsening of diabetic control due to unnecessarily large p.m. insulin doses. Hormonal response to unrecognized hypoglycemia (i.e., release of epinephrine, glucagon, growth hormone, cortisol) causes insensitivity to insulin. Increasing the amount of insulin required to treat the hyperglycemia intensifies the hypoglycemia.

superinfection new infection by an organism different from the initial infection being treated by antimicrobial therapy manifested by one or more of the following: black, hairy tongue; glossitis, stomatitis; anal itching; loose, foul-smelling stools; vaginal itching or discharge; sudden fever; cough.

tachyphylaxis rapid decrease in response to a drug after administration of a few doses. Initial drug response cannot be restored by an increase in dose.

tardive dyskinesia extrapyramidal symptom manifested by involuntary rhythmic, bizarre movements of face, jaw, mouth, tongue, and sometimes extremities.

torsade de pointes a form of ventricular tachycardia nearly always due to drugs; characterized by a long QT interval.

vasovagal symptoms transient vascular and neurogenic reaction marked by pallor, nausea, vomiting, bradycardia, and rapid fall in arterial blood pressure.

water intoxication (dilutional hyponatremia) less than normal concentration of sodium in the blood resulting from excess extracellular and intracellular fluid and producing one or more of the following: lethargy, confusion, headache, decreased skin turgor, tremors, convulsions, coma, anorexia, nausea, vomiting, diarrhea, sternal fingerprinting, weight gain, edema, full bounding pulse, jugular vein distention, rales, signs and symptoms of pulmonary edema.

◆ APPENDIX F   ABBREVIATIONS

ABGs	arterial blood gases
ABW	adjusted body weight
a.c.	before meals (*ante cibum*)
ACD	acid-citrate-dextrose
ACE	angiotensin-converting enzyme
ACh	acetylcholine
ACIP	Advisory Committee on Immunization Practices
ACLS	advanced cardiac life support
ACS	acute coronary syndrome
ACT	activated clotting time
ACTH	adrenocorticotropic hormone
AD	Alzheimer's disease
ADCC	antibody-dependent cell-mediated cytotoxicity
ADD	attention deficit disorder
ADH	antidiuretic hormone
ADLs	activities of daily living
ad lib	as desired (*ad libitum*)
ADP	adenosine diphosphate
ADT	alternate-day drug (administration)
AED	antiepileptic drug
AF	atrial fibrillation
AFL	atrial flutter
AIDS	acquired immunodeficiency syndrome
AIP	acute intermittent porphyria
alpha1-PI	alpha1-proteinase inhibitor
ALS	amyotrophic lateral sclerosis
ALT	alanine aminotransferase (formerly SGPT)
AMI	acute myocardial infarction
AML	acute myelogenous leukemia
AMP	adenosine monophosphate
ANA	antinuclear antibody(ies)
ANC	absolute neutrophil count
ANG I	angiotensin I
ANG II	angiotensin II
ANH	atrial natriuretic hormone
ANLL	acute nonlymphocytic leukemia
AntiXa	antifactor Xa
APL	acute promyelotic leukemia
aPTT	activated partial thromboplastin time
ARC	AIDS-related complex
ARDS	adult respiratory distress syndrome
ASHD	arteriosclerotic heart disease
AST	aspartate aminotransferase (formerly SGOT)
ATIII	antithrombin III
AT$_1$	angiotensin II receptor subtype I
AT$_2$	angiotensin II receptor subtype II

1844

ATP	adenosine triphosphate
AUV	area under the curve
AV	atrioventricular
b.i.d.	two times a day
BMD	bone mineral density
BMI	body mass index
BMR	basal metabolic rate
BP	blood pressure
BPH	benign prostatic hypertrophy
bpm	beats per minute
BSA	body surface area
BSE	breast self-exam
BSP	bromsulphalein
BT	bleeding time
BUN	blood urea nitrogen
C	centigrade, Celsius
CAD	coronary artery disease
cAMP	cyclic adenosine monophosphate
CBC	complete blood count
CCR5	cellular chemokine coreceptor-5
CD	Crohn's disease
CDAD	clostridium difficile-associated diarrhea
CDC	Centers for Disease Control and Prevention
CDC	complement-dependent cytotoxicity
CF	cystic fibrosis
cGMP	cyclic guanosine monophosphate
CHC	chronic hepatitis C
CHF	congestive heart failure
CKD	chronic kidney disease
CLL	chronic lymphocytic leukemia
cm	centimeter
CML	chronic myeloid leukemia
CMV	cytomegalovirus-I
CNS	central nervous system
Coll	collyrium (eye wash)
COMT	catecholamine-O-methyl transferase
COPD	chronic obstructive pulmonary disease
COX-1	cyclooxygenase-1
COX-2	cyclooxygenase-2
CPK	creatinine phosphokinase
CPR	cardiopulmonary resuscitation
CRC	colorectal cancer
CrCl	creatinine clearance
CRF	chronic renal failure
CRFD	chronic renal failure disease
C&S	culture and sensitivity
CSF	cerebrospinal fluid
CSP	cellulose sodium phosphate

CSSSI	complicated skin and skin structure infections
CT	clotting time
CTZ	chemoreceptor trigger zone
CV	cardiovascular
CVA	cerebrovascular accident
CVP	central venous pressure
CYP	cytochrome P450 system of enzymes
CYP3A4	cytochrome 3A4
D5W	5% dextrose in water
D&C	dilation and curettage
DIC	disseminated intravascular coagulation
DKA	diabetic ketoacidosis
dL	deciliter (100 mL or 0.1 liter)
DM	diabetes mellitus
DMARD	disease-modifying antirheumatic drug
DNA	deoxyribonucleic acid
DPD	dihydropyrimidine dehydrogenase
DTC	differentiated thyroid cancer
DTRs	deep tendon reflexes
DVT	deep venous thrombosis
ECG, EKG	electrocardiogram
ECT	electroconvulsive therapy
EEG	electroencephalogram
EENT	eye, ear, nose, throat
e.g.	for example (*exempli gratia*)
EGFR	epidermal growth factor receptor
eGFR	estimated glomerular filtration rate
EIB	exercise-induced bronchoconstriction
ENT	ear, nose, throat
EPS	extrapyramidal symptoms (or syndrome)
ER	estrogen receptor
ESRF	end-stage renal failure
F	Fahrenheit
FBS	fasting blood sugar
FDA	Food and Drug Administration
FSH	follicle-stimulating hormone
FTI	free thyroxine index
5-FU	5-fluorouracil
FUO	fever of unknown origin
g	gram
G6PD	glucose-6-phosphate dehydrogenase
GABA	gamma-aminobutyric acid
GERD	gastroesophageal reflux disease
GFR	glomerular filtration rate
GGT	gamma-glutamyl transferase
GGTP	gamma-glutamyl transpeptidase
GH	growth hormone
GI	gastrointestinal

GIST	gastrointestinal stomal tumor
GLP-1	glucagon-like peptide-1
GM-CSF	granulocyte-macrophage colony-stimulating factor
GnRH	gonadotropic releasing hormone
GPIIb/IIIa	glycoprotein IIb/IIIa
GTT	glucose tolerance test
GU	genitourinary
GVHD	graft-versus-host disease
h	hour
HACA	human antichimeric antibody
HbA1C	glycosylated hemoglobin
hBNP	human B-type natriuretic peptide
HBV	viral hepatitis B
HCG	human chorionic gonadotropin
Hct	hematocrit
HCV	hepatitis C virus
HDD-CKD	hemodialysis-dependent chronic kidney disease
HDL-C	high-density-lipoprotein cholesterol
HER	human epidermal growth factor
HF	heart failure
Hgb	hemoglobin
5-HIAA	5-hydroxyindoleacetic acid
HIT	heparin-induced thrombocytopenia
HIV	human immunodeficiency virus
HMG-CoA	3-hydroxy-3-methyl-glutaryl coenzyme A
HPA	hypothalamic–pituitary–adrenocortical (axis)
HPV	human papillomavirus
HR	heart rate
HSV-1	herpes simplex virus type 1
HSV-2	herpes simplex virus type 2
5-HT	5-hydroxytryptamine (serotonin receptor)
IBD	inflammatory bowel disease
IBW	ideal body weight
IC	intracoronary
ICH	intracranial hemorrhage
ICP	intracranial pressure
ICU	intensive care unit
ID	intradermal
IFN	interferon
Ig	immunoglobulin
IGF-1	insulin-like growth factor 1
IL	interleukin
IM	intramuscular
INR	international normalized ratio
IOP	intraocular pressure
IPPB	intermittent positive pressure breathing
iPTH	idiopathic parathyroid hormone
IT	intrathecal
ITP	idiopathic thrombocytopenic purpura

IV	intravenous
JRA	juvenile rheumatoid arthritis
kg	kilogram
KGF	keratinocyte growth factor
17-KGS	17-ketogenic steroids
17-KS	17-ketosteroids
KVO	keep vein open
L	liter
LABA	long-acting beta-2 agonist
LDH	lactic dehydrogenase
LDL	low density lipoprotein
LDL-C	low-density-lipoprotein cholesterol
LE	lupus erythematosus
LFT	liver function test
LH	luteinizing hormone
LLN	lower limit of normal
LR	lactated Ringer's
LSD	lysergic acid diethylamide
LTRA	leukotriene receptor antagonist
LVEDP	left ventricular end diastolic pressure
LVEF	left ventricular ejection fraction
M	molar (strength of a solution)
m^2	square meter (of body surface area)
MAC	mycobacterium avium complex
MAO	monoamine oxidase
MAOI	monoamine oxidase inhibitor
MBD	minimal brain dysfunction
MCH	mean corpuscular hemoglobin
MCHC	mean corpuscular hemoglobin concentration
mCi	millicurie
MCL	mantle cell lymphoma
mcg	microgram (1/1000 of a milligram)
MDD	major depressive disorder
MDI	metered dose inhaler
MDR	minimum daily requirements
MDS	muscular dystrophy syndrome
mEq	milliequivalent
mg	milligram
MI	myocardial infarction
MIC	minimum inhibitory concentration
min	minute
mL	milliliter (0.001 liter)
mm	millimeter
mo	month
MPS I	mucopolysaccharidosis I
MRSA	methicillin-resistant *Staphylococcus aureus*
MS	multiple sclerosis
MTC	medullary thyroid cancer
mTOR	mammalian target or rapamycin

mu-m	micrometer
N	normal (strength of a solution)
NADH	reduced form of nicotine adenine dinucleotide
NAPA	*N*-acetyl procainamide
nb	note well (*nota bene*)
NDD	non-hemodialysis dependent
NDD-CKD	non-hemodialysis-dependent chronic kidney disease
ng	nanogram (1/1000 of a microgram)
NMDA	N-methyl-D-aspartic acid
NMS	neuroleptic malignant syndrome
NNRTI	nonnucleoside reverse transcriptase inhibitor
NON-PVC	nonpolyvinyl chloride IV bag or tubing
NPN	nonprotein nitrogen
NPO	nothing by mouth
NRTI	nucleoside reverse transcriptase inhibitor
NS	normal saline
NS 3/4A	nonstructural protein (NS) 3/4A protease inhibitor
NSAID	nonsteroidal anti-inflammatory drug
NSCLC	non-small-cell lung cancer
NSR	normal sinus rhythm
NVAF	non-valvular atrial fibrillation
NYHA Class I, II, III, IV	New York Heart Association classes of heart failure
OA	osteoarthritis
OAB	overactive bladder
OATP	organic anion transporting polypeptide
OC	oral contraceptive
OCD	obsessive compulsive disorder
ODT	oral disintegrating tablet
17-OHCS	17-hydroxycorticosteroids
OTC	over the counter (nonprescription)
P450	cytochrome P450 system of enzymes
PABA	*para*-aminobenzoic acid
PAR-1	protease-activated receptor-1
PAS	*para*-aminosalicylic acid
PAWP	pulmonary artery wedge pressure
PBI	protein-bound iodine
PBP	penicillin-binding protein
p.c.	after meals (*post cibum*)
PCI	percutaneous coronary intervention
PCP	*Pneumocystis carinii* pneumonia
PCWP	pulmonary capillary wedge pressure
PD-1	programmed cell death receptors
PDD	peritoneal dialysis dependent
PDD-CKD	peritoneal dialysis-dependent chronic kidney disease
PDE	phosphodiesterase
PDE5	phosphodiesterase type-5

PE	pulmonary embolism
PERRLA	pupils equal, round, react to light and accommodation
P-gp	P-glycoprotein transporter
PG	prostaglandin
PGE$_2$	prostaglandin E$_2$
pH	hydrogen ion concentration
Ph	Philadelphia (chromosome)
PI	protease inhibitor
PID	pelvic inflammatory disease
PJP	*Pneumocystis jirovecii* pneumonia
PKU	phenylketonuria
PMDD	premenstrual dysphoric disorder
PML	progressive multifocal leukoencephalopathy
PND	paroxysmal nocturnal dyspnea
PNE	primary nocturnal enuresis
PO	by mouth or orally (*per os*)
PPES	Plantar Palmar Erythrodysesthesia
PPI	proton pump inhibitor
PPM	parts per million
PR	rectally (*per rectum*)
PRES	posterior reversible encephalopathy syndrome
prn	when required (*pro re nata*)
PSA	prostate-specific antigen
PSP	phenolsulfonphthalein
PSVT	paroxysmal supraventricular tachycardia
PT	prothrombin time
PTCL	peripheral T-cell lymphocyte
PTH	parathyroid hormone
PTLD	post-transplant lymphoproliferative disorder
PTSD	post-traumatic stress disorder
PTT	partial thromboplastin time
PUD	peptic ulcer disease
PVC	polyvinyl chloride IV bag or tubing
PVC	premature ventricular contraction
PVD	peripheral vascular disease
PZI	protamine zinc insulin
q.i.d.	four times daily
RA	rheumatoid arthritis
RAAS	renin angiotensin aldosterone system
RAI	radioactive iodine
RAR	retinoic acid receptor
RAST	radioallergosorbent test
RBC	red blood (cell) count
RDA	recommended (daily) dietary allowance
RDS	respiratory distress syndrome
REM	rapid eye movement
rem	radiation equivalent man
RES	reticuloendothelial system

RIA	radioimmunoassay
RNA	ribonucleic acid
ROM	range of motion
RSV	respiratory syncytial virus
RT	reverse transcriptase
RTK	receptor tyrosine kinase
RT_3U	total serum thyroxine concentration
S&S	signs and symptoms
SA	sinoatrial
SARA	selective aldosterone receptor antagonist
SBE	subacute bacterial endocarditis
SC	subcutaneous
S_{cr}	serum creatinine
SE	systemic embolism
sec	second
SERMs	selective estrogen receptor modulators
SGGT	serum gamma-glutamyl transferase
SGLT2	sodium-glucose cotransporter 2 in proximal tubule of kidney
SGOT	serum glutamic–oxaloacetic transaminase (*see* AST)
SGPT	serum glutamic–pyruvic transaminase (*see* ALT)
SIADH	syndrome of inappropriate antidiuretic hormone
SI Units	International System of Units
SK	streptokinase
SL	sublingual
SLE	systemic lupus erythematosus
SLL	small lymphocytic lymphoma
SMA	sequential multiple analysis
SMZ/TMP	sulfamethoxazole/trimethoprim
SNRI	serotonin norepinephrine reuptake inhibitor
SOS	if necessary (*si opus cit*)
sp	species
SPF	sun protection factor
sq	square
SR	sedimentation rate
SRS-A	slow-reactive substance of anaphylaxis
SSRI	selective serotonin reuptake inhibitor
stat	immediately
STD	sexually transmitted disease
STEMI	ST elevated MI
SVT	supraventricular tachyarrhythmias
SW	sterile water
$t_{1/2}$	half-life
T_3	triiodothyronine
T_4	thyroxine
TCA	tricyclic antidepressant
TG	total triglycerides
TIA	transient ischemic attack

t.i.d.	three times a day (*ter in die*)
TKI	tyrosine kinase inhibitor
TNF	tumor necrosis factor
tPA	tissue plasminogen activator
TPN	total parenteral nutrition
TPR	temperature, pulse, respirations
TSH	thyroid-stimulating hormone
TSS	toxic shock syndrome
TT	thrombin time
TTP	thrombotic cyclopenic purpura
UA	urinary analysis
UC	ulcerative colitis
ULN	upper limit of normal
URI	upper respiratory infection
USP	United States Pharmacopeia
USPHS	United States Public Health Service
UTI	urinary tract infection
UV-A, UVA	ultraviolet A wave
VDRL	Venereal Disease Research Laboratory
VEGF	vascular endothelial growth factor
VEGFR2	vascular endothelial growth factor receptor 2
VLDL	very low density lipoprotein
VMA	vanillylmandelic acid
VREF	vancomycin-resistant *Enterococcus faecium*
VRSA	vancomycin-resistant *Staphylococcus aureus*
VS	vital signs
wk	week
WBC	white blood (cell) count
WBCT	whole blood clotting time
y	year

◆ APPENDIX G   HERBAL AND DIETARY SUPPLEMENT TABLE

As patient interest in dietary supplements and other natural products increases, there is an increased need for information on this topic. These products are not standardized or stringently regulated by FDA guidelines; therefore, caution should be used when discussing these products. Consumers should note that since rigid quality control standards are not required for these products, substantial variability can occur in both potency and purity of a given product, especially between different commercial companies.

Many of these products have limited research on safety; thus, side effects and potential drug interactions are not well understood. Dietary supplements may either increase or decrease the level of a drug in the patient's body.

This table provides basic information on some of the most commonly sold dietary supplements. For additional information, a specialty resource on herbal and/or dietary supplements should be consulted.

Name	Common Use	Significant Safety Concerns
Bilberry	Eye health	Long-term, high-dose use can cause liver problems
Black cohosh	Menopausal symptoms	Should be avoided in pregnant patients
Cranberry	Urinary tract infections	Considered safe at usual doses; high dose may increase bleeding risk
Echinacea	Infections	May cause allergic reactions; should be used only short-term
Eleuthera (Siberian ginseng)	Energy	Avoid use with digoxin
Evening primrose	Menopausal symptoms	May affect seizure threshold
Garcinia cambogia	Weight loss	Mild GI side effects
Flax	Cholesterol	Minor GI side effects
Garlic	Cholesterol	Significant drug interactions with drugs metabolized by CYP system
Ginger	Nausea	Overdoses may cause cardiac arrhythmias

Name	Common Use	Significant Safety Concerns
Ginkgo	Memory enhancement	Potential increased bleeding risk
Ginseng (American ginseng)	Energy	Should not be used with MAO inhibitors; may affect anticoagulants
Glucosamine	Osteoarthritis	Considered safe at usual doses; at higher doses, possible interaction with warfarin and other coumarin anticoagulants
Green tea	Energy, weight loss	High doses may cause cardiovascular side effects
Horny goat weed	Sexual function	Should be avoided in pregnant/lactating women
Horse chestnut	Congestive heart failure	Potential hepatotoxicity
Milk thistle	Liver function	May affect CYP metabolism and interact with drugs metabolized by this system
Saw palmetto	Benign prostatic hyperplasia	Adverse effects appear mild
Soy	Menopausal symptoms	GI-related side effects may be significant for some patients
St. John's wort	Depression	Significant drug interactions with several drugs metabolized by CYP system
Turmeric	Arthritis, inflammatory conditions	May reduce blood glucose levels and have additive effect with other ANTIDIABETEIC AGENTS
Valerian	Sleep disorder	Potentially hepatotoxic
Yohimbe	Sexual function	Do not use with drugs affecting serotonin system

The Centers for Disease Control and Prevention (CDC) contains detailed listings of what vaccinations are recommended for various age groups as well as patients with multiple concurrent disease states. The full recommendations are available at: https://www.cdc.gov/vaccines/.

Dosing information is provided for some common vaccines. There are many other vaccines and vaccine formulations. Please consult the package insert for specific details regarding each of the following:

BCG (BACILLUS CALMETTE-GUERIN) VACCINE
Tice, TheraCys

USES To protect groups with excessive rates of TB infection.

Adult/Adolescent/Child (1 mo or older): **Percutaneous** 0.2–0.3 mL of a 50 mg/mL vaccine **Intradermal** 0.1 mL. If tuberculin test is negative post-vaccination and indications for immunization remain, administer full vaccine dose after 2 to 3 months.
Child (younger than 1 mo): **Percutaneous** 0.2 to 0.3 mL of 25 mg/mL solution for 1 dose. If tuberculin test is negative post-vaccination and indications for immunization remain, administer full vaccine dose when older than 1 year.
Children (1 month to 1 year): 0.2 to 0.3 mL of a 50 mg/mL solution for 1 dose. If tuberculin test is negative post-vaccination and indications for immunization remain, administer full vaccine dose when older than 1 year.

CONTRAINDICATIONS Hypersensitivity to any vaccine component; active or past mycobacterial infection; immunosuppressed patients, biopsy, transurethral resection or traumatic catheterization, active tuberculosis.

DIPHTHERIA TOXOID/TETANUS TOXOID/ACELLULAR PERTUSSIS VACCINE, ADSORBED (DTaP/Tdap)
Adacel, Boostrix, Daptacel, Infanrix

USES Prevention of tetanus, diphtheria, and pertussis.

Adult/Adolescent/Child (10 y or older): **IM** 0.5 mL

CONTRAINDICATIONS Severe allergic reaction to any component of the formulation; encephalopathy within 7 days of a previous dose of pertussis antigen; progressive neurologic disorder.

HAEMOPHILUS B CONJUGATE VACCINE (HIB)
ActHIB, Hiberix, Liquid PedvaxHIB

USES To provide active immunity to H. influenzae type b (Hib) infection.

Infant: **IM** 0.5 mL at 2, 4, and 6 mo (ActHIB)
Infant/Child: **IM** 0.5 mL at 2 and 4 mo and again at 12 to 15 mo (Liquid PedvaxHIB)

Child (15–71 mo): **IM** 0.5 mL as booster (PedvaxHIB(R)

CONTRAINDICATIONS Hypersensitivity to any vaccine components; fever of unknown etiology; infants younger than 6 weeks.

HEPATITIS A VACCINE
Havrix, Vaqta

USES To provide active immunity to hepatitis A.

Adult: **IM** 1 mL dose then 1 mL 6–12 mo later
Child (1–18 y): **IM** 0.5 mL then 0.5 mL booster dose 6–12 mo later

CONTRAINDICATIONS Hypersensitivity to any vaccine component; neomycin hypersensitivity.

HEPATITIS B IMMUNE GLOBULIN
HepaGam B, HyperHep, Nabi-HB

USES To provide passive immunity to hepatitis B infections in individuals exposed to HBV or Hbs Ag-positive materials; to prevent hepatitis B recurrence in post-liver transplant (HepaGam B).

Adult/Child: **IM** 0.06 mL/kg as soon as possible (preferably within 7 days) post-exposure, then repeat 28–30 day post-exposure
Neonate: **IM** 0.5 mL within 12 h of birth, then repeat at 3 and 6 mo
Adult: **HepaGam B IV** 20,000 U/dose daily every 2 wk (2–12 wk) then monthly

CONTRAINDICATIONS Hypersensitivity to any vaccine component.

HEPATITIS B VACCINE (RECOMBINANT)
Engerix-B, Recombivax HB, Heplisav-B

USES To provide active immunity to individuals at high risk for exposure.

Adult (older than 20 yo): **Engerix-B:** 20 mcg/1 mL IM as a 3-dose series: zero, 1–2, and 4–6 months. *Recombivax HB:* 10 mcg/mL 1 dose (1 mL) IM as a 3-dose series given on a 0, 1–2, and 4–6-month schedule. *Heplisav – B (only for 18 yo or older):* 0.5 mL IM at 0 and 1 month.
Adult (younger than 20 yo)/Adolescent/ Child/Infant: Engerix-B: **IM** 10 mcg/0.5mL within 24 hours of birth and at 1–2 months, 4 months and 6 months; for older children that did not start the series at birth: 0, 1–2, 4–6 months. *Recombivax HB:* 5mcg/0.5 mL 1 dose (0.5 1 mL) **IM** as 3-dose series given within 24 hours of birth, 1–2 months, 4-6-months, and 6-18 months schedule. For older children that did not start the series at birth: 0, 1–2 months and 4-6 months. For teens age 11–15 years, 1.0 mL at 0 and 1–2 months.

CONTRAINDICATIONS Hypersensitivity to any vaccine component; yeast hypersensitivity.

HUMAN PAPILLOMAVIRUS BIVALENT (RECOMBINANT)
Cervarix for females only

USES To prevent disease associated with HPV exposure.

Adult/Adolescent/Child (9 y or older): **IM** 0.5 mL dose at 0 (before the 15 yo birthday), 1, and 6–12 months. If an adolescent receives two doses less than 5 months apart, a third dose of HPV vaccine will be required. For teens and adults ages 15 through 26 years old, 3-dose schedule at 0, 1-2 month and 6 months is recommended. For immunocompromised individuals (including those with HIV), the 3-dose schedule is recommended for ages 9 through 26 years of age.

CONTRAINDICATIONS Hypersensitivity to any vaccine component; yeast hypersensitivity, pregnancy, moderate or severe acute illness.

HUMAN PAPILLOMAVIRUS QUADRIVALENT VACCINE (RECOMBINANT)
Gardasil females, transgender persons and males

USES To prevent HPV-related disease; to prevent genital warts; to prevent anal cancer.

Adult/Child (11 y or older): **IM** 0.5 mL followed by doses at 2 and 6 months.

CONTRAINDICATIONS Hypersensitivity to any vaccine component; yeast hypersensitivity; monitor for 15 minutes after vaccine because episodes of syncope have been reported that could result in fall and injury.

HUMAN PAPILLOMAVIRUS 9-VALENT VACCINE
Gardasil 9 females and males

USES To prevent HPV-related disease; to prevent genital warts; to prevent anal cancer.

Adult/Child (9-26 y): **IM** 0.5 mL for first dose and followed by doses at 2 and 6 months: make sure there is at least 4 weeks between the first and second interval, a 12-week interval between the second and third interval, and a 5-month minimum interval between the first and third dose.

CONTRAINDICATIONS Hypersensitivity to any vaccine component; yeast hypersensitivity; previous use of other brand of HPV vaccine, monitor for 15 minutes after vaccine because episodes of syncope have been reported that could result in fall and injury.

INFLUENZA VACCINE
Afluria Quadrivalent, FLUAD, Fluarix, Flublok, FluLaval, Fluzone, Flumist, FluMist Quadrivalent

USES To prevent influenza.

Adult & child (2-49 y): **Intranasal** *Flumist* 0.2 mL dose (0.1 per nostril); Afluria, *Fluarix Quadravalent, FluLaval Quadravalent* **IM** 0.5 mL; *Geriatric: FLUAD* formulation **IM** 0.5mL
Child (> 3 y): Afluria **IM** 0.5 mL
Infant/Child (6-35 mo): Fluzone Quadrivalent **IM** 0.25 mL dose.

CONTRAINDICATIONS Hypersensitivity to egg, kanamycin, neomycin or polymyxin' concomitant aspirin or salicylate-containing therapy in children and adolescents: children age 2y – 4y with diagnosis of asthma; children and adults who are immunocompromised; close contact with those that are severely immunocompromised; pregnancy; receipt of influenza antiviral medication within the past 48 hours.

MENINGOCOCCAL DIPHTHERIA TOXOID CONJUGATE
Menveo, Menactra

USES To provide prophylaxis against meningococcal infection.

Adult (younger than 55 y)/Adolescent/Child (2 y or older): **IM** 0.5 mL injection
Infant/Child (9 mo to 2 years): Menactra only: 0.5 mL injection (2 dose series); *Menveo (2 months to less than 7 months) IM 0.5 mL/dose given as a 4-dose series at 2,4,6 and 12 months of age.*

CONTRAINDICATIONS Hypersensitivity to any vaccine component; history of Guillain-Barré syndrome, latex hypersensitivity, moderate to severe illness.

MEASLES, MUMPS AND RUBELLA VIRUS VACCINE
M-M-R II

USES Vaccination against measles, mumps, and rubella.

Child (over 12 mo): **Subcutaneous** 0.5 mL at ages 12–15 mo; second dose at ages 4–6 y

CONTRAINDICATIONS Hypersensitivity to any component of the vaccine, including gelatin. Do not administer to patients who are pregnant, receiving immunosuppressive therapy, currently ill with febrile illness.

MENINGOCOCCAL GROUP B VACCINE
Bexsero, Trumenba

USES To provide prophylaxis against meningococcal infection.

Adult/Adolescent/Child (ages 10–25 y): **IM** 0.5 mL/dose as part of a 2 or 3 dose series

CONTRAINDICATIONS Hypersensitivity to the meningococcal group B vaccine or any component of the formulation.

PNEUMOCOCCAL 13-VALENT VACCINE, DIPHTHERIA
Prevnar 13

USES To provide routine prophylaxis for infants and children as part of the primary childhood immunization schedule.

Adult (19 to 64 y): **IM** 0.5 mL as a single dose

Geriatric (≥65 y): Only in special circumstances; not routine. **IM** 0.5 mL as a single dose.

Child/Adolescent (6–17 y): **IM** 0.5 mL as single dose
Infant and children (6 wk–15 mo): **IM** 0.5 mL dose initiated between 6 and 8 wk, then repeated at 4 mo, 6 mo., 12 mo to 15 mo. (total of 4 doses); see CDC guidelines for catch-up schedule if infant did not receive this recommended schedule.

CONTRAINDICATIONS Hypersensitivity to any vaccine component.

PNEUMOCOCCAL POLYSACCHARIDE VACCINE, 23-VALENT
Pneumovax 23

USES Pneumococcal disease prevention

Adult/Adolescent/Child (2 y or older): **Subcutaneous/IM** 0.5 mL; revaccination may be necessary in some patients with concurrent immunocompromised disease states.

CONTRAINDICATIONS Severe allergic reaction to pneumococcal vaccine or any component of the formulation.

RABIES VACCINE
RabAvert, Imovax

USES Pre-exposure rabies prophylaxis

Adult/Adolescent/Children/Infant: **IM** Series of 3 injections 1 mL on days 0, 7, 21, or 28

CONTRAINDICATIONS Anaphylaxis to vaccine or vaccine component.

ROTAVIRUS VACCINE
Rotarix, RotaTeq

USES To prevent gastroenteritis caused by rotavirus infection.

Infant (6–32 wk) (RotaTeq only): **PO** 2 mL at 6–2 wk, followed by 2 other doses given at 4–10 wk intervals and to be completed by 32 wk.

Infant (6–24 wk) (Rotarix only): **PO** 1 mL at 6 wk; then second dose to follow at least 4 wk later and completed by 24 wk.

CONTRAINDICATIONS Hypersensitivity to any vaccine component, history of intussusception, or severe combined immunodeficiency.

VARICELLA VACCINE
Varivax

USES To provide vaccination against varicella.

Adult/Adolescent: **Subcutaneous** 0.5 mL followed by a second dose 4–8 wk later
Child (1–12 y): **Subcutaneous** 0.5 mL and allow at least 3 months to elapse before a second 0.5 mL dose is given.

CONTRAINDICATIONS Hypersensitivity to any vaccine component; febrile illness; untreated tuberculosis; AIDS; bone marrow suppression; concurrent chemotherapy or corticosteroid therapy; gelatin hypersensitivity; hypogammaglobulinemia; current leukemia or lymphoma; neomycin hypersensitivity; pregnancy (avoid pregnancy for 3 months following vaccination); tuberculosis; concurrent radiation therapy.

ZOSTER VACCINE LIVE
Zostavax

USES To prevent herpes zoster in people over 50 y old.

Adult (50 y or older): **Subcutaneous** Administer 0.65 mL as single dose.

CONTRAINDICATIONS Hypersensitivity to any vaccine component; AIDS; gelatin hypersensitivity; immunosuppression; leukemia; lymphoma; neomycin hypersensitivity; pregnancy; people receiving antitumor necrosis factors.

BIBLIOGRAPHY

American Hospital Formulary Service (AHFS) Drug Information. 2020. Bethesda, MD: American Society of Health-System Pharmacists.

Food and Drug Administration. http://www.fda.gov. 2020.

Lexi-Drugs. Lexicomp [Online database]. Hudson, OH: Wolters Kluwer Health, Inc.; 2020. http://online.lexi.com/.

Micromedex [Online database]. Greenwood Village, CO: Truven Health Analytics; 2020. http://www.micromedexsolutions.com/

National Institute of Health. *Daily Med*. http://daily med.nlm.gov. 2020.

Trissel's 2 Clinical Pharmaceutics [Online database]. Hudson, OH: Wolters Kluwer 2020. https://online.lexi.com/lco/action/ivcompatibility/trissels

INDEX

Drug categories are in SMALL CAPS. Prototypes are in **bold.**
Generic drug names are given in parentheses.

Drug categories are in SMALL CAPS. Prototypes are in **bold.**
Generic drug names are given in parentheses.

Drug categories are in SMALL CAPS. Prototypes are in **bold.**
Generic drug names are given in parentheses.

1863

Drug categories are in SMALL CAPS. Prototypes are in **bold.**
Generic drug names are given in parentheses.

Drug categories are in SMALL CAPS. Prototypes are in **bold.**
Generic drug names are given in parentheses.

1865

Drug categories are in SMALL CAPS. Prototypes are in **bold.**
Generic drug names are given in parentheses.

Drug categories are in SMALL CAPS. Prototypes are in **bold.**
Generic drug names are given in parentheses.

1867

Drug categories are in SMALL CAPS. Prototypes are in **bold**.
Generic drug names are given in parentheses.

Drug categories are in SMALL CAPS. Prototypes are in **bold**.
Generic drug names are given in parentheses.

1869

Drug categories are in SMALL CAPS. Prototypes are in **bold.**
Generic drug names are given in parentheses.

Drug categories are in SMALL CAPS. Prototypes are in **bold.**
Generic drug names are given in parentheses.

Drug categories are in SMALL CAPS. Prototypes are in **bold.**
Generic drug names are given in parentheses.

1872

Drug categories are in SMALL CAPS. Prototypes are in **bold.**
Generic drug names are given in parentheses.

1873

Drug categories are in SMALL CAPS. Prototypes are in **bold.**
Generic drug names are given in parentheses.

Drug categories are in SMALL CAPS. Prototypes are in **bold**.
Generic drug names are given in parentheses.

1875

Drug categories are in SMALL CAPS. Prototypes are in **bold.**
Generic drug names are given in parentheses.

Drug categories are in SMALL CAPS. Prototypes are in **bold.**
Generic drug names are given in parentheses.

Drug categories are in SMALL CAPS. Prototypes are in **bold.**
Generic drug names are given in parentheses.

¹878

Drug categories are in SMALL CAPS. Prototypes are in **bold.**
Generic drug names are given in parentheses.

1879

Drug categories are in SMALL CAPS. Prototypes are in **bold.**
Generic drug names are given in parentheses.

Drug categories are in SMALL CAPS. Prototypes are in **bold.**
Generic drug names are given in parentheses.

1882

Drug categories are in SMALL CAPS. Prototypes are in **bold.**
Generic drug names are given in parentheses.

Drug categories are in SMALL CAPS. Prototypes are in **bold.**
Generic drug names are given in parentheses.

Drug categories are in SMALL CAPS. Prototypes are in **bold**.
Generic drug names are given in parentheses.

Drug categories are in SMALL CAPS. Prototypes are in **bold.**
Generic drug names are given in parentheses.

Drug categories are in SMALL CAPS. Prototypes are in **bold.**
Generic drug names are given in parentheses.

Drug categories are in SMALL CAPS. Prototypes are in **bold.**
Generic drug names are given in parentheses.

Drug categories are in SMALL CAPS. Prototypes are in **bold.**
Generic drug names are given in parentheses.

Drug categories are in SMALL CAPS. Prototypes are in **bold**.
Generic drug names are given in parentheses.

Drug categories are in SMALL CAPS. Prototypes are in **bold.**
Generic drug names are given in parentheses.

1891

Drug categories are in SMALL CAPS. Prototypes are in **bold.**
Generic drug names are given in parentheses.

Drug categories are in SMALL CAPS. Prototypes are in **bold.**
Generic drug names are given in parentheses.

Drug categories are in SMALL CAPS. Prototypes are in **bold.**
Generic drug names are given in parentheses.

lubiprostone, 1004–1005
Lucemyra (lofexidine), 988–990
luliconazole, 1006, 1820
Lumigan (bimatoprost), 197, 1808
Luminal (phenobarbital sodium), 1329–1332
Lunesta (eszopiclone), 664–665
LUNG SURFACTANT
  poractant alfa, 1369–1370
Lupron (leuprolide acetate), 952–954
Lupron Depot (leuprolide acetate), 952–954
Lupron Depot-Ped (leuprolide acetate), 952–954
lurasidone, 1006–1008
Lustra (hydroquinone), 818–819
LUTEINIZING HORMONE-RELEASING HORMONE RECEPTOR ANTAGONIST
  cetrorelix, 329–330
Luvox (fluvoxamine), 739–740
Luxiq (betamethasone valerate), 186–188, 1817
Luzu (luliconazole), 1006
Lybrel (estrogen-progestin combination), 655–658
Lyderm (fluocinonide), 726
LYMPHOCYTE FUNCTION-ASSOCIATED ANTIGEN-1 (LFA-1) ANTAGONIST
  lifitegrast, 968–969
Lyrica (pregabalin), 1393–1395
Lysodren (mitotane), 1111–1112

M

MACROLIDE ANTIBIOTICS. See ANTIBIOTICS, MACROLIDE
mafenide acetate, 1008–1009
Magnesia (magnesium hydroxide), 1011–1012
Magnesia Magma (magnesium hydroxide), 1011–1012
magnesium citrate, 1010–1011
magnesium hydroxide, 1011–1012
magnesium oxide, 1012–1013
magnesium salicylate, 1013–1014
magnesium sulfate, 1014–1016
Mag-Ox (magnesium oxide), 1012–1013
Makena (hydroxyprogesterone caproate), 822–823
Malarone (atovaquone/proguanil hydrochloride), 138–139
Malarone (combination drug), 1831
Mallamint (calcium carbonate), 249–251
Mallazine (tetrahydrozoline hydrochloride), 1647–1648

Malogex (testosterone enanthate), 1639–1642
Malotuss (guaifenesin), 793–794
MAMMALIAN TARGET OF RAPAMYCIN (MTOR) INHIBITOR
  temsirolimus, 1624–1625
mannitol, 1016–1018
MAO-B (MONOAMINE OXIDASE-B) INHIBITOR
  rasagiline, 1459–1461
MAOIS. See ANTIDEPRESSANTS, MONOAMINE OXIDASE INHIBITOR
Maox (magnesium oxide), 1012–1013
maraviroc, 1019–1021
Marplan (isocarboxazid), 895–896
MAST CELL STABILIZER
  cromolyn sodium, 413–415
Matonia (metoclopramide hydrochloride), 1079–1082
Matulane (procarbazine hydrochloride), 1403–1406
Matzim LA (diltiazem), 515–516
Maxalt (rizatriptan benzoate), 1500–1502
Maxalt-MLT (rizatriptan benzoate), 1500–1501
Maxidex (dexamethasone), 481–484
Maxiflor (diflorasone diacetate), 507, 1818
Maxitrol (combination drug), 1831
Maxivate (betamethasone dipropionate), 1817
Maxzide (combination drug), 1831
Maxzide 25 (combination drug), 1831
Mazepine (carbamazepine), 266–269
Mazicon (flumazenil), 724–726
measles, mumps and rubella virus vaccine, 1858
Measurin (aspirin), 126–129
mechlorethamine hydrochloride, 1021–1023
meclizine hydrochloride, 1023–1024
meclofenamate sodium, 1024–1026
Mediquell (dextromethorphan hydrobromide), 493–494
Medrol (methylprednisolone), 1075–1078
medroxyprogesterone acetate, 1026–1028
mefenamic acid, 1028–1029
mefloquine hydrochloride, 1029–1031
Mega-Cal (calcium carbonate), 249–251

Megace (megestrol acetate), 1031–1032
Megace ES (megestrol acetate), 1031–1032
Megacillin (penicillin G potassium), 1305–1308
Mega Twin EPA (omega-3 fatty acids EPA & DHA), 1217–1218
megestrol acetate, 1031–1032
MEGLITINIDES
  nateglinide, 1148–1149
  repaglinide, 1466–1467
MEK (MITOGEN-ACTIVATED EXTRACELLULAR KINASE)
  trametinib, 1705–1707
Mekinist (trametinib), 1705–1707
Melanex (hydroquinone), 818–819
MELATONIN RECEPTOR AGONISTS
  ramelteon, 1453–1454
  tasimelteon, 1611–1612
meloxicam, 1032–1034
melphalan, 1034–1036
memantine, 1036–1037
Menactra (meningococcal diphtheria toxoid conjugate), 1858
Menest (estrogens, esterified), 660–662
meningococcal diphtheria toxoid conjugate, 1858
meningococcal group B vaccine, 1858
Menostar (estradiol), 650–653
Menrium (estrogens, esterified), 660–662
Mentax (busulfan), 230–232
Menveo (meningococcal diphtheria toxoid conjugate), 1858
meperidine hydrochloride, 1037–1040
Mephyton (phytonadione), 1341–1343
mepolizumab, 1040–1041
meprobamate, 1041–1043
Mepron (atovaquone), 136–138
mequinol/tretinoin, 1043–1044. See also TRETINOIN
MEQUINOL/TRETINOIN. See also TRETINOIN
mercaptopurine, 1044–1045
meropenem, 1045–1047
Merrem (meropenem), 1045–1047
mesalamine, 1047–1048
mesna, 1048–1050
Mesnex (mesna), 1048–1050
Mestinon (pyridostigmine bromide), 1434–1436
METABOLISM REGULATOR, BONE. See also BISPHOSPHONATES
  calcitonin (salmon), 246–247

Drug categories are in SMALL CAPS. Prototypes are in **bold.**
Generic drug names are given in parentheses.

1895

Drug categories are in SMALL CAPS. Prototypes are in **bold.**
Generic drug names are given in parentheses.

Drug categories are in SMALL CAPS. Prototypes are in **bold.**
Generic drug names are given in parentheses.

Drug categories are in SMALL CAPS. Prototypes are in **bold.**
Generic drug names are given in parentheses.

Drug categories are in SMALL CAPS. Prototypes are in **bold.**
Generic drug names are given in parentheses.

1899

Drug categories are in SMALL CAPS. Prototypes are in **bold.**
Generic drug names are given in parentheses.

Drug categories are in SMALL CAPS. Prototypes are in **bold.**
Generic drug names are given in parentheses.

Drug categories are in SMALL CAPS. Prototypes are in **bold.**
Generic drug names are given in parentheses.

Drug categories are in SMALL CAPS. Prototypes are in **bold**.
Generic drug names are given in parentheses.

prucalopride, 1428–1429
pseudoephedrine hydrochloride, 1429–1430
Pseudofrin (pseudoephedrine hydrochloride), 1429–1430
PSORALEN
  methoxsalen, 1064–1067
Psorcon (diflorasone diacetate), 507–509, 1818
Psorcon E (diflorasone diacetate), 1818
Psorion (betamethasone valerate), 1817
psyllium hydrophilic mucilloid, 1431–1432
Pulmicort (budesonide), 221–223, 1815
PULMONARY ANTIHYPERTENSIVES. *See* ANTIHYPERTENSIVES, PULMONARY
Pulmophylline (theophylline), 1648–1650
Pulmozyme (dornase alfa), 549–550
PURINE ANTAGONIST
  thioguanine, 1652–1653
PURINE ANTIMETABOLITES. *See* ANTINEOPLASTICS, ANTIMETABOLITE (PURINE)
PURINE NUCLEOSIDE
  ganciclovir, 764–766
Purixan (mercaptopurine), 1044–1045
pyrantel pamoate, 1432–1433
pyrethrins, 1433–1434
Pyridiate (phenazopyridine hydrochloride), 1325–1326
Pyridium (phenazopyridine hydrochloride), 1325–1326
Pyridium Plus (combination drug), 1833
pyridostigmine bromide, 1434–1436
Pyridoxine (vitamin B₄), 1774–1776
pyridoxine hydrochloride, 1436–1437
pyrimethamine, 1437–1439
PYRIMIDINE SYNTHESIS INHIBITOR
  teriflunomide, 1635–1637
Pyrinate (pyrethrins), 1433–1434
Pyrinyl (pyrethrins), 1433–1434
Pyronium (phenazopyridine hydrochloride), 1325–1326

Q

Qbrelis (lisinopril), 983–985
Qnasl (beclomethasone dipropionate), 1815
Qsymia (combination drug), 1833
Qtren (combination drug), 1833

Qualaquin (quinine sulfate), 1446–1448
Quartette (combination drug), 1833
Quartette (estrogen-progestin combination), 655–658
quazepam, 1439–1440
Qudexy XR (topiramate), 1699–1700
Quelicin (succinylcholine chloride), 1585–1587
Questran (cholestyramine resin), 353–355
Questran Light (cholestyramine resin), 353–355
quetiapine fumarate, 1440–1442
Quick Pep (caffeine), 243–244
Quilivant XR (methylphenidate hydrochloride), 1073–1075
quinapril hydrochloride, 1442–1444
quinidine sulfate, 1444–1446
quinine sulfate, 1446–1448
quinupristin/dalfopristin, 1448–1450
Qutenza (capsaicin), 263–264
QVAR (beclomethasone dipropionate), 171–173, 1815

R

RabAvert (rabies vaccine), 1859
rabeprazole sodium, 1450–1451
rabies vaccine, 1859
racemic epinephrine, 609–613
raloxifene hydrochloride, 1451–1452
raltegravir, 1452–1453
ramelteon, 1453–1454
ramipril, 1455–1456
ramucirumab, 1456–1458
Ranexa (ranolazine), 1458–1459
RANK LIGAND INHIBITOR
  denosumab, 474–475
ranolazine, 1458–1459
Rapaflo (silodosin), 1545–1546
Rapamune (sirolimus), 1552–1554
Rapivab (peramivir), 1317–1318
rasagiline, 1459–1461
rasburicase, 1461–1462
Rasuvo (methotrexate sodium), 1062–1064
Rayos (prednisolone), 1389–1390
Razadyne (galantamine hydrobromide), 763–764
Razadyne ER (galantamine hydrobromide), 763–764
R & C (pyrethrins), 1433–1434
Reactine (cetirizine), 328–329
Rebetol (ribavirin), 1473–1475
Rebetron (combination drug), 1833

Rebif (interferon beta-1a), 879–880
Recarbrio (combination drug), 1833
Reclast (zoledronic acid), 1799–1801
Recombivax HB (hepatitis B vaccine), 1856
Recothrom (thrombin), 1659
Rectacort (hydrocortisone), 1817
Rectocort (hydrocortisone), 812–816
RED BLOOD CELL MODIFIER
  pentoxifylline, 1316–1317
Redoxon (ascorbic acid), 122–124
Refissa (tretinoin), 1714–1716
Regimex (benzphetamine hydrochloride), 182–184
Regitine (phentolamine mesylate), 1333–1334
Reglan (metoclopramide hydrochloride), 1048–1051
Regonol (pyridostigmine bromide), 1434–1436
regorafenib, 1462–1465
Regranex (becaplermin), 170–171
Regular Insulin (insulin), 871–874
Regulax (docusate sodium), 538–539
Reguloid (psyllium hydrophilic mucilloid), 1431–1432
Regutol (docusate sodium), 538–539
Relenza (zanamivir), 1789–1790
ReliOn N (insulin, isophane), 874–875
Relistor (methylnaltrexone bromide), 1072–1073
Remeron (mirtazapine), 1106–1108
Remeron SolTab (mirtazapine), 1106–1108
Remicade (infliximab), 861–863
remifentanil hydrochloride, 1465–1466
Renagel (sevelamer hydrochloride), 1542–1543
RENIN ANGIOTENSIN SYSTEM ANTAGONIST. *See* ANGIOTENSIN SYSTEM ANTAGONISTS, RENIN
  benazepril hydrochloride, 176–177
RENIN INHIBITOR, DIRECT
  aliskiren, 46–47
Renova (tretinoin), 1714–1716
Renvela (sevelamer hydrochloride), 1542–1543
ReoPro (abciximab), 5–6
repaglinide, 1466–1467
Repatha (evolocumab), 682–683

Drug categories are in SMALL CAPS. Prototypes are in **bold.**
Generic drug names are given in parentheses.

1905

Drug categories are in SMALL CAPS. Prototypes are in **bold.**
Generic drug names are given in parentheses.

1906

Drug categories are in SMALL CAPS. Prototypes are in **bold.**
Generic drug names are given in parentheses.

1907

Drug categories are in SMALL CAPS. Prototypes are in **bold.**
Generic drug names are given in parentheses.

Drug categories are in SMALL CAPS. Prototypes are in **bold.**
Generic drug names are given in parentheses.

1909

1910

Drug categories are in SMALL CAPS. Prototypes are in **bold.**
Generic drug names are given in parentheses.

Drug categories are in SMALL CAPS. Prototypes are in **bold.**
Generic drug names are given in parentheses.

1911

Drug categories are in SMALL CAPS. Prototypes are in **bold.**
Generic drug names are given in parentheses.

Drug categories are in SMALL CAPS. Prototypes are in **bold.**
Generic drug names are given in parentheses.

Drug categories are in SMALL CAPS. Prototypes are in **bold.**
Generic drug names are given in parentheses.

1914

Drug categories are in SMALL CAPS. Prototypes are in **bold.**
Generic drug names are given in parentheses.

1915

COMMON DRUG IV-SITE COMPATIBILITY CHART

	AMINOPHYLLINE	DOBUTAMINE	DOPAMINE	HEPARIN	MEPERIDINE	MORPHINE	NITROGLYCERIN	ONDANSETRON	POTASSIUM CL
acyclovir	C	–	–	C	I/C	I/C		I	C
alteplase		–	–	–			–		
amikacin	C	C	C	I/C	C	C	C	I/C	C
amino acids (TPN)	I/C	C	I/C	I/C	C	C	C	–	C
aminophylline		–	C	C	C	C	C	–	C
amiodarone	–	I/C	C	–	C	C	C		I/C
ampicillin	–	–	I/C	I/C	I/C	I/C	I/C	–	I/C
ampicillin/sulbactam	I/C	–	I/C	I/C	I/C	I/C	I/C	–	I/C
aztreonam	C	C	C	C	C	C	C	C	C
bretylium	C	C	C	C	C	C	C	C	C
bumetanide	C	C	C	C	C	C	C	C	C
calcium chloride	C	C	C	C	C	C	C	C	C
cefazolin	C	–	–	C	C	C	C	C	C
cefotaxime	C	–	C	C	C	C	C	C	C
cefotetan	C	–	C	C	I/C	C	C	I/C	C
cefoxitin	C	–	C	C	C	C	C	C	C
ceftazidime	C	I/C	C	C	C	C	C	I/C	C
ceftizoxime	C	C	C	C	C	C	C	C	C
ceftriaxone	C	–	C	C	C	C	C	I/C	C
cefuroxime	C	–	C	C	C	C	C	C	C
chloramphenicol	C	–	–	C	I/C	C	C	–	C
cimetidine	C	C	C	C	C	C	C	C	C
ciprofloxacin	–	C	C	–	C	C		C	C
clindamycin	C	C	C	C	C	C	C	C	C
dexamethasone	C	–	C	C	I/C	C	C	C	C
diazepam	–	I/C	–	–	–	I/C	–	I/C	–
digoxin	C	C	C	C	C	C	C	C	C

COMMON DRUG IV-SITE COMPATIBILITY CHART

	AMINOPHYLLINE	DOBUTAMINE	DOPAMINE	HEPARIN	MEPERIDINE	MORPHINE	NITROGLYCERIN	ONDANSETRON	POTASSIUM CL
diltiazem	I/C	C	C	I/C	C	C	C	C	C
diphenhydramine	−	C	C	I/C	C	C	C	C	C
dobutamine	−	C	C	I/C	C	C	C	C	C
dopamine	C	C	C	−	C	C	C	C	C
doxycycline	C	C	C	−	C	C	C	C	C
enalaprilat	C	C	C	C	C	C	C	C	C
epinephrine	I/C	C	C	C	C	C	C	C	C
eptifibatide	C	C	C	C	C	C	C	C	C
eryhtromycin	C	C	C	I/C	C	C	C	C	C
esmolol	C	C	C	C	C	C	C	C	C
famotidine	C	C	C	−	C	C		−	C
filgrastim	C							−	
fluconazole	C	C	C	C	C	C	C	C	C
foscarnet	C	−	C	C	C	C	C	−	C
furosemide	C	I/C	I/C	I/C	I/C	I/C	I/C	−	C
ganciclovir	−	−	−	C	−	−	C	−	C
gentamicin	C	C	C	I/C	C	C	C	C	C
heparin	C	I/C	C	C	I/C	C	C	C	I/C
hydrocortisone	C	−	C	C	I/C	C	C	C	I/C
hydromorphone	C	C	C	C	C	C	C	C	C
imipenem/cilastatin	I/C	I/C	C	C	I/C	C	C	C	C
inamrinone	I/C	I/C	I/C	−	I/C	−	I/C	I/C	C
insulin (regular)	C	I/C	I/C	I/C	C	I/C	C	I/C	C
isoproterenol	I/C	C	C	C	C	C	C	I/C	C
labetolol	C	C	C	I/C	C	C	C	−	−
lansoprazole	−	−	−	C	−	−	−	−	−
lidocaine	C	C	C	C	C	C	C	C	C
lorazepam	C	C	C	I/C	−	−	C	C	C
magnesium	−	C	C	C	I/C	C	C	C	C
meperidine	C	C	C	I/C	C	C	C	C	C

methylprednisolone	C	C	C	I/C	C	C	C	I/C	C
metoclopramide	C	C	C	C	C	C	C	C	C
metoprolol	C	C	C	C	I/C	C	C	C	C
metronidazole	C	C	C	C	C	C	C	C	C
micofungin	C	–	C	–	C	–	C	C	C
midazolam	–	I/C	C	C	C	C	C	–	–
milrinone	C	C	C	C	C	C	C	C	C
morphine	C	C	C	–	C	–	C	–	C
nafcillin	C	C	C	C	C	C	C	C	I/C
nitroglycerin	C	C	C	C	C	C	C	C	C
nitroprusside	C	I/C	C	C	C	C	C	C	C
norepinephrine	I/C	C	I/C	–	C	C	C	C	C
ondansetron	–	C	–	C	C	C	C	C	C
pantoprazole	I/C	I/C	I/C	I/C	I/C	I/C	I/C	I/C	I/C
penicillin G	I/C	C	C	C	C	C	C	C	–
phenylephrine	C	C	C	–	C	–	C	–	C
phenytoin	–	–	–	–	–	–	–	–	–
piperacillin	C	C	C	C	C	C	C	I/C	C
piperacillin/tazobactam	C	–	C	C	C	C	C	C	I/C
potassium Cl	C	C	C	C	C	C	C	C	C
procainamide	C	C	C	C	C	C	C	C	C
propofol	C	I/C	C	I/C	C	I/C	I/C	I/C	I/C
ranitidine	C	C	C	C	C	C	C	C	C
sargramostim	C	C	C	–	C	–	I/C	I/C	I/C
sodium bicarbonate	C	–	–	–	C	C	C	C	C
sulfamethoxazole-trimethoprim	–	–	I/C	I/C	C	I/C	–	–	C
ticarcillin/clavulanate	C	C	C	C	C	C	C	–	I/C
tobramycin	C	C	I/C	I/C	C	C	C	C	C
vancomycin	I	C	I/C	I/C	C	C	C	C	C

C = compatible; I = incompatible; I/C = conflicting data.